the MuRDer bAg

TONY PARSONS

the MuRDer bAg

CENTURY

Published by Century 2014

5 7 9 10 8 6

First published in Great Britain in 2014 by
Century
Random House, 20 Vauxhall Bridge Road,
London SW1V 2SA

www.randomhouse.co.uk

Addresses for companies within The Random House Group Limited can be found at:
www.randomhouse.co.uk/offices.htm

The Random House Group Limited Reg. No. 954009

A CIP catalogue record for this book
is available from the British Library

ISBN 9781780892337 (Hardback)
ISBN 9781780892344 (Trade paperback)

The Random House Group Limited supports the Forest Stewardship Council® (FSC®), the leading international forest-certification organisation. Our books carrying the FSC label are printed on FSC®-certified paper. FSC is the only forest-certification scheme supported by the leading environmental organisations, including Greenpeace. Our paper procurement policy can be found at www.randomhouse.co.uk/environment

Typeset in Fournier by Palimpsest Book Production Ltd,
Falkirk, Stirlingshire
Printed and bound in Great Britain by Clays Ltd, St Ives PLC

For David Morrison, Barry Hoy and Kevin Steel.
Somewhere East of Suez.

Crimes as serious as murder should have strong emotions behind them.

George Orwell, *The Decline of the English Murder*

And nothing in life shall sever
The chain that is round us now.

Eton Boating Song

PROLOGUE

1988

When they had finished with her they left her face down on the mattress and it was as if she was already dead.

The pack of boys in the basement room, boys with the strength of men and the cruelty of children. They had taken all they wanted, and now it was as if there was nothing left.

Their voices were no longer in her face, leering above her, pressed hard against her ear. Now they were coming from the long dining table where they smoked and laughed and congratulated each other on what they had done.

There was her T-shirt. If she could only get her T-shirt. Somehow she found the strength to reach it, pull it on and roll from the mattress. She was not meant to stay in this room. She began to crawl towards the basement stairs.

The voices at the table fell silent. The pipe, she thought. The pipe makes them slow and stupid and sleepy. God bless the pipe.

There was blood in her mouth and her face hurt. Everything hurt. The blood was coming from her nose and it caught in her throat and made her choke back the sickness.

She stopped, gagged, then began to move again.

The muscles in her legs were heavy slabs of pain. Nothing worked as it should. Nothing felt like it would ever work again.

Everything was ruined.

She could have wept with frustration. But she bit back the tears and gritted her teeth and kept edging to the door, an inch at a time, no more than that, feeling the torn skin on her elbows and knees as she dragged them across the basement floor, doing it again and again and again.

There was evil in this room.

But she was not meant to die tonight.

She was not meant to die in this room.

At first she thought they hadn't noticed. Because of what the pipe did to them. Because of the way the pipe made them slow and stupid. God bless the pipe. Then she stopped to rest at the foot of the stairs and she heard their laughter.

And when she looked, she saw they were all watching her, and that they had been watching all along.

Some of them gave her a round of mocking applause.

Then the one who had been the worst, the fat one who had talked to her all the time, and called her names, and taken pleasure in hearing her cry out, and left his marks on her from tooth and nail – the worst bastard in that bunch of rotten bastards – he yawned widely, revealing a mouth full of expensive orthodontic work, and said, 'We can't just let her go, man.'

She took a deep breath and placed the palms of her hands on the bottom step.

There was something wrong with her breathing. Because of her nose.

A single bead of livid red blood fell on to the back of her hand.

She ran her fingers across her top lip and with great effort struggled from her hands and knees on to her feet, leaning against the wall, closing her eyes and longing for sleep.

The pain revived her.

And the fear.

And the presence of the boy.

One of them was standing right next to her, a look of wicked amusement on his face. The one who had spoken to her first, and stopped her with a smile, and pretended to be nice, and brought her to this place.

Now he took a fistful of her hair and pulled her head to one side. Then, tightening his grip as he turned away, he began to drag her from the stairs and back into the room, that underground room where she was not meant to die.

Without the prompting of conscious thought, her hands flew to his face and she pressed her thumbs into his eye sockets as hard as she could.

Deep and deep and deep.

His turn to feel the pain.

Rotten bastards. Rotten bastards the lot of them.

The two of them stood there, locked together in the intimacy of dance partners, his fist still in her hair while she summoned all her remaining strength to push into the mocking blue eyes, her fingers with their nails cracked and bloody and suddenly stinging as she scrabbled for purchase in his thick black hair, gripping his ears, losing the grip, finding it again, pushing the thumbs deeper, then her left hand falling away as he reeled backwards with a rising shriek of agony, lashing out at her, and missing, but her right thumb still there, still pushed into his left eye socket as he tried to shove her away, her thumb pressing against his eyeball for a few more crucial seconds until she suddenly felt it give with a soft wet squelch and sink towards the back of his head.

He screamed.

His scream filled the basement, filled her head, filled the

night. They were on their feet at the table but paralysed by the screams of the boy who had just lost an eye.

Then she ran.

How she ran.

Flying up the stairs.

The door locked from the inside but with the key mercifully still in the lock – *thank God for the key* – fumbling with it, the cries behind her, and then she was out into the air, stunned to find the night had almost gone.

How long had they kept her there?

In the distance was the road, on the far side of playing fields with a misty shroud hanging over the great white H-shapes of the rugby posts.

She began to run across the playing fields, the fog wet on her face, her bare feet sliding on grass slick with the dawn, and the beautiful buildings of the famous old school rising up black and timeless behind her.

She ran without looking back, expecting to hear their voices at any moment, waiting for the pack to come and run her down and rip her to pieces.

But they did not come.

On the far side of the playing fields there was a tiny stone cottage, as unlikely as a woodman's house in a fairy tale, but its lights were out and she made no attempt to run towards it. Instead she headed for the road. If she could make it to the road then she would not die tonight.

Halfway to the road, she rested against a rugby goalpost and dared to look back. They had not followed her.

A leather strap slapped against her side, and she remembered that at some point they had put a dog collar and lead around her neck. She tore them off and threw them aside.

A solitary car had stopped by the road, headlights on, engine running.

Someone had seen her.

She stumbled towards it, waving, calling, crying out for the car to please wait for her, don't-go-don't-go, running alongside a wire mesh fence, looking for a gap, the wet grass of the playing fields no longer under her bare feet, asphalt now, then through a hole in the fence and running on the road's rough tarmac, crying oh please don't go; and then the passenger door opened and the fat one got out, the one who had been the worst, his face not laughing now, but clenched with absolute murderous fury, and for the first time she knew with total certainty that she would die in this place tonight.

More of them were getting out of the car.

The fat one flipped open the boot and the black hole waited for her like an open grave.

Some part of her mind registered that someone was screaming in the back of the car, screaming about his eye.

The one she had hurt. The one she had blinded.

She wished she could have hurt them all. She wished she could have blinded them all. God knows they deserved it.

But it was too late. She was done now. She felt the weakness and exhaustion flood her body, overwhelming her. They had won.

Angry hands on her, touching her, squeezing the last juice out of her, and then the hands lifting her off the ground and forcing her into the boot of the car.

The lid slammed down on her and she was lost in darkness as the car drove slowly back to the grand old school where she would die on the mattress in the basement where she was never meant to die.

In her last moments she saw the family who would never see her again, and – beyond them, like a road briefly glimpsed but never taken – she saw quite clearly the husband she would never meet, and the children who would never be born, and the good life full of love that had been taken away.

And as her soul passed over, her last breath was a silent cry of rage and grief for everything they had stolen on the night she died.

OCTOBER

#killallpigs

1

I was waiting for a man who was planning to die.

I had parked the old BMW X5 just up the road from the entrance to the railway station and I drank a triple espresso as I watched the commuters rushing off to work. I drank quickly.

He would be here soon.

I placed three photographs on the dashboard. One of my wife and daughter. The other two of the man who was planning to die. A passport photo from the Home Office and what we called a snatch shot taken from some CCTV footage.

I slipped the photo of my family inside my wallet and put the wallet inside my leather jacket. Then I taped the two photos of the man who was planning to die to the dashboard.

And I watched the street.

I was parked with my back to the station so I could face the busy main road. It was washed in thin autumn sunshine that was like a fading memory of summer days. One hundred metres away there was a young woman who was dressed for the gym looking in the window of the newsagent's, a large German Shepherd sitting patiently by her side, its lead loose, its intelligent face carefully watching her, the dog totally at ease among the rush hour crowds.

'Now that's a beautiful dog,' I said.

The woman smiled and scratched the back of the dog's ears

in response, and then there was a man's voice in my ear, although he was not addressing me.

'Reception's good for Delta 1.'

Then there were more voices in my ear as they checked transmission for the other radio call signs and all over the surveillance chatter I could hear the studied calm that the police use at moments of extreme tension, like a pilot talking to his passengers when all his engines are on fire. Nothing at all to worry about, folks.

I scanned the street for the spotter vans and unmarked cars and plainclothes officers on foot. But they were good at their job. All I could see was the woman with the beautiful German Shepherd.

'Delta 1?' the surveillance officer said to me. 'We see you and we hear you, Max. You're running point. We're waiting on your positive visual ID when Bravo 1 is in the grab zone. Stay in the car.'

Bravo 1 was the man who was planning to die.

'Copy that,' I said.

And then a voice I knew: 'DC Wolfe, it's the chief super.'

Detective Chief Superintendent Elizabeth Swire. My boss.

'Ma'am,' I said.

'Good luck, Wolfe,' she said. Then there was a little smile in her voice as she played to the gallery: 'And you heard the man. Stay in the car. Let the big boys do the heavy lifting.'

I stared at the street. It would not be long now.

'Ma'am,' I said, as nice and calm as the German Shepherd.

If I tilted my rear-view mirror I could look up at the grand Victorian façade of the station hotel. It was like a castle in a fairy story, the turrets and spires rising up to a blue sky full of billowy white clouds. The kind of place where you blink your eye and a hundred years go by. I could not see any of the big boys. But inside the railway station hotel there were enough of them to start a small war.

Somewhere beyond the net curtains and drapes, SCO19 were waiting, the firearms unit of the Metropolitan Police. Every one of them would be armed with a Heckler & Koch G36 assault rifle and two Glock SLP 9mm pistols. But no matter how hard I stared I still couldn't see them.

There would also be bomb disposal squads seconded from the RAF in there. Negotiators. Chemical and biological warfare specialists. And someone to order pizza. We also had maybe twenty people around the station but I could still only see the woman and the dog. The surveillance chatter continued.

'All units report. Echo 1?'

'No sign.'

'Victor 1?'

'Nothing.'

'Tango 1?'

'Contact,' said a woman's voice.

For the first time the piece of plastic stuffed in my ear was totally silent.

'I have visual with Bravo 1,' said the same voice. 'Contact.' And then a terrible pause. 'Possible,' she said. 'Repeat – possible contact.'

'Possible,' the surveillance officer said. 'Checking. Stand by.' His voice was winding tighter now.

And then the woman's voice again, and all the doubt creeping in: 'Possible. Red backpack. Just passing the British Library. Proceeding on foot in an easterly direction towards the station. Approaching the grab zone.'

'Delta 1?'

'Copy that,' I said.

'And I'm off,' Tango 1 said, meaning she had lost visual contact with the target.

I glanced quickly at the two photographs taped to my dashboard. I didn't really need to because I knew exactly what he looked like. But I looked one last time anyway. Then back at the crowds.

'I don't see him,' I said.

Then a more urgent voice in my ear. Another woman. The officer with the dog. It watched her intently as her mouth moved.

'This is Whisky 1, Whisky 1. I have possible visual contact. Bravo 1 coming now. Two hundred metres. Far side of the road. Easterly direction. Red backpack. Possible contact.'

A babble of voices and a sharp call for silence.

'Possible. Checking. Checking. Stand by, all units. Stand by, Delta 1.'

Then there was just the silence, crackling with static. Waiting for me now.

At first I stared straight through him.

Because he was different.

I looked quickly at the two photographs on the dashboard and he was nothing like them. The black hair was light brown. The wispy beard had gone. But it was far more than that. His face had changed. It was filled out, puffed up, almost the face of someone else.

But one thing was the same.

'Delta 1?'

'Contact,' I said.

The red backpack was exactly the same as the one in the CCTV snatch shot on the day he bought hydrogen peroxide in a chemist's wholesale warehouse.

He was wearing that red backpack when he wheeled out the 440 litres of hair bleach to the cash desk. Wearing it when he counted out the £550 in fifty-pound notes. Wearing it when he unloaded his van at the lock-up garage where we had put our cameras.

You couldn't miss that red backpack. It looked like the kind of bag you would use to climb Everest. Big and bright – safety red, they called that colour.

But his face was not the same. That threw me. It was meant to. The face had been pumped full of something. He was planning to go to his death with the face of another man.

But I could see it now.

There was no doubt.

'That's him,' I said. 'Contact. He's had something done. I don't know. Some work to his face. But that's him. Contact. Confirming visual identification. Contact.'

'Sniper 1 in range,' said a voice, and across the street I saw the shooters for the first time, three figures moving on the rooftops above a shabby strip of shops and restaurants, their weapons winking in the sunlight. Police marksmen, settling into position.

Our last resort, if it all went wrong. And it was already starting to go wrong.

'Sniper 2 in range. But I don't have a trigger. No clear shot. It's crowded down there.'

The man with the red backpack had paused on the far side of the road, waiting for the lights to change. Traffic thundered by, and in the gaps there were flashes of safety red. I touched my earpiece. Suddenly nobody was talking to me any more.

'That's our boy,' I said. 'Positive ID. Contact. Contact. Over.'

The lights changed and the traffic reluctantly stopped. The commuters began to shuffle across the road. The man with the red backpack went with them.

I spoke slowly and clearly: 'This is Delta 1 confirming contact. The target is about to enter the grab zone. Do you copy me? Over.'

And nothing but the white noise in response.

And then: 'Possible. Checking. Stand by.'

I shook my head and was about to speak again when the calm voice of DCS Swire said, 'It's a negative, Wolfe. That's not him. Negative. Cancel.'

And then the voice of the surveillance officer: 'Negative. Cancel. Stand down all stations.'

The lights changed again.

The man with the red backpack had crossed the road.

He was heading for the railway station.

'Do you expect him to wear a burka?' I said. 'That's Bravo 1. That's the target. That's our boy. His face—'

'We do not have visual confirmation,' the surveillance officer said. 'We do not have positive ID, Delta 1.'

And then Swire. 'That's not him,' she repeated. 'Stop talking, Wolfe.' A note of steel now. 'You had one task. It is concluded. No further action necessary. We're standing down all units. Negative. Cancel. Thank you everyone.'

The crowd slowed outside the station as it merged with the flow of commuters coming over from King's Cross. I figured that I had one minute to stop him before he disappeared inside the station. Once on a mainline train or down on the tube or on the concourse of the station itself, the man with the red backpack would simply touch his hands together and the world would blow apart.

The battery he probably already held in one hand would create an electric current connecting it to a simple terminal held in the other. The current would then pass down two wires and into that red backpack – a discreet slit would have been cut in the side – where a modified light bulb would trip a detonator stored inside a small tube. This would trigger the main charge – the hydrogen peroxide I had watched him buy with eleven £50 notes on CCTV.

At the same time he had bought a bulk supply of six-inch steel nails. Sacks of them. They would be taped to the outside of the main charge to inflict enough misery to last for several hundred lifetimes.

If it detonated.

If he was that smart.

If he hadn't messed up the cook.

I choked down a lump of hot bitter nausea as it rose in my throat.

'You're wrong,' I said. 'That's him. Contact.'

I had been inside his lock-up. I had seen the hundreds of empty bottles of hair bleach. I had watched the CCTV footage of the day he bought them until my eyes were burning with the sight of him.

I didn't need the photographs taped to the dash. I knew him. He was in my head.

He could not hide from me.

'Stand down all units,' a self-consciously calm voice was saying. 'Do you copy me, Delta 1?'

'No,' I said. 'You're breaking up.'

Thirty seconds now.

And among all those crowds, and surrounded by all those firearms, I was on my own with the man who was planning to die.

* * *

I once attended a lecture at the police academy in Bramshill, Hampshire – the Oxford and Cambridge of police higher education.

An FBI agent had been flown over to help us combat terrorism. I had been impressed by the whiteness of the agent's teeth. They were a fine set of teeth. Very American teeth. But what impressed me more was that the man knew his business.

His teeth shining, he told us that the FBI had identified twenty-five threat areas for terrorist activity. It wasn't quite an A to Z, but it was close – it was an A to T, from airports to tattoo parlours.

Everywhere, basically.

The Fed also suggested what possible terrorists might look like.

Everyone, basically.

The students at Bramshill, the brightest and the best, all these fast-tracked cops, the next generation of CID, young and tough and smart, had almost wet themselves with laughter. But unlike the rest of them, I did not find the talk useless. Just the opposite. Because I remembered the FBI man's number one point of potential indicators.

The suspect significantly alters his appearance.

Although my colleagues had smirked and rolled their eyes, I thought that was a point well worth making. Never overlook the obvious. Don't expect him to look like the photographs and the CCTV images. Be ready for him to look like someone else.

And here was another thing the FBI agent could have mentioned. The target who significantly alters his appearance will probably not bother to get a new bag.

* * *

'The same backpack,' I said, opening the car door. 'In the CCTV. Red backpack. When he bought the gear. Red backpack. All the way through. That's the red backpack. And that's him.'

'You can't park here, mate,' an Afro-Cockney voice said through my window, and I jumped to hear a voice that did not come from somewhere inside my head.

A traffic warden was writing me a parking ticket. I got out of the car. He was a tall man with West African tribal scars on his cheeks, and he reared back slightly, expecting trouble. I looked past him and could see the man with the red backpack.

The crowds had thinned now.

He was about to enter the station.

Fifteen seconds.

Then a voice inside my head: 'This is DCS Swire. Get back in the bloody car, Wolfe.'

All pretence at calm now gone.

I hesitated for a moment.

Then I got back into the car.

The traffic warden was tucking a ticket under my windscreen wiper. I shook my head and looked in the rear-view mirror. The man with the red backpack was directly behind me now, standing right outside the main entrance to the station. The crowds were melting away. There was nothing stopping him entering. But he had paused directly outside the station.

He was talking to himself.

No.

He was praying.

Ten seconds.

The man with the red backpack moved forward.

Nine seconds.

I stuck the car into reverse.

Eight seconds.

I twisted in my seat and slammed my foot to the ground.

The car shot backwards and I stared at the man with the red backpack as I hurtled towards him. I had one arm braced across the passenger seat for the shock of impact and the hand on the wheel pressed down hard on the horn, keeping it there, scattering the stray commuters.

He did not move.

But he looked into my eyes as the old X5 shot towards him, his mouth no longer praying.

Five seconds.

The car ploughed into him, striking him just above the kneecaps, shattering the thigh bones of both legs as it whipped his torso forward against the back of the car. His face shattered the rear window and the rear window did the same to his face.

Then the impact threw him backwards into a wall of red Victorian brick where the back of his head erupted like a soft-boiled egg being hit with a sledgehammer.

Three seconds.

I stuck the car in drive and tore back across the forecourt to where the traffic warden was staring at me, motionless, open-mouthed, his ticket machine still in his hand.

I put the car into reverse, ready to go again.

But there was no need to go again.

Zero.

I slowly got out of the car.

People were screaming. Some of them were commuters. Some of them were the voices in my head. A dog, getting closer every second, was barking wildly.

One voice in my ear was shouting about gross misconduct and manslaughter. Another was shouting about murder.

'*Wolfe!*'

Swire.

I tore out the earpiece and threw it away.

The man with the red backpack was sitting up against the brick wall, staring straight at me with a baffled expression on his ruined face. One hand still twitched with the surprise of sudden death. Both of his hands were empty.

I was not expecting his hands to be empty.

Suddenly there were armed men in balaclavas. Guns were trained on the dead man. Glock SLP 9mm pistols. Heckler & Koch submachine guns. Then I saw that some of them were pointing at me.

'He was the target,' I said.

Armed officers from SCO19 were everywhere. Commuters were running and crawling for cover. A lot of people were screaming and crying because these men with guns did not look remotely like police officers. They wore Kevlar body armour. They had metal carabiners on their shoulders so they could more easily be dragged away if they were down. The black balaclavas they wore had the eyes and mouths cut out. They looked like paramilitary bank robbers.

People thought it was to protect their identity but I knew it was to spread terror.

And it worked.

They were shouting into the radios attached just above their hearts. The masked faces were bawling at me to get down and stay down and lie on my face.

Now. Now. Now. Do it now!

Slowly I took my warrant card out of my jeans, showed it,

and tossed it at them. Then I held up my hands. But I wasn't getting on my knees for them. I wasn't getting down on my face. I kept walking towards the man on the ground.

Because I had to know if I was right.

Last chance! Do it now!

Crouching above the dead man on the ground, I saw that the impact had not cracked the back of his skull. It had removed it.

A huge slick of fresh blood was already spreading across the pavement.

All around there were the screams of terror and fury. The dog was so close now that I could smell it, so close now that I could feel its breath.

I could see the strange flat-nosed Glocks in the corner of my vision, aimed at the dead man on the ground and also at my face. The safety catches were released.

But this was our boy, wasn't it?

I looked at my hands with wonder.

They were covered in the dead man's blood.

But they were not shaking as I tore open the red backpack and looked inside.

2

'Sorry,' I said, my body clenched tight inside the suit I had not worn since my wedding day.

The office was crowded with the full cast of a murder investigation. A SOCO was standing directly in front of me, trying to get past, all in white apart from the blue facemask that covered everything but the irritation in her eyes. I was in a big corner room near the top of a shining glass tower, but I flashed briefly on the many school playgrounds of my childhood, and how you can feel both invisible and in the way just because you are new.

And then there was a spark of recognition in the SOCO's eyes.

'I know you,' she said.

'I'm the new man,' I said.

'No,' she said. 'You're the hero. At the railway station. When did you start working Homicide?'

'Today.'

Now she was smiling behind her blue facemask.

'Cool. What did they call you in court?'

'Officer A.'

'You kill anybody this week, Officer A?'

'Not yet,' I said. 'But it's only Monday morning.'

She laughed and left me standing by the dead man's

desk. There wasn't much on it. Just fresh blood and an old photograph.

In the photograph, seven young men in military uniform smiled for the camera as if they were looking at their unbreakable future. Blood had splattered across one corner of the glass. But it did nothing to hide their cocky faces.

It was a strange photograph to have on an office desk. No wife, no kids, no dog. Just seven young soldiers, defaced now with a bright spurt of blood.

Travel blood. Fresh from an artery.

I looked closer and saw the photograph was taken in the eighties, judging by the washed-out colours and the mullet haircuts of the cocky lads. Their hair was from another decade and their uniforms were from another century. They looked like Duran Duran at Waterloo.

And I saw that they were not men. These were boys who would be boys for perhaps one more summer. And despite the military uniforms, they were not real soldiers. Just students dressed as soldiers. Two of them looked like twins. One of them was the dead man on the far side of the desk. He had grown up to be a banker. He had grown up to be murdered.

I stood aside as a forensic photographer started taking pictures of the desk's bloody mess.

'Who would want to kill a banker?' the photographer said.

It got a laugh. Mostly among the SOCOs, chuckling away behind their facemasks. Spend your life collecting microscopic samples of blood, semen and dirt and you are grateful for any laugh you can get. But the senior detective standing on the far side of the desk did not smile, although I could not tell if he had not heard the remark, or if he was preoccupied with the corpse before him, or if he disapproved of levity in the presence of death.

He was waiting patiently while a small man with a briefcase – the divisional surgeon, here to pronounce death – knelt over the body.

The detective's large head was shaved so clean it shined, and despite his extravagantly broken nose – and it had been broken so often that it looked like a wonky ski run – he had enough vanity to keep his pale goatee beard neatly trimmed.

He turned his piercing blue eyes on me and I thought that he looked like a Viking. I could imagine that pale, fierce face coming up the beach for a spot of pillaging and monk bothering. But Vikings didn't wear glasses and the detective's were round and rimless, John Lennon Imagine specs; they softened his ferocious appearance and gave his hard face a kindly, slightly perplexed expression.

My new boss.

'DC Wolfe, sir,' I said.

'Ah, our new man,' he said, the quiet voice precise and clipped with the vowels of the distant north, Aberdeen or beyond, the kind of Highlands accent that sounds as if every word is carved from granite. 'I'm DCI Mallory.'

I already knew his name. I had never met him before but I had heard of him enough. Detective Chief Inspector Victor Mallory was one of the reasons I wanted the transfer to Homicide and Serious Crime Command.

We were both wearing thin blue gloves and made no attempt to reach across the desk and shake hands. But we smiled, and took a second to size each other up.

DCI Mallory looked very fit, not just for a man in his early fifties but for a man of any age, and it looked like the kind of fitness that comes from natural athleticism rather than hours in the gym. He watched me with his blue eyes as the divisional surgeon fussed briskly over the corpse.

'You're just in time,' Mallory said. 'We're about to begin. Welcome to Homicide.'

Friendly, but skipping all small talk.

The divisional surgeon was standing up.

'He's dead all right,' he said, snapping his bag shut.

Mallory thanked him and gave me the nod. I stepped forward. 'Come and have a look at our body, Wolfe,' he said, 'and tell me if you've ever seen anything like it.'

I joined DCI Mallory on the far side of the desk and we stood above the dead man. At first all I saw was the blood. Lavish arterial sprays with a man in a shirt and tie somewhere beneath it all.

'The deceased is Hugo Buck,' Mallory said. 'Thirty-five years old. Investment banker with ChinaCorps. Body discovered by cleaning staff at six a.m. He gets in early. Works with the Asian markets. While he was having his first coffee, somebody cut his throat.' Mallory looked at me keenly. 'Ever seen one of these?'

I did not know how to respond.

The banker's throat had been more than cut. It had been ripped wide open. The front half of his neck was cleaved away, sliced out with clean precision. He was flat on his back but it felt like only a bit of bony gristle was keeping his head attached to his body. The blood had erupted from his neck in great spurts; his shirt and tie looked like some monstrous red bib. I could smell it now, the copper stink of freshly spilt blood. I shut my mind to it.

Hugo Buck's jacket was still on the back of his chair. Somehow the fountains of blood had not touched it.

I looked quickly at Mallory and then back at the dead man.

'I've seen three cut throats, sir,' I said.

I hesitated and he nodded once, telling me to carry on.

'First week in uniform, there was a husband who saw a text message on his wife's phone from his best friend and reached for a carving knife. Maybe a year later I attended a robbery in a jewellery shop where a gun failed to discharge and the thief produced an axe and went for the man who pushed the security button. And then there was a wedding reception where the father of the bride objected to the best man's speech and shoved a champagne flute into his neck. Three cut throats.'

'Did any of them look anything like this?'

'No, sir.'

'This is almost a decapitation,' Mallory said.

I looked around.

'Somebody must have heard something,' I said.

'Nobody heard a thing,' Mallory said. 'There are people around in a building like this even at that time of day. But nobody hears a thing when a man almost gets his head chopped off.'

He considered me with his pale blue eyes. But I didn't get it.

'Because the victim's windpipe was cut,' he said. 'The trachea. There was no air. And you need air to scream. Nobody heard anything because there was nothing to hear.'

We contemplated the body in silence while all over the large office the SOCOs moved in slow motion like scientists examining the aftermath of a biological catastrophe. They were identical in their masks and gloves and white suits, patiently hunting for prints, placing tiny fibres in evidence bags and taking samples of blood from the desk, the carpet and the glass walls. There was a lot of blood to choose from. One SOCO was drawing a sketch. The photographer who had wondered why anyone would want to kill a banker had stopped taking stills and was now filming the room. Small numbered yellow plastic markers were blooming all over the lush carpet as SOCOs harvested footprints for forensics to match against SICAR, the Shoeprint Image Capture and Retrieval database.

Mallory watched them. 'Most professional hits are very amateur, Wolfe. Is that an irony or a paradox? They're carried out by thugs hired in the pub. Morons who will kill anyone for some cash in hand. Most professional hits come with a guarantee – they guarantee to do it badly. But not this one. You see how clean that cut is? Most people, cutting someone's throat, they slash and chop and saw. They make a mess, don't they? You saw that with your three. About as big a mess as an enraged human being can make to flesh and blood with something sharp. But this looks like just one cut. It almost took his head off, but it's just one cut. Now who cuts a throat like that?'

'Someone who knew what they were doing.' I thought about it. 'A butcher. A surgeon. A soldier.'

'You think we've got Rambo running around out there?'

'I don't know if he's running around, sir. Maybe he's sleeping on the streets.'

Mallory nodded beyond the glass walls to the city thirty floors below, spangled with autumn sunshine around the old grey serpent of a river.

'How many ex-servicemen are sleeping on those streets?' he asked.

'Too many,' I said. I tried to imagine it. 'He comes in here during the night. To find somewhere warm to sleep. To find something worth stealing. Gets disturbed.' I couldn't make it work. 'But he has to get past security.'

'Butcher, surgeon, soldier,' Mallory said. 'Or perhaps it was someone who had no idea what they were doing. One of Mr Buck's fellow bankers. One of the cleaning staff. Perhaps it was just beginner's luck. Or perhaps it was his wife. Apparently she didn't like him much. Officers were called out to a domestic dispute between Mr and Mrs Buck three nights ago. There was some violence. Did you see the marital bed?'

A mattress was leaning against one of the glass walls, a king-sized bed still wrapped in courier's cellophane and bearing the purple and orange FedEx markings.

'That's their bed?' I said. 'His wife sent their bed to his office?'

'Mrs Buck returned home early from a business trip and discovered Mr Buck with the housekeeper.' Mallory frowned with embarrassed disapproval. 'And he wasn't helping her to unload the dishwasher. So Mrs Buck went for Mr Buck with an oyster knife.'

'An oyster knife?'

'Yes, an oyster knife. It has a short, broad blade. These are affluent people. They like oysters. Anyway, she threatened to cut his testicles off and shove them up his back passage. Responding to sounds of a violent struggle, the neighbours call 999. Officers restrain both of them. Mr Buck hasn't slept at home since.'

We looked at the marital bed in its FedEx wrapping.

'You think the wife did this, sir?' I said.

Mallory shrugged. 'Right now she's all we've got. She's on record as making a threat to remove her husband's testicles.'

He looked down at the banker's mutilated throat. 'Although nobody's aim is that bad.'

'She may have delegated,' I said. 'She has the money to hire someone good.'

'That was my thought,' Mallory agreed. 'But then there would be glove prints. And we can't find any glove prints. And unless she hired someone who didn't have any idea what they were doing, there should certainly be glove prints in this room. As you know, glove prints can be as distinctive as fingerprints. If the gloves are thin enough, fingerprints can pass through the material. Fingerprints can also be present inside the gloves. Few villains take their gloves home, preferring to ditch them close to the crime scene. So we're looking for a pair of gloves as well as glove prints.'

'And what happens if we can't find glove prints?'

'Then we have to eliminate every print in the room.'

I looked again at the photograph on the desk. And I could see it now – the boy the man had been. Hugo Buck was standing on the far right of the photograph and one tiny spot from the spray of blood had flecked his image. Twenty years had gone by but the smooth good looks of the future banker were there, buried under a shallow layer of puppy fat. The boys become the men, I thought, and the living become the dead.

'Did you see his hands?' Mallory said.

Buck's hands had fallen by his side but still gripped the vial of pills he had been holding in the last moment of his life. It was another thing I was seeing for the first time.

'Cadaveric spasm,' Mallory said. Smiling now, perhaps happy to show me that I hadn't seen everything yet. That I hadn't seen anything yet. 'Instant rigor, caused by shock of sudden death, locking the body in its final second of life. That Pompeii moment. Can you make the pills out?'

I crouched by the corpse and peered at the label, trying to shut out the copper stink of his blood.

'Zestoretic,' I read. 'Take one daily as directed. Prescription only. Made out to Mr Hugo Randolph Buck. Zestoretic?'

'For hypertension,' Mallory replied. 'Blood pressure pills.'

'He was a bit young to be taking blood pressure pills, wasn't he?' I said, standing up. 'Must be a lot of stress working in banking.'

'And more stress at home,' Mallory added.

We stared at the dead man in silence.

'Why didn't they just shoot him?' Mallory asked suddenly.

I looked at him. 'The banker?'

'The bomber,' Mallory said. 'Your bomber. The chief super panics. The surveillance officer freezes. Nobody's sure if it's the man they want. I understand all of that. Nobody wants Jean Charles de Menezes on their CV. Everyone's jumpy because any fatal shooting has to go before an IPCC inquiry now. You've got the Crown Prosecution Service waiting in the wings. The human rights lawyers.' Mallory smiled shyly, blue eyes twinkling. 'But you confirmed a positive ID. You overruled the surveillance officer. It was your call. You had seen the man. Watched him. Followed him. Studied him. It was your career on the line. Your liberty. Why didn't they shoot him?'

'They can only shoot him in the head, sir,' I said. 'New rules of engagement. Everything else is too risky. Can't shoot him in the torso because he could be wearing a vest. Can't shoot him in the arms or legs because then he still has a chance to detonate whatever he's carrying.' I shrugged. 'Maybe they didn't feel confident they could get a clean head shot. Maybe they believed the SO and the chief super and not me. All I can say is, there was a genuine element of doubt. And maybe shooting a man in the head when there was an element of doubt seemed . . . rash.'

Mallory nodded. 'And maybe we're becoming afraid to do our job. How do you like this for a robbery?'

'This wasn't robbery,' I said. 'The Rolex on Mr Buck's wrist has to be worth fifteen grand.'

'Unless it was a robbery that was disturbed,' Mallory said.

I looked beyond the banker's door to the vast open-plan office.

'This place must take some cleaning,' I said.

'All authorised personnel,' Mallory said. 'You can't take a leak in this building without a laminated card and photo ID. We're waiting for a translator so we can interview the cleaner who found Mr Buck. He's fresh from Vilnius.'

'I thought everyone spoke English now.'

'He can't speak it today. Just Lithuanian. Finding the body shook him up. The rest of the cleaning staff are down in the underground car park. We can't let them go until we've had a word. My two DIs are down there – Detective Inspector Gane and Detective Inspector Whitestone. If you can give them a hand . . .'

'Yes, sir,' I said.

At the door of the banker's office two uniformed officers had established an entry and exit corridor where they logged everyone who came and went from the crime scene. Two PCs, one male and one female, both young, both of them with dark red hair. They could have been brother and sister despite the fact that the woman was small and whippet-thin, and the man tall and gangly. From the state of them they had to be the officers who had answered the call.

The man – a boy, I thought, although he was in his mid-twenties and only a few years younger than me – looked on the verge of passing out. As I approached he leaned against the wall and choked back the urge to be sick. The woman – and she looked like a girl, despite the Metropolitan Police uniform – placed one small hand on her colleague's shoulder.

She looked up at me as I signed out of the crime scene.

'His first body, sir,' she explained, almost apologetic. She hesitated for a moment. 'Mine, too.'

She was dealing with it better than the boy. But both of their startled faces were wide open and frozen with shock, like children who had just come downstairs and found their pet dead in its cage, or seen through Santa's disguise, and got their first real glimpse of this wicked world.

'Breathe,' I told him. I inhaled deeply through my nose, released it through my mouth with a controlled sigh. Showing him how to do it.

'Sir,' he said.

There were six lifts for the office workers and one, much larger and much dirtier, for the help. I took the stairs, thinking I might find gloves. Thirty flights. By the time I was halfway down I was starting to sweat but my breathing was still even.

I stopped at a sound in the stairwell, a hundred metres below.

Looking down, I glimpsed a blur of movement. There was the hint of a shadow and then a distant door slammed shut. I called out but there was no response and I took the final flights more slowly, stopping when I saw something written on the wall.

One word in black.
The shade of black that blood dries to.

P I G

Not taking my eyes from the three letters, I took out my phone and photographed the black word on the filthy wall. Then I went down the rest of the stairs, hearing a babble of voices now, rising up from below ground, the sound getting louder every second.

On the basement floor I shoved open the door and looked out at an underground car park that was full of cleaning staff. They had been invisible from the street. Men and women, young and old, talking in twenty different languages, the unseen people who came every day to clean the floors and the windows and the toilets in the shining glass tower.

And I saw that they were beyond number.

The armies of the poor.

3

When I arrived home that night I knew something was wrong even before I got through the front door.

We lived in a big top-floor loft and the stench filled every corner of it. I knew immediately where the stink came from because the clues were everywhere. A single shoe in the hallway, studded with teeth marks. Wooden floorboards that had been scrubbed clean to conceal evidence. A rubbish bin stuffed with stained kitchen roll. And everywhere there was that smell, meaty and musty and peaty. The smell of animal.

The dog had been bad again.

On the far side of the loft an elderly woman with white hair was sitting at one end of a sofa with a little red dog on her lap. At the other end of the sofa was a fresh wet stain that would now be there for ever.

Mrs Murphy was watching TV with the sound turned off, which was always her custom when my daughter Scout was sleeping.

Without moving his tennis ball-sized head from his front paws, the red dog – Stan was his name – rolled his huge round eyes up to look at me. You could see the whites of his bulging eyes around the blackness, as though the sockets were too small to contain such a pair of headlamps.

He caught my eye and quickly looked away.

'Mrs Murphy,' I said, 'you've had so much work again.'

'Don't worry none,' she said, scratching the dog behind his ears, her soft accent sounding as if she had never left County Cork a lifetime ago. 'Stan's still little. And the good news is that Scout ate her dinner. Some of it, anyway. She doesn't eat much, does she? There's nothing of her.'

I nodded and went off to look in on my daughter.

Scout was five years old and still slept in the baby fashion with her hands held up in loose fists by the side of her head, like a tiny weightlifter. The light was on in her room, although she must have been sleeping for hours.

She had slept with the light on ever since we lost her mother.

I picked up a school sweater from the floor, folded it and placed it on the back of a chair where Mrs Murphy had tomorrow's school uniform all neatly folded and waiting. I hesitated, wanting to turn off her light. She couldn't keep it on for ever. But in the end, I didn't have the nerve.

Mrs Murphy was putting on her coat.

'It will get better,' she told me.

I woke before dawn.

I always woke before dawn.

In the dreaming period of sleep, the lightest phase of sleep, REM sleep, I surfaced, waking on my side of the double bed, the left side, chased from my rest by yesterday's coffee and my dreams of the dead.

I was always right there waiting for the day before the day ever had a chance to begin.

Turning off my alarm before it had the chance to ring, I slipped out of bed without making a sound. I brushed my teeth and went back into the bedroom, got down on my hands and knees and quickly pumped out twenty-five press-ups. Then I sipped the water by my bedside, looking out of the window at the October sky – six in the morning and still black over the nearby dome of St Paul's Cathedral.

I got down and did twenty-five more press-ups, slower and more deliberate this time, thinking about technique. I gave myself a minute's break then did twenty-five more, starting to feel it now, my arms shaking with the build-up of lactic acid in the muscles. I stayed on the ground, found my breath and forced out the final twenty-five – an act of will, not strength.

I padded quietly to the kitchen, anxious not to wake daughter or dog, but hearing Stan breathing in the dark, a snorting, snuffling sound coming out of a nose that did not really resemble anything up to the difficult task of breathing. I stood there listening to him, enjoying the sound. He was wiped out after another busy night destroying our home. Then he stirred at my presence, the large ears falling across his face like silky curtains, the soulful eyes blinking open and glittering behind his lavish ears. And then he was awake too, staring at me through the bars of his cage, hopeful of an early release.

I got him out. Held him against my chest. Stan pressing a nose like a squashed prune against my fingers, sniffing them with interest.

Stan had been with us for a month (it felt much longer) – my present to Scout on her fifth birthday. I had found the breeder online, collected Stan on the day he turned eight weeks old, and carried him into the loft with a blanket over his head like a guilty man heading for the high court.

Every time I thought I had made a mistake, that the dog was my pitiful attempt to give Scout a proper family life, I remembered the first time she had seen Stan. Her smile was like the sun coming up. That's how I knew the dog was not a mistake.

In the kitchen I drank a triple espresso with him on my lap, the only light coming from my laptop as I searched medical sites for information on how to cut a windpipe.

Stan went back to sleep as I learned that either side of the windpipe are the carotid arteries, bringing blood from the heart to the brain, and that severing them is one of the most fatal head injuries known to man.

But no matter how many surgical websites I looked at, and no matter how many times I typed 'cut throat' into the search engine, I could find no weapon that looked remotely capable of doing the job.

In the end the search engine gave up on me, directing me to shaving websites where they sold foam, balm, gel and a variety of old-fashioned straight razors. They were interesting-looking blades, vicious enough to put a smile on Sweeney Todd's face. But I couldn't see how any of them could have cut deep enough to remove most of Hugo Buck's throat.

At seven the sky finally started to lighten. I snapped shut the laptop as Scout appeared, padding into the kitchen still in her pyjamas and puffy with sleep.

Stan struggled down from my lap and flew at her. Our loft was huge. Far too big for a man, child and dog. Our family had grown smaller while the loft seemed to get bigger. Now we rattled around in all that empty space under the exposed wooden beams and brickwork, the dog's paws skidding on the polished wooden floorboards as he chased towards Scout, sniffing and licking and nuzzling, clambering up her leg, crazy with love.

'Stan was bad,' she said, absent-mindedly scratching the top of his small head.

'I know.'

'On the sofa.'

'I saw.'

'And in the kitchen. And by the door.' She thought about it. 'Everywhere really.'

'Mrs Murphy took care of it.'

'I helped her.'

'Thank you for that.'

A pause.

'Do we have to give him back?' she said.

I squatted down to be level with her head. Her light brown hair, her dark brown eyes, the sweeping curve of her face – they all came straight from her mother. Even her name was from a character in a book that my wife loved. My wife was gone, but every time I looked at my daughter, I saw her face.

'This is our dog,' I said, and found myself quoting Mrs Murphy. 'It will all get better, OK?'

'OK.'

We slipped into our breakfast routine. Toast for Scout. Porridge for me. Nature's Menu dog food for Stan. After carrying her plate to the sink, Scout went off to brush her teeth. That had been one of her mother's rules – teeth are brushed after the meal, not before, and we really did our best to stick to her rules.

We lived opposite the great old meat market of Smithfield. At this time of the morning, the men were ending their long night shift. The butchers and porters were finishing the last of their loading and making their way to cafés and pubs that had opened long before dawn. A few were already outside the early morning pubs with pints of lager in their red fists, big men wilting in the daylight and blurry with exhaustion, white aprons smeared with blood and gore. As we walked through their world, some called out a greeting to Stan, and Scout and I smiled with pride.

He was a striking dog. In the pale daylight you could see the beauty of his colour – a rich chestnut somewhere between rusty red and old gold. His fur was wavy, and on the tips of those oversized ears there were ringlets of extravagant curls, as though he'd spent the previous evening with a fancy hair-dresser rather than urinating on our furniture. Held in check by Scout, who had his leather lead wrapped twice around the wrist of her right hand, Stan trotted happily by her side, his small head up and alert, his tail stiff with anticipation and then whipping like a windscreen wiper in a thunderstorm when something caught his eye.

And Stan was amazed by everything. He stared with awe at a porter across the street having a cigarette outside the market. A jogger went by and Stan stood stock still, his head tilted to one side, as if witnessing an alien landing. Scout and I laughed. Most of our laughs came from the dog. He looked at a piece of chewing gum, or a discarded cup, or a shard of broken glass, and instantly lurched towards it, dragging Scout with him.

The sun was up now and making me squint: fresh autumn light can be more crystal clear than summer's haze. I felt the rawness of the day and the bad sleeper's burden – the knowledge that every hour would have its own weight and no amount of coffee would ever take the place of lost sleep. Yet I still needed more coffee, immediately.

There was an all-night stall near the market, serving mostly black cab drivers and meat porters, and I got in line while men with shaved heads and fierce faces fussed over the chestnut-coloured dog at my daughter's feet. Stan leapt like a salmon, overcome with excitement, and they laughed, all the hard men of the London night, and I was happy then, knowing that our dog had yet to learn fear.

As we neared the school gates Scout fell into step with another little girl. The girl's mother turned away to talk to another mother and I waited at the gates with Stan and soothed him as he whimpered to see Scout leave. We waited in case she turned round to wave but she was with her friend now and she had forgotten all about us.

Before she disappeared into her own world I reflected that her school uniform was too big and it would be too big for a long time.

Mrs Murphy was right. There was almost nothing of my daughter.

There was almost nothing of her, and she was my everything.

Hugo Buck's home was in a portered apartment overlooking Regent's Park.

The porter must have been on his tea break when I got there because the double glass doors were locked. I stood outside, leaning on the bell and watching the dogs in the park. They were all off lead. Big, good-looking dogs, Labradors and Retrievers and Airedales, and some small fry, Beagles and Westies, all of them panting and confident as they sniffed piles of leaves and each other, coming back when their owner called. I could not imagine a time when Stan would come when I called.

'Detective?'

A young woman and man in their twenties were walking towards me. I had clocked the pair of them when I was parking, taken them for a couple of local rich kids. A pair of good-looking scruffs, carefully unkempt, passing a single cigarette between them as they sat on a low wall by the manicured gardens. Only the children of the wealthy can afford to be that laid back at that age.

On the driveway there was a chauffeur lounging in a big black Merc, squeezed in tight between a couple of Porsche 911s, and he eyed up the girl as he played with his peaked cap. I saw now the young guy had a camera slung around his neck. Press, then, I thought. It was the girl who did the talking.

'You're here to speak to Mrs Buck? Is she a suspect? Do you expect to make an arrest soon?'

I pressed my thumb on the buzzer and left it there.

'Is this a hate crime, detective?'

I looked at her.

'Every murder is a hate crime,' I said. 'Who did you say you write for?'

'I didn't,' she said.

She dug a card out of her bag, and when she gave it to me I saw that there was a tiny digital voice recorder in her other hand. A red light was shining. *Scarlet Bush*, I read. *The Daily Post*. Then her mobile phone number, email address and four or five social network accounts. That seemed like a lot to me.

'Scarlet Bush,' she laughed. 'Sounds like a porn star, right?'

When I looked up she nodded at the photographer and, almost lazily, he swung his camera towards me and pulled the trigger. It took photographs like a machine gun.

'Hey,' I said, raising a hand to protect myself.

'Have you seen what the online community are saying?' The little voice recorder was in my face. 'They're calling Bob the Butcher a hero.'

I stared at her. 'Bob the Butcher?'

'He's all over the social networks. He's been trending for twenty-four hours.' Scarlet Bush had a disbelieving little smile on her face. 'You genuinely weren't aware of that?'

The porter was finally opening the door. I pressed my warrant card against the glass and said my name and rank. So she knew my name, too.

'And how does that feel for you, DC Wolfe?' she asked. 'When the social networks are calling the murderer a hero and the victim a scumbag?'

'Sorry, sorry,' the porter said, finally opening up.

I paused in the open doorway.

'Murderers are never heroes,' I said.

Scarlet Bush smiled at me, more broadly now, as if we both knew that wasn't quite true.

Mrs Natasha Buck, widow of the dead banker, was in dark glasses and wet from the shower. Tall, early thirties, still in her bathrobe.

The strange combination of robe and shades made her look as though she was on holiday, heading for the pool. Her damp hair was blonde – very blonde, the white-gold you see on black-and-white film stars. She looked like a natural blonde, but maybe not that natural. She had the worked-on thinness that you see with a lot of wealthy women, and the same sense of entitlement.

Towelling her long blonde hair, she frowned at my warrant card as if it was junk mail from Pepe's Pizza Parlour.

'I'm very sorry for your loss, Mrs Buck. I know this must be a very distressing time.'

'I already told the police what I know,' she said. 'A young black man and an older white woman.' She had the carefully clipped enunciation of a foreigner who has spent ten years around serious English money.

'DI Gane and DI Whitestone,' I said. 'I know.'

'They even swabbed my mouth.'

'They do that for your DNA. To rule you out. We just need to double-check some details, if that's convenient.'

'Not *really*.' She glanced at her watch, shining like a diamond-encrusted bauble on her thin wrist. 'Actually I'm about to go out.'

She was strikingly attractive, with the kind of face that you would not look away from until you found yourself staring. And perhaps not even then. But it felt like a lot of men had told her she was beautiful.

'We do have an appointment, Mrs Buck. If it's inconvenient now we can do it at some later date.' A pause. 'At the station.'

She looked at me properly for the first time. Then she laughed.

The more money they have, I thought, the less they fear the police.

'Should I call my lawyer?' she said.

'We're just talking, Mrs Buck.'

Her hair fell across her face. She looked at me through the damp veil as she lazily pulled it back.

'Am I a suspect?'

Her voice had become lower and slower. I liked it more.

'Not yet,' I said.

We stared at each other.

'Oh, let's get it over with,' she said. 'Coffee? I'll have to make it myself. I had to let our housekeeper go when I found her with my late husband's penis in her mouth.' She stood up with a sigh. 'It's so hard to get good help.'

It was a lovely apartment. Clean, expensive, uncluttered. Big budget, good taste, no children. I thought of the office with all the blood and tried to feel her husband's presence in this place. But if his spirit was near, I couldn't sense him. It felt like the home of a woman who had been living alone for a long time.

There were two paintings on the wall, clearly by the same artist. City scenes with a kind of Sunday morning stillness about them. One was of deserted railway lines, the other some kind of tunnel, and they were both misty and dream-like, bathed in the soft light of dawn or twilight. There were no people in them and that gave them a strange kind of peace. I felt like I almost recognised these places.

I leaned in close to the painting of the tunnel, looking for the artist's name, but there were just two lower-case initials.

j s

A miniature dog came into the room while Mrs Buck was making the coffee. Looked like a Pekingese-Chihuahua cross. I let her sniff my hand and then picked her up and placed her on my thigh. She stood there shivering, as weightless as an insect.

When I tried to stroke her she ambled off to the far end of the sofa and stared at me defiantly as she emptied her bladder.

Mrs Buck came back into the room with a cafetière on a silver tray.

'Susan, you bad girl,' she said. 'You know you're meant to do that on the carpet.'

Mrs Buck dropped a silk cushion over the stain, pushed the dog on to the floor and then sat opposite me, leaning back, crossing her long legs, and sighing as her robe slid open. She pulled it shut as an iPhone on the coffee table between us began to vibrate. The dog barked at it, quaking with rage as Mrs Buck picked it up and began reading a message. She made me feel like I wasn't there at all.

I cleared my throat.

'Who would want to kill your husband?' I said.

Her pretty face was frowning at the iPhone.

'Apart from you,' I added.

Now she looked at me.

'Mrs Buck,' I said. 'Please try to concentrate on me for the next little while.'

She took a final look at her phone and turned it off, her face tight with anger.

'Do you really think I wanted my husband dead?' she said. 'You stupid little man!'

I took a breath.

'Officers were called to this address three days before he died.'

'That? A lover's tiff.'

'You made threats on your husband's life.'

'What do you expect me to say when I find the help blowing him? You say all sorts of things in the heat of the moment.'

'You FedExed your bed to his office.'

'I wanted to embarrass him. I wanted to humiliate him. I wanted him to know what it feels like.'

'And then someone cut his throat.'

She exhaled as she poured out coffee.

'I can see it looks bad. Sugar? Milk?'

'Black, please.'

'I didn't want him to die. I just wanted him to *stop*. To stop . . . what's the nice way of saying it? Sleeping around.'

It was good coffee.

'Did your husband have many friends?'

'You know what the English are like. Or at least that kind of upper-class Englishman. Hugo came from a family where they let their dogs get in their beds and send their children to kennels. He was shipped off to boarding school at the age of seven, made friends there and kept them for ever. He didn't have much use for the rest of the world. Including his wife.'

I thought about the photograph on his desk.

'Where did he go to school?'

'Trinity College Cambridge. Prince Charles went there.'

She was smiling with wistful pride.

'Before that,' I said.

'Potter's Field,' she said. 'His father went there. And his grandfather. Hugo called it the Eton for athletes, musicians and thugs. He meant it as a compliment.'

'Which one was he?'

'An athlete. My husband was good at games, detective.'

'Did he enjoy his years at Potter's Field?'

'Sadistic masters. Stodgy food. Cold showers. That constant obsession with sport. Casual bullying. A lot of homosexual sex. He always said they were the best days of his life.'

'Did your husband have lovers?'

She snorted.

'Apart from your housekeeper,' I said.

'Plenty.'

'And did the lovers have husbands?'

'Some of them. You think a jealous husband might have killed him? Possible, I suppose. But Hugo was fond of the help. He stayed away from my friends, I'll give him that. Although I don't think he did it out of any sense of morality. He just preferred his entertainment below stairs.'

'I'll need the name and contact details of the housekeeper. You told my colleagues you didn't have them.'

The anger flared. 'Because the bitch caught a plane back to Kiev. I *told* them. Do I have to say everything twice?'

'Did he fall out with any business partners? Did he receive any threatening phone calls, emails, letters?'

She shook her head. She had had enough. She took out her phone.

'Where were you between the hours of five and seven a.m. yesterday? I am going to need your credit card records, mobile phone bills, computers and their passwords. Laptops, desktops, tablets, the lot. Are you listening to me, Mrs Buck?'

She stood up.

'Do you really want to know about my husband?'

We stared at each other.

'Yes.'

'Then let me tell you about my husband,' she said.

With a shrug she let the robe fall from her shoulders and to the floor.

I saw the bruises on her arms and legs. On her long limbs there were fresh, livid marks and there were old and fading marks. All the signs of systematic and regular beatings that carefully avoided the face.

'This was my husband.'

'Mrs Buck—'

'*He* was the violent one, not me. When I picked up that little oyster knife he laughed in my face. He laughed at me, detective. But I didn't want him dead, no matter what I told him.' The tears finally came and they seemed real enough to me. 'I wanted him to be *kind*,' she continued. 'I wanted him to stop running around. I wanted him to stop humiliating me with women too poor and too stupid to tell him no. I wanted him to *stop*.'

I was on my feet. 'Please, Mrs Buck—'

'Natasha.'

I picked up her robe and draped it around her shoulders. She put her arms around my waist. I think she just wanted to be held for a while. I think she was sick of all the questions. I think she was just lonely. Our faces were next to each other. I could feel her breath. And I felt the blood flood into me unbidden.

Because I was lonely too.

After a long moment I pulled myself away, cracking my shin against the coffee table and waking up the dog.

Natasha Buck smiled sadly as she slipped the robe back on and tied the belt around her slim waist.

'Ah, that rare breed,' she said, nodding towards my left hand. My wedding ring had caught the soft light as I picked up my cup. 'A married man who loves his wife!'

'Drink your coffee,' I said.

The porter was nowhere to be seen when I left. The journalist and the photographer had disappeared. The chauffeur was dozing at the wheel of the Mercedes, his peaked cap pulled over his eyes. The dogs in the park had all gone home and the day was dark far too soon.

I was walking to the car, kicking through the piles of autumn leaves and thinking of Natasha Buck's long naked limbs, when DCI Mallory called.

'It wasn't beginner's luck,' he said. 'We've got another one.'

4

A blacked-out mortuary van waited at the mouth of the alley as the swirling blue lights of a dozen response cars lit up the Soho night. Uniformed officers were still unreeling spools of blue and white crime scene tape across Shaftesbury Avenue and shoving back crowds hopeful of glimpsing fresh corpse.

I ducked under the tape.

The Airwave digital radios chattered and clacked. The SOCOs were putting on their head-to-toe white body suits while Mallory's two detective inspectors, Gane and Whitestone, were already ripping off their protective gear. They were excited.

'It's a good body,' Gane said to me. He was young and black, his head shaved fashionably clean, and under his protective clothes he was far better dressed than he needed to be.

I pulled on thin blue latex gloves. 'A good body?'

'A bad body is one that's found by the public,' Whitestone said. 'Some drunk who needs a pee or a puke. A dog walker clomping through the gore before it's had a chance to get cold. Destroying evidence, tampering with the scene before we've even confirmed death.' Whitestone was in her middle thirties, a thoughtful-looking blonde woman with black-rimmed glasses. You might not have guessed she had more than ten years on murder investigation teams. 'A good body is one that's found by the police when it's definitely dead. A good body keeps things simple. Saves us work.'

'And this is a good body,' Gane said. And then, 'We read about you. You're famous, Wolfe. What did they call you in court?'

'Officer A,' I said.

'Officer A. You were in SO15?'

I nodded. 'Surveillance officer, Counter Terrorism Command.'

'You were a surveillance officer?' he said, clearly underwhelmed.

I could see how a Homicide detective like Gane would think surveillance was life in the slow lane. It's true there was a lot of hanging around, following people on foot and in cars and watching endless hours of CCTV footage, whereas Homicide and Serious Crime's work is carried out by Murder Investigation Teams, the Metropolitan Police's specialised murder squads, and is one of the Met's elite units, investigating nothing but murder, manslaughter and the threat of murder. But Gane made it sound like I had spent my time asking people if they wanted fries with that shake.

'I heard that it would never have detonated,' he said with a grin. 'Because the bomber ruined the cook.'

'I heard that too,' I said, flexing my fingers inside the latex gloves. 'In court the tech guy said the perp didn't distil the hydrogen peroxide to the correct concentration. Simmered when he should have stirred. Forgot to whisk his egg white. Maybe it's true. Maybe they're just trying to cheer us up. Anyone who makes a bomb in their old mum's kitchen can't be that bright, can they?'

'And what did they give you?' Gane asked.

'The Queen's Police Medal.'

He almost whistled. 'A QPM? Was it for exceptional courage, skill, exhibiting conspicuous devotion to duty, or all three?' He laughed. 'Lucky he had a bomb in his bag. Or they would have given you twenty years to life.'

'It's good to have you, Wolfe,' Whitestone told me, ending the chat. 'The boss is waiting for you.'

SOCOs were putting up arc lights at the end of the alley where Mallory stood next to a black shape lying on the ground by giant recycling bins, his long lean figure stock still in the blazing white glare as the scene was carefully prepared, looking like an actor waiting for his cue to step on stage. The filthy alley felt like it was light years away from the shining tower where we had found Hugo Buck.

'I thought we had another one,' I said.

'We do,' Mallory said.

There's a look that you see in all boxers and in certain breeds of dog – German Shepherds have it. It is a look that reveals knowledge of how serious the world is. Mallory had that look now.

'Different postcode, same killer,' he said. 'Look.'

The dead man wore the sad rags of homelessness. And someone had cut his throat out.

All of it.

The fierce white lights revealed a neck that had been ripped open, torn out, the front half of the victim's neck cleaved clean away. Again. It felt like only the spine was keeping the head attached to the body. Again. Mallory was right. The homeless man in the stinking alley was a world away from the banker in his glass tower.

But he was another one.

Even under the arc lights the alley was cold, and through

the thin rubber gloves I could feel the sweat tingle on my palms.

I turned on my torch to look beyond the reach of the lights' glare, and let the thin beam trace slowly across the great spurts of arterial blood covering the walls and the recycling bins. I turned the torch off as I looked at the blood that soaked and stained the top half of the body.

The blood stank with that distinctive metallic odour that is also sickeningly human, and the smell mixed with the fuel and food and alcohol scents of the West End.

I tried to look beyond the blood and the horror. I tried to look at what had once been a man.

His hair was long and matted, the clothes rags, blackened by the grinding toll of living on the streets. It was hard to estimate his age because he looked all used up, as though he had lived an entire lifetime long before this brutal death.

'There will be needle marks on his arms,' I said, 'and perhaps on the legs, and even between the toes.'

Mallory said, 'But why kill a man who was so busy killing himself?'

There were a few pitiful belongings by the dead man's side. A black rubbish bag secured by an elastic band holding his worldly goods. A woollen cap still full of coins. And a musical instrument. A thin piece of black wood with a complicated tangle of silver metal buttons and keys.

'A clarinet?' I said.

'Not a clarinet,' Mallory said. 'Too small. An oboe.'

'Nobody's busking is that bad,' said one of the SOCOs.

Nobody laughed.

Mallory's gaze took in the bloodied body, the untouched

money, and the musical instrument. He shook his head with what looked like real sadness.

'Looks like he was on the streets for a while,' I said. 'Plenty of addicts and former addicts around Soho. But the homeless don't often kill each other.'

'No,' Mallory agreed. 'It's the people with homes to go to who are the problem.'

I looked back at the street. The SOCOs moved in slow motion now, plodding white ghosts, falling into their routine of photographing footprints, gathering cigarette butts, collecting fibres, prints, and samples of blood. One of them was drawing a sketch. The photographer stopped taking stills and started filming the scene. The usual crop of small numbered yellow markers were blooming on the ragged ground and the SOCOs trod carefully between them, like scientists tiptoeing through the aftermath of nuclear Armageddon. Beyond them, in the festive swirl of the blue lights of our cars, uniformed officers were pushing back the crowds recording the drama on their phones.

'They think we're putting on *Les Misérables* down here,' Mallory sighed. 'This is a strange space, isn't it?'

I lifted my head. Mallory was right. It was not really an alley at all, more of a crevice between two of the grand old theatres of Shaftesbury Avenue. At the end of the alley, above the heads of the gawping crowd, I could see the bright lights of the very heart of the city. The white neon of the theatre marquees, the reds and golds of Chinatown.

'And nobody heard a thing,' Mallory said, reading my mind.

'Because his trachea had been cut,' I said. 'No windpipe, no scream.'

As the crowds were moved to the far side of the street their voices rose in protest. They craned their necks for a better view and held their little phones even higher above their heads.

'God spare us from stupid people with smartphones,' Mallory muttered.

The SOCOs began to erect a tent over the dead man to shield the scene from the public and to protect the thousand tiny scraps of evidence from the weather. Mallory's gaze settled on the beanie cap full of coins, then moved on to the musical instrument.

'What kind of heroin addict busks with an oboe?' he said.

I thought about it. 'One who comes from money. One who had all the chances. One who comes from privilege. The music teacher coming round once a week to practise the oboe. The lessons going on for years. Money never a problem.'

Mallory ran the palm of one large hand over his bald head and then pushed his John Lennon glasses a bit further up his broken nose. 'Or maybe he just stole it.' A beat. 'But I don't think so. I think you're right. I think there was all kind of care lavished on him. A long time ago now.'

The flash from a SOCO's camera lit up a part of the alley wall that the arc lights had not reached. Among the fresh spurts of travel blood there was a tangle of graffiti I had missed. One word shouted at me and I stepped closer to see, although I already knew what it said.

P I G

On the far side of the street I could see perhaps a hundred mobile phones, held above the shoulders of the uniformed officers who stood on the far side of the POLICE DO NOT CROSS tape. The crowds had been pushed right back now but the numbers were growing, stretching our officers, and as their excitement mounted the white lights on their phones glowed like the eyes of wolves in winter.

A SOCO came down the alley, carrying a laptop in one hand and pulling off her facemask with the other.

'Good body, sir,' she said to Mallory.

'No witness, no weapon, no CCTV, no ID and no glove prints,' he said. 'I've seen better.'

In the morning I took care of my daughter and my dog and then I drove to work – 27 Savile Row, London W1. The Met call it West End Central.

27 Savile Row is a modern block of offices with one of those ancient blue police lamps outside – the kind of blue lamp that makes you think of Sherlock Holmes hunting Jack the Ripper through the London fog. But although Savile Row is famous for two things, West End Central isn't one of them.

For hundreds of years Savile Row has been home to the most exclusive men's tailors in the world. The short Mayfair street is also where, on the rooftop high above number 3, the Beatles played their final gig, attracting the attention of the local police. The attending officers from West End Central let the Beatles finish their last ever set because they were all music fans. That's what they tell you in West End Central.

Carrying the triple espresso I had bought at Bar Italia in Soho, I went up to the Major Incident Room, MIR-1, on the top floor. MIR-1 would be the centre of Homicide's murder investigation. It was a large suite of connecting rooms with a computer station at every desk and it was now completely empty apart from DCI Mallory, who stood cradling a carton of takeaway tea as he stared at a blank whiteboard.

'You're early,' he said. 'Morning briefing's not for an hour.'

'I thought I'd be the first to arrive, sir,' I said. 'Look keen and all that.'

He laughed. 'I like to spend a bit of time figuring before I start opening my mouth,' he said. 'What could possibly connect a wealthy investment banker and a homeless heroin addict?' He shook his head. 'I don't know. I have no idea. And I need to know. At least I need to have a theory.' He sipped his tea. 'Have you heard of the Golden Hour principle?'

I nodded. 'It means early action can secure material that would otherwise be lost. Witnesses remember things more clearly. Offenders can still be nearby. CCTV footage hasn't been deleted. The longer we leave it, the harder it all gets.'

'I believe in the Golden Hour principle as much as the next man,' Mallory said. 'But I also believe in what the old SIOs call "creating slow time". Meaning you need to put your foot on the ball and have a figure; meaning you have to leave time for figuring as well as action.'

He was such a soft-spoken man that it took me a moment to realise that by coming in early I had intruded upon his private time – his figuring time. He must have seen the alarm on my face.

'Why don't you go down to the basement?' he suggested kindly. 'See if you can find our weapon.' He held out an A4 file. 'Take this with you.'

'Sir.'

I bolted my coffee and went down to the basement. The lift doors opened on to a low-ceilinged room where row upon row of canteen dining tables were covered with knives.

A young uniformed officer was filming them and making notes on a clipboard. He looked like a tourist in some exotic marketplace.

'Help you, sir?' he said.

'I'm looking for a knife,' I said.

'What kind of knife, sir?'

'A knife that can do this.'

There were four photographs inside the file. Two of Hugo Buck's corpse and the other two of the homeless man. They were all graphic close-ups of the fatal wounds. I held them up for the constable and saw the blood drain from his face.

'Go ahead, sir,' he said. 'We've got all sorts here.'

It was true. There were hundreds, perhaps thousands, of knives glinting under the harsh strip lighting. Knives that had been seized, found, dumped, bagged as evidence or surrendered during an amnesty. So many knives that I didn't see how I could fail to find a suitable candidate for the one that had cut the throats of the banker and the unknown man.

The uniformed officer had fallen into step beside me. He cleared his throat nervously.

'It's PC Greene, sir,' he said. 'PC Billy Greene? From that morning at the bank? You told me to breathe. When I came over all funny.'

I looked at him properly and remembered the young officer who was good for nothing after finding the body.

'PC Greene,' I said. 'You don't call me *sir* just because I'm in plain clothes.' I was wearing my black Paul Smith wedding suit. Savile Row being still a bit beyond my pay grade. 'I'm a detective constable – DC Wolfe. Exactly the same rank as you. You can call me Wolfe. You can call me Max. You can call me pretty much whatever you like. But if you call me *sir* then you make both of us look stupid. You do know that a DC has exactly the same powers and authority as a uniformed PC, don't you?'

He looked embarrassed. 'Of course, sir— Max, er, DC Wolfe. But anyway, I didn't thank you. A lot of them were laughing at me for wimping out that day. You helped. It definitely helps. The breathing.'

'You're not on the street any more?'

His white face flushed red. 'They've put me on desk duties. Reassigned. A canteen cowboy.' He laughed miserably. 'They think I fell to bits.'

I grimaced. 'That's a bit hard.'

Greene gestured at the knives, changing the subject. 'See what you're looking for?'

'Not yet.'

I walked between the tables, looking at the knives in their careful lines. Throwing knives. Hunting knives. Bowie knives. Knives so small and thin they could fit into a credit card holder. Samurai swords. Carpet cutters. Gurkha kukris. Rust-dappled Stanley knives. And the height of knife fashion – compact semi-automatic folding knives, with titanium handles and stainless steel blades, knives that whipped out like a gunslinger drawing his Colt 45.

I picked one up and looked at it in my hand.

'We're getting a lot of those,' Greene said. 'Gang members like them. You think it might be something like that?'

'I don't see how it can be,' I said, replacing the knife. 'It's not long enough. I figure what I'm looking for is about twelve inches long. Most of it blade. It has to be a blade that's long and thin and I guess double-edged. Something that's made to cut throats.'

He swallowed hard. 'This is about Bob the Butcher, isn't it?'

'Who *is* Bob the Butcher?'

He fetched his laptop and found the page. A newspaper's website.

BOB THE BUTCHER STALKS SCARED CITY BOYS

by Scarlet Bush

Crime correspondent

Champagne-swilling City boys are living in mortal terror after a senior detective revealed that the death of investment banker Hugo Buck was a hate crime.

'Yes, Bob the Butcher murdering that innocent young banker was a hate crime,' confirmed Detective Constable Max Wolfe. 'But then all murder is a hate crime.'

In the bars all over the financial district, high-flying young City boys busy blowing their bonuses are now living in abject terror of Bob the Butcher.

'It's terrible to think that Bob the Butcher is targeting bankers,' said Bruno Mancini in fashionable Cheapside watering hole The Lucky Cripple. 'What's wrong with being rich? We work hard for our success.'

I cursed under my breath. 'I didn't say any of that,' I said, then glanced at the piece again. 'Well, maybe just a bit of it.'

There was a small photograph next to the article. It was the young woman outside the flat in Regent's Park. I wasn't sure what this meant, but I knew it wasn't good. The one good thing was that she had not connected the murder of Hugo Buck with the unknown man in the alley. But it was the only good thing.

I carried on walking between the tables, somehow knowing that the knife I was looking for would not be found here.

'Thanks for your help, Billy. I'm sorry they took you off the street.'

He brightened. 'It's actually not so bad. I like the nights. And you get a sense of the history down here. Have you got a minute? Have a look at this.'

Greene opened the door to a storage room. It was as small and cluttered as an attic that had been abandoned around the time the Beatles were playing on a rooftop at the other end of Savile Row.

'It's full of stuff that nobody knows what to do with,' Greene said. 'It's not evidence so they can't bag it. It's not junk so they can't chuck it out. And it's not important enough to be in a museum. I think they've all just forgotten about it. Have a look, DC Wolfe.'

We stepped into the dusty room and I looked around in disbelief. There was a stovepipe hat, half eaten away by moths and mould. Cardboard boxes overflowing with old-fashioned rubber truncheons. A collapsed stack of elderly riot shields. Metropolitan Police baseball caps that had never quite caught on. A rack of heavyweight Kevlar jackets, nothing like the wafer-thin stab-proof numbers that we had these days. And there were other bits and pieces of uniform – helmets with the badge gone, jackets with their brass buttons missing, abandoned kit that had to be twenty, fifty, a hundred years old. Police junk that nobody quite had the heart or the energy or the permission to chuck away.

So they stuck it in here.

'Have you heard of the Black Museum?' Greene said. 'It's in New Scotland Yard. It's closed to the public. This is just like the Black Museum.'

I smiled. 'This is a bit more of a mess than the Black Museum. It's true that the Black Museum has a lot of old kit. Guns. Knives. Walking sticks that turn into swords. Umbrellas that turn into guns. They've got a sword that turns into a knife called a Cop Killer. But the Black Museum is not really a museum at all. It's more of a classroom. A training aid.'

Greene's eyes were wide. 'You've seen it?'

I nodded. 'Part of my training. They've got a display about Met officers killed in the line of duty. They show you around the Black Museum so that it doesn't happen to you.'

Greene took a deep breath and let it out slowly as he turned to point at a dusty shelf in the darkest corner of that strange little room.

'Look,' he said.

'I can't see anything,' I said, taking a step closer to where he was indicating.

And then I saw it.

It was an ancient leather bag sitting all by itself on a shelf tangled with cobwebs. The dark brown cowhide was worn and cracked. The brass hardware and locks were blackened with rust. Greene lifted it up for my inspection and at the back of the shelf a spider scuttled away as if late for an urgent appointment.

'It looks like an old doctor's bag,' I said.

'It's a Gladstone bag,' Greene said. 'What makes this one special is that it's a Murder Bag. I think it's one of the originals. Did you ever hear of Murder Bags?'

I shook my head.

'Murder Bags were where modern detective work began,' he explained. 'They had two of them in the Yard from 1925. Always packed and ready to go. They contained rubber gloves, magnifying glasses, containers for holding blood, test tubes for fingerprinting, all sorts of gear. The Murder Bags came in when Sir Bernard Spilsbury saw a detective handling a dismembered body with his bare hands. They were the start of modern homicide investigation.' He looked at me shyly. 'What you do.'

He gently replaced the ruined old bag as if it was priceless. 'The history,' he said. 'I love all the history.'

'One thing I don't understand,' I said.

Greene looked at me.

'Your colleague – the woman PC – told me that the dead banker was your first dead body.'

'PC Wren,' he said. 'Edie. Yes.'

'But that can't be true,' I said. 'How long have you been in uniform, Greene?'

'Six years.'

'You must have seen more dead bodies than me,' I said. 'You must have averaged a dead person every day. Motorists who went through their windscreens while sending a text. Cyclists who got hit by a bus. Pedestrians who got hit by the cyclists and the motorists.' I shook my head. 'I can't believe that Hugo Buck was your first dead body.'

Greene thought about it.

'It's true,' he said. 'I've seen a lot of dead people. But what Edie— what PC Wren and I found that morning, on the floor of that man's office, it wasn't rotten luck or fate or stupidity. It didn't happen because somebody was drunk or stoned or sending a text message. What happened to that man, that banker, was the most deliberate thing in the world. It felt like a violation of everything. It's not like the daily slaughter on the roads. I don't know how to explain it. It's just *different*, isn't it?'

I nodded. 'You're right. Murder's different.'

* * *

I wake too soon.

It is the sharp point of the night – too late to go back to sleep, too early to get up.

I slip out of bed and go to the window. The lights are blazing in the meat market. I come back and sit on the bed and I still haven't looked at the alarm clock. It feels like catching the eye of a mad man.

And then I look.

03:50

I walk across to the big cupboard built into the wall and push the double doors. They spring open, and the collection of belts and necklaces hanging on the back of the door jangle softly in the dark.

There are shoes on the left-hand side. All kinds of women's shoes. Strappy sandals and spike heels. On the right are stacks of drawers. Knitwear. Carefully folded jeans that will never be worn again.

And directly in front of me there are all the hangers with her dresses and skirts and shirts and jackets and tops. Lots of white cotton but splashes of colour too, although you can't see it in this light. But there are orange silks and blue batik and gauzy things spangled with silver. Soft as a feather, light as a sigh.

I spread my arms wide and sort of gently fall against it, pressing my face into her clothes, her essence, the old life.

I breathe her in.

And then I sleep.

5

The children had painted their families. An entire wall in the classroom was covered with pictures of brightly coloured stick figures. At five they were starting to make sense of the world and their place in it.

The stick-figure mothers had long flowing hair, squiggly lines of black, brown and yellow, and some of them held a sausage-shaped package with a circle for its head – a baby brother or sister. The fathers were mostly bigger stick-insect figures, and nearly all of them carried brown squares and rectangles – briefcases. All of the pictures seemed to be full of life, crowded with parents, siblings, stick figures of assorted shapes and sizes.

Apart from Scout's.

'Look, that's my one,' she said.

How could I miss it?

In Scout's picture there was just an unsmiling stick-figure daddy with no briefcase, a little stick-figure girl with huge brown eyes, and at our feet a small red four-legged daub – Stan.

We had left the dog at home that morning, to his high-pitched howls of rage and despair, because once a month the parents were allowed into the classroom to look at the children's work. It was meant to be a happy time. But I looked at her picture as parents and children jostled around us and I did not know what to say.

Most of the dads were dressed in suits and ties and carrying briefcases, while the mothers were either dressed for the office or for exercise, and some of the ones who were dressed for the gym were carrying babies or shepherding toddlers. So there was definitely a social realism about the pictures.

A young teacher, a blonde New Zealander, Miss Davies, watched us all with a kindly smile.

'Do you like it?' Scout said, disturbed by my silence.

'I love it,' I said.

The truth was it tore at my heart. The surrounding whiteness in Scout's picture seemed to overwhelm the three little figures. And I felt it again, as I knew I would feel it for ever. The completeness of other families, and the shattered nature of what was left of ours.

I placed my hand on Scout's shoulder and she looked up at me with her mother's eyes.

'Good work, Scout,' I said.

'Miss Davies said just family,' she said and, suddenly losing interest, wandered off to her desk to prepare for the first lesson.

It was time to go. Mothers and fathers were kissing their children goodbye and exchanging a few smiley words with the teacher.

But I stood there until the bell went, looking up at Scout's picture of our family, surrounded by all that empty white space.

Stan didn't like being left at home. He had upended his water dish, torn the puppy pad in his cage to shreds, and for an encore climbed on to the coffee table and contemptuously batted away the mouse of my laptop, so it dangled just above the floorboards like a hanging man.

We stared at each other.

A Cavalier would not have been my first choice for a dog. Or even my fifth or sixth choice. I would have gone for something larger. A Labrador or a Golden Retriever. A German Shepherd. Stan considered me with his bulging eyes, absent-mindedly gnawing on a TV cable as I cleaned up his mess. Something larger and smarter, I thought.

But Scout had done her research and she knew what she wanted. Stan was her dog.

And even if he had burned the place down, I couldn't be angry with him today. Without Stan in our lives all the white space around us might have swallowed us alive.

It was still early as Stan and I cut through Charterhouse Square on our way home from our walk. Mallory would be alone up in MIR-1, drinking his tea and figuring. Stan and I still had some time together before I put him in the custody of Mrs Murphy and went to work.

He was squatting for his wet when I became aware of the men on a bench. Three of them. Still up from last night. We got a lot of committed drinkers round our way, drawn by the all-night pubs surrounding Smithfield meat market. Two pasty-faced white boys in cheap grey sports gear, and an Asian man, older and larger, wearing a T-shirt despite the early morning chill. A weightlifter. He was the one who made a kissing noise at my dog.

I smiled.

The three men stared back.

It wasn't a good moment.

Then Stan was scampering happily towards them, mad with excitement, pulling me, incredulous at the coincidence that they happened to be here at exactly the same time as him.

I dropped the lead to allow him to greet them.

And that was my mistake.

The weightlifter picked Stan up – and picked him up all wrong, with both hands wrapped around the dog's chest, not supporting his weight with one hand under his butt – and recoiled with disgust when Stan attempted to lick his face.

As his milky-faced mates laughed, the weightlifter dropped Stan heavily. He twisted as he fell, landing hard and yelping. Stan was whimpering now, his tail rigid between his legs, ears flattened – all the hallmarks of dog terror.

He came back to me and I picked him up, one hand around his chest and the other under his bottom, the way you should hold a dog, and I held him to me, feeling the frantic drumbeat of his heart.

Because now he had learned fear.

'That's not a dog,' the weightlifter said, 'that's a rat.'

'Man, you freaked it out because you wouldn't give it a kiss!' said one of his mates.

'It's a dog!' the other said. 'But it's a gay dog!'

They all laughed.

I put Stan down and he prostrated himself on the ground, his tail tucked up, his ears flattened, big eyes bulging. I placed a reassuring hand on his flank, feeling the fragile ribs under the silky chestnut fur, the small heart still pounding wildly. I held the lead loosely in my hand.

The three men were still laughing on the bench. Tough guys, I thought. Tough guys who are only having a laugh.

I tried to walk away as they chuckled and chatted among

themselves but Stan stopped for a sniff of a bin. Then he squatted on his hind legs, looking shyly at me as he emptied his bowels. I scooped the three little droppings up in a bag, tied a knot, and placed the bag in the bin. They turned their attention back to my dog, pointing and leering. They had decided that Stan was here for their amusement.

And that was their big mistake.

'Walk on,' I said.

Stan's melancholy eyes rolled up to look at me. He made no attempt to move.

The men roared.

'Walk on!' the weightlifter said. 'Do you hear him? Walk on, he says! Hey, mate, does he bite? Or does he just suck your cock?'

I was looking down at Stan. He had never taken his eyes off me, and he seemed to flatten himself even lower now, his tail stiff and quivering between his legs, the paws either side of his head, the giant ears hanging down like shoulder-length hair, his chin pressed against the concrete.

It had to happen one day.

He had to learn fear sooner or later.

We all have to learn fear.

But it seemed a crying shame that it was today when I felt so grateful to him, genuinely grateful, for joining me and Scout in our family portrait on her classroom wall.

'Walk on,' I said.

Still Stan did not move.

'Not very obedient, is he, man?' the weightlifter said.

There was a confusion of cities in his accent. London and Los Angeles and Islamabad. And the very worst of all of those places.

I wrapped the old leather dog lead around an empty bench in a loose knot and turned to the men.

'I wasn't talking to the dog,' I said, walking towards them.

The weightlifter stood up, his smile fading, and he opened his mouth to say something just as I punched him in the heart.

One punch.

Right hand.

Full force.

They don't do it in the movies. But the heart is the very worst place to be hit hard. You really don't want to get hit in the heart.

It was a punch that began in the pivoting sole of my left boot and travelled up the muscles in my left leg, gaining full momentum with my twisting torso and then racing down my right arm into the first two knuckles on my right fist.

Less than a second after it had begun its journey, the punch slammed with enormous force against the man's sternum, right on the flat bone at the front of the chest where the upper ribs are attached by cartilage just in front of the heart.

I can never understand why nobody ever punches the heart. Drunks in a bar fight would not think of punching their opponent's heart. Street fighters at closing time would never dream of hitting a man in his heart. The average yob, like these three very average yobs in Charterhouse Square, know nothing about a blow to the heart.

But I knew.

The heart is everything.

The weightlifter staggered backwards, his hands on his heart, reeling from the trauma of chest compression. He sat back down on the bench, between his dumb friends, the fight all out of him. The punch had collapsed his sternum maybe an inch, no more, but it was devastating enough to shock the heart.

I looked at the other two, their faces already frozen. They didn't know what to do now. I didn't expect them to. And I looked at the weightlifter, clutching his chest, pawing at his collapsed sternum, and I could see that he lacked the will to get back up.

It was more than just the shock of being punched in the heart. The punch had induced tachycardia – an abrupt and terrifying increase in the heart rate.

He felt like his heart was about to explode.

He felt like he was dying.

I walked back to my dog and rubbed his neck.

'This is Stan,' I told them. 'Stan is a Cavalier King Charles Spaniel. Cavs are the most peace-loving dogs in the world. They are famous for being mild-mannered and polite. Great with children. They were the favourite dog of the Tudor and Stuart kings because of their gentle nature – the gentle nature that you can still see with Stan.'

'We don't want any trouble, man,' one of them said.

I looked at him sharply. 'Can you see Stan's gentle nature or not?'

'Yes,' he said.

I needed coffee immediately. A triple espresso that you could stand your spoon up in. Stan gazed at me with bashful love. He would sit on my lap outside the café and I would drink the short black coffee while I fed him Nature's Menu chicken treats until it was time to go to work.

I nodded at the men, glad that they understood at last.

'He's not the one who bites,' I said.

* * *

'Let's visit the dead,' Mallory said at the morning briefing.

If you cut across St James's Park it is a brisk ten-minute walk from 27 Savile Row to the Westminster Public Mortuary on Horseferry Road, and the Iain West Forensic Suite.

'Iain West was the Elvis of forensic pathologists,' Mallory told me as Gane, Whitestone and I struggled to keep pace with him. 'A genius who changed everything. Proved WPC Yvonne Fletcher was shot from the Libyan Embassy. Located exactly where the Brighton bomb was placed in the Grand Hotel by interpreting the injuries of the victims. Examined the victims of the IRA atrocities at Harrods and Hyde Park. Single-handedly improved rail safety with his autopsies of the King's Cross fire. And taught us all an invaluable lesson before dying while he was still a young man.'

'What's that, sir?'

'The dead can't lie.'

Deep inside the Iain West Forensic Suite we waited patiently in our blue scrubs and hairnets as Elsa Olsen, forensic pathologist, smiled and spoke with all the polite good grace of a hostess of a dinner party who was about to make the introductions.

Elsa had a lovely smile, I thought, as she turned her friendly gaze from our faces to the two naked corpses on the stainless steel tables before us.

'Our mystery man,' she said, indicating the drug-withered body of the homeless man. 'Adam Jones. Born New Year's Day, 1973. Died tenth of October 2008.' She indicated his neighbour, the over-fed body of the banker. 'And Hugo Buck, who I think you know already. Born on the seventh of January 1973, died ninth of October 2008.'

Elsa let the dates sink in. Mallory and I stared hard at the bodies. Born within seven days of each other. And died within twenty-four hours of each other. But what else connected them? Apart from the livid wounds that had opened up their throats, now gaping black slits, they looked as though they were from different planets.

Even in death, Hugo Buck's body looked like that of a good amateur sportsman who was only just starting to run to expense-account fat. It was the body of a man who had serious gym sessions a few times a week, probably a personal trainer screaming at him for fifty quid an hour, no matter how busy he got at work; but the years were passing and there were plenty of meals at good restaurants during the working day, and a steady social drinking habit.

You wife-beating bastard.

In comparison, the shell of Adam Jones looked totally depleted, a pathetic sack of bones blotted with bad tattoos and veins scarred by damaged tissue – the squalid souvenirs of a thousand needles. He already looked on the cusp of old age, as if he had shot not just opiates into his veins but all his future years.

I shuddered.

The temperature was kept just above zero in here. Beyond an impatience to get started, I felt nothing when I looked at the bodies. Their spirits had flown. Now there were just the living in this freezing room, and two brutalised empty husks.

'The four questions of death,' Elsa Olsen continued. 'Cause? Mechanism? Manner? Time?' She smiled pleasantly. 'Death's fifth and final question – who? – I leave to you gentlemen.' A smile for DI Whitestone. 'And lady.'

Elsa stepped between the two steel tables.

'Cause of death for both men was suffocation,' she said.

Mallory said, 'They didn't bleed to death?'

Elsa shook her head. 'The single wound to the neck caused a massive haemorrhage. Death would have been quick, quiet and messy. An initial spray, perhaps several, as the artery was cut and then massive bleeding. As you noted, DCI Mallory, the trachea was severed, so screaming was a physical impossibility – there was nothing left to scream with. But it wasn't just the trachea that was cut. The carotid artery was also severed along with the internal jugular vein. Death would have been almost immediate, but neither man had the chance to bleed to death. They suffocated before they had the chance to bleed out.'

Elsa spoke the effortlessly perfect English of the Scandinavian abroad. She was fortyish, Norwegian, tall and slim and dark, one of those black-haired, blue-eyed Norwegians who defied the Nordic stereotype. Mallory had told me that she was his favourite pathologist because she talked about the dead as if they had once been among the living. He said they did not all do that.

'We don't have a weapon,' Mallory said. 'We don't even have an idea of a weapon. What kind of blade can cut a throat like that, Elsa?'

'The mechanism would need to be long and thin and razor-sharp,' Elsa answered. She peered at the gaping black letterbox in Hugo Buck's neck which extended from ear to ear. 'The assailant was standing behind the victim, as we can see from the classic long sweep of the wound. The mechanism would be something like a short double-edged sword, a long scalpel, something similar. Something with a sharp stabbing point and good cutting edges. These are remarkably clean cuts. A torn artery tends to contract and stem the bleeding. But a cleanly cut artery starts bleeding and it doesn't stop.' And then, almost as an afterthought, she said, 'Manner of death was murder.'

'Time of death?' Whitestone said.

'Hugo Buck had an algor mortis or temperature of death of ninety-seven degrees Fahrenheit,' Elsa said. 'Not far below normal body temperature of 98.6. Adam Jones was ninety-five degrees. But Mr Jones died on the street and Mr Buck died in a climate-controlled office.'

'And bodies lose temperature more quickly in the open air,' Whitestone said, looking at Gane.

'Adam Jones was found just after seven p.m.,' Elsa said. 'I would estimate the time of death was between five and seven p.m. Hugo Buck was found at six a.m. and I would estimate time of death between four a.m. and six.'

Mallory smiled. 'Two-hour windows, Elsa? Not taking many chances, are you?' He looked at his detectives. 'I think we just missed them – both of them. I think they both died just before we got there.'

The pathologist raised her hands – the perfect hostess trying to avoid an unpleasant scene. 'Time of death is only ever a best guess,' she said. 'You know that as well as I do.'

'We have to cut Elsa some slack,' Mallory said, still smiling. 'Time of death can eliminate subjects or damn them. So time of death is where our forensic colleagues are at their most cagey, and least willing to speculate.'

'And where the investigating detectives are most desperate for accuracy,' Elsa added.

'Defensive wounds?' Gane said. 'I can't see anything obvious.'

'Nothing,' the pathologist said. 'Neither of them had the will or the chance to put up a fight. There are no defensive wounds on the hands, arms, wrists, legs or feet.' She peered at the body of Adam Jones. 'Although on the body of Mr Jones I did discover some old cuts, bruises and abrasions from minor, earlier incidents.'

'Life on the streets,' I said. 'Takes its toll. No sign of recent substance abuse? He wasn't using at the time of death?'

Elsa shook her head. 'Surprisingly not.' There was a note of pity in her voice. 'Mr Jones was drug free. He was trying to change his ways, despite what you can see.'

What we could see were the exhausted veins on the man's arms – track marks, the miniature railway lines of heroin abuse. They were fading now.

'I think he was trying to kick the habit,' Elsa continued. 'I think he had tried more than once.' She smiled apologetically. 'Do stop me if I start doing your job.'

Mallory said, 'Star sign?'

Elsa stared at him. 'Taurus,' she said. 'The oboe you mention in your notes gave it away. Taureans are lovers of music and song.' Then she smiled. 'Oh bugger off, Mallory!'

We all laughed.

I leaned close to the dead men, looking at the neck of first Adam Jones and then Hugo Buck. In length, depth and darkness, the wounds were absolutely identical.

'One cut,' I said, shaking my head. 'Just one cut in the right place.'

'Sometimes one cut is all it takes,' Mallory said. 'The assassination squad stabbed Julius Caesar twenty-three times. But the Roman physician who examined him concluded that Caesar would have survived the assault if not for the wound to his heart.'

Elsa pointed at the wounds where she had cut open, examined and then closed up their stomachs.

'As you noted from his locked fists, Mr Buck had a cadaveric spasm in the moment of his death – instant rigor,' she said. 'What you like to call that Pompeii moment, Mallory. But Mr Jones is different. There was rigor in his legs but only in the legs. As you know, rigor mortis usually takes two hours to kick in unless there's a cadaveric spasm – as in the case of Mr Buck – or a loss of energy in a part of the body. That causes a chemical reaction, a loss of adenosine triphosphate – ATP – that makes the muscles stiffen and contract. So rigor in the legs means one thing: there was strenuous muscular activity in the legs prior to death.'

We considered the corpse of Adam Jones.

'So Jones was running,' Mallory said.

'He was being chased,' I said.

Elsa Olsen smiled at me, like a teacher looking at her star student. She held out her hand, as if I had won a prize.

'And this belonged to Mr Buck,' she said, and dropped something into my palm.

A small blue thing, round and hard and staring at me from beyond the grave.

'Hugo Buck had a glass eye,' she announced.

6

It was late afternoon with the day's light already fading when I parked outside the block of flats in Regent's Park. The trees in the park were at their most beautiful now, a riot of red and gold leaves that had not yet become serious about falling. But it wouldn't be long, I thought as I walked to the glass doors, wishing I had a coat. You could feel the world turning.

The porter let me in. Natasha Buck opened her door in her robe again. I couldn't decide if it was a bit early to be in a robe, or very late. But this time her hair wasn't wet. And this time she wasn't alone.

A man moved across the living room, glaring at me, with a frosted champagne flute in one hand and a cigarette in the other. I recognised the chauffeur who had been lounging in the big black Merc. I recognised him even in his underpants. It must have been all my training.

'You're too late,' Mrs Buck said.

'This will only take a minute,' I said.

The chauffeur came to the door, sipping his drink. He had come up in the world.

'Is there a problem?' he said.

'Not yet,' I said. 'Would you like one?'

'I'll be in the other room,' he said.

Smart chauffeur.

He went away and took his iced champagne flute with him.

'Tell me about your husband's eye,' I said. 'The one he lost.'

'What do you want to know?'

'How it happened.'

'At school,' she said. 'At Potter's Field. He told me he was kicked in the eye when scoring a try. Hugo was a natural athlete.' She sounded proud of him. 'All those sports the English invented. Rugby. Cricket. Tennis. Football. They came easy to him.'

'So it's something that happened when he was a boy?'

Natasha Buck nodded. 'He was very good at games.'

The next morning I left West End Central after our morning briefing and one hour later I was parking the X5 on a sweeping gravel drive and looking up at a large detached house. It felt like the countryside.

Adam Jones had fallen a long way, I thought, as a Filipina housekeeper let me in. She left me in the hall and I stared through glass doors at the back garden while I waited for the dead man's mother.

There was a neglected swimming pool out there, the surface coated with dead leaves, and the huge garden was wild and overgrown. A fox dozed undisturbed on the far side of the pool, as if he knew that no gardener was coming round any time soon. The house felt abandoned. But there had been money here once. Maybe the money was still here. Maybe it wasn't the money that had run out.

There was one painting on the wall. A shaft of dying

sunlight striking the side of a skyscraper. It was a city street but the people had all gone home. It was clearly by the same artist as the one on the wall in Hugo Buck's apartment. And there in the corner I found the same two lower-case initials:

j s

'Thank you so much for coming,' Mrs Jones said, coming down the stairs with her hands outstretched as if I was paying a social call.

I tried not to look shocked but I recognised the function of the colourful scarf she had tied around her head, and the pale, puffy look that comes with long months of intensive chemotherapy.

This lady was dying.

And yet there was an undeniable youthful beauty about her appearance. Under the headscarf, beyond the cancer and the chemo, there was an unlined face, preserved in time like some enchanted creature from a magic land.

'Mrs Jones,' I said. 'I'm DC Wolfe. We spoke briefly on the phone.' I offered my warrant card and she smiled at it politely. 'Mrs Jones, I'm so sorry for the loss of your son.'

She flexed her mouth with a spasm of pain, nodded once and composed herself. She was a proud woman and determined not to show her heart to a man she would probably never see again.

'Please,' she said, gesturing towards the living room.

I followed her. She moved with the careful deliberation of someone whose body has betrayed them. I waited until she had sunk into an armchair, and then took my place on the sofa opposite. An ancient black Labrador padded silently into the room, sniffed the hand that I offered and then ambled over to settle on its owner's feet.

The Filipina housekeeper appeared.

'Tea, please, Rosalita,' said Mrs Jones. Then she looked at me with her shining eyes, bright blue behind her spectacles, intelligent eyes that were still shocked with grief. 'I do appreciate you coming,' she said. 'And how are your enquiries progressing? Have you arrested anyone yet?'

'No, ma'am,' I said. 'But if you could answer some questions, that would be an enormous help to our investigation.'

She nodded, her hand absent-mindedly stroking the back of the black Lab's neck. The dog grunted with contentment.

'Your son,' I said, 'Adam. It would be helpful if you could tell me about Adam.' I hesitated. 'He had no fixed abode at the time of his death?'

His mother smiled, remembering an earlier time.

'He was a very gifted boy,' she said. 'Enormously talented. Sensitive. A wonderful musician. Wonderful!'

She looked around the room, and now I saw that it was a shrine to her dead son. On the bookshelves were trophies, prizes, and small white busts of men having bad hair days. Beethoven and the boys. Between the shelves the walls were covered with framed certificates. And massed on top of a small piano was an array of silver-framed photographs.

'My son was at the Royal Academy of Music,' Mrs Jones told me. 'For one term. Before they asked him to leave.'

Rosalita brought our tea. Mrs Jones lifted a hand and the housekeeper understood that we would serve ourselves. I waited until she had left the room.

'Why did they ask Adam to leave?'

Mrs Jones ruffled the dog between the ears, her face

clenched with tension, and I saw that she was in what must have been constant pain.

'Because,' she said, 'there was a darkness in him.' She smiled with an old sadness. 'I don't know how else to explain it. There was a darkness in my son, and that led him to the drugs. And then the drugs took away everything.'

'I think he was trying to stop,' I said. 'The autopsy showed there were no drugs in Adam's body at the time of his death.'

'Yes, he was trying to stop. He was trying very hard.' She looked at me. 'Thank you,' she said.

I wasn't sure what she was thanking me for, and I didn't know how to respond.

Mrs Jones poured our tea. I looked out of the windows. The fox had gone.

'When was the last time you saw your son?'

'A month ago. He came to borrow some money.' She laughed. 'Borrow – that's a good one! His father died two years ago and it was easier for my son to come home and ask for money – to borrow money – after that. When his father was alive, it was difficult. Arguments. Refusals. Raised voices. Tearful promises to change his ways. You can imagine. And things disappeared. A watch left by a bedside. Money in a wallet. That made relations with his father very difficult. But he never stole from me. Not from me. And some do, I know. Some heroin addicts – and my son was certainly a heroin addict – do steal from the people who love them most.'

I sipped my tea. Already Adam Jones had become more than a homeless junkie found dead in an alley, more than a naked corpse on a freezing bed of stainless steel. He had become somebody's son.

'And I saw him last night,' Mrs Jones said. 'My son. Adam. In my dreams. Or in my sleep. But it didn't *feel* like a dream. He was very sad. Have you ever heard of such a thing?' She laughed again. The dog sat up, and then settled. 'Am I going dotty in my old age?'

'I think it happens all the time,' I said. 'A loved one appearing in a dream. Especially at the start. Especially when you have just lost them. I think it takes a while before the dead rest easy.'

She looked at me. 'I get so tired,' she said. She gestured impatiently at her headscarf. 'All this business.'

I nodded.

'Perhaps you're not eating as you should, Mrs Jones,' I said. I hesitated for a moment. 'Chemotherapy makes food taste awful.'

'Yes, it does,' she said. 'They tell you about the hair loss and the nausea. Everyone knows about that. But they don't warn you about what it does to your sense of taste.' She looked at me levelly. 'You seem to know something about the subject.'

'Not really. My grandmother went through the same thing. But it was a long time ago.'

'You must have been close to your grandmother.'

'She brought me up,' I said. 'She raised me. After my parents died. She was more like my mother.'

'I see. Your grandmother sounds like a wonderful woman.'

'She was the kindest person I've ever met,' I said.

'And then she died.'

'Yes. Please tell me some more about Adam. Did he have enemies?'

She raised her eyebrows. 'Somebody killed him. Somebody

did *that* to him. But he was a gentle boy. Everyone loved him. Everyone who ever met him. As far as I know.'

'Mrs Jones, most murder victims know their killer. Can you think of anyone who would want to harm Adam? When he came home, did he talk about his money problems? Money that he owed? Outstanding debts?'

'Money problems were a way of life for my son,' she replied. 'But there was no malice in him. He was one of those people who make the world a better place. Then he lost his way and he never found his way back. And it didn't do any good – however much we loved him, however much it hurt us, however much we wanted him to be well. However much he wanted it for himself. None of it mattered. But under it all he was a good boy. A happy boy. There wasn't always that sadness in him. There wasn't always that darkness.'

She suddenly seemed very tired. She nodded towards the piano and the silver-framed photographs. 'Look for yourself. Look at my son. Go on.' It was more than an invitation. 'Look,' she said.

I went across to the piano where there were dozens of photographs. But they were all of a baby and a boy. It was as if Adam Jones had never made it beyond his middle teens. There were shots of a bonny baby, in his cot and in the arms of Mrs Jones, when she was young and pretty and healthy, in love with life and her newborn son, laughing with delight at the miracle of this baby; and then Adam as a chubby-legged toddler, holding hands with his father, both of them smiling on some sunny English beach; and Adam a bit older, six or seven, long-haired and grinning to reveal the gaps in his front teeth, holding a child's violin. The boy grew before my eyes. But he did not grow to manhood. Not in these photographs.

I looked across at Mrs Jones. Her eyes were closed. The dog had seized the opportunity to climb on to the sofa and snuggle up to her. Her head was dropping forward.

'I get so very tired,' she said, looking up at me sharply. 'Did your grandmother experience that tiredness?'

'Yes, ma'am.'

I picked up a photograph of Adam at the age of about ten, on stage in an evening suit standing before an audience of adults and children who were on their feet and clapping. He held a child-sized oboe in his hands.

I put it back down.

'Chemotherapy makes you exhausted,' I said.

I looked at her, and she was sleeping. I turned back to the piano, my eyes ranging over the photographs, waiting for them to tell me something. No brothers, no sisters. Adam as a little boy in his Superman pyjamas. A posed picture of a youth orchestra. And another, a year or two later. And sitting in front of his mother on a carousel, both of them grinning and waving as their horse rode past the camera.

Goodbye, Daddy, goodbye.

I was holding the photograph in my hands before I knew it. The silver frame was flecked with the first signs of age. And I held it for a long moment before I realised that the Filipina housekeeper, Rosalita, was standing in the doorway, watching me. She came into the room and began to clear away the tea things. I looked back at the photograph in my hands.

Soldiers, I saw.

Young men in uniform, I saw.

This was the same photograph I had seen in the shining tower, sitting all alone on the desk of Hugo Buck, splashed with his fresh blood. The same seven with the same unbreakable smiles.

And again I saw that it was only at first glance that it looked like a photograph of soldiers. Despite the old-fashioned military uniforms, these were boys, not men. Schoolboys dressed as warriors. No, not men, but boys who would not be boys for much longer.

One of them was the young unspoilt Adam Jones and the other, on the far side of the photograph, was the teenage Hugo Buck.

I had only known them a couple of decades later, as dead men, murder victims, drowned in their own blood. I had only ever seen them as corpses on stainless steel slabs in the cold room of the Iain West Forensic Suite.

But when you looked, when you really looked, they were both unmistakable.

'I must have nodded off,' Mrs Jones said, suddenly standing next to me, and so close and so unexpected that I almost gasped out loud.

She took the frame from me, looked at the photograph as if she had not seen it for a while, then replaced it exactly where it had been, in its little groove of dust on the black lacquer of the piano.

She'd wanted me to see, and she'd wanted me to understand, but I saw now that this courteous, kind and dying woman would really prefer it if I did not actually touch her photographs.

'Did you ever meet Hugo Buck, Mrs Jones?'

'Hugo? I haven't seen him for, what, must be nearly twenty

years. He went into the City. I understand he's doing very well.'

'And your son knew Hugo Buck,' I said. 'They were friends, weren't they?'

She nodded. 'At Potter's Field. They were at school together.'

7

I drove back to 27 Savile Row and for the rest of that day and for most of the next our team never left Major Incident Room One.

The discovery of the second photograph changed everything. It gave us our MLOE – main line of enquiry – and focused all of the double homicide investigation on seven schoolboys in military uniform, grinning at a camera twenty years ago.

'Work out from the photograph applying the ABC principle at all times,' DCI Mallory warned us, moving between the workstations where we hunted, our phones on permanent charge and HOLMES2 – the Home Office Large Major Enquiry System, the mainframe police computer – flickering on the screens in front of us. 'Assume nothing. Believe nothing. Challenge and check everything.'

The sky was flat and white above the rooftops of Mayfair when Mallory faced us for his afternoon briefing. He ran a hand across his scalp and took a joyless gulp of cold takeaway tea.

'Right,' he said. 'What are we looking at?'

We were looking at the large flat plasma screen on the wall of MIR-1, and on the screen was the photograph that had been in the home of Adam Jones's mother, and also on Hugo Buck's desk.

DI Whitestone, the MIT's deputy SIO, cleared her throat and said, 'Sir, this photograph was taken at Potter's Field College in the spring of 1988. Potter's Field College is a boarding school for boys aged thirteen to eighteen on the border of Berkshire and Buckinghamshire. The seven boys in the photograph are all wearing the uniform of the school's Combined Cadet Force. On the far left of the picture is Adam Jones. And on the far right is Hugo Buck.'

Next to the screen was Mallory's wall – a massive whiteboard with the physical photograph of the seven smiling boys, eight inches by ten inches out of its frame, looking tiny tacked up there, and next to it a selection of pictures of Jones and Buck taken at the scenes of their murder and again at their autopsy at the Iain West.

'The Combined Cadet Force is the Potter's Field version of the Officer Training Corps,' Whitestone continued, 'which they still go in for at a lot of these old public schools.'

'And Potter's Field is one of the oldest,' Mallory said. 'Five hundred years old? It has to be as old as Harrow, St Paul's, Westminster, Winchester, Rugby and Marlborough. And of course Slough Comprehensive.' He glanced at our blank faces. 'Eton,' he explained. 'They call themselves Slough Comprehensive. It's their little joke. What's our source for the photograph?'

I said, 'Sir, this is the copy I obtained from the mother of Adam Jones.'

'And we're absolutely certain it's the same one that was on the desk of Hugo Buck?'

DI Gane looked up from his laptop. 'The one at the bank had some superficial damage, sir. There was a blood trace that had seeped under the glass. But it's the same photograph all right.'

'And were Jones and Buck in contact after leaving school?' Mallory asked.

'Looks like they went their separate ways, sir,' I replied. 'Jones's mother hadn't seen Hugo Buck in nearly twenty years. She wasn't aware of his death.'

Gane said, 'Doesn't she read the papers?'

'She's in the last stage of terminal cancer,' I said. 'I think she has other things on her mind.'

'Because the mother wasn't aware of contact doesn't mean there wasn't any,' Gane reasoned.

'Natasha Buck, Hugo Buck's widow, has no recollection of ever meeting Adam Jones,' I said. 'She would have remembered a homeless heroin addict turning up at their door or their wedding.'

'Jones tried to make contact with Buck at his office,' Whitestone said. 'I spoke to the PA at ChinaCorps and she can remember a man claiming to be an old friend of Buck's turning up at the office wanting to see him. This is two or three years back. She described the man as looking like a tramp. Sounds like Jones. But Buck wouldn't see him and security had to escort the unknown visitor from the building. Apparently it was an ugly little scene.'

'The junkie tapping his rich mate for money and getting a knockback,' Gane said.

'That's a reasonable assumption,' Mallory said.

'So we're definitely treating this as a double homicide, sir?' Gane asked. 'We're working on the theory that it's the same perp? Even without contact since – what's the school? – Potter's Field?'

'Yes,' Mallory confirmed. 'The killer's MO. The manner of death. The school connection. It's enough. It's more than enough. How are we doing with prints?'

'We've identified and eliminated all the prints found in the ChinaCorps office,' Gane said. 'The alley where Jones was found is a forensic nightmare. Full of prints that we can't identify and never will.'

'Glove prints?' Mallory said.

'No, boss. Sorry, boss.'

Mallory shook his bald head. 'There should be glove prints.' He stared up at the photograph. 'Who are the other five boys?'

'We're chasing that down, sir,' Whitestone said. 'Should have names by the end of play today. DC Wolfe's going to talk to Adam Jones's mother again and I've sounded out the school. The Head Master's calling me.'

'And I want the photographer, please,' Mallory said. 'Find out who took the photograph, will you, DI Whitestone? And give us a close-up, would you, DI Gane?'

Gane tapped some keys and the camera seemed to move in for a better look. Seven faces swam out of the past and into vivid close-up.

We looked at them in silence.

The boys had all looked the same to me at first. Seven smiling sons of privilege, cocky and smug in their military uniforms and their mullet haircuts, certain that tomorrow belonged to them. But now they were starting to look like individuals.

Adam Jones on the left – a skinny kid with an open, guileless face, looking far younger than the rest. The only one who still looked like a child.

Hugo Buck on the right – dark and mannish, already looking like he needed to shave every day, confident in his looks and his strength and his place in the world.

I was looking harder at the photo, really seeing it for the first time. They were not all the same.

They were not even all smiling.

In the middle of the group was a serious, delicate-looking boy in dark glasses, his fringe swept back off a high forehead.

He was flanked by the twins – identical, I could now see. Tall, good-looking and cold. One of them had a jumble of jagged scars running down one side of his face.

Next to the twin with the scars, between him and Adam Jones, there was a chubby, leering adolescent, the tip of his tongue exploring a corner of his mouth.

And on the other side, next to Buck, there was a grinning dark-skinned youth, possibly Indian, far taller than the rest.

Only their uniforms were the same.

'So what exactly is this Combined Cadet Force?' Gane said. 'Posh rich kids playing soldiers?'

'They take it seriously,' Mallory said. 'A significant number of boys take up commissions in these schools. I bet the British Army is still the biggest employer of Old Potter's Field Boys. Even now. They say that Old Etonians go into the army, politics and acting while Old Potters go into the army, banking and jail.'

I wondered how Mallory knew so much about it.

'But what's the point of them?' Gane persisted. 'The Officer Training Corps. The Combined Cadet Force. Why do a bunch of public schoolboys need to dress up as soldiers?'

Whitestone looked at her notes. 'It's been around for quite a while. The Potter's Field Combined Cadet Force was founded in 1805 as the Potter's Field Rifles.'

Mallory smiled with affection at Gane, his round John Lennon glasses glinting in the overhead lights. 'That year ring any bells, DI Gane? No? The country thought that Napoleon was about to invade. He had an army of two hundred thousand men on the coast of France. These grand old schools were preparing a home guard. A youth movement to repel the invaders.'

'And did Napoleon bottle it, sir?' Gane asked. 'Excuse my ignorance.'

'Yes, Gane, Napoleon seriously bottled it.' Mallory looked at the screen. 'But whether they called them an Officer Training Corps or a Combined Cadet Force or something else, the public schools all kept their Rifles.'

'They join at fifteen,' Whitestone said, 'around the age of the boys in the photograph. And they're taught by regular serving army officers. Leadership skills, signals. And how to shoot. They have a range weekend where they use live ammunition.'

'Any other business?' Mallory said.

'Bob the Butcher, sir,' Gane said.

And then he turned on me.

'You don't talk to the press, OK? You just never do it. We have people to do that for us. The media liaison officers – leave it to them, all right? Because as soon as you start talking to journalists, as soon as you start mouthing off with your little theories, then every mummy's boy with an iMac and a grudge against society starts crawling out of the woodwork, boasting on all the social network sites about how antisocial they've been. And once they do – once they start claiming to be Bob the Butcher – then we have to follow it up, chase down their IP addresses, go round to their house and tell them they've been very, very naughty. So we don't talk to the press, the MLOs do. OK?'

'Fair enough,' I said.

He saw that I wasn't going to argue with him, and he softened.

'Especially to this Scarlet Bush,' he continued. 'She's poison. They say she's got a tabloid brain and a broadsheet mouth. Or is it the other way round?'

I hesitated. 'But you're taking Bob the Butcher seriously?'

'We have no choice,' Gane said. 'If someone claims to have committed murder, then we have to take them seriously. And run them down. It's sort of our job.'

Mallory said, 'You've got the IP address for this Bob the Butcher?'

'Not yet, sir,' Gane replied. 'He's running his messages through some kind of anonymiser or anonymous proxy. Probably Tor or I2P. It's an intermediary that's meant to act as a wall between the user and the rest of the digital world. Most of the child pornography online is run through anonymisers. It's the deep web, designed to bury an IP address. Bob's been in touch again, if anybody's interested.'

Gane hit a couple of keys. On the big TV screen a social network site replaced the photograph of the seven boys. A black-and-white photograph the size of a postage stamp featuring a thin-faced man in a suit, tie and hat, an insolent cigarette dangling from one corner of his mouth. A face from history.

Mallory read the message aloud: 'I am become Death, the destroyer of worlds. Behold the dark angel of the people, righteous avenger of the dispossessed. Bob the Butcher is coming. Kill all bankers. Kill all pigs. #killallpigs.'

Gane laughed. 'Now there's someone who has played one too many computer games.'

Mallory wasn't laughing. 'The first part is from Robert

Oppenheimer, the father of the atomic bomb,' he said. '"I am become Death, the destroyer of worlds". The photograph is of Oppenheimer. He was quoting a Hindu scripture, the Bhagavad-Gita. He said it after they tested the first nuclear weapon. After the world changed for ever.'

'I'll find him,' Gane said, stabbing some keys.

The photograph of the seven boys returned to the screen.

'The school is the key,' Mallory said. 'Potter's Field.'

'Potter's Field,' Whitestone said. 'The school was founded by King Henry VIII in 1509, the first year of his reign. The name is taken from the Bible. A potter's field is a piece of land that's good for nothing but burial. The priests bought the potter's field with Judas's blood money. Matthew 27:3–8. "And the chief priests took the silver pieces and said; It is not lawful to put them into the treasury, because it is the price of blood. And they took counsel and bought with them the potter's field, to bury strangers in. Wherefore that field was called – The Field of Blood. Unto this day."'

She smiled modestly.

'Sunday school?' Gane said.

'Google,' Whitestone replied.

'They're more of a mixed bunch than I thought they would be,' I said. 'Hugo Buck comes from an old banking family. Adam Jones was at Potter's Field on a music scholarship. They didn't just die in different worlds. They came from different worlds.'

Mallory nodded. 'Old money. New money. And no money. But who hates them?'

We stared at the photograph of the Potter's Field Combined Cadet Force, class of 1988. The only sound was the traffic crawling along Savile Row five floors below. And I saw how

Mallory used the silence, how it created a space for the truth to seep in.

'Maybe they hate each other,' I said.

I was late. Horribly late.

Scout had an extra class after school. Fashion illustration, whatever that was. Something for kids who loved to draw and whose parents were stuck in an office. But I was still late.

Scout was waiting with her teacher, Miss Davies, just inside the school gates. Everyone else had gone home long ago. The pair of them were chatting happily – or Scout was talking and the blonde young New Zealander was listening, smiling and nodding and unable to get a word in edgeways. Scout really loved Miss Davies.

I parked the car as close as I could get to the school gates and ran to them.

'Sorry,' I said. 'The traffic.'

Miss Davies was all smiles and Kiwi cool and very understanding. Scout was poker-faced, revealing nothing.

In the car on the way home I looked at her in my rear-view mirror, watching her watching the street.

'Scout,' I said.

She looked at my eyes in the mirror. 'Yes?'

'I'm sorry.'

'It was one of your days to pick me up. Not one of Mrs Murphy's days. One of your days.'

'I'll work it out better,' I said. 'Maybe Mrs Murphy can do more days. But I'll never be late again.'

She wasn't looking at me any more.

'Scout?'

'What?'

'Forgive me?'

She looked back at the street.

'I always forgive you,' she said.

And I thought about that all the way home.

Scout rolled on the floor with the dog.

'He cries in the night sometimes,' she said. 'Stan does. I hear him.'

I nodded. 'I hear him too,' I said.

'I think he misses his old home.'

'No,' I said. 'He misses his mother's heartbeat. But there's a trick for young dogs that miss their mothers. I'll show you.'

I found an old alarm clock and slipped it under the blanket in the dog's basket.

'He'll think it's his old mum dog,' I said. 'He'll hear the tick-tock of the clock and he'll think it's her heartbeat.'

Scout looked so doubtful that the idea suddenly seemed ridiculous to me.

But it worked.

That night I lay awake until just before dawn, turning my pillow over until the meat market fell silent and the light in the room was milky grey. Stan did not whimper once.

8

The Black Museum of Scotland Yard is not a museum at all. It is not open to the public and its contents are guarded behind heavily locked doors. Officially, it is not even called the Black Museum. After complaints from officers working in areas with large ethnic minorities, it was renamed the Metropolitan Police Crime Museum, an enforced change that ensured we would always and forever call it the Black Museum.

As I had told PC Greene, the Black Museum is a teaching aide. That was why it was established in the Victorian era, that was why it still existed – to save the lives of policemen by educating them in the criminal's tools of the trade.

And that was why DCI Mallory and I went to the Black Museum. I had spent a full day on HOLMES2, slogging through just one item on the MLOE checklist – identifying modus operandi suspects, murderers who killed by cutting throats and who were neither dead nor in prison. It was a long, frustrating day of too many dead ends and too much caffeine.

So when the day's light was fading, we went looking for a murder weapon.

DCI Mallory and I stood outside Room 101 in New Scotland Yard. He was grinning broadly.

'Room 101,' he chuckled. 'It's almost too perfect, isn't it?'

I must have looked baffled.

'Room 101,' he repeated, frowning with mild disappointment. 'The torture chamber in the Ministry of Love. George Orwell? *1984*?'

My brain scrambled to catch up. I had read *1984* when I was a kid. Somebody made me. 'Where the rats are,' I said. 'The rats in the cage that get strapped to Winston's face.'

'Room 101 is the place of your worst nightmare,' Mallory said. 'It's the room that contains the worst thing in the world. O'Brien tells Winston that we all know what is waiting for us inside.'

Mallory knocked on the door and a voice told us to come in.

Even for a detective chief inspector in Homicide and Serious Crime, visits to the Black Museum were meant to be by appointment only. But the curator in Room 101 – a Sergeant John Caine with thirty years' service on his face and not a gram of flab on his body – greeted Mallory like an old friend.

'What can we do you for, sir?' the keeper of the Black Museum said as they shook hands.

'We're looking for a knife, John,' Mallory said. 'Or at least some kind of double-edged blade.' He was opening his briefcase. 'I figure it has to be less than a sword but more than a knife.' He removed a file containing a sheaf of photographs and spread them on the curator's desk. 'Something that could have done this.'

Sergeant Caine calmly studied half a dozen photographs, copies of the same murder scene and autopsy pictures that were on Mallory's wall in the Major Incident Room, while I looked around me. The walls were covered with bookshelves and badges from police forces around the world, presumably showing their gratitude for a glimpse inside the Black Museum.

I picked up an elderly hardback book from Caine's desk. There was no dust jacket. *Forty Years of Scotland Yard*, it said. *The Record of a Lifetime's Service in the Criminal Investigation Department* by Frederick Porter Wensley.

'Don't touch that,' Sergeant Caine said, not even looking at me.

I put the book down.

To Mallory he said, 'These are the Bob the Butcher killings.'

'We've yet to make that connection,' Mallory said.

'But you're treating it as a double homicide, sir?'

Mallory nodded. 'Same killer, same MO. But I'm not convinced it's Bob.'

Sergeant Caine looked at me without warmth or welcome. Mallory had warned me that he was wary of strangers. Although wary didn't quite cover his cold, gimlet-eyed hostility.

'This is DC Wolfe, the newest member of my MIT.'

I held out my hand but Caine didn't seem to see it. Happy to remind me that, as a sergeant, even one in uniform, he outranked me.

'Right,' he said. 'Ground rules. No photographs. No touching, unless I say so for the purpose of demonstration. And absolutely nothing I say is for the record. Got it?'

'Got it, sergeant,' I said.

'Good. Then let's go.'

There was a locked door inside Room 101. Sergeant Caine unlocked it and we went inside. It was a living room from the distant past. There was a fireplace, a bay window, gaslights. It took me a moment to register that although these were false, there were weapons everywhere, and these were very real. A glass case full of firearms. A desk covered with what looked like the results of a sword armistice. A hangman's noose dangled from the ceiling, which I thought was overdoing it a bit.

'What was the name of the detective who founded the museum?' Mallory asked.

'Inspector Neame, sir,' Caine said. 'In 1874. Do you want to have a wander round in here? There are plenty of blades.'

Mallory was peering at what looked like a pirate's cutlass. 'Please,' he said. 'You go ahead with DC Wolfe.'

I followed the curator through a doorway with no door.

'I heard they might open this place up,' I said, filling the silence.

He stopped to look at me sharply. 'Open it up?'

'To the public,' I said. 'To raise money.'

'The public?' he said with some distaste, as if it was the public who were largely responsible for the human misery on display in Room 101. 'Who wants to open it up to the public?'

'The council,' I said, wishing I had kept my cakehole shut.

'Over their dead bodies,' said Sergeant Caine.

'Don't you mean—'

'I know whose bodies I mean,' he said. Then he clapped his hands, his mood brightening as he gave me an evil grin. 'Not one of those queasy types, are you? Let me know if you're going to bring up your Weetabix.'

'I've been here before,' I said. 'A Crime Academy visit.'

'Ah, an expert. An old hand. Let's see how much of an expert you are, sonny.' He picked up a walking stick. 'What does this look like?'

'A sword,' I guessed. 'A sword disguised as a walking stick.'

Sergeant Caine smiled. 'Clever boy.' He pulled apart the walking stick to reveal twelve inches of gleaming Sheffield steel. Then closed it up again.

'So if I came at you . . .'

He swung the stick towards my face. I caught it with both hands.

'I would grab it before you had a chance to use it as a sword,' I said, twisting my grip and pulling the walking stick from his hand.

I allowed myself a small smile that immediately faded when I saw that he was still holding the handle. It was a handgun.

'Which would leave me with nothing but my firearm,' he said, pointing it at my face. 'Bang, bang, you're dead.'

'Does it work?' I asked, handing him the walking stick.

'Oh, they all work,' Caine said. He carefully attached the walking stick to the handle. 'That's the point.'

Mallory came into the room.

'See anything you fancy, sir?' Caine asked.

Mallory shook his head.

'Probably here somewhere,' the curator said cheerfully.

You would think so. The Black Museum contains every murder weapon you can imagine and plenty more that you can't. More than a hundred years' worth of explosives, firearms and poison. And every item in there has seen active service.

On the counter in front of me was a cutlass used by the Kray brothers. Next door was a rocket launcher used by the IRA. At first I thought Caine had a mini-kitchen in here, but it turned out to be the cooking pot where serial killer Dennis Nilsen boiled the meat off his victims before pouring it down the drains. And there were more knives than I had seen in the basement of West End Central.

The Black Museum was spread over several large, neat rooms full of glass display cases and exhibits and shelves with the facemasks of men who stole lives. Blank, ordinary, banal-looking men who shot, poisoned, stabbed, chopped up, boiled and ate their victims. All these pathetic little men who had abruptly aborted the happiness of countless lifetimes, all these savage creeps who had built a mountain of human misery.

Yes, I had been here before.

But this time was different.

Now I was not with my peers.

There was no hiding in a crowd, and no easy laughter to relieve the tension. This did not feel like a school trip. This time the Black Museum confronted me with all its horror, and its collection of human cruelty, and it was just too much for me.

Or perhaps it was something else. The first time I had been here, on that visit with the Crime Academy, I was a cocky unmarried kid who knew nothing about loss. And now I knew.

First came the sweat, and then suddenly I was crouching over a wastepaper basket, quietly being sick. Mallory and Sergeant Caine came into the room. If they saw my discomfort then they gave no sign.

'Your weapon could be custom-made,' Caine was saying. 'Some kind of knife that's made to cut a man's throat – and only that. Something that's made for that purpose and that purpose alone.'

Outside, Big Ben was chiming six. Mrs Murphy would have picked up Scout and would be making their dinner while my daughter and our dog chased each other across the great open space of our loft.

I stood up, looking with embarrassment and disgust at the yellow bile I had brought up. Mallory lightly patted my shoulder.

I couldn't look at him just yet.

'Nice cup of tea?' he said.

Mallory took me to his home.

His wife appeared at the door as we pulled up outside a terraced house on a quiet street in Pimlico. A tall, slim, grey-haired woman with an amused twinkle in her eye and carpet slippers on her feet. A West Highland White Terrier stood watch between them as Mr and Mrs Mallory communicated in the shorthand of the long-term married.

'Done for the day then?' she said, folding her arms.

'Not quite, hen,' he said, pecking her cheek.

'Going out again then.'

'Spruce up a bit first.'

'Something to eat?'

'Tea would be lovely.'

She had the same Aberdeen accent as her husband. They could have been born in the same street.

'Who's this?'

'New man. DC Wolfe.'

'Hello, hen,' Mrs Mallory said, her face breaking into a broad smile. 'Come on in.'

She brought us tea and biscuits, and I began to feel better with sugar and caffeine inside me. Mallory bolted his tea quickly and disappeared, shoving in a ginger nut.

'Five minutes,' he told me.

The Westie followed him, panting with pleasure.

Their home was a small, neat maisonette. The photographs on the mantelpiece and bookshelves, their colours fading now, showed the Mallorys' old life under some tropical sun. The pair of them, fifteen, twenty, twenty-five years younger, raising glasses and smiling shyly at some café table. And Mallory, his hair already gone at thirty, grinning in shorts, short-sleeve shirt and a black peaked cap, two Asian men in the same uniform grinning either side of him. And the Mallorys smiling again for the camera with a city built by a harbour behind and far below them.

'Hong Kong,' Mrs Mallory said. 'My husband was in the Royal Hong Kong Police Force for fifteen years. "We serve with pride and care". Maybe he told you.'

'No, ma'am.'

She laughed. 'You can call me Margaret.'

'DCI Mallory hasn't told me anything, ma'am – Margaret.'

'We came back in 1997. After the changeover. When it lost the royal bit. The British went home and so did we. Bit of a shock to the system. We miss it. Although of course that old Hong Kong is not there any more.'

The photographs ran the course of two lifetimes. But I could see no pictures of children.

'And do you have a family?' Mrs Mallory asked me.

'I have a little girl,' I said. 'My parents are long gone. No brothers, no sisters.' A beat. 'I lost my wife.'

She waited for more, but there wasn't any more.

'I see,' she said.

'I have my daughter. Scout. She's five.' I stirred my tea. 'But there's just me and her.'

Mrs Mallory nodded. 'Then you have a family,' she said, and she had me for life.

We crossed the river as the sun set, the groups of tourists on the bridge taking photographs of the Palace of Westminster, Big Ben and Westminster Abbey, all majestic in the dying light, as the London commuters hurried home, not even noticing the everyday magic of this place.

'And now you've met my wife,' Mallory said. 'Take the Lambeth Road on the far side of the bridge.'

'Sir.'

I drove south until two giant cannon reared out of the twilight. They sat before a domed building flying the Union Jack.

'We're going to the Imperial War Museum?'

'It was once the Bethlem Royal Hospital,' Mallory said. 'Bedlam. The lunatic asylum. Did you know that? You can park round the back in St George's Road. We're not going through the front door.'

A security guard emerged as we were coming through the gardens. He stared at us with suspicion until a woman's voice called out to him: 'It's all right, Charlie, they're with me.'

The security guard stepped back, and there was a young woman in a wheelchair. She smiled when she saw Mallory.

'Sir,' she said, and her smile grew bigger as she saluted.

'Hello, Carol,' he said, leaning forward to kiss her on each cheek.

He introduced me and we waited while she turned her wheelchair in a tight space. I went to help but she stopped me with a curt, 'I've got it'.

We followed her down a narrow corridor that led to the main hall. The lights were off. In the darkness Spitfires and Messerschmitts and Hurricanes and V2 flying bombs hung above us, frozen in mid-flight, frozen in time.

'How can I help you, sir?' Carol said.

Mallory was opening his briefcase. 'We're looking for a murder weapon, Carol.' He handed her the file.

She slowly leafed through it.

'Our conjecture is that the weapon was designed for cutting a man's throat,' Mallory said.

'Your conjecture is right, sir,' she said, smiling again. 'I know just the thing. We should have one in storage. Please follow me.'

The knife was just under twelve inches long, most of it blade, a blade that was long and thin and double-edged, designed to slip easily into human flesh and then cut through it without fuss. Mallory handed it to me, and I was surprised to find that it weighed next to nothing. The handle had a comforting ring grip, sitting easy in my closed right fist, and the thing conveyed a sense of terrible power.

'The Fairbairn-Sykes fighting knife,' Carol said. 'Developed by William Ewart Fairbairn and Eric Anthony Sykes when they were policing in Shanghai before the war.'

'The commando knife,' Mallory said. 'Of course.'

I could not get used to how light it felt in my hand. It was so easy to hold. A sharp stabbing point, a good cutting edge. The double-edged blade glinted in the half-light of the storage room.

'This was invented by two policemen?' I said.

Carol nodded. 'W. E. Fairbairn was an expert in close-combat fighting. This was designed to be the perfect fighting knife but it turned out to be the perfect killing knife. Standard-issue sidearm for all World War Two commandos. If the Nazis caught you with one of these, you were shot on the spot as a spy. Most knives are not specifically designed to kill – apart from the Fairbairn-Sykes. It looks easy to use, but it's not. You have to know which arteries are closest to the surface and unprotected by clothing. Give it here, will you?'

The young woman in the wheelchair gave us a demonstration. With the fingers on her left hand spread wide she mimed pulling a man's head to one side. With the knife in her right hand she stabbed the point sideways and then quickly pushed it forward.

'Punch and pull,' she said. 'Punch the tip of the knife through the side of the neck and then pull the blade out of the front. You can't patch that up with a couple of stitches and some Nurofen Plus. Most people who want to cut a throat start on the outside. They hack and saw and chop.'

She mimed hacking and sawing and chopping.

'That's all right if you want to hurt their feelings,' she said. 'That's all right if you want to put a crimp in their day. But not if you want to be certain of killing them.'

'The punch and pull,' Mallory said. 'It cuts the windpipe and then you have a good chance of cutting the carotid arteries.'

'More than a good chance,' Carol said. 'That move is called the carotid thrust. Cutting the carotid arteries is the whole point, sir. If the shock doesn't immediately kill them, then they die because the carotids have been severed and there's no blood being pumped from the heart to the brain.'

'How long?' I asked.

'Brain-dead immediately,' she said. 'Unconscious in five seconds and dead in twelve seconds.'

'And when did they stop making these knives?'

'They've never stopped making these knives. It's been evolving for almost a hundred years. There's a contemporary version used by the Special Forces – the UK-SFK. It's the greatest combat knife ever invented.' She looked at Mallory, and I wondered how they knew each other. 'And now Bob the Butcher's got one.'

Mallory smiled. 'We don't know if it's Bob,' he said. 'What we do know is that it's someone with training who has access to specialist weapons.' He looked at me. 'Presumably you can get a Fairbairn-Sykes online?'

'You can buy anything online,' I said.

'Apart from training and knowledge and the expertise you would need to execute the carotid thrust,' Carol said. 'That takes years to accumulate. And there's something else.'

We watched her feel the weight of the Fairbairn-Sykes fighting knife.

'To kill someone with one of these – to stick the stabbing point in the side of their neck and then pull it clean out the front . . .' She paused and looked up at Mallory from her wheelchair. 'You would have to really hate their guts, sir.'

I was in the ring and my legs were gone.

We were only a minute into the third round of sparring but already I was weak with exhaustion, flat-footed and breathing through my mouth, sagging against the ropes, my elbows pressed protectively against my lower ribcage, my hands raised to protect my head, the black leather of the fourteen-ounce Lonsdale gloves slick with sweat against my face.

The punches kept coming.

They were being thrown by a small man with long silver hair poking out of his old Everlast headguard. He grinned broadly at my exhaustion, revealing both a mean streak and a blue mouthguard. Hunched behind his tight, high guard, risking nothing, he moved in for the finish.

With my face buried deep into my gloves, I felt his body

shots rip into my side with blinding speed. The small man was both skinny and muscle-packed, and hit very hard. Left ribs, right ribs. Left ribs, right ribs. I dug my elbows in deeper, but I could still feel their whiplash sting.

We were face to face now. At six feet, I towered above my opponent – Fred was his name – but probably the first thing I had ever learned in a boxing ring is that speed beats power. The bigger you are, the more there is to hit.

A left hook came through my ragged defence and made me gasp as it struck the lowest rib. I dug my elbows in deeper, really not wanting another one, and the moment I lowered my gloves a few inches Fred smacked me in my poorly guarded head.

Upstairs downstairs, I thought, cursing my basic mistake – leaving one area undefended while another is being attacked. I rolled against the ropes, willing my legs to work, trying to get back up on the balls of my feet.

But a left hook cracked against the right side of my headguard, and then a right hook cracked harder against the left side, making my ears ring despite the thick protective leather of my headguard.

I must have instinctively lifted my gloves a fraction to protect my head because Fred whipped in a wicked left hook, digging me low in the right ribs.

He was flagging too. Hitting someone non-stop takes it out of you. His combinations were slowing down, but a body shot is the hardest punch to recover from and I felt my dead legs sagging. Everything was telling me to go down. But I didn't go down. I stayed on my feet, kept up by nothing but the ropes behind me and the will inside.

Fred grinned at me, revealing that old blue mouthguard. I

watched him lift the elbow of his left arm, preparing for a left hook. But such is the beautiful balance of boxing that if your opponent can hit you then you are in a position to hit them back.

I saw my chance and took it.

Before Fred could slam a short hard left hook into my aching body, or my ringing head, I whipped a short left uppercut on to the point of his chin, jerking back his head just as the buzzer went to end the third and final round.

We fell into each other's arms, totally spent, both laughing.

When we broke from the embrace, I stood there bent double, fighting for breath. I could hear the sound of skipping ropes, the business news on the TV by the treadmills, and a trainer chanting yoga instructions. When I looked up, Fred was taking off his battered headguard and his long silver hair was tumbling down – the hair of a veteran pirate. He pulled out his mouthguard.

'You're so lucky to be training,' he said.

He lifted a glove in salute and I touched it with my own glove.

'Good,' he told me. 'But keep those elbows tucked in and don't be a statue. When you've thrown your punches, get out of there. Don't stand around taking pictures. Even when you're knackered. Especially when you're knackered.'

My breath was slowly returning. 'It's hard,' I managed.

Fred laughed. 'It's supposed to be hard. If it was easy, then everyone would do it.' He patted my back. 'Warm down with thirty minutes on the bike and don't forget your stretching.'

Fred climbed out of the ring. He wandered over to the sound system and put on The Jam. This was Smithfield Amateur

Boxing Club, and Fred ran the place, so he got to choose the music. 'Going Underground' began to belt out.

I was feeling better already. My ribs might be sore in the morning but the ringing in my head had already calmed down and nothing else had sustained serious damage. It was not the pain itself that wore you out so much as the shock of being hit. Yet I was always surprised how little being punched in the face actually hurt. It was those body shots that killed you.

Then I was aware of someone watching me.

He was by the free weights, and had gloves on, those fingerless gloves for lifting weights, and his meaty shoulders looked as though he had lifted a lot of them. You don't see many Asians that heavily into their weights. But I guess you see more than you used to.

He held my gaze for a long moment, then removed his gloves and walked to the cupboards where Fred stored the boxing kit. He took out a black headguard and a pair of bright yellow gloves. Then he walked back across the gym and climbed into the ring. And by now I knew him. Just poking out of the top of his training vest I could see the bruise where I had punched him in the heart because he'd laughed at my dog.

'I'll fight you,' he said, pulling on the gloves.

'We call it sparring,' I said, 'not fighting.'

'But it's full contact, right?' he said. 'You're trying to punch each other's lights out, right?'

I shrugged. 'Of course.'

I saw no point explaining that there was an etiquette involved in sparring, an unwritten and unspoken code of honour, and a deep degree of trust. He didn't look as though he would be very interested in any of that stuff. I had been sparring with Fred for five years, but neither of us had ever been hit with a low blow, neither of us had ever left the ring feeling angry. Our friendship had been forged in the rough intimacy of sparring. But it was true what the weightlifter said: when we sparred, we didn't hold anything back.

'You sucker-punched me,' the weightlifter said, the anger flaring.

'You were rude to my dog.'

'I wasn't ready then. But I'm ready now.'

'I just did three rounds,' I said.

'I want to see how tough you really are,' he said. 'Unless you're chicken.'

I was looking at his yellow gloves – a pair of ten-ounce Cleto Reyes gloves, the best boxing gloves in the world, hand-made in Mexico, but far too light for hard sparring. But that wasn't what bothered me.

'I'm not sparring with you,' I said, taking my gloves off.

When I moved to get out of the ring, he blocked my path.

'Why not?'

'Because you don't have a mouthguard.'

'I don't need a mouthguard.'

'Yes you do,' I said. 'Everybody needs a mouthguard. Because I could catch you with my elbow. Or I could bang you with my forehead. And there's even an outside chance that I might actually punch you in the mouth.'

Then Fred was there. He took the weightlifter by the elbow and easily turned the far bigger man around. Fred had worked the doors at some point.

'See that sign?'

On the walls of Smithfield ABC gym there were framed photographs of boxers. They were a certain kind of boxer – natural-born fighters, all grit and glory, the kind of boxers Fred loved. Jack Dempsey. Jake La Motta. Joe Frazier. Marvin Hagler. The hard men of the sport. And there were other framed photographs – pictures of kids boxing in Cuba, a dozen of them in the ring at a time, shirtless and skinny and sparring with gloves that looked as though they had just been dug up. And above them all there was a sign.

NO SPARRING WITHOUT PERMISSION

'You don't have permission,' Fred said.

Fred was the smallest man in the gym. But in that place of assorted hard nuts – where policemen came to keep fit, and rough boys from sink estates came to learn the sweet science of bruising, and young women came to learn self-defence, and white-collar City types came to push themselves to the limit – nobody argued with him.

The weightlifter got out of the ring.

'There are many bad things about steroid abuse,' observed Fred, who was the kind of boxer who is also a philosopher. 'Shrunken balls. Acne. Hair loss. But the worst thing is that it wipes out the part of the brain that inhibits aggression. In the end they want to kill someone.'

There was a heavy bag near the exit door. Just before the weightlifter walked out of Smithfield ABC, he hit the bag as hard as he could.

Fred laughed with contempt.

'It's not about how hard you can hit,' he said.

9

Stan knew something was up.

The dog was the only member of the family who had eaten breakfast, but Scout was standing at the window with her palms pressed against the glass, watching the street, occasionally flinching with anticipation at the sight of a car pulling up, while I kept checking the clock, my watch, my mobile.

She should have been here by now.

Stan lay Sphinx-like in the middle of the loft, his front paws demurely crossed, his huge round eyes watching us with suspicion.

Something you want to tell me?

'Oh – oh – oh!' Scout said, and when I went to the window I saw a white van that was stuffed full of dogs.

An Irish Wolfhound occupied the passenger seat, staring with interest at a white-coated porter emerging from the meat market, arms stained red up to the elbow. A pair of Pugs pressed their flat faces against the rear windows, while behind them a forest of tails were erect and wagging as small faces sniffed large bottoms and large faces sniffed small bottoms.

A young woman in muddy combat fatigues got out of the driver's seat. A Labradoodle got out with her. She placed it back in the van and closed the door.

'Stan,' I said, 'it's your ride.'

She was a cheerful young Czech called Jana, and Stan welcomed her like an old friend. It was nothing personal. Stan welcomed everyone like an old friend.

Scout was saying goodbye when without further ceremony the dog walker snapped a lead on Stan's collar and headed for the door.

We returned to the window. A Bichon Frise had somehow squeezed through the van's half-open window and was sniffing the pavement as the Irish Wolfhound considered it with lofty disdain. Stan and Jana appeared on the street. The dog walker put the runaway Bichon Frise under one arm and Stan under the other and delivered them both to the back of the van. Then they were off. We stood at the window until the tail lights had disappeared.

'I hope Stan's all right,' Scout said.

'Are you kidding?' I said. 'He'll have the time of his life with the rest of the pack.'

We went down to Smiths of Smithfield for our breakfast. I was just getting the bill when Stan walked past the window, his lead trailing behind him. Scout went outside to collect him as I got Jana on the phone. I could hear furious barking, sounds of terror and fear, human and canine howls of protest.

'How's Stan doing?' I said.

'Ah,' Jana said. 'Ah, yes. Sam is very fine.'

Scout came into SOS with Stan. He was wild-eyed and panting with thirst and exhaustion. A kindly SOS waiter brought him a large silver bowl of water. Scout set him down and he began to lap it up, very loudly.

'You're sure Stan's fine?' I said.

At the sound of his name, Stan looked up at me, his huge

eyes bulging with outrage. Then he went back to his water, Scout's small hands fussing over him.

'Ah,' said Jana. 'Yes, Sam – lovely little Sam – is very fine. Sam is – ah – enjoying the beautiful park with his friends. There he goes now! Ha ha! Into the trees! Good boy, Sam!'

I looked at Scout and Stan, down on the floor and delighted to see each other, and I knew that from now on we would be walking our own dog.

At the morning briefing in MIR-1, DI Whitestone stood with her back to Mallory's wall. A blown-up photograph of the seven boy soldiers was visible just behind her. She had a list of names in her hand.

'Then there were four,' she said.

She turned to face the wall and carefully drew a red cross over the face of the boy on the extreme left.

'Adam Jones – deceased.'

She drew another red cross over the face of the boy on the extreme right.

'Hugo Buck – deceased.'

And finally she drew a red cross over the boy in the dead centre. The one in dark glasses. The one who wasn't smiling.

'This is the Honourable James Sutcliffe,' Whitestone said. 'Younger son of the Earl of Broughton. Or rather, this *was* the Honourable James Sutcliffe. Two years after this photograph was taken he committed suicide. Walked into the sea off the Amalfi coast where his parents were renting a villa.'

We were all silent.

'The summer he turned eighteen,' Whitestone added.

Mallory said, 'He has a daughter, doesn't he? The boy's father, I mean. The Earl of Broughton.'

Whitestone nodded. 'The Honourable Cressida. She was a bit of a wild young thing in the eighties. Took a pee on the Cenotaph during an anti-capitalism riot.'

'That's the one,' Mallory said.

'Ran off with some German artist thirty years her senior. Reconciled with her parents now, all forgiven.'

'When the boy killed himself, did the carabinieri find a suicide note?' Mallory asked.

'No, sir,' Whitestone said. 'They didn't even find a body. Just his clothes folded on the beach and a half-finished sketch. He was an artist. Apparently the most brilliant of the bunch.'

'Why was there an assumption of suicide if no note was found?'

'James Sutcliffe suffered from clinical depression. He was on quite a cocktail of medication.' DI Whitestone read from her notes. 'Prozac. Luvox. Lustral. Cipralex. He had a history of self-harm.'

Gane said, 'What does a rich kid like that have to be depressed about?'

'Perhaps we need to ask his friends,' Mallory said.

There were four of them left alive.

The twins – identical apart from the starburst of facial scarring on one of them.

The tall, dark, whippet-thin, foreign-looking youth.

And the leering fat boy with the stub of his tongue poking out.

The three red crosses did something to the old photograph. Whitestone picked up a sheaf of eight-by-ten photographs. Photographs of the living. She tapped the image of the unscarred twin standing between James Sutcliffe and the dark-skinned boy.

'Ben King,' she said. 'He's famous.'

She pinned a head-and-shoulders shot to Mallory's wall. A serious, well-groomed man in a suit and tie smiling for some kind of official photograph. It was recognisably the boy in the picture, twenty years on. His face looked vaguely familiar from late-night news shows glimpsed and turned over.

'I know him,' Mallory said. 'Ben King. He's a politician, isn't he?'

'Yes,' Whitestone said. 'His late father was the libel lawyer Quentin King. Ben King is MP for Hillingdon North. Educated at Potter's Field and Balliol, Oxford. PPE first class. On his party's fast track.'

Gane said, 'Which party?'

'Have a guess.'

Gane guessed the wrong one. I would have got it wrong, too.

'There's talk of him as a future Prime Minister,' Whitestone said.

'Independently wealthy, privately educated, slick on TV,' Mallory said. 'Never employed anyone, never run a business, never done a real job.' He thought about it for a moment. 'He'd be perfect. What about his brother? The one with the scars.'

'Ned King,' Whitestone replied, pinning a photograph of a soldier to the wall. 'Serving officer in the British Army. Captain in the Royal Gurkha Rifles. Two tours of Helmand Province. Decorations for valour. He also has a conviction for assault, fifteen years ago.'

The scar tissue on the left side of Ned King's face looked like the price of the medals on his dress uniform.

Next to him Whitestone put up a photograph of a thin balding man in a tuxedo, his bow tie hanging around his scrawny neck like something that had died. He had lost so much weight since his teenage years that he was almost unrecognisable from the fat boy he had been at school.

'Guy "Piggy" Philips,' Whitestone said. 'Known the King brothers since prep school. Father made a fortune in the property market. Played tennis at a high level – junior Wimbledon semi-finals. Then his knee blew up. Teaches sport at his alma mater – Potter's Field.'

'What sports?' Gane asked.

'Tennis. Fencing. Cricket. Skiing. Posh sports, Gane, OK? And distance running.'

'That's how he dropped the weight,' Mallory said.

There was one left. Whitestone pinned a portrait of an intense, unsmiling man to Mallory's wall. He was posing for some kind of company photograph and he considered the camera with eyes that looked black.

'Salman Khan,' Whitestone said. 'From a wealthy Anglo-Indian family. Builders, funnily enough, defying all the racial stereotypes. His father made a pile building estates in the sixties and seventies. Khan has also known the King brothers and Philips since prep school. Works as a human rights lawyer in the London offices of Butterfield, Hunt and West. Considered one of the rising stars of the legal profession. Successfully sued the Ministry of Defence on behalf of disabled servicemen.'

'You mentioned a conviction of assault for Ned King,' Mallory said. 'Anything else on their records?'

'Adam Jones had multiple convictions for drug offences and vagrancy. Six months after the school picture was taken, he was expelled for selling controlled substances behind the tuck shop. Pills. Dope. And plenty of it.'

'The upper class are always a greater mix than they are given credit for,' Mallory noted. 'What was he doing? Supplementing his personal use with some dealing?'

'Looks like it, sir. Adam went off the rails early. He was getting into heroin when the others were getting into Oxford, Sandhurst and Goldman Sachs.'

'DC Wolfe, was Jones expelled from the Royal Academy of Music for dealing?'

'No, sir,' I said. 'Not for dealing. He was smacked out of his brain during an Albinoni concert in Duke Hall. Nodded off during the adagio.'

'Don't you hate it when that happens?' said Gane.

'Our two victims,' Mallory said. 'They were both living dangerously, weren't they? One had a long-term commitment to opiates. The other was a violent, serial philanderer. Either one of those lifestyles would shorten life expectancy.'

He left the rest unsaid, but it hung in the air: their lifestyle choices did nothing to explain their identically butchered throats.

I looked down at a slim red volume I had before me. *Get Tough! How to Win in Hand-to-Hand Fighting – As Taught to the British Commandos and the U.S. Armed Forces.* The author was Captain W. E. Fairbairn, co-inventor of the commando knife. On its front was a drawing of two grappling soldiers. It looked like some old-fashioned *Boy's Own*-style comic. But inside was a manifesto for murder. I had placed a yellow Post-it note on the page I wanted, the one where they taught you how to execute the carotid thrust.

> Artery #3. Knife in right hand, edges parallel to the ground, seize opponent around the neck from behind with your left arm, pulling his head to the left. Thrust point well in; then cut sideways. See Fig. C.

'Piggy Philips has three convictions for criminal damage in an eighteen-month period in the late eighties,' Whitestone continued. 'As far as I can tell, the boys enjoyed smashing up the odd restaurant. Seems they couldn't always buy their way out.'

'Boys will be boys,' Gane said. 'Especially when Daddy's picking up the bill.' He snorted with contempt. 'My dog could get five A levels at Potter's Field. While licking his bollocks.'

'Piggy Philips seemed happy to always take the rap,' Whitestone said. 'According to the local rag, he nearly went down for contempt of court one time. "Disorderly, contemptuous and insolent behaviour towards the magistrate".'

We stared at the photographs, at the boys they had been, and then at the men they had become.

'So they were a gang?' Gane said.

'It's more than that, isn't it?' I said. 'Most of them had known each other pretty much all their lives. One of them sounds as if he was happy to take the rap for the rest of them. It sounds like they were – I don't know – almost brothers.'

'But did that relationship end with their school days or did it endure?' Mallory said. 'That's the next question. And we can start answering it by going to a funeral.'

He stepped closer to the wall.

'What does it say on their jackets? The Latin just above the crest. I can't make it out.'

Whitestone closed her notebook. 'Aut vincere aut mori,' she said. 'Their school motto.'

'Conquer or die,' Mallory said. 'Good motto.'

I found my eyes drifting to the boy in the centre. James Sutcliffe. The one without a smile, the one with the hidden eyes. The boy with the marks of self-harm on his arms who folded his clothes neatly and walked into the sea off the Amalfi coast. He was the only one not represented on the wall by a photograph of the man he had become. Dead by his own hand at eighteen. Even more than the pictures of the two murdered men, Sutcliffe's unsmiling presence made the old school photograph seem heavy with mortality.

These boys are not growing up, I thought. They are rushing to their graves.

The late afternoon light was dying over Highgate Cemetery when the soldier rose from his place on the front row of the crowded chapel, immaculate in the black dress uniform of an officer of the Royal Gurkha Rifles.

Captain Ned King was a big man and he moved slowly to the pulpit, glancing at the large black-and-white photograph of the late Hugo Buck that was placed before his coffin. As Captain King stood in the pulpit, looking at his notes, a bar of the waning light came through the high stained-glass windows and caught him, glinting on the medals he wore on his black jacket and highlighting the white starburst of scar tissue on the left side of his face.

Someone in the packed congregation cleared their throat. Captain King began to speak.

'Death is nothing at all,' he said, reading with the clipped, careful delivery of a man accustomed to public speaking. 'I have only slipped away into the next room. I am I, and you are you.'

My eyes drifted to where he had been sitting. The other three were all there.

Ben King.

Salman Khan.

Guy Philips.

The dead man's oldest friends, in their places of honour, in the front row with the parents of Hugo Buck and his widow, Natasha, her face hidden by a long black veil. Buck's parents were in their late sixties but tanned, attractive, looking as though nothing bad had ever happened to them in their lives before now.

Natasha turned her head and stared at me. Behind the veil her face was impassive and showed absolutely no sign of recognition. I had seen her chauffeur when Mallory and I had arrived at the cemetery, sneaking a cigarette out on the street as he waited with the other drivers. Even now he had seemed like her driver rather than her date. I wondered why the hell that even mattered to me.

'Whatever we were to each other, that we still are,' Captain King said, his voice rising in the high vaulted chapel. 'Call me by my old familiar name. Speak to me in the easy way which you always used. Put no difference in your tone. Wear no forced air of solemnity.'

Mallory leaned his head towards me and his one word was less than a whisper: 'Look.'

Salman Khan was crying. I could not see his face, but the man's shoulders were clearly juddering with sobs, and his hands were over his face to hide his grief. I watched as Ben King slowly turned his head, muttered something consoling in Khan's ear, then turned back to watch his brother. Guy Philips watched the exchange with a kind of cool indifference.

Khan swabbed his face with the palm of one hand. His crying seemed to stop.

'Life means all that it ever meant,' said Captain King, and I saw the shadow of a smile flit across his handsome, ruined face. 'It is the same as it ever was – there is unbroken continuity. Why should I be out of mind because I am out of sight?' He paused. 'I am waiting for you – for an interval – somewhere very near – just round the corner.' King folded his notes. 'All is well,' he said.

I looked at the mourners. Almost all of them were young. Men and women in their thirties, some of them carrying new babies or trying to control toddlers, all of their faces white with shock at the early and brutal death of one of their own generation.

Captain King had returned to his seat. The vicar was talking.

'Come, ye blessed children of my Father, receive the kingdom prepared for you from the beginning of the world.'

Hugo Buck had friends. Many friends. But it was the four men in the front row who flanked his coffin at the end of the service. And now, for the first time, I saw the other three faces clearly.

Salman Khan – a fit, prosperous businessman, in control now but clearly carrying a sadness that pressed on him like a physical weight.

Guy Philips – the top button of his shirt undone, sleepy-eyed, perhaps slightly bored, his face criss-crossed with the broken veins of the hardened drinker. He looked like a sports master from central casting – there was exactly that kind of hearty cruelty about him.

And Ben King – calm, self-contained, an impressive man, his smooth, unmarked face making his brother's image look like a defaced mirror.

At Ben King's word, the four men – the brothers at the front, Philips and Khan behind – crouched, linked arms, and stood up as one with the coffin on their shoulders. They began to walk slowly down the aisle, Buck's parents and his widow behind them.

Music was playing. People were crying. One of them was Salman Khan. With the weight of his dead friend on his left shoulder, grief seemed suddenly to overwhelm him. This time his friends let him weep. All over the chapel, men and women were doing the same. For their friend and for themselves. But Hugo Buck's widow looked straight ahead, passing by without looking left or right, her green eyes dry and unflinching behind that long black veil.

A youngish blonde woman who looked as though she knew her way around a horse was giving out single red roses at the door to the chapel. Mallory and I held back, letting the crowd go, and by the time we left the chapel the woman and the roses were gone, and the congregation were making their way to the grave.

By special request from the family, Hugo Buck was being buried in the West Cemetery, and it looked like a graveyard in a dream. As we followed the mourners up a steep winding path, we walked between row upon row of massive vaults, giant granite crosses and a host of stone angels whose faces were worn away by the years. A colossal stone dog slept for ever by the resting place of his master. An angel carried a sleeping child to heaven. All of it seemed consumed by nature. Ancient trees had grown between the graves and blotted out the dying sun. Ivy clung to tombs, as if claiming ownership. Everywhere wild flowers bloomed among the dead.

I shuddered as the committal prayer drifted through the trees. You could feel winter coming.

'Behold, I show you a mystery,' said the vicar.

'Corinthians,' Mallory said, with some approval. 'The resurrection of the dead. Let's see if we can get a little closer.'

'We shall not all sleep – but we shall all be changed. In a moment – in the twinkling of an eye – at the last trumpet.'

We skirted the back of the crowd. The sound of crying was louder now, in the open air at the edge of the freshly dug grave. Small children had joined in the wailing, upset at seeing grown-ups cry for the first time. The red roses were splashes of colour in a sea of black.

'For the trumpet shall sound – and the dead shall be raised incorruptible – and we shall be changed. For this corruptible must put on incorruption – and this mortal must put on immortality.'

We stopped when we were behind the vicar and directly opposite the mourners at the graveside. I could see the faces of the principal mourners over the shoulders of the crowd. Hugo Buck's parents were unravelling at the task of burying a child. Ben King stood with his arm around them. The politician had a consoling thought for everyone. Only Natasha Buck seemed drained of all emotion, numbed by the rituals of grief.

'Death is swallowed up in victory. Oh death, where is thy sting? Oh grave, where is thy victory?'

There was an electronic buzz as the coffin was automatically lowered.

When the sound stopped, Ned King casually dropped his red rose into the grave. Then they were all dropping their roses. Something inside the parents of the dead man seemed to break as they let go of theirs. They threw them in the grave and turned away, their legs uncertain. Guy Philips was next. Then Salman Khan, composed now. But Ben King paused, and with a gentle smile motioned Natasha to come forward.

'He stands in the presence of the Lord, the same Jesus who said to the dying man on a cross – Today you shall be with me in Paradise.'

Natasha took a step towards him. I saw her lift her veil, stay a moment with her memories, and then very carefully spit into her husband's grave.

Almost as an afterthought, she tossed in the rose.

There was a sudden burst of activity at the graveside. I saw Natasha's head twist towards the red features of Guy Philips, her face suddenly contorted with anger and pain as he expertly did something to her arm and marched her away. Erect and unresisting, Natasha came through the crowd with her hand held by Philips in a grotesque parody of caring, as if she might fall or run away or return once more to the grave of his dead friend.

'My hand,' she said. 'You're fucking hurting me, Piggy.'

I started forward but was stopped by Mallory's hand on my arm. I looked at him and he shook his head once. I felt a stab of shame for doing nothing. But we were here to observe. That was all. I nodded briefly, showing Mallory that I understood, and we followed Natasha and Philips down the path to the cemetery gate.

Out on the street, drivers were springing to attention. Philips opened the back door of Natasha's car. I thought of her as a strong woman, perhaps a hard woman, and it shocked me to see her so passive as he herded her inside.

Philips leaned into the driver's window and gave some instructions, and I saw the chauffeur's face torn between alarm and anger, but he nodded with mute obedience and drove her away. Philips watched them go.

Mallory and I walked back to the graveside. Most of the

congregation seemed oblivious to what had happened. Heads had turned briefly to watch the overcome widow being helped away by her husband's friend, but soon they had returned to see the flowers falling on the coffin. Only one mourner had kept his eyes on the ugly little scene – a freakishly tall man in his sixties who had the hooked, unblinking face of a bird of prey. Now he too stared at the open grave, a single rose in his hand.

Mallory and I watched as Guy Philips returned expressionless, and I knew Mallory had seen it too – how efficiently Philips had dispensed with the problem of the woman.

The crowd was forming a queue to offer their condolences to Buck's parents. Ben King was still by their side, every inch the politician, dispensing handshakes and soft words.

'No, Natasha's fine,' he said. 'She's not herself today. Yes, thank you so much.'

He caught my eye and smiled.

Then suddenly it was over. The prayers were all said, the coffin lowered, the roses in the grave. The living mopped their eyes and returned to their cars and their lives, even the mother and father who had buried their son.

But as Mallory and I walked away, I caught a glimpse through the trees of four men still standing at the open grave, wiping dirt from their hands, bound by something so strong that death could not touch it.

Scout cried out in the deep of the night.

Although I believed that I never really slept, I was aware of the sensation of waking, and surprised by it, the abrupt surfacing from a dream I would never remember.

I glanced at the numbers on the clock – 03:10 – and stumbled to her bedroom. She was sitting up in bed, her face wet with wailing, shielding her eyes with the sleeve of her pyjamas.

I put my arms around her, held her for a bit, then placed the back of my hand on her forehead. She felt a little warm.

'Monsters,' she said.

'Angel,' I said. 'There are no monsters.'

Stan was awake now, whimpering in the darkness. I let him out of his cage and he padded after me as I returned to Scout's bedroom. He was up on her bed with one silent bound and she automatically reached out to scratch behind his ears. The dog stemmed her crying in a way I could not. But it didn't stop completely and I felt the flutter of panic that her tears always made me feel. I was afraid that if she started crying then she would never stop.

'Why are you crying, Scout?'

'I don't know. I don't know.'

We both knew but neither of us had the words, neither of us knew where to begin. There was a hole in my daughter's life and no matter how much I loved her, no matter how hard I tried, I would never be able to fill it. The thought clawed at my heart and made me feel like weeping too.

'Don't go,' she said.

I smiled in the darkness.

'I'm not going anywhere.'

Neither was Stan, who had curled up by her side, seeking the warmth, and I decided to leave him there. Soon they were both sleeping, Scout grasping the dog like a hot-water bottle, the dog letting her.

I looked at Scout's alarm clock. It was far too early to get up and far too late to go back to bed.

I knew that I would not sleep now. So I sat on the side of

Scout's bed, watching my child and her dog, and I let the night crawl by as I had done so many nights before. But watching my daughter sleep made the small dark hours seem very different tonight. They did not feel wasted.

10

Bob the Butcher had aged thirty years overnight.

His new photograph showed a much older man, the cockiness of youth and the rakish hat both gone, a black pipe stuck into his set mouth in place of the cigarette. In the new photograph Robert Oppenheimer stared straight at the camera, his hair thinning now, his eyes huge and full of a terrible knowledge that had not been there before.

The destroyer of worlds.

The large screen on Mallory's wall showed Bob the Butcher's timeline but we stared at our laptops as Gane read the new message.

'The rich have known sin,' he said. 'And this is a knowledge which they cannot lose.' He sat back in his chair. 'Kill all pigs. #killallpigs.'

I had already chased down the quote.

'What Oppenheimer actually said was "the physicists have known sin; and this is a knowledge which they cannot lose".' I looked over at Gane. 'Not the rich, the physicists.'

He nodded briefly. Then cursed.

'This should be simple. We sent a search warrant to the social network and received an IP audit within twenty-four hours. As I expected, Bob's got an anonymiser. It's a proxy server that acts as a privacy shield between the user and the rest of the digital world. Unless he's a complete idiot – always a possibility – he was bound to have one. He might even have multiple anonymisers. I can usually work around them once I have the IP audit.' He shook his head. 'Usually. But Bob's using some kind of enhanced security architecture. Onion routing, they call it. Tor or something similar, some beefed-up anonymity network that I've never seen. It routes data through multiple relays, encrypting and re-encrypting every time. It's designed to make the web safe for whistleblowers – users reporting corporate or government corruption, and people living in dictatorships. Not serial killers.'

'What are you telling us?' Mallory said.

'He's gone deeper,' Gane said. 'Bob's digital footprints are exactly like his fingerprints or glove prints.' He shook his head. 'Invisible.'

'Turn it off,' Whitestone said. 'I'm sick of these idiots treating him like some kind of hero.'

The Bob the Butcher timeline had exploded with activity as the social network reacted to his message. The screen on Mallory's wall unrolled a constant stream of fan mail, marriage proposals and slavish compliments. Gane stabbed a key and it was instantly gone from the screen, replaced with the still photograph of the seven boys at Potter's Field.

'I don't know how they can make a hero of him,' Whitestone said. 'Someone who kills school friends.'

Mallory almost smiled.

'But they don't think he's killing school friends,' he said. 'They think he's killing the rich.'

* * *

After the morning briefing, Mallory and I walked from Savile Row to Hanover Square, where tall thin young women stood smoking in glamorous packs outside Vogue House.

We were expected at the law firm of Butterfield, Hunt and West, who had their offices on the north side of the great green expanse of Hanover Square. Salman Khan's PA showed us into his office, then offered us coffee, tea or mineral water, sparkling or still. We were spoilt for choice. But before we could reply, Khan was rising up from behind his desk and telling us how to do our job.

'But you must do more!' Khan said, his upper-class English laced with just a trace of India. 'This is simply not good enough! Two men murdered and no arrest? It's appalling! I intend to take the matter up with Detective Chief Superintendent Swire, who is a friend of my father. Do I make myself absolutely clear?'

Mallory turned politely to the PA, who was still waiting in the doorway. 'Tea, please, miss. A dash of milk and two sugars.'

He glanced at me.

'Coffee, please,' I said. 'Short and black.'

She closed the door without making a sound and we turned to look at Salman Khan. He was staring at us with open belligerence. You see that kind of aggression in poorly socialised dogs, I thought. They don't bark because they are angry. They bark because they are afraid.

He ranted for a minute or so. We let him get it out of his system. A big part of our job was talking to people who were scared. Scared of getting in trouble. Scared of getting hurt. Scared of getting more hurt than they were already. But I had never seen a man quite as scared as Salman Khan. He looked like a man who was scared of having his throat cut.

When Khan paused to catch his breath, Mallory introduced us in his mild-mannered way, and we both showed our warrant cards. Khan slumped back down in his big leather swivel chair as we took a seat opposite him, Mallory making reassuring noises about various leads being pursued while I watched Khan fiddle with an unlit cigarette in his hand. The offices of the law firm Butterfield, Hunt and West were non-smoking, but there was a silver cigarette case on Khan's desk. He worried the cigarette in his fingers like a set of rosary beads.

'We realise this is a traumatic time, Mr Khan,' Mallory said.

'You shouldn't be talking to me,' Khan said, placing the cigarette in its silver coffin. 'You should be out there finding the killer.'

'Why do you think someone wanted to kill Hugo Buck and Adam Jones, Mr Khan?'

'Because they were addicts,' Khan said. 'One of them was a sex addict and the other was a drug addict. Hugo was a dear friend. Adam – I hadn't seen Adam since leaving school. But they were both, in their own way, hopeless addicts. And that's what killed them.'

It was a credible theory on the surface. One man was a sexual adventurer and the other was a junkie. They were the victims of random murders, acts as senseless and irrational as most murders. Very sad and all that, but they were living dangerously and they died because they had it coming.

But the theory did not explain Khan's naked terror.

'You knew both men for many years,' Mallory prompted. 'Since you were at school.'

'I remember the first time I met Adam,' Khan said, shaking

his head. 'Thirteen years old. We were coming in from the playing fields. All of us. The six of us. Ben and Ned. Piggy Philips and Jimmy Sutcliffe. Hugo and me. The First Fifteen rugby trials. Covered in mud and blood. And there was Adam in his nice new uniform carrying his bloody oboe in its case. Waiting for some music tutorial. And somebody – probably the Pig – said, come on, give us a tune, new boy. Give us a tune, will you? Making fun of him, of course. But Adam took his instrument out of its case and he gave us the sweetest smile – and he played Bach. "Sheep May Safely Graze". And it was the most beautiful thing I had ever heard.'

There were photographs on the walls of Khan's office. I stood up to get a closer look. It is always worth studying a man's shrine to himself.

Khan smiling in a dinner jacket receiving an award from another man in a dinner jacket.

Khan making a speech at a podium that bore the words 'Aut vincere aut mori' – the Potter's Field school motto: Conquer or die.

The teenage Khan on a cricket field flanked by the King brothers, and Piggy Philips grinning behind them, all of them in immaculate whites, Philips resting his bat on his shoulder like a caveman with his club.

I did not see the photograph of the seven boys in their Combined Cadet Force uniforms.

'Can I help you?' Khan said sharply.

'Do you get back to your old school much, sir?' I said, smiling at him.

He was immune to my charms. 'I speak to the boys. There are various events. I still have friends at the school. Among the masters, I mean. There are various military charities the school helps this firm support. Look, what's your point?'

'Best days of your life, eh, sir?'

'Indeed.'

There was one lone painting on the wall. A hidden corner of the city, a canyon of office blocks glazed with a shining haze, like a city seen in a dream, or remembered far from home. There were no people. I already knew what the initials would be in the right-hand corner.

j s

'James Sutcliffe,' I said. 'James Sutcliffe painted this picture.'

'James was a genius,' Khan said. 'He could have achieved more than any of us.'

'Why did he kill himself?'

'James was troubled. His parents thought that having those Harley Street doctors stuff him with happy pills would make everything all right. But it pushed him over the edge.'

'You made some close friends at Potter's Field,' Mallory said.

Khan picked up an unlit cigarette, put it into his mouth, then took it out. He shivered with undisguised contempt.

'That's what school's *for*,' he said.

For a moment I thought he was going to ask us where we had gone, but he decided against it. He knew we hadn't gone anywhere. And suddenly he was furious.

'Resentment killed them,' he said. 'Jealousy – this country reeks of it now.' He put the unlit cigarette back between his lips. 'Isn't it bloody obvious? Envy killed them.'

* * *

The Officers' Mess at RAF Brize Norton overlooks the airfield, and from the window I could see a huge fat-bellied aircraft waiting on the runway, its four turboprop engines idle as all around its great bulk men in sleeveless yellow tabards made the last of their checks.

A wide ramp was open under the tail of the aircraft – a Lockheed C-130 Hercules – but the troops in their camouflage fatigues stood patiently on the tarmac, as though waiting was one of the things they were trained for, and good at. The Royal Gurkha Rifles were shipping out tonight.

I watched the faces of the men, all those small golden-faced warriors who somehow looked both gentle and fierce, and far off in the darkness I could see the distant lights of Oxford glinting and glittering in the night. It had only taken us ninety minutes to drive from Savile Row to Brize Norton after the afternoon briefing, but London felt far away.

I turned at the sound of a man's harsh laughter.

Captain Ned King and DCI Mallory sat facing each other on red leather sofas in the red-carpeted room. Mallory was leaning forward, his face impassive, unsmiling, letting the other man fill the silence. Like the men on the runway, Captain King was dressed in camouflage fatigues.

'Forgive me,' he said, grinning broadly, 'but there's no great mystery here. Adam, who I hadn't seen in many years, was a drug addict. And Hugo was a sex addict. These are high-risk hobbies, detective.'

'But who would want to kill them?' Mallory said.

'Off the top of my head? Try Adam's fellow drug addicts. Try Hugo's Russian wife – or possibly some of her Russian friends.'

Mallory nodded, as if giving the matter some thought.

'You really think Hugo Buck's wife is capable of killing someone?' I said.

King turned his scarred face towards me. He was not smiling now.

'I think that anyone in the world is capable of killing someone else,' he said.

'But your friends died in exactly the same way,' I said. 'All the evidence suggests the same killer. Do you really think that's just coincidence?'

Captain King shrugged. 'What I think is that death is random. That's what I think. And that's what I know.'

From the back of the mess came the sound of snooker balls kissing. Two officers were laughing easily together.

'Helmand is the only place I've ever seen a man eat his lunch and defecate his breakfast at the same time,' one of them was saying.

'Yes, they're four hours and thirty minutes ahead of us,' said the other. 'And a thousand years behind.'

Outside on the runway, the engines of the Hercules air transport started up. King suddenly had to raise his voice.

'I would very much like all those men out there to come back,' he said. 'I don't want them crippled. I don't want them killed. I don't want to see them repatriated – in the hideous modern parlance.' His broken face twisted with disgust, as if the word physically sickened him. 'I don't want those good brave men brought back to face the pity of the Darrens and the Sharons who stand outside Tesco.' He smiled without mirth. '"You smug-faced crowds with kindling eye who cheer when soldier lads march by—"'

'"Sneak home and pray you'll never know,"' Mallory said, '"the hell where youth and laughter go."'

King chuckled. 'Very good, detective. Where did you go?'

'Where did I go?'

'Your school.'

Mallory smiled. 'I didn't go anywhere. I went to a state school in Banff. In the Highlands. Get to Aberdeen and keep going. But we liked our First World War poets.'

'Siegfried Sassoon, of course,' King said. 'Lived to a ripe old age. Died in 1967. But his great friend Wilfred Owen was killed just one week before the Armistice. The fate of our two greatest war poets perfectly illustrates the random nature of death. I want all those men out there to come home. That will not happen. We arrive in Afghanistan at night so they can't kill us immediately. But they always get around to it eventually. The really unlucky ones will be wounded and live. Single amputees, double amputees, triple amputees and – full house – both arms and both legs gone. Or no balls, no cock, no face. Phallic reconstruction is a growth industry, I'm told. And no cheering crowds for those lads. There will be roadside bombs. There will be friendly fire from our American chums and our Afghan allies. There will be the local policeman who decides that his god wants him to blow up as many of my men as possible. My men will be killed by IEDs. They will step on bombs left behind by the Russians as well as the Taliban. Some of those men out there will come home in wheelchairs, and some will come home in a coffin. Death is the price we pay for life, gentlemen, and sometimes the bill arrives early. And it will not be fair. It will not be rational. You both know that as policemen. Death doesn't play the game, does it?'

He stood up. Outside, the soldiers were preparing to board the plane.

'We arrive on Sunday, and Sundays are the most dangerous. They pray on Friday, plan on Saturday and attack on Sunday. Holy Shit Sundays, we call them. But, you know, people are polite there. People are decent. There is no litter at Camp Bastion. Now, if you will excuse me, gentlemen.'

'Thank you for your time, Captain King,' Mallory said.

We followed him to the door of the mess.

As King stepped outside into the chill of the October night, every one of his men turned to look at him. Some of them smiled shyly, and I was struck by their youth, the jumble of equipment they all carried, and their obvious love for their commanding officer.

'Why did James Sutcliffe kill himself?'

King winced at Mallory's question.

'Well,' he said. 'That was all a long time ago.'

'But you must have some thoughts.'

'Why does anyone kill himself? Because he was weak.'

'I thought he was your friend.'

'James Sutcliffe was more than my friend. Far more. And I think about him every day of my life. But James was weak.'

Mallory nodded thoughtfully. 'My apologies for detaining you, Captain King.'

He shook our hands. 'I wish I could have been more helpful.'

'Just one final thing,' Mallory said.

King waited.

'What happened to your face?'

King laughed out loud.

'Ben did it,' he said. 'When we were boys. Threw a glass at my head at the breakfast table. Must have said something that annoyed him. Nobody ever asks me that,' he added cheerfully, his spirits rising now that he was joining his men. 'They all assume I copped it in the line of duty.'

Mallory shook his head. 'No, those marks are too old. I know what scars look like.'

11

Scout was silent over breakfast.

I knew there was a time coming, maybe not that long from now, when she would be able to hide her feelings from me. But at five years old we were not there yet.

I sat down opposite her, moved aside a cereal packet with grinning monkeys on the side, and looked into her eyes.

'Something's wrong, Scout,' I said. 'What's wrong, angel?'

Scout glanced down at the milky brown gloop in her bowl, then back at me.

'You have to make me a costume,' she said.

I leaned back in my chair, trying to take it in.

'Why do I have to do that?'

'A costume for our play. Our Christmas play.'

'A Nativity play?'

She nodded. 'The mummies all have to make the costumes for the children.' A moment of doubt. 'And the daddies. Miss Davies said so.'

If Miss Davies said something then it was burned into tablets of stone and carried down from the mountain in the trembling hands of Moses.

'What's the play?'

'*The Grumpy Sheep*. It's about the sheep that doesn't want to go to see the baby Jesus getting born in the manger.

Everybody goes to see the baby Jesus. The wise men, and the angels, and all the other sheep. But he doesn't want to go, the grumpy sheep. Do you know that story?'

'No.'

'He's grumpy, the sheep. Then he's sad. Then he's sorry. He's very, very sorry in the end. He sees the mistake he made.'

A costume, I thought. How do you make a costume? What stuff do you need?

'What part do you play, Scout?'

'The grumpy sheep.'

I was impressed. 'You've got the lead – the big part?'

A flicker of pride. 'Miss Davies chose me for the grumpy sheep,' she confirmed.

'That's a good part, Scout. That's the best.'

She refused to be distracted by flattery.

'I need my costume,' she said. 'You're going to have to make it.'

'I will,' I promised, not knowing how to do it, not even knowing where to start.

Instead of going to the morning briefing I drove off the edge of the *A to Z*, the BMW X5 alone on the road north as massed ranks of commuter traffic crawled into town in the other direction. It felt like nobody in the world was going where I was going.

It felt the same way when I sat in the back row of the crematorium waiting for the crowd to come.

And they never did.

Finally a handful of lost souls wandered slowly in. Tattooed faces, missing teeth and the pallid flesh of addiction. So few of them that everybody had their own row. They sat well back, avoiding close proximity to the simple coffin awaiting the flames.

When Guy Philips arrived, ruddy-faced from double games or a hard night on the tiles, he sat across the aisle from me in the other back row. I got up and sat next to him.

'Morning, Piggy.'

He reared back in his seat.

'I know you,' he said. 'You were at Hugo's funeral. The two plods. Spot you a mile off. Big feet, small dicks.'

'Have you been drinking, sir?'

'Not nearly enough.'

'And I saw you. You were a bit rough with the girl, Piggy. I think you hurt her.'

He smirked. 'Natasha? She was tired and emotional, that's all. Took her in hand. For the best.' He took a better look at me. 'You were up at Pak's office, weren't you?'

'Pak?'

'Paki Khan.'

'I understood Mr Khan was Anglo-Indian.'

'I don't want to split hairs, constable, but that's a kind of Paki, isn't it? Not that I'm racist. It's just an old school name. An affectionate nickname. I *adore* Indians.' He surveyed his fellow mourners and sighed. 'Christ, this place looks like a convention of *Big Issue* sellers.' And then to himself, shaking his large red head: 'What happened to you, Adam?'

'Why aren't the others here? The old gang.'

'Well, Ned must be in Helmand by now. Ben's a public figure, of course. Might not look good in the *Daily Mail* hanging out at the AGM of Junkies Anonymous. And I believe the Pak's in court, probably defending some gyppo's human rights.'

'Excuses, excuses.'

'I know. Dreadful, isn't it? But as you can see from his new chums, Adam was always a bit different.'

'Because he was a heroin addict? Cut him off, did you, Piggy?'

Philips chuckled. 'Do you think we care about that? Some of the best families have drug *issues*. Dreadful word. No, Adam was always an outsider. Adam was always different. Even more than Paki Khan – who was, lest we forget, a Paki. Thing about old Pak – bloody good cricketer, the Pak. *Bloody* good. Opened the first eleven's batting three years in a row. Hitting sixes gets you accepted, see. But Adam was a different creature entirely. Not because of the drugs. Because he was a scholarship boy. The rest of us, our parents paid for us to be there. Poor little Adam had to get there on merit. Strumming his banjo. Blowing his flute. Oh, I've offended you now. You think I'm a snob.'

'When did you last see him, Piggy?'

'Could you please stop calling me that? It was mildly amusing the first three or four times. But it's what we call unearned intimacy, constable.'

'Detective.'

'Of course. Sorry, constable.'

'Piggy is just an old school name,' I said. 'An affectionate nickname.'

'I don't remember you at school,' he said. 'Were you cleaning the lavatories?'

'Come on, Piggy. When did you last see Adam Jones?'

'Not for years. He came to me, begging for money. Boo hoo hoo. Poor little me. Look what a mess I've made of my veins. Don't know where my next fix is coming from. All of that. I gave him what I had. And he went away.'

'It didn't concern you that he would spend the money on heroin?'

'Not really. I wasn't expecting him to spend it on low fat yoghurt.'

'But why would anyone want to kill him? Hugo Buck I can understand. The woman-beating bastard.'

Philips gave me a sly look. 'Not soft on our Natasha, are you? Bit rich for your blood, I reckon. Out of your pay grade.'

I gently touched his arm. 'I'll ask you again. Very politely. Why would anyone want to kill a homeless heroin addict, Piggy?'

He shot me a furious look. 'Look, you've not earned the right to call me that name. It's a stupid name. A childish name. Give me *your* name. Give me your warrant card number. What exactly are you doing here?'

'I'm trying to understand. You must have some thoughts. And don't give me the line about Hugo Buck banging the help. Don't tell me that Adam Jones had it coming. Your friend Captain King told us that the deaths are unrelated. Mr Khan told us the same thing. But I don't think they believe it. And I don't think you do, Piggy.'

But he wasn't listening to me. Mrs Jones had entered the crematorium with Rosalita. They sat down in the front row directly in front of the coffin. I thought that Philips was shocked by the sight of Adam's mother. I had seen her far more recently and she shocked me. Her face was swollen with chemotherapy and twisted with grief. The coffin she stood before could have been her own.

But Guy Philips wasn't looking at Mrs Jones. He was looking at Rosalita.

'Christ,' he said, 'it's the same housekeeper. She's aged a bit.'

The minister was talking: 'Man that is born of a woman hath but a short time to live, and is full of misery.'

When the coffin had slid into the flames and the curtains had primly swished across the mouth of the furnace, I stood up.

'Are you off?' Philips said. 'Very pleasant talking to you, constable.'

'We haven't talked yet, Piggy,' I said.

As I walked down the aisle to the front the few mourners coming in the opposite direction eased out of my path with the instinctive cringe of people who are used to getting out of the way.

I found Mrs Jones contemplating the empty spaces.

'We should have waited before starting the service,' she said. 'More people might have come.'

'Ma'am,' Rosalita said. 'We had our time slot, ma'am. Forty-five minutes, ma'am. We had to begin, didn't we?'

Mrs Jones smiled weakly when she saw me. 'You came,' she said. 'How thoughtful.' She took my hands. 'I enjoyed our talk.'

'I'd like to talk to you again,' I said. 'About the old days. When Adam was a boy.'

She was suddenly distressed. 'It's all so long ago,' she said, pulling her hands away, turning to the woman by her side. 'I don't remember. Rosalita, tell him, will you?'

Rosalita put her arm around Mrs Jones, and glared at me.

'You upset her now.'

'I just don't remember,' Mrs Jones said.

'Of course not, ma'am, why should you?' Rosalita said. 'That's all right.'

They disappeared into a side room to collect the sad little pot containing the final remains of Adam Jones. I looked back for Guy Philips, but he had gone. Everyone had gone. I sat in the front row for a long time, feeling my face burning with the heat of the flames.

The crematorium's car park was almost empty by the time I drove away. But at the end of a quiet green lane I saw Rosalita waiting at a bus stop.

I stopped, rolled down my window.

'I remember,' she said.

I took her to a small café in Golders Green and bought her tea. She said she had to send a text message.

'My son,' she explained. 'He pick me up.'

I sipped a triple espresso as she typed and sent it. Then I watched her staring at her tea. I thought she was already regretting speaking to me.

'What do you remember, Rosalita?'

She nodded, relieved to begin.

'Adam's friends. The brothers. The Indian one. I remember all of them. And the one who died. And the one who was there today. I saw him. A man now. I saw him sitting at the back with you. And I remember.'

'But what do you remember?'

She nodded again.

'They would come in the summer. The boys. All the boys would come. When Mr and Mrs Jones were away.'

'When Adam's parents were on holiday, his friends would come? They stayed at the house when his parents were away?'

'Yes.'

'What did they do?'

Silence. Then she shook her head.

'They were not good boys.' How old was she? Mid forties.

Two decades ago she would have been in her twenties. Two decades ago she would have been young herself.

'Adam was a good boy. When he was little. A sweet boy. But he was not good when he was with them.'

'What happened? Did something happen?'

She stared at her tea.

She wouldn't look at me.

'Did they – did they do something to *you*?'

She looked up as a young man walked into the café. Early twenties, the blue overalls of a garage mechanic. He spoke to his mother in Tagalog.

'We don't want no trouble,' he said, taking his mother's arm, lifting her from her seat.

'Wait,' I said. 'Where are you going? What's wrong?'

'We don't want to talk to the police,' he said. 'We don't want any trouble.'

'What are you worried about?' I said to him. 'You don't have anything to worry about.'

But they were not listening to me now. They were arguing in their own language. Rosalita's son still had her by the arm.

'Are you worried about your visa status?' I tried. 'You don't have to worry about that. I don't care about that stuff. I can help you with all that.'

But they were leaving.

'Rosalita,' I said, 'what happened at that school?'

She turned at the door of the small café.

'It all went to hell,' she said.

12

PC Billy Greene lifted the twelve-ounce gloves in front of his face and marched slowly across the ring in a totally straight line. Fred was waiting for him. My heart sank as I watched from ringside.

It was the Charge of the Light Brigade in there.

Fred stuck out a jab and Greene, looking heavier after long days on desk duty, blocked it high on his gloves. There wasn't much force behind the blow but it was hard enough to slap Greene's gloves back against his face.

Above the gloves and inside the thick leather headguard, I saw Greene's eyes blink with surprise, the bridge of his nose grazed red. Fred danced sideways, light and springy as a dancer on the balls of his feet, arms dangling loosely by his side. Greene plodded after him.

Fred fired a flurry of jabs. They all detonated harmlessly on Greene's tight, high guard. Emboldened, he stuck out a shy jab of his own. Fred's head seemed to whip sideways as if on a string and the punch sailed harmlessly over his shoulder.

Now Fred was in the corner. He waved Greene forward, grinning, the blue mouthguard showing. Flat-footed, Greene accepted the invitation. He threw another jab. When he wanted to, Fred had a guard as cosy as a nuclear bunker – hands held high and close together, elbows tucked into his ribcage, chin down. He bounced against the ropes, inviting Greene to hit him. And he did. Jab. Hook. Jab. All of it unanswered by Fred.

Greene's confidence visibly rose.

He unloaded a right, as slow as a fat man leaving a buffet. Fred slipped the punch and, more from instinct than malice, dug a short left hook into Greene's ribcage. The air came out of him with a whoosh and he sank to one knee, his head hanging down, his elbow tucked into his side, as if trying to understand the source of this sudden and terrible pain.

Fred was immediately kneeling by the bigger man's side, a protective arm around his shoulder.

'I know I should be able to hit a bit harder,' Greene said, his face contorted with pain. 'Sorry.'

'It's not about how hard you can hit,' Fred said. 'It's about how hard you can *get* hit and then keep going.'

At this hour the gym was almost empty. They went on the pads, Fred holding up the worn leather mitts for Greene to hit, all the while giving him instructions.

'Get that jab out faster. Don't let the punch fade away. Harder, faster, sharper. Keep your guard up. You're so lucky to be training!'

And behind it all, there was the secret knowledge that boxing gives you. *There is good stuff inside you. You are better than you know.*

Outside Fred's gym, I shuddered in the cold night air, and hunched my shoulders inside my leather jacket. On the far side of Charterhouse Street the men of Smithfield had begun their night's work, and as they laughed and shouted at each other, their breath came out as steam. Winter was no longer coming. Winter was here. The full yellow moon of October hung low over the dome of St Paul's. You only see that moon once a year. A hunter's moon, they call it.

I turned up my collar and hurried home to take over from Mrs Murphy.

The next day I left Savile Row in plenty of time to make my two p.m. appointment with the Right Honourable Ben King, MP.

The address I had was just the other side of Piccadilly on St James's Street and it should not have taken me more than a few minutes to get there. But I walked up and down the street staring at windows and doors and the address in my hand, feeling like a fool.

Because Ben King's club was behind one of the many unmarked doors on St James's Street and if you did not know it was there then you were never meant to find it.

Through one window I glimpsed silver heads, all men, dipped behind newspapers. I took a chance, and this was the place. Inside there was a counter where a uniformed porter took my coat. He had hung it up on what looked like a row of old school pegs before he noticed I was still waiting.

'Anything else, sir?' he said.

'Ticket?' I said, already sensing that I had made some stupid mistake.

'Sir?'

'Don't I need some sort of ticket for my coat?'

There was another porter behind the front desk and I saw him smiling to himself. The porter who had hung up my coat grinned with hideous good humour.

'Oh, no tickets in here, sir,' he said. 'Your coat is quite safe with us.'

I was escorted into the dining area with my face burning. It was more like a room in a private house than a restaurant. Solitary diners muttered to themselves behind broadsheets. An elderly man in a three-piece pinstripe suit sipped a glass of red wine. Another dozed peacefully, a bowl of rhubarb and custard cooling before him.

And Ben King, the youngest man in the room, Member of Parliament for Hillingdon North, was rising with a smile to greet me.

He was alone at the table but the waiter was clearing away two places. Because of the timing, I had assumed I was going to be offered lunch. Apparently not. The clean-picked bones of a grilled fish were on one plate, a scrap of bloody steak on the other.

'DC Wolfe,' he said. 'I'm sorry this was so difficult to schedule. My apologies. Please.'

We ordered coffee, black for both of us – I couldn't risk asking for my favourite, a triple espresso, fearing more blank stares followed by suppressed laughter – and King fixed me with a frank but friendly gaze, leaning forward, giving me his full attention.

'My office is here to help your investigation in any way it can,' he said. 'As, of course, am I.'

He had a smooth, clean-cut, untouched version of his brother's face. He was a reassuring presence. I could understand why someone would vote for him.

'This must be a very traumatic time for you,' I said, 'losing two close friends in a short space of time.'

He smiled sadly. 'We lost Adam many years ago.'

There was a pause as the coffee was placed before us.

'I had been dreading that phone call for years – the one telling me he had gone. But Hugo – that was a blow, yes.'

'So you were not in contact with Adam Jones?'

'A few years ago he approached me for money – or rather my office. I didn't see him.'

'And you didn't give him any money?'

'I would have given him money for rehabilitation. I would have given him money for treatment. I wasn't giving him money for heroin. I think he approached a number of old friends. Guy saw him.'

'He told me,' I said, and the thought rushed in – *but you knew that already.* 'It's a tragedy that he couldn't get help. What a waste.'

Ben King looked at me. And I saw that he had a way of looking at someone as if he was suddenly seeing them clearly for the first time. He cocked his head to one side, as if re-adjusting his gaze, as if I had just said something unique, or momentous, or true. As if I were suddenly a man of substance in his eyes, coming out with things that had never been said before. He looked at me as if I were the last man left alive. That was the way he looked at me. But perhaps all politicians do that.

'That's three of your old school friends who have died before their time,' I pointed out.

He thought about it for a moment.

'You mean James? That was a tragedy. As I get older, I find myself thinking of James constantly.' For the first time he seemed genuinely moved, the eighteen-year-old suicide somehow a wound that was more raw than the two recent murders. 'Hugo and Adam,' he said. 'Are their deaths connected?'

'That's our conjecture,' I said, echoing Mallory. 'We're going to be visiting Potter's Field in due course.'

He sipped his coffee before speaking again. 'But why would you go to our old school?' His voice was calm and quiet.

'It's just one of the leads we're pursuing. As far as we know there's only one thing that links Mr Buck and Mr Jones – the past. Did anything happen during your school days that—'

'Might make someone want to kill them?' King said. The practised smile drew some of the sting from his words. He was trying not to laugh at me. 'You're talking as if their murders were somehow justified, detective.'

'I didn't mean to give that impression.'

'I'm sure you didn't,' he said, forgiving me. He let his eyes drift away, as if remembering. 'We were just ordinary boys,' he said. And then back at me. 'But if anything occurs, then of course I will immediately get in touch. I want what you want. Could I possibly have your card?'

I gave it to him, and realised that I was being very politely dismissed. And that there was someone else being brought in to see him. A dishevelled, overweight man blinking with awe behind his greasy specs, some kind of journalist, there for an interview, looking like a tourist. All hot and flustered, as if it had not been easy to find the unmarked door of a gentlemen's club on St James's Street. And then I was standing up and shaking Ben King's hand and thanking him for his time and the coffee.

I collected my coat from the smirking porters and I was back on St James's Street before it sank in that the MP for Hillingdon North had scheduled a meeting for every course of his lunch.

I was dessert.

'That little gang,' I said back at the incident room. 'It was all about the King brothers, Ben and Ned. They were the alpha males. Ben looks like the pack leader.'

'Why do you think that?' Mallory said.

'The mess he made of his brother's face. Guy Philips was their pit bull. Salman Khan was their poodle. Hugo Buck was their jock, their star athlete. Adam Jones – I think he just tagged along. Let them run wild at his house when his parents were away. Adam was their mascot. Their lapdog.'

'And what about the one who killed himself? James Sutcliffe.'

'They all seem to love him,' I said. 'Died young. Good-looking corpse and all that. I doubt if it was so different when he was alive. And he was the one genuine aristocrat among them. The Honourable James Sutcliffe, younger son of the Earl of Broughton. These boys – these men – they all come from money. Even Adam, with his music scholarship, grew up with money. But Sutcliffe was the only true toff, the only one of them that came from a family where the money had been there for generations. He was their hero.'

We looked up at the photograph of the seven soldiers, and at the boy dead centre, dark glasses, unsmiling, hair swept back off that high forehead. I pictured him folding his clothes on the beach at Amalfi and walking into the sea.

'If they don't hate each other,' I said, 'then who does?'

Mallory said, 'Oh, everyone hates them.'

'Sir?'

'It's that very British hatred with class resentment at its core. We pity the small boys packed off to their boarding schools where they wet the beds and cry for their mothers but we end up wanting to be them, because they have something that the rest of us will never have.'

Mallory considered the big screen and the grinning boys in their uniforms.

'It's more than confidence,' he continued. 'It's more than

the sense of entitlement. It's the total and unequivocal certainty that tomorrow belongs to them.' He smiled at me. 'Who wouldn't want to feel like that?'

The next day I drove us to Potter's Field.

13

'Now get down on the ground,' Guy Philips said.

Fifty boys, shivering in their running shorts and vests, stared at their sports master. They grinned foolishly at each other, still hoping that he might be joking. A bitter wind whipped across the school playing fields. Three in the afternoon and it already seemed to be getting dark.

'*Now!*' he screamed.

And they saw he wasn't joking.

Slowly they got down on all fours. The rugby pitch had been churned to mud by ten thousand studmarks and their hands and knees made squelching sounds as they tested the ground. Philips walked between them in his pristine white tracksuit, a grin spreading across his red face. He was enjoying himself.

'Not doggy style, toads. On your bellies. On your backs. Roll around in it. That's good. Now on your back, Knowles. Give it a good old wriggle, Jenkins. Come on, Patel, you big girl, rub it a bit harder than that!'

Soon their running gear – white shorts and vests trimmed with the purple and green of Potter's Field – was rank with mud and damp. But Philips left them down there as he strode across to where we were watching.

'A five-miler through the woods and I'll be with you after a shower,' he said to Mallory. 'Should be an hour plus another thirty minutes or so for the retards. That all right?'

Mallory nodded, and Philips jogged back to his boys. The sports master was in a good mood.

'Get up, get up!' he barked, as if it had been their idea to roll around in the mud. 'Now you don't have to worry about getting your knees dirty, do you?'

'Sir, no, sir,' they chorused.

'Then let's get cracking. Across the fields, through the woods to the Old Mill and back in time for evensong.'

They took off across the playing fields, Philips pristine in his tracksuit among the small muddy figures. By the time they reached the woods he was flanked only by the fastest runners while the bespectacled, the fat and the surly trailed behind.

We started back to the school.

Potter's Field was mostly a great jumble of redbrick Victorian buildings but there were also more modern blocks that were clearly residential, and some more ancient buildings, black and crumbling, that looked like something from the Middle Ages. You blinked your eye and a hundred years went by.

Flocks of boys drifted past. They wore straw boaters – the hats on the older boys threadbare and falling to pieces – green blazers trimmed with purple and light grey trousers. All of them lugged books or sports gear or both.

'It hasn't changed since Hugo Buck and Adam Jones were here in the eighties,' Mallory said. 'A thousand pupils. All boys. All boarding. Three resident staff in every boarding house – House Master, house tutor and matron.'

We paused to look at the statue of the school's founder in the courtyard of the main building. Not Henry VIII as a fat, bearded king, but as a long-haired scholar and athlete, a lean young man clutching a book, two stone spaniels at his feet – the King Henry VIII who wouldn't hurt a fly.

'And it probably hasn't changed very much since he founded the place,' Mallory added. 'Did you know he buried his greatest love here in the school grounds?'

'What wife was that, sir?'

'Not a wife. His dogs.' Mallory indicated the spaniels. 'Henry buried his favourite dogs at Potter's Field. We should have a look at their grave. I wouldn't want to miss it.'

Five hundred years. I couldn't imagine anything lasting for five hundred years. I was always happy to make it to the weekend.

There was a small graveyard behind the church chapel. Crumbling tombstones, many of the inscriptions wiped clean by time and weather. But the grave of the dogs was easy to find. It was a large square tomb in the very centre of the graveyard with a short epitaph.

Brothers and sisters,
I bid you beware
Of giving your heart
To a dog to tear.

As we walked back to the main buildings a coach was unloading visitors from a local state school's rugby team. The state school kids grinned with bewildered amusement at the boys from Potter's Field in their boaters and their green and purple blazers. But the Potter's Field boys gave no indication that they had noticed, which made the smiles on the faces of the state school kids look like some kind of defensive wound.

A towering man in a gown moved among the visitors,

nodding and smiling at nobody in particular with his hands behind his back, like royalty inspecting Third World troops. I had seen him before – the impossibly tall man at the funeral of Hugo Buck.

'That's the Head Master,' Mallory said. 'He's expecting us.'

Peregrine Waugh, Head Master of Potter's Field College, stood at the window of his study and stared across the playing fields.

'Three Prime Ministers, twelve Victoria Crosses and four Nobel Prizes,' he said. 'Two in physiology and two in physics. Fifteen Olympic medallists, forty-four Members of Parliament and six BAFTAs. Our drama department has always been very active. The boys were treading the boards, as it were, long before the first Old Etonian was admitted to RADA.'

'And two murders,' I said.

He stared at me over his rimless glasses.

'What's that?' he barked.

'Hugo Buck and Adam Jones,' Mallory said. 'They were Potter's Field old boys too.'

'Yes, yes. A terrible tragedy. Both of them. Did you arrest anyone yet?'

'Not yet,' Mallory said.

Waugh returned to his desk with a release of breath that might have been a sigh.

'Although Jones left the school under a cloud,' he said. 'And they are not the first old boys to be murdered, sadly. Persian chap in the seventies. Filthy rich. Oil money. Mistress clobbered him with an empty bottle of Bollinger on The Bishops Avenue.' He offered us a thin smile. 'Privilege is no guarantee of a happy life, or even a long one. And we do know we're privileged at Potter's Field, gentlemen. But we give something back, you know – it's part of the Potter's Field tradition. Part of our ethos. Always has been. Remembrance Day service. A carol concert for the people of the town. We pay for a street cleaner. Potter's Field Lawn Tennis Club uses our courts. And the school's facilities – the playing fields, the swimming pool – are used extensively by local schools and various charities.'

He rose from his chair and returned to the window.

'In fact, I think – ah yes.' He looked at us with a delighted smile. 'Look.'

We joined him at the window, the great green playing fields of Potter's Field spread out before us. They were deserted apart from three figures who hovered by the touchline of the nearest rugby field. There was a man in a wheelchair, another with a walking stick, and a third, their physiotherapist, was demonstrating a stretching exercise. They all wore T-shirts. The physio's face looked somehow unnatural, as if he were wearing some kind of mask.

The man in the wheelchair had no legs. Where his legs should have been there was simply nothing. What looked like two white bowls were attached just below his waist. One of his arms was a far lighter colour than his black skin and it was only the weak sun glinting on a curved piece of metal where a hand had once been that made me understand he was wearing a prosthesis.

The man with a walking stick had also lost his legs. Or most of his legs. Two thin black poles stuck out of his long baggy blue shorts. What remained of his right leg had some kind of white bandage around the knee area. He appeared to need the stick to stand up but his upper body was incredibly muscular.

They were all laughing.

'The British Army is still the biggest employer of Potter's

Field old boys,' Waugh said. 'Despite what the general public may think, not all the old boys go into investment banking in the City and the RSC in Stratford. We never forget our debt to our country.'

We watched the three men perform a few gentle exercises, the man in the wheelchair and the one with the stick taking their directions from the physio, the man who looked as though he was wearing a mask.

'Splendid, splendid,' Waugh said, turning away when he decided we had seen enough.

'You knew them,' Mallory said. It wasn't a question. 'You knew Hugo Buck and Adam Jones. When they were at Potter's Field. You were here too, were you not? Twenty years ago. In fact, you were their House Master.'

'Yes, yes,' Waugh said. 'Did I not mention that?'

Mallory let him fill the silence.

'Buck and Jones were both in The Abbey. It's the oldest and smallest house at Potter's Field. Not the most obvious of friendships – the athlete and the musician. But sharing a house throws boys together.'

'Could you explain the role of a House Master at Potter's Field?' I said.

Waugh sniffed.

'A boarding school is really just a day school with hotels attached,' he said. 'The House Master is in charge of the hotel where the boys live. He assumes a parental role – encouraging, supporting and making sure they participate fully in the life of the school. Disciplining when necessary.' The thin smile. 'Although of course there's not so much of that these days. Boys don't get flogged and they don't learn so much. So what they gain at one end they lose at the other.'

There were bird-like noises from the far side of the playing fields.

'Hark,' said Waugh. 'I believe Mr Philips and the boys are coming home.'

The soldiers saw it first.

Mallory and I had left the Head Master's office and were standing on the touchline of the main rugby pitch, watching the state school boys getting thrashed by their hosts, not really noticing the boys as they poured out of the tree line, covered in mud, their thin limbs flying.

But the soldiers had stopped their gentle exercise regime and were staring. And then we saw it too.

The boys were crying.

They ran past us, some of them locked in silence as tears streamed down their faces, some of them making the animal noises of shocked grief.

I grabbed one of them by the arm.

'What's happened?' I said.

'Please, sir,' he sobbed. 'It's Mr Philips, sir. Please, sir, someone's killing him.'

Then Guy Philips came out of the tree line with his hands around his neck and his white tracksuit livid with fresh blood. He stumbled across the playing fields, his legs on the edge of going, his eyes telling us that he was drowning.

We ran to meet him, and as he collapsed in Mallory's arms, the blood began pumping out of his wound.

Mallory tore off his tie, already covered in blood, and I saw the wound, a far deeper red than the blood that was flowing. Then Mallory was winding the tie around the sports master's ravaged throat, pressing it against the wound, trying to staunch the terrible flood, crouching beside him in the mud. Mallory had his phone in one hand but it slithered away from him, slick with blood.

And I heard him call my name as I began running towards the woods.

I was alone in the woods. I kept running until I came to an open field, as barren as the surface of the moon. There I stopped, finding my breath, uncertain if I should turn back to the woods or cross the ploughed field. There was a farm on the far side.

I saw the tree I was standing next to had a perfect bloody handprint on its trunk.

I looked across at the farm. There was nothing moving. And then something seemed to stir inside. There was a glimpse of a shadow. I didn't know if it was my imagination or a man or a trick of the dying light. But I began jogging towards it.

There was some kind of square brick pen, crumbling with age, and as I paused by it I saw that the windows of the farmhouse had all been joyfully smashed. Nobody had lived here for years.

I leaned against the low brick wall and jolted when I heard the noise. Like a baby's cry. I looked into the pen and I saw the pig. Its hind legs had been tied with some kind of twine, as if in preparation for slaughter, and fearing for its life it had crawled on its belly across the dirt of the pen. I stepped over some broken brickwork and crouched down beside the pig. It squealed with terror as I pulled at the twine with my bare hands until I had set it free. It scampered away, wild-eyed with panic.

And as I made to stand up there was a sudden explosion of pain at the back of my skull.

And then, following each other so closely that it felt like one blow, the inner edge of a forearm smashed into my throat and a fist hammered into the small of my back.

Now strong arms were around me, and he was right behind me, forcing my head back. He was near enough for me to kick him in the shins but I was suddenly not strong enough to do it, and he was close enough for me to rip his balls off, but suddenly I was too drained by shock and pain to even try.

Then he had me.

The palm of his left hand pulled hard against my right cheek, his fingertips pressing through the flesh and into my teeth as he twisted my face to one side. I looked down and glimpsed the knife.

The Fairbairn-Sykes commando dagger. The only knife ever designed to sever the carotid arteries of a man's neck.

The long thin blade moved a fraction and the steel tip pressed into the side of my neck, found a muscle it didn't like, edged forward, prodded the Adam's apple for a moment and then slipped back to the fleshy, resistant part of my neck and settled there, pressing harder.

The knife broke my skin with a sharp prick of pain.

I could feel his steady breath on the back of my throbbing head.

The wet warmth of fresh blood slid down my neck.

I tried to drop my centre of gravity. Terrified now, I lashed out with the heels of my shoes. I fought him and I fought my exhaustion, I bit and I cursed, refusing to let either overwhelm me.

But he held me tighter, and I was weak with pain, and the tip of his knife went in deeper, and the blade was buried in my flesh now.

I felt myself sag in his arms.

'Please,' I said. 'I have a daughter.'

He stopped.

The stump of metal at the knife handle's base banged once against my right temple. And then once against my left temple. It must have put me out for a few seconds because the next thing I knew I was down on my knees, dizzy and sick.

'Please,' I said, and when I looked up I saw the bag.

A worn-leather Gladstone bag.

A Murder Bag.

Waiting for him on a dry patch of ground inside the pigpen.

A boot's steel toecap slammed with full force into the base of my spine. The pain was blinding. I saw yellow light and exploding stars. I felt my back go into spasms of agony.

I realised I was screaming.

There were noises and lights but they were all inside my head. I dragged myself away on my hands and knees. I could not stand. I kept crawling. My muscles were paralysed slabs of pain and only my fear kept me moving. Time meant nothing but I knew it was passing because the ground changed beneath me, from the hard churned mud of the ploughed field to the carpet of dead leaves that covered the woods. And finally I was on grass. Now I heard voices that were not inside my head.

Then there was hot breath on the side of my face and I reared away in mortal panic.

'Please,' I said.

And I stared into the terrified face of the pig.

NOVEMBER

DreAms of the deAd

14

I lay on my bed in the darkness and the sound of my daughter playing with the dog in the main room edged me closer to sleep. It was a soothing sound, their play – Scout's laughter like temple bells, and the soft padding of the dog as he chased after whatever chewed-up old toy she was trailing. But then another spasm of pain would grip my back and I would jolt awake.

When they found me at the edge of the playing fields they had taken me to the nearest A&E to Potter's Field. The doctor wanted to keep me in overnight but that was impossible. I had to get home to Scout. So, after the usual routine – lights in the eyes, questions about being sick, checking for broken bones – the doctor reluctantly let a uniformed officer drive me home where Mrs Murphy took one look at me and packed me off to bed, saying she would call her family, take care of Scout and sleep on our sofa. For a night and a day I stayed in my bed, true rest always just out of reach, the pain never far away.

The tremors began at the bottom of my spine and rolled all the way to the base of my skull, and it was like every muscle in my back, shoulders and neck was clenching at once. At first the pain had an exact centre – the spot in my back where he had kicked me. But as the hours dragged by in that exhausting place between sleeping and waking, that centre point seemed to migrate, up to a shoulder, across to my ribs, to my neck, to the very middle of my back, as if it was seeking a happier home. I never knew where it would be next.

But the muscle spasms were the worst. They made me arch my back whenever another wave of blinding pain rolled through me. I almost cried out loud with the latest one.

'Daddy?'

Scout was in the doorway. I thought I had frightened her. But she was holding the phone.

'It's some lady,' she said.

I waited until she was in the other room and I could hear Mrs Murphy quietly talking to her, telling her they needed to fix her hair.

'Wolfe,' I said.

'Scarlet Bush.' I could hear the excitement in the reporter's voice. 'You met him. You met Bob the Butcher.'

'I don't know who I met.'

'It has to be Bob.'

'How did you get this number?'

'We want to help you find him,' she said. 'My editor has spoken to our proprietor. We have his full backing to help you bring Bob the Butcher to justice.'

'You stitched me up. Your bloody story put words in my mouth that I never said.'

She remained completely calm. 'E. L. Doctorow said, "I am led to the proposition that there is no fiction or non-fiction as we commonly understand the distinction, there is only narrative."'

'You mean you make stuff up?'

'Not quite. I mean there are facts and then there's the truth.'

She paused. 'Was that your little girl who answered the phone? Was that Scout?'

I struggled to contain my anger. 'Never call my home again.'

'Did you see his face?'

'Never speak to my daughter.'

'Did he talk to you?'

'Stay right away from her.'

'Did you say something to him?'

A spasm of pain clenched my back. I bit down against it, my mouth tight shut, and ragged breath came from my nose. It made the reporter feel like she was on to something.

'You did, didn't you?'

Please. I have a daughter.

Begging him.

Begging a murderer for my life.

Sick with the fear. Unmanned by the terror.

Please.

'What did you say to him, detective? Did you reason with him? Did you threaten him? How did you feel? We are hearing reports about the murder weapon. Some kind of Special Forces knife? Old school.' I could hear her tapping a keyboard. 'A Fairbairn-Sykes commando dagger. Is that what you saw?'

I cursed under my breath. Where did they get this from?

'One final question,' she said. 'Technical point. A third murder is the game changer, isn't it?' Her tone was lighter now. She was happy. 'Because when we have three murders, it's official: we have a serial killer. That's true, isn't it?'

I hung up.

Stan padded into the room and watched with interest as I tried to get dressed. He cocked his head to one side as I struggled to get my socks on. There was no longer enough give in my back for me to bend forward.

'You're not allowed in this room,' I said. 'Go on, Stan, get out.'

He lay down, still watching me. Sitting on the bed, I pulled my shirt on. Stan rested his chin on his front paws. I buttoned up the shirt and had another go at my socks. But it was no good. The muscles in my back were petrified.

Apparently bored with my pathetic efforts, the dog got up and yawned. Then he stretched, first lifting his tailbone in the air, his chest almost touching the ground, and then rocking forward on to his front legs, his hind legs and back almost a straight line.

Then he looked at me.

You try it.

But I knew if I got down on the floor I would need the fire brigade to get me up. So I stood with my forearms resting on the bed and pushed back with my tailbone, feeling the stretch in my lower back. Then I rocked forward, and there it was in my hamstrings – that sweet feeling of muscles that had been sleeping suddenly waking up.

I kept doing it – rocking back, rocking forward, a modest approximation of my dog's stretches – until I was sweating and breathless but finally loose enough to sit on the bed and pull on my socks.

Stan watched me.

Yeah, he seemed to say. *You got it.*

Scarlet Bush was right – three deaths and we were no longer hunting a murderer. We were hunting a serial killer.

But we were not there yet.

Piggy Philips was lying in a hospital bed, breathing through a ventilator because of the puncture wound in his windpipe, uniformed officers outside his door twenty-four hours a day as he stubbornly clung to life.

15

There is a canteen in 27 Savile Row, but just the other side of Regent Street all of Soho is waiting for you with every kind of food in the world. So if you work out of West End Central, the backstreets of Soho are your real canteen.

I found Elsa Olsen in a Korean restaurant at the top of Glasshouse Street. The forensic pathologist was just polishing off a bowl of dak bulgogi and steamed rice.

'You look like death warmed up, Max.'

I eased myself into the chair opposite her.

'Coming from someone in your job, Elsa, I'm going to consider that a compliment.'

She waved her chopsticks. 'You want something to eat?'

I shook my head.

'If you don't want lunch then you're here to ask me about a man with a knife wound in his windpipe,' she said.

I smiled at her. 'You know me so well.'

'You want to know if he's going to live.'

'It had crossed my mind.'

'That depends entirely on the severity of the penetrating trauma.'

'It's a puncture wound, Elsa. A knife was stuck in Guy Philips' throat but his throat was not cut open. I'm giving you the edited highlights, you understand.'

'I understand. But *you* have to understand that there are puncture wounds and there are puncture wounds, Max. Tracheal perforation ranges from a small wound to complete avulsion. He's survived for, what, forty-eight hours?'

'Yes.'

'Then I would think he has every chance. But not even his doctors will know for certain. If you don't like dak bulgogi, you'd be far better off talking to them.'

'There's something more, Elsa.'

She placed her chopsticks across her rice bowl and waited.

I leaned forward. My back throbbed in protest.

'Would he have lost consciousness?' I said. 'He had a knife stuck in his throat – the assailant was disturbed, we don't know why – and the victim somehow stemmed the blood for long enough to save his life, long enough to get up and get away. Was he awake through all of that? I got a couple of taps on the head and there were whole seconds when I was out for the count. This man had his throat cut. Would he have blacked out?'

She thought about it.

'I don't know.'

'Please, Elsa. Have a guess.'

'I doubt it. Because if he had blacked out then he would have bled to death. But, like you, there may have been moments when he was not fully conscious.'

'What's the timetable?'

'There is no timetable! There are only a series of approximations.'

'But we know that Hugo Buck and Adam Jones died almost instantly.'

'Yes, because if you cut the carotid artery then loss of consciousness is within five seconds. But even that's an approximation. And the killer didn't get the chance to cut the carotid artery this time, did he?'

'Because he was disturbed. Or he panicked. There were fifty kids in those woods. Or maybe he was spooked by a bird. Whatever happened, he didn't finish the job. So did Guy Philips lose consciousness?'

'What I'm telling you is that severing any artery will eventually result in loss of consciousness. *Eventually*. Suicides who cut their radial arteries – slash their wrists, in plain English – have approximately thirty seconds to regret it before they black out and then another two minutes before they die. But it is entirely dependent on the severity of the trauma. Or, more specifically, the loss of blood plasma.'

'So how about a punctured windpipe, Elsa? My guess is that the victim was awake all the time. Even with an open wound in his windpipe. He was always awake. That's what I think. What do you think, Elsa?'

'I know exactly what you're asking, Max, and I'm not going to give you an answer. Because I just don't know! And there's no way I could possibly know for certain.'

A waiter brought a bowl of kim chi and placed it in front of Elsa. She did not look at the waiter, the kim chi or me. She stared out at Glasshouse Street, which is really little more than a glorified alley that runs parallel to Regent Street, and she sighed, shaking her head.

I did what I had seen Mallory do. I let the silence between us grow and waited for her to fill it. And eventually she did.

'A body only has to lose approximately a fifth of its normal blood volume to produce hypovolemic shock. Lose that amount of blood and the heart stops pumping. Veins dilate, blood pressure drops, and eventually—'

'You flake out.'

'Yes. If we're going to use the medical term, you flake out.'

'But that didn't happen to Piggy because he didn't lose enough blood. He lost a lot of blood – a hell of a lot of blood – but not enough to put him out.'

'That's a reasonable supposition.'

'So the killer sticks the blade in his neck, cuts through the windpipe, but doesn't finish the job – something spooks him – and he lets the man slide from his arms. But Philips doesn't black out. Just so we're clear, he doesn't black out, right?'

Elsa reluctantly nodded.

And then finally she gave me what I had come to Soho to find.

'I know what you are asking, and the answer is yes,' she said. She picked up her chopsticks and selected a slice of kim chi. The chilli soaking the napa cabbage was as bright as fresh blood. 'There's a good chance Guy Philips saw his assailant's face.'

A uniformed sergeant was outside the main entrance to the hospital, red-faced and stamping his boots.

'He's still alive,' I said.

It wasn't a question.

The PS gave me a grin, indicating the deserted street outside the private hospital. 'You'll know soon enough when he's snuffed it,' he said. 'They'll all come running.'

I nodded. The death of Guy Philips would swamp the street with cameras and microphones because then we would have a serial killer.

There was another uniformed officer outside the lifts. I didn't recognise him and I had my warrant card in my hand before I reached him.

'All quiet?' I said.

'These nurses keep bothering me, sir,' he said. 'They love a man in uniform.'

I stepped into the lift. 'You'll just have to try to be strong,' I said, thinking that they should teach mindless banter at Hendon, the Training School of the Metropolitan Police.

The gangly figure of PC Billy Greene was waiting outside the Intensive Care Unit. He looked half asleep but snapped to attention when he saw me coming.

'Back on the beat,' I said.

He grinned. 'Yes, DC Wolfe.'

'Visitors?'

'The same gentleman,' Greene said. 'His friend. The politician. Mr King. It's still restricted visitors but Mr King must have had a word.'

The door to the ICU opened and a doctor emerged.

'Doctor,' I said, 'DC Wolfe. When can I talk to your patient?'

'Detective,' he said. 'Mr Philips has a severe tracheal rupture. Someone, as you know, stuck a knife through his windpipe. Thirty per cent of patients with tracheal tears die, most of them within one hour.'

'I get it,' I said. 'I understand the severity of the injury.'

'I'm not convinced you do. Mr Philips is currently sedated and breathing through a ventilator. If he survives, he will need extensive surgery to repair the severed windpipe. If he has surgery, even surgery that is successful, he will have breathing difficulties for the rest of his life, due to a narrowing of the airways in his throat.' He looked up from his notes. 'And you're seriously asking me when you can talk to him?'

'Because we believe he may have seen his assailant's face,'

I said. 'He wouldn't have to speak. He could write something down.'

The doctor looked at me with open hostility. 'He's not well enough for visitors,' he said. 'And I'll let you know when you can talk to him.'

He walked off.

I gave Greene my card.

'If he wakes, you call me. If his condition changes, you call me. And if there are any problems, what do you do?'

'I call you.'

'Good.'

Then I entered the Intensive Care Unit. PC Greene followed me inside, concern flitting across his face as he watched me scrub my hands in one of those big deep sinks you only find in ICUs.

'Don't worry,' I said, 'I'm not going to operate on him. And I'll be quick.'

I went inside Philips' room. In the gloom I could see a figure propped up in bed. I could not recognise him as the man I had last seen emerging from the woods at Potter's Field with blood pouring through hands around his neck. Guy Philips looked like the sole survivor of some catastrophic disaster. He looked like someone I had never met.

Three tubes, two fat and corrugated and one thin and smooth, snaked over the side of the bed like tentacles, and were connected to another tube, which in turn was connected to his nose and throat. The doctor had told me that the puncture in his trachea meant that he could only breathe through a ventilator. And the doctor was right – I didn't really understand what that meant until I saw him and heard him. The ventilator made every single breath Piggy took sound like a small war.

His neck was swathed in bandages which made him look like a relic from an Egyptian tomb, or as if someone had tried to decapitate him. There was no blood.

'Detective Wolfe,' a voice said, and only now did I see Ben King sitting on the far side of the room, hunched up in the solitary chair. 'I want to thank you for saving Guy's life.'

His voice was very soft, and although there was no chance of us waking the man in the bed, I responded in the same hushed tones.

'I don't deserve any credit for that,' I said. 'Thank DCI Mallory. He stopped him bleeding to death.'

'Of course. And I will thank him personally. Have you any leads?'

'No.' I hesitated for a moment. 'But we think he saw a face. We think he can identify whoever attacked him. And we believe he will. When he wakes.'

'When he wakes,' Ben King said. 'Then let's hope he wakes soon.'

He stood up in the darkness and I thought he was leaving. But he just wanted to shake my hand. There were tears in his eyes as he held my gaze.

'This has to end,' he said. 'These senseless murders. This unspeakable violence.'

'I want to end it,' I said.

His eyes blazed at me in the twilight of the hospital room, and that was when I felt the full force of his personality, and I understood exactly why he had climbed so far so fast.

'And I want what you want,' he told me.

16

I recognised her as soon as I walked into MIR-1 the next morning.

She was alone in the room, having arrived even before Mallory, sitting on a desk, looking at a laptop that was open on a PDF of the Murder Investigation Manual.

She turned to look at me with the cool, steady gaze that I remembered from my first day in Homicide, up at the bank, Hugo Buck on the shag carpet with his throat opened up. It was the rebellious red hair that really gave her away. Everything else seemed different, because this time she was not in uniform.

'DC Wolfe?' she said. 'I don't know if you remember me. From the one-oh-one at ChinaCorps. TDC Edie Wren?'

'I remember. You're a trainee detective constable now? How did that happen?'

'The usual way. I passed my National Investigations Exam. I'm working towards my PIP Level 2 Portfolio. You know – demonstrating competence, all of that?'

'What you doing here?'

'I'm the bagman on the double homicide.'

'Our bagman? The bagman's usually a detective sergeant or detective constable.'

'Cuts,' she said.

The bagman was the lowest rank of the investigation,

answering directly to the senior investigating officer, DCI Mallory, and giving assistance wherever it was needed. I remembered how calm Wren had been on the day she and Greene found Buck's body and I had no doubt she could do the job.

'So this is where it all happens,' she said.

'This is where some of it happens,' I said. 'There's plenty of legwork outside. I've learned that murder is labour intensive. In the Yorkshire Ripper case, the law checked over five million car registration numbers.'

'Yes, and they still cocked it up,' she said. 'Did you see the new Bob the Butcher post?'

She stabbed a few buttons on her laptop. The social network site came up. It was nothing I hadn't seen before. The later photograph of Robert Oppenheimer. The same apocalyptic boasting: 'I am become Death, the destroyer of worlds. Kill the protectors of the rich. Kill all pigs.'

'Seen it,' I said.

'But did you see the link?' Wren said. 'That's new. And you're in it.'

She clicked on the link. And there I was on my hands and knees, a thin trickle of blood running down the side of my face from a wound in my temple. Another sliding down the side of my neck. My mouth was open and my eyes were fixed on nothing.

And I was crawling.

There was only a few seconds of footage, but it kept repeating, and looping back on itself, so it looked like I was crawling forward, and then reversing, as if doing some comic jig. In one corner of the screen the pig edged towards me, its eyes bulging with terror. Our faces would almost touch and then we would back away from each other. And then the mad dance would begin again.

There was music, I realised. Not really music at all. Just mad laughter, on and on, hysterical screams of laughter over an oompah-oompah beat as the pig and I crawled towards each other and then backed away. And did it again. Laughter in the dark, laughter from the grave.

'Who filmed you out there?' Wren said.

'I don't know.'

'Did he film you, the killer? Did Bob make this film?'

'I doubt it,' I said. 'Not his style.'

'I would have thought it was exactly his style,' Wren said. 'I Shazamed it. That song. It's some old music-hall number. "The Laughing Policeman" by Charles Jolly.'

As if on cue, Charles Jolly stopped laughing and started singing.

He said, 'I must arrest you.'
He didn't know what for.
And then he started laughing
Until he cracked his jaw!
Ah ha ha ha ha ha ha ha ha ha ha ha ha ha!

'It's gone viral,' Wren said. 'You see how many hits you've got?'

My phone went.

It was the chief super.

I pictured her in one of those top-floor offices at New Scotland Yard where they either have a view of the river or a view of the park. And I knew from the ice-cold ferocity in her voice that she was looking at neither. Detective Chief

Superintendent Swire was looking at my little film. I was no longer flavour of the month. I was a flavour that had been discontinued.

'I think you've been promoted beyond your ability and experience,' she said. 'That day at the railway station – you were right and I was wrong. You got your medal and your pay rise and your transfer to Mallory's outfit. But here's the thing: I think nothing could have stopped you running that man down. I think that is who you are, Wolfe. I think you would have run him down if he'd had a bag full of onion bhajis. I think because of your personal history – don't be surprised, it's all in your file – you are completely out of control. Do you know why we don't have guns, detective?'

I knew the answers off by heart.

'Because we don't need them, ma'am. Because we have trained firearms officers. Because the public do not want their police to be armed. And because if every officer had a firearm, then standards would slip from their current high level.'

'No,' she said. 'The real reason we don't have guns is because of reckless bastards like you. In a war of smart bombs, you're an unexploded device. You're not even a loose cannon, Wolfe.'

She hung up, and I saw that Mallory was standing in the doorway of MIR-1, holding his takeaway tea and staring at me.

I couldn't look at him.

Not because the world was laughing at me.

Please. I have a daughter.

But because the world had seen me crawl.

* * *

I did not feel like going to the gym. But I knew I needed to. I knew I had to. I knew I must exhaust my body tonight, that muscle and blood and bone must be so weary by the time I got into bed that a few hours of sleep was at least a possibility. And I had to fill my head with something other than my humiliating new career as an internet sensation.

There was a sign in Fred's, and as the gym emptied near closing time I stood looking up at it. It was placed between a posed black-and-white photograph of Sonny Liston and a picture of a dozen Cuban kids sparring in a ring with ropes like snapped elastic.

PAIN IS JUST WEAKNESS LEAVING THE BODY

It was a good message, and there had been times when I'd believed in it, and it had helped me. But not today. Today I did not feel that the thick burning knot of pain in my lower back was just weakness leaving the body.

Today, pain was just pain.

Fred walked in. He went over to the music system and fiddled about with it until he found some early Clash. The gym was filled with the crashing guitar chords of Mick Jones and Joe Strummer's machine-gun bark. Fred picked up a towel that somebody had dropped on the floor and went off to put it in the laundry. When he came back I was leaning against the ropes and staring at the square that we call a ring. My back was stiff with pain, and I reflected on the fact that the things that hurt me the most were a source of entertainment for others.

Fred and I leaned on the ropes, the sweet stink of a boxing gym all around us, The Clash at full volume, and the silence between us was not awkward.

And then he spoke.

'It's not about how hard you can hit,' he said. 'It's about how hard you can get hit and then keep going – for just long enough to hit the bastards back.'

17

'Let him go!'

On the far side of a field that glittered with early morning frost, Scout released the dog and he began tearing towards me.

Hampstead Heath, early Sunday morning. The forest at the top of London. We were in a meadow high on the Heath and my daughter and my dog seemed giddy with all the sunlight, fresh air and freedom. All around us were trees that still clung to the last of the red and gold leaves of autumn. Beyond them you could see the city from Canary Wharf to the BT Tower. It felt like it all belonged to us.

We should do this more often, I thought. We should do this all the time.

The field we were in looked perfectly flat until Stan began racing across it. With him in top gear I suddenly became aware of all the dips and bumps and rabbit holes. As he came to one sudden drop in the ground he extended his front legs before him and his hind legs behind to dramatically bound across. He looked like he was flying.

Scout shouted with delight. 'Superdog!'

Stan raced towards me, his large ears streaming behind him, bright eyes shining and mouth open, panting, going flat out. It was his first time off lead and he was almost hysterical with excitement. And so were we.

I got down on my knees, my back moaning in protest, and held my arms wide to greet him.

Then he was on me, breathing hard and snuffling for the chicken treats I held in my fists. I fed him the treats, his nose a wet button in my palm, and I kept hold of his harness until Scout gave me the signal.

And he flew back to her side.

Hampstead Heath was dog heaven. Dogs of all sizes passed through this meadow on their walks, some of them coming over to give Stan an investigative sniff, others lost in their own world of smells, uninterested in the little red squirt off lead for the first time.

Dogs paced along the perimeter of the meadow where the trees began, noses pressed to the ground on the trail of some long-gone rabbit or fox. But Scout and I stayed on the meadow with Stan running between us, until he was gasping with exhaustion and our bags of chicken treats were almost empty.

We were both grinning with happy relief. Stan had gone off lead and he hadn't been lost. I took out his dog lead. It was time to go home.

And then he saw the birds.

Two fat crows, pecking the ground just beyond the tree line, and they took flight as Stan hurtled towards them. Scout and I chased after him, calling his name, but the birds had touched some ancient nerve and suddenly he was not interested in chicken treats or us.

The elm trees were old and huge on that part of the Heath, and their spreading boughs formed a thick canopy that made it impossible for the birds to take to the sky. So they flew low, flapping wildly, unable to break free.

And Stan went after them.

Within seconds we had lost sight of him. We staggered among the trees, calling his name, and within minutes we too had completely lost our bearings. The Heath was dense and wild up here, although we could hear the distant buzz of traffic on Hampstead Lane and could easily imagine our dog under their wheels. Scout began to cry. Silently, hopelessly. I put my arm around her and called Stan's name again, though it felt useless. The traffic was closer now. There was a tight knot of fear and grief in my stomach.

And then we saw them.

The woman coming through the trees with a little red dog in her arms and another dog scampering off lead by her side. A Pekingese-Chihuahua cross. I recognised the dog before I recognised Natasha Buck in her flat cap, green Hunter boots and black waterproofs, a city girl dressed for the country.

Scout and I choked out our thanks for Stan's safe return.

'Don't thank me,' she said. She pointed at the Pekingese-Chihuahua cross daintily snacking on rabbit droppings by her boots. 'Thank Susan.'

We thanked Susan.

I clipped on Stan's lead and we walked back to the meadow, while Natasha told us how they had been walking back from Kenwood House when they came across a young Cavalier King Charles Spaniel shivering alone under the elms. Then she asked us if we wanted a cup of hot chocolate.

I looked at Scout, and Scout looked at me.

'Yes, please,' we said.

We walked back to our cars with our dogs on their leads, and I thought that we looked like one of the families who take their dogs on the Heath at the weekend, one of those lucky families. Not perfect, but intact.

At first I thought she was moving out. There were boxes in the hallway of Natasha's flat, some of them sealed and some of them open, piled high with clothes and sports equipment, and shoeboxes overflowing with old photos. But she was only shipping out her husband's things.

She brought us our hot chocolate.

'First time off lead?' she asked.

'Yes,' Scout said. 'I don't like it. Off lead is scary. I don't like it when he can just run away.'

Natasha laughed. It was the first time I had seen her laugh properly, without anything behind it.

'But you have to let him go,' she said. 'You have to give him that freedom. He's a dog.'

'I know he's a dog,' Scout said. 'But I don't like it.'

Stan roamed the perimeter of the flat, sniffing the skirting board. Susan followed him, sniffing his backside. Natasha and Scout followed the pair of them, laughing together.

Some people who don't have children themselves try too hard. But Natasha wasn't like that. She was easy and friendly, and I thought I saw her for the first time. This wild girl who wanted to settle down but picked the wrong man. She looked back at me and smiled. They paused at the window, looking across Regent's Park. Natasha slipped her arm around Scout's shoulder. My daughter lifted her face to say something.

I sipped my hot chocolate. Hugo Buck had owned a lot of stuff, I thought, looking at the boxes. The two paintings of the empty city were no longer on the wall. I could see them sitting alone in an old champagne box.

I went over and picked one of them up. The style was very familiar to me now. The secret corners of the city, empty of people, changed by twilight. I'd seen it here, I had seen it on the wall of the Jones family home, and I had seen it again in Salman Khan's office. The abandoned city in soft half-light; London – I took it to be London – as a place of loneliness and shadows and sadness, full of the Sunday morning stillness that James Sutcliffe saw in the world.

The one I'd picked up featured the deserted railway lines. I looked in the corner for his initials.

But they were not there.

Instead there was a name I did not recognise.

Edward Duncan

I stared at the unknown signature, and then I picked up the other painting, the tunnel in the soft light of dawn or twilight.

j s

James Sutcliffe. Then who was Edward Duncan?

I placed the paintings side by side. And I saw what I had not seen before. The style was similar – so alike that it was easy to assume they were by the same artist. But the painting by Edward Duncan was different. It was different from the painting that had 'j s' in the corner, it was different from the painting on the wall of the Jones family home, and it was different from the painting on the wall of Khan's office. It was something to do with the artist's use of light.

Natasha was saying something to me. The dogs were at my

feet and Scout tugged at my sleeve. But I could not tear my eyes from the painting.

Edward Duncan's world was darker than the one James Sutcliffe knew. The light was not fading in his painting of an abandoned city.

It was dying.

18

First thing Monday morning I found TDC Edie Wren alone in MIR-1 reading a new post from Bob the Butcher on her laptop.

'"If the radiance of a thousand suns were to burst at once into the sky, that would be like the splendour of The Mighty One. #killallpigs." A shy, unassuming fellow, isn't he? You seen how many followers he's got now?'

Wren had her laptop plugged into a workstation and on the desk screen I could see that she was logged into HOLMES. Every scrap of evidence produced during the investigation – Operation Fat Boy, they were calling it, after the attack on Guy 'Piggy' Philips – had been entered into HOLMES: witness statements, forensic reports, crime scene photographs, autopsy records, every bit of it tagged with a number, a security level and a priority status. Wren had HOLMES open at the Action Management page, a yellow document that would allocate the day's work schedule for our team. But it was the social network site on her laptop that she was focused on.

'Just sending Bob a message telling him how much I love him,' she said. 'Not much chance of getting a response, I know. But if he replies I can find his IP address in sixty seconds.'

I watched her sending Bob the Butcher some fan mail.

'You're good at this stuff,' I said. 'The whole digital thing.'

She shrugged with false modesty. 'Good enough.'

'Do you think we've done all we can to find him?' I said.

'Bob or the perp?'

'I was thinking of Bob.'

'Everyone in here talks as if they're one and the same. But you don't think so.'

I shrugged. 'It comes down to this. If Jack the Ripper was around today, would he Tweet? Would the Boston Strangler be updating his single status on Facebook? I don't think so.'

Wren laughed. 'You're dead wrong. I think that's *exactly* what they'd be doing. Are you kidding? Jack the Ripper would have *loved* social media. The Boston Strangler, the Yorkshire Ripper – they would have got a big bang out of the digital community. Taunting the law, puffing out their little chests, revelling in the horror, the horror. The digital world is made for sociopaths. As long as you don't get caught.'

'Then you don't think we've done enough to find Bob.'

She pushed a strand of red hair from her face. 'Clearly not, because we haven't found him, have we? But it's not necessarily DI Gane's fault, and I'm not being diplomatic. Bob's hiding behind multiple firewalls, and IDS – intrusion detection systems, like a burglar alarm for computers – and Tor, the onion router, where every message is encrypted and re-encrypted multiple times through countless servers. So it will probably take more than a love letter to flush him out.'

Wren pushed back her chair and picked up what looked like a thick exercise book – the Action Book, which logs the tasks that have been done and the tasks that are yet to be done, and who should do them. It was the real-world equivalent of the Action Management page on HOLMES. Mallory still liked to have a paper record of everything.

'I see you're going back to Potter's Field today with a Specialist Search Unit, and taking more statements from the boys who were out running with Philips,' Wren observed.

I nodded.

As well as monitoring the Action Book, Wren was responsible for all the statements coming in, logging them into HOLMES, and for maintaining the integrity of the chain of evidence, the paper trail leading from the crime scenes to MIR-1 and all the way to court.

It was a big job, and I could see that it bored the hell out of her.

I indicated the laptop.

'Is it true what they say?' I asked. 'Does everyone leave a digital footprint?'

'Now I wouldn't go that far,' she said. 'Everybody leaves a digital *shadow*. We all live two lives – our physical life, and our digital life. All of us. And the finest minds of my generation are currently working out how to sell you stuff you've already bought. So there's pixel tracking, page tagging, tracking codes – it's why all these ads seem to follow you around, to magically know it's *you*.' She laughed. 'At its hollow heart, the internet doesn't really *want* anyone to be anonymous. Because it wants to sell you stuff.'

'So everyone leaves a shadow.'

'Yes.'

'Good,' I said. 'Because there's someone I want you to find.'

'Bob the Butcher,' she said. 'Because he broke your back. Because he made you the laughing stock of millions. And because he could have killed you if he wanted to.'

'Not Bob,' I said. 'I don't think Bob has anything to do with these murders. But the man I want to find just might. He would be somewhere in his mid thirties. Name of Edward Duncan.'

She found herself a pen. 'Edward Duncan,' she said as she wrote. 'Do we have a date of birth?'

'I can get you a possible one but I don't want you to treat it like gospel.'

'OK. What does he do, this Edward Duncan?'

'He paints.'

'Houses?'

'Cities.'

'Should I put it in the Action Book?'

I smiled at her. She wasn't bored now.

'This one's off the book,' I said.

As the afternoon grew colder and darker I stood on the edge of the ploughed field, watching twelve uniformed officers from the Specialist Search Unit inching across it on their hands and knees, fingertip-searching for evidence, the manual labour of police work.

A photographer was standing in the middle of the field staring at something on the ground. I walked over to him and we both looked at a dip in the field containing a single perfect footprint. On one side of it the photographer had placed a yellow marker with the number 1, and on the other side a plastic ruler. He hummed to himself, as cheerful as a wedding photographer, as he began setting up his tripod, lights and ladder.

'Not you, is it?' he grinned, nodding at the footprint.

'I don't think so,' I said.

'Well,' he said, adjusting his tripod. 'Maybe it's the farmer's wife. And maybe it's our man. You never know your luck, do you?'

I agreed that you never knew your luck and headed towards the woods, my back aching in protest at being forced to cross a ploughed field.

The SSU van was parked just beyond the tree line and another dozen officers were sitting around it gulping down tea and bars of chocolate, their clothes filthy from the fingertip search, their exhausted faces as black with sweat-streaked dirt as coal miners'.

I came out of the trees and on to the playing fields of Potter's Field. In the distance the wind whipped the flag of St George that flew above the main building. I'd just started towards it when I was caught by the smell of burning leaves. Smoke was drifting up from behind a tiny stone cottage at the edge of the rugby pitch. I walked round the back of it and found an old man unloading a wheelbarrow piled with dead leaves on to a small bonfire.

'Excuse me, sir?'

I showed him my warrant card. He peered at it and nodded. Then carried on with what he was doing. Whatever you do, get their name and address, they tell you at Hendon. It's the very first thing they tell you.

'May I ask your name, sir?'

'I'm nobody. I'm just the groundsman.'

A strange accent that contained both Eastern Europe and the West Country. I watched him unload the wheelbarrow. There was something wrong with his hands. He glanced at me and saw that I was still waiting for an answer.

'Len Zukov,' he said.

'Where you from, Len?'

He gave me a sharp look. 'I'm from here. How about you? Where you from?'

The accent was Russian, maybe.

'I'm from here, too,' I said.

'Then we're both from here.'

'Worked here long, Len?'

He was silent for a moment, as if adding it up.

'Thirty years,' he said.

'Do you remember these boys?'

I was holding out a photograph of the seven boys in their Combined Cadet Force uniforms.

He shook his head. Too quickly?

'Many boys come and go,' he said.

'This was taken in 1988. In your time. You don't remember them? Have a closer look. The King twins? You don't remember identical twins?'

'No.'

The worst thing about being a policeman? People lie to you. They lie all the time. They lie because they are afraid of getting into trouble, they lie because they are afraid of getting into deeper trouble, and most of all they lie so that you will go away.

But maybe he was telling the truth. It was a long time ago, and boys had come and gone in their thousands.

'But you know Mr Philips,' I said. 'The sports master. And you know that someone tried to kill him.'

The old man looked at me as if I was some kind of idiot.

'Everybody knows,' he said.

I watched him load more leaves on the fire and then saw what was wrong with his hands. The fingers did not open. He was building his fire with two fists closed by what looked like the advanced stages of rheumatoid arthritis.

'It was in the woods,' he said. 'Far from here.'

When the last of the leaves were on the fire he brushed his

closed fists on his trousers and we walked to the front of the cottage. There was a figure standing in the doorway – the physiotherapist Mallory and I had seen on the playing fields with the disabled men. Now I saw that he was not wearing a mask. Most of his face had been lost to burns.

I held out my hand.

'Sergeant Tom Monk,' he said. 'Formerly of the Royal Green Jackets.'

His shockingly burned face split with a wide white grin. He looked like a member of some lost race; I could not believe there would be a time when his face would not shock me. He clicked the heels of his Asics trainers, and Zukov smiled for the first time. He seemed much more relaxed in the presence of Monk.

'You do rehab here?' I asked Monk.

'One afternoon a week,' he said. 'I'm mostly down the road. I'm the senior physio at Barrington Court. Or the senior physio's assistant. Yeah, that's more like it.'

I had heard of Barrington Court. It was a rehabilitation centre for severely wounded veterans, most of them victims of IED blasts in Afghanistan.

'Mr Waugh lets us use the running track on Thursday afternoons,' Monk said. 'Quite funny really, lending us a running track when most of us don't have any legs.'

I automatically looked down at his faded jeans. Monk laughed.

'Oh, not me,' he said. 'I've still got all my parts. Some of them are just a bit overcooked.'

I smiled weakly.

'How's he doing?' Monk said, suddenly serious. 'Mr Philips.'

I shook my head. 'You know what? I really don't know, Tom.'

Because on the other side of the playing fields I could see the flag of St George being lowered, and stopping when it reached half-mast. The phone in my jacket began to vibrate.

I pulled it out and saw that it was PC Greene, and that he had already tried to call me five times.

Peregrine Waugh was crossing the playing fields towards me, his gown flowing behind him.

But I already knew.

Piggy Philips was dead.

19

I was waiting for Ben King in the central lobby of the Palace of Westminster, the most beautiful space in London – a high-vaulted octagonal hall with a giant central chandelier and an intricately tiled floor, lit by natural light that pours through massive windows.

The central lobby bustled with life. Constituents waited to talk to their MP. Political journalists gossiped and snickered and fawned. MPs and peers came and went from the corridors that led to their chambers – the Lords to the south, the MPs to the north.

With its statues of kings and queens and a national saint over each of the four exits – St George for England, St David for Wales, St Andrew for Scotland, St Patrick for Northern Ireland – the central lobby felt like more than the core of Parliament, more than the place where all the corridors of power converged.

It felt like the ultimate seat of British power.

I watched Ben King emerge from the corridor that led to the House of Commons. He was in a group of men surrounding the Prime Minister. King saw me and peeled away from the crowd.

We shook hands and walked out to the Terrace Pavilion, where there were white tables and chairs and people drinking tea. We stood with our backs to them all, the Palace of Westminster rising above us, and the Thames flowing far below.

'My condolences,' I said.

'Thank you.'

'You were with Guy Philips when he died.'

'Yes. I spent the last night in his room.'

'Did he say anything? I'm sorry but I have to ask you.'

Ben King stared at the river without seeing it.

'It was four in the morning. He was sleeping. I was sleeping. I awoke because the machine that monitored his heart rate was making a different sound. I called the nurse. She was sleeping too. When she came to the room she immediately called the doctor. But it was too late.' At last he looked at me. 'Guy died in his sleep. I know what you're asking. But he never woke, he never said anything about who attacked him and he passed away peacefully. And I am profoundly grateful for that small mercy, detective.'

'And you were with him every night he was in the hospital?'

'Yes. Guy never married. His parents were dead. My brother and I – all of his friends – were what he had instead of family.'

'I think he saw his killer's face. I'm certain of it.'

'He didn't say a word.'

A young blonde woman was standing in the entrance to the Terrace Pavilion, trying to attract King's attention. He raised his hand to show that he understood. But his manners were too good to rush me.

'There's something else,' I said. 'You – and your brother, and Mr Khan – you're all going to be issued with Osman Warnings.'

'Osman Warnings?'

'If the police have reason to believe that someone is at risk of being murdered or seriously injured we issue an Osman Warning – it's both an official warning and an offer of police protection.'

King almost smiled. 'It sounds rather like a way of the police trying to protect themselves from future accusations of negligence.'

'There's an element of that,' I agreed. 'My superiors will be writing to you to offer protection and to give advice on the steps you can take to ensure your safety.'

'Is that really necessary? Perhaps for Salman – who, I understand, is now too afraid to leave his house. But I'm surrounded by high security in the House. And Ned is out of the country and has the entire British Army watching over him. I think he's more at risk from the Taliban.'

'We have a duty of care to warn people when they are in mortal danger,' I said. 'On Hugo Buck's desk there was a photograph of seven boys at Potter's Field. You probably know the photograph.'

'Yes, I know it.'

'Now only four of you are still alive.'

He was watching the river again.

'Three,' he said. 'James Sutcliffe killed himself in Italy.'

'Of course. My apologies. Three of you.'

Then he looked at me. 'I want to put an end to this,' he said. 'I want to help you in any way I can. I want to assist you in apprehending this murderer.' He gripped my hand and he held my eyes.

'I know,' I said. 'I know you do.'

We walked back inside and said goodbye.

As he crossed the central lobby, people approached him – lobby journalists, other MPs, women and men, all of them with the half-smile of the truly smitten – and he had a word for each of them. But he kept walking, he never broke that long easy stride, eventually disappearing into the northern corridor that leads to the House of Commons; and for the first time I appreciated his true power, and how much he had to lose.

It's a five-minute walk from the Palace of Westminster to New Scotland Yard, and even though I did not have an appointment in Room 101, I thought it would be all right. They don't get many visitors in the Black Museum.

'I saw your film,' said Sergeant John Caine, the keeper of the gate. He looked at me with his hard eyes, but there was no mockery in them. 'Everybody saw your film, didn't they?'

'Will you watch it with me again?'

He was startled. 'Why?'

'It only lasts a minute. I want to ask your advice about something. I know you've seen it already, but will you watch it with me?'

There was an old computer on his desk. He pressed some keys and it wheezed into life.

'My one might be quicker,' I said.

He snorted. 'All mod cons at West End Central, eh?'

I took out my Mac and we waited in silence as it powered up. We remained silent as I went to the social network site and found the profile page of Bob the Butcher. I began scrolling down all his postings about killing pigs and destroying worlds.

'This one,' I said.

I clicked on the link, and there it was, the mirth with no mercy of 'The Laughing Policeman' as the camera watched me crawl. Just as the pig appeared, I hit pause.

'You see that?' I asked Sergeant Caine. 'By my right hand?'

He leaned closer. 'A white line.'

'A straight white line painted on grass,' I said. 'It's a touch-line. It's the edge of a rugby field. The rugby field that's closest to the trees at Potter's Field.'

We stared at the image together. Then he shrugged.

'So what?' he said.

'Doesn't it prove that Bob the Butcher isn't the killer?'

'Why does it prove that?'

'That film wasn't shot when I got a good hiding. Whatever Bob tells his devoted followers, he had nothing to do with it.'

Sergeant Caine had a think.

Then he said, 'You reckon that whoever had a knife to your throat is not the same person who stuck a camera in your face.'

'He can't be, can he?' I said. 'Whoever put me down wouldn't have followed me across a ploughed field and through some woods just to shoot this funny little film, would he?'

'How far did you crawl?'

'I was running through those woods for perhaps five minutes. It would have taken a lot longer to crawl back. But that film wasn't taken anywhere near where I was attacked. It wasn't taken at the pigpen at the farm. It wasn't taken in the ploughed field. It was filmed when I was back at Potter's Field. It was filmed on the edge of the playing fields.'

'So who put it on the internet? Where did Bob get it from?'

'I don't know. It doesn't matter. That school has a thousand boys and they all have phones with cameras. There are reporters crawling all over the place. The staff. Everybody's walking around with a camera crew in their back pocket. What it proves – what I *think* it proves – is that Bob the Butcher is full of bullshit. Whoever took that film didn't kill anyone. And neither did he.'

I closed my laptop and we looked at each other. Sergeant Caine folded his heavy arms. Then he nodded once.

'Yes,' he said, 'I think you're probably right.'

'Thank you.'

'You're welcome. What's the problem?'

'The problem is they're chucking everything they've got at Bob,' I said. 'All of our resources are being poured into looking for Bob the Butcher, serial killer of the year. Operation Fat Boy is being led up a dead end.'

A spasm of pain travelled up my spine and I ground my teeth together, arching my back until it passed.

'You want to find whoever messed up your back,' Sergeant Caine said.

'I want to find the killer.' I took a breath and let it go. 'And you can help me.'

'How can I do that?'

'I want to see the From Hell letter,' I said.

He looked away, then looked back at me. Suddenly he was angry.

'The From Hell letter? Do you know what you're asking? The From Hell letter was lost.'

'I don't think so,' I said. 'I think it's here. I think it's somewhere in this room. I think it's in your possession.'

'What do you know about the From Hell letter, detective?'

'I know that it was also known as the Lusk letter,' I replied. 'It was a letter posted in 1888 by a person unknown who claimed to be Jack the Ripper. What made the police think it was the one genuine correspondence from Jack the Ripper was that it arrived with part of an internal organ from a human body.'

'Where do you think you are,' Sergeant Caine said, shaking his head with disbelief, 'Madame Tussaud's? This is a training facility for officers who put themselves in harm's way. Not a freak show.'

'I just want to see the letter.'

'What makes you think it's here?'

'I just don't believe it was lost. I can't believe that. The only letter from Jack the Ripper? Come on. I think it would have been filed, saved, preserved.'

'Why lie about it?'

'Don't want the public getting too excited about some unholy relic, do we? Don't need them turning a serial killer into a bigger cult hero than he is already. But I think we would have saved it.'

'We?'

'The law. The Met. The good guys. And I think that if it is anywhere in London, then it will be in some secret corner of the Black Museum.'

He laughed. 'I suppose you might just make a detective one day. But why do you want to see it – assuming it's in my power to show it to you?'

'I want to see what the real thing looks like.'

He moved towards the door and I thought he was going to call for some help and have me kicked out. But Sergeant Caine wouldn't have needed any help to kick me out.

I watched him lock Room 101.

'There were hundreds of letters claiming to be from Jack the Ripper,' he said. 'The Dear Boss letter. The Saucy Jacky postcard. The Openshaw letter. What made the From Hell letter different was that, as you say, it came with a small box containing half a human kidney.'

I watched him remove a calendar from the wall that said MERRY CHRISTMAS AND A HAPPY NEW YEAR FROM THE METROPOLITAN POLICE.

There was a safe in the wall.

'Turn away, detective,' he said, and I turned my head as he tapped some numbered keys. 'It was addressed to George Lusk, the head of the Whitechapel Vigilance Committee. You can turn back now.'

There was a dark green folder on his desk.

He opened it. Inside the folder was a plastic envelope. Inside the envelope was a single sheet of paper, rust-coloured with age, as brittle as something scorched, like something pulled from the fire at the very last moment.

Large red letters, a dozen lines, words written quickly, words written in a fever.

'Somebody slung out the kidney,' Sergeant Caine said. 'Sorry about that.'

From hell

Mr Lusk
Sor
I send you half the
Kidne I took from one women
Prasarved it for you tother piece
I fried and ate it was very nice, I
may send you the bloody knif that
took it out if you only wate a whil
longer.

Signed
Catch me when
You Can
Mishter Lusk

'It's real, isn't it?' I said. 'You can tell. It's from him. It's from Jack the Ripper.'

Caine nodded. 'It's at a much lower literacy level than the other letters they received, but back in the day they thought that was deliberate. What's fake about it is the pretence of illiteracy. Look. He apparently can't spell to save his life but he manages to observe the silent "k" in knife and the silent "h" in while. Unlike all the other letters, he doesn't sign it "Jack the Ripper". And I'll say this for him – he did include a human kidney.'

'He was sick of the fakes,' I said. 'He was tired of all the nutcases claiming credit for crimes they didn't have the skill and the madness to commit. And it's going to be the same this time. Sooner or later, the real killer will show himself.'

Sergeant Caine watched me staring at the letter.

'Bob the Butcher is not real,' I said. 'But this is real. May I touch it?'

The keeper of the Black Museum stared at me.

'Be careful,' he said.

20

'One murder is a tragedy,' said Detective Chief Superintendent Elizabeth Swire. 'Two murders are a tragic coincidence. And three murders are prime-time entertainment.'

The call from the chief super had come just as Mallory was about to start the morning briefing at West End Central. Fifteen minutes later we were in a conference room on the top floor of New Scotland Yard. This high up the brass had a picture-postcard view of either St James's Park or the Thames. This room overlooked the park. But nobody noticed the view.

The death of Guy Philips had put Operation Fat Boy on all the front pages. Bob the Butcher was being called a serial killer and treated like a national celebrity. The popular press were going wild, but with a sneaking regard for Bob's dysfunctional social conscience. BOB THE BUTCHER – FEARED BY THE RICH, LOVED BY THE POOR? asked the *Sun*. The unpopular press saw Bob as the embodiment of the seething resentments at the rotten core of an unfair society. BUTCHER BOB – IS HE A ONE MAN RIOT? pondered the *Guardian*, as if all Bob was doing was kicking in store windows and stealing plasma TVs.

The chief super was not happy. And DCS Swire had a genius for registering her displeasure. She was a fifty-year-old woman with a ferocious blonde haircut, hair sprayed as stiff as a Spartan helmet. Swire looked like Mrs Thatcher's recently exhumed corpse, but with slightly less human warmth.

She considered DCI Mallory with dead eyes.

'You initially expressed doubts that Bob the Butcher was the perpetrator,' she said.

'That's correct, ma'am.'

'So have you eliminated him from your enquiries?'

'Not yet, ma'am,' Mallory said.

'Not yet, ma'am,' she said, her tone so caustic you could have used it to strip paint.

DI Gane spoke up, his voice shaking just a little. He talked about anonymity networks, onion routers and layers of encryption.

Swire cut him off with a short jerk of her head.

'Let's skip the tech talk, shall we?' she said. 'But tell me this: how likely is it that the average social network psycho would have security architecture that elaborate?'

'It would be . . . unusual,' Gane answered.

Swire may not have cocked a disbelieving eyebrow. But that was the impression she gave.

'Only unusual?' she said quietly. 'Really? No more than that?'

'It would be unprecedented, ma'am.'

Swire nodded, as if we were at last getting somewhere.

'What's the latest on prints?' she said. 'Are we working the prints?'

Mallory's fingertips brushed his SIO policy book. He cleared his throat.

'The situation is unchanged, ma'am. We have no prints at any of the crime scenes.'

Swire stared hard at him.

'You mean you have smooth glove prints?'

'No prints, ma'am. No smooth glove prints, no partials – no prints at all. The absence of prints remains . . . unexplained.'

Swire let this sink in.

'So he's a ghost?' she said.

The base of my spine pulsed with pain.

'He's no ghost,' I said. 'Ma'am.'

She nodded, as if she had only just decided something.

'We're rebooting Operation Fat Boy,' she said. 'I'm bringing in three new bodies.'

Swire was flanked by two men who had remained silent throughout the meeting, avoiding eye contact with the incompetent Murder Investigation Team from West End Central: a young East Asian in glasses with digital geek written all over him, and a much older man, about sixty, with soft white hair who couldn't possibly have been a part of the Met because he was wearing a suit but no tie.

Now they stirred.

Swire nodded curtly at Mallory and told him, 'You will remain as SIO for the time being. But I'll be sitting in at the morning briefings and you will be reporting directly to me.'

Gane and Whitestone exchanged a look. Mallory's time was passing. He was still senior investigating officer but this no longer felt like his investigation. Operation Fat Boy now felt like it was being run from Broadway, SW1 – New Scotland Yard – not 27 Savile Row.

Mallory was a good man, but the world was beating him down. Suddenly his authority felt like a fragile thing that could be taken away by one gesture from the woman at the top of the conference table. I saw that Gane and Whitestone could not look at him.

Swire gestured to the digital geek on her left. 'This is Colin Cho of the Police Central e-crime Unit. As you know, the PCeU is jointly funded by the Home Office and the Met to provide a national response to the most serious incidents of cyber-crime. Bob the Butcher comes under their remit.'

'Hopefully we might be able to show you a few new tricks,' Cho said to Gane, his accent somewhere between Hong Kong and London.

Gane said nothing.

'I want Bob flushed out,' Swire said. 'I want him dragged out from behind his firewall. I want him taken *seriously*. We're becoming a laughing stock.' She nodded sharply at me. Her hair did not move. 'Especially after DC Wolfe's recent stroll in the country.'

'We *have* taken Bob seriously, ma'am,' Mallory insisted.

She did not slap the table. She did not need to. She fixed Mallory with a look cold enough to give a snowman hypothermia.

'Not seriously enough,' she said. 'The MP for Hillingdon North is highly thought of in Whitehall and Westminster.' She inhaled deeply, exhaled slowly. 'I am receiving phone calls.'

So that was it, I thought. The murders were too close to Ben King, and Swire had the full weight of Downing Street and Whitehall pressing on her back.

She turned to the older man on her right. 'And this is Dr Joe Stephen of King's College London. Introduce yourself, Dr Stephen?'

'I'm a forensic psychologist and I'm here to give assistance in any way I can,' Dr Stephen said. He had the smooth sing-song vowels of a Californian who had lived in London for twenty years. The Hollywood Hills meets Muswell Hill.

'What can you tell us so far?' Swire asked.

'Well,' he said. 'Forensic psychology is more art than science. All I can do is look at the evidence, and estimate what kind of individual would commit these crimes.' There was a file before him and he glanced down at it without, I sensed, really needing to. 'To apprehend the unsub – sorry, the unknown subject – you need to understand that he is re-ordering the world. When women kill, they almost always kill someone they know. When men kill more than once, it's almost always strangers. Serial killers are invariably male.'

Gane folded his arms. 'So we're looking for a man?' he said. He smirked at Whitestone but she wouldn't return his look, or his smile. 'That narrows it down,' he muttered.

Dr Stephen stared at him. 'A white man,' he added.

'And why's that?' said the black DI.

'Because the dead men are all white,' Dr Stephen said, 'and serial killers almost always kill within their own race. That's not universal, but close enough to be considered a given.'

He looked a little rattled. He had come in wanting to be our friend and he was being forced to defend himself.

'What kind of white man, Dr Stephen?' Whitestone said, far friendlier than Gane. 'Any guess as to age, motive, social group?'

'A white man who is trying to right some perceived wrong,' Dr Stephen said. 'A man who is punishing his victims. These are all planned attacks. Very carefully planned attacks. These are not confrontational homicides, these are revenge homicides. The unsub is trying to right a wrong by the only means at his disposal – extreme violence. He is the product of a place where violence is the means of achieving your aims.'

The resentment was coming off Gane like steam, but to me Dr Stephen was making sense. I thought of the terrible neatness of those carotid thrusts and the ease with which they opened arteries that could never be closed again. It was the work of a man who was remaking the world.

'Maybe he's just a nutter,' Gane said.

Dr Stephen smiled at him with a kind of embarrassed pity. 'Then he is a nutter – your term, detective, not mine – who is restoring control over what he perceives to be a mad world. Honour. Power. Control. That's what matters to him. And when you find him, as you no doubt will, you will find a man who needs to control other men, a man who needs that more than anything in the world.'

'So you don't really know anything about him at all?' Gane persisted.

'Look, the reason I'm in this room is because these are stranger killings,' Dr Stephen said. 'Most of the homicides you attend, the killer and the victim are known to each other. The husband who murders his wife because of her infidelity, the mother who murders her child, the drug dealer who murders his business associate.' He paused. 'That link does not exist with a serial killer. He is not known to the victim. He is not a husband, a business associate, a friend. But the unknown sub leaves evidence. Psychiatric evidence. Behavioural evidence. Ritualistic evidence. The remnants of fantasy and madness.'

On the other side of the glass walls I saw Scarlet Bush being escorted to the conference room.

'Ah, this is Ms Bush,' Swire said when she entered the room, 'who some of you will know already as crime correspondent for the *Daily Post*.'

The reporter circled the table, shaking hands and making smiling eye contact with everyone, including me. She played it as if we had never met. Then she took her place at the top of the conference table, next to Dr Stephen.

'This is the plan,' Swire said.

The shock of these words jolted Mallory upright and made the pain at the base of my spine pulse with alarm. Whitestone and Gane exchanged a startled look.

What plan?

'Dr Stephen is going to provide a detailed profile of Bob the Butcher,' the chief super continued. 'Then, based on this profile, Ms Bush is going to write a comment piece in the *Post* designed to tempt Bob into explaining himself in an online interview. And Mr Cho will be waiting to drive a very large hole through his firewall.'

'Press his buttons,' said Scarlet Bush. 'Make Bob stop hiding behind the grandiose Robert Oppenheimer sound bites and raise his head above the parapet.'

Mallory shifted uncomfortably in his seat. 'You really think he'll respond if you – what? – insult him in print?'

'If I do it in the right way,' Bush said. 'Bob wouldn't be preening on a social network site if he wasn't vain, and if he didn't want attention, and if he wasn't a narcissist, and if he didn't want to justify himself to the world. Not necessarily insults – we have agreed that Dr Stephen will have copy approval – more observations. Just enough that Bob will feel the need to explain himself. Just a little. Just enough.'

A look of disbelief must have passed across my face. Bush stared at me, not smiling now.

'He'll talk to me for the same reason that, in the end, they all talk to me,' she continued. 'Not because it would be great to hear his side of the story. But because I'm going to tell his story anyway. So he can either have his say or stay quiet and let the world have its say.'

'That's the way it works, is it?' I said.

'That's exactly the way it works, detective.'

I turned to Swire.

'Ma'am, we're throwing everything we've got at this Bob the Butcher and—'

'And that's what we're going to keep throwing until we bury him,' the chief super responded, cutting me off. She turned to Cho. 'Colin?'

'I'm confident that PCeU have the kit to find cracks in whatever encryption systems, anonymisers and onion routers he's using.'

Swire's eyes swept across the subdued MIT from West End Central.

'And then you're going to bring me his head on a spike,' she told us.

Mallory was staring bleakly at his SIO policy book. The strength seemed to be visibly draining from him. The chief super had made it sound easy, so it felt like a betrayal when I looked out over St James's Park and thought – *why shouldn't it work?* Trace, interview, eliminate – the TIE process was standard police procedure in any major investigation. Maybe Swire's plan was for the best. Flush the preening little bastard out from under his digital rock.

Scarlet Bush leaned back in her chair.

'So, Dr Stephen, what kind of guy is Bob the Butcher?' she said.

'I can tell you about the unsub,' the American said. 'I can – I believe – also tell you something about Bob the Butcher. What I can't tell you is that they are one and the same.'

Swire and Bush glanced at each other. And I saw just how desperately they both wanted Bob to be the same man – our killer.

'Society struggles to understand the repeat serious offender,' Dr Stephen continued. 'The serial rapist and the serial killer. Often they are the same thing but at different stages on the road to madness.'

'But there's no sexual element to Bob's crimes,' Swire said.

'My point is that the serial rapist and the serial killer tend to share the same basic characteristics. Because transgression is a way of life, they tend to be charming, manipulative, vain, ruthless, morally numb and devoid of even a shred of human empathy. The unsub will have a rich fantasy life – a fantasy life so rewarding that it will have come to have more substance than the real world. The unsub is likely to be a liar of near genius. As you know, serial killers often sail through lie detector tests. Trauma in his background is a given. Frequently, but not always, they come from backgrounds of mental and sexual abuse.'

Scarlet Bush perked up. 'You think Bob the Butcher was the victim of child abuse?'

'It's possible. The rational mind struggles to understand the psychopathology of the irrational. These murders are an expression of the killer's masculinity. As I said, these homicides are displays of honour, power and control. Their sole purpose is punishment – for some perceived wrong done against the killer himself or a third party. The killer almost certainly doesn't know his victims. He is simply righting a wrong – or a series of wrongs.'

Scarlet Bush was jotting down notes.

'So you're saying that Bob the Butcher has a fragile masculinity?' she said.

'Not necessarily. But the unsub has a limited means of expressing his masculinity. He can't do it, for example, in the business world. So he does it with violence. He does it with murder.'

'What if I – I mean *we* – implied that there was, for example, a gay element to the crimes?'

Dr Stephen looked at her levelly. 'I doubt you will endear yourself to him. Look, he's seeking to gain control of a situation that is totally *beyond* his control. Unlike the overwhelming majority of murderers, he fully intends his victims to die. What's unusual is that most homicides, as you know far better than me, are simply a by-product of extreme violence. Most murder victims are just unlucky.'

'I'll say,' said Gane.

Dr Stephen had become good at ignoring him.

'Medical help is delayed,' he continued. 'A vital organ is accidentally severed. A fatal injury is sustained when a head hits the pavement.'

A sharp point of pain in my neck began to throb. *Please.* The cut beneath the scab where I had felt his knife. *Please.* I slowed my breathing before it was out of control.

Please. I have a daughter.

'Our unsub sets out with the intention to kill,' said Dr Stephen. 'Honour. Power. Control. If I can tell you anything at all, it is that: honour, power, control. There's your motive. These murders are an expression of affronted masculinity.'

Bob and the killer no longer sounded to me like people who were just different. They sounded like polar opposites.

Dr Stephen smiled pleasantly.

'And I can tell you one more thing for nothing,' he said.

We all looked at him.

'He won't stop.'

21

The fox had the playing fields to himself.

I had driven out to Potter's Field for Guy Philips' memorial service, and with an hour to kill I had wandered out to the playing fields, remembering when Piggy had come running from the woods with the life draining out of him.

The rugby and football pitches were all empty now. There was just the lone fox, which I'd watched come out of the trees and mooch along the touchline of the far rugby field, heading towards the little stone cottage.

There was no sign of Len Zukov, the groundsman, but the fox moved more warily near this sign of civilisation, slowing his pace and raising his head to sniff the air. My phone began to vibrate as I saw the fox veer away from the cottage and move into the great muddy green expanse of the playing fields.

Wren was calling. She wasn't in MIR-1. I could hear street noises, voices I didn't know.

'Edward Duncan,' she said.

'Yes?'

'He doesn't have a criminal record. He doesn't have a driving licence. He doesn't have a national insurance number. He doesn't have a passport. And he doesn't have a credit card, a bank account or a wife.'

She was pleased with herself. I could almost see her grinning with pleasure, brushing a strand of red hair from her pale face.

'What does he have?' I said.

'Edward Duncan has an art dealer.'

I let it sink in. 'Well done, Wren.'

'Nereus Fine Art. Small place. North London, right at the top of Heath Street, Hampstead way. I drove past it.'

'I didn't ask you to do that, did I?'

'Relax, detective, I didn't go in. It was closed anyway. It's tiny.'

'Nereus Fine Art,' I said.

'It's a Greek myth,' Wren explained. 'Nereus was a god of the sea. He was kind and just and he had a special power.'

'Go on.'

'He had the power to change his shape.'

The fox was trotting towards me, taking his time.

'Thank you,' I said.

'See? Everyone leaves a shadow.'

I took down the details of Nereus Fine Art.

'When are you going to check it out?' she said.

'When I get back to town,' I said. 'Tonight.'

'Pick me up at West End Central?'

'Why would I do that?'

'Because I'm coming with you.'

I almost laughed. 'You're not coming with me. This is off the book.'

'And that's exactly why I'm coming with you,' she said. 'It's off the book and I found him and I'm coming with you.'

I figured we could argue about it later.

'Who is he?' she said. 'Who's Edward Duncan?'

The fox had paused in the centre circle of the football pitch.

He sniffed the air, then pointed his face at the dirt and began to dig furiously.

'Edward Duncan is a dead man,' I said.

It was a shock to see Captain Ned King again.

He wore the immaculate black dress uniform of an officer in the Royal Gurkha Rifles, but he was unshaven and red-eyed, as if he had come to the Potter's Field College Chapel straight from Brize Norton, as if he had spent last night on a Hercules transport plane. But what shocked me was how alike Ned King was to his brother, yet how totally different. They sat side by side in the ancient chapel, as Peregrine Waugh glared out from the lectern. Ben King with his smooth politician's face, Captain King with his scarred soldier's face. Although I remembered it wasn't soldiering that had scarred his face.

Salman Khan was by Ben King's side, and he was looking up at the stupendously tall Head Master, as if he might be asked questions later.

'We gather today to remember Mr Philips,' Waugh said. 'An old boy. A master. A friend.'

Like most good public speakers, Waugh was a bit of a ham. He told us to look at the memorial leaflet. He told us to look at the year when Guy Philips was born, and the year when he died. And he said that they were not important. That what mattered most was what came between them. What mattered most was 'the dash'. His life.

He talked about Philips as if he had been a cross between Mother Teresa and Jesus Christ.

I thought of poor dead Piggy. I saw him hurting Natasha at Hugo Buck's funeral. I saw him making his pupils roll in the mud. It seemed to me that he had spent the dash bullying.

But Waugh was a commanding speaker, and I could hear the wet noses and choked throats of emotion behind me. Yet as I looked at the Head Master's stone-hard face I could not decide if Guy Philips had meant everything to Peregrine Waugh.

Or nothing at all.

The Potter's Field College Chapel was packed with what felt like the entire school. Black-robed masters in the first few rows, a great mass of boys in green and purple behind them and, under the stained-glass window, six rows of the choir facing another six rows. More boys and masters lined the perimeter of the chapel, and spilled through the open doorways.

The place was much smaller than I had expected. I had read online that building work had been interrupted during the War of the Roses and had yet to resume, and I had the feeling I always got at Potter's Field – that you could blink your eye and a hundred years would go by.

Captain King walked to the lectern.

'Our revels now are ended,' he read. 'These our actors, as I foretold you, were all spirits and are melted into air, into thin air. And, like the baseless fabric of this vision, the cloud-capped towers, the gorgeous palaces, the solemn temples, the great globe itself – yea, all which it inherit, shall dissolve and, like this insubstantial pageant faded, leave not a rack behind.'

Salman Khan hung his head and wept. Ben King kept his eyes on the shattered face of his brother as Captain King's words filled the ancient chapel.

'We are such stuff as dreams are made on, and our little life is rounded with a sleep.'

Captain King's delivery was matter of fact, yet the words carried real meaning. He was composed and yet replete with emotion. He was good at that. But then he had had a lot of practice.

Captain King returned to the front row, touching Khan once on the shoulder before taking his place next to his brother. Their wives sat behind them – pretty women, sleek and sexy even in their mourning clothes – shepherding well-behaved children with braces on their teeth. The ladies' fat jewels glistened. There was plenty of money and time for their children's bodies, minds and orthodontics.

The King brothers and Khan all had families. And I guessed that they loved those families.

But the real bonds, the unbreakable bonds, the bonds of a lifetime, they were different.

Because they were with each other.

After the memorial service I walked across the playing fields, skirting the rugby pitch where a games lesson was taking place. The boys all wore black armbands for their murdered sports master.

The sounds of flesh crashing into flesh, stud on to bone, cries and laughter faded behind me as I headed towards the stone cottage where Len Zukov lived. I knocked on the door. There was no answer. I walked round the back of the cottage, turning up my collar against the bitter wind. I stopped when I saw the fox.

It lay on top of the compost heap, a ragged sack of fur and bone, waiting for the fire.

Its neck had been neatly broken.

I got back to town at five in the afternoon, the November day already as dark as midnight and London's 180-minute rush hour starting to get mad. I sent Wren a text when I was on Piccadilly and she was waiting for me outside 27 Savile Row when I arrived. She got into the X5 with a triumphant smile.

'If it wasn't for me,' she said, 'you'd still be dicking about on Google. I'd go through Regent's Park, if I were you. The traffic is always surprisingly light around the park.'

I took the park route and within fifteen minutes we were on the Finchley Road, the traffic heavy but moving steadily; and then it was thinning and the road was rising steeply towards the end of Heath Street as we climbed to the highest point of the city.

I realised that we were close to the meadow where Scout and I had let Stan off his lead and lost him. I had never noticed all the art galleries before. You drive out of Hampstead and they are the last thing you see, a cluster of them, all shapes and sizes, just before you are surrounded by the wild green expanse of the Heath.

As the car crawled higher, I saw that some of these galleries were high end, great lavish spaces with large, expensively lit canvases displayed in the window; other places were far more modest, local artists selling their work to a local clientele. The one we were looking for was little more than a darkened hole in the wall.

'This is it,' Wren said.

NEREUS

Fine Art

I slowed as we drove past and caught a glimpse of a tiny space behind wrought-iron railings glinting under the street-lights. A recycling bin was overturned, its contents spilled over the narrow pavement. Wren was already unclipping her seat belt as I crested the hill. I found a parking space behind Jack Straw's Castle.

But when we walked back to the gallery we found that Nereus Fine Art was closed. Two small landscapes were displayed in the window. A wave of junk mail was washed up inside the glass door. BACK SOON lied a sign.

I stood back. It was a three-storey building: the small gallery had a basement flat below and a flat above. I leaned over the wrought-iron railings, looking down and then up. Both of the flats were in darkness. Broken glass crunched beneath my feet and the recycling bin looked as though it had been rifled through by a fox that had come down from the Heath. He had been out of luck. It was just beer bottles and empty pizza boxes.

I looked up and down the street. We were on the edge of Hampstead affluence. Businesses were either booming or going bust. Apart from the galleries, there were a few restaurants and clothes stores, but over half of them had closed down. The buildings all had exactly the same wrought-iron railings as Nereus. The blue and red lights of burglar alarms blinked on even the most modest buildings.

'Let's go,' I said. 'I've got another call to make. Where should I drop you?'

'I'll come with you.'

I looked at her. How old was she? Twenty-five? Younger?

'Don't you have a life to go to?' I said.

'I can't see my boyfriend tonight.' A beat. 'He has to have dinner with his wife.' Another beat. 'It's her birthday.'

She toed the broken beer bottles, then pushed aside an empty pizza box with fossilised cheese on its side.

'A man lives here,' she said.

'How do you know it's a man?'

'Only men live like this. Men and pigs.'

Holloway was a few miles and several light years away from Hampstead.

Wren and I stood before a large dusty shop window where pride of place was given to a showroom dummy dressed as a German soldier from World War Two.

'How'd you know about this place?' Wren said.

'I dicked about on Google,' I said.

Under its coalscuttle helmet the mannequin had the gently pouting features of a young male model. But the clothes he wore were heavy and harsh and made for invading Russia. A thick wool greatcoat was draped over a rough tunic, both far too large for the delicate, snake-hipped dummy, and baggy trousers were tucked into leather boots. It all looked impossibly old and fragile, as if it would disintegrate with one touch.

'Is any of this stuff real?' I wondered.

'Those boots aren't,' Wren said. 'Everything else might be. But the boots – never. The Krauts wore their boots out. On the Eastern Front the Germans used to saw the legs off dead Russian soldiers and defrost them in some lucky peasant's oven, just to get at the boots.'

I stared at her.

'My dad,' she said. 'He liked World War Two. Is that the expression? Liking it? He was interested, let's say. *The World at War* boxed set and all that.'

The rest of the window was full of lovingly presented junk. Buttons. Posters. Faded scraps of metal and cloth and card and leather, all of it displayed like holy relics. SECOND FRONT, it said above the store. COLLECTIBLE MILITARIA.

The lights were going out inside.

I cop-knocked on the door. A long-haired man, not young, stuck his head around the door.

'I'm just closing up,' he said.

'Don't let us stop you.'

He stood to one side at the sight of our warrant cards and we went in.

'DC Wolfe and TDC Wren,' I said.

'Nick Cage,' he said, reluctantly.

I saw rags in glass cases, rusty medals in presentation cases, framed photographs of smiling men who had died screaming a lifetime ago.

'Nice place,' Wren said. 'My old man would love it. Is that a real Luger P08?'

She was indicating a handgun in a dark stained-glass box.

'Replica,' he replied, looking at me. 'It doesn't fire.'

I opened my bag and removed a file. Inside it was a collection of eight-by-ten photographs. I spread them on top of a glass cabinet and felt a pulse of pain freeze my lower back. The photographs were all of a knife that was designed to cut a man's throat. I leaned forward, my palms on the glass case, easing my tailbone and my breath out at the same time. It wasn't a proper dog stretch, but it made me feel better.

'I know you,' Cage said. 'Where was it?' He clicked his fingers. 'The Laughing Policeman film on YouTube.'

'He's dead famous,' Wren said, flicking through a rack of ragged army jackets as if she was in Miss Selfridge. 'He went viral.'

I looked at Cage. 'You don't know me, OK?' I said.

'OK,' he said.

'Do you know what these are?'

He looked at the photos one by one.

'It's a Fairbairn-Sykes commando dagger. They're all Fairbairn-Sykes commando daggers. These are all different generations of the same weapon. I could be more specific if I could see the knives. This one with the green handle is marked PPCLI. That's Canadian – Princess Patricia's Canadian Light Infantry. This one with the French writing – LE COMMANDO INOX, see that? – was used by French Special Forces in Algeria between 1954 and 1962. Laymen think that the Fairbairn-Sykes was only used in World War Two. But Wilkinson's kept producing them after the war and sold them to Special Forces all over the world. This is about Bob the Butcher, isn't it?'

'Did you ever sell one of these knives?'

He shook his head. 'The only place I ever saw one was in a museum.'

'The Imperial War Museum?'

'Yes.'

'What kind of clients do you get in here?'

He was watching Wren browsing the store.

'Collectors,' he said.

The sound of muffled laughter. Wren had put on a gas mask.

'My dad would love this,' she said. 'Christmas is coming.'

'It's six hundred quid,' Cage said. 'You break it, you bought it.'

Wren removed the gas mask. 'Maybe I'll stick to socks and aftershave.'

'What's the appeal?' I said.

Cage looked at me as if he couldn't believe what he was hearing.

'The Second World War was the greatest conflagration in human history,' he said. 'It killed millions of people. It reshaped Europe and the world. We live with its legacy today. We will live with its legacy for ever. The men who come here – and they are all men – think they would have been improved by war. They believe they missed something by being born too late. And they're right. They did miss something. They missed everything. They missed the great test of the twentieth century – perhaps of all time.'

'But let me ask you this,' Wren said. 'Why is so much of this stuff about the Nazis? They lost, didn't they? Yet so much of the war memorabilia industry is about them. It's like wanting the replica shirt of the side that lost the cup final.'

'I think the general consensus is that they had the strongest sense of aesthetics.'

'They had the best kit?' Wren smiled.

'Yes.'

'If only it were that simple,' she said, not smiling at him now. 'If only it were that innocent.'

I smoothed the photographs on the glass case.

'Do you recall ever being asked about one of these knives?' I said.

'Well, of course,' Cage said. 'This is one of the great collector's items of World War Two.' A flicker of pleasure in his eyes. 'And the enquiries have been on the rise lately. What with all the publicity.'

'Can you give me a list of people who wanted to buy one?'

'No.'

'Why not?'

'Client confidentiality.'

Wren and I grinned at each other.

'You have to take the Hippocratic oath just to flog a bit of Nazi memorabilia?' I said.

He licked his lips and said nothing.

'Look,' I said. 'I'm not interested in busting you.'

He bridled at that. 'What could you bust me for?'

I didn't know where to start. 'Offensive weapons. Knives. Bayonets. These firearms. Incitement to racial hatred.'

'The idea that all my clients are Nazi fetishists is simply not true!'

'Not all of them. But some of them, I bet. And I bet there's some stuff in the back room or under the counter that you wouldn't necessarily put on display in the shop window. Am I right? Look, I don't want to stop you doing your job—'

'Thanks.'

'Unless you stop me from doing mine.'

I left him my card and a few simple instructions. The shop went dark as Wren and I got into the car across the street. The Wehrmacht dummy stared out into the Holloway night.

'You don't really think that Bob bought a knife here, do you?' Wren said.

'No,' I said. 'But I think he might.'

I dropped off Wren at her car in Savile Row and drove south of the river to where two hundred-ton cannons sat in a little green garden. I parked round the back of the museum and rang the buzzer at the service entrance. An elderly security guard who looked as though he had been roused from his slumbers answered the door. Beyond him I could see Carol negotiating her wheelchair down the tight corridor.

'It's all right,' she said. 'He's with me.'

She looked as if she had been expecting me.

22

We went back to Nereus Fine Art the next evening and this time it was open. It did not look so different from when it was closed. But a woman with short fair hair stood stock still in the gallery, staring out at the empty Hampstead street. She had not sold either of the two small landscapes.

'I don't mind you coming in,' I told Wren as I parked behind Jack Straw's Castle.

'Big of you,' she said.

'But let me ask the questions.'

'And what do I do?' she said.

'You tell me if I'm missing something.'

'Mr Duncan doesn't produce much work,' the gallery woman said. She was a slight blonde in black-rimmed glasses, attractive in a brittle sort of way, and with just as much charm as was necessary she was getting rid of me. 'He's a bit of a recluse, I'm afraid. He doesn't exhibit, he doesn't talk to the press. He doesn't need to. All his work is sold to private collectors. Very little of it comes on the market. But if you would like to leave me your card, I'll put your details on file.'

'Because I love his work,' I said, not for the first time.

And it was true. I had never seen anyone paint like that. It was a city that I recognised, if only from dreams.

But she didn't care what I loved.

'Please leave your details,' she said, with the warmth turned down a notch.

Wren was looking at the canvases on the walls. There was a lot of lush green countryside. I guessed there was a big market for that stuff.

'How does he survive?' Wren said.

'Excuse me?'

'How does he make a living? If he doesn't paint much, and if he doesn't sell much, and if he doesn't make much of an effort, how does he pay the rent?'

'Pay the rent?'

The gallery woman stared at Wren. Wren stared right back.

'I understand there's some family money,' the woman said.

'Ah.'

'We have some other interesting contemporary work,' she said to me, handing me her card.

'Do you own the gallery?' Wren said.

'Nereus is owned by my mother.'

Wren thought about it.

'So if your father is an earl, then what does that make your mother? A lady, right?'

The woman had stopped smiling. 'You're not collectors, you're fucking journalists. Get out. Get out now or I'll call the police.'

I was looking at the card.

HON. KRIS HUETLIN

Nereus Fine Art

And I saw what Wren had seen: that the Kris was short for Cressida and the Huetlin came from the German artist she had married at nineteen and divorced five years later. It was the 'Hon.' that she couldn't resist that gave her away.

The Honourable Cressida Sutcliffe, only daughter of the Earl of Broughton, sister of the late James Sutcliffe.

Then I was out on the street, gripping the wrought-iron railings, looking up. Wren had followed me outside and was watching me crouch in the broken glass from the recycling bin. The smashed glass was all from beer bottles.

Peroni. Italian beer.

'We're missing something,' I said, the sound of broken glass beneath our feet. 'Upstairs,' I said. 'A dead man lives there.'

Up a narrow flight of stairs.

The door was unlocked.

Behind me I could hear the Hon. Kris Huetlin arguing with Wren, then falling silent when she produced her warrant card. And then arguing some more.

I went into a room full of canvases, all of them turned to face the wall. I could smell fresh paint. A man was standing in the centre of the small room, next to a canvas on an easel.

The canvas before him was blank.

'Hello, James,' I said.

James Sutcliffe was heavy, bearded, with the weight of the long-term committed drinker. I could see no trace of the delicate boy in dark glasses who would not smile for the camera when he posed in his Combined Cadet Force uniform at Potter's Field. The hair that had been thick and black and slicked back straight off his forehead was now long and grey and thinning. It fell around his shoulders, and over the baggy smock he wore.

'Hello,' he said.

'I'm DC Wolfe,' I said, hearing footsteps on the stairs and then stopping behind me. 'This is TDC Edie Wren. Can we talk?'

'Yes.'

His sister was right behind Wren.

'Even lower than I thought,' she said. 'Not hacks. Pigs.'

I looked at her, remembering her radical past. Then I turned back to her brother.

'I love your paintings,' I said. 'I love the early ones. And I love the later ones, where the city gets darker.'

'Thank you.'

'Do you know why I'm here?'

He looked over my shoulder at his sister.

'Someone's killing your friends,' I said. 'Hugo Buck. Adam Jones. Guy Philips. They're all dead. Did you know that?'

A small shake of his head that could have meant anything.

'I'm going to find the killer,' I said. 'Don't you want to help me catch the bastard who's murdering your friends?'

He focused on me again.

'They're not my friends,' he said.

'You faked your death, didn't you? That summer in Italy. The clothes left on the beach. It was very convincing. But why did you do that, James?'

He closed his eyes and released some breath that sounded as if it had been trapped for a long time. When he opened his eyes I saw the ancient pain inside the man.

'Starting again?' I said. 'A clean slate? Was that it? And who knew? Your sister here. How many of your friends? All of them?'

'None of them.'

'Hugo Buck knew.'

'No.'

'He had two of your paintings on the wall of his home. One by James Sutcliffe. And another by Edward Duncan.'

He looked shocked.

'I'm not interested in exposing you,' I said. 'Unless you've done something wrong. Unless you've broken the law. Unless you've hurt someone. Is that what you did, James?'

And at last there was panic in his eyes.

'I know how you got away with your disappearing act,' I said. 'They believed you because you were suffering from depression. I saw what you were on. Prozac. Luvox. Lustral. Cipralex. That's quite a cocktail of happy pills, James. But what were you depressed about? What happened at that school?'

He took a deep breath. Let it out.

'When you're young, you try things,' he said. 'You experiment. You're a sponge. You soak it up – all of it, any of it. Dear Mr Waugh – he was more than just a House Master. He was our friend. And he taught us about so many things. Wonderful things. Artists. Writers.' A beat. 'To get beyond the self. "If the doors of perception were cleansed, everything would appear as it is – infinite." Who doesn't want to get beyond their sad, shoddy little self at sixteen? "To be shaken out of the rut of ordinary perception." Sacramental visions. Experimentation.'

'Drugs.'

A short laugh.

'Drugs? My God. Drugs were just the start.'

'Keep talking, James,' I said.

I could see that he remembered it all now, that it was almost a relief to talk about it.

'There was a girl,' he said.

There was silence in the room.

'There was a girl,' I said.

'James?' his sister said. 'I'm going to call Mother. And Mother is going to call Burke. Do you remember Peter Burke? The lawyer, darling. Don't say anything else to these people.'

'It was meant to be . . . not *fun*,' he continued. 'An experiment. Pushing the boundaries of experience.'

He was less certain of himself now.

I glimpsed the pale bracelet of self-harm on his wrists, as wide as a sweatband and as white as a dead fish.

He tugged at his shirtsleeves, knowing what I had seen.

'Who was the girl?' I said. 'What was her name? Where did you find her?'

'How many of you?' Wren added.

'Six of us,' he said. 'No – seven. And she was nice.'

'She was *nice*?' Wren said.

'She was. In another life, you might have loved her. The night is a blur.' He looked at the floor and then at me. 'Did you ever take opium— I'm sorry, I've forgotten your name?'

His sister crossed the room and slapped his face. 'Shut up! Shut up! Shut up! I'm so sick of carrying you. I am so sick of covering up for you. Just shut up when I tell you to shut up!' Then she hit him again.

He ducked away, cowering, taking a step back. Wren stepped between them, and it was enough to restrain the sister.

'Who was in that room?' I said. 'You said seven, right?'

'Six,' he said. 'Seven . . .'

'Seven? Concentrate. You, Hugo Buck, Adam Jones, Salman Khan, Guy Philips, Ben King, Ned King. Were they all there? Who else was there? What happened to the girl?'

'We were going to let her go,' he said. 'That was the plan.'

'You bastards,' Wren said, to herself.

'We were going to let her go but she hurt someone. Very badly. It got out of hand. All of it.'

'She hurt someone,' I said, and I remembered the morning in the Iain West Forensic Suite, and I recalled what Elsa Olsen had placed in the palm of my hand. 'She hurt someone's eye, didn't she?'

He looked at me with wonder. 'Yes, she hurt someone's eye. Really hurt it, I mean . . .'

'She hurt Hugo Buck, didn't she?'

He looked confused. 'Hugo? Was it Hugo? I don't think—'

'Yes, Hugo Buck. He had a glass eye.'

James Sutcliffe covered his face with his hands. 'I don't remember. It was a long time ago. It was another lifetime.'

'Do you know how I know, James?' I said. 'I held it in my hand. I held the glass eye in my hand when they were cutting Hugo up on the slab.'

Wren said, 'Do you want back-up? I think we should get back-up now. Wolfe?'

'We can handle this,' I said. 'What happened to the girl, James? And what was her name?'

He hung his head. He shook his head. There were no words.

'I think we are going to have to take you in, James,' I said. 'You're part of a murder investigation.'

His sister said, 'You'll kill him!'

But he looked at me, his eyes clear, strangely calm now that he knew for certain it would soon all be over.

'All right,' he said, his voice steady. 'I suppose I'm ready to go.'

He glanced towards the window. Outside the evening was

cold and foggy, the street shrouded in the misty lights of winter. It looked like one of his paintings.

'It's a lovely day today,' he said, walking over to the window.

And then he broke into a kind of run, the shambling run of the badly out-of-shape man.

I called out to Wren.

But it was too late.

He went through the closed window with an eruption of glass and fell into thin air. I heard his sister scream and I heard Wren cry out and just a second later we heard a hideous thump as he landed one floor below.

I was already running for the stairs.

The wrought-iron railings had broken his fall, impaling his great bulk, one spike speared into his groin and another through his cheek. A couple more had torn open his guts and buried themselves deep inside.

I heard Wren calling it in at the same awful moment I recoiled backwards as if struck in the face, choking on the sewer stink of a man's spilt intestines.

23

I sat in my car on Prince Albert Road, the lights of the mansion blocks rising up on one side of me and the black vastness of Regent's Park on the other, and I felt the sickness rise in me as Ben King came out of Natasha Buck's block. I grimaced at the smooth Westminster smile as the fawning porter let him out, actually touching his head in salute, as if seeking a forelock to tug.

Even when he was sneaking around his friend's widow after dark, King looked every inch the visiting dignitary.

She must have thought there was time enough to get him off the premises before I arrived. But for some reason there is never much traffic around the park, and I was early.

Natasha was dressed for a date. Candles on the table. Al Green singing about staying together. The smell of roasting red meat. And the perfumed smell of her as she kissed me on one cheek and then the other and then, finally, on the mouth. A smell to make a man want to start inhaling and never stop.

I was carrying a bottle of wine and she took it with elaborate grace as I thought how wrong, how grotesque, how inappropriate.

A date, I thought. We're on a date.

The rage inside me was directed at myself as well as her.

On the sofa the dog opened its bleary eyes, clocked me and

then closed them again, deeply unimpressed, as Natasha brought me a bottle of Asahi Super Dry and a frosted glass that had been sitting in the freezer, waiting for me.

'Scout,' she said. 'She went with her friend? To her playover?'

'Sleepover,' I said. 'Yes, her friend's mother picked them up after school.'

Natasha bit her bottom lip. Laughed. Shook her head.

'Then we can have a sleepover too,' she said, coming in close, holding my arm, looking up at me. 'You must think I'm bad.'

I laughed. Then she wasn't smiling.

'What's wrong?'

I walked towards the sofa but I didn't sit down. I wasn't staying long.

I took a pull on the Japanese beer and said, 'Do you know what it does to a murder case if an investigating officer sleeps with a material witness?'

She took a step back. 'What?'

'Of course you do,' I said. 'Of course you know.'

She had her hands on me and I froze so she stood back, keeping her distance.

'Max,' she said. 'Please.'

Her eyes were shining.

'Spare me the tears,' I said.

She angrily wiped her eyes with the back of her hand. 'All right,' she said. 'I'll spare you the tears if you tell me what's wrong with you. I thought we were going to have a lovely night—'

'Meeting us on the Heath – that wasn't a coincidence, was it?'

She looked away.

'No.'

'You don't walk your dog on the Heath, do you?'

'No.'

'You don't walk your dog at all, do you?'

'*No* – I'm another rich bitch who gets some little Eastern European scrubber to walk her dog.'

'And your husband didn't lose his eye playing rugby, did he?'

'What?'

'Your husband. Old Hugo. That story about how he lost his eye. That was all bullshit, wasn't it?'

She looked genuinely surprised. 'No, that's true.'

'Were you there? Did you see it happen?'

'Of course not.'

'Then you don't know, do you?'

'But I do. I do know.'

Maybe she believed it, I thought. Maybe she really believed in the sports injury lie.

'What was Ben King doing here?'

She laughed with disbelief. 'Is that what this is about? You saw Ben leaving? Don't you think it's a little early to be getting possessive?'

'You fucking him too?'

Her open palm cracked hard against my cheek.

The dog sat up, finally looking impressed.

'I'm not *fucking* anybody. Especially not you. Ben came to collect some of Hugo's personal things.'

'A couple of paintings?'

'I want you to go now.'

'What happened at that school?'

'Please leave.'

'Do you want to know how your husband lost his eye? Do you really want to know?'

She suddenly seemed very tired.

'I don't care,' she said. 'He's dead. It doesn't matter.'

She swallowed hard, and looked around the flat, taking it all in – the candles, the smell of prime beef, Al Green. She ran her hands through her hair. It was all ruined now.

'You're using me, Natasha,' I said. 'You're setting me up. You're telling me lies.'

'You're the liar,' she said, angry at last. 'You wear a wedding ring but you're not married.'

'What happened at that school? What did they do? Who was the girl?'

'I don't know what you're talking about. Where's your wife? What happened to her? You have a ring but no wife? What's all that about, detective? You liar. You fucking liar.'

She was pushing me out of the apartment and I was letting her. And I saw that she was as stupid as me. Another mug.

'You're wrong about everything,' she said, closing the door in my face.

In the morning, just inside the communal front door of our block of flats, half covered with flyers for pizza, there was a package waiting on the mat with my name on it.

As Stan sniffed at the junk mail, I tore the package open and pulled out a VHS videotape. It felt cheap, plastic, rickety. Incredibly old-fashioned. I looked at the spine. There was printed felt-tip writing, written very carefully, as if by a bright child.

Our 1st XV v Harrow 1st XV 10-10-88

I searched inside. No note. I looked back at the VHS I was holding, then down at the dog.

'How am I meant to play this?' I said out loud.

'Vice,' Wren told me when I got to work. 'Down on the third floor. Vice has video recorders from back in the day.'

MIR-1 was still deserted. Wren always got in early.

'I've been looking on HOLMES for missing persons,' she said. 'I started with female mispers between the ages of fifteen and thirty within a ten-mile radius of Potter's Field in 1988.'

'Keep looking.'

'I will – but you need to talk to the SIO,' she said. 'You need to talk to Mallory. About what James Sutcliffe said before he died.' A beat. 'About the school.'

'Mallory has the chief super breathing down his neck. And the chief super is anxious to protect Ben King.'

'You still need to talk to him.'

I looked at the VHS tape in my hand.

'I know,' I said. 'But what did Sutcliffe really tell us? We don't even know who we're talking about, do we? Who was in that room?'

'He told us enough,' Wren said. 'They're not dying because they're rich, are they? They're not dying because they're sons of privilege or symbols of social injustice or any of that Bob the Butcher stuff.'

'No,' I said. 'They're dying because of the past.'

We found a quiet corner of Vice with a couple of dusty video recorders and settled down to watch our videotape.

All around us young men and women were watching writhing bodies on their computer screens, and trying to separate standard filth from criminal obscenity that was likely to corrupt and deprave.

'Is that vulva open?' said one young man.

'I think it's only slightly ajar,' said a young woman.

'Definitely a grey area,' said the young man, making a note.

They were friendly enough but neither Wren or I knew any of the twenty-something officers in the department.

'They change personnel every six months down here,' Wren whispered. 'In case it does something to their sex drive. One way or the other.'

She posted the VHS into the video recorder and pressed play. The remote had been lost in time.

'Do you want to watch it on fast forward?' she said.

'Just let it roll,' I said.

I recognised the playing fields of Potter's Field. The tree line, the stone cottage, the endless expanse of green churned to mud down the centre of the pitches. Only the haircuts of the boys were different.

It was easy to spot Hugo Buck. Big, proud, confident. A good-looking bully. Calling for the ball. Exhorting his friends. Arguing with the referee. After twenty minutes he scored a try and preened before the camera, his big grin in our faces. I heard the laughter of the cameraman as he said 'Played, Bucko!' and it sounded like Ben King.

Five minutes later it happened.

The ball was kicked deep into the Harrow half. The Potter's Field First XV flew after it, Buck in the vanguard. A Harrow defender caught the ball, fumbled, dropped it, picked it up again. Voices screamed with excitement. The defender made to kick the ball just as Buck reached him.

Buck hurled himself at the Harrow defender.

The Harrow defender lashed wildly at the ball.

Buck beat it down.

And the point of the Harrow defender's right boot speared into Buck's left eye.

He screamed.

The game stopped. Players and pupils and teachers gathered around the boy on the ground.

He was silent now. But the teachers were shouting for an ambulance. The cameraman kept filming. And just before the tape stopped he went on to the pitch and looked over the shoulders of the boys and men gathered around Hugo Buck.

His eye was a ruined pulp.

The footage abruptly ended on that last bloody image.

'So,' Wren said, 'Hugo Buck lost his eye playing rugby.'

'Yes,' I said.

'James Sutcliffe told us he was hurt by a girl, didn't he?'

I paused, considered.

'Is that what he told us? Sutcliffe was doped up to the eyeballs for years. He was doped up when he was at school. He was doped up on the day he died. James Sutcliffe was a poor little rich boy who spent his entire life on medication.'

'Come on, Wolfe. You're the one who said Hugo Buck's wife was lying. You're the one who held Buck's fake eye in your hand. But she wasn't lying, was she?'

I stared at the frozen image on the screen.

We went back up to MIR-1. Suddenly the suite was heaving with people. Swire and Mallory. Cho and Dr Stephen. Gane and Whitestone. Faces were flushed with the fever of a chase that was nearing its end.

'What's happening?' I said.

'We've got Bob,' Gane said.

24

Behind the John Lennon glasses, Mallory's eyes were burning with quiet rage.

'Setting a trap with human bait,' he said quietly, each word chipped from Aberdeen granite, his bald head gleaming under the lights of MIR-1, 'was never the plan.'

'Change of plan,' said Swire.

'I'm not wearing a bullet-proof vest,' Scarlet Bush was telling DI Whitestone. 'Bob was very specific: "Come alone. No tapes I can't see." He might think a bullet-proof vest is a wire. I'm not wearing it.'

'It's not a bullet-proof vest,' Whitestone said patiently, 'it's a Kevlar Stealth. Lightweight, the thinnest we have. Invisible under the clothes you're wearing. I'd wear it if I were you.'

Gane's laptop was open on Bob the Butcher's timeline. Bob had changed his picture again. Instead of Robert Oppenheimer's thoughtful, pipe-smoking skull, there was now a mushroom cloud.

> In sleep – in confusion – in the depths of shame – the good deeds a man has done before defend him. #killallpigs

'Where's his response?' I said.

'He didn't respond online,' Gane said. 'He called her.' He laughed. 'On a *telephone*. A *landline*.'

Gane grinned, and I saw that Cho and his techie pals from the PCeU were looking sour.

'Stick around, boys!' Gane said. 'We might be able to show you a few tricks!'

'Give DI Gane your phone and he'll fit a GPS tracking device,' Whitestone told Bush.

'I don't want to carry anything bulky,' the journalist said.

'It's either a SIM card or some software,' Gane said, cutting her off. 'You're not going to notice it. The only people who will know it's even there are us, OK? But it means we know where you are. It means we can pinpoint your movements to within ten metres. If you go beyond a prescribed area, it sends us an alarm.'

Bush gave Gane her phone.

'The Kevlar Stealth and the tracking device,' she said. 'Is that it?'

Whitestone nodded. 'That's it. Belt and braces.'

'What did Bob say to you?' I said.

I saw the pride in the journalist's eyes.

'He said he liked my piece,' she said. 'And he said he'd be in touch.'

'How do you know it was him?'

'He told me he would post an Oppenheimer quote in the Bob the Butcher timeline. "In sleep – in confusion – in the depths of shame – the good deeds a man has done before defend him." And then he did.'

There were a dozen copies of her paper scattered across the workstations of MIR-1. In the end she had not goaded Bob the Butcher. There had been no references to sexual preference, childhood trauma or bed-wetting. She had stuck to Dr Stephen's script. Bob was presented as a mixed-up homicidal maniac who was operating by his own rules ('Honour, power and control are clearly motivating factors for this most complex of serial killers') and choosing victims who were something less than totally innocent ('It seems hardly a coincidence that Bob the Butcher selected as his targets a wealthy investment banker, a drug dealer and an inveterate bully'), and also as a slightly volatile folk hero to the dispossessed ('These are horrible crimes, certainly – but they are also a cry of rage in a society where the obscene gap between rich and poor is the new apartheid').

It was more of a press release than journalism. You could see why Bob the Butcher would want to cut it out and stick it in his scrapbook. It made him sound like a psycho Robin Hood.

'He's calling my paper's switchboard some time over the next twenty-four hours,' Bush said.

'We've got call analytics set up on your switchboard,' Gane said. 'The longer you can keep him talking the better. But as soon as he calls we will have the number of whatever disposable or payphone he's using. A landline or a mobile is too much to hope for. But it will give us more than we have right now. And when he gives you the meet you're going to lead us to him.'

Mallory was still not happy.

'I want you to have police protection from this moment on,' he told Scarlet Bush. 'I want two officers to escort you back to your office, and to accompany you to the meeting point, where we'll be waiting.'

'No chance,' she said. 'This is the most important story of my career and I am not going to let you screw it up for me.'

Mallory looked helplessly at Swire, who shrugged.

'The meet is going to be surrounded with ARVs and SFOs,'

the chief super said. 'There's going to be enough Special Firearms Officers to keep her from harm. And I'm all for making sure we don't frighten Bob away.'

'Then I want officers in the room an hour before you arrive at the meet,' Mallory told Bush. 'And I want roadblocks at fifty metres, five hundred metres and a mile. And make sure you're wearing the Kevlar.'

'Bob cuts throats.' Bush laughed, and for the first time I saw the raw courage in her. 'What good is a stab-proof vest going to do me?'

Swire chuckled approvingly.

'And I'll tell you what I want,' Bush added. 'When I get to the meet I want to talk to him before you move in and arrest him.'

'Five minutes,' Mallory said.

'Fuck that!'

Mallory visibly flinched at the profanity.

'I want at least an hour with him.'

'We'll give you five minutes,' Swire said. 'But any sign of aggression and he's coming down.'

Gane returned the reporter's mobile with the tracking device.

'What's in there?' Mallory said.

'In the end I went for the handset-based software,' Gane said. 'It's more accurate than a SIM card with an iPhone.'

Mallory still didn't look happy.

'Let us know as soon as he makes contact,' he said. 'Don't wait for us to pick it up on your switchboard.'

'Of course,' Bush said. She threw her phone into her bag. 'I'll tell you where we're meeting and I'll see you there.'

She left, escorted by the chief super, and for a moment I thought I was going to hear Mallory curse for the first time.

Instead he ran his hand over his polished skull and said angrily, 'And I want the lot of you in a Kevlar Stealth!'

In the only quiet corner of MIR-1, Dr Stephen was at his laptop. I walked over to him and saw that he was staring at Bob the Butcher's timeline. The forensic psychologist looked thoughtful. The mushroom cloud was still there.

'Those people in Hiroshima,' Dr Stephen said. 'They had been expecting a massive bombing raid for months. But what they got was the end of all things. What they got was a new world.'

'So what does it mean?' I said. 'The cloud. What's he trying to tell us?'

He shook his head.

'I'd be making a guess,' he said.

'Go ahead.'

'The designated target,' he said. 'It's been chosen.'

The internet café was on the Holloway Road. Wren and I sat on opposite sides of the room while half a dozen weary-looking foreign students checked their mail and Skyped home. It seemed a strange location for Scarlet Bush to meet Bob the Butcher.

And when I heard Gane curse in my earpiece, I knew they never would.

Wren heard it too. She looked over at me and I shook my head.

In the back room was a group of armed officers looking like soldiers from the next century. They wore black rubber goggles, Ballistic Kevlar helmets and shiny boots. They carried Heckler & Koch assault rifles, Taser X26 guns and CS gas spray. Their mouths were thin lines of frustrated adrenalin. Mallory and Whitestone were to one side hunched over Gane and his laptop.

'What's happening?' I asked them.

'We've lost Scarlet,' Mallory said. 'Not the signal from her phone. Just her.'

'She gave our officers the slip at her paper,' Gane said, not looking up from the screen. 'Went out the fire exit, we think. That easy.'

'Wanted some quality time on her own with Bob,' Whitestone said.

'The tracer on her phone told us she was on her way here,' Gane said. 'And now it seems she's not. The signal hasn't moved for ten minutes. Look.'

A red dot pulsed steadily in the map's spider web of streets.

'Where is it?' Mallory said. 'That looks like somewhere near St Paul's.'

'East Poultry Avenue, EC1,' Gane said. 'It's the Barbican.'

'That's not the Barbican,' I said. 'That's the meat market.'

Mallory shook his head.

'That stupid girl,' he said. 'Oh, that stupid girl.'

The hooks hung around the storage room like stainless steel bunting and our breath made steaming clouds in the freezing fog. Huge slabs of bloody meat hung everywhere in the sub-zero air. I could hear Wren and Whitestone calling her name.

'Scarlet! Scarlet! Scarlet!'

Mallory pushed aside a great headless carcass of beef.

'She's not here, is she?' he said.

Gane rubbed a hand over the misty screen of his laptop.

'Well, the phone's here,' he said.

And then I saw the pig's head sitting on a marble slab. The pig's head with its giant, floppy Dumbo ears. Comical and tragic all at once. The albino skin, more white than pink, with just a few delicate smears of blood. The eyes shut as if overwhelmed with exhaustion. And the monstrous snout, squashed flat and rich with blood.

Figures moved in the mist of the cold room, cursing and bumping into each other. Unable to find the thing they sought. They kept calling her name.

My spine throbbed with pain as I reached under the snout and into the pig's mouth and pulled out a phone, its screen smeared with milky blood.

'Sir?' I said.

Mallory took the phone from me. He looked across at Gane, who nodded and closed his laptop.

'He has her,' Mallory said.

My own phone began to vibrate. I took it out. SECOND FRONT CALLING it said, and I saw that the blood of the pig's head was on my hands now, and on my phone, and on my clothes, getting on everything.

'It's Cage from the war memorabilia shop,' a very distant voice said.

'What happened?' I said.

'I sold a knife.'

25

'This big guy walked into my shop,' Nick Cage said. 'Well, not big – pumped up. Weights. Maybe steroids. A little man but pumped up, you know?'

We had him in an interview room in West End Central. Mallory and Gane and me. Mallory didn't like him.

'I'm trying to help you,' Cage said, looking at me.

'I know,' I said.

'You sell knives,' Mallory said. 'You sell swords. Daggers.'

'Yes.'

'Did you ever see what a knife can do to someone?'

'I sell to collectors.'

'Ever heard of the Offensive Weapons Act?'

Cage's mouth tightened. 'Chapter and verse. This country has the most restrictive knife laws in the world. Not that you'd know it from all the kids in A&E with their stab wounds, their guts hanging out. Look, I don't sell flick knives, sword canes, butterfly knives, throwing stars or gravity knives, OK? I sell to *collectors*. I've got a *licence*. And I want to keep it. That's why I got a photocopy of his ID, all right? Now, do you want to talk about him or me?'

We were running the ID Cage had brought us through the Police National Computer. It was a UK driver's licence for what the PNC database would recognise as an IC1 – a male of white-skinned European appearance. There was a face and a name and a DOB. A young man around thirty with thinning hair. An attempt at a smile that never quite made it past the hint of a sneer. And there was an address. Right at the edge of the city.

'Do you buy this ID?' Gane said to Mallory. 'Bob's up to his neck in security architecture online but he doesn't have a fake photo ID? You know how many sites there are flogging fake photo IDs?'

'Not good ones,' Cage said. 'It's easy to get a bad one. Not so easy to get a good one. That's the real thing. Or better than anything I've ever seen.'

'Did he know his stuff?' I said.

'How do you mean?' Cage said.

'Did he know what he was buying?'

'He was very specific. The men who come in Second Front are collectors. They *all* know their stuff. He wanted a Fairbairn-Sykes commando dagger. Prepared to pay top dollar. I sourced it for him. Found a nice Second Pattern F-S made by Wilkinson.'

'And where did you get it from?' Mallory said.

'I'm not telling you,' Cage said, folding his arms.

Gane made a move towards him as Whitestone appeared in the doorway.

'We've got him,' she said.

The chief super walked into MIR-1, her face tight with tension beneath the helmet of blonde hair. It could have been Mrs Thatcher getting ready to send the Task Force to the South Atlantic, horribly aware that this thing could go either way.

The crowd parted for her and she did not look at any of us

until she came to Edie Wren, sitting on her desk at her workstation, a man's face on the screen behind her, like something she had just caught.

'What have we got?' DCS Swire said.

The face on the screen was the same photograph as the one on the driving licence but now it was life-size; now you could see the wary spite in the eyes, the thin scars from ancient acne, the way he had brushed his hair to cover the growing expanse of forehead.

'Ian Peck,' Wren said. 'Multiple convictions. The first one ten years ago for possession of class C drugs – anabolic steroids – and class B – cannabis. Peck was buying in Amsterdam and mailing the stuff to his home address with the name of the previous occupant on the package.'

'That old trick,' somebody said.

Wren dropped into her seat.

'Twelve months suspended,' she said, scrolling down. She shook her head. 'Four – no, five convictions for domestic violence against his girlfriend. She has a restraining order. Peck's a freelance software consultant. After the split with his girlfriend he moved back home with Mum and Dad.'

Wren turned to look at the chief super.

'And that's Bob the Butcher,' she said.

Swire's mouth twisted with triumph. 'Well done, everybody. Start making your preparations. We'll lift him at dawn.'

'A man who beats women?' I said. 'You really think that our perp is a man who beats up women?'

I was looking at Dr Stephen. He had his hands stuffed deep inside his pockets. I believed that he could see it too.

'The perp doesn't attack women,' I said.

Dr Stephen still wasn't looking at me.

'What did you say, Dr Stephen? Honour. Power. Control.' I gestured at the face that stared at us from the screen.

They were all looking at me.

Swire was very calm.

'Did you ever hear of a copper called George Oldfield?' she said.

I nodded. Everybody had heard of Assistant Chief Constable George Oldfield. He was the head of the hunt for the Yorkshire Ripper. Letters and a tape claiming 'I'm Jack' had Oldfield searching the north-east while Peter Sutcliffe was killing women in other parts of the country.

'I'm not going to play the part of George Oldfield here,' Swire said. 'I'm not letting our killer slip through my hands.'

She brushed past me as MIR-1 burst into activity.

But I stayed where I was, looking at the face on the screen.

Honour. Power. Control.

A man who hits women, I thought. Where's the honour in that?

In the first light of the new day we gathered on a suburban street of modest terraced houses and all I could hear was the sound of my blood. It sounds like the sea, a red rushing sound, when it's pumped hard enough. And as we crouched below a little garden wall and fiddled with our kit in those last few seconds – adjusting the straps on Kevlars, the firearms officers checking their safety catches, listening to the subdued murmurs of the Airwave radios – that is what mine sounded like.

It told me what was at stake. A young woman's life. The jobs of all of us who had let her slip away. And something else, something more personal. Because you never know what is on the other side of that door, and what it will do to you.

The officer with the worn red battering ram slung over his shoulder walked briskly down the garden path.

It didn't take long.

Two, three steps and he was at the door, hauling the battering ram from his shoulder and swinging it at the lock in one smooth and brutal motion. The door popped open with the rip and splinter of cheap wood and the officer stood to one side as the rest of us charged into the house, screaming as loud as we could – screaming to pour fear into whoever was on the inside, and screaming to hide the fear in our own hearts.

The two armed officers who went in ahead of me suddenly stopped, still shouting behind their Heckler & Koch assault rifles.

Over the shoulders of their body armour I could see a sickly cat at the end of a suburban hall. It arched its back and hissed, full of cancer and contempt.

A door opened at the end of the hall.

We were screaming again.

An old woman in house slippers slowly shuffled across the hall, ignoring all orders to halt. She did not even look our way.

I saw an old-fashioned hearing aid tucked behind her ear, as huge and pink as a wad of chewed bubblegum. She disappeared through a door on the other side of the hall, the old cat rubbing against her legs as it followed her.

We followed her down the hall and through the door.

In the living room the old woman sat on a sofa with an old man, a biscuit held halfway to his mouth. He elbowed her, and at last she registered our presence. The pair of them stared slack-jawed at the assault rifles that were aimed at their faces. The cat spat at us.

'Mr and Mrs Peck?' I said. 'Where's your son? Where's Ian?'

Still they didn't talk.

There was a small kitchen on the other side of the hall.

'Clear,' said an armed officer, coming out of it.

Boots thundered on the staircase. I could hear them moving around upstairs, screaming as they went through doors, and then the silence of disappointment and relief.

I went into the kitchen. There was a small garden out the back. Beyond the high garden fence I could see more black Kevlar helmets and rubber goggles, mouths tight with tension, the dull gleam of Heckler & Koch assault rifles.

Mallory came out of the garden and into the kitchen. Whitestone and a uniformed officer were with him. When the uniform took off his helmet I saw it was PC Billy Greene, his pale face slick with sweat and fear, but controlling it well. The boxing was doing him some good.

The shouting had stopped.

'Nothing,' I said.

'Did anyone check the basement?' Mallory said.

There was a wooden door just outside the kitchen. No lock, paint flaking. I opened it, reached inside and found the switch for the light.

Somewhere deeper down, a bare electric bulb came on.

I went carefully down a short flight of steps, smelling damp and dust, and then I was under the house itself, the ceiling so low that I had to stoop.

Mallory's voice was right behind me: 'Anything?'

The basement was more than half full with scrap, smashed

chunks of concrete and broken bricks, a ragged pile of rubble that almost reached to the ceiling.

'What is all this stuff?' I said.

'Looks like someone dreamed of converting this place into flats,' Mallory said. 'They have to fill the basement. Fire regulations. Then the property bubble burst and the dream got cancelled.' He peered into the darkness. 'Excuse me,' he said, easing past. 'There's something right at the back.'

'Clear,' I heard someone call at the top of the house. Then a brief gale of laughter, like a collective sigh of relief. They seemed very far away.

Mallory moved towards the back wall of the basement. There was a scuttle of something small but living across the rubble and I felt my heart lurch. The tail of a fat rat slithered over the rusted frame of a child's bicycle.

'There's a door,' Mallory said, and he suddenly had his torch in his hand, a sharp white beam in the dull yellow darkness.

PC Greene was now halfway down the steps, staring at Mallory's back. We both followed him.

Mallory was trying the door.

Locked.

Then the lights went out. All of them. The mains. A switch had been thrown. I could hear voices protesting far above us.

Mallory had some sort of blade in his hand and was running it inside the doorjamb. I took his torch and held it on the door as he moved the blade left and right, left and right, lifting the lock tongue from the doorframe socket until he had it.

The door opened with a crack of wood. Beyond it was a metal grille. And from somewhere beyond that came the screams of a woman.

Help me help me help me help me help me.

The rattle of a metal grille in the blackness.

'You hear that?' Mallory said.

'Yes.'

We were talking in whispers now. Mallory was reaching through the grille. It was locked from the inside. But a set of keys jangled on a nail; and then he had them and the grille suddenly slid open.

'You smell it?' Mallory said.

'Yes, sir, I can smell it.'

The stink of shit and petrol.

'Careful in here,' he said, stepping inside.

I followed him and I felt the ground beneath my feet, rough and uneven, and the screaming was louder now and it was recognisably Scarlet Bush, and we moved more quickly because the space suddenly opened up and I was between Mallory and Greene when Mallory seemed to lurch forward and I grabbed a fistful of his jacket and stopped him falling.

There was a ragged hole beneath us, perhaps two metres deep, and Scarlet Bush at the bottom of it, shielding her eyes from the white light of the torch, naked and wet with petrol.

A barbecue pit for cooking human flesh.

A light flared and I saw a man coming round the pit just before it fell – *whoooooosh* – into the pit, and Billy Greene seemed to fall with it as the flames erupted with a sickening pop, and then Greene was in the pit with Scarlet, beating at the flames with his bare hands.

The man was small and powerful, long-haired and simian, and when he punched me in the heart I felt the air go out of me as I went backwards, falling, smashing my back hard against some sort of work table that collapsed under my full weight.

I felt the pain explode in my back, and then the blow on the back of my skull as my head hit the wall.

I clutched at my heart and felt the rip in my shirt and suddenly I knew that he had not punched me.

He had stabbed me.

I touched the dent in the Kevlar Stealth that had saved my life, felt the sting of the bruise beyond.

I closed my eyes, dizzy and sick from the pain in the back of my head, the rest of it coming in broken fragments.

Screams from the pit. A man's screams now. Greene with his jacket in his hands, beating wildly at the fire. Scarlet Bush scrambling out, her eyes wide with the horror. Light in the room from the fire in the hole. A lot of light, but dancing and uneven, making ghosts of us all.

And the man – Bob the Butcher – punching Mallory in the chest, and in the arm, and in the side of the head. Mallory going down, his John Lennon glasses falling from his face. His face without his glasses no longer as hard as some old Viking, but vulnerable and lost and very easy to hurt.

Then Bob the Butcher gone. Out of the secret space. Past us all. Getting away with it.

And Whitestone waiting for him in the basement.

Bob walking into her forearm smash, the blow turning his head almost 180 degrees, and Whitestone, tiny woman that she was, perched on his back, cuffing him and punctuating his rights by bouncing his face against the ground.

'You are under arrest.' Smash. 'You do not have to say anything.' Smash.

I remembered a line from training days: a formal arrest will always be accompanied by physically taking control. She was doing that all right.

'But it may harm your defence if you do not mention when questioned something you later rely on in court.' Smash. 'Anything you do say may be given in evidence.'

Smash smash smash.

Bob the Butcher finally starting to beg.

And then I heard someone scream Mallory's name as the lights came on and I blacked out.

26

The pain in my back kicked me awake.

It started in the lower ribs and worked its way round to the spine, like some new pain meeting up with the pain that was already there. A bright bar of winter sunshine came through the crack in the curtains, telling me I had not been out for more than a few hours.

I groaned and slowly got out of bed.

They had me in one of those hospital smocks that reveal your behind to the world. I tore it off and found my clothes in the small room's wardrobe. I was sitting on the bed struggling to put my socks on when the nurse came in, a large-bosomed bossy matron – the type that expect to be obeyed. This one was Jamaican.

'How's the boy?' I said, my skin crawling at the thought of PC Greene alone in the pit, trying to put out the fire with nothing but his bare hands and his jacket. The effort of speaking set off a leaden throb at the back of my skull and I touched my head, expecting bandages or blood. There was nothing. Only the thud of pain.

'You're getting back in bed right this minute,' the nurse said.

I couldn't get my socks on. My back would not bend forward far enough. So I tossed them away. Slipped my shoes on. Stood up.

'How's the boy?' I said.

Now I had upset her.

'Do you think I've got all day for this nonsense? You have possible concussion. We're keeping you here for observation. Do you want me to get the doctor? Is that what I have to do?'

I was fully dressed by the time she came back with the doctor. Fully dressed apart from my socks. The doctor was young and Indian. Far too tired and busy to argue with me. Or too experienced. But he clearly thought I was stupid.

'I'm not discharging you,' he said. 'Is that quite clear? You're leaving at your own risk.'

'I get it. Where's the boy?'

'Intensive Care Unit. Top floor. Let me take you.'

PC Greene slept the sleep of the heavily drugged. Both his hands were wrapped in bandages. There was an IV drip by his side.

That was it. Just his hands. But it was probably enough to end his life as a copper.

'He has second-degree burns on both hands,' the doctor said. 'That means the burns penetrated the deeper skin but as far as we can tell there's no damage to muscle and bone. When he's well enough to be moved, we'll get him down to the Queen Victoria in West Sussex. It's the best burns hospital in the south-east of England.' The doctor turned to leave. 'He's a very brave young man,' he said, almost as an afterthought.

I thought of the day I met Billy Greene, almost unable to stand after a look at his first body, and the raw shame he had felt when they had made him a canteen cowboy. I wondered if he knew how much good stuff there was inside him. And I wondered how he would make a living for the rest of his life.

Then I went to work.

They had Bob the Butcher in an interview room.

In the observation room you could watch through a one-way mirror or on a CCTV feed. There were lots of people I didn't know crowding in front of the mirror. I looked up at the screen.

Whitestone and Gane were sitting across from Bob and his lawyer. She was pretty and prim, dressed in business black.

The lawyers are getting younger, I thought.

Bob had a broken nose and the two black eyes that came with it but none of it had wiped the smirk from his face.

He looked like a cocky little ape.

'Ian Peck,' Whitestone said, and her voice seemed changed as it came through the speaker. 'We are charging you with murder.'

I couldn't believe what I was hearing.

'But it's not him,' I said.

Some of the crowd standing in front of the mirror turned to look at me. But then they looked away.

'This is bullshit,' I said.

There was a big duty sergeant on the door of the interview room.

'You can't go in there,' he said as I came towards him.

I shoved him aside. He didn't fight back.

They all looked up as I came in. Whitestone and Gane. Bob and his pretty lawyer. Somebody said my name.

I reached in my pocket and took out the FS commando dagger I had borrowed from Carol at the Imperial War Museum. It clattered across the table.

'Show me how you did it,' I said.

The duty sergeant was in the room now and, after getting the nod from Whitestone, he put his hands on me. I pushed him away. He was a stronger man than me but he held back.

The lawyer was on her feet, whining about some legal point that I didn't quite catch. The pain was in my spine, and my skull, and directly behind my eyes.

The knife was right in front of Bob.

'Come on, tough guy,' I said. 'Show me how you cut all those throats. You lying bastard, you fucking fantasist, you pathetic little man.'

Gane was shouting at me. They were all shouting at me. Apart from Bob. He looked at me, and at the knife, and back at me, as if weighing something in his mind.

He licked his lips. He stood up.

The room suddenly fell silent.

'Come on,' I said, quietly now, and I smiled to give him encouragement. 'Show me how you did it.'

Bob – Peck, whatever his name was – picked up the knife.

They all started shouting again.

There were hands on me, and my hands were shoving them away, and Bob was looking at me with the knife in his hand. He essayed a slashing movement in slow motion.

'I cut them.'

I stepped forward.

'You lying piece of shit,' I said.

I took his wrist in one fist and punched his bicep with the other. The knife fell to the table.

'Wolfe,' Whitestone said. 'Max, please listen to me.'

'He didn't kill those men,' I said. 'Hugo Buck. Adam Jones. Guy Philips. I'm telling you, he doesn't know how. It's not him.'

Then I saw the tears in Whitestone's eyes.

'We're arresting him for the murder of DCI Mallory,' she said. 'He bled out on the way to the hospital.'

The duty sergeant was holding me now.

'I'm sorry, Max,' Whitestone said. 'The boss didn't make it.'

MIR-1 was deserted apart from Wren.

She looked up as I walked in.

'You have to see this, Wolfe.'

I walked to the window and stared down at Savile Row.

I thought of Margaret Mallory and how she had told me that Scout and I were a family when it felt like the entire world wanted to tell us something else, that we were not a real family at all, and the tears came then, blurring the traffic on the street far below and twisting my mouth into a rictus of raw, hopeless grief.

They would have told her by now, I thought; she would know that her husband was never coming home again by now; she would be alone in the small house in Pimlico with her dog and her photographs and her memories and her smashed heart. The knowledge choked up my throat and clawed at my insides and made my useless tears feel as though they were without end.

'Max?' Wren said.

I looked out across the rooftops of Savile Row. I wiped my eyes with the palm of my hands. I didn't turn around.

'DCI Mallory died,' I said, and my voice sounded strange to me, as if I was somebody else now. 'Stab wound in the neck. Dead before they could get him to the hospital.'

'I know,' she said. 'He was the kindest man I ever met. And the best copper. But you really need to see this. It's Bob's last post online. Before we went in and got him. Are you listening to me?'

I shook my head. 'No, I'm not listening to you, Edie. I don't care. Whatever it is, I really don't care. I don't want to see it. I don't care what he said.'

'You need to, Max. Because the killer is still out there. Because a world full of vicious little creeps is still out there. Will you please look at me?'

Silence.

Then Wren was suddenly by my side, dragging me to her workstation.

'Look, will you?' she said, not gently.

I looked.

The final message on Bob the Butcher's timeline.

There was no picture of Robert Oppenheimer.

There was no mushroom cloud.

In their place was a small black-and-white photograph. At first sight it looked like nothing – an abstract little squiggle of broken planes. But when I looked closer I saw that it was a city. It was an entire city, destroyed in an instant. My eye flicked across the hashtag, like a command to his one million followers.

#killallpigs

And then I read the message, and I did not understand, so I read it again, the rhythm of the numbers and words so familiar to me that at first I thought they were not on the screen but only in my head.

'Isn't that your home address?' Wren said.

I was gone.

* * *

They were coming back from school. Scout and Mrs Murphy and Stan. My daughter and Mrs Murphy looking down at the dog and laughing. Stan trotting happily by their side. Something in his mouth. A scrap of bagel. The smiles vanishing when they saw me.

'What's wrong?' Mrs Murphy said.

'We have to go,' I said. 'I'm sorry.'

I got Scout and Stan into the back of the X5, told Scout to put her seat belt on, and then I drove, pushing down hard, just ahead of the evening rush, Mrs Murphy standing on the street in my rear-view mirror, watching us go.

'But where are we going?' Scout said as we crossed Waterloo Bridge.

'We're going to see your mother,' I said.

She was standing on the lawn of a house on a road in a part of town where you could believe that nothing bad ever happened.

There was a small toddler crawling at her feet and a baby growing inside her.

Not my children. From her new man.

Anne.

It is such an ordinary, old-fashioned English name and I do not think I will ever be able to hear it without it pulling at my heart.

Anne, Anne, Anne.

You might not believe it – I could hardly believe it myself – but there had been a world, not so long ago, when we were as close to each other as we had been to anyone we had ever known in our young lives. When we laughed all the time; when a good life together was before us; when every night we lit a candle in the corner of our bedroom because we were unable to sleep, because it would have meant a kind of parting for a few hours. And now all that was gone; now that is all over, she told me, with one small stroke of the belly that was round with another man's child.

Anne, I thought. And looking at her now on the lawn, happy in this new place without me, I was shocked by something that I could not admit was the remains of our love.

You remember the pain and the anger and the grief of coming apart. You remember the raised voices and worries about money and the tears of a woman who finds that she is living a different life to the one she was expecting. You remember all of that, and you remember the letter that came two days after she said she had to go to stay with her parents to clear her head.

Dear Max, I am sorry but I have to go. I never wanted this to happen. But I love him and I am expecting his baby. He has moved so don't try looking for him . . .

You remember all of that, but you forget the love. It is a shock to be reminded of it, to admit to yourself that it existed at all, and perhaps still does.

I was parked across the road from her house on a beautiful street in a leafy south London suburb. Scout and the dog slept on the back seat.

I did not wake them.

And when another car pulled into the drive, and another man got out, and Anne smiled and kissed him on the mouth, I knew I was not going to.

I watched them go back inside the house, the new man with his arm around Anne's pregnant waist. She looked straight at me as she closed the door. But of course by then it was far too late for anything.

What about Scout? People sometimes ask me how a mother could leave a child. All I can say is, some people get a new home. And some people get a new family. And some people – mostly they are men, but not always – they make a lifetime of excuses for themselves, and they do what my wife did.

They get a new life.

Panic drove me out there. Reality drove me back. But as the night fell black and cold, I still wanted the same thing.

I wanted my daughter to be safe.

And as I drove back to Smithfield I saw that the safest place in the world for Scout would always be with me. Because I would kill for her and I would die for her. I would do anything for Scout because Scout was my everything.

There was a crowd outside our apartment block. Friday night men and women, red faces and white teeth, loud and laughing, bottles and glasses in their hands, making no attempt to move out of the way for a man with a sleeping child in his arms and a dog on a lead beside him.

I barged my way through them, sharp elbows and dipped shoulders, putting my weight into it, daring them to say something, to do something, to reveal themselves. To let me know they were for me, they had come for me, and now was the time. But there was blood in my eyes, murder in my face, and they said nothing. They got out of my way.

Across the street from our loft, the men of the meat market were just going to work as I put Scout to bed without her waking. Stan hopped up beside her, curled against her warmth, and I left them to their rest.

But I watched from the window, waiting for someone wicked

to come for us, knowing at last that pure evil was out there, knowing we would meet one day soon, and I saw that the lights of the meat market burned all night long, wiping out the sky and blinding the stars.

DECEMBER

Lost contActs

27

Two weeks later she came to see me.

Anne. My ex-wife.

Surprise visit.

Her old set of keys got her through the communal street-level door but they didn't work on our front door because I had changed the locks when she left me. I heard her key rattling in the lock and I saw her through the spy hole. It took me a while to unbolt the door. Then she was standing there. A knock-out, basically. The same woman but changed by all the time that had gone by, all the time we had not shared.

'Hello, Max.'

'Anne.'

She wore no make-up apart from a light touch of war paint on her lips. The light from the hall caught her shoulder-length hair and there was one single strand of silver running through the dark brown. She was dark-eyed, pale-skinned, and you could see where Scout got the heartbreaking curve of her face. It's hard to purge someone from your heart when you can see a child you love in their features.

Anne didn't bring her new life with her. Apart from the baby inside her, which she reassured and soothed with a hand rolled across her belly. The silence between us terrified me.

'Where's your little boy?' I said.

'Nanny,' she said, and she made it sound like a destination.

I followed her into the loft, fascinated by that single strand of silver in her hair. Not because it confirmed she was getting older – and she would one day be old, something that had never crossed my mind before now – but because I knew she would lose the special shine I had fallen in love with when we were kids. The shine was always going to go, and it wouldn't have made any difference. I would have kept on loving her without the special shine of youth. Maybe I would have truly loved her for the first time. But of course now I would never get the chance.

'Don't look at me like that, Max. It's giving me the creeps.'

'Sorry.'

Scout and Stan came out of her bedroom. We all stared at our visitor as if she had come from some other planet and not just down the road in London's leafy money-belt. Then Anne was on her knees and all over Scout. That's the trouble with not seeing much of your child. Acting naturally around them becomes impossible. And I felt a flood of resentment that I could taste in my mouth.

Scout should have mattered to you. Scout should have mattered to you more than anything.

Stan mooched towards Anne, tail high and swishing. He sniffed hopefully at her legs and she stood up, one hand at the base of her spine, the other fanning the air, her lovely, ageing face twisted down with distaste.

'I don't do dogs,' she said. 'You never know where their mouth has been.'

I picked Stan up and took him to Scout's bedroom. He gave me a mournful look as I closed the door.

When I got back, Scout was showing Anne the junior boxing gloves I had bought her. In truth Scout had shown zero interest in putting on boxing gloves. She preferred drawing, or hanging out with Stan, or talking to her dolls (Scout insisted she was *not* playing with them – 'just talking'). But I could see that she felt some nameless compulsion to show her mother something new.

So that this time she might stay.

They talked. Mother and daughter. I went into the kitchen and I was in the middle of making coffee when a great wave of grief rolled over me and sucked me down. The feeling gripped my throat and stung my eyes and made me feel that I would never move again.

Then it was gone.

I went back into the main room with a tray. Two coffees and an orange juice.

'I'm not drinking caffeine any more,' Anne said.

I was confused. But she loved her coffee.

'I'll get water,' I said.

'Don't push the boat out on my account,' she said, and that made me laugh. She could always make me laugh.

'Do you want to see my drawings?' Scout said.

'Yes!' Anne's hand rolling over her belly. 'Yes, Scout! Yes!'

Scout went to her room to get her drawings. Anne and I looked at each other. I could see the effort she was making. We turned our faces to the sound of Scout's voice. Stan was making an unsuccessful attempt to escape.

'*No*, Stan,' Scout told him, closing the door behind her as she went into her room.

'Dogs?' Anne said. 'Boxing?'

She made it sound as though I was running a crack den.

Anne moved slowly around the loft, as if checking to see if she had left anything of importance behind, and stepped on a stuffed monkey that gave an outraged squeak.

'There's junk all over the floor,' she said. 'And it's not even Scout's junk.'

It was true. Stan had his own junk. A dog of that age is exactly like a toddler. Stan had junk scattered all over our flat – a squeaky duck, a spiky rubber ball, a bear in a Union Jack bib, assorted bits of chewed bone and gnawed rope.

'And this is really your dog?' she continued, with the amused contempt that I remembered so well. 'You're not looking after it for somebody?'

'Dogs are great,' I said.

Stan was back, having escaped from the bedroom when Scout came out with her drawings, and he shot me a furtive glance.

'Dogs don't care if you're rich or poor,' I said. 'Dogs don't care if you're beautiful or plain, smart or dumb, or what kind of car you drive.'

'That's right,' Anne said. 'Because dogs are stupid. What's that strange smell?'

'Scrambled omelette,' Scout said, placing a stack of drawings before her mother. 'Daddy burned the pan.'

'Scrambled omelette?' Anne said. 'There's no such thing!'

'No, scrambled omelettes are good,' Scout said, and I nearly wept at her loyalty to my simple meals. 'Because you can have what you want in them. Ham. Cheese. And you can eat them with Paul Newman's barbecue sauce.'

Anne touched her hair and laughed. 'Darling, there's omelette and then there's scrambled eggs. There's not scrambled omelette.'

Scout was wide-eyed.

'Lots of great chefs are men,' she said.

Anne shook her head, smiling. She studied the top drawing. 'What's this one?'

'This one's from school,' Scout said. She carefully read the title: 'My Family'.

Anne inhaled. 'But there's only you, Daddy and the dog, darling. Where's Mummy? And your baby brother? Where's Oliver?'

The new man. At least she doesn't call him Uncle Oliver, I thought. At least we are spared that ugly fate.

'I've got more drawings,' Scout said, before Anne could complain any more, and she went back to her bedroom.

'Look,' Anne said to me. 'If you're finding it difficult to adjust . . .'

I stared at her. I didn't know what to say. Adjusting? Is getting on with it the same as adjusting?

A burst of sudden pain throbbed in my lower back.

'What's wrong with you?' she said.

'Daddy's not at work today,' Scout said, her arms full of drawings. 'He hurt his back.'

'How long has your back been bad, Max?'

'I'm fine,' I said.

'Are you sleeping?'

'Like a baby.'

'What – you wake up wet and screaming in the middle of the night?'

We smiled at each other.

'I'm going to be the grumpy sheep,' Scout announced, dumping her drawings on the floor.

'The grumpy sheep?' Anne said. 'What's that?'

'The sheep that didn't want to see Jesus. The story's called

The Grumpy Sheep. The part I play is the grumpy sheep. It's in the Bible.'

'Scout's Nativity play,' I said. 'At Christmas. I'm not sure the grumpy sheep is in the Bible, angel.'

'Daddy's going to make my costume.'

Anne raised an eyebrow. 'Good luck with that,' she said.

It was time to go. There were promises to see Scout soon. Promises to come again. Promises to have her down, and put her up, and show her a good time. Talk of baby brother and unborn sister that meant nothing to Scout. Promises, promises. If they were kept then everything would be better. Not perfect. Not remade. But better.

And, despite everything that had happened, I knew that Anne loved Scout. But she hadn't made space for her in the new life, with the new man, in the new place. And unless and until she did, Scout would be lost to her, and our beautiful daughter would carry those wounds with her for ever.

'Oh,' Anne said. 'There was a young woman waiting for you downstairs.'

'I get that a lot,' I said.

'I can believe it,' Anne said, walking away from us and back to her new family, her new life. 'They probably like your dog.'

'Hello, Sick Note,' Wren said. 'I thought you were never going to let me in. What's wrong with you now?'

'Torn internal intercostal muscles,' I said.

Wren shook her head. 'You're going to have to give me a clue.'

'The intercostal muscles lift your ribcage when you inhale and exhale.'

'Does it hurt?'

'Only when I breathe.'

'We missed you at Mallory's funeral. It would have been good if you were there, Max. His wife, Margaret, she was asking after you.'

I hung my head and choked something down. 'I can't see her,' I said. 'I wouldn't know what to say.'

'You don't have to say anything, stupid.'

Scout and Stan came out to meet her.

'His hair is the same colour as mine!' Wren told Scout.

All three of them were delighted. Stan began hopping around. Wren offered him the back of her hand to sniff before she started stroking him, and I could tell she was raised around dogs.

'What's your name?' Scout asked.

'Edie,' Wren replied.

'Look at this, Edie,' Scout said. And then to Stan, 'Play dead.'

Stan flopped down on his side, his head lifted from the ground, his eyes wide open and fixed on the Nature's Menu chicken treats gripped in Scout's little fist. He licked his lips. His head quivered with anticipation. In truth, he didn't look very dead. He didn't even look sleepy.

'That . . . is . . . incredible,' Wren said. 'Never seen anything like it. The pair of you should be on TV. Whatever that show's called. Well done.'

Beaming with pride, Scout and Stan went off to her room.

'When are you coming back?' Wren said.

'Tomorrow,' I said. 'Maybe the day after.'

'It doesn't matter. Because this would be off the book.'

There was an A4-sized file in her hand. Small and thin and green. She held it out to me but I made no attempt to take it.

'Mispers,' Wren said.

'What?'

'I was looking for missing persons, remember? Missing girls from twenty years ago.' A glint in her eye. '*You asked me.* Remember?'

I nearly laughed out loud. A spasm of pain shot through my lower back.

'It's over,' I said. 'Case closed. Murders solved. The perp convicted. They got their killer, didn't they?'

Ian Peck, aka Bob the Butcher, was standing up for all the murders. Not just Mallory. Not just the one he actually did, but also the murders of Hugo Buck, Adam Jones and Guy 'Piggy' Philips. Peck was an official serial killer, a superstar of real-life crime. Bob the Butcher's followers were still lighting up the social network sites.

I suddenly felt somewhere beyond exhausted.

'I heard Whitestone made DCI,' I said.

'That's right,' Wren said. 'And she deserves it.'

'And they're giving Mallory a posthumous QPM.'

'And Scarlet Bush has got a book out called *Pigslayer*.'

'A book? Already?'

'*Pigslayer* is an e-book, Grandad.' She flicked her fingers. 'They do 'em fast. Haven't read it myself. The chief super's happy. Looks like everybody in our team is going up at least one pay grade. While you're at home with your busted back feeling sorry for yourself.'

I shook my head. 'It's over,' I repeated.

'No,' Wren said. 'It's only just starting. Because there are still the missing.'

'You know how many people go missing in this country?' I said. 'Every single day of the year?'

'Yes,' Wren said. 'One every three minutes. Most of them young. Many of them female. Girls running away from care homes. Girls who are being abused by dear old mum's brand-new boyfriend. Girls with drug problems, drink problems and body issues. Self-harmers and addicts of every kind. The waifs and strays. The unlucky ones who fall through the net – who fall through all the nets. Girls who are pregnant. Girls who think they are in love. Girls whose parents are religious fanatics who think they are whores if they listen to pop music.'

'That just about covers it,' I said.

'You know how many girls went missing in the country that year, 1988, the year we're looking at?'

I was silent for a moment.

'I guess it was a lot,' I said.

'You wouldn't believe how many.'

'And you're going to find them all, are you, Edie? Avenge them all? Make it right?'

'Not all of them. Just one. I narrowed it right down. The net – the net you gave me – was much too wide. It turned up too many names. Too many missing girls. So I looked in the immediate vicinity of Potter's Field. During school time. In the spring and summer of 1988.'

'But not all mispers are murder victims, Edie. Some of them – most of them – are just lost contacts. You heard of lost contacts? Did you do lost contacts yet in detective school?'

'Fine.' She began to gather up the contents of her thin little file. 'I'll do it by myself.'

'Mispers are sometimes just lost contacts who got out and moved on and changed their name and were bloody happy to get away from whatever nightmare they were stuck in,' I said.

'That's true,' she conceded. 'But some mispers end up dead in a basement. Or alive – and that's even worse. Alive in some bastard's basement for ten years or more. Chained naked to some fucking wall. And you know that's true too, don't you, Max?'

I was silent for a moment.

'Yes,' I said.

'And you were there. You heard what James Sutcliffe told us. There was a girl, Max. It all starts with a girl! Find the girl and you find the killer and you find the motive for it all. But first you have to find the girl. And we have to find the girl, don't we? We can't just . . . leave her.' She stared at me. 'You really want me to do this thing alone, Max? I can't believe it. I don't think that's who you are.'

'You don't know me.'

'Probably not.'

I walked her to the door.

'You know the worst thing about being on your own with a kid?' I said. 'You care a lot less about the rest of the world. You really wouldn't believe how much less you care. You just do. Your heart gets hardened. Your world narrows down to you and your child. You want to do this thing off the book?'

She nodded.

'But why?' I said. 'The missing will still be missing. Mallory will still be dead. Bob the Butcher will still be getting marriage proposals sent to his cell.'

'We do it because if we don't, they get away with it,' Wren said. 'We do it because if we don't, we're just like the worst of our kind – too scared to do our job. And we do it because it matters. We do it because it's *right*.'

The file slapped hard against my chest.

This time I took it.

'You have a daughter, Max,' Wren said. 'Do it for her.'

When Mrs Murphy arrived I went down to Smiths of Smithfield to look at the file.

There wasn't much in it. Three sheets of paper.

The first featured a passport-sized photograph of a fair-haired girl in her mid teens holding an uncertain smile for the camera, a name, Anya Bauer – German? – and a date of birth: 4 July 1973.

I looked at the photograph and saw that Anya Bauer had teased her hair into some elaborate approximation of some unknown hero. It could have been anything from a pop star to a princess. It could have been Madonna or Princess Diana. No, it was Madonna. Early on, when Madonna's hair was still quite short. Anya Bauer trying to look older, trying to look pretty – trying to do what every teenager in the world tried to do. Anya Bauer was in her mid teens in the late eighties, so she would be on the cusp of middle age by now.

If she had lived.

The second page was a printout from a contemporary missing persons website with the same photograph and a disclaimer:

> Note: the child may look significantly different now to these images due to the age and stylistic differences.

The third and final sheet carried the same image of the smiling girl. Page seven of the *Potter's Field Post*, dated 21 August 1988. One sentence: 'Anya Bauer, 15, has been missing from her home for two months and police are anxious to contact her.' And there was a telephone number that had probably been defunct for the best part of two decades.

I looked at Anya Bauer's photograph for a long time, and when I climbed the stairs to my home, just before I opened the door I heard the sound of Stan barking and the untouched joy of Scout's laughter.

28

WELCOME TO POTTER'S FIELD said the ornate wooden sign on the edge of town. FINAL RESTING PLACE OF THE ROYAL DOGS.

Wren snorted. 'They make it sound like the Taj Mahal or Victoria Falls,' she said. 'It's not even all the royal dogs, is it? Just Henry's. They haven't got any of the Queen's corgis in there, have they? And probably not all of Henry's dogs.'

The sign featured the Henry VIII of popular imagination – the portly wife-killer in his middle years, not the athletic young king whose statue adorned the school he had founded five hundred years ago. Some goggle-eyed spaniels frolicked by his silken club-toe shoes. They all looked like Stan's relatives.

It was always a shock to see that there was a town beyond the world of the school. Like a lot of small English towns, Potter's Field hovered somewhere between gentility and poverty. With Wren at the wheel of a pool car, a little unmarked Hyundai, we passed a pretty village green where a group of local youths sat drinking from cans and smoking, their mountain bikes scattered around them.

'DCI Mallory's wife came in,' Wren said. 'After the medal ceremony. Margaret. She was really nice. She wanted to thank everyone. She's a class act, that lady. She was asking after you.' A pause. 'You should go and see her.'

'You want to take the police station or the local newspaper?' I said.

Wren stared at me.

'Did you hear me?'

'I heard you. Police station or the local rag?'

She looked at me for a moment longer, then looked away.

We were on the high street now. There were quaint little teashops among the chain coffee shops and mobile phone stores and supermarkets. I pulled up outside one of the teashops. A life-sized effigy of Henry VIII and his dogs guarded the offer of afternoon cream tea and a taste of English summer.

'I'll take the local rag,' Wren said.

They were not expecting me. But my warrant card got me into an interview room with the duty sergeant, Sergeant Lane, a big red-faced copper with the hint of a rural accent. He handed me back my warrant card with a smirking mixture of deference and derision. But he shook my hand and gave me a paper cup of scalding black coffee.

'CID are back?' he said. 'We haven't seen you out here since that unfortunate business with the sports master. But the perpetrator went down, didn't he?'

'This is another matter,' I said. 'A missing person.' I slid the thin file across the table. 'You've always worked in Potter's Field?'

'Born and bred here,' he said. 'The big city never appealed. It's beautiful out here. Very green. You get out in the fields, it's like the last few centuries never happened.'

'Do you remember a missing person called Anya Bauer?'

He was half-heartedly leafing through the file.

'And why would I?' he said. He closed the file and raised

his eyebrows. 'Not much of a missing person, was she? More of a lost contact.'

The file slid back towards me.

'So she was reported missing but you never followed it up?' I said.

A slow smile. 'You think we've got plenty of time on our hands? The local yokels.'

I smiled back at him. 'Not at all. You must get busy. All those spoilt rich kids at Potter's Field.'

'Oh, they're no trouble,' he said, bridling. 'We have a good relationship with the school. Always have done. If those kids are smashing up restaurants, then they're doing it in Chelsea and Knightsbridge, not round here.' He gestured at the file. 'Foreign girl, was she?'

I nodded. 'German. From Munich. Would you have tried a bit harder to find her if she'd been a local?'

He laughed. 'Wouldn't have had a choice, would we?' Then his face grew serious. 'Have you got a body? Is that what this is about?'

'We don't have a body. It's more of a hunch.'

I was on my feet, gathering the file with one hand and reaching out to shake his hand with the other. He took it and gripped it for just long enough to demonstrate that despite my age and warrant card and fancy big city ways, he was by far the stronger man.

'Forgive me, but I don't quite understand why you're here,' he said. 'This is an official inquiry, is it?

'Just some old business we're trying to clear up,' I said. 'I appreciate your time.'

'My pleasure,' he said.

Before I was out of the door, he was reaching for the phone.

* * *

The offices of the *Potter's Field Post* were located on the high street above an antique shop but Wren had left a text message changing our meet, and directing me to a small thatched cottage on the edge of town where a sprightly woman in her early eighties was tending an immaculate garden.

'She's inside,' she called, 'with my husband. It's not locked!'

An old Golden Retriever lumbered up to me as I went into the cottage. It sniffed my hand sleepily and then trailed after me down the hall as I followed the sound of Wren's excited voice.

She was on her knees in the living room, peering through a magnifying glass at an old contact sheet of photographs. The floor was entirely covered with contact sheets. In an armchair was a white-haired old man with what looked like a large Scotch in his hand. The dog went over to him and collapsed on his tartan slippers.

'Be good, Fanta,' said the old man. And to me, 'Hello, young man. Would you like a wee dram?'

'Single malt,' Wren said. 'Twenty years old. It's very good.' There was a glass on the table but it didn't look as though she had touched it.

The old gentleman started to rise from his chair but I held up my hands, thanking him, but no. Wren pressed the magnifying glass against her eye, and then against the contact sheet in her hand.

'There's nothing at the paper,' she said. 'It's on its last legs. They don't even have proper files. They haven't even digitally converted their old filing system. I found dry rot in their microfiche. Can you believe it?'

'The *Potter's Field Post*?' said the old man. 'They give it away these days! Give it away! A free sheet, they call it!'

'But they directed me to Mr Cooper here,' Wren said.

'Monty!' the old man erupted.

'Monty!' agreed Wren. 'Monty was the staff photographer on the paper for forty years.'

'Man and boy,' he chortled.

I got the impression that Monty mightily enjoyed Wren's company, and was happy to produce his stacks of old contact sheets. He didn't even seem to mind the red felt-tip pen she was waving around for emphasis, and using to circle images of interest.

I sat down beside her.

'Nightmare at the local rag,' she said. 'As far as I can tell, they did nothing on Anya Bauer beyond that one piece when she went missing. They never followed it up.'

'Neither did the law,' I said.

'But look at this,' Wren said, and held out the magnifying glass.

'I photographed this town all my working life,' Monty said, and I could hear an even stronger echo of the old lost countryside that I had heard in Sergeant Lane's voice. 'And once a year, on Potter's Fifth, I photographed the school.'

I was looking at images of boys in military uniform. It was the uniform worn by the seven boys in the Combined Cadet Force of Potter's Field. But here there was an entire army of them, and they marched across the decades.

'Potter's Fifth is the school's big day,' Wren explained.

Monty barked with laughter. Fanta the Golden Retriever sat up sharply and then slowly curled itself back into sleep.

'On the fifth of May every year the school opens its doors to the great unwashed,' Monty said. 'And the town opens its heart to the school. Or pretends it does. It's the Potter's Field equivalent of the fourth of June at Eton. Of course they've got the river at Eton and we don't have a river.'

'Do you see them?' Wren said.

'No.'

She punched my arm. 'Jesus, Wolfe! Look harder!'

I saw hundreds of boys in uniform. Marching past the statue of the young King Henry. Saluting the raising of the flag. Eyes snapped right as they marched past the camera. And then I concentrated on one central image on the contact sheet that was circled with red and the mist cleared.

They were not as I remembered them – cocky and grinning and unbreakable, as they had been in that first photograph. Now they were serious, upright, stern, in a line of boy soldiers being inspected by Her Majesty the Queen when she and they were twenty years younger.

Seven of them together in a line that stretched beyond the frame of the camera: Guy Philips, Salman Khan, Ben King, Ned King, James Sutcliffe, Hugo Buck, Adam Jones. And towering by the side of the Queen as Her Majesty frowned at James Sutcliffe, there was Peregrine Waugh, the line of his mouth suggesting that he was about to detonate with pride.

'And this one,' Wren said.

There was another contact sheet she had placed by her side. It too had a red circle around one image.

It was night in the picture. A long shot of some kind of party in a large white tent. Waiters hovered with trays of champagne flutes. Parents and boys and masters and guests stood around grinning and swilling. Another Potter's Fifth had gone well. And on the far side of the party I could see a boy and a girl half turning away from the camera with a smile.

'It's Ben King,' I said.

'It's Ned King,' Wren said. 'Look closer. You can just about see the scars on his face where his brother glassed him over the Coco Pops.'

'And the girl?'

She was young, blonde, pretty. A ponytail bobbing, the shadow of a secret smile as she turned away. She was in T-shirt and jeans, far too casual for an event like the one in the big white tent, far too casual for Potter's Fifth.

Wren smiled and shook her head. 'I don't know. It could be just a girl. You talked to Ned King, right? You and Mallory.'

I remembered the night out at Brize Norton when Captain King and his regiment were about to get on the Hercules for Afghanistan.

'The killings had only just begun,' I said. 'Ned King was leaving. Mallory was gentle with him. Impressed by him.' I stared through the magnifying glass at the image of the boy and girl at a party long ago. 'We both were.'

'Well, someone has to talk to Captain King again,' Wren said. 'When he gets back.'

'Monty,' I said, 'would that have been your only reason to go to the school? Potter's Fifth?'

He nodded and eased himself out of the chair. 'Apart from pictures we needed for the files,' he said. 'When there was a new Head Master, they would always want a shot of him. And the statue of Henry. The mainstay of our tourist industry.' He was bent over the coffee table, not risking getting down on his knees. 'And the grave, of course. The grave of the royal dogs.' He tapped a ragged cardboard file. 'There you go.'

These were not contact sheets. These were glossy eight-by-ten shots. Some of them were of the Head Masters of Potter's Field, formal portraits. Peregrine Waugh was the most recent but there were also men long retired, long dead. And there were close-up shots of the grave of the royal dogs, taken in all kinds of weather, and all kinds of seasons.

I held one in each hand. One was black and white, the stone slick with rain, the grass around it untrimmed. The other was in colour, the stone reflecting a white bar of summer sunshine, the grass border neat and cut.

But that wasn't the only difference between the two photographs.

'Look at the inscription,' I said. 'Look at the epitaph on the grave.' I held up the black-and-white shot. 'The words are missing on this one.'

On the photograph of the grave taken in summer, the epitaph was there. But on the rain-slick shot, it was missing.

The old photographer smiled, and he didn't need to look at the words to recite them. '"Brothers and sisters, I bid you beware of giving your heart to a dog to tear." Well, they could hardly put that on the original grave, now could they?'

'Why not?'

'Because the grave is nearly five hundred years old,' he said. 'But those words were written in the early twentieth century by Rudyard Kipling. By my time the grave was literally falling to bits. Collapsing in on itself.'

Wren said, 'Do you have any pictures?'

He looked doubtful but eventually found one image of a small yellow bulldozer parked next to the cracked tomb. You could clearly make out the name of the company on the side: V. J. Khan & Sons.

'The grave was always unmarked,' Monty said. 'Or at least the inscription had worn clean away. I never saw anything on it. It's five hundred years old, remember. But when they restored it, he added the words from Kipling.'

'Who did?' Wren said.

'The Head Master,' he said, sipping his single malt. 'Mr Waugh said he didn't want to leave the grave unmarked.'

29

I left Wren tucking into cheese on toast with Monty, his wife and their Golden Retriever and drove the pool car to Potter's Field. The school seemed shut up and silent already but the main gates were open and I left the Hyundai in the staff car park. I could make out a figure moving around in the twilight of the playing fields and I was starting towards him when I heard the sound of the first shot.

A large-gauge gun, some distance away, the shot seeming to contain its own echo. And then there was silence and I started off again towards the playing fields, the buildings looking so lifeless that you would never guess they contained one thousand souls.

The old caretaker, Len Zukov, was moving slowly along a rugby pitch with what looked like a lawnmower. It was only when I got closer that I saw he was leaving a long straight white line in his wake as he marked out a touchline.

I called out a greeting, raising my hand.

'Don't step on that!' he replied. 'Still wet!'

'Remember me? DC Wolfe from West End Central.'

I was reaching for my warrant card. But he couldn't have cared less about my warrant card.

'I remember you.'

'I'm just following up a few details of our ongoing investigation.'

But he wasn't interested. He was already moving off, his machine drowning my words, the straight white line trailing behind him.

'Don't step on my lines,' he shouted over his shoulder, a man accustomed to bawling at generations of boys. 'Got to get this done before dark.'

I walked back across the main courtyard, round the side of the college chapel and into the graveyard. There was a flurry of sound and movement. A squirrel skittered across my path and swiftly up a tree. I reached the grave of Henry's dogs as another shot split the silence. And there was the epitaph.

Brothers and sisters,
I bid you beware
Of giving your heart
To a dog to tear.

Weather and time had etched the words in green moss.

I turned at a shuffling sound behind me and saw Len Zukov coming slowly down the path. Checking up on me.

'What you want?' he said. 'You shouldn't be in here. You should tell someone you're coming. Get permission.'

'Those words on the grave,' I said. 'I never realised until today that they're only a hundred years old. But the grave is five hundred years old. So they had to be put there within the last century.'

His mouth moved as if to say *and so what?*

'I just wondered how I missed it,' I said, talking to myself as much as him, and looking up at the sound of another gunshot. 'Noticing things – it's sort of what I do, Len.'

He didn't take his eyes from me.

'What's that shooting?' I said. 'Twelve-bore?'

'Sounds more like a .410,' he said. 'Better for close range, thick-cover shooting. Vermin.' He rubbed his hands on his overalls. They were locked in permanent fists by his arthritis. He saw me looking at his hands and pushed them deep into his pockets. 'Rats, rabbit and fox,' he added.

'Where you from, Len?'

He frowned at me. 'I told you – I'm from here,' he said.

'Originally, I mean.'

'Russia.'

'Russia? They didn't call you Len over there, I bet.'

'Lev,' he said. 'Near enough.'

'What part of Russia?'

We both looked up at the sound of another gunshot. Closer now. The long, drawn-out, rolling sound of a large-gauge shotgun fired in open countryside. The noise just went on and on.

'Who's shooting?' I said.

He shrugged, like that was another subject he couldn't care less about.

'Farmer,' he suggested.

'So you came over after the Second World War?'

'No,' he said, not quite smiling. 'I came over after the Great Patriotic War.'

I smiled. 'Same war. Different names.'

'No,' he said, unsmiling. 'Very different wars. Very different wars for your people and my people. In Russia there were twenty-five million dead.'

We both stared at the grave. I wondered what he thought about an English king who built a tomb for his pet spaniels. Not much, probably. Not if he had been in Russia during the war. He had to be somewhere in his seventies, I guessed. That would have made him a boy of eleven or twelve at the end.

'You must have been too young for the war,' I said.

He laughed. 'Nobody in Russia was too young for the war.'

I nodded.

'I'm away now,' I said, and offered him my hand to shake.

It was a mistake. He took his arthritic hands from his overalls and brushed his clenched right fist briefly against my open palm, and we both turned away with our own private shame.

He made no attempt to follow me this time.

Perhaps he figured that I wouldn't be able to poke my nose in where it wasn't wanted. Certainly everywhere seemed locked up, and despite the falling darkness few lights appeared in any of the ancient windows. I looked up at the room where Mallory and I had stared across the playing fields with Peregrine Waugh but I could see no sign of life even there.

But I saw Len Zukov again as I walked back to the car park. He was in front of his little stone cottage with another man and it took me a moment to recognise Sergeant Tom Monk, the burns on his face a smooth black mask from so far away.

As the old caretaker watched, a cigarette clutched in one balled-up fist, Monk raked a pile of newly mown grass, shovelled it into a wheelbarrow and carried the load round the side of the cottage to where the smoke from a small bonfire was rising. Easing the old man's burden.

I raised my hand in farewell but they did not appear to see me.

Then there was another gunshot as I reached the car, much

closer now, coming from somewhere just beyond the tree line. The stuttering shot tore through leaves and took its time to crack the sky. Len was wrong. Whatever they were killing, they were not using a .410 to do it. I know what a twelve-bore shotgun sounds like.

That's big vermin someone's hunting, I thought, happy to get back into the car.

There was something wrong with the silence.

It jolted me from my shallow sleep, and before I was even awake I was sitting by the side of the bed, staring straight into the eye of the madman who sat on my bedside table.

12:05, he told me. Five minutes after midnight?

Outside I could hear the hum and roar of the meat market as it began its night. The clamour of the trolleys, the shouts of the men, still laughing with the long hours of the night ahead of them.

What had woken me?

I pulled on my pants and a pair of lightweight knuckle-dusters that sat in the drawer by the bed. They weighed nothing but would crack open a skull like a boiled egg if you could get close enough. I stepped out of my bedroom, resisting the urge to call Scout's name. Inside his cage, Stan stirred in his sleep.

Our front door was shut. Our windows were unbroken. There was no fresh air coming from somewhere it shouldn't be.

I looked at Stan's cage. It was not a sound that had broken my sleep. It was the absence of a sound.

I knelt beside Stan, felt under him and beneath the blanket that covered his basket and pulled out the alarm clock we had put there to stand in place of his mother's heartbeat. The battery had died some time ago. I smiled at him in the darkness and touched his soft red coat. Then I walked into the kitchen and dropped the old alarm clock into the bin.

Stan didn't need it any more. He was home.

But under the door to my daughter's bedroom, I could see that Scout still slept with all the lights on.

30

Salman Khan opened his front door unshaven and squinting in the pale morning sunlight, a baseball bat in one hand and a cigarette in the other. He held them both loosely, as if either might slip from his hand in a strong wind. He was in a dress shirt, open to his waist, with a black bow tie hanging around his neck like fresh roadkill. He looked like he had been wearing black tie to bed for a week.

'Mr Khan,' Wren said. 'DCI Whitestone received a complaint—'

'Because they're not here any more!' Khan gestured with his baseball bat. 'The officers who were protecting me! The ones who were here after the – what is it? The Osman Warning!'

Wren smiled sympathetically. 'Because the threat to your life is over,' she said, all professional calm. 'The perpetrator has been convicted.'

He laughed viciously.

We just stared at him, letting the laughter fade and then the silence grow.

Khan looked over our shoulders. There was a young Nepalese security guard on the drive. You were starting to see them all across London's money-belt – private policemen hired to watch over just one wealthy street. The rich were getting scared.

But nobody was more scared than Salman Khan.

'Thank you, Padam,' Khan said.

The Gurkha saluted. 'Sir.'

We followed Khan inside his house. A midget motorbike was resting against a double-sided winding staircase. Through glass panels in the marble floor you could see down into the basement area and the impossible blue world of an indoor swimming pool. You could feel its heat, taste the chlorine. Wren looked at me and I knew she felt it too.

These people have so much.

'Your family are away?' I said.

'They can't stay here! It's too dangerous! If anything should happen to them . . .'

This was meant to be routine, one of the last jobs on the Action Book in the winding up of Operation Fat Boy. But Salman Khan could still smell murder in the air.

'What are you afraid of, Mr Khan?' I asked.

'Are you serious? Some of my closest friends have died.'

He stubbed out his cigarette and immediately lit another one.

'Mr Khan,' I said. 'Look at me.'

He looked at me, looked away, and threw his baseball bat aside with a scream. 'Fuck!'

'How's your father's business doing? A building firm, isn't it?'

It took him a moment to recover.

'My father died ten years ago. The company was sold at the time of his death. Why do you ask?'

Wren said, 'Who was Anya Bauer?'

The name seemed to mean nothing to him. He shook his head. 'I don't know what's going on,' he said. 'I don't know what you're talking about. You're supposed to be—'

'What happened at that school?' I said.

'How long are you going to keep asking that question?'

'Until I get the truth.'

'What happened? Nothing. High jinks. Nothing more. I can't deny that we did things. Irresponsible things.'

'Like what?' Wren said.

'God, I don't know! Smashed some glass. Made some noise. Bought some charlie.'

'That's it?' Wren said. 'Petty vandalism and recreational drugs? Come on.'

Khan shot her a wary look. 'But none of it was at our instigation. And all of it was done in a spirit of experimentation and adventure.' He seemed to stop himself, then clenched his teeth. 'We fell under his spell, you see.'

'You mean Peregrine Waugh? He was your House Master twenty years ago, wasn't he?'

Khan shook his head. 'I mean the Master's favourite.' He laughed. 'I mean Peregrine's representative on earth.'

And I suddenly saw who had the most to lose.

'You're talking about Ben King, aren't you? Was he the Master's favourite?'

He couldn't look at me. 'I didn't say that,' he said. 'I didn't give you any names.' He gripped a fistful of his hair. 'You're meant to be here to *help* me!'

'Would you like to make a statement?' I said.

Khan's mouth twisted into a grotesque parody of coquettishness. 'Would you like me to, detective?'

'I think you're ready to talk to us, Mr Khan,' I said. 'I think you know that it's really the only option you have left.' I looked around at all the useless luxury. 'This is no life, is it?'

He sucked hungrily on his cigarette.

'I need to talk to a few people. I need to talk to my wife,

my beautiful—' He choked up. Hung his head. Then gathered himself. 'And my lawyer. And my children, God help me. After that, I'll come to your station.' He was starting to compose himself now. 'I believe there's a possibility that I can help you with your enquiries.'

'And when will that be?' Wren asked.

'When I am fucking ready, young lady.'

I shook my head. 'Not good enough, sir,' I said. 'And watch your mouth when you're addressing my colleague. We have reason to believe that a serious crime was committed during the period when you were a student at Potter's Field. I could take you in now if I wanted to.'

He laughed. 'Really? And by this time next year you would be waiting outside in your new security guard's uniform, watching over my children as they unload their mountain bikes from my wife's Porsche Cayenne. Wouldn't you?' He paused, took a breath. 'Tomorrow morning,' he said. 'Afternoon at the latest. I promise. I want it to be over.'

'It will be,' I assured him. 'We can help you. But you have to help us: what happened at that school?'

'What happened? I'll tell you what happened. They break you down and then they build you up. That's what they do at those fine old English schools. That's what your parents are paying them for. They take you apart bit by bit and they put you together again in their image. They take scared little boys and they turn them into captains of industry, leaders of the land, future Prime Ministers.'

He took a long pull on his cigarette.

'The first day I met Peregrine Waugh – I was thirteen years old, he was just an English master – he drew a single chalk mark on the wall just above the blackboard. "That is

Shakespeare," he said. And then he drew another chalk mark, at the very top of the blackboard. "That is T. E. Lawrence." And then he got down on his knees – we were all laughing madly, of course – and drew a third chalk mark just above the floorboards. "And that is you."' Salman Khan smiled a crooked smile as he waved his cigarette. 'And we took it from there.'

It was a busy morning at the Black Museum. A dozen young cadets in uniform were squeezed into Room 101. Sergeant John Caine contemplated them without pleasure or pity.

'Ground rules,' he said. 'You do not touch anything. You do not photograph anything. You do not take a souvenir that you think nobody will miss. Believe me, I will miss it. Everything here is far older and far more valuable than you are.'

A few guffaws. But Sergeant Caine wasn't laughing.

'So show respect,' he continued. 'And keep your sticky paws in your pockets at all times.'

He unlocked the door to the Black Museum.

'Go on. Off you go.'

They set off, excited and laughing, like big kids on a school trip. When the last of them had shuffled into the first room, the one mocked up to look like the original museum in Whitehall, Sergeant Caine turned his attention to me.

'They've come down from Hendon,' he said. 'This spotty shower are coming to the end of their course and sending them to me is an attempt to prepare them for the real world. A new initiative.'

'I'll wait, if that's OK.'

He nodded. 'Best to wait. Join them if you like.'

I followed them through into the Victorian sitting room, nine young men and three young women who were happy to be on a field trip, snickering at the fake fireplace and fake sash window.

They passed under the hangman's noose and reached the table covered with weapons. Shotguns and rifles, replicas and the real thing, walking sticks that were really swords, umbrellas that were really handguns, and a glass case full of automatic weapons. By the time they went through the doorless opening into the museum proper, their laughter had stopped.

They saw the walking stick that turned into a sword that then turned into a knife – the Cop Killer. There was every kind of gun, every kind of knife – some of them dark with prehistoric blood. They paused longest before the display about the officers of the Metropolitan Police who had been killed in the line of duty.

By the end of their visit – and it doesn't take very long to see the Black Museum – they were silent and shaken.

'This place is a learning centre,' Sergeant Caine told them, leaning against his cluttered desk and holding a mug that said BEST DAD IN THE WORLD. 'I hope the lesson that you have learned today is that there are many ways to kill a policeman.'

They said nothing.

'Thank you for visiting the Crime Museum at New Scotland Yard,' Caine concluded with a formality I had not heard before. 'Before you graduate from Hendon, I suggest you go to your school's Simpson Hall where you will find the Metropolitan Police Book of Remembrance. Her Majesty the Queen has signed it and, before your studies come to an end, so should you.' He looked at their serious young faces and nodded once. 'Take care of yourself and take care of each other. Thank you, good luck and goodbye.'

* * *

When we were alone I opened my kitbag. Inside was a large evidence bag containing the Kevlar Stealth that had been worn by DCI Mallory on the night he died. It was almost new apart from the large stain on the right shoulder from the neck wound that had killed him.

Handling it with great care, I entrusted it to the safe keeping of Sergeant John Caine of the Black Museum, New Scotland Yard.

31

Stan's favourite café in Regent's Park was The Honest Sausage, just off The Broadwalk near London Zoo. We were at an outside table sharing a bacon sandwich, my dog on my lap, when she walked in. Sooner or later, every dog person in central London walks into The Honest Sausage.

'You again,' Natasha said.

She didn't sit down. Susan and Stan did the dog dance, moving in tight, excited circles as they sniffed at each other's rear end. Then the Pekingese-Chihuahua cross had suddenly had enough and turned and yapped in his face. Stan backed off immediately, tail between his legs, edging closer to me for protection.

'Fancy bumping into you,' Natasha said. 'What's the lovely old English saying? Accidentally on purpose. Hello, Stan.'

At least she was pleased to see my dog.

'It's a good saying,' I said. 'I went to your old apartment block but they said you had moved.'

'Just across the park. Marylebone. I downsized.'

I held out the manila envelope to her. 'Your videotape. I wanted to return it.'

She took it from me without speaking, her mouth tightening. She still hadn't sat down. She wasn't going to now. Not with the videotape of that old rugby match in her hand.

'I also wanted to say that you were right, and I was wrong. About how your late husband lost his eye. I was rough and rude. And I'm sorry, I really am.' I shrugged. 'That's it.'

'And what did you think might happen? Did you think you were going to return my VHS tape and say sorry and then I would take you home with me and have wild sex?'

'Well,' I said, 'it crossed my mind.'

She shook her head. 'We missed our moment,' she said.

I was surprised how sad that made me.

'Did we really?'

'Yes. Men and women have a moment and sometimes they just miss it. Bad timing.'

'Like missing a flight?'

'Exactly like missing a flight.'

My phone was in front of me on the table. It began to vibrate. WREN CALLING, it said.

Natasha laughed. 'We don't even know each other.'

'I know you,' I said. 'You're one of those party girls with a good heart who wants to settle down but chooses the wrong man and then it all falls to pieces. You can see yourself getting harder and more cynical and you don't like it because you were expecting a better life. Stop me if I'm getting warm.'

My phone was still vibrating.

'Story of my life,' Natasha said. 'But what kind of man are you? Are you one of those men who stop looking at a woman so he can look at his little phone? The world is full of those men. That's not what I want.'

'No,' I said. 'That's not me. I can't stand guys like that. I'm actually thinking of getting rid of this phone.' WREN CALLING. 'But you know what? I do have to take this call.'

'Of course you do.'

Natasha scooped up her Pekingese-Chihuahua cross and walked away on those long legs. Without turning round, she raised one hand in farewell.

I picked up the phone.

'Whitestone heard from Salman Khan's lawyer,' Wren told me. 'Khan's not coming in.'

'He's not coming in today?'

I could hear her breathing.

'Max, Khan's never coming in.'

Salman Khan's beautiful home had burned for most of the night and the wealthy street stank of smoke and death. A body had been recovered and taken away before I arrived.

Where the house had stood on the leafy St John's Wood avenue there was now a blackened husk, sodden and steaming – a five-million-pound monument to ruin. The great pyre had collapsed in on itself at some point, taking the roof with it, and among the wreckage you could just make out what had once been the subterranean swimming pool, now heaped with collapsed brick, bent steel, burned wood.

Fire Officer Mike Truman stood between two fire engines and watched his men carefully picking their way through the ruin. DI Gane and I were with him, Gane taking notes, while beyond the police tape uniformed officers kept back a small crowd wielding camera phones. They seemed to be mostly hired help walking dogs to the park or children to school. You didn't see the locals walking about round here.

'There's evidence of some kind of accelerant,' Truman said. 'A petroleum distillate like diesel fuel or gasoline. But we also found a small motorbike – a child's motorbike, if you can believe that – at the foot of the staircase, so that could explain the traces of accelerant.'

Gane said, 'That's the fire's point of origin?'

Truman nodded. 'Looks like it.'

'But how did he die?' I said.

'You mean was it the fire or the smoke that killed him?'

Gane was staring at me. 'No. DC Wolfe's asking, did someone cut his throat?'

I had never seen a burned corpse before. I had never seen how death by fire seems to coat a body in a black substance that comes from the very centre of the earth. I had never experienced the double shock of seeing what a fire takes away, and what it leaves behind.

Every inch of living flesh on Salman Khan's body had been replaced by something that resembled a rough black overcoat yet you could clearly see his ribcage, his teeth and the fine bones of his hands, the fingers now long and tapered with all the flesh burned away, like the fingers of a concert pianist.

The fire took away everything but left the shadow of some unimaginable pain. His mouth was open, as if crying out in agony, and his elegant hands were placed over his heart and genitalia, as if protecting himself in the last instant of life.

Whitestone and I were in a viewing room at the Iain West Forensic Suite watching on CCTV as Elsa Olsen examined Khan's charred remains.

'Did you ever see pictures of Pompeii?' Whitestone said, more to herself than to me. 'They look like they're screaming, don't they? They look like they're going to be screaming for ever.'

'He was going to come in,' I said. 'He was going to make a statement.'

Whitestone looked at me and shook her head. 'Mr Khan agreed to be interviewed in the presence of his lawyer,' she said. 'That's all.'

'But how did he die?'

Whitestone gestured angrily at the screen. 'How do you think he died? He died in the fire.'

Then I was through the door and into the mortuary, and Elsa Olsen was looking up from the burned cadaver on the stainless steel slab before her.

'Scrubs and hairnets, Wolfe. You know that.'

'How did he die, Elsa?'

Whitestone was right behind me.

'How did he die, Elsa?' I said again. 'Was it like the rest of them? Did someone cut his throat?'

'DC Wolfe,' Whitestone said calmly, 'get out of here.'

I ignored her.

'Elsa? You have twenty years of experience. You're in a million-pound state-of-the-art mortuary. You *must* know how he died.'

Whitestone gripped my shoulder hard enough to turn me around. How could such a slight woman summon up such reserves of physical strength? There was a rage in Whitestone, and she let me glimpse it now.

'You think someone cut his carotid arteries, don't you, Max?' she said. 'You think someone stuck a commando dagger in his neck and then torched the house. You think our killer is still out there.'

'That's exactly what I think.'

Whitestone gestured at the blackened corpse. 'But why would they bother? I mean, really – look at the state of him. Why would anyone bother cutting the poor bastard's throat?'

'Because he wouldn't commit murder with fire,' I said. 'Too unpredictable.'

'Why is this murder? I saw TDC Wren's report. I've spoken to Gane and Fire Officer Truman. A rich, chain-smoking drunk drops a cigarette butt near a fuel tank. The next thing you know – smoked Salman. Why exactly does that surprise you?'

'Do you know what oxidation is, Max?' Elsa said gently. 'It's what fire does. It's what fire *is*. Oxidation is what happens when a fuel substance combines with oxygen to produce light and heat. It's what makes fire a living, destructive entity.' She looked at the burned piece of meat on the stainless steel slab. 'There's no evidence that someone cut his throat. Because fire destroys everything.'

At the Cromwell Green entrance to the Palace of Westminster, I showed them my warrant card.

I kept it in my hand as I went through the security turnstiles, Big Ben ringing in the sky high above, then past the armed officers in twos and fours cradling their Heckler & Koch assault rifles and finally through the search point just before you enter the great expanse of Westminster Hall.

Under the hammer-beam roof, the thousand-year-old hall teemed with life – guides and tourist groups, journalists and lobbyists, MPs and their constituents. I walked quickly past them all and up the stairs at the far end, where a security guard stopped me under the great medieval window that spilled winter light into the hall. I showed him my warrant card too and told him that I was here to see the MP for Hillingdon North.

'And is Mr King expecting you, sir?'

'Probably.'

He hesitated for just a moment.

'Central Lobby, sir.'

I turned left and walked down to the Central Lobby, where great Prime Ministers get full-sized statues and mediocre Prime Ministers get life-sized busts. I spoke to the doorkeeper and he went off to find the MP for Hillingdon North.

He came back with a cool blonde in glasses and a business suit.

'DC Wolfe? I'm Siri Voss, Mr King's PA.' Just the hint of a Scandinavian accent. She was the woman who had called King in when we spoke out on the terrace. We shook hands. 'As you can appreciate, this is not a good day.'

And then I saw him. Coming out of the corridors that led to the House of Commons.

Ben King looked at me, white-faced and shaken.

'Detective Wolfe,' he said. 'I thought it was over.'

'It's just getting started,' I said. 'What did you do twenty years ago?'

He kept walking, trying to shake me off the way he shook off the world. I fell into step beside him. I could feel the light touch of his blonde PA on my arm. People were staring at us. Everyone was staring at us.

'What happened to Anya Bauer?' I said. 'What was Salman Khan going to tell me? What happened at that school?'

He stopped, a powerful man in his prime, accustomed to being in control but suddenly badly rattled by events.

'Can we do this some other time?' he said.

'How about when your brother comes back?'

'My brother? You want to talk to my brother?' His eyes blazed with something I could not read. 'I don't think that will be possible.'

Then he was walking away, and I was suddenly aware of Siri Voss standing right in front of me.

'Please,' she said. 'Oh, please leave him.'

And I saw the two coppers she had brought with her, holding their assault rifles and looking at me with embarrassment more than anything else.

'It's not over!' I shouted at King's back. 'You know that, don't you?'

But there was something in the face of Siri Voss that made me let him go.

I was at home making scrambled omelette for Scout's tea when DCS Swire called.

'You're suspended and under investigation by the police Professional Standards Department pending an IPPC inquiry,' the chief super told me.

'Charges?' I said, stirring the eggs.

'Neglect or failure in duty. Oppressive conduct or harassment. Whatever sticks. There's already more than enough.' A pause. 'Have you seen the news? You haven't even seen it, have you? You don't even *know*.' Swire sighed with disbelief. 'Do yourself a favour, Wolfe, you dumb bastard. Turn on the TV.'

She hung up.

I served up Scout's scrambled omelette then turned on the BBC. It looked like the news looked every night. A bomb in Iraq. A riot in Athens. A meeting in Brussels. A missing child. A flatlining economy. And then came photographs of three soldiers.

'. . . Private Himal Sameer, twenty-two, Corporal Bibek Prabin, twenty-three, and Captain Ned King, thirty-five, of the Royal Gurkha Rifles—'

'Daddy?'

'Wait, wait. Let me watch this, angel.'

'. . . in Helmand when their armoured vehicle was hit by an improvised explosive device. All three died of their injuries in the hospital at Camp Bastion.'

The two young Gurkhas wore serious expressions in their official portraits, their features rigid with fierce pride and there was Ned King, smiling broadly for the camera, as if he held a secret the world could never share.

32

Peregrine Waugh walked down Potter's Field High Street, his tremendous height raising that gaunt bony head above the crowds and almost brushing the bunting and Union Jacks that fluttered above the streets.

It was just three days since the smiling face of Captain Ned King had appeared on the evening news, and now every boy from the old school was there, gathered in their houses, youngest at the front, but the Head Master said not a word to any of them. He did not need to, for he could make a boy straighten his slovenly tie with just his towering presence; he could kill idle chatter with one fierce look.

Waugh paused when he reached the boy soldiers of the Combined Cadet Force, four lines of them at the end of the high street, self-consciously rigid with military discipline, and for the first time that day he smiled.

The school and the town had turned out for the homecoming of Captain Ned King.

I saw Sergeant Lane, the local copper who had been no help with my enquiry about Anya Bauer's disappearance, taking his duties more seriously today. He patrolled down the empty street, closed to traffic for the day, and greeted the Head Master with something like a cringing bow.

I glimpsed faces I knew in the crowd. On the far side of the high street I saw Mrs Jones, the mother of Adam Jones, the second victim, her face skull-like under her headscarf, almost totally consumed by her cancer now, supported by Rosalita, the Filipina housekeeper, who had a protective arm wrapped around her employer.

A little further down I saw Len Zukov standing with Sergeant Tom Monk, the burned features of the physio from Barrington Court making him look like some exotic foreign guest among the uniformly white faces of the Potter's Field townsfolk. Did I see some of them shiver at the sight of the injured soldier? Did I see fathers and mothers lift their staring small children and carry them away to a less disturbing part of the high street? Tom Monk gave no sign that he had noticed. He stared at the empty road, waiting for the homecoming of another soldier.

And I saw Natasha, standing alone at the end of the street where the crowds thinned out.

Then all heads turned to watch a lone vehicle coming down the empty high street. Murmurs of resentment. It was a sleek black Mercedes saloon and not a hearse.

Sergeant Lane stepped forward, barking commands at the uniformed officers who stood watch over the docile crowds, holding up one hand, commanding the Mercedes to stop. When it did, a uniformed chauffeur sprang from the driver's seat and opened the rear door.

Ben King got out of the car and the crowd let out an audible gasp at the sight of the MP.

He was wearing the jacket his brother had worn on the day he died. A British Army desert camouflage jacket in two colours – swirls of sand and stone – stained with a third colour, a deep bloody red that was already turning brown.

And now I realised that there were cameras for the homecoming. There was TV, press photographers, and journalists. I saw Scarlet Bush stick a sharp elbow in a photographer's eye as the media broke through the loose police cordon and spilled on to the street, swarming around Ben King.

'Dear Ben,' said Peregrine Waugh, suddenly right next to me. 'He always was an exhibitionist.'

'Get them *back*!' Sergeant Lane was shouting at his officers, red-faced with fury.

Ben King walked slowly from the street to the pavement, his face expressionless, his brother's jacket hanging limply on his shoulders and radiating another world of pure horror.

Was he wearing the army jacket over a suit and tie? It was impossible to say. All anyone saw was the jacket.

He stood in front of the Combined Cadet Force. The young soldiers stared straight ahead, trying not to look at him. Cameras capered before them as young police officers tried to restore order.

'Let them see what they have done,' murmured Waugh. 'The words of Jacqueline Kennedy when she refused to change out of the pink Chanel suit that was stained with the blood of her assassinated husband. *Let them see what they have done!* Yes, let them see.'

A scrum was forming on the pavement. Officers had pushed the press back and King's PA, Siri Voss, was handing out a press release. Two journalists walked behind us, each with one of the A4 sheets in their hands.

'So it's a British Army DPM desert camouflage jacket,' said the first. 'Does it say what DPM is?'

'Yeah, there, look – disruptive pattern material,' said the second. 'There's the front page tomorrow, mate.'

'He should have worn the full kit. Better shot with the full kit.'

'Siri says there was nothing left of the trousers.'

They were silent for a moment.

'God.'

'Yeah.'

There were tears, now. Some emotional dam had broken in the women and the men of the town, and their children took their cue, confused and upset by the unravelling of the adults.

The boys from Potter's Field gritted their teeth, set their jaws and held out for longer.

I looked at Peregrine Waugh. The Head Master was dry-eyed.

'A terrible day for you, sir,' I said.

'Ned was a soldier,' he said. 'I could not wish for a better death for him, only a better war. When did the first British soldier die in that wretched country? 1839? "When you're wounded and left on Afghanistan plains – and the women come out to cut up what remains – just roll to your rifle and blow out your brains – and go to your god like a soldier."'

'Suicide?'

He looked at me with disdain. 'Kipling, actually. But there's no shame in suicide, detective. It's only milksop Christianity that clucks with disapproval. The Romans and the Greeks saw suicide largely as a pragmatic act. A graceful and courageous exit when life has become unendurable. Ah – I think Captain King's coming now.'

A black hearse was moving slowly down the high street. In the back was a coffin wrapped in the Union Jack.

'Suicide didn't seem like a pragmatic act for James Sutcliffe,' I said, watching the first of the flowers being tossed from the pavement. They fell on the windscreen, they fell on the gleaming black hood, and they fell under the slowly turning wheels. 'For him, suicide seemed like an act of despair. Both times.'

Waugh sighed, his eyes never leaving the hearse.

'I'm afraid I have no idea what goes on in the mind of every disturbed adolescent,' he said. 'But I'm with the Romans and the Greeks – every human body is the property of the gods. Good day, detective.'

I thought that the Head Master was going to join Ben King in his bloodstained army jacket. Then I thought he might stand with the stiff fierce lines of the Combined Cadet Force. Instead he disappeared into the crowd, and the next time I saw him he was standing beside a small, snivelling Potter's Field boy. Waugh had placed a large white hand on the shoulder of the boy's green and purple blazer. I saw the Head Master's mouth move.

'There, there,' he seemed to be saying. 'There, there.'

The hearse was passing now, the windscreen wipers swishing once, twice, three times to clear the driver's view of the flowers that threatened to cover the glass. Roses, orchids, lilies – expensive flowers bought and thrown by the people of the town.

The boys of Potter's Field brought no flowers for the homecoming of Captain Ned King.

But later, as I walked through the deserted school grounds, past the chapel and into the small graveyard, I saw that someone had placed a single lily on the tomb of King Henry's dogs.

33

Saturday morning in Smithfield ABC.

I was down on the mat stretching my back. Upward-facing dog – hold it; downward-facing dog – hold it. The pain seemed to release itself. It still hurt but I was not contained in one tight slab. It was looser. It was better. I could feel it.

This was the quiet time in Fred's gym. Otis Redding on the sound system and the sound of fourteen-ounce gloves smacking pads.

There was a young woman banging the heavy bag, an older woman watching the business news as she ran on the treadmill, and, up in the ring, Fred wearing a T-shirt that told you PLAY HARD OR GO HOME as he took some kid in his late teens on the pads. North African, a big toothy grin, either a pro or thinking about it. The kid was fast, slick, hitting the pads very hard without apparently making much of an effort.

'Get that right all the way back to the chin,' Fred was telling him. 'Don't let it fade away. And don't stand there taking photographs. Get out when you've done your work. And throw punches in bunches, punches in bunches.'

When the bell rang Fred would look down at me, the pads still on his hands, and he would name the part of my body that needed to be stretched.

'Hamstring . . . calves . . . abductors . . . Did you do your abductors? Do your abductors.'

I laid the front of my left leg on a bench, placed my right foot on the floor and gently eased my shoulders back, feeling the stretch in the muscles at the top of my leg and the bottom of my spine.

Then Ben King walked in.

The woman on the heavy bag looked at him, then looked again. It had been a week since he was the lead item on the news, since he was on every front page, since he wore his brother's bloodstained camouflage jacket on the rolling news. Satisfied it was really him, the woman looked away and went back to her work on the heavy bag.

He was dressed for a run.

'I wasn't party to anything that happened at Potter's Field,' he said to me. A beat. 'But I know who was.'

I eased myself out of the stretch and sat on the bench.

'You're coming forward with new information?'

'Yes.'

'Why didn't you come forward before now?'

King turned his head as a buzzer sounded in the ring.

'Time!' shouted Fred.

Ben King looked back at me. 'Because I loved my brother.'

'Do you know the identity of the man who killed Hugo Buck?'

'No.'

'Adam Jones? Guy Philips?'

'No.'

'Salman Khan?'

'That was an accident, wasn't it? A fire.'

'What happened to Anya Bauer?'

'Who's Anya Bauer?'

I stood up and took a fistful of his T-shirt near the neck. He didn't flinch.

'Are you wasting my time?' I said.

He shook his head. 'No.'

'Who was Anya Bauer?' I said. 'What happened to her?'

'I don't know that name. I never knew any name. I never even saw the girl you're talking about. But I know that . . . questionable acts were done at that school. I know – to my eternal regret – that my brother Ned was a party to them. And, yes, my friends, too. And I know the name of the adult who instigated those questionable acts. Because he was the same man who sexually abused us for years.'

I still had his T-shirt in my fist. I twisted it until our faces were almost touching.

'Don't lie to me,' I said.

'I'm past lying,' he said. 'People get lost. My brother Ned got lost. When we were boys, I threw a glass at his face across the breakfast table. Why do you think I threw that glass at his face? Because I loved him. Because of the unspeakable things he was doing. Because of what was happening to him. Because of that man.'

'The Head Master,' I said. 'Peregrine Waugh.'

'Oy!' Fred called. He was talking to me. I still had a fistful of Ben King's T-shirt in my hand. 'Take it in the ring or take it outside.'

I let go of King's T-shirt. He was smiling.

'I haven't boxed since school,' he said.

'You boxed at school?' I said.

'Of course! All good schools teach their boys to box. May I borrow these?'

He was pointing at a pair of yellow fourteen-ounce Cleto Reyes gloves.

I shook my head. 'I don't think that's a good idea,' I said.

His mouth twisted with amusement. 'I'm sure you're right.'

I stared at him for a moment.

'Find a headguard,' I said.

He was a boxer not a fighter. He kept his distance, up on the balls of his feet, dancing sideways as I advanced, and for a moment I thought he had lost his nerve and did not want to fight.

Then I stuck out a left jab that fell short and he came back with a stiff counter that went straight through my guard and smacked hard against my nose. By the time I had angrily swung back, he had skipped away.

We repeated our little dance. He would wait for me to strike, then slip, block or move out of range, and come back with a fast, straight counter.

The sweat was pouring under my headguard. I had not sparred for weeks and I could feel my ring rust, that tiny loss of pace you get when you haven't boxed for a while. I was one second too slow in everything I did, and nothing is more draining than being hit without having the chance to hit back.

A buzzer sounded. One minute gone and his confidence was growing. And that was good because I jabbed, he countered with a jab, and stayed close to smack me with a right cross. It caught me high on the headguard but not hard enough to stop me slipping inside and burying a left hook into his bottom rib.

King went down on one knee, one glove pressed against his ribs, and his face contorted with pain. A body shot sticks around in a way a head shot never does, and when he got to his feet he was less cocky, keeping his distance, happy to get in the odd counter, happy to stay away from another dig in the ribs.

The buzzer counted down from ten and it was over. We had sparred for three minutes and were both totally spent.

'Christ,' he said. 'That's harder than squash.'

Fred was smiling at us.

'Nice spar,' he said. And to Ben King, 'Keep those elbows tucked in. Going to do another couple of rounds?'

'Perhaps some other time,' King said, still breathing hard.

Fred laughed and went off to collect the towels that were strewn around the gym. King and I sat there saying nothing, drenched in sweat, locked in the strange intimacy of two men who have just shared a boxing ring.

'What do you want, Max?' he said.

'I want justice,' I said. 'And I want the truth. And I want it to be over.'

He fixed me with his politician's look – that look that suddenly saw you, the look that endlessly flattered you, the look that saw you in your true light for the first time.

'And I want what you want,' he said.

'The abuse started as soon as we arrived,' King said. 'Mental abuse before the sexual abuse. "Shakespeare is here, T. E. Lawrence is here, and you are here because you are nothing, you are specks of dirt on my shoes". And then the building up – feeling you were special, almost acolytes – by this God-like and punitive father figure who knew everything there was to know about history, art, literature, war and the ways of the flesh. We were thirteen years old! There was, shall we say, a disparity of power. We wanted to please him. My God – we wanted that more than anything in the world.'

The grey ribbon of motorway hummed and unfurled ahead of me, eating up the miles. I let him talk.

'And he gave us all what we were looking for. The insecure – Adam, Salman – were made to feel as if they belonged, as if they were part of a family, a country, a secret world. The strong – Hugo, Ned, Guy – were made to feel they were clever. The exceptional – James, of course – were made to feel that they were touched by God. And he told us we were special, and he taught us to sneer at the rest of the world, and he talked of beauty and truth as he put us in his mouth.'

He was silent for miles.

'I bailed out,' King said eventually. 'I don't know why it was possible for me and not the others. Some basic survival instinct I had and they lacked. They were all exceptional boys, in their own way. James – James was brilliant, truly gifted. Adam was a child prodigy. Hugo was the school's athlete. Guy – Piggy – was a force of nature. And Salman – Salman was so touching, trying so hard to fit in, so determined, so much more English than the rest of us. And everyone loved Ned. Ned was *good*.'

'Why did you throw the glass at his face?'

'They were getting older. It was no longer enough to perform sexual acts on the Head Master in his study and then sit down for a chapter of *The Seven Pillars of Wisdom*. They were curious, they were growing boys. Hugo and Guy had been caught in town with a couple of local girls. Women – grown women – went wild at the sight of James.' He laughed. 'And Piggy was masturbating himself into a coma every night.' He chewed his bottom lip. 'It was a world without women. So he told them that he would find them one. A woman. A girl. And let them see how little they were missing.'

'What did your brother tell you about the girl?'

'He told me she was being given as a special treat.' A pause. 'Which was the exact moment I threw the glass at Ned's face. And after that, he told me nothing.'

I turned off the motorway. In the distance, across the empty fields, you could already see the black towers of Potter's Field.

The boy was small for his age and he wore a Potter's Field school blazer over his fencing whites. He sat on the steps of the main building, pushing back his mop of dark hair as he stared at the paperback in his hands.

'Any good?' Ben King said.

The boy looked up, startled. 'Sir?'

'Book any good?'

King held out his hand and the boy passed him the paperback, standing up as he did so, self-consciously smoothing his green and purple blazer.

'*The Seven Pillars of Wisdom* by T. E. Lawrence,' King said. He opened it up and read, as if to himself. '"But at last Dahoum drew me: 'Come and smell the very sweetest scent of all,' and we went into the main lodging, to the gaping window sockets of its eastern face, and there drank with open mouths of the effortless, empty, eddyless wind of the desert, throbbing past." I read this one when I was your age. How you getting on with it?'

'Just started it, sir. Pretty good stuff, sir.'

King nodded at him. 'Waiting to see the Master?'

'Sir.'

'Private lesson today?'

A red flush flooded the boy's pale face. 'Yes, sir. Every Saturday morning this half. Immediately after fencing club.'

King handed the boy his book. 'Lesson's cancelled.'

'Sir?'

'Go back to your house. Practise your lunge and parry. Do your prep. Write to your mother.'

The boy looked doubtful.

King clapped his hands once. 'Go on then!'

The boy went, and we climbed the stairs to the Head Master's rooms.

Peregrine Waugh answered the door in a plain white kimono. His bliss-heavy eyes took a moment to focus. A smile leapt to his face at the sight of Ben King and died when he saw me.

'Ah,' he said.

We followed him inside. Heavy brocade curtains, pulled shut at noon. A thick fug of smoke from whatever had been in the water pipe that sat unlit on an oak desk. Piles of books everywhere.

'To what do I owe—'

'Actually we've come here for the truth, Perry,' King told him. 'Finally.'

I couldn't breathe in this place. I pulled back the curtains, opened the windows as wide as they would go. On the playing fields, there was the First XV playing rugby against another school watched by a scattering of pupils and two sports masters, and more boys in bright training bibs carrying cones and five-a-side nets to the football pitch. Their shouts and laughter drifted up to me.

'The truth? You wouldn't dare! Think of your career, Benjamin. The Right Honourable Member for . . . what's the name of that dreary little suburb you represent? It's slipped my mind.'

'Hillingdon North,' King said.

Waugh dropped backwards on to a red velvet sofa, pulling primly at his kimono as one hairy leg with the dimensions of a small tree popped into view. And then, again, the savagery of the despot who has no experience of being challenged: 'You would not dare.'

'The world is changing, Perry,' King said calmly.

'Really?' Waugh said. 'How unfortunate.'

'It is for you, Perry. Because we're finally learning not to despise the victims of abuse.' He let it sink in. 'You broke a bond of trust. You abused the children in your care.'

'Genius makes its own rules.'

King shook his head. 'If you have a genius, Perry, then it is for destroying the lives of children. How many would you say? Over the years.'

'Ratting me out, are you, Benjamin? You little snitch. You little shit. You *grass*. Is that the correct term? Everybody hates a tell-tale, King.'

'Hundreds?'

'Oh, more. Thousands. An *MP*.' Waugh laughed. 'A *politician*. And I wanted greatness for you! Remember?' Measuring the air with a languid hand. 'The good old days. "Shakespeare is here. T. E. Lawrence is here. And you boys are here."'

'Oh, Perry,' King said. 'Then where does that leave you?'

I picked up the pipe and breathed in, inhaling something that stank like a curry made of gasoline and flowers. A heavy, musky, strangely beautiful smell. I had never smelled it before. I had only heard tales.

'Opium?' I said.

Waugh sniffed. 'The honey of the gods,' he said, smiling to reveal a jumble of crumbling teeth, like the mouth of an elderly weasel. 'The keys of paradise. The gardens of gold. "Boy – as you love me – I charge you to fold – pipe over pipe into gardens of gold". Did you ever read Aleister Crowley, detective? No? Not your *thing*?'

I crossed the room.

'What happened to the girl?' I said.

The Head Master looked genuinely perplexed. 'I thought we were talking about *the boys*. I thought that's what you were going to arrest me for. *The boys*. I thought that's why I was being thrown to the baying mob. The thousands of *boys*. What bloody girl?'

The open palm of my hand cracked against his cheek.

'Ouch,' he said, recoiling as if I had hurt feelings more than flesh. 'That was very painful.'

'Anya Bauer,' I said. 'German. Blonde. Pretty. Around fifteen years old when she passed through your hands some twenty years ago.'

'Oh,' he said. '*That* girl.' His eyes darted across the floor. Then he closed them. 'She rests. She sleeps. Perchance to dream.'

'Where?' I said.

He was looking at Ben King.

'What do you expect me to *do*, Benjamin? Beg for forgiveness? Seek counselling? Repent my sins?'

'What would the Romans have recommended, Perry?' King said. 'Or the Greeks? Or T. E. Lawrence?'

'I don't know. A cup of tea and a nice lie down?'

I slapped him again. Harder this time, leaving my red mark livid on his skull-like head.

'Where?' I said.

'With the *dogs*,' he said. 'With the bloody *dogs*.'

'The dogs?'

'You've hurt me now,' he said, edging away from me, gathering his kimono in his long bony fingers. 'Truly. I'm very upset. Police brutality.' And then he began to snivel with self-pity. He turned to King, pleading. 'May I change? Before we leave? Ben?'

'Look at me,' I said quietly.

Waugh looked at me.

'What did you do to her?' I said.

He gathered the neck of his kimono. 'I never touched the little tart!' he said. 'Not until it was time to put her down. Nobody else had the stomach for it.'

King was looking at me, struggling to breathe.

'My God,' he said, white-faced with shock. 'My God.'

'Your keys,' I said to Waugh. 'I need all the keys to this place. Move!'

He moved stiffly across to his desk, rummaged for a while in a drawer then gave me two sets of keys. One was a little domestic set for Waugh's front door and car. The other could have been a gaoler's keys from a fairy tale, perhaps two dozen of every shape and age on a rust-flecked metal hoop – apparently the means of access to every door in Potter's Field.

When I had double-locked them inside Waugh's rooms I stuffed both sets of keys in my pockets and went quickly down to the chapel and round the back to the old graveyard.

I saw now, and for the first time, that there were many gravestones so old that time and weather had erased every word of their epitaphs. Their blank faces stared back at me. My pace slowed and faltered when I saw what someone had done to the tomb of Henry's dogs.

I could see it through the ancient trees and the rusting iron railings that guarded the grander tombs; I could see it quite clearly waiting for me on the far side of the leaning headstones and the forest of crosses and the cracked grey vaults. Watched by the sightless eyes of stone angels, I walked towards a great splash of red and black.

Poppies.

Someone had completely covered the tomb of King Henry VIII's dogs with poppies.

There were poppies in the shape of a cross, and poppies in round wreaths of every size, the wreaths of old soldiers and young children, all of them coming apart after spending long winter weeks out in the elements resting against monuments to the glorious dead.

And there were single poppies that had come astray from the wreaths, or perhaps been worn for that week of remembrance in November and then discarded.

Where had they all come from? Some must have been collected from the war memorial at Potter's Field, but others must have come from war memorials in the town itself, and in surrounding towns.

My vision filled with the red and black of the poppies, and even as my mind raced to understand, their message was clear.

You are never forgotten.

Fighting back an overwhelming urge to turn and run away,

I pulled out my phone and called Elsa Olsen, reaching her voicemail.

'Elsa,' I said. 'It's me, Wolfe. Sorry – Saturday, and all that.' I knelt by the tomb, touched the stone beneath the poppies, so suddenly and unexpectedly cold that it made my blood shiver. 'And I'll clear this with Whitestone and Swire as soon as I hang up, but I wanted you to be the first to know.' I picked up a single poppy and held it in my hand. 'I need an exhumation certificate.'

There was a red Lexus parked outside the main building. King's PA, Siri Voss, sat in the driver's seat tapping away on a phone. She got out when she saw me, wearing jeans and leather jacket, off duty now, her quick smile changing to a frown of concern.

'You all right?'

'Sorry,' I said, confused. 'What are you doing here?'

'I'm Mr King's ride back into town,' she said. 'He called me. He doesn't want to waste your time, or police resources.' Her hand was on my arm. 'Can I get you anything?'

'I have to go,' I said. 'Upstairs.'

'Of course.' She hesitated. 'When you have a chance – when things are better – when this ghastly business is over – I would love to talk to you. Mr King wants to start a charity in the name of your late colleague, DCI Mallory. A fund for the families of policemen killed in the line of duty. Is that something you would be interested in?'

Her hand was on my arm again. It was a strange touch. It stayed there a little too long, yet somehow not long enough.

'How's Mrs Mallory coping?' she tried. 'How's Margaret?'

'I don't know,' I said, and felt a stab of real shame.

She smiled and fell in behind me as I climbed the stairs and made my way to the Head Master's rooms. Ben King was sitting at Waugh's desk, his head in his hands, and when he looked up I saw the tears on his face.

'I knew that boy,' he said. 'The boy outside. I knew that boy. Because he was me. And he was Ned. And he was all of us.'

Siri flew to his side.

'Where is he?' I said, but King was good for nothing now, the pretty PA rocking him like a child as he wept.

I moved quickly through the rooms, a feeling of dread rising in my stomach.

And then I saw the water coming from under the bathroom door.

It was locked from inside so I slammed my shoulder into it – nothing. And again. Nothing.

The water was through my shoes and soaking my feet. I felt an icy calm descend on me as I remembered how to open a locked door quickly. I took a step back to give myself room and kicked the lock as hard as I could. The door flew open with a crack of metal and wood and I saw one of Waugh's long white arms hanging over the side of the bath, fresh blood pouring from the open veins on his wrists, staining the side of the bathtub and the white tiles of the floor with long crimson streaks.

There were soft white towels on heated rails and in little piles stacked neatly under the sink. I snatched them up and, sliding on the sopping floor, pressed them against his open wrists, and tied them tight around his limp white arms, and then threw them aside and started all over again when, in what seemed like seconds, his blood soaked through.

I was screaming and cursing and calling for help as I pressed the towels against the open veins of Peregrine Waugh. It was only when I ran out of towels that I saw the lifeblood had drained from his body, that his eyes were staring at the ceiling without seeing. I stood there with no breath and no strength to move until I finally remembered to turn off the hot and cold running water.

In the sudden silence the only sound was the boys down on the playing fields and, from the room behind me, the subdued sobbing of a grown man.

'Open it up,' DCI Whitestone said.

By now the December night was cold and black but the lamps of the SOCOs encircled the tomb and drenched it in blazing light. A bitter wind whipped through the graveyard, rustling dead leaves and the poppies that someone had swept from the grave.

A forklift truck was slightly tilted on the slope of the old graveyard, and it seemed to rock dangerously as its long metal fork eased beneath the grey stone of Henry's tomb.

The Murder Investigation Team from West End Central stood just behind the SOCOs, their mufti evidence of their interrupted weekends. Whitestone was in a parka thrown over jeans and T-shirt, as if she had come straight from home. Gane was in a tracksuit, as if he had come straight from the gym. And Edie Wren was in a short dress and killer heels and complicated hair, as if she had come straight from seeing her married man, or maybe trying to forget about him.

I saw the chief super exchanging words with Sergeant Lane of Potter's Field, their faces ghost-like in the fierce artificial light.

And then I looked back at the tomb as the wheels of the bulldozer fought for purchase in the soft soil. All at once the great slab of stone came away with the crack of torn granite. It rose in the air, clumps of dirt and cement falling away, and the grave was suddenly open.

A dozen officers in protective clothing moved quickly forward, and there were shouts and groans and protests as they heaved the lid of the tomb on its side and eased it up against an ancient oak. The white-suited SOCOs and the uniformed officers edged forward, but the grave was pitch black, buried in the darkness.

Somebody adjusted a light.

And there in the earth were the small bones of perhaps a dozen spaniels, their legs as thin as fish bones, their skulls the size of tennis balls, locked for eternity in the embrace of what were unmistakably human remains.

34

Natasha came down The Broadwalk in Regent's Park, her perfect face impassive behind dark glasses, long of hair and arms and legs, the little Pekingese-Chihuahua cross trotting by her side with a stick in its mouth, and she looked like the one for me.

It was sixty hours since we'd found the lonely bones of Anya Bauer. I had not slept and I had not eaten since we'd opened the grave, but after taking Scout to school on the third morning I knew that I desperately needed to do both. You can go without food and sleep for three nights and then you begin to fall apart. A single parent can't afford to fall apart.

Then I saw Natasha coming towards me as I was finishing my second bacon sandwich at a table outside The Honest Sausage, and I saw that I needed her even more.

'My stalker,' she said.

'The merry widow,' I said. 'Sorry.'

'No daughter? No dog?'

I looked under the table. 'I knew I'd forgotten something.'

'Too bad,' she said. 'I like your dog and daughter.'

Susan had abandoned her stick and was snuffling at my hand.

'They like you,' I said, wondering if it was too much. 'My daughter and my dog.'

'I can't think why.'

'Me neither.'

She indicated the little Pekingese-Chihuahua cross who was eating out of my empty hand.

'I didn't know Susan cared for you.'

'Nothing to do with me. Everything to do with my bacon sandwich.'

Natasha took off her dark glasses. She seemed younger than I remembered, and not quite as tough as she wanted to be.

'Listen,' she said.

Later, as we lay side by side, and I knew her for the first time, my hands moved across those long limbs and skin that was as white and unbroken as snow. And I remembered that I had seen her naked body once before, long ago, the first time we met.

She kissed my mouth and read my thoughts, and the traffic down on Marylebone High Street seemed to be coming from some other world. She held my hands and made me feel her, made me know her properly, made me understand what had changed.

The bruises were gone.

'I healed,' Natasha said.

We loved and slept the day away.

I had not slept by someone's side for a long time. It was a delicious feeling, a private world of warmth and safety and longing. But then, too soon, it was time for me to go.

I slipped out of the sheets, and the dog at the foot of the bed stirred with annoyance and then went back to sleep.

Natasha was half awake, and I sat by her side and smoothed her hair and very softly ran my hands over the smooth warmth of her skin and all of that seemed to make her more sleepy and smiley.

'Oh, come back to bed,' she said. 'Don't make me call the cops.'

I kissed her arm.

'I have to pick up my daughter.'

'Then come back tonight. Both of you. I'm not a cook but there are some great restaurants round here. What does Scout like?'

'We have to do something tonight. Family stuff.'

She hugged me.

'OK,' she said, waking up a bit now, the real world creeping into this secret room. 'I know you're a father. I know a dad has to do what a dad has to do, right?'

I kissed her cheek, her neck, her mouth.

'Right,' I said.

'But we'll work it out,' she said, and I believed her.

I parked the X5 outside a terraced house on a quiet street in Pimlico.

Scout was in the passenger seat, holding Stan and a bouquet of white flowers that was almost as big as her – lilies and roses and flowers that neither of us knew the name of.

Bringing flowers always felt like an imposition to me. A vase had to be found. Stems cut, water added, topped up at regular intervals, and one week later the dead flowers had to be thrown out, the stinking green water poured away, the vase washed clean.

It felt like you were asking a lot of someone when you gave them flowers.

Then Scout grinned at me as we got out of the car – a new

smile, a gappy smile, because she had lost two teeth at the bottom, the first of her milk teeth to go – and I knew the flowers didn't matter a damn. What mattered was her, and us, and knowing that coming here was the right thing to do.

Scout rang the bell. Stan barked once, then again, his feathery tail revolving with excitement. From beyond the door's frosted glass I heard the excited yap of a West Highland Terrier.

Then I saw the shape of Mrs Margaret Mallory coming down the hall, and the outline of her face through the frosted glass, and the start of her smile.

35

Soho was our canteen.

It meant that odd, unexpected couples were sometimes seen sharing a meal together in the backstreet restaurants.

PC Billy Greene and Dr Stephen were in a corner table of the Siam Café on Frith Street. Greene's hands were no longer bandaged. He was in uniform. I was about to join them when I realised that this was not a chance encounter. This was therapy.

'Please,' Dr Stephen said. 'Our fifty minutes are just about up. So you're no longer suspended, Max?'

I shook my head. 'One day you're the cock of the walk and the next you're a feather duster,' I said. 'Or is it the other way round?'

I joined them.

'You found the missing girl,' Dr Stephen said.

I nodded. 'We just got the results of the forensic autopsy from Elsa Olsen. Identified her body from dental records sent over from Germany. Cause of death was a broken neck. Peregrine Waugh snapped Anya Bauer's neck like she was some kind of wounded animal.'

'And twenty years later,' Greene said, 'he opens up his veins.'

'And gets off too lightly,' I said. 'I wanted to see him in court. I wanted to see him in a cell.'

We were silent until I nodded at Greene's hands.

'How are you doing, Billy?'

'Doing good,' he said. 'The pain is easing off. The physio is coming along. My fingers are working better, although the right hand is still a bit stiff. The more exercises I do, the better I feel.'

The waitress brought a plate of fruit. I saw that Greene's hands were stained black with burns, and that he held a fork with difficulty.

'Stick with it, Billy,' I said. 'Stick with all of it.'

But he didn't want my pity.

When a piece of mango slipped from his fork and slid across the table, he stabbed at it repeatedly until he finally speared it. He popped the mango in his mouth and laughed.

'Lunch takes a bit longer,' he said.

Dr Stephen stared at his plate and then back at Greene.

'Funny thing is, they gave me sick leave,' Greene said. 'After the night we got Bob. And I went to Vegas – because I always fancied Vegas. So I flew to Vegas.' He paused dramatically. 'But they wouldn't let me in!'

Dr Stephen had obviously heard the anecdote before. I had the impression that Greene had told the story many times, and that his fellow uniformed policemen had enjoyed the punchline. It was the kind of punchline that coppers would find amusing.'They wouldn't let you in?' I said. 'You mean, into the country? When you landed?'

He nodded, still looking cheery, still seeing the funny side and assuming that I would see it too.

'The Americans fingerprint everyone when they pass through immigration – part of the tightened security after 9/11, right?'

I shrugged. 'OK.'

Greene held up his hands like it was a conjuring trick. 'And guess who doesn't have fingerprints any more! They put me on the first flight home!'

I stared at Billy Greene's blackened hands and I kept on staring until he placed them on his lap, below the table, where I could no longer see them.

'Harry Jackson,' said Sergeant John Caine. 'People tend to walk right past old Harry Jackson.'

It was true.

The Black Museum was so full of gory artefacts, from the endless variety of firearms and blades that had claimed policemen's lives to the pots and pans in which serial killers had cooked the flesh of their victims, that it was easy to walk past the small, unassuming display devoted to Harry Jackson.

There wasn't much. A glass frame containing a short newspaper clipping, yellow with age. Two typewritten paragraphs of explanation.

And the whorls of a dead man's thumbprint.

'Harry Jackson was the first man to be convicted in England because of fingerprint evidence,' Sergeant Caine said. 'Harry was a burglar. In the summer of 1902 he climbed through a window in Denmark Hill, stole some billiard balls and left his thumbprint in wet paint on the windowsill.' Sergeant Caine chuckled. 'Silly bugger. He got seven years.'

I peered closer at the newspaper clipping. It was a letter to *The Times*, signed by someone calling himself A Disgusted Magistrate.

> Sir, Scotland Yard, once known as the world's finest police organisation, will be the laughing stock of Europe if it insists on trying to trace criminals by the odd ridges on their skins.

'Eight years later, the rest of the world was catching up,' said Caine. 'Thomas Jennings of Chicago became the first person in America to be convicted by fingerprint evidence.'

'Another burglar?'

'No – Jennings was a murderer. And soon the French were at it, nicking a reprobate by the name of Vincenzo Perugia – doesn't sound very French, does he? – on the basis of a left thumbprint.'

'What had he done?'

'He stole the Mona Lisa from the Louvre. Took the Frogs two years to find him because they only had his right thumbprint on file. I hear you solved your case. DCI Mallory would be very happy.'

I nodded, staring at Harry Jackson's thumbprint.

'Twenty years ago, a girl called Anya Bauer was the victim of a gang rape at Potter's Field,' I said. 'The Head Master, Peregrine Waugh, killed her to stop her talking. Bob the Butcher – Ian Peck – cut the throats of the men who had been the boys who attacked Anya. We got two murderers. We got their motives. The pieces all fit. The trouble is, John, when you look at them, those pieces don't make much sense.'

'Why not?'

'Peck is going to get life for Mallory's murder,' I said. 'And his prints were everywhere in his parents' house.'

'I heard.'

'But they were not at the murder scenes of Hugo Buck, Adam Jones and Guy Philips, the other murders he confessed to. No prints there. Not even a partial. Not even a glove print.'

'Yes,' said Sergeant Caine. 'I heard that, too.'

'But why would he lie?' I said. 'Why would Ian Peck confess to murders that he didn't commit?'

'Because he's nobody,' said the keeper of the Black Museum. 'And he wants to be somebody. They're all the same. Serial killers – you think they're criminal masterminds? They're not Hannibal Lecter, Max! They're all just grubby little men. They're all psychopathic losers. Who are they? Albert DeSalvo, Peter Sutcliffe and Ian Peck. They're germs, they're insects. But their crimes make them the Boston Strangler, the Yorkshire Ripper and Bob the Butcher. It wouldn't surprise me if Bob the Butcher is standing up for murders that he didn't do. It's what Albert DeSalvo did. He wasn't even in jail for killing those thirteen women in Boston. He was in jail for rape. That's the kind of vicious little woman-hating creep we're talking about. But then he becomes the Boston Strangler and suddenly you've got Tony Curtis playing you in a movie.'

I was still staring at Harry Jackson's thumbprint.

'No prints,' I said. 'Who has no prints, John?'

Sergeant John Caine of the Black Museum reached out and straightened the frame on his neglected Harry Jackson display.

'Only a man with no hands, Max,' he said.

36

Midnight on the school playing fields, the black silhouette of Potter's Field behind me, a jumble of towers and spires and architecture from the last five centuries.

Blink your eye and a hundred years go by.

It felt like the world was dead.

I checked my phone one last time – no new calls, although I had left urgent messages for Whitestone, Gane and Wren on my drive out here – and then began across the playing fields.

The wind whistled through the trees in the distant woods and I shuddered, as if the eyes of Anya Bauer were watching me. Soon you will be at rest, I thought. Soon you will be at peace at last.

There were no lights on in the little stone cottage as I felt in my pocket for the Head Master's keys, the large set that looked like they were from a fairy tale, holding the key to every lock in every door in Potter's Field.

There were two locks on the front door of the cottage. A standard Yale lock and a flush bolt. Nothing complicated. But I still had to try a dozen keys before the door swung silently open and I stepped inside.

I stood there listening for a moment, my eyes adjusting to the light, slowing my breath, and then I quietly eased the door shut.

On the table there was an empty teacup, a copy of the local newspaper and a .410 shotgun.

It was a small cottage. A servant's quarters given a quick coat of rural comfort. To the left was the bedroom and the bathroom, both doors shut. To the right the small living area ran into an L-shaped kitchen only large enough for one person at a time.

I stood there, seeing in the darkness now, but not knowing what I was looking for until I glimpsed it under the sink.

I moved quickly to the little kitchen, crouched down and pulled the door all the way open. An ancient leather bag was sitting with the bleach and disinfectant and insecticide. Its dark brown cowhide was worn and cracked, the brass hardware and locks blackened with rust.

But somehow you knew it was still being used.

As something very small scuttled away in the skirting board, I reached in and took out the worn-leather Gladstone bag.

A Murder Bag.

I turned to carry the bag back to the living space and there he was, old Len Zukov, sitting at the table with the .410 shotgun in his arthritic hands.

I held up the bag for his inspection, as if he had asked me to retrieve it.

'Your bag, Len?'

He sniffed. 'Of course.'

I set it on the table, saying nothing.

'You don't believe me,' he said, the accent forever caught somewhere between rural England and his Russian homeland. 'You never believe a word I say, do you?'

I watched his hands on the .410. Despite his condition the shotgun rested easily in his strong arms and those locked, arthritic fists. He was more comfortable than I had ever seen him. And I looked towards the door, wondering if the .410 was even loaded, and how much mobility he needed in his fingers to pull the trigger.

Not much, I thought. The .410 is the lightest shotgun, often used for teaching children how to shoot.

'Sit down now,' he said, interrupting my calculations.

'My colleagues will be here soon,' I said, hearing the doubt in my voice.

He liked that. 'Perhaps not soon enough,' he said. 'I told you to sit down.'

I remained standing.

'You didn't come forward to claim the body,' I said. 'Anya's body, Len. Anya Bauer. We know it was her remains in the grave with the dogs. No doubt about it. We obtained dental records from Germany. What stopped you coming forward and claiming the body? What were you afraid of? You knew her, Len.'

'Did you ever see what a shotgun does to a man's face?' he said.

I joined him at the table. There were only two chairs. He wasn't one for doing a lot of socialising.

'Poking around in the night,' he said, shaking his head. 'What you looking for?' He indicated the Gladstone bag that I had placed on the table. 'That old thing?'

'Not you,' I said. 'I'm not looking for you, Len.'

'Maybe you should be,' he said, and he shifted the shotgun in his paralysed hands.

'Why don't you put the gun down, Len. Then we can talk.'

He gripped the .410 tighter.

'You asked me how I came here,' he said. 'I came with the

soldiers. I rode on the back of a T-34. Do you know the T-34?'

'It was a tank in the war. The Second World War. The Great Patriotic War, you call it. The T-34 was a Russian tank.'

'No,' he said. '*The* Russian tank. The T-34 was *the* Russian tank. The tank that bought your freedom. The tank that paid for your democracy. Britain, America. You said once that I was too young for the war. You were right. I was eleven years old, too young for a war of annihilation. The Germans were coming and I was in the fields and I ran away. Then the Red Army took our town and I returned. But the town was not there any more. Because we were sub-humans. To them. You understand? My mother. My father. My grandmother. My sisters. Sub-humans. I never cried so much as at that time. The last days of my childhood passed in this way.'

He was silent, lost in memory, or listening to the night.

'I went west with our soldiers,' he said. 'West, west, west. The First Belorussian. The *frontoviki* – frontline troops. Through a world in ruins. Do you know why they kept me? Because I had almost the same name as their leader. General Georgy Zhukov. What do you call it?'

'A mascot,' I said.

'A mascot. I wanted to live. I wanted to stay alive. But I wanted to see Germany destroyed. I closed my heart to pity.' He shook his head with wonder. 'They had so much! The Germans were so rich! The farms, the animals – why did they come to us when they already had so much?'

'They wanted more, Len,' I said soothingly. 'They wanted the world. It was madness.'

But he wasn't listening to me now.

'Our soldiers wanted women,' he said. '"*Frau, frau, frau!*"

I wanted something else. For my dead family. For my grandparents. For my sisters. For my parents. For my gone family. Our *frontoviki* placed me inside a cellar. One by one, a dozen Waffen-SS men who had destroyed their papers and ripped off their badges were sent inside. I could hear them screaming on the other side of the door. "*Nix SS! Nix SS!*" Our soldiers had showed me what to do. You know? The knife through the neck, then pull, then kick the Nazi down the stairs. A dozen of them. So, you see an old man. But you're looking at a killer.'

We stared at each other.

'I think it's been a while since you killed anyone,' I said quietly. 'I think it's been a lifetime.'

He pointed the .410 at my face.

'You hate the Germans,' I said. 'But Anya Bauer was German, wasn't she? And you didn't hate Anya, did you? You loved her.'

'Anya's father was German,' he said. 'But her mother was Russian. My daughter.'

'And Anya came to stay with you when she was fifteen years old. Your granddaughter came to stay with you at Potter's Field. What was that? A summer holiday? Trouble at home? A bit of both? I bet there was some kind of trouble at home, wasn't there?'

'Stop talking about her,' he said.

His voice flat and hard, levelling the .410 at my chest, giving himself a bigger target.

'And then one day Anya was gone,' I said. 'Somewhere between a missing person and a lost contact. And you didn't know what happened – or maybe you suspected, but you were never sure until you saw what was in Henry's grave. When it was collapsing. When it was falling to bits. You saw her bones, didn't you? Human bones in there with the bones of Henry's dogs. Or maybe you saw them later, when the grave was being renovated. But at some point you saw inside the grave and you knew it had to be Anya.'

'Shut up now,' he said, the shotgun moving between my face and my chest.

'And you put it all together,' I continued. 'Anya coming to stay. The boys who were sniffing around. Hugo Buck and his little gang. And then Anya gone – for a night, and then a year, and then for ever. Were there rumours, Len? Did you hear anything about what Peregrine Waugh's followers had done to some girl? Were they afraid of the truth coming out? There must have been talk after James Sutcliffe killed himself – or pretended to. Somehow you suddenly knew what had happened to her – what they had done. And you drew up a list of the boys who must have been in that room when Waugh broke her neck and they treated your beautiful girl like something to be thrown away. And you wanted revenge. Is that what happened?'

The .410 seemed to seek out my heart, and stay there, steady at last in his paralysed hands.

'What matters,' he said, 'what matters is that I avenged her. Do you believe me at last?'

'I believe all of it, Len,' I said. 'I truly do. Except the last part. I don't believe that you've killed anyone since you were a boy.'

The door opened and Tom Monk came in, an old army jacket slung over jeans, carrying a twelve-bore shotgun and a lifeless brace of rabbits. Behind the terrible burns on his ruined face I saw his eyes widen and grow cold.

'Ah,' he said. 'I was wondering when you might turn up.'

'A young policeman I know burned his hands when we

collared Bob the Butcher,' I said. 'A brave young lad called Billy Greene. He was going to spend his sick leave in Las Vegas. Champagne cocktails by the pool in Caesar's, chorus girls, all that.'

'Very nice,' Monk said.

'But guess what? They wouldn't let him in. Sent Billy straight back to Gatwick. Because the Americans fingerprint everyone at the border now. And they couldn't get any prints off him.'

Monk held up his hands, a mocking gesture of surrender. And for the first time I saw that the reason we could never find any prints at the crime scenes was because the flesh on his hands was as destroyed as the flesh on his face.

'Remind me to steer clear of Las Vegas,' he said.

'So what was in it for you, Tom?' I said. 'Keeping your hand in? Spot of vigilante work? Never kicked the killing habit?'

He stopped smiling.

'Justice,' he said.

I tried to smile but my mouth merely twisted, and my heart began to hammer in my chest as I realised what was going to happen to me tonight.

'You're right,' he said. 'It's a joke. How can there be justice in a land where they let the bravest and the best sleep on the streets until they work up the nerve to top themselves?'

'So you cut the throats of Hugo Buck and Adam Jones,' I said. 'Botched it with Piggy Philips, didn't you?'

'Oh, I don't know,' he said. 'I don't think he's going to be taking double games for a while, do you?'

'But you missed out on Captain King, didn't you? The Taliban beat you to it.'

Monk's mask-like face clenched with sudden fury. 'You're

just another stupid policeman. Captain King was a brave man. A warrior. One more lion led by yet more donkeys. Same story in this country for a hundred years.' He leaned against the door and shook his head. 'Captain Ned King was never on my list.'

'What about Salman Khan?' I said. 'Was he still alive when that big house went up in flames? Or did you break in there, open up his throat and then torch the place?'

'One of his kids had a motorbike,' Monk said. 'Have you ever heard of such a thing? A child with his own little motorbike? I served my country for ten years and all I've got is a second-hand bicycle.'

'What outfit were you with in Afghanistan, Tom?'

'I told you. The Royal Green Jackets.'

'I don't think so. You're too handy with a knife. Too good at creeping around, unarmed combat and covering your tracks. I reckon you were with the Special Forces Support Group. Or maybe the SAS? Or the SBS?'

'You calling me a liar?'

I nodded.

'You going to cut my throat, Tom?' I said, knowing that was exactly what he was going to do.

'Should have done it when I had the chance the first time.'

I looked at the old man opposite me. 'You should have gone to the police, Len. If you wanted justice for your granddaughter. You should have come to us. Not waited for Rambo here to turn up.'

Monk laughed. 'Who was going to get justice for Anya? Or for Len here? The police? The courts? You? You with your soft judges and weak laws and tricky lawyers selling rich man's justice? You with your bad back!'

'Enough,' Len said.

And I turned my head just in time to see the old man shoot me in the chest.

The roar of the .410 split the air.

I was blown backwards and over and flat on my back with my head in the open fireplace, the deafening sound of the .410 fired in a tiny space still ringing somewhere deep inside my eardrums, and I was calling for Jesus and God to help me as my fingers scrabbled at my heart.

The excruciating pain of two cracked ribs beneath massive bruising told me that I was not yet dead.

The .410 shell had ripped a hole in my leather jacket and my T-shirt but had not passed through the lightweight CV1 body armour.

I kept calling for Jesus and God.

'You're better off shooting him in the head,' Monk said. 'I need to go home now.'

'Yes,' Len said. 'Go to them now. Go to your family. It is time. Your work here is done. Thank you, my beloved friend. Thank you, my brother.'

I struggled to sit up but the pain in the top half of my body held me down. I could not move.

Oh God . . . oh Jesus . . .

I realised that the chair I had been sitting on was underneath me, smashed to pieces.

I saw Zukov kiss Tom Monk hard on the mouth and I saw Monk leave the cottage without looking back.

Len shuffled off to his bedroom, and when he came back he had a box of shells with him. I saw him break the .410, laboriously push in a three-inch red shell, then snap it shut.

Oh God . . . oh Jesus . . .

He shuffled across to where I was lying and pointed the shotgun at my face.

Oh God . . . oh Jesus . . .

'No!'

Edie Wren was in the doorway.

Len Zukov swung the shotgun at her and paused.

'Please,' she said. 'What do you want? Talk to me. Please talk to me, sir.'

He looked at her face for a moment and then, as if in answer, he placed the shotgun on the floor and, half crouching, set the barrel under his chin.

I heard Edie scream and I heard the shotgun roar but then the darkness overwhelmed me and the night was black.

37

We drove back to the city. DCI Whitestone at the wheel of my X5. DI Gane beside her in the passenger seat. Edie Wren and me in the back. Every time I was drifting off, thinking I might steal some sleep, the road rushing under our wheels and the white-hot pain in my cracked ribs shoved me awake.

'Sergeant Tom Monk came back from Afghanistan and he never went home,' Whitestone said, her eyes not leaving the road ahead. 'I spoke to the people at Barrington Court. Monk returned from Helmand with a Conspicuous Gallantry Cross and third-degree burns on his face and hands. He spent a few months in an ICU and then went to Barrington Court for his final rehab. Treatment for his burns. Extensive physio. Therapy sessions with a psychoanalyst. The usual routine for a veteran with his injuries. When he had recovered, he stayed on helping out at Barrington Court. And they were glad for an extra pair of hands. Nobody seems to know what happened. But just before he was due to leave Barrington Court, Monk put on his dress uniform and had his photo taken at a small studio in Potter's Field High Street. Then he mailed the photo to his fiancée back in Stratford.'

Whitestone fell silent. I thought of the face that had been

burned beyond recognition, and I thought of his girl back home, seeing a posed photograph of the damage for the first time.

The road kept slipping past, lit by nothing but the high winter moon.

'Nobody knows if she ever wrote back. Or sent him a text, email or message on Facebook. Monk never talked about it. Maybe she told him that it was over. Maybe she never contacted him again and that told him all he needed to know. Who knows? But Monk never left Barrington Court. He stayed on – unpaid, unofficial, helping out with the rehab of other badly injured veterans. Taking the men to Potter's Field for exercise.'

'Where he met another old soldier,' I said. 'Len Zukov. The start of a beautiful friendship.'

'I understand why Len Zukov wanted payback for what they did to his granddaughter,' Wren said. 'And I get why his friend would want to help him. But – did Monk want to kill evil bastards? Or did he just want to kill somebody?'

Whitestone glanced at me in the rear-view mirror. I had no answers. All I knew was that the state had trained Monk to be a killer and in the end that was all he had left, and all he could do, all he could offer, even when the state wanted him to stop.

'Edie,' Whitestone said. 'Some stuff we never get to know.'

You could see the piercing blue lights of our cars cutting up the night from a mile away. They illuminated the sleek, futuristic buildings of the Olympic Park and the urban wasteland that surrounded them.

'Now Monk's returned to the place you go when you've run out of places to go,' Whitestone said. 'He's finally come home.'

* * *

In the shadow of Olympic Park, a dozen armed response vehicles surrounded a shabby block of flats that managed to be both modern and derelict. They were out of place in a neighbourhood where the buildings were either neat little flats and small houses that promised a nice life in the new East End, or they had been wiped from the face of the Earth. It looked like the surface of the moon after a few years of serious gentrification.

We lowered the windows of the X5 and dug out our warrant cards. Beyond the police tape you could hear the digital cackle of the Airwave radios, the occasional bark from one of the police dogs, and the shouts of officers who were pulled tight by nerves.

Armed officers waited between the ARVs, their Heckler & Koch assault rifles held at their favourite forty-five-degree angle, butt high and business end pointing down, sweating hard in all that kit despite the chill of the December night. They looked like the future.

Tom Monk was standing alone on a scrappy patch of grass outside the block of flats, looking up, his gaze unswerving. And I saw now that there were half a dozen Glock 17 pistols pointing at the back of his head.

They had evacuated most of the residents from the flats. In almost every window the only signs of life were the fairy lights of Christmas, twinkling, white and red and green.

A young woman appeared briefly in one window, a toddler under her arm, and then she was gone. But Monk kept looking up at her window, even after the light in the room had gone out.

'That's her,' said Edie Wren, and the tears on her face shone bright in the riot of flashing blue lights. 'That's Monk's family. That poor girl. That poor man.'

'No,' DCI Whitestone said. 'That's our killer. Let's nick the bastard.'

The armed officers stood aside as the K9 unit came forward with their German Shepherds. The handlers knelt by the flanks of their dogs, fingers scratching the back of those noble heads, whispering their final words of encouragement.

Monk turned at the sound of the dogs. His old army coat swung open and I saw his weapon sticking out of the lining, stuffed inside what looked like one of those big secret pockets that shoplifters use – the 12-bore shotgun that he had carried all the way from Potter's Field.

Then voices were shouting all around and someone screamed 'I have the shot!' and Whitestone said 'Take the shot!' and the crack of gunfire tore the night, ripped it wide open, shockingly loud, one single shot that was so stretched-out and jagged it made your heart leap, and Tom Monk was falling backwards, his head twisting sideways as if suddenly and savagely punched, the top of it flying away in a clump of blood and hair and skin and bone and brain, and then he was lying very still on the scrappy piece of grass looking like what he was now – a fallen British soldier.

I moved towards the lifeless body, any hatred I had felt for him suddenly turned to a sour kind of sadness; but I felt Whitestone's hand on my arm, making me wait, taking no more chances.

'Enough for one night, Max,' she said. 'It's almost Christmas.'

She gave the command and they let loose the dogs.

38

Sunday morning.

Scout sat at the window, waiting for her mother. Across the street the great meat market of Smithfield was closed for the weekend, the crowds all gone, and the white dome of St Paul's Cathedral rose above a scene of perfect stillness.

On TV, the MP for Hillingdon North was entering 10 Downing Street, Siri Voss one pace behind, cradling a thick file of papers. Ben King smiled shyly at the journalists who called out to him.

'Congratulations on the promotion! A few words, Minister?'

'The youngest Parliamentary Secretary to the Treasury in history – how does that feel?'

'What kind of Chief Whip are you going to be, Mr King? Are you going to put it about a bit? Are you going to give them some stick?'

There was a policeman on the door. King murmured good morning to him. The policeman touched his helmet in salute. Ben King and Siri Voss disappeared inside as a spasm of pain racked my lower back.

Stan was sleeping at Scout's feet. But as I flinched the dog stirred and stretched – downward-facing dog, then upward-facing dog – all the while watching me with those massive round eyes, as if to say *you must do the stretching every day of your life, don't you even know that?*

Or maybe he just wanted some food.

In the pocket of my jeans, my phone began to vibrate. Then it was still. And then it began to vibrate again. I took it out and read the message from Anne, and I thought, there is no greater stranger than someone we used to love.

'Angel,' I said to Scout, with a lightness that I did not feel. 'Your mother's not coming today. Something came up. I'm sorry.'

Scout watched me with impassive eyes.

'She's very busy,' my daughter said.

I nodded, and I could not tear my eyes from her as she went to the table and took out her box of pens and opened her drawing book. I walked over to her and watched her work for a bit. She was drawing Stan's head, and she had captured him very well. The bulging beauty of the eyes, the extravagant ears flowing like the hair of a girl in an old-fashioned painting, the nose like a squashed prune, the feathered glory of his tail.

I touched her hand and her eyes met mine.

'Scout,' I said, 'it's just you and me now. But we're all right, aren't we?'

She looked at her drawing and then back at me.

'Yes,' she said. 'We're all right.'

I breathed again.

'Scout?'

'What?'

'I'm very, very proud that you're my daughter.'

She got up and gave me an awkward embrace, her arm around my waist as I kissed her on top of her head. Then she broke off and went off to her bedroom, Stan trailing behind her, his tail up like a periscope.

I turned to the TV as Ben King came out of Number Ten and began walking towards the camera. Siri Voss was beside him, hugging her papers, but as they reached the camera she stepped aside with a smile, waiting for him just out of shot.

Ben King smiled. Then he cocked his head at the camera, and looked into it the way he had so often looked at me – a penetrating, lopsided look, disarmed and disarming, as if he saw something in you the rest of the world had yet to see.

Something glinted for a moment but I couldn't tell if the fragment of light was on the TV screen or just inside my head.

And then I realised that Ben King had a glass eye.

And I saw that what James Sutcliffe had claimed was true. Someone had lost an eye in that room twenty years ago – a small forfeit for a young girl's life. But it wasn't Hugo Buck.

How had I missed it?

You, I thought, as Ben King smiled for the cameras in Downing Street. *You*.

And I saw a vision of two boys at a breakfast table, twin brothers, arguing with a fury that neither of them had known before, identical in every way apart from their hearts, and one of the brothers threw a glass with full force at the other's face. And I knew it wasn't Ned who was in that basement room the night they stole Anya Bauer's life.

It was his brother, Ben.

'Daddy?' Scout said.

She was holding the junior boxing gloves I had bought her – one of those unsuccessful presents that parents so often buy for their children, when they still hold on to the vain hope that their mutual interests might possibly coincide; one of those presents that are admired for the sake of politeness and then tossed into a drawer, never to be seen again.

'I want to know how,' she said. 'Show me.'

I helped her to put on the gloves. They were the smallest size available and they were still comically enormous on her. But we did not smile. I held up my palms.

'When you throw a punch,' I said, 'it should be like catching a fly. You ever catch a fly?'

She shivered. 'I saw Stan catch a wasp once.'

'Well, think of that. The hand should snap back as fast as it snaps forward.'

I demonstrated, and then held up my palms again.

'You try.'

Scout frowned.

'I can't hit very hard,' she said.

I touched her shoulder.

'Angel,' I said. 'It's got nothing to do with how hard you can hit.'

Scout started punching.

Then suddenly there were just a few days to Christmas and there was the promise of snow in the grey city skies.

I sat in a dark school hall and I watched angels in bed sheets with sellotaped paper wings, five-year-old wise men with wonky cotton-wool beards, stuffed toys standing in for the animals in the manger in Bethlehem and, at the centre of it all, a grumpy sheep waving her small fist at the heavens.

'It's all right for the angels!' the grumpy sheep said bitterly. 'The angels can *fly* to the manger! But I must *walk*!'

The grumpy sheep – Scout under an old white rug superglued to an even older rucksack, her nose blackened with make-up – narrowed her eyes at the heavens.

'Why must I walk to the manger? It means nothing to me! I don't even want to see this baby they call Jesus.'

She regretted it in the end. On her knees in the centre of the stage, shaking her head as the wise men and angels milled around in the background.

'Oh *why* was I so grumpy! Why did I complain? I see clearly now! At last, I see it all.' She raised her head and stared out into the darkness. 'This is a special child!'

Mrs Mallory – Margaret – was sitting next to me and she reached across and squeezed my hand as I sat there in the darkness with all the other parents, choking down wild laughter, and the hot tears streaming down my face.

AUTHOR'S NOTE

The first grown-up piece of journalism I ever wrote – the first article that did not involve staying up all night with rock stars – was out of 27 Savile Row, London W1 – West End Central.

The young men and women I met there were among the finest people I have ever met. They are real, but this book, which roams freely about their place of work, is a work of fiction.

I have taken the liberty of using real life to give *The Murder Bag* some grit – for example, the Black Museum really is at Room 101, New Scotland Yard, and the 'From Hell' letter by someone claiming to be Jack the Ripper is quoted accurately from contemporary photographs.

The letter itself is said to be lost, and its location in this book is a product of the author's imagination.

Tony Parsons
September 2013

MAX WOLFE RETURNS IN 2015 . . .

the SlaughTer MAn

TONY PARSONS

CENTURY

Further information

In some cases, we have judged that a derivation is too long, too detailed, or too different in level for it to be included in the text. There are also topics that extend the material which are useful to have available but would also be too intrusive. We have moved both types of information to *Further information* sections at the end of the relevant chapter.

Appendices

Physical chemistry draws on a lot of background material, especially in mathematics and physics (and increasingly from biology). We have included a set of *Appendices* to provide a quick survey of some of the information that we draw on in the text.

CHECKLIST OF KEY IDEAS

You should now be familiar with the following concepts:

☐ 1 A system is classified as open, closed, or isolated.

☐ 2 The surroundings remain at constant temperature and either constant volume or constant pressure when processes occur in the system.

☐ 3 An exothermic process releases energy as heat, q, to the surroundings; an endothermic process absorbs energy as heat.

☐ 4 The work of expansion against constant external pressure is $w = -p_{ex}\Delta V$.

☐ 5 Maximum expansion work is achieved in a reversible change.

☐ 6 The work of reversible, isothermal expansion of a perfect gas is $w = -nRT\ln(V_f/V_i)$.

☐ 7 The change in internal energy may be calculated from $\Delta U = w + q$, where U is a state function.

☐ 8 The First Law of thermodynamics states that the internal energy of an isolated system is constant.

☐ 9 The enthalpy is defined as $H = U + pV$.

☐ 10 A change in internal energy is equal to the energy transferred as heat at constant volume ($\Delta U = q_V$); a change in enthalpy is equal to the energy transferred as heat at constant pressure ($\Delta H = q_p$).

☐ 11 The constant-volume heat capacity is the slope of the tangent to the graph of the internal energy of a constant-volume system plotted against temperature ($C_V = \Delta U/\Delta T$).

☐ 12 The constant-pressure heat capacity is the slope of the tangent to the graph of the enthalpy of a constant-pressure system plotted against temperature ($C_p = \Delta H/\Delta T$).

☐ 13 The molar constant-volume and constant-pressure heat capacities of a perfect gas are related by $C_{p,m} - C_{V,m} = R$.

Checklist of key ideas

Here we collect together the major concepts that we have introduced in the chapter. You might like to check off the box that precedes each entry when you feel that you are confident about the topic.

Mathematics support

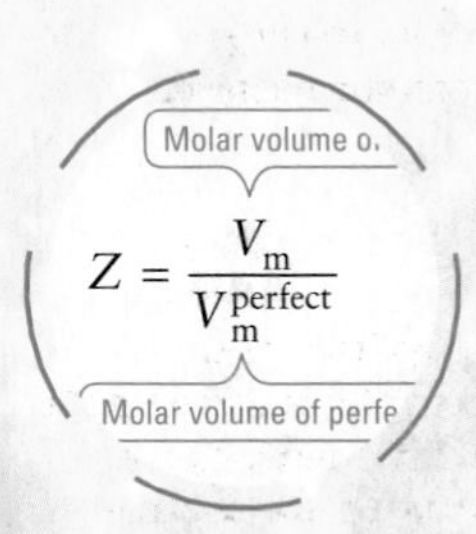

Bubbles

You often need to know how to develop a mathematical expression, but how do you go from one line to the next? A 'bubble' is a little reminder about the approximation that has been used, the terms that have been taken to be constant, the substitution of an expression, and so on.

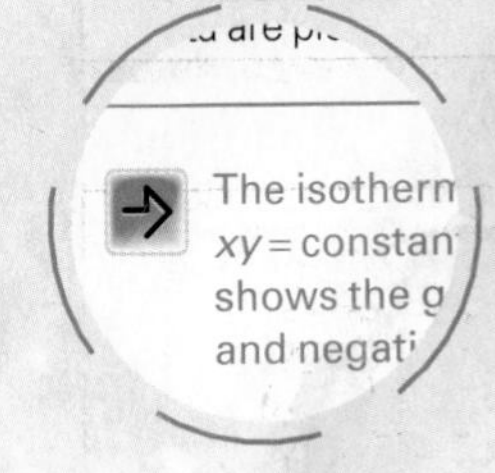

Mathematics commentaries

We often need to draw on a mathematical procedure, such as the expansion of a function; a *Mathematics commentary* is a quick reminder of the procedure. Don't forget Appendix 2 on mathematical procedures where some of these *Commentaries* are discussed greater length.

Problem solving

190 CHAPTER 8: CONSEQUENCES OF EQUILIBRIUM

and then, by taking negative common logarithms, to the **Henderson–Hasselbalch equation**

$$pH = pK_a - \log\frac{[\text{acid}]}{[\text{base}]} \qquad (8.11)$$

Example 8.5

Estimating the pH at an intermediate stage in a titration

Calculate the pH of the solution after the addition of 5.00 cm^3 of the titrant to the analyte in the titration described above.

Strategy The first step involves deciding the amount of OH^- ions added in the titrant, and then to use that amount to calculate the amount of CH_3COOH remaining. Note that because the ratio of acid to base molar concentrations occurs in eqn 8.11, the volume of solution cancels, and we can equate the ratio of concentrations to the ratio of amounts.

Solution The addition of 5.00 cm^3, or 5.00×10^{-3} dm^3 (because 1 $cm^3 = 10^{-3}$ dm^3), of titrant corresponds to the addition of

$$n_{OH^-} = (5.00 \times 10^{-3}\ dm^3) \times (0.200\ mol\ dm^{-3}) = 1.00 \times 10^{-3}\ mol$$

This amount of OH^- (1.00 mmol) converts 1.00 mmol CH_3COOH to the base $CH_3CO_2^-$. The initial amount of CH_3COOH in the analyte is

$$n_{CH_3COOH} = (25.00 \times 10^{-3}\ dm^3) \times (0.200\ mol\ dm^{-3}) = 2.50 \times 10^{-3}\ mol$$

so the amount remaining after the addition of titrant is 1.50 mmol. It then follows from the Henderson–Hasselbalch equation that

$$pH = 4.75 - \log\frac{1.50 \times 10^{-3}}{1.00 \times 10^{-3}} = 4.6$$

As expected, the addition of base has resulted in an increase in pH from 2.9. You should not take the value 4.6 too seriously because we have already pointed out that such calculations are approximate. However, it is important to note that the pH has increased from its initial acidic value.

Self-test 8.10

Calculate the pH after the addition of a further 5.00 cm^3 of titrant.

[Answer: 5.4]

Halfway to the stoichiometric point, when enough base has been added to neutralize half the acid, the concentrations of acid and base are equal and because log 1 = 0 the Henderson–Hasselbalch equation gives

$$pH = pK_a \qquad (8.12)$$

In the present titration, we see that at this stage of the titration, pH ≈ 4.75. Note from the pH curve in Fig. 8.4 how much more slowly the pH is changing compared with initially: this point will prove important shortly. Equation 8.12 implies that we can determine the pK_a of the acid directly from the pH of the mixture. Indeed, an approximate value of the pK_a may be calculated by recording the pH during a titration and then examining the record for the pH halfway to the stoichiometric point.

At the stoichiometric point, enough base has been added to convert all the acid to its base, so the solution consists—nominally—only of $CH_3CO_2^-$ ions. These ions are Brønsted bases, so we can expect the solution to be basic with a pH of well above 7. We have already seen how to estimate the pH of a solution of a weak base in terms of its concentration B (Example 8.2), so all that remains to be done is to calculate the concentration of $CH_3CO_2^-$ at the stoichiometric point.

Illustration 8.3

Calculating the pH at the stoichiometric point

Because the analyte initially contained 2.50 mmol CH_3COOH, the volume of titrant needed to neutralize it is the volume that contains the same amount of base:

$$V_{base} = \frac{2.50 \times 10^{-3}\ mol}{0.200\ mol\ dm^{-3}} = 1.25 \times 10^{-2}\ dm^3$$

or 12.5 cm^3. The total volume of the solution at this stage is therefore 37.5 cm^3, so the concentration of base is

$$[CH_3CO_2^-] = \frac{2.50 \times 10^{-3}\ mol}{37.5 \times 10^{-3}\ dm^3} = 6.67 \times 10^{-2}\ mol\ dm^{-3}$$

It then follows from a calculation similar to that in Example 8.2 (with $pK_b = 9.25$ for $CH_3CO_2^-$) that the pH of the solution at the stoichiometric point is 8.8.

It is very important to note that the pH at *the stoichiometric point of a weak-acid–strong-base*

Illustrations

An *Illustration* (don't confuse this with a diagram!) is a short example of how to use an equation that has just been introduced in the text. In particular, we show how to use data and how to manipulate units correctly.

Worked examples

A *Worked Example* is a much more structured form of Illustration, often involving a more elaborate procedure. Every *Worked Example* has a Strategy section to suggest how you might set up the problem (you might prefer another way: setting up problems is a highly personal business). Then there is the worked-out Answer.

Self tests

Every *Worked Example* and many *Illustrations* have a *Self-test*, with the answer provided, so that you can check whether you have understood the procedure. There are also free-standing *Self-tests* where we thought it a good idea to provide a question for you to check your understanding. Think of *Self-tests* as in-chapter *Exercises* designed to help you to monitor your progress.

from $\Delta U = w + q$, where U is a state function.

pressure heat capacities of a perfect gas are related by $C_{p,m} - C_{V,m} = R$.

DISCUSSION QUESTIONS

2.1 Provide molecular interpretations for work and heat.

2.2 Distinguish between expansion work against constant pressure and work of reversible expansion.

2.3 Explain the difference between the change in internal energy and the change in enthalpy of a chemical or physical process.

2.4 Explain the limitations of the following expressions: (a) $q = nRT\ln(V_f/V_i)$; (b) $\Delta H = \Delta U + p\Delta V$; (c) $C_{p,m} - C_{V,m} = R$.

EXERCISES

Assume all gases are perfect unless stated otherwise. The sign ‡ indicates that calculus is required.

2.5 Calculate the work that a person must do to raise a mass of 1.0 kg through 10 m on the surface of (a) the Earth ($g = 9.81$ m s^{-2}) and (b) the Moon ($g = 1.60$ m s^{-2}).

2.6 How much metabolic energy must a bird of mass 200 g exert to fly to a height of 20 m? Neglect all losses due to friction, physiological imperfection, and the acquisition of kinetic energy.

2.7 Calculate the work needed for a person of mass 65 kg to climb through 4.0 m on the surface of the Earth.

2.8 The centre of mass of a cylindrical column of liquid lies halfway along its length. Calculate the work required to raise a column of mercury (density 13.6 g cm^{-3}) of diameter 1.00 cm through 760 mm on the surface of the Earth ($g = 9.81$ m s^{-2}).

2.9 ‡The gravitational force acting on an object of mass m is $-Gmm_E/r^2$, where m_E is the mass of the Earth (6.0×10^{24} kg) and G is the gravitational constant. (a) Calculate the work

Discussion questions

The end-of-chapter material starts with a short set of questions that are intended to encourage you to think about the material you have encountered and to view it in a broader context than is obtained by solving numerical problems.

Exercises

The real core of testing your progress is the collection of end-of-chapter Exercises. We have provided a wide variety at a range of levels. When you see the sign ‡ you should be aware that calculus is needed to answer the question.

Answers to exercises are available on the companion web site.

About the companion web site

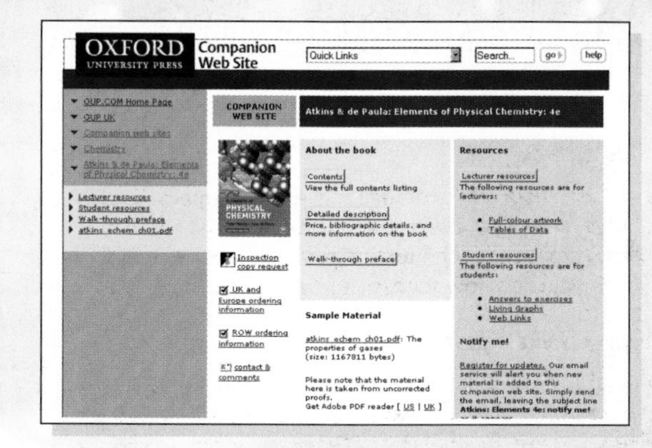

Companion web sites are developed to provide students and lecturers with ready-to-use teaching and learning resources. They are free-of-charge, designed to complement the textbook and offer additional materials, which are suited to electronic delivery.

You will find this material at:
www.oup.com/uk/booksites/chemistry
and
www.whfreeman.com/elements4e

Student resources

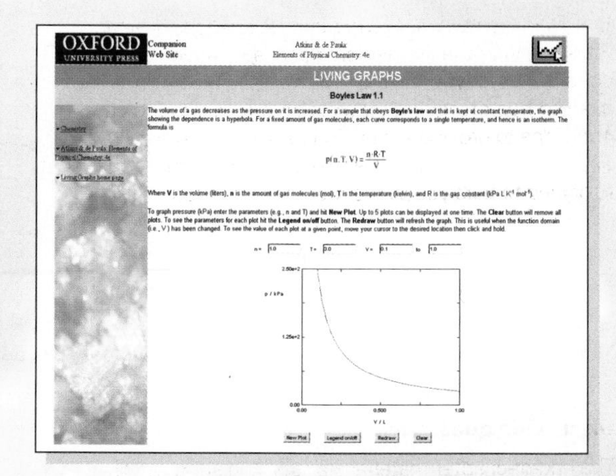

Living graph icon

A *Living Graph* is indicated in the text by the icon attached to the legend of a graph. If you go to the web site, you will be able to explore how a graph changes as you change a variety of parameters.

Web links

There is a huge network of information available about physical chemistry, and it can be bewildering to find your way to it. Also, you often need a piece of information that we have not included in the text. Where you see this icon in the text, you should go to the web site to find the data you require, or at least to receive information about where additional data can be found.

Answers to Exercises

Numerical answers are available so that you can check your calculations.

Lecturer resources

Artwork

Your instructor may wish to use the illustrations from this text in a lecture. Almost all the illustrations are available in full colour and can be used for lectures without charge (but not for commercial purposes without specific permission).

Tables of data

Your instructor may also wish to display the tables of data that occur in the test. All the data tables are also available in downloadable form and may be used under the same conditions as the artwork.

Contents

Contents

Introduction

Chemistry is the science of matter and the changes it can undergo. The branch of the subject called **physical chemistry** is concerned with the physical principles that underlie chemistry. Physical chemistry seeks to account for the properties of matter in terms of fundamental concepts such as atoms, electrons, and energy. It provides the basic framework for all other branches of chemistry—for inorganic chemistry, organic chemistry, biochemistry, geochemistry, and chemical engineering. It also provides the basis of modern methods of analysis, the determination of structure, and the elucidation of the manner in which chemical reactions occur. To do all this, it draws on two of the great foundations of modern physical science, thermodynamics and quantum mechanics. This text introduces the central concepts of these two subjects and shows how they are used in chemistry. This *Introduction* reviews material fundamental to the whole of physical chemistry, much of which will be familiar from introductory courses.

We begin by thinking about matter in bulk. The broadest classification of matter is into one of three **states of matter**, or forms of bulk matter, namely, gas, liquid, and solid. Later we shall see how this classification can be refined, but these three broad classes are a good starting point.

The mathematical techniques required in physical chemistry are reviewed in Appendix 2.

0.1 The states of matter

We distinguish the three states of matter by noting the behaviour of a substance enclosed in a container:

A **gas** is a fluid form of matter that fills the container it occupies.

A **liquid** is a fluid form of matter that possesses a well-defined surface and (in a gravitational field) fills the lower part of the container it occupies.

A **solid** retains its shape regardless of the shape of the container it occupies.

One of the roles of physical chemistry is to establish the link between the properties of bulk matter and the behaviour of the particles—atoms, ions, or molecules—of which it is composed. A physical chemist formulates a **model**, a simplified description, of each physical state and then shows how the state's properties can be understood in terms of this model. The existence of different states of matter is a first illustration of this procedure, as the properties of the three states suggest that they are composed of particles with different degrees of freedom of movement. Indeed, as we work through this text, we shall gradually establish and elaborate the following models:

A gas is composed of widely separated particles in continuous rapid, disordered motion. A particle travels several (often many) diameters before colliding with another particle. For most of the time the particles are so far apart that they interact with each other only very weakly.

A liquid consists of particles that are in contact but are able to move past each other in a restricted manner. The particles are in a continuous state of motion, but travel only a fraction of a diameter before bumping into a neighbour. The overriding image is one of movement, but with molecules jostling one another.

A solid consists of particles that are in contact and unable to move past one another. Although the particles oscillate around an average location, they are essentially trapped in their initial positions, and typically lie in ordered arrays.

The essential difference between the three states of matter is the freedom of the particles to move past one another. If the average separation of the particles is large, there is hardly any restriction on their motion, and the substance is a gas. If the particles interact strongly with one another that they are locked together rigidly, then the substance is a solid. If the particles have an intermediate mobility between these extremes, then the substance is a liquid. We can understand the melting of a solid and the vaporization of a liquid in terms of the progressive increase in the liberty of the particles as a sample is heated and the particles become able to move more freely.

0.2 Physical state

The term 'state' has many different meanings in chemistry, and it is important to keep them all in mind. We have already met one meaning in the expression 'the states of matter' and, specifically, 'the gaseous state'. Now we meet a second: by **physical state** (or just 'state') we shall mean a specific condition of a sample of matter that is described in terms of its physical form (gas, liquid, or solid) and the volume, pressure, temperature, and amount of substance present. (The precise meanings of these terms are described later.) So, 1 kg of hydrogen gas in a container of volume 10 dm^3 at a specified pressure and temperature is in a particular state. The same mass of gas in a container of volume 5 dm^3 is in a different state. Two samples of a given substance are in the same state if they are the same state of matter (that is, are both present as gas, liquid, or solid) *and* if they have the same mass, volume, pressure, and temperature.

To see more precisely what is involved in specifying the state of a substance, we need to define the terms we have used. The **mass**, m, of a sample is a measure of the quantity of matter it contains. Thus, 2 kg of lead contains twice as much matter as 1 kg of lead and indeed twice as much matter as 1 kg of anything. The *Système International* (SI) unit of mass is the **kilogram** (kg), with 1 kg currently defined as the mass of a certain block of platinum–iridium alloy preserved at Sèvres, outside Paris. For typical laboratory-sized samples it is usually more convenient to use a smaller unit and to express mass in grams (g), where 1 kg = 10^3 g.

The text's web site contains additional information about the international system of units.

The **volume**, V, of a sample is the amount of space it occupies. Thus, we write $V = 100\ cm^3$ if the sample occupies 100 cm^3 of space. The units used to express volume (which include cubic metres, m^3; cubic decimetres, dm^3, or litres, L; millilitres, mL), and units and symbols in general, are reviewed in Appendix 1.

The other properties we have mentioned (pressure, temperature, and amount of substance) need more introduction as, even though they may be familiar from everyday life, they need to be defined carefully for use in science.

0.3 Force

One of the most basic concepts of physical science is that of *force*. In classical mechanics, the mechanics originally formulated by Isaac Newton at the end of the seventeenth century, a body of mass m travels in a straight line at constant speed until a force acts on it. Then it undergoes an acceleration, a rate of change of velocity, given by Newton's second law of motion:

$$\text{Force} = \text{mass} \times \text{acceleration} \qquad F = ma$$

The acceleration of a freely falling body at the surface of the Earth is close to 9.81 m s^{-2}, so the gravitational force acting on a mass of 1.0 kg is

$$F = (1.0\ \text{kg}) \times (9.81\ \text{m s}^{-2}) = 9.8\ \text{kg m s}^{-2}$$

The derived unit of force is the newton, N:

$$1\ \text{N} = 1\ \text{kg m s}^{-2}$$

Therefore, we can report the force we have just calculated as 9.8 N. It might be helpful to note that a force of 1 N is approximately the gravitational force exerted on a small apple (of mass 100 g).

Force is a directed quantity, in the sense that it has direction as well as magnitude. For a body on the surface of the Earth, the force of gravitational attraction is directed towards the centre of the Earth.

When an object is moved through a distance s against an opposing force, we say that **work** is done. The magnitude of the work (we worry about signs later) is the product of the distance moved and the opposing force:

$$\text{Work} = \text{force} \times \text{distance}$$

Therefore, to raise a body of mass 1.0 kg on the surface of the Earth through a vertical distance of 1.0 m requires us to do the following amount of work:

$$\text{Work} = (9.8\ \text{N}) \times (1.0\ \text{m}) = 9.8\ \text{N m}$$

As we see more formally in a moment, the unit 1 N m (or, in terms of base units, 1 kg m^2 s^{-2}) is called 1 joule (1 J). So, 9.8 J is needed to raise a mass of 1.0 kg through 1.0 m on the surface of the Earth.

0.4 Energy

A property that will occur in just about every chapter of the following text is the *energy*, E. Everyone uses the term 'energy' in everyday language, but in science it has a precise meaning, a meaning that we shall draw on throughout the text. **Energy** is the capacity to do work. A fully wound spring can do more work than a half-wound spring (that is, it can raise a weight through a greater height, or move a greater weight through a given height). A hot object, when attached to some kind of heat engine (a device for converting heat into work), can do more work than the same object when it is cool, and therefore a hot object has a higher energy than the same cool object.

The SI unit of energy is the joule (J), named after the nineteenth-century scientist James Joule, who helped to establish the concept of energy (see Chapter 2). It is defined as

$$1\ \text{J} = 1\ \text{kg m}^2\ \text{s}^{-2}$$

A joule is quite a small unit, and in chemistry we often deal with energies of the order of kilojoules (1 kJ = 10^3 J).

There are two contributions to the total energy of a collection of particles. The **kinetic energy**, E_K, is the energy of a body due to its motion. For a body of mass m moving at a speed v,

$$E_K = \tfrac{1}{2}mv^2 \qquad (0.1)$$

That is, a heavy object moving at the same speed as a light object has a higher kinetic energy, and doubling the speed of any object increases its kinetic energy by a factor of 4. A ball of mass 1 kg travelling at 1 m s^{-1} has a kinetic energy of 0.5 J.

The **potential energy**, E_P, of a body is the energy it possesses due to its position. The precise dependence on position depends on the type of force acting on the body. For a body of mass m on the surface of the Earth, the potential energy depends on its height, h, above the surface as

$$E_P = mgh \tag{0.2}$$

where g is a constant known as the **acceleration of free fall**, which is close to 9.81 m s^{-2} at sea level. Thus, doubling the height, doubles the potential energy. This expression is based on the convention of taking the potential energy to be zero at sea level. A ball of mass 1.0 kg at 1.0 m above the surface of the Earth has a potential energy of 9.8 J. Another type of potential energy is that of one electric charge in the vicinity of another electric charge: we specify and use this hugely important 'Coulombic' potential energy in Section 13.2. As we shall see as the text develops, most contributions to the potential energy that we need to consider in chemistry are due to this Coulombic interaction.

The **total energy,** E, of a body is the sum of its kinetic and potential energies:

$$E = E_K + E_P \tag{0.3}$$

Provided no external forces are acting on the body, its total energy is constant. This remark is elevated to a central statement of classical physics known as the **law of the conservation of energy**. Potential and kinetic energy may be freely interchanged: for instance, a falling ball loses potential energy but gains kinetic energy as it accelerates, but its value remains constant provided the body is isolated from external influences.

0.5 Pressure

Pressure, p, is force, F, divided by the area, A, on which the force is exerted:

$$\text{Pressure} = \frac{\text{force}}{\text{area}} \qquad p = \frac{F}{A} \tag{0.4}$$

When you stand on ice, you generate a pressure on the ice as a result of the gravitational force acting on your mass and pulling you towards the centre of the Earth. However, the pressure is low because the downward force of your body is spread over the area equal to that of the soles of your shoes. When you stand on skates, the area of the blades in contact with the ice is much smaller, so although your downward *force* is the same, the *pressure* you exert is much greater (Fig. 0.1).

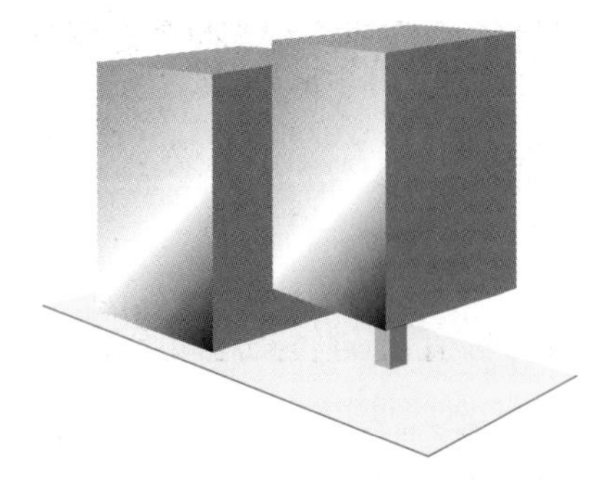

Fig. 0.1 These two blocks of matter have the same mass. They exert the same force on the surface on which they are standing, but the block on the right exerts a stronger pressure because it exerts the same force over a smaller area than the block on the left.

Pressure can arise in ways other than from the gravitational pull of the Earth on an object. For example, the impact of gas molecules on a surface gives rise to a force and hence to a pressure. If an object is immersed in the gas, it experiences a pressure over its entire surface because molecules collide with it from all directions. In this way, the atmosphere exerts a pressure on all the objects in it. We are incessantly battered by molecules of gas in the atmosphere, and experience this battering as the atmospheric pressure. The pressure is greatest at sea level because the density of air and hence the number of colliding molecules are greatest there. The atmospheric pressure is very considerable: it is the same as would be exerted by loading 1 kg of lead (or any other material) on to a surface of area 1 cm^2. We go through our lives under this heavy burden pressing on every square centimetre of our bodies. Some deep-sea creatures are built to withstand even greater pressures: at 1000 m below sea level the pressure is 100 times greater than at the surface. Creatures and submarines that operate at these depths must withstand the equivalent of 100 kg of lead loaded on to each square centimetre of their surfaces. The pressure of the air in our lungs helps us to withstand the relatively low but still substantial pressures that we experience close to sea level.

When a gas is confined to a cylinder fitted with a movable piston, the position of the piston adjusts until the pressure of the gas inside the cylinder is

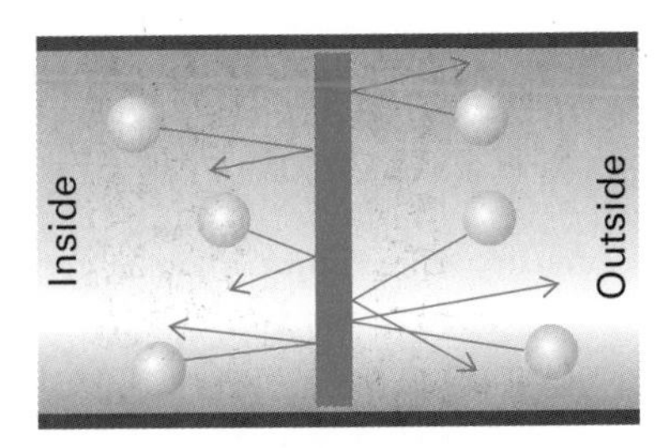

Fig. 0.2 A system is in mechanical equilibrium with its surroundings if it is separated from them by a movable wall and the external pressure is equal to the pressure of the gas in the system.

equal to that exerted by the atmosphere. When the pressures on either side of the piston are the same, we say that the two regions on either side are in **mechanical equilibrium**. The pressure of the confined gas arises from the impact of the particles: they batter the inside surface of the piston and counter the battering of the molecules in the atmosphere that is pressing on the outside surface of the piston (Fig. 0.2). Provided the piston is weightless (that is, provided we can neglect any gravitational pull on it), the gas is in mechanical equilibrium with the atmosphere whatever the orientation of the piston and cylinder, because the external battering is the same in all directions.

The SI unit of pressure is called the **pascal**, Pa:

$$1 \text{ Pa} = 1 \text{ N m}^{-2} = 1 \text{ kg m}^{-1} \text{ s}^{-2}$$

The pressure of the atmosphere at sea level is about 10^5 Pa (100 kPa). This fact lets us imagine the magnitude of 1 Pa, as we have just seen that 1 kg of lead resting on 1 cm^2 on the surface of the Earth exerts about the same pressure as the atmosphere; so $1/10^5$ of that mass, or 10 mg (1 mg = 10^{-3} g), will exert about 1 Pa; we see that the pascal is a fairly small unit of pressure. Table 0.1 lists the other units commonly used to report pressure.[1] One of the most important in modern physical chemistry is the **bar**, where 1 bar = 10^5 Pa exactly; the bar is not an SI unit, but it is an accepted and widely used abbreviation for 10^5 Pa. Normal atmospheric pressure is close to 1 bar.

Table 0.1
*Pressure units and conversion factors**

pascal, Pa	1 Pa = 1 N m^{-2}
bar	1 bar = 10^5 Pa
atmosphere, atm	1 atm = **101.325** kPa = **1.013 25** bar
torr, Torr†	**760** Torr = 1 atm 1 Torr = 133.32 Pa

* Values in bold are exact.
† The name of the unit is torr, its symbol is Torr.

Example 0.1
Converting between units

A scientist was exploring the effect of atmospheric pressure on the rate of growth of a lichen, and measured a pressure (p) of 1.115 bar. What is the pressure in atmospheres?

Strategy Write the relation between the 'old units' (the units to be replaced) and the 'new units' (the units required) in the form

1 old unit = x new units

then replace the 'old unit' everywhere it occurs by 'x new units', and multiply out the numerical expression.

Solution From Table 0.1 we have

1.013 25 bar = 1 atm

with atm the 'new unit' and bar the 'old unit'. As a first step we write

$$1 \text{ bar} = \frac{1}{1.013\,25} \text{ atm}$$

Then we replace bar wherever it appears by (1/1.013 25) atm:

$$p = 1.115 \text{ bar} = 1.115 \times \left(\frac{1}{1.013\,25} \text{ atm}\right) = 1.100 \text{ atm}$$

A note on good practice The number of significant figures in the answer (four in this instance) is the same as the number of significant figures in the data; the relation between old and new numbers in this case is exact.

Self-test 0.1

The pressure in the eye of a hurricane was recorded as 723 Torr. What is the pressure in kilopascals?

[*Answer:* 96.4 kPa]

[1] See Appendix 1 for a fuller description of the units and their manipulation.

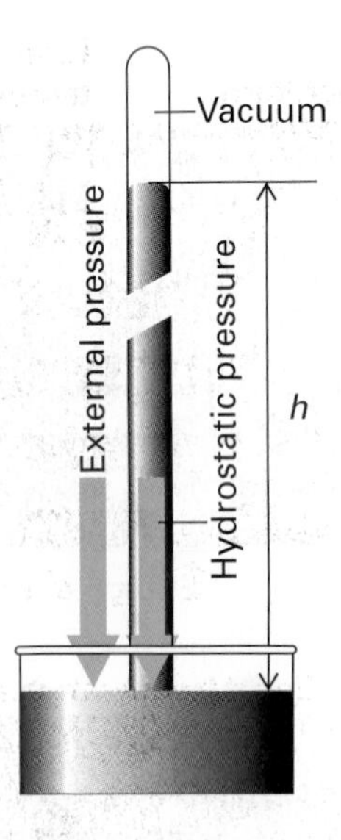

Fig. 0.3 The operation of a mercury barometer. The space above the mercury in the vertical tube is a vacuum, so no pressure is exerted on the top of the mercury column; however, the atmosphere exerts a pressure on the mercury in the reservoir, and pushes the column up the tube until the pressure exerted by the mercury column is equal to that exerted by the atmosphere. The height, h, reached by the column is proportional to the external pressure, so the height can be used as a measure of this pressure.

Atmospheric pressure (a property that varies with altitude and the weather) is measured with a **barometer**, which was invented by Torricelli, a student of Galileo. A mercury barometer consists of an inverted tube of mercury that is sealed at its upper end and stands with its lower end in a bath of mercury. The mercury falls until the pressure it exerts at its base is equal to the atmospheric pressure (Fig. 0.3). We can determine the atmospheric pressure, p, by measuring the height, h, of the mercury column and using the relation (see Derivation 0.1)

$$p = \rho g h \tag{0.5}$$

where ρ (rho) is the mass density (commonly just 'density'), the mass of a sample divided by the volume it occupies:

$$\rho = \frac{m}{V} \tag{0.6}$$

With the mass measured in kilograms and the volume in cubic metres, d[illegible]sity is reported in kilograms per cubic metre (kg [illegible]; however, it is equally acceptable and often [illegible] convenient to report mass density in grams per cubic centimetre (g cm^{-3}). The relation between these units is

$$1\ \text{g cm}^{-3} = 10^3\ \text{kg m}^{-3}$$

Thus, the density of mercury may be reported as either 13.6 g cm^{-3} or 1.36×10^4 kg m^{-3}.

Derivation 0.1

Hydrostatic pressure

The strategy of the calculation is to relate the mass of the column to its height, to calculate the downward force exerted by that mass, and then to divide the force by the area over which it is exerted.

Consider Fig. 0.4. The volume of a cylinder of liquid of height h and cross-sectional area A is hA. The mass, m, of this cylinder of liquid is the volume multiplied by the density, ρ, of the liquid, or $m = \rho \times hA$. The downward force exerted by this mass is mg, where g is the acceleration of free fall. Therefore, the force exerted by the column is $\rho \times hA \times g$. This force acts over the area A at the foot of the column so, according to eqn 0.4, the pressure at the base is ρhAg divided by A, which is eqn 0.5.

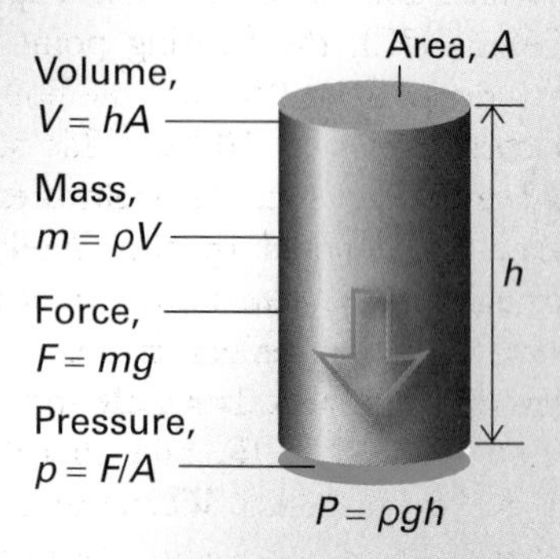

Fig. 0.4 The calculation of the hydrostatic pressure exerted by a column of height h and cross-sectional area A.

Illustration 0.1

Calculating hydrostatic pressure

The pressure at the foot of a column of mercury of height 760 mm (0.760 m) and density 13.6 g cm^{-3} (1.36×10^4 kg m^{-3}) is

$$p = (9.81\ \text{m s}^{-2}) \times (1.36 \times 10^4\ \text{kg m}^{-3}) \times (0.760\ \text{m})$$
$$= 1.01 \times 10^5\ \text{kg m}^{-1}\ \text{s}^{-2} = 1.01 \times 10^5\ \text{Pa}$$

This pressure corresponds to 101 kPa (1.00 atm).

A note on good practice. Write units at *every* stage of a calculation and do not simply attach them to a final numerical value. Also, it is often sensible to express all numerical quantities in terms of base units when carrying out a calculation.

0.6 Temperature

In everyday terms, the temperature is an indication of how 'hot' or 'cold' a body is. In science, **temperature**, T, is the property of an object that determines in which direction energy will flow when it is in contact with another object. Energy flows from higher temperature to lower temperature. When the two bodies have the same temperature, there is no net flow of energy between them. In that case we say that the bodies are in **thermal equilibrium** (Fig. 0.5).

Temperature in science is measured on either the Celsius scale or the Kelvin scale. On the **Celsius scale**, in which the temperature is expressed in degrees Celsius (°C), the freezing point of water at 1 atm corresponds to 0°C and the boiling point at 1 atm corresponds to 100°C. This scale is in widespread everyday use. Temperatures on the Celsius scale are denoted by the Greek letter θ (theta) throughout this text. However, it turns out to be much more convenient in many scientific applications to adopt the **Kelvin scale** and to express the temperature in kelvin (K; note that the degree sign is not used for this unit). *Whenever we use T to denote a temperature, we mean a temperature on the Kelvin scale.* The Celsius and Kelvin scales are related by

$$T\text{ (in kelvin)} = \theta\text{ (in degrees Celsius)} + 273.15$$

That is, to obtain the temperature in kelvins, add 273.15 to the temperature in degrees Celsius. Thus, water at 1 atm freezes at 273 K and boils at 373 K; a warm day (25°C) corresponds to 298 K.

A more sophisticated way of expressing the relation between T and θ, and one that we shall use in other contexts, is to regard the value of T as the product of a number (such as 298) and a unit (K), so that T/K (that is, the temperature divided by K) is a pure number. For example, if $T = 298$ K, then $T/\text{K} = 298$. Likewise, $\theta/°\text{C}$ is also a pure number.

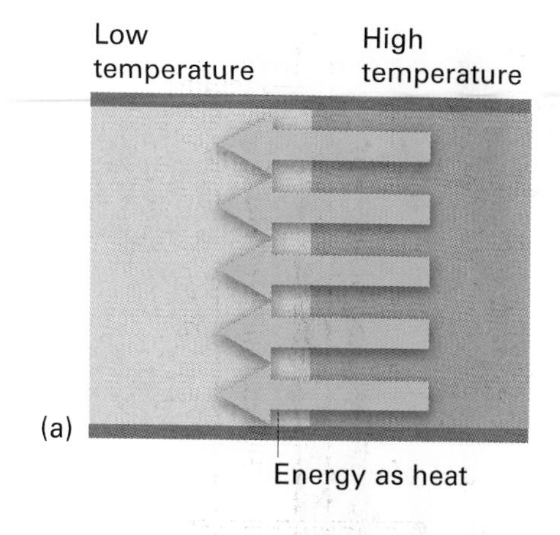

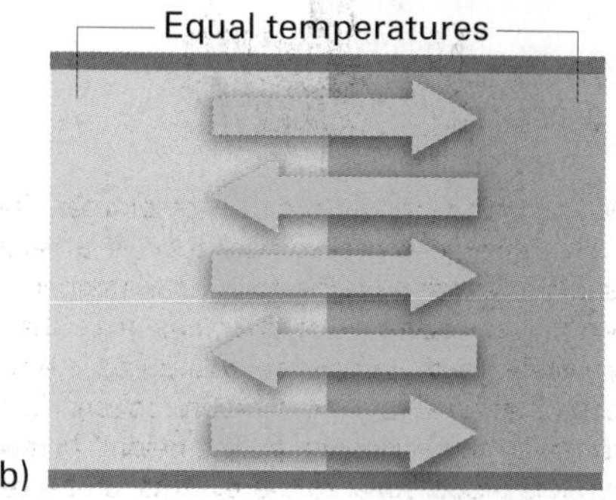

Fig. 0.5 The temperatures of two objects act as a signpost showing the direction in which energy will flow as heat through a thermally conducting wall. (a) Heat always flows from high temperature to low temperature. (b) When the two objects have the same temperature, although there is still energy transfer in both directions, there is no net flow of energy.

For example, if $\theta = 25°\text{C}$, then $\theta/°\text{C} = 25$. With this convention, we can write the relation between the two scales as

$$T/\text{K} = \theta/°\text{C} + 273.15 \quad (0.7)$$

This expression is a relation between pure numbers.[2]

Self-test 0.2

Use eqn 0.7 to express body temperature, 37°C, in kelvins.

[*Answer:* 310 K]

[2] Equation 0.7, in the form $\theta/°\text{C} = T/\text{K} - 273.15$, also defines the Celsius scale in terms of the more fundamental Kelvin scale.

A note on good practice. We write $T = 0$, not $T = 0$ K. There are other 'absolute' scales of temperature, all of which set their lowest value at zero. In so far as it is possible, all expressions in science should be independent of the units being used, and in this case the lowest attainable temperature is $T = 0$ regardless of the scale we are using.

0.7 Amount of substance

Mass is a measure of the quantity of matter in a sample regardless of its chemical identity. Thus, 1 kg of lead is the same quantity of matter as 1 kg of butter. In chemistry, where we focus on the behaviour of atoms, it is usually more useful to know the quantity of each specific kind of atom, molecule, or ion in a sample rather than the quantity of matter (the mass) itself. However, because even 10 g of water consists of about 10^{23} H_2O molecules, it is clearly appropriate to define a new unit that can be used to express such large numbers simply. As will be familiar from introductory chemistry, chemists have introduced the **mole** (mol; the name is derived, ironically, from the Latin word meaning 'massive heap'), which is defined as follows:

1 mol of specified particles is equal to the number of atoms in exactly 12 g of carbon-12.

This number is determined experimentally by dividing 12 g by the mass of one atom of carbon-12. Because the mass of one carbon-12 atom is measured by using a mass spectrometer as $1.992\,65 \times 10^{-23}$ g, the number of atoms in exactly 12 g of carbon-12 is

$$\text{Number of atoms} = \frac{\text{total mass of sample}}{\text{mass of one atom}} = \frac{12\,\text{g}}{1.992\,65 \times 10^{-23}\,\text{g}} = 6.022 \times 10^{23}$$

This number is the number of particles in 1 mol of any substance.[3] For example, a sample of hydrogen gas that contains 6.022×10^{23} hydrogen molecules consists of 1.000 mol H_2, and a sample of water that contains 1.2×10^{24} $(= 2.0 \times 6.022 \times 10^{23})$ water molecules consists of 2.0 mol H_2O.

A note on good practice. Always specify the identity of the particles when using the unit mole, to avoid any ambiguity. If, improperly, we report that a sample consisted of 1 mol of hydrogen, it would not be clear whether it consisted of 6×10^{23} hydrogen atoms (1 mol H) or 6×10^{23} hydrogen molecules (1 mol H_2).

The mole is the unit used when reporting the value of the physical property called the **amount of substance**, n, in a sample. Thus, we can write $n = 1$ mol H_2 or $n_{H_2} = 1$ mol, and say that the amount of hydrogen molecules in a sample is 1 mol. The term 'amount of substance', however, has not yet found wide acceptance among chemists and in casual conversation they commonly refer to 'the number of moles' in a sample. The term **chemical amount**, however, is becoming more widely used as a convenient synonym for amount of substance, and we shall often use it in this book.

There are various useful concepts that stem from the introduction of the chemical amount and its unit the mole. One is **Avogadro's constant**, N_A, the number of particles (of any kind) per mole of substance:

$$N_A = 6.022 \times 10^{23}\,\text{mol}^{-1}$$

Avogadro's constant makes it very simple to convert from the number of particles N (a pure number) in a sample to the chemical amount n (in moles) it contains:

Number of particles

= chemical amount × number of particles per mole

$$N = n \times N_A \qquad (0.8)$$

Illustration 0.2

Relating amount and number

From $n = N/N_A$, a sample of copper containing 8.8×10^{22} Cu atoms corresponds to

$$n_{Cu} = \frac{N}{N_A} = \frac{8.8 \times 10^{22}}{6.022 \times 10^{23}\,\text{mol}^{-1}} = 0.15\,\text{mol}$$

Note how much easier it is to report the amount of Cu atoms present rather than their actual number.

[3] The currently accepted value is $6.022\,141\,99 \times 10^{23}$; see the end papers.

A note on good practice. As noted above, always ensure that the use of the unit mole refers unambiguously to the entities intended. This may be done in a variety of ways: here we have labelled the amount n with the entities (Cu atoms), as in n_{Cu}.

The second very important concept that should be familiar from introductory courses is the **molar mass**, M, the mass per mole of substance: that is, the mass of a sample of the substance divided by the chemical amount of atoms, molecules, or formula units it contains. When we refer to the molar mass of an element we always mean the mass per mole of its *atoms*. When we refer to the molar mass of a compound, we always mean the molar mass of its molecules or, in the case of ionic compounds, the mass per mole of its formula units. The molar mass of a typical sample of carbon, the mass per mole of carbon atoms (with carbon-12 and carbon-13 atoms in their typical abundances), is 12.01 g mol^{-1}. The molar mass of water is the mass per mole of H_2O molecules, with the isotopic abundances of hydrogen and oxygen those of typical samples of the elements, and is 18.02 g mol^{-1}. The informal unit **dalton** (1 Da) is commonly used as an abbreviation for 1 g mol^{-1}, especially in biophysical applications. The molar mass of a biological macromolecule measured as 1.2×10^4 g mol^{-1}, for instance, could be reported as 12 kDa (where 1 kDa = 1 kg mol^{-1}).

The terms *atomic weight* (AW) or *relative atomic mass* (RAM) and *molecular weight* (MW) or *relative molecular mass* (RMM) are still commonly used to signify the numerical value of the molar mass of an element or compound, respectively. More precisely (but equivalently), the RAM of an element or the RMM of a compound is its average atomic or molecular mass relative to the mass of an atom of carbon-12 set equal to 12. The atomic weight (or RAM) of a natural sample of carbon is 12.01 and the molecular weight (or RMM) of water is 18.02.

The molar mass of an element is determined by mass spectrometric measurement of the mass of its atoms and then multiplication of the mass of one atom by Avogadro's constant (the number of atoms per mole). Care has to be taken to allow for the isotopic composition of an element, so we must use a suitably weighted mean of the masses of the isotopes present. The values obtained in this way are printed on the periodic table inside the back cover. The molar mass of a compound of known composition is calculated by taking a sum of the molar masses of its constituent atoms. The molar mass of a compound of unknown composition is determined experimentally by using mass spectrometry in a similar way to the determination of atomic masses, but allowing for the fragmentation of molecules in the course of the measurement.

Molar mass is used to convert from the mass, m, of a sample (which we can measure) to the amount of substance, n (which, in chemistry, we often need to know):

Mass of sample = chemical amount × molar mass

$$m = n \times M \qquad (0.9)$$

Illustration 0.3

Converting from mass to amount

To find the amount of C atoms present in 21.5 g of carbon, given that the molar mass of carbon is 12.01 g mol^{-1}, from $n = m/M$ we write (taking care to specify the species)

$$n_C = \frac{m}{M_C} = \frac{21.5\ \text{g}}{12.01\ \text{g mol}^{-1}} = 1.79\ \text{mol}$$

That is, the sample contains 1.79 mol C.

Self-test 0.3

What amount of H_2O molecules is present in 10.0 g of water?

[*Answer:* 0.555 mol H_2O]

0.8 Extensive and intensive properties

A distinction is made in chemistry between extensive properties and intensive properties. An **extensive property** is a property that depends on the amount of substance in the sample. An **intensive property** is a property that is independent of the amount of substance in the sample. Two examples of extensive properties are mass and volume. Examples of intensive properties are temperature and pressure.

Some intensive properties are ratios of two extensive properties. Consider the mass density of a substance, the ratio of two extensive properties—the mass and the volume (eqn 0.6). The mass density of a substance is independent of the size of the sample because doubling the volume also doubles the mass, so the ratio of mass to volume remains the same. The mass density is therefore an intensive property.

CHECKLIST OF KEY IDEAS

You should now be familiar with the following concepts:

☐ 1 Physical chemistry is the branch of chemistry that establishes and develops the principles of chemistry in terms of the underlying concepts of physics and the language of mathematics.

☐ 2 The states of matter are gas, liquid, and solid.

☐ 3 Work is done when a body is moved against an opposing force.

☐ 4 Energy is the capacity to do work.

☐ 5 The contributions to the energy of matter are the kinetic energy (the energy due to motion) and the potential energy (the energy due to position).

☐ 6 The total energy of an isolated system is conserved, but kinetic and potential energy may be interchanged.

☐ 7 Pressure, p, is force divided by the area on which the force is exerted.

☐ 8 Two systems in contact through movable walls are in mechanical equilibrium when their pressures are equal.

☐ 9 Two systems in contact through thermally conducting walls are in thermal equilibrium when their temperatures are equal.

☐ 10 Temperatures on the Kelvin and Celsius scales are related by $T/\mathrm{K} = \theta/{}^\circ\mathrm{C} + 273.15$.

☐ 11 Chemical amounts, n, are expressed in moles of specified entities.

☐ 12 An extensive property is a property that depends on the amount of substance in the sample. An intensive property is a property that is independent of the amount of substance in the sample.

DISCUSSION QUESTIONS

0.1 Explain the differences between gases, liquids, and solids.

0.2 Define the terms: force, work, energy, kinetic energy, and potential energy.

0.3 Distinguish between mechanical and thermal equilibrium.

0.4 Identify whether the following properties are extensive or intensive: (a) volume, (b) mass density, (c) temperature, (d) molar volume, (e) amount of substance.

EXERCISES

The symbol ‡ signifies that calculus is required.

0.5 Calculate the work that a person of mass 65 kg must do to climb between two floors of a building separated by 3.5 m.

0.6 What is the kinetic energy of a tennis ball of mass 58 g served at 30 m s^{-1}?

0.7 A car of mass 1.5 t (1 t = 10^3 kg) travelling at 50 km h^{-1} must be brought to a stop. How much kinetic energy must be dissipated?

0.8 Consider a region of the atmosphere of volume 25 dm^3 that at 20°C contains about 1.0 mol of molecules. Take the average molar mass of the molecules as 29 g mol^{-1} and their average speed as about 400 m s^{-1}. Estimate the energy stored as molecular kinetic energy in this volume of air.

0.9 What is the difference in potential energy of a mercury atom between the top and bottom of a column of mercury in a barometer when the pressure is 1.0 atm?

0.10 Calculate the minimum energy that a bird of mass 25 g must expend to reach a height of 50 m.

0.11 The gravitational potential energy of a body of mass m at a distance r from the centre of the Earth is $-Gmm_E/r$, where m_E is the mass of the Earth and G is the gravitational constant (see inside front cover). Consider the difference in potential energy of the body when it is moved from the surface of the Earth (radius r_E) to a height h above the surface, with $h \ll r_E$, and find an expression for the acceleration of free fall, g, in terms of the mass and radius of the Earth. (*Hint.* Use the approximation $(1 + h/r_E)^{-1} = 1 - h/r_E + \cdots$. See Appendix 2 for more information on series expansions.)

0.12 You need to assess the fuel needed to send the robot explorer *Spirit*, which has a mass of 185 kg, to Mars. (a) What was the energy needed to raise the vehicle itself from the surface of the Earth to a distant point where the Earth's gravitational field was effectively zero? The mean radius of the Earth is 6371 km and its average mass density is 5.5170 g cm^{-3}. (*Hint.* Use the full expression for gravitational potential energy in Exercise 0.11.)

0.13 ‡Given the expression for gravitational potential energy in Exercise 0.11, (a) what is the gravitational force on an object of mass m at a distance r from the centre of the Earth? (b) What is the gravitational force that you are currently experiencing? For data on the Earth, see Exercise 0.12.

0.14 Express (a) 110 kPa in torr, (b) 0.997 bar in atmospheres, (c) 2.15×10^4 Pa in atmospheres, (d) 723 Torr in pascals.

0.15 Calculate the pressure in the Mindañao trench, near the Philippines, the deepest region of the oceans. Take the depth there as 11.5 km and for the average mass density of sea water use 1.10 g cm^{-3}.

0.16 The atmospheric pressure on the surface of Mars, where $g = 3.7$ m s^{-2}, is only 0.0060 atm. To what extent is that low pressure due to the low gravitational attraction and not to the thinness of the atmosphere? What pressure would the same atmosphere exert on Earth, where $g = 9.81$ m s^{-2}?

0.17 What pressure difference must be generated across the length of a 15 cm vertical drinking straw to drink a water-like liquid of mass density 1.0 g cm^{-3} (a) on Earth, (b) on Mars? For data, see Exercise 0.16.

0.18 The unit 'millimetre of mercury' (mmHg) has been replaced by the unit torr (Torr): 1 mmHg is defined as the pressure at the base of a column of mercury exactly 1 mm high when its density is 13.5951 g cm^{-3} and the acceleration of free fall is 9.806 65 m s^{-2}. What is the relation between the two units?

0.19 Given that the Celsius and Fahrenheit temperature scales are related by $\theta_{\text{Celsius}}/°\text{C} = \frac{5}{9}(\theta_{\text{Fahrenheit}}/°\text{F} - 32)$, what is the temperature of absolute zero ($T = 0$) on the Fahrenheit scale?

0.20 Imagine that Pluto is inhabited and that its scientists use a temperature scale in which the freezing point of liquid nitrogen is 0°P (degrees Plutonium) and its boiling point is 100°P. The inhabitants of Earth report these temperatures as −209.9°C and −195.8°C, respectively. What is the relation between temperatures on (a) the Plutonium and Kelvin scales, (b) the Plutonium and Fahrenheit scales?

0.21 The *Rankine scale* is used in some engineering applications. On it, the absolute zero of temperature is set at zero but the size of the Rankine degree (°R) is the same as that of the Fahrenheit degree (°F). What is the boiling point of water on the Rankine scale?

0.22 The molar mass of the oxygen-storage protein myoglobin is 16.1 kDa. How many myoglobin molecules are present in 1.0 g of the compound?

0.23 The mass of a red blood cell is about 33 pg, and it contains typically 3×10^8 haemoglobin molecules. Each haemoglobin molecule is a tetramer of myoglobin (see preceding exercise). What fraction of the mass of the cell is due to haemoglobin?

0.24 Express the mass density of a compound, which is defined as $\rho = m/V$, in terms of its molar mass and its molar volume.

Chapter 1

The properties of gases

Although gases are simple, both to describe and in terms of their internal structure, they are of immense importance. We spend our whole lives surrounded by gas in the form of air, and the local variation in its properties is what we call the 'weather'. To understand the atmospheres of this and other planets we need to understand gases. As we breathe, we pump gas in and out of our lungs, where it changes composition and temperature. Many industrial processes involve gases, and both the outcome of the reaction and the design of the reaction vessels depend on a knowledge of their properties.

Equations of state

We can specify the state of any sample of substance by giving the values of the following properties (all of which are defined in the *Introduction*):

V, the volume of the sample

p, the pressure of the sample

T, the temperature of the sample

n, the amount of substance in the sample

However, an astonishing experimental fact is that *these four quantities are not independent of one another*. For instance, we cannot arbitrarily choose to have a sample of 0.555 mol H_2O in a volume of 100 cm^3 at 100 kPa and 500 K: it is found *experimentally* that the state simply does not exist. If we select the amount, the volume, and the temperature, then we find that we have to accept a particular pressure (in this case, close to 230 kPa). The same is true of all substances, but the pressure in general will be different for each one. This experimental generalization is summarized by saying the substance obeys an **equation of state**, an equation of the form

$$p = f(n,V,T) \qquad (1.1)$$

This expression tells us that the pressure is some function of amount, volume, and temperature and that if we know those three variables, then the pressure can have only one value.

The equations of state of most substances are not known, so in general we cannot write down an explicit expression for the pressure in terms of the other variables. However, certain equations of state are known. In particular, the equation of state of a low-pressure gas is known, and proves to be very simple and very useful. This equation is used to describe the behaviour of gases taking part in reactions, the behaviour of the atmosphere, as a starting point for problems in chemical engineering, and even in the description of the structures of stars.

1.1 The perfect gas equation of state

The equation of state of a low-pressure gas was among the first results to be established in physical chemistry. The original experiments were carried out by Robert Boyle in the seventeenth century and there was a resurgence in interest later in the century when people began to fly in balloons. This technological progress demanded more knowledge about the response of gases to changes of pressure and temperature and, like technological advances in other fields today, that interest stimulated a lot of experiments.

The experiments of Boyle and his successors led to the formulation of the following **perfect gas equation of state:**

$$pV = nRT \qquad (1.2)$$

In this equation (which has the form of eqn 1.1 when we rearrange it into $p = nRT/V$), the **gas constant** R is an experimentally determined quantity that turns out to have the same value for all gases. It may be determined by evaluating $R = pV/nRT$ as the pressure is allowed to approach zero or by measuring the speed of sound (which depends on R). Values of R in different units are given in Table 1.1.

Table 1.1
The gas constant in various units

$R =$	8.314 47	$dm^3\ K^{-1}\ mol^{-1}$
	8.314 47	$dm^3\ kPa\ K^{-1}\ mol^{-1}$
	$8.205\ 74 \times 10^{-2}$	$dm^3\ atm\ K^{-1}\ mol^{-1}$
	62.364	$dm^3\ Torr\ K^{-1}\ mol^{-1}$
	1.987 21	$cal\ K^{-1}\ mol^{-1}$

$1\ dm^3 = 10^{-3}\ m^3$.

The perfect gas equation of state—more briefly, the 'perfect gas law'—is so-called because it is an idealization of the equations of state that gases actually obey. Specifically, it is found that all gases obey the equation ever more closely as the pressure is reduced towards zero. That is, eqn 1.2 is an example of a **limiting law**, a law that becomes increasingly valid as the pressure is reduced and is obeyed exactly in the limit of zero pressure.

A hypothetical substance that obeys eqn 1.2 at *all* pressures is called a **perfect gas.**[1] From what has just been said, an actual gas, which is termed a **real gas**, behaves more and more like a perfect gas as its pressure is reduced towards zero. In practice, normal atmospheric pressure at sea level ($p \approx 100$ kPa) is already low enough for most real gases to behave almost perfectly, and unless stated otherwise we shall always assume in this text that the gases we encounter behave like a perfect gas. The reason why a real gas behaves differently from a perfect gas can be traced to the attractions and repulsions that exist between actual molecules and which are absent in a perfect gas (Chapter 16).

The perfect gas law summarizes three sets of experimental observations. One is **Boyle's law:**

At constant temperature, the pressure of a fixed amount of gas is inversely proportional to its volume.

Mathematically:

$$\textit{Boyle's law: at constant temperature, } p \propto \frac{1}{V}$$

We can easily verify that eqn 1.2 is consistent with Boyle's law: by treating n and T as constants, the perfect gas law becomes pV = constant, and hence $p \propto 1/V$. Boyle's law implies that if we compress (reduce the volume of) a fixed amount of gas at constant temperature into half its original volume, then its pressure will double. Figure 1.1 shows the

[1] The term 'ideal gas' is also widely used.

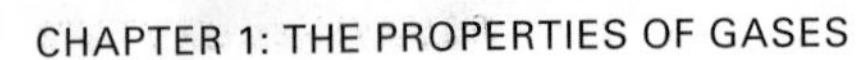

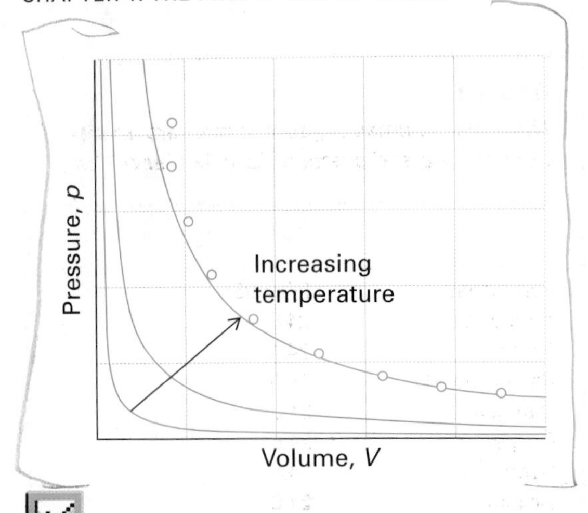

Fig. 1.1 The volume of a gas decreases as the pressure on it is increased. For a sample that obeys Boyle's law and that is kept at constant temperature, the graph showing the dependence is a hyperbola, as shown here. Each curve corresponds to a single temperature, and hence is an isotherm.

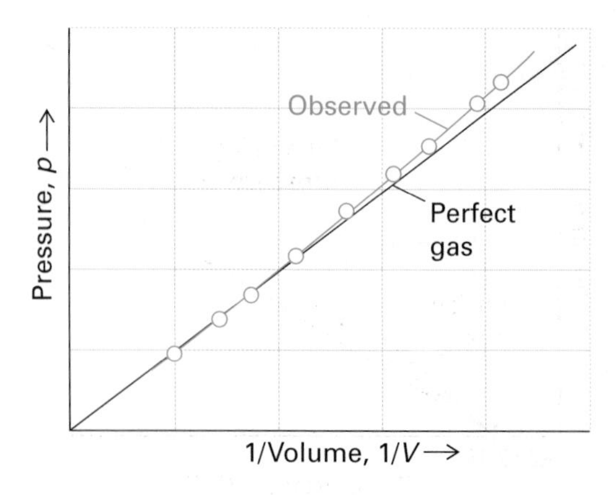

Fig. 1.2 A good test of Boyle's law is to plot the pressure against $1/V$ (at constant temperature), when a straight line should be obtained. This diagram shows that the observed pressures (the blue line) approach a straight line as the volume is increased and the pressure reduced. A perfect gas would follow the straight line at all pressures; real gases obey Boyle's law in the limit of low pressures.

graph obtained by plotting experimental values of p against V for a fixed amount of gas at different temperatures and the curves predicted by Boyle's law. Each curve is called an **isotherm** because it depicts the variation of a property (in this case, the pressure) at a single constant temperature. It is difficult, from this graph, to judge how well Boyle's law is obeyed. However, when we plot p against $1/V$, we get straight lines, just as we would expect from Boyle's law (Fig. 1.2).

A note on good practice. It is generally the case that a proposed relation is easier to verify if the experimental data are plotted in a form that should give a straight line.

The isotherms are *hyperbolas*, graphs of xy = constant, or y = constant/x. The illustration shows the graphs of $xy = 1$ and $xy = 2$ for positive and negative values of x and y.

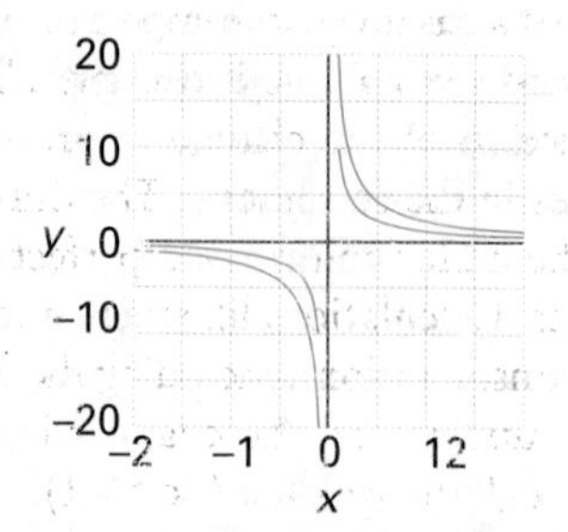

The second experimental observation summarized by eqn 1.2 is **Charles's law:**

At constant pressure, the volume of a fixed amount of gas varies linearly with the temperature.

Mathematically:

$$\text{Charles's law: at constant pressure, } V = A + B\theta$$

where θ is the temperature on the Celsius scale and A and B are constants that depend on the amount of gas and the pressure. Figure 1.3 shows typical plots of volume against temperature for a series of samples of gases at different pressures and confirms that (at low pressures, and for temperatures that are not too low) the volume varies linearly with the Celsius temperature. We also see that all the volumes extrapolate to zero as θ approaches the same very low temperature (−273.15°C, in fact), regardless of the identity of the gas. Because a volume cannot be negative, this common temperature must represent the **absolute zero** of temperature, a temperature below which it is impossible to cool an object. Indeed, the Kelvin scale ascribes the value $T = 0$ to this absolute zero of temperature. In terms of the Kelvin temperature, therefore, Charles's law takes the simpler form

$$\text{Charles's law: at constant pressure, } V \propto T$$

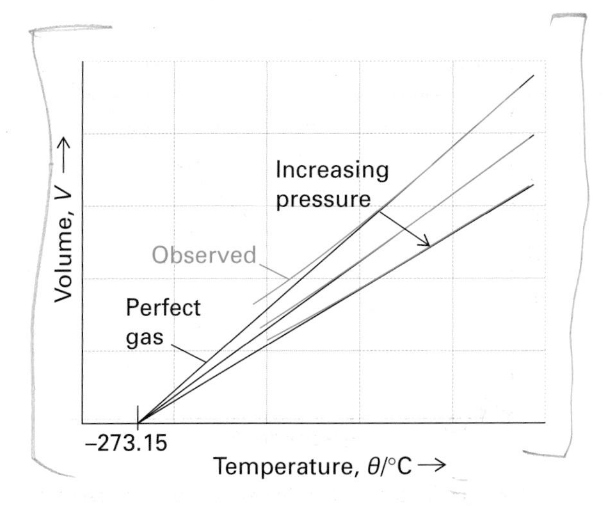

Fig. 1.3 This diagram illustrates the content and implications of Charles's law, which asserts that the volume occupied by a gas (at constant pressure) varies linearly with the temperature. When plotted against Celsius temperatures (as here), all gases give straight lines that extrapolate to $V = 0$ at −273.15°C. This extrapolation suggests that −273.15°C is the lowest attainable temperature.

It follows that doubling the temperature (on the Kelvin scale, such as from 300 K to 600 K, corresponding to an increase from 27°C to 327°C) doubles the volume, provided the pressure remains the same. Now we can see that eqn 1.2 is consistent with Charles's law. First, we rearrange it into $V = nRT/p$, and then note that when the amount n and the pressure p are both constant, we can write $V \propto T$, as required.

The third feature of gases summarized by eqn 1.2 is **Avogadro's principle**:

At a given temperature and pressure, equal volumes of gas contain the same numbers of molecules.

That is, 1.00 dm^3 of oxygen at 100 kPa and 300 K contains the same number of molecules as 1.00 dm^3 of carbon dioxide, or any other gas, at the same temperature and pressure. The principle implies that if we double the number of molecules, but keep the temperature and pressure constant, then the volume of the sample will double. We can therefore write:

Avogadro's principle: at constant temperature and pressure, $V \propto n$

This result follows easily from eqn 1.2 if we treat p and T as constants. Avogadro's suggestion is a principle rather than a law (a direct summary of experience), because it is based on a model of a gas, in this case as a collection of molecules.

Table 1.2

The molar volumes of gases at standard ambient temperature and pressure (298.15 K and 1 bar)

Gas	$V_m/(dm^3\ mol^{-1})$
Perfect gas	24.7896*
Ammonia	24.8
Argon	24.4
Carbon dioxide	24.6
Nitrogen	24.8
Oxygen	24.8
Hydrogen	24.8
Helium	24.8

* At STP (0°C, 1 atm), $V_m = 24.4140\ dm^3\ mol^{-1}$.

The **molar volume**, V_m, of any substance (not just a gas) is the volume it occupies per mole of molecules. It is calculated by dividing the volume of the sample by the amount of molecules it contains:

$$V_m = \frac{V}{n} \quad (1.3)$$

With volume in cubic decimetres and amount in moles, the units of molar volume are cubic decimetres per mole ($dm^3\ mol^{-1}$). Avogadro's principle implies that the molar volume of a gas should be the same for all gases at the same temperature and pressure. The data in Table 1.2 show that this conclusion is approximately true for most gases under normal conditions (normal atmospheric pressure of about 100 kPa and room temperature).

1.2 Using the perfect gas law

Here we review three elementary applications of the perfect gas equation of state. The first is the prediction of the pressure of a gas given its temperature, its chemical amount, and the volume it occupies. The second is the prediction of the change in pressure arising from changes in the conditions. The third is the calculation of the molar volume of a perfect gas under any conditions. Calculations like these underlie more advanced considerations, including the way that meteorologists understand the changes in the atmosphere that we call the weather (Box 1.1).

Box 1.1 *The gas laws and the weather*

The biggest sample of gas readily accessible to us is the atmosphere, a mixture of gases with the composition summarized in the table. The composition is maintained moderately constant by diffusion and convection (winds, particularly the local turbulence called *eddies*) but the pressure and temperature vary with altitude and with the local conditions, particularly in the troposphere (the 'sphere of change'), the layer extending up to about 11 km.

One of the most variable constituents of air is water vapour, and the humidity it causes. The presence of water vapour results in a *lower* density of air at a given temperature and pressure, as we may conclude from Avogadro's principle. The numbers of molecules in 1 m^3 of moist air and dry air are the same (at the same temperature and pressure), but the mass of an H_2O molecule is less than that of all the other major constituents of air (the molar mass of H_2O is 18 g mol^{-1}, the average molar mass of air molecules is 29 g mol^{-1}), so the density of the moist sample is less than that of the dry sample.

The pressure and temperature vary with altitude. In the troposphere the average temperature is 15°C at sea level, falling to –57°C at the bottom of the tropopause at 11 km. This variation is much less pronounced when expressed on the Kelvin scale, ranging from 288 K to 216 K, an average of 268 K. If we suppose that the temperature has its average value all the way up to the edge of the troposphere, then the pressure varies with altitude, h, according to the *barometric formula*:

$$p = p_0 e^{-h/H}$$

where p_0 is the pressure at sea level and H is a constant approximately equal to 8 km. More specifically, $H = RT/Mg$, where M is the average molar mass of air and T is the temperature. The barometric formula fits the observed pressure distribution quite well even for regions well above the troposphere (see the first illustration). It implies that the pressure of the air and its density fall to half their sea-level value at $h = H \ln 2$, or 6 km.

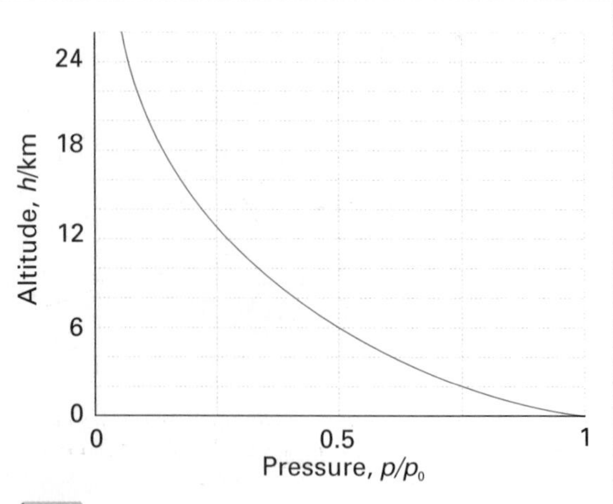

The variation of atmospheric pressure with altitude as predicted by the barometric formula.

The composition of the Earth's atmosphere

Substance		Percentage By volume	By mass
Nitrogen, N_2		78.08	75.53
Oxygen, O_2		20.95	23.14
Argon, Ar		0.93	1.28
Carbon dioxide, CO_2		0.031	0.047
Hydrogen, H_2		5.0×10^{-3}	2.0×10^{-4}
Neon, Ne		1.8×10^{-3}	1.3×10^{-3}
Helium, He		5.2×10^{-4}	7.2×10^{-5}
Methane, CH_4		2.0×10^{-4}	1.1×10^{-4}
Krypton, Kr		1.1×10^{-4}	3.2×10^{-4}
Nitric oxide, NO		5.0×10^{-5}	1.7×10^{-6}
Xenon, Xe		8.7×10^{-6}	3.9×10^{-5}
Ozone, O_3	summer:	7.0×10^{-6}	1.2×10^{-5}
	winter:	2.0×10^{-6}	3.3×10^{-6}

Local variations of pressure, temperature, and composition in the troposphere are manifest as 'weather'. A small region of air is termed a *parcel*. First, we note that a parcel of warm air is less dense than the same parcel of cool air. As a parcel rises, it expands without transfer of heat from its surroundings and so it cools (see Section 1.14 for an explanation). Cool air can absorb lower concentrations of water vapour than warm air, so the moisture forms clouds. Cloudy skies can therefore be associated with rising air and clear skies are often associated with descending air.

The motion of air in the upper altitudes may lead to an accumulation in some regions and a loss of molecules from other regions. The former result in the formation of

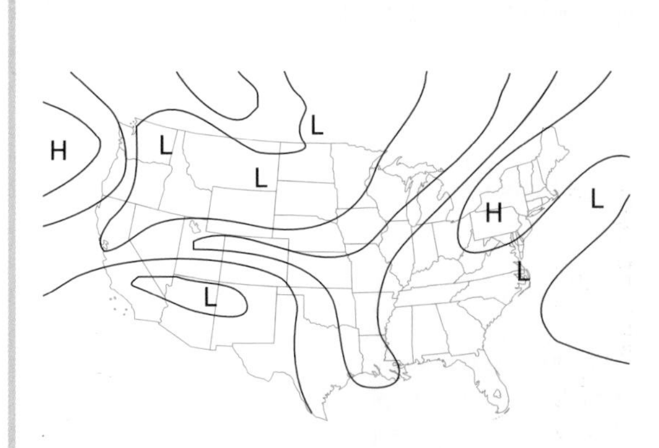

A typical weather map; this one for the continental United States on 14 July 1999. Regions of high pressure are denoted H and those of low pressure L.

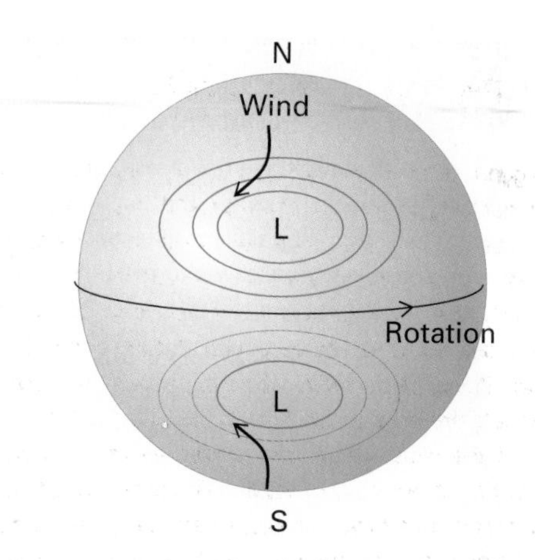

The horizontal flow of air relative to an area of low pressure in the northern and southern hemispheres.

regions of high pressure ('highs' or anticyclones) and the latter result regions of low pressure ('lows', depressions, or cyclones). These regions are shown as H and L on the accompanying weather map. The lines of constant pressure—differing by 4 mbar (400 Pa, about 3 Torr)—marked on it are called *isobars*. The elongated regions of high and low pressure are known, respectively, as *ridges* and *troughs*.

In meteorology, large-scale vertical movement is called *convection*. Horizontal pressure differentials result in the flow of air that we call *wind*. Because the Earth is rotating from west to east, winds are deflected towards the right in the northern hemisphere and towards the left in the southern hemisphere. Winds travel nearly parallel to the isobars, with low pressure to their left in the northern hemisphere and to the right in the southern hemisphere. At the surface, where wind speeds are lower, the winds tend to travel perpendicular to the isobars from high to low pressure. This differential motion results in a spiral outward flow of air clockwise in the northern hemisphere around a high and an inward counterclockwise flow around a low.

The air lost from regions of high pressure is restored as an influx of air converges into the region and descends. As we have seen, descending air is associated with clear skies. It also becomes warmer by compression as it descends, so regions of high pressure are associated with high surface temperatures. In winter, the cold surface air may prevent the complete fall of air, and result in a temperature *inversion*, with a layer of warm air over a layer of cold air. Geographical conditions may also trap cool air, as in Los Angeles, and the photochemical pollutants we know as *smog* may be trapped under the warm layer. A less dramatic manifestation of an inversion layer is the presence of hazy skies, particularly in industrial areas. Hazy skies also form over vegetation that generate aerosols of terpenes or other plant transpiration products. These hazes give rise to the various 'Blue Mountains' of the world, such as the Great Dividing Range in New South Wales, the range in Jamaica, and the range stretching from central Oregon into southeastern Washington, which are dense with eucalyptus, tree ferns, and pine and fir, respectively. The Blue Ridge section of the Appalachians is another example.

Exercise 1 Balloons were used to obtain much of the early information about the atmosphere and continue to be used today to obtain weather information. In 1782, Jacques Charles used a hydrogen-filled balloon to fly from Paris 25 km into the French countryside. What is the mass density of hydrogen relative to air at the same temperature and presure? What mass of payload can be lifted by 10 kg of hydrogen, neglecting the mass of the balloon?

Exercise 2 Atmospheric pollution is a problem that has received much attention. Not all pollution, however, is from industrial sources. Volcanic eruptions can be a significant source of air pollution. The Kilauea volcano in Hawaii emits 200–300 t of SO_2 per day. If this gas is emitted at 800°C and 1.0 atm, what volume of gas is emitted?

Example 1.1

Predicting the pressure of a sample of gas

A chemist is investigating the conversion of atmospheric nitrogen to usable form by the bacteria that inhabit the root systems of certain legumes, and needs to know the pressure in kilopascals exerted by 1.25 g of nitrogen gas in a flask of volume 250 cm^3 at 20°C.

Strategy For this calculation we need to arrange eqn 1.2 ($pV = nRT$) into a form that gives the unknown (the pressure, p) in terms of the information supplied:

$$p = \frac{nRT}{V}$$

To use this expression, we need to know the amount of molecules (in moles) in the sample, which we can obtain from the mass and the molar mass (by using $n = m/M$) and to convert the temperature to the Kelvin scale (by adding 273.15 to the Celsius temperature). Select the value of R from Table 1.1 using the units that match the data and the information required (pressure in kilopascals and volume in cubic decimetres).

Solution The amount of N_2 molecules (of molar mass 28.02 g mol^{-1}) present is

$$n_{N_2} = \frac{m}{M_{N_2}} = \frac{1.25\text{ g}}{28.02\text{ g mol}^{-1}} = \frac{1.25}{28.02}\text{ mol}$$

The temperature of the sample is

$$T/\text{K} = 20 + 273.15$$

Therefore, from $p = nRT/V$,

$$p = \frac{\overbrace{(1.25/28.02)\text{ mol}}^{n} \times \overbrace{(8.314\,47\text{ J K}^{-1}\text{ mol}^{-1})}^{R} \times \overbrace{(20 + 273.15\text{ K})}^{T = 293\text{ K}}}{\underbrace{2.50 \times 10^{-3}\text{ m}^3}_{V = 250\text{ cm}^3}}$$

$$= \frac{(1.25/28.02) \times (8.314\,47) \times 293}{2.50 \times 10^{-3}}\,\frac{\text{J}}{\text{m}^3}$$

$$= 4.35 \times 10^5\text{ Pa} = 435\text{ kPa}$$

We have used the relations 1 J = 1 Pa m^3 and 1 kPa = 10^3 Pa. Note how the units cancel like ordinary numbers.

A note on good practice. It is best to postpone the actual numerical calculation to the last possible stage, and carry it out in a single step. This procedure avoids rounding errors.

Self-test 1.1

Calculate the pressure exerted by 1.22 g of carbon dioxide confined to a flask of volume 500 dm^3 at 37°C.

[Answer: 143 kPa]

In some cases, we are given the pressure under one set of conditions and are asked to predict the pressure of the same sample under a different set of conditions. We use the perfect gas law as follows. Suppose the initial pressure is p_1, the initial temperature is T_1, and the initial volume is V_1. Then by dividing both sides of eqn 1.2 by the temperature we can write

$$\frac{p_1V_1}{T_1} = nR$$

Suppose now that the conditions are changed to T_2 and V_2, and the pressure changes to p_2 as a result. Then under the new conditions eqn 1.2 tells us that

$$\frac{p_2V_2}{T_2} = nR$$

The nR on the right of these two equations is the same in each case, because R is a constant and the amount of gas molecules has not changed. It follows that we can combine the two equations into a single equation:

$$\frac{p_1V_1}{T_1} = \frac{p_2V_2}{T_2} \tag{1.4}$$

This expression is known as the **combined gas equation.** We can rearrange it to calculate any one unknown (such as p_2, for instance) in terms of the other variables.

Self-test 1.2

What is the final volume of a sample of gas that has been heated from 25°C to 1000°C and its pressure increased from 10.0 kPa to 150.0 kPa, given that its initial volume was 15 cm^3?

[Answer: 4.3 cm^3]

Finally, we see how to use the perfect gas law to calculate the molar volume of a perfect gas at any temperature and pressure. Equation 1.3 expresses the molar volume in terms of the volume of a sample; eqn 1.2 in the form $V = nRT/p$ expresses the volume in terms of the pressure. When we combine the two, we get

$$V_m = \frac{V}{n} = \overbrace{\frac{nRT/p}{n}}^{V = nRT/p} = \frac{RT}{p} \tag{1.5}$$

This expression lets us calculate the molar volume of any gas (provided it is behaving perfectly) from its pressure and its temperature. It also shows that, for a given temperature and pressure, provided they are behaving perfectly, all gases have the same molar volume.

Chemists have found it convenient to report much of their data at a particular set of 'standard' conditions. By **standard ambient temperature and pressure** (SATP) they mean a temperature of 25°C (more precisely, 298.15 K) and a pressure of exactly 1 bar (100 kPa). The **standard pressure** is denoted $p^{\ominus}$, so $p^{\ominus} = 1$ bar exactly. The molar volume of a perfect gas at SATP is 24.79 $dm^3\ mol^{-1}$, as can be verified by substituting the values of the temperature and pressure into eqn 1.5. This value implies that at SATP, 1 mol of perfect gas molecules occupies about 25 dm^3 (a cube of about 30 cm on a side). An earlier set of standard conditions, which is still encountered, is **standard temperature and pressure** (STP), namely 0°C and 1 atm. The molar volume of a perfect gas at STP is 22.41 $dm^3\ mol^{-1}$.

1.3 Mixtures of gases: partial pressures

We are often concerned with mixtures of gases, such as when we are considering the properties of the atmosphere in meteorology, the composition of exhaled air in medicine, or the mixtures of hydrogen and nitrogen used in the industrial synthesis of ammonia. We need to be able to assess the contribution that each component of a gaseous mixture makes to the total pressure.

In the early nineteenth century, John Dalton carried out a series of experiments that led him to formulate what has become known as **Dalton's law:**

The pressure exerted by a mixture of perfect gases is the sum of the pressures that each gas would exert if it were alone in the container at the same temperature:

$$p = p_A + p_B + \cdots \tag{1.6}$$

In this expression, p_J is the pressure that the gas J (J = A, B, ...) would exert if it were alone in the container at the same temperature. Dalton's law is strictly valid only for mixtures of perfect gases (or for real gases at such low pressures that they are behaving perfectly), but it can be treated as valid under most conditions we encounter.

Illustration 1.1

Dalton's law

Suppose we were interested in the composition of inhaled and exhaled air, and we knew that a certain mass of carbon dioxide exerts a pressure of 5 kPa when present alone in a container, and that a certain mass of oxygen exerts 20 kPa when present alone in the same container at the same temperature. Then, when both gases are present in the container, the carbon dioxide in the mixture contributes 5 kPa to the total pressure and oxygen contributes 20 kPa; according to Dalton's law, the total pressure of the mixture is the sum of these two pressures, or 25 kPa (Fig. 1.4).

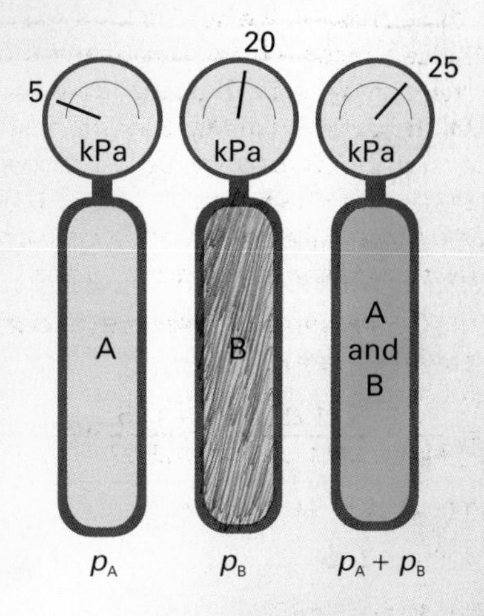

Fig. 1.4 The partial pressure p_A of a perfect gas A is the pressure that the gas would exert if it occupied a container alone; similarly, the partial pressure p_B of a perfect gas B is the pressure that the gas would exert if it occupied the same container alone. The total pressure p when both perfect gases simultaneously occupy the container is the sum of their partial pressures.

For any type of gas (real or perfect) in a mixture, the **partial pressure**, p_J, of the gas J is defined as

$$p_J = x_J p \tag{1.7}$$

where x_J is the **mole fraction** of the gas J in the mixture. The mole fraction of J is the amount of J molecules expressed as a fraction of the total amount of molecules in the mi... i a mixture that consists of n_A A molecules, ... ec... nd so on (where the n_J are amounts in moles), the mole fraction of J (where J = A, B, ...) is

$$x_J = \frac{n_J}{n} \quad \text{(Amount of J; Total amount of molecules)} \qquad (1.8a)$$

where $n = n_A + n_B + \cdots$. Mole fractions are unitless because the unit mole in numerator and denominator cancels. For a **binary mixture**, one that consists of two species, this general expression becomes

$$x_A = \frac{n_A}{n_A + n_B} \quad x_B = \frac{n_B}{n_A + n_B} \quad x_A + x_B = 1 \qquad (1.8b)$$

When only A is present, $x_A = 1$ and $x_B = 0$. When only B is present, $x_B = 1$ and $x_A = 0$. When both A and B are present in the same amounts, $x_A = \frac{1}{2}$ and $x_B = \frac{1}{2}$ (Fig. 1.5).

Self-test 1.3

Calculate the mole fractions of N_2, O_2, and Ar in dry air at sea level, given that 100.0 g of air consists of 75.5 g of N_2, 23.2 g of O_2, and 1.3 g of Ar. (*Hint.* Begin by converting each mass to an amount in moles.)

[*Answer:* 0.780, 0.210, 0.009]

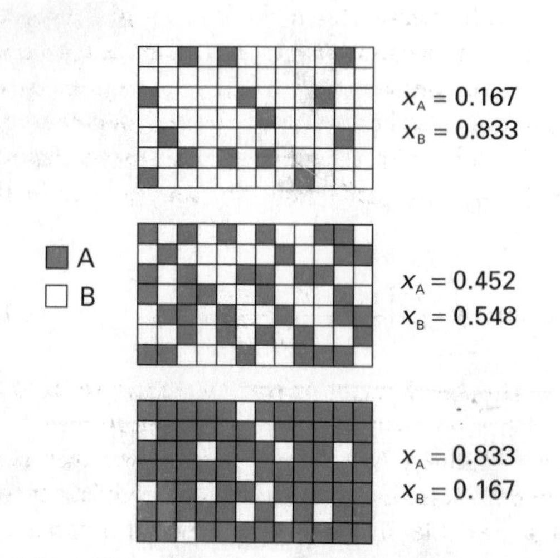

Fig. 1.5 A representation of the meaning of mole fraction. In each case, a small square represents one molecule of A (coloured squares) or B (white squares). There are 84 squares in each sample.

For a mixture of perfect gases, we can identify the partial pressure of J with the contribution that J makes to the total pressure. Thus, if we introduce $p = nRT/V$ into eqn 1.7, we get

$$p_J = x_J p = x_J \times \frac{nRT}{V} = \frac{n_J RT}{V} \quad (p = nRT/V;\ x_J = n_J/n)$$

The value of $n_J RT/V$ is the pressure that an amount n_J of J would exert in the otherwise empty container. That is, the partial pressure of J as defined by eqn 1.7 is the pressure of J used in Dalton's law, provided all the gases in the mixture behave perfectly. If the gases are real, their partial pressures are still given by eqn 1.7, as that definition applies to all gases, and the sum of these partial pressures is the total pressure (because the sum of all the mole fractions is 1); however, each partial pressure is no longer the pressure that the gas would exert when alone in the container.

Illustration 1.2

Calculating partial pressures

From Self-test 1.3, we have $x_{N_2} = 0.780$, $x_{O_2} = 0.210$, and $x_{Ar} = 0.009$ for dry air at sea level. It then follows from eqn 1.7 that when the total atmospheric pressure is 100 kPa, the partial pressure of nitrogen is

$$p_{N_2} = x_{N_2} p = 0.780 \times (100 \text{ kPa}) = 78.0 \text{ kPa}$$

Similarly, for the other two components we find p_{O_2} = 21.0 kPa and p_{Ar} = 0.9 kPa. Provided the gases are perfect, these partial pressures are the pressures that each gas would exert if it were separated from the mixture and put in the same container on its own.

Self-test 1.4

The partial pressure of oxygen in air plays an important role in the aeration of water, to enable aquatic life to thrive, and in the absorption of oxygen by blood in our lungs (see Box 6.1). Calculate the partial pressures of a sample of gas consisting of 2.50 g of oxygen and 6.43 g of carbon dioxide with a total pressure of 88 kPa.

[*Answer:* 31 kPa, 57 kPa]

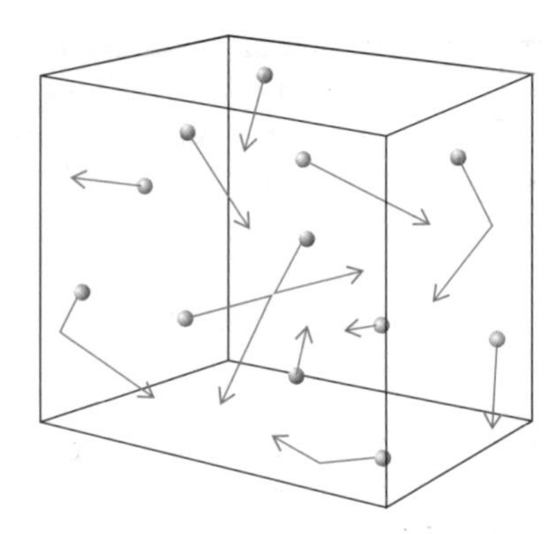

Fig. 1.6 The model used for discussing the molecular basis of the physical properties of a perfect gas. The point-like molecules move randomly with a wide range of speeds and in random directions, both of which change when they collide with the walls or with other molecules.

The kinetic model of gases

We saw in the *Introduction* that a gas may be pictured as a collection of particles in ceaseless, random motion (Fig. 1.6). Now we develop this model of the gaseous state of matter to see how it accounts for the perfect gas law. One of the most important functions of physical chemistry is to convert qualitative notions into quantitative statements that can be tested experimentally by making measurements and comparing the results with predictions. Indeed, an important component of science as a whole is its technique of proposing a qualitative model and then expressing that model mathematically. The 'kinetic model' (or the 'kinetic molecular theory', KMT) of gases is an excellent example of this procedure: the model is very simple, and the quantitative prediction (the perfect gas law) is experimentally verifiable.

The **kinetic model of gases** is based on three assumptions:

1. A gas consists of molecules in ceaseless random motion.
2. The size of the molecules is negligible in the sense that their diameters are much smaller than the average distance travelled between collisions.
3. The molecules do not interact, except during collisions.

The assumption that the molecules do not interact unless they are in contact implies that the potential energy of the molecules (their energy due to their position) is independent of their separation and may be set equal to zero. The total energy of a sample of gas is therefore the sum of the kinetic energies (the energy due to motion) of all the molecules present in it. It follows that the faster the molecules travel (and hence the greater their kinetic energy), the greater the total energy of the gas.

1.4 The pressure of a gas according to the kinetic model

The kinetic model accounts for the steady pressure exerted by a gas in terms of the collisions the molecules make with the walls of the container. Each collision gives rise to a brief force on the wall, but as billions of collisions take place every second, the walls experience an almost constant force, and hence the gas exerts a steady pressure. On the basis of this model, the pressure exerted by a gas of molar mass M in a volume V is[2]

$$p = \frac{nMc^2}{3V} \tag{1.9}$$

Here c is the **root-mean-square speed** (rms speed) of the molecules. This quantity is defined as the square root of the mean value of the squares of the speeds, v, of the molecules. That is, for a sample consisting of N molecules with speeds $v_1, v_2, \ldots, v_N$, we square each speed, add the squares together, divide by the total number of molecules (to get the mean, denoted by $\langle \ldots \rangle$), and finally take the square root of the result:

$$c = \langle v^2 \rangle^{1/2} = \left(\frac{v_1^2 + v_2^2 + \cdots + v_N^2}{N} \right)^{1/2} \tag{1.10}$$

The rms speed might at first encounter seem to be a rather peculiar measure of the mean speeds of the molecules, but its significance becomes clear when we make use of the fact that the kinetic energy of a molecule of mass m travelling at a speed v is $E_K = \frac{1}{2}mv^2$, which implies that the mean kinetic

[2] See *Further information* 1.1 for a derivation of eqn 1.9.

energy, $\langle E_K \rangle$, is the average of this quantity, or $\frac{1}{2}mc^2$. It follows that

$$c = \left(\frac{2\langle E_K \rangle}{m}\right)^{1/2} \qquad (1.11)$$

Therefore, wherever c appears, we can think of it as a measure of the mean kinetic energy of the molecules of the gas. The rms speed is quite close in value to another and more readily visualized measure of molecular speed, the **mean speed**, $\bar{c}$, of the molecules:

$$\bar{c} = \frac{v_1 + v_2 + \cdots + v_N}{N} \qquad (1.12)$$

For samples consisting of large numbers of molecules, the mean speed is slightly smaller than the rms speed. The precise relation is

$$\bar{c} = \left(\frac{8}{3\pi}\right)^{1/2} c \approx 0.921c \qquad (1.13)$$

For elementary purposes, and for qualitative arguments, we do not need to distinguish between the two measures of average speed, but for precise work the distinction is important.

Self-test 1.5

Cars pass a point travelling at 45.00 (5), 47.00 (7), 50.00 (9), 53.00 (4), 57.00 (1) km h^{-1}, where the number of cars is given in parentheses. Calculate (a) the rms speed and (b) the mean speed of the cars. (*Hint.* Use the definitions directly; the relation in eqn 1.13 is unreliable for such small samples.)

[*Answer:* (a) 49.06 km h^{-1}, (b) 48.96 km h^{-1}]

Equation 1.9 already resembles the perfect gas equation of state, as we can rearrange it into

$$pV = \tfrac{1}{3}nMc^2 \qquad (1.14)$$

and compare it to $pV = nRT$. This conclusion is a major success of the kinetic model, as the model implies an experimentally verified result.

1.5 The average speed of gas molecules

We now suppose that the expression for pV derived from the kinetic model is indeed the equation of state of a perfect gas. That being so, we can equate the expression on the right of eqn 1.14 to nRT, which gives

$$\tfrac{1}{3}nMc^2 = nRT$$

The ns now cancel. The great usefulness of this expression is that we can rearrange it into a formula for the rms speed of the gas molecules at any temperature:

$$c = \left(\frac{3RT}{M}\right)^{1/2} \qquad (1.15)$$

Substitution of the molar mass of O_2 (32.0 g mol^{-1}) and a temperature corresponding to 25°C (that is, 298 K) gives an rms speed for these molecules of 482 m s^{-1}. The same calculation for nitrogen molecules gives 515 m s^{-1}. Both these values are not far off the speed of sound in air (346 m s^{-1} at 25°C). That similarity is reasonable, because sound is a wave of pressure variation transmitted by the movement of molecules, so the speed of propagation of a wave should be approximately the same as the speed at which molecules can adjust their locations.

The important conclusion to draw from eqn 1.15 is that *the rms speed of molecules in a gas is proportional to the square root of the temperature*. Because the mean speed is proportional to the rms speed, the same is true of the mean speed too. Therefore, doubling the temperature (on the Kelvin scale) increases the mean and the rms speed of molecules by a factor of $2^{1/2} = 1.414\ldots$.

Illustration 1.3

The effect of temperature on mean speeds

Cooling a sample of air from 25°C (298 K) to 0°C (273 K) reduces the original rms speed of the molecules by a factor of

$$\left(\frac{273\text{ K}}{298\text{ K}}\right)^{1/2} = \left(\frac{273}{298}\right)^{1/2} = 0.957$$

So, on a cold day, the average speed of air molecules (which is changed by the same factor) is about 4 per cent less than on a warm day.

1.6 The Maxwell distribution of speeds

So far, we have dealt only with the *average* speed of molecules in a gas. Not all molecules, however, travel at the same speed: some move more slowly than the average (until they collide, and get accelerated to a high speed, like the impact of a bat on a ball), and others may briefly move at much higher speeds than the average, but be brought to a sudden stop when they collide. There is a ceaseless redistribution of speeds among molecules as they undergo collisions. Each molecule collides once every nanosecond (1 ns = 10^{-9} s) or so in a gas under normal conditions.

The mathematical expression that tells us the fraction of molecules that have a particular speed at any instant is called the **distribution of molecular speeds**. Thus, the distribution might tell us that at 20°C, 19 out of 1000 O_2 molecules have a speed in the range between 300 and 310 m s^{-1}, that 21 out of 1000 have a speed in the range 400 to 410 m s^{-1}, and so on. The precise form of the distribution was worked out by James Clerk Maxwell towards the end of the nineteenth century, and his expression is known as the **Maxwell distribution of speeds**. According to Maxwell, the fraction f of molecules that have a speed in a narrow range between s and $s + \Delta s$ (for example, between 300 m s^{-1} and 310 m s^{-1}, corresponding to s = 300 m s^{-1} and Δs = 10 m s^{-1}) is

$$f = F(s)\Delta s \quad \text{with} \quad F(s) = 4\pi\left(\frac{M}{2\pi RT}\right)^{3/2} s^2\, e^{-Ms^2/2RT} \qquad (1.16)$$

This formula was used to calculate the values quoted above.

Although eqn 1.16 looks complicated, its features can be picked out quite readily. One of the skills to develop in physical chemistry is the ability to interpret the message carried by equations. Equations convey information, and it is far more important to be able to read that information than simply to remember the equation. Let's read the information in eqn 1.16 piece by piece.

Before we begin, and in preparation for a large number of occurrences of exponential functions throughout the text, it will be useful to know the shape of exponential functions. Here we deal with two types, e^{-ax} and e^{-ax^2}. An exponential function of the form e^{-ax} starts off at 1 when $x = 0$ and decays towards zero, which it reaches as x approaches infinity (Fig. 1.7). This function approaches zero more rapidly as a increases. The function e^{-ax^2} is called a **Gaussian function**. It also starts off at 1 when $x = 0$ and decays to zero as x increases; however, its decay is initially slower but then plunges down more rapidly than e^{-ax}. The illustration also shows the behaviour of the two functions for negative values of x. The exponential function e^{-ax} rises rapidly to infinity, but the Gaussian function falls back to zero and traces out a bell-shaped curve.

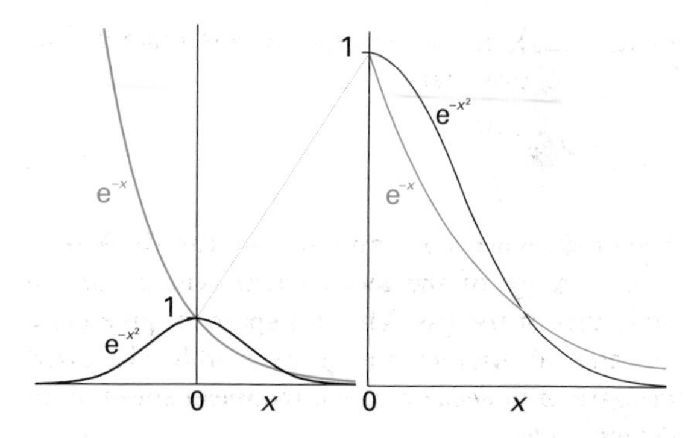

Fig. 1.7 The exponential function, e^{-x}, and the bell-shaped Gaussian function, e^{-x^2}. Note that both are equal to 1 at $x = 0$ but the exponential function rises to infinity as $x \to -\infty$. The enlargement in the right shows the behaviour for $x > 0$ in more detail.

Now let's consider the content of eqn 1.16.

1 Because f is proportional to the range of speeds Δs, we see that the fraction in the range Δs increases in proportion to the width of the range. If at a given speed we double the range of interest (but still ensure that it is narrow), then the fraction of molecules in that range doubles too.

2 Equation 1.16 includes a decaying exponential function, the term $e^{-Ms^2/2RT}$. Its presence implies that the fraction of molecules with very high speeds will be very small because e^{-x^2} becomes very small when x^2 is large.

3 The factor $M/2RT$ multiplying s^2 in the exponent is large when the molar mass, M, is large, so the exponential factor goes most rapidly towards zero when M is large. That tells us that heavy molecules are unlikely to be found with very high speeds.

4 The opposite is true when the temperature, T, is high: then the factor $M/2RT$ in the exponent is small, so the exponential factor falls towards zero relatively slowly as s increases. This tells us that at high temperatures, a greater fraction of the molecules can be expected to have high speeds than at low temperatures.

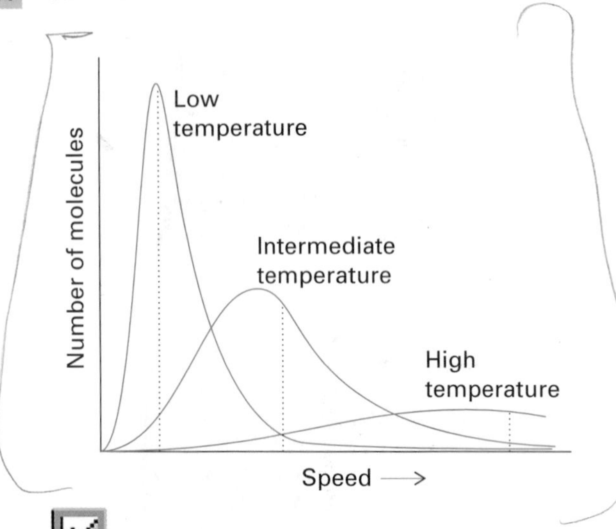

Fig. 1.8 The Maxwell distribution of speeds and its variation with the temperature. Note the broadening of the distribution and the shift of the rms speed (denoted by the locations of the vertical lines) to higher values as the temperature is increased.

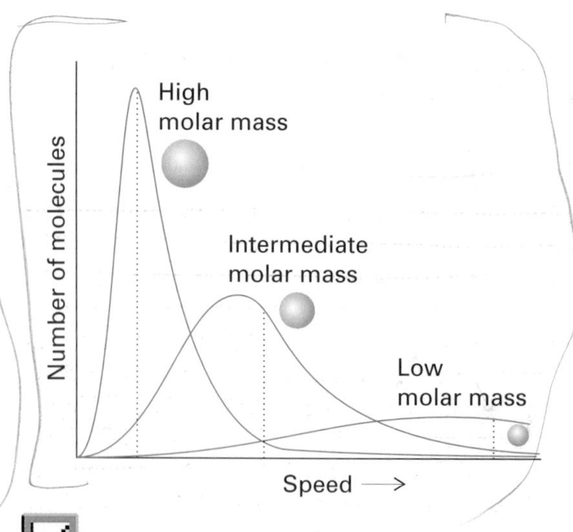

Fig. 1.9 The Maxwell distribution of speeds also depends on the molar mass of the molecules. Molecules of low molar mass have a broad spread of speeds, and a significant fraction may be found travelling much faster than the rms speed. The distribution is much narrower for heavy molecules, and most of them travel with speeds close to the rms value (denoted by the locations of the vertical lines).

5 A factor s^2 (the term before the e) multiplies the exponential. This factor goes to zero as s goes to zero, so the fraction of molecules with very low speeds will also be very small.

The remaining factors (the term in parentheses in eqn 1.16 and the 4π) simply ensure that when we add together the fractions over the entire range of speeds from zero to infinity, we get 1.

Figure 1.8 is a plot of the Maxwell distribution, and shows these features pictorially for the same gas (the same value of M) but different temperatures. As we deduced from the equation, we see that only small fractions of molecules in the sample have very low or very high speeds. However, the fraction with very high speeds increases sharply as the temperature is raised, as the tail of the distribution reaches up to higher speeds. This feature plays an important role in the rates of gas-phase chemical reactions because (as we shall see in Section 10.10) the rate of a reaction in the gas phase depends on the energy with which two molecules crash together, which in turn depends on their speeds.

Figure 1.9 is a plot of the Maxwell distribution for molecules with different molar masses at the same temperature. As can be seen, not only do heavy molecules have lower average speeds than light molecules at a given temperature, but they also have a significantly narrower spread of speeds. That narrow spread means that most molecules will be found with speeds close to the average. By contrast, light molecules (such as H_2) have high average speeds and a wide spread of speeds: many molecules will be found travelling either much more slowly or much more quickly than the average. This feature plays an important role in determining the composition of planetary atmospheres, because it means that a significant fraction of light molecules travel at sufficiently high speeds to escape from the planet's gravitational attraction. The ability of light molecules to escape is one reason why hydrogen (molar mass 2.02 g mol^{-1}) and helium (4.00 g mol^{-1}) are very rare in the Earth's atmosphere.

The Maxwell distribution has been verified experimentally by passing a beam of molecules from an oven at a given temperature through a series of coaxial slotted discs. The speed of rotation of the discs brings the slots into line for molecules travelling at a particular speed, so only molecules with that speed pass through and are detected. By varying the rotation speed, the shape of the speed distribution can be explored and is found to match that predicted by eqn 1.16.

1.7 Diffusion and effusion

Diffusion is the process by which the molecules of different substances mingle with each other. The atoms of two solids diffuse into each other when the two solids are in contact, but the process is very slow. The diffusion of a solid through a liquid solvent is much faster but mixing normally needs to be encouraged by stirring or shaking the solid in the liquid (the process is then no longer pure diffusion). Gaseous diffusion is much faster. It accounts for the largely uniform composition of the atmosphere because, if a gas is produced by a localized source (such as carbon dioxide from the respiration of animals, oxygen from photosynthesis by green plants, and pollutants from vehicles and industrial sources), then the molecules of gas will diffuse from the source and in due course be distributed throughout the atmosphere. In practice, the process of mixing is accelerated by winds: such bulk motion of matter is called **convection**. The process of **effusion** is the escape of a gas through a small hole, as in a puncture in an inflated balloon or tyre (Fig. 1.10).

The rates of diffusion and effusion of gases increase with increasing temperature, as both processes depend on the motion of molecules, and molecular speeds increase with temperature. The rates also decrease with increasing molar mass, as molecular speeds decrease with increasing molar mass. The dependence on molar mass, however, is simple only in the case of effusion. In effusion, only a single substance is in motion, not the two or more intermingling gases involved in diffusion.

The experimental observations on the dependence of the rate of effusion of a gas on its molar mass are summarized by **Graham's law of effusion,** proposed by Thomas Graham in 1833:

At a given pressure and temperature, the rate of effusion of a gas is inversely proportional to the square root of its molar mass:

$$\text{Rate of effusion} \propto \frac{1}{M^{1/2}} \quad (1.17)$$

Rate in this context means the number (or number of moles) of molecules that escape per second.

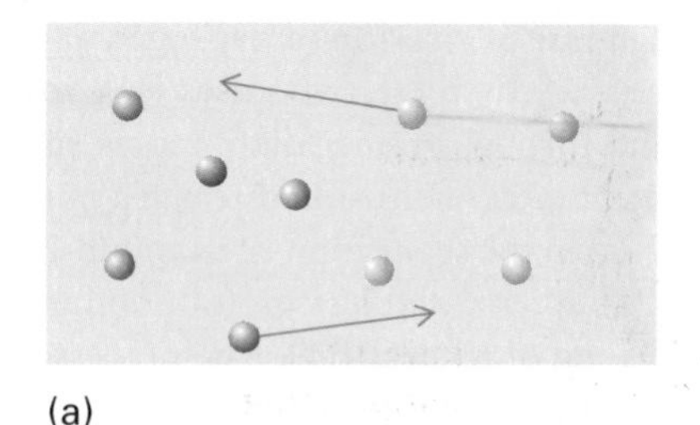

(a)

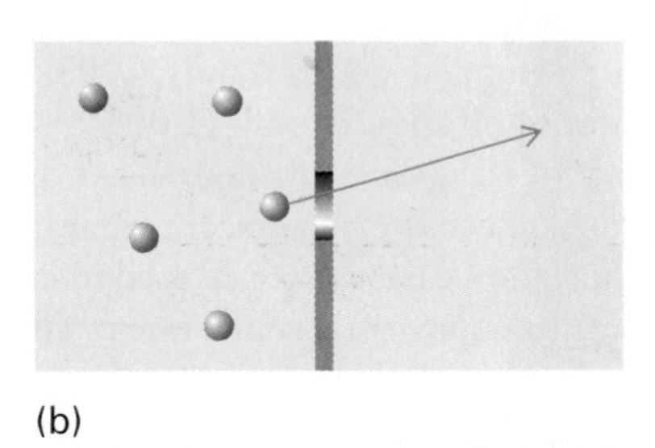

(b)

Fig. 1.10 (a) Diffusion is the spreading of the molecules of one substance into the region initially occupied by another species. Note that molecules of both substances move, and each substance diffuses into the other. (b) Effusion is the escape of molecules through a small hole in a confining wall.

Illustration 1.4

Relative rates of effusion

The rates (in terms of amounts of molecules) at which hydrogen (molar mass 2.016 g mol^{-1}) and carbon dioxide (44.01 g mol^{-1}) effuse under the same conditions of pressure and temperature are in the ratio

$$\frac{\text{Rate of effusion of } H_2}{\text{Rate of effusion of } CO_2} = \left(\frac{M_{CO_2}}{M_{H_2}}\right)^{1/2} = \left(\frac{44.01\text{ g mol}^{-1}}{2.016\text{ g mol}^{-1}}\right)^{1/2} = \left(\frac{44.01}{2.016}\right)^{1/2} = 4.672$$

The *mass* of carbon dioxide that escapes in a given interval is greater than the mass of hydrogen, because although nearly 5 times as many hydrogen molecules escape, each carbon dioxide molecule has over 20 times the mass of a molecule of hydrogen.

A note on good practice. Always make it clear what terms mean: in this instance 'rate' alone is ambiguous; you need to specify that it is the rate in terms of amount of molecules.

The high rate of effusion of hydrogen and helium is one reason why these two gases leak from containers and through rubber diaphragms so readily. The different rates of effusion through a porous barrier are used in the separation of uranium-235 from the more abundant and less useful uranium-238 in the processing of nuclear fuel. The process depends on the formation of uranium hexafluoride, a volatile solid. However, because the ratio of the molar masses of $^{238}UF_6$ and $^{235}UF_6$ is only 1.008, the ratio of the rates of effusion is only $(1.008)^{1/2} = 1.004$. Thousands of successive effusion stages are therefore required to achieve a significant separation. The rate of effusion of gases was once used to determine molar mass by comparison of the rate of effusion of a gas or vapour with that of a gas of known molar mass. However, there are now much more precise methods available, such as mass spectrometry.

Graham's law is explained by noting that the rms speed of molecules of a gas is inversely proportional to the square root of the molar mass (eqn 1.15). Because the rate of effusion through a hole in a container is proportional to the rate at which molecules pass through the hole, it follows that the rate should be inversely proportional to $M^{1/2}$, which is in accord with Graham's law.

1.8 Molecular collisions

The average distance that a molecule travels between collisions is called its **mean free path**, λ (lambda). The mean free path in a liquid is less than the diameter of the molecules, because a molecule in a liquid meets a neighbour even if it moves only a fraction of a diameter. However, in gases, the mean free paths of molecules can be several hundred molecular diameters. If we think of a molecule as the size of a tennis ball, then the mean free path in a typical gas would be about the length of a tennis court.

The **collision frequency**, z, is the average rate of collisions made by one molecule. Specifically, z is the average number of collisions one molecule makes in a given time interval divided by the length of the interval. It follows that the inverse of the collision frequency, $1/z$, is the **time of flight**, the average time that a molecule spends in flight between two collisions (for instance, if there are 10 collisions per second so the collision frequency is 10 s^{-1}, then the average time between collisions is $\frac{1}{10}$ of a second and the time of flight is $\frac{1}{10}$ s). As we shall see, the collision frequency in a typical gas is about 10^9 s^{-1} at 1 atm and room temperature, so the time of flight in a gas is typically 1 ns.

Because speed is distance travelled divided by the time taken for the journey, the rms speed c, which we can think of loosely as the average speed, is the average length of the flight of a molecule between collisions (that is, the mean free path, λ) divided by the time of flight ($1/z$). It follows that the mean free path and the collision frequency are related by

$$c = \frac{\text{mean free path}}{\text{time of flight}} = \frac{\lambda}{1/z} = \lambda z \qquad (1.18)$$

Therefore, if we can calculate either λ or z, then we can find the other from this equation and the value of c given in eqn 1.15.

To find expressions for λ and z we need a slightly more elaborate version of the kinetic model. The basic kinetic model supposes that the molecules are effectively point-like; however, to obtain collisions, we need to assume that two 'points' score a hit whenever they come within a certain range d of each other, where d can be thought of as the diameter of the molecules (Fig. 1.11). The **collision cross-section**, σ (sigma), the target area presented by one molecule to another, is therefore the area of a circle of radius d, so $\sigma = \pi d^2$. When this quantity is built into the kinetic model, we find that

$$\lambda = \frac{RT}{2^{1/2} N_A \sigma p} \qquad z = \frac{2^{1/2} N_A \sigma c p}{RT} \qquad (1.19)$$

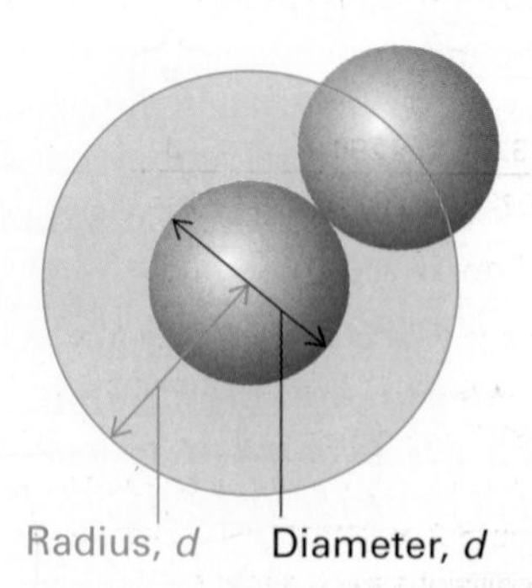

Fig. 1.11 To calculate features of a perfect gas that are related to collisions, a point is regarded as being surrounded by a sphere of diameter d. A molecule will hit another molecule if the centre of the former lies within a circle of radius d. The collision cross-section is the target area, πd^2.

Table 1.3

Collision cross-sections of atoms and molecules

Species	σ/nm^2
Argon, Ar	0.36
Benzene, C_6H_6	0.88
Carbon dioxide, CO_2	0.52
Chlorine, Cl_2	0.93
Ethene, C_2H_4	0.64
Helium, He	0.21
Hydrogen, H_2	0.27
Methane, CH_4	0.46
Nitrogen, N_2	0.43
Oxygen, O_2	0.40
Sulfur dioxide, SO_2	0.58

1 nm^2 = 10^{-18} m^2.

Table 1.3 lists the collision cross-sections of some common atoms and molecules.

Illustration 1.5

Calculating a mean free path

From the information in Table 1.3 we can calculate that the mean free path of O_2 molecules in a sample of oxygen at SATP (25°C, 1 bar) is

$$\lambda = \frac{\overbrace{(8.314\,47\ \mathrm{J\,K^{-1}\,mol^{-1}})}^{R} \times \overbrace{(298\ \mathrm{K})}^{T}}{2^{1/2} \times \underbrace{(6.022 \times 10^{23}\ \mathrm{mol^{-1}})}_{N_A} \times \underbrace{(0.40 \times 10^{-18}\ \mathrm{m^2})}_{\sigma} \times \underbrace{(1.00 \times 10^{5}\ \mathrm{Pa})}_{p}}$$

$$= \frac{8.314\,47 \times 298}{2^{1/2} \times 6.022 \times 0.40 \times 1.00 \times 10^{10}} \frac{\mathrm{J}}{\mathrm{Pa\,m^2}}$$

$$= 7.3 \times 10^{-8}\ \mathrm{m} = 73\ \mathrm{nm}$$

We have used R in one of its SI unit forms: this form is usually appropriate in calculations based on the kinetic model; we have also used 1 J = 1 Pa m^3 and 1 nm = 10^{-9} m. Under the same conditions, the collision frequency is 6.2×10^9 s^{-1}, so each molecule makes 6.2 billion collisions each second.

Once again, we should *interpret the essence* of the two expressions in eqn 1.19 rather than trying to remember them.

1 Because $\lambda \propto 1/p$, we see that *the mean free path decreases as the pressure increases*. This decrease is a result of the increase in the number of molecules present in a given volume as the pressure is increased, so each molecule travels a shorter distance before it collides with a neighbour.

For example, the mean free path of an O_2 molecule decreases from 73 nm to 36 nm when the pressure is increased from 1.0 bar to 2.0 bar at 25°C.

2 Because $\lambda \propto 1/\sigma$, *the mean free path is shorter for molecules with large collision cross-sections.*

For example, the collision cross-section of a benzene molecule (0.88 nm^2) is about four times greater than that of a helium atom (0.21 nm^2), and at the same pressure and temperature its mean free path is four times shorter.

3 Because $z \propto p$, *the collision frequency increases with the pressure of the gas.* This dependence follows from the fact that, provided the temperature is the same, the molecules take less time to travel to its neighbour in a denser, higher-pressure gas.

For example, although the collision frequency for an O_2 molecule in oxygen gas at SATP is 6.2×10^9 s^{-1}, at 2.0 bar and the same temperature the collision frequency is doubled, to 1.2×10^{10} s^{-1}.

4 Because eqn 1.19 shows that $z \propto c$, and we know that $c \propto 1/M^{1/2}$, *heavy molecules have lower collision frequencies than light molecules*, providing their collision cross-sections are the same. Heavy molecules travel more slowly on average than light molecules do (at the same temperature), so they collide with other molecules less frequently.

Real gases

So far, everything we have said applies to perfect gases, in which the average separation of the molecules is so great that they move independently of one another. In terms of the quantities introduced in the previous section, a perfect gas is a gas for which the mean free path, λ, of the molecules in the sample is much greater than d, the separation at which they are regarded as being in contact:

Condition for perfect gas behaviour: λ

Box 1.2 *The Sun as a ball of perfect gas*

The kinetic theory of gases is valid when the size of the particles is negligible compared with their mean free path. It may seem absurd, therefore, to expect the kinetic theory and, as a consequence, the perfect gas law, to be applicable to the dense matter of stellar interiors. In the Sun, for instance, the density is 1.50 times that of liquid water at its centre and comparable to that of water about halfway to its surface. However, we have to realize that the state of matter is that of a *plasma*, in which the electrons have been stripped from the atoms of hydrogen and helium that make up the bulk of the matter of stars. As a result, the particles making up the plasma have diameters comparable to those of nuclei, or about 10 fm. Therefore, a mean free path of only 0.1 pm satisfies the criterion for the validity of the kinetic theory and the perfect gas law. We can therefore use $pV = nRT$ as the equation of state for the stellar interior.

As for any perfect gas, the pressure in the interior of the Sun is related to the mass density, $\rho = m/V$, by

$$p = \frac{nRT}{V} = \frac{mRT}{MV} = \frac{\rho RT}{M}$$

The problem is to know the molar mass to use. Atoms are stripped of their electrons in the interior of stars, so if we suppose that the interior consists of ionized hydrogen atoms, the mean molar mass is one-half the molar mass of hydrogen, or 0.5 g mol^{-1} (the mean of the molar mass of H^+ and e^-, the latter being almost 0). Halfway to the centre of the Sun, the temperature is 3.6 MK and the mass density is 1.20 g cm^{-3} (slightly denser than water); so the pressure there is

$$p = \frac{(1.20 \times 10^3\ \text{kg m}^{-3}) \times (8.3145\ \text{J K}^{-1}\ \text{mol}^{-1}) \times (3.6 \times 10^6\ \text{K})}{0.50 \times 10^{-3}\ \text{kg mol}^{-1}}$$

$$= 7.2 \times 10^{13}\ \text{Pa}$$

or 720 Mbar (about 720 million atmospheres).

We can combine this result with the expression for the pressure from kinetic theory ($p = \frac{1}{3}NMc^2/V$). Because the total kinetic energy of the particles is $E_K = \frac{1}{2}Nmc^2$, we can write $p = \frac{2}{3}E_K/V$. That is, the pressure of the plasma is related to the *kinetic energy density*, $\rho_K = E_K/V$, the kinetic energy of the molecules in a region divided by the volume of the region, by

$$p = \tfrac{2}{3}\rho_K$$

It follows that the kinetic energy density halfway to the centre of the Sun is

$$\rho_K = \tfrac{3}{2}p = \tfrac{3}{2} \times (7.2 \times 10^{13}\ \text{Pa}) = 1.1 \times 10^{14}\ \text{J m}^{-3}$$

or 0.11 GJ cm^{-3}. By contrast, on a warm day (25°C) on Earth, the (translational) kinetic energy density of our atmosphere is only 1.5×10^5 J m^{-3} (corresponding to 0.15 J cm^{-3}).

Exercise 1 A star eventually depletes some of the hydrogen in its core, which contracts and results in higher temperatures. The increased temperature results in an increase in the rates of nuclear reaction, some of which result in the formation of heavier nuclei, such as carbon. The outer part of the star expands and cools to produce a red giant. Assume that halfway to the centre a red giant has a temperature of 3500 K, is composed primarily of fully ionized carbon atoms and electrons, and has a mass density of 1200 kg m^{-3}. What is the pressure at this point?

Exercise 2 If the red giant in Exercise 1 consisted of neutral carbon atoms, what would be the pressure at the same point under the same conditions?

As a result of this large average separation, a perfect gas is a gas in which the only contribution to the energy comes from the kinetic energy of the motion of the molecules and there is no contribution to the total energy from the potential energy arising from the interaction of the molecules with one another. However, all molecules do in fact interact with one another provided they are close enough together, so the 'kinetic energy only' model is only an approximation. Nevertheless, under most conditions the criterion $\lambda \gg d$ is satisfied and the gas can be treated as though it is perfect; the criterion is also satisfied under some other rather surprising conditions (Box 1.2).

1.9 Molecular interactions

There are two types of contribution to the interaction between molecules. At relatively large separations (a few molecular diameters), molecules attract each other. This attraction is responsible for the condensation of gases into liquids at low temperatures. At low-enough temperatures the molecules of a gas have insufficient kinetic energy to escape from each other's attraction and they stick together. Second, although molecules attract each other when they are a few diameters apart, as soon as they come into contact they repel each other. This repulsion is responsible for the fact that liquids and solids have a definite bulk and do not collapse to an infinitesimal point.

Molecular interactions—the attractions and repulsions between molecules—give rise to a potential energy that contributes to the total energy of a gas. Because attractions correspond to a lowering of total energy as molecules get closer together, they make a *negative* contribution to the potential energy. Repulsions, however, make a positive contribution to the total energy as the molecules squash together. Figure 1.12 illustrates the general form of the variation of the intermolecular potential energy. At large separations, the energy-lowering interactions are dominant, but at short distances the energy-raising repulsions dominate.

Molecular interactions affect the bulk properties of a gas and, in particular, their equations of state.

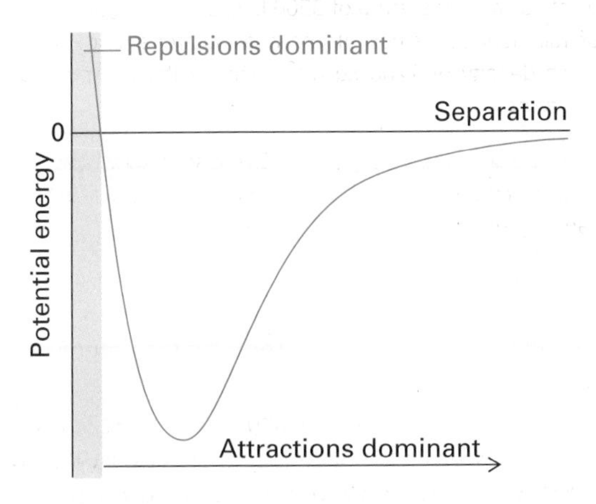

Fig. 1.12 The variation of the potential energy of two molecules with their separation. High positive potential energy (at very small separations) indicates that the interactions between them are strongly repulsive at these distances. At intermediate separations, where the potential energy is negative, the attractive interactions dominate. At large separations (on the right) the potential energy is zero and there is no interaction between the molecules.

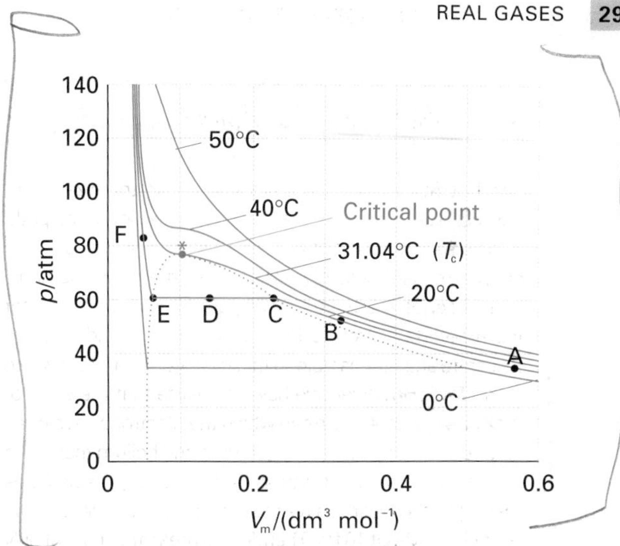

Fig. 1.13 The experimental isotherms of carbon dioxide at several temperatures. The critical isotherm is at 31.04°C.

For example, the isotherms of real gases have shapes that differ from those implied by Boyle's law, particularly at high pressures and low temperatures when the interactions are most important. Figure 1.13 shows a set of experimental isotherms for carbon dioxide. They should be compared with the perfect gas isotherms shown in Fig. 1.1. Although the experimental isotherms resemble the perfect gas isotherms at high temperatures (and at low pressures, off the scale on the right of the graph), there are very striking differences between the two at temperatures below about 50°C and at pressures above about 1 bar.

1.10 The critical temperature

To understand the significance of the isotherms in Fig. 1.13, let's begin with the isotherm at 20°C. At point A the sample is a gas. As the sample is compressed to B by pressing in a piston, the pressure increases broadly in agreement with Boyle's law, and the increase continues until the sample reaches point C. Beyond this point, we find that the piston can be pushed in without any further increase in pressure, through D to E. The reduction in volume from E to F requires a very large increase in pressure. This variation of pressure with volume is exactly what we expect if the gas at C condenses to a compact liquid at E. Indeed, if we could observe the sample

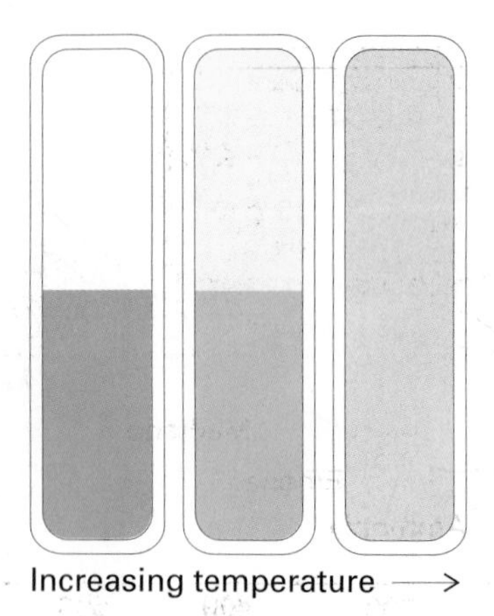

Fig. 1.14 When a liquid is heated in a sealed container, the density of the vapour phase increases and that of the liquid phase decreases, as depicted here by the changing density of shading. There comes a stage at which the two densities are equal and the interface between the two fluids disappears. This disappearance occurs at the critical temperature. The container needs to be strong: the critical temperature of water is at 373°C and the vapour pressure is then 218 atm.

Table 1.4

The critical temperatures of gases

	Critical temperature/°C
Noble gases	
Helium, He	–268 (5.2 K)
Neon, Ne	–229
Argon, Ar	–123
Krypton, Kr	–64
Xenon, Xe	17
Halogens	
Chlorine, Cl_2	144
Bromine, Br_2	311
Small inorganic molecules	
Ammonia, NH_3	132
Carbon dioxide, CO_2	31
Hydrogen, H_2	–240
Nitrogen, N_2	–147
Oxygen, O_2	–118
Water, H_2O	374
Organic compounds	
Benzene, C_6H_6	289
Methane, CH_4	–83
Tetrachloromethane, CCl_4	283

we would see it begin to condense to a liquid at C, and the condensation would be complete when the piston was pushed in to E. At E, the piston is resting on the surface of the liquid. The subsequent reduction in volume, from E to F, corresponds to the very high pressure needed to compress a liquid into a smaller volume. In terms of intermolecular interactions, the step from C to E corresponds to the molecules being so close on average that they attract each other and cohere into a liquid. The step from E to F represents the effect of trying to force the molecules even closer together when they are already in contact, and hence trying to overcome the strong repulsive interactions between them.

If we could look inside the container at point D, we would see a liquid separated from the remaining gas by a sharp surface (Fig. 1.14). At a slightly higher temperature (at 30°C, for instance), a liquid forms, but a higher pressure is needed to produce it. It might be difficult to make out the surface because the remaining gas is at such a high pressure that its density is similar to that of the liquid. At the special temperature of 31.04°C (304.19 K) the gaseous state appears to transform continuously into the condensed state and at no stage is there a visible surface between the two states of matter. At this temperature, which is called the **critical temperature**, T_c, and at all higher temperatures, a single form of matter fills the container at all stages of the compression and there is no separation of a liquid from the gas. We have to conclude that *a gas cannot be condensed to a liquid by the application of pressure unless the temperature is below the critical temperature*.

Table 1.4 lists the critical temperatures of some common gases. The data there imply, for example, that liquid nitrogen cannot be formed by the application of pressure unless the temperature is below 126 K (–147°C). The critical temperature is sometimes used to distinguish between the terms 'vapour' and 'gas': a vapour is the gaseous phase of a substance below its critical temperature (and which can therefore be liquefied by compression); a gas is the gaseous phase of a substance above its critical temperature (and which cannot therefore be liquefied by compression alone). Oxygen at room temperature is therefore a true gas; the gaseous phase of water at room temperature is a vapour.

The text's web site contains links to online databases of properties of gases.

The dense fluid obtained by compressing a gas when its temperature is higher than its critical temperature is not a true liquid, but it behaves like a liquid in many respects—it has a density similar to that of a liquid, for instance, and can act as a solvent. However, despite its density, the fluid is not strictly a liquid because it never possesses a surface that separates it from a vapour phase. Nor is it much like a gas, because it is so dense. It is an example of a **supercritical fluid**. Supercritical fluids (SCFs) are currently being used as solvents. For example, supercritical carbon dioxide is used to extract caffeine in the manufacture of decaffeinated coffee where, unlike organic solvents, it does not result in the formation of an unpleasant and possibly toxic residue. Supercritical fluids are also currently of great interest in industrial processes, as they can be used instead of chlorofluorocarbons (CFCs) and hence avoid the environmental damage that CFCs are known to cause. Because supercritical carbon dioxide is obtained either from the atmosphere or from renewable organic sources (by fermentation), its use does not increase the net load of atmospheric carbon dioxide.

1.11 The compression factor

A useful quantity for discussing the properties of real gases is the **compression factor**, Z, which is the ratio of the actual molar volume of a gas to the molar volume of a perfect gas under the same conditions:

Molar volume of the gas

$$Z = \frac{V_m}{V_m^{\text{perfect}}} \tag{1.20a}$$

Molar volume of perfect gas

The molar volume of a perfect gas is RT/p (recall eqn 1.3), so we can rewrite this definition as

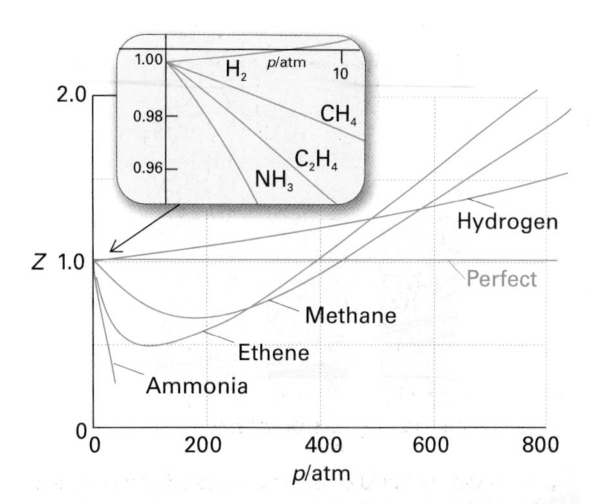

Fig. 1.15 The variation of the compression factor, Z, with pressure for several gases at 0°C. A perfect gas has $Z = 1$ at all pressures. Of the gases shown, hydrogen shows positive deviations at all pressures (at this temperature); all the other gases show negative deviations initially but positive deviations at high pressures. The negative deviations are a result of the attractive interactions between molecules and the positive deviations are a result of the repulsive interactions.

$$Z = \frac{V_m}{RT/p} = \frac{pV_m}{RT} \tag{1.20b}$$

where V_m is the molar volume of the gas we are studying. For a perfect gas, $Z = 1$, so deviations of Z from 1 are a measure of how far a real gas departs from behaving perfectly.

When Z is measured for real gases, it is found to vary with pressure as shown in Fig. 1.15. At low pressures, some gases (methane, ethane, and ammonia, for instance) have $Z < 1$. That is, their molar volumes are smaller than that of a perfect gas, suggesting that the molecules are pulled together slightly. We can conclude that for these molecules and these conditions, the attractive interactions are dominant. The compression factor rises above 1 at high pressures whatever the identity of the gas, and for some gases (hydrogen in Fig. 1.15) $Z > 1$ at all pressures.[3] The observation that $Z > 1$ tells us that the molar volume of the gas is now greater than that expected

[3] The type of behaviour exhibited depends on the temperature.

for a perfect gas of the same temperature and pressure, so the molecules are pushed apart slightly. This behaviour indicates that the repulsive forces are dominant. For hydrogen, the attractive interactions are so weak that the repulsive interactions dominate even at low pressures.

1.12 The virial equation of state

We can use the deviation of Z from its 'perfect' value of 1 to construct an *empirical* (observation-based) equation of state. To do so, we suppose that, for real gases, the relation $Z = 1$ is only the first term of a lengthier expression, and write instead

$$Z = 1 + \frac{B}{V_m} + \frac{C}{V_m^2} + \cdots \tag{1.21}$$

The coefficients B, C, ..., are called **virial coefficients**; B is the second virial coefficient, C, the third, and so on; the unwritten $A = 1$ is the first.[4] They vary from gas to gas and depend on the temperature. This technique, of taking a limiting expression (in this case, $Z = 1$, which applies to gases at very large molar volumes) and supposing that it is the first term of a more complicated expression, is quite common in physical chemistry. The limiting expression is the first approximation to the true expression, whatever that may be, and the additional terms progressively take into account the secondary effects that the limiting expression ignores.

The most important additional term on the right in eqn 1.21 is the one proportional to B (more precisely, under most conditions $C/V_m^2 \ll B/V_m$ and can therefore be neglected). From the graphs in Fig. 1.15, it follows that, for the temperature to which the data apply, B must be positive for hydrogen (so that $Z > 1$) but negative for methane, ethane, and ammonia (so that $Z < 1$). However, regardless of the sign of B, the positive term C/V_m^2 becomes large for highly compressed gases (when V_m^2 is very small) and the right-hand side of eqn 1.21 becomes greater than 1, just as in the curves for the other gases in Fig. 1.15. The values of the virial coefficients for many gases are known from measurements of Z over a range of molar volumes and fitting the data to eqn 1.21 by varying the coefficients until a good match is obtained.

To convert eqn 1.21 into an equation of state, we combine it with eqn 1.20b ($Z = pV_m/RT$), which gives

$$\frac{pV_m}{RT} = 1 + \frac{B}{V_m} + \frac{C}{V_m^2} + \cdots$$

We then multiply both sides by RT/V_m and replace V_m by V/n throughout to get an expression for p in terms of the other variables:

$$p = \frac{nRT}{V}\left(1 + \frac{nB}{V} + \frac{n^2C}{V^2} + \cdots\right) \tag{1.22}$$

Equation 1.22 is the **virial equation of state.** When the molar volume is very large, the terms nB/V and n^2C/V^2 are both very small, and only the 1 inside the parentheses survives. In this limit, the equation of state approaches that of a perfect gas.

1.13 The van der Waals equation of state

Although it is the most reliable equation of state, the virial equation does not give us much immediate insight into the behaviour of gases and their condensation to liquids. The **van der Waals equation,** which was proposed in 1873 by the Dutch physicist Johannes van der Waals, is only an approximate equation of state but it has the advantage of showing how the intermolecular interactions contribute to the deviations of a gas from the perfect gas law. We can view the van der Waals equation as another example of taking a soundly based qualitative idea and building up a mathematical expression that can be tested quantitatively.

The repulsive interaction between two molecules implies that they cannot come closer than a certain distance. Therefore, instead of being free to travel anywhere in a volume V, the actual volume in which the molecules can travel is reduced to an extent proportional to the number of molecules present and the volume they each exclude (Fig. 1.16). We can therefore model the effect of the repulsive, volume-excluding forces by changing V in the perfect gas equation to $V - nb$, where b is the proportionality constant between the reduction in volume and the

[4] The word 'virial' comes from the Latin word for force, and it reflects the fact that intermolecular forces are now significant. Virial coefficients are also denoted B_2, B_3, etc. in place of B, C, etc.

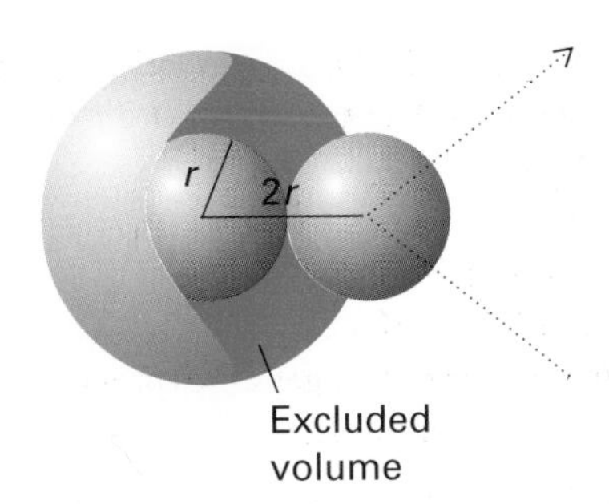

Fig. 1.16 When two molecules, each of radius r and volume $v_{mol} = \frac{4}{3}\pi r^3$ approach each other, the centre of one of them cannot penetrate into a sphere of radius $2r$ and therefore volume $8v_{mol}$ surrounding the other molecule.

amount of molecules present in the container. With this modification, the perfect gas equation of state changes from $p = nRT/V$ to

$$p = \frac{nRT}{V - nb}$$

This equation of state—it is not yet the full van der Waals equation—should describe a gas in which repulsions are important. Note that when the pressure is low, the volume is large compared with the volume excluded by the molecules (which we write $V \gg nb$). The nb can then be ignored in the denominator and the equation reduces to the perfect gas equation of state. It is always a good plan to verify that an equation reduces to a known form when a plausible physical approximation is made.

The effect of the attractive interactions between molecules is to reduce the pressure that the gas exerts. We can model the effect by supposing that the attraction experienced by a given molecule is proportional to the concentration, n/V, of molecules in the container. Because the attractions slow the molecules down,[5] the molecules strike the walls less frequently *and* strike it with a weaker impact. We can therefore expect the reduction in pressure to be proportional to the *square* of the molar concentration, one factor of n/V reflecting the reduction in frequency of collisions and the other factor the reduction in the strength of their impulse. If the constant of proportionality is written a, we can write

$$\text{Reduction in pressure} = a \times \left(\frac{n}{V}\right)^2$$

It follows that the equation of state allowing for both repulsions and attractions is

$$p = \frac{nRT}{V - nb} - a\left(\frac{n}{V}\right)^2 \qquad (1.23a)$$

This expression is the **van der Waals equation of state.** To show the resemblance of this equation to the perfect gas equation $pV = nRT$, eqn 1.23a is sometimes rearranged into

$$\left(p + \frac{an^2}{V^2}\right)(V - nb) = nRT \qquad (1.23b)$$

We have built the van der Waals equation by using physical arguments about the volumes of molecules and the effects of forces between them. It can be derived in other ways, but the present method has the advantage of showing how to derive the form of an equation out of general ideas. The derivation also has the advantage of keeping imprecise the significance of the **van der Waals parameters**, the constants a and b: they are much better regarded as empirical parameters than as precisely defined molecular properties. The van der Waals parameters depend on the gas, but are taken as independent of temperature (Table 1.5). It follows from the way we have constructed the equation that a (the parameter representing the role of attractions) can be expected to be large when the molecules attract each other strongly, whereas b (the parameter representing the role of repulsions) can be expected to be large when the molecules are large.

We can judge the reliability of the van der Waals equation by comparing the isotherms it predicts, which are shown in Fig. 1.17, with the experimental isotherms already shown in Fig. 1.13. Apart from the waves below the critical temperature, they do resemble experimental isotherms quite well. The waves, which are called **van der Waals loops**, are unrealistic because they suggest that under some conditions compression results in a decrease of pressure. The loops are therefore trimmed away and replaced by horizontal lines (Fig. 1.18).[6] The

[5] This slowing does not mean that the gas is cooler close to the walls: the simple relation between T and mean speed in eqn 1.15 is valid only in the absence of intermolecular forces.

[6] Theoretical arguments show that the horizontal line should trim equal areas of loop above and below where it lies.

Table 1.5 *van der Waals parameters of gases*

Substance	a/(atm dm^6 mol^{-2})	b/(10^{-2} dm^3 mol^{-1})
Air	1.4	0.039
Ammonia, NH_3	4.169	3.71
Argon, Ar	1.338	3.20
Carbon dioxide, CO_2	3.610	4.29
Ethane, C_2H_6	5.507	6.51
Ethene, C_2H_4	4.552	5.82
Helium, He	0.0341	2.38
Hydrogen, H_2	0.2420	2.65
Nitrogen, N_2	1.352	3.87
Oxygen, O_2	1.364	3.19
Xenon, Xe	4.137	5.16

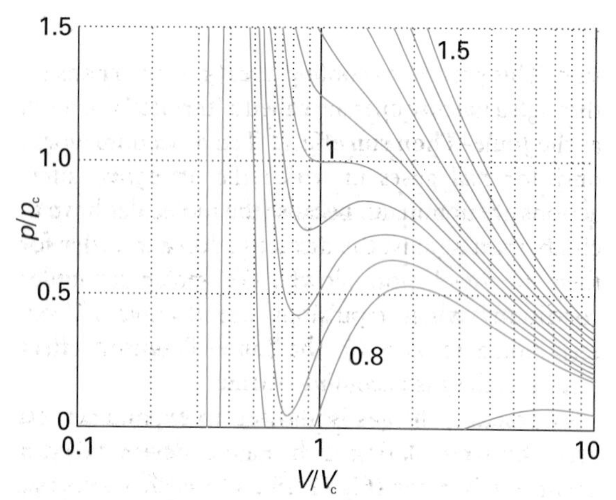

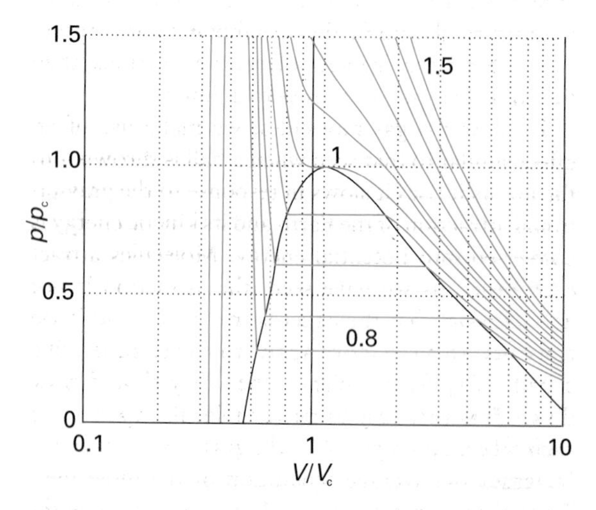

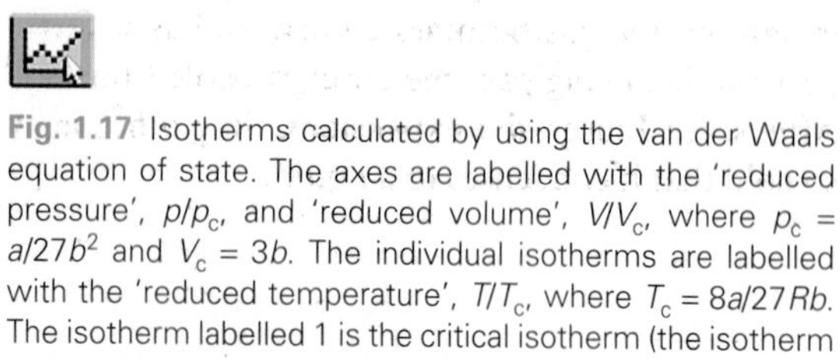

Fig. 1.17 Isotherms calculated by using the van der Waals equation of state. The axes are labelled with the 'reduced pressure', p/p_c, and 'reduced volume', V/V_c, where $p_c = a/27b^2$ and $V_c = 3b$. The individual isotherms are labelled with the 'reduced temperature', T/T_c, where $T_c = 8a/27Rb$. The isotherm labelled 1 is the critical isotherm (the isotherm at the critical temperature).

Fig. 1.18 The unphysical van der Waals loops are eliminated by drawing straight lines that divide the loops into areas of equal size. With this procedure, the isotherms strongly resemble the observed isotherms.

van der Waals parameters in Table 1.5 were found by fitting the calculated curves to experimental isotherms.

Perfect gas isotherms are obtained from the van der Waals equation at high temperatures and low pressures. To confirm this remark, we need to note that when the temperature is high, RT may be so large that the first term on the right in eqn 1.23a greatly exceeds the second, so the latter may be ignored. Furthermore, at low pressures, the molar volume is so large that $V - nb$ can be replaced by V. Hence, under these conditions (of high temperature and low pressure), eqn 1.23a reduces to $p = nRT/V$, the perfect gas equation.

1.14 The liquefaction of gases

A gas may be liquefied by cooling it below its boiling point at the pressure of the experiment. For example, chlorine at 1 atm can be liquefied by cooling it to below −34°C in a bath cooled with dry ice (solid carbon dioxide). For gases with very low boiling points (such as oxygen and nitrogen, at −183°C and −186°C, respectively), such a simple technique is not practicable unless an even colder bath is available.

One alternative and widely used commercial technique makes use of the forces that act between molecules. We saw earlier that the rms speed of molecules in a gas is proportional to the square root of the temperature (eqn 1.15). It follows that reducing the rms speed of the molecules is equivalent to cooling the gas. If the speed of the molecules can be reduced to the point that neighbours can capture each other by their intermolecular attractions, then the cooled gas will condense to a liquid.

To slow the gas molecules, we make use of an effect similar to that seen when a ball is thrown into the air: as it rises it slows in response to the gravitational attraction of the Earth and its kinetic energy is converted into potential energy. Molecules attract each other, as we have seen (the attraction is not gravitational, but the effect is the same), and if we can cause them to move apart from each other, like a ball rising from a planet, then they should slow down. It is very easy to move molecules apart from each other: we simply allow the gas to expand, which increases the average separation of the molecules. To cool a gas, therefore, we allow it to expand without allowing any heat to enter from outside. As it does so, the molecules move apart to fill the available volume, struggling as they do so against the attraction of their neighbours. Because some kinetic energy must be converted into potential energy to reach greater separations, the molecules travel more slowly as their separation increases. Therefore, because the average speed of the molecules has been reduced, the gas is now cooler than before the expansion. This process of cooling a real gas by expansion through a narrow opening called a 'throttle' is known as the **Joule–Thomson effect.**[7] The procedure works only for real gases in which the attractive interactions are dominant, because the molecules have to climb apart against the attractive force in order for them to travel more slowly. For molecules under conditions when repulsions are dominant (corresponding to $Z > 1$), the Joule–Thomson effect results in the gas becoming warmer.

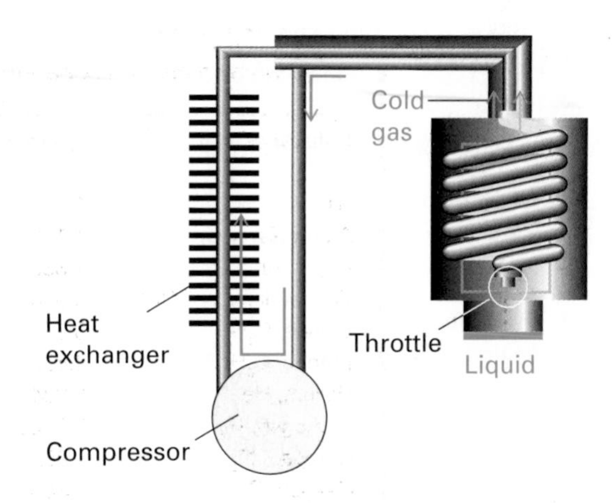

Fig. 1.19 The principle of the Linde refrigerator. The gas is recirculated and cools the gas that is about to undergo expansion through the throttle. The expanding gas cools still further. Eventually, liquefied gas drips from the throttle.

In practice, the gas is allowed to expand several times by recirculating it through a device called a *Linde refrigerator* (Fig. 1.19). On each successive expansion the gas becomes cooler, and as it flows past the incoming gas, the latter is cooled further. After several successive expansions, the gas becomes so cold that it condenses to a liquid.

[7] The effect was first observed and analysed by James Joule (whose name is commemorated in the unit of energy) and William Thomson (who later became Lord Kelvin).

CHECKLIST OF KEY IDEAS

You should now be familiar with the following concepts:

☐ 1 An equation of state is an equation relating pressure, volume, temperature, and amount of a substance.

☐ 2 The perfect gas equation of state, $pV = nRT$, is a limiting law applicable as $p \to 0$.

☐ 3 The perfect gas equation of state is based on Boyle's law ($p \propto 1/V$), Charles's law ($V \propto T$), and Avogadro's principle ($V \propto n$).

☐ 4 Dalton's law states that the total pressure of a mixture of perfect gases is the sum of the pressures that each gas would exert if it were alone in the container at the same temperature.

☐ 5 The partial pressure of any gas is defined as $p_J = x_J \times p$, where x_J is its mole fraction in a mixture and p is the total pressure.

☐ 6 The kinetic model of gases expresses the properties of a perfect gas in terms of a collection of mass points in ceaseless random motion.

☐ 7 The mean speed and root-mean-square (rms) speed of molecules is proportional to the square root of the (absolute) temperature and inversely proportional to the square root of the molar mass.

☐ 8 The properties of the Maxwell distribution of speeds are summarized in Figs 1.8 and 1.9.

☐ 9 Diffusion is the spreading of one substance through another; effusion is the escape of a gas through a small hole.

☐ 10 Graham's law states that the rate of effusion is inversely proportional to the square root of the molar mass.

☐ 11 The collision frequency, z, and mean free path, λ, of molecules in a gas are related by $c = \lambda z$.

☐ 12 In real gases, molecular interactions affect the equation of state; the true equation of state is expressed in terms of virial coefficients $B, C, \ldots$: $p = (nRT/V)(1 + nB/V + n^2C/V^2 + \cdots)$.

☐ 13 The van der Waals equation of state is an approximation to the true equation of state in which attractions are represented by a parameter a and repulsions are represented by a parameter b: $p = nRT/(V - nb) - a(n/V)^2$.

☐ 14 The Joule–Thomson effect is the cooling of gas that occurs when it expands through a throttle without the influx of heat.

FURTHER INFORMATION 1.1

Kinetic molecular theory

One of the essential skills of a physical chemist is the ability to turn simple, qualitative ideas into rigid, testable, quantitative theories. The kinetic model of gases is an excellent example of this technique, as it takes the concepts set out in the text and turns them into precise expressions. As usual in model building, there are a number of steps, but each one is motivated by a clear appreciation of the underlying physical picture, in this case a swarm of mass points in ceaseless random motion. The key quantitative ingredients we need are the equations of classical mechanics. So we begin with a brief review of velocity, momentum, and Newton's second law of motion.

The velocity, $\boldsymbol{v}$, is a vector, a quantity with both magnitude and direction. The magnitude of the velocity vector is the speed, v, given by $v = (v_x^2 + v_y^2 + v_z^2)^{1/2}$, where v_x, v_y, and v_z are the components of the vector along the x-, y-, and z-axes, respectively (Fig. 1.20). The magnitude of each component, its value without a sign, is denoted $|\cdots|$. For example, $|v_x|$ means the magnitude of v_x. The linear momentum, $\boldsymbol{p}$, of a particle of mass m is the vector $\boldsymbol{p} = m\boldsymbol{v}$ with magnitude $p = mv$. Newton's second law of motion states that the force acting on a particle is equal to the rate

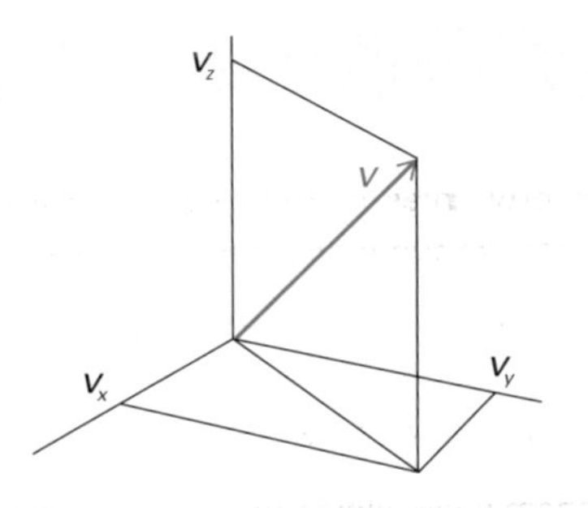

Fig. 1.20 A vector $\boldsymbol{v}$ and its three components on a set of perpendicular axes.

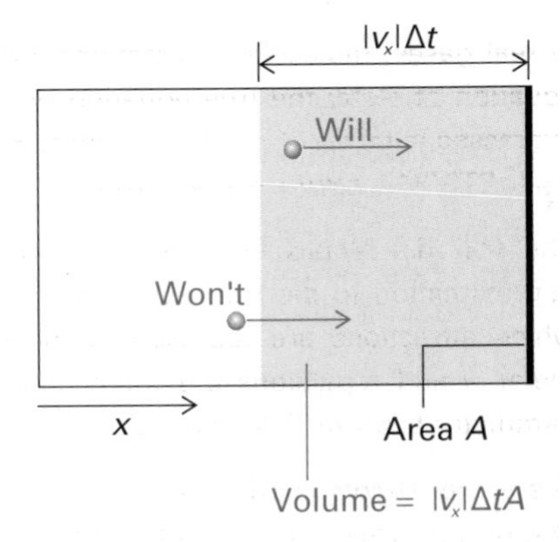

Fig. 1.21 The model used for calculating the pressure of a perfect gas according to the kinetic molecular theory. Here, for clarity, we show only the x-component of the velocity (the other two components are not changed when the molecule collides with the wall). All molecules within the shaded area will reach the wall in an interval Δt provided they are moving towards it.

of change of the momentum, the change of momentum divided by the interval during which it occurs.

Now we begin the derivation of eqn 1.9 by considering the arrangement in Fig. 1.21. When a particle of mass m that is travelling with a component of velocity v_x parallel to the x-axis ($v_x > 0$ corresponding to motion to the right and $v_x < 0$ to motion to the left) collides with the wall on the right and is reflected, its linear momentum changes from $+m|v_x|$ before the collision to $-m|v_x|$ after the collision (when it is travelling in the opposite direction at the same speed). The x-component of the momentum therefore changes by $2m|v_x|$ on each collision (the y- and z-components are unchanged). Many molecules collide with the wall in an interval Δt, and the total change of momentum is the product of the change in momentum of each molecule multiplied by the number of molecules that reach the wall during the interval.

Next, we need to calculate that number. Because a molecule with velocity component v_x can travel a distance $|v_x|\Delta t$ along the x-axis in an interval Δt, all the molecules within a distance $|v_x|\Delta t$ of the wall will strike it if they are travelling towards it. It follows that if the wall has area A, then all the particles in a volume $A \times |v_x|\Delta t$ will reach the wall (if they are travelling towards it). The number density, the number of particles divided by the total volume, is nN_A/V (where n is the total amount of molecules in the container of volume V and N_A is Avogadro's constant), so the number of molecules in the volume $A|v_x|\Delta t$ is $(nN_A/V) \times A|v_x|\Delta t$. At any instant, half the particles are moving to the right and half are moving to the left. Therefore, the average number of collisions with the wall during the interval Δt is $\frac{1}{2}nN_A A|v_x|\Delta t/V$.

The total momentum change in the interval Δt is the product of the number we have just calculated and the change $2m|v_x|$:

$$\text{Momentum change} = \frac{nN_A A|v_x|\Delta t}{2V} \times 2m|v_x|$$
$$= \frac{nmAN_A v_x^2 \Delta t}{V} = \frac{nMAv_x^2 \Delta t}{V}$$

where $M = mN_A$. Next, to find the force, we calculate the rate of change of momentum:

$$\text{Force} = \frac{\text{Change of momentum}}{\text{Time interval}} = \frac{nMAv_x^2}{V}$$

It follows that the pressure, the force divided by the area, is

$$\text{Pressure} = \frac{nMv_x^2}{V}$$

Not all the molecules travel with the same velocity, so the detected pressure, p, is the average (denoted $\langle\cdots\rangle$) of the quantity just calculated:

$$p = \frac{nM\langle v_x^2\rangle}{V}$$

To write an expression of the pressure in terms of the rms speed, c, we begin by writing the speed of a single molecule, v, as $v^2 = v_x^2 + v_y^2 + v_z^2$. Because the rms speed, c, is defined as $c = \langle v^2\rangle^{1/2}$ (eqn 1.10), it follows that

$$c^2 = \langle v^2\rangle = \langle v_x^2\rangle + \langle v_y^2\rangle + \langle v_z^2\rangle$$

However, because the molecules are moving randomly, all three averages are the same. It follows that $c^2 = 3\langle v_x^2\rangle$. Equation 1.9 follows immediately by substituting $\langle v_x^2\rangle = \frac{1}{3}c^2$ into $p = nM\langle v_x^2\rangle/V$.

DISCUSSION QUESTIONS

1.1 Explain how the experiments of Boyle, Charles, and Avogadro led to the formulation of the perfect gas equation of state.

1.2 Explain the term 'partial pressure' and why Dalton's law is a limiting law.

1.3 Provide a molecular interpretation for the variation of the rates of diffusion and effusion of gases with temperature.

1.4 Describe the formulation of the van der Waals equation state.

EXERCISES

Treat all gases as perfect unless instructed otherwise.
The symbol ‡ indicates that calculus is required.

1.5 What pressure is exerted by a sample of nitrogen gas of mass 2.045 g in a container of volume 2.00 dm^3 at 21°C?

1.6 A sample of neon of mass 255 mg occupies 3.00 dm^3 at 122 K. What pressure does it exert?

1.7 Much to everyone's surprise, nitrogen monoxide (NO) has been found to act as a neurotransmitter. To prepare to study its effect, a sample was collected in a container of volume 250.0 cm^3. At 19.5°C its pressure is found to be 24.5 kPa. What amount (in moles) of NO has been collected?

1.8 A domestic water-carbonating kit uses steel cylinders of carbon dioxide of volume 250 cm^3. They weigh 1.04 kg when full and 0.74 kg when empty. What is the pressure of gas in the cylinder at 20°C?

1.9 The effect of high pressure on organisms, including humans, is studied to gain information about deep-sea diving and anaesthesia. A sample of air occupies 1.00 dm^3 at 25°C and 1.00 atm. What pressure is needed to compress it to 100 cm^3 at this temperature?

1.10 You are warned not to dispose of pressurized cans by throwing them on to a fire. The gas in an aerosol container exerts a pressure of 125 kPa at 18°C. The container is thrown on a fire, and its temperature rises to 700°C. What is the pressure at this temperature?

1.11 Until we find an economical way of extracting oxygen from sea water or lunar rocks, we have to carry it with us to inhospitable places, and do so in compressed form in tanks. A sample of oxygen at 101 kPa is compressed at constant temperature from 7.20 dm^3 to 4.21 dm^3. Calculate the final pressure of the gas.

1.12 To what temperature must a sample of helium gas be cooled from 22.2°C to reduce its volume from 1.00 dm^3 to 100 cm^3?

1.13 Hot-air balloons gain their lift from the lowering of density of air that occurs when the air in the envelope is heated. To what temperature should you heat a sample of air, initially at 340 K, to increase its volume by 14 per cent?

1.14 At sea level, where the pressure was 104 kPa and the temperature 21.1°C, a certain mass of air occupied 2.0 m^3. To what volume will the region expand when it has risen to an altitude where the pressure and temperature are (a) 52 kPa, −5.0°C, (b) 880 Pa, −52.0°C?

1.15 A diving bell has an air space of 3.0 m^3 when on the deck of a boat. What is the volume of the air space when the bell has been lowered to a depth of 50 m? Take the mean density of sea water to be 1.025 g cm^{-3} and assume that the temperature is the same as on the surface.

1.16 A meteorological balloon had a radius of 1.0 m when released at sea level at 20°C and expanded to a radius of 3.0 m when it had risen to its maximum altitude where the temperature was −20°C. What is the pressure inside the balloon at that altitude?

1.17 A gas mixture being used to simulate the atmosphere of another planet consists of 320 mg of methane, 175 mg of argon, and 225 mg of nitrogen. The partial pressure of nitrogen at 300 K is 15.2 kPa. Calculate (a) the volume and (b) the total pressure of the mixture.

1.18 The vapour pressure of water at blood temperature is 47 Torr. What is the partial pressure of dry air in our lungs when the total pressure is 760 Torr?

1.19 A determination of the density of a gas or vapour can provide a quick estimate of its molar mass even though for practical work mass spectrometry is far more precise. The density of a gaseous compound was found to be 1.23 g dm^{-3} at 330 K and 25.5 kPa. What is the molar mass of the compound?

1.20 In an experiment to measure the molar mass of a gas, 250 cm^3 of the gas was confined in a glass vessel. The pressure was 152 Torr at 298 K and the mass of the gas was 33.5 mg. What is the molar mass of the gas?

1.21 A vessel of volume 22.4 dm^3 contains 2.0 mol H_2 and 1.0 mol N_2 at 273.15 K. Calculate (a) their partial pressures and (b) the total pressure.

1.22 The composition of planetary atmospheres is determined in part by the speeds of the molecules of the constituent gases, because the faster-moving molecules can reach escape velocity and leave the planet. Calculate the mean speed of (a) He atoms, (b) CH_4 molecules at (i) 77 K, (ii) 298 K, (iii) 1000 K.

1.23 ‡Use the Maxwell distribution of speeds to confirm that the mean speed of molecules of molar mass M at a temperature T is equal to $(8RT/\pi M)^{1/2}$. (*Hint.* You will need an integral of the form $\int_0^\infty x^3 e^{-ax^2} dx = n!/2a^2$.)

1.24 ‡Use the Maxwell distribution of speeds to confirm that the rms speed of molecules of molar mass M at a temperature T is equal to $(3RT/M)^{1/2}$ and hence confirm eqn 1.13. (*Hint.* You will need an integral of the form $\int_0^\infty x^4 e^{-ax^2} dx = (3/8a^2)(\pi/a)^{1/2}$.)

1.25 ‡Use the Maxwell distribution of speeds to find an expression for the most probable speed of molecules of molar mass M at a temperature T. (*Hint.* Look for a maximum in the Maxwell distribution (the maximum occurs as $dF/ds = 0$).)

1.26 ‡Use the Maxwell distribution of speeds to estimate the fraction of N_2 molecules at 500 K that have speeds in the range 290 to 300 m s^{-1}.

1.27 At what pressure does the mean free path of argon at 25°C become comparable to the diameter of a spherical vessel of volume 1.0 dm^3 that contains it? Take $\sigma = 0.36$ nm^2.

1.28 At what pressure does the mean free path of argon at 25°C become comparable to 10 times the diameter of the atoms themselves? Take $\sigma = 0.36$ nm^2.

1.29 When we are studying the photochemical processes that can occur in the upper atmosphere, we need to know how often atoms and molecules collide. At an altitude of 20 km the temperature is 217 K and the pressure 0.050 atm. What is the mean free path of N_2 molecules? Take $\sigma = 0.43$ nm^2.

1.30 How many collisions does a single Ar atom make in 1.0 s when the temperature is 25°C and the pressure is (a) 10 bar, (b) 100 kPa, (c) 1.0 Pa?

1.31 Calculate the total number of collisions per second in 1.0 dm^3 of argon under the same conditions as in Exercise 1.30.

1.32 How many collisions per second does an N_2 molecule make at an altitude of 20 km? (See Exercise 1.29 for data.)

1.33 The spread of pollutants through the atmosphere is governed partly by the effects of winds but also by the natural tendency of molecules to diffuse. The latter depends on how far a molecule can travel before colliding with another molecule. Calculate the mean free path of diatomic molecules in air using $\sigma = 0.43$ nm^2 at 25°C and (a) 10 bar, (b) 103 kPa, (c) 1.0 Pa.

1.34 How does the mean free path in a sample of a gas vary with temperature in a constant-volume container?

1.35 Calculate the pressure exerted by 1.0 mol C_2H_6 behaving as (a) a perfect gas, (b) a van der Waals gas when it is confined under the following conditions: (i) at 273.15 K in 22.414 dm^3, (ii) at 1000 K in 100 cm^3. Use the data in Table 1.5.

1.36 How reliable is the perfect gas law in comparison with the van der Waals equation? Calculate the difference in pressure of 10.00 g of carbon dioxide confined to a container of volume 100 cm^3 at 25.0°C between treating it as a perfect gas and a van der Waals gas.

1.37 Express the van der Waals equation of state as a virial expansion in powers of $1/V_m$ and obtain expressions for B and C in terms of the parameters a and b. (*Hint.* The expansion you will need is $(1-x)^{-1} = 1 + x + x^2 + \cdots$. Series expansions are discussed in Appendix 2.)

1.38 Measurements on argon gave $B = -21.7$ cm^3 mol^{-1} and $C = 1200$ cm^6 mol^{-2} for the virial coefficients at 273 K. What are the values of a and b in the corresponding van der Waals equation of state?

1.39 Show that there is a temperature at which the second virial coefficient, B, is zero for a van der Waals gas, and calculate its value for carbon dioxide. (*Hint.* Use the expression for B derived in Exercise 1.37.)

1.40 ‡The critical point of a van der Waals gas occurs where the isotherm has a flat inflexion, which is where $dp/dV_m = 0$ (zero slope) and $d^2p/dV_m^2 = 0$ (zero curvature). (a) Evaluate these two expressions using eqn 1.23b, and find expressions for the critical constants in terms of the van der Waals parameters. (b) Show that the value of the compression factor at the critical point is $\frac{3}{8}$.

Chapter 2

Thermodynamics: the First Law

The branch of physical chemistry known as **thermodynamics** is concerned with the study of the transformations of energy: in particular, the transformation of heat into work and vice versa. That concern might seem remote from chemistry; indeed, thermodynamics was originally formulated by physicists and engineers interested in the efficiency of steam engines. However, thermodynamics has proved to be of immense importance in chemistry. Not only does it deal with the energy output of chemical reactions but also it helps to answer questions that lie right at the heart of the subject, such as why reactions reach equilibrium, what their composition is at equilibrium, and how reactions in electrochemical (and biological) cells can be used to generate electricity.

Classical thermodynamics, the thermodynamics developed during the nineteenth century, stands aloof from any models of the internal constitution of matter: we could develop and use thermodynamics without ever mentioning atoms and molecules. However, the subject is greatly enriched by acknowledging that atoms and molecules do exist and interpreting thermodynamic properties and relations in terms of them. Wherever it is appropriate, we shall cross back and forth between thermodynamics, which provides useful relations between observable properties of bulk matter, and the properties of atoms and molecules, which are ultimately responsible for these bulk properties. The theory of the connection between atomic and bulk thermodynamic properties is called **statistical thermodynamics** and is treated in Chapter 22.

Chemical thermodynamics is a tree with many branches. **Thermochemistry** is the branch that deals with the heat output of chemical reactions. As we elaborate the content of thermodynamics, we shall see that we can also discuss the output of energy in the form of work. This leads us into the fields of **electrochemistry**, the interaction between electricity and chemistry, and **bioenergetics**, the deployment of energy in living organisms. The whole of equilibrium chemistry—the formulation of equilibrium constants, and the very special case of the equilibrium composition of solutions of acids and bases—is an aspect of thermodynamics.

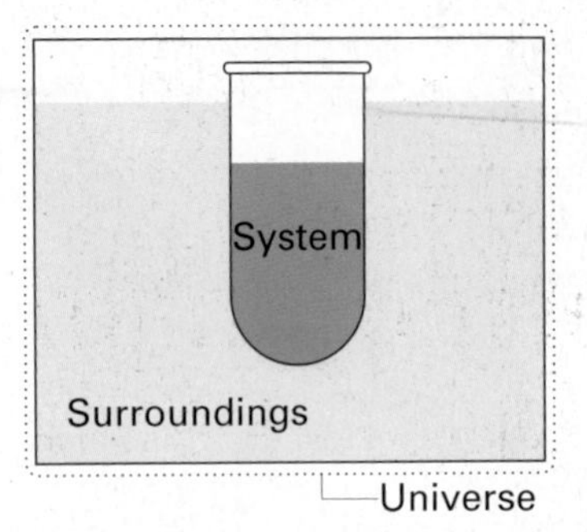

Fig. 2.1 The sample is the system of interest; the rest of the world is its surroundings. The surroundings are where observations are made on the system. They can often be modelled, as here, by a large water bath. The universe consists of the system and surroundings.

The conservation of energy

Almost every argument and explanation in chemistry boils down to a consideration of some aspect of a single property: the *energy*. Energy determines what molecules may form, what reactions may occur, how fast they may occur, and—with a refinement in our conception of energy that we explore in Chapter 4 —in which direction a reaction has a tendency to occur.

As we saw in the *Introduction*:

Energy is the capacity to do work

Work is motion against an opposing force

These definitions imply that a raised weight of a given mass has more energy than one of the same mass resting on the ground because the former has a greater capacity to do work: it can do work as it falls to the level of the lower weight. The definition also implies that a gas at high temperature has more energy than the same gas at a low temperature: the hot gas has a higher pressure and can do more work in driving out a piston.

People struggled for centuries to create energy from nothing, as they believed that if they could create energy, then they could produce work (and wealth) endlessly. However, without exception and despite strenuous efforts, many of which degenerated into deceit, they failed. As a result of their failed efforts, we have come to recognize that energy can be neither created nor destroyed but merely converted from one form into another or moved from place to place. This 'law of the conservation of energy' is of great importance in chemistry. Most chemical reactions release energy or absorb it as they occur; so according to the law of the conservation of energy, we can be confident that all such changes must result only in the conversion of energy from one form into another or its transfer from place to place, not its creation or annihilation. The detailed study of that conversion and transfer is the domain of thermodynamics.

2.1 Systems and surroundings

In thermodynamics, a **system** is the part of the world in which we have a special interest. The **surroundings** are where we make our observations (Fig. 2.1). The surroundings, which can be modelled as a large water bath, remain at constant temperature regardless of how much energy flows into or out of them. They are so huge that they also have either constant volume or constant pressure regardless of any changes that take place to the system. Thus, even though the system might expand, the surroundings remain effectively the same size.

We need to distinguish three types of systems (Fig. 2.2):

An **open system** can exchange both energy and matter with its surroundings and hence can undergo changes of composition.

A **closed system** can exchange energy but not matter with its surroundings.

An **isolated system** can exchange neither matter nor energy with its surroundings.

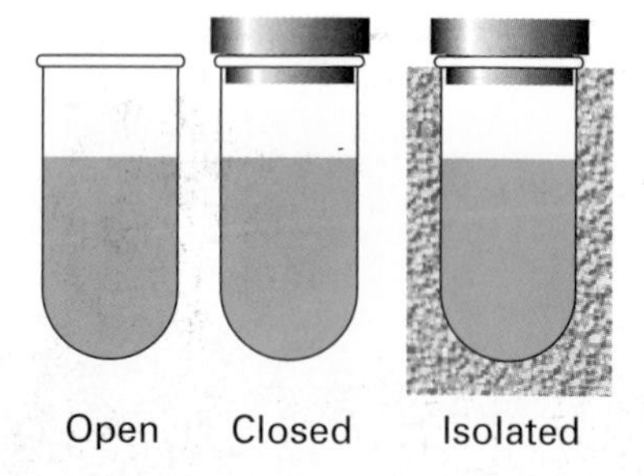

Fig. 2.2 A system is *open* if it can exchange energy and matter with its surroundings, *closed* if it can exchange energy but not matter, and *isolated* if it can exchange neither energy nor matter.

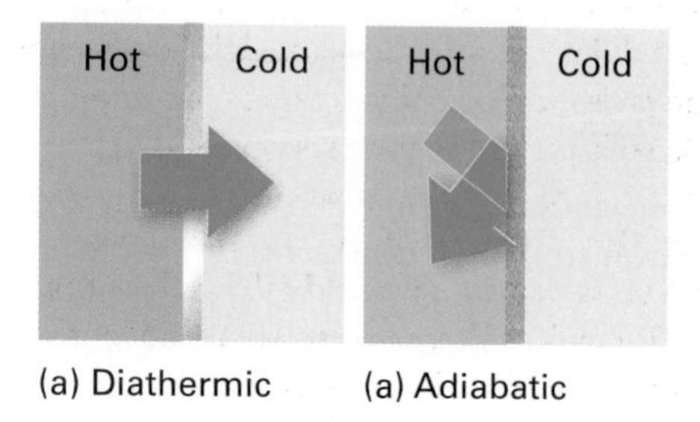

Fig. 2.3 (a) A diathermic wall permits the passage of energy as heat; (b) an adiabatic wall does not, even if there is a temperature difference across the wall.

An example of an open system is a flask that is not stoppered and to which various substances can be added. A biological cell is an open system because nutrients and waste can pass through the cell wall. You and I are open systems: we ingest, respire, perspire, and excrete. An example of a closed system is a stoppered flask: energy can be exchanged with the contents of the flask because the walls may be able to conduct heat. An example of an isolated system is a sealed flask that is thermally, mechanically, and electrically insulated from its surroundings.

2.2 Work and heat

Energy can be exchanged between a closed system and its surroundings by doing work or by the process called 'heating'. A system does work when it causes motion against an opposing force. We can identify when a system does work by noting whether the process can be used to change the height of a weight somewhere in the surroundings. **Heating** is the process of transferring energy as a result of a temperature difference between the system and its surroundings. To avoid a lot of awkward circumlocution, it is common to say that 'energy is transferred as work' when the system does work, and 'energy is transferred as heat' when the system heats its surroundings (or vice versa). However, we should always remember that 'work' and 'heat' are *modes of transfer* of energy, not *forms* of energy.

Walls that permit heating as a mode of transfer of energy are called **diathermic** (Fig. 2.3). A metal container is diathermic. Walls that do not permit heating even though there is a difference in temperature are called **adiabatic**.[1] The double walls of a vacuum flask are adiabatic to a good approximation.

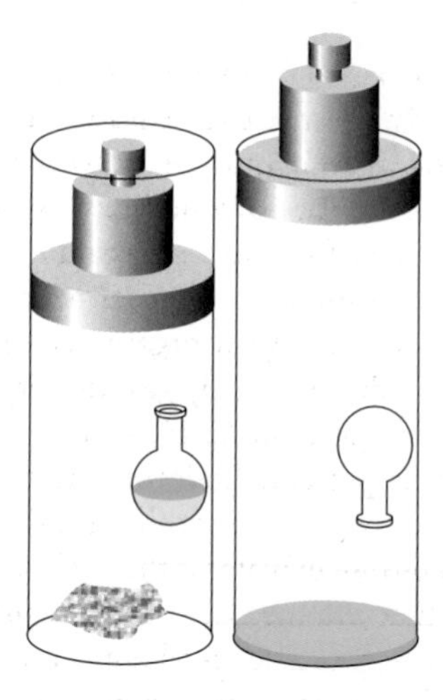

Fig. 2.4 When hydrochloric acid reacts with zinc, the hydrogen gas produced must push back the surrounding atmosphere (represented by the weight resting on the piston), and hence must do work on its surroundings. This is an example of energy leaving a system as work.

As an example of the different ways of transferring energy, consider a chemical reaction that produces gases, such as the reaction of an acid with zinc:

$$\mathrm{Zn(s) + 2\,HCl(aq) \rightarrow ZnCl_2(aq) + H_2(g)}$$

Suppose first that the reaction takes place inside a cylinder fitted with a piston, then the gas produced drives out the piston and raises a weight in the surroundings (Fig. 2.4). In this case, energy has

[1] The word is derived from the Greek words for 'not passing through'.

migrated to the surroundings as a result of the system doing work because a weight has been raised in the surroundings: that weight can now do more work, so it possesses more energy. Some energy also migrates into the surroundings as heat. We can detect that transfer of energy by immersing the reaction vessel in an ice bath and noting how much ice melts. Alternatively, we could let the same reaction take place in a vessel with a piston locked in position. No work is done, because no weight is raised. However, because it is found that more ice melts than in the first experiment, we can conclude that more energy has migrated to the surroundings as heat.

A process in a system that heats the surroundings (we commonly say 'releases heat into the surroundings') is called **exothermic.** A process in a system that is heated by the surroundings (we commonly say 'absorbs heat from the surroundings') is called **endothermic.** Examples of exothermic reactions are all combustions, in which organic compounds are completely oxidized to CO_2 gas and liquid H_2O if the compounds contain C, H, and O, and also to N_2 gas if N is present. Endothermic reactions are much less common. The endothermic dissolution of ammonium nitrate in water is the basis of the instant cold-packs that are included in some first-aid kits. They consist of a plastic envelope containing water dyed blue (for psychological reasons) and a small tube of ammonium nitrate, which is broken when the pack is to be used.

The clue to the molecular nature of work comes from thinking about the motion of a weight in terms of its component atoms. When a weight is raised, all its atoms move in the same direction. This observation suggests that *work is the mode of transfer of energy that achieves or utilizes uniform motion in the surroundings* (Fig. 2.5). Whenever we think of work, we can always think of it in terms of uniform motion of some kind. Electrical work, for instance, corresponds to electrons being pushed in the same direction through a circuit. Mechanical work corresponds to atoms being pushed in the same direction against an opposing force.

Now consider the molecular nature of heat. When energy is transferred as heat to the surroundings, the atoms and molecules oscillate more rapidly around their positions or move from place to place more vigorously. The key point is that the motion stimulated by the arrival of energy from the system as heat is disorderly, not uniform as in the case of doing work. This observation suggests that *heat is the mode of transfer of energy that achieves or utilizes disorderly motion in the surroundings* (Fig. 2.6). A fuel burning, for example, generates disorderly molecular motion in its vicinity.

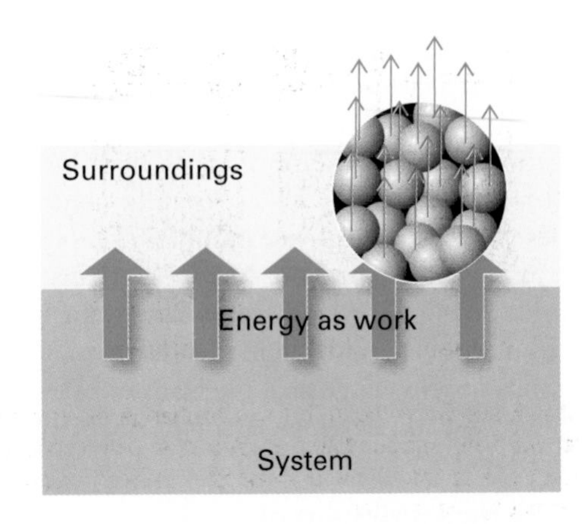

Fig. 2.5 Work is transfer of energy that causes or utilizes uniform motion of atoms in the surroundings. For example, when a weight is raised, all the atoms of the weight (shown magnified) move in unison in the same direction.

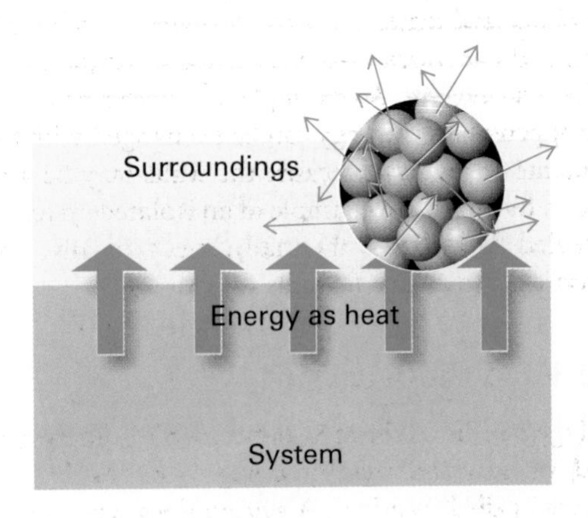

Fig. 2.6 Heat is the transfer of energy that causes or utilizes chaotic motion in the surroundings. When energy leaves the system (the shaded region), it generates chaotic motion in the surroundings (shown magnified).

An interesting historical point is that the molecular difference between work and heat correlates with the chronological order of their application. The release of energy when a fire burns is a relatively unsophisticated procedure because the energy emerges in a disordered fashion from the burning fuel. It was developed—stumbled upon—early in the history of civilization. The generation of work by a burning fuel, by contrast, relies on a carefully controlled transfer of energy so that vast numbers of molecules move in unison. Apart from Nature's achievement of work through the evolution of muscles, the large-scale transfer of energy by doing work was achieved thousands of years later than the transfer of energy by heating, with the development of the steam engine.

2.3 The measurement of work

We saw in Section 0.3 that if the force is the gravitational attraction of the Earth on a mass m, then the force opposing raising the mass vertically is mg, where g is the acceleration of free fall (9.81 m s^{-2}). Therefore, the work needed to raise the mass through a height h on the surface of the Earth is

$$\text{Work} = mgh \tag{2.1}$$

For example, raising a book like this one (of mass about 1.0 kg) from the floor to the table 75 cm above requires

$$\begin{aligned}\text{Work} &= (1.0\text{ kg}) \times (9.81\text{ m s}^{-2}) \times (0.75\text{ m}) \\ &= 7.4\text{ kg m}^2\text{ s}^{-2} = 7.4\text{ J}\end{aligned}$$

It follows that we have a simple way of measuring the work done by or on a system: we measure the height through which a weight is raised or lowered in the surroundings and then use eqn 2.1.

When a system does work, such as by raising a weight in the surroundings or forcing an electric current through a circuit, the energy transferred, w, is reported as a negative quantity. For instance, if a system raises a weight in the surroundings and in the process does 100 J of work (that is, 100 J of energy leaves the system by doing work), then we write $w = -100$ J. When work is done on the system—for example, when we wind a spring inside a clockwork mechanism—w is reported as a positive quantity. We write $w = +100$ J to signify that 100 J of work has been done on the system (that is, 100 J of energy has been transferred to the system by doing work). The sign convention is easy to follow if we think of changes to the energy of the system: its energy decreases (w is negative) if energy leaves it and its energy increases (w is positive) if energy enters it (Fig. 2.7).

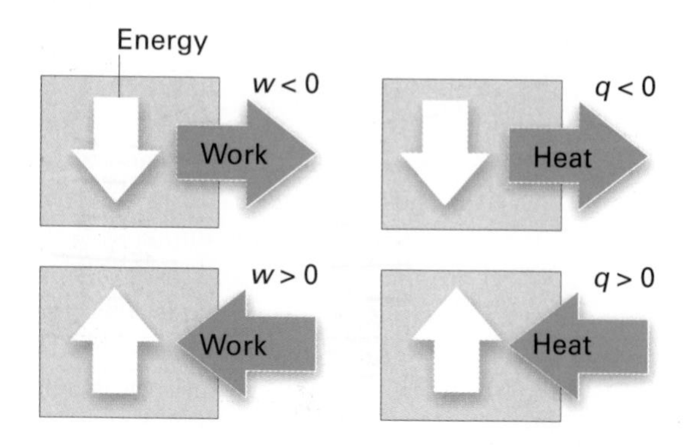

Fig. 2.7 The sign convention in thermodynamics: w and q are positive if energy enters the system (as work and heat, respectively), but negative if energy leaves the system.

We use the same convention for energy transferred by heating, q. We write $q = -100$ J if 100 J of energy leaves the system by heating its surroundings, so reducing the energy of the system, and $q = +100$ J if 100 J of energy enters the system when it is heated by the surroundings.

Because many chemical reactions produce gas, one very important type of work in chemistry is **expansion work**, the work done when a system expands against an opposing pressure. The action of acid on zinc illustrated in Fig. 2.4 is an example of a reaction in which expansion work is done in the process of making room for the gaseous product, hydrogen in this case. We show in Derivation 2.1 that when a system expands through a volume ΔV against a constant external pressure p_{ex} the work done is

$$w = -p_{ex}\,\Delta V \tag{2.2}$$

Derivation 2.1

Expansion work

To calculate the work done when a system expands from an initial volume V_i to a final volume V_f, a change $\Delta V = V_f - V_i$, we consider a piston of area A moving out through a distance h (Fig. 2.8). There need not be an actual piston: we can think of the piston as representing the boundary between the expanding gas and the surrounding atmosphere. However, there may be an actual piston, such as when the expansion takes place inside an internal combustion engine.

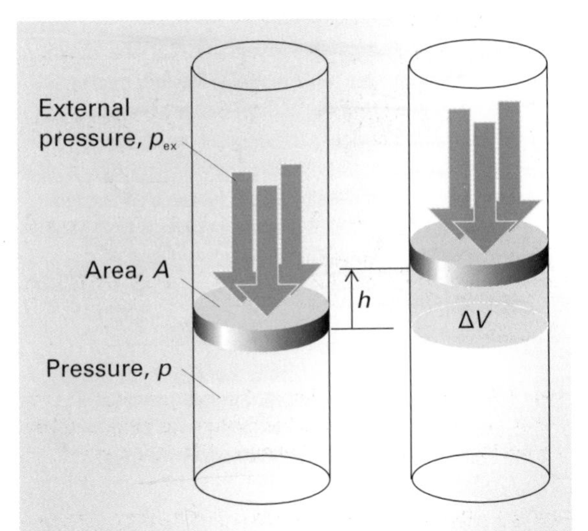

Fig. 2.8 When a piston of area A moves out through a distance h, it sweeps out a volume $\Delta V = Ah$. The external pressure p_{ex} opposes the expansion with a force $p_{ex}A$.

The force opposing the expansion is the constant external pressure p_{ex} multiplied by the area of the piston (because force is pressure times area, Section 0.5). The work done is therefore

Work done by the system
= distance moved × opposing force
$= h \times (p_{ex} A) = p_{ex} \times (hA) = p_{ex} \times \Delta V$

The last equality follows from the fact that hA is the volume of the cylinder swept out by the piston as the gas expands, so we can write $hA = \Delta V$. That is, for expansion work,

Work done by the system $= p_{ex} \Delta V$

Now consider the sign. A system does work and thereby loses energy (that is, w is negative) when it expands (when ΔV is positive). Therefore, we need a negative sign in the equation to ensure that w is negative when ΔV is positive, so we obtain eqn 2.2.

A note on good practice. Always keep track of signs by considering whether the stored energy has decreased when the system does work (w is then negative) or has increased when work has been done on the system (w is then positive).

According to eqn 2.2, the *external* pressure determines how much work a system does when it expands through a given volume: the greater the external pressure, the greater the opposing force and the greater the work that a system does. When the external pressure is zero, $w = 0$. In this case, the system does no work as it expands because it has nothing to push against. Expansion against zero external pressure is called **free expansion.**

Self-test 2.1

Calculate the work done by a system in which a reaction results in the formation of 1.0 mol CO_2(g) at 25°C and 100 kPa. (*Hint.* The increase in volume will be 25 dm^3 under these conditions if the gas is treated as perfect; use the relations 1 dm^3 = 10^{-3} m^3 and 1 Pa m^3 = 1 J.)

[Answer: 2.5 kJ]

Equation 2.2 shows us how to get the *least* expansion work from a system: we just reduce the external pressure to zero. But how can we achieve the *greatest* work for a given change in volume? According to eqn 2.2, the system does maximum work when the external pressure has its maximum value. The force opposing the expansion is then the greatest and the system must exert most effort to push the piston out. However, that external pressure cannot be greater than the pressure, p, of the gas inside the system, otherwise the external pressure would compress the gas instead of allowing it to expand. Therefore, *maximum work is obtained when the external pressure is only infinitesimally less than the pressure of the gas in the system*. In effect, the two pressures must be adjusted to be the same at all stages of the expansion. In Chapter 1 we called this balance of pressures a state of mechanical equilibrium. Therefore, we can conclude that *a system that remains in mechanical equilibrium with its surroundings at all stages of the expansion does maximum expansion work*.

There is another way of expressing this condition. Because the external pressure is infinitesimally less than the pressure of the gas at some stage of the expansion, the piston moves out. However, suppose we increase the external pressure so that it became infinitesimally greater than the pressure of the gas; now the piston moves in. That is, *when a system is in a state of mechanical equilibrium, an infinitesimal change in the pressure results in opposite directions of change*. A change that can be reversed by an *infinitesimal* change in a variable—in this case, the pressure—is said to be **reversible**. In everyday life

'reversible' means a process that can be reversed; in thermodynamics it has a stronger meaning—it means that a process can be reversed by an *infinitesimal* modification in some variable (such as the pressure).

We can summarize this discussion by the following remarks:

1. A system does maximum expansion work when the external pressure is equal to that of the system at every stage of the expansion ($p_{ex} = p$).
2. A system does maximum expansion work when it is in mechanical equilibrium with its surroundings at every stage of the expansion.
3. Maximum expansion work is achieved in a reversible change.

All three statements are equivalent, but they reflect different degrees of sophistication in the way the point is expressed.

We cannot write down the expression for maximum expansion work simply by replacing p_{ex} in eqn 2.2 by p (the pressure of the gas in the cylinder) because, as the piston moves out, the pressure inside the system falls. To make sure the entire process occurs reversibly, we have to adjust the external pressure to match the internal pressure at each stage. To calculate the work, we must take into account the fact that the external pressure must change as the system expands. Suppose that we conduct the expansion isothermally (that is, at constant temperature) by immersing the system in a water bath held at a specified temperature. As we show in Derivation 2.2, the work of isothermal, reversible expansion of a perfect gas from an initial volume V_i to a final volume V_f at a temperature T is

$$w = -nRT \ln \frac{V_f}{V_i} \qquad (2.3)$$

where n is the amount of gas molecules in the system.

Derivation 2.2

Reversible, isothermal expansion work

Because (to ensure reversibility) the external pressure must be adjusted in the course of the expansion, we have to think of the process as taking place in series of small steps during each one of which the external pressure is constant. We calculate the work done in each step for the prevailing external pressure, and then add all these values together. To ensure that the overall result is accurate, we have to make the steps as small as possible—infinitesimal, in fact—so that the pressure is truly constant during each one. In other words, we have to use the calculus, in which case the sum over an infinite number of infinitesimal steps becomes an integral.

When the system expands through an infinitesimal volume dV, the infinitesimal work, dw, done is:

$$dw = -p_{ex}\,dV$$

For a review of calculus, see Appendix 2. As indicated there, the replacement of Δ by d always indicates an infinitesimal change: dV is positive for an infinitesimal increase in volume and negative for an infinitesimal decrease.

This is eqn 2.2, rewritten for an infinitesimal expansion. However, at each stage, we ensure that the external pressure is the same as the current pressure, p, of the gas (Fig. 2.9), in which case

$$dw = -p\,dV$$

We can use the system's pressure to calculate the expansion work only for a reversible change, because then the external pressure is matched to the internal pressure for each infinitesimal change in volume.

The total work when the system expands from V_i to V_f is the sum (integral) of all the infinitesimal changes between the limits V_i and V_f, which we write

$$w = -\int_{V_i}^{V_f} p\,dV$$

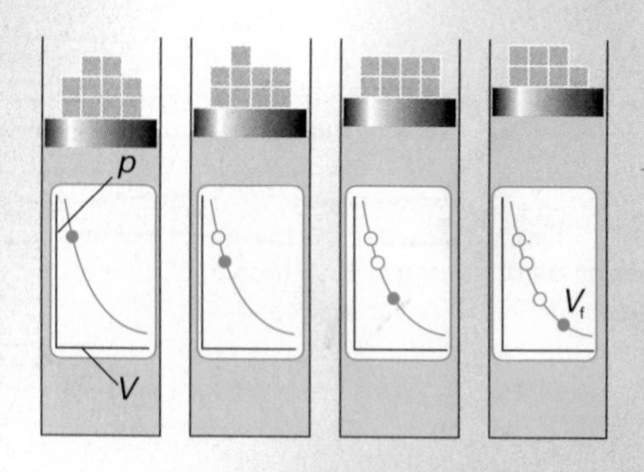

Fig. 2.9 For a gas to expand reversibly, the external pressure must be adjusted to match the internal pressure at each stage of the expansion. This matching is represented in this illustration by gradually unloading weights from the piston as the piston is raised and the internal pressure falls. The procedure results in the extraction of the maximum possible work of expansion.

To evaluate the integral, we need to know how p, the pressure of the gas in the system, changes as it expands. For this step, we suppose that the gas is perfect, in which case we can use the perfect gas law to write[2]

$$p = \frac{nRT}{V}$$

At this stage we have

For the reversible expansion of a perfect gas,

$$w = -\int_{V_i}^{V_f} \frac{nRT}{V}\, dV$$

In general, the temperature might change as the gas expands, so in general T depends on V, and T changes as V changes. For isothermal expansion, however, the temperature is held constant and we can take n, R, and T outside the integral and write

For the isothermal, reversible expansion of a perfect gas, $w = -nRT \int_{V_i}^{V_f} \frac{dV}{V}$

A very useful integral in physical chemistry is

$$\int \frac{dx}{x} = \ln x + \text{constant}$$

where $\ln x$ is the natural logarithm of x. To evaluate the integral between the limits $x = a$ and $x = b$, we write

$$\int_a^b \frac{dx}{x} = (\ln x + \text{constant})|_a^b = (\ln b + \text{constant}) - (\ln a + \text{constant}) = \ln b - \ln a = \ln \frac{b}{a}$$

We shall encounter integrals of this form throughout this text.

It will be helpful to bear in mind that we can always interpret a 'definite' integral (an integral with the two limits specified, in this case a and b) as the area under a graph of the function being integrated (in this case the function $1/x$) between the two limits. For instance, the area under the graph of $1/x$ lying between $a = 2$ and $b = 3$ in the illustration is $\ln(3/2) = 0.41$.

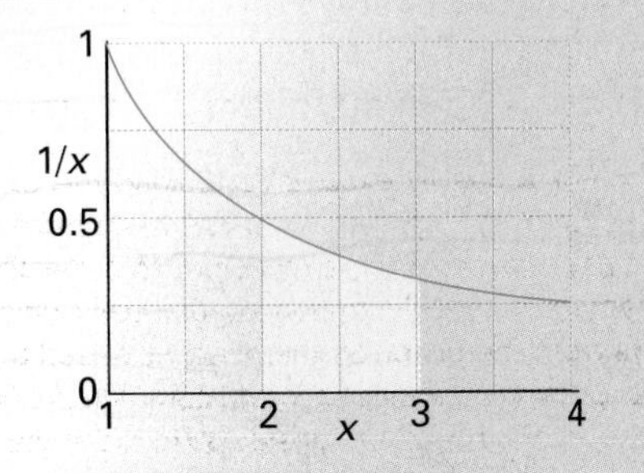

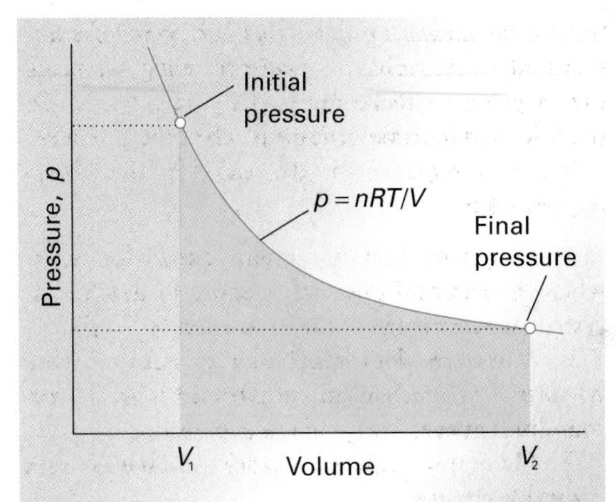

Fig. 2.10 The work of reversible isothermal expansion of a gas is equal to the area beneath the corresponding isotherm evaluated between the initial and final volumes (the tinted area). The isotherm shown here is that of a perfect gas, but the same relation holds for any gas.

The integral is the area under the isotherm $p = nRT/V$ between V_i and V_f (Fig. 2.10) and evaluates to

$$\int_{V_i}^{V_f} \frac{dV}{V} = \ln \frac{V_f}{V_i}$$

When we insert this result into the preceding one, we obtain eqn 2.3.

A note on good practice. Introduce (and keep note of) the restrictions only as they prove necessary, as you might be able to use a formula without needing to restrict it in some way.

Equation 2.3 will turn up in various disguises throughout this text. Once again, it is important to be able to interpret it rather than just remember it. First, we note that in an expansion $V_f > V_i$, so $V_f/V_i > 1$ and the logarithm is positive ($\ln x$ is positive if $x > 1$). Therefore, in an expansion, w is negative. That is what we should expect: energy *leaves* the system as the system does expansion work. Second, for a given change in volume, we get more work the higher the temperature of the confined gas (Fig. 2.11). That is also what we should expect: at high temperatures, the pressure of the gas is high, so we have to use a high external pressure,

[2] If we were considering a real gas, we could use, for instance, the van der Waals equation of state introduced in Section 1.13.

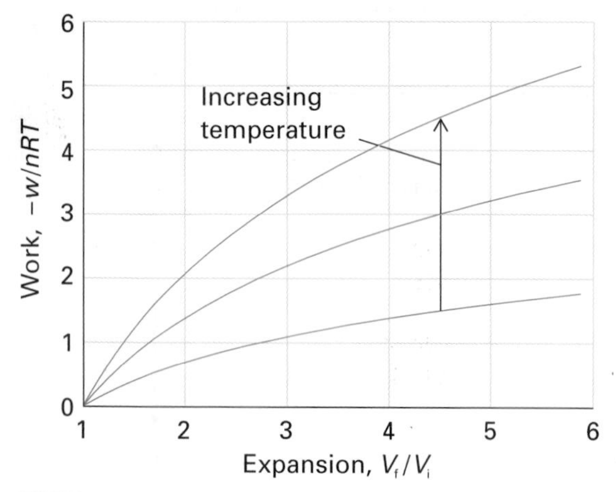

Fig. 2.11 The work of reversible, isothermal expansion of a perfect gas. Note that for a given change of volume and fixed amount of gas, the work is greater the higher the temperature.

and therefore a stronger opposing force, to match the internal pressure at each stage.

Self-test 2.2

Calculate the work done when 1.0 mol Ar(g) confined in a cylinder of volume 1.0 dm^3 at 25°C expands isothermally and reversibly to 2.0 dm^3.

[*Answer:* $w = -1.7$ kJ]

2.4 The measurement of heat

When a substance is heated, its temperature typically rises.[3] However, for a specified energy, q, transferred by heating, the size of the resulting temperature change, ΔT, depends on the 'heat capacity' of the substance. The **heat capacity, C,** is defined as:

$$C = \frac{q}{\Delta T} \quad (2.4a)$$

(Energy supplied as heat; Change in temperature)

The temperature change may be expressed in kelvins (ΔT) or degrees Celsius ($\Delta\theta$); the same numerical value is obtained but with the units joules per kelvin (J K^{-1}) and joules per degree Celsius (J °C^{-1}), respectively. It follows that we have a simple way of measuring the energy absorbed or released by a system as heat: we measure a temperature change and then use the appropriate value of the heat capacity and eqn 2.4a rearranged into

$$q = C\,\Delta T \quad (2.4b)$$

For instance, if the heat capacity of a beaker of water is 0.50 kJ K^{-1}, and we observe a temperature rise of 4.0 K, then we can infer that the heat transferred to the water is

$$q = (0.50 \text{ kJ K}^{-1}) \times (4.0 \text{ K}) = 2.0 \text{ kJ}$$

Heat capacities will occur extensively in the following sections and chapters, and we need to be aware of their properties and how their values are reported. First, we note that the heat capacity is an extensive property, a property that depends on the amount of substance in the sample (Section 0.7): 2 kg of iron has twice the heat capacity of 1 kg of iron, so twice as much heat is required to raise its temperature by a given amount. It is more convenient to report the heat capacity of a substance as an intensive property, a property that is independent of the amount of substance in the sample (Section 0.8). We therefore use either the **specific heat capacity, C_s,** the heat capacity divided by the mass of the sample ($C_s = C/m$, in joules per kelvin per gram, J K^{-1} g^{-1}) or the **molar heat capacity, C_m,** the heat capacity divided by the amount of substance ($C_m = C/n$, in joules per kelvin per mole, J K^{-1} mol^{-1}). In common usage, the specific heat capacity is often called the *specific heat*.

The text's web site contains links to online databases of heat capacities.

For reasons that will be explained shortly, the heat capacity of a substance depends on whether the sample is maintained at constant volume (like a gas in a sealed vessel) as it is heated, or whether the sample is maintained at constant pressure (like water in an open container), and is free to change its volume. The latter is a more common arrangement, and the values given in Table 2.1 are for the **heat capacity at constant pressure, C_p.** The **heat capacity at constant volume** is denoted C_V.

[3] We say 'typically' because the temperature does not always rise. The temperature of boiling water, for instance, remains unchanged as it is heated (see Chapter 5).

Table 2.1 *Heat capacities of common materials*

Substance	Heat capacity	
	Specific, $C_{p,s}$/(J K^{-1} g^{-1})	Molar, $C_{p,m}$/(J K^{-1} mol^{-1})*
Air	1.01	29
Benzene, C_6H_6(l)	1.05	136.1
Brass (Cu/Zn)	0.37	
Copper, Cu(s)	0.38	24.44
Ethanol, C_2H_5OH(l)	2.42	111.46
Glass (Pyrex)	0.78	
Granite	0.80	
Marble	0.84	
Polyethylene	2.3	
Stainless steel	0.51	
Water, H_2O(s)	2.03	37
H_2O(l)	4.18	75.29
H_2O(g)	2.01	33.58

* Molar heat capacities are given only for air and well-defined pure substances; see also the *Data section.*

Illustration 2.1

Using the heat capacity

The molar heat capacity of water at constant pressure, $C_{p,m}$, is 75 J K^{-1} mol^{-1}. It follows that the increase in temperature of 100 g of water (5.55 mol H_2O) when 1.0 kJ of energy is supplied by heating a sample free to expand is approximately

$$\Delta T = \frac{q}{C_p} = \frac{q}{nC_{p,m}}$$

$$= \frac{1.0 \times 10^3 \text{ J}}{(5.55 \text{ mol}) \times (75 \text{ J K}^{-1} \text{ mol}^{-1})} = +2.4 \text{ K}$$

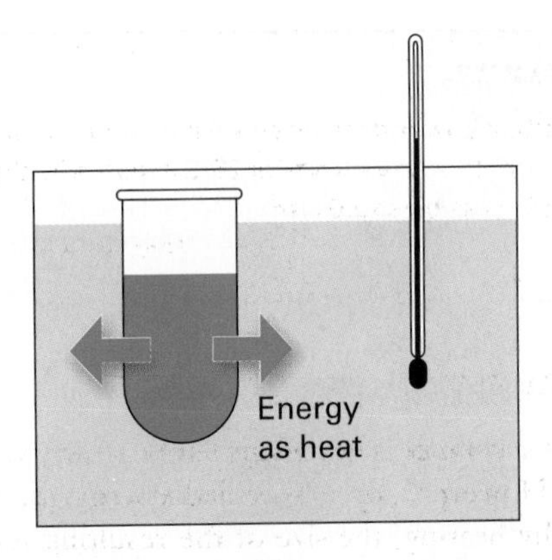

Fig. 2.12 The loss of energy into the surroundings can be detected by noting whether the temperature rises.

One way to measure the energy transferred as heat in a process is to use a **calorimeter** (Fig. 2.12),[4] which consists of a container in which the reaction or physical process occurs, a thermometer, and a surrounding water bath. The entire assembly is insulated from the rest of the world. The principle of a calorimeter is to use the rise in temperature to determine the energy released as heat by the process occurring inside it. To interpret the rise in temperature, we must first calibrate the calorimeter by comparing the observed change in temperature with a change in temperature brought about by the transfer of a known quantity of energy as heat. One procedure is to heat the calorimeter electrically by passing a known current for a measured time through a heater, and record the increase in temperature. The energy provided electrically is

$$q = IVt \tag{2.5}$$

[4] The name comes from 'calor', the Latin word for heat.

where I is the current (in amperes, A), V is the potential of the supply (in volts, V), and t is the time (in seconds, s) for which the current flows.

Electrical charge is measured in *coulombs*, C. The motion of charge gives rise to an electric current, I, measured in coulombs per second, or *amperes*, A, where

$$1\ \text{A} = 1\ \text{C s}^{-1}$$

If current flows through a potential difference V (measured in volts, V), the total energy supplied in an interval t is

$$\text{Energy supplied} = IVt$$

Because

$$1\ \text{A V s} = 1\ (\text{C s}^{-1})\ \text{V s} = 1\ \text{C V} = 1\ \text{J}$$

the energy is obtained in joules with the current in amperes, the potential difference in volts, and the time in seconds. For instance, if a current of 0.50 A from a 12 V source is passed for 360 s,

$$\begin{aligned}\text{Energy supplied} &= (0.50\ \text{A}) \times (12\ \text{V}) \times (360\ \text{s})\\ &= 2.2 \times 10^3\ \text{J, or } 2.2\ \text{kJ}\end{aligned}$$

The *rate of change of energy* is the power, expressed as joules per second, or *watts*, W:

$$1\ \text{W} = 1\ \text{J s}^{-1}$$

Because 1 J = 1 A V s, in terms of electrical units 1 W = 1 A V. We write the electrical power, P, as

$$P = (\text{energy supplied})/t = IVt/t = IV$$

The heater in the example above is therefore rated at

$$P = (0.50\ \text{A}) \times (12\ \text{V}) = 6.0\ \text{A V} = 6.0\ \text{W}$$

The observed rise in temperature lets us calculate the heat capacity of the calorimeter (which in this context is also called the *calorimeter constant*) from eqn 2.4. Then we use this heat capacity to interpret a temperature rise due to a reaction in terms of the heat released or absorbed. An alternative procedure is to calibrate the calorimeter by using a reaction of known heat output, such as the combustion of benzoic acid (C_6H_5COOH), for which the heat output is 3227 kJ per mole of C_6H_5COOH consumed.

Example 2.1

Calibrating a calorimeter and measuring a heat transfer

In an experiment to measure the heat released by the combustion of a sample of nutrient, the compound was burned in a calorimeter and the temperature rose by 3.22°C. When a current of 1.23 A from a 12.0 V source flows through a heater in the same calorimeter for 123 s, the temperature rose by 4.47°C. What is the heat released by the combustion reaction?

Strategy We calculate the heat supplied electrically by using eqn 2.5 with 1 A V s = 1 J. Then we use the observed rise in temperature to find the heat capacity of the calorimeter. Finally, we use this heat capacity to convert the temperature rise observed for the combustion into a heat output by writing $q = C\Delta T$ (or $q = C\Delta\theta$ if the temperature is given on the Celsius scale).

Solution The heat supplied during the calibration step is

$$\begin{aligned}q = IVt &= (1.23\ \text{A}) \times (12.0\ \text{V}) \times (123\ \text{s})\\ &= 1.23 \times 12.0 \times 123\ \text{J}\end{aligned}$$

This product works out as 1.82 kJ, but to avoid rounding errors we save the numerical work to the final stage. The heat capacity of the calorimeter is

$$\begin{aligned}C = \frac{q}{\Delta\theta} &= \frac{1.23 \times 12.0 \times 123\ \text{J}}{4.47°\text{C}}\\ &= \frac{1.23 \times 12.0 \times 123}{4.47}\ \text{J °C}^{-1}\end{aligned}$$

The numerical value of C is 406 J °C^{-1}, but we don't evaluate it yet in the actual calculation. The heat output of the combustion is therefore

$$\begin{aligned}q = C\,\Delta\theta &= \left(\frac{1.23 \times 12.0 \times 123}{4.47}\ \text{J °C}^{-1}\right) \times (3.22°\text{C})\\ &= 1.31\ \text{KJ}\end{aligned}$$

A note on good practice. As well as keeping the numerical evaluation to the final stage, we show the units at each stage of the calculation.

Self-test 2.3

In an experiment to measure the heat released by the combustion of a sample of fuel, the compound was burned in an oxygen atmosphere inside a calorimeter and the temperature rose by 2.78°C. When a current of 1.12 A from an 11.5 V source flows through a heater in the same calorimeter for 162 s, the temperature rose by 5.11°C. What is the heat released by the combustion reaction?

[*Answer:* 1.1 kJ]

2.5 Heat influx during expansion

In certain cases, we can relate the value of q to the change in volume of a system, and so can calculate, for instance, the flow of energy as heat into the system when a gas expands.

The simplest case is that of a perfect gas undergoing isothermal expansion. Because the expansion is isothermal, the temperature of the gas is the same at the end of the expansion as it was initially. Therefore, the mean speed of the molecules of the gas is the same before and after the expansion. That implies in turn that the total kinetic energy of the molecules is the same. But for a perfect gas, the *only* contribution to the energy is the kinetic energy of the molecules (recall Section 1.5), so we have to conclude that the *total* energy of the gas is the same before and after the expansion. Energy has left the system as work; therefore, a compensating amount of energy must have entered the system as heat. We can therefore write:

For the isothermal expansion of a perfect gas:

$$q = -w \tag{2.6}$$

For instance, if we find that $w = -100$ J for a particular expansion (meaning that 100 J has left the system as a result of the system doing work), then we can conclude that $q = +100$ J (that is, 100 J must enter as heat). For free expansion, $w = 0$, so we conclude that $q = 0$ too: there is no influx of energy as heat when a perfect gas expands against zero pressure.

If the isothermal expansion is also reversible, we can use eqn 2.3 for the work in eqn 2.6, and write

For the isothermal, reversible expansion of a perfect gas:

$$q = nRT \ln \frac{V_f}{V_i} \tag{2.7}$$

When $V_f > V_i$, as in an expansion, the logarithm is positive and we conclude that $q > 0$, as expected: energy flows as heat into the system to make up for the energy lost as work. We also see that the greater the ratio of the final and initial volumes, the greater the influx of energy as heat.

Internal energy and enthalpy

Heat and work are *equivalent* ways of transferring energy into or out of a system in the sense that once the energy is inside, it is stored simply as 'energy'. Regardless of how the energy was supplied, as work or as heat, it can be released in either form. The experimental evidence for this **equivalence of heat and work** goes all the way back to the experiments done by James Joule, who showed that the same rise in temperature of a sample of water is brought about by transferring a given quantity of energy either by heating or by doing work.

2.6 The internal energy

We need some way of keeping track of the energy changes in a system. This is the job of the property called the **internal energy**, U, of the system, the sum of all the kinetic and potential contributions to the energy of all the atoms, ions, and molecules in the system. The internal energy is the grand total energy of the system with a value that depends on the temperature and, in general, the pressure. It is an extensive property because 2 kg of iron at a given temperature and pressure, for instance, has twice the internal energy of 1 kg of iron under the same conditions. The **molar internal energy**, $U_m = U/n$, the internal energy per mole of material, is an intensive property.

In practice, we do not know and cannot measure the total energy of a sample, because it includes the kinetic and potential energies of all the electrons and all the components of the atomic nuclei. Nevertheless, there is no problem with dealing with the *changes* in internal energy, ΔU, because we can determine those changes by monitoring the energy supplied or lost as heat or as work. All practical applications of thermodynamics deal with ΔU, not with U itself. A change in internal energy is written

$$\Delta U = w + q \tag{2.8}$$

where w is the energy transferred to the system by doing work and q the energy transferred to it by heating. The internal energy is an accounting device, like a country's gold reserves for monitoring transactions with the outside world (the surroundings) using either currency (heat or work).

Illustration 2.2

Changes in internal energy

When a system releases 10 kJ of energy into the surroundings by doing work (that is, when $w = -10$ kJ), the internal energy of the system decreases by 10 kJ, and we write $\Delta U = -10$ kJ. The minus sign signifies the reduction in internal energy that has occurred. If the system loses 20 kJ of energy by heating its surroundings (so $q = -20$ kJ), we write $\Delta U = -20$ kJ. If the system loses 10 kJ as work *and* 20 kJ as heat, as in an inefficient internal combustion engine, the internal energy falls by a total of 30 kJ, and we write $\Delta U = -30$ kJ. However, if we do 10 kJ of work on the system ($w = +10$ kJ), for instance, by winding a spring it contains or pushing in a piston to compress a gas (Fig. 2.13), then the internal energy of the system increases by 10 kJ, and we write $\Delta U = +10$ kJ. Likewise, if we supply 20 kJ of energy by heating the system ($q = +20$ kJ), then the internal energy increases by 20 kJ, and we write $\Delta U = +20$ kJ.

A note on good practice. Note that ΔU always carries a sign explicitly, even if it is positive: we never write $\Delta U = 20$ kJ, for instance, but always +20 kJ.

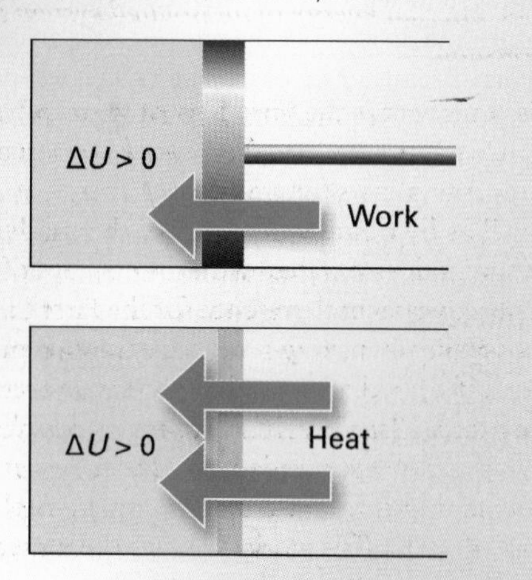

Fig. 2.13 When work is done on a system, its internal energy rises ($\Delta U > 0$). The internal energy also rises when energy is transferred into the system as heat.

We have seen that a feature of a perfect gas is that for any *isothermal* expansion, the total energy of the sample remains the same, and therefore, because $\Delta U = 0$, that $q = -w$. That is, any energy lost as work is restored by an influx of energy as heat. We can express this property in terms of the internal energy, as it implies that the internal energy remains constant when a perfect gas expands isothermally: from eqn 2.8 we can write

Isothermal expansion of a perfect gas:

$$\Delta U = 0 \tag{2.9}$$

In other words, *the internal energy of a sample of perfect gas at a given temperature is independent of the volume it occupies*. We can understand this independence by realizing that when a perfect gas expands isothermally the only feature that changes is the average distance between the molecules; their average speed and therefore total kinetic energy remains the same. However, as there are no intermolecular interactions, the total energy is independent of the average separation, so the internal energy is unchanged by expansion.

Example 2.2

Calculating the change in internal energy

Nutritionists are interested in the use of energy by the human body and we can consider our own body as a thermodynamic 'system'. Calorimeters have been constructed that can accommodate a person to measure (non-destructively!) their net energy output. Suppose in the course of an experiment someone does 622 kJ of work on an exercise bicycle and loses 82 kJ of energy as heat. What is the change in internal energy of the person? Disregard any matter loss by perspiration.

Strategy This example is an exercise in keeping track of signs correctly. When energy is lost from the system, w or q is negative. When energy is gained by the system, w or q is positive.

Solution To take note of the signs we write $w = -622$ kJ (622 kJ is lost by doing work) and $q = -82$ kJ (82 kJ is lost by heating the surroundings). Then eqn 2.8 gives us

$$\Delta U = w + q = (-622 \text{ kJ}) + (-82 \text{ kJ}) = -704 \text{ kJ}$$

We see that the person's internal energy falls by 704 kJ. Later, that energy will be restored by eating.

A note on good practice. Always attach the correct signs: use a positive sign when there is a flow of energy into the system and a negative sign when there is a flow of energy out of the system.

Self-test 2.4

An electric battery is charged by supplying 250 kJ of energy to it as electrical work (by driving an electric current through it), but in the process it loses 25 kJ of energy as heat to the surroundings. What is the change in internal energy of the battery?

[*Answer*: +225 kJ]

An important characteristic of the internal energy is that it is a **state function**, a physical property that depends only on the present state of the system and is independent of the path by which that state was reached. If we were to change the temperature of the system, then change the pressure, then adjust the temperature and pressure back to their original values, the internal energy would return to its original value too. A state function is very much like altitude: each point on the surface of the Earth can be specified by quoting its latitude and longitude, and (on land areas, at least) there is a unique property, the altitude, that has a fixed value at that point. In thermodynamics, the role of latitude and longitude is played by the pressure and temperature (and any other variables needed to specify the state of the system), and the internal energy plays the role of the altitude, with a single, fixed value for each state of the system.

The fact that U is a state function implies that *a change, ΔU, in the internal energy between two states of a system is independent of the path between them* (Fig. 2.14). Once again, the altitude is a helpful analogy. If we climb a mountain between two fixed points, we make the same change in altitude regardless of the path we take between the two points. Likewise, if we compress a sample of gas until it reaches a certain pressure and then cool it to a certain temperature, the change in internal energy has a particular value. If, on the contrary, we changed the temperature and then the pressure, but ensured that the two final values were the same as in the first experiment, then the overall change in internal energy would be exactly the same as before. This path independence of the value of ΔU is of the greatest importance in chemistry, as we shall soon see.

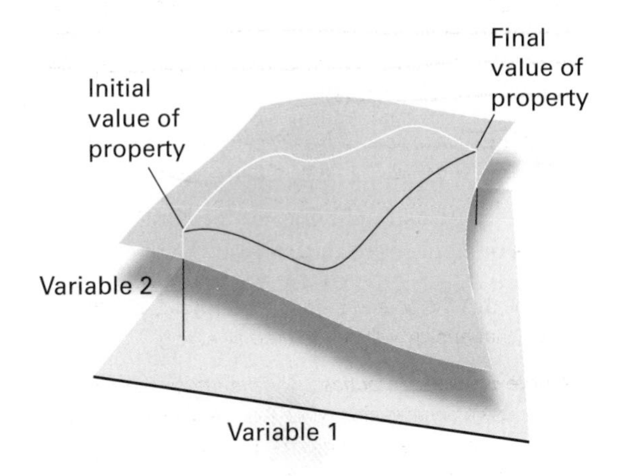

Fig. 2.14 The curved sheet shows how a property (for example, the altitude) changes as two variables (for example, latitude and longitude) are changed. The altitude is a state property, because it depends only on the current state of the system. The change in the value of a state property is independent of the path between the two states. For example, the difference in altitude between the initial and final states shown in the diagram is the same whatever path (as depicted by the dark and light lines) is used to travel between them.

Suppose we now consider an isolated system. Because an isolated system can neither do work nor heat its surroundings (or acquire energy by either process), it follows that its internal energy cannot change. That is,

The internal energy of an isolated system is constant.

This statement is the **First Law of thermodynamics**. It is closely related to the law of conservation of energy, but allows for transfers of energy by heating as well as by doing work. Unlike thermodynamics, mechanics does not deal with the concept of heat.

The experimental evidence for the First Law is the impossibility of making a 'perpetual motion machine', a device for producing work without consuming fuel. As we have already remarked, try as people might, they have never succeeded. No device has ever been made that creates internal energy to replace the energy drawn off as work. We cannot extract energy as work, leave the system isolated for some time, and hope that when we return the internal energy will have become restored to its original value.

The definition of ΔU in terms of w and q points to a very simple method for measuring the change in internal energy of a system when a reaction takes place. We have seen already that the work done by a system when it pushes against a fixed external pressure is proportional to the change in volume. Therefore, if we carry out a reaction in a container of constant volume, the system can do no expansion work and, provided it can do no other kind of work (so-called 'non-expansion work', such as electrical work), we can set $w = 0$. Then eqn 2.8 simplifies to

At constant volume, no non-expansion work:

$$\Delta U = q \qquad (2.10a)$$

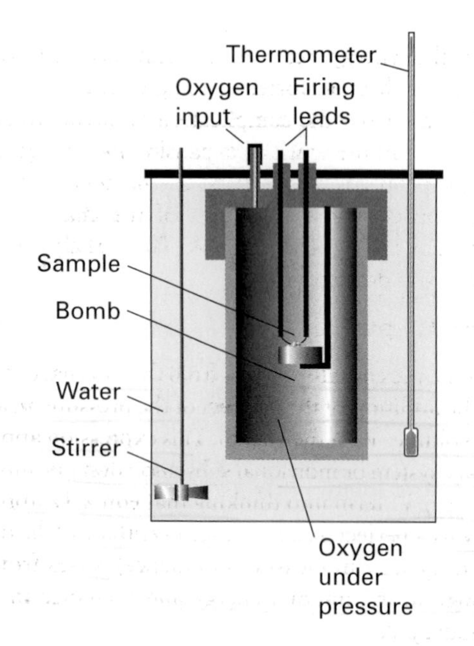

Fig. 2.15 A constant-volume bomb calorimeter. The 'bomb' is the central, sturdy vessel, which is strong enough to withstand moderately high pressures. The calorimeter is the entire assembly shown here. To ensure that no heat escapes into the surroundings, the calorimeter may be immersed in a water bath with a temperature that is continuously adjusted to that of the calorimeter at each stage of the combustion.

This relation is commonly written

$$\Delta U = q_V \tag{2.10b}$$

The subscript V signifies that the volume of the system is constant. An example of a chemical system that can be approximated as a constant-volume container is an individual biological cell.

To measure a change in internal energy, we should use a calorimeter that has a fixed volume, and monitor the energy released ($q < 0$) or supplied ($q > 0$) as heat. A **bomb calorimeter** is an example of a constant-volume calorimeter: it consists of a sturdy, sealed, constant-volume vessel in which the reaction takes place, and a surrounding water bath (Fig. 2.15). To ensure that no heat escapes unnoticed from the calorimeter, it is immersed in a water bath with a temperature adjusted to match the rising temperature of the calorimeter. The fact that the temperature of the bath is the same as that of the calorimeter ensures that no heat flows from one to the other. That is, the arrangement is adiabatic.

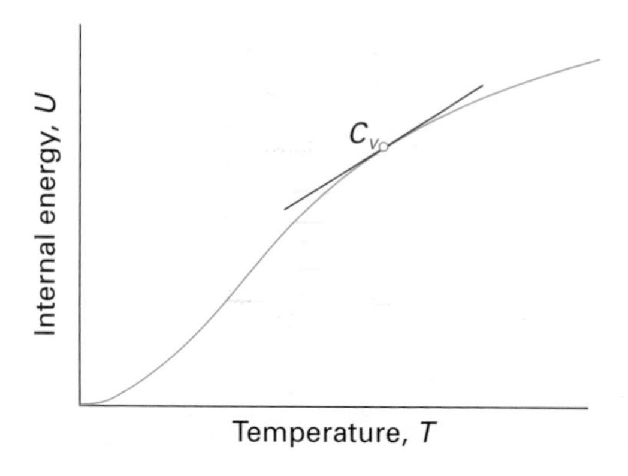

Fig. 2.16 The constant-volume heat capacity is the slope of a curve showing how the internal energy varies with temperature. The slope, and therefore the heat capacity, may be different at different temperatures.

We can use eqn 2.10 to obtain more insight into the heat capacity of a substance. The definition of heat capacity is given in eqn 2.4 ($C = q/\Delta T$). At constant volume, q may be replaced by the change in internal energy of the substance, so

$$C_V = \frac{\Delta U}{\Delta T} \text{ at constant volume} \tag{2.11}$$

The expression on the right is the slope of the graph of internal energy plotted against temperature, with the volume of the system held constant, so C_V tells us how the internal energy of a constant-volume system varies with temperature. If, as is generally the case, the graph of internal energy against temperature is not a straight line, we interpret C_V as the slope of the tangent to the curve at the temperature of interest (Fig. 2.16).

2.7 The enthalpy

Much of chemistry, and most of biology, takes place in vessels that are open to the atmosphere and subjected to constant pressure, not maintained at constant volume. In general, when a change takes place in a system open to the atmosphere, the volume of the system changes. For example, the thermal decomposition of 1.0 mol $CaCO_3(s)$ at 1 bar results in an increase in volume of nearly 90 dm^3 at 800°C on account of the carbon dioxide gas produced. To create this large volume for the carbon dioxide to occupy, the surrounding atmosphere must be pushed

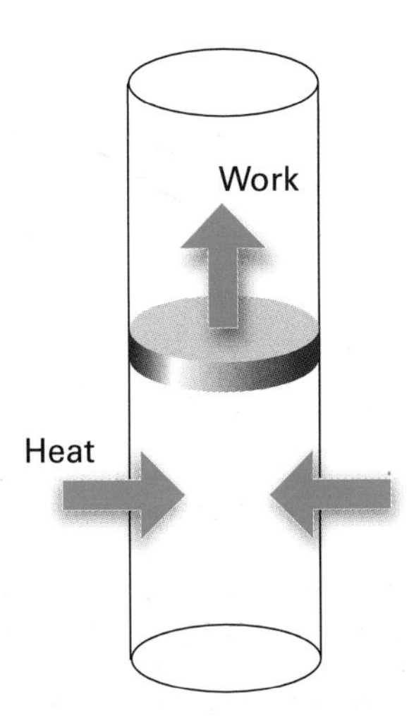

Fig. 2.17 The change in internal energy of a system that is free to expand or contract is not equal to the energy supplied as heat because some energy may escape back into the surroundings as work. However, the change in enthalpy of the system under these conditions *is* equal to the energy supplied as heat.

back. That is, the system must perform expansion work of the kind treated in Section 2.3. Therefore, although a certain quantity of heat may be supplied to bring about the endothermic decomposition, the increase in internal energy of the system is not equal to the energy supplied as heat because some energy has been used to do work of expansion (Fig. 2.17). In other words, because the volume has increased, some of the heat supplied to the system has leaked back into the surroundings as work.

Another example is the oxidation of a fat, such as tristearin, to carbon dioxide in the body. The overall reaction is

$$2\,C_{57}H_{110}O_6(s) + 163\,O_2(g) \rightarrow 114\,CO_2(g) + 110\,H_2O(l)$$

In this exothermic reaction there is a net *decrease* in volume equivalent to the elimination of (163 – 114) mol = 49 mol of gas molecules for every 2 mol of tristearin molecules that react. The decrease in volume at 25°C is about 600 cm^3 for the consumption of 1 g of fat. Because the volume of the system decreases, the atmosphere does work *on* the system as the reaction proceeds. That is, energy is transferred *to* the system as it contracts.[5] For this reaction, the decrease in the internal energy of the system is less than the energy released as heat because some energy has been restored by doing work.

We can avoid the complication of having to take into account the work of expansion by introducing a new property that will be at the centre of our attention throughout the rest of the chapter and will recur throughout the book. The **enthalpy**, H, of a system is defined as

$$H = U + pV \tag{2.12}$$

That is, the enthalpy differs from the internal energy by the addition of the product of the pressure, p, and the volume, V, of the system. This expression applies to *any* system or individual substance: don't be misled by the 'pV' term into thinking that eqn 2.12 applies only to a perfect gas. A change in enthalpy (the only quantity we can measure in practice) arises from a change in the internal energy and a change in the product pV:

$$\Delta H = \Delta U + \Delta(pV) \tag{2.13a}$$

where $\Delta(pV) = p_f V_f - p_i V_i$. If the change takes place at constant pressure p, the second term on the right simplifies to

$$\Delta(pV) = pV_f - pV_i = p(V_f - V_i) = p\Delta V$$

and we can write

$$\text{At constant pressure: } \Delta H = \Delta U + p\Delta V \tag{2.13b}$$

We shall often make use of this important relation for processes occurring at constant pressure, such as chemical reactions taking place in containers open to the atmosphere.

Enthalpy is an extensive property. The **molar enthalpy**, $H_m = H/n$, of a substance, an intensive property, differs from the molar internal energy by an amount proportional to the molar volume, V_m, of the substance:

$$H_m = U_m + pV_m \tag{2.14a}$$

This relation is valid for all substances. For a perfect gas we can go on to write $pV_m = RT$, and obtain

$$\text{For a perfect gas: } H_m = U_m + RT \tag{2.14b}$$

[5] In effect, a weight has been lowered in the surroundings, so the surroundings can do less work after the reaction has occurred. Some of their energy has been transferred into the system.

At 25°C, $RT = 2.5$ kJ mol^{-1}, so the molar enthalpy of a perfect gas differs from its molar internal energy by 2.5 kJ mol^{-1}. Because the molar volume of a solid or liquid is typically about 1000 times less than that of a gas, we can also conclude that the molar enthalpy of a solid or liquid is only about 2.5 J mol^{-1} (note: joules, not kilojoules) more than its molar internal energy, so the numerical difference is negligible.

Although the enthalpy and internal energy of a sample may have similar values, the introduction of the enthalpy has very important consequences in thermodynamics. First, note that because H is defined in terms of state functions (U, p, and V), *the enthalpy is a state function*. The implication is that the change in enthalpy, ΔH, when a system changes from one state to another is independent of the path between the two states. Second, we show in Derivation 2.3 that the change in enthalpy of a system can be identified with the heat transferred to it at constant pressure:

At constant pressure, no non-expansion work:

$$\Delta H = q \tag{2.15a}$$

This relation is commonly written

$$\Delta H = q_p \tag{2.15b}$$

The subscript p signifies that the pressure is held constant.

Derivation 2.3

Heat transfers at constant pressure

Consider a system open to the atmosphere, so that its pressure p is constant and equal to the external pressure p_{ex}. From eqn 2.13b we can write

$$\Delta H = \Delta U + p\,\Delta V = \Delta U + p_{ex}\,\Delta V$$

However, we know that the change in internal energy is given by eqn 2.8 ($\Delta U = w + q$) with $w = -p_{ex}\,\Delta V$ (provided the system does no other kind of work). When we substitute that expression into this one we obtain

$$\Delta H = (-p_{ex}\,\Delta V + q) + p_{ex}\,\Delta V = q$$

which is eqn 2.15.

The result expressed by eqn 2.15, that *at constant pressure, no non-expansion work, we can identify the energy transferred by heating with a change in enthalpy of the system*, is enormously powerful. It relates a quantity we can measure (the energy transferred as heat at constant pressure) to the change in a state function (the enthalpy). Dealing with state functions greatly extends the power of thermodynamic arguments, because we don't have to worry about how we get from one state to another: all that matters is the initial and final states.

Illustration 2.3

Interpreting a heat transfer in terms of enthalpy

Equation 2.15 implies that if 10 kJ of energy is supplied as heat to the system that is free to change its volume at constant pressure, then the enthalpy of the system increases by 10 kJ regardless of how much energy enters or leaves by doing work, and we write $\Delta H = +10$ kJ. However, if the reaction is exothermic and releases 10 kJ of energy as heat when it occurs, then $\Delta H = -10$ kJ regardless of how much work is done. For the particular case of the combustion of tristearin mentioned at the beginning of the section, in which 90 kJ of energy is released as heat, we would write $\Delta H = -90$ kJ.

An endothermic reaction ($q > 0$) taking place at constant pressure results in an increase in enthalpy ($\Delta H > 0$) because energy enters the system as heat. An exothermic process ($q < 0$) taking place at constant pressure corresponds to a decrease in enthalpy ($\Delta H < 0$) because energy leaves the system as heat. All combustion reactions, including the controlled combustions that contribute to respiration, are exothermic and are accompanied by a decrease in enthalpy. These relations are consistent with the name 'enthalpy', which is derived from the Greek words meaning 'heat inside': the 'heat inside' the system is increased if the process is endothermic and absorbs energy as heat from the surroundings; it is decreased if the process is exothermic and releases energy as heat into the surroundings.[6] **Differential scanning calorimetry**, discussed in Box 2.1, is a common technique for the measurement of the enthalpy change that accompanies a physical or chemical change occurring at constant pressure.

[6] But heat does not actually 'exist' inside: only energy exists in a system; heat is a means of recovering that energy or increasing it.

Box 2.1 *Differential scanning calorimetry*

A *differential scanning calorimeter* (DSC) is used to measure the heat transferred to or from a sample at constant pressure during a physical or chemical change. The term 'differential' refers to the fact that the behaviour of the sample is compared to that of a reference material that does not undergo a physical or chemical change during the analysis. The term 'scanning' refers to the fact that the temperatures of the sample and reference material are increased, or scanned, systematically during the analysis.

A DSC consists of two small compartments that are heated electrically at a constant rate (see the first illustration). The temperature, T, at time t during a linear scan is $T = T_0 + \alpha t$, where T_0 is the initial temperature and α is the temperature scan rate (in kelvin per second, K s^{-1}). A computer controls the electrical power output in order to maintain the same temperature in the sample and reference compartments throughout the analysis.

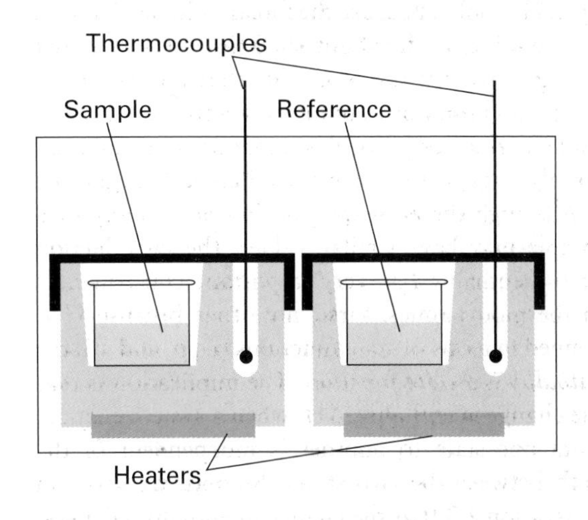

A differential scanning calorimeter. The sample and a reference material are heated in separate but identical compartments. The output is the difference in power needed to maintain the compartments at equal temperatures as the temperature rises.

The temperature of the sample changes significantly relative to that of the reference material if a chemical or physical process involving heat transfer occurs in the sample during the scan. To maintain the same temperature in both compartments, excess heat is transferred to the sample during the process. For example, an endothermic process lowers the temperature of the sample relative to that of the reference and, as a result, the sample must be supplied with more heat than the reference to maintain equal temperatures.

If no physical or chemical change occurs in the sample at temperature T, we can use eqn 2.4 to write the heat transferred to the sample at constant pressure as $q_p = C_p \Delta T$, where $\Delta T = T - T_0 = \alpha t$ and we have assumed that C_p is independent of temperature. If an endothermic process occurs in the sample, we have to supply additional 'excess' heat, $q_{p,\text{ex}}$, to achieve the same change in temperature of the sample, and can express this excess heat in terms of an additional contribution to the heat capacity, $C_{p,\text{ex}}$, by writing $q_{p,\text{ex}} = C_{p,\text{ex}} \Delta T$. It follows that

$$C_{p,\text{ex}} = \frac{q_{p,\text{ex}}}{\Delta T} = \frac{q_{p,\text{ex}}}{\alpha t} = \frac{P_{\text{ex}}}{\alpha}$$

where $P_{\text{ex}} = q_{p,\text{ex}}/t$ is the excess electrical power necessary to equalize the temperature of the sample and reference compartments.

A DSC trace, also called a *thermogram*, consists of a plot of P_{ex} or $C_{p,\text{ex}}$ against T (see the second illustration). Broad peaks in the thermogram indicate processes requiring heat transfer. To see how an enthalpy change can

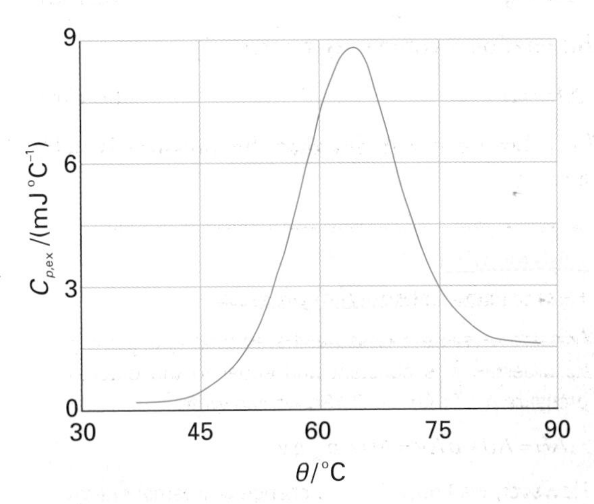

A thermogram for the protein ubiquitin. The protein retains its native structure up to about 45°C and then undergoes an endothermic conformational change. (Adapted from B. Chowdhry and S. LeHarne, *J. Chem. Educ.* **74**, 236 (1997).)

be calculated from the thermogram, we rewrite eqn 2.16 as $\Delta H = C_{p,\text{ex}} \Delta T$ and then consider only infinitesimally small changes, so

$$dH = C_{p,\text{ex}} dT$$

To find the change in enthalpy, we integrate both sides of this expression from an initial temperature T_1 and initial enthalpy H_1, to a final temperature T_2 and enthalpy H_2. But we cannot regard the heat capacity as a constant, so the integral of interest is

$$\int_{H_1}^{H_2} dH = \int_{T_1}^{T_2} C_{p,ex}\, dT$$

The left-hand side of the expression evaluates to

$$\int_{H_1}^{H_2} dH = H_2 - H_1 = \Delta H$$

It then follows that

$$\Delta H = \int_{T_1}^{T_2} C_{p,ex}\, dT$$

The integral on the right-hand side of this expression is the area under the curve of $C_{p,ex}$ against T between T_1 and T_2. Therefore, the enthalpy change of the process is the area under the thermogram between the temperatures at which the process begins and ends.

With a DSC, enthalpy changes may be determined in samples of masses as low as 0.5 mg. This is a significant advantage over bomb calorimeters (Section 2.6), which require several grams of material. The DSC is used in biochemistry laboratories to assess the stability of proteins, nucleic acids, and membranes. Large molecules, such as biological polymers, attain complex three-dimensional structures due to intra- and intermolecular interactions, such as hydrogen bonding and hydrophobic interactions (Chapter 17). Disruption of these interactions is an endothermic process that can be studied with a DSC. For example, the thermogram shown in the second illustration indicates that the protein ubiquitin retains its native structure up to about 45°C. At higher temperatures, the protein undergoes an endothermic conformational change that results in the loss of its three-dimensional structure.

Exercise 1 In many experimental thermograms, such as that shown in the illustration, the baseline below T_1 is at a different level from that above T_2. Explain this observation.

Exercise 2 You have at your disposal a sample of pure polymer P and a sample of P that has just been synthesized in a large chemical reactor and that may contain impurities. Describe how you would use differential scanning calorimetry to determine the mole percentage composition of P in the allegedly impure sample.

2.8 The temperature variation of the enthalpy

We have seen that the internal energy of a system rises as the temperature is increased. The same is true of the enthalpy, which also rises when the temperature is increased (Fig. 2.18). For example, the enthalpy of 100 g of water is greater at 80°C than at 20°C. We can measure the change by monitoring the energy that we must supply as heat to raise the temperature through 60°C when the sample is open to the atmosphere (or subjected to some other constant pressure); it is found that $\Delta H \approx +25$ kJ in this instance.

Just as we saw that the constant-volume heat capacity tells us about the temperature dependence of the internal energy at constant volume, so the constant-pressure heat capacity tells us how the enthalpy of a system changes as its temperature is raised at constant pressure. To derive the relation,

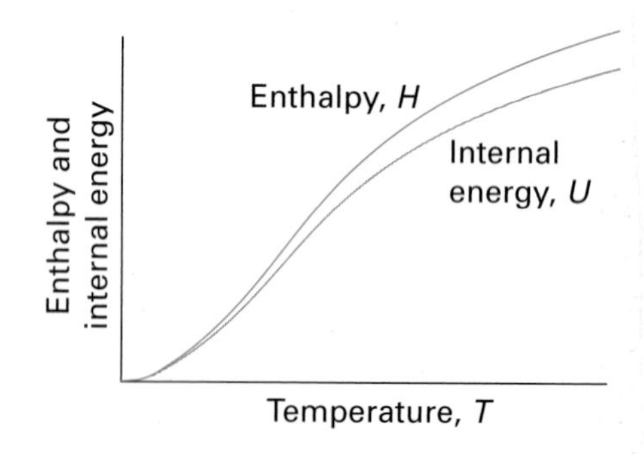

Fig. 2.18 The enthalpy of a system increases as its temperature is raised. Note that the enthalpy is always greater than the internal energy of the system, and that the difference increases with temperature.

we combine the definition of heat capacity in eqn 2.4 ($C = q/\Delta T$) with eqn 2.15 and obtain

$$C_p = \frac{\Delta H}{\Delta T} \quad \text{at constant pressure} \qquad (2.16)$$

That is, the constant-pressure heat capacity is the slope of a plot of enthalpy against temperature of a system kept at constant pressure. Because the plot might not be a straight line, in general we interpret C_p as the slope of the tangent to the curve at the temperature of interest (Fig. 2.19, Table 2.1).

Illustration 2.4

Using the constant-pressure heat capacity

Provided the heat capacity is constant over the range of temperatures of interest, we can write eqn 2.16 as $\Delta H = C_p \Delta T$. This relation means that when the temperature of 100 g of water (5.55 mol H_2O) is raised from 20°C to 80°C (so $\Delta T = +60$ K) at constant pressure, the enthalpy of the sample changes by

$$\begin{aligned}\Delta H &= C_p \Delta T = nC_{p,m} \Delta T \\ &= (5.55\ \text{mol}) \times (75.29\ \text{J K}^{-1}\ \text{mol}^{-1}) \times (60\ \text{K}) \\ &= +25\ \text{kJ}\end{aligned}$$

The greater the temperature rise, the greater the change in enthalpy and therefore the more heating required to bring it about. Note that this calculation is only approximate, because the heat capacity depends on the temperature, and we have used an average value for the temperature range of interest.

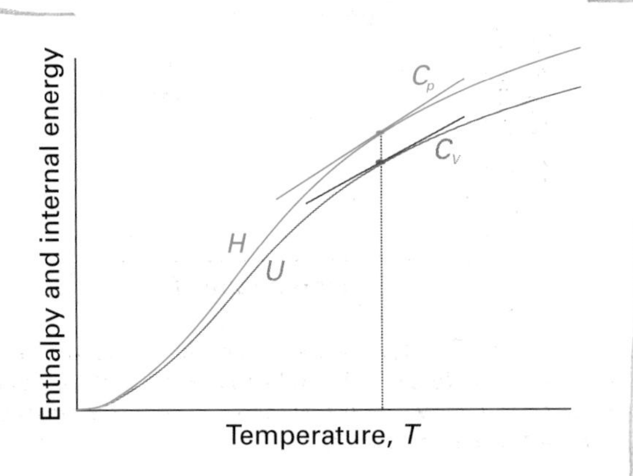

Fig. 2.19 The heat capacity at constant pressure is the slope of the curve showing how the enthalpy varies with temperature; the heat capacity at constant volume is the corresponding slope of the internal energy curve. Note that the heat capacity varies with temperature (in general), and that C_p is greater than C_V.

Because we know that the difference between the enthalpy and internal energy of a perfect gas depends in a very simple way on the temperature (eqn 2.14), we can suspect that there is a simple relation between the heat capacities at constant volume and constant pressure. We show in Derivation 2.4 that, in fact, for a perfect gas:

$$C_{p,m} - C_{V,m} = R \tag{2.17}$$

Derivation 2.4

The relation between heat capacities

The molar internal energy and enthalpy of a perfect gas are related by eqn 2.14 ($H_m = U_m + RT$), which we can write as

$$H_m - U_m = RT$$

When the temperature increases by ΔT, the molar enthalpy increases by ΔH_m and the molar internal energy increases by ΔU_m, so

$$\Delta H_m - \Delta U_m = R\Delta T$$

Now divide both sides by ΔT, which gives

$$\frac{\Delta H_m}{\Delta T} - \frac{\Delta U_m}{\Delta T} = R$$

We recognize the first term on the left as the molar constant-pressure heat capacity, $C_{p,m}$, and the second term as the molar constant-volume heat capacity, $C_{V,m}$. Therefore, this relation can be written as in eqn 2.17.

Equation 2.17 shows that the molar heat capacity of a perfect gas is greater at constant pressure than at constant volume. This difference is what we should expect. At constant volume, all the energy supplied as heat to the system remains inside and the temperature rises accordingly. At constant pressure, though, some of the energy supplied as heat escapes back into the surroundings when the system expands and does work. As less energy remains in the system, the temperature does not rise as much, which corresponds to a greater heat capacity. The difference is significant for gases (for oxygen, $C_{V,m} = 20.8\ \text{J K}^{-1}\ \text{mol}^{-1}$ and $C_{p,m} = 29.1\ \text{J K}^{-1}\ \text{mol}^{-1}$), which undergo large changes of volume when heated, but is negligible for most solids and liquids.

CHECKLIST OF KEY IDEAS

You should now be familiar with the following concepts:

- ☐ 1 A system is classified as open, closed, or isolated.
- ☐ 2 The surroundings remain at constant temperature and either constant volume or constant pressure when processes occur in the system.
- ☐ 3 An exothermic process releases energy as heat, q, to the surroundings; an endothermic process absorbs energy as heat.
- ☐ 4 The work of expansion against constant external pressure is $w = -p_{ex}\Delta V$.
- ☐ 5 Maximum expansion work is achieved in a reversible change.
- ☐ 6 The work of reversible, isothermal expansion of a perfect gas is $w = -nRT\ln(V_f/V_i)$.
- ☐ 7 The change in internal energy may be calculated from $\Delta U = w + q$, where U is a state function.
- ☐ 8 The First Law of thermodynamics states that the internal energy of an isolated system is constant.
- ☐ 9 The enthalpy is defined as $H = U + pV$.
- ☐ 10 A change in internal energy is equal to the energy transferred as heat at constant volume ($\Delta U = q_V$); a change in enthalpy is equal to the energy transferred as heat at constant pressure ($\Delta H = q_p$).
- ☐ 11 The constant-volume heat capacity is the slope of the tangent to the graph of the internal energy of a constant-volume system plotted against temperature ($C_V = \Delta U/\Delta T$).
- ☐ 12 The constant-pressure heat capacity is the slope of the tangent to the graph of the enthalpy of a constant-pressure system plotted against temperature ($C_p = \Delta H/\Delta T$).
- ☐ 13 The molar constant-volume and constant-pressure heat capacities of a perfect gas are related by $C_{p,m} - C_{V,m} = R$.

DISCUSSION QUESTIONS

2.1 Provide molecular interpretations for work and heat.

2.2 Distinguish between expansion work against constant pressure and work of reversible expansion.

2.3 Explain the difference between the change in internal energy and the change in enthalpy of a chemical or physical process.

2.4 Explain the limitations of the following expressions: (a) $q = nRT\ln(V_f/V_i)$; (b) $\Delta H = \Delta U + p\Delta V$; (c) $C_{p,m} - C_{V,m} = R$.

EXERCISES

Assume all gases are perfect unless stated otherwise. The sign ‡ indicates that calculus is required.

2.5 Calculate the work that a person must do to raise a mass of 1.0 kg through 10 m on the surface of (a) the Earth ($g = 9.81$ m s^{-2}) and (b) the Moon ($g = 1.60$ m s^{-2}).

2.6 How much metabolic energy must a bird of mass 200 g exert to fly to a height of 20 m? Neglect all losses due to friction, physiological imperfection, and the acquisition of kinetic energy.

2.7 Calculate the work needed for a person of mass 65 kg to climb through 4.0 m on the surface of the Earth.

2.8 The centre of mass of a cylindrical column of liquid lies halfway along its length. Calculate the work required to raise a column of mercury (density 13.6 g cm^{-3}) of diameter 1.00 cm through 760 mm on the surface of the Earth ($g = 9.81$ m s^{-2}).

2.9 ‡The gravitational force acting on an object of mass m is $-Gmm_E/r^2$, where m_E is the mass of the Earth (6.0×10^{24} kg) and G is the gravitational constant. (a) Calculate the work needed to raise an aircraft of mass 100 t to its cruising altitude of 11.0 km. (b) What is the percentage error in assuming that eqn 2.1 may be used?

2.10 ‡The force opposing the stretching and compression of a spring is given by *Hooke's law*, $F = -kx$, where x is the displacement from equilibrium. What work must be done to stretch the spring through a displacement x? Draw a graph of your conclusion.

2.11 Calculate the work done by a gas when it expands through (a) 1.0 cm^3 and (b) 1.0 dm^3 against an atmospheric pressure of 100 kPa. What work must be done to compress the gas back to its original state in each case?

2.12 Calculate the work of expansion accompanying the complete combustion of 1.0 g of glucose to carbon dioxide and (a) liquid water, (b) water vapour at 20°C when the external pressure is 1.0 atm.

2.13 We are all familiar with the general principles of operation of an internal combustion engine: the combustion of fuel drives out the piston. It is possible to imagine engines that use reactions other than combustions, and we need to assess the work they can do. A chemical reaction takes place in a container of cross-sectional area 100 cm^2; the container has a piston at one end. As a result of the reaction, the piston is pushed out through 10.0 cm against a constant external pressure of 100 kPa. Calculate the work done by the system.

2.14 The work done by an engine may depend on its orientation in a gravitational field, because the mass of the piston is relevant when the expansion is vertical. A chemical reaction takes place in a container of cross-sectional area 55.0 cm^2; the container has a piston of mass 250 g at one end. As a result of the reaction, the piston is pushed out (a) horizontally, (b) vertically through 155 cm against an external pressure of 105 kPa. Calculate the work done by the system in each case.

2.15 A sample of methane of mass 4.50 g occupies 12.7 dm^3 at 310 K. (a) Calculate the work done when the gas expands isothermally against a constant external pressure of 30.0 kPa until its volume has increased by 3.3 dm^3. (b) Calculate the work that would be done if the same expansion occurred isothermally and reversibly.

2.16 In the isothermal reversible compression of 52.0 mmol of a perfect gas at 260 K, the volume of the gas is reduced from 300 cm^3 to 100 cm^3. Calculate w for this process.

2.17 A sample of blood plasma occupies 0.550 dm^3 at 0°C and 1.03 bar, and is compressed isothermally by 0.57 per cent by being subjected to a constant external pressure of 95.2 bar. Calculate w.

2.18 A strip of magnesium metal of mass 12.5 g is dropped into a beaker of dilute hydrochloric acid. Given that the magnesium is the limiting reactant, calculate the work done by the system as a result of the reaction. The atmospheric pressure is 1.00 atm and the temperature 20.2°C.

2.19 ‡Derivation 2.2 showed how to calculate the work of reversible, isothermal expansion of a perfect gas. Suppose that the expansion is reversible but not isothermal and that the temperature decreases as the expansion proceeds. (a) Find an expression for the work when $T = T_i - c(V - V_i)$, with c a positive constant. (b) Is the work greater or smaller than for isothermal expansion?

2.20 ‡Graphical displays often enhance understanding. Take your result from Exercise 2.19 and use mathematical software to plot the work done by the system against the final volume for a selection of values of c. Include negative values of c (corresponding to the temperature rising as the expansion occurs).

2.21 What is the heat capacity of a sample of liquid that rose in temperature by 5.23°C when supplied with 124 J of energy as heat?

2.22 The high heat capacity of water is ecologically benign because it stabilizes the temperatures of lakes and oceans: a large quantity of energy must be lost or gained before there is a significant change in temperature. Conversely, it means that a lot of heat must be supplied to achieve a large rise in temperature. The molar heat capacity of water is 75.3 J K^{-1} mol^{-1}. What energy is needed to heat 250 g of water (a cup of coffee, for instance) through 40°C?

2.23 A current of 1.34 A from a 110 V source was passed through a heater for 5.0 min. The heater was immersed in a water bath. What quantity of energy was transferred to the water as heat?

2.24 When 229 J of energy is supplied as heat to 3.00 mol Ar(g), the temperature of the sample increases by 2.55 K. Calculate the molar heat capacities at constant volume and constant pressure of the gas.

2.25 The heat capacity of air is much smaller than that of water, and relatively modest amounts of heat are needed to change its temperature. This is one of the reasons why desert regions, though very hot during the day, are bitterly cold at night. The heat capacity of air at room temperature and pressure is approximately 21 J K^{-1} mol^{-1}. How much energy is required to raise the temperature of a room of dimensions 5.5 m × 6.5 m × 3.0 m by 10°C? If losses are neglected, how long will it take a heater rated at 1.5 kW to achieve that increase given that 1 W = 1 J s^{-1}?

2.26 In an experiment to determine the calorific value of a food, a sample of the food was burned in an oxygen atmosphere and the temperature rose by 2.89°C. When a current of 1.27 A from a 12.5 V source flowed through the same calorimeter for 157 s, the temperature rose by 3.88°C. What energy is released as heat by the combustion?

2.27 The transfer of energy from one region of the atmosphere to another is of great importance in meteorology as it affects the weather. Calculate the heat needed to be supplied to a parcel of air containing 1.00 mol air molecules to maintain its temperature at 300 K when it expands reversibly and isothermally from 22 dm^3 to 30.0 dm^3 as it ascends.

2.28 A laboratory animal exercised on a treadmill that, through pulleys, raised a 200 g mass through 1.55 m. At the same time, the animal lost 5.0 J of energy as heat. Disregarding all other losses, and regarding the animal as a closed system, what is its change in internal energy?

2.29 In preparation for a study of the metabolism of an organism, a small, sealed calorimeter was prepared. In the initial phase of the experiment, a current of 15.22 mA from a 12.4 V source was passed for 155 s through a heater inside the calorimeter. What is the change in internal energy of the calorimeter?

2.30 The internal energy of a perfect gas does not change when the gas undergoes isothermal expansion. What is the change in enthalpy?

2.31 Carbon dioxide, although only a minor component of the atmosphere, plays an important role in determining the weather and the composition and temperature of the atmosphere. Calculate the difference between the molar enthalpy and the molar internal energy of carbon dioxide regarded as a real gas at 298.15 K. For this calculation treat carbon dioxide as a van der Waals gas and use the data in Table 1.5.

2.32 A sample of a serum of mass 25 g is cooled from 290 K to 275 K at constant pressure by the extraction of 1.2 kJ of energy as heat. Calculate q and ΔH and estimate the heat capacity of the sample.

2.33 When 3.0 mol $O_2(g)$ is heated at a constant pressure of 3.25 atm, its temperature increases from 260 K to 285 K. Given that the molar heat capacity of O_2 at constant pressure is 29.4 J K^{-1} mol^{-1}, calculate q, ΔH, and ΔU.

2.34 The molar heat capacity at constant pressure of carbon dioxide is 29.14 J K^{-1} mol^{-1}. What is the value of its molar heat capacity at constant volume?

2.35 Use the information in Exercise 2.34 to calculate the change in (a) molar enthalpy, (b) molar internal energy when carbon dioxide is heated from 15°C (the temperature when air is inhaled) to 37°C (blood temperature, the temperature in our lungs).

2.36 ‡Suppose that the molar internal energy of a substance over a limited temperature range could be expressed as a polynomial in T as $U_m(T) = a + bT + cT^2$. Find an expression for the constant-volume molar heat capacity at a temperature T.

2.37 ‡The heat capacity of a substance is often reported in the form $C_{p,m} = a + bT + c/T^2$. Use this expression to make a more accurate estimate of the change in molar enthalpy of carbon dioxide when it is heated from 15°C to 37°C (as in the preceding exercise), given a = 44.22 J K^{-1} mol^{-1}, $b = 8.79 \times 10^{-3}$ J K^{-2} mol^{-1}, and $c = -8.62 \times 10^5$ J K mol^{-1}. *Hint.* You will need to integrate $dH = C_p\,dT$.

2.38 ‡Exercise 2.37 gives an expression for the temperature dependence of the constant-pressure molar heat capacity over a limited temperature range. (a) How does the molar enthalpy of the substance change over that range? (b) Plot the molar enthalpy as a function of temperature using the data in Exercise 2.37.

2.39 ‡The exact expression for the relation between the heat capacities at constant volume and constant pressure is $C_p - C_V = \alpha^2 TV/\kappa$, where α is the expansion coefficient, $\alpha = (dV/dT)/V$ at constant pressure, and κ (kappa) is the isothermal compressibility, $\kappa = -(dV/dp)/V$. Confirm that this general expression reduces to that in eqn 2.17 for a perfect gas.

Chapter 3

Thermochemistry

This chapter is an extended illustration of the role of enthalpy in chemistry. There are three properties of enthalpy to keep in mind. One is that a change in enthalpy can be identified with the heat supplied at constant pressure ($\Delta H = q_p$). Second, enthalpy is a state function, so we can calculate the change in its value ($\Delta H = H_f - H_i$) between two specified initial and final states by selecting the most convenient path between them. Third, the slope of a plot of enthalpy against temperature is the constant-pressure heat capacity of the system ($C_p = \Delta H/\Delta T$). All the material in this chapter is based on these three properties.

Physical change

First, we consider physical change, such as when one form of a substance changes into another form of the same substance, as when ice melts to water. We shall also include changes of a particularly simple kind, such as the ionization of an atom or the breaking of a bond in a molecule.

The numerical value of a thermodynamic property depends on the conditions, such as the states of the substances involved, the pressure, and the temperature. Chemists have therefore found it convenient to report their data for a set of standard conditions at the temperature of their choice:

The standard state *of a substance is the pure substance at exactly 1 bar.*[1]

[1] Remember that 1 bar = 10^5 Pa exactly. Solutions are a special case, and are dealt with in Section 6.6.

We denote the standard state value by the superscript $^\ominus$ on the symbol for the property, as in $H_m^\ominus$ for the standard molar enthalpy of a substance and $p^\ominus$ for the standard pressure of 1 bar. For example, the standard state of hydrogen gas is the pure gas at 1 bar and the standard state of solid calcium carbonate is the pure solid at 1 bar, with either the calcite or aragonite form specified. The physical state needs to be specified because we can speak of the standard states of the solid, liquid, and vapour forms of water, for instance, which are the pure solid, the pure liquid, and the pure vapour, respectively, at 1 bar in each case.

In older texts you might come across a standard state defined for 1 atm (101.325 kPa) in place of 1 bar. That is the old convention. In most cases, data for 1 atm differ only a little from data for 1 bar. You might also come across standard states defined as referring to 298.15 K. That is incorrect: temperature is not a part of the definition of standard state, and standard states may refer to any temperature (but it should be specified). Thus, it is possible to speak of the standard state of water vapour at 100 K, 273.15 K, or any other temperature. It is conventional, though, for data to be reported at the so-called 'conventional temperature' of 298.15 K (25.00°C), and from now on, unless specified otherwise, all data will be for that temperature. For simplicity, we shall often refer to 298.15 K as '25°C'. Finally, a standard state need not be a stable state and need not be realizable in practice. Thus, the standard state of water vapour at 25°C is the vapour at 1 bar, but water vapour at that temperature and pressure would immediately condense to liquid water.

3.1 The enthalpy of phase transition

A **phase** is a specific state of matter that is uniform throughout in composition and physical state. The liquid and vapour states of water are two of its phases. The term 'phase' is more specific than 'state of matter' because a substance may exist in more than one solid form, each one of which is a solid phase. Thus, the element sulfur may exist as a solid. However, as a solid it may be found as rhombic sulfur or as monoclinic sulfur; these two solid phases differ in the manner in which the crownlike S_8 molecules stack together. No substance has more than one gaseous phase, so 'gas phase' and 'gaseous state' are effectively synonyms. The only substance that exists in more than one liquid phase is helium, although evidence is accumulating that water may also have two liquid phases. Most substances exist in a variety of solid phases. Carbon, for instance, exists as graphite, diamond, and a variety of forms based on fullerene structures; calcium carbonate exists as calcite and aragonite; there are at least twelve forms of ice.

The conversion of one phase of a substance to another phase is called a **phase transition**. Thus, vaporization (liquid → gas) is a phase transition, as is a transition between solid phases (such as rhombic sulfur → monoclinic sulfur). Most phase transitions are accompanied by a change of enthalpy, for the rearrangement of atoms or molecules usually requires or releases energy.[2]

The vaporization of a liquid, such as the conversion of liquid water to water vapour when a pool of water evaporates at 20°C or a kettle boils at 100°C, is an endothermic process ($\Delta H > 0$), because heat must be supplied to bring about the change. At a molecular level, molecules are being driven apart from the grip they exert on one another, and this process requires energy. One of the body's strategies for maintaining its temperature at about 37°C is to use the endothermic character of the vaporization of water, because the evaporation[3] of perspiration requires heat and withdraws it from the skin.

The energy that must be supplied as heat at constant pressure per mole of molecules that are vaporized under standard conditions (that is, pure liquid at 1 bar changing to pure vapour at 1 bar) is called the **standard enthalpy of vaporization** of the liquid, and is denoted $\Delta_{vap}H^\ominus$ (Table 3.1).[4] For example, 44 kJ of heat is required to vaporize 1 mol $H_2O(l)$ at 1 bar and 25°C, so $\Delta_{vap}H^\ominus = 44\ kJ\ mol^{-1}$. All enthalpies of vaporization are positive, so the sign is not normally given. Alternatively, we can report

[2] Note the 'most' and the 'usually'; there are exceptions.

[3] Evaporation is almost synonymous with vaporization, but commonly denotes vaporization to dryness.

[4] The attachment of the subscript vap to the Δ is the modern convention; however, the older convention in which the subscript is attached to the H, as in ΔH_{vap}, is still widely used.

Table 3.1 *Standard enthalpies of transition at the transition temperature**

Substance	Freezing point, T_f/K	$\Delta_{fus}H^{\ominus}$/(kJ mol^{-1})	Boiling point, T_b/K	$\Delta_{vap}H^{\ominus}$/(kJ mol^{-1})
Ammonia, NH_3	195.3	5.65	239.7	23.4
Argon, Ar	83.8	1.2	87.3	6.5
Benzene, C_6H_6	278.7	9.87	353.3	30.8
Ethanol, C_2H_5OH	158.7	4.60	351.5	43.5
Helium, He	3.5	0.02	4.22	0.08
Mercury, Hg	234.3	2.292	629.7	59.30
Methane, CH_4	90.7	0.94	111.7	8.2
Methanol, CH_3OH	175.5	3.16	337.2	35.3
Propanone, CH_3COCH_3	177.8	5.72	329.4	29.1
Water, H_2O	273.15	6.01	373.2	40.7

* For values at 298.15 K, use the information in the *Data section*.

the same information by writing the **thermochemical equation**[5]

$$H_2O(l) \rightarrow H_2O(g) \qquad \Delta H^{\ominus} = +44 \text{ kJ}$$

A thermochemical equation shows the standard enthalpy change (including the sign) that accompanies the conversion of an amount of reactant equal to its stoichiometric coefficient in the accompanying chemical equation (in this case, 1 mol H_2O). If the stoichiometric coefficients in the chemical equation are multiplied through by 2, then the thermochemical equation would be written

$$2\, H_2O(l) \rightarrow 2\, H_2O(g) \qquad \Delta H^{\ominus} = +88 \text{ kJ}$$

This equation signifies that 88 kJ of heat is required to vaporize 2 mol $H_2O(l)$ at 1 bar and (recalling our convention) at 298.15 K.

Example 3.1

Determining the enthalpy of vaporization of a liquid

Ethanol, C_2H_5OH, is brought to the boil at 1 atm. When an electric current of 0.682 A from a 12.0 V supply is passed for 500 s through a heating coil immersed in the boiling liquid, it is found that the temperature remains constant but 4.33 g of ethanol is vaporized. What is the enthalpy of vaporization of ethanol at its boiling point at 1 atm?

Strategy Because the heat is supplied at constant pressure, we can identify the heat supplied, q, with the change in enthalpy of the ethanol when it vaporizes. We need to calculate the heat supplied and the amount of ethanol molecules vaporized. Then the enthalpy of vaporization is the heat supplied divided by the amount. The heat supplied is given by eqn 2.5 ($q = IVt$; recall that 1 A V s = 1 J). The amount of ethanol molecules is determined by dividing the mass of ethanol vaporized by its molar mass ($n = m/M$).

Solution The energy supplied by heating is

$$q = IVt = (0.682 \text{ A}) \times (12.0 \text{ V}) \times (500 \text{ s})$$
$$= 0.682 \times 12.0 \times 500 \text{ J}$$

This value is the change in enthalpy of the sample. The amount of ethanol molecules (of molar mass 46.07 g mol^{-1}) vaporized is

$$n = \frac{m}{M} = \frac{4.33 \text{ g}}{46.07 \text{ g mol}^{-1}} = \frac{4.33}{46.07} \text{ mol}$$

The molar enthalpy change is therefore

$$\Delta_{vap}H = \frac{0.682 \times 12.0 \times 500 \text{ J}}{(4.33/46.07) \text{ mol}} = 4.35 \times 10^4 \text{ J mol}^{-1}$$

corresponding to 43.5 kJ mol^{-1}.

Because the pressure is 1 atm, not 1 bar, the enthalpy of vaporization calculated here is not the standard value. However, 1 atm differs only slightly from 1 bar, so we

[5] Unless otherwise stated, all data in this text are for 298.15 K.

can expect the standard enthalpy of vaporization to be very close to the value found here. Note also that the value calculated here is for the boiling point of ethanol, which is 78°C (351 K): we convey this information by writing $\Delta_{vap}H^{\ominus}(351\ K) = 43.5\ kJ\ mol^{-1}$.

A note on good practice Molar quantities are expressed as a quantity per mole (as in kilojoules per mole, kJ mol^{-1}). Distinguish them from the magnitude of a property *for* 1 mol of substance, which is expressed as the quantity itself (as in kilojoules, kJ). All enthalpies of transition, denoted $\Delta_{trs}H$, are molar quantities.

Self-test 3.1

In a similar experiment, it was found that 1.36 g of boiling benzene, C_6H_6, is vaporized when a current of 0.835 A from a 12.0 V source is passed for 53.5 s. What is the enthalpy of vaporization of benzene at its boiling point?

[*Answer:* 30.8 kJ mol^{-1}]

There are some striking differences in standard enthalpies of vaporization: although the value for water is 44 kJ mol^{-1}, that for methane, CH_4, at its boiling point is only 8 kJ mol^{-1}. Even allowing for the fact that vaporization is taking place at different temperatures, the difference between the enthalpies of vaporization signifies that water molecules are held together in the bulk liquid much more tightly than methane molecules are in liquid methane.[6] The high enthalpy of vaporization of water has profound ecological consequences, as it is partly responsible for the survival of the oceans and the generally low humidity of the atmosphere. If only a small amount of heat had to be supplied to vaporize the oceans, the atmosphere would be much more heavily saturated with water vapour than is in fact the case.

Another common phase transition is **fusion,** or melting, as when ice melts to water or iron becomes molten. The change in molar enthalpy that accompanies fusion under standard conditions (pure solid at 1 bar changing to pure liquid at 1 bar) is called the **standard enthalpy of fusion,** $\Delta_{fus}H^{\ominus}$. Its value for water at 0°C is 6.01 kJ mol^{-1} (all enthalpies of fusion are positive, and the sign need not be given), which signifies that 6.01 kJ of energy is needed to melt 1 mol $H_2O(s)$ at 0°C and 1 bar. Note that the enthalpy of fusion of water is much less than its enthalpy of vaporization. In vaporization the molecules become completely separated from each other, whereas in melting the molecules are merely loosened without separating completely (Fig. 3.1).

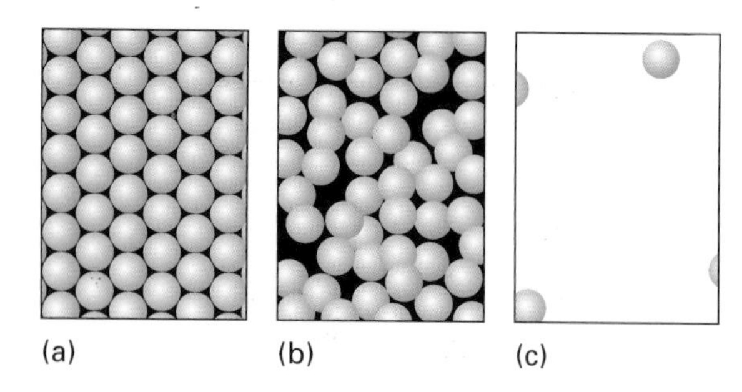

Fig. 3.1 When a solid (a) melts to a liquid (b), the molecules separate from one another only slightly, the intermolecular interactions are reduced only slightly, and there is only a small change in enthalpy. When a liquid vaporizes (c), the molecules are separated by a considerable distance, the intermolecular forces are reduced almost to zero, and the change in enthalpy is much greater.

The text's web site contains links to animations illustrating this point.

The reverse of vaporization is **condensation** and the reverse of fusion (melting) is **freezing.** The molar enthalpy changes are, respectively, the negative of the enthalpies of vaporization and fusion, because the heat that is supplied to vaporize or melt the substance is released when it condenses or freezes.[7] It is always the case that *the enthalpy change of a reverse transition is the negative of the enthalpy change of the forward transition* (under the same conditions of temperature and pressure):

$$H_2O(s) \rightarrow H_2O(l) \qquad \Delta H^{\ominus} = +6.01\ kJ$$

$$H_2O(l) \rightarrow H_2O(s) \qquad \Delta H^{\ominus} = -6.01\ kJ$$

and in general

$$\Delta_{forward}H^{\ominus} = -\Delta_{reverse}H^{\ominus} \tag{3.1}$$

This relation follows directly from the fact that H is a state property, because H must return to the same value if a forward change is followed by the reverse

[6] We shall see in Chapter 17 that the interaction responsible for the low volatility of water is the hydrogen bond.

[7] This relation is the origin of the obsolescent terms 'latent heat' of vaporization and fusion for what are now termed the enthalpy of vaporization and fusion.

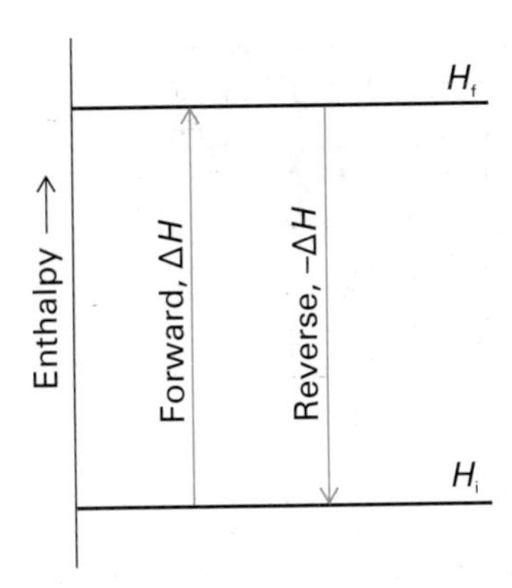

Fig. 3.2 An implication of the First Law is that the enthalpy change accompanying a reverse process is the negative of the enthalpy change for the forward process.

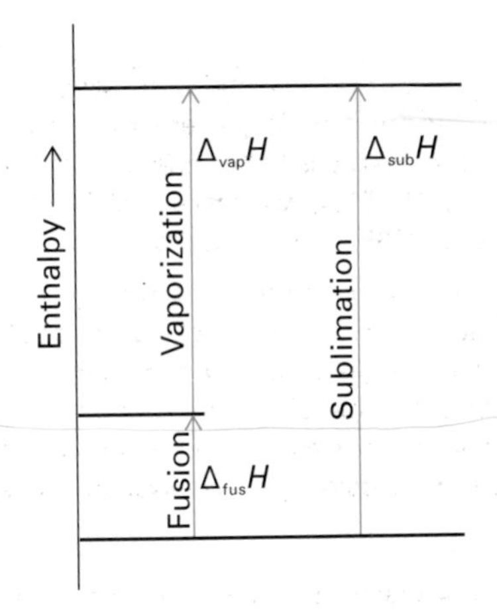

Fig. 3.3 The enthalpy of sublimation at a given temperature is the sum of the enthalpies of fusion and vaporization at that temperature. Another implication of the First Law is that the enthalpy change of an overall process is the sum of the enthalpy changes for the possibly hypothetical steps into which it may be divided.

of that change (Fig. 3.2). The high standard enthalpy of vaporization of water (44 kJ mol^{-1}), signifying a strongly endothermic process, implies that the condensation of water (−44 kJ mol^{-1}) is a strongly exothermic process. That exothermicity is the origin of the ability of steam to scald severely, because the energy is passed on to the skin.

The direct conversion of a solid to a vapour is called **sublimation**. The reverse process is called **vapour deposition**. Sublimation can be observed on a cold, frosty morning, when frost vanishes as vapour without first melting. The frost itself forms by vapour deposition from cold, damp air. The vaporization of solid carbon dioxide ('dry ice') is another example of sublimation. The standard molar enthalpy change accompanying sublimation is called the **standard enthalpy of sublimation**, $\Delta_{sub}H^{\ominus}$. Because enthalpy is a state property, the same change in enthalpy must be obtained both in the *direct* conversion of solid to vapour and in the *indirect* conversion, in which the solid first melts to the liquid and then that liquid vaporizes (Fig. 3.3):

$$\Delta_{sub}H^{\ominus} = \Delta_{fus}H^{\ominus} + \Delta_{vap}H^{\ominus} \tag{3.2}$$

The two enthalpies that are added together must be for the same temperature, so to get the enthalpy of sublimation of water at 0°C we must add together the enthalpies of fusion and vaporization for this temperature. Adding together enthalpies of transition for different temperatures gives a meaningless result.

Self-test 3.2

Calculate the standard enthalpy of sublimation of ice at 0°C from its standard enthalpy of fusion at 0°C (6.01 kJ mol^{-1}) and the standard enthalpy of vaporization of water at 0°C (45.07 kJ mol^{-1}).

[*Answer:* 51.08 kJ mol^{-1}]

The result expressed by eqn 3.2 is an example of a more general statement that will prove useful time and again during our study of thermochemistry:

The enthalpy change of an overall process is the sum of the enthalpy changes for the steps (observed or hypothetical) into which it may be divided.

3.2 Atomic and molecular change

One group of enthalpy changes that we shall use frequently in the following pages are those accompanying changes to individual atoms and molecules. Among the most important is the **standard enthalpy of ionization**, $\Delta_{ion}H^{\ominus}$, the standard molar enthalpy change accompanying the removal of an electron from a gas-phase atom (or ion). For example, because

$$H(g) \rightarrow H^+(g) + e^-(g) \qquad \Delta H^{\ominus} = +1312 \text{ kJ}$$

Table 3.2 *First and second (and some higher) standard enthalpies of ionization, $\Delta_{ion}H/(\text{kJ mol}^{-1})$*

1	2	13	14	15	16	17	18
H							**He**
1312							2370
							5250
Li	**Be**	**B**	**C**	**N**	**O**	**F**	**Ne**
519	900	799	1 090	1400	1310	1680	2080
7300	1760	2 420	2 350	2860	3390	3370	3950
		14 800	3 660				
			25 000				
Na	**Mg**	**Al**	**Si**	**P**	**S**	**Cl**	**Ar**
494	738	577	786	1060	1000	1260	1520
4560	1451	1 820					
	7740	2 740					
		11 600					
K	**Ca**	**Ga**	**Ge**	**As**	**Se**	**Br**	**Kr**
418	590	577	762	966	941	1140	1350
3070	1150						
	4940						
Rb	**Sr**	**In**	**Sn**	**Sb**	**Te**	**I**	**Xe**
402	548	556	707	833	870	1010	1170
2650	1060						
	4120						
Cs	**Ba**	**Tl**	**Pb**	**Bi**	**Po**	**At**	**Rn**
376	502	812	920	1040	812	920	1040
2420	966						
3300	3390						

Strictly, these are the values of $\Delta_{ion}U(0)$. For more precise work, use $\Delta_{ion}H(T) = \Delta_{ion}U(0) + \frac{5}{2}RT$, with $\frac{5}{2}RT = 6.20\ \text{J mol}^{-1}$ at 298 K.

the standard enthalpy of ionization of hydrogen atoms is reported as 1312 kJ mol^{-1}. This value signifies that 1312 kJ of energy must be supplied as heat to ionize 1 mol H(g) at 1 bar (and 298.15 K). Table 3.2 gives values of the ionization enthalpies for a number of elements; note that all enthalpies of ionization are positive.[8]

We often need to consider a succession of ionizations, such as the conversion of magnesium atoms to Mg^+ ions, the ionization of these Mg^+ ions to Mg^{2+} ions, and so on. The successive molar enthalpy changes are called, respectively, the **first ionization enthalpy**, the **second ionization enthalpy**, and so on. For magnesium, these enthalpies refer to the processes

$$Mg(g) \rightarrow Mg^+(g) + e^-(g) \qquad \Delta H^\ominus = +738\ \text{kJ}$$

$$Mg^+(g) \rightarrow Mg^{2+}(g) + e^-(g) \qquad \Delta H^\ominus = +1451\ \text{kJ}$$

Note that the second ionization enthalpy is larger than the first: more energy is needed to separate an electron from a positively charged ion than from the neutral atom. Note also that enthalpies of ionization refer to the ionization of the gas-phase atom or ion, not to the ionization of an atom or ion in a solid. To determine the latter, we need to combine two or more enthalpy changes.

[8] The enthalpy of ionization is closely related to the ionization energy; see Section 13.15.

Example 3.2
Combining enthalpy changes

The standard enthalpy of sublimation of magnesium at 25°C is 148 kJ mol^{-1}. How much energy as heat (at constant temperature and pressure) must be supplied to 1.00 g of solid magnesium metal to produce a gas composed of Mg^{2+} ions and electrons?

Strategy The enthalpy change for the overall process is a sum of the steps, sublimation followed by the two stages of ionization, into which it can be divided. Then the heat required for the specified process is the product of the overall molar enthalpy change and the amount of atoms; the latter is calculated from the given mass and the molar mass of the substance.

Solution The overall process is

$$Mg(s) \rightarrow Mg^{2+}(g) + 2\,e^-(g)$$

The thermochemical equation for this process is the sum of the following thermochemical equations:

		$\Delta H^{\ominus}$/kJ
Sublimation:	$Mg(s) \rightarrow Mg(g)$	+148
First ionization:	$Mg(g) \rightarrow Mg^+(g) + e^-(g)$	+738
Second ionization:	$Mg^+(g) \rightarrow Mg^{2+}(g) + e^-(g)$	+1451
Overall (sum):	$Mg(s) \rightarrow Mg^{2+}(g) + 2\,e^-(g)$	+2337

These processes are illustrated diagrammatically in Fig. 3.4. It follows that the overall enthalpy change per mole of Mg is 2337 kJ mol^{-1}. Because the molar mass of magnesium is 24.31 g mol^{-1}, 1.0 g of magnesium corresponds to

$$n_{Mg} = \frac{m_{Mg}}{M_{Mg}} = \frac{1.00\text{ g}}{24.31\text{ g mol}^{-1}} = \frac{1.00}{24.31}\text{ mol}$$

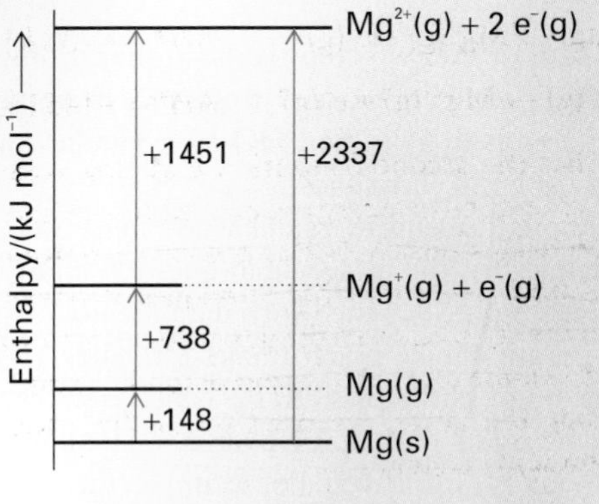

Fig. 3.4 The contributions to the enthalpy change treated in Example 3.2.

Therefore, the energy that must be supplied as heat (at constant pressure) to ionize 1.00 g of magnesium metal is

$$q = \left(\frac{1.00}{24.31}\text{ mol}\right) \times (2337\text{ kJ mol}^{-1}) = 96.1\text{ kJ}$$

This quantity of energy is approximately the same as that needed to vaporize about 43 g of boiling water.

Self-test 3.3

The enthalpy of sublimation of aluminium is 326 kJ mol^{-1}. Use this information and the ionization enthalpies in Table 3.2 to calculate the energy that must be supplied as heat (at constant pressure) to convert 1.00 g of solid aluminium metal to a gas of Al^{3+} ions and electrons at 25°C.

[*Answer:* +203 kJ]

The reverse of ionization is **electron gain**, and the corresponding molar enthalpy change under standard conditions is called the **standard electron gain enthalpy**, $\Delta_{eg}H^{\ominus}$.[9] For example, because experiments show that

$$Cl(g) + e^-(g) \rightarrow Cl^-(g) \qquad \Delta H^{\ominus} = -349\text{ kJ}$$

it follows that the electron gain enthalpy of Cl atoms is −349 kJ mol^{-1}. Note that electron gain by Cl is an exothermic process, so heat is released when a Cl atom captures an electron and forms an ion. It can be seen from Table 3.3, which lists a number of electron gain enthalpies, that some electron gains are exothermic and others are endothermic, so we need to include their sign. For example, electron gain by an O^- ion is strongly endothermic because it takes energy to push an electron on to an already negatively charged species:

$$O^-(g) + e^-(g) \rightarrow O^{2-}(g) \qquad \Delta H^{\ominus} = +844\text{ kJ}$$

The final atomic and molecular process to consider at this stage is the **dissociation**, or breaking, of a chemical bond, as in the process

$$HCl(g) \rightarrow H(g) + Cl(g) \qquad \Delta H^{\ominus} = +431\text{ kJ}$$

The corresponding standard molar enthalpy change is called the **bond enthalpy**, so we would report the

[9] This term is closely related to the electron affinity; see Section 13.15.

Table 3.3 *Electron gain enthalpies of the main-group elements, $\Delta_{eg}H/(kJ\ mol^{-1})$**

1	2	13	14	15	16	17	18
H							**He**
−73							+21
Li	**Be**	**B**	**C**	**N**	**O**	**F**	**Ne**
−60	+18	−27	−122	+7	−141 +844	−328	+29
Na	**Mg**	**Al**	**Si**	**P**	**S**	**Cl**	**Ar**
−53	+232	−43	−134	−44	−200 +532	−349	+35
K	**Ca**	**Ga**	**Ge**	**As**	**Se**	**Br**	**Kr**
−48	+186	−29	−116	−78	−195	−325	+39
Rb	**Sr**	**In**	**Sn**	**Sb**	**Te**	**I**	**Xe**
−47	+146	−29	−116	−103	−190	−295	+41
Cs	**Ba**	**Tl**	**Pb**	**Bi**	**Po**	**At**	
−46	+46	−19	−35	−91	−183	−270	

* Where two values are given, the first refers to the formation of the ion X^- from the neutral atom X and the second to the formation of X^{2-} from X^-.

H–Cl bond enthalpy as 431 kJ mol^{-1}. All bond enthalpies are positive.

Some bond enthalpies are given in Table 3.4. Note that the nitrogen–nitrogen bond in molecular nitrogen, N_2, is very strong, at 945 kJ mol^{-1}, which helps to account for the chemical inertness of nitrogen and its ability to dilute the oxygen in the atmosphere without reacting with it. By contrast, the fluorine–fluorine bond in molecular fluorine, F_2, is relatively weak, at 155 kJ mol^{-1}; the weakness of this bond contributes to the high reactivity of elemental fluorine. However, bond enthalpies alone do not account for reactivity because, although the bond in molecular iodine is even weaker than that in fluorine, I_2 is less reactive than F_2, and the bond in CO is stronger than the bond in N_2, but CO forms many carbonyl compounds, such as $Ni(CO)_4$. The types and strengths of the bonds that the elements can make to other elements are additional factors.

A complication when dealing with bond enthalpies is that their values depend on the molecule in which the two linked atoms occur. For instance, the total standard enthalpy change for the atomization (the complete dissociation into atoms) of water

$$H_2O(g) \rightarrow 2\,H(g) + O(g) \qquad \Delta H^{\ominus} = +927\text{ kJ}$$

is not twice the O–H bond enthalpy in H_2O even though two O–H bonds are dissociated. There are, in fact, two different dissociation steps. In the first step, an O–H bond is broken in an H_2O molecule:

$$H_2O(g) \rightarrow HO(g) + H(g) \qquad \Delta H^{\ominus} = +499\text{ kJ}$$

In the second step, the O–H bond is broken in an OH radical:

$$HO(g) \rightarrow H(g) + O(g) \qquad \Delta H^{\ominus} = +428\text{ kJ}$$

The sum of the two steps is the atomization of the molecule. As can be seen from this example, the O–H bonds in H_2O and HO have similar but not identical bond enthalpies.

Although accurate calculations must use bond enthalpies for the molecule in question and its successive fragments, when such data are not available there is no choice but to make estimates by using **mean bond enthalpies**, ΔH_B, which are the averages of bond enthalpies over a related series of compounds (Table 3.5). For example, the mean HO bond enthalpy, $\Delta H_B(H\text{–}O)$ = 463 kJ mol^{-1}, is the mean of the O–H bond enthalpies in H_2O and several other similar compounds, including methanol, CH_3OH.

Table 3.4 *Selected bond enthalpies, $\Delta H(AB)/(\text{kJ mol}^{-1})$*

Diatomic molecules							
H–H	436	O=O	497	F–F	155	H–F	565
		N≡N	945	Cl–Cl	242	H–Cl	431
		O–H	428	Br–Br	193	H–Br	366
		C≡O	1074	I–I	151	H–I	299
Polyatomic molecules							
H–CH_3	435	H–NH_2	431			H–OH	492
H–C_6H_5	469	O_2N–NO_2	57			HO–OH	213
H_3C–CH_3	368	O=CO	531			HO–CH_3	377
H_2C=CH_2	699					Cl–CH_3	452
HC≡CH	962					Br–CH_3	293
						I–CH_3	234

Table 3.5 *Mean bond enthalpies, $\Delta H_B/(\text{kJ mol}^{-1})$*

	H	C	N	O	F	Cl	Br	I	S	P	Si
H	436										
C	412	348 (1) 612 (2) 838 (3) 518 (a)									
N	388	305 (1) 613 (2) 890 (3)	163 (1) 409 (2) 945 (3)								
O	463	360 (1) 743 (2)	157	146 (1) 497 (2)							
F	565	484	270	185	155						
Cl	431	338	200	203	254	242					
Br	366	276				219	193				
I	299	238				210	178	151			
S	338	259			496	250	212		264		
P	322									200	
Si	318		374	466							226

Values are for single bonds except where otherwise stated (in parentheses).
(a) Denotes aromatic.

Example 3.3

Using mean bond enthalpies

Estimate the standard enthalpy change for the reaction

$$C(s, graphite) + 2\,H_2(g) + \tfrac{1}{2}\,O_2(g) \rightarrow CH_3OH(l)$$

in which liquid methanol is formed from its elements at 25°C. Use information from the *Data section* and bond enthalpy data from Tables 3.4 and 3.5.

Strategy In calculations of this kind, the procedure is to break the overall process down into a sequence of steps such that their sum is the chemical equation required. Always ensure, when using bond enthalpies, that all the species are in the gas phase. That may mean including the appropriate enthalpies of vaporization or sublimation. One approach is to atomize all the reactants and then to build the products from the atoms so produced. When explicit bond enthalpies are available (that is, data are given in the tables available), use them; otherwise, use mean bond enthalpies to obtain estimates. It is often helpful to display the enthalpy changes diagrammatically.

Solution The following steps are required (Fig. 3.5):

		$\Delta H^\ominus$/kJ
Atomization of graphite:	$C(s, graphite) \rightarrow C(g)$	+716.68
Dissociation of 2 mol $H_2(g)$:	$2\,H_2(g) \rightarrow 4\,H(g)$	+871.88
Dissociation of $\tfrac{1}{2}O_2(g)$:	$\tfrac{1}{2}O_2(g) \rightarrow O(g)$	+249.17
Overall, so far:	$C(s) + 2\,H_2(g) + \tfrac{1}{2}O_2(g) \rightarrow C(g) + 4\,H(g) + O(g)$	+1837.73

These values are accurate. In the second step, three CH bonds, one CO bond, and one OH bond are formed, and we estimate their enthalpies from mean values. The standard enthalpy change for bond formation (the reverse of dissociation) is the negative of the mean bond enthalpy (obtained from Table 3.5):

	$\Delta H^\ominus$/kJ
Formation of 3 C–H bonds:	−1236
Formation of 1 C–O bond:	−360
Formation of 1 O–H bond:	−463
Overall, in this step: $C(g) + 4\,H(g) + O(g) \rightarrow CH_3OH(g)$	−2059

These values are estimates. The final stage of the reaction is the condensation of methanol vapour:

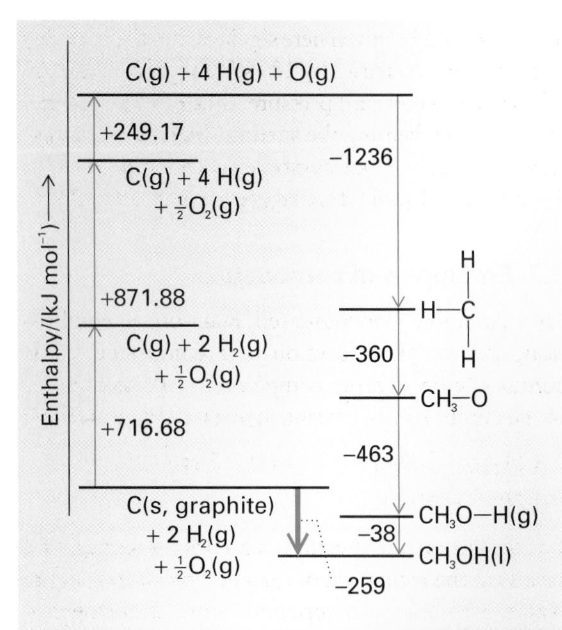

Fig. 3.5 The enthalpy changes used to estimate the enthalpy change accompanying the formation of liquid methanol from its elements. The bond enthalpies are mean values, so the final value is only approximate.

$$CH_3OH(g) \rightarrow CH_3OH(l) \qquad \Delta H^\ominus = -38.00\ \text{kJ}$$

The sum of the enthalpy changes is

$$\Delta H^\ominus = (+1837.73\ \text{kJ}) + (-2059\ \text{kJ}) + (-38.00\ \text{kJ}) = -259\ \text{kJ}$$

The experimental value is −239.00 kJ.

Self-test 3.4

Estimate the enthalpy change for the combustion of liquid ethanol to carbon dioxide and liquid water under standard conditions by using the bond enthalpies, mean bond enthalpies, and the appropriate standard enthalpies of vaporization.

[*Answer:* −1348 kJ; the experimental value is −1368 kJ]

Chemical change

In the remainder of this chapter we concentrate on enthalpy changes accompanying chemical reactions, such as the hydrogenation of ethene:

$$CH_2{=}CH_2(g) + H_2(g) \rightarrow CH_3CH_3(g)$$
$$\Delta H^\ominus = -137\ \text{kJ}$$

The value of $\Delta H^{\ominus}$ given here signifies that the enthalpy of the system decreases by 137 kJ (and, if the reaction takes place at constant pressure, that 137 kJ of energy is released by heating the surroundings) when 1 mol $CH_2{=}CH_2(g)$ at 1 bar combines with 1 mol $H_2(g)$ at 1 bar to give 1 mol $CH_3CH_3(g)$ at 1 bar, all at 25°C.

3.3 Enthalpies of combustion

One commonly encountered reaction is **combustion**, the complete reaction of a compound, most commonly an organic compound, with oxygen, as in the combustion of methane in a natural gas flame:

$$CH_4(g) + 2\,O_2(g) \rightarrow CO_2(g) + 2\,H_2O(l) \quad \Delta H^{\ominus} = -890\text{ kJ}$$

By convention, combustion of an organic compound results in the formation of carbon dioxide gas, liquid water, and—if the compound contains nitrogen—nitrogen gas. The **standard enthalpy of combustion**, $\Delta_c H^{\ominus}$, is the change in standard enthalpy per mole of combustible substance. In this example, we would write $\Delta_c H^{\ominus}(CH_4, g) = -890$ kJ mol^{-1}. Some typical values are given in Table 3.6. Note that $\Delta_c H^{\ominus}$ is a molar quantity, and is obtained from the value of $\Delta H^{\ominus}$ by dividing by the amount of organic reactant consumed (in this case, by 1 mol CH_4). We see in Box 3.1 that the enthalpy of combustion is a useful measure of the efficiency of fuels.

Enthalpies of combustion are commonly measured by using a bomb calorimeter, a device in which energy is transferred as heat at constant volume. According to the discussion in Section 2.6 and the relation $\Delta U = q_V$, the energy transferred as heat at constant volume is equal to the change in internal energy, ΔU, not ΔH. To convert from ΔU to ΔH we need to note that the molar enthalpy of a substance is related to its molar internal energy by $H_m = U_m + pV_m$ (eqn 2.14a). For condensed phases, pV_m is so small it may be ignored. For example, the molar volume of liquid water is 18 cm^3 mol^{-1}, and at 1.0 bar

$$pV_m = (1.0 \times 10^5\text{ Pa}) \times (18 \times 10^{-6}\text{ m}^3\text{ mol}^{-1}) = 1.8\text{ Pa m}^3\text{ mol}^{-1} = 1.8\text{ J mol}^{-1}.$$

However, the molar volume of a gas, and therefore the value of pV_m, is about 1000 times greater and cannot be ignored. For gases treated as perfect, pV_m may be replaced by RT. Therefore, if in the chemical equation the difference (products – reactants) in the stoichiometric coefficients of *gas-phase* species is $\Delta\nu_{gas}$, we can write

$$\Delta_c H = \Delta_c U + \Delta\nu_{gas} RT \qquad (3.3)$$

Note that $\Delta\nu_{gas}$ (where ν is nu) is a dimensionless quantity.

Table 3.6
Standard enthalpies of combustion

Substance	$\Delta_c H^{\ominus}$/(kJ mol^{-1})
Benzene, $C_6H_6(l)$	−3268
Carbon monoxide, $CO(g)$	−394
Carbon, C(s,graphite)	−394
Ethanol, $C_2H_5OH(l)$	−1368
Ethyne, $C_2H_2(g)$	−1300
Glucose, $C_6H_{12}O_6(s)$	−2808
Hydrogen, $H_2(g)$	−286
iso-Octane*, $C_8H_{18}(l)$	−5461
Methane, $CH_4(g)$	−890
Methanol, $CH_3OH(l)$	−726
Methylbenzene, $C_6H_5CH_3(l)$	−3910
Octane, $C_8H_{18}(l)$	−5471
Propane, $C_3H_8(g)$	−2220
Sucrose, $C_{12}H_{22}O_{11}(s)$	−5645
Urea, $CO(NH_2)_2(s)$	−632

* 2,2,4-Trimethylpentane.

Illustration 3.1
Converting between $\Delta_c H$ and $\Delta_c U$

The energy released as heat when glycine is burned in a bomb calorimeter is 969.6 kJ mol^{-1} at 298.15 K, so $\Delta_c U = -969.6$ kJ mol^{-1}. From the chemical equation

$$NH_2CH_2COOH(s) + \tfrac{9}{4}O_2(g) \rightarrow 2\,CO_2(g) + \tfrac{5}{2}H_2O(l) + \tfrac{1}{2}N_2(g)$$

we find that $\Delta\nu_{gas} = (2 + \frac{1}{2}) - \frac{9}{4} = \frac{1}{4}$. Therefore,

$$\begin{aligned}\Delta_c H &= \Delta_c U + \tfrac{1}{4}RT \\ &= -969.6\text{ kJ mol}^{-1} + \tfrac{1}{4} \times (8.3145 \times 10^{-3}\text{ J K}^{-1}\text{ mol}^{-1}) \times (298.15\text{ K}) \\ &= -969.6\text{ kJ mol}^{-1} + 0.62\text{ kJ mol}^{-1} \\ &= -969.0\text{ kJ mol}^{-1}\end{aligned}$$

Box 3.1 *Fuels, food, and energy reserves*

We shall see in Chapter 4 that the best assessment of the ability of a compound to act as a fuel to drive many of the processes occurring in the body makes use of the 'Gibbs energy'. However, a useful guide to the resources provided by a fuel, and the only one that matters when its heat output is being considered, is the enthalpy, particularly the enthalpy of combustion. The thermochemical properties of fuels and foods are commonly discussed in terms of their *specific enthalpy*, the enthalpy of combustion divided by the mass of material (typically in kilojoules per gram), or the *enthalpy density*, the magnitude of the enthalpy of combustion divided by the volume of material (typically in kilojoules per cubic decimetre). Thus, if the standard enthalpy of combustion is $\Delta_c H^\ominus$ and the molar mass of the compound is M, then the specific enthalpy is $\Delta_c H^\ominus/M$. Similarly, the enthalpy density is $\Delta_c H^\ominus/V_m$, where V_m is the molar volume of the material.

The table lists the specific enthalpies and enthalpy densities of several fuels. The most suitable fuels are those with high specific enthalpies, as the advantage of a high molar enthalpy of combustion may be eliminated if a large mass of fuel is to be transported. We see that H_2 gas compares very well with more traditional fuels such as methane (natural gas), iso-octane (gasoline), and methanol. Furthermore, the combustion of H_2 gas does not generate CO_2 gas, a pollutant implicated in the mechanism of global warming (Box 19.1). As a result, H_2 gas has been proposed as an efficient, clean alternative to fossil fuels, such as natural gas and petroleum. However, we also see that H_2 gas has a very low enthalpy density, which arises from the fact that hydrogen is a very light gas. So, the advantage of a high specific enthalpy is undermined by the large volume of fuel to be transported and stored. Strategies are being developed to solve the storage problem. For example, the small H_2 molecules can travel through holes in the crystalline lattice of a sample of metal, such as titanium, where they bind as metal hydrides. In this way it is possible to increase the effective density of hydrogen atoms to a value that is higher than that of liquid H_2. Then the fuel can be released on demand by heating the metal.

We now assess the factors that optimize the heat output of carbon-based fuels, with an eye toward understanding such biological fuels as carbohydrates, fats, and proteins. Let's consider the combustion of 1 mol $CH_4(g)$, the main constituent of natural gas. The reaction involves changes in the oxidation numbers of carbon from −4 to +4, an oxidation, and of oxygen from 0 to −2, a reduction.[1] From the thermochemical equation, we see that 890 kJ of energy is released as heat per mole of carbon atoms that are oxidized. Now consider the oxidation of 1 mol $CH_3OH(g)$:

$$CH_3OH(g) + \tfrac{3}{2}\,O_2(g) \rightarrow CO_2(g) + 2\,H_2O(l)$$

$$\Delta H^\ominus = -764\ \text{kJ}$$

This reaction is also exothermic, but now only 764 kJ of energy is released as heat per mole of carbon that undergoes oxidation. Much of the observed change in energy output between the reactions can be explained by noting that the carbon in methanol has an oxidation number of −2, and not −4 as in methane. That is, the replacement

Thermochemical properties of some fuels

Fuel	Combustion equation	$\Delta_c H^\ominus/(\text{kJ mol}^{-1})$	Specific enthalpy/(kJ g^{-1})	Enthalpy density*/(kJ dm^{-3})
Hydrogen	$2\,H_2(g) + O_2(g) \rightarrow 2\,H_2O(l)$	−286	142	13
Methane	$CH_4(g) + 2\,O_2(g) \rightarrow CO_2(g) + 2\,H_2O(l)$	−890	55	40
iso-Octane†	$2\,C_8H_{18}(l) + 25\,O_2(g) \rightarrow 16\,CO_2(g) + 18\,H_2O(l)$	−5461	48	3.3×10^4
Methanol	$2\,CH_3OH(l) + 3\,O_2(g) \rightarrow 2\,CO_2(g) + 4\,H_2O(l)$	−726	23	1.8×10^4

* At atmospheric pressures and room temperature.
† 2,2,4-Trimethylpentane.

[1] See Appendix 4 for a review of oxidation numbers and oxidation–reduction reactions.

of a C–H bond by a C–O bond renders the carbon in methanol more oxidized than the carbon in methane, so it is reasonable to expect that less energy is released to complete the oxidation of carbon to CO_2 in methanol. In general, we find that the presence of partially oxidized carbon atoms (that is, carbon atoms bonded to oxygen atoms) in a material makes it a less suitable fuel than a similar material containing more highly reduced carbon atoms.

Another factor that determines the heat output of combustion reactions is the number of carbon atoms in hydrocarbon compounds. For example, from the value of the standard enthalpy of combustion for methane we know that for each mole of CH_4 supplied to a furnace, 890 kJ of heat can be released, whereas for each mole of iso-octane molecules (C_8H_{18}, 2,2,4-trimethylpentane, a typical component of gasoline) supplied to an internal combustion engine, 5461 kJ of heat is released (see the table). The much larger value for iso-octane is a consequence of each molecule having eight C atoms to contribute to the formation of carbon dioxide whereas methane has only one.

Now we turn our attention to biological fuels, the foods we ingest to meet the energy requirements of daily life. A typical 18–20-year-old man requires a daily input of about 12 MJ (1 MJ = 10^6 J); a woman of the same age needs about 9 MJ. If the entire consumption were in the form of glucose, which has a specific enthalpy of 16 kJ g^{-1}, meeting energy needs would require the consumption of 750 g of glucose by a man and 560 g by a woman. In fact, the complex carbohydrates (polymers of carbohydrate units, such as starch) more commonly found in our diets have slightly higher specific enthalpies (17 kJ g^{-1}) than glucose itself, so a carbohydrate diet is slightly less daunting than a pure glucose diet, as well as being more appropriate in the form of fibre, the indigestible cellulose that helps to move digestion products through the intestine.

The specific enthalpy of fats, which are long-chain esters such as tristearin (beef fat), is much greater than that of carbohydrates, at around 38 kJ g^{-1}, slightly less than the value for the hydrocarbon oils used as fuel (48 kJ g^{-1}). This is because many of the carbon atoms in carbohydrates are bonded to oxygen atoms and are already partially oxidized, whereas most of the carbon atoms in fats are bonded to hydrogen and other carbon atoms and hence have lower oxidation numbers. As we saw above, the presence of partially oxidized carbons lowers the heat output of a fuel. Fats are commonly used as an energy store, to be used only when the more readily accessible carbohydrates have fallen into short supply. In Arctic species, the stored fat also acts as a layer of insulation; in desert species (such as the camel), the fat is also a source of water, one of its oxidation products.

Proteins are also used as a source of energy, but their components, the amino acids, are often too valuable to squander in this way, and are used to construct other proteins instead. When proteins are oxidized (to urea, $CO(NH_2)_2$), the equivalent enthalpy density is comparable to that of carbohydrates.

We have already mentioned that not all the energy released by the oxidation of foods is converted to work. The heat that is also released needs to be discarded in order to maintain body temperature within its typical range of 35.6–37.8°C. A variety of mechanisms contribute to this aspect of homeostasis, the ability of an organism to counteract environmental changes with physiological responses. The general uniformity of temperature throughout the body is maintained largely by the flow of blood. When heat needs to be dissipated rapidly, warm blood is allowed to flow through the capillaries of the skin, so producing flushing. Radiation is one means of discarding heat; another is evaporation and the energy demands of the enthalpy of vaporization of water. Evaporation removes about 2.4 kJ per gram of water perspired. When vigorous exercise promotes sweating (through the influence of heat detectors on the hypothalamus), 1–2 dm^3 of perspired water can be produced per hour, corresponding to a heat loss of 2.4–5.0 MJ h^{-1}.

Exercise 1 1.0 dm^3 of water is perspired by a runner in order to maintain body temperature. Assume evaporation of 1.0 dm^3 of water dissipates the heat generated by metabolism. (a) What is the change in enthalpy of the runner? (b) Assume that none of the 1.0 dm^3 of sweat evaporated and instead an increase in body temperature resulted. If the runner weighs 60 kg and has a heat capacity approximately equal to that of water, what is the runner's body temperature?

Exercise 2 There are no dietary recommendations for consumption of carbohydrates. Some nutritionists recommend diets that are largely devoid of carbohydrates, with most of the energy needs being met by fats, whereas others recommend that at least 65 per cent of our food calories should come from carbohydrates. A $\frac{3}{4}$-cup serving of pasta contains 40 g of carbohydrates. What percentage of the daily calorie requirement for a person on a 2200 Calorie diet (1 Cal = 1 kcal) does this serving represent?

3.4 The combination of reaction enthalpies

It is often the case that a reaction enthalpy is needed but is not available in tables of data. Now the fact that enthalpy is a state function comes in handy, because it implies that we can construct the required reaction enthalpy from the reaction enthalpies of known reactions. We have already seen a primitive example when we calculated the enthalpy of sublimation from the sum of the enthalpies of fusion and vaporization. The only difference is that we now apply the technique to a sequence of chemical reactions. The procedure is summarized by **Hess's law**:

The standard enthalpy of a reaction is the sum of the standard enthalpies of the reactions into which the overall reaction may be divided.

Although the procedure is given the status of a law, it hardly deserves the title because it is nothing more than a consequence of enthalpy being a state function, which implies that an overall enthalpy change can be expressed as a sum of enthalpy changes for each step in an indirect path. The individual steps need not be actual reactions that can be carried out in the laboratory—they may be entirely hypothetical reactions, the only requirement being that their equations should balance. Each step must correspond to the same temperature.

Example 3.4

Using Hess's law

Given the thermochemical equations

$$C_3H_6(g) + H_2(g) \rightarrow C_3H_8(g) \qquad \Delta H^\ominus = -124\ kJ$$

$$C_3H_8(g) + 5\ O_2(g) \rightarrow 3\ CO_2(g) + 4H_2O(l) \qquad \Delta H^\ominus = -2220\ kJ$$

where C_3H_6 is propene and C_3H_8 is propane, calculate the standard enthalpy of combustion of propene.

Strategy We need to add or subtract the thermochemical equations, together with any others that are needed (from the *Data section*), so as to reproduce the thermochemical equation for the reaction required. In calculations of this type, it is often necessary to use the synthesis of water to balance the hydrogen or oxygen atoms in the overall equation. Once again, it may be helpful to express the changes diagrammatically.

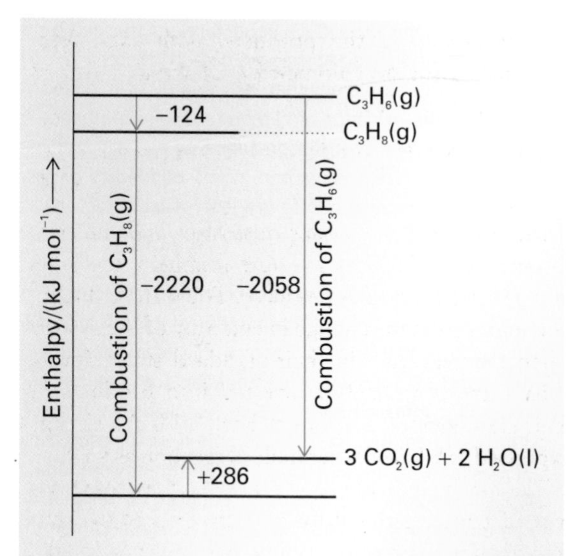

Fig. 3.6 The enthalpy changes used in Example 3.4 to illustrate Hess's law.

Solution The overall reaction is

$$C_3H_6(g) + \tfrac{9}{2}O_2(g) \rightarrow 3\ CO_2(g) + 3\ H_2O(l) \qquad \Delta H^\ominus$$

We can recreate this thermochemical equation from the following sum (Fig. 3.6):

	$\Delta H^\ominus$/kJ
$C_3H_6(g) + H_2(g) \rightarrow C_3H_8(g)$	−124
$C_3H_8(g) + 5\ O_2(g) \rightarrow 3\ CO_2(g) + 4\ H_2O(l)$	−2220
$H_2O(l) \rightarrow H_2(g) + \tfrac{1}{2}O_2(g)$	+286
Overall: $C_3H_6(g) + \tfrac{9}{2}O_2(g) \rightarrow 3\ CO_2(g) + 3\ H_2O(l)$	−2058

It follows that the standard enthalpy of combustion of propene is −2058 kJ mol⁻¹.

Self-test 3.5

Calculate the standard enthalpy of the reaction $C_6H_6(l) + 3\ H_2(g) \rightarrow C_6H_{12}(l)$ from the standard enthalpies of combustion of benzene (Table 3.6) and cyclohexane (−3930 kJ mol⁻¹).

[*Answer:* −196 kJ]

3.5 Standard enthalpies of formation

The **standard reaction enthalpy, $\Delta_r H^\ominus$,** is the difference between the standard molar enthalpies of the reactants and the products, with each term weighted by the stoichiometric coefficient, ν (nu), in the chemical equation:

$$\Delta_r H^\ominus = \sum \nu H_m^\ominus(\text{products}) - \sum \nu H_m^\ominus(\text{reactants}) \quad (3.4)$$

Because the $H_m^\ominus$ are molar quantities and the stoichiometric coefficients are pure numbers, the units of $\Delta_r H^\ominus$ are kilojoules per mole. The standard reaction enthalpy is the change in enthalpy of the system when the reactants in their standard states (pure, 1 bar) are completely converted into products in their standard states (pure, 1 bar), with the change expressed in kilojoules per mole of reaction as written.

The problem with eqn 3.4 is that we have no way of knowing the absolute enthalpies of the substances. To avoid this problem, we can imagine the reaction as taking place by an indirect route, in which the reactants are first broken down into the elements and then the products are formed from the elements (Fig. 3.7). Specifically, the **standard enthalpy of formation, $\Delta_f H^\ominus$**, of a substance is the standard enthalpy (per mole of the substance) for its formation from its elements in their reference states. The **reference state** of an element is its most stable form under the prevailing conditions (Table 3.7). Don't confuse 'reference state' with 'standard state': the reference state of carbon at 25°C is graphite; the standard state of carbon is any specified phase of the element at 1 bar. For example, the standard enthalpy of formation of liquid water (at 25°C, as always in this text) is obtained from the thermochemical equation

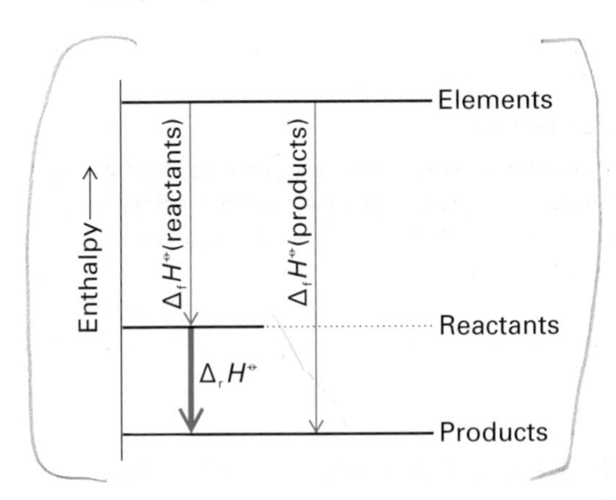

Fig. 3.7 An enthalpy of reaction may be expressed as the difference between the enthalpies of formation of the products and the reactants.

Table 3.7
Reference states of some elements

Element	Reference state
Arsenic	Grey arsenic
Bromine	Liquid
Carbon	Graphite
Hydrogen	Gas
Iodine	Solid
Mercury	Liquid
Nitrogen	Gas
Oxygen	Gas
Phosphorus	White phosphorus
Sulfur	Rhombic sulfur
Tin	White tin, α-tin

$$H_2(g) + \tfrac{1}{2}O_2(g) \rightarrow H_2O(l) \qquad \Delta H^\ominus = -286 \text{ kJ}$$

and is $\Delta_f H^\ominus(H_2O, l) = -286$ kJ mol^{-1}. Note that enthalpies of formation are molar quantities, so to go from $\Delta H^\ominus$ in a thermochemical equation to $\Delta_f H^\ominus$ for that substance, divide by the amount of substance formed (in this instance, by 1 mol H_2O).

With the introduction of standard enthalpies of formation, we can write

$$\Delta_r H^\ominus = \sum \nu \Delta_f H^\ominus(\text{products}) - \sum \nu \Delta_f H^\ominus(\text{reactants}) \quad (3.5)$$

The first term on the right is the enthalpy of formation of all the products from their elements; the second term on the right is the enthalpy of formation of all the reactants from their elements. The fact that the enthalpy is a state function means that a reaction enthalpy calculated in this way is identical to the value that would be calculated from eqn 3.4 if absolute enthalpies were available.

The text's web site contains links to online databases of thermochemical data, including enthalpies of combustion and standard enthalpies of formation.

The values of some standard enthalpies of formation at 25°C are given in Table 3.8, and a longer list

Table 3.8

*Standard enthalpies of formation at 298.15 K**

Substance	$\Delta_f H^\ominus/(\text{kJ mol}^{-1})$
Inorganic compounds	
Ammonia, $NH_3(g)$	−46.11
Ammonium nitrate, $NH_4NO_3(s)$	−365.56
Carbon monoxide, $CO(g)$	−110.53
Carbon disulfide, $CS_2(l)$	+89.70
Carbon dioxide, $CO_2(g)$	−393.51
Dinitrogen tetroxide, $N_2O_4(g)$	+9.16
Dinitrogen monoxide, $N_2O(g)$	+82.05
Hydrogen chloride, $HCl(g)$	−92.31
Hydrogen fluoride, $HF(g)$	−271.1
Hydrogen sulfide, $H_2S(g)$	−20.63
Nitric acid, $HNO_3(l)$	−174.10
Nitrogen dioxide, $NO_2(g)$	+33.18
Nitrogen monoxide, $NO(g)$	+90.25
Sodium chloride, $NaCl(s)$	−411.15
Sulfur dioxide, $SO_2(g)$	−296.83
Sulfur trioxide, $SO_3(g)$	−395.72
Sulfuric acid, $H_2SO_4(l)$	−813.99
Water, $H_2O(l)$	−285.83
$H_2O(g)$	−241.82
Organic compounds	
Benzene, $C_6H_6(l)$	+49.0
Ethane, $C_2H_6(g)$	−84.68
Ethanol, $C_2H_5OH(l)$	−277.69
Ethene, $C_2H_4(g)$	+52.26
Ethyne, $C_2H_2(g)$	+226.73
Glucose, $C_6H_{12}O_6(s)$	−1268
Methane, $CH_4(g)$	−74.81
Methanol, $CH_3OH(l)$	−238.86
Sucrose, $C_{12}H_{22}O_{11}(s)$	−2222

* A longer list is given in the *Data section* at the end of the book.

is given in the *Data section*. The standard enthalpies of formation of elements in their reference states are zero by definition (because their formation is the null reaction: element → element). Note, however, that the standard enthalpy of formation of an element in a state other than its reference state is not zero:

$$\text{C(s, graphite)} \rightarrow \text{C(s, diamond)}$$
$$\Delta H^\ominus = +1.895 \text{ kJ}$$

Therefore, although $\Delta_f H^\ominus(\text{C, graphite}) = 0$, $\Delta_f H^\ominus(\text{C, diamond}) = +1.895 \text{ kJ mol}^{-1}$.

Example 3.5

Using standard enthalpies of formation

Calculate the standard enthalpy of combustion of liquid benzene from the standard enthalpies of formation of the reactants and products.

Strategy We write the chemical equation, identify the stoichiometric numbers of the reactants and products, and then use eqn 3.5. Note that the expression has the form 'products − reactants'. Numerical values of standard enthalpies of formation are given in the *Data section*. The standard enthalpy of combustion is the enthalpy change per mole of substance, so we need to interpret the enthalpy change accordingly.

Solution The chemical equation is

$$C_6H_6(l) + \tfrac{15}{2} O_2(g) \rightarrow 6\,CO_2(g) + 3\,H_2O(l)$$

It follows that

$$\begin{aligned}\Delta_r H^\ominus &= \{6\,\Delta_f H^\ominus(CO_2, g) + 3\,\Delta_f H^\ominus(H_2O, l)\} \\ &\quad - \{\Delta_f H^\ominus(C_6H_6, l) + \tfrac{15}{2}\,\Delta_f H^\ominus(O_2, g)\} \\ &= \{6 \times (-393.51 \text{ kJ mol}^{-1}) \\ &\quad + 3 \times (-285.83 \text{ kJ mol}^{-1})\} - \{(49.0 \text{ kJ mol}^{-1}) + 0\} \\ &= -3268 \text{ kJ mol}^{-1}\end{aligned}$$

Inspection of the chemical equation shows that, in this instance, the 'per mole' is per mole of C_6H_6, which is exactly what we need for an enthalpy of combustion. It follows that the standard enthalpy of combustion of liquid benzene is −3268 kJ mol^{-1}.

A note on good practice. The standard enthalpy of formation of an element in its reference state (oxygen gas in this example) is written 0 not 0 kJ mol^{-1}, because it is zero whatever units we happen to be using.

Self-test 3.6

Use standard enthalpies of formation to calculate the enthalpy of combustion of propane gas to carbon dioxide and water vapour.

[*Answer:* −2220 kJ mol^{-1}]

The reference states of the elements define a thermochemical 'sea level', and enthalpies of formation can be regarded as thermochemical 'altitudes' above or below sea level (Fig. 3.8). Compounds that have negative standard enthalpies of formation (such as water) are classified as **exothermic compounds**, as

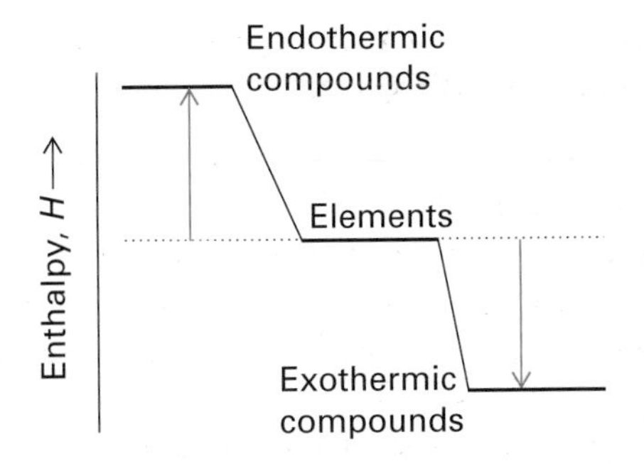

Fig. 3.8 The enthalpy of formation acts as a kind of thermochemical 'altitude' of a compound with respect to the 'sea level' defined by the elements from which it is made. Endothermic compounds have positive enthalpies of formation; exothermic compounds have negative energies of formation.

they lie at a lower enthalpy than their component elements (they lie below thermochemical sea level). Compounds that have positive standard enthalpies of formation (such as carbon disulfide) are classified as **endothermic compounds**, and possess a higher enthalpy than their component elements (they lie above sea level).

3.6 Enthalpies of formation and molecular modelling

It is difficult to estimate standard enthalpies of formation of different conformations of molecules. For example, we obtain the same enthalpy of formation for the equatorial (**1**) and axial (**2**) conformations of methylcyclohexane if we proceed as in Example 3.3. However, it has been observed experimentally that molecules in these two conformations have different standard enthalpies of formation as a result of the greater steric repulsion when the methyl group is in an axial position than when it is equatorial.

Computer-aided molecular modelling using commercially available software is now widely used to estimate standard enthalpies of formation of molecules with complex three-dimensional structures, and can distinguish between different conformations of the same molecule. In the case of methylcyclohexane, for instance, the calculated difference in enthalpy of formation ranges from 5.9 to 7.9 kJ mol^{-1}, which compares favourably with the experimental value of 7.5 kJ mol^{-1}. However, good agreement between calculated and experimental values is relatively rare. Computational methods almost always predict correctly which conformation of a molecule is most stable but do not always predict the correct numerical values of the difference in enthalpies of formation.

A calculation performed in the absence of solvent molecules estimates the properties of the molecule of interest in the gas phase. Computational methods are available that allow for the inclusion of several solvent molecules around a solute molecule, thereby taking into account the effect of molecular interactions with the solvent on the enthalpy of formation of the solute. Again, the numerical results are only estimates and the primary purpose of the calculation is to predict whether interactions with the solvent increase or decrease the enthalpy of formation. As an example, consider the amino acid glycine, which can exist in a neutral or zwitterionic form, H_2NHCH_2COOH and $^+H_3NCH_2CO_2^-$, respectively, in which in the latter the amino group is protonated and the carboxyl group is deprotonated. Molecular modelling shows that in the gas phase the neutral form has a lower enthalpy of formation than the zwitterionic form. However, in water the opposite is true on account of the strong interactions between the polar solvent and the charges on the zwitter ion.

3.7 The variation of reaction enthalpy with temperature

It often happens that we have data at one temperature but need them at another temperature. For example, we might want to know the enthalpy of a particular reaction at body temperature, 37°C, but may have data available for 25°C. Another type of question that might arise might be whether the oxidation of glucose is more exothermic when it takes place inside an Arctic fish that inhabits water at 0°C than when it takes place at mammalian body temperatures. Similarly, we may need to predict whether the synthesis of ammonia is more exothermic at a typical industrial temperature of 450°C than at 25°C. In precise work, every attempt would be made to measure the reaction enthalpy at the temperature of interest, but it is useful to have a 'back-of-the-envelope' way of estimating the direction of change and even a moderately reliable numerical value.

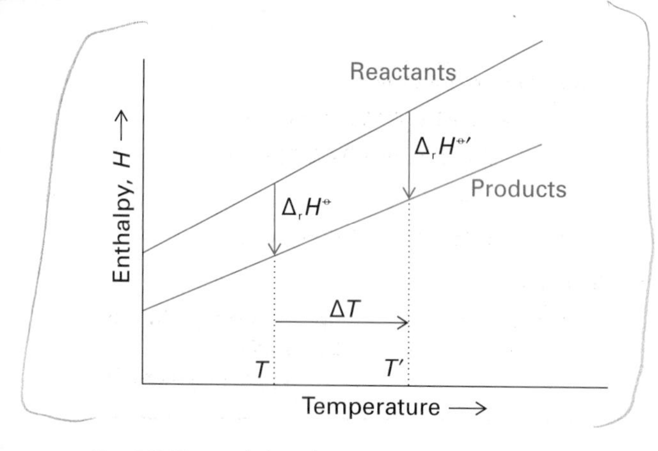

Fig. 3.9 The enthalpy of a substance increases with temperature. Therefore, if the total enthalpy of the reactants increases by a different amount from that of the products, the reaction enthalpy will change with temperature. The change in reaction enthalpy depends on the relative slopes of the two lines and hence on the heat capacities of the substances.

Figure 3.9 illustrates the technique we use. As we have seen, the enthalpy of a substance increases with temperature; therefore, the total enthalpy of the reactants and the total enthalpy of the products increase as shown in the illustration. Provided the two total enthalpy increases are different, the standard reaction enthalpy (their difference) will change as the temperature is changed. The change in the enthalpy of a substance depends on the slope of the graph and therefore on the constant-pressure heat capacities of the substances (recall Fig. 2.18). We can therefore expect the temperature dependence of the reaction enthalpy to be related to the difference in heat capacities of the products and the reactants.

As a simple example, consider the reaction

$$2\,H_2(g) + O_2(g) \rightarrow 2\,H_2O(l)$$

where the standard enthalpy of reaction is known at one temperature (for example, at 25°C from the tables in this book). According to eqn 3.5, we can write

$$\Delta_r H^{\ominus}(T) = 2H^{\ominus}_m(H_2O, l) - \{2H^{\ominus}_m(H_2, g) + H^{\ominus}_m(O_2, g)\}$$

for the reaction at a temperature T. If the reaction takes place at a higher temperature T', the molar enthalpy of each substance is increased because it stores more energy and the standard reaction enthalpy becomes

$$\Delta_r H^{\ominus}(T') = 2H^{\ominus\prime}_m(H_2O, l) - \{2H^{\ominus\prime}_m(H_2, g) + H^{\ominus\prime}_m(O_2, g)\}$$

where the primes signify the values at the new temperature. Equation 2.16 ($C_p = \Delta H/\Delta T$) implies that the increase in molar enthalpy of a substance when the temperature is changed from T to T' is $C^{\ominus}_{p,m} \times (T' - T)$, where $C^{\ominus}_{p,m}$ is the standard molar constant-pressure heat capacity of the substance, the molar heat capacity measured at 1 bar. For example, the molar enthalpy of water changes to

$$H^{\ominus\prime}_m(H_2O, l) = H^{\ominus}_m(H_2O, l) + C^{\ominus}_{p,m}(H_2O, l) \times (T' - T)$$

When we substitute terms like this into the expression above, we find

$$\Delta_r H^{\ominus}(T') = \Delta_r H^{\ominus}(T) + \Delta_r C^{\ominus}_p \times (T' - T) \qquad (3.6)$$

where

$$\Delta_r C^{\ominus}_p = 2C^{\ominus}_{p,m}(H_2O, l) - \{2C^{\ominus}_{p,m}(H_2, g) + C^{\ominus}_{p,m}(O_2, g)\}$$

Note that this combination has the same pattern as the reaction enthalpy, and the stoichiometric numbers occur in the same way. In general, $\Delta_r C^{\ominus}_p$ is the difference between the weighted sums of the standard molar heat capacities of the products and the reactants:

$$\Delta_r C^{\ominus}_p = \sum \nu C^{\ominus}_{p,m}(\text{products}) - \sum \nu C^{\ominus}_{p,m}(\text{reactants}) \qquad (3.7)$$

Equation 3.6 is **Kirchhoff's law**. We see that, just as we anticipated, the standard reaction enthalpy at one temperature can be calculated from the standard reaction enthalpy at another temperature provided we know the standard molar constant-pressure heat capacities of all the substances. These values are given in the *Data section*. The derivation of Kirchhoff's law supposes that the heat capacities are constant over the range of temperature of interest, so the law is best restricted to small temperature differences (of no more than 100 K or so).

Example 3.6

Using Kirchhoff's law

The standard enthalpy of formation of gaseous water at 25°C is −241.82 kJ mol^{-1}. Estimate its value at 100°C.

Strategy First, write the chemical equation and identify the stoichiometric numbers. Then calculate the value of $\Delta_r C_p^{\ominus}$ from the data in the *Data section* by using eqn 3.7 and use the result in eqn 3.6.

Solution The chemical equation is

$$H_2(g) + \tfrac{1}{2} O_2(g) \rightarrow H_2O(g)$$

and the molar constant-pressure heat capacities of $H_2O(g)$, $H_2(g)$, and $O_2(g)$ are 33.58 J K^{-1} mol^{-1}, 28.84 J K^{-1} mol^{-1}, and 29.37 J K^{-1} mol^{-1}, respectively. It follows that

$$\begin{aligned}\Delta_r C_p^{\ominus} &= C_{p,m}^{\ominus}(H_2O, g) - \{C_{p,m}^{\ominus}(H_2, g) + \tfrac{1}{2} C_{p,m}^{\ominus}(O_2, g)\} \\ &= (33.58\ \text{J K}^{-1}\ \text{mol}^{-1}) - \{(28.84\ \text{J K}^{-1}\ \text{mol}^{-1}) \\ &\quad + \tfrac{1}{2} \times (29.37\ \text{J K}^{-1}\ \text{mol}^{-1})\} \\ &= -9.95\ \text{J K}^{-1}\ \text{mol}^{-1} \\ &= -9.95 \times 10^{-3}\ \text{kJ K}^{-1}\ \text{mol}^{-1}\end{aligned}$$

Then, because $T' - T = +75$ K, from eqn 3.6 we find

$$\begin{aligned}\Delta_r H^{\ominus\prime} &= (-241.82\ \text{kJ mol}^{-1}) \\ &\quad + (-9.95 \times 10^{-3}\ \text{kJ K}^{-1}\ \text{mol}^{-1}) \times (75\ \text{K}) \\ &= (-241.82\ \text{kJ mol}^{-1}) - (0.75\ \text{kJ mol}^{-1}) \\ &= -242.57\ \text{kJ mol}^{-1}\end{aligned}$$

The experimental value is −242.58 kJ mol^{-1}.

Self-test 3.7

Estimate the standard enthalpy of formation of $NH_3(g)$ at 400 K from the data in the *Data section*.

[*Answer:* −48.4 kJ mol^{-1}]

The calculation in Example 3.6 shows that the standard reaction enthalpy at 100°C is only slightly different from that at 25°C. The reason is that the change in reaction enthalpy is proportional to the *difference* between the molar heat capacities of the products and the reactants, which is usually not very large. It is generally the case that, provided the temperature range is not too wide, enthalpies of reactions vary only slightly with temperature. A reasonable first approximation is that standard reaction enthalpies are independent of temperature.

CHECKLIST OF KEY IDEAS

You should now be familiar with the following concepts:

☐ **1** The standard state of a substance is the pure substance at 1 bar.

☐ **2** The standard enthalpy of transition, $\Delta_{trs}H^{\ominus}$, is the change in molar enthalpy when a substance in one phase changes into another phase, both phases being in their standard states.

☐ **3** The standard enthalpy of the reverse of a process is the negative of the standard enthalpy of the forward process, $\Delta_{reverse}H^{\ominus} = -\Delta_{forward}H^{\ominus}$.

☐ **4** The standard enthalpy of a process is the sum of the standard enthalpies of the individual processes into which it may be regarded as divided, as in $\Delta_{sub}H^{\ominus} = \Delta_{fus}H^{\ominus} + \Delta_{vap}H^{\ominus}$.

☐ **5** Hess's law states that the standard enthalpy of a reaction is the sum of the standard enthalpies of the reactions into which the overall reaction may be divided.

☐ **6** The standard enthalpy of formation of a compound, $\Delta_f H^{\ominus}$, is the standard reaction enthalpy for the formation of the compound from its elements in their reference states.

☐ **7** The standard reaction enthalpy, $\Delta_r H^{\ominus}$, is the difference between the standard enthalpies of formation of the products and reactants, weighted by their stoichiometric coefficients ν: $\Delta_r H^{\ominus} = \sum \nu \Delta_f H^{\ominus}(\text{products}) - \sum \nu \Delta_f H^{\ominus}(\text{reactants})$.

☐ **8** At constant pressure, exothermic compounds are those for which $\Delta_f H^{\ominus} < 0$; endothermic compounds are those for which $\Delta_f H^{\ominus} > 0$.

☐ **9** Kirchhoff's law states that the standard reaction enthalpies at different temperatures are related by $\Delta_r H^{\ominus}(T') = \Delta_r H^{\ominus}(T) + \Delta_r C_p^{\ominus} \times (T' - T)$, where $\Delta_r C_p^{\ominus} = \sum \nu C_{p,m}^{\ominus}(\text{products}) - \sum \nu C_{p,m}^{\ominus}(\text{reactants})$.

DISCUSSION QUESTIONS

3.1 A primitive air-conditioning unit for use in places where electrical power is not available can be made by hanging up strips of linen soaked in water. Explain why this strategy is effective.

3.2 Describe at least two calculational methods by which standard reaction enthalpies may be predicted. Discuss the advantages and disadvantages of each method.

3.3 Distinguish between: (a) standard state and reference state of an element; (b) endothermic and exothermic compounds.

3.4 Discuss the limitations of the expressions:

(a) $\Delta_r H = \Delta_r U + \Delta \nu_{gas} RT$;

(b) $\Delta_r H^{\ominus}(T') = \Delta_r H^{\ominus}(T) + \Delta_r C_p^{\ominus} \times (T' - T)$.

EXERCISES

Assume all gases are perfect unless stated otherwise. All thermochemical data are for 298.15 K.
The symbol ‡ signifies that calculus is required.

3.5 Estimate the difference between the standard enthalpy of formation of $H_2O(l)$ as currently defined (at 1 bar) and its value using the former definition (at 1 atm).

3.6 Liquid mixtures of sodium and potassium are used in some nuclear reactors as coolants that can survive the intense radiation inside reactor cores. Calculate the energy required as heat to melt 224 kg of sodium metal at 371 K.

3.7 Calculate the heat required to evaporate 1.00 kg of water at (a) 25°C, (b) 100°C.

3.8 Isopropanol (2-propanol) is commonly used as 'rubbing alcohol' to relieve sprain injuries in sport: its action is due to the cooling effect that accompanies its rapid evaporation when applied to the skin. In an experiment to determine its enthalpy of vaporization, a sample was brought to the boil. It was then found that when an electric current of 0.812 A from a 11.5 V supply was passed for 303 s, then 4.27 g of the alcohol was vaporized. What is the (molar) enthalpy of vaporization of isopropanol?

3.9 Refrigerators make use of the heat absorption required to vaporize a volatile liquid. A fluorocarbon liquid being investigated to replace a chlorofluorocarbon has $\Delta_{vap}H^{\ominus} = +26.0\ \text{kJ mol}^{-1}$. Calculate q, w, ΔH, and ΔU when 1.50 mol is vaporized at 250 K and 750 Torr.

3.10 Use the information in Tables 3.1 and 3.2 to calculate the total heat required to melt 100 g of ice at 0°C, heat it to 100°C, and then vaporize it at that temperature. Sketch a graph of temperature against time on the assumption that the sample is heated at a constant rate.

3.11 The enthalpy of sublimation of calcium at 25°C is 178.2 kJ mol^{-1}. How much energy (at constant temperature and pressure) must be supplied as heat to 10.0 g of solid calcium to produce a plasma (an ionic gas) composed of Ca^{2+} ions and electrons?

3.12 Estimate the difference between the enthalpy of ionization of Mg(g) to Mg^{2+}(g) and the change in internal energy at 25°C.

3.13 Estimate the difference between the electron gain enthalpy of Cl(g) and the corresponding change in internal energy at 25°C.

3.14 How much energy (at constant temperature and pressure) must be supplied as heat to 10.0 g of chlorine gas (as Cl_2) to produce a plasma (an ionic gas) composed of Cl^- and Cl^+ ions? The enthalpy of ionization of Cl(g) is +1257.5 kJ mol^{-1} and its electron gain enthalpy is −354.8 kJ mol^{-1}.

3.15 Use the data in Exercise 3.14 to identify (a) the enthalpy of ionization of Cl^-(g) and (b) the accompanying change in molar internal energy.

3.16 The enthalpy changes accompanying the dissociation of successive bonds in NH_3(g) are 460, 390, and 314 kJ mol^{-1}, respectively. (a) What is the mean enthalpy of an N–H bond? (b) Do you expect the mean bond internal energy to be larger or smaller than the mean bond enthalpy?

3.17 Use bond enthalpies and mean bond enthalpies to estimate (a) the enthalpy of the glycolysis reaction adopted by anaerobic bacteria as a source of energy, $C_6H_{12}O_6(aq) \rightarrow 2\ CH_3CH(OH)COOH(aq)$, lactic acid, which is produced via the formation of pyruvic acid, $CH_3COCOOH$, and the action of lactate dehydrogenase and (b) the enthalpy of combustion of glucose. Ignore the contributions of enthalpies of fusion and vaporization.

3.18 The efficient design of chemical plants depends on the designer's ability to assess and use the heat output in one process to supply another process. The standard enthalpy of reaction for $N_2(g) + 3\ H_2(g) \rightarrow 2\ NH_3(g)$ is -92.22 kJ mol^{-1}. What is the change in enthalpy when (a) 1.00 mol $N_2(g)$ is consumed, (b) 1.00 mol $NH_3(g)$ is formed?

3.19 Ethane is flamed off in abundance from oil wells, because it is unreactive and difficult to use commercially. But would it make a good fuel? The standard enthalpy of reaction for $2\ C_2H_6(g) + 7\ O_2(g) \rightarrow 4\ CO_2(g) + 6\ H_2O(l)$ is -3120 kJ mol^{-1}. (a) What is the standard enthalpy of combustion of ethane? (b) What is the change in enthalpy when 3.00 mol CO_2 is formed in the reaction?

3.20 Standard enthalpies of formation are widely available, but we might need a standard enthalpy of combustion instead. The standard enthalpy of formation of ethylbenzene is -12.5 kJ mol^{-1}. Calculate its standard enthalpy of combustion.

3.21 Combustion reactions are relatively easy to carry out and study, and their data can be combined to give enthalpies of other types of reaction. As an illustration, calculate the standard enthalpy of hydrogenation of cyclohexene to cyclohexane given that the standard enthalpies of combustion of the two compounds are -3752 kJ mol^{-1} (cyclohexene) and -3953 kJ mol^{-1} (cyclohexane).

3.22 Estimate the standard internal energy of formation of liquid methyl acetate (methyl ethanoate, CH_3COOCH_3) at 298 K from its standard enthalpy of formation, which is -442 kJ mol^{-1}.

3.23 The standard enthalpy of combustion of naphthalene is -5157 kJ mol^{-1}. Calculate its standard enthalpy of formation.

3.24 When 320 mg of naphthalene, $C_{10}H_8(s)$, was burned in a bomb calorimeter, the temperature rose by 3.05 K. Calculate the heat capacity of the calorimeter. By how much will the temperature rise when 100 mg of phenol, $C_6H_5OH(s)$, is burned in the calorimeter under the same conditions?

3.25 The energy resources of glucose are of major concern for the assessment of metabolic processes. When 0.3212 g of glucose was burned in a bomb calorimeter of heat capacity 641 J K^{-1} the temperature rose by 7.793 K. Calculate (a) the standard molar enthalpy of combustion, (b) the standard internal energy of combustion, and (c) the standard enthalpy of formation of glucose.

3.26 The complete combustion of fumaric acid in a bomb calorimeter released 1333 kJ per mole of HOOCCH=CHCOOH(s) at 298 K. Calculate (a) the internal energy of combustion, (b) the enthalpy of combustion, (c) the enthalpy of formation of fumaric acid.

3.27 Calculate the standard enthalpy of solution of AgBr(s) in water from the standard enthalpies of formation of the solid and the aqueous ions.

3.28 The standard enthalpy of decomposition of the yellow complex NH_3SO_2 into NH_3 and SO_2 is $+40$ kJ mol^{-1}. Calculate the standard enthalpy of formation of NH_3SO_2.

3.29 Given that the enthalpy of combustion of graphite is -393.5 kJ mol^{-1} and that of diamond is -395.41 kJ mol^{-1}, calculate the standard enthalpy of the C(s, graphite) $\rightarrow$ C(s, diamond) transition.

3.30 The pressures deep within the Earth are much greater than those on the surface, and to make use of thermochemical data in geochemical assessments we need to take the differences into account. Use the information in Exercise 3.29 together with the densities of graphite (2.250 g cm^{-3}) and diamond (3.510 g cm^{-3}) to calculate the internal energy of the transition when the sample is under a pressure of 150 kbar.

3.31 The mass of a typical sugar (sucrose) cube is 1.5 g. Calculate the energy released as heat when a cube is burned in air. To what height could a person of mass 68 kg climb on the energy a cube provides assuming 20 per cent of the energy is available for work?

3.32 Camping gas is typically propane. The standard enthalpy of combustion of propane gas is -2220 kJ mol^{-1} and the standard enthalpy of vaporization of the liquid is $+15$ kJ mol^{-1}. Calculate (a) the standard enthalpy and (b) the standard internal energy of combustion of the liquid.

3.33 Classify as endothermic or exothermic (a) a combustion reaction for which $\Delta_r H^\circ = -2020$ kJ mol^{-1}, (b) a dissolution for which $\Delta H^\circ = +4.0$ kJ mol^{-1}, (c) vaporization, (d) fusion, (e) sublimation.

3.34 Standard enthalpies of formation are very useful because they can be used to calculate the standard enthalpies of a wide range of reactions of interest in chemistry, biology, geology, and industry. Use information in the *Data section* to calculate the standard enthalpies of the following reactions:

(a) $2\ NO_2(g) \rightarrow N_2O_4(g)$

(b) $NO_2(g) \rightarrow \frac{1}{2}\ N_2O_4(g)$

(c) $3\ NO_2(g) + H_2O(l) \rightarrow 2\ HNO_3(aq) + NO(g)$

(d) Cyclopropane(g) $\rightarrow$ propene(g)

(e) $HCl(aq) + NaOH(aq) \rightarrow NaCl(aq) + H_2O(l)$

3.35 Calculate the standard enthalpy of formation of N_2O_5 from the following data:

$2\ NO(g) + O_2(g) \rightarrow 2\ NO_2(g)$ $\quad \Delta_r H^\circ = -114.1$ kJ mol^{-1}

$4\ NO_2(g) + O_2(g) \rightarrow 2\ N_2O_5(g)$ $\quad \Delta_r H^\circ = -110.2$ kJ mol^{-1}

$N_2(g) + O_2(g) \rightarrow 2\ NO(g)$ $\quad \Delta_r H^\circ = +180.5$ kJ mol^{-1}

3.36 Heat capacity data can be used to estimate the reaction enthalpy at one temperature from its value at another. Use the information in the *Data section* to predict the standard reaction enthalpy of $2\ NO_2(g) \rightarrow N_2O_4(g)$ at 100°C from its value at 25°C.

3.37 Estimate the enthalpy of vaporization of water at 100°C from its value at 25°C (44.01 kJ mol^{-1}) given the constant-pressure heat capacities of 75.29 J K^{-1} mol^{-1} and 33.58 J K^{-1} mol^{-1} for liquid and gas, respectively.

3.38 It is often useful to be able to anticipate, without doing a detailed calculation, whether an increase in temperature will result in a raising or a lowering of a reaction enthalpy. The constant-pressure molar heat capacity of a gas of linear molecules is approximately $\frac{7}{2}R$ whereas that of a gas of non-linear molecules is approximately $4R$. Decide whether the standard enthalpies of the following reactions will increase or decrease with increasing temperature:

(a) $2\ H_2(g) + O_2(g) \rightarrow 2\ H_2O(g)$

(b) $N_2(g) + 3\ H_2(g) \rightarrow 2\ NH_3(g)$

(c) $CH_4(g) + 2\ O_2(g) \rightarrow CO_2(g) + 2\ H_2O(g)$

3.39 The molar heat capacity of liquid water is approximately $9R$. Decide whether the standard enthalpy of the reactions (a) and (c) in Exercise 3.38 will increase or decrease with a rise in temperature if the water is produced as a liquid.

3.40 Is the standard enthalpy of combustion of glucose likely to be higher or lower at blood temperature than at 25°C?

3.41 Derive a version of Kirchhoff's law (eqn 3.6) for the temperature dependence of the internal energy of reaction.

3.42 ‡The formulation of Kirchhoff's law given in eqn 3.6 is valid when the difference in heat capacities is independent of temperature over the temperature range of interest. Suppose instead that $\Delta_r C_p^\ominus = a + bT + c/T^2$. Derive a more accurate form of Kirchhoff's law in terms of the parameters a, b, and c. (*Hint*. The change in the reaction enthalpy for an infinitesimal change in temperature is $\Delta_r C_p^\ominus \mathrm{d}T$. Integrate this expression between the two temperatures of interest.)

Chapter 4

Thermodynamics: the Second Law

Some things happen; some things don't. A gas expands to fill the vessel it occupies; a gas that already fills a vessel does not suddenly contract into a smaller volume. A hot object cools to the temperature of its surroundings; a cool object does not suddenly become hotter than its surroundings. Hydrogen and oxygen combine explosively (once their ability to do so has been liberated by a spark) and form water; water left standing in oceans and lakes does not gradually decompose into hydrogen and oxygen. These everyday observations suggest that changes can be divided into two classes. A **spontaneous change** is a change that has a tendency to occur without work having to be done to bring it about. A spontaneous change has a natural tendency to occur. A **non-spontaneous change** is a change that can be brought about only by doing work. A non-spontaneous change has no natural tendency to occur. Non-spontaneous changes can be *made* to occur by doing work: gas can be compressed into a smaller volume by pushing in a piston, the temperature of a cool object can be raised by forcing an electric current through a heater attached to it, and water can be decomposed by the passage of an electric current. However, in each case we need to act in some way on the system to bring about the non-spontaneous change. There must be some feature of the world that accounts for the distinction between the two types of change.

Throughout this chapter we use the terms 'spontaneous' and 'non-spontaneous' in their thermodynamic sense. That is, we use them to signify that a change does or does not have a natural *tendency* to occur. In thermodynamics the term spontaneous has nothing to do with speed. Some spontaneous changes are very fast, such as the precipitation reaction that occurs when solutions of sodium chloride and silver nitrate are mixed. However, some spontaneous changes are so slow that there may be no observable change even after millions of years. For example, although the decomposition of benzene into carbon and hydrogen is spontaneous, it does not occur at a measurable rate under normal conditions, and benzene is a common laboratory commodity with a shelf-life of (in principle) millions of years. Thermodynamics deals with the tendency to change; it is silent on the rate at which that tendency is realized.

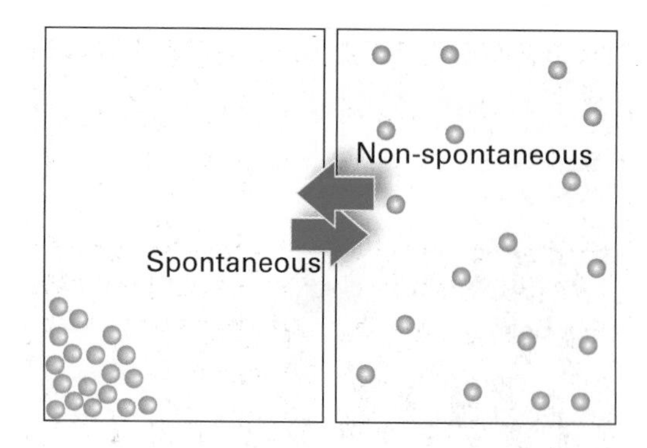

Fig. 4.1 One fundamental type of spontaneous process is the chaotic dispersal of matter. This process accounts for the spontaneous tendency of a gas to spread into and fill the container it occupies. It is extremely unlikely that all the particles will collect into one small region of the container. (In practice, the number of particles is of the order of 10^{23}.)

Entropy

A few moments' thought is all that is needed to identify the reason why some changes are spontaneous and others are not. That reason is *not* the tendency of the system to move towards lower energy. This point is easily established by identifying an example of a spontaneous change in which there is no change in energy. The isothermal expansion of a perfect gas into a vacuum is spontaneous, but the total energy of the gas does not change because the molecules continue to travel at the same average speed and so keep their same total kinetic energy. Even in a process in which the energy of a system does decrease (as in the spontaneous cooling of a block of hot metal), the First Law requires the total energy to be constant. Therefore, in this case the energy of another part of the world must increase if the energy decreases in the part that interests us. For instance, a hot block of metal in contact with a cool block cools and loses energy; however, the second block becomes warmer, and increases in energy. It is equally valid to say that the second block moves spontaneously to higher energy as it is to say that the first block has a tendency to go to lower energy!

4.1 The direction of spontaneous change

We shall now show that *the apparent driving force of spontaneous change is the tendency of energy and matter to become disordered*. For example, the molecules of a gas may all be in one region of a container initially, but their ceaseless disorderly motion ensures that they spread rapidly throughout the entire volume of the container (Fig. 4.1). Because their motion is so disorderly, there is a negligibly small probability that all the molecules will find their way back simultaneously into the region of the container they occupied initially. In this instance, the natural direction of change corresponds to the dispersal of matter.

A similar explanation accounts for spontaneous cooling, but now we need to consider the dispersal of energy rather than matter. In a block of hot metal, the atoms are oscillating vigorously and, the hotter the block, the more vigorous their motion. The cooler surroundings also consist of oscillating atoms, but their motion is less vigorous. The vigorously oscillating atoms of the hot block jostle their neighbours in the surroundings, and the energy of the atoms in the block is handed on to the atoms in the surroundings (Fig. 4.2). The process continues until the vigour with which the atoms in the system are oscillating has fallen to that of the surroundings. The opposite flow of energy is very unlikely. It is highly improbable that there will be a net flow of energy into the system as a result of jostling from less vigorously oscillating molecules in the surroundings. In this case, the natural direction of change corresponds to the dispersal of energy.

The tendency towards dispersal of energy also explains why, despite numerous attempts, it has

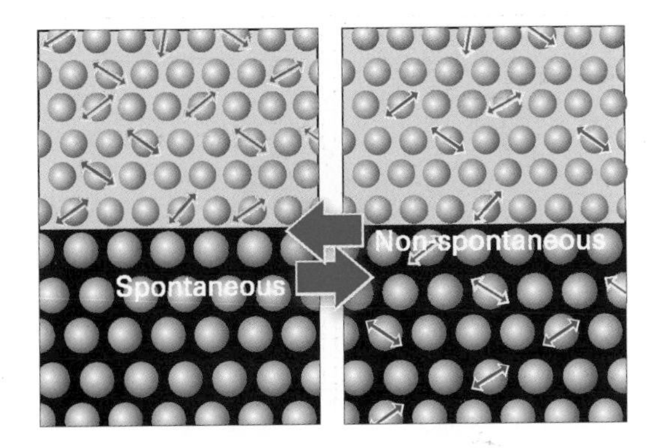

Fig. 4.2 Another fundamental type of spontaneous process is the chaotic dispersal of energy (represented by the small arrows). In these diagrams, the small spheres (top) represent the system and the large spheres (bottom) represent the surroundings. The double-headed arrows represent the thermal motion of the atoms.

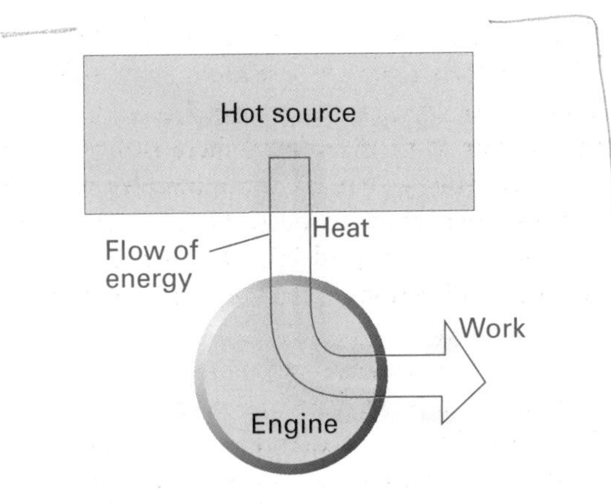

Fig. 4.3 The Second Law denies the possibility of the process illustrated here, in which heat is changed completely into work, there being no other change. The process is not in conflict with the First Law, because the energy is conserved.

proved impossible to construct an engine like that shown in Fig. 4.3, in which heat, perhaps from the combustion of a fuel, is drawn from a hot reservoir and completely converted into work, such as the work of moving an automobile. All actual heat engines have both a hot region, the 'source', and a cold region, the 'sink', and it has been found that some energy must be discarded into the cold sink as heat and not used to do work. In molecular terms, only some of the energy stored in the atoms and molecules of the hot source can be used to do work and transferred to the surroundings in an orderly way. For the engine to do work, some energy must be transferred to the cold sink as heat, to stimulate disorderly motion of its atoms and molecules.

In summary, we have identified two basic types of spontaneous physical processes:

1 Matter tends to become disordered.

2 Energy tends to become disordered.

We must now see how these two primitive types of spontaneous physical change result in some chemical reactions being spontaneous and others not. It may seem very puzzling that collapse into disorder can account for the formation of such ordered systems as proteins and biological cells. Nevertheless, in due course we shall see that organized structures can emerge as energy and matter disperse. We shall see, in fact, that collapse into disorder accounts for change in all its forms.

4.2 Entropy and the Second Law

The measure of disorder used in thermodynamics is called the **entropy**, S. Initially, we can take entropy to be a synonym for the extent of disorder, but shortly we shall see that it can be defined precisely and quantitatively, measured, and then applied to chemical reactions. At this point, all we need to know is that, when matter and energy become disordered, the entropy increases. That being so, we can combine the two remarks above into a single statement known as the **Second Law of thermodynamics:**

The entropy of an isolated system tends to increase.

The 'isolated system' may consist of a system in which we have a special interest (a beaker containing reagents) and that system's surroundings: the two components jointly form a little 'universe' in the thermodynamic sense.

To make progress and turn the Second Law into a quantitatively useful statement, we need to define entropy precisely. We shall use the following definition of a *change* in entropy:

$$\Delta S = \frac{q_{\text{rev}}}{T} \tag{4.1}$$

That is, the change in entropy of a substance is equal to the energy transferred as heat to it *reversibly* divided by the temperature at which the transfer takes place.

This definition can be justified thermodynamically, but we shall confine ourselves to showing that it is plausible and then show how to use it to obtain numerical values for a range of processes.

There are three points we need to understand about the definition in eqn 4.1: the significance of the term 'reversible', why heat (not work) appears in the numerator, and why temperature appears in the denominator.

We met the concept of reversibility in Section 2.3, where we saw that it refers to the ability of an infinitesimal change in a variable to change the direction of a process. Mechanical reversibility refers to the equality of pressure acting on either side of a movable wall. Thermal reversibility, the type involved in eqn 4.1, refers to the equality of temperature on either side of a thermally conducting wall. Reversible transfer of heat is smooth, careful, restrained transfer between two bodies at the same temperature. By making the transfer reversible we ensure that there are no hot spots generated in the object that later disperse spontaneously and hence add to the entropy.

Now consider why heat and not work appears in eqn 4.1. Recall from Section 2.2 that to transfer energy as heat we make use of the disorderly motion of molecules, whereas to transfer energy as work we make use of orderly motion. It should be plausible that the change in entropy—the change in the degree of disorder—is proportional to the energy transfer that takes place by making use of disorderly motion rather than orderly motion.

Finally, the presence of the temperature in the denominator in eqn 4.1 takes into account the disorder that is already present. If a given quantity of energy is transferred as heat to a hot object (one in which the atoms have a lot of disorderly thermal motion), then the additional disorder generated is less significant than if the same quantity of energy is transferred as heat to a cold object in which the atoms have less thermal motion. The difference is like sneezing in a busy street (an environment analogous to a high temperature) and sneezing in a quiet library (an environment analogous to a low temperature).

The entropy (it can be proved) is a state function, a property with a value that depends only on the present state of the system. The entropy is a measure of the current state of disorder of the system, and how that disorder was achieved is not relevant to its current value. A sample of liquid water of mass 100 g at 60°C and 98 kPa has exactly the same degree of molecular disorder—the same entropy—regardless of what has happened to it in the past. The implication of entropy being a state function is that a change in its value when a system undergoes a change of state is independent of how the change of state is brought about. One practical application of entropy is to the discussion of the efficiencies of heat engines, refrigerators, and heat pumps (Box 4.1).

Illustration 4.1

Calculating a change in entropy

Transferring 100 kJ of heat to a large mass of water at 0°C (273 K) results in a change in entropy of[1]

$$\Delta S = \frac{q_{rev}}{T} = \frac{100 \times 10^3 \text{ J}}{273 \text{ K}} = +366 \text{ J K}^{-1}$$

The same transfer at 100°C (373 K) results in

$$\Delta S = \frac{100 \times 10^3 \text{ J}}{373 \text{ K}} = +268 \text{ J K}^{-1}$$

The increase in entropy is greater at the lower temperature.

A note on good practice. The units of entropy are joules per kelvin (J K^{-1}). Entropy is an extensive property. When we deal with molar entropy, an intensive property, the units will be joules per kelvin per mole ($\text{J K}^{-1}\text{ mol}^{-1}$).

4.3 The entropy change accompanying expansion

We can often rely on intuition to judge whether the entropy increases or decreases when a substance undergoes a physical change. For instance, the entropy of a sample of gas increases as it expands because the molecules get to move in a greater volume and so have a greater degree of disorder. However, the advantage of eqn 4.1 is that it lets us express the increase *quantitatively* and make numerical calculations. For instance, we can use the definition to calculate the

[1] We use a large mass of water to ensure that the temperature of the sample does not change as heat is transferred.

Box 4.1 *Heat engines, refrigerators, and heat pumps*

As remarked in the text, to achieve spontaneity—an engine is less than useless if it has to be driven—some energy must be discarded as heat into the cold sink. It is quite easy to calculate the minimum energy that must be discarded in this way by thinking about the flow of energy and the changes in entropy of the hot source and cold sink. To simplify the discussion, we shall express it in terms of the magnitudes of the heat and work transactions, which we write as $|q|$ and $|w|$, respectively (so, if $q = -100$ J, $|q| = 100$ J). Maximum work—and therefore maximum efficiency—is achieved if all energy transactions take place reversibly, so we assume that to be the case in the following.

Suppose that the hot source is at a temperature T_{hot}. Then when energy $|q|$ is released from it reversibly as heat, its entropy changes by $-|q|/T_{hot}$. Suppose that we allow an energy $|q'|$ to flow reversibly as heat into the cold sink at a temperature T_{cold}. Then the entropy of that sink changes by $+|q'|/T_{cold}$ (see the first illustration). The total change in entropy is therefore

$$\Delta S_{total} = -\frac{|q|}{T_{hot}} + \frac{|q'|}{T_{cold}}$$

The engine will not operate spontaneously if this change in entropy is negative, and just becomes spontaneous as ΔS_{total} becomes positive. This change of sign occurs when $\Delta S_{total} = 0$, which is achieved when

$$|q'| = \frac{T_{cold}}{T_{hot}} \times |q|$$

If we have to discard an energy $|q'|$ into the cold sink, the maximum energy that can be extracted as work is $|q| - |q'|$. It follows that the *efficiency*, ε (epsilon), of the engine, the ratio of the work produced to the heat absorbed, is

$$\varepsilon = \frac{\text{work produced}}{\text{heat absorbed}} = \frac{|q| - |q'|}{|q|} = 1 - \frac{|q'|}{|q|}$$

$$= 1 - \frac{T_{cold}}{T_{hot}}$$

This remarkable result tells us that the efficiency of a perfect heat engine (one working reversibly and without mechanical defects such as friction) depends only on the temperatures of the hot source and cold sink. It shows that maximum efficiency (closest to $\varepsilon = 1$) is achieved by using a sink that is as cold as possible and a source that is as hot as possible. For example, the maximum efficiency of an electrical power station using steam at 200°C (473 K) and discharging at 20°C (293 K) is

$$\varepsilon = 1 - \frac{293\text{ K}}{473\text{ K}} = 1 - \frac{293}{473} = 0.381$$

or 38.1 per cent.

A refrigerator can be analysed similarly (see the second illustration). The entropy change when an energy $|q|$ is withdrawn reversibly as heat from the cold interior at a temperature T_{cold} is $-|q|/T_{cold}$. The entropy change when an energy $|q'|$ is deposited reversibly as heat in the

The flow of energy in a heat engine. For the process to be spontaneous, the decrease in entropy of the hot source must be offset by the increase in entropy of the cold sink. However, because the latter is at a lower temperature, not all the energy removed from the hot source need be deposited in it, leaving the difference available as work.

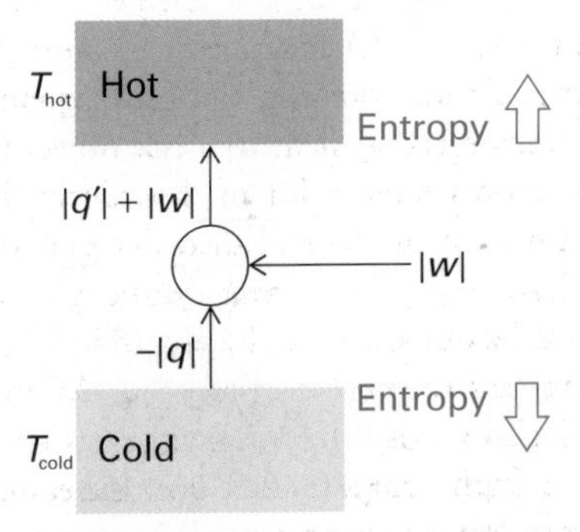

The flow of energy as heat from a cold source to a hot sink becomes feasible if work is provided to add to the energy stream. Then the increase in entropy of the hot sink can be made to cancel the entropy decrease of the hot source.

outside world at a temperature T_{hot} is $+|q'|/T_{hot}$. The total change in entropy would be negative if $|q'| = |q|$, and the refrigerator would not work. However, if we increase the flow of energy into the warm exterior by doing work on the refrigerator, then the entropy change of the warm exterior can be increased to the point at which it overcomes the decrease in entropy of the cold interior, and the refrigerator operates. The calculation of the maximum efficiency of this process is left as an exercise (see below).

A heat pump is simply a refrigerator, but one in which we are more interested in the supply of heat to the exterior than the cooling achieved in the interior. You are invited to show (see the second exercise), that the efficiency of a perfect heat pump, as measured by the heat produced divided by the work done, also depends on the ratio of the two temperatures.

Exercise 1 Show that the best *coefficient of cooling performance*, c_{cool}, the ratio of the energy extracted as heat at T_{cold} to the energy supplied as work in a perfect refrigerator, is $c_{cool} = T_{cold}/(T_{hot} - T_{cold})$. What is the maximum rate of extraction of energy as heat in a domestic refrigerator rated at 200 W operating at 5.0°C in a room at 22°C?

Exercise 2 Show that the best *coefficient of heating performance*, c_{warm}, the ratio of the energy produced as heat at T_{hot} to the energy supplied as work in a perfect heat pump, is $c_{warm} = T_{hot}/(T_{hot} - T_{cold})$. What is the maximum power rating of a heat pump that consumes power at 2.5 kW operating at 18.0°C and warming a room at 22°C?

change in entropy when a perfect gas expands isothermally from a volume V_i to a volume V_f, and obtain

$$\Delta S = nR \ln \frac{V_f}{V_i} \tag{4.2}$$

Derivation 4.1

The variation of the entropy of a perfect gas with volume

We need to know q_{rev}, the energy transferred as heat in the course of a *reversible* change at the temperature T. From eqn 2.7 we know that the energy transferred as heat to a perfect gas when it undergoes reversible, isothermal expansion from a volume V_i to a volume V_f at a temperature T is

$$q_{rev} = nRT \ln \frac{V_f}{V_i}$$

It follows that

Definition

$$\Delta S = \frac{q_{rev}}{T} = \frac{nRT \ln(V_f/V_i)}{T} = nR \ln \frac{V_f}{V_i}$$

Isothermal, reversible, perfect gas

which is eqn 4.2.

We have already stressed the importance of reading equations for their physical content. In this case we see that if $V_f > V_i$, as in an expansion, then $V_f/V_i > 1$ and the logarithm is positive. Consequently, eqn 4.2 predicts a positive value for ΔS, corresponding to an increase in entropy, just as we anticipated (Fig. 4.4). Perhaps surprisingly, though, the equation shows that the change in entropy is independent of the temperature at which the isothermal expansion occurs. The explanation is that more work is done if the temperature is high (because the external pressure must be matched to a higher value of the pressure of the gas), so more energy must be supplied as heat to maintain the temperature. The temperature in the denominator of eqn 4.1 is higher, but the 'sneeze' (in

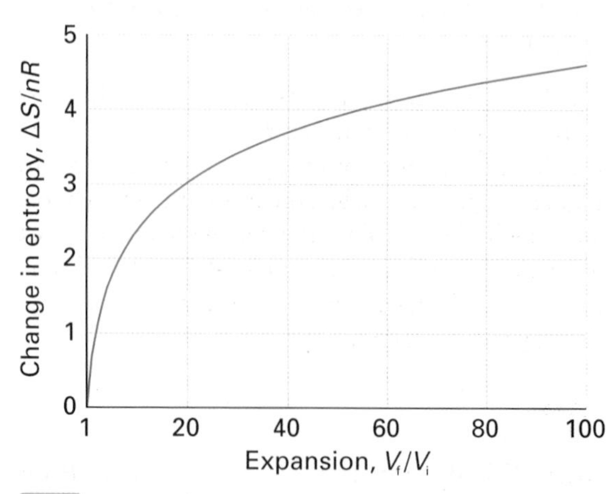

Fig. 4.4 The entropy of a perfect gas increases logarithmically (as ln V) as the volume is increased.

terms of the analogy introduced earlier) is greater too, and the two effects cancel.

Self-test 4.1

Calculate the change in molar entropy when a sample of hydrogen gas expands isothermally to twice its initial volume.

[*Answer:* $+5.8\ \text{J K}^{-1}\ \text{mol}^{-1}$]

Here is a subtle but important point. The definition in eqn 4.1 makes use of a *reversible* transfer of heat, and that is what we used in the derivation of eqn 4.2. However, entropy is a state function, so its value is independent of the path between the initial and final states. This independence of path means that although we have used a reversible path to calculate ΔS, the same value applies to an irreversible change (for instance, free expansion) between the same two states. We cannot use an irreversible path to calculate ΔS, but the value calculated for a reversible path applies however the path is traversed in practice between the specified initial and final states. You may have noticed that in Self-test 4.1 we did not specify how the expansion took place other than that it is isothermal.

4.4 The entropy change accompanying heating

We should expect the entropy of a sample to increase as the temperature is raised from T_i to T_f, because the thermal disorder of the system is greater at the higher temperature, when the molecules move more vigorously. To calculate the change in entropy, we go back to the definition in eqn 4.1 and find that, provided the heat capacity is constant over the range of temperatures of interest,

$$\Delta S = C \ln \frac{T_f}{T_i} \tag{4.3}$$

where C is the heat capacity of the system. If the pressure is held constant during the heating, we use the constant-pressure heat capacity, C_p, and if the volume is held constant, we use the constant-volume heat capacity, C_V.

Derivation 4.2

The variation of entropy with temperature

Equation 4.1 refers to the transfer of heat to a system at a temperature T. In general, the temperature changes as we heat a system, so we cannot use eqn 4.1 directly. Suppose, however, that we transfer only an infinitesimal energy, dq, to the system, then there is only an infinitesimal change in temperature and we introduce negligible error is we keep the temperature in the denominator of eqn 4.1 equal to T during that transfer. As a result, the entropy increases by an infinitesimal amount dS given by

$$dS = \frac{dq_{rev}}{T}$$

To calculate dq, we recall from Section 2.4 that the heat capacity C is

$$C = \frac{q}{\Delta T}$$

where ΔT is macroscopic change in temperature. For the case of an infinitesimal change dT, we write

$$C = \frac{dq}{dT}$$

This relation also applies when the transfer of energy is carried out reversibly. It follows that

$$dq_{rev} = C\,dT$$

Infinitesimally small quantities may be treated like any other quantity in algebraic manipulations. Thus, the expression $dy/dx = a$ may be rewritten as $dy = a\,dx$, $dx/dy = 1/a$, and so on. For instance, if $dy/dx = 2$, then $dy = 2dx$ and $dx/dy = \frac{1}{2}$.

and therefore that

$$dS = \frac{C\,dT}{T}$$

The total change in entropy, ΔS, when the temperature changes from T_i to T_f is the sum (integral) of all such infinitesimal terms:

$$\Delta S = \int_{T_i}^{T_f} \frac{C\,dT}{T}$$

For many substances and for small temperature ranges we may take C to be constant. This assumption is strictly true for a monatomic perfect gas. Then C may be taken outside the integral, and the latter evaluated as follows:

Constant heat capacity

$$\Delta S = \int_{T_i}^{T_f} \frac{C\,dT}{T} = C\int_{T_i}^{T_f} \frac{dT}{T} = C \ln \frac{T_f}{T_i}$$

We have used the same standard integral as in Derivation 2.2, and evaluated the limits similarly.

Equation 4.3 is in line with what we expect. When $T_f > T_i$, $T_f/T_i > 1$, which implies that the logarithm is positive, that $\Delta S > 0$, and therefore that the entropy increases (Fig. 4.5). Note that the relation also shows a less obvious point, that the higher the heat capacity of the substance, the greater the change in entropy for a given rise in temperature. A moment's thought shows that that conclusion is reasonable too. A high heat capacity implies that a lot of heat is required to produce a given change in temperature, so the 'sneeze' must be more powerful than for the case when the heat capacity is low, and the entropy increase is correspondingly high.

Self-test 4.2

Calculate the change in molar entropy when hydrogen gas is heated from 20°C to 30°C at constant volume. ($C_{V,m} = 22.44$ J K^{-1} mol^{-1}.)

[*Answer:* +0.75 J K^{-1} mol^{-1}]

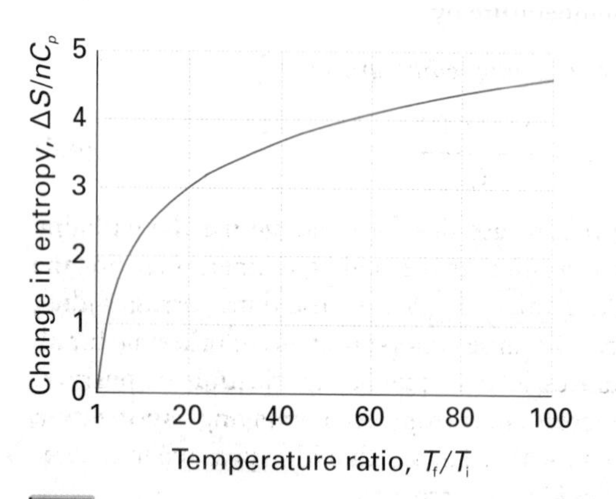

Fig. 4.5 The entropy of a sample with a heat capacity that is independent of temperature, such as a monatomic perfect gas, increases logarithmically (as ln T) as the temperature is increased. The increase is proportional to the heat capacity of the sample.

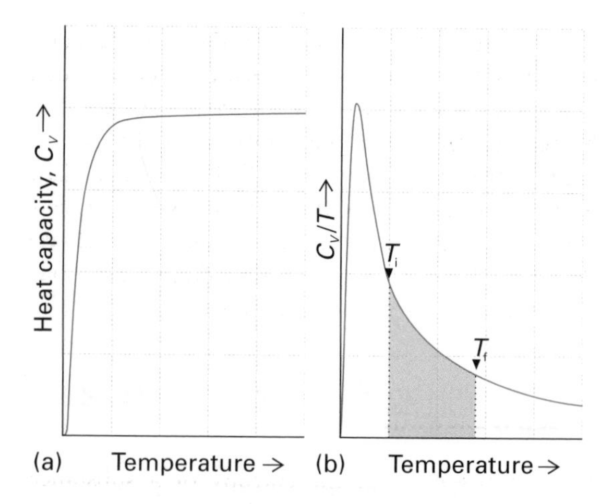

Fig. 4.6 The experimental determination of the change in entropy of a sample that has a constant-volume heat capacity that varies with temperature involves measuring the heat capacity over the range of temperatures of interest, then plotting C_V/T against T and determining the area under the curve (the tinted area shown here). The heat capacity of all solids decreases towards zero as the temperature is reduced.

When we cannot assume that the heat capacity is constant over the temperature range of interest, which is the case for all solids at low temperatures, we have to allow for the variation of C with temperature. As we show below, the result is

$$\Delta S = \text{area under the graph of } C/T \text{ plotted against } T, \text{ between } T_i \text{ and } T_f \qquad (4.4)$$

This rule is illustrated in Fig. 4.6.

Derivation 4.3

The entropy change when the heat capacity varies with temperature

In Derivation 4.2 we found, before making the assumption that the heat capacity is constant, that

$$\Delta S = \int_{T_i}^{T_f} \frac{C\,dT}{T}$$

This is our starting point in this Derivation. All we need to recognize is the standard result from calculus illustrated in Derivation 2.2, that the integral of a function between two limits is the area under the graph of the function between the two limits. In this case, the function is C/T, the heat capacity at each temperature divided by that temperature.

To use eqn 4.4, we measure the heat capacity throughout the range of temperatures of interest, and make a list of values. Then we divide each one by the corresponding temperature, to get C/T at each temperature, plot these C/T against T, and evaluate the area under the graph between the temperatures T_i and T_f. The simplest way to evaluate the area is to count squares on the graph paper, but a more accurate way is to use a computer.

4.5 The entropy change accompanying a phase transition

We can suspect that the entropy of a substance increases when it melts and when it boils because its molecules become more disordered as it changes from solid to liquid and from liquid to vapour.

The transfer of energy as heat occurs reversibly when a solid is at its melting temperature. If the temperature of the surroundings is infinitesimally lower than that of the system, then energy flows out of the system as heat and the substance freezes. If the temperature is infinitesimally higher, then energy flows into the system as heat and the substance melts. Moreover, because the transition occurs at constant pressure, we can identify the heat transferred per mole of substance with the enthalpy of fusion (melting). Therefore, the **entropy of fusion**, $\Delta_{fus}S$, the change of entropy per mole of substance, at the melting temperature, T_f (with f now denoting fusion), is

At the melting temperature:

$$\Delta_{fus}S = \frac{\Delta_{fus}H(T_f)}{T_f} \qquad (4.5)$$

Note how we must use the enthalpy of fusion *at the melting temperature*. We get the standard entropy of fusion, $\Delta_{fus}S^\ominus$, if the solid and liquid are both at 1 bar; we use the melting temperature at 1 bar and the corresponding standard enthalpy of fusion at that temperature. All enthalpies of fusion are positive (melting is endothermic: it requires heat), so all entropies of fusion are positive too: disorder increases on melting (Fig. 4.7). The entropy of water, for example, increases when it melts because the orderly structure of ice collapses as the liquid forms.

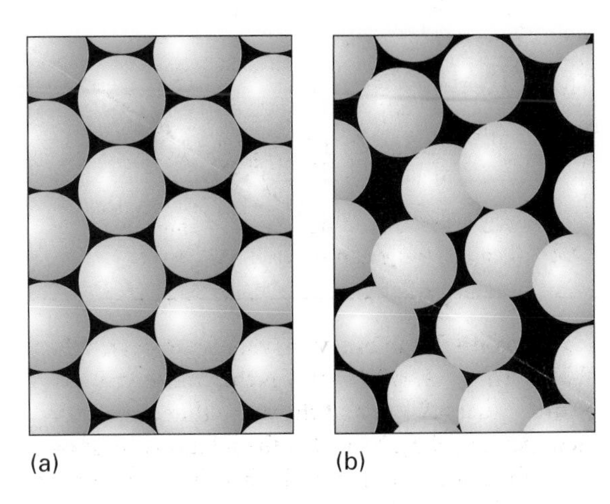

Fig. 4.7 When a solid, depicted by the orderly array of spheres (a), melts, the molecules form a more chaotic liquid, the disorderly array of spheres (b). As a result, the entropy of the sample increases.

Self-test 4.3

Calculate the standard entropy of fusion of ice at 0°C from the information in Table 3.1.

[*Answer:* +22 J K^{-1} mol^{-1}]

The entropy of other types of transition may be discussed similarly. Thus, the **entropy of vaporization**, $\Delta_{vap}S$, at the boiling temperature, T_b, of a liquid is related to its enthalpy of vaporization at that temperature by

At the boiling temperature:

$$\Delta_{vap}S = \frac{\Delta_{vap}H(T_b)}{T_b} \qquad (4.6)$$

Note that to use this formula, we use the enthalpy of vaporization at the boiling temperature. For the standard value, $\Delta_{vap}S^\ominus$, we use data corresponding to 1 bar. Because vaporization is endothermic for all substances, all entropies of vaporization are positive. The increase in entropy accompanying vaporization is in line with what we should expect when a compact liquid turns into a gas.

Self-test 4.4

Calculate the entropy of vaporization of water at 100°C.

[*Answer:* +109 J K^{-1} mol^{-1}]

Table 4.1
Entropies of vaporization at 1 atm and the normal boiling point

	$\Delta_{vap}S/(J\ K^{-1}\ mol^{-1})$
Ammonia, NH_3	97.4
Benzene, C_6H_6	87.2
Bromine, Br_2	88.6
Carbon tetrachloride, CCl_4	85.9
Cyclohexane, C_6H_{12}	85.1
Hydrogen sulfide, H_2S	87.9
Mercury, Hg	94.2
Water, H_2O	109.1

Entropies of vaporization shed light on an empirical relation known as **Trouton's rule.** Trouton noticed that $\Delta_{vap}H(T_b)/T_b$ is approximately the same (and equal to about 85 J K^{-1} mol^{-1}) for all liquids except when hydrogen bonding or some other kind of specific molecular interaction is present (see Table 4.1). We know that the quantity $\Delta_{vap}H(T_b)/T_b$, however, is the entropy of vaporization of the liquid at its boiling point, so Trouton's rule is explained if all liquids have approximately the same entropy of vaporization. This near equality is to be expected because, when a liquid vaporizes, the compact condensed phase changes into a widely dispersed gas that occupies approximately the same volume whatever its identity. To a good approximation, therefore, we expect the increase in disorder, and therefore the entropy of vaporization, to be almost the same for all liquids at their boiling temperatures.

A hydrogen bond is an attractive interaction between two species that arises from a link of the form A–H ··· B, where A and B are highly electronegative elements and B possesses a lone pair of electrons. See Section 17.6 for a more detailed description.

The exceptions to Trouton's rule include liquids in which the interactions between molecules result in the liquid being less disordered than a random jumble of molecules. For example, the high value for water implies that the H_2O molecules are linked together in some kind of ordered structure by hydrogen bonding, with the result that the entropy change is greater when this relatively ordered liquid forms a disordered gas. The high value for mercury has a similar explanation but stems from the presence of metallic bonding in the liquid, which organizes the atoms into more definite patterns than would be the case if such bonding were absent.

Illustration 4.2
Using Trouton's rule

We can estimate the enthalpy of vaporization of liquid bromine from its boiling temperature, 59.2°C. No hydrogen bonding or other kind of special interaction is present, so we use the rule after converting the boiling point to 332.4 K:

$$\Delta_{vap}H \approx (332.4\ K) \times (85\ J\ K^{-1}\ mol^{-1}) = 28\ kJ\ mol^{-1}$$

The experimental value is 29 kJ mol^{-1}.

Self-test 4.5

Estimate the enthalpy of vaporization of ethane from its boiling point, which is −88.6°C.

[*Answer:* 16 kJ mol^{-1}]

To calculate the entropy of phase transition at a temperature other than the transition temperature, we have to do additional calculations, as shown in Illustration 4.3.

Illustration 4.3
The entropy of vaporization of water at 25°C

Suppose we want to calculate the entropy of vaporization of water at 25°C. The most convenient way to proceed is to perform three calculations. First, we calculate the entropy change for heating liquid water from 25°C to 100°C (using eqn 4.3 with data for the liquid from Table 2.1):

$$\Delta S_1 = C_{p,m}(H_2O, \text{liquid}) \ln \frac{T_f}{T_i}$$
$$= (75.29\ J\ K^{-1}\ mol^{-1}) \times \ln \frac{373\ K}{298\ K}$$
$$= +16.9\ J\ K^{-1}\ mol^{-1}$$

Then, we use eqn 4.6 and data from Table 3.1 to calculate the entropy of transition at 100°C:

$$\Delta S_2 = \frac{\Delta_{vap}H(T_b)}{T_b} = \frac{4.07 \times 10^4 \text{ J mol}^{-1}}{373 \text{ K}} = +1.09 \times 10^2 \text{ J K}^{-1} \text{ mol}^{-1}$$

Finally, we calculate the change in entropy for cooling the vapour from 100°C to 25°C (using eqn 4.3 again, but now with data for the vapour from Table 2.1):

$$\Delta S_3 = C_{p,m}(H_2O, \text{vapour}) \ln \frac{T_f}{T_i} = (33.58 \text{ J K}^{-1} \text{ mol}^{-1}) \times \ln \frac{298 \text{ K}}{373 \text{ K}} = -7.54 \text{ J K}^{-1} \text{ mol}^{-1}$$

The sum of the three entropy changes is the entropy of transition at 25°C:

$$\Delta_{vap}S\,(298 \text{ K}) = \Delta S_1 + \Delta S_2 + \Delta S_3 = +118 \text{ J K}^{-1} \text{ mol}^{-1}$$

4.6 Entropy changes in the surroundings

We can use the definition of entropy in eqn 4.1 to calculate the entropy change of the surroundings in contact with the system at the temperature T:

$$\Delta S_{sur} = \frac{q_{sur,rev}}{T}$$

The surroundings are so extensive that they remain at constant pressure regardless of any events taking place in the system, so $q_{sur,rev} = \Delta H_{sur}$. The enthalpy is a state function, so a change in its value is independent of the path and we get the same value of ΔH_{sur} regardless of how the heat is transferred. Therefore, we can drop the label 'rev' from q and write

$$\Delta S_{sur} = \frac{q_{sur}}{T} \qquad (4.7)$$

We can use this formula to calculate the entropy change of the surroundings regardless of whether the change in the system is reversible or not.

Example 4.1

Estimating the entropy change of the surroundings

A typical resting person heats the surroundings at a rate of about 100 W. Estimate the entropy you generate in the surroundings in the course of a day at 20°C.

Strategy We can estimate the approximate change in entropy from eqn 4.7 once we have calculated the energy transferred as heat. To find this quantity, we use 1 W = 1 J s^{-1} and the fact that there are 86 400 s in a day. Convert the temperature to kelvins.

Solution The heat transferred to the surroundings in the course of a day is

$$q_{sur} = (86\,400 \text{ s}) \times (100 \text{ J s}^{-1}) = 86\,400 \times 100 \text{ J}$$

The increase in entropy of the surroundings is therefore

$$\Delta S_{sur} = \frac{q_{sur}}{T} = \frac{86\,400 \times 100 \text{ J}}{293 \text{ K}} = +2.95 \times 10^4 \text{ J K}^{-1}$$

That is, the entropy production is about 30 kJ K^{-1}. Just to stay alive, each person on the planet contributes about 30 kJ K^{-1} each day to the entropy of their surroundings. The use of transport, machinery, and communications generates far more in addition.

Self-test 4.6

Suppose a small reptile operates at 0.50 W. What entropy does it generate in the course of a day in the water in the lake that it inhabits, where the temperature is 15°C?

[*Answer:* +150 J K^{-1}]

Equation 4.7 is expressed in terms of the energy supplied to the *surroundings* as heat, q_{sur}. Normally, we have information about the energy supplied to or escaping from the *system* as heat, q. The two quantities are related by $q_{sur} = -q$. For instance, if $q = +100$ J (an influx of 100 J), then $q_{sur} = -100$ J, indicating that the surroundings have lost that 100 J. Therefore, at this stage we can replace q_{sur} in eqn 4.7 by $-q$ and write

$$\Delta S_{sur} = -\frac{q}{T} \qquad (4.8)$$

This expression is in terms of the properties of the system. Moreover, it applies whether or not the process taking place in the system is reversible.

Illustration 4.4

Total entropy changes accompanying expansion

Suppose a perfect gas expands isothermally and reversibly from V_i to V_f. The entropy change of the gas itself (the system) is given by eqn 4.2. To calculate the entropy change in the surroundings, we note that q, the heat required to keep the temperature constant, is given in Derivation 4.1. Therefore,

$$\Delta S_{sur} = -\frac{q}{T} = -\frac{nRT\ln(V_f/V_i)}{T} = -nR\ln\frac{V_f}{V_i}$$

The change of entropy in the surroundings is therefore the negative of the change in entropy of the system, and the total entropy change for the reversible process is zero. Now suppose that the gas expands isothermally but freely ($p_{ex} = 0$) between the same two volumes. The change in entropy of the system is the same, because entropy is a state function. However, because $\Delta U = 0$ for the isothermal expansion of a perfect gas and no work is done, no heat is taken in from the surroundings. Because $q = 0$, it follows from eqn 4.8 (which, remember, can be used for either reversible or irreversible heat transfers) that $\Delta S_{sur} = 0$. The total change in entropy is therefore equal to the change in entropy of the system, which is positive. We see that for this irreversible process, the entropy of the universe has increased, in accord with the Second Law.

If a chemical reaction or a phase transition takes place at constant pressure, we can identify q in eqn 4.8 with the change in enthalpy of the system, and obtain

For a process at constant pressure:

$$\Delta S_{sur} = -\frac{\Delta H}{T} \quad (4.9)$$

This enormously important expression will lie at the heart of our discussion of chemical equilibria. We see that it is consistent with common sense: if the process is exothermic, ΔH is negative and therefore ΔS_{sur} is positive. The entropy of the surroundings increases if heat is released into them. If the process is endothermic ($\Delta H > 0$), then the entropy of the surroundings decreases.

4.7 Absolute entropies and the Third Law of thermodynamics

The graphical procedure summarized by Fig. 4.6 and eqn 4.4 for the determination of the difference in entropy of a substance at two temperatures has a very important application. If $T_i = 0$, then the area under the graph between $T = 0$ and some temperature T gives us the value of $\Delta S = S(T) - S(0)$.[2] However, at $T = 0$, all the motion of the atoms has been eliminated, and there is no thermal disorder. Moreover, if the substance is perfectly crystalline, with every atom in a well-defined location, then there is no spatial disorder either. We can therefore suspect that at $T = 0$, the entropy is zero.

The thermodynamic evidence for this conclusion is as follows. Sulfur undergoes a phase transition from rhombic to monoclinic at 96°C (369 K) and the enthalpy of transition is +402 J mol^{-1}. The entropy of transition is therefore +1.09 J K^{-1} mol^{-1} at this temperature. We can also measure the molar entropy of each phase relative to its value at $T = 0$ by determining the heat capacity from $T = 0$ up to the transition temperature (Fig. 4.8). At this stage, we do not know the values of the entropies at $T = 0$. However, as we see from the illustration, to match

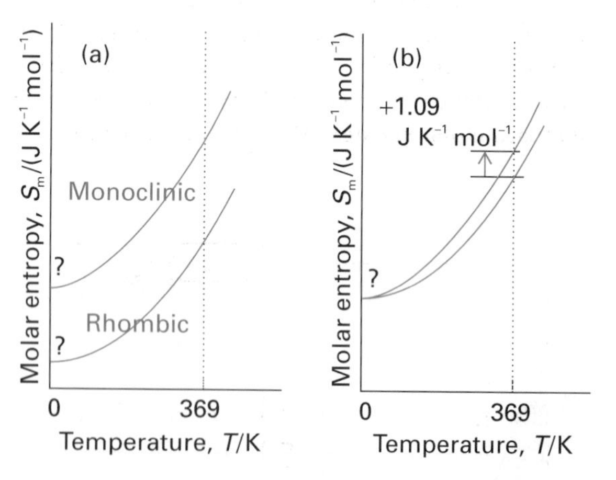

Fig. 4.8 (a) The molar entropies of monoclinic and rhombic sulfur vary with temperature as shown here. At this stage we do not know their values at $T = 0$. (b) When we slide the two curves together by matching their separation to the measured entropy of transition at the transition temperature, we find that the entropies of the two forms are the same at $T = 0$.

[2] We are supposing that there are no phase transitions below the temperature T. If there are any phase transitions (for example, melting) in the temperature range of interest, then the entropy of each transition at the transition temperature is calculated like that in eqn 4.5.

the observed entropy of transition at 369 K, the molar entropies of the two crystalline forms must be the same at $T = 0$. We cannot say that the entropies are zero at $T = 0$, but from the experimental data we do know that they are the same. This observation is generalized into the **Third Law of thermodynamics:**

The entropies of all perfectly crystalline substances are the same at $T = 0$.

For convenience (and in accord with our understanding of entropy as a measure of disorder), we take this common value to be zero. Then, with this convention, according to the Third Law, $S(0) = 0$ *for all perfectly ordered crystalline materials.*

The **Third-Law entropy** at any temperature, $S(T)$, is equal to the area under the graph of C/T between $T = 0$ and the temperature T (Fig. 4.9). If there are any phase transitions (for example, melting) in the temperature range of interest, then the entropy of each transition at the transition temperature is calculated like that in eqn 4.5 and its contribution added to the contributions from each of the phases, as shown in Fig. 4.10. The Third-Law entropy, which is commonly called simply 'the entropy', of a substance depends on the pressure; we therefore select a standard pressure (1 bar) and report the **standard molar entropy**, $S^{\ominus}_{m}$, the molar entropy of a substance in its standard state at the temperature of interest. Some values at 298.15 K (the conventional temperature for reporting data) are given in Table 4.2.

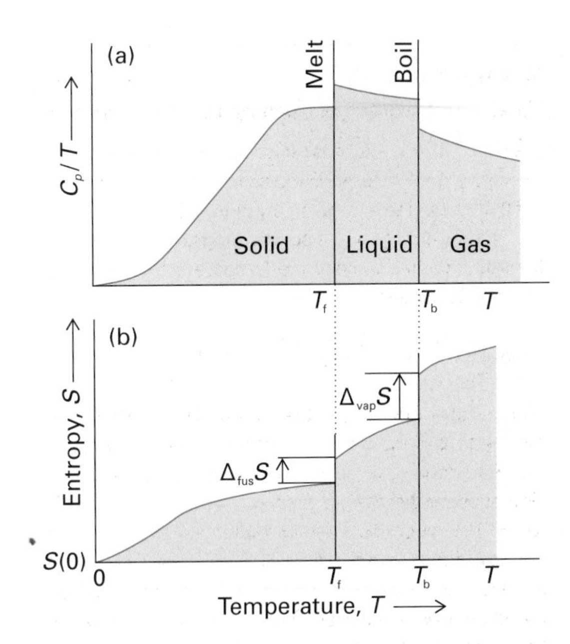

Fig. 4.10 The determination of entropy from heat capacity data. (a) Variation of C_p/T with the temperature of the sample. (b) The entropy, which is equal to the area beneath the upper curve up to the temperature of interest plus the entropy of each phase transition between $T = 0$ and the temperature of interest.

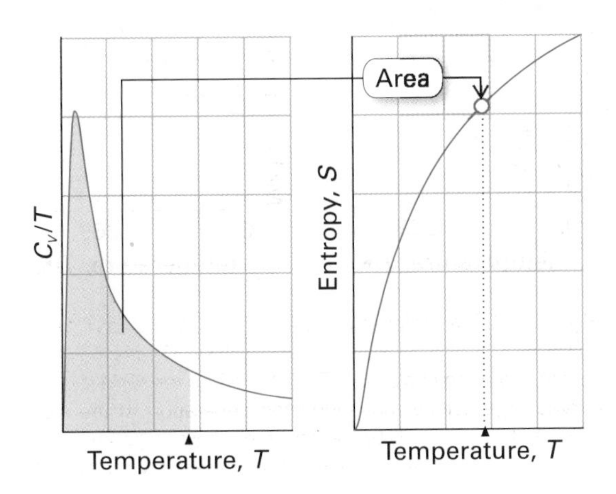

Fig. 4.9 The absolute entropy (or Third-Law entropy) of a substance is calculated by extending the measurement of heat capacities down to $T = 0$ (or as close to that value as possible), and then determining the area of the graph of C_V/T against T up to the temperature of interest. The area is equal to the absolute entropy at the temperature T.

The text's web site contains links to online databases of thermochemical data, including tabulations of standard molar entropies.

It is worth spending a moment to look at the values in Table 4.2 to see that they are consistent with our understanding of entropy. All standard molar entropies are positive, because raising the temperature of a sample above $T = 0$ invariably increases its entropy above the value $S(0) = 0$. Another feature is that the standard molar entropy of diamond (2.4 J K^{-1} mol^{-1}) is lower than that of graphite (5.7 J K^{-1} mol^{-1}). This difference is consistent with the atoms being linked less rigidly in graphite than in diamond and their thermal disorder being correspondingly greater. The standard molar entropies of ice, water, and water vapour at 25°C are, respectively, 45, 70, and 189 J K^{-1} mol^{-1}, and the increase in values corresponds to the increasing disorder on going from a solid to a liquid and then to a gas.

Table 4.2

Standard molar entropies of some substances at 298.15 K

Substance	$S_m^{\ominus}$/J K^{-1} mol^{-1}
Gases	
Ammonia, NH_3	192.5
Carbon dioxide, CO_2	213.7
Helium, He	126.2
Hydrogen, H_2	130.7
Neon, Ne	146.3
Nitrogen, N_2	191.6
Oxygen, O_2	205.1
Water vapour, H_2O	188.8
Liquids	
Benzene, C_6H_6	173.3
Ethanol, CH_3CH_2OH	160.7
Water, H_2O	69.9
Solids	
Calcium oxide, CaO	39.8
Calcium carbonate, $CaCO_3$	92.9
Copper, Cu	33.2
Diamond, C	2.4
Graphite, C	5.7
Lead, Pb	64.8
Magnesium carbonate, $MgCO_3$	65.7
Magnesium oxide, MgO	26.9
Sodium chloride, NaCl	72.1
Sucrose, $C_{12}H_{22}O_{11}$	360.2
Tin, Sn (white)	51.6
Sn (grey)	44.1

See the *Data section* for more values.

Heat capacities can be measured only with great difficulty at very low temperatures, particularly close to $T = 0$. However, it has been found that many non-metallic substances have a heat capacity that obeys the **Debye T^3-law:**

At temperatures close to $T = 0$,

$$C_{V,m} = aT^3 \tag{4.10a}$$

where a is an empirical constant that depends on the substance and is found by fitting eqn 4.10a to a series of measurements of the heat capacity close to $T = 0$. With a determined, it is easy to deduce the molar entropy at low temperatures, because

At temperatures close to $T = 0$,

$$S_m(T) = \tfrac{1}{3}C_{V,m}(T) \tag{4.10b}$$

That is, the molar entropy at the low temperature T is equal to one-third of the constant-volume heat capacity at that temperature.

Derivation 4.4

Entropies close to $T = 0$

Once again, we use the general expression for the entropy change accompanying a change of temperature deduced in Derivation 4.2, with ΔS interpreted as $S(T_f) - S(T_i)$, taking molar values, and supposing that the heating takes place at constant volume:

$$S_m(T_f) - S_m(T_i) = \int_{T_i}^{T_f} \frac{C_{V,m}}{T}\, dT$$

If we set $T_i = 0$ and T_f at some general temperature T, we can rearrange this expression into

$$S_m(T) - S_m(0) = \int_0^T \frac{C_{V,m}}{T}\, dT$$

According to the Third Law, $S(0) = 0$, and according to the Debye T^3-law, $C_{V,m} = aT^3$, so

$$S_m(T) = \int_0^T \frac{aT^3}{T}\, dT = a\int_0^T T^2\, dT$$

At this point we can use the standard integral

$$\int x^2\, dx = \tfrac{1}{3}x^3 + \text{constant}$$

to write

$$\begin{aligned}\int_0^T T^2\, dT &= (\tfrac{1}{3}T^3 + \text{constant})\big|_0^T \\ &= (\tfrac{1}{3}T^3 + \text{constant}) - \text{constant} \\ &= \tfrac{1}{3}T^3\end{aligned}$$

We can conclude that

$$S_m(T) = \tfrac{1}{3}aT^3 = \tfrac{1}{3}C_{V,m}(T)$$

as in eqn 4.10b.

4.8 The standard reaction entropy

Now we move into the arena of chemistry, where reactants are transformed into products. When there is a net formation of a gas in a reaction, as in many combustions, we can usually anticipate that the entropy increases. When there is a net consumption of gas it is usually safe to predict that the entropy decreases. However, for a quantitative value of the change in entropy, and to predict the sign of the change when no gases are involved, we need to make an explicit calculation.

The difference in molar entropy between the products and the reactants in their standard states is called the **standard reaction entropy, $\Delta_r S^\ominus$**. It can be expressed in terms of the molar entropies of the substances in much the same way as we have already used for the standard reaction enthalpy:

$$\Delta_r S^\ominus = \sum \nu S_m^\ominus(\text{products}) - \sum \nu S_m^\ominus(\text{reactants}) \quad (4.11)$$

where the ν are the stoichiometric coefficients in the chemical equation.

Illustration 4.5

Calculating a standard reaction entropy

For the reaction $2\,H_2(g) + O_2(g) \rightarrow 2\,H_2O(l)$ we expect a negative entropy of reaction as gases are consumed. To find the explicit value we use the values in the *Data section* to write

$$\begin{aligned}\Delta_r S^\ominus &= 2S_m^\ominus(H_2O, l) - \{2S_m^\ominus(H_2, g) + S_m^\ominus(O_2, g)\}\\ &= 2(70\ \text{J K}^{-1}\ \text{mol}^{-1}) - \{2(131\ \text{J K}^{-1}\ \text{mol}^{-1})\\ &\qquad + (205\ \text{J K}^{-1}\ \text{mol}^{-1})\}\\ &= -327\ \text{J K}^{-1}\ \text{mol}^{-1}\end{aligned}$$

A note on good practice. Do not make the mistake of setting the standard molar entropies of elements equal to zero: they have non-zero values (provided $T > 0$), as we have already discussed.

Self-test 4.7

(a) Calculate the standard reaction entropy for $N_2(g) + 3\,H_2(g) \rightarrow 2\,NH_3(g)$ at 25°C. (b) What is the change in entropy when 2 mol H_2 reacts?

[*Answer:* (a) (using values from Table 4.2) $-198.7\ \text{J K}^{-1}\ \text{mol}^{-1}$; (b) $-132.5\ \text{J K}^{-1}$]

4.9 The spontaneity of chemical reactions

The result of the calculation in Illustration 4.5 should be rather surprising at first sight. We know that the reaction between hydrogen and oxygen is spontaneous and, once initiated, that it proceeds with explosive violence. Nevertheless, the entropy change that accompanies it is negative: the reaction results in less disorder, yet it is spontaneous!

The resolution of this apparent paradox underscores a feature of entropy that recurs throughout chemistry: *it is essential to consider the entropy of both the system and its surroundings when deciding whether a process is spontaneous or not.* The reduction in entropy by 327 J K^{-1} mol^{-1} relates only to the system, the reaction mixture. To apply the Second Law correctly, we need to calculate the *total* entropy, the sum of the changes in the system and the surroundings that jointly compose the 'isolated system' referred to in the Second Law. It may well be the case that the entropy of the system decreases when a change takes place, but there may be a more than compensating increase in entropy of the surroundings so that overall the entropy change is positive. The opposite may also be true: a large decrease in entropy of the surroundings may occur when the entropy of the system increases. In that case we would be wrong to conclude from the increase of the system alone that the change is spontaneous.

Whenever considering the implications of entropy, we must always consider the total change of the system and its surroundings.

To calculate the entropy change in the surroundings when a reaction takes place at constant pressure, we use eqn 4.9, interpreting the ΔH in that expression as the reaction enthalpy. For example, for the water formation reaction in Illustration 4.5, with $\Delta_r H^\ominus = -572$ kJ mol^{-1}, the change in entropy of the surroundings (which are maintained at 25°C, the same temperature as the reaction mixture) is

$$\begin{aligned}\Delta_r S_{\text{sur}} &= -\frac{\Delta_r H}{T} = -\frac{(-572\ \text{kJ mol}^{-1})}{298\ \text{K}}\\ &= +1.92\times10^3\ \text{J K}^{-1}\ \text{mol}^{-1}\end{aligned}$$

Now we can see that the total entropy change is positive:

$$\Delta_r S_{total} = (-327\,\mathrm{J\,K^{-1}\,mol^{-1}}) + (1.92\times10^3\,\mathrm{J\,K^{-1}\,mol^{-1}}) = +1.59\times10^3\,\mathrm{J\,K^{-1}\,mol^{-1}}$$

This calculation confirms that the reaction is spontaneous. In this case, the spontaneity is a result of the considerable disorder that the reaction generates in the surroundings: water is dragged into existence, even though $H_2O(l)$ has a lower entropy than the gaseous reactants, by the tendency of energy to disperse into the surroundings.

The Gibbs energy

One of the problems with entropy calculations is already apparent: we have to work out two entropy changes, the change in the system and the change in the surroundings, and then consider the sign of their sum. The great American theoretician J. W. Gibbs (1839–1903), who laid the foundations of chemical thermodynamics towards the end of the nineteenth century, discovered how to combine the two calculations into one. The combination of the two procedures in fact turns out to be of much greater relevance than just saving a little labour, and throughout this text we shall see consequences of the procedure he developed.

4.10 Focusing on the system

The total entropy change that accompanies a process is

$$\Delta S_{total} = \Delta S + \Delta S_{sur}$$

where ΔS is the entropy change for the system; for a spontaneous change, $\Delta S_{total} > 0$. If the process occurs at constant pressure and temperature, we can use eqn 4.9 to express the change in entropy of the surroundings in terms of the enthalpy change of the system, ΔH. When the resulting expression is inserted into this one, we obtain

At constant temperature and pressure:

$$\Delta S_{total} = \Delta S - \frac{\Delta H}{T} \qquad (4.12)$$

The great advantage of this formula is that it expresses the total entropy change of the system and its surroundings in terms of properties of the system alone. The only restriction is to changes at constant pressure and temperature.

Now we take a very important step. First, we introduce the **Gibbs energy**, G, which is defined as[3]

$$G = H - TS \qquad (4.13)$$

Because H, T, and S are state functions, G is a state function too. A change in Gibbs energy, ΔG, at constant temperature arises from changes in enthalpy and entropy, and is

At constant temperature:

$$\Delta G = \Delta H - T\Delta S \qquad (4.14)$$

By comparing eqns 4.12 and 4.14 we obtain

At constant temperature and pressure:

$$\Delta G = -T\Delta S_{total} \qquad (4.15)$$

We see that at constant temperature and pressure, the change in Gibbs energy of a system is proportional to the overall change in entropy of the system plus its surroundings.

4.11 Properties of the Gibbs energy

The difference in sign between ΔG and ΔS_{total} implies that the condition for a process being spontaneous changes from $\Delta S_{total} > 0$ in terms of the total entropy (which is universally true) to $\Delta G < 0$ in terms of the Gibbs energy (for processes occurring at constant temperature and pressure). That is, *in a spontaneous change at constant temperature and pressure, the Gibbs energy decreases* (Fig. 4.11).

It may seem more natural to think of a system as falling to a lower value of some property. However, it must never be forgotten that to say that a system tends to fall towards lower Gibbs energy is only a modified way of saying that a system and its surroundings jointly tend towards a greater total entropy. The *only* criterion of spontaneous change is the total entropy of the system and its surroundings;

[3] The Gibbs energy is commonly referred to as the 'free energy'.

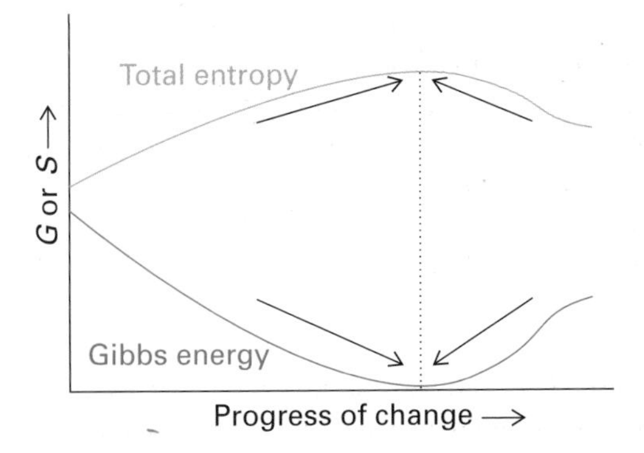

Fig. 4.11 (a) The criterion of spontaneous change is the increase in total entropy of the system and its surroundings. (b) Provided we accept the limitation of working at constant pressure and temperature, we can focus entirely on properties of the system, and express the criterion as a tendency to move to lower Gibbs energy.

the Gibbs energy merely contrives a way of expressing that total change in terms of the properties of the system alone, and is valid only for processes that occur at constant temperature and pressure. Every chemical reaction that is spontaneous under conditions of constant temperature and pressure, including those that drive the processes of growth, learning, and reproduction, are reactions that change in the direction of lower Gibbs energy, or—another way of expressing the same thing—result in the overall entropy of the system and its surroundings becoming greater.

A second feature of the Gibbs energy is that *the value of* ΔG *for a process gives the maximum non-expansion work that can be extracted from the process at constant temperature and pressure.* By **non-expansion work,** w', we mean any work other than that arising from the expansion of the system. It may include electrical work, if the process takes place inside an electrochemical or a biological cell, or other kinds of mechanical work, such as the winding of a spring or the contraction of a muscle (we saw examples in Section 2.3). To demonstrate this property, we need to combine the First and Second Laws, and then we find

At constant temperature and pressure:

$$\Delta G = w'_{\text{max}} \tag{4.16}$$

Derivation 4.5

Maximum non-expansion work

We need to consider infinitesimal changes, because dealing with reversible processes is then much easier. Our aim is to derive the relation between the infinitesimal change in Gibbs energy, dG, accompanying a process and the maximum amount of non-expansion work that the process can do, dw'. We start with the infinitesimal form of eqn 4.14,

At constant temperature: $dG = dH - T\,dS$

where, as usual, d denotes an infinitesimal difference. A good rule in the manipulation of thermodynamic expressions is to feed in definitions of the terms that appear. We do this twice. First, we use the expression for the change in enthalpy at constant pressure (eqn 2.13; $dH = dU + p\,dV$), and obtain

At constant temperature and pressure:
$dG = dU + p\,dV - T\,dS$

Then we replace dU in terms of infinitesimal contributions from work and heat ($dU = dw + dq$):

$$dG = dw + dq + p\,dV - T\,dS$$

The work done on the system consists of expansion work, $-p_{\text{ex}}\,dV$, and non-expansion work, dw'. Therefore,

$$dG = -p_{\text{ex}}\,dV + dw' + dq + p\,dV - T\,dS$$

This derivation is valid for any process taking place at constant temperature and pressure.

Now we specialize to a reversible change. For expansion work to be reversible, we need to match p and p_{ex}, in which case the first and fourth terms on the right cancel. Moreover, because the heat transfer is also reversible, we can replace dq by $T\,dS$, in which case the third and fifth terms also cancel. We are left with

At constant temperature and pressure, for a reversible process: $dG = dw'_{\text{rev}}$

Maximum work is done during a reversible change (Section 2.3), so another way of writing this expression is

At constant temperature and pressure: $dG = dw'_{\text{max}}$

Because this relation holds for each infinitesimal step between the specified initial and final states, it applies to the overall change too. Therefore, we obtain eqn 4.16.

Illustration 4.6

Calculating the maximum non-expansion work

Experiments show that for the formation of 1 mol $H_2O(l)$ at 25°C and 1 bar, $\Delta H = -286$ kJ and $\Delta G = -237$ kJ. It follows that up to 237 kJ of non-expansion work can be extracted from the reaction between hydrogen and oxygen to produce 1 mol $H_2O(l)$ at 25°C. If the reaction takes place in a fuel cell—a device for using a chemical reaction to produce an electric current, like those used on the space shuttle—then up to 237 kJ of electrical energy can be generated for each mole of H_2O produced. This energy is enough to keep a 60 W light bulb shining for about 1.1 h. If no attempt is made to extract any energy as work, then 286 kJ (in general, ΔH) of energy will be produced as heat. If some of the energy released is used to do work, then up to 237 kJ (in general, ΔG) of non-expansion work can be obtained.

Example 4.2

Estimating a change in Gibbs energy

Suppose a certain small bird has a mass of 30 g. What is the minimum mass of glucose that it must consume to fly to a branch 10 m above the ground? The change in Gibbs energy that accompanies the oxidation of 1.0 mol $C_6H_{12}O_6(s)$ to carbon dioxide and water vapour at 25°C is −2828 kJ.

Strategy First, we need to calculate the work needed to raise a mass m through a height h on the surface of the Earth. As we saw in eqn 2.1, this work is equal to mgh, where g is the acceleration of free fall. This work, which is non-expansion work, can be identified with ΔG. We need to determine the amount of substance that corresponds to the required change in Gibbs energy, and then convert that amount to a mass by using the molar mass of glucose.

Solution The non-expansion work to be done is

$$w' = (30 \times 10^{-3}\ \text{kg}) \times (9.81\ \text{m s}^{-2}) \times (10\ \text{m})$$
$$= 3.0 \times 9.81 \times 1.0 \times 10^{-1}\ \text{J}$$

(because 1 kg m^2 s^{-2} = 1 J). The amount, n, of glucose molecules required for oxidation to give a change in Gibbs energy of this value given that 1 mol provides 2828 kJ is

$$n = \frac{3.0 \times 9.81 \times 1.0 \times 10^{-1}\ \text{J}}{2.828 \times 10^{6}\ \text{J mol}^{-1}}$$
$$= \frac{3.0 \times 9.81 \times 1.0 \times 10^{-7}}{2.828}\ \text{mol}$$

Therefore, because the molar mass, M, of glucose is 180 g mol^{-1}, the mass, m, of glucose that must be oxidized is

$$m = nM$$
$$= \left(\frac{3.0 \times 9.81 \times 1.0 \times 10^{-7}}{2.828}\ \text{mol}\right) \times (180\ \text{g mol}^{-1})$$
$$= 1.9 \times 10^{-4}\ \text{g}$$

That is, the bird must consume at least 0.19 mg of glucose for the mechanical effort (and more if it thinks about it).

Self-test 4.8

A hard-working human brain, perhaps one that is grappling with physical chemistry, operates at about 25 W (1 W = 1 J s^{-1}). What mass of glucose must be consumed to sustain that power output for an hour?

[*Answer:* 5.7 g]

The great importance of the Gibbs energy in chemistry is becoming apparent. At this stage, we see that it is a measure of the non-expansion work resources of chemical reactions: if we know ΔG, then we know the maximum non-expansion work that we can obtain by harnessing the reaction in some way. In some cases, the non-expansion work is extracted as electrical energy. This is the case when the reaction takes place in an electrochemical cell, of which a fuel cell is a special case, as we see in Chapter 9. In other cases, the reaction may be used to build other molecules. This is the case in biological cells, where the Gibbs energy available from the hydrolysis of ATP (adenosine triphosphate) to ADP is used to build proteins from amino acids, to power muscular contraction, and to drive the neuronal circuits in our brains.

Some insight into the physical significance of G itself comes from its definition as $H - TS$. The enthalpy is a measure of the energy that can be obtained from the system as heat. The term TS is a measure of the quantity of energy stored in the *random* motion of the molecules making up the sample. Work, as we have seen, is energy transferred in an orderly way, so we cannot expect to obtain work from the energy stored randomly. The difference between the total stored energy and the energy stored randomly, $H - TS$, is available for doing work, and we recognize that difference as the Gibbs energy. In other words, the Gibbs energy is the energy stored in the orderly motion and arrangement of the molecules in the system.

CHECKLIST OF KEY IDEAS

You should now be familiar with the following concepts:

☐ 1 A spontaneous change is a change that has a tendency to occur without work having to be done to bring it about.

☐ 2 Matter and energy tend to disperse.

☐ 3 The Second Law states that the entropy of an isolated system tends to increase.

☐ 4 A change in entropy is defined as $\Delta S = q_{rev}/T$.

☐ 5 The entropy change accompanying the isothermal expansion of a perfect gas is $\Delta S = nRT\ln(V_f/V_i)$.

☐ 6 The entropy change accompanying heating a system of constant heat capacity is $\Delta S = C\ln(T_f/T_i)$.

☐ 7 In general, the entropy change accompanying the heating of a system is equal to the area under the graph of C/T against T between the two temperatures of interest.

☐ 8 The entropy of transition at the transition temperature is given by $\Delta_{trs}S = \Delta_{trs}H(T_{trs})/T_{trs}$.

☐ 9 The change in entropy of the surroundings is given by $\Delta S_{sur} = -q/T$.

☐ 10 The Third Law of thermodynamics states that the entropies of all perfectly crystalline substances are the same at $T = 0$ (and may be taken to be zero).

☐ 11 The standard reaction entropy is the difference in standard molar entropies of the products and reactants weighted by their stoichiometric coefficients, $\Delta_r S^\ominus = \sum \nu S_m^\ominus(\text{products}) - \sum \nu S_m^\ominus(\text{reactants})$.

☐ 12 The Gibbs energy is defined as $G = H - TS$ and is a state function.

☐ 13 At constant temperature, the change in Gibbs energy is $\Delta G = \Delta H - T\Delta S$.

☐ 14 At constant temperature and pressure, a system tends to change in the direction of decreasing Gibbs energy.

☐ 15 At constant temperature and pressure, the change in Gibbs energy accompanying a process is equal to the maximum non-expansion work the process can do.

DISCUSSION QUESTIONS

4.1 The following expressions have been used to establish criteria for spontaneous change: $\Delta S_{\text{isolated system}} > 0$ and $\Delta G < 0$. Discuss the origin, significance, and applicability of each criterion.

4.2 Justify Trouton's rule. What are the sources of discrepancies?

4.3 The evolution of life requires the organization of a very large number of molecules into biological cells. Does the formation of living organisms violate the Second Law of thermodynamics? State your conclusion clearly and present detailed arguments to support it.

4.4 Without performing a calculation, estimate whether the standard entropies of the following reactions are positive or negative:

(a) Ala–Ser–Thr–Lys–Gly–Arg–Ser $\xrightarrow{\text{trypsin}}$ Ala–Ser–Thr–Lys + Gly–Arg

(b) $N_2(g) + 3\,H_2(g) \rightarrow 2\,NH_3(g)$

(c) $ATP^{4-}(aq) + 2\,H_2O(l) \rightarrow ADP^{3-}(aq) + HPO_4^{2-}(aq) + H_3O^+(aq)$

EXERCISES

The symbol ‡ indicates that calculus is required.

4.5 A goldfish swims in a bowl of water at 20°C. Over a period of time, the fish transfers 120 J to the water as a result of its metabolism. What is the change in entropy of the water?

4.6 Suppose you put a cube of ice of mass 100 g into a glass of water at just above 0°C. When the ice melts, about 33 kJ of energy is absorbed from the surroundings as heat. What is the change in entropy of (a) the sample (the ice), (b) the surroundings (the glass of water)?

4.7 A sample of aluminium of mass 1.25 kg is cooled at constant pressure from 300 K to 260 K. Calculate the energy that must be removed as heat and the change in entropy of the sample. The molar heat capacity of aluminium is 24.35 J K^{-1} mol^{-1}.

4.8 Calculate the change in entropy of 100 g of ice at 0°C as it is melted, heated to 100°C, and then vaporized at that temperature. Suppose that the changes are brought about by a heater that supplies energy at a constant rate, and sketch a graph showing (a) the change in temperature of the system, (b) the enthalpy of the system, (c) the entropy of the system as a function of time.

4.9 Calculate the change in molar entropy when carbon dioxide expands isothermally from 1.5 dm^3 to 4.5 dm^3.

4.10 A sample of carbon dioxide that initially occupies 15.0 dm^3 at 250 K and 1.00 atm is compressed isothermally. Into what volume must the gas be compressed to reduce its entropy by 10.0 J K^{-1}?

4.11 Whenever a gas expands—when we exhale, when a flask is opened, and so on—the gas undergoes an increase in entropy. A sample of methane gas of mass 25 g at 250 K and 185 kPa expands isothermally and (a) reversibly, (b) irreversibly until its pressure is 2.5 kPa. Calculate the change in entropy of the gas.

4.12 What is the change in entropy of 100 g of water when it is heated from room temperature (20°C) to body temperature (37°C)? Use $C_{p,m} = 75.5$ J K^{-1} mol^{-1}.

4.13 Calculate the change in molar entropy when a sample of argon is compressed from 2.0 dm^3 to 500 cm^3 and simultaneously heated from 300 K to 400 K. Take $C_{V,m} = \frac{3}{2}R$.

4.14 A monatomic perfect gas at a temperature T_i is expanded isothermally to twice its initial volume. To what temperature should it be cooled to restore its entropy to its initial value? Take $C_{V,m} = \frac{3}{2}R$.

4.15 In a certain cyclic engine (technically, a *Carnot cycle*), a perfect gas expands isothermally and reversibly, then adiabatically ($q = 0$) and reversibly. In the adiabatic expansion step the temperature falls. At the end of the expansion stage, the sample is compressed reversibly first isothermally and then adiabatically in such a way as to end up at the starting volume and temperature. Draw a graph of entropy against temperature for the entire cycle.

4.16 Estimate the molar entropy of potassium chloride at 5.0 K, given that its molar heat capacity at that temperature is 1.2 mJ K^{-1} mol^{-1}.

4.17 ‡Equation 4.3 is based on the assumption that the heat capacity is independent of temperature. Suppose, instead, that the heat capacity depends on temperature as $C = a + bT + a/T^2$. Find an expression for the change of entropy accompanying heating from T_i to T_f. (*Hint.* See Derivation 4.2.)

4.18 Calculate the change in entropy when 100 g of water at 80°C is poured into 100 g of water at 10°C in an insulated vessel given that $C_{p,m} = 75.5$ J K^{-1} mol^{-1}.

4.19 The enthalpy of the graphite → diamond phase transition, which under 100 kbar occurs at 2000 K, is +1.9 kJ mol^{-1}. Calculate the entropy of transition.

4.20 The enthalpy of vaporization of chloroform (trichloromethane), $CHCl_3$, is 29.4 kJ mol^{-1} at its normal boiling point of 334.88 K. (a) Calculate the entropy of vaporization of chloroform at this temperature. (b) What is the entropy change in the surroundings?

4.21 Calculate the entropy of fusion of a compound at 25°C given that its enthalpy of fusion is 32 kJ mol^{-1} at its melting point of 146°C and the molar heat capacities (at constant pressure) of the liquid and solid forms are 28 J K^{-1} mol^{-1} and 19 J K^{-1} mol^{-1}, respectively.

4.22 Octane is typical of the components of gasoline. Estimate (a) the entropy of vaporization, (b) the enthalpy of vaporization of octane, which boils at 126°C.

4.23 Calculate the standard reaction entropy at 298 K of

(a) $2\ CH_3CHO(g) + O_2(g) \rightarrow 2\ CH_3COOH(l)$

(b) $2\ AgCl(s) + Br_2(l) \rightarrow 2\ AgBr(s) + Cl_2(g)$

(c) $Hg(l) + Cl_2(g) \rightarrow HgCl_2(s)$

(d) $Zn(s) + Cu^{2+}(aq) \rightarrow Zn^{2+}(aq) + Cu(s)$

(e) $C_{12}H_{22}O_{11}(s) + 12\ O_2(g) \rightarrow 12\ CO_2(g) + 11\ H_2O(l)$

4.24 The constant-pressure molar heat capacities of linear gaseous molecules are approximately $\frac{7}{2}R$ and those of non-linear gaseous molecules are approximately $4R$. Estimate the change in standard reaction entropy of the following two reactions when the temperature is increased by 10 K at constant pressure:

(a) $2\ H_2(g) + O_2(g) \rightarrow 2\ H_2O(g)$

(b) $CH_4(g) + 2\ O_2(g) \rightarrow CO_2(g) + 2\ H_2O(g)$

4.25 Suppose that when you exercise, you consume 100 g of glucose and that all the energy released as heat remains in your body at 37°C. What is the change in entropy of your body? Use $\Delta_c H = -2808$ kJ mol^{-1}.

4.26 In a particular biological reaction taking place in the body at 37°C, the change in enthalpy was −125 kJ mol^{-1} and the change in entropy was −126 J K^{-1} mol^{-1}. (a) Calculate the change in Gibbs energy. (b) Is the reaction spontaneous? (c) Calculate the total change in entropy of the system and the surroundings.

4.27 The change in Gibbs energy that accompanies the oxidation of $C_6H_{12}O_6(s)$ to carbon dioxide and water vapour at 25°C is −2828 kJ mol^{-1}. How much glucose does a person of mass 65 kg need to consume to climb through 10 m?

4.28 The formation of glutamine from glutamate and ammonium ions requires 14.2 kJ mol^{-1} of energy input. It is driven by the hydrolysis of ATP to ADP mediated by the enzyme glutamine synthetase. (a) Given that the change in Gibbs energy for the hydrolysis of ATP corresponds to $\Delta G =$ −31 kJ mol^{-1} under the conditions prevailing in a typical cell, can the hydrolysis drive the formation of glutamine? (b) How many moles of ATP molecules must be hydrolysed to form 1 mol glutamine?

4.29 The hydrolysis of acetyl phosphate has $\Delta G = -42$ kJ mol^{-1} under typical biological conditions. If acetyl phosphate were to be synthesized by coupling to the hydrolysis of ATP, what is the minimum number of ATP molecules that would need to be involved for the formation of one acetyl phosphate molecule?

4.30 Suppose that the radius of a typical cell is 10 μm and that inside it 10^6 ATP molecules are hydrolysed each second. What is the power density of the cell in watts per cubic metre (1 W = 1 J s^{-1}). A computer battery delivers about 15 W and has a volume of 100 cm^3. Which has the greater power density, the cell or the battery? (For data, see Exercise 4.29.)

Chapter 5

Phase equilibria: pure substances

Boiling, freezing, and the conversion of graphite to diamond are all examples of **phase transitions**, or changes of phase without change of chemical composition. Many phase changes are common everyday phenomena and their description is an important part of physical chemistry. They occur whenever a solid changes into a liquid, as in the melting of ice, or a liquid changes into a vapour, as in the vaporization of water in our lungs. They also occur when one solid phase changes into another, as in the conversion of graphite into diamond under high pressure, or the conversion of one phase of iron into another as it is heated in the process of steel-making. The tendency of a substance to form a liquid crystal, a phase intermediate between solid and liquid, guides the design of displays for electronic devices. Phase changes are important geologically too; for example, calcium carbonate is typically deposited as aragonite, but then gradually changes into another crystal form, calcite.

The thermodynamics of transition

The Gibbs energy, $G = H - TS$, of a substance will be at centre stage in all that follows. We need to know how its value depends on the pressure and temperature. As we work out these dependencies, we shall acquire deep insight into the thermodynamic properties of matter and the transitions it can undergo.

5.1 The condition of stability

First, we need to establish the importance of the *molar* Gibbs energy, $G_m = G/n$, in the discussion of phase transitions of a pure substance. The molar Gibbs energy, an intensive property, depends on the phase of the substance. For instance, the molar Gibbs energy of liquid water is in general different from that of water vapour at the same temperature and pressure. When an amount n of the substance changes from phase 1 (for instance, liquid), with molar Gibbs energy $G_m(1)$, to phase 2 (for instance, vapour), with molar Gibbs energy $G_m(2)$, the change in Gibbs energy is

$$\Delta G = nG_m(2) - nG_m(1) = n\{G_m(2) - G_m(1)\}$$

We know that a spontaneous change at constant temperature and pressure is accompanied by a negative value of ΔG. This expression shows, therefore, that a change from phase 1 to phase 2 is spontaneous if the molar Gibbs energy of phase 2 is lower than that of phase 1. In other words, *a substance has a spontaneous tendency to change into the phase with the lowest molar Gibbs energy.*

If at a certain temperature and pressure the solid phase of a substance has a lower molar Gibbs energy than its liquid phase, then the solid phase is thermodynamically more stable and the liquid will (or at least has a tendency to) freeze. If the opposite is true, the liquid phase is thermodynamically more stable and the solid will melt. For example, at 1 atm, ice has a lower molar Gibbs energy than liquid water when the temperature is below 0°C, and under these conditions water converts spontaneously to ice.

Self-test 5.1

The Gibbs energy of transition from metallic white tin (α-Sn) to nonmetallic grey tin (β-Sn) is +0.13 kJ mol^{-1} at 298 K. Which is the reference state (Section 3.5) of tin at this temperature?

[*Answer:* white tin]

5.2 The variation of Gibbs energy with pressure

To discuss how phase transitions depend on the pressure, we need to know how the molar Gibbs energy varies with pressure. We show in Derivation 5.1 that when the temperature is held constant and the pressure is changed by a small amount Δp, the molar Gibbs energy of a substance changes by

$$\Delta G_m = V_m \Delta p \qquad (5.1)$$

where V_m is the molar volume of the substance. This expression is valid when the molar volume is constant in the pressure range of interest.

Derivation 5.1

The variation of the Gibbs energy with pressure

We start with the definition of Gibbs energy, $G = H - TS$, and change the temperature, volume, and pressure by an infinitesimal amount. As a result, H changes to $H + dH$. T changes to $T + dT$, S changes to $S + dS$, and G changes to $G + dG$. After the change

$$G + dG = H + dH - (T + dT)(S + dS)$$
$$= H + dH - TS - T\,dS - S\,dT - dT\,dS$$

The G on the left cancels the $H - TS$ on the right, the doubly infinitesimal $dTdS$ can be neglected, and we are left with

$$dG = dH - T\,dS - S\,dT$$

To make progress, we need to know how the enthalpy changes. From its definition $H = U + pV$, in a similar way (letting U change to $U + dU$, and so on, and neglecting the doubly infinitesimal term $dpdV$) we can write

$$dH = dU + p\,dV + V\,dp$$

At this point we need to know how the internal energy changes, and write

$$dU = dq + dw$$

If initially we consider only reversible changes, we can replace dq by $T\,dS$ (because $dS = dq_{rev}/T$) and dw by $-p\,dV$ (because $dw = -p_{ex}\,dV$ and $p_{ex} = p$ for a reversible change), and obtain

$$dU = T\,dS - p\,dV$$

Now we substitute this expression into the expression for dH and that expression into the expression for dG and obtain

$$dG = T\,dS - p\,dV + p\,dV + V\,dp - T\,dS - S\,dT$$
$$= V\,dp - S\,dT$$

Now here is a subtle but important point. To derive this result we have supposed that the changes in conditions have been made reversibly. However, G is a state function, and so the change in its value is independent of path. Therefore, the expression is valid for any change, not just a reversible change.

At this point we decide to keep the temperature constant, and set $dT = 0$; this leaves $dG = V dp$ and, for molar quantities, $dG_m = V_m dp$. This expression is exact, but applies only to an infinitesimal change in the pressure. For an observable change, we replace dG_m and dp by ΔG_m and Δp, respectively, and obtain eqn 5.1, provided the molar volume is constant over the range of interest.

A note on good practice. When confronted with a proof in thermodynamics, go back to fundamental definitions (as we did three times in succession in this derivation: first of G, then of H, and finally of U).

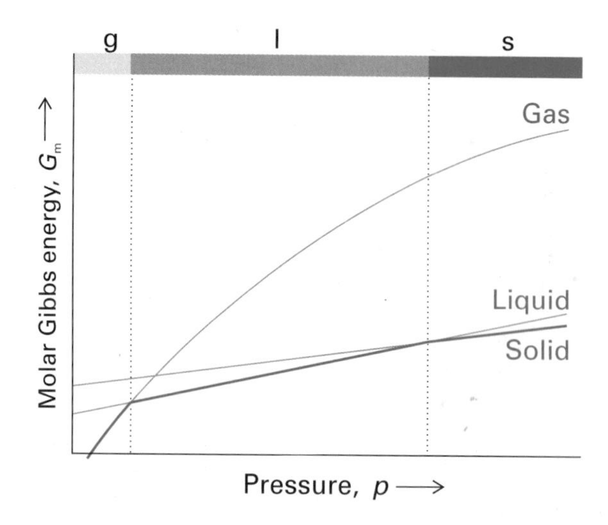

Fig. 5.1 The variation of molar Gibbs energy with pressure. The region where the molar Gibbs energy of a particular phase is least is shown by a dark line and the corresponding region of stability of each phase is indicated in the band at the top of the illustration.

Equation 5.1 tells us that, because all molar volumes are positive, *the molar Gibbs energy increases* ($\Delta G_m > 0$) *when the pressure increases* ($\Delta p > 0$). We also see that, for a given change in pressure, the resulting change in molar Gibbs energy is greatest for substances with large molar volumes. Therefore, because the molar volume of a gas is much larger than that of a condensed phase (a liquid or a solid), the dependence of G_m on p is much greater for a gas than for a condensed phase. For most substances (water is an important exception), the molar volume of the liquid phase is greater than that of the solid phase. Therefore, for most substances, the slope of a graph of G_m against p is greater for a liquid than for a solid. These characteristics are illustrated in Fig. 5.1.

As we see from Fig. 5.1, when we increase the pressure on a substance, the molar Gibbs energy of the gas phase rises above that of the liquid, then the molar Gibbs energy of the liquid rises above that of the solid. Because the system has a tendency to convert into the state of lowest molar Gibbs energy, the graphs show that at low pressures the gas phase is the most stable, then at higher pressures the liquid phase becomes the most stable, followed by the solid phase. In other words, under pressure the substance condenses to a liquid, and then further pressure can result in the formation of a solid.

We can use eqn 5.1 to predict the actual shape of graphs like those in Fig. 5.1. For a solid or liquid, the molar volume is almost independent of pressure, so eqn 5.1 is an excellent approximation to the change in molar Gibbs energy and with $\Delta G_m = G_m(p_f) - G_m(p_i)$ and $\Delta p = p_f - p_i$ we can write

$$G_m(p_f) = G_m(p_i) + V_m(p_f - p_i) \qquad (5.2a)$$

This equation shows that the molar Gibbs energy of a solid or liquid increases linearly with pressure. However, because the molar volume of a condensed phase is so small, the dependence is very weak, and for the typical ranges of pressure normally of interest to us we can ignore the pressure dependence of G. The molar Gibbs energy of a gas, however, does depend on the pressure, and because the molar volume of a gas is large, the dependence is significant. We show in Derivation 5.2 that

$$G_m(p_f) = G_m(p_i) + RT \ln \frac{p_f}{p_i} \qquad (5.2b)$$

This equation shows that the molar Gibbs energy increases logarithmically (as $\ln p$) with the pressure (Fig. 5.2). The flattening of the curve at high pressures reflects the fact that as V_m gets smaller, G_m becomes less responsive to pressure.

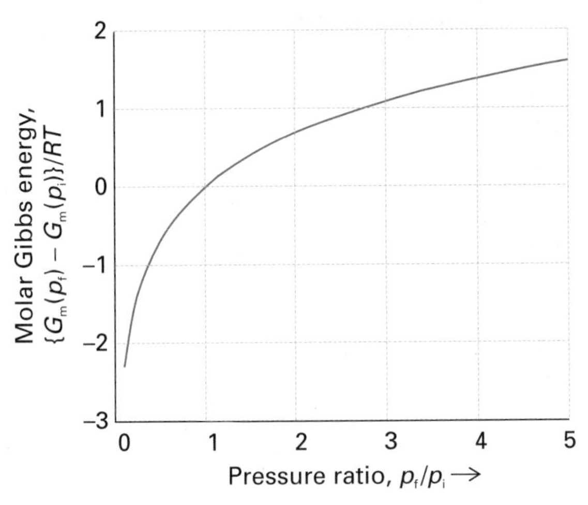

Fig. 5.2 The variation of the molar Gibbs energy of a perfect gas with pressure.

Derivation 5.2

The pressure variation of the Gibbs energy of a perfect gas

We start with the exact expression for the effect of an infinitesimal change in pressure obtained in Derivation 5.1, that $dG_m = V_m\,dp$. For a change in pressure from p_i to p_f, we need to add together (integrate) all these infinitesimal changes, and write

$$\Delta G_m = \int_{p_i}^{p_f} V_m\,dp$$

To evaluate the integral, we must know how the molar volume depends on the pressure. For a perfect gas $V_m = RT/p$. Then

Perfect gas — Constant temperature

$$\Delta G_m = \int_{p_i}^{p_f} V_m\,dp = \int_{p_i}^{p_f} \frac{RT}{p}\,dp = RT\int_{p_i}^{p_f} \frac{dp}{p}$$

$$= RT \ln \frac{p_f}{p_i}$$

We have used the standard integral described in Derivation 2.2. Finally, with $\Delta G_m = G_m(p_f) - G_m(p_i)$, we get eqn 5.2b.

5.3 The variation of Gibbs energy with temperature

Now we consider how the molar Gibbs energy varies with temperature. For small changes in temperature, the change in molar Gibbs energy at constant pressure is

$$\Delta G_m = -S_m\,\Delta T \qquad (5.3)$$

where $\Delta G_m = G_m(T_f) - G_m(T_i)$ and $\Delta T = T_f - T_i$. This expression is valid provided the entropy of the substance is unchanged over the range of temperatures of interest.

Derivation 5.3

The variation of the Gibbs energy with temperature

The starting point for this short derivation is the expression obtained in Derivation 5.1 for the change in molar Gibbs energy when both the pressure and the temperature are changed by infinitesimal amounts:

$$dG_m = V_m\,dp - S_m\,dT$$

If we hold the pressure constant, $dp = 0$, and

$$dG_m = -S_m\,dT$$

This expression is exact. If we suppose that the molar entropy is unchanged in the range of temperatures of interest, we can replace the infinitesimal changes by observable changes, and so obtain eqn 5.3.

Equation 5.3 tells us that, because molar entropy is positive, *an increase in temperature* ($\Delta T > 0$) *results in a decrease in* G_m ($\Delta G_m < 0$). We see that for a given change of temperature, the change in molar Gibbs energy is proportional to the molar entropy. For a given substance, there is more spatial disorder in the gas phase than in a condensed phase, so the molar entropy of the gas phase is greater than that for a condensed phase. It follows that the molar Gibbs energy falls more steeply with temperature for a gas than for a condensed phase. The molar entropy of the liquid phase of a substance is greater than that of its solid phase, so the slope is least steep for a solid. Figure 5.3 summarizes these characteristics.

Figure 5.3 also reveals the thermodynamic reason why substances melt and vaporize as the temperature

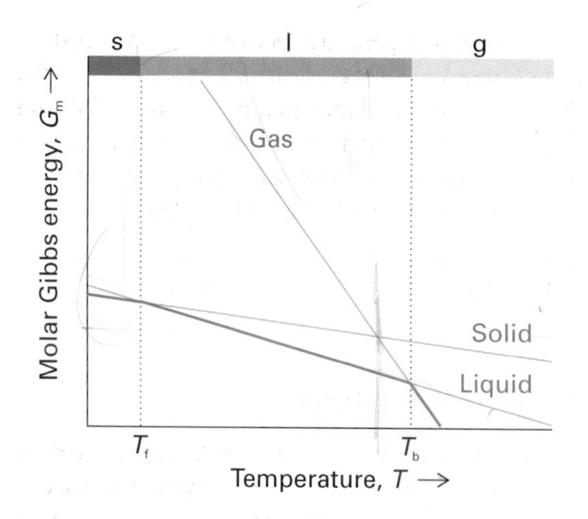

Fig. 5.3 The variation of molar Gibbs energy with temperature. All molar Gibbs energies decrease with increasing temperature. The regions of temperature over which the solid, liquid, and gaseous forms of a substance have the lowest molar Gibbs energy are indicated in the band at the top of the illustration.

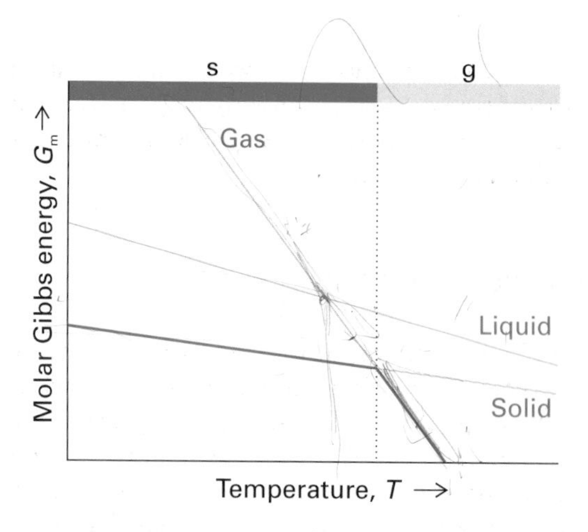

Fig. 5.4 If the line for the Gibbs energy of the liquid phase does not cut through the line for the solid phase (at a given pressure) before the line for the gas phase cuts through the line for the solid, the liquid is not stable at any temperature at that pressure. Such a substance sublimes.

is raised. At low temperatures, the solid phase has the lowest molar Gibbs energy and is therefore the most stable. However, as the temperature is raised, the molar Gibbs energy of the liquid phase falls below that of the solid phase, and the substance melts. At even higher temperatures, the molar Gibbs energy of the gas phase plunges down below that of the liquid phase, and the gas becomes the most stable phase. In other words, above a certain temperature, the liquid vaporizes to a gas.

We can also start to understand why some substances, such as carbon dioxide, sublime to a vapour without first forming a liquid. There is no fundamental requirement for the three lines to lie exactly in the positions we have drawn them in Fig. 5.3: the liquid line, for instance, could lie where we have drawn it in Fig. 5.4. Now we see that at no temperature (at the given pressure) does the liquid phase have the lowest molar Gibbs energy. Such a substance converts spontaneously directly from the solid to the vapour. That is, the substance sublimes.

The **transition temperature** between two phases, such as between liquid and solid or between ordered and disordered states of a protein, is the temperature, at a given pressure, at which the molar Gibbs energies of the two phases are equal. Above the solid–liquid transition temperature the liquid phase is thermodynamically more stable; below it, the solid phase is more stable. For example, at 1 atm, the transition temperature for ice and liquid water is 0°C and that for grey and white tin is 13°C. At the transition temperature itself, the molar Gibbs energies of the two phases are identical and there is no tendency for either phase to change into the other. At this temperature, therefore, the two phases are in equilibrium. At 1 atm, ice and liquid water are in equilibrium at 0°C and the two allotropes of tin are in equilibrium at 13°C.

As always when using thermodynamic arguments, it is important to keep in mind the distinction between the spontaneity of a phase transition and its rate. *Spontaneity is a tendency, not necessarily an actuality.* A phase transition predicted to be spontaneous may occur so slowly as to be unimportant in practice. For instance, at normal temperatures and pressures the molar Gibbs energy of graphite is 3 kJ mol^{-1} lower than that of diamond, so there is a thermodynamic tendency for diamond to convert into graphite. However, for this transition to take place, the carbon atoms of diamond must change their locations, and because the bonds between the atoms are so strong and large numbers of bonds must change simultaneously, this process is unmeasurably slow except at high temperatures. In gases and liquids the mobilities of the molecules normally allow phase transitions to occur rapidly, but in solids thermodynamic instability may be frozen in and a thermodynamically unstable phase may persist for thousands of years.

Phase diagrams

The **phase diagram** of a substance is a map showing the conditions of temperature and pressure at which its various phases are thermodynamically most stable (Fig. 5.5). For example, at point A in the illustration, the vapour phase of the substance is thermodynamically the most stable, but at C the liquid phase is the most stable.

The boundaries between regions in a phase diagram are called **phase boundaries**; they show the values of p and T at which the two neighbouring phases are in equilibrium. For example, if the system is arranged to have a pressure and temperature represented by point B, then the liquid and its vapour are in equilibrium (like liquid water and water vapour at 1 atm and 100°C). If the temperature is reduced at constant pressure, the system moves to point C where the liquid is stable (like water at 1 atm and at temperatures between 0°C and 100°C). If the temperature is reduced still further to D, then the solid and the liquid phases are in equilibrium (like ice and water at 1 atm and 0°C). A further reduction in temperature takes the system into the region where the solid is the stable phase.

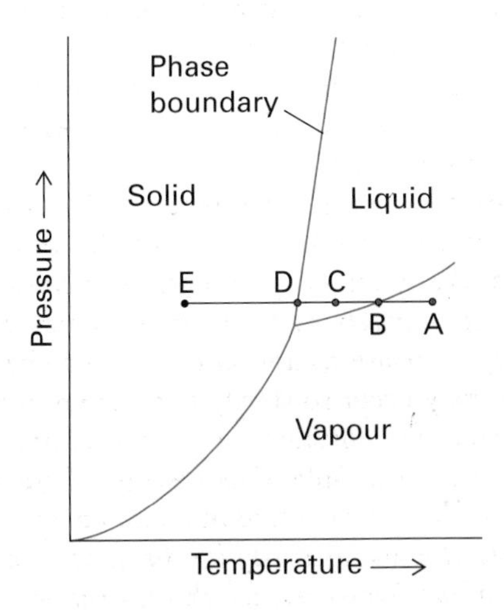

Fig. 5.5 A typical phase diagram, showing the regions of pressure and temperature at which each phase is the most stable. The phase boundaries (three are shown here) show the values of pressure and temperature at which the two phases separated by the line are in equilibrium. The significance of the letters A, B, C, D, and E (also referred to in Fig. 5.8) is explained in the text.

The text's web site contains links to online databases of data on phase transitions.

5.4 Phase boundaries

The pressure of the vapour in equilibrium with its condensed phase is called the **vapour pressure** of the substance. Vapour pressure increases with temperature because, as the temperature is raised, more molecules have sufficient energy to leave their neighbours in the liquid.

The liquid–vapour boundary in a phase diagram is a plot of the vapour pressure against temperature. To determine the boundary, we can introduce a liquid into the near vacuum at the top of a mercury barometer and measure by how much the column is depressed (Fig. 5.6). To ensure that the pressure exerted by the vapour is truly the vapour pressure, we have to add enough liquid for some to remain after the vapour forms, as only then are the liquid and vapour phases in equilibrium. We can change the temperature and determine another point on the curve, and so on (Fig. 5.7).

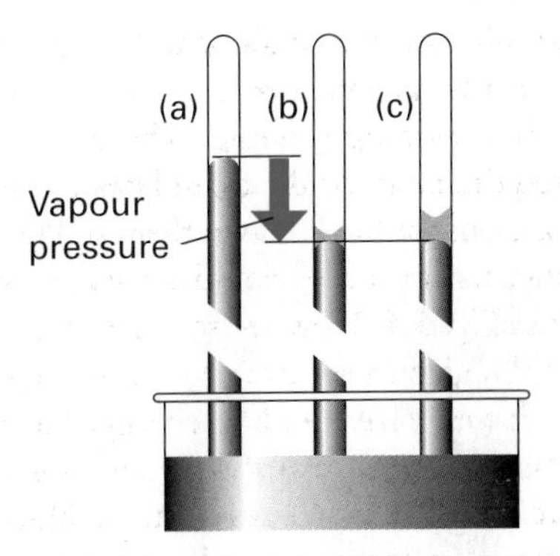

Fig. 5.6 When a small volume of water is introduced into the vacuum above the mercury in a barometer (a), the mercury is depressed (b) by an amount that is proportional to the vapour pressure of the liquid. (c) The same pressure is observed however much liquid is present (provided some is present).

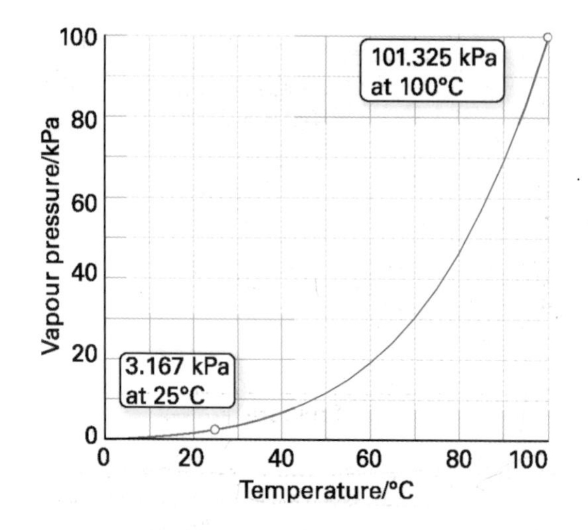

Fig. 5.7 The experimental variation of the vapour pressure of water with temperature.

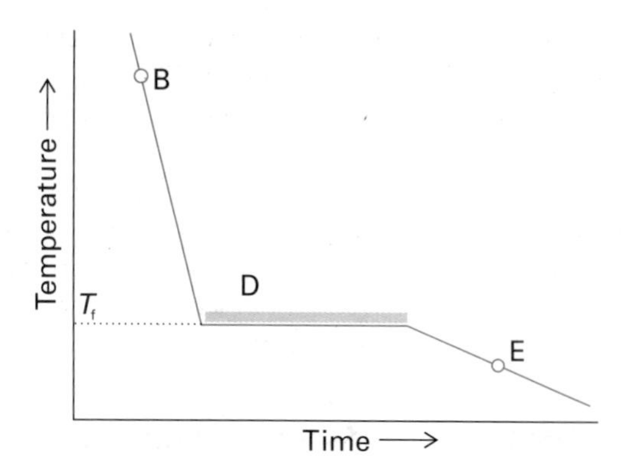

Fig. 5.8 The cooling curve for the B–E section of the horizontal line in Fig. 5.5. The halt at D corresponds to the pause in cooling while the liquid freezes and releases its enthalpy of transition. The halt lets us locate T_f even if the transition cannot be observed visually.

Now suppose we have a liquid in a cylinder fitted with a piston. If we apply a pressure greater than the vapour pressure of the liquid, the vapour is eliminated, the piston rests on the surface of the liquid, and the system moves to one of the points in the 'liquid' region of the phase diagram. Only a single phase is present. If instead we reduce the pressure on the system to a value below the vapour pressure, the system moves to one of the points in the 'vapour' region of the diagram. Reducing the pressure will involve pulling out the piston a long way, so that all the liquid evaporates; while any liquid is present, the pressure in the system remains constant at the vapour pressure of the liquid.

Self-test 5.2

What would be observed when a pressure of 7.0 kPa is applied to a sample of water in equilibrium with its vapour at 25°C, when its vapour pressure is 3.2 kPa?

[*Answer:* the sample condenses entirely to liquid]

The same approach can be used to plot the solid–vapour boundary, which is a graph of the vapour pressure of the solid against temperature. The **sublimation vapour pressure** of a solid, the pressure of the vapour in equilibrium with a solid at a particular temperature, is usually much lower than that of a liquid.

A more sophisticated procedure is needed to determine the locations of solid–solid phase boundaries like that between calcite and aragonite, for instance, because the transition between two solid phases is more difficult to detect. One approach is to use **thermal analysis**, which takes advantage of the heat released during a transition. In a typical thermal analysis experiment, a sample is allowed to cool and its temperature is monitored. When the transition occurs, energy is released as heat and the cooling stops until the transition is complete (Fig. 5.8). The transition temperature is obvious from the shape of the graph and is used to mark a point on the phase diagram. The pressure can then be changed, and the corresponding transition temperature determined.

Any point lying on a phase boundary represents a pressure and temperature at which there is a 'dynamic equilibrium' between the two adjacent phases. A state of **dynamic equilibrium** is one in which a reverse process is taking place at the same rate as the forward process. Although there may be a great deal of activity at a molecular level, there is no net change in the bulk properties or appearance of the sample. For example, any point on the liquid–vapour boundary represents a state of dynamic equilibrium in which vaporization and condensation continue at matching rates. Molecules are leaving the surface of the liquid at a certain rate, and molecules already in the gas phase are returning to the liquid at the same rate; as a result, there in no net change in the number of molecules in the vapour and hence no net change in its pressure. Similarly, a point on the solid–liquid curve represents conditions of pressure and temperature at which molecules are ceaselessly breaking away from the surface of the solid and contributing to the liquid. However, they are doing so at a rate that exactly matches that at which molecules already in the liquid are settling on to the surface of the solid and contributing to the solid phase.

5.5 The location of phase boundaries

Thermodynamics provides us with a way of predicting the location of the phase boundaries. Suppose two phases are in equilibrium at a given pressure and temperature. Then, if we change the pressure, we must adjust the temperature to a different value to ensure that the two phases remain in equilibrium. In other words, there must be a relation between the change in pressure, Δp, that we exert and the change in temperature, ΔT, we must make to ensure that the two phases remain in equilibrium. The relation between the change in temperature and the change in pressure needed to maintain equilibrium is given by the **Clapeyron equation:**

$$\Delta p = \frac{\Delta_{trs}H}{T\Delta_{trs}V} \times \Delta T \qquad (5.4a)$$

where $\Delta_{trs}S$ is the entropy of transition and $\Delta_{trs}V$ is the volume of transition (the change in molar volume when the transition occurs). This form of the Clapeyron equation is valid for small changes in pressure and temperature.

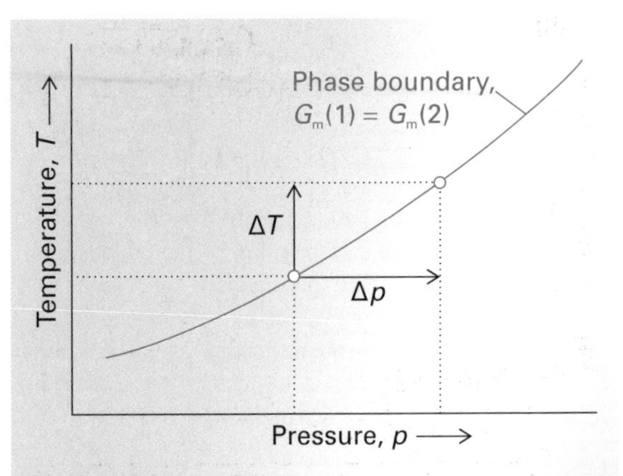

Fig. 5.9 At equilibrium, two phases have the same molar Gibbs energy. When the temperature is changed, for the two phases to remain in equilibrium, the pressure must be changed so that the Gibbs energies of the two phases remain equal.

Derivation 5.4

The Clapeyron equation

This derivation is also based on the relation obtained in Derivation 5.1, that for infinitesimal changes in pressure and temperature, the molar Gibbs energy changes by $dG_m = V_m\,dp - S_m\,dT$.

Consider two phases 1 (for instance, a liquid) and 2 (a vapour). At a certain pressure and temperature the two phases are in equilibrium and $G_m(1) = G_m(2)$, where $G_m(1)$ is the molar Gibbs energy of phase 1 and $G_m(2)$ that of phase 2 (Fig. 5.9). Now change the pressure by an infinitesimal amount dp and the temperature by dT. The molar Gibbs energies of each phase change as follows:

$$dG_m(1) = V_m(1)\,dp - S_m(1)\,dT$$
$$dG_m(2) = V_m(2)\,dp - S_m(2)\,dT$$

where $V_m(1)$ and $S_m(1)$ are the molar volume and molar entropy of phase 1 and $V_m(2)$ and $S_m(2)$ are those of phase 2. The two phases were in equilibrium before the change, so the two molar Gibbs energies were equal. The two phases are still in equilibrium after the pressure and temperature are changed, so their two molar Gibbs energies are still equal. Therefore, the two *changes* in molar Gibbs energy must be equal, $dG_m(1) = dG_m(2)$, and we can write

$$V_m(1)\,dp - S_m(1)\,dT = V_m(2)\,dp - S_m(2)\,dT$$

This equation can be rearranged to

$$\{V_m(2) - V_m(1)\}\,dp = \{S_m(2) - S_m(1)\}\,dT$$

The entropy of transition, $\Delta_{trs}S$, is the difference between the two molar entropies, and the volume of transition, $\Delta_{trs}V$, is the difference between the molar volumes of the two phases:

$$\Delta_{trs}V = V_m(2) - V_m(1) \qquad \Delta_{trs}S = S_m(2) - S_m(1)$$

We can therefore write

$$\Delta_{trs}V\,dp = \Delta_{trs}S\,dT$$

We saw in Chapter 4 that the transition entropy is related to the enthalpy of transition by $\Delta_{trs}S = \Delta_{trs}H/T_{trs}$, so

$$T\Delta_{trs}V\,dp = \Delta_{trs}H\,dT$$

We have dropped the 'trs' subscript from the temperature because all the points on the phase boundary—the only points we are considering—are transition temperatures. For small variations in pressure and temperature, the infinitesimal changes can be replaced by observable changes, and we obtain eqn 5.4a. For future reference, the thermodynamically exact form of the Clapeyron equation is

$$\frac{dp}{dT} = \frac{\Delta_{trs}H}{T\Delta_{trs}V} \quad (5.4b)$$

The Clapeyron equation tells us the slope (the value of $\Delta p/\Delta T$) of any phase boundary in terms of the enthalpy and volume of transition. For the solid–liquid phase boundary, the enthalpy of transition is the enthalpy of fusion, which is positive because melting is always endothermic. For most substances, the molar volume increases slightly on melting, so $\Delta_{trs}V$ is positive but small. It follows that the slope of the phase boundary is large and positive (up from left to right), and therefore that a large increase in pressure brings about only a small increase in melting temperature. Water, however, is quite different, for although its melting is endothermic, its molar volume decreases on melting (liquid water is denser than ice at 0°C, which is why ice floats on water), so $\Delta_{trs}V$ is small but negative. Consequently, the slope of the ice–water phase boundary is steep but negative (down from left to right). Now a large increase in pressure brings about a small lowering of the melting temperature of ice.

We cannot use eqn 5.4a to discuss the liquid–vapour phase boundary, except over very small ranges of temperature and pressure, because we cannot assume that the volume of the vapour, and therefore the volume of transition, is independent of pressure. However, if we suppose that the vapour behaves as a perfect gas, then it turns out (see Derivation 5.5) that the relation between a change in pressure and a change in temperature is given by the **Clausius–Clapeyron equation:**

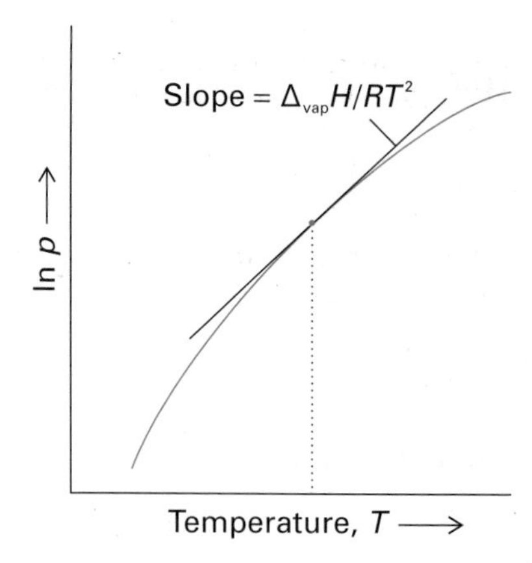

Fig. 5.10 The Clausius–Clapeyron equation gives the slope of a plot of the logarithm of the vapour pressure of a substance against the temperature. That slope at a given temperature is proportional to the enthalpy of vaporization of the substance.

$$\Delta(\ln p) = \frac{\Delta_{vap}H}{RT^2} \times \Delta T \quad (5.5)$$

The Clausius–Clapeyron equation is an approximate equation for the slope of a plot of the logarithm of the vapor pressure against temperature ($\Delta(\ln p)/\Delta T$, Fig. 5.10). Moreover, it follows from eqn 5.5 that the vapour pressure p' at a temperature T' is related to the vapour pressure p at a temperature T by

$$\ln p' = \ln p + \frac{\Delta_{vap}H}{R}\left(\frac{1}{T} - \frac{1}{T'}\right) \quad (5.6)$$

Derivation 5.5

The Clausius–Clapeyron equation

For the liquid–vapour boundary the 'trs' label in the exact form of the Clapeyron equation, eqn 5.4b in Derivation 5.4, becomes 'vap':

$$\frac{dp}{dT} = \frac{\Delta_{vap}H}{T\Delta_{vap}V}$$

Because the molar volume of a gas is much larger than the molar volume of a liquid, the volume of vaporization, $\Delta_{vap}V = V_m(g) - V_m(l)$, is approximately equal to the molar volume of the gas itself. Therefore, to a good approximation,

$$\frac{dp}{dT} = \frac{\Delta_{vap}H}{TV_m(g)}$$

To make further progress, we can treat the vapour as a perfect gas and write its molar volume as $V_m = RT/p$. Then

$$\frac{dp}{dT} = \frac{\Delta_{vap}H}{T(RT/p)} = \frac{p\Delta_{vap}H}{RT^2}$$

Upon dividing both sides by p and using $dp/p = d \ln p$, we obtain the Clausius–Clapeyron equation:

$$\frac{d \ln p}{dT} = \frac{\Delta_{vap}H}{RT^2}$$

 A standard result of calculus is

$$\frac{d \ln x}{dx} = \frac{1}{x}$$

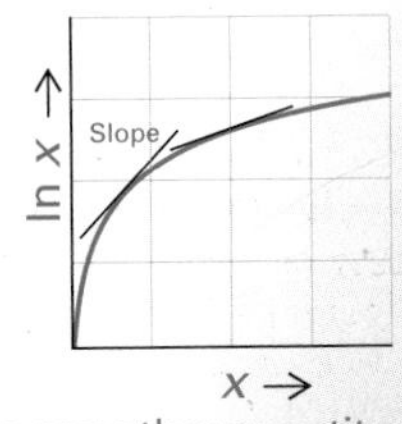

This relation tells us that the slope of a graph of $\ln x$ against x decreases as x increases, as shown here. Because infinitesimally small quantities are treated like any other quantity in algebraic manipulations (see Derivation 4.2), we may rearrange this expression into $dx/x = d \ln x$.

Provided the range of temperature and pressure is small, the infinitesimal changes $d \ln p$ and dT can be replaced by measurable changes, and we obtain eqn 5.5.

To obtain the explicit expression for the vapour pressure at any temperature (eqn 5.6) we rearrange the equation we have just derived into

$$d \ln p = \frac{\Delta_{vap}H}{RT^2} dT$$

and integrate both sides. If the vapour pressure is p at a temperature T and p' at a temperature T', this integration takes the form

$$\int_{\ln p}^{\ln p'} d \ln p = \int_T^{T'} \frac{\Delta_{vap}H}{RT^2} dT$$

A note on good practice When setting up an integration, make sure the limits match on each side of the expression. Here, the lower limits are $\ln p$ on the left and T on the right, and the upper limits are $\ln p'$ and T', respectively.

The integral on the left evaluates to $\ln p' - \ln p$, which simplifies to $\ln(p'/p)$. To evaluate the integral on the right, we suppose that the enthalpy of vaporization is constant over the temperature range of interest, so together with R it can be taken outside the integral:

$$\ln \frac{p'}{p} = \frac{\Delta_{vap}H}{R} \int_T^{T'} \frac{1}{T^2} dT = \frac{\Delta_{vap}H}{R}\left(\frac{1}{T} - \frac{1}{T'}\right)$$

which is eqn 5.6. To obtain this result we have used the standard integral

$$\int \frac{dx}{x^2} = -\frac{1}{x} + \text{constant}$$

A note on good practice. Keep a note of any approximations made in a derivation. In this lengthy pair of derivations we have made three: (1) the molar volume of a gas is much greater than that of a liquid, (2) the vapour behaves as a perfect gas, (3) the enthalpy of vaporization is independent of temperature in the range of interest. Approximations limit the ways in which an expression may be used to solve problems.

Equation 5.5 shows that as the temperature of a liquid is raised ($\Delta T > 0$), its vapour pressure increases (an increase in the logarithm of p, $\Delta(\ln p) > 0$, implies that p increases). Equation 5.6 lets us calculate the vapour pressure at one temperature provided we know it at another temperature. The equation tells us that, for a given change in temperature, the larger the enthalpy of vaporization, the greater the change in vapour pressure. The vapour pressure of water, for instance, responds more sharply to a change in temperature than that of benzene does. Note too that we can rearrange eqn 5.6 into the form

$$\log p = A - \frac{B}{T} \tag{5.7}$$

where A and B are constants.[1] This is the form in which vapour pressures are commonly reported (Table 5.1 and Fig. 5.11).

Example 5.1

Interpreting an empirical expression

The vapour pressure of benzene in the range 0–42°C can be expressed in the form of eqn 5.7:

$$\log(p/\text{kPa}) = 7.0871 - \frac{1785\ \text{K}}{T}$$

What is the enthalpy of vaporization of liquid benzene?

Strategy Compare eqns 5.6 and 5.7 to identify the values of A and B in terms of the quantities that appear in eqn 5.6, then use the values given here to solve for $\Delta_{vap}H$.

[1] The value of A depends on the units adopted for p.

Table 5.1 *Vapour pressure**

Substance	A	B/K	Temperature range/°C
Benzene, C_6H_6(l)	7.0871	1785	0 to +42
	6.7795	1687	42 to 100
Hexane, C_6H_{14}(l)	6.849	1655	−10 to +90
Methanol, CH_3OH(l)	7.927	2002	−10 to +80
Methylbenzene, $C_6H_5CH_3$(l)	7.455	2047	−92 to +15
Phosphorus, P_4(s, white)	8.776	3297	20 to 44
Sulfur trioxide, SO_3(l)	9.147	2269	24 to 48
Tetrachloromethane, CCl_4(l)	7.129	1771	−19 to +20

* A and B are the constants in the expression $\log(p/\text{kPa}) = A - B/T$.

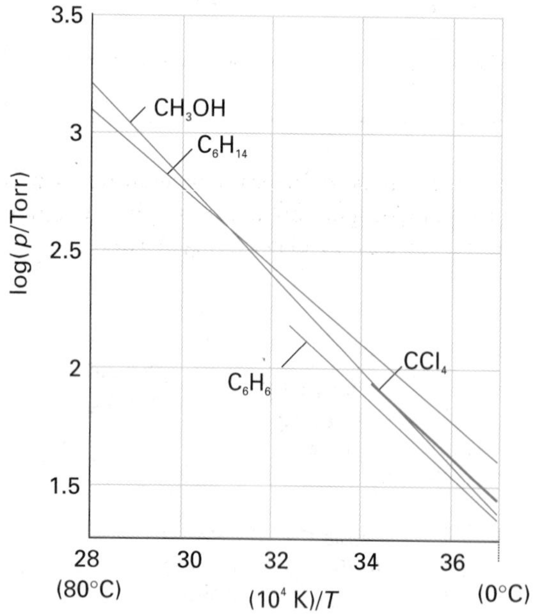

Fig. 5.11 The vapour pressures of some substances based on the data in Table 5.1.

Solution We begin by writing eqn 5.6 as

$$\ln\frac{p}{p'} = \ln\left(\frac{p}{\text{kPa}}\frac{\text{kPa}}{p'}\right) = \ln\left(\frac{p}{\text{kPa}}\right) - \ln\left(\frac{p'}{\text{kPa}}\right)$$

$$= \frac{\Delta_{\text{vap}}H}{RT'} - \frac{\Delta_{\text{vap}}H}{RT}$$

A note on good practice. It is meaningless to take the logarithm of a quantity with units: note how in the first step we have expressed pressures in dimensionless form (as p/kPa), where the choice of pressure units is arbitrary, and then separated the logarithm using $\ln(x/y) = \ln x - \ln y$, with x and y both dimensionless numbers. Writing $\ln(p/p') = \ln p - \ln p'$ is only a formal manipulation.

Next, because $\ln x = \ln 10 \times \log x$ (where $\log x$ is a logarithm to base 10), we can write (by dividing through by ln 10)

$$\log\frac{p}{\text{kPa}} = \log\frac{p'}{\text{kPa}} + \frac{\Delta_{\text{vap}}H}{RT'\ln 10} - \frac{\Delta_{\text{vap}}H}{RT\ln 10}$$

This expression has the form of eqn 5.7 with p in kilopascals if we make the following identifications:

$$A = \ln\frac{p'}{\text{kPa}} + \frac{\Delta_{\text{vap}}H}{RT'\ln 10} \qquad B = \frac{\Delta_{\text{vap}}H}{R\ln 10}$$

We infer that, because $B = 1785$ K,

$$\Delta_{\text{vap}}H = BR\ln 10$$
$$= (1785\text{ K}) \times (8.3145\text{ J K}^{-1}\text{ mol}^{-1}) \times \ln 10$$
$$= 34.2\text{ kJ mol}^{-1}$$

A note on good practice. You will sometimes see the equation in the question written without units, or with the units in parentheses. It is much better practice to include the units in such a way as to make all the quantities unitless: p/kPa is a dimensionless number. You will also often see ln 10 replaced by its numerical value, which is approximately 2.303; however, to keep the expressions more accurate and to avoid rounding errors, it is better to keep it as ln 10 and to enter that value into your calculator.

Self-test 5.3

For benzene in the range 42–100°C, B = 1687 K and A = 6.7795. Estimate the normal boiling point of benzene. (The normal boiling point is the temperature at which the vapour pressure is 1 atm; see below.)

[*Answer:* 80.2°C; the actual value is 80.1°C]

5.6 Characteristic points

As we have seen, as the temperature of a liquid is raised, its vapour pressure increases. First, consider what we would observe when we heat a liquid in an open vessel. At a certain temperature, the vapour pressure becomes equal to the external pressure. At this temperature, the vapour can drive back the surrounding atmosphere and expand indefinitely. Moreover, because there is no constraint on expansion, bubbles of vapour can form throughout the body of the liquid, a condition known as **boiling**. The temperature at which the vapour pressure of a liquid is equal to the external pressure is called the **boiling temperature**. When the external pressure is 1 atm, the boiling temperature is called the **normal boiling point**, T_b. It follows that we can predict the normal boiling point of a liquid by noting the temperature on the phase diagram at which its vapour pressure is 1 atm.[2]

Now consider what happens when we heat the liquid in a closed vessel. Because the vapour cannot escape, its density increases as the vapour pressure rises and in due course the density of the vapour becomes equal to that of the remaining liquid. At this stage the surface between the two phases disappears, as was depicted in Fig. 1.14. The temperature at which the surface disappears is the critical temperature, T_c, which we first encountered in Section 1.10. The vapour pressure at the critical temperature is called the **critical pressure**, p_c, and the critical temperature and critical pressure together identify the **critical point** of the substance (see Table 5.2). If we exert pressure on a sample that is above its critical temperature, we produce a denser fluid. However, no surface appears to separate the two parts of the sample and a single uniform phase, a supercritical fluid, continues to fill the container (Box 5.1). That is, we have to conclude that *a liquid cannot be produced by the application of pressure to a substance if it is at or above its critical temperature*. That is why the liquid–vapour boundary in a phase diagram terminates at the critical point (Fig. 5.12).

Table 5.2
*Critical constants**

	p_c/atm	V_c/(cm^3 mol^{-1})	T_c/K
Ammonia, NH_3	111	73	406
Argon, Ar	48	75	151
Benzene, C_6H_6	49	260	563
Bromine, Br_2	102	135	584
Carbon dioxide, CO_2	73	94	304
Chlorine, Cl_2	76	124	417
Ethane, C_2H_6	48	148	305
Ethene, C_2H_4	51	124	283
Hydrogen, H_2	13	65	33
Methane, CH_4	46	99	191
Oxygen, O_2	50	78	155
Water, H_2O	218	55	647

* The critical volume, V_c, is the molar volume at the critical pressure and critical volume.

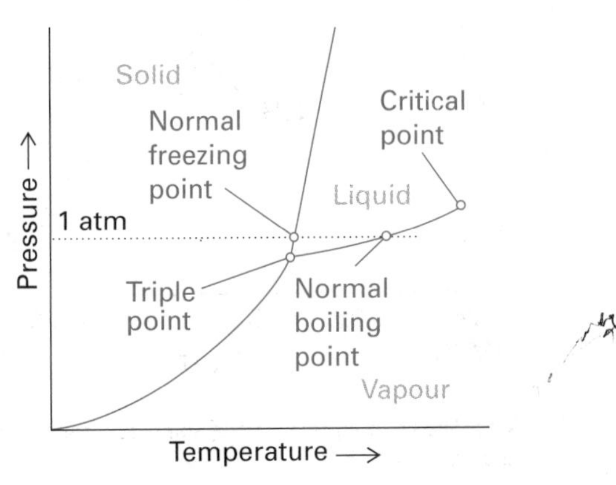

Fig. 5.12 The significant points of a phase diagram. The liquid–vapour phase boundary terminates at the *critical point*. At the *triple point*, solid, liquid, and vapour are in dynamic equilibrium. The *normal freezing point* is the temperature at which the liquid freezes when the pressure is 1 atm; the *normal boiling point* is the temperature at which the vapour pressure of the liquid is 1 atm.

[2] The use of 1 atm in the definition of normal boiling point rather than 1 bar is historical. The boiling temperature at 1 bar is called the *standard boiling point*.

Box 5.1 *Supercritical fluids*

Supercritical carbon dioxide, $scCO_2$, is the centre of attention for an increasing number of solvent-based processes. The critical temperature 304.2 K (31.0°C) and pressure (72.9 atm) are readily accessible and carbon dioxide is cheap. The density of $scCO_2$ at its critical point is 0.45 g cm^{-3}. However, the transport properties of any supercritical fluid depend strongly on its density, which in turn is sensitive to the pressure and temperature. For instance, densities may be adjusted from a gas-like 0.1 g cm^{-3} to a liquid-like 1.2 g cm^{-3}. A useful rule of thumb is that the solubility of a solute is an exponential function of the density of the supercritical fluid, so small increases in pressure, particularly close to the critical point, can have very large effects on solubility.

A great advantage of $scCO_2$ is that there are no noxious residues once the solvent has been allowed to evaporate, so, coupled with its low critical temperature, $scCO_2$ is ideally suited to food processing and the production of pharmaceuticals. It is used, for instance, to remove caffeine from coffee. The supercritical fluid is also increasingly being used for dry cleaning, which avoids the use of carcinogenic and environmentally deleterious chlorinated hydrocarbons.

Supercritical CO_2 has been used since the 1960s as a mobile phase in *supercritical fluid chromatography* (SFC), but it fell out of favour when the more convenient technique of high-performance liquid chromatography (HPLC) was introduced. However, interest in SFC has returned, and there are separations possible in SFC that cannot easily be achieved by HPLC, such as the separation of lipids and phospholipids. Samples as small as 1 pg can be analysed. The essential advantage of SFC is that diffusion coefficients in supercritical fluids are an order of magnitude greater than in liquids, so there is less resistance to the transfer of solutes through the column, with the result that separations may be effected rapidly or with high resolution.

The principal problem with $scCO_2$, however, is that the fluid is not a very good solvent and surfactants are needed to induce many potentially interesting solutes to dissolve. Indeed, $scCO_2$-based dry cleaning depends on the availability of cheap surfactants, so too does the use of $scCO_2$ as a solvent for homogeneous catalysts, such as metal complexes. There appear to be two principal approaches to solving the solubilizing problem. One solution is to use fluorinated and siloxane-based polymeric stabilizers, which allow polymerization reactions to proceed in $scCO_2$. The disadvantage of these stabilizers for commercial use is their great expense. An alternative and much cheaper approach is to use poly(ether-carbonate) copolymers. The copolymers can be made more soluble in $scCO_2$ by adjusting the ratio of ether and carbonate groups.

The critical temperature of water is 374°C and its pressure is 218 atm. The conditions for using scH_2O are therefore much more demanding than for $scCO_2$ and the properties of the fluid are highly sensitive to pressure. Thus, as the density of scH_2O decreases, the characteristics of a solution change from those of an aqueous solution through those of a non-aqueous solution and eventually to those of a gaseous solution. One consequence is that reaction mechanisms may change from ionic to radical.

Exercise 1 The use of supercritical fluids for the extraction of a component from a complicated mixture is not confined to the decaffeination of coffee. Consult library and internet resources and prepare a discussion of the principles, advantages, disadvantages, and current uses of supercritical fluid extraction technology.

Exercise 2 Show that a substance that is described by the equation of state $p = nRT/V - an^2/V^2 + bn^3/V^3$ shows critical behaviour, and express the critical constants in terms of the parameters a and b. (*Hint.* At the critical point, $dp/dV = 0$ and $d^2p/dV^2 = 0$; use $dV^n/dV = nV^{n-1}$.) (This exercise requires calculus.)

The temperature at which the liquid and solid phases of a substance coexist in equilibrium at a specified pressure is called the **melting temperature** of the substance. Because a substance melts at the same temperature as it freezes, 'melting temperature' is synonymous with **freezing temperature**. The solid–liquid boundary therefore shows how the melting temperature of a solid varies with pressure. The melting temperature when the pressure on the sample is 1 atm is called the **normal melting point** or the **normal freezing point**, T_f. A liquid freezes when the energy of the molecules in the liquid is so low that they cannot escape from the attractive forces of their neighbours and lose their mobility.

There is a set of conditions under which three different phases (typically solid, liquid, and vapour) all simultaneously coexist in equilibrium. It is represented by the **triple point**, where the three phase boundaries meet. The triple point of a pure substance is a characteristic, unchangeable physical property of the substance. For water the triple point lies at 273.16 K and 611 Pa, and ice, liquid water, and water vapour coexist in equilibrium at no other combination of pressure and temperature.[3] At the triple point, the rates of each forward and reverse process are equal (but the three individual rates are not necessarily the same).

The triple point and the critical point are important features of a substance because they act as frontier posts for the existence of the liquid phase. As we see from Fig. 5.13a, if the slope of the solid–liquid phase boundary is as shown in the diagram:

The triple point marks the lowest temperature at which the liquid can exist.

The critical point marks the highest temperature at which the liquid can exist.

We shall see in the following section that for a few materials (most notably water) the solid–liquid phase boundary slopes in the opposite direction, and then only the second of these conclusions is relevant (see Fig. 5.13b).

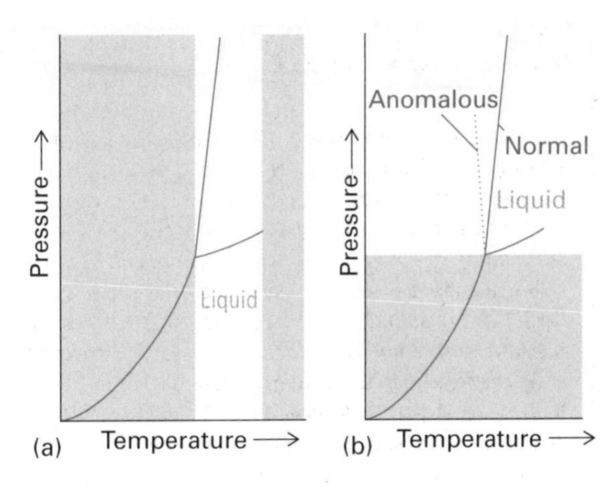

Fig. 5.13 (a) For substances that have phase diagrams resembling the one shown here (which is common for most substances, with the important exception of water), the triple point and the critical point mark the range of temperatures over which the substance may exist as a liquid. The shaded areas show the regions of temperature in which a liquid cannot exist as a stable phase. (b) A liquid cannot exist as a stable phase if the pressure is below that of the triple point for normal or anomalous liquids.

5.7 The phase rule

We might wonder whether *four* phases of a single substance could ever be in equilibrium (such as the two solid forms of tin, liquid tin, and tin vapour). To explore this question we think about the thermodynamic criterion for four phases to be in equilibrium. For equilibrium, the four molar Gibbs energies would all have to be equal and we could write

$$G_m(1) = G_m(2) \quad G_m(2) = G_m(3) \quad G_m(3) = G_m(4)$$

(The other equalities $G_m(1) = G_m(4)$, and so on, are implied by these three equations.) Each Gibbs energy is a function of the pressure and temperature, so we should think of these three relations as three equations for the two unknowns p and T. In general, three equations for two unknowns have no solution. For instance, the three equations $5x + 3y = 4$, $2x + 6y = 5$, and $x + y = 1$ have no solutions (try it). Therefore, we have to conclude that the four molar Gibbs energies cannot all be equal. In other words, *four phases of a single substance cannot coexist in mutual equilibrium.*

The conclusion we have reached is a special case of one of the most elegant results of chemical thermodynamics. The **phase rule** was derived by Gibbs and states that, for a system at equilibrium,

$$F = C - P + 2 \tag{5.8}$$

Here F is the number of degrees of freedom, C is the number of components, and P is the number of phases. The **number of components**, C, in a system is the minimum number of independent species necessary to define the composition of all the phases present in the system. The definition is easy to apply when the species present in a system do not react, for then we simply count their number. For instance, pure water is a one-component system ($C = 1$) and a mixture of ethanol and water is a two-component

[3] The triple point of water is used to define the Kelvin scale of temperatures: the triple point is defined as lying at 273.16 K exactly. The normal freezing point of water is found experimentally to lie approximately 0.01 K below the triple point, at very close to 273.15 K.

system ($C = 2$). The **number of degrees of freedom**, F, of a system is the number of intensive variables (such as the pressure, temperature, or mole fractions) that can be changed independently without disturbing the number of phases in equilibrium.[4]

For a one-component system, such as pure water, we set $C = 1$ and the phase rule simplifies to $F = 3 - P$. When only one phase is present, $F = 2$, which implies that p and T can be varied independently. In other words, a single phase is represented by an *area* on a phase diagram. When two phases are in equilibrium $F = 1$, which implies that pressure is not freely variable if we have set the temperature. That is, the equilibrium of two phases is represented by a *line* in a phase diagram: a line in a graph shows how one variable must change if another variable is varied (Fig. 5.14). Instead of selecting the temperature, we can select the pressure, but having done so the two phases come into equilibrium at a single definite temperature. Therefore, freezing (or any other phase transition of a single substance) occurs at a definite temperature at a given pressure. When three phases are in equilibrium $F = 0$. This special 'invariant condition' can therefore be established only at a definite temperature and pressure. The equilibrium of three phases is therefore represented by a *point*, the triple point, on the phase diagram. If we set $P = 4$, we get the absurd result that F is negative; that result is in accord with the conclusion at the start of this section that four phases cannot be in equilibrium in a one-component system.

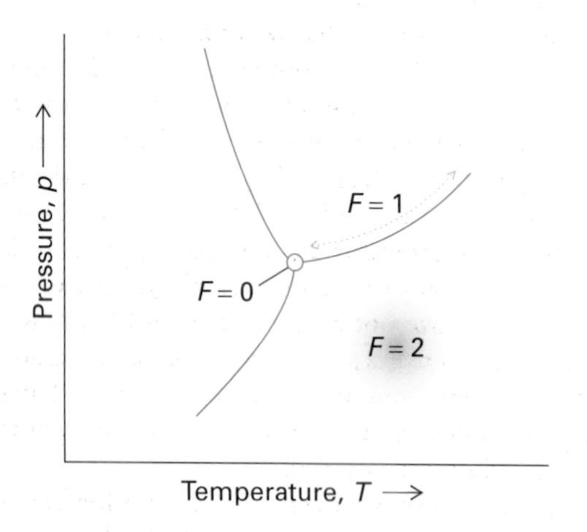

Fig. 5.14 The features of a phase diagram represent different degrees of freedom. When only one phase is present, $F = 2$ and the pressure and temperature can be varied at will. When two phases are present in equilibrium, $F = 1$: now, if the temperature is changed, the pressure must be changed by a specific amount. When three phases are present in equilibrium, $F = 0$ and there is no freedom to change either variable.

5.8 Phase diagrams of typical materials

We shall now see how these general features appear in the phase diagrams of a selection of pure substances.

Figure 5.15 is the phase diagram for water. The liquid–vapour phase boundary shows how the vapour pressure of liquid water varies with temperature. We can use this curve, which is shown in more detail in Fig. 5.7, to decide how the boiling temperature

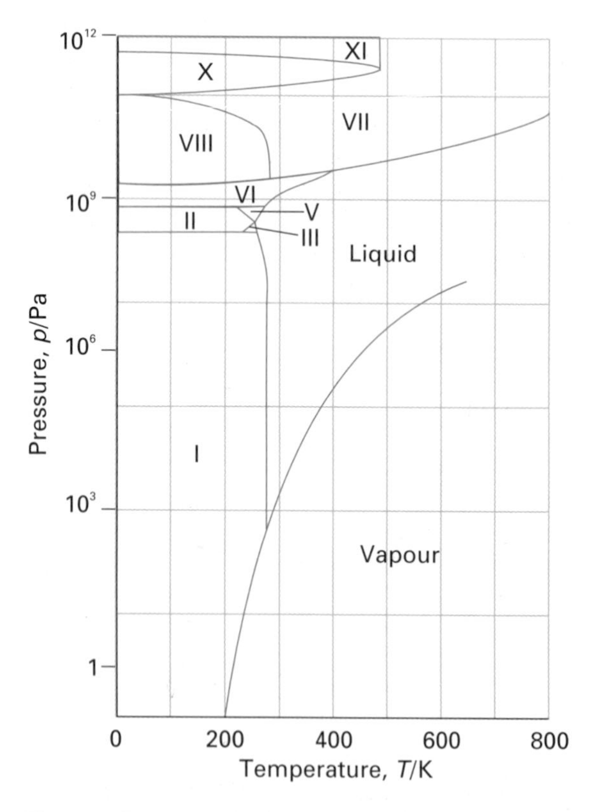

Fig. 5.15 The phase diagram for water showing the different solid phases.

[4] An intensive property, recall from Section 0.8, is one that is independent of the amount of material in the sample.

varies with changing external pressure. For example, when the external pressure is 19.9 kPa (at an altitude of 12 km), water boils at 60°C because that is the temperature at which the vapour pressure is 19.9 kPa.

Self-test 5.4

What is the minimum pressure at which liquid is the thermodynamically stable phase of water at 25°C?

[*Answer:* 3.17 kPa (see Fig. 5.7)]

The solid–liquid boundary line in Fig. 5.15, which is shown in more detail in Fig. 5.16, shows how the melting temperature of water depends on the pressure. For example, although ice melts at 0°C at 1 atm, it melts at −1°C when the pressure is 130 bar. The very steep slope of the boundary indicates that enormous pressures are needed to bring about significant changes. Note that the line slopes down from left to right, which—as we anticipated—means that the melting temperature of ice falls as the pressure is raised. As pointed out in Section 5.5, we can trace the reason for this unusual behaviour to the decrease in volume that occurs when ice melts: it is favourable for the solid to transform into the denser liquid as the pressure is raised. The decrease in volume is a result of the very open structure of the crystal structure of ice: as shown in Fig. 5.17, the water molecules are held apart, as well as together, by the hydrogen bonds between them but the structure partially collapses on melting and the liquid is denser than the solid.

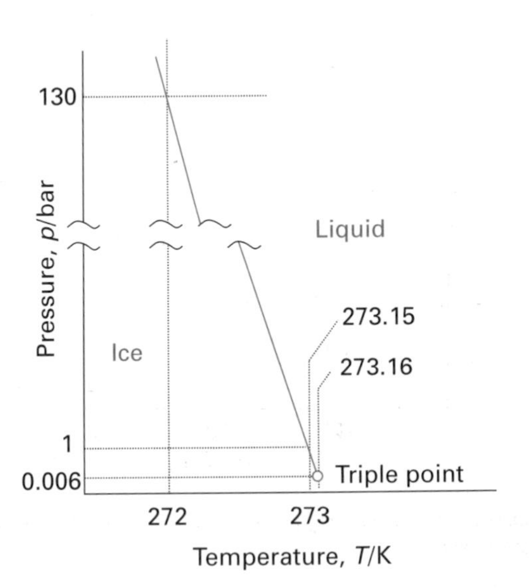

Fig. 5.16 The solid–liquid boundary of water in more detail. The graph is schematic, and not to scale.

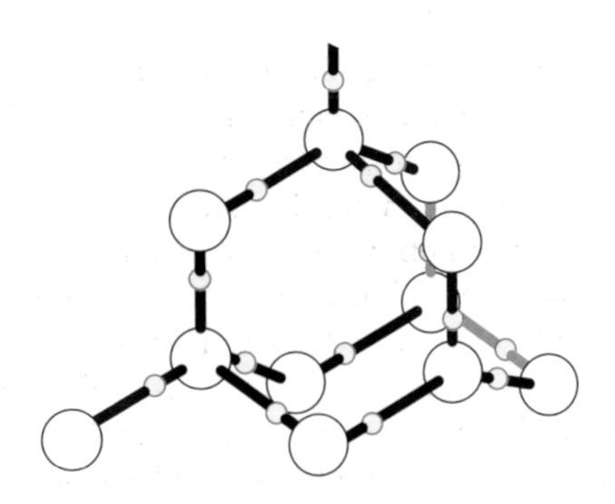

Fig. 5.17 The structure of ice-I. Each O atom is at the centre of a tetrahedron of four O atoms at a distance of 276 pm. The central O atom is attached by two short O—H bonds to two H atoms and by two long hydrogen bonds to the H atoms of two of the neighbouring molecules. Overall, the structure consists of planes of puckered hexagonal rings of H_2O molecules (like the chair form of cyclohexane). This structure collapses partially on melting, leading to a liquid that is denser than the solid.

Figure 5.15 shows that water has many different solid phases other than ordinary ice ('ice-I', shown in Fig. 5.17). These solid phases differ in the arrangement of the water molecules: under the influence of very high pressures, hydrogen bonds buckle and the H_2O molecules adopt different arrangements. These **polymorphs**, or different solid phases, of ice may be responsible for the advance of glaciers, as ice at the bottom of glaciers experiences very high pressures where it rests on jagged rocks. The sudden apparent explosion of Halley's comet in 1991 may have been due to the conversion of one form of ice into another in its interior.

Figure 5.18 shows the phase diagram for carbon dioxide. The features to note include the slope of the solid–liquid boundary: this positive slope is typical of almost all substances. The slope indicates that the melting temperature of solid carbon dioxide rises as the pressure is increased. As the triple point (217 K, 5.11 bar) lies well above ordinary atmospheric pressure, liquid carbon dioxide does not exist at

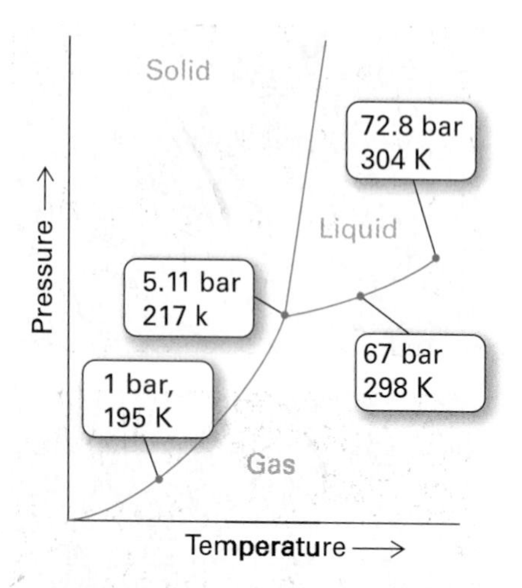

Fig. 5.18 The phase diagram of carbon dioxide. Note that, as the triple point lies well above atmospheric pressure, liquid carbon dioxide does not exist under normal conditions (a pressure of at least 5.11 bar must be applied).

normal atmospheric pressures whatever the temperature, and the solid sublimes when left in the open (hence the name 'dry ice'). To obtain liquid carbon dioxide, it is necessary to exert a pressure of at least 5.11 bar.

Cylinders of carbon dioxide generally contain the liquid or compressed gas; if both gas and liquid are present inside the cylinder, then at 20°C the pressure must be about 65 atm. When the gas squirts through the throttle it cools by the Joule–Thomson effect, so when it emerges into a region where the pressure is only 1 atm, it condenses into a finely divided snow-like solid.

Figure 5.19 shows the phase diagram of helium. Helium behaves unusually at low temperatures. For instance, the solid and gas phases of helium are never in equilibrium however low the temperature: the atoms are so light that they vibrate with a large-amplitude motion even at very low temperatures and the solid simply shakes itself apart. Solid helium can be obtained, but only by holding the atoms together by applying pressure. A second unique feature of helium is that pure helium-4 has two liquid phases. The phase marked He-I in the diagram behaves like a normal liquid; the other phase, He-II, is a **superfluid**; it is so called because it flows without viscosity. Helium is the only known substance with a liquid–liquid boundary in its phase diagram.[5]

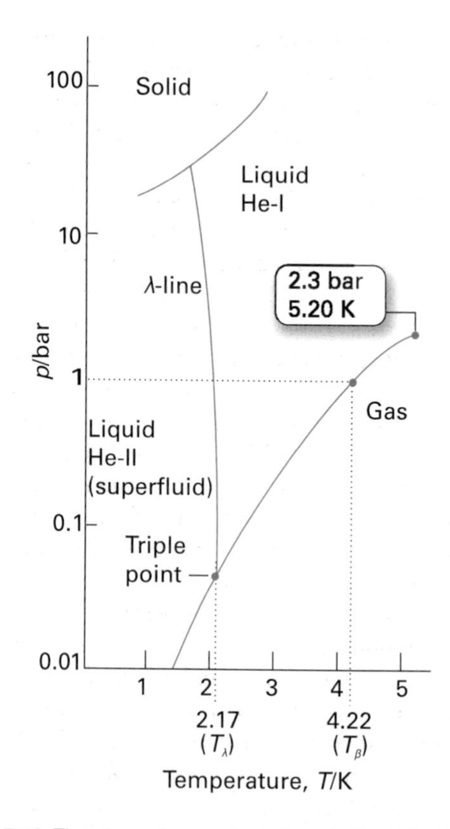

Fig. 5.19 The phase diagram for helium-4. The 'λ-line' marks the conditions under which the two liquid phases are in equilibrium. Helium-I is a conventional liquid and helium-II is a superfluid. Note that a pressure of at least 20 bar must be exerted before solid helium can be obtained.

5.9 The molecular structure of liquids

One question that should arise in your mind is what is the molecular basis of the material we have been discussing: in particular, what is the molecular nature of a pure liquid phase? That is the question we address here.

The starting point for the discussion of gases is the totally random distribution of the molecules of a perfect gas. The starting point for the discussion of solids is the well-ordered structure of perfect crystals (Chapter 15). The liquid state is between these extremes: there is some structure and some disorder. The particles of a liquid are held together by intermolecular forces of the kind we discuss in Chapter 17, but their kinetic energies are comparable to their

[5] Recent work has suggested that water may also have a superfluid liquid phase.

potential energies. As a result, although the molecules are not free to escape completely from the bulk, the whole structure is very mobile. The flow of molecules is like a crowd of spectators leaving a stadium.

What do we mean by the molecular structure of a liquid? The average locations of the particles in the liquid are described in terms of the **pair distribution function**, $g(r)$. This function is defined so that $g(r)\delta r$ is the probability that a molecule will be found at a distance between r and $r + \delta r$ from another molecule. It follows that if $g(r)$ passes through a maximum at a radius of, for instance, 0.5 nm, then the most probable distance (regardless of direction) at which a second molecule will be found will be at 0.5 nm from the first molecule. At large distances, $g(r)$ settles down to a constant value because the first molecule no longer influences the arrangement of molecules.

In a crystal, $g(r)$ is an array of sharp spikes, representing the certainty (in the absence of defects and thermal motion) that particles lie at definite locations. This regularity continues out to large distances (to the edge of the crystal, billions of molecules away), so we say that crystals have **long-range order**. When the crystal melts, the long-range order is lost and wherever we look at long distances from a given particle there is equal probability of finding a second particle. Close to the first particle, however, there may be a remnant of order (Fig. 5.20). Its nearest neighbours might still adopt approximately their original positions, and even if they are displaced by newcomers the new particles might adopt their vacated positions. It may still be possible to detect, on average, a sphere of nearest neighbours at a distance r_1, and perhaps beyond them a sphere of next-nearest neighbours at r_2. The existence of this **short-range order** means that $g(r)$ can be expected to have a broad but pronounced peak at r_1, a smaller and broader peak at r_2, and perhaps some more structure beyond that. This short-range order is due largely to short-range repulsive forces, and is quite well reproduced in a simple model of a liquid in which the molecules are represented by hard spheres ('ball-bearings').

The pair distribution function can be determined experimentally by some of the same techniques used to determine the structures of crystals (Chapter 15). The results show that the shells of local structure in water are unmistakable (Fig. 5.21). Closer analysis shows that any given H_2O molecule is surrounded by other molecules at the corners of a tetrahedron, similar to the arrangement in ice. The form of $g(r)$ at 100°C shows that the intermolecular forces (in this case, largely hydrogen bonds) are strong enough to affect the local structure right up to the boiling point.

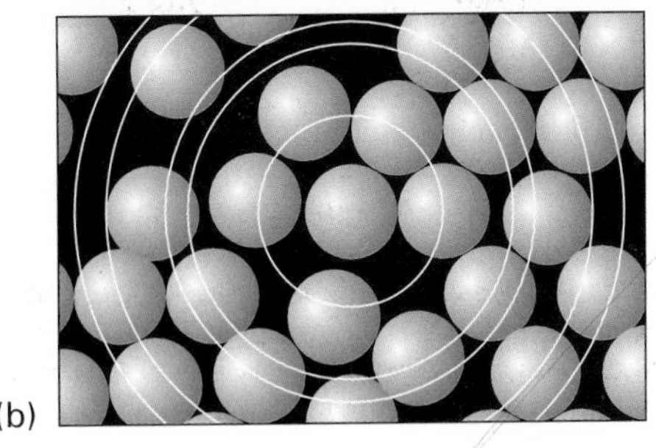

Fig. 5.20 (a) In a perfect crystal at $T = 0$, the distribution of molecules (or ions) is highly regular, and the pair distribution function shows a series of sharp peaks showing the regular organization of rings of neighbours around any selected central molecule or ion. (b) In a liquid, there remain some elements of structure close to each molecule, but the further the distance, the less the correlation. The pair distribution function now shows a pronounced (but broadened) peak corresponding to the nearest neighbours of the molecule of interest (which are only slightly more disordered than in the solid), and a suggestion of a peak for the next ring of molecules, but little structure at greater distances.

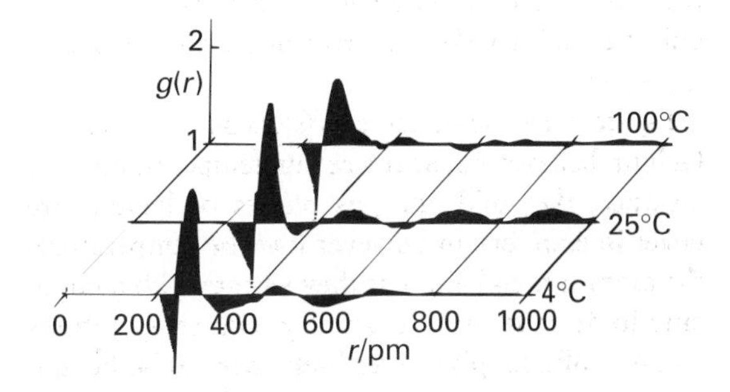

Fig. 5.21 The experimentally determined pair distribution function of the oxygen atoms in liquid water at three temperatures. Note the expansion as the temperature is raised.

CHECKLIST OF KEY IDEAS

You should now be familiar with the following concepts:

☐ 1 The molar Gibbs energy of a liquid or a solid is almost independent of pressure ($\Delta G_m = V_m \Delta p$).

☐ 2 The molar Gibbs energy of a perfect gas increases logarithmically with pressure: $\Delta G_m = RT \ln(p_f/p_i)$.

☐ 3 The molar Gibbs energy of a substance decreases as the temperature is increased ($\Delta G_m = -S_m \Delta T$).

☐ 4 A phase diagram of a substance shows the conditions of pressure and temperature at which its various phases are most stable.

☐ 5 A phase boundary depicts the pressures and temperatures at which two phases are in equilibrium.

☐ 6 The slope of a phase boundary is given by the Clapeyron equation, $\Delta p/\Delta T = \Delta_{trs}H/T\Delta_{trs}V$.

☐ 7 The slope of the liquid–vapour phase boundary is given by the Clausius–Clapeyron equation, $\Delta(\ln p)/\Delta T = \Delta_{trs}H/RT^2$.

☐ 8 The vapour pressure of a liquid is the pressure of the vapour in equilibrium with the liquid; it depends on temperature as $\log p = A - B/T$.

☐ 9 The boiling temperature is the temperature at which the vapour pressure is equal to the external pressure; the normal boiling point is the temperature at which the vapour pressure is 1 atm.

☐ 10 The critical temperature is the temperature above which a substance does not form a liquid.

☐ 11 The triple point is the condition of pressure and temperature at which three phases are in mutual equilibrium.

☐ 12 The phase rule for a system of C components, P phases, and F degrees of freedom is $F = C - P + 2$.

☐ 13 The arrangement of molecules in liquids is expressed in terms of the pair distribution function.

DISCUSSION QUESTIONS

5.1 Discuss the implication for phase stability of the variation of molar Gibbs energy with temperature and pressure.

5.2 Without doing a calculation, decide whether the presence of (a) attractive, (b) repulsive interactions between gas molecules will raise of lower the molar Gibbs energy of a gas relative to its 'perfect' value.

5.3 Explain the significance of the Clapeyron equation and of the Clausius–Clapeyron equation.

5.4 Use the phase rule to discuss the form of the phase diagram of sulfur, which has two solid phases, one liquid phase, and one vapour phase. Identify the number of degrees of freedom for each possible combination of phase equilibria.

EXERCISES

The symbol ‡ indicates that the question requires calculus.

5.5 The standard Gibbs energy of formation of rhombic sulfur is 0 and that of monoclinic sulfur is +0.33 kJ mol^{-1} at 25°C. Which polymorph is the more stable at that temperature?

5.6 The density of rhombic sulfur is 2.070 g cm^{-3} and that of monoclinic sulfur is 1.957 g cm^{-3}. Can the application of pressure be expected to make monoclinic sulfur more stable than rhombic sulfur? (See Exercise 5.5.)

5.7 What is the difference in molar Gibbs energy due to pressure alone of (a) water (density 1.03 g cm^{-3}), at the ocean surface and in the Mindañao trench (depth 11.5 km), (b) mercury (density 13.6 g cm^{-3}), at the top and bottom of the column in a barometer? (*Hint.* At the very top, the pressure on the mercury is equal to the vapour pressure of mercury, which at 20°C is 160 mPa.)

5.8 The density of the fat tristearin is 0.95 g cm^{-3}. Calculate the change in molar Gibbs energy of tristearin when a deep-sea creature is brought to the surface (p = 1.0 atm) from a depth of 2.0 km. To calculate the hydrostatic pressure, take the mean density of water to be 1.03 g cm^{-3}.

5.9 Calculate the change in molar Gibbs energy of carbon dioxide (treated as a perfect gas) at 20°C when its pressure is changed isothermally from 1.0 bar to (a) 2.0 bar, (b) 0.000 27 atm, its partial pressure in air.

5.10 A sample of water vapour at 200°C is compressed isothermally from 300 cm^3 to 100 cm^3. What is the change in its molar Gibbs energy?

5.11 ‡Suppose that a gas obeys the van der Waals equation of state with the repulsive effects much greater than the attractive effects (that is, neglect the parameter a). (a) Find an expression for the change in molar Gibbs energy when the pressure is changed from p_i to p_f. (b) Is the change greater or smaller than for a perfect gas? (c) Estimate the percentage difference between the van der Waals and perfect gas calculations for carbon dioxide undergoing a change from 1.0 atm to 10.0 atm at 298.15 K. (*Hint.* For the first part, use calculus as in Derivation 5.2.)

5.12 The standard molar entropy of rhombic sulfur is 31.80 J K^{-1} mol^{-1} and that of monoclinic sulfur is 32.6 J K^{-1} mol^{-1}. (a) Can an increase in temperature be expected to make monoclinic sulfur more stable than rhombic sulfur? (b) If so, at what temperature will the transition occur at 1 bar? (See Exercise 5.5 for data.)

5.13 The standard molar entropy of benzene is 173.3 J K^{-1} mol^{-1}. Calculate the change in its standard molar Gibbs energy when benzene is heated from 20°C to 50°C.

5.14 The standard molar entropies of water ice, liquid, and vapour are 37.99, 69.91, and 188.83 J K^{-1} mol^{-1}, respectively. On a single graph, show how the Gibbs energies of each of these phases varies with temperature.

5.15 An open vessel containing (a) water, (b) benzene, (c) mercury stands in a laboratory measuring 6.0 m × 5.3 m × 3.2 m at 25°C. What mass of each substance will be found in the air if there is no ventilation? (The vapour pressures are (a) 3.2 kPa, (b) 14 kPa, (c) 0.23 Pa.)

5.16 (a) Use the Clapeyron equation, eqn 5.4, to estimate the slope of the solid–liquid phase boundary of water given the enthalpy of fusion is 6.008 kJ mol^{-1} and the densities of ice and water at 0°C are 0.916 71 and 0.999 84 g cm^{-3}, respectively. (*Hint.* Express the entropy of fusion in terms of the enthalpy of fusion and the melting point of ice.) (b) Estimate the pressure required to lower the melting point of ice by 1°C.

5.17 ‡Equation 5.6 has been derived on the assumption that the enthalpy of vaporization is independent of temperature in the range of interest. Derive an improved version of the equation on the basis that the enthalpy of vaporization has the form $\Delta_{vap}H = a + bT$.

5.18 Given the parametrization of the vapour pressure in eqn 5.7 and Table 5.1, what is (a) the enthalpy of vaporization, (b) the normal boiling point of hexane?

5.19 Suppose we wished to express the vapour pressure in eqn 5.7 in torr. What would be the values of A and B for methylbenzene?

5.20 The vapour pressure of mercury is at 20°C is 160 mPa; what is its vapour pressure at 50°C given that its enthalpy of vaporization is 59.30 kJ mol^{-1}?

5.21 The vapour pressure of pyridine is 50.0 kPa at 365.7 K and the normal boiling point is 388.4 K. What is the enthalpy of vaporization of pyridine?

5.22 Estimate the boiling point of benzene given that its vapour pressure is 20 kPa at 35°C and 50.0 kPa at 58.8°C.

5.23 On a cold, dry morning after a frost, the temperature was –5°C and the partial pressure of water in the atmosphere fell to 2 Torr. Will the frost sublime? What partial pressure of water would ensure that the frost remained?

5.24 (a) Refer to Fig. 5.15 and describe the changes that would be observed when water vapour at 1.0 bar and 400 K is cooled at constant pressure to 260 K. (b) Suggest the appearance of a plot of temperature against time if energy is removed at a constant rate. To judge the relative slopes of the cooling curves, you need to know that the constant-pressure molar heat capacities of water vapour, liquid, and solid are approximately 4R, 9R, and 4.5R, respectively; the enthalpies of transition are given in Table 3.1.

5.25 Refer to Fig. 5.15 and describe the changes that would be observed when cooling takes place at the pressure of the triple point.

5.26 Use the phase diagram in Fig. 5.18 to state what would be observed when a sample of carbon dioxide, initially at 1.0 atm and 298 K, is subjected to the following cycle: (a) constant-pressure heating to 320 K, (b) isothermal compression to 100 atm, (c) constant-pressure cooling to 210 K, (d) isothermal decompression to 1.0 atm, (e) constant-pressure heating to 298 K.

5.27 Infer from the phase diagram for helium in Fig. 5.19 whether helium-I is more or less dense than helium-II given that the molar entropy of helium-I is greater than that of helium-II.

Chapter 6

The properties of mixtures

We now leave pure materials and the limited but important changes they can undergo and examine mixtures. We shall consider only **homogeneous mixtures**, or solutions, in which the composition is uniform however small the sample. The component in smaller abundance is called the **solute** and that in larger abundance is the **solvent**. These terms, however, are normally but not invariably reserved for solids dissolved in liquids; one liquid mixed with another is normally called simply a 'mixture' of the two liquids. In this chapter we consider mainly **non-electrolyte solutions**, where the solute is not present as ions. Examples are sucrose dissolved in water, sulfur dissolved in carbon disulfide, and a mixture of ethanol and water. We delay until Chapter 9 the special problems of **electrolyte solutions**, in which the solute consists of ions that interact strongly with one another.

The thermodynamic description of mixtures

We need a set of concepts that enable us to apply thermodynamics to mixtures of variable composition. We have already seen how to use the partial pressure, the contribution of one component in a gaseous mixture to the total pressure, to discuss the properties of mixtures of gases. For a more general description of the thermodynamics of mixtures we have to introduce other 'partial' properties, each one being the contribution that a particular component makes to the mixture.

6.1 Measures of concentration

There are three measures of concentration commonly used to describe the composition of mixtures. One, the *molar concentration*, is used when we need to know the amount of solute in a sample of known volume of solution. The other two, the *molality* and the *mole fraction*, are used when we need to know the relative numbers of solute and solvent molecules in a sample.

The **molar concentration**, [J] or c_J, of a solute J in a solution (more formally, the 'amount of substance concentration') is the chemical amount of J divided by the volume of the solution:[1]

$$[\mathrm{J}] = \frac{n_\mathrm{J}}{V} \quad \begin{matrix}\text{Amount of J (mol)} \\ \text{Volume of solution (dm}^3\text{)}\end{matrix} \tag{6.1}$$

Molar concentration is typically reported in moles per cubic decimetre (mol dm^{-3}; more informally, as moles per litre, mol L^{-1}). The unit 1 mol dm^{-3} is commonly denoted 1 M (and read 'molar'). Once we know the molar concentration of a solute, we can calculate the amount of that substance in a given volume, V, of solution by writing

$$n_\mathrm{J} = [\mathrm{J}]V \tag{6.2}$$

Self-test 6.1

Suppose that 0.282 g of glycine, NH_2CH_2COOH, is dissolved in enough water to make 250 cm^3 of solution. What is the molar concentration of the solution?

[*Answer:* 0.0150 M $NH_2CH_2COOH(aq)$]

The **molality**, b_J, of a solute J in a solution is the amount of substance divided by the mass of solvent used to prepare the solution:

$$b_\mathrm{J} = \frac{n_\mathrm{J}}{m_\mathrm{solvent}} \quad \begin{matrix}\text{Amount of J (mol)} \\ \text{Mass of solvent (kg)}\end{matrix} \tag{6.3}$$

Molality is typically reported in moles of solute per kilogram of solvent (mol kg^{-1}). This unit is sometimes (but unofficially) denoted m, with 1 m = 1 mol kg^{-1}. An important distinction between molar concentration and molality is that whereas the former is defined in terms of the volume of the *solution*, the molality is defined in terms of the mass of *solvent* used to prepare the solution. A distinction to remember is that molar concentration varies with temperature as the solution expands and contracts but the molality does not. For dilute solutions in water, the numerical values of the molality and molar concentration differ very little because 1 dm^3 of solution is mostly water and has a mass close to 1 kg; for concentrated aqueous solutions and for all non-aqueous solutions with densities different from 1 g cm^{-3}, the two values are very different.

As we have indicated, we use molality when we need to emphasize the relative amounts of solute and solvent molecules. To see why this is so, we note that the mass of solvent is proportional to the amount of solvent molecules present, so from eqn 6.3 we see that the molality is proportional to the ratio of the amounts of solute and solvent molecules. For example, any 1.0 m aqueous nonelectrolyte solution contains 1.0 mol solute particles per 55.5 mol H_2O molecules, so in each case there is 1 solute molecule per 55.5 solvent molecules.

Closely related to the molality of a solute is the mole fraction, x_J, which was introduced in Chapter 1 in connection with mixtures of gases:

$$x_\mathrm{J} = \frac{n_\mathrm{J}}{n} \quad \begin{matrix}\text{Amount of J (mol)} \\ \text{Total amount of molecules (mol)}\end{matrix} \tag{6.4}$$

As noted in Chapter 1, $x_J = 0$ corresponds to the absence of J molecules and $x_J = 1$ corresponds to pure J.

Example 6.1

Relating mole fraction and molality

What is the mole fraction of glycine molecules in 0.140 m $NH_2CH_2COOH(aq)$? Ignore ionization.

Strategy We consider a sample that contains (exactly) 1 kg of solvent, and hence an amount $n_J = b_J \times (1\ \mathrm{kg})$ of solute molecules. The amount of solvent molecules in exactly 1 kg of solvent is

$$n_\mathrm{solvent} = \frac{1\ \mathrm{kg}}{M}$$

[1] Molar concentration is still widely called 'molarity'.

where M is the molar mass of the solvent. Once these two amounts are available, we can calculate the mole fraction by using eqn 6.4 with $n = n_J + n_{solvent}$.

Solution It follows from the discussion in the *Strategy* that the amount of glycine (gly) molecules in exactly 1 kg of solvent is

$$n_{gly} = (0.140 \text{ mol kg}^{-1}) \times (1 \text{ kg}) = 0.140 \text{ mol}$$

The amount of water molecules in exactly 1 kg (10^3 g) of water is

$$n_{water} = \frac{10^3 \text{ g}}{18.02 \text{ g mol}^{-1}} = \frac{10^3}{18.02} \text{ mol}$$

The total amount of molecules present is

$$n = 0.140 \text{ mol} + \frac{10^3}{18.02} \text{ mol}$$

The mole fraction of glycine molecules is therefore

$$x_{gly} = \frac{0.140 \text{ mol}}{0.140 + (10^3/18.02) \text{ mol}} = 2.52 \times 10^{-3}$$

A note on good practice. We refer to *exactly* 1 kg of solvent to avoid problems with significant figures.

Self-test 6.2

Calculate the mole fraction of sucrose molecules in 1.22 m $C_{12}H_{22}O_{11}$(aq).

[*Answer:* 2.15×10^{-2}]

6.2 Partial molar properties

A **partial molar property** is the contribution (per mole) that a substance makes to an overall property of a mixture. The easiest partial molar property to visualize is the **partial molar volume,** V_J, of a substance J, the contribution J makes to the total volume of a mixture.[2] We have to be alert to the fact that although 1 mol of a substance has a characteristic volume when it is pure, 1 mol of that substance can make different contributions to the total volume of a mixture because molecules pack together in different ways in the pure substances and in mixtures.

Illustration 6.1

Partial molar volume

To grasp the meaning of the concept of partial molar volume, imagine a huge volume of pure water. When a further 1 mol H_2O is added, the volume increases by 18 cm^3. However, when we add 1 mol H_2O to a huge volume of pure ethanol, the volume increases by only 14 cm^3. The quantity 18 cm^3 mol^{-1} is the volume occupied per mole of water molecules in pure water; 14 cm^3 mol^{-1} is the volume occupied per mole of water molecules in almost pure ethanol. In other words, the partial molar volume of water in pure water is 18 cm^3 mol^{-1} and the partial molar volume of water in pure ethanol is 14 cm^3 mol^{-1}. In the latter case there is so much ethanol present that each H_2O molecule is surrounded by ethanol molecules and the packing of the molecules results in 1 mol of water molecules occupying only 14 cm^3.

The partial molar volume at an intermediate composition of the water/ethanol mixture is an indication of the volume the H_2O molecules occupy when they are surrounded by a mixture of molecules representative of the overall composition (half water, half ethanol, for instance, when the mole fractions are both 0.5). The partial molar volume of ethanol varies as the composition of the mixture is changed, because the environment of an ethanol molecule changes from pure ethanol to pure water as the proportion of water increases and the volume occupied by the ethanol molecules varies accordingly. Figure 6.1 shows the variation of the two partial molar volumes across the full composition range at 25°C.

Once we know the partial molar volumes V_A and V_B of the two components A and B of a mixture at the composition (and temperature) of interest, we can state the total volume V of the mixture by using

$$V = n_A V_A + n_B V_B \tag{6.5}$$

[2] Partial molar quantities are also commonly denoted by a bar over the symbol, as in $\bar{V}_J$.

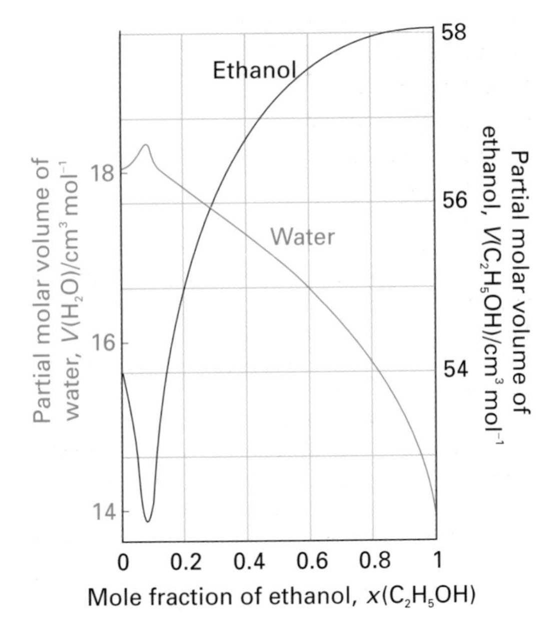

Fig. 6.1 The partial molar volumes of water and ethanol at 25°C. Note the different scales (water on the left, ethanol on the right).

Derivation 6.1

Total volume and partial molar volume

Consider a very large sample of the mixture of the specified composition. Then, when an amount n_A of A is added, the composition remains (almost) unchanged but the volume of the sample increases by $n_A V_A$. Similarly, when an amount n_B of B is added, the volume increases by $n_B V_B$. The total increase in volume is $n_A V_A + n_B V_B$. The mixture now occupies a larger volume but the proportions of the components are still the same. Next, scoop out of this enlarged volume a sample containing n_A of A and n_B of B. Its volume is $n_A V_A + n_B V_B$. Because volume is a state function, the same sample could have been prepared simply by mixing the appropriate amounts of A and B.

Example 6.2

Using partial molar volumes

What is the total volume of a mixture of 50.0 g of ethanol and 50.0 g of water at 25°C?

Strategy To use eqn 6.5, we need the mole fractions of each substance and the corresponding partial molar volumes. We calculate the mole fractions in the same way as in Self-test 1.3, by using the molar masses of the components to calculate the amounts. We can then find the partial molar volumes corresponding to these mole fractions by referring to Fig. 6.1.

Solution We find first that $n_{ethanol} = 1.09$ mol and $n_{water} = 2.77$ mol, and hence that $x_{ethanol} = 0.282$ and $x_{water} = 0.718$. According to Fig. 6.1, the partial molar volumes of the two substances in a mixture of this composition are 55 $cm^3\ mol^{-1}$ and 18 $cm^3\ mol^{-1}$, respectively, so from eqn 6.5 the total volume of the mixture is

$$V = (1.09\ \text{mol}) \times (55\ \text{cm}^3\ \text{mol}^{-1}) + (2.77\ \text{mol}) \times (18\ \text{cm}^3\ \text{mol}^{-1})$$

$$= 1.09 \times 55 + 2.77 \times 18\ \text{cm}^3 = 110\ \text{cm}^3$$

Self-test 6.3

Use Fig. 6.1 to calculate the mass density of a mixture of 20 g of water and 100 g of ethanol.

[*Answer:* 0.86 g cm^{-3}]

Now we extend the concept of a partial molar quantity to other state functions. The most important for our purposes is the **partial molar Gibbs energy**, G_J, of a substance J, which is the contribution of J (per mole of J) to the total Gibbs energy of a mixture. It follows in the same way as for volume that, if we know the partial molar Gibbs energies of two substances A and B in a mixture of a given composition, then we can calculate the total Gibbs energy of the mixture by using an expression like eqn 6.5:

$$G = n_A G_A + n_B G_B \tag{6.6}$$

The partial molar Gibbs energy has exactly the same significance as the partial molar volume. For instance, ethanol has a particular partial molar Gibbs energy when it is pure (and every molecule is surrounded by other ethanol molecules), and it has a different partial molar Gibbs energy when it is in an aqueous solution of a certain composition (because then each ethanol molecule is surrounded by a mixture of ethanol and water molecules).

The partial molar Gibbs energy is so important in chemistry that it is given a special name and symbol. From now on, we shall call it the **chemical potential** and denote it μ (mu). Then, eqn 6.6 becomes

$$G = n_A \mu_A + n_B \mu_B \tag{6.7}$$

where μ_A is the chemical potential of A in the mixture and μ_B is the chemical potential of B. In the course of this chapter and the next we shall see that the name 'chemical potential' is very appropriate, for it will become clear that μ_J is a measure of the ability of J to bring about physical and chemical change. A substance with a high chemical potential has a high ability, in a sense we shall explore, to drive a reaction or some other physical process forward.

To make progress, we need an explicit formula for the variation of the chemical potential of a substance with the composition of the mixture. Our starting point is eqn 5.2b, which shows how the molar Gibbs energy of a perfect gas depends on pressure:

$$G_m(p_f) = G_m(p_i) + RT \ln \frac{p_f}{p_i}$$

First, we set $p_f = p$, the pressure of interest, and $p_i = p^{\ominus}$, the standard pressure (1 bar). At the latter pressure, the molar Gibbs energy has its standard value, $G_m^{\ominus}$, so we can write

$$G_m(p) = G_m^{\ominus} + RT \ln \frac{p}{p^{\ominus}} \qquad (6.8)$$

Next, for a *mixture* of perfect gases, we interpret p as the *partial* pressure of the gas, and the G_m is the *partial* molar Gibbs energy, the chemical potential. Therefore, for a mixture of perfect gases, for each component J present at a partial pressure p_J,

$$\mu_J = \mu_J^{\ominus} + RT \ln \frac{p_J}{p^{\ominus}} \qquad (6.9a)$$

In this expression, $\mu_J^{\ominus}$ is **standard chemical potential** of the gas J, which is identical to its standard molar Gibbs energy, the value of G_m for the pure gas at 1 bar. If we adopt the convention that, whenever p_J appears in a formula it is to be interpreted as $p_J/p^{\ominus}$ (so, if the pressure is 2.0 bar, $p_J = 2.0$), we can write eqn 6.9a more simply as

$$\mu_J = \mu_J^{\ominus} + RT \ln p_J \qquad (6.9b)$$

Figure 6.2 illustrates the pressure dependence of the chemical potential of a perfect gas predicted by this equation. Note that the chemical potential becomes negatively infinite as the pressure tends to zero, rises to its standard value at 1 bar (because ln 1 = 0), and then increases slowly (logarithmically, as ln p) as the pressure is increased further.

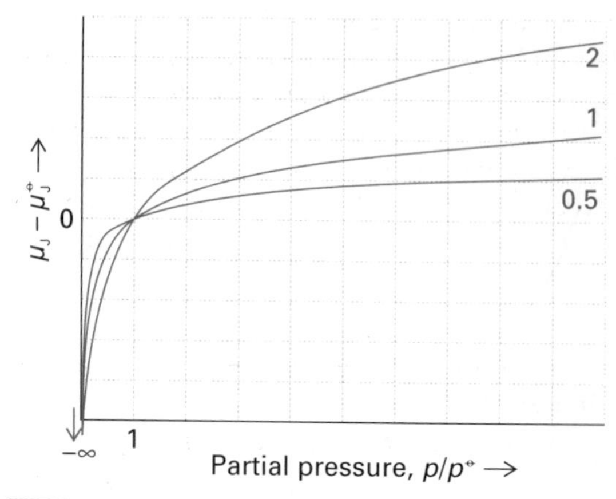

Fig. 6.2 The variation with partial pressure of the chemical potential of a perfect gas at three different temperatures (in the ratios 0.5:1:2). Note that the chemical potential increases with pressure and, at a given pressure, with temperature.

As always, we can become familiar with an equation by listening to what it tells us. In this case, we note that as p_J increases, so does ln p_J. Therefore, eqn 6.9 tells us that *the higher the partial pressure of a gas, the higher its chemical potential*. This conclusion is consistent with the interpretation of the chemical potential as an indication of the potential of a substance to be active chemically: the higher the partial pressure, the more active chemically the species. In this instance the chemical potential represents the tendency of the substance to react when it is in its standard state (the significance of the term $\mu^{\ominus}$) plus an additional tendency that reflects whether it is at a different pressure. A higher partial pressure gives a substance more chemical 'punch', just like winding a spring gives a spring more physical punch (that is, enables it to do more work).

Self-test 6.4

Suppose that the partial pressure of a perfect gas falls from 100 kPa to 50 kPa as it is consumed in a reaction at 25°C. What is the change in chemical potential of the substance?

[*Answer:* −1.7 kJ mol^{-1}]

We saw in Section 5.1 that the molar Gibbs energy of a pure substance is the same in all the phases at equilibrium. We can use the same argument to show that *a system is at equilibrium when the chemical potential of each substance has the same value in every phase in which it occurs*. We can think of the chemical potential as the pushing power of each substance, and equilibrium is reached only when each substance pushes with the same strength in any phase it occupies.

Derivation 6.2

The uniformity of chemical potential

Suppose a substance J occurs in different phases in different regions of a system. For instance, we might have a liquid mixture of ethanol and water and a mixture of their vapours. Let the substance J have chemical potential $\mu_J(l)$ in the liquid mixture and $\mu_J(g)$ in the vapour. We could imagine an infinitesimal amount, dn_J, of J migrating from the liquid to the vapour. As a result, the Gibbs energy of the liquid phase falls by $\mu_J(l)dn_J$ and that of the vapour rises by $\mu_J(g)dn_J$. The net change in Gibbs energy is

$$dG = \mu_J(g)dn_J - \mu_J(l)dn_J = \{\mu_J(g) - \mu_J(l)\}\, dn_J$$

There is no tendency for this migration (and the reverse process, migration from the vapour to the liquid) to occur if $dG = 0$. The argument applies to each component of the system. Therefore, *for a substance to be at equilibrium throughout the system, its chemical potential must be the same everywhere.*

6.3 Spontaneous mixing

All gases mix spontaneously with one another because the molecules of one gas can mingle with the molecules of the other gas. But how can we show *thermodynamically* that mixing is spontaneous? At constant temperature and pressure, we need to show that $\Delta G < 0$. The first step is therefore to find an expression for ΔG when two gases mix, and then to decide whether it is negative. As we see in Derivation 6.3, when an amount n_A of A and n_B of B of two gases mingle at a temperature T,

$$\Delta G = nRT\{x_A \ln x_A + x_B \ln x_B\} \qquad (6.10)$$

with $n = n_A + n_B$ and the x_J the mole fractions in the mixture.

Derivation 6.3

The Gibbs energy of mixing

Suppose we have an amount n_A of a perfect gas A at a certain temperature T and pressure p, and an amount n_B of a perfect gas B at the same temperature and pressure. The two gases are in separate compartments initially (Fig. 6.3). The Gibbs energy of the system (the two unmixed gases) is the sum of their individual Gibbs energies:

$$\begin{aligned} G_i &= n_A\mu_A + n_B\mu_B \\ &= n_A\{\mu_A^\ominus + RT \ln p\} + n_B\{\mu_B^\ominus + RT \ln p\} \end{aligned}$$

The chemical potentials are those for the two gases, each at a pressure p. When the partition is removed, the total pressure remains the same, but according to Dalton's law (Section 1.3), the partial pressures fall to $p_A = x_A p$ and $p_B = x_B p$, where the x_J are the mole fractions of the two gases in the mixture ($x_J = n_J/n$, with $n = n_A + n_B$). The final Gibbs energy of the system is therefore

$$\begin{aligned} G_f &= n_A\{\mu_A^\ominus + RT \ln p_A\} + n_B\{\mu_B^\ominus + RT \ln p_B\} \\ &= n_A\{\mu_A^\ominus + RT \ln x_A p\} + n_B\{\mu_B^\ominus + RT \ln x_B p\} \end{aligned}$$

The difference $G_f - G_i$ is the change in Gibbs energy that accompanies mixing. The standard chemical potentials cancel, and by making use of the relation

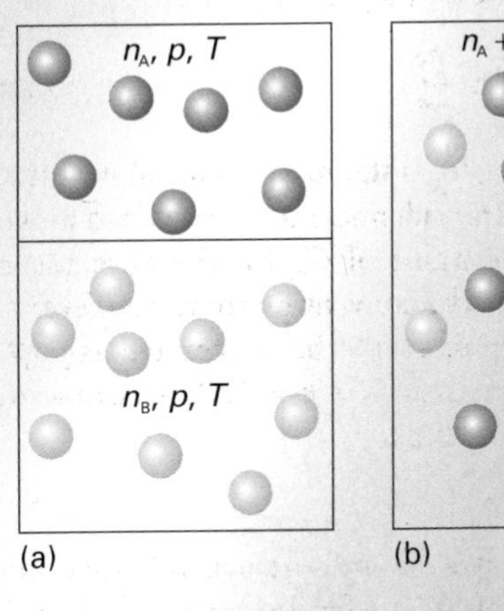

Fig. 6.3 The (a) initial and (b) final states of a system in which two perfect gases mix. The molecules do not interact, so the enthalpy of mixing is zero. However, because the final state is more disordered than the initial state, there is an increase in entropy.

$$\ln x_J p - \ln p = \ln \frac{x_J p}{p} = \ln x_J$$

for each gas, we obtain

$$\Delta G = RT\{n_A \ln x_A + n_B \ln x_B\} = nRT\{x_A \ln x_A + x_B \ln x_B\}$$

which is eqn 6.10.

A useful relation involving logarithms is $\ln x - \ln y = \ln(x/y)$. For example, because $\ln 2 = 0.693$ and $\ln 3 = 1.099$, $\ln 2 - \ln 3 = -0.405$; we note that $\ln \frac{2}{3} = -0.405$ too.

Equation 6.10 tells us the change in Gibbs energy when two gases mix at constant temperature and pressure (Fig. 6.4). The crucial feature is that because x_A and x_B are both less than 1, the two logarithms are negative ($\ln x < 0$ if $x < 1$), so $\Delta G < 0$ at all compositions. Therefore, *perfect gases mix spontaneously in all proportions*. Furthermore, if we compare eqn 6.10 with $\Delta G = \Delta H - T\Delta S$, we can conclude that:

1 *Because eqn 6.10 does not have a term that is independent of temperature,*

$$\Delta H = 0 \tag{6.11a}$$

2 *Because* $\Delta G = 0 - T\Delta S = nRT\{x_A \ln x_A + x_B \ln x_B\}$,

$$\Delta S = -nR\{x_A \ln x_A + x_B \ln x_B\} \tag{6.11b}$$

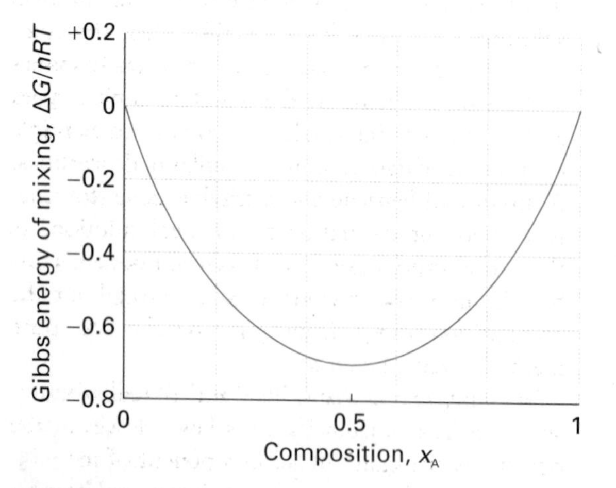

Fig. 6.4 The variation of the Gibbs energy of mixing with composition for two perfect gases at constant temperature and pressure. Note that $\Delta G < 0$ for all compositions, which indicates that two gases mix spontaneously in all proportions.

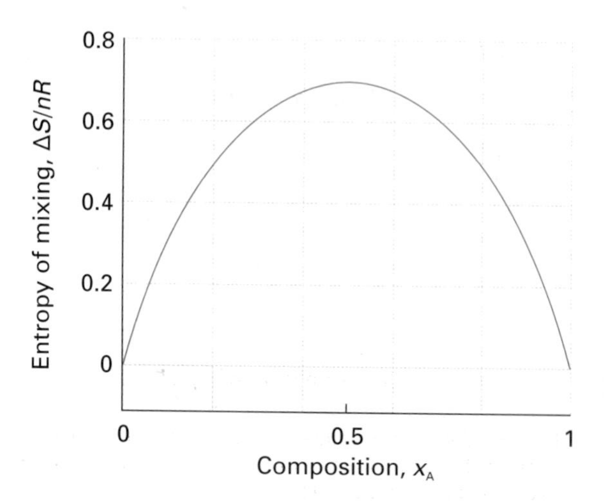

Fig. 6.5 The variation of the entropy of mixing with composition for two perfect gases at constant temperature and pressure.

That is, there is no change in enthalpy when two perfect gases mix, which reflects the fact that there are no interactions between the molecules. There is an increase in entropy, because the mixed gas is more disordered than the unmixed gases (Fig. 6.5). The entropy of the surroundings is unchanged because the enthalpy of the system is constant, so no energy escapes as heat into the surroundings. It follows that the increase in entropy of the system is the 'driving force' of the mixing.

6.4 Ideal solutions

In chemistry we are concerned with liquids as well as gases, so we need an expression for the chemical potential of a substance in a liquid solution. We can anticipate that the chemical potential of a species ought to increase with concentration, because the higher its concentration the greater its chemical 'punch'. In the following, we use J to denote a substance in general, A to denote a solvent, and B a solute.

The key to setting up an expression for the chemical potential of a solute is the work done by the French chemist François Raoult (1830–1901), who spent most of his life measuring the vapour pressures of solutions. He measured the **partial vapour pressure**, p_J, of each component in the mixture, the partial pressure of the vapour of each component in

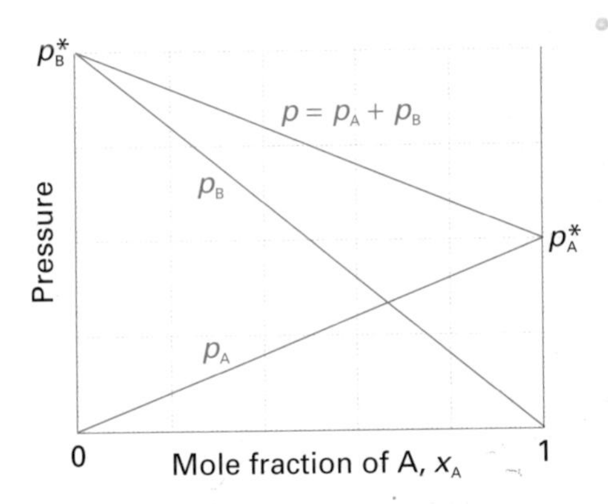

Fig. 6.6 The partial vapour pressures of the two components of an ideal binary mixture are proportional to the mole fractions of the components in the liquid. The total pressure of the vapour is the sum of the two partial vapour pressures.

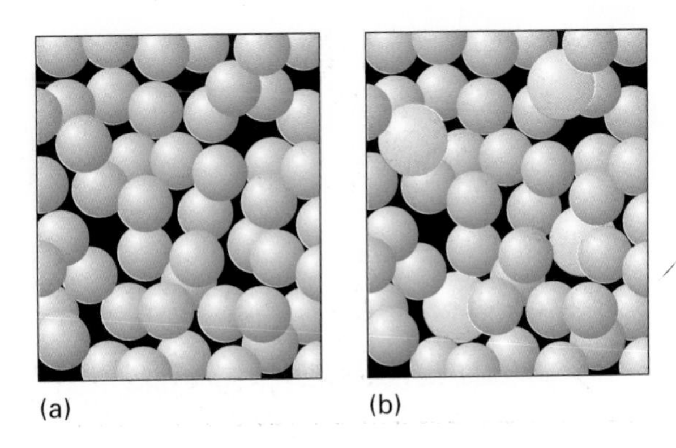

Fig. 6.7 (a) In a pure liquid, we can be confident that any molecule selected from the sample is a solvent molecule. (b) When a solute is present, we cannot be sure that blind selection will give a solvent molecule, so the entropy of the system is greater than in the absence of the solute.

dynamic equilibrium with the liquid mixture, and established what is now called **Raoult's law:**

The partial vapour pressure of a substance in a liquid mixture is proportional to its mole fraction in the mixture and its vapour pressure when pure:

$$p_J = x_J p_J^* \tag{6.12}$$

In this expression, p_J^* is the vapour pressure of the pure substance. For example, when the mole fraction of water in an aqueous solution is 0.90, then, provided Raoult's law is obeyed, the partial vapour pressure of the water in the solution is 90 per cent that of pure water. This conclusion is approximately true whatever the identity of the solute and the solvent (Fig. 6.6).

Self-test 6.5

A solution is prepared by dissolving 1.5 mol $C_{10}H_8$ (naphthalene) in 1.00 kg of benzene. The vapour pressure of pure benzene is 12.6 kPa at 25°C. What is the partial vapour pressure of benzene in the solution?

[*Answer:* 11.3 kPa]

The molecular origin of Raoult's law is the effect of the solute on the entropy of the solution. In the pure solvent, the molecules have a certain disorder and a corresponding entropy; the vapour pressure then represents the tendency of the system and its surroundings to reach a higher entropy. When a solute is present, the solution has a greater disorder than the pure solvent because we cannot be sure that a molecule chosen at random will be a solvent molecule (Fig. 6.7). Because the entropy of the solution is higher than that of the pure solvent, the solution has a lower tendency to acquire an even higher entropy by the solvent vaporizing. In other words, the vapour pressure of the solvent in the solution is lower than that of the pure solvent.

A hypothetical solution of a solute B in a solvent A that obeys Raoult's law throughout the composition range from pure A to pure B is called an **ideal solution.** The law is most reliable when the components of a mixture have similar molecular shapes and are held together in the liquid by similar types and strengths of intermolecular forces. An example is a mixture of two structurally similar hydrocarbons. A mixture of benzene and methylbenzene (toluene) is a good approximation to an ideal solution, as the partial vapour pressure of each component satisfies Raoult's law reasonably well throughout the composition range from pure benzene to pure methylbenzene (Fig. 6.8).

No mixture is perfectly ideal and all real mixtures show deviations from Raoult's law. However, the deviations are small for the component of the mixture that is in large excess (the solvent) and become smaller as the concentration of solute decreases (Fig. 6.9). We can usually be confident that Raoult's law is reliable for the solvent when the solution is

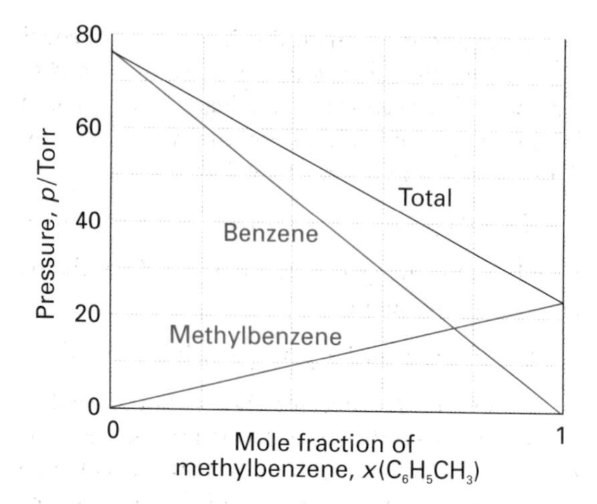

Fig. 6.8 Two similar substances, in this case benzene and methylbenzene (toluene) behave almost ideally and have vapour pressures that closely resemble those for the ideal case depicted in Fig. 6.6.

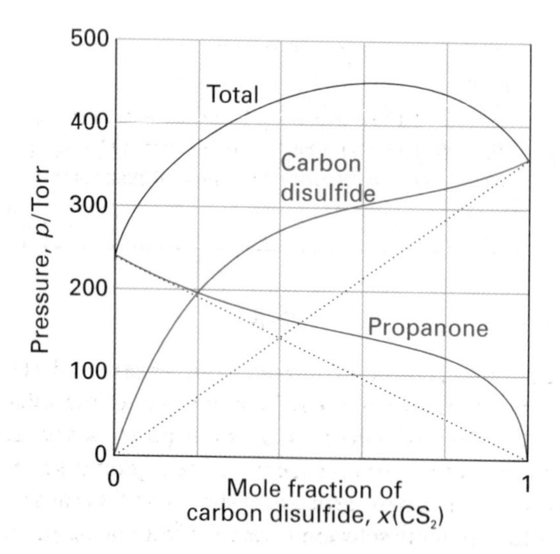

Fig. 6.9 Strong deviations from ideality are shown by dissimilar substances, in this case carbon disulfide and acetone (propanone). Note, however, that Raoult's law is obeyed by propanone when only a small amount of carbon disulfide is present (on the left) and by carbon disulfide when only a small amount of propanone is present (on the right).

very dilute. More formally, Raoult's law is a *limiting law* (like the perfect gas law), and is strictly valid only in the limit of zero concentration of solute.

The theoretical importance of Raoult's law is that, because it relates vapour pressure to composition, and we know how to relate pressure to chemical potential, we can use the law to relate chemical potential to the composition of a solution. As we show in Derivation 6.4, the chemical potential of a solvent A present in solution at a mole fraction x_A is

$$\mu_A = \mu_A^* + RT \ln x_A \tag{6.13}$$

where μ_A^* is the chemical potential of pure A.[3] This expression is valid throughout the concentration range for either component of a binary ideal solution. It is valid for the solvent of a real solution the closer the composition approaches pure solvent (pure A).

Derivation 6.4

The chemical potential of a solvent

We have seen that when a liquid A in a mixture is in equilibrium with its vapour at a partial pressure p_A, the chemical potentials of the two phases are equal (Fig. 6.10), and we can write $\mu_A(l) = \mu_A(g)$. However, we already have an expression for the chemical potential of a vapour, eqn 6.9; so at equilibrium

$$\mu_A(l) = \mu_A^\ominus(g) + RT \ln p_A$$

According to Raoult's law, $p_A = x_A p_A^*$, so we can write

$$\begin{aligned}\mu_A(l) &= \mu_A^\ominus(g) + RT \ln x_A p_A^* \\ &= \mu_A^\ominus(g) + RT \ln p_A^* + RT \ln x_A\end{aligned}$$

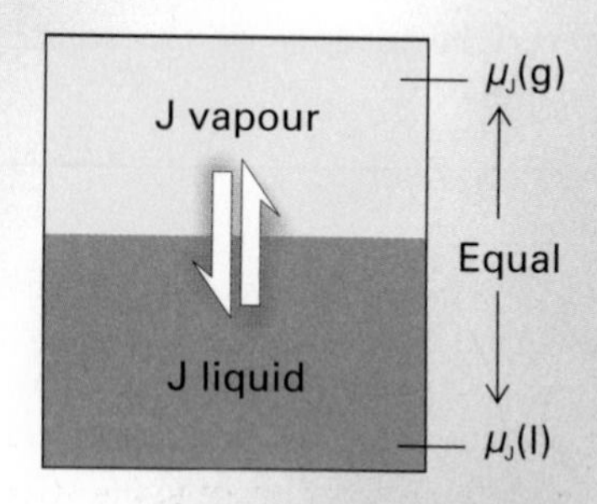

Fig. 6.10 At equilibrium, the chemical potential of a substance in its liquid phase is equal to the chemical potential of the substance in its vapour phase.

[3] If the pressure is 1 bar, μ_A^* can be identified with the standard chemical potential of A, $\mu_A^\ominus$.

A useful relation involving logarithms is $\ln xy = \ln x + \ln y$. For example, $\ln 2 = 0.693$, $\ln 3 = 1.099$, so $\ln 2 + \ln 3 = 1.792$, the same value we get by evaluating $\ln 6$.

The first two terms on the right, $\mu_A^\ominus(g)$ and $RT \ln p_A^*$, are independent of the composition of the mixture. We can write them as the constant μ_A^*, the standard chemical potential of pure liquid A. Then eqn 6.13 follows.

Figure 6.11 shows the variation of chemical potential of the solvent predicted by this expression. Note that the chemical potential has its pure value at $x_A = 1$ (when only A is present). The essential feature of eqn 6.13 is that, because $x_A < 1$ implies that $\ln x_A < 0$, *the chemical potential of a solvent is lower in a solution than when it is pure*. Provided the solution is almost ideal, a solvent in which a solute is present has less chemical 'punch' (including a lower ability to generate a vapour pressure) than when it is pure.

Self-test 6.6

What is the change in chemical potential of benzene at 25°C caused by a solute that is present at a mole fraction of 0.10?

[*Answer:* −0.26 kJ mol^{-1}]

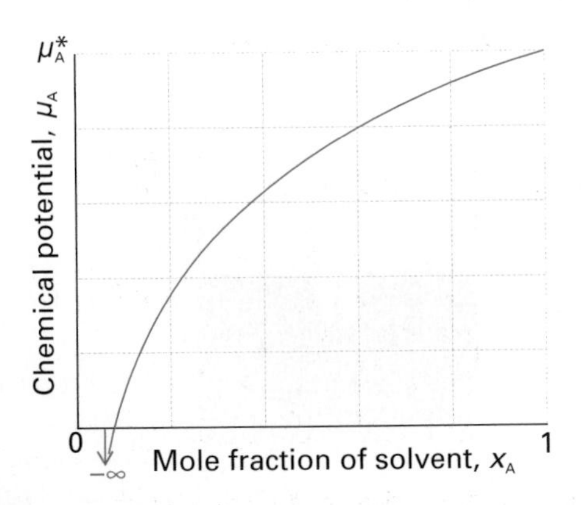

Fig. 6.11 The variation of the chemical potential of the solvent with the composition of the solution. Note that the chemical potential of the solvent is lower in the mixture than for the pure liquid (for an ideal system). This behaviour is likely to be shown by a dilute solution in which the solvent is almost pure (and obeys Raoult's law).

Is mixing to form an ideal solution spontaneous? To answer this question, we need to discover whether ΔG is negative for mixing. The calculation is essentially the same as for the mixing of two perfect gases, and we conclude that

$$\Delta G = nRT\{x_A \ln x_A + x_B \ln x_B\} \qquad (6.14)$$

exactly as for two gases. As for gases, the enthalpy and entropy of mixing are

$$\Delta H = 0 \quad \Delta S = -nR\{x_A \ln x_A + x_B \ln x_B\} \qquad (6.15)$$

The value of ΔH indicates that, although (unlike for perfect gases) there are interactions between the molecules, the solute–solute, solvent–solvent, and solute–solvent interactions are all the same, so the solute slips into solution without a change in enthalpy. The driving force for mixing is the increase in entropy of the system as one component mingles with the other (as in Fig. 6.5).

Self-test 6.7

Derive eqn 6.14 by following Derivation 6.3: the initial Gibbs energy of the unmixed components is $G_i = n_A\mu_A^* + n_B\mu_B^*$; after mixing, use the chemical potentials in eqn 6.13.

6.5 Ideal-dilute solutions

Raoult's law provides a good description of the vapour pressure of the *solvent* in a very dilute solution, when the solvent A is almost pure. However, we cannot in general expect it to be a good description of the vapour pressure of the solute B because a solute in dilute solution is very far from being pure. In a dilute solution, each solute molecule is surrounded by nearly pure solvent, so its environment is quite unlike that in the pure solute and, except when solute and solvent are very similar (such as benzene and methylbenzene), it is very unlikely that its vapour pressure will be related in a simple manner to that of the pure solute. However, it is found experimentally that in dilute solutions the vapour pressure of the solute is in fact proportional to its mole fraction, just as for the solvent. Unlike the solvent, however, the constant of proportionality is not in general the vapour pressure of the pure solute.

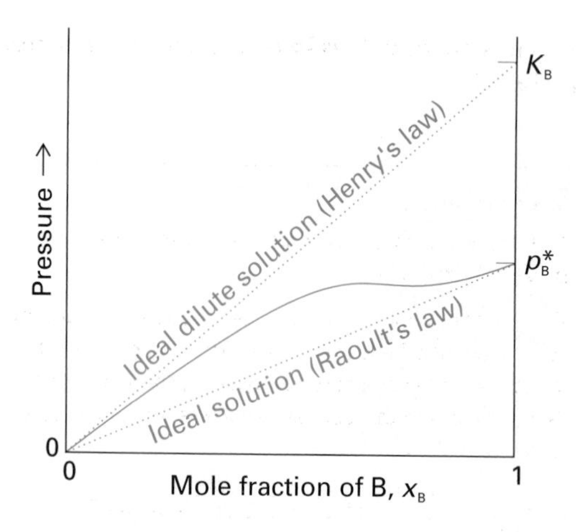

Fig. 6.12 When a component (the solvent) is almost pure, it behaves in accord with Raoult's law and has a vapour pressure that is proportional to the mole fraction in the liquid mixture, and a slope p^*, the vapour pressure of the pure substance. When the same substance is the minor component (the solute), its vapour pressure is still proportional to its mole fraction, but the constant of proportionality is now K.

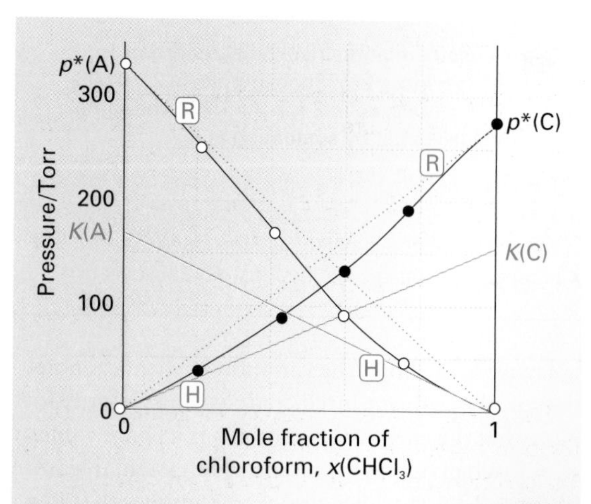

Fig. 6.13 The experimental partial vapour pressures of a mixture of trichloromethane, $CHCl_3$ (chloroform, C), and propanone, CH_3COCH_3 (acetone, A), based on the data in Example 6.3. Henry's or Raoult's law behaviour is denoted H or R, respectively.

This linear but different dependence was discovered by the English chemist William Henry (1775–1836), and is summarized as **Henry's law:**

The vapour pressure of a volatile solute B is proportional to its mole fraction in a solution:

$$p_B = x_B K_B \qquad (6.16)$$

Here K_B, which is called **Henry's law constant,** is characteristic of the solute and chosen so that the straight line predicted by eqn 6.16 is tangent to the experimental curve at $x_B = 0$ (Fig. 6.12).

Henry's law is usually obeyed only at low concentrations of the solute (close to $x_B = 0$). Solutions that are dilute enough for the solute to obey Henry's law are called **ideal-dilute solutions.**

Example 6.3

Verifying Raoult's and Henry's laws

The partial vapour pressures of each component in a mixture of propanone (acetone, A) and trichloromethane (chloroform, C) were measured at 35°C with the following results:

x_C	0	0.20	0.40	0.60	0.80	1
p_C/Torr	0	35	82	142	219	293
p_A/Torr	347	270	185	102	37	0

Confirm that the mixture conforms to Raoult's law for the component in large excess and to Henry's law for the minor component. Find the Henry's law constants.

Strategy We need to plot the partial vapour pressures against mole fraction. To verify Raoult's law, we compare the data to the straight line $p_J = x_J p_J^*$ for each component in the region in which it is in excess and therefore acting as the solvent. We verify Henry's law by finding a straight line $p_J = x_J K_J$ that is tangent to each partial vapour pressure at low x_J where the component can be treated as the solute.

Solution The data are plotted in Fig. 6.13 together with the Raoult's law lines. Henry's law requires K_A = 175 Torr and K_C = 165 Torr. Note how the data deviate from both Raoult's and Henry's laws for even quite small departures from $x = 1$ and $x = 0$, respectively.

A note on good practice In a more professional approach, the data are fitted to a polynomial function (using a computer) and then the tangent is calculated by evaluating the first derivative of the polynomial at $x_J = 0$. We have in fact used that approach here.

Self-test 6.8

The vapour pressure of chloromethane at various mole fractions in a mixture at 25°C was found to be as follows:

x	0.005	0.009	0.019	0.024
p/Torr	205	363	756	946

Estimate Henry's law constant.

[*Answer:* 4×10^4 Torr]

The Henry's law constants of some gases are listed in Table 6.1. The values given there are for the law written in terms of the molar concentration

$$p_J = K_H[J] \qquad (6.17)$$

The web site contains links to online databases of Henry's law constants.

Henry's constant, K_H, is commonly reported in kilopascals metre-cubed per mole (kPa m^3 mol^{-1}). This form of the law and these units make it very easy to calculate the molar concentration of the dissolved gas, simply by multiplying the partial pressure of the gas (in kilopascals) by the appropriate constant. Equation 6.17 is used, for instance, to estimate the concentration of O_2 in natural waters or the concentration of carbon dioxide in blood plasma. A knowledge of Henry's law constants for gases in fats and lipids is important for the discussion of respiration, especially when the partial pressure of oxygen is abnormal, as in diving and mountaineering (Box 6.1).

Table 6.1

Henry's law constants for gases dissolved in water at 25°C

	K_H/(kPa m^3 mol^{-1})
Ammonia, NH_3	5.69
Carbon dioxide, CO_2	2.937
Helium, He	282.7
Hydrogen, H_2	121.2
Methane, CH_4	67.4
Nitrogen, N_2	155
Oxygen, O_2	74.68

Illustration 6.2

Determining whether a natural water can support aquatic life

The concentration of O_2 in water required to support aerobic aquatic life is about 4 mg dm^{-3}. To calculate the minimum partial pressure of oxygen in the atmosphere that can achieve this concentration we use eqn 6.17 to write

$$[O_2] = \frac{4 \times 10^{-3}\ \text{g dm}^{-3}}{32\ \text{g mol}^{-1}} = \frac{4 \times 10^{-3}}{32}\ \text{mol dm}^{-3}$$

From Table 6.1, K_H for oxygen in water is 74.68 kPa m^3 mol^{-1}; therefore the partial pressure needed to achieve the stated concentration is

$$p_{O_2} = (74.68\ \text{kPa m}^3\ \text{mol}^{-1}) \times \left(\frac{4 \times 10^{-3}}{32}\ \text{mol dm}^{-3}\right)$$

$$= \frac{74.68 \times 4 \times 10^{-3}}{32}\ \frac{\text{kPa m}^3}{\text{dm}^3}$$

$$= \frac{74.68 \times 4}{32}\ \text{kPa} = 9\ \text{kPa}$$

(We have used 1 dm^3 = 10^{-3} m^3.) The partial pressure of oxygen in air at sea level is 21 kPa, which is greater than 9 kPa, so the required concentration can be maintained under normal conditions.

A note on good practice The number of significant figures in the result of a calculation should not exceed the number in the data (only 1 in this case).

Self-test 6.9

What partial pressure is needed to dissolve 21 g of carbon dioxide in 100 g of water at 25°C?

[*Answer:* 14 kPa]

Henry's law lets us write an expression for the chemical potential of a solute in a solution. By exactly the same reasoning as in Derivation 6.4, but with the empirical constant K_B used in place of the vapour pressure of the pure solute, p_B^*, the chemical potential of the solute when it is present at a mole fraction x_B is

$$\mu_B = \mu_B^* + RT \ln x_B \qquad (6.18)$$

Box 6.1 *Gas solubility and breathing*

We inhale about 500 cm^3 of air with each breath we take. The influx of air is a result of changes in volume of the lungs as the diaphragm is depressed and the chest expands, which results in a decrease in pressure of about 100 Pa relative to atmospheric pressure. Expiration occurs as the diaphragm rises and the chest contracts, and gives rise to a differential pressure of about 100 Pa above atmospheric pressure. The total volume of air in the lungs is about 6 dm^3, and the additional volume of air that can be exhaled forcefully after normal expiration is about 1.5 dm^3. Some air remains in the lungs at all times to prevent the collapse of the alveoli.

The effect of gas exchange between blood and the air inside the alveoli of the lungs means that the composition of the air in the lungs changes throughout the breathing cycle. Alveolar gas is in fact a mixture of newly inhaled air and air about to be exhaled. The concentration of oxygen present in arterial blood is equivalent to a partial pressure of about 5 kPa, whereas the partial pressure of freshly inhaled air is about 14 kPa. Arterial blood remains in the capillary passing through the wall of an alveolus for about 0.75 s, but such is the steepness of the pressure gradient that it becomes fully saturated with oxygen in about 0.25 s. If the lungs collect fluids (as in pneumonia), the respiratory membrane thickens, diffusion is greatly slowed, and body tissues begin to suffer from oxygen starvation. Carbon dioxide moves in the opposite direction across the respiratory tissue, but the partial pressure gradient is much less, corresponding to about 700 Pa in blood and 5 kPa in air at equilibrium. However, because carbon dioxide is much more soluble in the alveolar fluid than oxygen is, equal amounts of oxygen and carbon dioxide are exchanged in each breath.

A hyperbaric oxygen chamber, in which oxygen is at an elevated partial pressure, is used to treat certain types of disease. Carbon monoxide poisoning can be treated in this way, as can the consequences of shock. Diseases that are caused by anaerobic bacteria, such as gas gangrene and tetanus, can also be treated because the bacteria cannot thrive in high oxygen concentrations.

In scuba diving (where *scuba* is an acronym formed from 'self-contained underwater breathing apparatus'), air is supplied at a higher pressure, so that the pressure within the diver's chest matches the pressure exerted by the surrounding water. The latter increases by about 1 atm for each 10 m of descent. One unfortunate consequence of breathing air at high pressures is that nitrogen is much more soluble in fatty tissues than in water, so it tends to dissolve in the central nervous system, bone marrow, and fat reserves. The result is *nitrogen narcosis*, with symptoms like intoxication. If the diver rises too rapidly to the surface, the nitrogen comes out of its lipid solution as bubbles, which causes the painful and sometimes fatal condition known as *the bends*. Many cases of scuba drowning appear to be consequences of arterial embolisms (obstructions in arteries caused by gas bubbles) and loss of consciousness as the air bubbles rise into the head.

Exercise 1 Haemoglobin, the red blood protein responsible for oxygen transport, binds about 1.34 cm^3 of oxygen per gram. Normal blood has a haemoglobin concentration of 150 g dm^{-3}. Haemoglobin in the lungs is about 97 per cent saturated with oxygen, but only about 75 per cent saturated in the capillaries of the tissues to which the blood is supplied. What volume of oxygen is given up by 100 cm^3 of blood flowing from the lungs in the capillaries?

Exercise 2 Breathing air at high pressures, such as in scuba diving, results in an increased concentration of dissolved nitrogen. The Henry's law constant in the form $c = Kp$ for the solubility of nitrogen is 0.18 μg/(g H_2O atm). What mass of nitrogen is dissolved in 100 g of water saturated with air at 4.0 atm and 20°C? Compare your answer to that for 100 g of water saturated with air at 1.0 atm. (Air is 78.08 mole per cent N_2.) If nitrogen is four times as soluble in fatty tissues as in water, what is the increase in nitrogen concentration in fatty tissue in going from 1 atm to 4 atm?

This expression, which is illustrated in Fig. 6.14, applies when Henry's law is valid, in very dilute solutions. The chemical potential of the solute has its pure value when it is present alone ($x_B = 1$, $\ln 1 = 0$) and a smaller value when dissolved (when $x_B < 1$, $\ln x_B < 0$).

We often express the composition of a solution in terms of the molar concentration of the solute, [B], rather than as a mole fraction. The mole fraction and the molar concentration are proportional to each other in dilute solutions, so we write x_B = constant × [B]. To avoid complications with units,

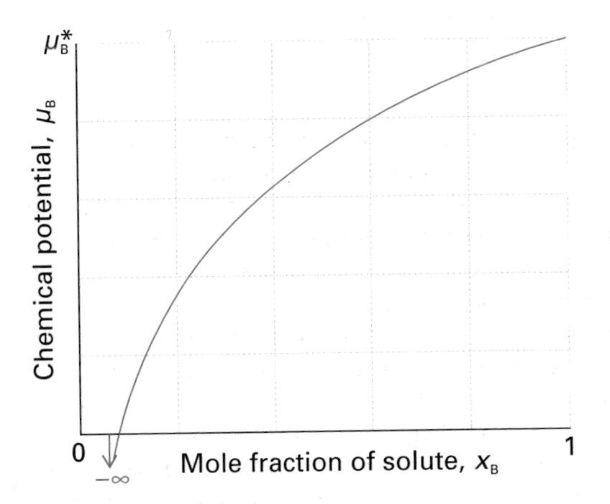

Fig. 6.14 The variation of the chemical potential of the solute with the composition of the solution expressed in terms of the mole fraction of solute. Note that the chemical potential of the solute is lower in the mixture than for the pure solute (for an ideal system). This behaviour is likely to be shown by a dilute solution in which the solvent is almost pure and the solute obeys Henry's law.

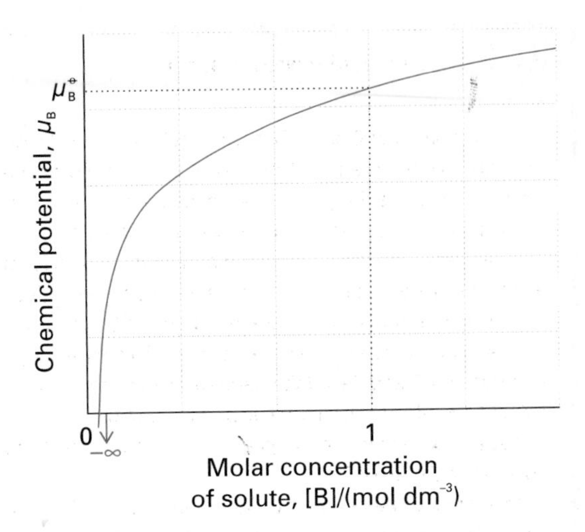

Fig. 6.15 The variation of the chemical potential of the solute with the composition of the solution that obeys Henry's law expressed in terms of the molar concentration of solute. The chemical potential has its standard value at [B] = 1 mol dm^{-3}.

we shall interpret [B] wherever it appears as the numerical value of the molar concentration in moles per cubic decimetre.[4] Then eqn 6.18 becomes

$$\mu_B = \mu_B^* + RT \ln(\text{constant}) + RT \ln [B]$$

We can combine the first two terms into a single constant, which we denote $\mu_B^\ominus$, and write this relation as

$$\mu_B = \mu_B^\ominus + RT \ln [B] \qquad (6.19)$$

Figure 6.15 illustrates the variation of chemical potential with concentration predicted by this equation. The chemical potential of the solute has its standard value when the molar concentration of the solute is 1 mol dm^{-3}.

6.6 Real solutions: activities

No actual solutions are ideal, and many solutions deviate from ideal-dilute behaviour as soon as the concentration of solute rises above a small value. In thermodynamics we try to preserve the form of equations developed for ideal systems so that it becomes easy to step between the two types of system.[5] This is the thought behind the introduction of the **activity**, a_J, of a substance, which is a kind of effective concentration. The activity is defined so that the expression

$$\mu_J = \mu_J^\ominus + RT \ln a_J \qquad (6.20)$$

is true at *all* concentrations and for both the solvent and the solute.

For ideal solutions, $a_J = x_J$, and the activity of each component is equal to its mole fraction. For ideal-dilute solutions using the definition in eqn 6.19, a_B = [B], and the activity of the solute is equal to the numerical value of its molar concentration. For *non*-ideal solutions we write

$$a_A = \gamma_A x_A \qquad a_B = \gamma_B [B] \qquad (6.21)$$

where the γ (gamma) in each case is the **activity coefficient**. Activity coefficients depend on the composition of the solution and we should note that:

because the solvent behaves more in accord with Raoult's law as it becomes pure, $\gamma_A \to 1$ as $x_A \to 1$;

because the solute behaves more in accord with Henry's law as the solution becomes very dilute, $\gamma_B \to 1$ as $[B] \to 0$.

[4] Thus, if the molar concentration of B is 1.0 mol dm^{-3}, [B] = 1.0.

[5] An added advantage is that there are fewer equations to remember!

Table 6.2
*Activities and standard states**

Substance	Standard state	Activity, *a*
Solid	Pure solid, 1 bar	1
Liquid	Pure liquid, 1 bar	1
Gas	Pure gas, 1 bar	$p/p^{\ominus}$
Solute	Molar concentration of 1 mol dm^{-3}	$[J]/c^{\ominus}$

$p^{\ominus} = 1$ bar ($= 10^5$ Pa), $c^{\ominus} = 1$ mol dm^{-3}.
* Activities are for perfect gases and ideal-dilute solutions; all activities are dimensionless.

These conventions and relations are summarized in Table 6.2.

Activities and activity coefficients are often branded as 'fudge factors'. To some extent that is true. However, their introduction does allow us to derive thermodynamically exact expressions for the properties of non-ideal solutions. Moreover, in a number of cases it is possible to calculate or measure the activity coefficient of a species in solution. In this text we shall normally derive thermodynamic relations in terms of activities, but when we want to make contact with actual measurements, we shall set the activities equal to the 'ideal' values in Table 6.2.

Colligative properties

An ideal solute has no effect on the enthalpy of a solution in the sense that the enthalpy of mixing is zero. However, it does affect the entropy by introducing a degree of disorder that is not present in the pure solvent, and we found in eqn 6.15 that $\Delta S > 0$ when two components mix to give an ideal solution. We can therefore expect a solute to modify the physical properties of the solution. Apart from lowering the vapour pressure of the solvent, which we have already considered, a non-volatile solute has three main effects: it raises the boiling point of a solution, it lowers the freezing point, and it gives rise to an osmotic pressure. (The meaning of the last will be explained shortly.) Because these properties all stem from changes in the disorder of the solvent, and the increase in disorder is independent of the identity of the species we use to bring it about, all of them depend only on the number of solute particles present, not their chemical identity. For this reason they are called **colligative properties.**[6] Thus, a 0.01 mol kg^{-1} aqueous solution of any non-electrolyte should have the same boiling point, freezing point, and osmotic pressure.

6.7 The modification of boiling and freezing points

As indicated above, the effect of a solute is to raise the boiling point of a solvent and to lower its freezing point. It is found empirically, and can be justified thermodynamically, that the **elevation of boiling point**, ΔT_B, and the **depression of freezing point**, ΔT_f, are both proportional to the molality, b_B, of the solute:

$$\Delta T_B = K_B b_B \qquad \Delta T_f = K_f b_B \tag{6.22}$$

K_B is the **ebullioscopic constant** and K_f is the **cryoscopic constant** of the solvent.[7] The two constants can be estimated from other properties of the solvent, but both are best treated as empirical constants (Table 6.3).

Table 6.3
Cryoscopic and ebullioscopic constants

Solvent	K_f/(K kg mol^{-1})	K_b/(K kg mol^{-1})
Acetic acid	3.90	3.07
Benzene	5.12	2.53
Camphor	40	
Carbon disulfide	3.8	2.37
Naphthalene	6.94	5.8
Phenol	7.27	3.04
Tetrachloromethane	30	4.95
Water	1.86	0.51

[6] Colligative denotes 'depending on the collection'.
[7] They are also called the 'boiling-point constant' and the 'freezing-point constant', respectively.

Self-test 6.10

Estimate the lowering of the freezing point of the solution made by dissolving 3.0 g (about one cube) of sucrose in 100 g of water.

[*Answer:* −0.16 K]

To understand the origin of these effects we shall make two simplifying assumptions:

1 The solute is not volatile, and therefore does not appear in the vapour phase.

2 The solute is insoluble in the solid solvent, and therefore does not appear in the solid phase.

For example, a solution of sucrose in water consists of a solute (sucrose, $C_{12}H_{22}O_{11}$) that is not volatile and therefore never appears in the vapour, which is therefore pure water vapour. The sucrose is also left behind in the liquid solvent when ice begins to form, so the ice remains pure.

The origin of colligative properties is the lowering of chemical potential of the solvent by the presence of a solute, as expressed by eqn 6.13. We saw in Section 5.3 that the freezing and boiling points correspond to the temperatures at which the graph of the molar Gibbs energy of the liquid intersects the graphs of the molar Gibbs energy of the solid and vapour phases, respectively. Because we are now dealing with mixtures, we have to think about the *partial* molar Gibbs energy (the chemical potential) of the solvent. The presence of a solute lowers the chemical potential of the liquid but, because the vapour and solid remain pure, their chemical potentials remain unchanged. As a result, we see from Fig. 6.16 that the freezing point moves to lower values; likewise, from Fig. 6.17 we see that the boiling point moves to higher values. In other words, the freezing point is depressed, the boiling point is elevated, and the liquid phase exists over a wider range of temperatures.

The elevation of boiling point is too small to have any practical significance. A practical consequence of the lowering of freezing point, and hence the lowering of the melting point of the pure solid, is its use in organic chemistry to judge the purity of a sample, because any impurity lowers the melting point of a substance from its accepted value. The

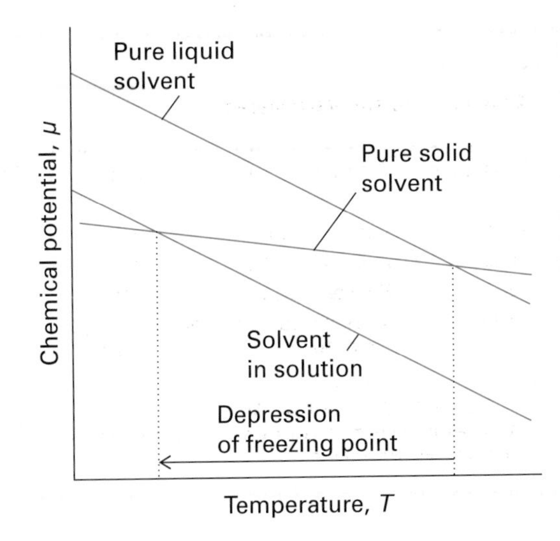

Fig. 6.16 The chemical potentials of pure solid solvent and pure liquid solvent decrease with temperature, and the point of intersection, where the chemical potential of the liquid rises above that of the solid, marks the freezing point of the pure solvent. A solute lowers the chemical potential of the solvent but leaves that of the solid unchanged. As a result, the intersection point lies further to the left and the freezing point is therefore lowered.

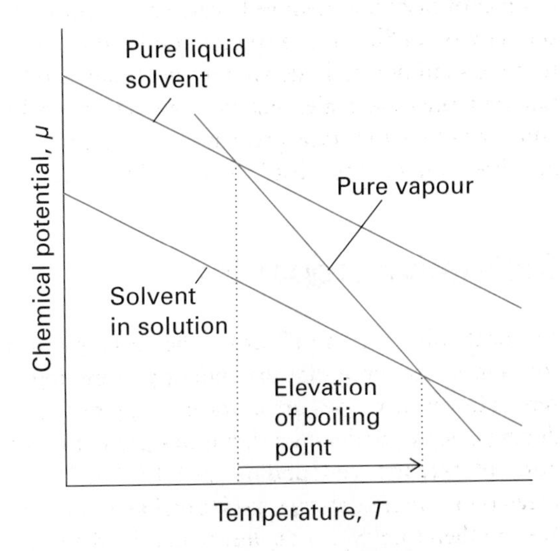

Fig. 6.17 The chemical potentials of pure solvent vapour and pure liquid solvent decrease with temperature, and the point of intersection, where the chemical potential of the vapour falls below that of the liquid, marks the boiling point of the pure solvent. A solute lowers the chemical potential of the solvent but leaves that of the vapour unchanged. As a result, the intersection point lies further to the right, and the boiling point is therefore raised.

salt water of the oceans freezes at temperatures lower than that of fresh water, and salt is spread on highways to delay the onset of freezing. The addition of 'antifreeze' to car engines and, by natural processes, to arctic fish, is commonly held up as an example of the lowering of freezing point, but the concentrations are far too high for the arguments we have used here to be applicable. The 1,2-ethanediol ('glycol') used as antifreeze and the proteins present in fish body fluids probably simply interfere with bonding between water molecules.

6.8 Osmosis

The phenomenon of **osmosis** is the passage of a pure solvent into a solution separated from it by a semipermeable membrane.[8] A **semipermeable membrane** is a membrane that is permeable to the solvent but not to the solute. The membrane might have microscopic holes that are large enough to allow water molecules to pass through, but not ions or carbohydrate molecules with their bulky coating of hydrating water molecules. The **osmotic pressure**, Π (uppercase pi), is the pressure that must be applied to the solution to stop the inward flow of solvent.

In the simple arrangement shown in Fig. 6.18, the pressure opposing the passage of solvent into the solution arises from the hydrostatic pressure of the column of solution that the osmosis itself produces.

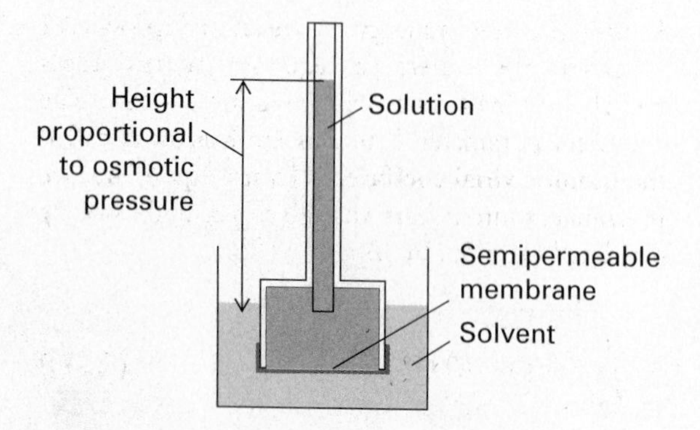

Fig. 6.18 In a simple osmosis experiment, a solution is separated from the pure solvent by a semipermeable membrane. Pure solvent passes through the membrane and the solution rises in the inner tube. The net flow ceases when the pressure exerted by the column of liquid is equal to the osmotic pressure of the solution.

This column is formed when the pure solvent flows through the membrane into the solution and pushes the column of solution higher up the tube. Equilibrium is reached when the downward pressure exerted by the column of solution is equal to the upward osmotic pressure. A complication of this arrangement is that the entry of solvent into the solution results in dilution of the latter, so it is more difficult to treat mathematically than an arrangement in which an externally applied pressure opposes any flow of solvent into the solution.

The osmotic pressure of a solution is proportional to the concentration of solute. In fact, we show in Derivation 6.5 that the expression for the osmotic pressure of an ideal solution, which is called the **van 't Hoff equation**, bears an uncanny resemblance to the expression for the pressure of a perfect gas:

$$\Pi V \approx n_B RT \quad (6.23a)$$

Because $n_B/V = [B]$, the molar concentration of the solute, a simpler form of this equation is

$$\Pi \approx [B]RT \quad (6.23b)$$

This equation applies only to solutions that are sufficiently dilute to behave as ideal-dilute solutions.

Derivation 6.5

The van 't Hoff equation

The thermodynamic treatment of osmosis makes use of the fact that, at equilibrium, the chemical potential of the solvent A is the same on each side of the membrane (Fig. 6.19). The starting relation is therefore

$$\mu_A(\text{pure solvent at pressure } p)$$
$$= \mu_A(\text{solvent in the solution at pressure } p+\Pi)$$

The pure solvent is at atmospheric pressure, p, and the solution is at a pressure $p + \Pi$ on account of the additional pressure, Π, that has to be exerted on the solution to establish equilibrium. We shall write the chemical potential of the pure solvent at the pressure p as $\mu_A^*(p)$. The chemical potential of the solvent in the solution is lowered by the solute but it is raised on account of the greater pressure, $p+\Pi$, acting on the solution. We denote this chemical potential by $\mu_A(x_A, p+\Pi)$. Our task

[8] The name *osmosis* is derived from the Greek word for 'push'.

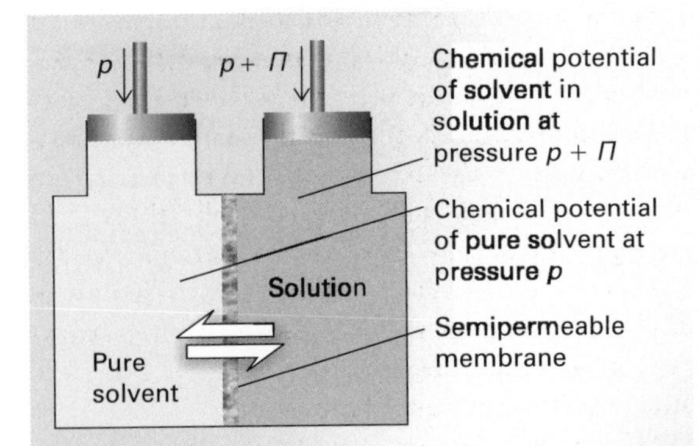

Fig. 6.19 The basis of the calculation of osmotic pressure. The presence of a solute lowers the chemical potential of the solvent in the right-hand compartment, but the application of pressure raises it. The osmotic pressure is the pressure needed to equalize the chemical potential of the solvent in the two compartments.

is to find the extra pressure Π needed to balance the lowering of chemical potential caused by the solute.

The condition for equilibrium is

$$\mu_A^*(p) = \mu_A(x_A, p+\Pi)$$

We take the effect of the solute into account by using eqn 6.13:

$$\mu_A(x_A, p+\Pi) = \mu_A^*(p+\Pi) + RT\ln x_A$$

The effect of pressure on an (assumed incompressible) liquid is given by eqn 5.1 ($\Delta G_m = V_m \Delta p$) but now expressed in terms of the chemical potential and the partial molar volume of the solvent:

$$\mu_A^*(p+\Pi) = \mu_A^*(p) + V_A \Delta p$$

At this point we identify the difference in pressure Δp as Π. When the last three equations are combined we get

$$\mu_A^*(p) = \mu_A^*(p) + V_A\Pi + RT\ln x_A$$

and therefore

$$-RT\ln x_A = \Pi V_A$$

The mole fraction of the solvent is equal to $1 - x_B$, where x_B is the mole fraction of solute molecules. In dilute solution, $\ln(1 - x_B)$ is approximately equal to $-x_B$, so this equation becomes

$$RTx_B \approx \Pi V_A$$

The series expansion of a natural logarithm (see Appendix 2) is

$$\ln(1-x) = -x - \tfrac{1}{2}x^2 - \tfrac{1}{3}x^3 \cdots$$

If $x \ll 1$, then the terms involving x raised to a power greater than 1 are much smaller than x, so $\ln(1-x) \approx -x$. For example, $\ln(1-0.050) = \ln 0.950 = -0.051$, which is close to -0.050.

When the solution is dilute, $x_B = n_B/n \approx n_B/n_A$. Moreover, because $n_AV_A \approx V$, the total volume of the solution, this equation becomes eqn 6.23.

Osmosis helps biological cells to maintain their structure. Cell membranes are semipermeable and allow water, small molecules, and hydrated ions to pass, while blocking the passage of biopolymers synthesized inside the cell. The difference in concentrations of solutes inside and outside the cell gives rise to an osmotic pressure, and water passes into the more concentrated solution in the interior of the cell, carrying small nutrient molecules. The influx of water also keeps the cell swollen, whereas dehydration causes the cell to shrink.

One of the most common applications of osmosis is **osmometry**, the measurement of molar masses of proteins and synthetic polymers from the osmotic pressure of their solutions. As these huge molecules dissolve to produce solutions that are far from ideal, we assume that the van 't Hoff equation is only the first term of an expansion:

$$\Pi = [B]RT\{1 + B[B] + \cdots\} \qquad (6.24a)$$

Exactly the same strategy was used in Section 1.12 to extend the perfect gas equation to real gases and there it led to the virial equation of state. The empirical parameter B in this expression is called the **osmotic virial coefficient**. To use eqn 6.24a, we rearrange it into a form that gives a straight line by dividing both sides by [B]:

$$\frac{\Pi}{[B]} = \underbrace{RT}_{\text{Intercept}} + \underbrace{BRT}_{\text{Slope}}[B] + \cdots \qquad (6.24b)$$

As we illustrate in the following example, we can find the molar mass of the solute B by measuring the osmotic pressure at a series of mass concentrations and making a plot of $\Pi/[B]$ against [B] (Fig. 6.20).

Example 6.4

Using osmometry to determine molar mass

The osmotic pressures of solutions of an enzyme in water at 298 K are given below. Determine the molar mass of the enzyme.

$c/(\mathrm{g\ dm^{-3}})$	1.00	2.00	4.00	7.00	9.00
Π/Pa	27	70	197	500	785

Strategy First, we need to express eqn 6.24b in terms of the mass concentration, *c*. The molar concentration [B] of the solute is related to the mass concentration $c_B = m_B/V$ by

$$c_B = \frac{m_B}{V} = \frac{m_B}{n_B} \times \frac{n_B}{V}$$

$$= M \times [\mathrm{B}]$$

where M is the molar mass of the solute (its mass, m_B, divided by its amount in moles, n_B), so $[\mathrm{B}] = c_B/M$. With these substitutions, eqn 6.24b becomes

$$\frac{\Pi}{c_B/M} = RT + \frac{BRTc_B}{M} + \cdots$$

Division through by M gives

$$\frac{\Pi}{c_B} = \frac{RT}{M} + \left(\frac{RTB}{M^2}\right)c_B + \cdots$$

It follows that, by plotting Π/c_B against c_B, the results should fall on a straight line with intercept RT/M on the vertical axis at $c_B = 0$. Therefore, by locating the intercept by extrapolation of the data to $c_B = 0$, we can find the molar mass of the solute.

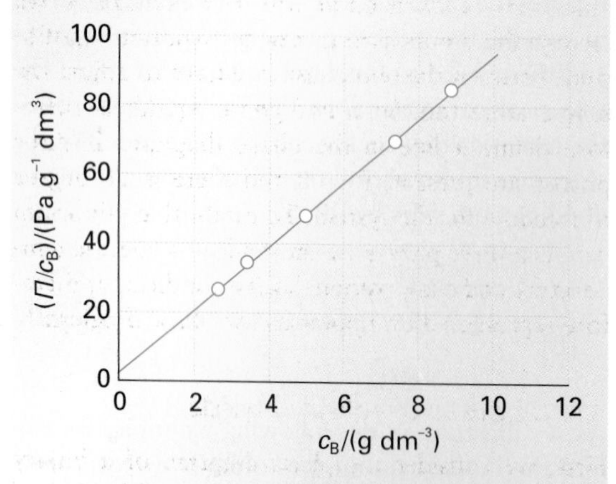

Fig. 6.21 The plot of the data in Example 6.4. The molar mass is determined from the intercept at $c_B = 0$.

Solution The following values of Π/c_B can be calculated from the data:

$c_B/(\mathrm{g\ dm^{-3}})$	1.00	2.00	4.00	7.00	9.00
$(\Pi/c_B)/(\mathrm{Pa\ g^{-1}\ dm^3})$	27	35	49.2	71.4	87.2

The points are plotted in Fig. 6.21. The intercept with the vertical axis at $c_B = 0$ is at

$$(\Pi/c_B)/(\mathrm{Pa\ g^{-1}\ dm^3}) = 19.6$$

which we can rearrange into

$$\Pi/c_B = 19.6\ \mathrm{Pa\ g^{-1}\ dm^3}$$

$$= 19.6\ \frac{\mathrm{Pa\ dm^3}}{\mathrm{g}}$$

$$= 19.6\ \frac{\mathrm{kg\ m^{-1}\ s^{-2}} \times 10^{-3}\ \mathrm{m^3}}{10^{-3}\ \mathrm{kg}}$$

$$= 19.6\ \mathrm{m^2\ s^{-2}}$$

Therefore, because this intercept is equal to RT/M, we can write

$$M = \frac{RT}{19.6\ \mathrm{m^2\ s^{-2}}}$$

It follows that

$$M = \frac{(8.314\,47\ \mathrm{J\ K^{-1}\ mol^{-1}}) \times (298\ \mathrm{K})}{19.6\ \mathrm{m^2\ s^{-2}}}$$

$$= \frac{8.314\,47 \times 298}{19.6}\ \frac{\mathrm{J\ mol^{-1}}}{\mathrm{m^2\ s^{-2}}}$$

$$= 126\ \mathrm{kg\ mol^{-1}}$$

(To get the last line, we have used $1\ \mathrm{J} = 1\ \mathrm{kg\ m^2\ s^{-2}}$.) The molar mass of the enzyme is therefore close to 130 kDa.

A note on good practice. Graphs should be plotted on axes labelled with pure numbers. Note how the plotted quantities are divided by their units, so that $c_B/(\mathrm{g\ dm^{-3}})$, for instance, is a dimensionless number. By carrying the units through every stage of the calculation, we end up with the correct units for M.

Self-test 6.11

The osmotic pressures of a solution of poly(vinyl chloride), PVC, in dioxane at 25°C were as follows:

$c/(\mathrm{g\ dm^{-3}})$	0.50	1.00	1.50	2.00	2.50
Π/Pa	33.6	35.2	36.8	38.4	40.0

Determine the molar mass of the polymer.

[*Answer:* 73 kg mol^{-1}]

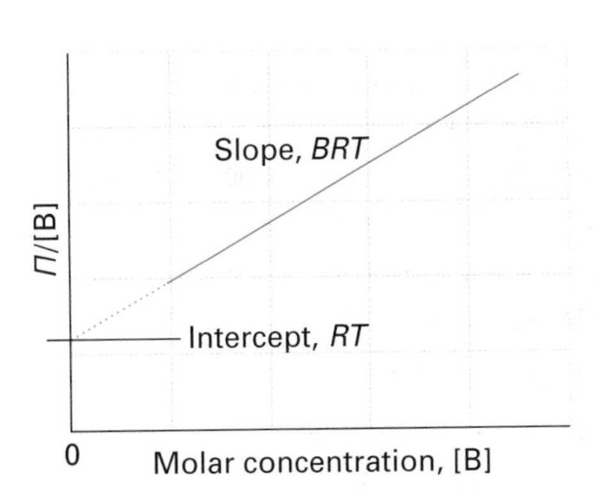

Fig. 6.20 The plot and extrapolation made to analyse the results of an osmometry experiment.

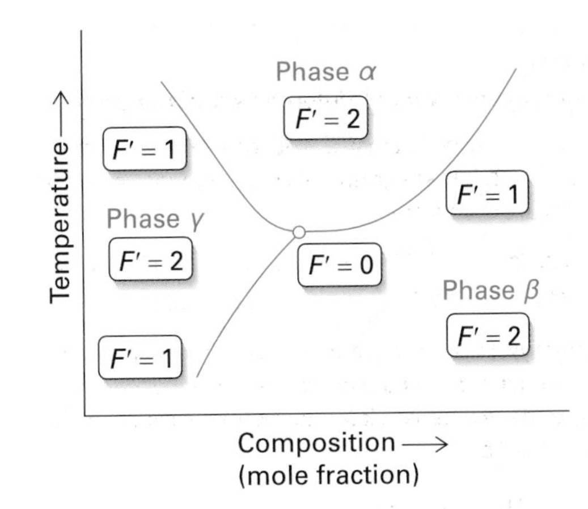

Fig. 6.22 The interpretation of a temperature–composition phase diagram at constant pressure. In a region where only one phase is present, $F' = 2$ and both composition and temperature can be varied. On a phase boundary, where two phases are in equilibrium, $F' = 1$ and only one variable can be changed independently. At a point where three phases are present in equilibrium, $F' = 0$, and the temperature and composition are fixed.

When pressure greater than the osmotic pressure is applied to the solution, there is a thermodynamic tendency for the solvent to flow out of the solution and into the pure solvent. This process is called **reverse osmosis.** Reverse osmosis is of great importance for the purification of sea water so that it is potable (drinkable) and can be used for irrigation, and many reverse osmosis plants are in operation around the world to supply fresh water to arid or water-deficient regions. The principal technical problem is to manufacture semipermeable membranes that are strong enough to withstand the high pressures required but still allow an economic flow.

Phase diagrams of mixtures

As in the discussion of pure substances (Chapter 5), the phase diagram of a mixture shows which phase is most stable for the given conditions. However, composition is now a variable in addition to the pressure and temperature.

It will be useful to keep in mind the implications of the phase rule ($F = C - P + 2$, Section 5.7). We shall consider only **binary mixtures,** which are mixtures of two components (such as ethanol and water) and may therefore set $C = 2$. Then $F = 4 - P$. For simplicity we keep the pressure constant (at 1 atm, for instance), which uses up one of the degrees of freedom, and write $F' = 3 - P$ for the number of degrees of freedom remaining. One of these degrees of freedom is the temperature, the other is the composition. Hence we should be able to depict the phase equilibria of the system on a **temperature–composition diagram** in which one axis is the temperature and the other axis is the mole fraction. In a region where there is only one phase, $F' = 2$ and both the temperature and the composition can be varied (Fig. 6.22). If two phases are present at equilibrium, $F' = 1$, and only one of the two variables may be changed at will. For example, if we change the composition, then to maintain equilibrium between the two phases we have to adjust the temperature too. Such two-phase equilibria therefore define a line in the phase diagram. If three phases are present, $F' = 0$ and there is no degree of freedom for the system. To establish equilibrium between three phases we must adopt a specific temperature and composition. Such a condition is therefore represented by a point on the phase diagram.

6.9 Mixtures of volatile liquids

First, we consider the phase diagram of a binary mixture of two volatile components. This kind of system is important for understanding fractional distillation, which is a widely used technique in

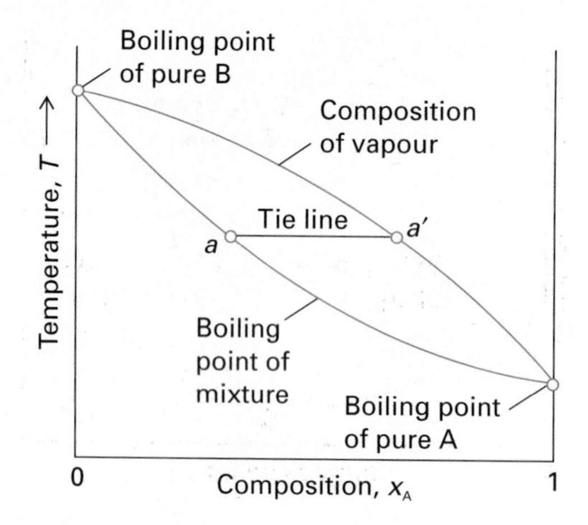

Fig. 6.23 A temperature–composition diagram for a binary mixture of volatile liquids. The tie line connects the points that represent the compositions of liquid and vapour that are in equilibrium at each temperature. The lower curve is a plot of the boiling point of the mixture against composition.

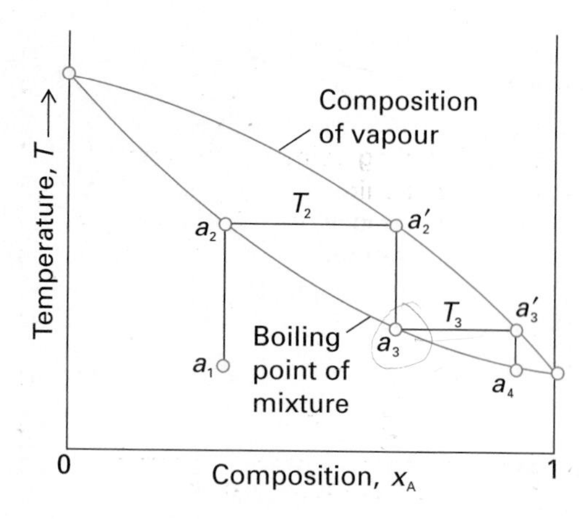

Fig. 6.24 The process of fractional distillation can be represented by a series of steps on a temperature–composition diagram like that in Fig. 6.23. The initial liquid mixture may be at a temperature and have a composition like that represented by point a_1. It boils at the temperature T_2, and the vapour in equilibrium with the boiling liquid has composition a_2'. If that vapour is condensed (to a_3 or below), the resulting condensate boils at T_3 and gives rise to a vapour of composition represented by a_3'. As the succession of vaporizations and condensations is continued, the composition of the distillate moves towards pure A (the more volatile component).

industry and the laboratory. Intuitively, we might expect the boiling point of a mixture of two volatile liquids to vary smoothly from the boiling point of one pure component when only that liquid is present to the boiling point of the other pure component when only that liquid is present. This expectation is often borne out in practice, and Fig. 6.23 shows a typical plot of boiling point against composition (the lower curve).

The vapour in equilibrium with the boiling mixture is also a mixture of the two components. We should expect the vapour to be richer than the liquid mixture in the more volatile of the two substances. This difference is also often found in practice, and the upper curve in the illustration shows the composition of the vapour in equilibrium with the boiling liquid. To identify the composition of the vapour, we note the boiling point of the liquid mixture (point a, for instance) and draw a horizontal **tie line**, a line joining two phases that are in equilibrium with each other, across to the upper curve. Its point of intersection (a') gives the composition of the vapour. In this example, we see that the mole fraction of A in the vapour is about 0.65. As expected, the vapour is richer than the liquid in the more volatile component. Graphs like these are determined empirically, by measuring the boiling points of a series of mixtures (to plot the lower curve of boiling point against composition), and measuring the composition of the vapour in equilibrium with each boiling mixture (to plot the corresponding points of the vapour-composition curve).

We can follow the changes that occur during the fractional distillation of a mixture of volatile liquids by following what happens when a mixture of composition a_1 is heated (Fig. 6.24). The mixture boils at a_2 and its vapour has composition a_2'. This vapour condenses to a liquid of the same composition when it has risen to a cooler part of the 'fractionating column', a vertical column packed with glass rings or beads to give a large surface area. This condensate boils at the temperature corresponding to the point a_3 and yields a vapour of composition a_3'. This vapour is even richer in the more volatile component. That vapour condenses to a liquid that boils at the temperature corresponding to the point a_4. The cycle is repeated until almost pure A emerges from the top of the column.

Whereas many binary liquid mixtures do have temperature–composition diagrams resembling that shown in Fig. 6.24, in a number of important cases

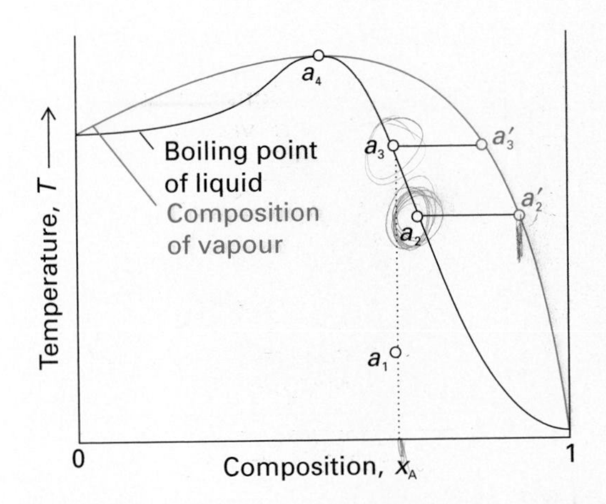

Fig. 6.25 The temperature–composition diagram for a high-boiling azeotrope. As fractional distillation proceeds, the composition of the remaining liquid moves towards a_4; however, once there, the vapour in equilibrium with that liquid has the same composition, so the mixture evaporates with an unchanged composition and no further separation can be achieved.

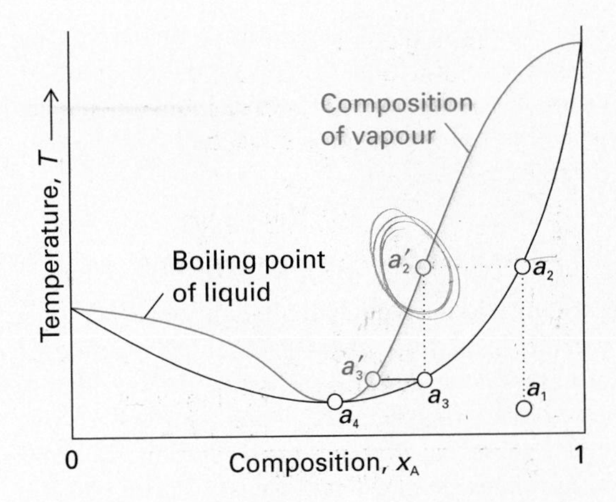

Fig. 6.26 The temperature–composition diagram for a low-boiling azeotrope. As fractional distillation proceeds, the composition of the vapour moves towards a_4; however, once there, the vapour in equilibrium with that liquid has the same composition, so no further separation of the distillate can be achieved.

there are marked differences. For example, a maximum in the boiling point curve is sometimes found (Fig. 6.25). This behaviour is a sign that favourable interactions between the molecules of the two components reduce the vapour pressure of the mixture below the ideal value. Examples of this behaviour include trichloromethane/propanone and nitric acid/water mixtures. Temperature–composition curves are also found that pass through a minimum (Fig. 6.26). This behaviour indicates that the (A,B) interactions are unfavourable and hence that the mixture is more volatile than expected on the basis of simple mingling of the two species. Examples include dioxane/water and ethanol/water.

There are important consequences for distillation when the temperature–composition diagram has a maximum or a minimum. Consider a liquid of composition a_1 on the right of the maximum in Fig. 6.25. It boils at a_2 and its vapour (of composition a_2') is richer in the more volatile component A. If that vapour is removed, the composition of the remaining liquid moves towards a_3. The vapour in equilibrium with this boiling liquid has composition a_3': note that the two compositions are more similar than the original pair (a_3 and a_3' are closer together than a_2 and a_2'). If that vapour is removed, the composition of the boiling liquid shifts towards a_4 and the vapour of that boiling mixture has a composition identical to that of the liquid. At this stage, evaporation occurs without change of composition. The mixture is said to form an **azeotrope**.[9] When the azeotropic composition has been reached, distillation cannot separate the two liquids because the condensate retains the composition of the liquid. One example of azeotrope formation is hydrochloric acid/water, which is azeotropic at 80 per cent water (by mass) and boils unchanged at 108.6°C.

The system shown in Fig. 6.26 is also azeotropic, but shows this character in a different way. Suppose we start with a mixture of composition a_1 and follow the changes in the composition of the vapour that rises through a fractionating column. The mixture boils at a_2 to give a vapour of composition a_2'. This vapour condenses in the column to a liquid of the same composition (now marked a_3). That liquid reaches equilibrium with its vapour at a_3', which condenses higher up the tube to give a liquid of the same composition. The fractionation therefore shifts the vapour towards the azeotropic composition at a_4, but the composition cannot move beyond a_4 because now the vapour and the liquid have the

9 The name comes from the Greek words for 'boiling without changing'.

same composition. Consequently, the azeotropic vapour emerges from the top of the column. An example is ethanol/water, which boils unchanged when the water content is 4 per cent and the temperature is 78°C.

6.10 Liquid–liquid phase diagrams

Partially miscible liquids are liquids that do not mix together in all proportions. An example is a mixture of hexane and nitrobenzene: when the two liquids are shaken together, the liquid consists of two liquid phases, one is a saturated solution of hexane in nitrobenzene and the other is a saturated solution of nitrobenzene in hexane. Because the two solubilities vary with temperature, the compositions and proportions of the two phases change as the temperature is changed. We can use a temperature–composition diagram to display the composition of the system at each temperature.

Suppose we add a small amount of nitrobenzene to hexane at a temperature T'. The nitrobenzene dissolves completely; however, as more nitrobenzene is added, a stage comes when no more dissolves. The sample now consists of two phases in equilibrium with each other, the more abundant one consisting of hexane saturated with nitrobenzene, the less abundant one a trace of nitrobenzene saturated with hexane. In the temperature–composition diagram drawn in Fig. 6.27, the composition of the former is represented by the point a' and that of the latter by the point a''. The relative abundances of the two phases are given by the **lever rule** (Fig. 6.28):

$$\frac{\text{Amount of phase of composition } a''}{\text{Amount of phase of composition } a'} = \frac{l'}{l''} \qquad (6.25)$$

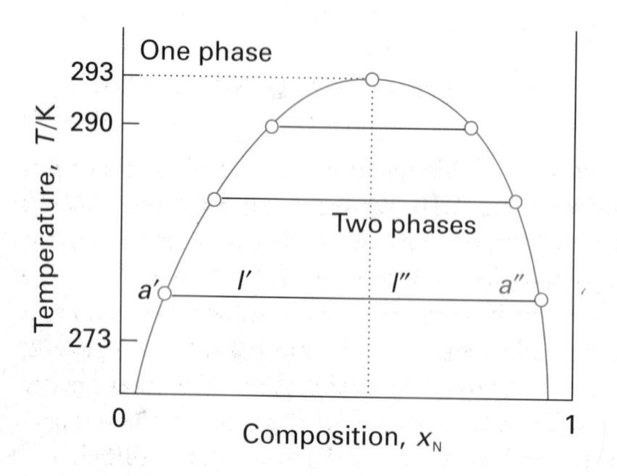

Fig. 6.27 The temperature–composition diagram for hexane and nitrobenzene at 1 atm. The upper critical solution temperature, T_{uc}, is the temperature above which no phase separation occurs. For this system it lies at 293 K (when the pressure is 1 atm).

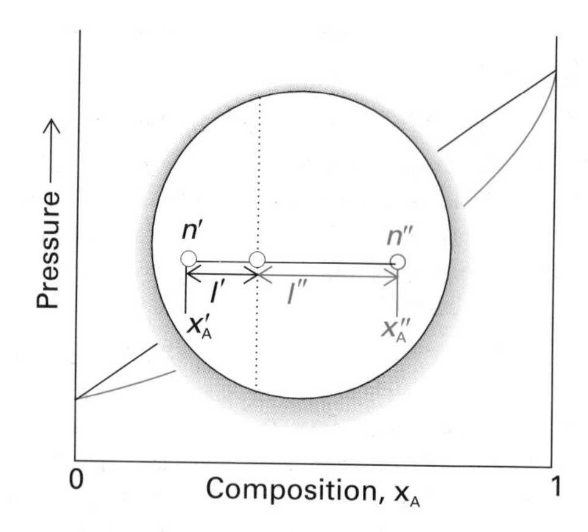

Fig. 6.28 The coordinates and compositions referred to by the lever rule.

Derivation 6.6

The lever rule

We write $n = n' + n''$, where n' is the total amount of molecules in the one phase, n'' is the total amount in the other phase, and n is the total amount of molecules in the sample. The total amount of A in the sample is nx_A, where x_A is the overall mole fraction of A in the sample (this is the quantity plotted along the horizontal axis). The overall amount of A is also the sum of its amounts in the two phases, where it has the mole fractions x'_A and x''_A, respectively:

$$nx_A = n'x'_A + n''x''_A$$

We can also multiply each side of the relation $n = n' + n''$ by x_A and obtain

$$nx_A = n'x_A + n''x_A$$

Then, by equating these two expressions and rearranging them slightly, it follows that

$$n'(x'_A - x_A) = n''(x_A - x''_A)$$

or (as can be seen by referring to Fig. 6.28)

$$n'l' = n''l''$$

which is eqn 6.25.

Example 6.5

Interpreting a liquid–liquid phase diagram

A mixture of 50 g (0.59 mol) of hexane and 50 g (0.41 mol) of nitrobenzene was prepared at 290 K. What are the compositions of the phases, and in what proportions do they occur? To what temperature must the sample be heated to obtain a single phase?

Strategy The answer is based on Fig. 6.27. First, we need to identify the tie line corresponding to the temperature specified: the points at its two ends give the compositions of the two phases in equilibrium. Next, we identify the location on the horizontal axis corresponding to the overall composition of the system and draw a vertical line. Where that line cuts the tie line it divides it into the two lengths needed to use the lever rule, eqn 6.25. For the final part, we note the temperature at which the same vertical line cuts through the phase boundary: at that temperature and above, the system consists of a single phase.

Solution We denote hexane by H and nitrobenzene by N. The horizontal tie line at 290 K cuts the phase boundary at $x_N = 0.37$ and at $x_N = 0.83$, so those mole fractions are the compositions of the two phases. The overall composition of the system corresponds to $x_N = 0.41$, so we draw a vertical line at that mole fraction. The lever rule then gives the ratio of amounts of each phase as

$$\frac{l'}{l''} = \frac{0.41 - 0.37}{0.83 - 0.41} = \frac{0.04}{0.42} = 0.1$$

We conclude that the hexane-rich phase is 10 times more abundant than the nitrobenzene-rich phase at this temperature. Heating the sample to 292 K takes it into the single-phase region.

Self-test 6.12

Repeat the problem for 50 g hexane and 100 g nitrobenzene at 273 K.

[*Answer:* $x_N = 0.09$ and 0.95 in the ratio 1:1.3; 290 K]

When more nitrobenzene is added to the two-phase mixture at the temperature T', hexane dissolves in it slightly. The overall composition moves to the right in the phase diagram, but the compositions of the two phases in equilibrium remain a' and a''. The difference is that the amount of the second phase increases at the expense of the first. A stage is reached when so much nitrobenzene is present that it can dissolve all the hexane, and the system reverts to a single phase. Now the point representing the overall composition and temperature lies to the right of the phase boundary in the illustration and the system is a single phase.

The **upper critical solution temperature**, T_{uc}, is the upper limit of temperatures at which phase separation occurs.[10] Above the upper critical solution temperature the two components are fully miscible. In molecular terms, this temperature exists because the greater thermal motion of the molecules leads to greater miscibility of the two components. In thermodynamic terms, the Gibbs energy of mixing becomes negative above a certain temperature, regardless of the composition.

To demonstrate this behaviour thermodynamically, we consider the properties of a **regular solution**, a model for a real solution in which solute particles are distributed randomly (as in an ideal solution), but for which the enthalpy of mixing is non-zero. The entropy of mixing is the same as for an ideal solution, so for ΔS we can use eqn 6.11b. We suppose that the enthalpy of mixing is

$$\Delta H = n\beta RT x_A x_B \qquad (6.26a)$$

with $\beta < 0$ for exothermic mixing and $\beta > 0$ for endothermic mixing; in an ideal solution, $\beta = 0$. The composition dependence of this enthalpy of mixing is shown in Fig. 6.29. Now we combine the enthalpy and entropy of mixing to get the Gibbs energy of mixing:

$$\Delta G = \Delta H - T\Delta S$$
$$= n\beta RT x_A x_B + nRT\{x_A \ln x_A + x_B \ln x_B\} \qquad (6.26b)$$

The shape of this function for several values of β is shown in Fig. 6.30. We see that if $\beta < 2$, then $\Delta G < 0$ for all compositions, so mixing is spontaneous for all compositions. However, if $\beta > 2$, then a mixture of composition $x_A = 0.5$, for instance, can acquire a lower Gibbs energy by separating into two phases, one of composition richer in A and the other poorer in A. The latter behaviour depends on the temperature, and as we see in Fig. 6.30, at a sufficiently high temperature, the two dips vanish, and the system can no longer reach a lower Gibbs energy by

[10] The upper critical solution temperature is also called the *upper consolute temperature*.

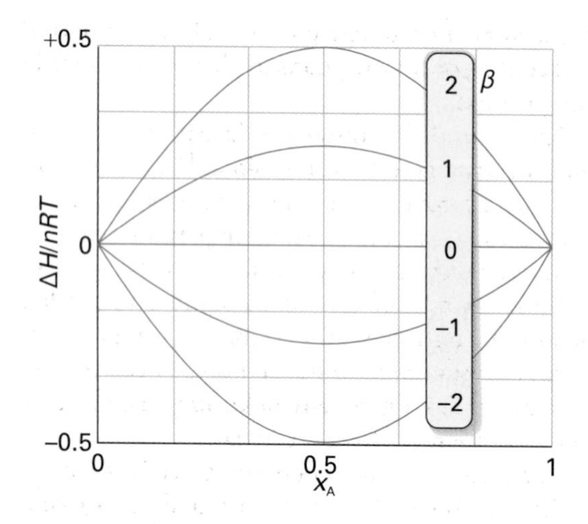

Fig. 6.29 The contribution to the enthalpy of mixing represented by the term $\Delta H = n\beta RTx_Ax_B$ for different values of β: negative values of β correspond to exothermic mixing.

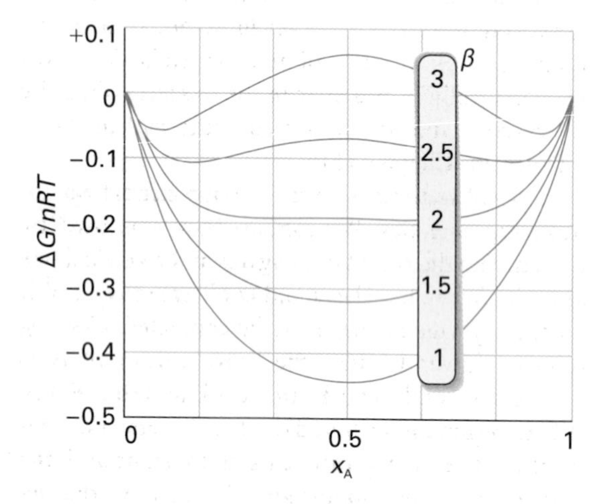

Fig. 6.30 The Gibbs energy of mixing of two substances to give a regular solution. The numbers are the values of the parameter β.

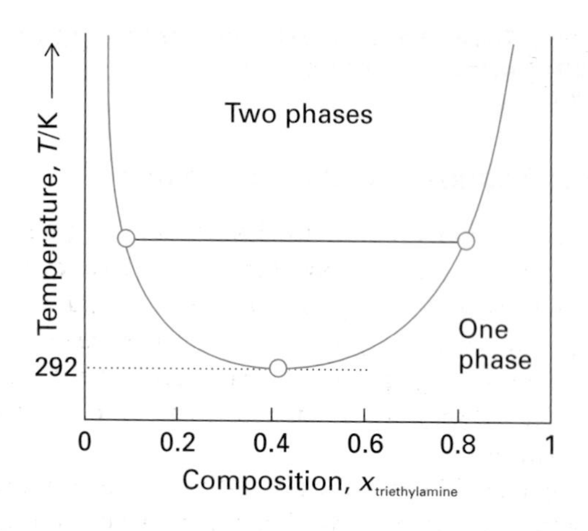

Fig. 6.31 The temperature–composition diagram for water and triethylamine. The lower critical solution temperature, T_{lc}, is the temperature below which no phase separation occurs. For this system it lies at 292 K (when the pressure is 1 atm).

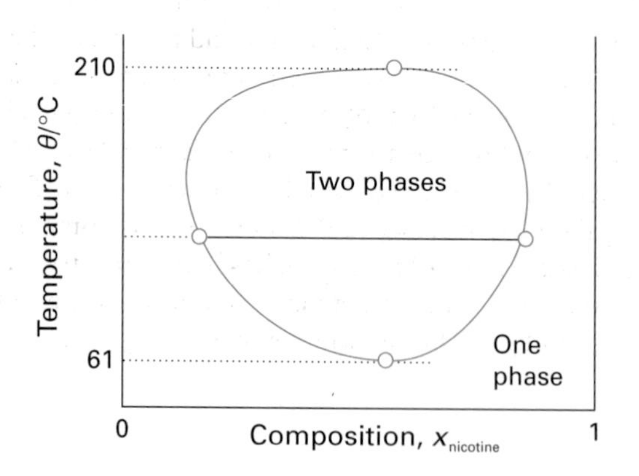

Fig. 6.32 The temperature–composition diagram for water and nicotine, which has both upper and lower critical solution temperatures. Note the high temperatures on the graph: the diagram corresponds to a sample under pressure.

separating into two phases. At this temperature and above, the two liquids are completely miscible.

Some systems show a **lower critical solution temperature**, T_{lc}, below which they mix in all proportions and above which they form two phases.[11] An example is water and triethylamine (Fig. 6.31). In this case, at low temperatures the two components are more miscible because they form a weak complex; at higher temperatures the complexes break up and the two components are less miscible.

A few systems have both upper and lower critical temperatures. The reason can be traced to the fact that, after the weak complexes have been disrupted, leading to partial miscibility, the thermal motion at higher temperatures homogenizes the mixture again, just as in the case of ordinary partially miscible liquids. One example is nicotine and water, which are partially miscible between 61°C and 210°C (Fig. 6.32).

[11] The lower critical solution temperature is also called the *lower consolute temperature*.

The textbook's web site contains links to online databases of phase diagrams.

6.11 Liquid–solid phase diagrams

Phase diagrams are also used to show the regions of temperature and composition at which solids and liquids exist in binary systems. Such diagrams are useful for discussing the techniques that are used to prepare the high-purity materials used in the electronics industry and are also of great importance in metallurgy.

Figure 6.33 shows the phase diagram for a system composed of two metals that are almost completely immiscible right up to their melting points (such as antimony and bismuth). Consider the molten liquid of composition a_1. When the liquid is cooled to a_2, the system enters the two-phase region labelled 'Liquid + A'. Almost pure solid A begins to come out of solution and the remaining liquid becomes richer in B. On cooling to a_3, more of the solid forms, and the relative amounts of the solid and liquid (which are in equilibrium) are given by the lever rule: at this stage there are nearly equal amounts of each. The liquid phase is richer in B than before (its composition is given by b_3) because A has been deposited. At a_4 there is less liquid than at a_3 and its composition is given by e. This liquid now freezes to give a two-phase system of almost pure A and almost pure B and cooling down to a_5 leads to no further change in composition.

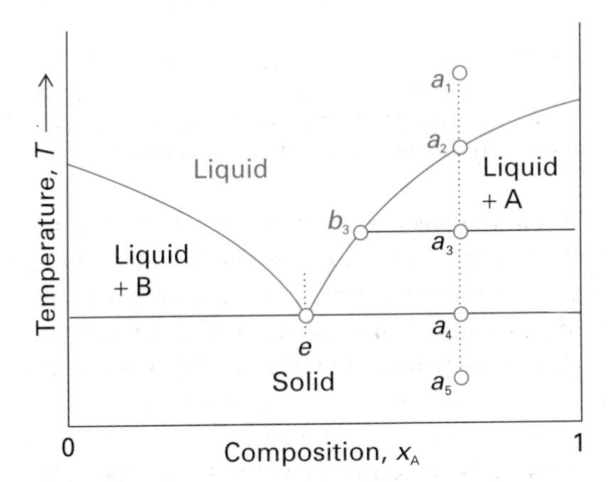

Fig. 6.33 The temperature–composition diagram for two almost immiscible solids and their completely immiscible liquids. The vertical line through e corresponds to the eutectic composition, the mixture with lowest melting point.

The vertical line through e in Fig. 6.33 corresponds to the **eutectic composition.**[12] A solid with the eutectic composition melts, without change of composition, at the lowest temperature of any mixture. Solutions of composition to the right of e deposit A as they cool, and solutions to the left deposit B: only the eutectic mixture (apart from pure A or pure B) solidifies at a single definite temperature without gradually unloading one or other of the components from the liquid.

One technologically important eutectic is solder, which consists of 67 per cent tin and 33 per cent lead by mass and melts at 183°C. Eutectic formation occurs in the great majority of binary alloy systems. It is of great importance for the microstructure of solid materials because, although a eutectic solid is a two-phase system, it crystallizes out in a nearly homogeneous mixture of microcrystals. The two microcrystalline phases can be distinguished by microscopy and structural techniques such as X-ray diffraction (Chapter 15).

Thermal analysis is a very useful practical way of detecting eutectics. We can see how it is used by considering the rate of cooling down the vertical line at a_1 in Fig. 6.33. The liquid cools steadily until it reaches a_2, when A begins to be deposited. Cooling is now slower because the solidification of A is exothermic and retards the cooling (Fig. 6.34). When the remaining liquid reaches the eutectic composition, the temperature remains constant until the whole sample has solidified: this pause in the decrease in temperature is known as the **eutectic halt.** If the liquid has the eutectic composition e initially, then the liquid cools steadily down to the freezing temperature of the eutectic, when there is a long eutectic halt as the entire sample solidifies just like the freezing of a pure liquid.

Monitoring the cooling curves at different overall compositions gives a clear indication of the structure of the phase diagram. The solid–liquid boundary is given by the points at which the rate of cooling changes. The longest eutectic halt gives the location

[12] The name comes from the Greek words for 'easily melted'.

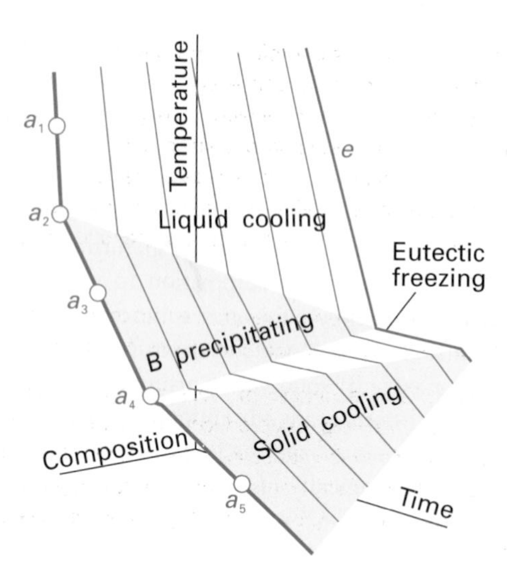

of the eutectic composition and its melting temperature. Phase diagrams are also important for representing the process used to get ultrapure materials for use in the semiconductor industry (Box 6.2).

Fig. 6.34 The cooling curves for the system shown in Fig. 6.33. For a sample of composition represented by the vertical line through a_1 to a_5, the rate of cooling decreases at a_2 because solid A comes out of solution. The curves between the vertical lines through *a* and *e* are for samples of intermediate composition. If the experiment is repeated using a sample of composition represented by the vertical line through *e*, then there is a complete halt at *e* when the eutectic solidifies without change of composition. The halt is longest for the mixture of eutectic composition. The cooling curves can be used to construct the phase diagram.

Box 6.2 *Ultrapurity and controlled impurity*

Advances in technology have called for materials of extreme purity. For example, semiconductor devices consist of almost perfectly pure silicon or germanium doped to a precisely controlled extent. For these materials to operate successfully, the impurity level must be kept down to less than 1 in 10^9. The technique of *zone refining* makes use of the non-equilibrium properties of mixtures. It relies on the impurities being more soluble in the molten sample than in the solid, and sweeps them up by passing a molten zone repeatedly from one end to the other along a sample (see the first illustration). In practice, a train of hot and cold zones are swept repeatedly from one end to the other. The zone at the end of the sample is the impurity dump: when the heater has gone by, it cools to a dirty solid that can be discarded.

We can use a phase diagram to discuss zone refining, but we have to allow for the fact that the molten zone moves along the sample and the sample is uniform in neither temperature nor composition. Consider a liquid (which represents the molten zone) on the vertical line at a_1 in the second illustration, and let it cool without the entire sample coming to overall equilibrium. If the temperature falls to a_2, a solid of composition b_2 is deposited and the remaining liquid (the zone where the heater has moved on) is at a_2'. Cooling that liquid down a vertical line passing through a_2' deposits solid of composition b_3 and leaves liquid at a_2'. The process continues until the last drop of liquid to solidify is heavily contaminated with A. There is plenty of everyday evidence that impure liquids freeze in this way. For example, an ice cube is clear near the surface but misty in the core. The water used to make ice normally contains dissolved air; freezing proceeds from the outside, and air is accumulated in the retreating liquid phase. The air cannot escape from the interior of the cube, so when that freezes the air is trapped in a mist of tiny bubbles.

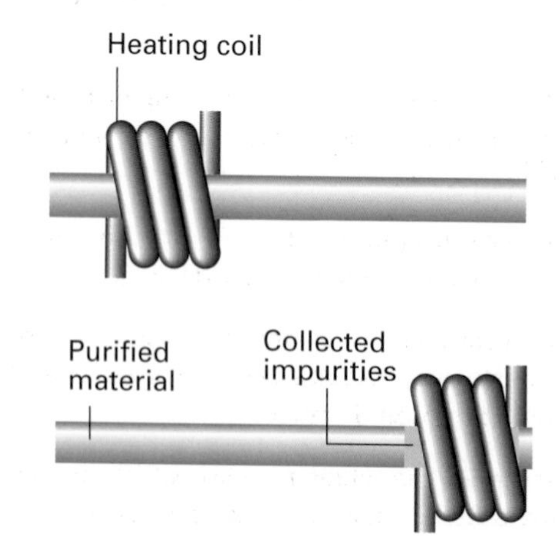

In the zone refining procedure, a heater is used to melt a small region of a long cylindrical sample of the impure solid, and that zone is swept to the other end of the rod. As it moves, it collects impurities. If a series of passes are made, the impurities accumulate at one end of the rod and can be discarded.

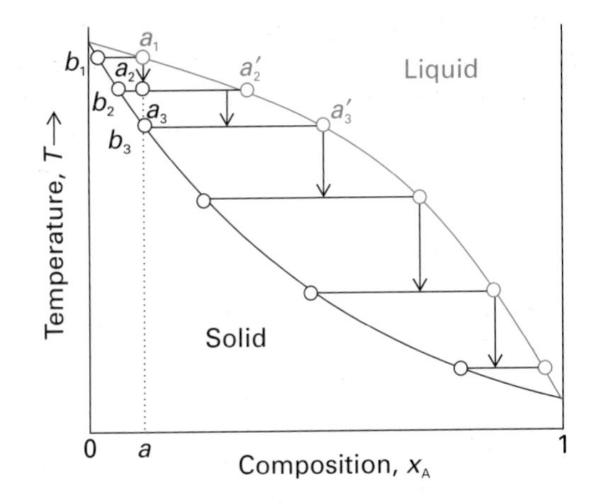

A binary temperature–composition diagram can be used to discuss zone refining, as explained in the text.

A modification of zone refining is *zone levelling*. This technique is used to introduce controlled amounts of impurity (for example, of indium into germanium). A sample rich in the required dopant is put at the head of the main sample, and made molten. The zone is then dragged repeatedly in alternate directions through the sample, where it deposits a uniform distribution of the impurity.

Exercise 1 Use a phase diagram like that in the illustration to indicate how zone levelling may be described.

Exercise 2 The technique of *float zoning*, which is similar to zone refining, has produced very pure samples of silicon for use in the semiconductor industry. Consult a textbook of materials science or metallurgy and prepare a discussion of the principles, advantages, and disadvantages of float zoning.

CHECKLIST OF KEY IDEAS

You should now be familiar with the following concepts:

☐ 1 Composition is commonly reported as molar concentration, molality, or mole fraction.

☐ 2 A partial molar quantity is the contribution of a component (per mole) to the overall property of a mixture.

☐ 3 The chemical potential of a component is the partial molar Gibbs energy of that component in a mixture, and $G = n_A\mu_A + n_B\mu_B$.

☐ 4 For a perfect gas, $\mu_J = \mu_J^{\ominus} + RT\ln p_J$; for a solute in an ideal solution, $\mu_J = \mu_J^{*} + RT\ln x_J$.

☐ 5 An ideal solution is one in which both components obey Raoult's law, $p_J = x_J p_J^{*}$, over the entire composition range.

☐ 6 An ideal-dilute solution is one in which the solute obeys Henry's law, $p_J = x_J K_J$; this law may also be written $[J] = K_H p_J$.

☐ 7 The activity of a substance is an effective concentration; see Table 6.2.

☐ 8 A colligative property is a property that depends on the number of solute particles, not their chemical identity; they arise from the effect of a solute on the entropy of the solution.

☐ 9 Colligative properties include lowering of vapour pressure, depression of freezing point, elevation of boiling point, and osmotic pressure.

☐ 10 The elevation of boiling point, ΔT_B, and the depression of freezing point, ΔT_f, are calculated from $\Delta T_B = K_B b_B$ and $\Delta T_f = K_f b_B$, respectively, where K_B is the ebullioscopic constant and K_f is the cryoscopic constant of the solvent.

☐ 11 The osmotic pressure, Π, of an ideal solution is given by the van 't Hoff equation, $\Pi V = n_B RT$.

☐ 12 The equilibria between phases (at constant pressure) are represented by lines on a temperature–composition phase diagram, and the relative abundance of phases is obtained by using the lever rule, $n'l' = n''l''$.

☐ 13 A regular solution is one in which the entropy of mixing, but not the enthalpy of mixing, is the same as for an ideal solution.

☐ 14 An azeotrope is a mixture that vaporizes and condenses without a change of composition; a eutectic is a mixture that freezes and melts without change of composition.

DISCUSSION QUESTIONS

6.1 State and justify the thermodynamic criterion for solution–vapour equilibrium.

6.2 Explain the origin of the colligative properties.

6.3 What is meant by the activity of a solute?

6.4 Explain how osmotic pressure measurements can be used to determine the molar mass of a polymer.

EXERCISES

The symbol ‡ indicates that the exercise requires calculus.

6.5 What mass of glucose should you use to prepare 250.0 cm^3 of 0.112 M $C_6H_{12}O_6$(aq)?

6.6 What mass of glucose should you use to prepare 0.112 *m* $C_6H_{12}O_6$(aq) using 250.0 g of water?

6.7 What is the mass of glycine in 25.00 cm^3 of 0.245 M NH_2CH_2COOH(aq)?

6.8 What is the mole fraction of alanine in 0.134 *m* $CH_3CH(NH_2)COOH$(aq)?

6.9 What mass of sucrose, $C_{12}H_{22}O_{11}$, should you dissolve in 100.0 g of water to obtain a solution in which the mole fraction of $C_{12}H_{22}O_{11}$ is 0.124?

6.10 A mixture was prepared consisting of 50.0 g of 1-propanol and 50.0 g of 2-propanol. What are the mole fractions of the two alcohols?

6.11 A mixture was prepared that consists of 40.0 g of 1-propanol and 60.0 g of 1-butanol. Calculate the mole fractions of the two components.

6.12 The partial molar volumes of propanone and trichloromethane in a mixture in which the mole fraction of $CHCl_3$ is 0.4693 are 74.166 $cm^3\ mol^{-1}$ and 80.235 $cm^3\ mol^{-1}$, respectively. What is the volume of a solution of total mass 1.000 kg?

6.13 Use Fig. 6.1 to estimate the total volume of a solution formed by mixing 50.0 cm^3 of ethanol with 50.0 cm^3 of water. The densities of the two liquids are 0.789 and 1.000 g cm^{-3}, respectively.

6.14 The partial molar volume of ethanol in a mixture at 25°C is

$$V_{\text{ethanol}}/(\text{cm}^3\ \text{mol}^{-1}) = 54.6664 - 0.727\,88b + 0.0847\,68b^2$$

where b is the numerical value of the molality of ethanol. Plot this quantity as a function of b and identify the composition at which the partial molar volume is a minimum. Express that composition as a mole fraction.

6.15 ‡Use differentiation to identify the minimum in Exercise 6.14.

6.16 The total volume of a water–ethanol mixture at 25°C fits the expression

$$V/\text{cm}^3 = 1002.93 + 54.6664b - 0.363\,94b^2 + 0.0282\,56b^3$$

where b is the numerical value of the molality of ethanol. With the information in Exercise 6.13, find an expression for the partial molar volume of water. Plot the curve. Show that the partial molar volume of water has a maximum value where the partial molar volume of ethanol is a minimum.

6.17 ‡Use calculus to plot the partial molar volumes of ethanol and water from the data in Exercise 6.16. (*Hint.* Convert b to a mole fraction, then use $V_J = dV/dx_J$.)

6.18 Calculate (a) the (molar) Gibbs energy of mixing, (b) the (molar) entropy of mixing when the two major components of air (nitrogen and oxygen) are mixed to form air at 298.15 K. The mole fractions of N_2 and O_2 are 0.78 and 0.22, respectively. Is the mixing spontaneous?

6.19 Suppose now that argon is added to the mixture in Exercise 6.18 to bring the composition closer to real air, with mole fractions 0.780, 0.210, and 0.0096, respectively. What is the additional change in molar Gibbs energy and entropy? Is the mixing spontaneous?

6.20 A solution is prepared by dissolving 1.23 g of C_{60} (buckminsterfullerene) in 100.0 g of toluene (methylbenzene). Given that the vapour pressure of pure toluene is 5.00 kPa at 30°C, what is the vapour pressure of toluene in the solution?

6.21 Estimate the vapour pressure of sea water at 20°C given that the vapour pressure of pure water is 2.338 kPa at that temperature and the solute is largely Na^+ and Cl^- ions, each present at about 0.50 mol dm^{-3}.

6.22 At 300 K, the vapour pressure of dilute solutions of HCl in liquid $GeCl_4$ are as follows:

x(HCl)	0.005	0.012	0.019
p/kPa	32.0	76.9	121.8

Show that the solution obeys Henry's law in this range of mole fractions and calculate Henry's law constant at 300 K.

6.23 Calculate the concentration of carbon dioxide in fat given that the Henry's law constant is 8.6×10^4 Torr and the partial pressure of carbon dioxide is 55 kPa.

6.24 What partial pressure of hydrogen results in a molar concentration of 1.0 mmol dm^{-3} in water at 25°C?

6.25 The rise in atmospheric carbon dioxide results in higher concentrations of dissolved carbon dioxide in natural waters. Use Henry's law and the data in Table 6.1 to calculate the solubility of CO_2 in water at 25°C when its partial pressure is (a) 4.0 kPa, (b) 100 kPa.

6.26 The mole fractions of N_2 and O_2 in air at sea level are approximately 0.78 and 0.21. Calculate the molalities of the solution formed in an open flask of water at 25°C.

6.27 A water-carbonating plant is available for use in the home and operates by providing carbon dioxide at 3.0 atm. Estimate the molar concentration of the CO_2 in the soda water it produces.

6.28 At 90°C the vapour pressure of toluene (methylbenzene) is 53 kPa and that of *o*-xylene (1,2-dimethylbenzene) is 20 kPa. What is the composition of the liquid mixture that boils at 25°C when the pressure is 0.50 atm? What is the composition of the vapour produced?

6.29 The vapour pressure of a sample of benzene is 53.0 kPa at 60.6°C, but it fell to 51.2 kPa when 0.125 g of an organic compound was dissolved in 5.00 g of the solvent. Calculate the molar mass of the compound.

6.30 Estimate the freezing point of 150 cm^3 of water sweetened with 7.5 g of sucrose.

6.31 The addition of 28.0 g of a compound to 750 g of tetrachloromethane, CCl_4, lowered the freezing point of the solvent by 5.40 K. Calculate the molar mass of the compound.

6.32 A compound A existed in equilibrium with its dimer, A_2, in propanone solution. Derive an expression for the equilibrium constant $K = [A_2]/[A]^2$ in terms of the depression in vapour pressure caused by a given concentration of compound. (*Hint.* Suppose that a fraction f of the A molecules are present as the dimer. The depression of vapour pressure is proportional to the total concentration of A and A_2 molecules regardless of their chemical identities.)

6.33 The osmotic pressure of an aqueous solution of urea at 300 K is 120 kPa. Calculate the freezing point of the same solution.

6.34 The osmotic pressure of a solution of polystyrene in toluene (methylbenzene) was measured at 25°C with the following results:

c/(g dm^{-3})	2.042	6.613	9.521	12.602
Π/Pa	58.3	188.2	270.8	354.6

Calculate the molar mass of the polymer.

6.35 The molar mass of an enzyme was determined by dissolving it in water, measuring the osmotic pressure at 20°C and extrapolating the data to zero concentration. The following data were used:

c/(mg cm^{-3})	3.221	4.618	5.112	6.722
h/cm	5.746	8.238	9.119	11.990

Calculate the molar mass of the enzyme. (*Hint.* Begin by expressing eqn 6.24 in terms of the height of the solution, by using $\Pi = \rho g h$; take $\rho = 1.000$ g cm^{-3}.)

6.36 The following temperature/composition data were obtained for a mixture of octane (O) and toluene (T) at 760 Torr, where x is the mole fraction in the liquid and y the mole fraction in the vapour at equilibrium.

θ/°C	110.9	112.0	114.0	115.8	117.3	119.0	120.0	123.0
x_T	0.908	0.795	0.615	0.527	0.408	0.300	0.203	0.097
y_T	0.923	0.836	0.698	0.624	0.527	0.410	0.297	0.164

The boiling points are 110.6°C for toluene and 125.6°C for octane. Plot the temperature–composition diagram of the mixture. What is the composition of the vapour in equilibrium with the liquid of composition (a) $x_T = 0.250$ and (b) $x_O = 0.250$?

6.37 Sketch the phase diagram of the system NH_3/N_2H_4 given that the two substances do not form a compound with each other, that NH_3 freezes at −78°C and N_2H_4 freezes at +2°C, and that a eutectic is formed when the mole fraction of N_2H_4 is 0.07 and that the eutectic melts at −80°C.

6.38 Figure 6.35 shows the phase diagram for two partially miscible liquids, which can be taken to be that for water (A) and 2-methyl-1-propanol (B). Describe what will be observed

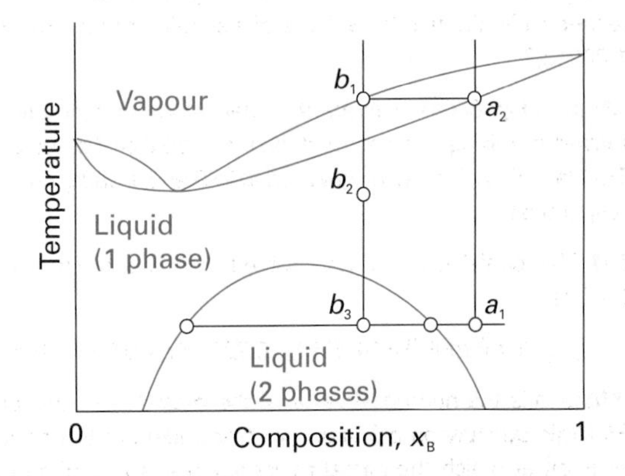

Fig. 6.35

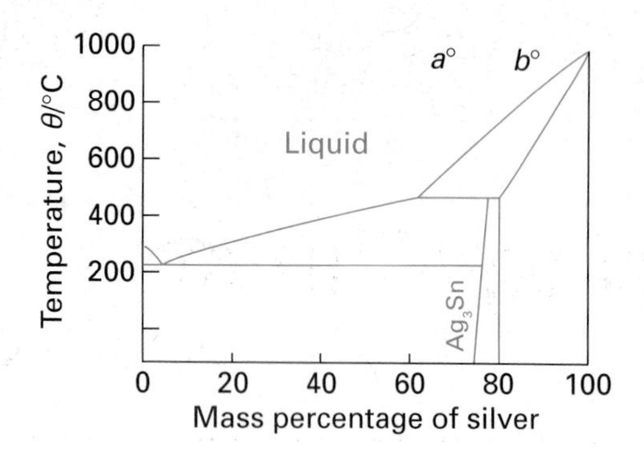

Fig. 6.36

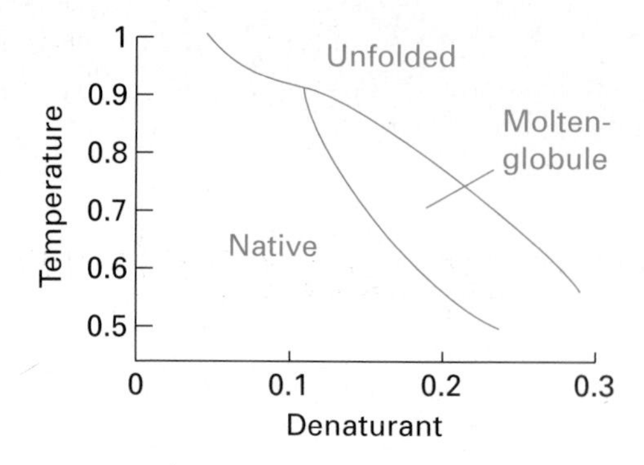

Fig. 6.37

when a mixture of composition b_3 is heated, at each stage giving the number, composition, and relative amounts of the phases present.

6.39 Figure 6.36 is the phase diagram for silver/tin. Label the regions, and describe what will be observed when liquids of compositions *a* and *b* are cooled to 200°C.

6.40 Sketch the cooling curves for the compositions *a* and *b* in Fig. 6.36.

6.41 Use the phase diagram in Fig. 6.36 to determine (a) the solubility of silver in tin at 800°C, (b) the solubility of Ag_3Sn in silver at 460°C, and (c) the solubility of Ag_3Sn in silver at 300°C.

6.42 Hexane and perfluorohexane (C_6F_{14}) show partial miscibility below 22.70°C. The critical concentration at the upper critical temperature is $x = 0.355$, where x is the mole fraction of C_6F_{14}. At 22.0°C the two solutions in equilibrium have $x = 0.24$ and $x = 0.48$ respectively, and at 21.5°C the mole fractions are 0.22 and 0.51. Sketch the phase diagram. Describe the phase changes that occur when perfluorohexane is added to a fixed amount of hexane at (a) 23°C, (b) 25°C.

6.43 In a theoretical study of protein-like polymers, the phase diagram shown in Fig. 6.37 was obtained. It shows three structural regions: the native form, the unfolded form, and a 'molten-globule' form. (a) Is the molten-globule form ever stable when the denaturant concentration is below 0.1? (b) Describe what happens to the polymer as the native form is heated in the presence of denaturant at concentration 0.15.

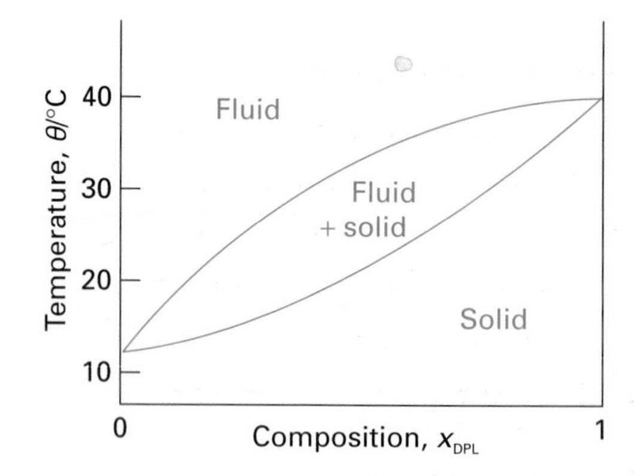

Fig. 6.38

6.44 In an experimental study of membrane-like assemblies of synthetic materials, a phase diagram like that shown in Fig. 6.38 was obtained. The two components are dielaidoylphosphatidylcholine (DEL) and dipalmitoylphosphatidylcholine (DPL). Explain what happens as a liquid mixture of composition $x_{DEL} = 0.5$ is cooled from 45°C.

Chapter 7

Principles of chemical equilibrium

Now we arrive at the point where real chemistry begins. Chemical thermodynamics is used to predict whether a mixture of reactants has a spontaneous tendency to change into products, to predict the composition of the reaction mixture at equilibrium, and to predict how that composition will be modified by changing the conditions. Although reactions in industry are rarely allowed to reach equilibrium, knowing whether equilibrium lies in favour of reactants or products under certain conditions is a good indication of the feasibility of a process. Much the same is true of biochemical reactions, where the avoidance of equilibrium is life and the attainment of equilibrium is death.

There is one proviso that is essential to remember: *thermodynamics is silent about the rates of reaction.* All it can do is to identify whether a particular reaction mixture has a tendency to form products, it cannot say whether that tendency will ever be realized. Chapters 10 and 11 explore what determines the rates of chemical reactions.

Thermodynamic background

The thermodynamic criterion for spontaneous change at constant temperature and pressure is $\Delta G < 0$. The principal idea behind this chapter, therefore, is that, *at constant temperature and pressure, a reaction mixture tends to adjust its composition until its Gibbs energy is a minimum.* If the Gibbs energy of a mixture varies as shown in Fig. 7.1a, very little of the reactants convert into products before G has reached its minimum value and the reaction 'does

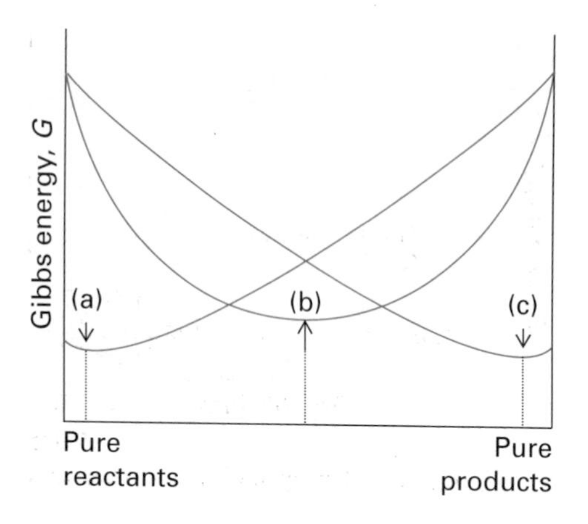

Fig. 7.1 The variation of Gibbs energy of a reaction mixture with progress of the reaction, pure reactants on the left and pure products on the right. (a) This reaction 'does not go': the minimum in the Gibbs energy occurs very close to reactants. (b) This reaction reaches equilibrium with approximately equal amounts of reactants and products present in the mixture. (c) This reaction goes almost to completion, as the minimum in Gibbs energy lies very close to pure products.

not go'. If G varies as shown in Fig. 7.1c, then a high proportion of products must form before G reaches its minimum and the reaction 'goes'. In many cases, the equilibrium mixture contains almost no reactants or almost no products. Many reactions have a Gibbs energy that varies as shown in Fig. 7.1b, and at equilibrium the reaction mixture contains substantial amounts of both reactants and products. One of our tasks is to see how to use thermodynamic data to predict the equilibrium composition and to see how that composition depends on the conditions.

7.1 The reaction Gibbs energy

To keep our ideas in focus, we consider two important reactions. One is the isomerism of glucose-6-phosphate (**1**, G6P) to fructose-6-phosphate (**2**, F6P), which is an early step in the anaerobic breakdown of glucose:

1 Glucose-6-phosphate **2** Fructose-6-phosphate

$$\text{G6P(aq)} \rightleftharpoons \text{F6P(aq)} \qquad \text{(A)}$$

This reaction takes place in the aqueous environment of the cell. The second is the synthesis of ammonia, which is of crucial importance for industry and agriculture:

$$\text{N}_2\text{(g)} + 3\,\text{H}_2\text{(g)} \rightarrow 2\,\text{NH}_3\text{(g)} \qquad \text{(B)}$$

These two reactions are specific examples of a general reaction of the form

$$a\,\text{A} + b\,\text{B} \rightarrow c\,\text{C} + d\,\text{D} \qquad \text{(C)}$$

with arbitrary physical states.

First, consider reaction A. Suppose that, in a short interval while the reaction is in progress, the amount of G6P changes by $-\Delta n$. As a result of this change in amount, the contribution of G6P to the total Gibbs energy of the system changes by $-\mu_{\text{G6P}}\Delta n$, where μ_{G6P} is the chemical potential (the partial molar Gibbs energy) of G6P in the reaction mixture. In the same interval, the amount of F6P changes by $+\Delta n$, so its contribution to the total Gibbs energy changes by $+\mu_{\text{F6P}}\Delta n$, where μ_{F6P} is the chemical potential of F6P. Provided Δn is small enough to leave the composition virtually unchanged, the net change in Gibbs energy of the system is

$$\Delta G = \mu_{\text{F6P}} \times \Delta n - \mu_{\text{G6P}} \times \Delta n$$

If we divide through by Δn, we obtain the **reaction Gibbs energy, $\Delta_r G$**:

$$\Delta_r G = \frac{\Delta G}{\Delta n} = \mu_{\text{F6P}} - \mu_{\text{G6P}} \qquad (7.1\text{a})$$

There are two ways to interpret $\Delta_r G$. First, it is the difference of the chemical potentials of the products and reactants *at the composition of the reaction mixture*. Second, because $\Delta_r G$ is the change in G divided by the change in composition, we can think of $\Delta_r G$ as being the slope of the graph of G plotted against the changing composition of the system (Fig. 7.2).

The synthesis of ammonia provides a slightly more complicated example. If the amount of N_2 changes by $-\Delta n$, then from the reaction stoichiometry we know that the change in the amount of H_2 will be $-3\Delta n$ and the change in the amount of NH_3 will be $+2\Delta n$. Each change contributes to the change in the total Gibbs energy of the mixture, and the overall change is

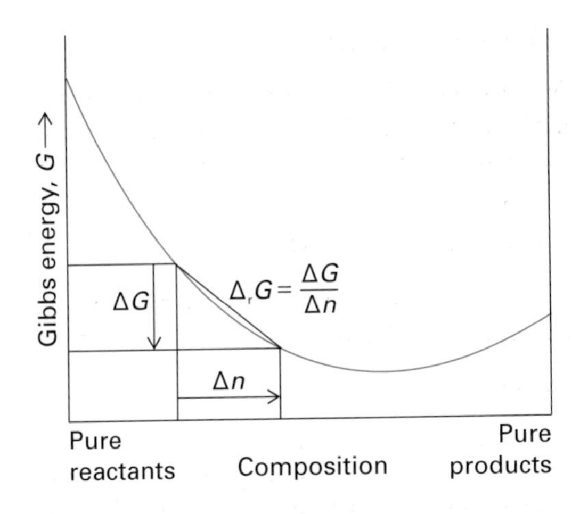

Fig. 7.2 The variation of Gibbs energy with progress of reaction showing how the reaction Gibbs energy, $\Delta_r G$, is related to the slope of the curve at a given composition.

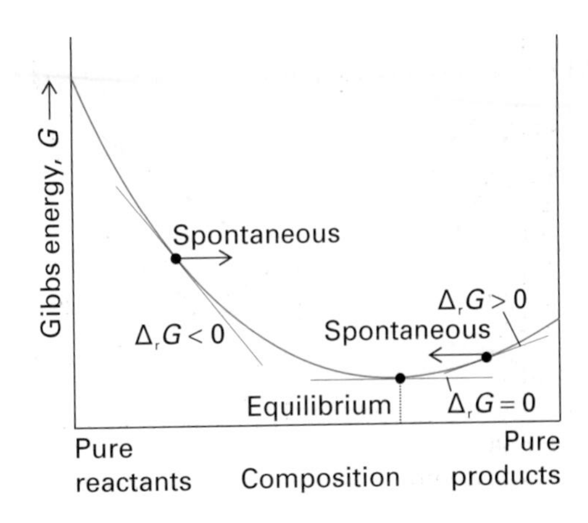

Fig. 7.3 At the minimum of the curve, corresponding to equilibrium, $\Delta_r G = 0$. To the left of the minimum, $\Delta_r G < 0$, and the forward reaction is spontaneous. To the right of the minimum, $\Delta_r G > 0$ and the reverse reaction is spontaneous.

$$\begin{aligned}\Delta G &= \mu_{NH_3} \times 2\Delta n - \mu_{N_2} \times \Delta n - \mu_{H_2} \times 3\Delta n \\ &= (2\mu_{NH_3} - \mu_{N_2} - 3\mu_{H_2})\Delta n\end{aligned}$$

where the μ_J are the chemical potentials of the species in the reaction mixture. In this case, therefore, the reaction Gibbs energy is

$$\Delta_r G = \frac{\Delta G}{\Delta n} = 2\mu_{NH_3} - (\mu_{N_2} + 3\mu_{H_2}) \qquad (7.1b)$$

Note that each chemical potential is multiplied by the corresponding stoichiometric coefficient and that reactants are subtracted from products. For the general reaction C,

$$\Delta_r G = (c\mu_C + d\mu_D) - (a\mu_A - b\mu_B) \qquad (7.1c)$$

The chemical potential of a substance depends on the composition of the mixture in which it is present, and is high when its concentration or partial pressure is high. Therefore, $\Delta_r G$ changes as the composition changes (Fig. 7.3). Remember that $\Delta_r G$ is the *slope of G plotted against composition*. We see that $\Delta_r G < 0$ and the slope of G is negative (down from left to right) when the mixture is rich in the reactants A and B because μ_A and μ_B are then high. Conversely, $\Delta_r G > 0$ and the slope of G is positive (up from left to right) when the mixture is rich in the products C and D because μ_C and μ_D are then high. At compositions corresponding to $\Delta_r G < 0$ the reaction tends to form more products; where $\Delta_r G > 0$, the *reverse* reaction is spontaneous, and the products tend to decompose into reactants. Where $\Delta_r G = 0$ (at the minimum of the graph where the slope is zero), the reaction has no tendency to form either products or reactants. In other words, the reaction is at equilibrium. That is, *the criterion for chemical equilibrium at constant temperature and pressure* is

$$\Delta_r G = 0 \qquad (7.2)$$

7.2 The variation of $\Delta_r G$ with composition

Our next step is to find how $\Delta_r G$ varies with the composition of the system. Once we know that, we shall be able to identify the composition corresponding to $\Delta_r G = 0$. Our starting point is the general expression for the composition dependence of the chemical potential derived in Section 6.6:

$$\mu_J = \mu_J^{\ominus} + RT \ln a_J \qquad (7.3)$$

where a_J is the activity of the species J. When we are dealing with ideal systems, which will be the case in this chapter, we use the identifications given in Table 6.2:

For solutes in an ideal solution, $a_J = [J]/c^{\ominus}$, the molar concentration of J relative to the standard value $c^{\ominus} = 1$ mol dm^{-3}.

For perfect gases, $a_J = p_J/p^{\ominus}$, the partial pressure of J relative to the standard pressure $p^{\ominus} = 1$ bar.

For pure solids and liquids, $a_J = 1$.

As in Chapter 6, to simplify the appearance of expressions in what follows, we shall not write $c^{\ominus}$ and $p^{\ominus}$ explicitly.

Substitution of eqn 7.3 into eqn 7.1c gives

$$\begin{aligned}\Delta_r G &= \{c(\mu_C^{\ominus} + RT\ln a_C) + d(\mu_D^{\ominus} + RT\ln a_D)\} \\ &\quad - \{a(\mu_A^{\ominus} + RT\ln a_A) + b(\mu_B^{\ominus} + RT\ln a_B)\} \\ &= \{(c\mu_C^{\ominus} + d\mu_D^{\ominus}) - (a\mu_A^{\ominus} + b\mu_B^{\ominus})\} \\ &\quad + RT\{c\ln a_C + d\ln a_D - a\ln a_A - b\ln a_B\}\end{aligned}$$

The first term on the right in the second equality is the **standard reaction Gibbs energy, $\Delta_r G^{\ominus}$**:

$$\Delta_r G^{\ominus} = \{c\mu_C^{\ominus} + d\mu_D^{\ominus}\} - \{a\mu_A^{\ominus} + b\mu_B^{\ominus}\} \quad (7.4a)$$

Because the standard states refer to the pure materials, the standard chemical potentials in this expression are the standard molar Gibbs energies of the (pure) species. Therefore, eqn 7.4a is the same as

$$\begin{aligned}\Delta_r G^{\ominus} &= \{cG_m^{\ominus}(C) + dG_m^{\ominus}(D)\} \\ &\quad - \{aG_m^{\ominus}(A) + bG_m^{\ominus}(B)\}\end{aligned} \quad (7.4b)$$

We consider this important quantity in more detail shortly. At this stage, therefore, we know that

$$\begin{aligned}\Delta_r G = \Delta_r G^{\ominus} + RT\{c\ln a_C + d\ln a_D \\ - a\ln a_A - b\ln a_B\}\end{aligned}$$

and the expression for $\Delta_r G$ is beginning to look much simpler.

To make further progress, we rearrange the remaining terms on the right as follows:

$$\begin{aligned}c\ln a_C &+ d\ln a_D - a\ln a_A - b\ln a_B \\ &= \ln a_C^c + \ln a_D^d - \ln a_A^a - \ln a_B^b \\ &= \ln a_C^c a_D^d - \ln a_A^a a_B^b \\ &= \ln \frac{a_C^c a_D^d}{a_A^a a_B^b}\end{aligned}$$

We have used the following relations:

$a\ln x = \ln x^a$ (for the first equality, for each term)

$\ln x + \ln y = \ln(xy)$ (for the second equality, for two pairs of terms)

$\ln x - \ln y = \ln(x/y)$ (for the third equality)

At this point, we have deduced that

$$\Delta_r G = \Delta_r G^{\ominus} + RT\ln \frac{a_C^c a_D^d}{a_A^a a_B^b}$$

To simplify the appearance of this expression still further we introduce the (dimensionless) **reaction quotient**, Q, for reaction C:

$$Q = \frac{a_C^c a_D^d}{a_A^a a_B^b} \quad (7.5)$$

Note that Q has the form of products divided by reactants, with the activity of each species raised to a power equal to its stoichiometric coefficient in the reaction. We can now write the overall expression for the reaction Gibbs energy at any composition of the reaction mixture as

$$\Delta_r G = \Delta_r G^{\ominus} + RT\ln Q \quad (7.6)$$

This simple but hugely important equation will occur several times in different disguises.

Illustration 7.1

Formulating a reaction quotient

The reaction quotient for reaction A is

$$Q = \frac{a_{F6P}}{a_{G6P}} = \frac{[F6P]/c^{\ominus}}{[G6P]/c^{\ominus}}$$

However, we are not writing the standard concentration explicitly, so this expression simplifies to

$$Q = \frac{[F6P]}{[G6P]}$$

with [J] the numerical value of the molar concentration of J in moles per cubic decimetre (so, if [F6P] = 2.0 mmol dm^{-3}, corresponding to 2.0×10^{-3} mol dm^{-3}, we just write [F6P] = 2.0×10^{-3} when using this expression). For reaction B, the synthesis of ammonia, the reaction quotient is

$$Q = \frac{(p_{NH_3}/p^{\ominus})^2}{(p_{N_2}/p^{\ominus})(p_{H_2}/p^{\ominus})^3}$$

However, we are not writing the standard pressure explicitly, so this expression simplifies to

$$Q = \frac{p_{NH_3}^2}{p_{N_2} p_{H_2}^3}$$

with p_J the numerical value of the partial pressure of J in bar (so, if $p_{NH_3} = 2$ bar, we just write $p_{NH_3} = 2$ when using this expression).

Self-test 7.1

Write the reaction quotient for the esterification reaction $CH_3COOH + C_2H_5OH \rightleftharpoons CH_3COOC_2H_5 + H_2O$. (All four components are present in the reaction mixture as liquids: the mixture is not an aqueous solution.)

[*Answer:* $Q \approx [CH_3COOC_2H_5][H_2O]/[CH_3COOH][C_2H_5OH]$]

7.3 Reactions at equilibrium

When the reaction has reached equilibrium, the composition has no further tendency to change because $\Delta_r G = 0$ and the reaction is spontaneous in neither direction. At equilibrium, the reaction quotient has a certain value called the **equilibrium constant**, K, of the reaction:

$$K = \left(\frac{a_C^c a_D^d}{a_A^a a_B^b}\right)_{\text{equilibrium}} \tag{7.7}$$

We shall not normally write 'equilibrium'; the context will always make it clear that Q refers to an *arbitrary* stage of the reaction whereas K, the value of Q at equilibrium, is calculated from the *equilibrium* composition. It now follows from eqn 7.6 that, at equilibrium,

$$0 = \Delta_r G^\ominus + RT \ln K$$

and therefore

$$\Delta_r G^\ominus = -RT \ln K \tag{7.8}$$

This is one of the most important equations in the whole of chemical thermodynamics. Its principal use is to predict the value of the equilibrium constant of any reaction from tables of thermodynamic data, like those in the *Data section*. Alternatively, we can use it to determine $\Delta_r G^\ominus$ by measuring the equilibrium constant of a reaction.

Illustration 7.2

Calculating an equilibrium constant

Suppose we know that $\Delta_r G^\ominus = +3.40$ kJ mol^{-1} for the reaction $H_2(g) + I_2(s) \rightleftharpoons 2\,HI(g)$ at 25°C; then to calculate the equilibrium constant we write

$$\ln K = -\frac{\Delta_r G^\ominus}{RT} = -\frac{3.40 \times 10^3 \text{ J mol}^{-1}}{(8.314\,47 \text{ J K}^{-1}\text{ mol}^{-1}) \times (298 \text{ K})} = -\frac{3.40 \times 10^3}{8.314\,47 \times 298}$$

This expression evaluates to $\ln K = -1.37$ but, to avoid rounding errors, we leave the evaluation until the next step, which is to use the relation $e^{\ln x} = x$ with $x = K$ to write

$$K = e^{-\frac{3.40\times10^3}{8.314\,47\times298}} = 0.25$$

A note on good practice All equilibrium constants and reaction quotients are dimensionless numbers.

Self-test 7.2

Calculate the equilibrium constant of the reaction $N_2(g) + 3\,H_2(g) \rightleftharpoons 2\,NH_3(g)$ at 25°C, given that $\Delta_r G^\ominus = -32.90$ kJ mol^{-1}.

[*Answer:* 5.8×10^5]

An important feature of eqn 7.8 is that it tells us that $K > 1$ if $\Delta_r G^\ominus < 0$. Broadly speaking, $K > 1$ implies that products are dominant at equilibrium, so we can conclude that *a reaction is thermodynamically feasible if* $\Delta_r G^\ominus < 0$ (Fig. 7.4). Conversely, because

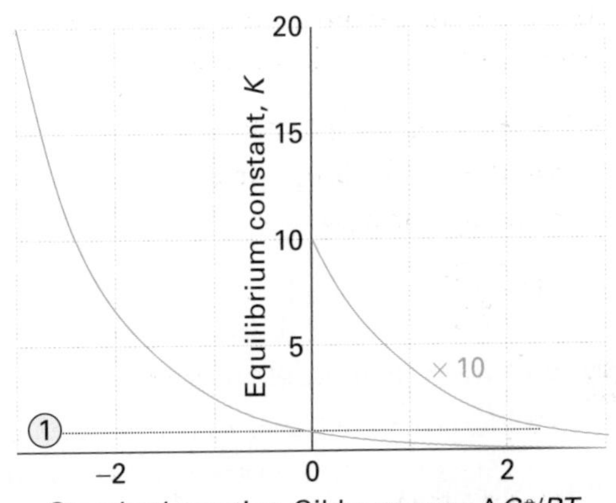

Fig. 7.4 The relation between standard reaction Gibbs energy and the equilibrium constant of the reaction. The pale curve is magnified by a factor of 10.

Table 7.1

Thermodynamic criteria of spontaneity

1 If the reaction is exothermic ($\Delta_r H^\ominus < 0$) and $\Delta_r S^\ominus > 0$

$\Delta_r G^\ominus < 0$ and $K > 1$ at all temperatures

2 If the reaction is exothermic ($\Delta_r H^\ominus < 0$) and $\Delta_r S^\ominus < 0$

$\Delta_r G^\ominus < 0$ and $K > 1$ provided that $T < \Delta_r H^\ominus/\Delta_r S^\ominus$

3 If the reaction is endothermic ($\Delta_r H^\ominus > 0$) and $\Delta_r S^\ominus > 0$

$\Delta_r G^\ominus < 0$ and $K > 1$ provided that $T > \Delta_r H^\ominus/\Delta_r S^\ominus$

4 If the reaction is endothermic ($\Delta_r H^\ominus > 0$) and $\Delta_r S^\ominus < 0$

$\Delta_r G^\ominus < 0$ and $K > 1$ at no temperature

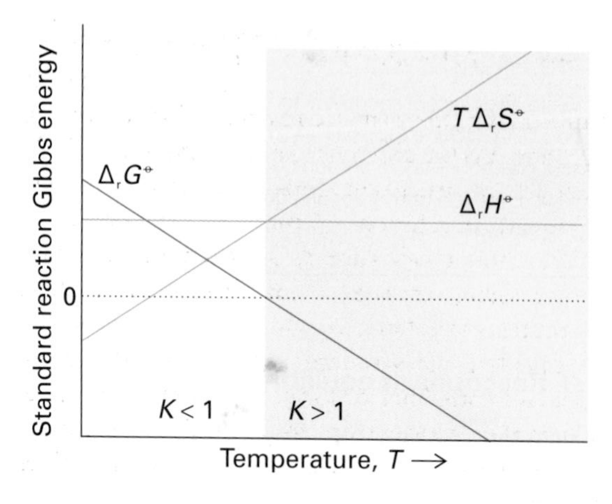

Fig. 7.5 An endothermic reaction may have $K > 1$ provided the temperature is high enough for $T\Delta_r S^\ominus$ to be large enough that, when subtracted from $\Delta_r H^\ominus$ the result is negative.

eqn 7.8 tells us that $K < 1$ if $\Delta_r G^\ominus > 0$, then we know that the reactants will be dominant in a reaction mixture at equilibrium if $\Delta_r G^\ominus > 0$. In other words, *a reaction with $\Delta_r G^\ominus > 0$ is not thermodynamically feasible.* Some care must be exercised with these rules, however, because the products will be significantly more abundant than reactants only if $K \gg 1$ (more than about 10^3) and even a reaction with $K < 1$ may have a reasonable abundance of products at equilibrium.

Table 7.1 summarizes the conditions under which $\Delta_r G^\ominus < 0$ and $K > 1$. Because $\Delta_r G^\ominus = \Delta_r H^\ominus - T\Delta_r S^\ominus$, the standard reaction Gibbs energy is certainly negative if both $\Delta_r H^\ominus < 0$ (an exothermic reaction) and $\Delta_r S^\ominus > 0$ (a reaction system that becomes more disorderly, such as by forming a gas). The standard reaction Gibbs energy is also negative if the reaction is endothermic ($\Delta_r H^\ominus > 0$) and $T\Delta_r S^\ominus$ is sufficiently large and positive. Note that for an endothermic reaction to have $\Delta_r G^\ominus < 0$, its standard reaction entropy *must* be positive. Moreover, the temperature must be high enough for $T\Delta_r S^\ominus$ to be greater than $\Delta_r H^\ominus$ (Fig. 7.5). The switch of $\Delta_r G^\ominus$ from positive to negative, corresponding to the switch from $K < 1$ (the reaction 'does not go') to $K > 1$ (the reaction 'goes'), occurs at a temperature given by equating $\Delta_r H^\ominus - T\Delta_r S^\ominus$ to 0, which gives:

$$T = \frac{\Delta_r H^\ominus}{\Delta_r S^\ominus} \qquad (7.9)$$

Illustration 7.3

Estimating a decomposition temperature

Consider the (endothermic) thermal decomposition of calcium carbonate:

$$CaCO_3(s) \rightarrow CaO(s) + CO_2(g)$$

For this reaction $\Delta_r H^\ominus = +178$ kJ mol^{-1} and $\Delta_r S^\ominus = +161$ J K^{-1} mol^{-1}. The decomposition temperature, the temperature at which the decomposition becomes spontaneous, is

$$T = \frac{1.78 \times 10^5 \text{ J mol}^{-1}}{161 \text{ J K}^{-1} \text{ mol}^{-1}} = 1.11 \times 10^3 \text{ K}$$

or about 832°C. Because the entropy of decomposition is similar for all such reactions (they all involve the decomposition of a solid into a gas), we can conclude that the decomposition temperatures of solids increase as their enthalpy of decomposition increases.

7.4 The standard reaction Gibbs energy

The standard reaction Gibbs energy, $\Delta_r G^\ominus$, is central to the discussion of chemical equilibria and the calculation of equilibrium constants. We have seen that it is defined as the difference in standard molar Gibbs energies of the products and the reactants weighted by the stoichiometric coefficients, ν, in the chemical equation:

$$\Delta_r G^\ominus = \sum \nu G_m^\ominus(\text{products}) - \sum \nu G_m^\ominus(\text{reactants}) \quad (7.10)$$

For example, the standard reaction Gibbs energy for reaction A is the difference between the molar Gibbs energies of fructose-6-phosphate and glucose-6-phosphate in solution at 1 mol dm^{-3} and 1 bar.

We cannot calculate $\Delta_r G^\ominus$ from the standard molar Gibbs energies themselves, because these quantities are not known. One practical approach is to calculate the standard reaction enthalpy from standard enthalpies of formation (Section 3.5), the standard reaction entropy from Third-Law entropies (Section 4.6), and then to combine the two quantities by using

$$\Delta_r G^\ominus = \Delta_r H^\ominus - T\Delta_r S^\ominus \quad (7.11)$$

Illustration 7.4

Evaluating the standard reaction Gibbs energy

To evaluate the standard reaction Gibbs energy at 25°C for the reaction $H_2(g) + \frac{1}{2} O_2(g) \rightarrow H_2O(l)$, we note that

$$\Delta_r H^\ominus = \Delta_f H^\ominus(H_2O, l) = -285.83 \text{ kJ mol}^{-1}$$

The standard reaction entropy, calculated as in Illustration 4.3, is

$$\Delta_r S^\ominus = -163.34 \text{ J K}^{-1} \text{ mol}^{-1}$$

which, because 163.34 J is the same as 0.163 34 kJ, corresponds to −0.163 34 kJ K^{-1} mol^{-1}. Therefore, from eqn 7.11,

$$\Delta_r G^\ominus = (-285.83 \text{ kJ mol}^{-1}) - (298.15 \text{ K}) \times (-0.163\,34 \text{ kJ K}^{-1} \text{ mol}^{-1}) = -237.13 \text{ kJ mol}^{-1}$$

Self-test 7.3

Use the information in the *Data section* to determine the standard reaction Gibbs energy for $3\,O_2(g) \rightarrow 2\,O_3(g)$ from standard enthalpies of formation and standard entropies.

[*Answer:* +326.4 kJ mol^{-1}]

We saw in Section 3.5 how to use standard enthalpies of formation of substances to calculate standard reaction enthalpies. We can use the same technique for standard reaction Gibbs energies. To do so, we list the **standard Gibbs energy of formation**, $\Delta_f G^\ominus$, of a substance, which is the standard reaction Gibbs energy (per mole of the species) for its formation from the elements in their reference states. The concept of reference state was introduced in Section 3.5; the temperature is arbitrary, but we shall almost always take it to be 25°C (298 K). For example, the standard Gibbs energy of formation of liquid water, $\Delta_f G^\ominus(H_2O, l)$, is the standard reaction Gibbs energy for

$$H_2(g) + \tfrac{1}{2} O_2(g) \rightarrow H_2O(l)$$

and is −237 kJ mol^{-1} at 298 K. Some standard Gibbs energies of formation are listed in Table 7.2 and more can be found in the *Data section*. It follows from the definition that the standard Gibbs energy of formation of an element in its reference state is zero because reactions such as

$$C(s, \text{graphite}) \rightarrow C(s, \text{graphite})$$

Table 7.2

*Standard Gibbs energies of formation at 298.15 K**

Substance	$\Delta_f G^\ominus/(\text{kJ mol}^{-1})$
Gases	
Ammonia, NH_3	−16.45
Carbon dioxide, CO_2	−394.36
Dinitrogen tetroxide, N_2O_4	+97.89
Hydrogen iodide, HI	+1.70
Nitrogen dioxide, NO_2	+51.31
Sulfur dioxide, SO_2	−300.19
Water, H_2O	−228.57
Liquids	
Benzene, C_6H_6	+124.3
Ethanol, CH_3CH_2OH	−174.78
Water, H_2O	−237.13
Solids	
Calcium carbonate, $CaCO_3$	−1128.8
Iron(III) oxide, Fe_2O_3	−742.2
Silver bromide, AgBr	−96.90
Silver chloride, AgCl	−109.79

* Additional values are given in the *Data section*.

are null (that is, nothing happens). The standard Gibbs energy of formation of an element in a phase different from its reference state is non-zero:

$$C(s, graphite) \rightarrow C(s, diamond)$$

$$\Delta_f G^{\ominus}(C, diamond) = +2.90 \text{ kJ mol}^{-1}$$

Many of the values in the tables have been compiled by combining the standard enthalpy of formation of the species with the standard entropies of the compound and the elements, as illustrated above, but there are other sources of data and we encounter some of them later.

Standard Gibbs energies of formation can be combined to obtain the standard Gibbs energy of almost any reaction. We use the now familiar expression

$$\Delta_r G^{\ominus} = \sum \nu \Delta_f G^{\ominus}(\text{products}) - \sum \nu \Delta_f G^{\ominus}(\text{reactants}) \quad (7.12)$$

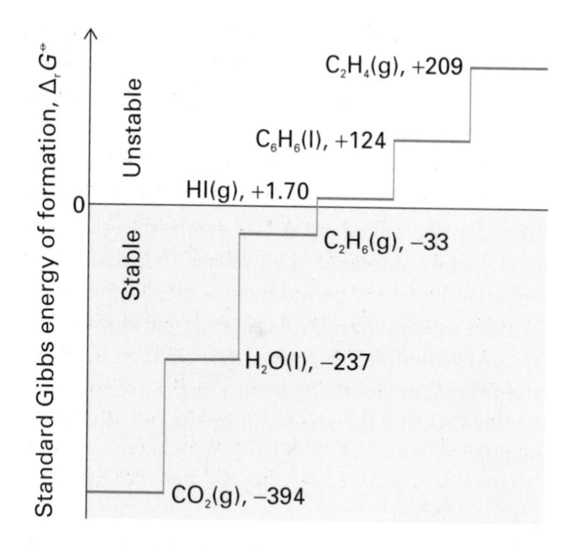

Fig. 7.6 The standard Gibbs energy of formation of a compound is like a measure of the compound's altitude above (or below) sea level: compounds that lie above sea level have a spontaneous tendency to decompose into the elements (and to revert to sea level). Compounds that lie below sea level are stable with respect to decomposition into the elements. The numerical values are in kilojoules per mole.

Illustration 7.5

Calculating a standard reaction Gibbs energy

To determine the standard reaction Gibbs energy for

$$2\,CO(g) + O_2(g) \rightarrow 2\,CO_2(g)$$

we carry out the following calculation:

$$\begin{aligned}\Delta_r G^{\ominus} &= 2\Delta_f G^{\ominus}(CO_2, g) - \{2\Delta_f G^{\ominus}(CO, g) + \Delta_f G^{\ominus}(O_2, g)\} \\ &= 2 \times (-394 \text{ kJ mol}^{-1}) - \{2 \times (-137 \text{ kJ mol}^{-1}) + 0\} \\ &= -514 \text{ kJ mol}^{-1}\end{aligned}$$

Self-test 7.4

Calculate the standard reaction Gibbs energy of the oxidation of ammonia to nitric oxide according to the equation $4\,NH_3(g) + 5\,O_2(g) \rightarrow 4\,NO(g) + 6\,H_2O(g)$.

[*Answer:* −959.42 kJ mol^{-1}]

Standard Gibbs energies of formation of compounds have their own significance as well as being useful in calculations of K. They are a measure of the 'thermodynamic altitude' of a compound above or below a 'sea level' of stability represented by the elements in their reference states (Fig. 7.6). If the standard Gibbs energy of formation is positive and the compound lies above 'sea level', then the compound has a spontaneous tendency to sink towards thermodynamic sea level and decompose into the elements. That is, $K < 1$ for their formation reaction. We say that a compound with $\Delta_f G^{\ominus} > 0$ is **thermodynamically unstable** with respect to its elements or that it is **endergonic**. Thus, the endergonic substance ozone, for which $\Delta_f G^{\ominus} = +163$ kJ mol^{-1}, has a spontaneous tendency to decompose into oxygen under standard conditions at 25°C. More precisely, the equilibrium constant for the reaction $\frac{3}{2}O_2(g) \rightleftharpoons O_3(g)$ is less than 1 (much less in fact, as $K = 2.7 \times 10^{-29}$). However, although ozone is thermodynamically unstable, it can survive if the reactions that convert it into oxygen are slow. That is the case in the upper atmosphere, and the O_3 molecules in the ozone layer survive for long periods. Benzene ($\Delta_f G^{\ominus} = +124$ kJ mol^{-1}) is also thermodynamically unstable with respect to its elements ($K = 1.8 \times 10^{-22}$). However, the fact that bottles of benzene are everyday laboratory commodities also reminds us of the point made at the start of the chapter, that *spontaneity is a thermodynamic tendency that might not be realized at a significant rate in practice*.

Another useful point that can be made about standard Gibbs energies of formation is that there is no point in searching for *direct* syntheses of a thermodynamically unstable compound from its elements (under standard conditions, at the temperature to which the data apply), because the reaction does not occur in the required direction: the *reverse* reaction, decomposition, is spontaneous. Endergonic compounds must be synthesized by alternative routes or under conditions for which their Gibbs energy of formation is negative and they lie beneath thermodynamic sea level.

Compounds with $\Delta_f G^\ominus < 0$ (corresponding to $K > 1$ for their formation reactions) are said to be **thermodynamically stable** with respect to their elements or **exergonic**. Exergonic compounds lie below the thermodynamic sea level of the elements (under standard conditions). An example is the exergonic compound ethane, with $\Delta_f G^\ominus = -33$ kJ mol^{-1}: the negative sign shows that the formation of ethane gas is spontaneous in the sense that $K > 1$ (in fact, $K = 7.1 \times 10^5$ at 25°C).

7.5 The equilibrium composition

The magnitude of an equilibrium constant is a good *qualitative* indication of the feasibility of a reaction regardless of whether the system is ideal or not. Broadly speaking, if $K \gg 1$ (typically $K > 10^3$, corresponding to $\Delta_r G^\ominus < -17$ kJ mol^{-1} at 25°C), then the reaction has a strong tendency to form products. If $K \ll 1$ (that is, for $K < 10^{-3}$, corresponding to $\Delta_r G^\ominus > +17$ kJ mol^{-1} at 25°C), then the equilibrium composition will consist of largely unchanged reactants. If K is comparable to 1 (typically lying between 10^{-3} and 10^3), then significant amounts of both reactants and products will be present at equilibrium.

An equilibrium constant expresses the composition of an equilibrium mixture as a ratio of products of activities. Even if we confine our attention to ideal systems it is still necessary to do some work to extract the actual equilibrium concentrations or partial pressures of the reactants and products given their initial values.

Example 7.1

Calculating an equilibrium composition 1

Estimate the fraction f of F6P in a solution, where f is defined as

$$f = \frac{[\text{F6P}]}{[\text{F6P}] + [\text{G6P}]}$$

in which G6P and F6P are in equilibrium at 25°C given that $\Delta_r G^\ominus = +1.7$ kJ mol^{-1} at that temperature.

Strategy Express f in terms of K. To do so, recognize that if the numerator and denominator in the expression for f are both divided by [G6P], then the ratios [F6P]/[G6P] can be replaced by K. Calculate the value of K by using eqn 7.8.

Solution Division of the numerator and denominator by [G6P] gives

$$f = \frac{[\text{F6P}]/[\text{G6P}]}{[\text{F6P}]/[\text{G6P}] + 1} = \frac{K}{K+1}$$

We find the equilibrium constant by using $K = e^{\ln K}$ and rearranging eqn 7.8 into

$$K = e^{-\Delta_r G^\ominus/RT}$$

First, note that because +1.7 kJ mol^{-1} is the same as $+1.7 \times 10^3$ J mol^{-1},

$$\frac{\Delta_r G^\ominus}{RT} = \frac{1.7 \times 10^3 \text{ J mol}^{-1}}{(8.3145 \text{ J K}^{-1} \text{ mol}^{-1}) \times (298 \text{ K})} = \frac{1.7 \times 10^3}{8.3145 \times 298}$$

Therefore,

$$K = e^{-\frac{1.7 \times 10^3}{8.3145 \times 298}} = 0.50$$

and

$$f = \frac{0.50}{1 + 0.50} = 0.33$$

That is, at equilibrium, 33 per cent of the solute is F6P and 67 per cent is G6P.

Self-test 7.5

Estimate the composition of a solution in which two isomers A and B are in equilibrium (A $\rightleftharpoons$ B) at 37°C and $\Delta_r G^\ominus = -2.2$ kJ mol^{-1}.

[*Answer*: the fraction of B at equilibrium is $f = 0.30$]

In more complicated cases it is best to organize the necessary work into a systematic procedure resembling a spreadsheet by constructing a table with columns headed by the species and, in successive rows:

1 The initial molar concentrations of solutes or partial pressures of gases.
2 The changes in these quantities that must take place for the system to reach equilibrium.
3 The resulting equilibrium values.

In most cases, we do not know the change that must occur for the system to reach equilibrium, so the change in the concentration or partial pressure of one species is written as x and the reaction stoichiometry is used to write the corresponding changes in the other species. When the values at equilibrium (the last row of the table) are substituted into the expression for the equilibrium constant, we obtain an equation for x in terms of K. This equation can be solved for x, and hence the concentrations of all the species at equilibrium may be found.

Example 7.2

Calculating an equilibrium composition 2

Suppose that in an industrial process, N_2 at 1.00 bar is mixed with H_2 at 3.00 bar and the two gases are allowed to come to equilibrium with the product ammonia (in the presence of a catalyst) in a reactor of constant volume. At the temperature of the reaction, it has been determined experimentally that $K = 977$. What are the equilibrium partial pressures of the three gases?

Strategy Proceed as set out above. Write down the chemical equation of the reaction and the expression for K. Set up the equilibrium table, express K in terms of x, and solve the equation for x. Because the volume of the reaction vessel is constant, each partial pressure is proportional to the amount of its molecules present ($p_J = n_J RT/V$), so the stoichiometric relations apply to the partial pressures directly. In general, solution of the equation for x results in several mathematically possible values of x. Select the chemically acceptable solution by considering the signs of the predicted concentrations or partial pressures: they must be positive. Confirm the accuracy of the calculation by substituting the calculated equilibrium partial pressures into the expression for the equilibrium constant to verify that the value so calculated is equal to the experimental value used in the calculation.

Solution The chemical equation is reaction B ($N_2(g) + 3\,H_2(g) \rightarrow 2\,NH_3(g)$), and the equilibrium constant is

$$K = \frac{p_{NH_3}^2}{p_{N_2}p_{H_2}^3}$$

with the partial pressures those at equilibrium (and, as usual, relative to $p^{\ominus}$). The equilibrium table is

	Species		
	N_2	H_2	NH_3
Initial partial pressure/bar	1.00	3.00	0
Change/bar	$-x$	$-3x$	$+2x$
Equilibrium partial pressure/bar	$1.00 - x$	$3.00 - 3x$	$2x$

The equilibrium constant for the reaction is therefore

$$K = \frac{(2x)^2}{(1.00 - x) \times (3.00 - 3x)^3}$$

Our task is to solve this equation for x. Because $K = 977$, this equation rearranges first to

$$977 = \tfrac{4}{27}\left(\frac{x}{(1.00 - x)^2}\right)^2$$

and then, after multiplying both sides by $\tfrac{27}{4}$ and taking the square root, to

$$\sqrt{\tfrac{27}{4} \times 977} = \frac{x}{(1.00 - x)^2}$$

To keep the appearance of this equation simple, we write $g = (\tfrac{27}{4} \times 977)^{1/2}$, when it becomes

$$g = \frac{x}{(1.00 - x)^2} = \frac{x}{1.00 - 2.00x + x^2}$$

This expression can now be rearranged into the quadratic equation

$$gx^2 - (2.00g + 1)x + 1.00g = 0$$

A quadratic equation of the form $ax^2 + bx + c = 0$ has solutions for values of x given by the quadratic formula:

$$x = \frac{-b \pm (b^2 - 4ac)^{1/2}}{2a}$$

More complex equations must be solved graphically or by using mathematical software; in some cases, approximations may be used.[1]

[1] For example, that x is very small when $K \ll 1$; examples are given in Section 8.2.

The quadratic formula gives the solutions $x = 1.12$ and $x = 0.895$. Because p_{N_2} cannot be negative, and $p_{N_2} = 1.00 - x$ (from the equilibrium table), we know that x cannot be greater than 1.00; therefore, we select $x = 0.895$ as the acceptable solution. It then follows from the last line of the equilibrium table that (with the units bar restored):

$$p_{N_2} = 0.10 \text{ bar} \qquad p_{H_2} = 0.31 \text{ bar} \qquad p_{NH_3} = 1.8 \text{ bar}$$

This is the composition of the reaction mixture at equilibrium. Note that, because K is large (of the order of 10^3), the products dominate. To verify the result, we calculate

$$\frac{p_{NH_3}^2}{p_{N_2}p_{H_2}^3} = \frac{(1.8)^2}{(0.10) \times (0.32)^3} = 9.9 \times 10^2$$

The result is close to the experimental value (the discrepancy stems from rounding errors).

Self-test 7.6

In an experiment to study the formation of nitrogen oxides in jet exhausts, N_2 at 0.100 bar is mixed with O_2 at 0.200 bar and the two gases are allowed to come to equilibrium with the product NO in a reactor of constant volume. Take $K = 3.4 \times 10^{-21}$ at 800 K. What is the equilibrium partial pressure of NO?

[*Answer:* 8.2 pbar]

7.6 The equilibrium constant in terms of concentration

An important point to appreciate is that the equilibrium constant K calculated from thermodynamic data refers to activities. For gas-phase reactions, that means partial pressures (and explicitly, $p_J/p^{\ominus}$). This requirement is sometimes emphasized by writing K as K_p, but the practice is unnecessary if the thermodynamic origin of K is remembered. In practical applications, however, we might wish to discuss gas-phase reactions in terms of molar concentrations. The equilibrium constant is then denoted K_c, and for reaction B is

$$K_c = \frac{[NH_3]^2}{[N_2][H_2]^3}$$

with, as usual, the molar concentration [J] interpreted as $[J]/c^{\ominus}$ with $c^{\ominus} = 1 \text{ mol dm}^{-3}$. To obtain the value of K_c from thermodynamic data, we must first calculate K and then convert K to K_c by using, as shown in Derivation 7.1,

$$K = K_c \times \left(\frac{c^{\ominus}RT}{p^{\ominus}}\right)^{\Delta\nu_{gas}} \tag{7.13a}$$

In this expression, $\Delta\nu_{gas}$ is the difference in the stoichiometric coefficients of the gas-phase species, products – reactants. We get a very convenient form of this expression by substituting the values of $c^{\ominus}$, $p^{\ominus}$, and R, which gives

$$K = K_c \times \left(\frac{T}{12.027 \text{ K}}\right)^{\Delta\nu_{gas}} \tag{7.13b}$$

The textbook's web site contains links to online tools for the estimation of equilibrium constants of gas-phase reactions.

Derivation 7.1

The relation between K and K_c

In this Derivation, we need to be fussy about units, and will write the equilibrium constants of reaction C in all their glory as

$$K = \frac{(p_C/p^{\ominus})^c(p_D/p^{\ominus})^d}{(p_A/p^{\ominus})^a(p_B/p^{\ominus})^b} \qquad K_c = \frac{([C]/c^{\ominus})^c([D]/c^{\ominus})^d}{([A]/c^{\ominus})^a([B]/c^{\ominus})^b}$$

The inclusion of $p^{\ominus}$ and $c^{\ominus}$ ensures that the two equilibrium constants are dimensionless. Now we use the perfect gas law to replace each partial pressure by

$$p_J = n_JRT/V = [J]RT$$

(because $[J] = n_J/V$). This substitution turns the expression for K into

$$K = \frac{([C]RT/p^{\ominus})^c([D]RT/p^{\ominus})^d}{([A]RT/p^{\ominus})^a([B]RT/p^{\ominus})^b}$$

$$= \frac{[C]^c[D]^d}{[A]^a[B]^b} \times \left(\frac{RT}{p^{\ominus}}\right)^{(c+d)-(a+b)}$$

Next, we recognize that

$$K_c = \frac{[C]^c[D]^d}{[A]^a[B]^b} \times \left(\frac{1}{c^{\ominus}}\right)^{(c+d)-(a+b)}$$

and so conclude that

$$K = K_c \times \left(\frac{c^{\ominus}RT}{p^{\ominus}}\right)^{(c+d)-(a+b)}$$

We obtain eqn 7.13 by writing $(c + d) - (a + b) = \Delta\nu_{gas}$.

Illustration 7.6

Converting from K to K_c

For reaction B we have $\Delta\nu_{gas} = 2 - (1 + 3) = -2$; therefore, from eqn 7.13b,

$$K_c = \frac{K}{(T/12.027\ \text{K})^{-2}} = K \times \left(\frac{T}{12.027\ \text{K}}\right)^2$$

At 298 K, $K = 5.8 \times 10^5$, so at this temperature

$$K_c = 5.8 \times 10^5 \times \left(\frac{298\ \text{K}}{12.027\ \text{K}}\right)^2 = 3.6 \times 10^8$$

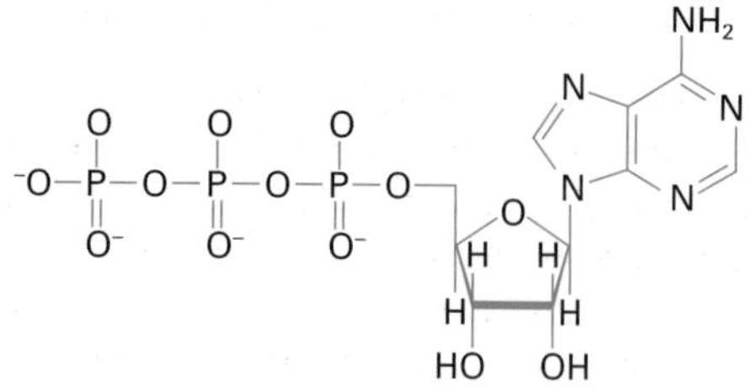

3 ATP

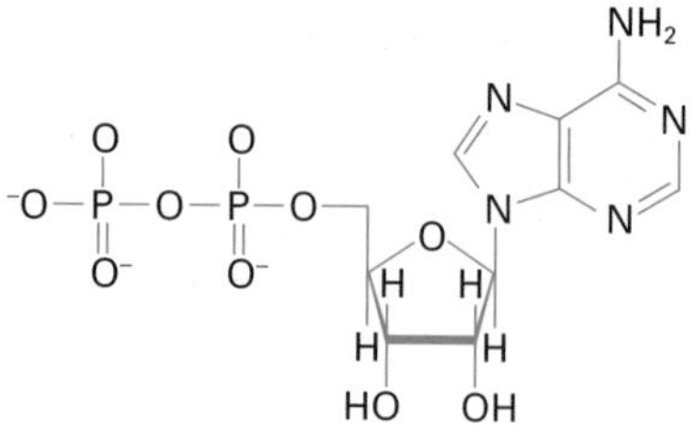

4 ADP

7.7 Coupled reactions

A reaction that is not spontaneous may be driven forward by coupling it to a reaction that is spontaneous. A simple mechanical analogy is a pair of weights joined by a string (Fig. 7.7): the lighter of the pair of weights will be pulled up as the heavier weight falls. Although the lighter weight has a natural tendency to move downwards, its coupling to the heavier weight results in it being raised. The thermodynamic analogue is an **endergonic reaction**, a reaction with a positive Gibbs energy, $\Delta_r G$ (the analogue of the lighter weight), being forced to occur by coupling it to an **exergonic reaction**, a reaction with a negative Gibbs energy, $\Delta_r G'$ (the analogue of the heavier weight falling to the ground). The overall reaction is spontaneous because the sum $\Delta_r G + \Delta_r G'$ is negative. The whole of life's activities depend on coupling of this kind, as the oxidation reactions of food act as the heavy weights that drive other reactions forward and result in the formation of proteins from amino acids, the actions of muscles for propulsion, and even the activities of the brain for reflection, learning, and imagination.

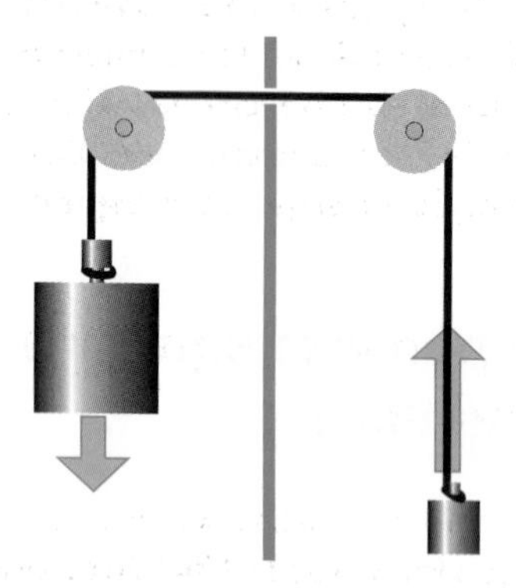

Fig. 7.7 If two weights are coupled as shown here, then the heavier weight will move the lighter weight in its non-spontaneous direction: overall, the process is still spontaneous. The weights are the analogues of two chemical reactions: a reaction with a large negative ΔG can force another reaction with a smaller ΔG to run in its non-spontaneous direction.

The function of adenosine triphosphate, ATP (**3**), for instance, is to store the energy made available when food is oxidized and then to supply it on demand to a wide variety of processes, including muscular contraction, reproduction, and vision. The essence of ATP's action is its ability to lose its terminal phosphate group by hydrolysis and to form adenosine diphosphate, ADP (**4**):

$$\text{ATP(aq)} + \text{H}_2\text{O(l)} \rightarrow \text{ADP(aq)} + \text{P}_i^-\text{(aq)} + \text{H}^+\text{(aq)}$$

where P_i^- denotes an inorganic phosphate group, such as $H_2PO_4^-$. This reaction is exergonic under the conditions prevailing in cells and can drive an endergonic reaction forward if suitable enzymes are available to couple the reactions. For example, the endergonic phosphorylation of glucose (Example 7.1) is coupled to the hydrolysis of ATP in the cell, so the net reaction

$$\text{glucose(aq)} + \text{ATP(aq)} \rightarrow \text{G6P(aq)} + \text{ADP(aq)}$$

is exergonic and initiates glycolysis.

Before discussing the hydrolysis of ATP quantitatively, we need to note that the conventional standard state of hydrogen ions ($a = 1$, corresponding to pH = 0, a strongly acidic solution) is not appropriate to normal biological conditions inside cells, where the pH is close to 7. Therefore, in biochemistry it is common to adopt the **biological standard state**, in which pH = 7, a neutral solution. We shall adopt this convention in this section, and label the corresponding standard quantities as $G^{\oplus}$, $H^{\oplus}$, and $S^{\oplus}$.[2]

The hydronium ion concentration is commonly expressed in terms of the pH, which is defined as pH = $-\log a_{H_3O^+}$. In elementary work, we replace the hydronium ion activity by the numerical value of its molar concentration, $[H_3O^+]$. For more details, see Chapter 8.

Example 7.3

Converting between thermodynamic and biological standard states

The standard reaction Gibbs energy for the hydrolysis of ATP (given above) is +10 kJ mol^{-1} at 298 K. What is the biological standard state value?

Strategy Because protons occur as products, lowering their concentration (from 1 mol dm^{-3} to 10^{-7} mol dm^{-3}) suggests that the reaction will have a higher tendency to form products. Therefore, we expect a more negative value of the reaction Gibbs energy for the biological standard than for the thermodynamic standard. The two types of standard are related by eqn 7.6, with the activity of hydrogen ions 10^{-7} in place of 1.

Solution The reaction quotient for the hydrolysis reaction when all the species are in their standard states except the hydrogen ions, which are present at 10^{-7} mol dm^{-3}, is

$$Q = \frac{a_{ADP}a_{P_i^-}a_{H^+}}{a_{ATP}a_{H_2O}} = \frac{1 \times 1 \times 10^{-7}}{1 \times 1} = 1 \times 10^{-7}$$

The thermodynamic and biological standard values are therefore related by eqn 7.6 in the form

$$\begin{aligned}\Delta_r G^{\oplus} &= \Delta_r G^{\ominus} + (8.314\,47 \times 10^{-3}\ \text{J K}^{-1}\ \text{mol}^{-1}) \\ &\quad \times (298\ \text{K}) \times \ln(1 \times 10^{-7}) \\ &= 10\ \text{kJ mol}^{-1} - 40\ \text{kJ mol}^{-1} = -30\ \text{kJ mol}^{-1}\end{aligned}$$

Note how the large change in pH changes the sign of the standard reaction Gibbs energy. Also, it follows from this discussion that there is no difference between thermodynamic and biological standard values if hydrogen ions are not involved in the reaction.

Self-test 7.7

The overall reaction for the glycolysis reaction is $C_6H_{12}O_6$(aq) + 2 NAD$^+$(aq) + 2 ADP(aq) + 2 P_i^-(aq) + 2 H_2O(l) → 2 $CH_3COCO_2^-$(aq) + 2 NADH(aq) + 2 ATP(aq) + 2 H_3O^+(aq). For this reaction, $\Delta_r G^{\oplus} = -80.6$ kJ mol^{-1} at 298 K. What is the value of $\Delta_r G^{\ominus}$?

[*Answer*: −0.7 kJ mol^{-1}]

The biological standard values for the hydrolysis of ATP at 37°C (310 K, body temperature) are

$$\Delta_r G^{\oplus} = -31\ \text{kJ mol}^{-1} \qquad \Delta_r H^{\oplus} = -20\ \text{kJ mol}^{-1}$$
$$\Delta_r S^{\oplus} = +34\ \text{kJ mol}^{-1}$$

The hydrolysis is therefore exergonic ($\Delta_r G < 0$) under these conditions, and 31 kJ mol^{-1} is available for driving other reactions. On account of its exergonic character, the ADP–phosphate bond has been called a 'high-energy phosphate bond'. The name is intended to signify a high tendency to undergo reaction and should not be confused with 'strong' bond in its normal chemical sense (that of a high bond enthalpy). In fact, even in the biological sense it is not of very 'high energy'. The action of ATP depends on the bond being intermediate in strength. Thus ATP acts as a phosphate donor to a number of acceptors (such as glucose), but is recharged with a new phosphate group by more powerful phosphate donors in the phosphorylation steps in the respiration cycle.

The response of equilibria to the conditions

In introductory chemistry, we meet the empirical rule of thumb known as **Le Chatelier's principle**:

When a system at equilibrium is subjected to a disturbance, the composition of the system adjusts so as to tend to minimize the effect of the disturbance.

[2] Another convention to denote the biological standard state is to write $X^{\circ\prime}$ or $X^{\ominus\prime}$.

For instance, if a system is compressed, then the equilibrium position can be expected to shift in the direction that leads to a reduction in the number of molecules in the gas phase, as that tends to minimize the effect of compression. Le Chatelier's principle, however, is only a rule of thumb, and to understand why reactions respond as they do, and to calculate the new equilibrium composition, we need to use thermodynamics. We need to keep in mind that some changes in conditions affect the value of $\Delta_r G^\ominus$ and therefore of K (temperature is the only instance) whereas others change the consequences of K having a particular fixed value without changing the value of K (the pressure, for instance).

7.8 The presence of a catalyst

A catalyst is a substance that accelerates a reaction without itself appearing in the overall chemical equation. Enzymes are biological versions of catalysts. We study the action of catalysts in Section 10.12, and at this stage do not need to know in detail how they work other than that they provide an alternative, faster route from reactants to products.

Although the new route from reactants to products is faster, the initial reactants and the final products are the same. The quantity $\Delta_r G^\ominus$ is defined as the difference of the standard molar Gibbs energies of the reactants and products, so it is independent of the path linking the two. It follows that an alternative pathway between reactants and products leaves $\Delta_r G^\ominus$ and therefore K unchanged. That is, *the presence of a catalyst does not change the equilibrium constant of a reaction.*

7.9 The effect of temperature

According to Le Chatelier's principle, we can expect a reaction to respond to a lowering of temperature by releasing heat and to respond to an increase of temperature by absorbing heat. That is, when the temperature is increased:

The equilibrium composition of an exothermic reaction will shift towards reactants.

The equilibrium composition of an endothermic reaction will shift towards products.

In each case, the response tends to minimize the effect of raising the temperature. But *why* do reactions at equilibrium respond in this way? Le Chatelier's principle is only a rule of thumb, and gives no clue to the reason for this behaviour. As we shall now see, the origin of the effect is the dependence of $\Delta_r G^\ominus$, and therefore of K, on the temperature.

First, we consider the effect of temperature on $\Delta_r G^\ominus$. We use the relation $\Delta_r G^\ominus = \Delta_r H^\ominus - T\Delta_r S^\ominus$ and make the assumption that neither the reaction enthalpy nor the reaction entropy varies much with temperature (over small ranges, at least). It follows that

$$\text{Change in } \Delta_r G^\ominus = -(\text{change in } T) \times \Delta_r S^\ominus \quad (7.14)$$

This expression is easy to apply when there is a consumption or formation of gas because, as we have seen (Section 4.6), gas formation dominates the sign of the reaction entropy.

Illustration 7.7

Predicting the effect of temperature

Consider the three reactions

(i) $\frac{1}{2}C(s) + \frac{1}{2}O_2(g) \rightarrow \frac{1}{2}CO_2(g)$

(ii) $C(s) + \frac{1}{2}O_2(g) \rightarrow CO(g)$

(iii) $CO(g) + \frac{1}{2}O_2(g) \rightarrow CO_2(g)$

all of which are important in the discussion of the extraction of metals from their ores. In reaction (i), the amount of gas is constant, so the reaction entropy is small and $\Delta_r G^\ominus$ for this reaction changes only slightly with temperature.[3] Because in reaction (ii) there is a net increase in the amount of gas molecules, from $\frac{1}{2}$ mol to 1 mol, the reaction entropy is large and positive; therefore, $\Delta_r G^\ominus$ for this reaction decreases sharply with increasing temperature. In reaction (iii), there is a similar net decrease in the amount of gas molecules, from $\frac{3}{2}$ mol to 1 mol, so $\Delta_r G^\ominus$ for this reaction increases sharply with increasing temperature. These remarks are summarized in Fig. 7.8.

[3] Note, however, that K changes, because $-\Delta_r G^\ominus/RT$ becomes less negative as T increases, so K decreases.

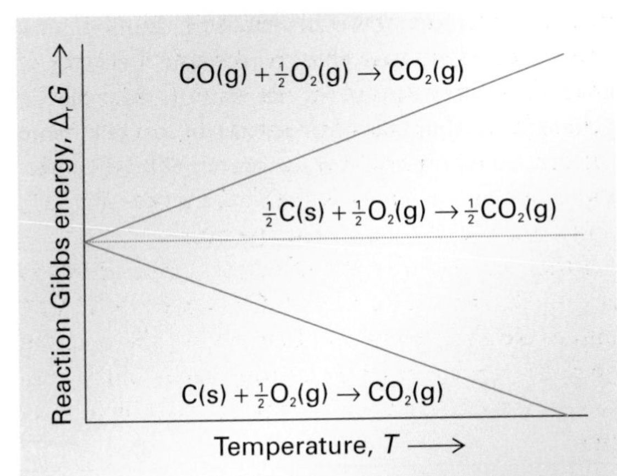

Fig. 7.8 The variation of reaction Gibbs energy with temperature depends on the reaction entropy and therefore on the net production or consumption of gas in a reaction. The Gibbs energy of a reaction that produces gas decreases with increasing temperature. The Gibbs energy of a reaction that results in a net consumption of gas increases with temperature.

Now consider the effect of temperature on K itself. At first, this problem looks troublesome, because both T and $\Delta_r G^{\ominus}$ appear in the expression for K. However, in fact, the effect of temperature can be expressed very simply as the **van 't Hoff equation:**[4]

$$\ln K' - \ln K = \frac{\Delta_r H^{\ominus}}{R}\left(\frac{1}{T} - \frac{1}{T'}\right) \quad (7.15)$$

where K is the equilibrium constant at the temperature T and K' is its value when the temperature is T'. All we need to know to calculate the temperature dependence of an equilibrium constant, therefore, is the standard reaction enthalpy.

Derivation 7.2

The van 't Hoff equation

As before, we use the approximation that the standard reaction enthalpy and entropy are independent of temperature over the range of interest, so the entire temperature dependence of $\Delta_r G^{\ominus}$ stems from the T in $\Delta_r G^{\ominus} = \Delta_r H^{\ominus} - T\Delta_r S^{\ominus}$. At a temperature T,

Substitute $\Delta G_r^{\ominus} = \Delta H_r^{\ominus} - T\Delta_r S^{\ominus}$

$$\ln K = -\frac{\Delta_r G^{\ominus}}{RT} = -\frac{\Delta_r H^{\ominus}}{RT} + \frac{\Delta_r S^{\ominus}}{R}$$

At another temperature T', when $\Delta_r G^{\ominus\prime} = \Delta_r H^{\ominus} - T'\Delta_r S^{\ominus}$ and the equilibrium constant is K', a similar expression holds:

$$\ln K' = -\frac{\Delta_r H^{\ominus}}{RT'} + \frac{\Delta_r S^{\ominus}}{R}$$

The difference between the two is

$$\ln K' - \ln K = \frac{\Delta_r H^{\ominus}}{R}\left(\frac{1}{T} - \frac{1}{T'}\right)$$

which is the van 't Hoff equation.

Let's explore the information in the van 't Hoff equation. Consider the case when $T' > T$. Then the term in parentheses in eqn 7.15 is positive. If $\Delta_r H^{\ominus} > 0$, corresponding to an endothermic reaction, the entire term on the right is positive. In this case, therefore, $\ln K' > \ln K$. That being so, we conclude that $K' > K$ for an endothermic reaction. In general, *the equilibrium constant of an endothermic reaction increases with temperature.* The opposite is true when $\Delta_r H^{\ominus} < 0$, so we can conclude that *the equilibrium constant of an exothermic reaction decreases with an increase in temperature.*

The conclusions we have outlined are of considerable commercial and environmental significance. For example, the synthesis of ammonia is exothermic, so its equilibrium constant decreases as the temperature is increased; in fact, K falls below 1 when the temperature is raised to above 200°C. Unfortunately, the reaction is slow at low temperatures and is commercially feasible only if the temperature exceeds about 750°C even in the presence of a catalyst; but then K is very small. We shall see shortly how Fritz Haber, the inventor of the Haber process for the commercial synthesis of ammonia, was able to overcome this difficulty. Another example is the oxidation of nitrogen:

$$N_2(g) + O_2(g) \rightarrow 2\,NO(g)$$

This reaction is endothermic ($\Delta_r H^{\ominus} = +180\ kJ\ mol^{-1}$) largely as a consequence of the very high bond enthalpy of N_2, so its equilibrium constant increases

4 There are several 'van 't Hoff equations'. To distinguish them, this one is sometimes called the *van 't Hoff isochore*.

with temperature. It is for this reason that nitrogen monoxide (nitric oxide) is formed in significant quantities in the hot exhausts of jet engines and in the hot exhaust manifolds of internal combustion engines, and then goes on to contribute to the problems caused by acid rain.

A final point in this connection is that to use the van 't Hoff equation for the temperature dependence of K_c, we first convert K_c to K by using eqn 7.13 at the temperature to which it applies, use eqn 7.15 to convert K to the new temperature, and then use eqn 7.13 again, but with the new temperature, to convert the new K to K_c. As you might appreciate, on the whole it is better to stick to using K.

7.10 The effect of compression

We have seen that Le Chatelier's principle suggests that the effect of compression (decrease in volume) on a gas-phase reaction at equilibrium is as follows:

When a system at equilibrium is compressed, the composition of a gas-phase equilibrium adjusts so as to reduce the number of molecules in the gas phase.

For example, in the synthesis of ammonia, reaction B, four reactant molecules give two product molecules, so compression favours the formation of ammonia. Indeed, this is the key to resolving Haber's dilemma: by working with highly compressed gases he was able to increase the yield of ammonia. Pressure plays an important role in governing the uptake and release of oxygen from oxygen transport and storage proteins (Box 7.1).

Self-test 7.8

Is the formation of products in the reaction $4\ NH_3(g) + 5\ O_2(g) \rightleftharpoons 4\ NO(g) + 6\ H_2O(g)$ favoured by compression or expansion of the reaction vessel?

[*Answer:* expansion]

Let's explore the thermodynamic basis of this dependence. First, we note that $\Delta_r G^{\ominus}$ is defined as the difference between the Gibbs energies of substances in their standard states and therefore at 1 bar. It follows that $\Delta_r G^{\ominus}$ has the same value whatever the actual pressure used for the reaction. Therefore, because $\ln K$ is proportional to $\Delta_r G^{\ominus}$, *K is independent of the pressure at which the reaction is carried out*. Thus, if the reaction mixture in which ammonia is being synthesized is compressed isothermally, the equilibrium constant remains unchanged.

This rather startling conclusion should not be misinterpreted. The value of K is independent of

Box 7.1 *Binding of oxygen to myoglobin and haemoglobin*

The protein myoglobin (Mb) stores O_2 in muscle and the protein haemoglobin (Hb) transports O_2 in blood; haemoglobin is composed of four myoglobin-like molecules. In each protein, the O_2 molecule attaches to an iron ion in a haem group, and each myoglobin-like component of haemoglobin responds to the change in shape of the others when O_2 binds to them.

First, consider the equilibrium between Mb and O_2:

$$\mathrm{Mb(aq)} + \mathrm{O_2(g)} \rightleftharpoons \mathrm{MbO_2(aq)} \qquad K = \frac{[\mathrm{MbO_2}]}{p[\mathrm{Mb}]}$$

where p is the numerical value of the partial pressure (in bar) of O_2 gas. It follows that the *fractional saturation*, s, the fraction of Mb molecules that are oxygenated, is

$$s = \frac{[\mathrm{MbO_2}]}{[\mathrm{Mb}]_{\mathrm{total}}} = \frac{[\mathrm{MbO_2}]}{[\mathrm{Mb}] + [\mathrm{MbO_2}]} = \frac{Kp}{1 + Kp}$$

The dependence of s on p is shown in the illustration.

Now consider the equilibria between Hb and O_2:

$$\mathrm{Hb(aq)} + \mathrm{O_2(g)} \rightleftharpoons \mathrm{HbO_2(aq)} \qquad K_1 = \frac{[\mathrm{HbO_2}]}{p[\mathrm{Hb}]}$$

$$\mathrm{HbO_2(aq)} + \mathrm{O_2(g)} \rightleftharpoons \mathrm{Hb(O_2)_2(aq)} \qquad K_2 = \frac{[\mathrm{Hb(O_2)_2}]}{p[\mathrm{HbO_2}]}$$

$$\mathrm{Hb(O_2)_2(aq)} + \mathrm{O_2(g)} \rightleftharpoons \mathrm{Hb(O_2)_3(aq)} \qquad K_3 = \frac{[\mathrm{Hb(O_2)_3}]}{p[\mathrm{Hb(O_2)_2}]}$$

$$\mathrm{Hb(O_2)_3(aq)} + \mathrm{O_2(g)} \rightleftharpoons \mathrm{Hb(O_2)_4(aq)} \qquad K_4 = \frac{[\mathrm{Hb(O_2)_4}]}{p[\mathrm{Hb(O_2)_3}]}$$

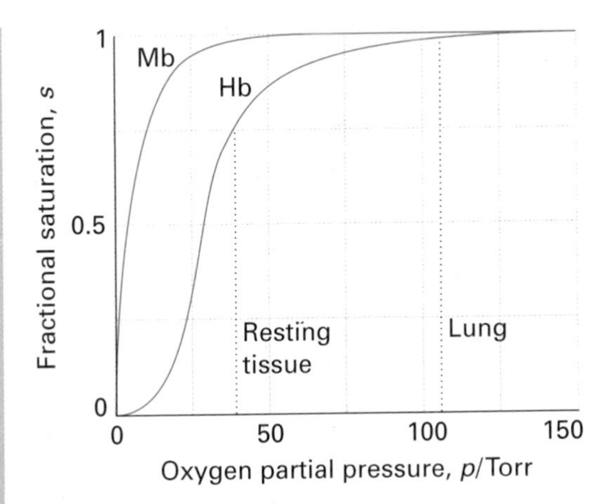

The variation of the fractional saturation of myoglobin and haemoglobin molecules with the partial pressure of oxygen. The different shapes of the curves account for the different biological functions of the two proteins.

To develop an expression for s, we express $[Hb(O_2)_2]$ in terms of $[HbO_2]$ by using K_2, then express $[HbO_2]$ in terms of [Hb] by using K_1, and likewise for all the other concentrations of $Hb(O_2)_3$ and $Hb(O_2)_4$. It follows that

$$[HbO_2] = K_1 p[Hb] \qquad [Hb(O_2)_2] = K_1K_2p^2[Hb]$$

$$[Hb(O_2)_3] = K_1K_2K_3p^3[Hb] \qquad [Hb(O_2)_4] = K_1K_2K_3K_4p^4[Hb]$$

The total concentration of bound O_2 is

$$[O_2]_{bound} = [HbO_2] + 2[Hb(O_2)_2] + 3[Hb(O_2)_3] + 4[Hb(O_2)_4]$$
$$= (1 + 2K_2p + 3K_2K_3p^2 + 4K_2K_3K_4p^3)K_1p[Hb]$$

and the total concentration of haemoglobin is

$$[Hb]_{total} = (1 + K_1p + K_1K_2p^2 + K_1K_2K_3p^3 + K_1K_2K_3K_4p^4)[Hb]$$

Because each Hb molecule has four sites at which O_2 can attach, the fractional saturation is

$$s = \frac{[O_2]_{bound}}{4[Hb]_{total}}$$
$$= \frac{(1 + 2K_2p + 3K_2K_3p^2 + 4K_2K_3K_4p^3)K_1p}{4(1 + K_1p + K_1K_2p^2 + K_1K_2K_3p^3 + K_1K_2K_3K_4p^4)}$$

A reasonable fit of the experimental data can be obtained with $K_1 = 0.01$, $K_2 = 0.02$, $K_3 = 0.04$, and $K_4 = 0.08$ when p is expressed in torr. The binding of O_2 to haemoglobin is an example of *cooperative binding*, in which the binding of a ligand (in this case O_2) to a biopolymer (in this case Hb) becomes more favourable thermodynamically (that is, the equilibrium constant increases) as the number of bound ligands increases up to the maximum number of binding sites. We see the effect of cooperativity in the illustration. Unlike the myoglobin saturation curve, the haemoglobin saturation curve is *sigmoidal* (S-shaped): the fractional saturation is small at low ligand concentrations, increases sharply at intermediate ligand concentrations, and then levels off at high ligand concentrations. Cooperative binding of O_2 by haemoglobin is explained by an *allosteric effect*, in which an adjustment of the conformation of a molecule when one substrate binds affects the ease with which a subsequent substrate molecule binds.

The differing shapes of the saturation curves for myoglobin and haemoglobin have important consequences for the way O_2 is made available in the body: in particular, the greater sharpness of the Hb saturation curve means that Hb can load O_2 more fully in the lungs and unload it more fully in different regions of the organism. In the lungs, where $p \approx 14$ kPa (100 Torr), $s \approx 0.98$, representing almost complete saturation. In resting muscular tissue, p is equivalent to about 5 kPa (40 Torr), corresponding to $s \approx 0.75$, implying that sufficient O_2 is still available should a sudden surge of activity take place. If the local partial pressure falls to 3 kPa (20 Torr), s falls to about 0.1. Note that the steepest part of the curve falls in the range of typical tissue oxygen partial pressure. Myoglobin, however, begins to release O_2 only when p has fallen below about 3 kPa (20 Torr), so it acts as a reserve to be drawn on only when the Hb oxygen has been used up.

Exercise 1 The saturation curves shown in the illustration may also be modelled mathematically by the equation

$$\log \frac{s}{1-s} = \nu \log p - \nu \log K$$

where s is the saturation, p is the partial pressure of O_2, K is a constant (not the binding constant for one ligand), and ν is the *Hill coefficient*, which varies from 1, for no cooperativity, to N for all-or-none binding of N ligands ($N = 4$ in Hb). The Hill coefficient for myoglobin is 1, and for haemoglobin it is 2.8. Determine the constant K for both Mb and Hb from the graph of fractional saturation (at $s = 0.5$) and then calculate the fractional saturation of Mb and Hb for the following values of p/kPa: 1.0, 1.5, 2.5, 4.0, 8.0.

Exercise 2 Using the information from the first exercise, calculate the value of s at the same p values assuming ν has the theoretical maximum value of 4.

the pressure to which the system is subjected, but because partial pressures occur in the expression for K in a rather complicated way, that does not mean that the *individual* partial pressures or concentrations are unchanged. Suppose, for example, the volume of the reaction vessel in which the reaction $H_2(g) + I_2(s) \rightleftharpoons 2\ HI(g)$ has reached equilibrium is reduced by a factor of 2 and the system is allowed to reach equilibrium again. If the partial pressures were simply to double (that is, there is no adjustment of composition by further reaction), the equilibrium constant would change from

$$K = \frac{p_{HI}^2}{p_{H_2}} \text{ to } K' = \frac{(2p_{HI})^2}{2p_{H_2}} = 2K$$

However, we have seen that compression leaves K unchanged. Therefore, the two partial pressures must adjust by different amounts. In this instance, K' will remain equal to K if the partial pressure of HI changes by a factor of less than 2 and the partial pressure of H_2 increases by more than a factor of 2. In other words, the equilibrium composition must shift in the direction of the reactants in order to preserve the equilibrium constant.

We can express this effect quantitatively by expressing the partial pressures in terms of the mole fractions and the total pressure. For the reaction above, we find

$$K = \frac{p_{HI}^2}{p_{H_2}} = \frac{x_{HI}^2 p^2}{x_{H_2} p} = \frac{x_{HI}^2 p}{x_{H_2}}$$

For K to remain constant as the pressure increases, the ratio of mole fractions must decrease, implying that the proportion of HI in the mixture must decrease. Because $x_{HI} + x_{H_2} = 1$, the explicit dependence of the mole fractions can be found by substituting $x_{H_2} = 1 - x_{HI}$ and solving the resulting quadratic equation for x_{HI}:

$$x_{HI} = \left(\frac{K}{2p}\right)\left\{\left(1 + \frac{4p}{K}\right)^{1/2} - 1\right\} \qquad (7.16)$$

The dependence of the mole fractions implied by this expression is shown in Fig. 7.9. Note that as p becomes zero, x_{HI} approaches 1; this limit is derived in Derivation 7.3.

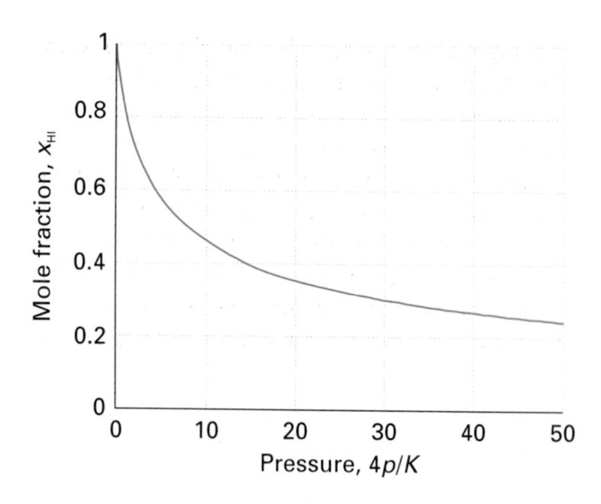

Fig. 7.9 The mole fraction of HI molecules in a gas-phase reaction mixture of H_2 and HI as a function of pressure (expressed as $4p/K$); the I_2 is present as a solid throughout.

Derivation 7.3

Taking a limit

To show that x_{HI} approaches 1 as p becomes zero, we cannot simply substitute $p = 0$ in eqn 7.16, because the first factor gives infinity and the second factor gives zero, and infinity times zero is not defined. Instead, we have to allow p to become very small and use the following expansion:

In this case, with $x = 4p/K$,

$$x_{HI} = \left(\frac{K}{2p}\right)\left\{\left(1 + \frac{2p}{K} + \cdots\right) - 1\right\} = \left(\frac{K}{2p}\right)\left\{\frac{2p}{K} + \cdots\right\}$$
$$= 1 + \cdots$$

and x_{HI} becomes 1 (the first of the unwritten terms is proportional to p, so all the other terms are zero when $p = 0$).

Series and expansions are discussed in Appendix 2.

$$(1 + x)^{1/2} = 1 + \tfrac{1}{2}x + \cdots$$

A note on good practice When one factor increases and another decreases, always evaluate the limit of an expression in this way: never rely on simply setting a term equal to zero.

Compression has no effect on the composition when the number of gas-phase molecules is the same in the reactants as in the products. An example is the synthesis of hydrogen iodide in which all three substances are present in the gas phase and the chemical equation is $H_2(g) + I_2(g) \rightleftharpoons 2\,HI(g)$.

A more subtle example is the effect of the addition of an inert gas to a reaction mixture contained inside a vessel of constant volume. The overall pressure increases as the gas (such as argon) is added, but the addition of a foreign gas does not affect the *partial* pressures of the other gases present.[5] Therefore, under these circumstances, not only does the equilibrium constant remain unchanged but also the partial pressures of the reactants and products remain the same whatever the stoichiometry of the reaction.

[5] The partial pressure of an ideal gas (Section 1.3) is the pressure a gas would exert if it alone occupied the vessel, so it is independent of the presence or absence of any other gases.

CHECKLIST OF KEY IDEAS

You should now be familiar with the following concepts:

☐ 1 The reaction Gibbs energy, $\Delta_r G$, is the slope of a plot of Gibbs energy against composition.

☐ 2 The condition of chemical equilibrium at constant temperature and pressure is $\Delta_r G = 0$.

☐ 3 The reaction Gibbs energy is related to the composition by $\Delta_r G = \Delta_r G^{\ominus} + RT \ln Q$, where Q is the reaction quotient.

☐ 4 The standard reaction Gibbs energy is the difference of the standard Gibbs energies of formation of the products and reactants weighted by the stoichiometric coefficients in the chemical equation, $\Delta_r G^{\ominus} = \sum \boldsymbol{\nu}\,\Delta_f G^{\ominus}(\text{products}) - \sum \boldsymbol{\nu}\,\Delta_f G^{\ominus}(\text{reactants})$.

☐ 5 The equilibrium constant is the value of the reaction quotient at equilibrium; it is related to the standard Gibbs energy of reaction by $\Delta_r G^{\ominus} = -RT \ln K$.

☐ 6 A compound is thermodynamically stable with respect to its elements if $\Delta_f G^{\ominus} < 0$.

☐ 7 The equilibrium constant K_c in terms of the molar concentrations of gases is related to the thermodynamic equilibrium constant K by $K = (c^{\ominus}RT/p^{\ominus})^{\Delta\nu_{\text{gas}}}K_c$.

☐ 8 The equilibrium constant of a reaction is independent of the presence of catalysts and independent of the pressure.

☐ 9 The variation of an equilibrium constant with temperature is expressed by the van 't Hoff equation, $\ln K' - \ln K = (\Delta_r H^{\ominus}/R)(1/T - 1/T')$.

☐ 10 The equilibrium constant K increases with temperature if $\Delta_r H^{\ominus} > 0$ (an endothermic reaction) and decreases if $\Delta_r H^{\ominus} < 0$ (an exothermic reaction).

☐ 11 When a system at equilibrium is compressed, the composition of a gas-phase equilibrium adjusts so as to reduce the number of molecules in the gas phase.

DISCUSSION QUESTIONS

7.1 Explain how the mixing of reactants and products affects the position of chemical equilibrium.

7.2 Explain how a reaction that is not spontaneous may be driven forward by coupling to a spontaneous reaction.

7.3 Explain Le Chatelier's principle in terms of thermodynamic quantities.

7.4 State the limits to the generality of the van't Hoff equation, written as

$$\ln K' - \ln K = \frac{\Delta_r H^{\ominus}}{R}\left(\frac{1}{T} - \frac{1}{T'}\right)$$

EXERCISES

The symbol ‡ indicates that calculus is required.

7.5 Write the reaction quotients for the following reactions making the approximation of replacing activities by molar concentrations or partial pressures:

(a) $G6P(aq) + H_2O(l) \rightarrow G(aq) + P_i(aq)$, where G6P is glucose 6-phosphate, G is glucose, and P_i is inorganic phosphate.

(b) $Gly(aq) + Ala(aq) \rightarrow Gly\text{–}Ala(aq) + H_2O(l)$

(c) $Mg^{2+}(aq) + ATP^{4-}(aq) \rightarrow MgATP^{2-}(aq)$

(d) $2\ CH_3COCOOH(aq) + 5\ O_2(g) \rightarrow 6\ CO_2(g) + 4\ H_2O(l)$

7.6 One of the most extensively studied reactions of industrial chemistry is the synthesis of ammonia, as its successful operation helps to govern the efficiency of the entire economy. The standard Gibbs energy of formation of $NH_3(g)$ is -16.5 kJ mol^{-1} at 298 K. What is the reaction Gibbs energy when the partial pressure of the N_2, H_2, and NH_3 (treated as perfect gases) are 3.0 bar, 1.0 bar, and 4.0 bar, respectively? What is the spontaneous direction of the reaction in this case?

7.7 Write the expressions for the equilibrium constants of the following reactions:

(a) $CO(g) + Cl_2(g) \rightleftharpoons COCl(g) + Cl(g)$

(b) $2\ SO_2(g) + O_2(g) \rightleftharpoons 2\ SO_3(g)$

(c) $H_2(g) + Br_2(g) \rightleftharpoons 2\ HBr(g)$

(d) $2\ O_3(g) \rightleftharpoons 3\ O_2(g)$

7.8 If the equilibrium constant for the reaction $A + B \rightleftharpoons C$ is reported as 0.224, what would be the equilibrium constant for the reaction written as $C \rightleftharpoons A + B$?

7.9 The equilibrium constant for the reaction $A + B \rightleftharpoons 2\ C$ is reported as 3.4×10^4. What would it be for the reaction written as (a) $2\ A + 2\ B \rightleftharpoons 4\ C$, (b) $\frac{1}{2}A + \frac{1}{2}B \rightleftharpoons C$?

7.10 The equilibrium constant for the isomerization of *cis*-2-butene to *trans*-2-butene is $K = 2.07$ at 400 K. Calculate the standard reaction Gibbs energy for the isomerization.

7.11 The standard reaction Gibbs energy of the isomerization of *cis*-2-pentene to *trans*-2-pentene at 400 K is -3.67 kJ mol^{-1}. Calculate the equilibrium constant of the isomerization.

7.12 One reaction has a standard Gibbs energy of -200 kJ mol^{-1} and a second reaction has a standard Gibbs energy of -100 kJ mol^{-1}. What is the ratio of their equilibrium constants at 300 K?

7.13 One enzyme-catalysed reaction in a biochemical cycle has an equilibrium constant that is 10 times the equilibrium constant of a second reaction. If the standard Gibbs energy of the former reaction is -300 kJ mol^{-1}, what is the standard reaction Gibbs energy of the second reaction?

7.14 What is the value of the equilibrium constant of a reaction for which $\Delta_r G^{\ominus} = 0$?

7.15 The standard reaction Gibbs energies (at pH = 7) for the hydrolysis of glucose-1-phosphate, glucose-6-phosphate, and glucose-3-phosphate are -21, -14, and -9.2 kJ mol^{-1}. Calculate the equilibrium constants for the hydrolyses at 37°C.

7.16 The standard Gibbs energy for the hydrolysis of ATP to ADP is -30.5 kJ mol^{-1}; what is the Gibbs energy of reaction in an environment at 37°C in which the ATP, ADP, and P_i concentrations are all (a) 1.0 mmol dm^{-3}, (b) 1.0 μmol dm^{-3}?

7.17 The distribution of Na^+ ions across a typical biological membrane is 10 mmol dm^{-3} inside the cell and 140 mmol dm^{-3} outside the cell. At equilibrium the concentrations are equal. What is the Gibbs energy difference across the membrane at 37°C? The difference in concentration must be sustained by coupling to reactions that have at least that difference in Gibbs energies.

7.18 Use the information in the *Data section* to estimate the temperature at which (a) $CaCO_3$ decomposes spontaneously and (b) $CuSO_4{\cdot}5H_2O$ undergoes dehydration.

7.19 The standard reaction enthalpy of $Zn(s) + H_2O(g) \rightarrow ZnO(s) + H_2(g)$ is approximately constant at $+224$ kJ mol^{-1} from 920 K up to 1280 K. The standard reaction Gibbs energy is $+33$ kJ mol^{-1} at 1280 K. Assuming that both quantities remain constant, estimate the temperature at which the equilibrium constant becomes greater than 1.

7.20 The equilibrium constant for the reaction $I_2(g) \rightarrow 2\ I(g)$ is 0.26 at 1000 K. What is the corresponding value of K_c?

7.21 The second step in glycolysis is the isomerization of glucose-6-phosphate (G6P) to fructose-6-phosphate (F6P). Example 7.1 considered the equilibrium between F6P and G6P. Draw a graph to show how the reaction Gibbs energy varies with the fraction *f* of F6P in solution. Label the regions of the graph that correspond to the formation of F6P and G6P being spontaneous, respectively.

7.22 Classify the following compounds as endergonic or exergonic: (a) glucose, (b) methylamine, (c) octane, (d) ethanol.

7.23 Combine the reaction entropies calculated in the following reactions with the reaction enthalpies and calculate the standard reaction Gibbs energies at 298 K:

(a) $HCl(g) + NH_3(g) \rightarrow NH_4Cl(s)$

(b) $2\ Al_2O_3(s) + 3\ Si(s) \rightarrow 3\ SiO_2(s) + 4\ Al(s)$

(c) $Fe(s) + H_2S(g) \rightarrow FeS(s) + H_2(g)$

(d) $FeS_2(s) + 2\ H_2(g) \rightarrow Fe(s) + 2\ H_2S(g)$

(e) $2\ H_2O_2(l) + H_2S(g) \rightarrow H_2SO_4(l) + 2\ H_2(g)$

7.24 Use the Gibbs energies of formation in the *Data section* to decide which of the following reactions have $K > 1$ at 298 K.

(a) $2\ CH_3CHO(g) + O_2(g) \rightleftharpoons 2\ CH_3COOH(l)$

(b) $2\ AgCl(s) + Br_2(l) \rightleftharpoons 2\ AgBr(s) + Cl_2(g)$

(c) $Hg(l) + Cl_2(g) \rightleftharpoons HgCl_2(s)$

(d) $Zn(s) + Cu^{2+}(aq) \rightleftharpoons Zn^{2+}(aq) + Cu(s)$

(e) $C_{12}H_{22}O_{11}(s) + 12\ O_2(g) \rightleftharpoons 12\ CO_2(g) + 11\ H_2O(l)$

7.25 Recall from Chapter 4 that the change in Gibbs energy can be identified with the maximum non-expansion work that can be extracted from a process. What is the maximum energy that can be extracted as (a) heat, (b) non-expansion work when 1.0 kg of natural gas (taken to be pure methane) is burned under standard conditions at 25°C? Take the reaction to be $CH_4(g) + 2\ O_2(g) \rightarrow CO_2(g) + 2\ H_2O(l)$.

7.26 In assessing metabolic processes we are usually more interested in the work that may be performed for the consumption of a given mass of compound than the heat it can produce (which merely keeps the body warm). What is the maximum energy that can be extracted as (a) heat, (b) non-expansion work when 1.0 kg of glucose is burned under standard conditions at 25°C with the production of water vapour? The reaction is $C_6H_{12}O_6(s) + 6\ O_2(g) \rightarrow 6\ CO_2(g) + 6\ H_2O(g)$.

7.27 Is it more energy effective to ingest sucrose or glucose? Calculate the non-expansion work, the expansion work, and the total work that can be obtained from the combustion of 1.0 kg of sucrose under standard conditions at 25°C when the product includes (a) water vapour, (b) liquid water.

7.28 The standard enthalpy of combustion of solid phenol, C_6H_5OH, is -3054 kJ mol^{-1} at 298 K and its standard molar entropy is 144.0 J K^{-1} mol^{-1}. Calculate the standard Gibbs energy of formation of phenol at 298 K.

7.29 Calculate the maximum non-expansion work per mole that may be obtained from a fuel cell in which the chemical reaction is the combustion of methane at 298 K.

7.30 Calculate the standard biological Gibbs energy for the reaction

$$\text{Pyruvate}^- + NADH + H^+ \rightarrow \text{lactate}^- + NAD^+$$

at 310 K given that $\Delta_r G^\ominus = -66.6$ kJ mol^{-1}. (NAD^+ is the oxidized form of nicotinamide dinucleotide.) This reaction occurs in muscle cells deprived of oxygen during strenuous exercise and can lead to cramp.

7.31 The standard biological reaction Gibbs energy for the removal of the phosphate group from adenosine monophosphate is -14 kJ mol^{-1} at 298 K. What is the value of the thermodynamic standard reaction Gibbs energy?

7.32 Show that if the logarithm of an equilibrium constant is plotted against the reciprocal of the temperature, then the standard reaction enthalpy may be determined.

7.33 Use the following data on the reaction $H_2(g) + Cl_2(g) \rightarrow 2\ HCl(g)$ to determine the standard reaction enthalpy:

T/K	300	500	1000
K	4.0×10^{31}	4.0×10^{18}	5.1×10^{8}

7.34 The equilibrium constant of the reaction $2\ C_3H_6(g) \rightleftharpoons C_2H_4(g) + C_4H_8(g)$ is found to fit the expression

$$\ln K = -1.04 - \frac{1088\ \text{K}}{T} + \frac{1.51 \times 10^5\ \text{K}^2}{T^2}$$

between 300 K and 600 K. Calculate the standard reaction enthalpy and standard reaction entropy at 400 K. (*Hint.* Begin by calculating ln K at 390 K and 410 K; then use eqn 7.14.)

7.35 ‡The thermodynamically exact form of the van 't Hoff equation (eqn 7.15) is $d(\ln K)/dT = -\Delta_r H^\ominus/RT^2$. Use the data in Exercise 7.34 to deduce an expression for the temperature dependence of the standard reaction enthalpy for the reaction treated there, and draw a graph to show the variation.

7.36 The van 't Hoff equation (eqn 7.15) applies to K, not to K_c. Find the corresponding expression for K_c. (*Hint.* Combine eqns 7.13 and 7.15.)

7.37 Borneol is a pungent compound obtained from the camphorwood tree of Borneo and Sumatra. The standard reaction Gibbs energy of the isomerization of borneol (**5**) to isoborneol (**6**) in the gas phase at 503 K is +9.4 kJ mol^{-1}. Calculate the reaction Gibbs energy in a mixture consisting of 0.15 mol of borneol and 0.30 mol of isoborneol when the total pressure is 600 Torr.

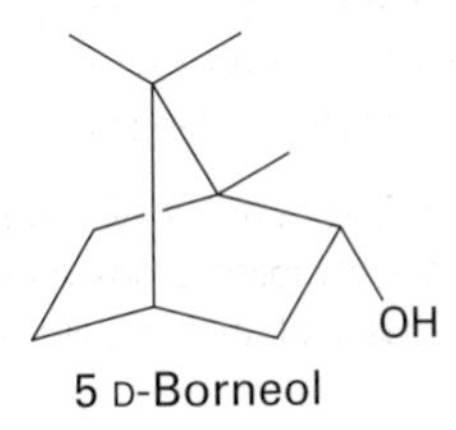

5 D-Borneol

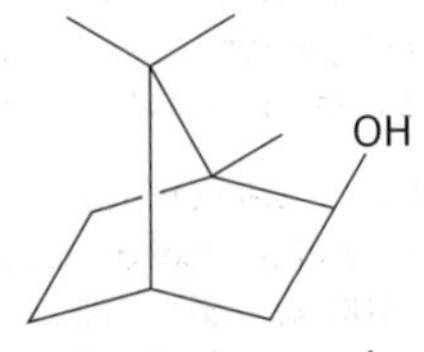

6 D-Isoborneol

7.38 The equilibrium constant for the gas-phase isomerization of borneol, $C_{10}H_{17}OH$, to isoborneol (see Exercise 7.37) at 503 K is 0.106. A mixture consisting of 7.50 g of borneol and 14.0 g of isoborneol in a container of volume 5.0 dm^3 is heated to 503 K and allowed to come to equilibrium. Calculate the mole fractions of the two substances at equilibrium.

7.39 Calculate the composition of a system in which nitrogen and hydrogen are mixed at partial pressures of 1.00 bar and 4.00 bar and allowed to reach equilibrium with their product, ammonia, under conditions when $K = 89.8$.

7.40 The bond in molecular iodine is quite weak, and hot iodine vapour contains a proportion of atoms. When 1.00 g of I_2 is heated to 1000 K in a sealed container of volume 1.00 dm^3, the resulting equilibrium mixture contains 0.830 g of I_2. Calculate K for the dissociation equilibrium $I_2(g) \rightleftharpoons 2\,I(g)$.

7.41 In a gas-phase equilibrium mixture of $SbCl_5$, $SbCl_3$, and Cl_2 at 500 K, $p_{SbCl_5} = 0.15$ bar and $p_{SbCl_3} = 0.20$ bar. Calculate the equilibrium partial pressure of Cl_2 given that $K = 3.5 \times 10^{-4}$ for the reaction $SbCl_5(g) \rightleftharpoons SbCl_3(g) + Cl_2(g)$.

7.42 The equilibrium constant $K = 0.36$ for the reaction $PCl_5(g) \rightleftharpoons PCl_3(g) + Cl_2(g)$ at 400 K. (a) Given that 2.0 g of PCl_5 was initially placed in a reaction vessel of volume 250 cm^3, determine the molar concentrations in the mixture at equilibrium. (b) What is the percentage of PCl_5 decomposed at 400 K?

7.43 In the Haber process for ammonia, $K = 0.036$ for the reaction $N_2(g) + 3\,H_2(g) \rightleftharpoons 2\,NH_3(g)$ at 500 K. If a reactor is charged with partial pressures of 0.020 bar of N_2 and 0.020 bar of H_2, what will be the equilibrium partial pressure of the components?

7.44 Express the equilibrium constant for $N_2O_4(g) \rightleftharpoons 2\,NO_2(g)$ in terms of the fraction α of N_2O_4 that has dissociated and the total pressure p of the reaction mixture, and show that when the extent of dissociation is small ($\alpha \ll 1$), α is inversely proportional to the square root of the total pressure ($\alpha \propto p^{-1/2}$).

7.45 The equilibrium pressure of H_2 over a mixture of solid uranium and solid uranium hydride at 500 K is 1.04 Torr. Calculate the standard Gibbs energy of formation of $UH_3(s)$ at 500 K.

7.46 Which of the products in Exercise 7.7 are favoured by a rise in temperature at constant pressure (in the sense that K increases)?

7.47 What is the standard enthalpy of a reaction for which the equilibrium constant is (a) doubled, (b) halved when the temperature is increased by 10 K at 298 K?

7.48 The dissociation vapour pressure (the pressure of gaseous products in equilibrium with the solid reactant) of NH_4Cl at 427°C is 608 kPa but at 459°C it has risen to 1115 kPa. Calculate (a) the equilibrium constant, (b) the standard reaction Gibbs energy, (c) the standard enthalpy, (d) the standard entropy of dissociation, all at 427°C. Assume that the vapour behaves as a perfect gas and that $\Delta H^{\ominus}$ and $\Delta S^{\ominus}$ are independent of temperature in the range given.

Chapter 8

Consequences of equilibrium

In this chapter we examine some consequences of dynamic chemical equilibria. We concentrate on the equilibria that exist in solutions of acids, bases, and their salts in water, where rapid proton transfer between species ensures that equilibrium is maintained at all times. The link between Chapter 7 and the discussion here is that, provided the temperature is held constant, *an equilibrium constant retains its value even though the individual activities may change*. So, if one substance is added to a mixture at equilibrium, the other substances adjust their abundances to restore the value of K.

Proton transfer equilibria

The reactions of acids and bases are central to chemistry and its applications, such as chemical analysis and synthesis. One particularly important application of proton transfer equilibrium is in living cells, as even small drifts in the equilibrium concentration of hydrogen ions can result in disease, cell damage, and death. Throughout this chapter, keep in mind that a free hydrogen ion (H^+, a proton) does not exist in water: it is always attached to a water molecule and exists as H_3O^+, a hydronium ion.

8.1 Brønsted–Lowry theory

According to the **Brønsted–Lowry theory** of acids and bases, an **acid** is a proton donor and a **base** is a proton acceptor. The proton, which in this context means a hydrogen ion, H^+, is highly mobile and acids and bases in water are always in equilibrium with their deprotonated and protonated counterparts and hydronium ions (H_3O^+). Thus, an acid HA, such as HCN, immediately establishes the equilibrium

$$HA(aq) + H_2O(l) \rightleftharpoons H_3O^+(aq) + A^-(aq)$$

$$K = \frac{a_{H_3O^+} a_{A^-}}{a_{HA} a_{H_2O}}$$

and a base B, such as NH_3, immediately establishes the equilibrium

$$B(aq) + H_2O(l) \rightleftharpoons BH^+(aq) + OH^-(aq)$$

$$K = \frac{a_{BH^+} a_{OH^-}}{a_B a_{H_2O}}$$

In these equilibria, A^- is the **conjugate base** of the acid HA, and BH^+ is the **conjugate acid** of the base B. Even in the absence of added acids and bases, proton transfer occurs between water molecules and the **autoprotolysis equilibrium**[1]

$$2\,H_2O(l) \rightleftharpoons H_3O^+(aq) + OH^-(aq)$$

$$K = \frac{a_{H_3O^+} a_{OH^-}}{a_{H_2O}^2}$$

is always present.

As will be familiar from introductory chemistry, the hydronium ion concentration is commonly expressed in terms of the pH, which is defined formally as

$$pH = -\log a_{H_3O^+} \qquad (8.1)$$

where the logarithm is to base 10. In elementary work, the hydronium ion activity is replaced by the numerical value of its molar concentration, $[H_3O^+]$, which is equivalent to setting the activity coefficient γ equal to 1. For example, if the molar concentration of H_3O^+ is 2.0 mmol dm^{-3} (where 1 mmol = 10^{-3} mol), then

$$pH \approx -\log(2.0 \times 10^{-3}) = 2.70$$

If the molar concentration were 10 times less, at 0.20 mmol dm^{-3}, then the pH would be 3.70. Note that *the higher the pH, the lower the concentration of hydronium ions in the solution* and that a change in pH by 1 unit corresponds to a 10-fold change in their molar concentration. However, it should never be forgotten that the replacement of activities by molar concentration is invariably hazardous. Because ions interact over long distances, the replacement is unreliable for all but the most dilute solutions.

Self-test 8.1

Death is likely if the pH of human blood plasma changes by more than ±0.4 from its normal value of 7.4. What is the approximate range of molar concentrations of hydrogen ions for which life can be sustained?

[*Answer:* 16 nmol dm^{-3} to 100 nmol dm^{-3} (1 nmol = 10^{-9} mol)]

8.2 Protonation and deprotonation

All the solutions we consider are so dilute that we can regard the water present as being a nearly pure liquid and therefore as having unit activity (see Table 6.2). When we set $a_{H_2O} = 1$ for all the solutions we consider, the resulting equilibrium constant is called the **acidity constant**, K_a, of the acid HA:[2]

$$K_a = \frac{a_{H_3O^+} a_{A^-}}{a_{HA}} \approx \frac{[H_3O^+][A^-]}{[HA]} \qquad (8.2)$$

Data are widely reported in terms of the negative common logarithm of this quantity:

$$pK_a = -\log K_a \qquad (8.3)$$

It follows from eqn 7.8 ($\Delta_r G^\ominus = -RT \ln K$) that pK_a is proportional to $\Delta_r G^\ominus$ for the proton transfer reaction. More explicitly, $pK_a = \Delta_r G^\ominus/(RT \ln 10)$, with ln 10 = 2.303 .... Therefore, manipulations of pK_a and related quantities are in fact manipulations of standard reaction Gibbs energies in disguise.

Self-test 8.2

Show that $pK_a = \Delta_r G^\ominus/(RT \ln 10)$. (*Hint.* $\ln x = \ln 10 \times \log x$.)

The value of the acidity constant indicates the extent to which proton transfer occurs at equilibrium in aqueous solution. The smaller the value of

[1] Autoprotolysis is also called *autoionization*.

[2] Acidity constants are also called *acid ionization constants* and, less appropriately, *dissociation constants*.

K_a, and therefore the larger the value of pK_a, the lower is the concentration of deprotonated molecules. Most acids have $K_a < 1$ (and usually much less than 1), with $pK_a > 0$, indicating only a small extent of deprotonation in water. These acids are classified as **weak acids.** A few acids, most notably, in aqueous solution, HCl, HBr, HI, HNO_3, H_2SO_4, and $HClO_4$, are classified as **strong acids,** and are commonly regarded as being completely deprotonated in aqueous solution.[3]

The corresponding expression for a base is called the **basicity constant,** K_b:

$$K_b = \frac{a_{BH^+}a_{OH^-}}{a_B} \approx \frac{[BH^+][OH^-]}{[B]}$$

$$pK_b = -\log K_b \qquad (8.4)$$

A **strong base** is fully protonated in solution in the sense that $K_b > 1$. One example is the oxide ion, O^{2-}, which cannot survive in water but is immediately and fully converted into its conjugate acid OH^-. A **weak base** is not fully protonated in water in the sense that $K_b < 1$ (and usually much less than 1). Ammonia, NH_3, and its organic derivatives the amines are all weak bases in water, and only a small proportion of their molecules exist as the conjugate acid (NH_4^+ or RNH_3^+).

The **autoprotolysis constant** for water, K_w, is

$$K_w = a_{H_3O^+}a_{OH^-} \qquad pK_w = -\log K_w \qquad (8.5)$$

At 25°C, the only temperature we consider in this chapter, $K_w = 1.0 \times 10^{-14}$ and $pK_w = 14.00$. As may be confirmed by multiplying the two constants together, the acidity constant of the conjugate acid, BH^+, of a base B (the equilibrium constant for the reaction $BH^+ + H_2O \rightleftharpoons H_3O^+ + B$) is related to the basicity constant of B (the equilibrium constant for the reaction $B + H_2O \rightleftharpoons BH^+ + OH^-$) by

$$K_aK_b = \frac{a_{H_3O^+}a_B}{a_{BH^+}} \times \frac{a_{BH^+}a_{OH^-}}{a_B}$$

$$= a_{H_3O^+}a_{OH^-} = K_w \qquad (8.6a)$$

The implication of this relation is that K_a increases as K_b decreases to maintain a product equal to the constant K_w. That is, *as the strength of a base decreases, the strength of its conjugate acid increases,* and vice versa. On taking the negative common logarithm of both sides of eqn 8.6a, we obtain

$$pK_a + pK_b = pK_w \qquad (8.6b)$$

The great advantage of this relation is that the pK_b values of bases may be expressed as the pK_a of their conjugate acids, so the strengths of all weak acids and bases may be listed in a single table (Table 8.1).

Illustration 8.1

The acidity and basicity constants of a base

If the acidity constant of the conjugate acid ($CH_3NH_3^+$) of the base methylamine (CH_3NH_2) is reported as $pK_a = 10.56$, we can infer that the basicity constant of methylamine itself is

$$pK_b = pK_w - pK_a = 14.00 - 10.56 = 3.44$$

Another useful relation is obtained by taking the negative common logarithm of both sides of the definition of K_w in eqn 8.5, which gives

$$pH + pOH = pK_w \qquad (8.7)$$

where $pOH = -\log a_{OH^-}$. This enormously important relation means that the activities (in elementary work, the molar concentrations) of hydronium and hydroxide ions are related by a see-saw relation: as one goes up, the other goes down to preserve the value of pK_w.

Self-test 8.3

The molar concentration of OH^- ions in a certain solution is 0.010 mmol dm^{-3}. What is the pH of the solution?

[*Answer:* 9.00]

The extent of deprotonation of a weak acid in solution depends on the acidity constant and the initial concentration of the acid, its concentration as prepared. The **fraction deprotonated,** the fraction of acid molecules HA that have donated a proton, is

$$\text{Fraction deprotonated} = \frac{\text{equilibrium molar concentration of conjugate base}}{\text{molar concentration of acid as prepared}}$$

$$f = \frac{[A^-]_{equilibrium}}{[HA]_{as\ prepared}} \qquad (8.8)$$

[3] Sulfuric acid, H_2SO_4, is strong with respect only to its first deprotonation; HSO_4^- is weak.

Table 8.1 *Acidity and basicity constants* at 298.15 K*

Acid/base	K_b	pK_b	K_a	pK_a
Strongest weak acids				
Trichloroacetic acid, CCl_3COOH	3.3×10^{-14}	13.48	3.0×10^{-1}	0.52
Benzenesulfonic acid, $C_6H_5SO_3H$	5.0×10^{-14}	13.30	2×10^{-1}	0.70
Iodic acid, HIO_3	5.9×10^{-14}	13.23	1.7×10^{-1}	0.77
Sulfurous acid, H_2SO_3	6.3×10^{-13}	12.19	1.6×10^{-2}	1.81
Chlorous acid, $HClO_2$	1.0×10^{-12}	12.00	1.0×10^{-2}	2.00
Phosphoric acid, H_3PO_4	1.3×10^{-12}	11.88	7.6×10^{-3}	2.12
Chloroacetic acid, $CH_2ClCOOH$	7.1×10^{-12}	11.15	1.4×10^{-3}	2.85
Lactic acid, $CH_3CH(OH)COOH$	1.2×10^{-11}	10.92	8.4×10^{-4}	3.08
Nitrous acid, HNO_2	2.3×10^{-11}	10.63	4.3×10^{-4}	3.37
Hydrofluoric acid, HF	2.9×10^{-11}	10.55	3.5×10^{-4}	3.45
Formic acid, HCOOH	5.6×10^{-11}	10.25	1.8×10^{-4}	3.75
Benzoic acid, C_6H_5COOH	1.5×10^{-10}	9.81	6.5×10^{-5}	4.19
Acetic acid, CH_3COOH	5.6×10^{-10}	9.25	5.6×10^{-5}	4.75
Carbonic acid, H_2CO_3	2.3×10^{-8}	7.63	4.3×10^{-7}	6.37
Hypochlorous acid, HClO	3.3×10^{-7}	6.47	3.0×10^{-8}	7.53
Hypobromous acid, HBrO	5.0×10^{-6}	5.31	2.0×10^{-9}	8.69
Boric acid, $B(OH)_3$†	1.4×10^{-5}	4.86	7.2×10^{-10}	9.14
Hydrocyanic acid, HCN	2.0×10^{-5}	4.69	4.9×10^{-10}	9.31
Phenol, C_6H_5OH	7.7×10^{-5}	4.11	1.3×10^{-10}	9.89
Hypoiodous acid, HIO	4.3×10^{-4}	3.36	2.3×10^{-11}	10.64
Weakest weak acids				
Weakest weak bases				
Urea, $CO(NH_2)_2$	1.3×10^{-14}	13.90	7.7×10^{-1}	0.10
Aniline, $C_6H_5NH_2$	4.3×10^{-10}	9.37	2.3×10^{-5}	4.63
Pyridine, C_5H_5N	1.8×10^{-9}	8.75	5.6×10^{-6}	5.35
Hydroxylamine, NH_2OH	1.1×10^{-8}	7.97	9.1×10^{-7}	6.03
Nicotine, $C_{10}H_{11}N_2$	1.0×10^{-6}	5.98	1.0×10^{-8}	8.02
Morphine, $C_{17}H_{19}O_3N$	1.6×10^{-6}	5.79	6.3×10^{-9}	8.21
Hydrazine, NH_2NH_2	1.7×10^{-6}	5.77	5.9×10^{-9}	8.23
Ammonia, NH_3	1.8×10^{-5}	4.75	5.6×10^{-10}	9.25
Trimethylamine, $(CH_3)_3N$	6.5×10^{-5}	4.19	1.5×10^{-10}	9.81
Methylamine, CH_3NH_2	3.6×10^{-4}	3.44	2.8×10^{-11}	10.56
Dimethylamine, $(CH_3)_2NH$	5.4×10^{-4}	3.27	1.9×10^{-11}	10.73
Ethylamine, $C_2H_5NH_2$	6.5×10^{-4}	3.19	1.5×10^{-11}	10.81
Triethylamine, $(C_2H_5)_3N$	1.0×10^{-3}	2.99	1.0×10^{-11}	11.01
Strongest weak bases				

* Values for polyprotic acids—those capable of donating more than one proton—refer to the first deprotonation.

† The proton transfer equilibrium is $B(OH)_3(aq) + 2\,H_2O(l) \rightleftharpoons H_3O^+(aq) + B(OH)_4^-(aq)$.

The extent to which a weak base B is protonated is reported in terms of the **fraction protonated:**

$$\text{Fraction protonated} = \frac{\text{equilibrium molar concentration of conjugate acid}}{\text{molar concentration of base as prepared}}$$

$$f = \frac{[BH^+]_{\text{equilibrium}}}{[B]_{\text{as prepared}}} \qquad (8.9)$$

We can estimate the pH of a solution of a weak acid or a weak base and calculate either of these fractions by using the equilibrium-table technique described in Section 7.6.

Example 8.1

Assessing the extent of deprotonation of a weak acid

Estimate the pH and the fraction of CH_3COOH molecules deprotonated in 0.15 M $CH_3COOH(aq)$.

Strategy The aim is to calculate the equilibrium composition of the solution. To do so, we use the technique illustrated in Example 7.3, with x the change in molar concentration of H_3O^+ ions required to reach equilibrium. We ignore the tiny concentration of hydronium ions present in pure water. Once x has been found, calculate $pH = -\log x$. Because we can anticipate that the extent of deprotonation is small (the acid is weak), use the approximation that x is very small to simplify the equations.

Solution We draw up the following equilibrium table:

	Species:		
	CH_3COOH	H_3O^+	$CH_3CO_2^-$
Initial concentration/(mol dm^{-3})	0.15	0	0
Change to reach equilibrium/(mol dm^{-3})	$-x$	$+x$	$+x$
Equilibrium concentration/(mol dm^{-3})	$0.15 - x$	x	x

The value of x is found by inserting the equilibrium concentrations into the expression for the acidity constant:

$$K_a = \frac{[H_3O^+][CH_3CO_2^-]}{[CH_3COOH]} = \frac{x \times x}{0.15 - x}$$

We could arrange the expression into a quadratic equation and use the solution in Example 7.3. However, it is more instructive to make use of the smallness of x to replace $0.15 - x$ by 0.15 (this approximation is valid if $x \ll 0.15$, which is likely because the acid is weak, but should be verified). Then the simplified equation rearranges first to $0.15 \times K_a = x^2$ and then to

$$x = (0.15 \times K_a)^{1/2} = (0.15 \times 1.8 \times 10^{-5})^{1/2} = 1.6 \times 10^{-3}$$

Therefore, pH = 2.80. Calculations of this kind are rarely accurate to more than one decimal place in the pH (and even that may be too optimistic) because the effects of ion–ion interactions have been ignored, so this answer would be reported as pH = 2.8. The fraction deprotonated, f, is

$$f = \frac{[CH_3CO_2^-]_{\text{equilibrium}}}{[CH_3COOH]_{\text{added}}} = \frac{x}{0.15} = \frac{1.6 \times 10^{-3}}{0.15} = 0.011$$

That is, only 1.1 per cent of the acetic acid molecules have donated a proton.

A note on good practice When an approximation has been assumed, verify at the end of the calculation that the approximation is consistent with the result obtained. In this case, we assumed that $x \ll 0.15$ and have found that $x = 0.011$, which is consistent.

Another note on good practice Acetic acid (ethanoic acid) is written CH_3COOH because the two O atoms are inequivalent; its conjugate base, the acetate ion (ethanoate ion) is written $CH_3CO_2^-$ because the two O atoms are now equivalent (by resonance).

Self-test 8.4

Estimate the pH of 0.010 M $CH_3CH(OH)COOH(aq)$ (lactic acid) from the data in Table 8.1. Before carrying out the numerical calculation, decide whether you expect the pH to be higher or lower than that calculated for the same concentration of acetic acid.

[*Answer:* 2.5]

Example 8.2

Assessing the extent of protonation of a weak base

The conjugate acid of the base quinoline (**1**) has $pK_a = 4.88$. Estimate the pH and the fraction of molecules protonated in a 0.010 M aqueous solution of quinoline.

N

1 Quinoline

Strategy The calculation of the pH of a solution of a base involves one more step than that for the pH of a solution of an acid. The first step is to calculate the concentration of OH^- ions in the solution by using the equilibrium-table technique, and to express it as the pOH of the solution. The additional step is to convert that pOH into a pH by using the water autoprotolysis equilibrium, eqn 8.7, in the form $pH = pK_w - pOH$, with $pK_w = 14.00$ at 25°C. We also need to compute $pK_b = pK_w - pK_a$.

Solution First, we write

$$pK_b = 14.00 - 4.88 = 9.12, \text{ corresponding to}$$
$$K_b = 10^{-9.12} = 7.6 \times 10^{-10}$$

Now draw up the following equilibrium table, denoting quinoline by Q and its conjugate acid by QH^+:

	Species		
	Q	OH^-	QH^+
Initial concentration/(mol dm^{-3})	0.010	0	0
Change to reach equilibrium/(mol dm^{-3})	$-x$	$+x$	$+x$
Equilibrium concentration/(mol dm^{-3})	$0.010 - x$	x	x

The value of x is found by inserting the equilibrium concentrations into the expression for the basicity constant:

$$K_b = \frac{[OH^-][QH^+]}{[Q]} = \frac{x \times x}{0.010 - x}$$

We suppose that $x \ll 0.010$. Then the simplified equation rearranges to

$$x = (0.010 \times K_b)^{1/2} = (0.010 \times 7.6 \times 10^{-10})^{1/2}$$
$$= 2.8 \times 10^{-6}$$

This value is consistent with the assumption that $x \ll 0.010$. Therefore, pOH = 5.55, and consequently pH = 14.00 − 5.55 = 8.45, or about 8.4. The fraction protonated, f, is

$$f = \frac{[QH^+]_{\text{equilibrium}}}{[Q]_{\text{added}}} = \frac{x}{0.010} = \frac{2.8 \times 10^{-6}}{0.010} = 2.8 \times 10^{-4}$$

or 1 molecule in about 3500.

Self-test 8.5

The pK_a for the first protonation of nicotine (**2**) is 8.02. What is the pH and the fraction of molecules protonated in a 0.015 M aqueous solution of nicotine?

[*Answer:* 10.1; 1/120]

2 Nicotine

8.3 Polyprotic acids

A **polyprotic acid** is a molecular compound that can donate more than one proton. Two examples are sulfuric acid, H_2SO_4, which can donate up to two protons, and phosphoric acid, H_3PO_4, which can donate up to three. A polyprotic acid is best considered to be a molecular species that can give rise to a series of Brønsted acids as it donates its succession of protons. Thus, sulfuric acid is the parent of two Brønsted acids, H_2SO_4 itself and HSO_4^-, and phosphoric acid is the parent of three Brønsted acids, namely H_3PO_4, $H_2PO_4^-$, and HPO_4^{2-}.

For a species H_2A with two acidic protons (such as H_2SO_4), the successive equilibria we need to consider are

$$H_2A(aq) + H_2O(l) \rightleftharpoons H_3O^+(aq) + HA^-(aq)$$

$$K_{a1} = \frac{a_{H_3O^+} a_{HA^-}}{a_{H_2A}}$$

$$HA^-(aq) + H_2O(l) \rightleftharpoons H_3O^+(aq) + A^{2-}(aq)$$

$$K_{a2} = \frac{a_{H_3O^+} a_{A^{2-}}}{a_{HA^-}}$$

In the first of these equilibria, HA^- is the conjugate base of H_2A. In the second, HA^- acts as the acid and A^{2-} is its conjugate base. Values are given in Table 8.2. In all cases, K_{a2} is smaller than K_{a1}, typically by three orders of magnitude for small molecular species, because the second proton is more difficult to remove, partly on account of the negative charge on HA^-. Enzymes are polyprotic acids; they possess many protons that can be donated to a substrate molecule or to the surrounding aqueous medium of the cell. For them, successive acidity constants vary much less because the molecules are so large that the loss of a proton from one part of the molecule has little effect on the ease with which another some distance away may be lost.

Table 8.2 *Successive acidity constants of polyprotic acids at 298.15 K*

Acid	K_{a1}	pK_{a1}	K_{a2}	pK_{a2}	K_{a3}	pK_{a3}
Carbonic acid, H_2CO_3	4.3×10^{-7}	6.37	5.6×10^{-11}	10.25		
Hydrosulfuric acid, H_2S	1.3×10^{-7}	6.88	7.1×10^{-15}	14.15		
Oxalic acid, $(COOH)_2$	5.9×10^{-2}	1.23	6.5×10^{-5}	4.19		
Phosphoric acid, H_3PO_4	7.6×10^{-3}	2.12	6.2×10^{-8}	7.21	2.1×10^{-13}	12.67
Phosphorous acid, H_2PO_3	1.0×10^{-2}	2.00	2.6×10^{-7}	6.59		
Sulfuric acid, H_2SO_4	Strong		1.2×10^{-2}	1.92		
Sulfurous acid, H_2SO_3	1.5×10^{-2}	1.81	1.2×10^{-7}	6.91		
Tartaric acid, $C_2H_4O_2(COOH)_2$	6.0×10^{-4}	3.22	1.5×10^{-5}	4.82		

Example 8.3

Calculating the concentration of carbonate ion in carbonic acid

Ground water contains dissolved carbon dioxide, carbonic acid, hydrogencarbonate ions, and a very low concentration of carbonate ions. Estimate the molar concentration of CO_3^{2-} ions in a solution in which water and CO_2(g) are in equilibrium. We must be very cautious in the interpretation of calculations involving carbonic acid because equilibrium between dissolved CO_2 and H_2CO_3 is achieved only very slowly. In organisms, attainment of equilibrium is facilitated by the enzyme carbonic anhydrase.

Strategy We start with the equilibrium that produces the ion of interest (such as A^{2-}) and write its activity in terms of the acidity constant for its formation (K_{a2}). That expression will contain the activity of the conjugate acid (HA^-), which we can express in terms of the activity of *its* conjugate acid (H_2A) by using the appropriate acidity constant (K_{a1}). This equilibrium dominates all the rest provided the molecule is small and there are marked differences between its acidity constants, so it may be possible to make an approximation at this stage.

Solution The CO_3^{2-} ion, the conjugate base of the acid HCO_3^-, is produced in the equilibrium

$$HCO_3^-(aq) + H_2O(l) \rightleftharpoons H_3O^+(aq) + CO_3^{2-}(aq)$$

$$K_{a2} = \frac{a_{H_3O^+}a_{CO_3^{2-}}}{a_{HCO_3^-}}$$

Hence,

$$a_{CO_3^{2-}} = \frac{a_{HCO_3^-}K_{a2}}{a_{H_3O^+}}$$

The HCO_3^- ions are produced in the equilibrium

$$H_2CO_3(aq) + H_2O(l) \rightleftharpoons H_3O^+(aq) + HCO_3^-(aq)$$

One H_3O^+ ion is produced for each HCO_3^- ion produced. These two concentrations are not exactly the same, because a little HCO_3^- is lost in the second deprotonation and the amount of H_3O^+ has been increased by it. Also, HCO_3^- is a weak base and abstracts a proton from water to generate H_2CO_3 (see Section 8.4). However, those secondary changes can safely be ignored in an approximate calculation. Because the molar concentrations of HCO_3^- and H_3O^+ are approximately the same, we can suppose that their activities are also approximately the same, and set $a_{HCO_3^-} \approx a_{H_3O^+}$. When this equality is substituted into the expression for $a_{CO_3^{2-}}$ and we make the approximation that $a_{CO_3^{2-}} = [CO_3^{2-}]$, then we obtain

$$[CO_3^{2-}] \approx K_{a2}$$

Because we know from Table 8.2 that $pK_{a2} = 10.25$, it follows that $[CO_3^{2-}] = 5.6 \times 10^{-11}$, and therefore, if equilibrium has in fact been achieved, that the molar concentration of CO_3^{2-} ions is 5.6×10^{-11} mol dm^{-3} and (within the approximations we have made) independent of the concentration of H_2CO_3 present initially.

Self-test 8.6

Calculate the molar concentration of S^{2-} ions in H_2S(aq).

[*Answer:* 7.1×10^{-15} mol dm^{-3}]

Example 8.4

Calculating the fractional composition of a solution

Oxalic acid, $H_2C_2O_4$ (ethandioic acid, HOOC–COOH), exists in solution in equilibrium with $HC_2O_4^-$ and $C_2O_4^{2-}$. Show how the composition of an aqueous solution that contains 0.010 mol dm^{-3} of oxalic acid varies with pH.

Strategy We expect the fully protonated species ($H_2C_2O_4$) at low pH, the partially protonated species ($HC_2O_4^-$) at intermediate pH, and the fully deprotonated species ($C_2O_4^{2-}$) at high pH. Set up the expressions for the two acidity constants, treating $H_2C_2O_4$ as the parent acid, and an expression for the total concentration of oxalic acid. Solve the resulting expressions for the fraction of each species in terms of the hydronium ion concentration.

Solution The two acidity constants are

$$H_2C_2O_4(aq) + H_2O(l) \rightleftharpoons H_3O^+(aq) + HC_2O_4^-(aq)$$

$$K_{a1} = \frac{[H_3O^+][HC_2O_4^-]}{[H_2C_2O_4]}$$

$$HC_2O_4^-(aq) + H_2O(l) \rightleftharpoons H_3O^+(aq) + C_2O_4^{2-}(aq)$$

$$K_{a2} = \frac{[H_3O^+][C_2O_4^{2-}]}{[HC_2O_4^-]}$$

We also know that the total concentration of oxalic acid in all its forms is

$$[H_2C_2O_4] + [HC_2O_4^-] + [C_2O_4^{2-}] = O_{total}$$

We now have three equations for three unknown concentrations. To solve the equations, we proceed systematically by using K_{a2} to express $[C_2O_4^{2-}]$ in terms of $[HC_2O_4^-]$, then K_{a1} to express $[HC_2O_4^-]$ in terms of $[H_2C_2O_4]$:

$$[HC_2O_4^-] = \frac{K_{a1}[H_2C_2O_4]}{[H_3O^+]}$$

$$[C_2O_4^{2-}] = \frac{K_{a2}[HC_2O_4^-]}{[H_3O^+]} = \frac{K_{a1}K_{a2}[H_2C_2O_4]}{[H_3O^+]^2}$$

The expression for the total concentration O_{total} can now be written in terms of $[H_2C_2O_4]$ and $[H_3O^+]$:

$$O_{total} = [H_2C_2O_4] + \frac{K_{a1}[H_2C_2O_4]}{[H_3O^+]} + \frac{K_{a1}K_{a2}[H_2C_2O_4]}{[H_3O^+]^2}$$

$$= \left\{1 + \frac{K_{a1}}{[H_3O^+]} + \frac{K_{a1}K_{a2}}{[H_3O^+]^2}\right\}[H_2C_2O_4]$$

$$= \frac{1}{[H_3O^+]^2}\{[H_3O^+]^2 + [H_3O^+]K_{a1} + K_{a1}K_{a2}\}[H_2C_2O_4]$$

It follows that the fractions of each species present in the solution are

$$f(H_2C_2O_4) = \frac{[H_2C_2O_4]}{O_{total}}$$

$$= \frac{[H_2C_2O_4]}{(1/[H_3O^+])\{[H_3O^+]^2 + [H_3O^+]K_{a1} + K_{a1}K_{a2}\}[H_2C_2O_4]}$$

$$= \frac{[H_3O^+]}{[H_3O^+]^2 + [H_3O^+]K_{a1} + K_{a1}K_{a2}}$$

and similarly

$$f(HC_2O_4^-) = \frac{[HC_2O_4^-]}{O_{total}} = \frac{[H_3O^+]K_{a1}}{[H_3O^+]^2 + [H_3O^+]K_{a1} + K_{a1}K_{a2}}$$

$$f(C_2O_4^{2-}) = \frac{[C_2O_4^{2-}]}{O_{total}} = \frac{K_{a1}K_{a2}}{[H_3O^+]^2 + [H_3O^+]K_{a1} + K_{a1}K_{a2}}$$

These fractions are plotted against pH $= -\log[H_3O^+]$ in Fig. 8.1. Note how $H_2C_2O_4$ is dominant for pH < pK_{a1}, that $H_2C_2O_4$ and $HC_2O_4^-$ have the same concentration at pH = pK_{a1}, and that $HC_2O_4^-$ is dominant for pH > pK_{a1}, until $C_2O_4^{2-}$ becomes dominant.

A note on good practice. Be ready to take advantage of symmetries in the expressions: inspection of the three expressions for the fractions of the species present shows a symmetry in the appearance of $[H_3O^+]$ and the *K*s. By noting this symmetry, it is possible to write

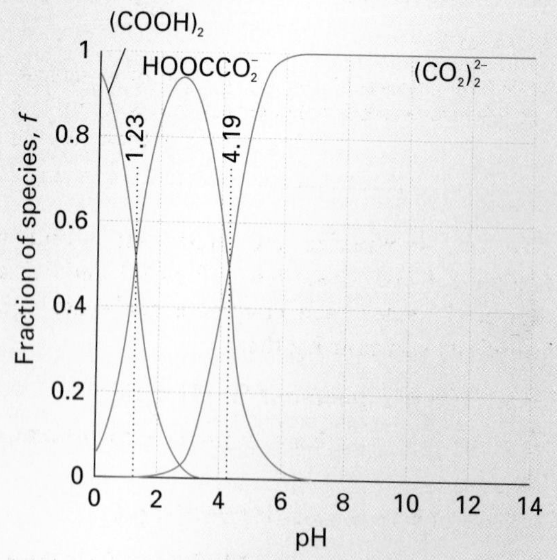

Fig. 8.1 The fractional composition of the protonated and deprotonated forms of oxalic acid in aqueous solution as a function of pH. Note that conjugate pairs are present at equal concentrations when the pH is equal to the pK_a of the acid member of the pair.

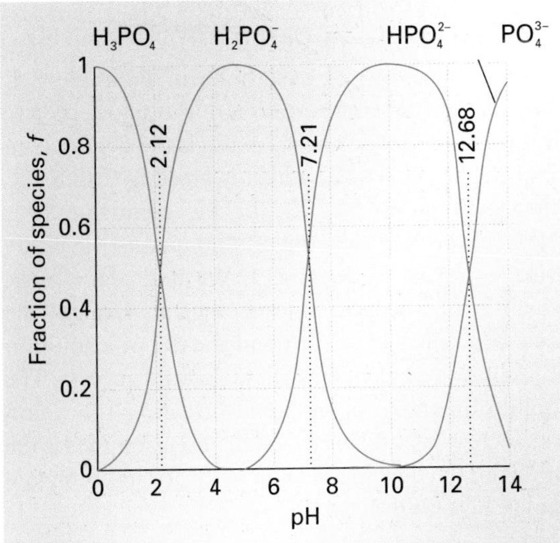

Fig. 8.2 The fractional composition of the protonated and deprotonated forms of phosphoric acid in aqueous solution as a function of pH.

down the expression for the species present in a solution of a triprotic acid without further calculation (see the following Self-test).

Self-test 8.7

Construct the diagram for the fraction of protonated species in an aqueous solution of phosphoric acid.

[*Answer:* Fig. 8.2]

We can summarize the behaviour found in Example 8.4 and illustrated in Figs 8.1 and 8.2 as follows. Consider each conjugate acid–base pair, with acidity constant K_a; then:

The acid form is dominant for $pH < pK_a$

The conjugate pair have equal concentrations at $pH = pK_a$

The base form is dominant for $pH > pK_a$

In each case, the other possible forms of a polyprotic system can be ignored, provided the pK_a values are not too close together.

8.4 Amphiprotic systems

An **amphiprotic** species is a molecule or ion that can both accept and donate protons. For instance, HCO_3^- can act as an acid (to form CO_3^{2-}) and as a base (to form H_2CO_3). The question we need to tackle is the pH of a solution of a salt with an amphiprotic anion, such as a solution of $NaHCO_3$. Is the solution acidic on account of the acid character of HCO_3^-, or is it basic on account of the anion's basic character? As we show in Derivation 8.1, the pH of such a solution is given by

$$pH = \tfrac{1}{2}(pK_{a1} + pK_{a2}) \qquad (8.10)$$

Derivation 8.1

The pH of an amphiprotic salt solution

Let's suppose that we make up a solution of the salt MHA, where HA^- is the amphiprotic anion (such as HCO_3^-) and M^+ is a cation (such as Na^+). The equilibrium table is as follows:

	Species			
	H_2A	HA^-	A^{2-}	H_3O^+
Initial molar concentration/(mol dm^{-3})	0	A	0	0
Change to reach equilibrium/(mol dm^{-3})	$+x$	$-(x+y)$	$+y$	$+(y-x)$
Equilibrium concentration/(mol dm^{-3})	x	$A-x-y$	y	$y-x$

The two acidity constants are

$$K_{a1} = \frac{[H_3O^+][HA^-]}{[H_2A]} = \frac{(y-x)(A-x-y)}{x}$$

$$K_{a2} = \frac{[H_3O^+][A^{2-}]}{[HA^-]} = \frac{(y-x)y}{A-x-y}$$

Multiplication of these two expressions, noting from the equilibrium table that at equilibrium $y - x = [H_3O^+]$, gives

$$K_{a1}K_{a2} = \frac{(y-x)^2 y}{x} = [H_3O^+]^2 \times \frac{y}{x}$$

Next, we show that, to a good approximation, $y/x \approx 1$ and therefore that $[H_3O^+] = (K_{a1}K_{a2})^{1/2}$. For this step we rearrange the expression for K_{a1} as follows:

$$xK_{a1} = Ay - y^2 - Ax + x^2$$

Because xK_{a1}, x^2, and y^2 are all very small compared with terms that have A in them, this expression reduces to

$$0 \approx Ay - Ax$$

We conclude that $x \approx y$, and therefore that $y/x \approx 1$, as required. Equation 8.10 now follows by taking the negative common logarithm of both sides of $[H_3O^+] = (K_{a1}K_{a2})^{1/2}$.

Illustration 8.2

The pH of an amphiprotic salt solution

If the dissolved salt is sodium hydrogencarbonate, we can immediately conclude that the pH of the solution *of any concentration* is

$$pH = \tfrac{1}{2}(6.37 + 10.25) = 8.31$$

The solution is basic. We can treat a solution of potassium dihydrogenphosphate in the same way, taking into account only the second and third acidity constants of H_3PO_4 because protonation as far as H_3PO_4 is negligible:

$$pH = \tfrac{1}{2}(7.21 + 12.67) = 9.94$$

Salts in water

The ions present when a salt is added to water may themselves be either acids or bases and consequently affect the pH of the solution. For example, when ammonium chloride is added to water, it provides both an acid (NH_4^+) and a base (Cl^-). The solution consists of a weak acid (NH_4^+) and a very weak base (Cl^-). The net effect is that the solution is acidic. Similarly, a solution of sodium acetate consists of a neutral ion (the Na^+ ion) and a base ($CH_3CO_2^-$). The net effect is that the solution is basic, and its pH is greater than 7.

Self-test 8.8

Is an aqueous solution of potassium lactate likely to be acidic or basic?

[*Answer:* basic]

To estimate the pH of the solution, we proceed in exactly the same way as for the addition of a 'conventional' acid or base, because in the Brønsted–Lowry theory, there is no distinction between 'conventional' acids like acetic acid and the conjugate acids of bases (like NH_4^+). For example, to calculate the pH of 0.010 M $NH_4Cl(aq)$ at 25°C, we proceed exactly as in Example 8.1, taking the initial concentration of the acid (NH_4^+) to be 0.010 mol dm^{-3}. The K_a to use is the acidity constant of the acid NH_4^+, which is listed in Table 8.1. Alternatively, we use K_b for the conjugate base (NH_3) of the acid and convert that quantity to K_a by using eqn 8.6a ($K_aK_b = K_w$). We find pH = 5.63, which is on the acid side of neutral. Exactly the same procedure is used to find the pH of a solution of a salt of a weak acid, such as sodium acetate. The equilibrium table is set up by treating the anion $CH_3CO_2^-$ as a base (which it is), and using for K_b the value obtained from the value of K_a for its conjugate acid (CH_3COOH).

Self-test 8.9

Estimate the pH of 0.0025 M $NH(CH_3)_3Cl(aq)$ at 25°C.

[*Answer:* 6.2]

8.5 Acid–base titrations

Acidity constants play an important role in acid–base titrations, as we can use them to decide the value of the pH that signals the **stoichiometric point**, the stage at which a stoichiometrically equivalent amount of acid has been added to a given amount of base.[4] The plot of the pH of the **analyte**, the solution being analysed, against the volume of **titrant**, the solution in the burette, added is called the **pH curve**. It shows a number of features that are still of interest even nowadays when many titrations are carried out in automatic titrators with the pH monitored electronically: automatic titration equipment is built to make use of the concepts we describe here.

First, consider the titration of a strong acid with a strong base, such as the titration of hydrochloric acid with aqueous sodium hydroxide. The reaction is

$$HCl(aq) + NaOH(aq) \rightarrow NaCl(aq) + H_2O(l)$$

Initially, the analyte (hydrochloric acid) has a low pH. The ions present at the stoichiometric point (the

[4] The stoichiometric point is widely called the *equivalence point* of a titration. The meaning of *end point* is explained in Section 8.7.

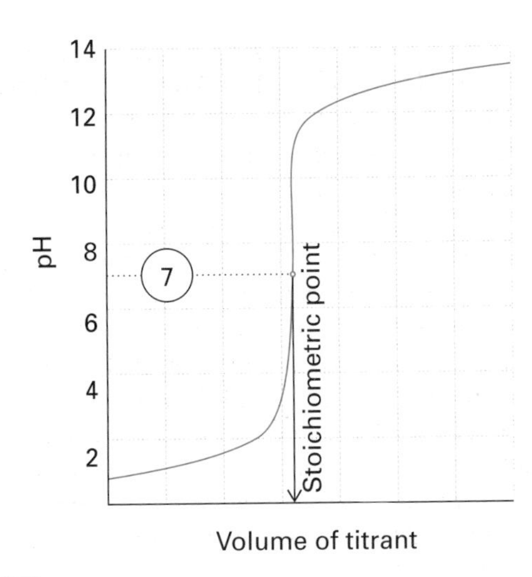

Fig. 8.3 The pH curve for the titration of a strong acid (the analyte) with a strong base (the titrant). There is an abrupt change in pH near the stoichiometric point at pH = 7. The final pH of the medium approaches that of the titrant.

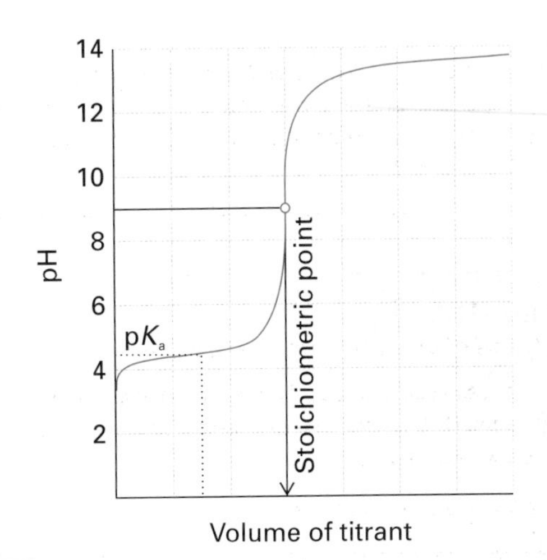

Fig. 8.4 The pH curve for the titration of a weak acid (the analyte) with a strong base (the titrant). Note that the stoichiometric point occurs at pH > 7 and that the change in pH near the stoichiometric point is less abrupt than in Fig. 8.3. The pK_a of the acid is equal to the pH halfway to the stoichiometric point.

Na^+ ions from the strong base and the Cl^- ions from the strong acid) barely affect the pH, so the pH is that of almost pure water, namely pH = 7. After the stoichiometric point, when base is added to a neutral solution, the pH rises sharply to a high value. The pH curve for such a titration is shown in Fig. 8.3.

Figure 8.4 shows the pH curve for the titration of a weak acid (such as CH_3COOH) with a strong base (NaOH). At the stoichiometric point the solution contains $CH_3CO_2^-$ ions and Na^+ ions together with any ions stemming from autoprotolysis. The presence of the Brønsted base $CH_3CO_2^-$ in the solution means that we can expect pH > 7. In a titration of a weak base (such as NH_3) and a strong acid (HCl), the solution contains NH_4^+ ions and Cl^- ions at the stoichiometric point. Because Cl^- is only a very weak Brønsted base and NH_4^+ is a weak Brønsted acid the solution is acidic and its pH will be less than 7.

Now we consider the shape of the pH curve in terms of the acidity constants of the species involved. The approximations we make are based on the fact that the acid is weak, and therefore that HA is more abundant than any A^- ions in the solution. Furthermore, when HA is present, it provides so many H_3O^+ ions, even though it is a weak acid, that they greatly outnumber any H_3O^+ ions that come from the very feeble autoprotolysis of water. Finally, when excess base is present after the stoichiometric point has been passed, the OH^- ions it provides dominate any that come from the water autoprotolysis.

To be specific, let's suppose that we are titrating 25.00 cm^3 of 0.10 M $CH_3COOH(aq)$ with 0.20 M NaOH(aq) at 25°C. We can calculate the pH at the start of a titration of a weak acid with a strong base as explained in Example 8.1, and find pH = 2.9. The addition of titrant converts some of the acid to its conjugate base in the reaction

$$CH_3COOH(aq) + OH^-(aq) \rightarrow H_2O(l) + CH_3CO_2^-(aq)$$

Suppose we add enough titrant to produce a concentration [base] of the conjugate base and simultaneously reduce the concentration of acid to [acid]. Then, because the solution remains at equilibrium,

$$K_a = \frac{a_{H_3O^+} a_{CH_3CO_2^-}}{a_{CH_3COOH}} \approx \frac{a_{H_3O^+}[\text{base}]}{[\text{acid}]}$$

which rearranges first to

$$a_{H_3O^+} \approx \frac{K_a[\text{acid}]}{[\text{base}]}$$

and then, by taking negative common logarithms, to the **Henderson–Hasselbalch equation**

$$pH \approx pK_a - \log\frac{[acid]}{[base]} \tag{8.11}$$

Example 8.5

Estimating the pH at an intermediate stage in a titration

Calculate the pH of the solution after the addition of 5.00 cm^3 of the titrant to the analyte in the titration described above.

Strategy The first step involves deciding the amount of OH^- ions added in the titrant, and then to use that amount to calculate the amount of CH_3COOH remaining. Note that because the ratio of acid to base molar concentrations occurs in eqn 8.11, the volume of solution cancels, and we can equate the ratio of concentrations to the ratio of amounts.

Solution The addition of 5.00 cm^3, or 5.00×10^{-3} dm^3 (because 1 $cm^3 = 10^{-3}$ dm^3), of titrant corresponds to the addition of

$$n_{OH^-} = (5.00 \times 10^{-3}\ dm^3) \times (0.200\ mol\ dm^{-3})$$
$$= 1.00 \times 10^{-3}\ mol$$

This amount of OH^- (1.00 mmol) converts 1.00 mmol CH_3COOH to the base $CH_3CO_2^-$. The initial amount of CH_3COOH in the analyte is

$$n_{CH_3COOH} = (25.00 \times 10^{-3}\ dm^3) \times (0.200\ mol\ dm^{-3})$$
$$= 2.50 \times 10^{-3}\ mol$$

so the amount remaining after the addition of titrant is 1.50 mmol. It then follows from the Henderson–Hasselbalch equation that

$$pH \approx 4.75 - \log\frac{1.50 \times 10^{-3}}{1.00 \times 10^{-3}} = 4.6$$

As expected, the addition of base has resulted in an increase in pH from 2.9. You should not take the value 4.6 too seriously because we have already pointed out that such calculations are approximate. However, it is important to note that the pH has increased from its initial acidic value.

Self-test 8.10

Calculate the pH after the addition of a further 5.00 cm^3 of titrant.

[*Answer:* 5.4]

Halfway to the stoichiometric point, when enough base has been added to neutralize half the acid, the concentrations of acid and base are equal and because log 1 = 0 the Henderson–Hasselbalch equation gives

$$pH \approx pK_a \tag{8.12}$$

In the present titration, we see that at this stage of the titration, pH ≈ 4.75. Note from the pH curve in Fig. 8.4 how much more slowly the pH is changing compared with initially: this point will prove important shortly. Equation 8.12 implies that we can determine the pK_a of the acid directly from the pH of the mixture. Indeed, an approximate value of the pK_a may be calculated by recording the pH during a titration and then examining the record for the pH halfway to the stoichiometric point.

At the stoichiometric point, enough base has been added to convert all the acid to its base, so the solution consists—nominally—only of $CH_3CO_2^-$ ions. These ions are Brønsted bases, so we can expect the solution to be basic with a pH of well above 7. We have already seen how to estimate the pH of a solution of a weak base in terms of its concentration B (Example 8.2), so all that remains to be done is to calculate the concentration of $CH_3CO_2^-$ at the stoichiometric point.

Illustration 8.3

Calculating the pH at the stoichiometric point

Because the analyte initially contained 2.50 mmol CH_3COOH, the volume of titrant needed to neutralize it is the volume that contains the same amount of base:

$$V_{base} = \frac{2.50 \times 10^{-3}\ mol}{0.200\ mol\ dm^{-3}} = 1.25 \times 10^{-2}\ dm^3$$

or 12.5 cm^3. The total volume of the solution at this stage is therefore 37.5 cm^3, so the concentration of base is

$$[CH_3CO_2^-] = \frac{2.50 \times 10^{-3}\ mol}{37.5 \times 10^{-3}\ dm^3} = 6.67 \times 10^{-2}\ mol\ dm^{-3}$$

It then follows from a calculation similar to that in Example 8.2 (with $pK_b = 9.25$ for $CH_3CO_2^-$) that the pH of the solution at the stoichiometric point is 8.8.

It is very important to note that the pH at *the stoichiometric point of a weak-acid–strong-base titration is on the basic side of neutrality* (pH > 7). At the stoichiometric point, the solution consists of a weak base (the conjugate base of the weak acid, here the $CH_3CO_2^-$ ions) and neutral cations (the Na^+ ions from the titrant).

The general form of the pH curve suggested by these estimates throughout a weak-acid–strong-base titration is illustrated in Fig. 8.4. The pH rises slowly from its initial value, passing through the values given by the Henderson–Hasselbalch equation when the acid and its conjugate base are both present, until the stoichiometric point is approached. It then changes rapidly to and through the value characteristic of a solution of a salt, which takes into account the effect on the pH of a solution of a weak base, the conjugate base of the original acid. The pH then climbs less rapidly towards the value corresponding to a solution consisting of excess base, and finally approaches the pH of the original base solution when so much titrant has been added that the solution is almost the same as the titrant itself. The stoichiometric point is detected by observing where the pH changes rapidly through the value calculated in Illustration 8.3 as described at the beginning of this section.

A similar sequence of changes occurs when the analyte is a weak base (such as ammonia) and the titrant is a strong acid (such as hydrochloric acid). In this case the pH curve is like that shown in Fig. 8.5: the pH falls as acid is added, plunges through the pH corresponding to a solution of a weak acid (the conjugate acid of the original base, such as NH_4^+), and then slowly approaches the pH of the original strong acid. The pH of the stoichiometric point is that of a solution of a weak acid, and is calculated as illustrated in Example 8.1.

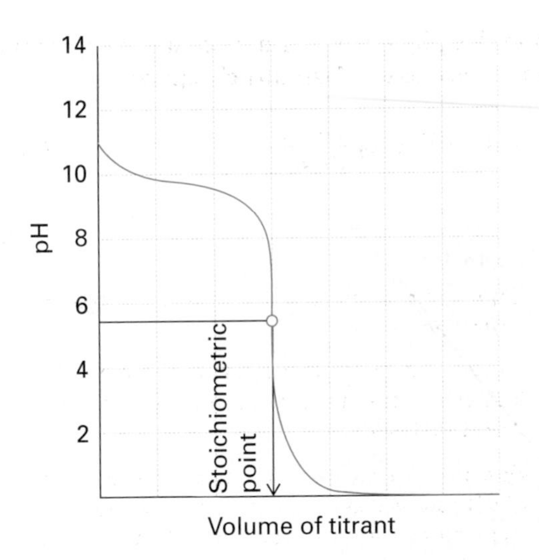

Fig. 8.5 The pH curve for the titration of a weak base (the analyte) with a strong acid (the titrant). The stoichiometric point occurs at pH < 7. The final pH of the solution approaches that of the titrant.

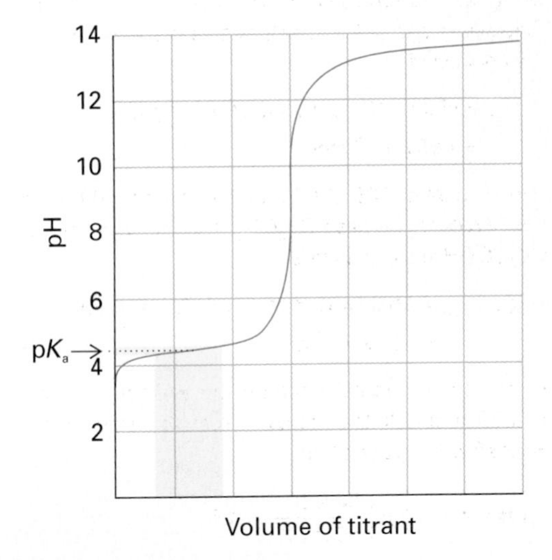

Fig. 8.6 The pH of a solution changes only slowly in the region of halfway to the stoichiometric point. In this region the solution is buffered to a pH close to pK_a.

8.6 Buffer action

The slow variation of the pH when the concentrations of the conjugate acid and base are equal, when pH = pK_a, is the basis of **buffer action**, the ability of a solution to oppose changes in pH when small amounts of strong acids and bases are added (Fig. 8.6). An **acid buffer** solution, one that stabilizes the solution at a pH below 7, is typically prepared by making a solution of a weak acid (such as acetic acid) and a salt that supplies its conjugate base (such as sodium acetate). A **base buffer**, one that stabilizes a solution at a pH above 7, is prepared by making a solution of a weak base (such as ammonia) and a salt that supplies its conjugate acid (such as ammonium chloride). Physiological buffers are responsible for maintaining the pH of blood within a narrow range of 7.37 to 7.43, thereby stabilizing the active conformations of biological macromolecules and optimizing the rates of biochemical reactions (Box 8.1).

An acid buffer stabilizes the pH of a solution because the abundant supply of A^- ions (from the salt) can remove any H_3O^+ ions brought by additional acid; furthermore, the abundant supply of HA molecules can provide H_3O^+ ions to react with any base that is added. Similarly, in a base buffer the weak base B can accept protons when an acid is added and its conjugate acid BH^+ can supply protons if a base is added.

Box 8.1 *Buffer action in blood*

The pH of blood in a healthy human being varies from 7.37 to 7.43. There are two buffer systems that help to maintain the pH of blood relatively constant: one arising from a carbonic acid/bicarbonate (hydrogencarbonate) ion equilibrium and another involving protonated and deprotonated forms of haemoglobin, the protein responsible for the transport of O_2 in blood (Box 7.1).

Carbonic acid forms in blood from the reaction between water and CO_2 gas, which comes from inhaled air and is also a by-product of metabolism:

$$CO_2(g) + H_2O(l) \rightleftharpoons H_2CO_3(aq)$$

In red blood cells, this reaction is catalysed by the enzyme carbonic anhydrase. Aqueous carbonic acid then deprotonates to form bicarbonate (hydrogencarbonate) ion:

$$H_2CO_3(aq) \rightleftharpoons H^+(aq) + HCO_3^-(aq)$$

The fact that the pH of normal blood is approximately 7.4 implies that $[HCO_3^-]/[H_2CO_3] \approx 20$. The body's control of the pH of blood is an example of *homeostasis*, the ability of an organism to counteract environmental changes with physiological responses. For instance, the concentration of carbonic acid can be controlled by respiration: exhaling air depletes the system of $CO_2(g)$ and $H_2CO_3(aq)$ so the pH of blood rises when air is exhaled. Conversely, inhalation increases the concentration of carbonic acid in blood and lowers its pH. The kidneys also play a role in the control of the concentration of hydronium ions. There, ammonia formed by the release of nitrogen from some amino acids (such as glutamine) combines with excess hydronium ions and the ammonium ion is excreted through urine.

The condition known as *alkalosis* occurs when the pH of blood rises above about 7.45. *Respiratory alkalosis* is caused by hyperventilation, or excessive respiration. The simplest remedy consists of breathing into a paper bag to increase the levels of inhaled CO_2. *Metabolic alkalosis* may result from illness, poisoning, repeated vomiting, and overuse of diuretics. The body may compensate for the increase in the pH of blood by decreasing the rate of respiration.

Acidosis occurs when the pH of blood falls below about 7.35. In *respiratory acidosis*, impaired respiration increases the concentration of dissolved CO_2 and lowers the blood's pH. The condition is common in victims of smoke inhalation and patients with asthma, pneumonia, and emphysema. The most efficient treatment consists of placing the patient in a ventilator. *Metabolic acidosis* is caused by the release of large amounts of lactic acid or other acidic by-products of metabolism, which react with hydrogencarbonate ion to form carbonic acid, thus lowering the blood's pH. The condition is common in patients with diabetes and severe burns.

The concentration of hydronium ions in blood is also controlled by haemoglobin, which can exist in deprotonated (basic) or protonated (acidic) forms, depending on the state of protonation of several amino acid residues on the protein's surface. The carbonic acid/bicarbonate ion equilibrium and proton equilibria in haemoglobin also regulate the oxygenation of blood. The key to this regulatory mechanism is the *Bohr effect*, the observation that haemoglobin binds O_2 strongly when it is deprotonated and releases O_2 when it is protonated. It follows that when dissolved CO_2 levels are high and the pH of blood falls slightly, haemoglobin becomes protonated and releases bound O_2 to tissue. Conversely, when CO_2 is exhaled and the pH rises slightly, haemoglobin becomes deprotonated and binds O_2.

Exercise 1 What are the values of the ratio $[HCO_3^-]/[H_2CO_3]$ at the onset of acidosis and alkalosis?

Exercise 2 The Bohr effect may be understood in terms of a dependence on pH of the degree of cooperativity in the binding of O_2 by haemoglobin. Based on the description of the Bohr effect given here and the information provided in Exercise 1 of Box 7.1, does the Hill coefficient of haemoglobin increase or decrease with pH?

Table 8.3 *Indicator colour changes*

Indicator	Acid colour	pH range of colour change	pK_{In}	Base colour
Thymol blue	Red	1.2–2.8	1.7	Yellow
Methyl orange	Red	3.2–4.4	3.4	Yellow
Bromophenol blue	Yellow	3.0–4.6	3.9	Blue
Bromocresol green	Yellow	4.0–5.6	4.7	Blue
Methyl red	Red	4.8–6.0	5.0	Yellow
Bromothymol blue	Yellow	6.0–7.6	7.1	Blue
Litmus	Red	5.0–8.0	6.5	Blue
Phenol red	Yellow	6.6–8.0	7.9	Red
Thymol blue	Yellow	9.0–9.6	8.9	Blue
Phenolphthalein	Colourless	8.2–10.0	9.4	Pink
Alizarin yellow	Yellow	10.1–12.0	11.2	Red
Alizarin	Red	11.0–12.4	11.7	Purple

Illustration 8.4

Estimating the pH of a buffer

Suppose we need to estimate the pH of a buffer formed from equal amounts of KH_2PO_4(aq) and K_2HPO_4(aq). We note that the two anions present are $H_2PO_4^-$ and HPO_4^{2-}. The former is the conjugate acid of the latter:

$$H_2PO_4^-(aq) + H_2O(l) \rightleftharpoons H_3O^+(aq) + HPO_4^{2-}(aq)$$

so we need the pK_a of the acid form, $H_2PO_4^-$. In this case we can take it from Table 8.1, or recognize it as the pK_{a2} of phosphoric acid, and take it from Table 8.2 instead. In either case, pK_a = 7.21. Hence, the solution should buffer close to pH = 7.

Self-test 8.11

Calculate the pH of an aqueous buffer solution that contains equal amounts of NH_3 and NH_4Cl.

[*Answer:* 9.25; more realistically: 9]

8.7 Indicators

The rapid change of pH near the stoichiometric point of an acid–base titration is the basis of indicator detection. An **acid–base indicator** is a water-soluble organic molecule with acid (HIn) and conjugate base (In^-) forms that differ in colour. The two forms are in equilibrium in solution:

$$HIn(aq) + H_2O(l) \rightleftharpoons H_3O^+(aq) + In^-(aq)$$

$$K_{In} = \frac{a_{H_3O^+}a_{In^-}}{a_{HIn}}$$

The pK_{In} values of some indicators are listed in Table 8.3. The ratio of the concentrations of the conjugate acid and base forms of the indicator is

$$\frac{[In^-]}{[HIn]} \approx \frac{K_{In}}{a_{H_3O^+}}$$

This expression can be rearranged (after taking common logarithms) to

$$\log\frac{[In^-]}{[HIn]} \approx pH - pK_{In} \qquad (8.13)$$

We see that as the pH swings from higher than pK_{In} to lower than pK_{In} as acid is added to the solution, the ratio of In^- to HIn swings from well above 1 to well below 1 (Fig. 8.7). For instance, if pH = pK_{In} − 1, then $[In^-]/[HIn] = 10$, but if pH = pK_{In} + 1, then $[In^-]/[HIn] = 10^{-1}$, a decrease of two orders of magnitude.

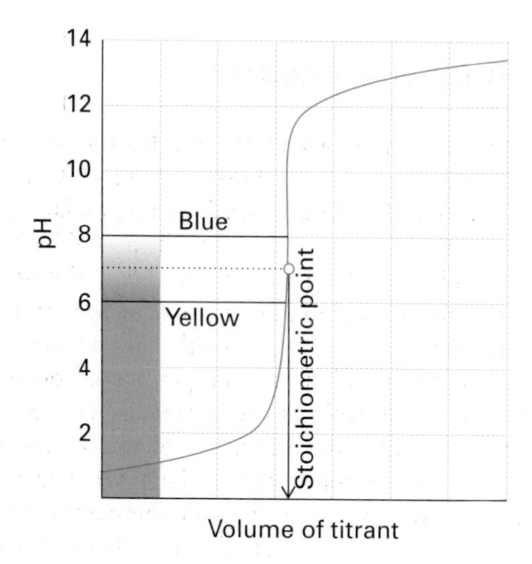

Fig. 8.7 The range of pH over which an indicator changes colour is depicted by the tinted band. For a strong acid–strong base titration, the stoichiometric point is indicated accurately by an indicator that changes colour at pH = 7 (such as bromothymol blue). However, the change in pH is so sharp that accurate results are also obtained even if the indicator changes colour in neighbouring values. Thus, phenolphthalein (which has $pK_{In} = 9.4$, see Table 8.3) is also often used.

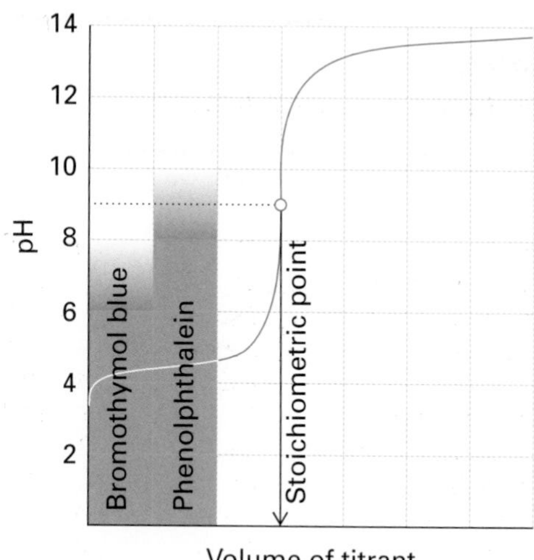

Fig. 8.8 In a weak acid–strong base titration, an indicator with $pK_{In} \approx 7$ (the lower band, like bromothymol blue) would give a false indication of the stoichiometric point; it is necessary to use an indicator that changes colour close to the pH of the stoichiometric point. If that lies at about pH = 9, then phenolphthalein would be appropriate.

Self-test 8.12

What is the ratio of the yellow and blue forms of bromocresol green in solution of pH (a) 3.7, (b) 4.7, and (c) 5.7?

[*Answer:* (a) 10:1, (b) 1:1, (c) 1:10]

At the stoichiometric point, the pH changes sharply through several pH units, so the molar concentration of H_3O^+ changes through several orders of magnitude. The indicator equilibrium changes so as to accommodate the change of pH, with HIn the dominant species on the acid side of the stoichiometric point, when H_3O^+ ions are abundant, and In^- dominant on the basic side, when the base can remove protons from HIn. The accompanying colour change signals the stoichiometric point of the titration. The colour in fact changes over a range of pH, typically from pH $\approx pK_{In} - 1$, when HIn is 10 times as abundant as In^-, to pH $\approx pK_{In} + 1$, when In^- is 10 times as abundant as HIn. The pH halfway through a colour change, when pH $\approx pK_{In}$ and the two forms, HIn and In^-, are in equal abundance, is the **end point** of the indicator. With a well-chosen indicator, the end point of the indicator coincides with the stoichiometric point of the titration.

Care must be taken to use an indicator that changes colour at the pH appropriate to the type of titration. Specifically, we need to match the end point to the stoichiometric point, and therefore select an indicator for which pK_{In} is close to the pH of the stoichiometric point. Thus, in a weak-acid–strong-base titration, the stoichiometric point lies at pH > 7, and we should select an indicator that changes at that pH (Fig. 8.8). Similarly, in a strong-acid–weak-base titration, we need to select an indicator with an end point at pH < 7. Qualitatively, we should choose an indicator with $pK_{In} \approx 7$ for strong-acid–strong-base titrations, one with $pK_{In} < 7$ for strong-acid–weak-base titrations, and one with $pK_{In} > 7$ for weak-acid–strong-base titrations.

Self-test 8.13

Vitamin C is a weak acid (ascorbic acid), and the amount in a sample may be determined by titration with sodium hydroxide solution. Should you use methyl red or phenolphthalein as the indicator?

[*Answer:* phenolphthalein]

Table 8.4
Solubility constants at 298.15 K

Compound	Formula	K_s
Aluminium hydroxide	$Al(OH)_3$	1.0×10^{-33}
Antimony sulfide	Sb_2S_3	1.7×10^{-93}
Barium carbonate	$BaCO_3$	8.1×10^{-9}
fluoride	BaF_2	1.7×10^{-6}
sulfate	$BaSO_4$	1.1×10^{-10}
Bismuth sulfide	Bi_2S_3	1.0×10^{-97}
Calcium carbonate	$CaCO_3$	8.7×10^{-9}
fluoride	CaF_2	4.0×10^{-11}
hydroxide	$Ca(OH)_2$	5.5×10^{-6}
sulfate	$CaSO_4$	2.4×10^{-5}
Copper(I) bromide	$CuBr$	4.2×10^{-8}
chloride	$CuCl$	1.0×10^{-6}
iodide	CuI	5.1×10^{-12}
sulfide	Cu_2S	2.0×10^{-47}
Copper(II) iodate	$Cu(IO_3)_2$	1.4×10^{-7}
oxalate	CuC_2O_4	2.9×10^{-8}
sulfide	CuS	8.5×10^{-45}
Iron(II) hydroxide	$Fe(OH)_2$	1.6×10^{-14}
sulfide	FeS	6.3×10^{-18}
Iron(III) hydroxide	$Fe(OH)_3$	2.0×10^{-39}
Lead(II) bromide	$PbBr_2$	7.9×10^{-5}
chloride	$PbCl_2$	1.6×10^{-5}
fluoride	PbF_2	3.7×10^{-8}
iodate	$Pb(IO_3)_2$	2.6×10^{-13}
iodide	PbI_2	1.4×10^{-8}
sulfate	$PbSO_4$	1.6×10^{-8}
sulfide	PbS	3.4×10^{-28}
Magnesium		
ammonium phosphate	$MgNH_4PO_4$	2.5×10^{-13}
carbonate	$MgCO_3$	1.0×10^{-5}
fluoride	MgF_2	6.4×10^{-9}
hydroxide	$Mg(OH)_2$	1.1×10^{-11}
Mercury(I) chloride	Hg_2Cl_2	1.3×10^{-18}
iodide	Hg_2I_2	1.2×10^{-28}
Mercury(II) sulfide	HgS black:	1.6×10^{-52}
	red:	1.4×10^{-53}
Nickel(II) hydroxide	$Ni(OH)_2$	6.5×10^{-18}
Silver bromide	$AgBr$	7.7×10^{-13}
carbonate	Ag_2CO_3	6.2×10^{-12}
chloride	$AgCl$	1.6×10^{-10}
hydroxide	$AgOH$	1.5×10^{-8}
iodide	AgI	1.5×10^{-16}
sulfide	Ag_2S	6.3×10^{-51}
Zinc hydroxide	$Zn(OH)_2$	2.0×10^{-17}
sulfide	ZnS	1.6×10^{-24}

Solubility equilibria

A solid dissolves in a solvent until the solution and the solid solute are in equilibrium. At this stage, the solution is said to be **saturated**, and its molar concentration is the **molar solubility** of the solid. That the two phases—the solid solute and the solution—are in dynamic equilibrium implies that we can use equilibrium concepts to discuss the composition of the saturated solution. The properties of aqueous solutions of electrolytes are commonly treated in terms of equilibrium constants, and in this section we shall confine our attention to them. We shall also limit our attention to **sparingly soluble** compounds, which are compounds that dissolve only slightly in water. This restriction is applied because the effects of ion–ion interactions are a complicating feature of more concentrated solutions and more advanced techniques are then needed before the calculations are reliable. Once again, we shall concentrate on general trends and properties rather than expecting to obtain numerically precise results.

8.8 The solubility constant

The equilibrium between a sparingly soluble ionic compound, such as calcium hydroxide, $Ca(OH)_2$, and its ions in aqueous solution is

$$Ca(OH)_2(s) \rightleftharpoons Ca^{2+}(aq) + 2\,OH^-(aq)$$

$$K_s = a_{Ca^{2+}} a_{OH^-}^2$$

The equilibrium constant for an ionic equilibrium such as this, bearing in mind that the solid does not appear in the equilibrium expression because its activity is 1, is called the **solubility constant.**[5] As usual, for very dilute solutions, we can replace the activity a_J of a species J by the numerical value of its molar concentration. Experimental values for solubility constants are given in Table 8.4.

We can interpret the solubility constant in terms of the numerical value of the **molar solubility**, S, of a sparingly soluble substance. For instance, it follows from the stoichiometry of the equilibrium equation written above that the molar concentration of Ca^{2+}

[5] Other common names are the 'solubility product constant' or simply the 'solubility product'.

ions in solution is equal to that of the $Ca(OH)_2$ dissolved in solution, so $S = [Ca^{2+}]$. Likewise, because the concentration of OH^- ions is twice that of $Ca(OH)_2$ formula units, it follows that $S = \frac{1}{2}[OH^-]$. Therefore, provided it is permissible to replace activities by molar concentrations,

$$K_s \approx S \times (2S)^2 = 4S^3$$

from which it follows that

$$S \approx (\tfrac{1}{4}K_s)^{1/3} \qquad (8.14)$$

This expression is only approximate because ion–ion interactions have been ignored. However, because the solid is sparingly soluble, the concentrations of the ions are low and the inaccuracy is moderately low. Thus, from Table 8.4, $K_s = 5.5 \times 10^{-6}$, so $S \approx 1 \times 10^{-2}$ and the molar solubility is 1×10^{-2} mol dm^{-3}. Solubility constants (which are determined by electrochemical measurements of the kind described in Chapter 9) provide a more accurate way of measuring solubilities of very sparingly soluble compounds than the direct measurement of the mass that dissolves.

Self-test 8.14

Copper occurs in many minerals, one of which is chalcocite, Cu_2S. What is the approximate solubility of this compound in water at 25°C? Use the data for Cu_2S in Table 8.4.

[*Answer:* 1.7×10^{-16} mol dm^{-3}]

8.9 The common-ion effect

The principle that an equilibrium constant remains unchanged whereas the individual concentrations of species may change is applicable to solubility constants, and may be used to assess the effect of the addition of species to solutions. An example of particular importance is the effect on the solubility of a compound of the presence of another freely soluble solute that provides an ion in common with the sparingly soluble compound already present. For example, we may consider the effect on the solubility of adding sodium chloride to a saturated solution of silver chloride, the common ion in this case being Cl^-.

The molar solubility of silver chloride in pure water is related to its solubility constant by $S \approx K_s^{1/2}$. To assess the effect of the common ion, we suppose that Cl^- ions are added to a concentration C mol dm^{-3}, which greatly exceeds the concentration of the same ion that stems from the presence of the silver chloride. Therefore, we can write

$$K_s = a_{Ag^+}a_{Cl^-} \approx [Ag^+]C$$

It is very dangerous to neglect deviations from ideal behaviour in ionic solutions, so from now on the calculation will only be indicative of the kinds of changes that occur when a common ion is added to a solution of a sparingly soluble salt: the qualitative trends are reproduced, but the quantitative calculations are unreliable. With these remarks in mind, it follows that the solubility S' of silver chloride in the presence of added chloride ions is

$$S' \approx \frac{K_s}{C}$$

The solubility is greatly reduced by the presence of the common ion. For example, whereas the solubility of silver chloride in water is 1.3×10^{-5} mol dm^{-3}, in the presence of 0.10 M NaCl(aq) it is only 2×10^{-9} mol dm^{-3}, which is nearly 10 000 times less. The reduction in the solubility of a sparingly soluble salt by the presence of a common ion is called the **common-ion effect**.

Self-test 8.15

Estimate the molar solubility of calcium fluoride, CaF_2, in (a) water, (b) 0.010 M NaF(aq).

[*Answer:* (a) 2.2×10^{-4} mol dm^{-3}; (b) 4.0×10^{-7} mol dm^{-3}]

CHECKLIST OF KEY IDEAS

You should now be familiar with the following concepts:

☐ 1 The strength of an acid HA is reported in terms of its acidity constant, $K_a = a_{H_3O^+}a_{A^-}/a_{HA}$, and that of a base B in terms of its basicity constant, $K_b = a_{BH^+}a_{OH^-}/a_B$.

☐ 2 The autoprotolysis constant of water is $K_w = a_{H_3O^+}a_{OH^-}$; this relation implies that pH + pOH = pK_w.

☐ 3 The basicity constant of a base is related to the acidity constant of its conjugate acid by $K_aK_b = K_w$ (or pK_a + pK_b = pK_w).

☐ 4 The acid form of a species is dominant if pH < pK_a and the base form is dominant if pH > pK_a.

☐ 5 The pH of the solution of an amphiprotic salt is pH = $\frac{1}{2}$(pK_{a1} + pK_{a2}).

☐ 6 The pH of a mixed solution of a weak acid and its conjugate base is given by the Henderson–Hasselbalch equation, pH = pK_a − log([acid]/[base]).

☐ 7 The pH of a buffer solution containing equal concentrations of a weak acid and its conjugate base is pH = pK_a.

☐ 8 The end point of the colour change of an indicator occurs at pH = pK_{In}; in a titration, choose an indicator with an end point that coincides with the stoichiometric point.

☐ 9 The solubility constant of a sparingly soluble salt M^+A^- is $K_s = a_{M^+}a_{A^-}$.

☐ 10 The common-ion effect is the reduction in solubility of a sparingly soluble salt by the presence of a common ion.

DISCUSSION QUESTIONS

8.1 Describe the changes in pH that take place during the titration of: (a) a weak acid with a strong base, (b) a weak base with a strong acid.

8.2 Describe the basis of buffer action and indicator detection.

8.3 State the limits to the generality of the following expressions: (a) pH = $\frac{1}{2}$(pK_{a1} + pK_{a2}), (b) pH = pK_a − log([acid]/[base]).

8.4 Explain the common-ion effect.

EXERCISES

8.5 Write the proton transfer equilibria for the following acids in aqueous solution and identify the conjugate acid–base pairs in each one: (a) H_2SO_4, (b) HF (hydrofluoric acid), (c) $C_6H_5NH_3^+$ (anilinium ion), (d) $H_2PO_4^-$ (dihydrogenphosphate ion), (e) HCOOH (formic acid), (f) $NH_2NH_3^+$ (hydrazinium ion).

8.6 Numerous acidic species are found in living systems. Write the proton transfer equilibria for the following biochemically important acids in aqueous solution: (a) lactic acid ($CH_3CHOHCOOH$), (b) glutamic acid ($HOOCCH_2CH_2CH(NH_2)COOH$), (c) glycine (NH_2CH_2COOH), (d) oxalic acid (HOOCCOOH).

8.7 For biological and medical applications we often need to consider proton transfer equilibria at body temperature (37°C). The value of K_w for water at body temperature is 2.5×10^{-14}. (a) What is the value of [H_3O^+] and the pH of neutral water at 37°C? (b) What is the molar concentration of OH^- ions and the pOH of neutral water at 37°C?

8.8 Suppose that something had gone wrong in the Big Bang, and instead of ordinary hydrogen there was an abundance of deuterium in the universe. There would be many subtle changes in equilibria, particularly the deuteron transfer equilibria of heavy atoms and bases. The K_w for D_2O, heavy water, at 25°C is 1.35×10^{-15}. (a) Write the chemical equation for the autoprotolysis (more precisely, autodeuterolysis) of D_2O. (b) Evaluate pK_w for D_2O at 25°C. (c) Calculate the molar concentrations of D_3O^+ and OD^- in neutral heavy water at 25°C. (d) Evaluate the pD and pOD of neutral heavy water at 25°C. (e) Formulate the relation between pD, pOD, and $pK_w(D_2O)$.

8.9 Use the van 't Hoff equation to derive an expression for the slope of a plot of pK_a against temperature.

8.10 The molar concentration of H_3O^+ ions in the following solutions was measured at 25°C. Calculate the pH and pOH of the solution: (a) 1.5×10^{-5} mol dm^{-3} (a sample of rain water), (b) 1.5 mmol dm^{-3}, (c) 5.1×10^{-14} mol dm^{-3}, (d) 5.01×10^{-5} mol dm^{-3}.

8.11 Calculate the molar concentration of H_3O^+ ions and the pH of the following solutions: (a) 25.0 cm^3 of 0.144 M HCl(aq) was added to 25.0 cm^3 of 0.125 M NaOH(aq), (b) 25.0 cm^3 of 0.15 M HCl(aq) was added to 35.0 cm^3 of 0.15 M KOH(aq), (c) 21.2 cm^3 of 0.22 M HNO_3(aq) was added to 10.0 cm^3 of 0.30 M NaOH(aq).

8.12 Determine whether aqueous solutions of the following salts have a pH equal to, greater than, or less than 7; if pH > 7 or pH < 7, write a chemical equation to justify your answer. (a) NH_4Br, (b) Na_2CO_3, (c) KF, (d) KBr, (e) $AlCl_3$, (f) $Co(NO_3)_2$.

8.13 (a) A sample of potassium acetate, KCH_3CO_2, of mass 8.4 g is used to prepare 250 cm^3 of solution. What is the pH of the solution? (b) What is the pH of a solution when 3.75 g of ammonium bromide, NH_4Br, is used to make 100 cm^3 of solution? (c) An aqueous solution of volume 1.0 dm^3 contains 10.0 g of potassium bromide. What is the percentage of Br^- ions that are protonated?

8.14 There are many organic acids and bases in our cells, and their presence modifies the pH of the fluids inside them. It is useful to be able to assess the pH of solutions of acids and bases and to make inferences from measured values of the pH. A solution of equal concentrations of lactic acid and sodium lactate was found to have pH = 3.08. (a) What are the values of pK_a and K_a of lactic acid? (b) What would the pH be if the acid had twice the concentration of the salt?

8.15 Sketch reasonably accurately the pH curve for the titration of 25.0 cm^3 of 0.15 M $Ba(OH)_2$(aq) with 0.22 M HCl(aq). Mark on the curve (a) the initial pH, (b) the pH at the stoichiometric point.

8.16 Determine the fraction of solute deprotonated or protonated in (a) 0.25 M C_6H_5COOH(aq), (b) 0.150 M NH_2NH_2(aq) (hydrazine), (c) 0.112 M $(CH_3)_3N$(aq) (trimethylamine).

8.17 Calculate the pH, pOH, and fraction of solute protonated or deprotonated in the following aqueous solutions: (a) 0.120 M $CH_3CH(OH)COOH$(aq) (lactic acid), (b) 1.4×10^{-4} M $CH_3CH(OH)COOH$(aq), (c) 0.10 M $C_6H_5SO_3H$(aq) (benzenesulfonic acid).

8.18 Show how the composition of an aqueous solution that contains 0.010 mol dm^{-3} glycine varies with pH.

8.19 Show how the composition of an aqueous solution that contains 0.010 mol dm^{-3} tyrosine varies with pH.

8.20 Deduce expressions for the fractions of each type of species present in an aqueous solution of lysine (**3**) as a function of pH and plot the appropriate speciation diagram. Use the following values of the acidity constants: $pK_a(H_3Lys^{2+}) = 2.18$, $pK_a(H_2Lys^+) = 8.95$, $pK_a(HLys) = 10.53$. (*Hint.* Although it is instructive to rework Example 8.4 for a triprotic species, the expressions for the fraction can easily be written down by analogy with those in the example.)

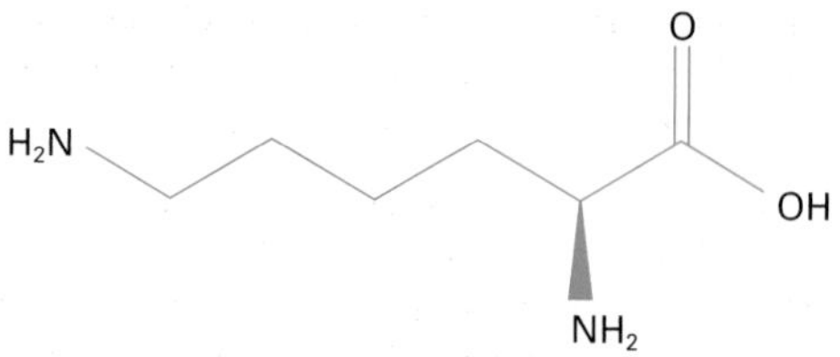

3 Lysine (Lys)

8.21 *Without doing a calculation,* sketch the speciation diagram for histidine (**4**) in water and label the the axes with the significant values of pH. Use $pK_a(H_3His^{2+}) = 1.77$, $pK_a(H_2His^+) = 6.10$, $pK_a(HHis) = 9.18$.

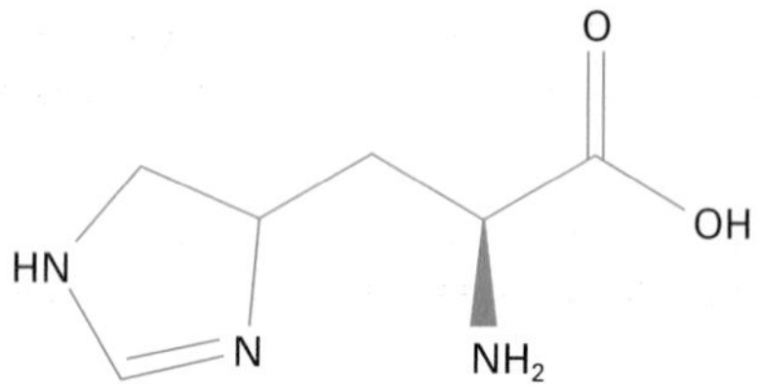

4 Histidine (His)

8.22 Calculate the pH of a solution of sodium hydrogenoxalate.

8.23 Calculate the pH of the following acid solutions at 25°C; ignore second deprotonations only when that approximation is justified. (a) 1.0×10^{-4} M H_3BO_3(aq) (boric acid acts as a monoprotic acid), (b) 0.015 M H_3PO_4(aq), (c) 0.10 M H_2SO_3(aq).

8.24 The weak base colloquially known as Tris, and more precisely as tris(hydroxymethyl)aminomethane, has $pK_a = 8.3$ at 20°C and is commonly used to produce a buffer for biochemical applications. At what pH would you expect Tris to act as a buffer in a solution that has equal molar concentrations of Tris and its conjugate acid?

8.25 The amino acid tyrosine has $pK_a = 2.20$ for deprotonation of its carboxylic acid group. What are the relative concentrations of tyrosine and its conjugate base at a pH of (a) 7, (b) 2.2, (c) 1.5?

8.26 (a) Calculate the molar concentrations of $(COOH)_2$, $HOOCCO_2^-$, $(CO_2)_2^{2-}$, H_3O^+, and OH^- in 0.15 M $(COOH)_2(aq)$. (b) Calculate the molar concentrations of H_2S, HS^-, S^{2-}, H_3O^+, and OH^- in 0.065 M $H_2S(aq)$.

8.27 A sample of 0.10 M $CH_3COOH(aq)$ of volume 25.0 cm^3 is titrated with 0.10 M NaOH(aq). The K_a for CH_3COOH is 1.8×10^{-5}. (a) What is the pH of 0.10 M $CH_3COOH(aq)$? (b) What is the pH after the addition of 10.0 cm^3 of 0.10 M NaOH(aq)? (c) What volume of 0.10 M NaOH(aq) is required to reach halfway to the stoichiometric point? (d) Calculate the pH at that halfway point. (e) What volume of 0.10 M NaOH(aq) is required to reach the stoichiometric point? (f) Calculate the pH at the stoichiometric point.

8.28 A buffer solution of volume 100 cm^3 consists of 0.10 M $CH_3COOH(aq)$ and 0.10 M $Na(CH_3CO_2)(aq)$. (a) What is its pH? (b) What is the pH after the addition of 3.3 mmol NaOH to the buffer solution? (c) What is the pH after the addition of 6.0 mmol HNO_3 to the initial buffer solution?

8.29 Predict the pH region in which each of the following buffers will be effective, assuming equal molar concentrations of the acid and its conjugate base: (a) sodium lactate and lactic acid, (b) sodium benzoate and benzoic acid, (c) potassium hydrogenphosphate and potassium phosphate, (d) potassium hydrogenphosphate and potassium dihydrogenphosphate, (e) hydroxylamine and hydroxylammonium chloride.

8.30 At the halfway point in the titration of a weak acid with a strong base the pH was measured as 4.66. What is the acidity constant and the pK_a of the acid? What is the pH of the solution that is 0.015 M in the acid?

8.31 Calculate the pH of (a) 0.15 M $NH_4Cl(aq)$, (b) 0.15 M $NaCH_3CO_2(aq)$, (c) 0.150 M $CH_3COOH(aq)$.

8.32 Calculate the pH at the stoichiometric point of the titration of 25.00 cm^3 of 0.100 M lactic acid with 0.175 M NaOH(aq).

8.33 Sketch the pH curve of a solution containing 0.10 M $NaCH_3CO_2(aq)$ and a variable amount of acetic acid.

8.34 From the information in Tables 8.1 and 8.2, select suitable buffers for (a) pH = 2.2 and (b) pH = 7.0.

8.35 Write the expression for the solubility constants of the following compounds: (a) AgI, (b) Hg_2S, (c) $Fe(OH)_3$, (d) Ag_2CrO_4.

8.36 Use the data in Table 8.4 to estimate the molar solubilities of (a) $BaSO_4$, (b) Ag_2CO_3, (c) $Fe(OH)_3$, (d) Hg_2Cl_2 in water.

8.37 Use the data in Table 8.4 to estimate the solubility in water of each sparingly soluble substance in its respective solution: (a) silver bromide in 1.4×10^{-3} M NaBr(aq), (b) magnesium carbonate in 1.1×10^{-5} M $Na_2CO_3(aq)$, (c) lead(II) sulfate in 0.10 M $CaSO_4(aq)$, (d) nickel(II) hydroxide in 2.7×10^{-5} M $NiSO_4(aq)$.

8.38 Thermodynamic data can be used to predict the solubilities of compounds that would be very difficult to measure directly. Calculate the solubility of mercury(II) chloride in water at 25°C from standard Gibbs energies of formation.

8.39 (a) Derive an expression for the ratio of solubilities of AgCl at two different temperatures; assume that the standard enthalpy of solution of AgCl is independent of temperature in the range of interest. (b) Do you expect the solubility of AgCl to increase or decrease as the temperature is raised?

Chapter 9

Electrochemistry

Such apparently unrelated processes as combustion, respiration, photosynthesis, and corrosion are in fact all closely related, as in each of them an electron, sometimes accompanied by a group of atoms, is transferred from one species to another. Indeed, together with the proton transfer typical of acid–base reactions, processes in which electrons are transferred, the so-called **redox reactions**, account for many of the reactions encountered in chemistry. Redox reactions—the principal topic of this chapter—are of immense practical significance, not only because they underlie many biochemical and industrial processes but also because they are the basis of the generation of electricity by chemical reactions and the investigation of reactions by making electrical measurements.

Measurements like the ones we describe in this chapter lead to a collection of data that are very useful for discussing the characteristics of electrolyte solutions and of a wide range of different types of equilibria in solution. They are also used throughout inorganic chemistry to assess the thermodynamic feasibility of reactions and the stabilities of compounds. They are used in physiology to discuss the details of the propagation of signals in neurons.

Before getting down to business, a word about notation. Throughout this chapter (and book) we use $\ln x$ for the natural logarithm of x (to the base e); this logarithm is sometimes written $\log_e x$. We use $\log x$ for the common logarithm of x (to the base 10); this logarithm is sometimes denoted $\log_{10} x$. The two logarithms are related by

$$\ln x = \ln 10 \times \log x \approx 2.303 \log x$$

Ions in solution

The most significant difference between the solution of an electrolyte and a non-electrolyte is that there are long-range Coulombic interactions between the ions in the former. As a result, electrolyte solutions exhibit non-ideal behaviour even at very low concentrations because the solute particles, the ions, do not move independently of one another. Some idea of the importance of ion–ion interactions is obtained by noting their average separations in solutions of different molar concentration c and, to appreciate the scale, the typical number of H_2O molecules that can fit between them:

$c/(\text{mol dm}^{-3})$	0.001	0.01	0.1	1	10
Separation/pm	90	40	20	9	4
Number of H_2O molecules	30	14	6	3	1

We see how to take the interactions between ions into account—which become very serious for concentrations of 0.01 mol dm^{-3} and more—in the first part of this chapter. A second difference is that an ion in solution responds to the presence of an electric field, migrates through the solution, and carries charge from one location to another. Our bodies are electric conductors and some of the thoughts you are currently having as you read this sentence can be traced to the migration of ions through membranes in the enormously complex electrical circuits of your brain.

The Coulomb interaction between two charges q_1 and q_2 separated by a distance r is described by the *Coulombic potential energy*:

$$E_P = \frac{q_1 q_2}{4\pi\varepsilon_0 r}$$

where $\varepsilon_0 = 8.854 \times 10^{-12}\ \text{J}^{-1}\ \text{C}^2\ \text{m}^{-1}$ is the vacuum permittivity. Note that the interaction is attractive ($E_p < 0$) when q_1 and q_2 have opposite signs and repulsive ($E_p > 0$) when their signs are the same. The potential energy of a charge is zero when it is at an infinite distance from the other charge. Concepts related to electricity are reviewed in Appendix 3.

9.1 The Debye–Hückel theory

We have seen that the thermodynamic properties of solutes are expressed in terms of their activity, a_J, which is a kind of effective concentration, and that activities are related to concentrations by multiplication by an activity coefficient, γ_J. There are various ways of expressing concentration; in the first part of this chapter we use the molality, b_J, and write

$$a_J = \gamma_J b_J / b^{\ominus} \qquad (9.1a)$$

where $b^{\ominus} = 1\ \text{mol kg}^{-1}$. For notational simplicity, we shall replace $b_J/b^{\ominus}$ by b itself, treat b as the numerical value of the molality, and write

$$a_J = \gamma_J b_J \qquad (9.1b)$$

Because the solution becomes more ideal as the molality approaches zero, we know that $\gamma_J \to 1$ as $b_J \to 0$. Once we know the activity of the species J, we can write its chemical potential by using

$$\mu_J = \mu_J^{\ominus} + RT \ln a_J \qquad (9.2)$$

The thermodynamic properties of the solution—such as the equilibrium constants of reactions involving ions—can then be derived in the same way as for ideal solutions but with activities in place of concentrations. However, when we want to relate the results we derive to observations, we need to know how to relate activities to concentrations. We ignored that problem when discussing acids and bases, and simply assumed that all activity coefficients were 1. In this chapter, we see how to improve that approximation.

One problem that confronts us from the outset is that cations and anions always occur together in solution. Therefore, there is no experimental procedure for distinguishing the deviations from ideal behaviour due to the cations from those of the anions: we cannot measure the activity coefficients of cations and anions separately. The best we can do experimentally is to ascribe deviations from ideal behaviour equally to each kind of ion and to talk in terms of a **mean activity coefficient**, $\gamma_\pm$. For a salt MX, such as NaCl, we show in Derivation 9.1 that the mean activity coefficient is related to the activity coefficients of the individual ions as follows:

$$\gamma_\pm = (\gamma_+ \gamma_-)^{1/2} \qquad (9.3a)$$

For a salt M_pX_q, such as $Mg_3(PO_4)_2$, where $p = 3$ and $q = 2$, the mean activity coefficient is related to the activity coefficients of the individual ions as follows:

$$\gamma_\pm = (\gamma_+^p \gamma_-^q)^{1/s} \qquad s = p + q \tag{9.3b}$$

Thus, for $Mg_3(PO_4)_2$, $s = 5$ and the mean activity coefficient for each type of ion is

$$\gamma_\pm = (\gamma_+^3 \gamma_-^2)^{1/5}$$

Derivation 9.1

Mean activity coefficients

In this Derivation, we use the relation $\ln xy = \ln x + \ln y$ several times (sometimes as $\ln x + \ln y = \ln xy$), and its implication (by setting $y = x$) that $\ln x^2 = 2 \ln x$. For a salt MX that dissociates completely in solution, the molar Gibbs energy of the ions is

$$G_m = \mu_+ + \mu_-$$

where μ_+ and μ_- are the chemical potentials of the cations and anions, respectively. Each chemical potential can be expressed in terms of a molality b and an activity coefficient γ by using eqn 9.2 ($\mu = \mu^\ominus + RT \ln a$) and then eqn 9.1b ($a = \gamma b$) together with $\ln \gamma b = \ln \gamma + \ln b$, which gives

$$G_m = (\mu_+^\ominus + RT \ln \gamma_+ b_+) + (\mu_-^\ominus + RT \ln \gamma_- b_-)$$
$$= (\mu_+^\ominus + RT \ln \gamma_+ + RT \ln b_+) + (\mu_-^\ominus + RT \ln \gamma_- + RT \ln b_-)$$

We now use $\ln x + \ln y = \ln xy$ again to combine the two terms involving the activity coefficients as

$$RT \ln \gamma_+ + RT \ln \gamma_- = RT(\ln \gamma_+ + \ln \gamma_-) = RT \ln \gamma_+\gamma_-$$

and write

$$G_m = (\mu_+^\ominus + RT \ln b_+) + (\mu_-^\ominus + RT \ln b_-) + RT \ln \gamma_+\gamma_-$$

We now write the term inside the logarithm as $\gamma_\pm^2$, and use $\ln x^2 = 2 \ln x$ to obtain

$$G_m = (\mu_+^\ominus + RT \ln b_+) + (\mu_-^\ominus + RT \ln b_-) + 2RT \ln \gamma_\pm$$
$$= (\mu_+^\ominus + RT \ln b_+ + RT \ln \gamma_\pm) + (\mu_-^\ominus + RT \ln b_- + RT \ln \gamma_\pm)$$
$$= (\mu_+^\ominus + RT \ln \gamma_\pm b_+) + (\mu_-^\ominus + RT \ln \gamma_\pm b_-)$$

We see that, with the mean activity coefficient defined as in eqn 9.3a, the deviation from ideal behaviour (as expressed by the activity coefficient) is now shared equally between the two types of ion. In exactly the same way, the Gibbs energy of a salt M_pX_q can be written

$$G_m = p(\mu_+^\ominus + RT \ln \gamma_\pm b_+) + q(\mu_-^\ominus + RT \ln \gamma_\pm b_-)$$

with the mean activity coefficient defined as in eqn 9.3b.[1]

Illustration 9.1

Using the mean activity coefficient

Suppose we found a way to calculate the actual activity coefficients of Na^+ and SO_4^{2-} ions in 0.010 m Na_2SO_4(aq) and found them to be 0.98 and 0.84, respectively (these values are invented), the mean activity coefficient would be

$$\gamma_\pm = \{(0.98)^2 \times (0.84)\}^{1/3} = 0.93$$

because $p = 2$ and $q = 1$ and $s = 3$. We would then write the activities of the two ions as

$$a_+ = \gamma_\pm b_+ = 0.93 \times (2 \times 0.010) = 0.019$$
$$a_- = \gamma_\pm b_- = 0.93 \times (0.010) = 0.0093$$

The question still remains, however, about how the mean activity coefficients may be estimated. A theory that accounts for their values in very dilute solutions was developed by Peter Debye and Erich Hückel in 1923. They supposed that each ion in solution is surrounded by an **ionic atmosphere** of counter charge. This 'atmosphere' is the slight imbalance of charge arising from the competition between thermal motion, which tends to keep all the ions distributed uniformly throughout the solution, and the Coulombic interaction between ions, which tends to attract counterions (ions of opposite charge) into each other's vicinity and repel ions of like charge (Fig. 9.1). As a result of this competition, there is a slight excess of cations near any anion, giving a positively charged ionic atmosphere around the anion, and a slight excess of anions near any cation, giving a negatively charged ionic atmosphere around the cation. Because each ion is in an atmosphere of opposite charge, its energy is lower than in a uniform, ideal solution, and therefore its chemical potential is lower than in an ideal solution. A lowering of the chemical potential of an ion below its ideal solution value is equivalent to the activity coefficient of the ion being less than 1 (because $\ln \gamma$ is negative when $\gamma < 1$). Debye and Hückel were able to derive an expression that is a limiting law in the sense that it becomes increasingly valid

[1] For the details of this general case, see P. Atkins and J. de Paula, *Physical chemistry*, 7th edn, Oxford University Press/W.H. Freeman (2002); see also Exercise 9.8.

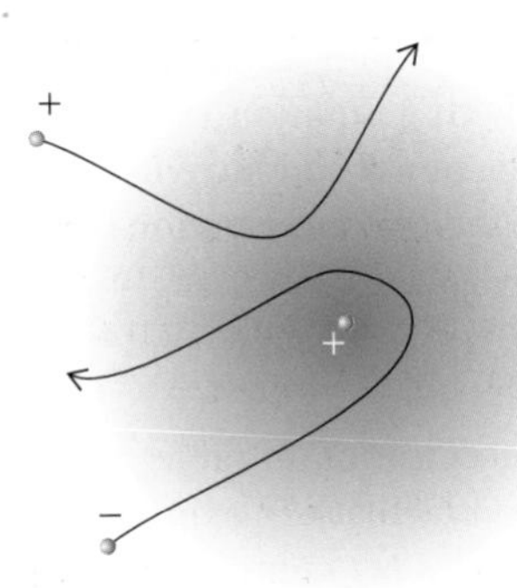

Fig. 9.1 The ionic atmosphere surrounding an ion consists of a slight excess of opposite charge as ions move through the vicinity of the central ion, with counterions lingering longer than ions of the same charge. The ionic atmosphere lowers the energy of the central ion.

as the concentration of ions approaches zero. The **Debye–Hückel limiting law**[2] is

$$\log \gamma_\pm = -A|z_+z_-|I^{1/2} \tag{9.4}$$

(Note the common logarithm.) In this expression, A is a constant that for water at 25°C works out as 0.509. The z_J are the charge numbers of the ions (so $z_+ = +1$ for Na^+ and $z_- = -2$ for SO_4^{2-}); the vertical bars mean that we ignore the sign of the product. The quantity I is the **ionic strength** of the solution, which is defined in terms of the numerical values of the molalities of the ions as

$$I = \tfrac{1}{2}(z_+^2 b_+ + z_-^2 b_-) \tag{9.5}$$

Illustration 9.2

Estimating an activity coefficient

To estimate the mean activity coefficient for the ions in 0.0010 m Na_2SO_4(aq) at 25°C, we first evaluate the ionic strength of the solution from eqn 9.5:

$$I = \tfrac{1}{2}\{(+1)^2 \times (2 \times 0.0010) + (-2)^2 \times (0.0010)\} = 0.0030$$

Then we use the Debye–Hückel limiting law, eqn 9.4, to write

$$\log \gamma_\pm = -0.509 \times |(+1)(-2)| \times (0.0030)^{1/2}$$
$$= -2 \times 0.509 \times (0.0030)^{1/2}$$

(This expression evaluates to −0.056.) On taking antilogarithms ($x = 10^{\log x}$), we conclude that

$$\gamma_\pm = 0.88$$

When using eqn 9.5, make sure to include all the ions present in the solution, not just those of interest. For instance, if you are calculating the ionic strength of a solution of silver chloride and potassium nitrate, there are contributions to the ionic strength from all four types of ion. When more than two ions contribute to the ionic strength, we write:

$$I = \tfrac{1}{2}\sum_i z_i^2 b_i$$

where the symbol Σ denotes a sum (in this case of all terms of the form $z_i^2 b_i$), z_i is the charge number of an ion i (positive for cations and negative for anions) and b_i is its molality.

As we have stressed, eqn 9.4 is a *limiting* law and is reliable only in very dilute solutions. For solutions more concentrated than about 10^{-3} mol dm^{-3} it is better to use an empirical modification known as the **extended Debye–Hückel law:**

$$\log \gamma_\pm = -\frac{A|z_+z_-|I^{1/2}}{1 + BI^{1/2}} + CI \tag{9.6}$$

with B and C empirically determined constants (Fig. 9.2).

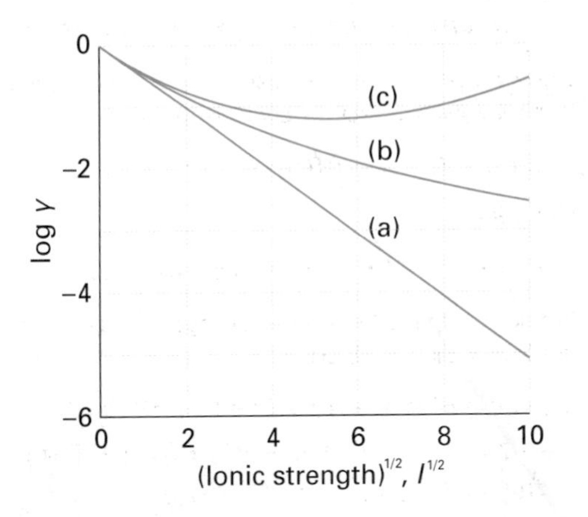

Fig. 9.2 The variation of the activity coefficient with ionic strength according to the extended Debye–Hückel theory. (a) The limiting law for a 1,1-electrolyte. (b) The extended law with $B = 0.5$. (c) The extended law, extended further by the addition of a term CI; in this case with $C = 0.02$. The last form of the law reproduces the observed behaviour reasonably well.

[2] For a derivation of the Debye–Hückel limiting law, see P. Atkins and J. de Paula, *Physical chemistry*, 7th edn, Oxford University Press/W.H. Freeman (2002).

9.2 The migration of ions

Ions are mobile in solution, and the study of their motion down a potential gradient gives an indication of their size, the effect of solvation, and details of the type of motion they undergo. The migration of ions in solution is studied by measuring the electrical resistance of a solution of known concentration in a cell like that in Fig. 9.3. The resistance, R (in ohms, Ω), of the solution is related to the current, I (in amperes, A), that flows when a potential difference, V (in volts, V), is applied between the two electrodes. Certain technicalities must be dealt with in practice, such as using an alternating current to minimize the effects of electrolysis, but the essential point is the determination of R.

Ohm's law states that $V = IR$. Additional concepts of electrostatics are discussed in Appendix 3.

It is found empirically that the resistance of a sample is proportional to its length, l, and inversely proportional to its cross-sectional area, A. The constant of proportionality is called the **resistivity**, ρ (rho), and we write $R = \rho l/A$. The units of resistivity are ohm metre (Ω m). The reciprocal of the resistivity is called the **conductivity**, κ (kappa), which is expressed in Ω^{-1} m^{-1}. Reciprocal ohms appear so widely in electrochemistry that they are given their own name, siemens (S, 1 S = 1 Ω^{-1}); then conductivities are expressed in siemens per metre (S m^{-1}).

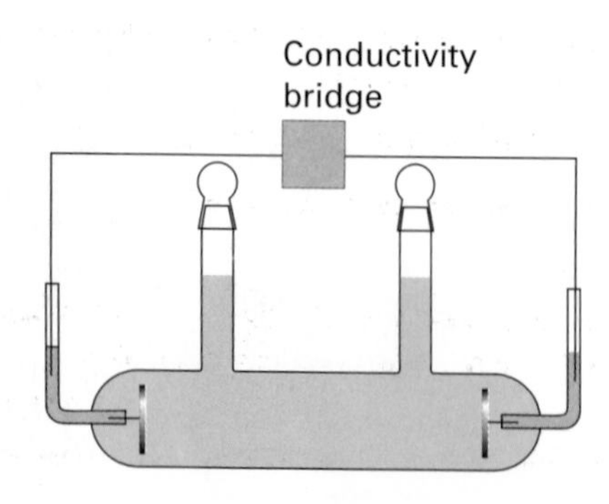

Fig. 9.3 A typical conductivity cell. The cell is made part of a 'bridge' and its resistance is measured. The conductivity is normally determined by comparison of its resistance to that of a solution of known conductivity. An alternating current is used to avoid the formation of decomposition products at the electrodes.

Once we have determined κ (in practice, by calibrating the cell with a solution of known conductivity), we find the **molar conductivity**, Λ_m (lambda), when the solute molar concentration is c by forming

$$\Lambda_m = \frac{\kappa}{c} \qquad (9.7)$$

With molar concentration in moles per cubic decimetre, molar conductivity is expressed in siemens per metre per (moles per cubic decimetre), or S m^{-1} (mol $dm^{-3})^{-1}$. These units can be simplified to siemens metre-squared per mole (S m^2 mol^{-1}).[3]

The molar conductivity of a *strong* electrolyte (one that is fully dissociated into ions in solution, such as the solution of a salt) varies with molar concentration in accord with the empirical law discovered by Friedrich Kohlrausch in 1876:

$$\Lambda_m = \Lambda_m^\circ - Kc^{1/2} \qquad (9.8)$$

The constant Λ_m°, the **limiting molar conductivity**, is the molar conductivity in the limit of such low concentration that the ions no longer interact with one another. The constant K takes into account the effect of these interactions when the concentration is non-zero. The fact that the interactions give rise to a square-root dependence on the concentration suggests that they arise from effects like those responsible for activity coefficients in the Debye–Hückel theory, and in particular the effect of an ionic atmosphere on the mobilities of ions. The fact that the molar conductivity *decreases* with increasing concentration can be traced to the retarding effect of the ions on the motion of one another. We shall concentrate on the limiting conductivity.

When the ions are so far apart that their interactions can be ignored, we can suspect that the molar conductivity is due to the independent migration of cations in one direction and of anions in the opposite direction, and write

$$\Lambda_m^\circ = \lambda_+ + \lambda_- \qquad (9.9)$$

where λ_+ and λ_- are the **ionic conductivities** of the individual cations and anions (Table 9.1).

The molar conductivity of a *weak* electrolyte varies in a more complex way with concentration.

[3] The relation between units is 1 S m^{-1} (mol $dm^{-3})^{-1}$ = 1 mS m^2 mol^{-1}, where 1 mS = 10^{-3} S.

Table 9.1

*Ionic conductivities, λ/(mS m^2 mol^{-1})**

Cations		Anions	
H^+ (H_3O^+)	34.96	OH^-	19.91
Li^+	3.87	F^-	5.54
Na^+	5.01	Cl^-	7.64
K^+	7.35	Br^-	7.81
Rb^+	7.78	I^-	7.68
Cs^+	7.72	CO_3^{2-}	13.86
Mg^{2+}	10.60	NO_3^-	7.15
Ca^{2+}	11.90	SO_4^{2-}	16.00
Sr^{2+}	11.89	$CH_3CO_2^-$	4.09
NH_4^+	7.35	HCO_2^-	5.46
$[N(CH_3)_4]^+$	4.49		
$[N(CH_2CH_3)_4]^+$	3.26		

* The same numerical values apply when the units are S m^{-1} (mol dm^{-3})$^{-1}$.

This variation reflects the fact that the degree of ionization (or, in the case of weak acids and bases, the degree of deprotonation or protonation) varies with the concentration, with relatively more ions present at low concentrations than at high. Because we can use simple equilibrium-table techniques to relate the ion concentrations to the nominal (initial) concentration, we can use measurements of molar conductivity to determine acidity constants. The same kind of measurements can also be used to monitor the progress of reactions in solution, provided that they involve ions.

Example 9.1

Determining the acidity constant from the conductivity of a weak acid

The molar conductivity of 0.010 M CH_3COOH(aq) is 1.65 mS m^2 mol^{-1}. What is the acidity constant of the acid?

Strategy Because acetic acid is weak, it is only partly deprotonated in aqueous solution. Only the fraction of acid molecules present as ions contributes to the conduction, so we need to express Λ_m in terms of the fraction deprotonated. To do so, we set up an equilibrium table, find the molar concentration of H_3O^+ and $CH_3CO_2^-$ ions, and relate those concentrations to the observed molar conductivity.

Solution The equilibrium table for CH_3COOH(aq) + H_2O(l) $\rightleftharpoons$ H_3O^+(aq) + $CH_3CO_2^-$(aq) is

	Species		
	CH_3COOH	H_3O^+	$CH_3CO_2^-$
Initial molar concentration/(mol dm^{-3})	0.010	0	0
Change/(mol dm^{-3})	$-x$	$+x$	$+x$
Equilibrium molar concentration/(mol dm^{-3})	$0.010-x$	x	x

The value of x is found by substituting the entries in the last line into the expression for K_a:

$$K_a = \frac{[H_3O^+][CH_3CO_2^-]}{[CH_3COOH]} = \frac{x^2}{0.010-x}$$

On the assumption that x is small, the solution is $x = (0.010K_a)^{1/2}$. The fraction, α, of CH_3COOH molecules present as ions is therefore $x/0.010$, or $\alpha = (K_a/0.010)^{1/2}$. The molar conductivity of the solution is therefore this fraction multiplied by the molar conductivity of acetic acid calculated on the assumption that deprotonation is complete:

$$\Lambda_m = \alpha\Lambda_m^\circ = \alpha(\lambda_{H_3O^+} + \lambda_{CH_3CO_2^-})$$

Because

$$\lambda_{H_3O^+} + \lambda_{CH_3CO_2} = 34.96 + 4.09 \text{ mS m}^2\text{ mol}^{-1}$$
$$= 39.05 \text{ mS m}^2\text{ mol}^{-1}$$

it follows that α = (1.65 mS m^2 mol^{-1})/(39.05 mS m^2 mol^{-1}) = 0.0423. Therefore,

$$K_a = 0.010\alpha^2 = 0.010 \times (0.0423)^2 = 1.8 \times 10^{-5}$$

This value corresponds to pK_a = 4.75.

Self test 9.1

The molar conductivity of 0.0250 M HCOOH(aq) is 4.61 mS m^2 mol^{-1}. What is the pK_a of formic acid?

[*Answer:* 3.49]

The ability of an ion to conduct electricity depends on its ability to move through the solution. When an ion is subjected to an electric field, $\mathcal{E}$, it accelerates. However, the faster it travels through the solution, the greater the retarding force it experiences from the viscosity of the medium. As a result, it settles down into a limiting velocity called its **drift velocity**, s, which is proportional to the strength of the applied field:

$$s = u\mathscr{E} \tag{9.10}$$

The **mobility**, u, depends on the radius, a, of the ion and the viscosity, η (eta), of the solution:

$$u = \frac{ez}{6\pi\eta a} \tag{9.11}$$

Derivation 9.2
The ionic mobility

An *electric field* is an influence that accelerates a charged particle. An ion of charge ze in an electric field $\mathscr{E}$ (typically, in volts per metre, V m^{-1}) experiences a force of magnitude $ze\mathscr{E}$, which accelerates it. However, the ion experiences a frictional force due to its motion through the medium, which increases the faster the ion travels. The retarding force due to the viscosity on a spherical particle of radius a travelling at a speed s is given by 'Stokes' law':

$$F = 6\pi\eta as$$

When the particle has reached its drift speed, the accelerating and viscous retarding forces are equal, so we can write

$$ez\mathscr{E} = 6\pi\eta as$$

and solve this expression for s:

$$s = \frac{ez\mathscr{E}}{6\pi\eta a}$$

At this point we can compare this expression for the drift speed with eqn 9.10, and hence find the expression for mobility given in eqn 9.11.

Equation 9.11 tells us that the mobility of an ion is high if it is highly charged, small, and in a solution with low viscosity. These features appear to contradict the trends in Table 9.2, which lists the mobilities of a number of ions. For instance, the mobilities of the Group 1 cations *increase* down the group despite their increasing radii. The explanation is that the radius to use in eqn 9.11 is the **hydrodynamic radius**, the *effective* radius for the migration of the ions taking into account the entire object that moves. When an ion migrates, it carries its hydrating water molecules with it, and as small ions are more extensively hydrated than large ions (because they give rise to a stronger electric field in their vicinity), ions of small radius have a large hydrodynamic radius. Thus, hydrodynamic radius *decreases* down Group 1 because the extent of hydration decreases with increasing ionic radius.

Table 9.2
Ionic mobilities in water at 298 K, $u/(10^{-8}$ m^2 s^{-1} V$^{-1})$

Cations		Anions	
H^+ (H_3O^+)	36.23	OH^-	20.64
Li^+	4.01	F^-	5.74
Na^+	5.19	Cl^-	7.92
K^+	7.62	Br^-	8.09
Rb^+	8.06	I^-	7.96
Cs^+	8.00	CO_3^{2-}	7.18
Mg^{2+}	5.50	NO_3^-	7.41
Ca^{2+}	6.17	SO_4^{2-}	8.29
Sr^{2+}	6.16		
NH_4^+	7.62		
$[N(CH_3)_4]^+$	4.65		
$[N(CH_2CH_3)_4]^+$	3.38		

One significant deviation from this trend is the very high mobility of the proton in water. It is believed that this high mobility reflects an entirely different mechanism for conduction, the **Grotthus mechanism**, in which the proton on one H_2O molecule migrates to its neighbour, the proton on that H_2O molecule migrates to its neighbour, and so on along a chain (Fig. 9.4). The motion is therefore an *effective* motion of a proton, not the actual motion of a single proton.[4] The motion of protons and other ions across biological membranes is even more complicated and makes use of special proteins called *ion channels* and *ion pumps* (Box 9.1).

[4] For a detailed account of the modern version of this mechanism, see P. Atkins and J. de Paula, *Physical chemistry*, 7th edn, Oxford University Press/W.H. Freeman (2002).

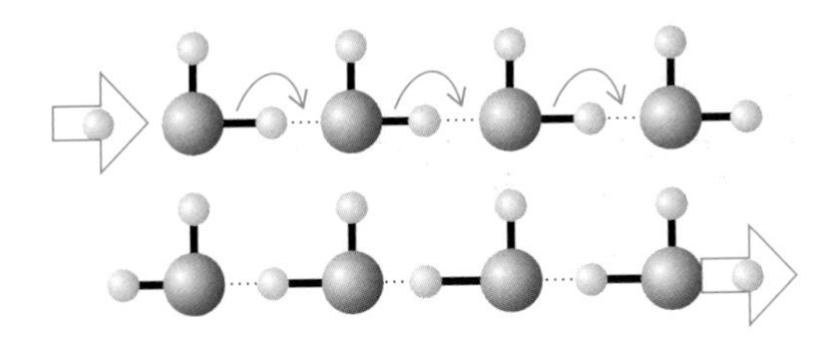

Fig. 9.4 A simplified version of the 'Grotthus mechanism' of proton conduction through water. The proton leaving the chain on the right is not the same as the proton entering the chain on the left.

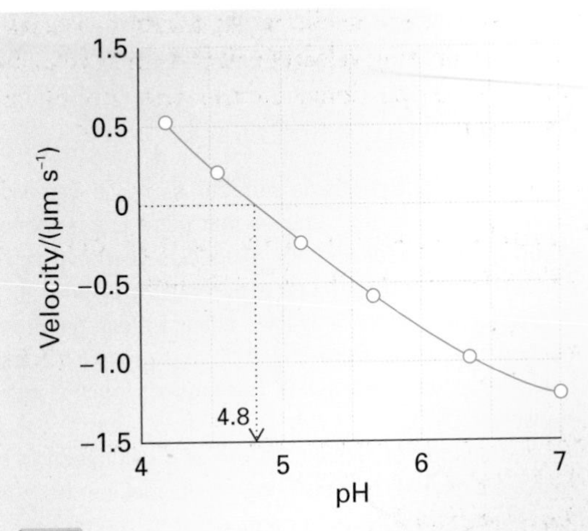

Fig. 9.5 The plot of the speed of a moving macromolecule against pH allows the isoelectric point to be detected as the pH at which the speed is zero.

Example 9.2

The isoelectric point of a protein

The mobility of an ion depends on its charge and if a large molecule, such as a protein, can be contrived to have zero net charge, then it does not respond to an electric field. This 'isoelectric point' can be reached by varying the pH of the medium. The speed with which bovine serum albumin (BSA) moves through water under the influence of an electric field was monitored at several values of pH, and the data are listed below. What is the isoelectric point of the protein?

pH	4.20	4.56	5.20	5.65	6.30	7.00
Velocity/(μm s^{-1})	0.50	0.18	−0.25	−0.65	−0.90	−1.25

Strategy If we plot speed against pH, we can use interpolation to find the pH at which the speed is zero, which is the pH at which the molecule has zero net charge.

Solution The data are plotted in Fig. 9.5. The velocity passes through zero at pH = 4.8; hence pH = 4.8 is the isoelectric point.

Self-test 9.2

The following data were obtained for another protein:

pH	4.5	5.0	5.5	6.0
Velocity/(μm s^{-1})	−0.10	−0.20	−0.30	−0.35

Estimate the pH of the isoelectric point.

[*Answer:* 4.1]

Box 9.1 *Ion channels and pumps*

Controlled transport of molecules and ions across biological membranes is at the heart of a number of key cellular processes, such as the transmission of nerve impulses, the transfer of glucose into red blood cells, and the synthesis of ATP. Here we examine in some detail the various ways in which ions cross the alien environment of the lipid bilayer.

Suppose that a membrane provides a barrier that slows down the transfer of molecules or ions into or out of the cell. The thermodynamic tendency to transport a species A through the membrane is partially determined by a concentration gradient (more precisely, an activity gradient) across the membrane, which results in a difference in molar Gibbs energy between the inside and the outside of the cell

$$\Delta G_m = G_{m,in} - G_{m,out} = RT \ln \frac{a_{in}}{a_{out}}$$

The equation implies that transport into the cell of either neutral or charged species is thermodynamically favourable if $a_{in} < a_{out}$ or, if we set the activity coefficients to 1, if $[A]_{in} < [A]_{out}$. If A is an ion, there is a second contribution to ΔG_m that is due to the different potential energy of the ions on each side of the bilayer, where the difference in electrostatic potential is $\Delta\phi = \phi_{in} - \phi_{out}$. The final expression for ΔG is then

$$\Delta G_m = RT \ln \frac{[A]_{in}}{[A]_{out}} + zF\Delta\phi$$

where z is the ion charge number and F is Faraday's constant. This equation implies that there is a tendency, called *passive transport*, for a species to move down concentration and membrane potential gradients. It is also possible to move a species against these gradients, but now the flow must be driven by an exergonic process, such as the hydrolysis of ATP. This process is called *active transport*.

The transport of ions into or out of a cell needs to be mediated (that is, facilitated by other species) because the hydrophobic environment of the membrane is inhospitable to ions. There are two mechanisms for ion transport: mediation by a carrier molecule and transport through a *channel former*, a protein that creates a hydrophilic pore through which the ion can pass. An example of a channel former is the polypeptide gramicidin A, which increases the membrane permeability to cations such as H^+, K^+, and Na^+.

Ion channels are proteins that effect the movement of specific ions down a membrane potential gradient. They are highly selective, so there is a channel protein for Ca^{2+}, another for Cl^-, and so on. The opening of the gate may be triggered by potential differences between the two sides of the membrane or by the binding of an *effector* molecule to a specific receptor site on the channel.

The *patch clamp technique* can be used to measure the transport of ions across cell membranes. One of many possible experimental arrangements is shown in the illustration. With mild suction, a 'patch' of membrane from a whole cell or a small section of a broken cell can be attached tightly to the tip of a micropipette containing an electrolyte solution and an electrode, the *patch electrode*. A potential difference (the 'clamp') is applied between the patch electrode and an intracellular electrode in contact with the cytosol of the cell. If the membrane is permeable to ions at the applied potential difference, a current flows through the completed circuit. Using sufficiently narrow micropipette tips with diameters of less than 1 μm, ion currents of a few picoamperes (1 pA = 10^{-12} A) have been measured across sections of membranes containing only one ion channel protein.

A striking example of the importance of ion channels is their role in the propagation of impulses by neurons, the fundamental units of the nervous system. The cell membrane of a neuron is more permeable to K^+ ions than to either Na^+ or Cl^- ions. The key to the mechanism of action of a nerve cell is its use of Na^+ and K^+ channels to move ions across the membrane, modulating its potential. For example, the concentration of K^+ inside an inactive nerve cell is about 20 times that on the outside, whereas the concentration of Na^+ outside the cell is about 10 times that on the inside. The difference in concentrations of ions results in a transmembrane potential difference of about −62 mV, with the negative sign denoting that the inside has a lower potential. This potential difference is also called the *resting potential* of the cell membrane.

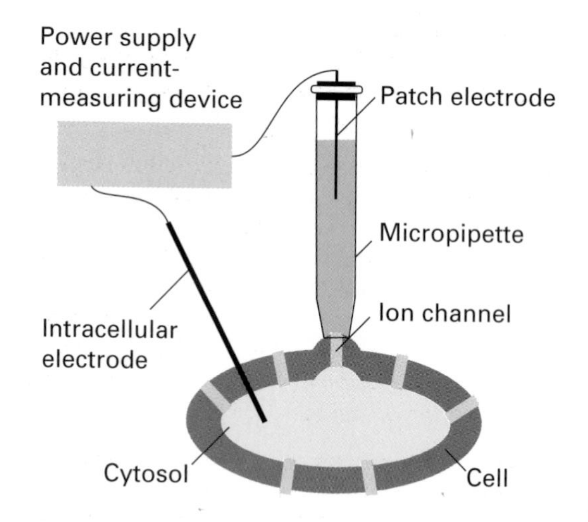

A representation of the patch clamp technique for the measurement of ionic currents through membranes in intact cells. A section of membrane containing an ion channel is in tight contact with the tip of a micropipette containing an electrolyte solution and the patch electrode. An intracellular electrode is inserted into the cytosol of the cell and the two electrodes are connected to a power supply and current-measuring device.

The transmembrane potential difference plays a particularly interesting role in the transmission of nerve impulses. Upon receiving an impulse, which is called an *action potential*, a site in the nerve cell membrane becomes transiently permeable to Na^+ and the transmembrane potential changes. To propagate along a nerve cell, the action potential must change the transmembrane potential by at least 20 mV to values that are less negative than −40 mV. Propagation occurs when an action potential in one site of the membrane triggers an action potential in an adjacent site, with sites behind the moving action potential returning to the resting potential.

Ions such as H^+, Na^+, K^+, and Ca^{2+} are often transported actively across membranes by integral proteins called *ion pumps*. Ion pumps are molecular machines that work by adopting conformations that are permeable to one ion but not others depending on the state of phosphorylation of the protein. Because protein phosphorylation requires dephosphorylation of ATP, the conformational change that opens or closes the pump is endergonic and requires the use of energy stored during metabolism.

Exercise 1 Estimate the resting potential, the membrane potential at equilibrium, of a neuron at 298 K by using the fact that the concentration of K^+ inside an inactive nerve cell is about 20 times that on the outside. Now repeat the calculation, this time using the fact that the concentration of Na^+ outside the inactive cell is about 10 times that on the inside. Are the two values the same or different? How do each of the calculated values compare with the observed resting potential of −62 mV?

Exercise 2 Your estimates of the resting potential from the previous exercise did not agree with the experimental value because the cell is never at equilibrium and ions continually cross the membrane, which is more permeable to some ions than others. To take into account membrane permeability, we use the *Goldman equation* to calculate the resting potential:

$$\Delta\phi = \frac{RT}{F}\ln\left(\frac{\sum_i P_i[M_i^+]_{out} + \sum_j P_j[X_j^-]_{in}}{\sum_i P_i[M_i^+]_{in} + \sum_j P_j[X_j^-]_{out}}\right)$$

where P_i and P_j are the relative permeabilities, respectively, for the cation M_i^+ and the anion X_j^-, and the sum is over all ions. Consider an experiment in which $[Na^+]_{in}$ = 50 mmol dm^{-3}, $[K^+]_{in}$ = 400 mmol dm^{-3}, $[Cl^-]_{in}$ = 50 mmol dm^{-3}, $[Na^+]_{out}$ = 440 mmol dm^{-3}, $[K^+]_{out}$ = 20 mmol dm^{-3}, and $[Cl^-]_{out}$ = 560 mmol dm^{-3}. Use the Goldman equation and the relative permeabilities $P_{K^+} = 1.0$, $P_{Na^+} = 0.04$, and $P_{Cl^-} = 0.45$ to estimate the resting potential at 298 K under the stated conditions. How does your calculated value agree with the experimental value of −62 mV?

Electrochemical cells

An **electrochemical cell** consists of two electronic conductors (metal or graphite, for instance) dipping into an electrolyte (an ionic conductor), which may be a solution, a liquid, or a solid. The electronic conductor and its surrounding electrolyte is an **electrode**. The physical structure containing them is called an **electrode compartment**. The two electrodes may share the same compartment (Fig. 9.6). If the electrolytes are different, then the two compartments may be joined by a **salt bridge**, which is an electrolyte solution that completes the electrical circuit by permitting ions to move between the compartments (Fig. 9.7). Alternatively, the two solutions may be in direct physical contact (for example, through a porous membrane) and form a **liquid junction**. However, a liquid junction introduces complications into the interpretation of measurements, and we shall not consider it further.

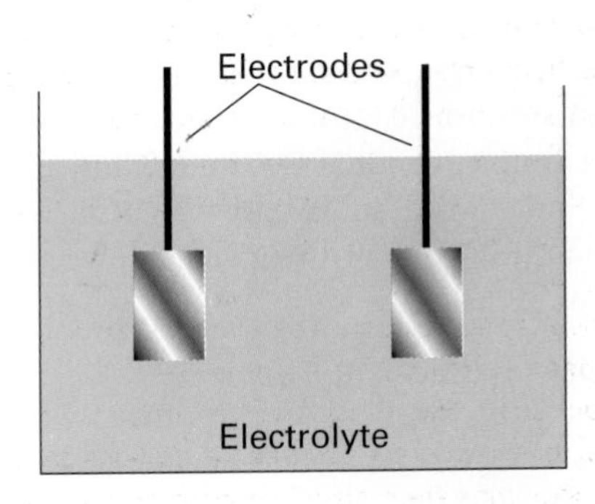

Fig. 9.6 The arrangement for an electrochemical cell in which the two electrodes share a common electrolyte.

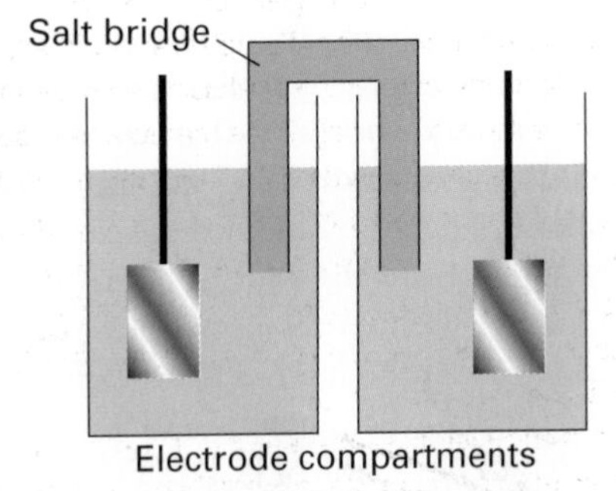

Fig. 9.7 When the electrolytes in the electrode compartments of a cell are different, they need to be joined so that ions can travel from one compartment to another. One device for joining the two compartments is a salt bridge.

A **galvanic cell** is an electrochemical cell that produces electricity as a result of the spontaneous reaction occurring inside it.[5] An **electrolytic cell** is an electrochemical cell in which a non-spontaneous reaction is driven by an external source of direct current. The commercially available dry cells, mercury cells, nickel–cadmium ('nicad') cells, and lithium ion cells used to power electrical equipment are all galvanic cells and produce electricity as a result of the spontaneous chemical reaction between the substances built into them at manufacture. A **fuel cell** is a galvanic cell in which the reagents, such as hydrogen and oxygen or methane and oxygen, are supplied continuously from outside. Fuel cells are used on manned spacecraft, are beginning to be considered for use in automobiles, and gas supply companies hope that one day they may be used as a convenient, compact source of electricity in homes (Box 9.2). Electric eels and electric catfish are biological versions of fuel cells in which the fuel is food and the cells are adaptations of muscle cells. Electrolytic cells include the arrangement used to electrolyse water into hydrogen and oxygen and to obtain aluminium from its oxide in the *Hall–Hérault process*. Electrolysis is the only commercially viable means for the production of fluorine. The electron transfer processes that occur in respiration and photosynthesis can be modelled by electrochemical cells in which electrons are transferred between proteins.

See Appendix 4 for a review of oxidation numbers.

Self-test 9.3

Identify the species that have undergone oxidation and reduction in the reaction $CuS(s) + O_2(g) \rightarrow Cu(s) + SO_2(g)$.

[*Answer:* Cu(+2) reduced to Cu(0), S(−2) oxidized to S(+4), O(0) reduced to O(−2)]

9.3 Half-reactions and electrodes

A redox reaction is the outcome of the loss of electrons, and perhaps atoms, from one species and their gain by another species. It will be familiar from introductory chemistry that we identify the loss of electrons (oxidation) by noting whether an element has undergone an increase in oxidation number. We identify the gain of electrons (reduction) by noting whether an element has undergone a decrease in oxidation number. The requirement to break and form covalent bonds in some redox reactions, as in the conversion of PCl_3 to PCl_5 or of NO_2^- to NO_3^-, is one of the reasons why redox reactions often achieve equilibrium quite slowly, often much more slowly than acid–base proton transfer reactions.

Any redox reaction may be expressed as the difference of two reduction **half-reactions**. Two examples are

Reduction of Cu^{2+}: $Cu^{2+}(aq) + 2\,e^- \rightarrow Cu(s)$

Reduction of Zn^{2+}: $Zn^{2+}(aq) + 2\,e^- \rightarrow Zn(s)$

Difference: $Cu^{2+}(aq) + Zn(s) \rightarrow Cu(s) + Zn^{2+}(aq)$ (A)

A half-reaction in which atom transfer accompanies electron transfer is

Reduction of MnO_4^-:

$$MnO_4^-(aq) + 8\,H^+(aq) + 5\,e^- \rightarrow Mn^{2+}(aq) + 4\,H_2O(l) \quad \text{(B)}$$

where oxygen atoms are lost from $MnO_4^-(aq)$ and form $H_2O(l)$. In the discussion of redox reactions, the hydrogen ion is commonly denoted simply $H^+(aq)$ rather than treated as a hydronium ion, $H_3O^+(aq)$, as proton transfer is less of an issue and the chemical equations are simplified.

Half-reactions are *conceptual*. Redox reactions normally proceed by a much more complex mechanism in which the electron is never free. The electrons in these conceptual reactions are regarded as being 'in transit' and are not ascribed a state. The oxidized and reduced species in a half-reaction form a **redox couple**, denoted Ox/Red. Thus, the redox couples mentioned so far are Cu^{2+}/Cu, Zn^{2+}/Zn, and $MnO_4^-,H^+/Mn^{2+},H_2O$. In general, we adopt the notation

Couple: Ox/Red

Half-reaction: $Ox + \nu\,e^- \rightarrow Red$

[5] The term *voltaic cell* is also used.

Box 9.2 *Fuel cells*

A fuel cell operates like a conventional galvanic cell with the exception that the reactants are supplied from outside rather than forming an integral part of its construction. A fundamental and important example of a fuel cell is the *hydrogen/oxygen cell*, such as the ones used in the Apollo Moon missions. One of the electrolytes used is concentrated aqueous potassium hydroxide maintained at 200°C and 20–40 atm; the electrodes may be porous nickel in the form of sheets of compressed powder. The cathode reaction is the reduction

$$O_2(g) + 2\,H_2O(l) + 4\,e^- \rightarrow 4\,OH^-(aq) \qquad E^\ominus = +0.40\text{ V}$$

and the anode reaction is the oxidation

$$H_2(g) + 2\,OH^-(aq) \rightarrow 2\,H_2O(l) + 2\,e^-$$

For the corresponding reduction, $E^\ominus = -0.83$ V. Because the overall reaction

$$2\,H_2(g) + O_2(g) \rightarrow 2\,H_2O(l) \qquad E^\ominus = +1.23\text{ V}$$

is exothermic as well as spontaneous, it is less favourable thermodynamically at 200°C than at 25°C, so the cell potential is lower at the higher temperature. However, the increased pressure compensates for the increased temperature, and at 200°C and 40 atm $E \approx +1.2$ V.

A property that determines the efficiency of an electrode is the *current density*, the electric current flowing through a region of an electrode divided by the area of the region. One advantage of the hydrogen/oxygen system is the large *exchange current density*, the magnitude of the equal but opposite current densities when the electrode is at equilibrium, of the hydrogen reaction. Unfortunately, the oxygen reaction has an exchange current density of only about 0.1 nA cm^{-2}, which limits the current available from the cell. One way round the difficulty is to use a catalytic surface with a large surface area. One type of highly developed fuel cell has phosphoric acid as the electrolyte and operates with hydrogen and air at about 200°C; the hydrogen is obtained from a reforming reaction on natural gas

Anode: $2\,H_2(g) \rightarrow 4\,H^+(aq) + 4\,e^-$

Cathode: $O_2(g) + 4\,H^+(aq) + 4\,e^- \rightarrow 2\,H_2O(l)$

This fuel cell has shown promise for *combined heat and power (CHP) systems*. In such systems, the waste heat is used to heat buildings or to do work. Efficiency in a CHP plant can reach 80 per cent. The power output of batteries of such cells has reached the order of 10 MW. Although hydrogen gas is an attractive fuel, it has disadvantages for mobile applications: it is difficult to store and dangerous to handle. One possibility for portable fuel cells is to store the hydrogen in carbon nanotubes. It has been shown that carbon nanofibres in herringbone patterns can store huge amounts of hydrogen and result in energy densities twice that of gasoline.

Cells with molten carbonate electrolytes at about 600°C can make use of natural gas directly. Until these materials have been developed, one attractive fuel is methanol, which is easy to handle and is rich in hydrogen atoms:

Anode: $CH_3OH(l) + 6\,OH^-(aq) \rightarrow 5\,H_2O(l) + CO_2(g) + 6\,e^-$

Cathode: $O_2(g) + 4\,e^- + 2\,H_2O(l) \rightarrow 4\,OH^-(aq)$

One disadvantage of methanol, however, is the phenomenon of 'electro-osmotic drag' in which protons moving through the polymer electrolyte membrane separating the anode and cathode carry water and methanol with them into the cathode compartment, where the potential is sufficient to oxidize CH_3OH to CO_2, so reducing the efficiency of the cell. Solid ionic conducting oxide cells operate at about 1000°C and can use hydrocarbons directly as fuel.

A *biofuel cell* is like a conventional fuel cell but in place of a platinum catalyst it uses enzymes or even whole organisms. The electricity will be extracted through organic molecules that can support the transfer of electrons. One application will be as the power source for medical implants, such as pacemakers, perhaps using the glucose present in the bloodstream as the fuel.

Exercise 1 A fuel cell develops an electric potential from the chemical reaction between reagents supplied from an outside source. What is the emf of a cell fuelled by (a) hydrogen and oxygen, (b) the complete oxidation of benzene at 1.0 bar and 298 K?

Exercise 2 A fuel cell is constructed in which both electrodes make use of the oxidation of methane. The left-hand electrode makes use of the complete oxidation of methane to carbon dioxide and water; the right-hand electrode makes use of the partial oxidation of methane to carbon monoxide and water. (a) Which electrode is the cathode? (b) What is the zero-current cell potential at 25°C when all gases are at 1 bar?

Example 9.3

Expressing a reaction in terms of half-reactions

Express the oxidation of NADH (nicotinamide adenine dinucleotide, **1**), which participates in the chain of oxidations that constitutes respiration, to NAD^+ (**2**) by oxygen, when the latter is reduced to H_2O_2, in aqueous solution as the difference of two reduction half-reactions. The overall reaction is $NADH(aq) + O_2(g) + H^+(aq) \rightarrow NAD^+(aq) + H_2O_2(aq)$.

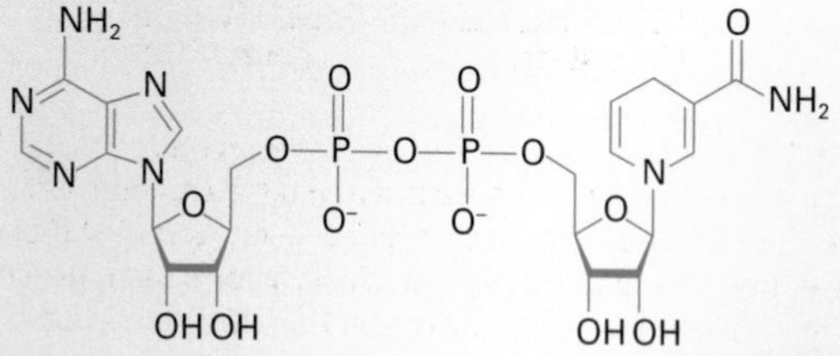

1 Nicotinamide adenine dinucleotide, reduced form (NADH)

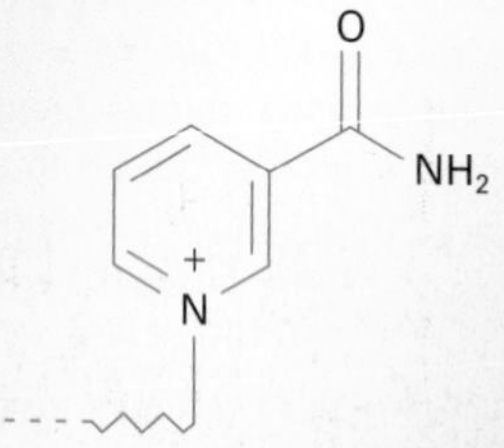

2 Nicotinamide adenine dinucleotide (NAD^+)

Strategy To express a reaction as the difference of two reduction half-reactions, identify one reactant species that undergoes reduction, its corresponding reduction product, and write the half-reaction for this process. To find the second half-reaction, subtract the first half-reaction from the overall reaction and rearrange the species so that all the stoichiometric coefficients are positive and the equation is written as a reduction.

Solution Oxygen is reduced to H_2O_2, so one half-reaction is

$$O_2(g) + 2\,H^+(aq) + 2\,e^- \rightarrow H_2O_2(aq)$$

Subtraction of this half-reaction from the overall equation gives

$$NADH(aq) - H^+(aq) - 2\,e^- \rightarrow NAD^+(aq)$$

Addition of $H^+(aq) + 2\,e^-$ to both sides gives

$$NADH(aq) \rightarrow NAD^+(aq) + H^+(aq) + 2\,e^-$$

This is an oxidation half-reaction. We reverse it to find the corresponding reduction half-reaction:

$$NAD^+(aq) + H^+(aq) + 2\,e^- \rightarrow NADH(aq)$$

Self-test 9.4

Express the formation of H_2O from H_2 and O_2 in acidic solution as the difference of two reduction half-reactions.

[*Answer:* $4\,H^+(aq) + 4\,e^- \rightarrow 2\,H_2(g)$, $O_2(g) + 4\,H^+(aq) + 4\,e^- \rightarrow 2\,H_2O(l)$]

A chemical reaction need not be a redox reaction for it to be expressed in terms of reduction half-reactions. For instance, the expansion of a gas

$$H_2(g, p_i) \rightarrow H_2(g, p_f)$$

can be expressed as the difference of two reductions:

$$2\,H^+(aq) + 2\,e^- \rightarrow H_2(g, p_f)$$

$$2\,H^+(aq) + 2\,e^- \rightarrow H_2(g, p_i)$$

The two couples are both H^+/H_2 with the gas at a different pressure in each case. Similarly, the dissolution of the sparingly soluble salt silver chloride

$$AgCl(s) \rightarrow Ag^+(aq) + Cl^-(aq)$$

can be expressed as the difference of the following two reduction half-reactions:

$$AgCl(s) + e^- \rightarrow Ag(s) + Cl^-(aq)$$

$$Ag^+(aq) + e^- \rightarrow Ag(s)$$

We saw in Chapter 7 that a natural way to express the composition of a system is in terms of the reaction quotient, Q. The quotient for a half-reaction is defined like the quotient for the overall reaction, but with the electrons ignored. Thus, for the half-reaction of the $NAD^+/NADH$ couple in Example 9.3 we would write

$$NAD^+(aq) + H^+(aq) + 2\,e^- \rightarrow NADH(aq)$$

$$Q = \frac{a_{NADH}}{a_{NAD^+}a_{H^+}} \approx \frac{[NADH]}{[NAD^+][H^+]}$$

In elementary work, and provided the solution is very dilute, the activities are interpreted as the numerical values of the molar concentrations (see Table 6.2). The replacement of activities by molar concentrations is very hazardous for ionic solutions,

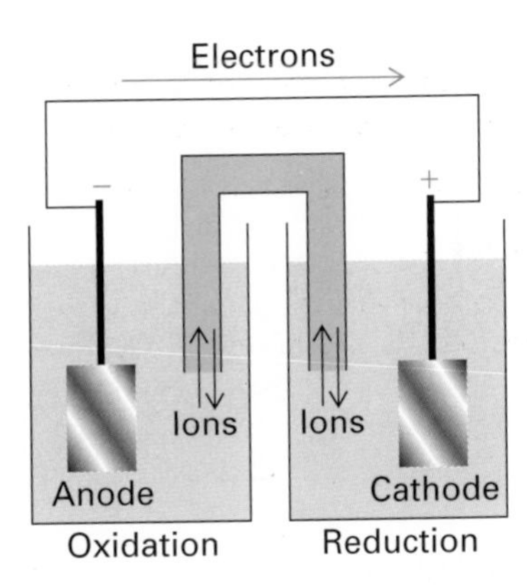

Fig. 9.8 The flow of electrons in the external circuit is from the anode of a galvanic cell, where they have been lost in the oxidation reaction, to the cathode, where they are used in the reduction reaction. Electrical neutrality is preserved in the electrolytes by the flow of cations and anions in opposite directions through the salt bridge.

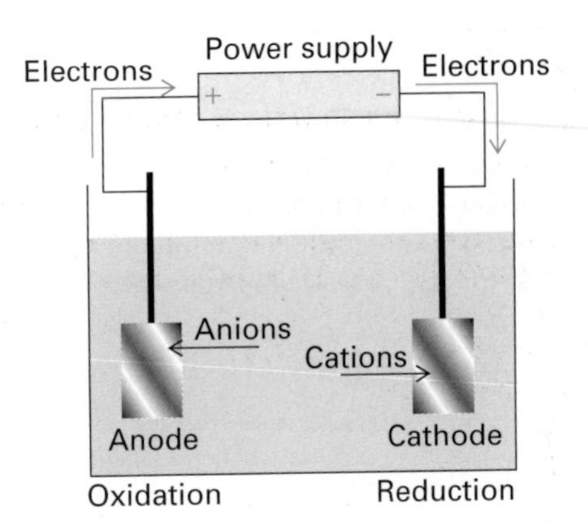

Fig. 9.9 The flow of electrons and ions in an electrolytic cell. An external supply forces electrons into the cathode, where they are used to bring about a reduction, and withdraws them from the anode, which results in an oxidation reaction at that electrode. Cations migrate towards the negatively charged cathode and anions migrate towards the positively charged anode. An electrolytic cell usually consists of a single compartment, but a number of industrial versions have two compartments.

as we have seen, so wherever possible we delay taking that final step.

9.4 Reactions at electrodes

In an electrochemical cell, the **anode** is where oxidation takes place and the **cathode** is where reduction takes place. As the reaction proceeds in a galvanic cell, the electrons released at the anode travel through the external circuit (Fig. 9.8). They re-enter the cell at the cathode, where they bring about reduction. This flow of current in the external circuit, from anode to cathode, corresponds to the cathode having a higher potential than the anode.[6] In an electrolytic cell, the anode is also the location of oxidation (by definition). Now, however, electrons must be withdrawn from the species in the anode compartment, so the anode must be connected to the positive terminal of an external supply. Similarly, electrons must pass from the cathode to the species undergoing reduction, so the cathode must be connected to the negative terminal of a supply (Fig. 9.9).

In a **gas electrode** (Fig. 9.10), a gas is in equilibrium with a solution of its ions in the presence of an inert metal. The inert metal, which is often platinum, acts as a source or sink of electrons but takes no other part in the reaction except perhaps acting as a catalyst. One important example is the

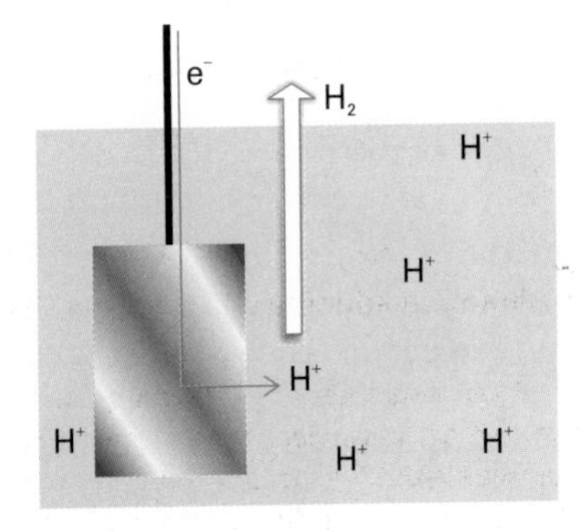

Fig. 9.10 The schematic structure of a hydrogen electrode, which is like other gas electrodes. Hydrogen is bubbled over a black (that is, finely divided) platinum surface that is in contact with a solution containing hydrogen ions. The platinum, as well as acting as a source or sink for electrons, speeds the electrode reaction because hydrogen attaches to (adsorbs on) the surface as atoms.

hydrogen electrode, in which hydrogen is bubbled through an aqueous solution of hydrogen ions and the redox couple is H^+/H_2. This electrode is denoted $Pt(s)|H_2(g)|H^+(aq)$. The vertical lines denote junctions

[6] Negatively charged electrons tend to travel to regions of higher potential.

between phases. In this electrode, the junctions are between the platinum and the gas and between the gas and the liquid containing its ions.

Example 9.4

Writing the half-reaction for a gas electrode

Write the half-reaction and the reaction quotient for the reduction of oxygen to water in acidic solution.

Strategy Write the chemical equation for the half-reaction. Then express the reaction quotient in terms of the activities and the corresponding stoichiometric coefficients, with products in the numerator and reactants in the denominator. Pure (and nearly pure) solids and liquids do not appear in Q; nor does the electron. The activity of a gas is set equal to the numerical value of its partial pressure in bar (more formally: $a_J = p_J/p^{\ominus}$).

Solution The equation for the reduction of O_2 in acidic solution is

$$O_2(g) + 4\,H^+(aq) + 4\,e^- \rightarrow 2\,H_2O(l)$$

The reaction quotient for the half-reaction is therefore

$$Q = \frac{1}{p_{O_2} a_{H^+}^4}$$

Note the very strong dependence of Q on the hydrogen ion activity.

Self-test 9.5

Write the half-reaction and the reaction quotient for a chlorine gas electrode.

[*Answer:* $Cl_2(g) + 2\,e^- \rightarrow 2\,Cl^-(aq)$, $Q = a_{Cl^-}^2/p_{Cl_2}$]

A **metal–insoluble-salt electrode** consists of a metal M covered by a porous layer of insoluble salt MX, the whole being immersed in a solution containing X^- ions (Fig. 9.11). The electrode is denoted M|MX|X^-, where the vertical line denotes a boundary across which electron transfer takes place. An example is the silver–silver-chloride electrode, Ag(s)|AgCl(s)|Cl^-(aq), for which the reduction half-reaction is

$$AgCl(s) + e^- \rightarrow Ag(s) + Cl^-(aq) \qquad Q = a_{Cl^-} \approx [Cl^-]$$

The activities of both solids are 1. Note that the reaction quotient (and therefore, as we see later, the potential of the electrode) depends on the activity of chloride ions in the electrolyte solution.

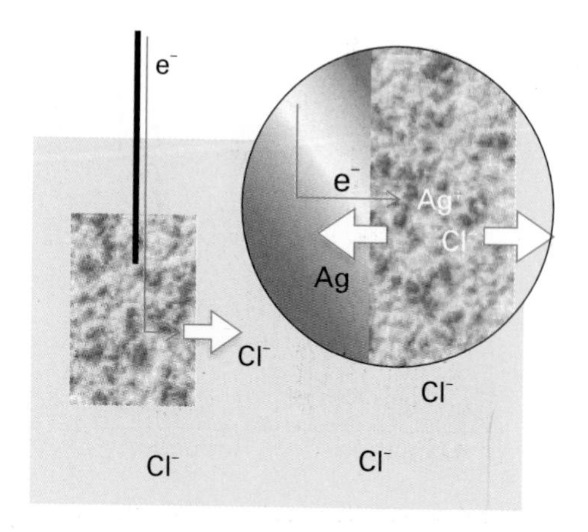

Fig. 9.11 The schematic structure of a silver–silver-chloride electrode (as an example of an insoluble-salt electrode). The electrode consists of metallic silver coated with a layer of silver chloride in contact with a solution containing Cl^- ions.

Example 9.5

Writing the half-reaction for a metal–insoluble-salt electrode

Write the half-reaction and the reaction quotient for the lead–lead-sulfate electrode of the lead–acid battery, in which Pb(II), as lead(II) sulfate, is reduced to metallic lead in the presence of hydrogensulfate ions in the electrolyte.

Strategy Begin by identifying the species that is reduced, and writing the half-reaction. Balance that half-reaction by using H_2O molecules if O atoms are required, hydrogen ions (because the solution is acidic) if H atoms are needed, and electrons for the charge. Then write the reaction quotient in terms of the stoichiometric numbers and activities of the species present. Products appear in the numerator, reactants in the denominator.

Solution The electrode is

$$Pb(s)|PbSO_4(s)|HSO_4^-(aq)$$

in which Pb(II) is reduced to metallic lead. The equation for the reduction half-reaction is therefore

$$PbSO_4(s) + H^+(aq) + 2\,e^- \rightarrow Pb(s) + HSO_4^-(aq)$$

and the reaction quotient is

$$Q = \frac{a_{HSO_4^-}}{a_{H^+}}$$

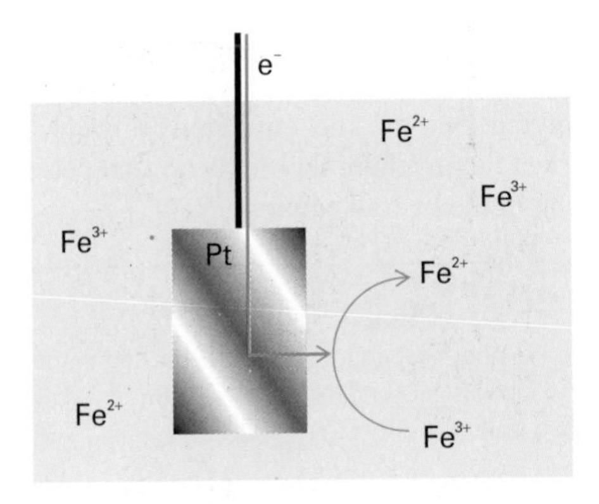

Fig. 9.12 The schematic structure of a redox electrode. The platinum metal acts as a source or sink for electrons required for the interconversion of (in this case) Fe^{2+} and Fe^{3+} ions in the surrounding solution.

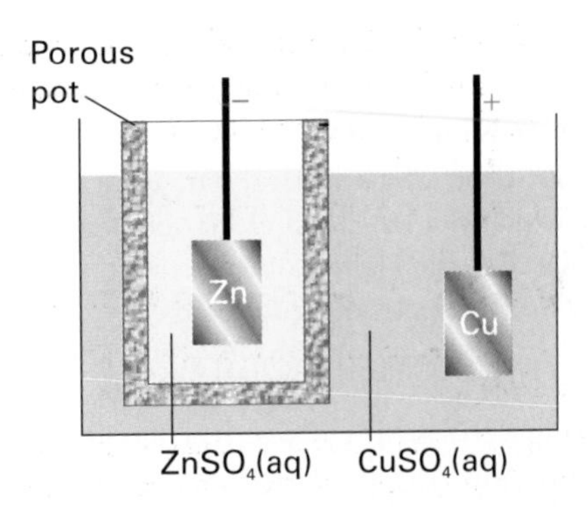

Fig. 9.13 A Daniell cell consists of copper in contact with copper(II) sulfate solution and zinc in contact with zinc sulfate solution; the two compartments are in contact through the porous pot that contains the zinc sulfate solution. The copper electrode is the cathode and the zinc electrode is the anode.

Self-test 9.6

Write the half-reaction and the reaction quotient for the *calomel electrode*, $Hg(l)|Hg_2Cl_2(s)|Cl^-(aq)$, in which mercury(I) chloride (calomel) is reduced to mercury metal in the presence of chloride ions. This electrode is a component of instruments used to measure pH, as explained later.

[*Answer:* $Hg_2Cl_2(s) + 2\,e^- \rightarrow 2\,Hg(l) + 2\,Cl^-(aq)$, $Q = a^2_{Cl^-}$]

The term **redox electrode** is normally reserved for an electrode in which the couple consists of the same element in two non-zero oxidation states (Fig. 9.12). An example is an electrode in which the couple is Fe^{3+}/Fe^{2+}. In general, the equilibrium is

$$\text{Ox} + \nu\,e^- \rightarrow \text{Red} \qquad Q = \frac{a_{\text{Red}}}{a_{\text{Ox}}}$$

A redox electrode is denoted M|Red,Ox, where M is an inert metal (typically platinum) making electrical contact with the solution. The electrode corresponding to the Fe^{3+}/Fe^{2+} couple is therefore denoted $Pt(s)|Fe^{2+}(aq),Fe^{3+}(aq)$ and the reduction half-reaction and reaction quotient are

$$Fe^{3+}(aq) + e^- \rightarrow Fe^{2+}(aq) \qquad Q = \frac{a_{Fe^{2+}}}{a_{Fe^{3+}}}$$

Another example of a similar kind is the electrode $Pt(s)|NADH(aq),NAD^+(aq),H^+(aq)$ used to study the $NAD^+/NADH$ couple.

9.5 Varieties of cell

The simplest type of galvanic cell has a single electrolyte common to both electrodes (as in Fig. 9.6). In some cases it is necessary to immerse the electrodes in different electrolytes, as in the *Daniell cell* (Fig. 9.13), in which the redox couple at one electrode is Cu^{2+}/Cu and at the other is Zn^{2+}/Zn. In an **electrolyte concentration cell**, which would be constructed like the cell in Fig. 9.7, the electrode compartments are of identical composition except for the concentrations of the electrolytes. In an **electrode concentration cell** the electrodes themselves have different concentrations, either because they are gas electrodes operating at different pressures or because they are amalgams (solutions in mercury) with different concentrations.

In a cell with two different electrolyte solutions in contact, as in the Daniell cell or an electrolyte concentration cell, the **liquid junction potential,** E_j, the potential difference across the interface of the two electrolytes, contributes to the overall potential difference generated by the cell. The contribution of the liquid junction to the potential can be decreased (to about 1 to 2 mV) by joining the electrolyte compartments through a salt bridge consisting of a saturated electrolyte solution (usually KCl) in agar jelly (as in Fig. 9.7). The reason for the success of the salt bridge is that the mobilities of the K^+ and Cl^- ions are very similar and the liquid junctions at each end of the bridge are minimized.

In the notation for cells, an interface between phases is denoted by a vertical bar, |. For example, a cell in which the left-hand electrode is a hydrogen electrode and the right-hand electrode is a silver–silver-chloride electrode is denoted

$$Pt(s)|H_2(g)|HCl(aq)|AgCl(s)|Ag(s)$$

A double vertical line || denotes an interface for which the junction potential has been eliminated. Thus a cell in which the left-hand electrode, in an arrangement like that in Fig. 9.7, is zinc in contact with aqueous zinc sulfate and the right-hand electrode is copper in contact with aqueous copper(II) sulfate is denoted

$$Zn(s)|ZnSO_4(aq)||CuSO_4(aq)|Cu(s)$$

9.6 The cell reaction

The current produced by a galvanic cell arises from the spontaneous reaction taking place inside it. The **cell reaction** is the reaction in the cell written on the assumption that the right-hand electrode is the cathode, and hence that reduction is taking place in the right-hand compartment. Later we see how to predict if the right-hand electrode is in fact the cathode; if it is, then the cell reaction is spontaneous as written. If the left-hand electrode turns out to be the cathode, then the reverse of the cell reaction is spontaneous.

To write the cell reaction corresponding to the cell diagram, we first write the half-reactions at both electrodes as reductions, and then subtract the equation for the left-hand electrode from the equation for the right-hand electrode. Thus, we saw in Example 9.3 that for the cell used to study the reaction between NADH and O_2,

$$Pt(s)|NADH(aq),NAD^+(aq),H^+(aq)||H_2O_2(aq),H^+(aq)|O_2(g)|Pt(s)$$

the two reduction half-reactions are

Right (R): $O_2(g) + 2\,H^+(aq) + 2\,e^- \rightarrow H_2O_2(aq)$

Left (L): $NAD^+(aq) + H^+(aq) + 2\,e^- \rightarrow NADH(aq)$

The equation for the cell reaction is the difference:

Overall (R – L): $NADH(aq) + O_2(g) + H^+(aq) \rightarrow NAD^+(aq) + H_2O_2(aq)$

In other cases, it may be necessary to match the numbers of electrons in the two half-reactions by multiplying one of the equations through by a numerical factor: there should be no spare electrons showing in the overall equation.

Self-test 9.7

Write the chemical equation for the reaction in the cell $Ag(s)|AgBr(s)|NaBr(aq)||NaCl(aq)|Cl_2(g)|Pt(s)$.

[*Answer:* $2\,Ag(s) + 2\,Br^-(aq) + Cl_2(g) \rightarrow 2\,AgBr(s) + 2\,Cl^-(aq)$]

9.7 The electromotive force

A galvanic cell does electrical work as the reaction drives electrons through an external circuit. The work done by a given transfer of electrons depends on the potential difference between the two electrodes. This potential difference is measured in volts (V, where $1\ V = 1\ J\ C^{-1}$). When the potential difference is large (for instance, 2 V), a given number of electrons travelling between the electrodes can do a large amount of electrical work. When the potential difference is small (such as 2 mV), the same number of electrons can do only a small amount of work. A cell in which the reaction is at equilibrium can do no work and the potential difference between its electrodes is zero.

According to the discussion in Section 4.11, we know that the maximum non-expansion work, w'_{max}, that a system (in this context, the cell) can do is given by the value of ΔG, and in particular that

At constant temperature and pressure:

$$w'_{max} = \Delta G \qquad (9.12)$$

Therefore, by measuring the potential difference and converting it to the electrical work done by the reaction, we have a means of determining a thermodynamic quantity, the reaction Gibbs energy. Conversely, if we know ΔG for a reaction, then we have a route to the prediction of the potential difference between the electrodes of a cell. However, to use eqn 9.12 we need to recall that maximum work is achieved only when a process occurs reversibly. In the present context, reversibility means that the cell should be connected to an external source of potential difference that opposes and exactly matches the potential difference generated by the cell. Then an infinitesimal change of the external potential difference will allow the reaction to proceed in its spontaneous direction and an opposite infinitesimal change will drive the reaction in its reverse direction.[7] The potential difference measured when a cell is balanced against an external source of potential is called the **electromotive force** (emf) of the cell and denoted E (Fig. 9.14). An alternative name for this quantity is the *zero-current cell potential.* In practice, all we need do is to measure the potential difference with a voltmeter that draws negligible current.

As we show in Derivation 9.3, the relation between the emf and the Gibbs energy of the cell reaction is

$$-\nu FE = \Delta_r G \quad (9.13)$$

where F is **Faraday's constant,** the magnitude of electric charge per mole of electrons:

$$F = eN_A = 96.485 \text{ kC mol}^{-1}$$

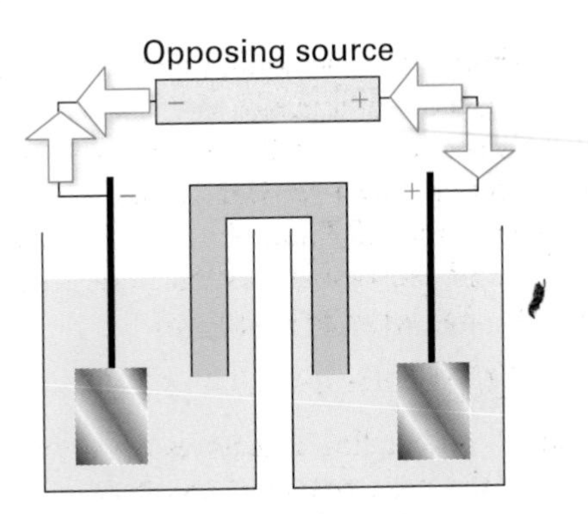

Fig. 9.14 The cell emf is measured by balancing the cell against an external potential that opposes the reaction in the cell. When there is no current flow, the external potential difference is equal to the cell emf.

Derivation 9.3

The cell emf

Suppose the cell reaction can be broken down into half-reactions of the form $A + \nu e^- \rightarrow B$. Then, when the reaction takes place, νN_A electrons are transferred from the reducing agent to the oxidizing agent per mole of reaction events, so the charge transferred between the electrodes is $\nu N_A \times (-e)$, or $-\nu F$. The electrical work w' done when this charge travels from the anode to the cathode is equal to the product of the charge and the potential difference E:

$$w' = -\nu F \times E$$

Provided the work is done reversibly at constant temperature and pressure, we can equate this electrical work to the reaction Gibbs energy and obtain eqn 9.13.

Equation 9.13 shows that the sign of the emf is opposite to that of the reaction Gibbs energy, which we should recall is the slope of a graph of G plotted against the composition of the reaction mixture (Section 7.1). When the reaction is spontaneous in the forward direction, $\Delta_r G < 0$ and $E > 0$. When $\Delta_r G > 0$, the reverse reaction is spontaneous and $E < 0$. At equilibrium $\Delta_r G = 0$ and therefore $E = 0$ too.

Equation 9.13 provides an electrical method for measuring a reaction Gibbs energy at any composition of the reaction mixture: we simply measure the cell's emf and convert it to $\Delta_r G$. Conversely, if we know the value of $\Delta_r G$ at a particular composition, then we can predict the emf.

Illustration 9.3

Estimating a typical emf

Suppose $\Delta_r G \approx -1 \times 10^2$ kJ mol^{-1} and $\nu = 1$, then

$$E = -\frac{\Delta_r G}{\nu F} = -\frac{(-1 \times 10^5 \text{ J mol}^{-1})}{1 \times (9.6485 \times 10^4 \text{ C mol}^{-1})} = 1 \text{ V}$$

Most electrochemical cells bought commercially are indeed rated at between 1 and 2 V.

Our next step is to see how E varies with composition by combining eqn 9.13 with eqn 7.6 showing how the reaction Gibbs energy varies with composition:

$$\Delta_r G = \Delta_r G^{\ominus} + RT \ln Q$$

In this expression, $\Delta_r G^{\ominus}$ is the standard reaction Gibbs energy and Q is the reaction quotient for

[7] We saw in Section 2.3 that the criterion of thermodynamic reversibility is the reversal of a process by an infinitesimal change in the external conditions.

the cell reaction. When we substitute this relation into eqn 9.13 written $E = -\Delta_r G/\nu F$ we obtain the **Nernst equation:**

$$E = E^\ominus - \frac{RT}{\nu F}\ln Q \qquad (9.14)$$

$E^\ominus$ is the **standard emf** of the cell:

$$E^\ominus = -\frac{\Delta_r G^\ominus}{\nu F} \qquad (9.15)$$

The standard emf is often interpreted as the emf of the cell when all the reactants and products are in their standard states (unit activity for all solutes, pure gases, and solids, at a pressure of 1 bar). However, because such a cell is not in general attainable, it is better to regard $E^\ominus$ simply as the standard Gibbs energy of the reaction expressed as a potential. Note that if all the stoichiometric coefficients in the equation for a cell reaction are multiplied by a factor, then $\Delta_r G^\ominus$ is increased by the same factor; but so too is ν, so the standard emf is unchanged. Likewise, Q is raised to a power equal to the factor (so if the factor is 2, Q is replaced by Q^2) and because $\ln Q^2 = 2\ln Q$, and likewise for other factors, the second term on the right-hand side of the Nernst equation is also unchanged. That is, E is independent of how we write the balanced equation for the cell reaction.

At 25.00°C,

$$\frac{RT}{F} = \frac{(8.31447\ \mathrm{J\ K^{-1}\ mol^{-1}}) \times (298.15\ \mathrm{K})}{9.6485 \times 10^4\ \mathrm{C\ mol^{-1}}} = 2.5693 \times 10^{-2}\ \mathrm{J\ C^{-1}}$$

Because 1 J = 1 V C, 1 J $\mathrm{C^{-1}}$ = 1 V, and 10^{-3} V = 1 mV, we can write this result as

$$\frac{RT}{F} = 25.693\,\mathrm{mV}$$

or approximately 25.7 mV. It follows from the Nernst equation that for a reaction in which $\nu = 1$, if Q is decreased by a factor of 10, then the emf of the cell becomes more positive by (25.7 mV) × ln 10 = 59.2 mV. The reaction has a greater tendency to form products. If Q is increased by a factor of 10, then the emf falls by 59.2 mV and the reaction has a lower tendency to form products.

9.8 Cells at equilibrium

A special case of the Nernst equation has great importance in chemistry. Suppose the reaction has reached equilibrium; then $Q = K$, where K is the equilibrium constant of the cell reaction. However, because a chemical reaction at equilibrium cannot do work, it generates zero potential difference between the electrodes. Setting $Q = K$ and $E = 0$ in the Nernst equation gives

$$\ln K = \frac{\nu F E^\ominus}{RT} \qquad (9.16)$$

This very important equation lets us predict equilibrium constants from the standard emf of a cell.[8] Note that

If $E^\ominus > 0$, then $K > 1$ and at equilibrium the cell reaction lies in favour of products.

If $E^\ominus < 0$, then $K < 1$ and at equilibrium the cell reaction lies in favour of reactants.

Illustration 9.4

Calculating an equilibrium constant

Because the standard emf of the Daniell cell is +1.10 V, the equilibrium constant for the cell reaction (reaction A) is

$$\ln K = \frac{2 \times (9.6485 \times 10^4\ \mathrm{C\ mol^{-1}}) \times (1.10\ \mathrm{V})}{(8.3145\ \mathrm{J\ K^{-1}\ mol^{-1}}) \times (298.15\ \mathrm{K})} = \frac{2 \times 9.6485 \times 1.10 \times 10^4}{8.3145 \times 298.15}$$

(we have used 1 C V = 1 J to cancel units) and therefore $K = 1.5 \times 10^{37}$. Hence, the displacement of copper by zinc goes nearly to completion in the sense that the ratio of concentrations of Zn^{2+} ions to Cu^{2+} ions at equilibrium is about 10^{37}. This value is far too large to be measured by classical analytical techniques but its electrochemical measurement is straightforward. Note that a standard emf of +1 V corresponds to a very large equilibrium constant (and −1 V would correspond to a very small one).

[8] Equation 9.16, of course, is simply eqn 7.8 expressed electrochemically.

9.9 Standard potentials

Each electrode in a galvanic cell makes a characteristic contribution to the overall emf. Although it is not possible to measure the contribution of a single electrode, one electrode can be assigned a value zero and the others assigned relative values on that basis. The specially selected electrode is the **standard hydrogen electrode** (SHE):

$$\mathrm{Pt(s)|H_2(g)|H^+(aq)} \qquad E^{\ominus} = 0 \text{ at all temperatures}$$

The **standard potential**, $E^{\ominus}$(Ox/Red), of a couple Ox/Red is then measured by constructing a cell in which the couple of interest forms the right-hand electrode and the standard hydrogen electrode is on the left.[9] For example, the standard potential of the Ag^+/Ag couple is the standard emf of the cell

$$\mathrm{Pt(s)|H_2(g)|H^+(aq)||Ag^+(aq)|Ag(s)}$$

and is +0.80 V. Table 9.3 lists a selection of standard potentials; a longer list will be found in the *Data section*.

To calculate the standard emf of a cell formed from any pair of electrodes we take the difference of their standard potentials:

$$E^{\ominus} = E^{\ominus}_{\mathrm{R}} - E^{\ominus}_{\mathrm{L}} \tag{9.17}$$

Here $E^{\ominus}_{\mathrm{R}}$ is the standard potential of the right-hand electrode and $E^{\ominus}_{\mathrm{L}}$ is that of the left. Once we have the numerical value of $E^{\ominus}$ we can use it in eqn 9.16 to calculate the equilibrium constant of the cell reaction.

Example 9.6

Calculating an equilibrium constant

Calculate the equilibrium constant for the disproportionation reaction $2\,Cu^+(aq) \rightleftharpoons Cu(s) + Cu^{2+}(aq)$ at 298 K.

Strategy The aim is to find the values of $E^{\ominus}$ and ν corresponding to the reaction; then we can use eqn 9.16. To do so, we express the equation as the difference of two reduction half-reactions. The stoichiometric number of the electron in these matching half-reactions is the value of ν we require. We then look up the standard potentials for the couples corresponding to the half-reactions and calculate their difference to find $E^{\ominus}$. Use $RT/F = 25.69$ mV (written as 2.569×10^{-2} V).

Solution The two half-reactions are

Right: $Cu^+(aq) + e^- \rightarrow Cu(aq)$ $\quad E^{\ominus}(Cu^+,Cu) = +0.52$ V

Left: $Cu^{2+}(aq) + e^- \rightarrow Cu^+(aq)$ $\quad E^{\ominus}(Cu^{2+},Cu^+) = +0.15$ V

The difference is

$$E^{\ominus} = (0.52\text{ V}) - (0.15\text{ V}) = +0.37\text{ V}$$

It then follows from eqn 9.16 with $\nu = 1$, that

$$\ln K = \frac{0.37\text{ V}}{2.569 \times 10^{-2}\text{ V}} = \frac{37}{2.569}$$

Therefore, because $K = e^{\ln K}$,

$$K = e^{37/2.569} = 1.8 \times 10^6$$

The equilibrium lies strongly in favour of products, so Cu^+ disproportionates almost totally in aqueous solution.

A note on good practice Evaluate antilogarithms right at the end of the calculation, because e^x is very sensitive to the value of x and rounding an earlier numerical result can have a significant effect on the final answer.

Self-test 9.8

Calculate the equilibrium constant for the reaction $Sn^{2+}(aq) + Pb(s) \rightleftharpoons Sn(s) + Pb^{2+}(aq)$ at 298 K.

[*Answer:* 0.46]

9.10 The variation of potential with pH

The half-reactions of many redox couples involve hydrogen ions. For example, the fumaric acid/succinic acid couple (HOOCCH=CHCOOH/$HOOCCH_2CH_2COOH$), which plays a role in the aerobic breakdown of glucose in biological cells, is

$$\mathrm{HOOCCH{=}CHCOOH(aq) + 2\,H^+(aq) + 2\,e^- \rightarrow HOOCCH_2CH_2COOH(aq)}$$

Half-reactions of this kind have potentials that depend on the pH of the medium. In this example, in which the hydrogen ions occur as reactants, an increase in pH, corresponding to a decrease in hydrogen ion activity, favours the formation of reactants, so the fumaric acid has a lower thermodynamic tendency to become reduced. We expect,

[9] Standard potentials are also called *standard electrode potentials* and *standard reduction potentials*. If in an older source of data you come across a 'standard oxidation potential', reverse its sign and use it as a standard reduction potential.

Table 9.3 *Standard reduction potentials at 25°C*

Reduction half-reaction				$E^{\ominus}$/V
Oxidizing agent			Reducing agent	
Strongly oxidizing				
F_2	$+ 2 e^-$	→	$2 F^-$	+2.87
$S_2O_8^{2-}$	$+ 2 e^-$	→	$2 SO_4^{2-}$	+2.05
Au^+	$+ e^-$	→	Au	+1.69
Pb^{4+}	$+ 2 e^-$	→	Pb^{2+}	+1.67
Ce^{4+}	$+ e^-$	→	Ce^{3+}	+1.61
$MnO_4^- + 8 H^+$	$+ 5 e^-$	→	$Mn^{2+} + 4 H_2O$	+1.51
Cl_2	$+ 2 e^-$	→	$2 Cl^-$	+1.36
$Cr_2O_7^{2-} + 14 H^+$	$+ 6 e^-$	→	$2 Cr^{3+} + 7 H_2O$	+1.33
$O_2 + 4 H^+$	$+ 4 e^-$	→	$2 H_2O$	+1.23, +0.81 at pH = 7
Br_2	$+ 2 e^-$	→	$2 Br^-$	+1.09
Ag^+	$+ e^-$	→	Ag	+0.80
Hg_2^{2+}	$+ 2 e^-$	→	2 Hg	+0.79
Fe^{3+}	$+ e^-$	→	Fe^{2+}	+0.77
I_2	$+ e^-$	→	$2 I^-$	+0.54
$O_2 + 2 H_2O$	$+ 4 e^-$	→	$4 OH^-$	+0.40, +0.81 at pH = 7
Cu^{2+}	$+ 2 e^-$	→	Cu	+0.34
AgCl	$+ e^-$	→	$Ag + Cl^-$	+0.22
$2H^+$	$+ 2 e^-$	→	H_2	0, by definition
Fe^{3+}	$+ 3 e^-$	→	Fe	−0.04
$O_2 + H_2O$	$+ 2 e^-$	→	$HO_2^- + OH^-$	−0.08
Pb^{2+}	$+ 2 e^-$	→	Pb	−0.13
Sn^{2+}	$+ 2 e^-$	→	Sn	−0.14
Fe^{2+}	$+ 2 e^-$	→	Fe	−0.44
Zn^{2+}	$+ 2 e^-$	→	Zn	−0.76
$2H_2O$	$+ 2 e^-$	→	$H_2 + 2 OH^-$	−0.83, −0.42 at pH = 7
Al^{3+}	$+ 3 e^-$	→	Al	−1.66
Mg^{2+}	$+ 2 e^-$	→	Mg	−2.36
Na^+	$+ e^-$	→	Na	−2.71
Ca^{2+}	$+ 2 e^-$	→	Ca	−2.87
K^+	$+ e^-$	→	K	−2.93
Li^+	$+ e^-$	→	Li	−3.05
			Strongly reducing	

For a more extensive table, see the *Data section*.

therefore, that the potential of the fumaric/succinic acid couple should decrease as the pH is increased.

We can establish the quantitative variation of reduction potential with pH for a reaction by using the Nernst equation for the half-reaction and noting that (see the note at the beginning of this chapter pointing out the relation between ln x and log x)

$$\ln a_{H^+} = \ln 10 \times \log a_{H^+} = -\ln 10 \times pH$$

with ln 10 = 2.303.... If we suppose that fumaric acid and succinic acid have fixed concentrations, the potential of the fumaric/succinic redox couple is

$$E = E^{\ominus} - \frac{RT}{2F}\ln\frac{a_{\text{suc}}}{a_{\text{fum}}a_{\text{H}^+}^2}$$

$$= \overbrace{E^{\ominus} - \frac{RT}{2F}\ln\frac{a_{\text{suc}}}{a_{\text{fum}}}}^{E'} + \frac{RT}{F}\ln a_{\text{H}^+}$$

which is easily rearranged into

$$E = E' - \frac{RT\ln 10}{F}\times \text{pH}$$

At 25°C,

$$E = E' - (59.2\ \text{mV})\times\text{pH}$$

We see that each increase of 1 unit in pH decreases the potential by 59.2 mV, which is in agreement with the remark above that the reduction of fumaric acid is discouraged by an increase in pH.

We use the same approach to convert standard potentials to **biological standard potentials**, $E^{\oplus}$, which correspond to neutral solution (pH = 7).[10] If the hydrogen ions appear as reactants in the reduction half-reaction, then the potential is decreased below its standard value (for the fumaric/succinic couple, by 7 × 59.2 mV = 414 mV, or about 0.4 V). If the hydrogen ions appear as products, then the biological standard potential is higher than the thermodynamic standard potential. The precise change depends on the number of electrons and protons participating in the half-reaction.

Example 9.7

Converting a standard potential to a biological standard value

Estimate the biological standard potential of the NAD^+/NADH couple at 25°C (Example 9.3). The reduction half-reaction is

$$NAD^+(aq) + H^+(aq) + 2\,e^- \rightarrow NADH(aq) \quad E^{\ominus} = -0.11\ \text{V}$$

Strategy Write the Nernst equation for the potential, and express the reaction quotient in terms of the activities of the species. All species except H^+ are in their standard states, so their activities are all equal to 1. The remaining task is to express the hydrogen ion activity in terms of the pH, exactly as was done in the text, and set pH = 7.

Solution The Nernst equation for the half-reaction, with $v = 2$, is

$$E = E^{\ominus} - \frac{RT}{2F}\ln\frac{\overbrace{a_{\text{NADH}}}^{1}}{a_{\text{H}^+}\underbrace{a_{\text{NAD}^+}}_{1}} = E^{\ominus} + \frac{RT}{2F}\ln a_{\text{H}^+}$$

We rearrange this expression to

$$E = E^{\ominus} + \frac{RT}{2F}\ln a_{\text{H}^+} = E^{\ominus} - \frac{RT\ln 10}{2F}\times\text{pH}$$

$$= E^{\ominus} - (29.58\ \text{mV})\times\text{pH}$$

The biological standard potential (at pH = 7) is therefore

$$E^{\oplus} = (-0.11\ \text{V}) - (29.58\times10^{-3}\ \text{V})\times 7 = -0.32\ \text{V}$$

Self-test 9.9

Calculate the biological standard potential of the half-reaction $O_2(g) + 4\,H^+(aq) + 4\,e^- \rightarrow 2\,H_2O(l)$ at 25°C given its value +1.23 V under thermodynamic standard conditions.

[*Answer*: +0.82 V]

9.11 The determination of pH

The potential of a hydrogen electrode is directly proportional to the pH of the solution. However, in practice, indirect methods are much more convenient to use than one based on the standard hydrogen electrode, and the hydrogen electrode is replaced by a *glass electrode* (Fig. 9.15). This electrode is sensitive to hydrogen ion activity and has a potential that depends linearly on the pH. It is filled with a phosphate buffer containing Cl^- ions, and conveniently has $E \approx 0$ when the external medium is at pH = 7. The glass electrode is much more convenient to handle than the gas electrode itself, and can be calibrated using solutions of known pH (for example, one of the buffer solutions described in Section 8.6).

[10] Biological standard states were introduced in Section 7.7.

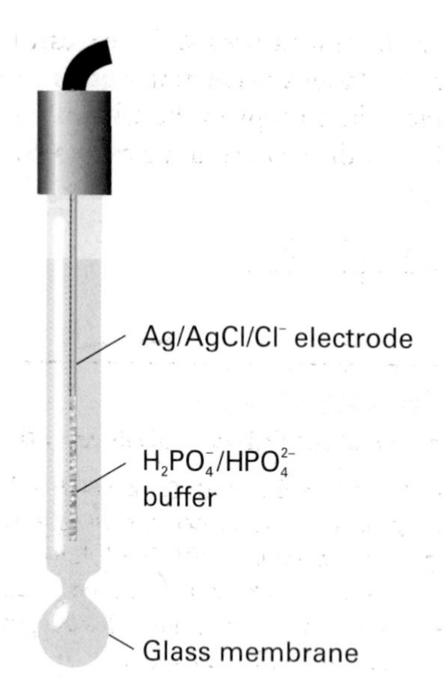

Fig. 9.15 A glass electrode has a potential that varies with the hydrogen ion concentration in the medium in which it is immersed. It consists of a thin glass membrane containing an electrolyte and a silver chloride electrode. The electrode is used in conjunction with a calomel (Hg_2Cl_2) electrode that makes contact with the test solution through a salt bridge.

Self-test 9.10

What range should a voltmeter have (in volts) to display changes of pH from 1 to 14 at 25°C if it is arranged to give a reading of zero when pH = 7?

[*Answer:* from −0.42 V to +0.35 V, a range of 0.77 V]

Finally, it should be noted that we now have a method for measuring the pK_a of an acid electrically. As we saw in Section 8.5, the pH of a solution containing equal amounts of the acid and its conjugate base is pH = pK_a. We now know how to determine pH and hence can determine pK_a in the same way.

Applications of standard potentials

The measurement of the emf of a cell is a convenient source of data on the Gibbs energies, enthalpies, and entropies of reactions. In practice, the standard values (and the biological standard values) of these quantities are the ones normally determined.

9.12 The electrochemical series

We have seen that a cell reaction has $K > 1$ if $E^\ominus > 0$, and that $E > 0$ corresponds to reduction at the right-hand electrode (using the conventions explained previously). We have also seen that $E^\ominus$ may be written as the difference of the standard potentials of the redox couples in the right and left electrodes (eqn 9.17, $E^\ominus = E_R^\ominus - E_L^\ominus$). A reaction corresponding to reduction at the right-hand electrode therefore has $K > 1$ if $E_L^\ominus < E_R^\ominus$, and we can conclude that

A couple with a low standard potential has a thermodynamic tendency to reduce a couple with a high standard potential.

More briefly: *low reduces high* and, equivalently, *high oxidizes low*. For example,

$$E^\ominus(Zn^{2+},Zn) = -0.76\ V < E^\ominus(Cu^{2+},Cu) = +0.34\ V$$

and Zn(s) has a thermodynamic tendency to reduce Cu^{2+}(aq) under standard conditions. Hence, the reaction

$$Zn(s) + CuSO_4(aq) \rightleftharpoons ZnSO_4(aq) + Cu(s)$$

can be expected to have $K > 1$ (in fact, as we have seen, $K = 1.5 \times 10^{37}$ at 298 K).

Self-test 9.11

Does acidified dichromate ($Cr_2O_7^{2-}$) have a thermodynamic tendency to oxidize mercury metal to mercury(I)?

[*Answer:* yes]

9.13 The determination of thermodynamic functions

We have seen that the standard emf of a cell is related to the standard reaction Gibbs energy by eqn 9.15 ($\Delta_r G^\ominus = -\nu F E^\ominus$). Therefore, by measuring the standard emf of a cell driven by the reaction of interest we can obtain the standard reaction Gibbs energy. If we were interested in the biological standard state, we would use the same expression but with the standard emf at pH = 7 ($\Delta_r G^\oplus = -\nu F E^\oplus$).

The relation between the standard emf and the standard reaction Gibbs energy is a convenient route for the calculation of the standard potential of a couple from two others. We make use of the fact that G is a state function, and that the Gibbs energy of an overall reaction is the sum of the Gibbs energies of the reactions into which it can be divided. In general, we cannot combine the $E^{\ominus}$ values directly because they depend on the value of ν, which may be different for the two couples.

Example 9.8
Calculating a standard potential from two others

Given the standard potentials $E^{\ominus}(Cu^{2+},Cu) = +0.340$ V and $E^{\ominus}(Cu^{+},Cu) = +0.522$ V, calculate $E^{\ominus}(Cu^{2+},Cu^{+})$.

Strategy We need to convert the two $E^{\ominus}$ to $\Delta_r G^{\ominus}$ by using eqn 9.15, adding them appropriately, and then converting the overall $\Delta_r G^{\ominus}$ so obtained to the required $E^{\ominus}$ by using eqn 9.15 again. Because the Fs cancel at the end of the calculation, carry them through.

Solution The electrode reactions are as follows:

(a) $Cu^{2+}(aq) + 2\,e^- \rightarrow Cu(s)$ $E^{\ominus} = +0.340$ V

$\Delta_r G^{\ominus}(a) = -2F \times (0.340\ \text{V}) = (-0.680\ \text{V}) \times F$

(b) $Cu^{+}(aq) + e^- \rightarrow Cu(s)$ $E^{\ominus} = +0.522$ V

$\Delta_r G^{\ominus}(b) = -F \times (0.522\ \text{V}) = (-0.522\ \text{V}) \times F$

The required reaction is

(c) $Cu^{2+}(aq) + e^- \rightarrow Cu^{+}(aq)$ $\Delta_r G^{\ominus}(c) = -FE^{\ominus}$

Because (c) = (a) – (b), it follows that

$$\Delta_r G^{\ominus}(c) = \Delta_r G^{\ominus}(a) - \Delta_r G^{\ominus}(b)$$

Therefore, from eqn 9.15,

$$FE^{\ominus}(c) = -\{(-0.680\ \text{V})F - (-0.522\ \text{V})F\}$$

The Fs cancel, and we are left with $E^{\ominus}(c) = +0.158$ V.

A note on good practice Whenever combining standard potentials to obtain the standard potential of a third couple, always work via the Gibbs energies because they are additive, whereas, in general, standard potentials are not.

Self-test 9.12

Given the standard potentials $E^{\ominus}(Fe^{3+},Fe) = -0.04$ V and $E^{\ominus}(Fe^{2+},Fe) = -0.44$ V, calculate $E^{\ominus}(Fe^{3+},Fe^{2+})$.

[*Answer*: +0.76 V]

Once we have measured $\Delta_r G^{\ominus}$ we can use thermodynamic relations to determine other properties. For instance, the entropy of the cell reaction can be obtained from the change in the cell potential with temperature:

$$\Delta_r S^{\ominus} = \frac{\nu F(E^{\ominus} - E^{\ominus\prime})}{T - T'} \qquad (9.18)$$

Derivation 9.4
The reaction entropy from the cell potential

The definition of the Gibbs energy is $G = H - TS$. This formula applies to all substances involved in a reaction, so at a given temperature $\Delta_r G^{\ominus}(T) = \Delta_r H^{\ominus} - T\Delta_r S^{\ominus}$. If we can ignore the weak temperature dependence of $\Delta_r H^{\ominus}$ and $\Delta_r S^{\ominus}$, at a temperature T' we can write $\Delta_r G^{\ominus}(T') = \Delta_r H^{\ominus} - T'\Delta_r S^{\ominus}$. Therefore,

$$\Delta_r G^{\ominus}(T') - \Delta_r G^{\ominus}(T) = -(T' - T)\Delta_r S^{\ominus}$$

Substitution of $\Delta_r G^{\ominus} = -\nu FE^{\ominus}$ then gives

$$-\nu FE^{\ominus\prime} + \nu FE^{\ominus} = -(T' - T)\Delta_r S^{\ominus}$$

which is easily rearranged into eqn 9.18.

We see from eqn 9.18 that the standard emf of a cell increases with temperature if the standard reaction entropy is positive, and that the slope of a plot of potential against temperature is proportional to the reaction entropy (Fig. 9.16). An implication is that, if the cell reaction produces a lot of gas, then

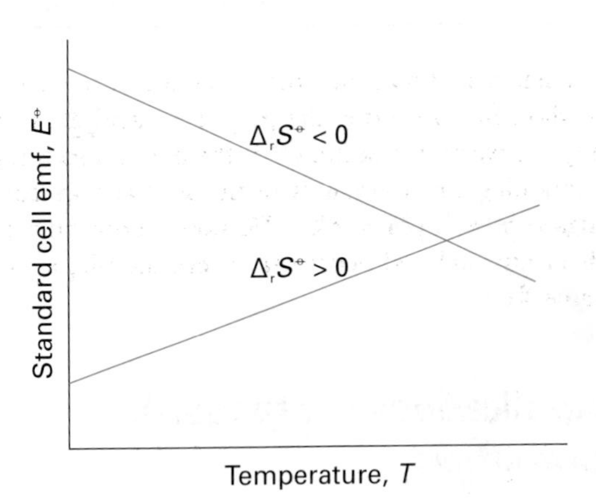

Fig. 9.16 The variation of the standard potential of a cell with temperature depends on the standard entropy of the cell reaction.

its potential will increase with temperature. The opposite is true for a reaction that consumes gas.

Finally, we can combine the results obtained so far by using $G = H - TS$ in the form $H = G + TS$ to obtain the standard reaction enthalpy:

$$\Delta_r H^{\ominus} = \Delta_r G^{\ominus} + T\Delta_r S^{\ominus} \quad (9.19)$$

with $\Delta_r G^{\ominus}$ determined from the cell potential and $\Delta_r S^{\ominus}$ from its temperature variation. Thus, we now have a non-calorimetric method of measuring a reaction enthalpy.

Example 9.9

Using the temperature dependence of the cell potential

The standard potential of the cell

$Pt(s)|H_2(g)|HCl(aq)|Hg_2Cl_2(s)|Hg(l)$

was found to be +0.2699 V at 293 K and +0.2669 V at 303 K. Evaluate the standard Gibbs energy, enthalpy, and entropy at 298 K of the reaction

$Hg_2Cl_2(s) + H_2(g) \rightarrow 2\,Hg(l) + 2\,HCl(aq)$

Strategy We find the standard reaction Gibbs energy from the standard emf by using eqn 9.15 and making a linear interpolation between the two temperatures (in this case, we take the mean $E^{\ominus}$ because 298 K lies midway between 293 K and 303 K). The standard reaction entropy is obtained by substituting the data into eqn 9.18. Then the standard reaction enthalpy is obtained by combining these two quantities by using eqn 9.19. Use 1 C V = 1 J.

Solution Because the mean standard cell emf is +0.2684 V and $\nu = 2$ for the reaction,

$$\begin{aligned}\Delta_r G^{\ominus} &= -\nu F E^{\ominus} \\ &= -2 \times (9.6485 \times 10^4\ \mathrm{C\ mol^{-1}}) \times (0.2684\ \mathrm{V}) \\ &= -51.79\ \mathrm{kJ\ mol^{-1}}\end{aligned}$$

Then, from eqn 9.18, the standard reaction entropy is

$$\begin{aligned}\Delta_r S^{\ominus} &= 2 \times (9.6485 \times 10^4\ \mathrm{C\ mol^{-1}}) \\ &\quad \times \left(\frac{0.2699\ \mathrm{V} - 0.2669\ \mathrm{V}}{293\ \mathrm{K} - 303\ \mathrm{K}}\right) \\ &= -57.9\ \mathrm{J\ K^{-1}\ mol^{-1}}\end{aligned}$$

For the next stage of the calculation it is convenient to write the last value as -5.79×10^{-2} kJ K^{-1} mol^{-1}. Then, from eqn 9.19 we find

$$\begin{aligned}\Delta_r H^{\ominus} &= (-51.79\ \mathrm{kJ\ mol^{-1}}) + (298\ \mathrm{K}) \times \\ &\qquad (-5.79 \times 10^{-2}\ \mathrm{kJ\ K^{-1}\ mol^{-1}}) \\ &= -69.0\ \mathrm{kJ\ mol^{-1}}\end{aligned}$$

One difficulty with this procedure lies in the accurate measurement of small temperature variations of cell potential. Nevertheless, it is another example of the striking ability of thermodynamics to relate the apparently unrelated, in this case to relate electrical measurements to thermal properties.

Self-test 9.13

Predict the standard potential of the *Harned cell*

$Pt(s)|H_2(g)|HCl(aq)|AgCl(s)|Ag(s)$

at 303 K from tables of thermodynamic data for 298 K.

[*Answer:* +0.2168 V]

CHECKLIST OF KEY IDEAS

You should now be familiar with the following concepts:

- ☐ 1 Deviations from ideal behaviour in ionic solutions are ascribed to the interaction of an ion with its ionic atmosphere.
- ☐ 2 According to the Debye–Hückel limiting law, the mean activity of ions in a solution is related to the ionic strength, I, of the solution by $\log \gamma_{\pm} = -A|z_+z_-|I^{1/2}$.
- ☐ 3 The molar conductivity of a strong electrolyte follows the Kohlrausch law, $\Lambda_m = \Lambda_m^{\circ} - Kc^{1/2}$.
- ☐ 4 The rate at which an ion migrates through solution is determined by its mobility, which depends on its charge, its hydrodynamic radius, and the viscosity of the solution.
- ☐ 5 Protons migrate by the Grotthus mechanism, Fig. 9.4.

☐ 6 A galvanic cell is an electrochemical cell in which a spontaneous chemical reaction produces a potential difference.

☐ 7 An electrolytic cell is an electrochemical cell in which an external source of current is used to drive a non-spontaneous chemical reaction.

☐ 8 A redox reaction is expressed as the difference of two reduction half-reactions.

☐ 9 A cathode is the site of reduction; an anode is the site of oxidation.

☐ 10 The electromotive force of a cell is the potential difference it produces when operating reversibly; $E = -\Delta_r G/\nu F$.

☐ 11 The Nernst equation for the emf of a cell is $E = E^{\ominus} - (RT/\nu F) \ln Q$.

☐ 12 The standard potential of a couple is the standard emf of a cell in which it forms the right-hand electrode and a hydrogen electrode is on the left.

☐ 13 The standard emf of a cell is the difference of its standard electrode potentials: $E^{\ominus} = E^{\ominus}_R - E^{\ominus}_L$.

☐ 14 The equilibrium constant of a cell reaction is related to the standard emf of the cell by $\ln K = \nu F E^{\ominus}/RT$.

☐ 15 The pH of a solution is determined by measuring the potential of a glass electrode.

☐ 16 A couple with a low standard potential has a thermodynamic tendency (in the sense $K > 1$) to reduce a couple with a high standard potential.

☐ 17 The entropy and enthalpy of a cell reaction are measured from the temperature dependence of the cell's emf: $\Delta_r S^{\ominus} = \nu F(E^{\ominus} - E^{\ominus\prime})/(T - T')$.

DISCUSSION QUESTIONS

9.1 Describe the general features of the Debye–Hückel theory of electrolyte solutions.

9.2 Discuss the mechanism of proton conduction in water.

9.3 Distinguish between galvanic, electrolytic, and fuel cells.

9.4 Describe a method for the determination of the standard potential of an electrochemical cell.

EXERCISES

9.5 Relate the ionic strengths of (a) KCl, (b) $FeCl_3$, and (c) $CuSO_4$ solutions to their molalities, b.

9.6 (a) Calculate the ionic strength of a solution that is 0.10 mol kg^{-1} in KCl(aq) and 0.20 mol kg^{-1} in $CuSO_4$(aq).

9.7 Calculate the masses of (a) $Ca(NO_3)_2$ and, separately, (b) NaCl to add to a 0.150 mol kg^{-1} solution of KNO_3(aq) containing 500 g of solvent to raise its ionic strength to 0.250.

9.8 Express the mean activity coefficient of the ions in a solution of $CaCl_2$ in terms of the activity coefficients of the individual ions.

9.9 Estimate the mean ionic activity coefficient and activity of a solution that is 0.010 mol kg^{-1} $CaCl_2$(aq) and 0.030 mol kg^{-1} NaF(aq).

9.10 The mean activity coefficients of HBr in three dilute aqueous solutions at 25°C are 0.930 (at 5.0 mmol kg^{-1}), 0.907 (at 10.0 mmol kg^{-1}), and 0.879 (at 20.0 mmol kg^{-1}). Estimate the value of B in the extended Debye–Hückel law.

9.11 The limiting molar conductivities of KCl, KNO_3, and $AgNO_3$ are 14.99 mS m^2 mol^{-1}, 14.50 mS m^2 mol^{-1}, and 13.34 mS m^2 mol^{-1}, respectively (all at 25°C). What is the limiting molar conductivity of AgCl at this temperature?

9.12 The mobility of a chloride ion in aqueous solution at 25°C is 7.91×10^{-8} m^2 s^{-1} V^{-1}. Calculate the molar ionic conductivity.

9.13 The mobility of a Rb^+ ion in aqueous solution is 7.92×10^{-8} m^2 s^{-1} V^{-1} at 25°C. The potential difference between two electrodes placed in the solution is 35.0 V. If the electrodes are 8.00 mm apart, what is the drift speed of the Rb^+ ion?

9.14 The resistances of a series of aqueous NaCl solutions, formed by successive dilution of a sample, were measured in a cell with cell constant (the constant C in the relation $\kappa = C/R$) equal to 0.2063 cm^{-1}. The following values were found:

c/(mol dm^{-3})	0.000 50	0.0010	0.0050	0.010	0.020	0.050
R/Ω	3314	1669	342.1	174.1	89.08	37.14

(a) Verify that the molar conductivity follows the Kohlrausch law and find the limiting molar conductivity. (b) Determine the coefficient K. (c) Use the value of K (which should depend only on the nature, not the identity, of the ions) and the information that $\lambda(Na^+) = 5.01$ mS m^2 mol^{-1} and $\lambda(I^-) = 7.68$ mS m^2 mol^{-1} to predict (i) the molar conductivity, (ii) the conductivity, (iii) the resistance it would show in the cell, of 0.010 mol dm^{-3} NaI(aq) at 25°C.

9.15 After correction for the water conductivity, the conductivity of a saturated aqueous solution of AgCl at 25°C was found to be 0.1887 mS m^{-1}. What is the solubility of silver chloride at this temperature?

9.16 The molar conductivity of 0.020 M HCOOH(aq) is 3.83 mS m^2 mol^{-1}. What is the value of pK_a for formic acid?

9.17 Is the conversion of pyruvate ion to lactate ion in the reaction $CH_3COCO_2^-$(aq) + NADH(aq) + H^+(aq) $\rightarrow$ $CH_3CH_2(OH)CO_2^-$(aq) + NAD^+(aq) a redox reaction?

9.18 Express the reaction in Exercise 9.17 as the difference of two half-reactions.

9.19 Express the reaction in which ethanol is converted to acetaldehyde (propanal) by NAD^+ in the presence of alcohol dehydrogenase as the difference of two half-reactions and write the corresponding reaction quotients for each half-reaction and the overall reaction.

9.20 Express the oxidation of cysteine ($HSCH_2CH(NH_2)COOH$) to cystine ($HOOCCH(NH_2)CH_2SSCH_2CH(NH_2)COOH$) as the difference of two half-reactions, one of which is O_2(g) + 4 H^+(aq) + 4 e$^-$ $\rightarrow$ 2 H_2O(l).

9.21 One of the steps in photosynthesis is the reduction of $NADP^+$ by ferredoxin (fd) in the presence of ferredoxin–NADP reductase: 2 fd$_{red}$(aq) + $NADP^+$(aq) + 2 H^+(aq) $\rightarrow$ 2 fd$_{ox}$(aq) + NADPH(aq). Express this reaction as the difference of two half-reactions. How many electrons are transferred in the reaction event?

9.22 From the biological standard half-cell potentials $E^{\oplus}(O_2,H^+,H_2O) = +0.82$ V and $E^{\oplus}(NADH^+,H^+,NADH) = -0.32$ V, calculate the standard potential arising from the reaction in which NADH is oxidized to NAD^+ and the corresponding biological standard reaction Gibbs energy.

9.23 Consider a hydrogen electrode in HBr(aq) at 25°C operating at 1.45 bar. Estimate the change in the electrode potential when the solution is changed from 5.0 mmol dm^{-3} to 25.0 mmol dm^{-3}.

9.24 A hydrogen electrode can, in principle, be used to monitor changes in the molar concentrations of weak acids in biologically active solutions. Consider a hydrogen electrode in a solution of lactic acid as part of an overall galvanic cell at 25°C and 1 bar. Estimate the change in the electrode potential when the concentration of lactic acid in the solution is changed from 5.0 mmol dm^{-3} to 25.0 mmol dm^{-3}.

9.25 Devise a cell in which the cell reaction is Mn(s) + Cl_2(g) $\rightarrow$ $MnCl_2$(aq). Give the half-reactions for the electrodes and from the standard cell potential of +2.54 V deduce the standard potential of the Mn^{2+}/Mn couple.

9.26 Write the cell reactions and electrode half-reactions for the following cells:

(a) Ag(s)|$AgNO_3$(aq,m_L)||$AgNO_3$(aq,m_R)|Ag(s)

(b) Pt(s)|H_2(g,p_L)|HCl(aq)|H_2(g,p_L)|Pt(s)

(c) Pt(s)|$K_3[Fe(CN)_6]$(aq),$K_4[Fe(CN)_6]$(aq)||Mn^{2+}(aq),H^+(aq)|MnO_2(s)|Pt(s)

(d) Pt(s)|Cl_2(g)|HCl(aq)||HBr(aq)|Br_2(l)|Pt(s)

(e) Pt(s)|Fe^{3+}(aq),Fe^{2+}(aq)||Sn^{4+}(aq),Sn^{2+}(aq)|Pt(s)

(f) Fe(s)|Fe^{2+}(aq)||Mn^{2+}(aq),H^+(aq)|MnO_2(s)|Pt(s)

9.27 Write the Nernst equations for the cells in the preceding exercise.

9.28 Devise cells in which the following are the reactions. In each case state the value for v to use in the Nernst equation.

(a) Fe(s) + $PbSO_4$(aq) $\rightarrow$ $FeSO_4$(aq) + Pb(s)

(b) Hg_2Cl_2(s) + H_2(g) $\rightarrow$ 2 HCl(aq) + 2 Hg(l)

(c) 2 H_2(g) + O_2(g) $\rightarrow$ 2 H_2O(l)

(d) H_2(g) + O_2(g) $\rightarrow$ H_2O_2(aq)

(e) H_2(g) + I_2(g) $\rightarrow$ 2 HI(aq)

(f) 2 CuCl(aq) $\rightarrow$ Cu(s) + $CuCl_2$(aq)

9.29 Devise cells to study the following biochemically important reactions. In each case state the value for v to use in the Nernst equation.

(a) CH_3CH_2OH(aq) + NAD^+(aq) $\rightarrow$ CH_3CHO(aq) + NADH(aq) + H^+(aq)

(b) ATP^{4-}(aq) + Mg^{2+}(aq) $\rightarrow$ $MgATP^{2-}$(aq)

(c) 2 Cyt-c(red, aq) + $CH_3COCO_2^-$(aq) + 2 H^+(aq) $\rightarrow$ 2 Cyt-c(ox, aq) + $CH_3CH(OH)CO_2^-$(aq)

(Cyt-c denotes cytochrome c, a protein containing an iron ion that can change oxidation states between +2 and +3.)

9.30 Use the standard potentials of the electrodes to calculate the standard potentials of the cells in Exercise 9.26.

9.31 Use the standard potentials of the electrodes to calculate the standard potentials of the cells devised in Exercise 9.28.

9.32 Use the standard potentials of the electrodes to calculate the standard potentials of the cells devised in Exercise 9.29.

9.33 Could the synthesis of ammonia be used as the basis of a fuel cell? What is the maximum electrical energy output for the consumption of 100 g of nitrogen?

9.34 The permanganate ion is a common oxidizing agent. What is the standard potential of the MnO_4^-,H^+/Mn^{2+} couple at (a) pH = 6.00, (b) general pH?

9.35 Consider the Harned cell Pt(s)|H_2(g)|HCl(aq)|AgCl(s)|Ag(s). Show that the standard potential of the silver–silver-chloride electrode may be determined by plotting $E - (RT/F)\ln b$ against $b^{1/2}$. (*Hint.* Express the cell emf in terms of activities, and use the Debye–Hückel law to estimate the mean activity coefficient.)

9.36 State what you would expect to happen to the cell potential when the following changes are made to the corresponding cells in Exercise 9.26. Confirm your prediction by using the Nernst equation in each case.

(a) The molar concentration of silver nitrate in the left-hand compartment is increased.

(b) The pressure of hydrogen in the left-hand compartment is increased.

(c) The pH of the right-hand compartment is decreased.

(d) The concentration of HCl is increased.

(e) Some iron(III) chloride is added to both compartments.

(f) Acid is added to both compartments.

9.37 State what you would expect to happen to the cell potential when the following changes are made to the corresponding cells devised in Exercise 9.28. Confirm your prediction by using the Nernst equation in each case.

(a) The molar concentration of $FeSO_4$ is increased.

(b) Some nitric acid is added to both cell compartments.

(c) The pressure of oxygen is increased.

(d) The pressure of hydrogen is increased.

(e) Some (i) hydrochloric acid, (ii) hydroiodic acid is added to both compartments.

(f) Hydrochloric acid is added to both compartments.

9.38 State what you would expect to happen to the cell potential when the following changes are made to the corresponding cells devised in Exercise 9.29. Confirm your prediction by using the Nernst equation in each case.

(a) The pH of the solution is raised.

(b) A solution of Epsom salts (magnesium sulfate) is added.

(c) Sodium lactate is added to the solution.

9.39 (a) Calculate the standard potential of the cell Hg(l)|$HgCl_2$(aq)||$TlNO_3$(aq)|Tl(s) at 25°C. (b) Calculate the cell potential when the molar concentration of the Hg^{2+} ion is 0.150 mol dm^{-3} and that of the Tl^+ ion is 0.93 mol dm^{-3}.

9.40 Calculate the standard Gibbs energies at 25°C of the following reactions from the standard potential data in the *Data section*.

(a) Ca(s) + 2 H_2O(l) → $Ca(OH)_2$(aq) + H_2(g)

(b) 2 Ca(s) + 4 H_2O(l) → 2 $Ca(OH)_2$(aq) + 2 H_2(g)

(c) Fe(s) + 2 H_2O(l) → $Fe(OH)_2$(aq) + H_2(g)

(d) $Na_2S_2O_8$(aq) + 2 NaI(aq) → I_2(s) + 2 Na_2SO_4(aq)

(e) $Na_2S_2O_8$(aq) + 2 KI(aq) → I_2(s) + Na_2SO_4(aq) + K_2SO_4(aq)

(f) Pb(s) + Na_2CO_3(aq) → $PbCO_3$(aq) + 2 Na(s)

9.41 Calculate the biological standard Gibbs energies of the following reactions and half-reactions:

(a) 2 NADH(aq) + O_2(g) + 2 H^+(aq) → 2 NAD^+(aq) + 2 H_2O(l) $\quad E^{\oplus} = +1.14$ V

(b) Malate(aq) + NAD^+(aq) → oxaloacetate(aq) + NADH(aq) + H^+(aq) $\quad E^{\oplus} = -0.154$ V

(c) O_2(g) + 4 H^+(aq) + 4 e^- → 2 H_2O(l) $\quad E^{\oplus} = +0.81$ V

9.42 Tabulated thermodynamic data can be used to predict the standard potential of a cell even if it cannot be measured directly. The standard Gibbs energy of the reaction K_2CrO_4(aq) + 2 Ag(s) + 2 $FeCl_3$(aq) → Ag_2CrO_4(s) + 2 $FeCl_2$(aq) + 2 KCl(aq) is −62.5 kJ mol^{-1} at 298 K. (a) Calculate the standard potential of the corresponding galvanic cell and (b) the standard potential of the Ag_2CrO_4/Ag,CrO_4^{2-} couple.

9.43 Estimate the potential of the cell

Ag(s)|AgCl(s)|KCl(aq, 0.025 mol kg^{-1})||$AgNO_3$(aq, 0.010 mol kg^{-1})|Ag(s)

at 25°C.

9.44 (a) Use the information in the *Data section* to calculate the standard potential of the cell Ag(s)|$AgNO_3$(aq)||$Cu(NO_3)_2$(aq)|Cu(s) and the standard Gibbs energy and enthalpy of the cell reaction at 25°C. (b) Estimate the value of $\Delta_r G^{\ominus}$ at 35°C.

9.45 (a) Calculate the standard potential of the cell Pt(s)|cystine(aq),cysteine(aq)||H^+(aq)|O_2(g)|Pt(s) and the standard Gibbs energy and enthalpy of the cell reaction at 25°C. (b) Estimate the value of $\Delta_r G^{\ominus}$ at 35°C. Use $E^{\ominus} = -0.34$ V for the cysteine/cystine couple.

9.46 The biological standard potential of the couple pyruvic acid/lactic acid is −0.19 V at 25°C. What is the thermodynamic standard potential of the couple? Pyruvic acid is $CH_3COCOOH$ and lactic acid is $CH_3CH(OH)COOH$.

9.47 One ecologically important equilibrium is that between carbonate and hydrogencarbonate (bicarbonate) ions in natural water. (a) The standard Gibbs energies of formation of CO_3^{2-}(aq) and HCO_3^-(aq) are −527.81 kJ mol^{-1} and −586.77 kJ mol^{-1}, respectively. What is the standard potential of the $HCO_3^-/CO_3^{2-},H_2$ couple? (b) Calculate the standard potential of a cell in which the cell reaction is Na_2CO_3(aq) + H_2O(l) → $NaHCO_3$(aq) + NaOH(aq). (c) Write the Nernst equation for the cell, and (d) predict and calculate the change in potential when the pH is change to 7.0. (e) Calculate the value of pK_a for HCO_3^-(aq).

9.48 Calcium phosphate is the principal inorganic component of bone. Its solubility characteristics are important for the stabilities of skeletons, and they can be assessed electrochemically. The solubility constant of $Cu_3(PO_4)_2$ is 1.3×10^{-37}. Calculate (a) the solubility of $Cu_3(PO_4)_2$, (b) the potential of the cell Pt(s)|H_2(g)|HCl(aq, pH = 0)||$Cu_3(PO_4)_2$(aq, satd.)|Cu(s) at 25°C.

9.49 Calculate the equilibrium constants of the following reactions at 25°C from standard potential data:

(a) Sn(s) + Sn^{4+}(aq) ⇌ 2 Sn^{2+}(aq)

(b) Sn(s) + 2 AgBr(s) ⇌ $SnBr_2$(aq) + 2 Ag(s)

(c) Fe(s) + $Hg(NO_3)_2$(aq) ⇌ Hg(l) + $Fe(NO_3)_2$(aq)

(d) Cd(s) + $CuSO_4$(aq) ⇌ Cu(s) + $CdSO_4$(aq)

(e) Cu^{2+}(aq) + Cu(s) ⇌ 2 Cu^+(aq)

(f) 3 Au^{2+}(aq) ⇌ Au(s) + 2 Au^{3+}(aq)

9.50 The molar solubilities of AgCl and $BaSO_4$ in water are 1.34×10^{-5} mol dm^{-3} and 9.51×10^{-4} mol dm^{-3}, respectively, at 25°C. Calculate their solubility constants from the appropriate standard potentials.

9.51 The dichromate ion in acidic solution is a common oxidizing agent for organic compounds. Derive an expression for the potential of an electrode for which the half-reaction is the reduction of $Cr_2O_7^{2-}$ ions to Cr^{3+} ions in acidic solution.

9.52 The emf of the cell Pt(s)|H_2(g)|HCl(aq)|AgCl(s)|Ag(s) is 0.312 V at 25°C. What is the pH of the electrolyte solution?

9.53 The molar solubility of AgBr is 2.6 μmol dm^{-3} at 25°C. What is the emf of the cell Ag(s)|AgBr(aq)|AgBr(s)|Ag(s) at that temperature?

9.54 The standard potential of the cell Ag(s)|AgI(s)|AgI(aq)|Ag(s) is +0.9509 V at 25°C. Calculate (a) the molar solubility of AgI and (b) its solubility constant.

9.55 Devise a cell in which the overall reaction is Bi(s) + Hg_2SO_4(s) → $BiSO_4$(s) + 2 Hg(l). What is its potential when the electrolyte is saturated with both salts at 25°C?

Chapter 10

The rates of reactions

The branch of physical chemistry called **chemical kinetics** is concerned with the rates of chemical reactions. Chemical kinetics deals with how rapidly reactants are consumed and products formed, how reaction rates respond to changes in the conditions or the presence of a catalyst, and the identification of the steps by which a reaction takes place.

One reason for studying the rates of reactions is the practical importance of being able to predict how quickly a reaction mixture approaches equilibrium. The rate might depend on variables under our control, such as the pressure, the temperature, and the presence of a catalyst, and we might be able to optimize it by the appropriate choice of conditions. Another reason is that the study of reaction rates leads to an understanding of the **mechanism** of a reaction, its analysis into a sequence of elementary steps. For example, we might discover that the reaction of hydrogen and bromine to form hydrogen bromide proceeds by the dissociation of a Br_2 molecule, the attack of a Br atom on an H_2 molecule, and several subsequent steps. By analysing the rate of a biochemical reaction we may discover how an enzyme, a biological catalyst, acts. **Enzyme kinetics**, the study of the effect of enzymes on the rates of reactions, is also an important window on how these macromolecules work.

We need to cope with a wide variety of different rates and a process that appears to be slow may be the outcome of many faster steps. That is particularly true in the chemical reactions that underlie life. Photobiological processes like those responsible for photosynthesis and the slow growth of a plant may take place in about 1 ps. The binding of a neurotransmitter can have an effect after about 1 μs. Once a gene has been activated, a protein may emerge in about 100 s; but even that time-scale incorporates many others, including the wriggling of a newly formed polypeptide chain into its working conformation, each step of which may take about 1 ps. On a grander view, some of the equations of chemical kinetics are applicable to the behaviour of whole populations of organisms; such societies change on time-scales of 10^7–10^9 s.

Table 10.1
Kinetic techniques for fast reactions

Technique	Range of time-scales/s
Femtochemistry	$>10^{-15}$
Flash photolysis	$>10^{-12}$
Fluorescence decay	10^{-10}–10^{-6}
Ultrasonic absorption	10^{-10}–10^{-4}
EPR*	10^{-9}–10^{-4}
Electric field jump	10^{-7}–1
Temperature jump	10^{-6}–1
Phosphorescence	10^{-6}–10
NMR*	10^{-5}–1
Pressure jump	$>10^{-5}$
Stopped flow	$>10^{-3}$

* EPR is electron paramagnetic resonance (or electron spin resonance); NMR is nuclear magnetic resonance; see Chapter 21.

Empirical chemical kinetics

The first step in the investigation of the rate and mechanism of a reaction is the determination of the overall stoichiometry of the reaction and the identification of any side reactions. The next step is to determine how the concentrations of the reactants and products change with time after the reaction has been initiated. Because the rates of chemical reactions are sensitive to temperature, the temperature of the reaction mixture must be held constant throughout the course of the reaction, otherwise the observed rate would be a meaningless average of the rates for different temperatures.

The method used to monitor the concentrations of reactants and products and their variation with time depends on the substances involved and the rapidity with which their concentrations change (Table 10.1). We shall see that **spectrophotometry**, the measurement of the absorption of light by a material, is used widely to monitor concentration. If a reaction changes the number or type of ions present in a solution, then concentrations may be followed by monitoring the conductivity of the solution. Reactions that change the concentration of hydrogen ions may be studied by monitoring the pH of the solution with a glass electrode. Other methods of monitoring the composition include the detection of light emission, titration, mass spectrometry, gas chromatography, and magnetic resonance (both EPR and NMR, Chapter 21). Polarimetery, the observation of the optical activity of a reaction mixture, is occasionally applicable.

10.1 Spectrophotometry

The key result for using the intensity of absorption of radiation at a particular wavelength to determine the concentration [J] of the absorbing species is the empirical **Beer–Lambert law** (Fig. 10.1):

In classical physics, light is treated as an electromagnetic wave which, in a vacuum, travels at the *speed of light*, *c*, which is about 3×10^8 m s^{-1}. The wavelength and frequency of the wave are related by $\lambda\nu = c$. See Appendix 3 for a review of electromagnetism.

$$\log \frac{I_0}{I} = \varepsilon[\mathrm{J}]l \qquad (10.1a)$$

$$I = I_0\, 10^{-\varepsilon[\mathrm{J}]l} \qquad (10.1b)$$

(Note: common logarithms, to the base 10.) In this expression, I_0 and I are the incident and transmitted intensities, respectively, and l is the length of the sample. The quantity ε (epsilon) is called the **molar absorption coefficient** (formerly, and still widely, the *extinction coefficient*): it depends on the wavelength of the incident radiation and is greatest where the absorption is most intense; the units of ε are typically cubic decimetres per mole per centimetre

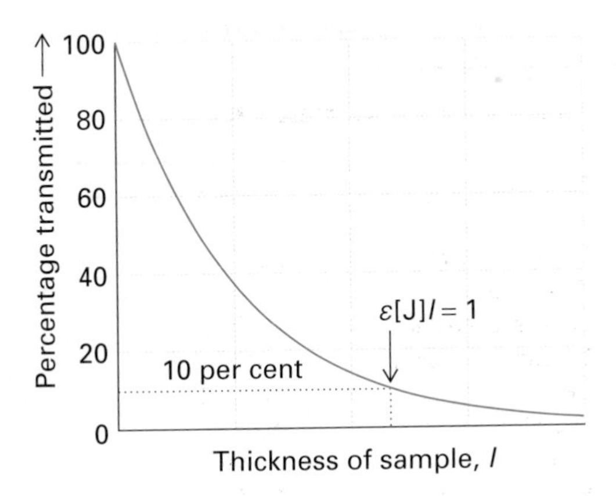

Fig. 10.1 The intensity of light transmitted by an absorbing sample decreases exponentially with the path length through the sample.

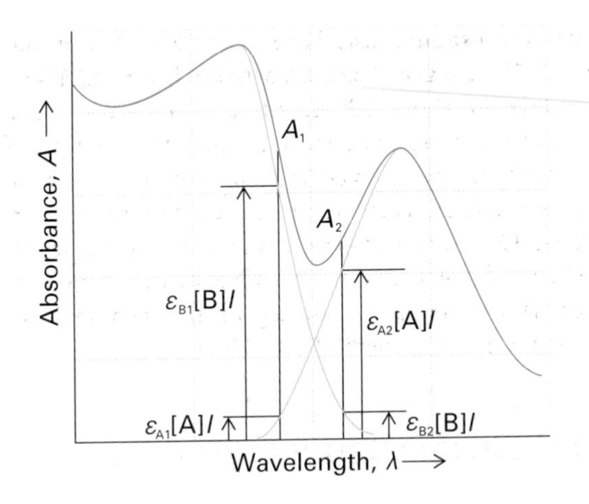

Fig. 10.2 The concentrations of two absorbing species in a mixture can be determined from their molar absorption coefficients and the measurement of their absorbances at two different wavelengths lying within their joint absorption region.

($dm^3\ mol^{-1}\ cm^{-1}$; which are sensible when [J] is expressed in moles per cubic decimetre and l is in centimetres). The dimensionless expression on the right of eqn 10.1a, $\varepsilon[J]l$, is called the **absorbance**, A, of the sample (formerly, the *optical density*):

$$A = \varepsilon[J]l \tag{10.2}$$

To use Beer's law (as it is normally called) to determine the concentrations of species of known molar absorption coefficients, we measure the absorbance of a sample and rearrange eqn 10.2 into

$$[J] = \frac{A}{\varepsilon l} \tag{10.3}$$

It follows from this equation that we can observe the appearance or depletion of a species during a reaction by monitoring changes in the absorbance of the reaction mixture.

We can also make measurements at two wavelengths and use them to find the individual concentrations of two components A and B in a mixture. For this analysis, we write the total absorbance at a given wavelength as

$$A = A_A + A_B = \varepsilon_A[A]l + \varepsilon_B[B]l = (\varepsilon_A[A] + \varepsilon_B[B])l$$

Then, for two measurements of the total absorbance at wavelengths λ_1 and λ_2 at which the molar absorption coefficients are ε_1 and ε_2 (Fig. 10.2), we have

$$A_1 = (\varepsilon_{A1}[A] + \varepsilon_{B1}[B])l \qquad A_2 = (\varepsilon_{A2}[A] + \varepsilon_{B2}[B])l$$

We can solve these two simultaneous equations for the two unknowns (the molar concentrations of A and B), and find

$$[A] = \frac{\varepsilon_{B2}A_1 - \varepsilon_{B1}A_2}{(\varepsilon_{A1}\varepsilon_{B2} - \varepsilon_{A2}\varepsilon_{B1})l}$$

$$[B] = \frac{\varepsilon_{A1}A_2 - \varepsilon_{A2}A_1}{(\varepsilon_{A1}\varepsilon_{B2} - \varepsilon_{A2}\varepsilon_{B1})l} \tag{10.4}$$

There may be a wavelength, λ°, called the **isosbestic wavelength**, at which the molar extinction coefficients of the two species are equal; we write this common value as ε°. The total absorbance of the mixture at the isosbestic wavelength is

$$A^\circ = \varepsilon^\circ([A] + [B])l \tag{10.5}$$

Even if A and B are interconverted in a reaction of the form A → B or its reverse, then because their total concentration remains constant, so does A°. As a result, one or more **isosbestic points**,[1] which are invariant points in the absorption spectrum, may be observed (Fig. 10.3). It is very unlikely that three or more species would have the same molar absorption coefficients at a single wavelength. Therefore, the observation of an isosbestic point, or at least not

[1] The name 'isosbestic' comes from the Greek words for 'the same' and 'extinguish'.

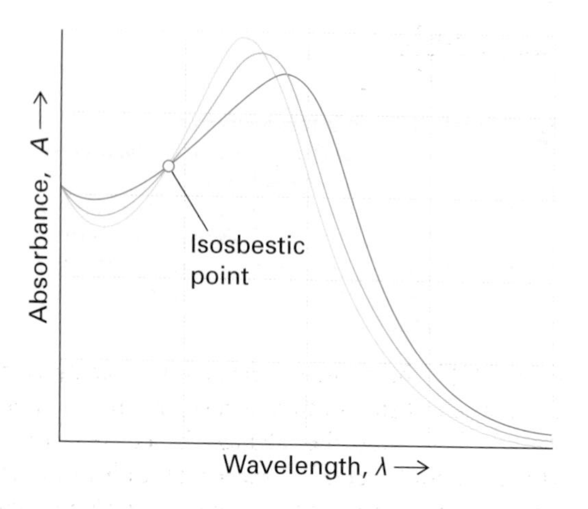

Fig. 10.3 One or more isosbestic points are formed when there are two interrelated absorbing species in solution. The three curves correspond to three different stages of the reaction A → B.

more than one such point, is compelling evidence that a solution consists of only two solutes in equilibrium with each other with no intermediates.

10.2 Applications of spectrophotometry

In a **real-time analysis**, the composition of a system is analysed while the reaction is in progress by direct spectroscopic observation of the reaction mixture. In the **flow method**, the reactants are mixed as they flow together in a chamber (Fig. 10.4). The reaction continues as the thoroughly mixed solutions flow through a capillary outlet tube at about 10 m s^{-1}, and different points along the tube correspond to different times after the start of the reaction. Spectrophotometric determination of the composition at different positions along the tube is equivalent to the determination of the composition of the reaction mixture at different times after mixing. This technique was originally developed in connection with the study of the rate at which oxygen combined with haemoglobin. Its disadvantage is that a large volume of reactant solution is necessary, because the mixture must flow continuously through the apparatus. This disadvantage is particularly important for reactions that take place very rapidly, because the flow must be rapid if it is to spread the reaction over an appreciable length of tube.

The **stopped-flow technique** avoids this disadvantage (Fig. 10.5). The two solutions are mixed very rapidly (in less than 1 ms) by injecting them into a mixing chamber designed to ensure that the flow is turbulent and that complete mixing occurs very quickly. Behind the reaction chamber there is an observation cell fitted with a plunger that moves back as the liquids flood in, but which comes up against a stop after a certain volume has been admitted. The filling of that chamber corresponds to the sudden creation of an initial sample of the reaction mixture. The reaction then continues in the thoroughly mixed solution and is monitored spectrophotometrically. Because only a small, single charge of the reaction chamber is prepared, the technique is

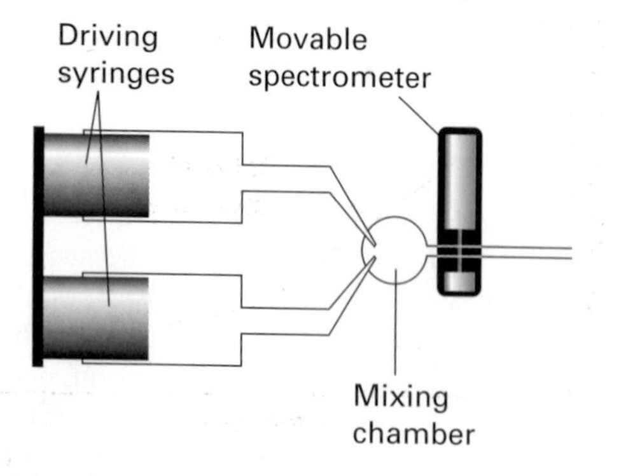

Fig. 10.4 The arrangement used in the flow technique for studying reaction rates. The reactants are squirted into the mixing chamber at a steady rate from the syringes or by using peristaltic pumps (pumps that squeeze the fluid through flexible tubes, as in our intestines). The location of the spectrometer corresponds to different times after initiation.

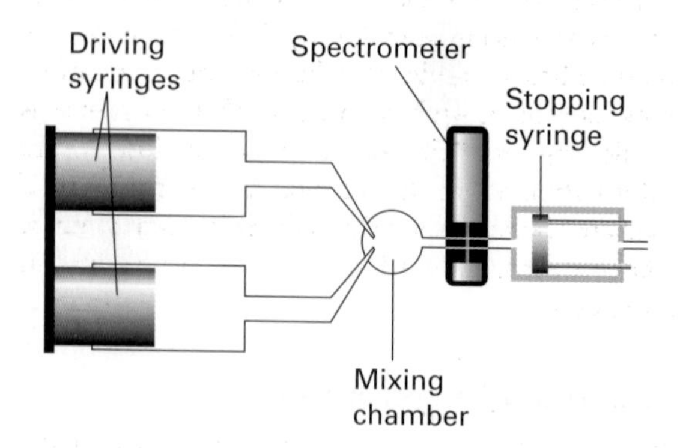

Fig. 10.5 In the stopped-flow technique the reagents are driven quickly into the mixing chamber and then the time dependence of the concentrations is monitored.

much more economical than the flow method. The suitability of the stopped-flow technique to the study of small samples means that it is appropriate for biochemical reactions, and it has been widely used to study the kinetics of enzyme action. Modern techniques of monitoring composition spectrophotometrically can span repetitively a wavelength range of 300 nm at 1 ms intervals.

Very fast reactions can be studied by **flash photolysis**, in which the sample is exposed to a brief flash of light that initiates the reaction, and then the contents of the reaction chamber are monitored spectrophotometrically. Lasers can be used to generate nanosecond flashes routinely, picosecond flashes quite readily, and flashes as brief as a few femtoseconds in special arrangements.

In contrast to real-time analysis, **quenching methods** are based on stopping, or quenching, the reaction after it has been allowed to proceed for a certain time and the composition is analysed at leisure. The quenching (of the entire mixture or of a sample drawn from it) can be achieved by cooling suddenly, by adding the mixture to a large volume of solvent, or by rapid neutralization of an acid reagent. This method is suitable only for reactions that are slow enough for there to be little reaction during the time it takes to quench the mixture.

Reaction rates

The raw data from experiments to measure reaction rates are the concentrations or partial pressures of reactants and products at a series of times after the reaction is initiated. Ideally, information on any intermediates should also be obtained, but often they cannot be studied because their existence is so fleeting or their concentration so low. More information about the reaction can be extracted if data are obtained at a series of different temperatures. The next few sections look at these observations in more detail.

10.3 The definition of rate

The rate of a reaction is defined in terms of the rate of change of the concentration of a designated species:

$$\text{Rate} = \frac{|\Delta[\text{J}]|}{\Delta t}$$

The rate defined in this expression is actually an average rate over the interval Δt. To be precise, reaction rates are defined as the derivative $|d[\text{J}]/dt|$, where the interval Δt has been allowed to become infinitesimal. This definition is the basis of identifying the instantaneous rate (see main text) with the slope of the graph of concentration against time.

where $\Delta[\text{J}]$ is the change in the molar concentration of the species J that occurs during the time interval Δt. We have put the change in concentration between modulus signs to ensure that all rates are positive: if J is a reactant, its concentration will decrease and $\Delta[\text{J}]$ will be negative, but $|\Delta[\text{J}]|$ is positive. However, because the rates at which reactants are consumed and products are formed change in the course of a reaction, it is necessary to consider the **instantaneous rate** of the reaction, its rate at a specific instant. The instantaneous rate of consumption of a reactant is the slope of a graph of its molar concentration plotted against the time, with the slope evaluated as the tangent to the graph at the instant of interest (Fig. 10.6) and reported as a positive quantity. The instantaneous rate of formation of a product is also the slope of the tangent to the

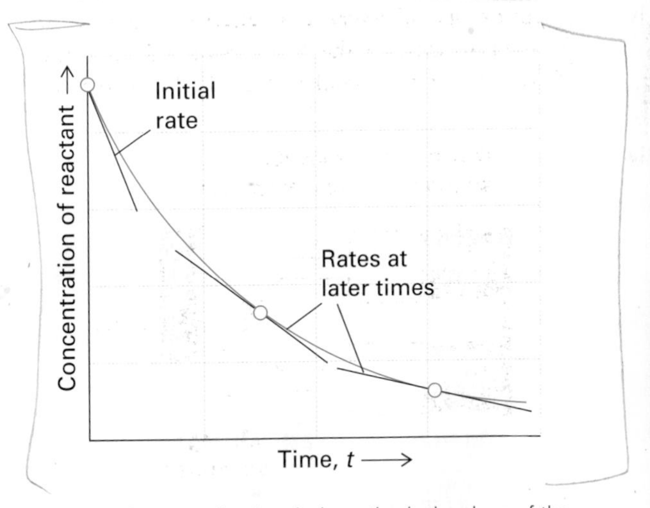

Fig. 10.6 The rate of a chemical reaction is the slope of the tangent to the curve showing the variation of concentration of a species with time. This graph is a plot of the concentration of a reactant, which is consumed as the reaction progresses. The rate of consumption decreases in the course of the reaction as the concentration of reactant decreases.

graph of its molar concentration plotted against time, and also reported as a positive quantity. The steeper the slope in either case, the greater the rate of the reaction. With the concentration measured in moles per cubic decimetre and the time in seconds, the reaction rate is reported in moles per cubic decimetre per second (mol dm^{-3} s^{-1}).

In general, the various reactants in a given reaction are consumed at different rates, and the various products are also formed at different rates. However, these rates are related by the stoichiometry of the reaction. For example, in the decomposition of urea, $(NH_2)_2CO$, in acidic solution

$$(NH_2)_2CO(aq) + 2\,H_2O(l) \rightarrow 2\,NH_4^+(aq) + CO_3^{2-}(aq)$$

provided any intermediates are not present in significant quantities the rate of formation of NH_4^+ is twice the rate of disappearance of $(NH_2)_2CO$, because for 1 mol $(NH_2)_2CO$ consumed, 2 mol NH_4^+ is formed. Once we know the rate of formation or consumption of one substance, we can use the reaction stoichiometry to deduce the rates of formation or consumption of the other participants in the reaction. In this example, for instance,

$$\text{Rate of formation of } NH_4^+ = 2 \times \text{rate of consumption of } (NH_2)_2CO$$

One consequence of this kind of relation is that we have to be careful to specify exactly what species we mean when we report a reaction rate.

Self-test 10.1

The rate of formation of NH_3 in the reaction $N_2(g) + 3\,H_2(g) \rightarrow 2\,NH_3(g)$ was reported as 1.2 mmol dm^{-3} s^{-1} under a certain set of conditions. What is the rate of consumption of H_2?

[*Answer:* 1.8 mmol dm^{-3} s^{-1}]

10.4 Rate laws and rate constants

An empirical observation of the greatest importance is that *the rate of reaction is often found to be proportional to the molar concentrations of the reactants raised to a simple power*. For example, it may be found that the rate is directly proportional to the concentrations of the reactants A and B, so

$$\text{Rate} = k[A][B] \qquad (10.6)$$

The coefficient k, which is characteristic of the reaction being studied, is called the **rate constant**. The rate constant is independent of the concentrations of the species taking part in the reaction but depends on the temperature. An *experimentally determined* equation of this kind is called the 'rate law' of the reaction. More formally, a **rate law** is an equation that expresses the rate of reaction in terms of the molar concentrations (or partial pressures) of the species in the overall reaction (including, possibly, the products).

The units of k are always such as to convert the product of concentrations into a rate expressed as a change in concentration divided by time. For example, if the rate law is the one shown above, with concentrations expressed in mol dm^{-3}, then the units of k will be dm^3 mol^{-1} s^{-1} because

$$\overbrace{dm^3\,mol^{-1}\,s^{-1}}^{k} \times \overbrace{mol\,dm^{-3}}^{[A]} \times \overbrace{mol\,dm^{-3}}^{[B]} = \overbrace{mol\,dm^{-3}\,s^{-1}}^{\text{rate}}$$

In gas-phase studies, concentrations are commonly expressed in molecules cm^{-3}, so the rate constant for the reaction above would be expressed in cm^3 $molecule^{-1}$ s^{-1}. We can use the approach just developed to determine the units of the rate constant from rate laws of any form. For example, the rate constant for a reaction with rate law of the form $k[A]$ is commonly expressed in s^{-1}.

Illustration 10.1

Converting between rate constants

The rate constant for the reaction $O(g) + O_3(g) \rightarrow 2\,O_2(g)$ is 8.0×10^{-15} cm^3 $molecule^{-1}$ s^{-1} at 298 K. To express this rate constant in dm^3 mol^{-1} s^{-1}, we make use of the fact that 1 mol = 6.022×10^{23} molecule, so 1 molecule = (1 mol)/(6.022×10^{23}) and 1 cm = 10^{-1} dm. It follows from the procedure described in Example 0.1 that

$$k = 8.0 \times 10^{-15}\,cm^3\,molecule^{-1}\,s^{-1}$$

$$= 8.0 \times 10^{-15}\left(\frac{1\,dm}{10}\right)^3\left(\frac{1\,mol}{6.022 \times 10^{23}}\right)^{-1} s^{-1}$$

$$= \frac{8.0 \times 10^{-15} \times 6.022 \times 10^{23}}{10^3}\,dm^3\,mol^{-1}\,s^{-1}$$

$$= 4.8 \times 10^6\,dm^3\,mol^{-1}\,s^{-1}$$

Self-test 10.2

A reaction has a rate law of the form $k[A]^2[B]$. What are the units of the rate constant k if the reaction rate was measured in mol dm^{-3} s^{-1}?

[*Answer:* dm^6 mol^{-2} s^{-1}]

Once we know the rate law and the rate constant of the reaction, we can predict the rate of the reaction for any given composition of the reaction mixture. We shall also see that we can use a rate law to predict the concentrations of the reactants and products at any time after the start of the reaction. Furthermore, a rate law is also an important guide to the mechanism of the reaction, for any proposed mechanism must be consistent with the observed rate law.

10.5 Reaction order

A rate law provides a basis for the classification of reactions according to their kinetics. The advantage of having such a classification is that reactions belonging to the same class have similar kinetic behaviour—their rates and the concentrations of the reactants and products vary with composition in a similar way. The classification of reactions is based on their **order**, the power to which the concentration of a species is raised in the rate law. For example, a reaction with the rate law in eqn 10.6 (rate = k[A][B]) is *first-order* in A and first-order in B. A reaction with the rate law

$$\text{Rate} = k[\text{A}]^2 \qquad (10.7)$$

is *second-order* in A.

The **overall order** of a reaction is the sum of the orders of all the components. The two rate laws just quoted both correspond to reactions that are *second-order* overall. An example of the first type of reaction is the reformation of a DNA double helix after the double helix has been separated into two strands by raising the temperature or the pH:

$$\text{Strand} + \text{complementary strand} \rightarrow \text{double helix}$$

$$\text{Rate} = k[\text{strand}][\text{complementary strand}]$$

This reaction is first-order in each strand and second-order overall. An example of the second type is the reduction of nitrogen dioxide by carbon monoxide,

$$NO_2(g) + CO(g) \rightarrow NO(g) + CO_2(g)$$

$$\text{Rate} = k[NO_2]^2$$

which is second-order in NO_2 and, because no other species occurs in the rate law, second-order overall. The rate of the latter reaction is independent of the concentration of CO provided that some CO is present. This independence of concentration is expressed by saying that the reaction is *zero-order* in CO, because a concentration raised to the power zero is 1 ($[CO]^0 = 1$, just as $x^0 = 1$ in algebra).

A reaction need not have an integral order, and many gas-phase reactions do not. For example, if a reaction is found to have the rate law

$$\text{Rate} = k[\text{A}]^{1/2}[\text{B}] \qquad (10.8)$$

then it is *half-order* in A, first-order in B, and three-halves order overall.

If a rate law is not of the form $[\text{A}]^x[\text{B}]^y[\text{C}]^z\ldots$ then the reaction does not have an overall order. Thus, the experimentally determined rate law for the gas-phase reaction $H_2(g) + Br_2(g) \rightarrow 2\,HBr(g)$ is

$$\text{Rate} = \frac{k[H_2][Br_2]^{3/2}}{[Br_2] + k'[HBr]} \qquad (10.9)$$

Although the reaction is first-order in H_2, it has an indefinite order with respect to both Br_2 and HBr and an indefinite order overall. Similarly, a typical rate law for the action of an enzyme E on a substrate S is (see Chapter 11)

$$\text{Rate} = \frac{k[\text{E}][\text{S}]}{[\text{S}] + K_M} \qquad (10.10)$$

where K_M is a constant. This rate law is first-order in the enzyme but does not have a specific order with respect to the substrate.

Under certain circumstances a complicated rate law without an overall order may simplify into a law with a definite order. For example, if the substrate concentration in the enzyme-catalysed reaction is so low that $[\text{S}] \ll K_M$, then eqn 10.10 simplifies to

$$\text{Rate} = \frac{k}{K_M}[\text{S}][\text{E}]$$

which is first-order in S, first-order in E, and second-order overall.

It is very important to note that *a rate law is established experimentally, and cannot in general be inferred from the chemical equation for the reaction*. The reaction of hydrogen and bromine, for example, has a very simple stoichiometry, but its rate law (eqn 10.9) is very complicated. In some cases, however, the rate law does reflect the reaction stoichiometry. This is the case with the reaction of hydrogen and iodine, which has the same stoichiometry as the reaction of hydrogen with bromine but a much simpler rate law:

$$H_2(g) + I_2(g) \rightarrow 2\,HI(g) \qquad \text{Rate} = k[H_2][I_2]$$

10.6 The determination of the rate law

The determination of a rate law is simplified by the **isolation method**, in which all the reactants except one are present in large excess. We can find the dependence of the rate on each of the reactants by isolating each of them in turn—by having all the other substances present in large excess—and piecing together a picture of the overall rate law.

If a reactant B is in large excess, for example, it is a good approximation to take its concentration as constant throughout the reaction. Then, although the true rate law might be

$$\text{Rate} = k[A][B]^2$$

we can approximate [B] by its initial value $[B]_0$ (from which it hardly changes in the course of the reaction) and write

$$\text{Rate} = k'[A], \text{ with } k' = k[B]_0^2$$

Because the true rate law has been forced into first-order form by assuming a constant B concentration, the effective rate law is classified as **pseudofirst-order** and k' is called the **effective rate constant** for a given, fixed concentration of B. If, instead, the concentration of A were in large excess, and hence effectively constant, then the rate law would simplify to

$$\text{Rate} = k''[B]^2, \text{ with } k'' = k[A]_0$$

This **pseudosecond-order rate law** is also much easier to analyse and identify than the complete law.

In a similar manner, a reaction may even appear to be zeroth-order. For instance, the oxidation of ethanol to acetaldehyde by NAD^+ in the liver in the presence of the enzyme liver alcohol dehydrogenase

$$CH_3CH_2OH(aq) + NAD^+(aq) + H_2O(l) \rightarrow CH_3CHO(aq) + NADH(aq) + H_3O^+(aq)$$

is zeroth-order overall as the ethanol is in excess and the concentration of the NAD^+ is maintained at a constant level by normal metabolic processes. Many reactions in aqueous solution that are reported as first- or second-order are in fact pseudofirst- or pseudosecond-order: the solvent water participates in the reaction but it is in such large excess that its concentration remains constant.

In the method of **initial rates**, which is often used in conjunction with the isolation method, the instantaneous rate is measured at the beginning of the reaction for several different initial concentrations of reactants. For example, suppose the rate law for a reaction with A isolated is

$$\text{Rate} = k'[A]^a$$

Then the initial rate of the reaction, rate_0, is given by the initial concentration of A:

$$\text{Rate}_0 = k'[A]_0^a$$

Taking logarithms gives

$$\log \text{rate}_0 = \log k' + a \log[A]_0 \qquad (10.11)$$

The following are useful relations involving logarithms:

$$\log xy = \log x + \log y$$

$$\log x/y = \log x - \log y$$

$$\log x^a = a \log x$$

This equation has the form of the equation for a straight line:

$$y = \text{intercept} + \text{slope} \times x$$

with $y = \log \text{rate}_0$ and $x = \log[A]_0$. It follows that, for a series of initial concentrations, a plot of the logarithms of the initial rates against the logarithms of the initial concentrations of A should be a straight line, and that the slope of the graph will be a, the order of the reaction with respect to the species A (Fig. 10.7).

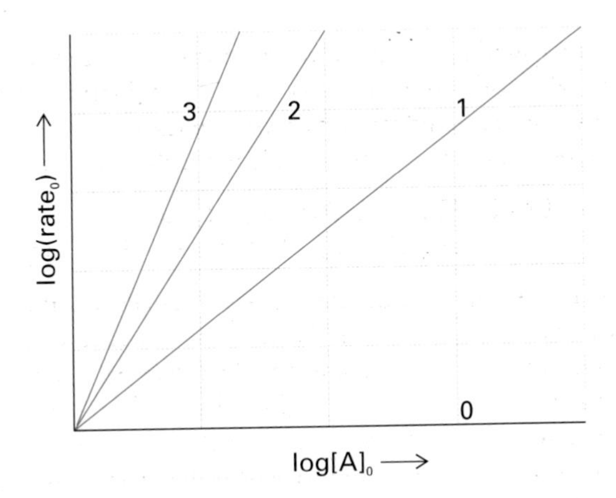

Fig. 10.7 The plot of log $rate_0$ against $\log[A]_0$ gives straight lines with slopes equal to the order of the reaction.

Example 10.1

Using the method of initial rates

The recombination of I atoms in the gas phase in the presence of argon (which removes the energy released by the formation of an I–I bond, and so prevents the immediate dissociation of a newly formed I_2 molecule) was investigated and the order of the reaction was determined by the method of initial rates. The initial rates of reaction of $2\,I(g) + Ar(g) \rightarrow I_2(g) + Ar(g)$ were as follows:

$[I]_0/(10^{-5}\ mol\ dm^{-3})$	1.0	2.0	4.0	6.0
$Rate_0/(mol\ dm^{-3}\ s^{-1})$				
(a)	8.70×10^{-4}	3.48×10^{-3}	1.39×10^{-2}	3.13×10^{-2}
(b)	4.35×10^{-3}	1.74×10^{-2}	6.96×10^{-2}	1.57×10^{-1}
(c)	8.69×10^{-3}	3.47×10^{-2}	1.38×10^{-1}	3.13×10^{-1}

The Ar concentrations are (a) 1.0×10^{-3} mol dm^{-3}, (b) 5.0×10^{-3} mol dm^{-3}, and (c) 1.0×10^{-2} mol dm^{-3}. Find the orders of reaction with respect to I and Ar and the rate constant.

Strategy For constant $[Ar]_0$, the initial rate law has the form $rate_0 = k'[I]_0^a$, with $k' = k[Ar]_0^b$, so

$$\log rate_0 = \log k' + a \log[I]_0$$

We need to make a plot of log $rate_0$ against $\log[I]_0$ for a given $[Ar]_0$ and find the rate from the slope and the value of k' from the intercept at $\log[I]_0 = 0$. Then, because

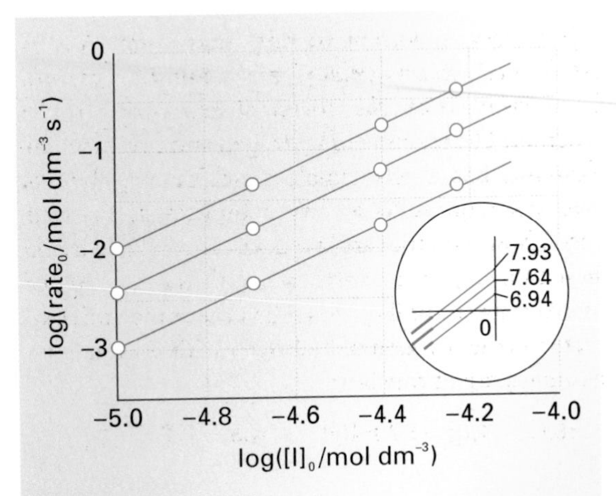

Fig. 10.8 The plots of the data in Example 10.1 for finding the order with respect to I.

$$\log k' = \log k + b \log[Ar]_0$$

plot $\log k'$ against $\log[Ar]_0$ to find $\log k$ from the intercept and b from the slope.

Solution The data give the following points for the graph:

$\log([I]_0/mol\ dm^{-3})$	−5.00	−4.70	−4.40	−4.22
$\log(rate_0/mol\ dm^{-3}\ s^{-1})$				
(a)	−2.971	−2.458	−1.857	−1.504
(b)	−2.362	−1.760	−1.157	−0.804
(c)	−1.971	−1.460	−0.860	−0.504

The graph of the data is shown in Fig. 10.8. The slopes of the lines are 2 and the effective rate constants k' are as follows:

$[Ar]_0/(mol\ dm^{-3})$	1.0×10^{-3}	5.0×10^{-3}	1.0×10^{-2}
$\log([Ar]_0/mol\ dm^{-3})$	−3.00	−2.30	−2.00
$\log(k'/mol^{-1}\ dm^3\ s^{-1})$	6.94	7.64	7.93

Figure 10.9 is the plot of $\log k'$ against $\log[Ar]_0$. The slope is 1, so $b = 1$. The intercept at $\log[Ar]_0 = 0$ is $\log k = 9.91$, so $k = 8.6 \times 10^9\ mol^{-2}\ dm^6\ s^{-1}$. The overall (initial) rate law is

$$Rate = k[I]_0^2[Ar]_0$$

A note on good practice When taking the common logarithm of a number of the form $x.xx \times 10^n$, there are *four* significant figures in the answer: the figure before

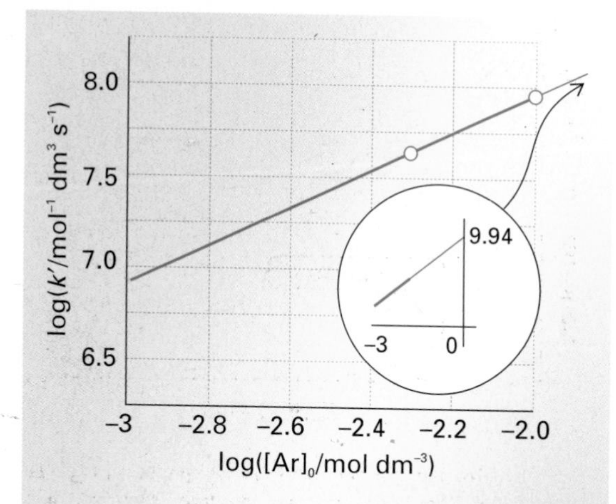

Fig. 10.9 The plots of the data in Example 10.1 for finding the order with respect to Ar.

the decimal point is simply the power of 10. Strictly, the logarithms are of the quantity divided by its units.

Self-test 10.3

The initial rate of a certain reaction depended on concentration of a substance J as follows:

$[J]_0/(10^{-3}$ mol dm$^{-3})$	5.0	10.2	17	30
Rate$_0/(10^{-7}$ mol dm^{-3} s$^{-1})$	3.6	9.6	41	130

Find the order of the reaction with respect to J and the rate constant.

[*Answer:* 2, 1.6×10^{-2} mol^{-1} dm^3 s^{-1}]

The method of initial rates might not reveal the entire rate law, as in a complex reaction the products themselves might affect the rate. That is the case for the synthesis of HBr, as eqn 10.9 shows that the rate law depends on the concentration of HBr, none of which is present initially.

10.7 Integrated rate laws

A rate law tells us the rate of the reaction at a given instant (when the reaction mixture has a particular composition). That is rather like being given the speed of a car at each point of its journey. For a car journey, we may want to know the distance that a car has travelled at a certain time given its varying speed. Similarly, for a chemical reaction, we may want to know the composition of the reaction mixture at a given time given the varying rate of the reaction. An **integrated rate law** is an expression that gives the concentration of a species as a function of the time.

Integrated rate laws have two principal uses. One is to predict the concentration of a species at any time after the start of the reaction. Another is to help to find the rate constant and order of the reaction. Indeed, although we have introduced rate laws through a discussion of the determination of reaction rates, these rates are rarely measured directly because slopes are so difficult to determine accurately. Almost all experimental work in chemical kinetics deals with integrated rate laws, their great advantage being that they are expressed in terms of the experimental observables of concentration and time. Computers can be used to find the integrated form of even the most complex rate laws numerically and in some cases can be used to obtain closed, algebraic expressions. However, in a number of simple cases solutions can be obtained by elementary techniques and prove to be very useful.

For a chemical reaction and first-order rate law of the form A → products,

$$\text{Rate of consumption of A} = k[\mathrm{A}] \qquad (10.12)$$

the integrated rate law is

$$\ln \frac{[\mathrm{A}]_0}{[\mathrm{A}]} = kt \qquad (10.13a)$$

where $[\mathrm{A}]_0$ is the initial concentration of A. Two alternative forms of this expression are

$$\ln[\mathrm{A}] = \ln[\mathrm{A}]_0 - kt \qquad (10.13b)$$

$$[\mathrm{A}] = [\mathrm{A}]_0\, \mathrm{e}^{-kt} \qquad (10.13c)$$

Equation 10.13c has the form of an **exponential decay** (Fig. 10.10). A common feature of all first-order reactions, therefore, is that *the concentration of the reactant decays exponentially with time.*

Derivation 10.1

First-order integrated rate laws

Our first step is to express the rate of consumption of a reactant A mathematically. In mathematics, the slope of a plot of [A] against *t* is the 'derivative' of [A] with respect to t, and denoted d[A]/dt. The rate of consumption of a reactant, a positive quantity, is defined as the negative of this slope, so we can interpret the rate as –d[A]/dt. It follows that a first-order rate equation has the form

$$-\frac{d[A]}{dt} = k[A]$$

The concepts of calculus used in this derivation are reviewed in Appendix 2.

This expression is an example of a 'differential equation'. Because the terms d[A] and dt may be manipulated like any algebraic quantity, we rearrange the differential equation into

$$\frac{d[A]}{[A]} = -k dt$$

and then integrate both sides. Integration from $t = 0$, when the concentration of A is $[A]_0$, to the time of interest, t, when the molar concentration of A is [A], is written as

$$\int_{[A]_0}^{[A]} \frac{d[A]}{[A]} = -k \int_0^t dt$$

We now use the standard integral

$$\int \frac{dx}{x} = \ln x + \text{constant}$$

and obtain the expression

$$\ln[A] - \ln[A]_0 = -kt$$

which rearranges into eqn 10.13a.

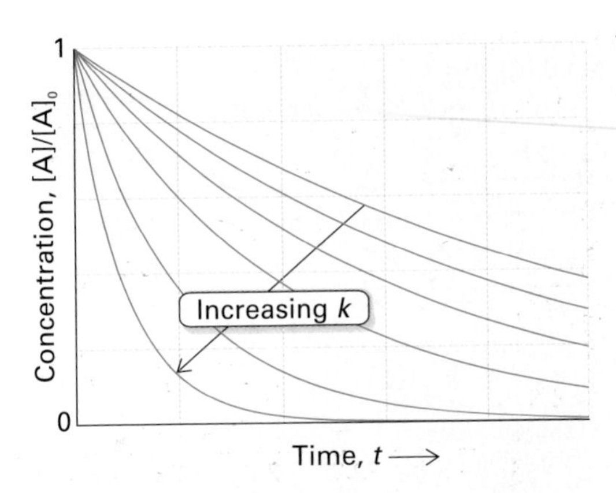

Fig. 10.10 The exponential decay of the reactant in a first-order reaction. The greater the rate constant, the more rapid is the decay.

Equation 10.13c lets us predict the concentration of A at any time after the start of the reaction. Equation 10.13b shows that if we plot ln [A] against t, then we will get a straight line if the reaction is first-order. If the experimental data do not give a straight line when plotted in this way, then the reaction is not first-order. If the line is straight, then it follows from eqn 10.13b that its slope is $-k$, so we can also determine the rate constant from the graph. Some rate constants determined in this way are given in Table 10.2.

The web site contains links to databases of rate constants of chemical reactions.

Table 10.2 *Kinetic data for first-order reactions*

Reaction	Phase	θ/°C	k/s^{-1}	$t_{1/2}$
$2\ N_2O_5 \rightarrow 4\ NO_2 + \mathbf{O_2}$	g	25	3.38×10^{-5}	2.85 h
$2\ N_2O_5 \rightarrow 4\ NO_2 + \mathbf{O_2}$	Br_2(l)	25	4.27×10^{-5}	2.25 h
$\mathbf{C_2H_6} \rightarrow 2\ CH_3$	g	700	5.46×10^{-4}	21.2 min
Cyclopropane → propene	g	500	6.17×10^{-4}	17.2 min

The rate constant is for the rate of formation or consumption of the species in bold type. The rate laws for the other species may be obtained from the reaction stoichiometry.

Example 10.2

Analysing a first-order reaction

The variation in the partial pressure p_A of azomethane with time was followed at 460 K, with the results given below. Confirm that the decomposition $CH_3N_2CH_3(g) \rightarrow CH_3CH_3(g) + N_2(g)$ is first-order in $CH_3N_2CH_3$, and find the rate constant at this temperature.

t/s	0	1000	2000	3000	4000
$p_A/(10^{-2}$ Torr)	10.20	5.72	3.99	2.78	1.94

Strategy The easiest procedure is to plot ln(p/Torr) against t/s and expect to obtain a straight line. If the graph is straight, then the slope is $-k$.

Solution We draw up the following table:

t/s	0	1000	2000	3000	4000
$p_A/(10^{-2}$ Torr)	10.20	5.72	3.99	2.78	1.94
ln(p_A/Torr)	−2.28	−2.86	−3.22	−3.58	−3.94

The graph of the data is shown in Fig. 10.11. The plot is straight, confirming a first-order reaction. Its least-squares best-fit slope is -4.04×10^{-4}, so $k = 4.04 \times 10^{-4}$ s^{-1}. Note that the total pressure, the sum of the partial pressures of the three substances, increases as the reaction proceeds, initially $p = 102.0$ mTorr and after 4000 s (over 1 h) is 184.6 mTorr.

The text's web site features interactive applets for data analysis.

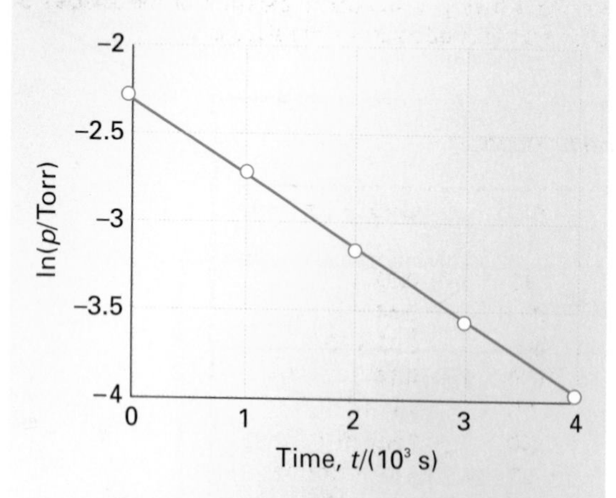

Fig. 10.11 The determination of the rate constant of a first-order reaction. A straight line is obtained when ln[A] (or ln p, where p is the partial pressure of the species of interest) is plotted against t; the slope is $-k$. The data are from Example 10.2.

Self-test 10.4

The concentration of N_2O_5 in liquid bromine varied with time as follows:

t/s	0	200	400	600	1000
$[N_2O_5]/(\text{mol dm}^{-3})$	0.110	0.073	0.048	0.032	0.014

Confirm that the reaction is first-order in N_2O_5 and determine the rate constant.

[*Answer:* 2.1×10^{-3} s^{-1}]

Now we need to see how the concentration varies with time for a reaction and second-order rate law of the form A → products,

$$\text{Rate of consumption of A} = k[\text{A}]^2 \qquad (10.14)$$

As before, we suppose that the concentration of A at $t = 0$ is $[\text{A}]_0$ and find that

$$\frac{1}{[\text{A}]_0} - \frac{1}{[\text{A}]} = kt \qquad (10.15\text{a})$$

Two alternative forms of eqn 10.15a are

$$\frac{1}{[\text{A}]} = \frac{1}{[\text{A}]_0} + kt \qquad (10.15\text{b})$$

$$[\text{A}] = \frac{[\text{A}]_0}{1 + kt[\text{A}]_0} \qquad (10.15\text{c})$$

Derivation 10.2

Second-order integrated rate laws

As before, the rate of consumption of the reactant A is $-\text{d}[\text{A}]/\text{d}t$, so the differential equation for the rate law is

$$-\frac{\text{d}[\text{A}]}{\text{d}t} = k[\text{A}]^2$$

To solve this equation, we rearrange it into

$$\frac{\text{d}[\text{A}]}{[\text{A}]^2} = -k\text{d}t$$

and integrate it between $t = 0$, when the concentration of A is $[\text{A}]_0$, and the time of interest t, when the concentration of A is [A]:

$$\int_{[\text{A}]_0}^{[\text{A}]} \frac{\text{d}[\text{A}]}{[\text{A}]^2} = -k\int_0^t \text{d}t$$

The term on the right is $-kt$. We evaluate the integral on the left by using the standard form

$$\int \frac{dx}{x^2} = -\frac{1}{x} + \text{constant}$$

which implies that

$$\int_a^b \frac{dx}{x^2} = \left\{-\frac{1}{x} + \text{constant}\right\}\Bigg|_b - \left\{-\frac{1}{x} + \text{constant}\right\}\Bigg|_a$$

$$= -\frac{1}{b} + \frac{1}{a}$$

and so obtain eqn 10.15a.

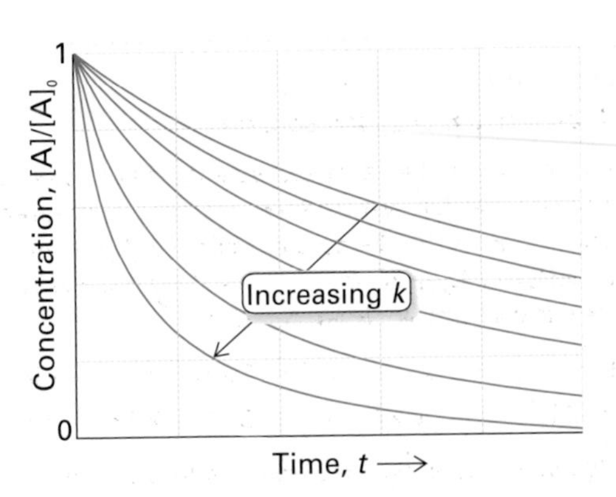

Fig. 10.12 The variation with time of the concentration of a reactant in a second-order reaction.

Equation 10.15c enables us to predict the concentration of A at any time after the start of the reaction (Fig. 10.12). Equation 10.15b shows that to test for a second-order reaction we should plot 1/[A] against t and expect a straight line. If the line is straight, the reaction is second-order in A and the slope of the line is equal to the rate constant (Fig. 10.13). Some rate constants determined in this way are given in Table 10.3.

From plots of [A] against t, we see that the concentration of A approaches zero more slowly in a second-order reaction than in a first-order reaction with the same initial rate (Fig. 10.14). That is, reactants that decay by a second-order process die away more slowly at low concentrations than would be

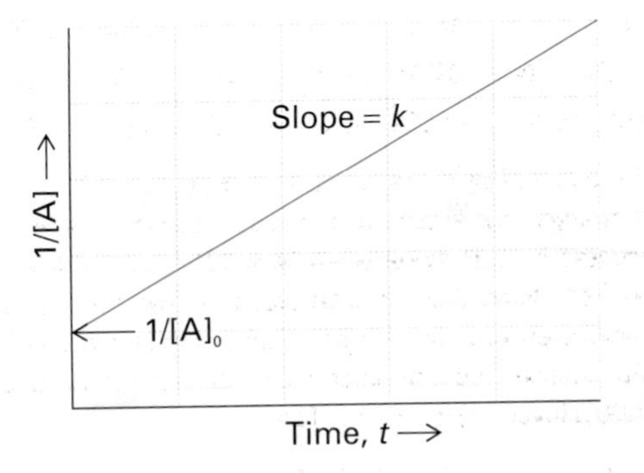

Fig. 10.13 The determination of the rate constant of a second-order reaction. A straight line is obtained when 1/[A] (or $1/p$, where p is the partial pressure of the species of interest) is plotted against t; the slope is k.

Table 10.3 *Kinetic data for second-order reactions*

Reaction	Phase	θ/°C	k/(dm^3 mol^{-1} s^{-1})
$2\,NOBr \rightarrow 2\,NO + \mathbf{Br_2}$	g	10	0.80
$2\,NO_2 \rightarrow 2\,NO + \mathbf{O_2}$	g	300	0.54
$H_2 + I_2 \rightarrow 2\,HI$	g	400	2.42×10^{-2}
$D_2 + HCl \rightarrow DH + DCl$	g	600	0.141
$2\,I \rightarrow I_2$	g	23	7×10^{9}
	hexane	50	1.8×10^{10}
$\mathbf{CH_3Cl} + CH_3O^-$	$CH_3OH(l)$	20	2.29×10^{-6}
$\mathbf{CH_3Br} + CH_3O^-$	$CH_3OH(l)$	20	9.23×10^{-6}
$H^+ + OH^- \rightarrow H_2O$	water	25	1.5×10^{11}

The rate constant is for the rate of formation or consumption of the species in bold type. The rate laws for the other species may be obtained from the reaction stoichiometry.

Table 10.4 *Integrated rate laws*

Order	Reaction type	Rate law	Integrated rate law
0	$A \rightarrow P$	rate = k	$[P] = kt$ for $kt \leq [A]_0$
1	$A \rightarrow P$	rate = $k[A]$	$[P] = [A]_0(1 - e^{-kt})$
2	$A \rightarrow P$	rate = $k[A]^2$	$[P] = \dfrac{kt[A]_0^2}{1 + kt[A]_0}$
	$A + B \rightarrow P$	rate = $k[A][B]$	$[P] = \dfrac{[A]_0[B]_0(1 - e^{([B]_0-[A]_0)kt})}{[A]_0 - [B]_0\, e^{([B]_0-[A]_0)kt}}$

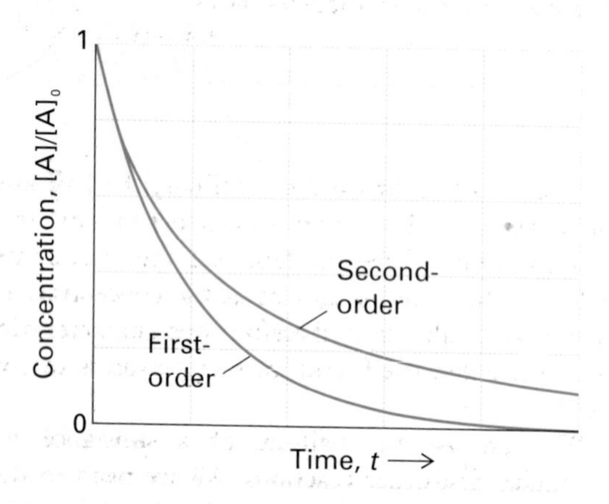

Fig. 10.14 Although the initial decay of a second-order reaction may be rapid, later the concentration approaches zero more slowly than in a first-order reaction with the same initial rate (compare Fig. 10.10).

expected if the decay was first-order. A point of interest in this connection is that pollutants commonly disappear by second-order processes, so it takes a very long time for them to decline to acceptable levels.

Table 10.4 summarizes the integrated rate laws for a variety of simple reaction types.

10.8 Half-lives and time constants

A useful indication of the rate of a first-order chemical reaction is the **half-life**, $t_{1/2}$, of a reactant, which is the time it takes for the concentration of the species to fall to half its initial value. We can find the half-life of a species A that decays in a first-order reaction (eqn 10.12) by substituting $[A] = \frac{1}{2}[A]_0$ and $t = t_{1/2}$ into eqn 10.13a:

$$kt_{1/2} = -\ln \frac{\frac{1}{2}[A]_0}{[A]_0} = -\ln \tfrac{1}{2} = \ln 2$$

It follows that

$$t_{1/2} = \frac{\ln 2}{k} \tag{10.16}$$

Illustration 10.2

Using a half-life I

Because the rate constant for the first-order reaction

$$N_2O_5(g) \rightarrow 2\,NO_2(g) + \tfrac{1}{2}\,O_2(g)$$

$$\text{Rate of consumption of } N_2O_5 = k[N_2O_5]$$

is equal to $6.76 \times 10^{-5}\ s^{-1}$ at 25°C, the half-life of N_2O_5 is 2.85 h. Hence, the concentration of N_2O_5 falls to half its initial value in 2.85 h, and then to half that concentration again in a further 2.85 h, and so on (Fig. 10.15).

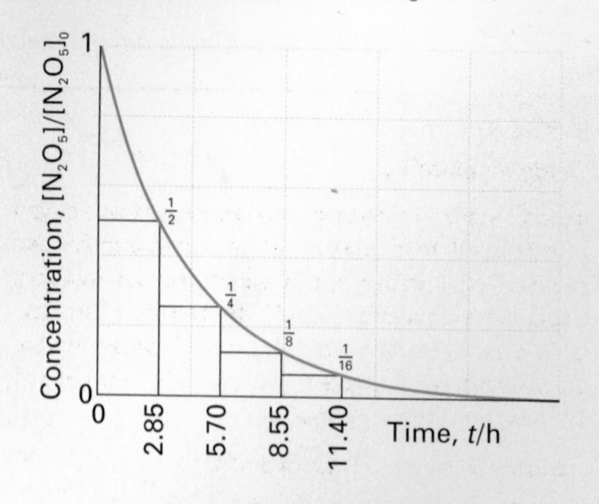

Fig. 10.15 The molar concentration of N_2O_5 after a succession of half-lives.

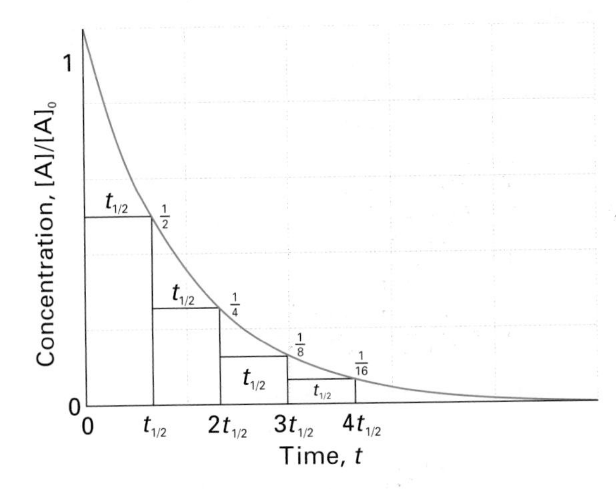

Fig. 10.16 In each successive period of duration $t_{1/2}$, the concentration of a reactant in a first-order reaction decays to half its value at the start of that period. After n such periods, the concentration is $(\frac{1}{2})^n$ of its initial concentration.

The main point to note about eqn 10.16 is that, *for a first-order reaction, the half-life of a reactant is independent of its concentration*. It follows that if the concentration of A at some arbitrary stage of the reaction is [A], then the concentration will fall to $\frac{1}{2}$[A] after an interval of $(\ln 2)/k$ whatever the actual value of [A] (Fig. 10.16). Some half-lives are given in Table 10.2.

Illustration 10.3

Using a half-life II

In acidic solution, the disaccharide sucrose (cane sugar) is converted to a mixture of the monosaccharides glucose and fructose in a pseudofirst-order reaction. Under certain conditions of pH, the half-life of sucrose is 28.4 min. To calculate how long it takes for the concentration of a sample to fall from 8.0 mmol dm^{-3} to 1.0 mmol dm^{-3} we note that

Molar concentration/(mmol dm^{-3}):

$$8.0 \xrightarrow{28.4\ \text{min}} 4.0 \xrightarrow{28.4\ \text{min}} 2.0 \xrightarrow{28.4\ \text{min}} 1.0$$

The total time required is 3 × 28.4 min = 85.2 min.

Self-test 10.5

The half-life of a substrate in a certain enzyme-catalysed first-order reaction is 138 s. How long is required for the concentration of substrate to fall from 1.28 mmol dm^{-3} to 0.040 mmol dm^{-3}?

[*Answer:* 690 s]

Self-test 10.6

Derive an expression for the half-life of a second-order reaction in terms of the rate constant k.

[*Answer:* $t_{1/2} = 1/k[A]_0$]

In contrast to first-order reactions, the half-life of a second-order reaction does depend on the concentration of the reactant (see the answer to Self-test 10.6), and lengthens as the concentration of reactant falls. It is therefore not characteristic of the reaction itself, and for that reason is rarely used.

We can use the half-life of a substance to recognize first-order reactions. All we need to do is inspect a set of data of composition against time. If we see that the initial concentration falls to half its value in a certain time, and that another concentration falls to half its value in the same time, then we can infer that the reaction is first-order. The first-order character can then be confirmed by plotting ln[A] against t and obtaining a straight line, as indicated earlier.

Another indication of the rate of a first-order reaction is the **time constant**, τ, the time required for the concentration of a reactant to fall to 1/e of its initial value. From eqn 10.13a it follows that

Set $[A] = [A]_0/e$

$$k\tau = -\ln\left(\frac{[A]_0/e}{[A]_0}\right) = -\ln\frac{1}{e} = \ln e = 1$$

Hence, the time constant is the reciprocal of the rate constant:

$$\tau = \frac{1}{k} \qquad (10.17)$$

The temperature dependence of reaction rates

The rates of most chemical reactions increase as the temperature is raised. Many organic reactions in solution lie somewhere in the range spanned by the hydrolysis of methyl ethanoate (for which the rate constant at 35°C is 1.8 times that at 25°C) and the hydrolysis of sucrose (for which the factor is 4.1). Enzyme-catalysed reactions may show a more complex temperature dependence because raising the temperature may provoke conformational changes that lower the effectiveness of the enzyme. Indeed, one of the reasons why we fight infection with a fever is to upset the balance of reaction rates in the infecting organism, and hence destroy it, by the increase in temperature. There is a fine line, though, between killing an invader and killing the invaded!

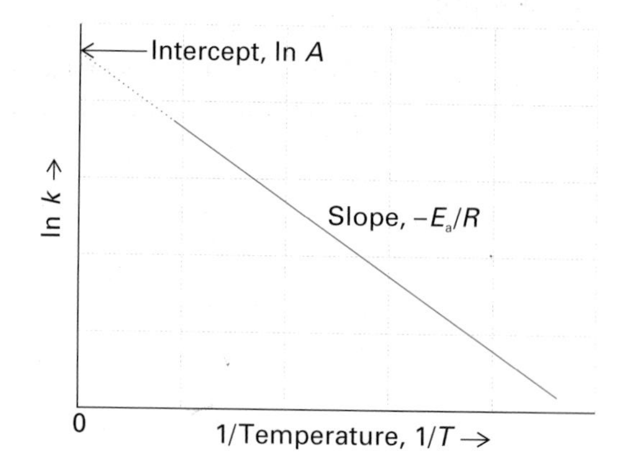

Fig. 10.17 The general form of an Arrhenius plot of $\ln k$ against $1/T$. The slope is equal to $-E_a/R$ and the intercept at $1/T = 0$ is equal to $\ln A$.

10.9 The Arrhenius parameters

As data on reaction rates were accumulated towards the end of the nineteenth century, the Swedish chemist Svante Arrhenius noted that almost all of them showed a similar dependence on the temperature. In particular, he noted that a graph of $\ln k$, where k is the rate constant for the reaction, against $1/T$, where T is the (absolute) temperature at which k is measured, gives a straight line with a slope that is characteristic of the reaction (Fig. 10.17). The mathematical expression of this conclusion is that the rate constant varies with temperature as

$$\ln k = \text{intercept} + \text{slope} \times \frac{1}{T}$$

This expression is normally written as the **Arrhenius equation**

$$\ln k = \ln A - \frac{E_a}{RT} \qquad (10.18)$$

or alternatively as

$$k = Ae^{-E_a/RT} \qquad (10.19)$$

The parameter A (which has the same units as k) is called the **pre-exponential factor**, and E_a (which is a molar energy and normally expressed as kilojoules per mole) is called the **activation energy**.

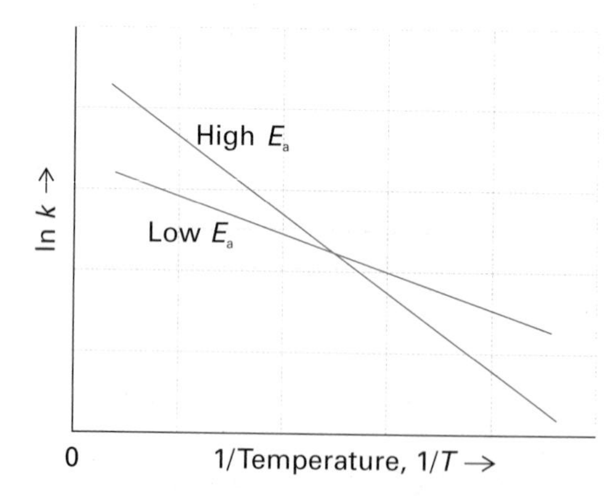

Fig. 10.18 These two Arrhenius plots correspond to two different activation energies. Note that the plot corresponding to the higher activation energy is steeper, indicating that the rate of that reaction is more sensitive to temperature.

Collectively, A and E_a are called the **Arrhenius parameters** of the reaction (Table 10.5).

A practical point to note from eqn 10.18 and illustrated in Fig. 10.18 is that a high activation energy corresponds to a reaction rate that is very sensitive to temperature (the Arrhenius plot has a steep slope). Conversely, a small activation energy indicates a reaction rate that varies only slightly with temperature (the slope is shallow). A reaction with zero activation energy, such as for some radical recombination reactions in the gas phase, has a rate that is largely independent of temperature.

Table 10.5 *Arrhenius parameters*

First-order reactions	A/s^{-1}	$E_a/(kJ\ mol^{-1})$
Cyclopropene → propane	1.58×10^{15}	272
$CH_3NC \rightarrow CH_3CN$	3.98×10^{13}	160
cis-CHD=CHD → *trans*-CHD=CHD	3.16×10^{12}	256
Cyclobutane → $2\ C_2H_4$	3.98×10^{15}	261
$2\ N_2O_5 \rightarrow 4\ NO_2 + O_2$	4.94×10^{13}	103
$N_2O + N_2 + O$	7.94×10^{11}	250

Second-order reactions	$A/(dm^3\ mol^{-1}\ s^{-1})$	$E_a/(kJ\ mol^{-1})$
Gas phase		
$O + N_2 \rightarrow NO + H$	1×10^{11}	315
$OH + H_2 \rightarrow H_2 + H$	8×10^{10}	42
$Cl + H_2 \rightarrow HCl + H$	8×10^{10}	23
$CH_3 + CH_3 \rightarrow C_2H_6$	2×10^{10}	0
$NO + Cl_2 \rightarrow NOCl + Cl$	4×10^{9}	85
Solution		
$NaC_2H_5O + CH_3I$ in ethanol	2.42×10^{11}	81.6
$C_2H_5Br + OH^-$ in water	4.30×10^{11}	89.5
$CH_3I + S_2O_3^{2-}$ in water	2.19×10^{12}	78.7
Sucrose + H_2O in acidic water	1.50×10^{15}	107.9

Example 10.3

Determining the Arrhenius parameters

The rate of the second-order decomposition of acetaldehyde (ethanal, CH_3CHO) was measured over the range 700–1000 K, and the rate constants that were found are reported below. Determine the activation energy and the pre-exponential factor.

T/K	700	730	760	790
$k/(mol^{-1}\ dm^3\ s^{-1})$	0.011	0.035	0.105	0.343
T/K	810	840	910	1000
$k/(mol^{-1}\ dm^3\ s^{-1})$	0.789	2.17	20.0	145

Strategy We plot ln k against $1/T$ and expect a straight line. The slope is $-E_a/R$ and the intercept of the extrapolation to $1/T = 0$ is ln A. It is best to do a least-squares fit of the data to a straight line. Note that A has the same units as k.

Solution The Arrhenius plot is shown in Fig. 10.19. The least-squares best fit of the line has slope -2.265×10^4

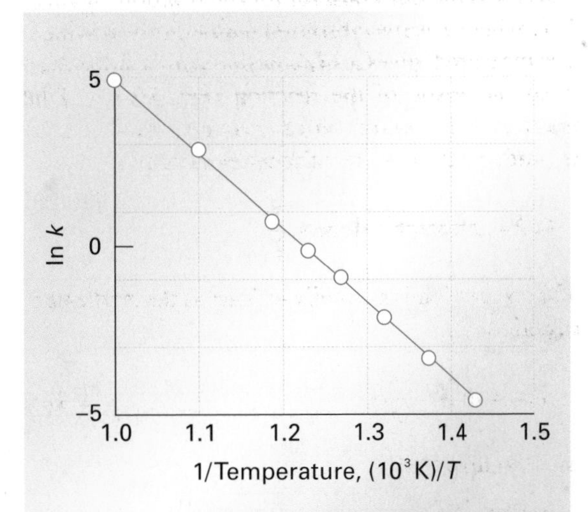

Fig. 10.19 The Arrhenius plot for the decomposition of CH_3CHO, and the best (least-squares) straight line fitted to the data points. The data are from Example 10.3.

and intercept (which is well off the graph) 27.7. Therefore,

$$E_a = -R \times \text{slope}$$
$$= -(8.3145 \text{ J K}^{-1} \text{ mol}^{-1}) \times (-2.265 \times 10^4 \text{ K})$$
$$= 188 \text{ kJ mol}^{-1}$$

and

$$A = e^{27.7} \text{ mol}^{-1} \text{ dm}^3 \text{ s}^{-1} = 1.1 \times 10^{12} \text{ mol}^{-1} \text{ dm}^3 \text{ s}^{-1}$$

Self-test 10.7

Determine A and E_a from the following data:

T/K	300	350	400
k/(mol^{-1} dm^3 s^{-1})	7.9×10^6	3.0×10^7	7.9×10^7

T/K	450	500
k/(mol^{-1} dm^3 s^{-1})	1.7×10^8	3.2×10^8

[*Answer:* 8×10^{10} mol^{-1} dm^3 s^{-1}, 23 kJ mol^{-1}]

Once the activation energy of a reaction is known, it is a simple matter to predict the value of a rate constant k' at a temperature T' from its value k at another temperature T. To do so, we write

$$\ln k = \ln A - \frac{E_a}{RT}$$

and then subtract eqn 10.18, so obtaining

$$\ln k' - \ln k = -\frac{E_a}{RT'} + \frac{E_a}{RT}$$

We can rearrange this expression to

$$\ln \frac{k'}{k} = \frac{E_a}{R}\left(\frac{1}{T} - \frac{1}{T'}\right) \quad (10.20)$$

Illustration 10.4

The temperature dependence of a rate constant

For a reaction with an activation energy of 50 kJ mol^{-1}, an increase in the temperature from 25°C to 37°C (body temperature) corresponds to

$$\ln \frac{k'}{k} = \frac{50 \times 10^3 \text{ J mol}^{-1}}{8.3145 \text{ J K}^{-1} \text{ mol}^{-1}}\left(\frac{1}{298 \text{ K}} - \frac{1}{310 \text{ K}}\right)$$
$$= \frac{50 \times 10^3}{8.3145}\left(\frac{1}{298} - \frac{1}{310}\right)$$

(The right-hand side evaluates to 0.7812..., but we take the next step before evaluating the answer.) By taking natural antilogarithms (that is, by forming e^x), $k' = 2.18k$. This result corresponds to slightly more than a doubling of the rate constant.

Self-test 10.8

The activation energy of one of the reactions in a biochemical process is 87 kJ mol^{-1}. What is the change in rate constant when the temperature falls from 37°C to 15°C?

[*Answer:* $k' = 0.076k$]

10.10 Collision theory

We can understand the origin of the Arrhenius parameters most simply by considering a class of gas-phase reactions in which reaction occurs when two molecules meet.[2] In this **collision theory** of reaction rates it is supposed that reaction occurs only if two molecules collide with a certain minimum kinetic energy along their line of approach (Fig. 10.20). In collision theory, a reaction resembles the collision of two defective billiard balls: the balls bounce apart if they collide with only a small energy, but might smash each other into fragments (products) if they collide with more than a certain

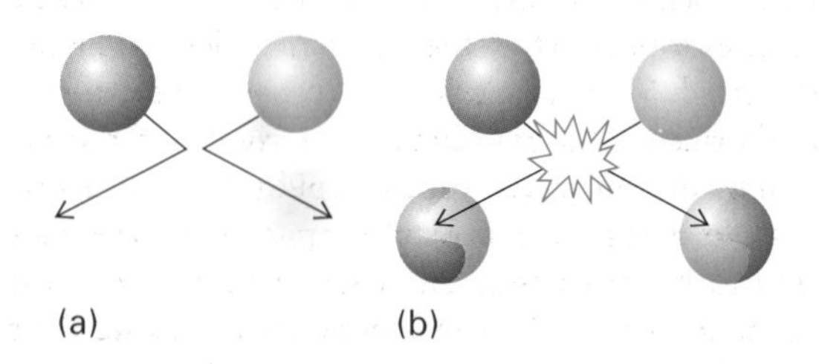

Fig. 10.20 In the collision theory of gas-phase chemical reactions, reaction occurs when two molecules collide, but only if the collision is sufficiently vigorous. (a) An insufficiently vigorous collision: the reactant molecules collide but bounce apart unchanged. (b) A sufficiently vigorous collision results in a reaction.

[2] In the terminology to be introduced in Section 11.4, we are considering bimolecular gas-phase reactions.

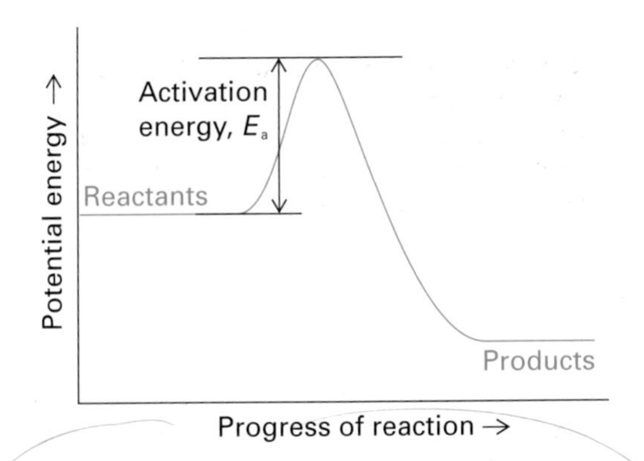

Fig. 10.21 A reaction profile. The graph depicts schematically the changing potential energy of two species that approach, collide, and then go on to form products. The activation energy is the height of the barrier above the potential energy of the reactants.

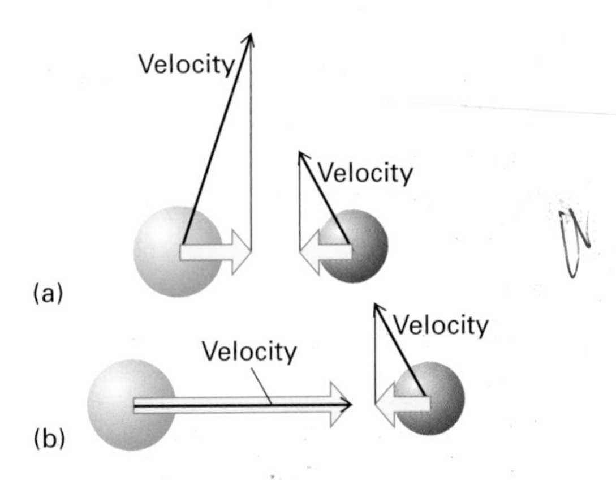

Fig. 10.22 The criterion for a successful collision is that the two reactant species should collide with a kinetic energy along their line of approach that exceeds a certain minimum value E_a that is characteristic of the reaction: (a) low kinetic energy of approach; (b) high kinetic energy of approach. The two molecules might also have components of velocity (and an associated kinetic energy) in other directions (for example, the two molecules depicted here might be moving up the page as well as towards each other); but only the energy associated with their mutual approach can be used to overcome the activation energy.

minimum kinetic energy. This model of a reaction is a reasonable first approximation to the types of process that take place in planetary atmospheres and govern their compositions and temperature profiles.

A **reaction profile** in collision theory is a graph showing the variation in potential energy as one reactant molecule approaches another and the products then separate (Fig. 10.21). On the left, the horizontal line represents the potential energy of the two reactant molecules that are far apart from one another. The potential energy rises from this value only when the separation of the molecules is so small that they are in contact, when it rises as bonds bend and start to break. The potential energy reaches a peak when the two molecules are highly distorted. Then it starts to decrease as new bonds are formed. At separations to the right of the maximum, the potential energy rapidly falls to a low value as the product molecules separate. For the reaction to be successful, the reactant molecules must approach with sufficient kinetic energy along their line of approach to carry them over the **activation barrier**, the peak in the reaction profile. As we shall see, we can identify the height of the activation barrier with the activation energy of the reaction.

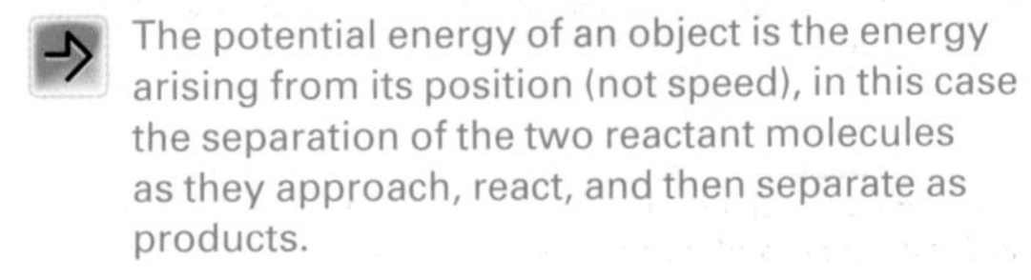

The potential energy of an object is the energy arising from its position (not speed), in this case the separation of the two reactant molecules as they approach, react, and then separate as products.

With the reaction profile in mind, it is quite easy to establish that collision theory accounts for Arrhenius behaviour. Thus, **collision frequency**, the rate of collisions between species A and B, is proportional to both their concentrations: if the concentration of B is doubled, then the rate at which A molecules collide with B molecules is doubled, and if the concentration of A is doubled, then the rate at which B molecules collide with A molecules is also doubled. It follows that the collision frequency of A and B molecules is directly proportional to the concentrations of A and B, and we can write

$$\text{Collision frequency} \propto [\mathrm{A}][\mathrm{B}]$$

Next, we need to multiply the collision frequency by a factor f that represents the fraction of collisions that occur with at least a kinetic energy E_a along the line of approach (Fig. 10.22), as only these collisions will lead to the formation of products. Molecules that approach with less than a kinetic energy E_a will behave like a ball that rolls towards the activation barrier, fails to surmount it, and rolls back. We saw in Section 1.6 that only small fractions of molecules in the gas phase have very high speeds and that the

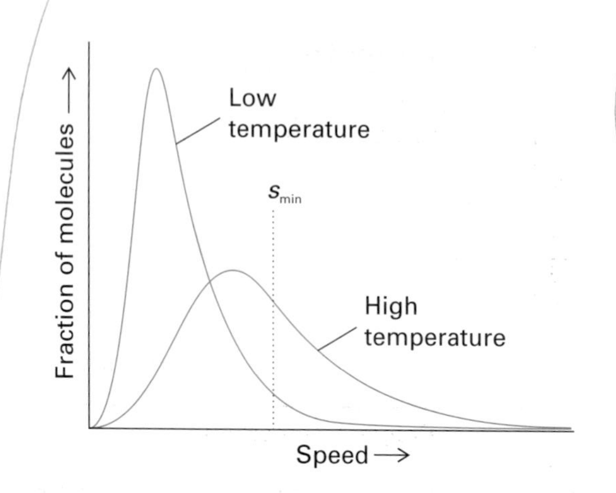

Fig. 10.23 According to the Maxwell distribution of speeds (Section 1.6), as the temperature increases, so does the fraction of gas-phase molecules with a speed that exceeds a minimum value s_{min}. Because the kinetic energy is proportional to the square of the speed, it follows that more molecules can collide with a minimum kinetic energy E_a (the activation energy) at higher temperatures.

fraction with very high speeds increases sharply as the temperature is raised. Because the kinetic energy increases as the square of the speed, we expect that, at higher temperatures, a larger fraction of molecules will have speed and kinetic energy that exceed the minimum values required for collisions that lead to formation of products (Fig. 10.23). The fraction of collisions that occur with at least a kinetic energy E_a can be calculated from general arguments developed in Chapter 22 concerning the probability that a molecule has a specified energy. The result is

$$f = e^{-E_a/RT} \quad (10.21)$$

which suggests, as we now expect, that f increases with increasing temperature.

For a body of mass m moving at a speed v, the kinetic energy is $E_K = \frac{1}{2}mv^2$.

Self-test 10.9

What is the fraction of collisions that have sufficient energy for reaction if the activation energy is 50 kJ mol^{-1} and the temperature is (a) 25°C, (b) 500°C?

[*Answer:* (a) 1.7×10^{-9}, (b) 4.2×10^{-4}]

At this stage we can conclude that the rate of reaction, which is proportional to the collision frequency multiplied by the fraction of successful collisions, is

$$\text{Rate} \propto [A][B]\, e^{-E_a/RT}$$

If we compare this expression with a second-order rate law,

$$\text{Rate} = k[A][B]$$

it follows that

$$k \propto e^{-E_a/RT}$$

This expression has exactly the Arrhenius form (eqn 10.19) if we identify the constant of proportionality with A. Collision theory therefore suggests the following interpretations:

The *pre-exponential factor*, A, is the constant of proportionality between the concentrations of the reactants and the rate at which the reactant molecules collide.

The *activation energy*, E_a, is the minimum kinetic energy required for a collision to result in reaction.

The value of A can be calculated from the kinetic theory of gases (Chapter 1):

$$A = \sigma\left(\frac{8kT}{\pi\mu}\right)^{1/2} N_A^2 \qquad \mu = \frac{m_A m_B}{m_A + m_B} \quad (10.22)$$

where m_A and m_B are the masses of the molecules A and B and σ is the collision cross-section (Section 1.8). However, it is often found that the experimental value of A is smaller than that calculated from the kinetic theory. One possible explanation is that not only must the molecules collide with sufficient kinetic energy, but they must also come together in a specific relative orientation (Fig. 10.24). It follows that the reaction rate is proportional to the probability that the encounter occurs in the correct relative orientation. The pre-exponential factor A should therefore include a **steric factor**, P, which usually lies between 0 (no relative orientations lead to reaction) and 1 (all relative orientations lead to reaction). As an example, for the reactive collision

$$NOCl + NOCl \rightarrow NO + NO + Cl_2$$

in which two NOCl molecules collide and break apart into two NO molecules and a Cl_2 molecule, $P \approx 0.16$. For the hydrogen addition reaction

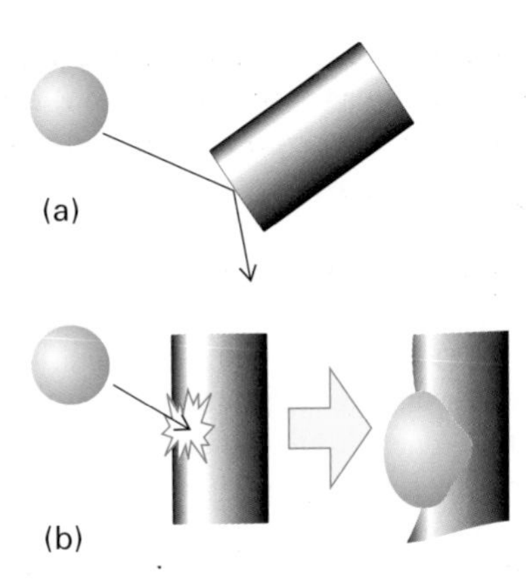

Fig. 10.24 Energy is not the only criterion of a successful reactive encounter, relative orientation may also play a role. (a) In this collision, the reactants approach in an inappropriate relative orientation, and no reaction occurs even though their energy is sufficient. (b) In this encounter, both the energy and the orientation are suitable for reaction.

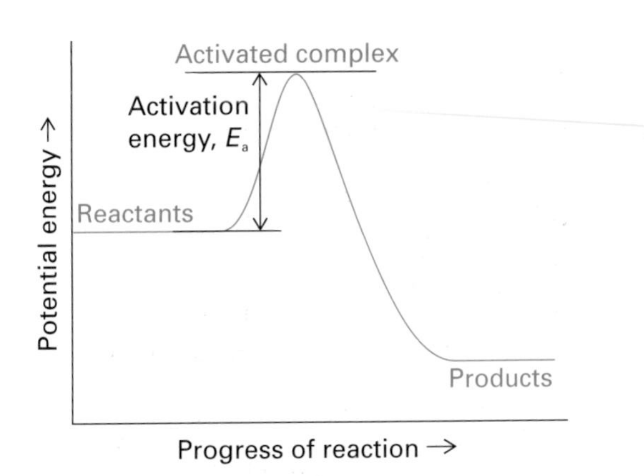

Fig. 10.25 The same type of graph as in Fig. 10.21 represents the reaction profile that is considered in activated complex theory. The activation energy is the potential energy of the activated complex relative to that of the reactants.

$$H_2 + H_2C{=}CH_2 \rightarrow H_3C{-}CH_3$$

in which a hydrogen molecule attaches directly to an ethene molecule to form an ethane molecule, P is only 1.7×10^{-6}, which suggests that the reaction has very stringent orientational requirements.

Some reactions have $P > 1$. Such a value may seem absurd, because it appears to suggest that the reaction occurs more often than the molecules meet! An example of a reaction of this kind is

$$K + Br_2 \rightarrow KBr + Br$$

in which a K atom plucks a Br atom out of a Br_2 molecule; for this reaction the experimental value of P is 4.10. In this reaction, the distance of approach at which reaction can occur seems to be considerably larger than the distance needed for deflection of the path of the approaching molecules in a non-reactive collision! To explain this surprising conclusion, it has been proposed that the reaction proceeds by a 'harpoon mechanism'. This brilliant name is based on a model of the reaction that pictures the K atom as approaching the Br_2 molecules, and when the two are close enough an electron (the harpoon) flips across to the Br_2 molecule. In place of two neutral particles there are now two ions, and so there is a Coulombic attraction between them: this attraction is the line on the harpoon. Under its influence the ions move together (the line is wound in), the reaction takes place, and KBr and Br emerge. The harpoon extends the cross-section for the reactive encounter and we would greatly underestimate the reaction rate if we used for the collision cross-section the value for simple mechanical contact between K and Br_2.

10.11 Transition state theory

There is a more sophisticated theory of reaction rates that can be applied to reactions taking place in solution as well as in the gas phase. In the **transition state theory** of reactions,[3] it is supposed that as two reactants approach, their potential energy rises and reaches a maximum, as illustrated by the reaction profile in Fig. 10.25. This maximum corresponds to the formation of an **activated complex**, a cluster of atoms that is poised to pass on to products or to collapse back into the reactants from which it was formed (Fig. 10.26). An activated complex is not a reaction intermediate that can be isolated and studied like ordinary molecules (Box 10.1). The concept of an activated complex is applicable to reactions in solution as well as in the gas phase, because we can think of the activated complex as perhaps involving any solvent molecules that may be present.

[3] The theory is also called *activated complex theory*.

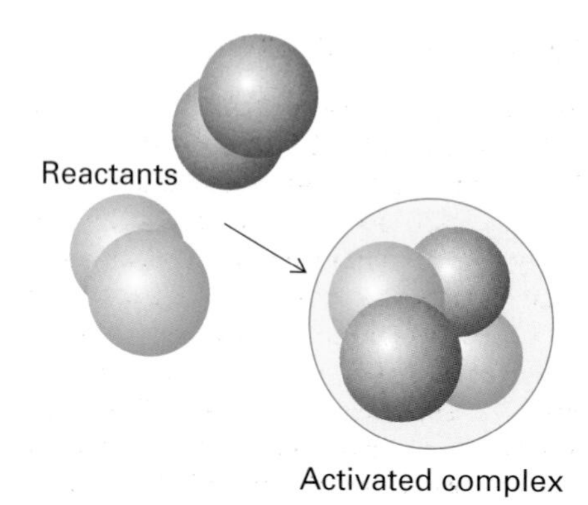

Fig. 10.26 In the activated complex theory of chemical reactions, two reactants encounter each other (either in a gas-phase collision or as a result of diffusing together through a solvent), and if they have sufficient energy, form an activated complex. The activated complex is depicted here by a relatively loose cluster of atoms that may undergo rearrangement into products. In an actual reaction, only some atoms—those at the actual reaction site—might be significantly loosened in the complex, the bonding of the others remaining almost unchanged. This would be the case for CH_3 groups attached to a carbon atom that was undergoing substitution.

Initially, only the reactants A and B are present. As the reaction event proceeds, A and B come into contact, distort, and begin to exchange or discard atoms. The potential energy rises to a maximum, and the cluster of atoms that corresponds to the region close to the maximum is the activated complex. The potential energy falls as the atoms rearrange in the cluster, and reaches a value characteristic of the products. The climax of the reaction is at the peak of the potential energy. Here, two reactant molecules have come to such a degree of closeness and distortion that a small further distortion will send them in the direction of products. This crucial configuration is called the **transition state** of the reaction. Although some molecules entering the transition state might revert to reactants, if they pass through this configuration it is probable that products will emerge from the encounter.

The **reaction coordinate** is an indication of the stage reached in this process. On the left, we have undistorted, widely separated reactants. On the right are the products. Somewhere in the middle is the stage of the reaction corresponding to the formation

Box 10.1 *Femtochemistry*

Until recently, activated complexes were not observed directly, as they have a very fleeting existence and often survive for only a few picoseconds. However, the development of femtosecond pulsed lasers (1 fs = 10^{-15} s) and their application to chemistry in the form of *femtochemistry* has made it possible to make observations on species that have such short lifetimes that in a number of respects they resemble activated complexes. Ahmed Zewail received the Nobel Prize for Chemistry in 1999 for his pioneering work in femtochemistry.

In a typical experiment, energy from a femtosecond pulse is used to dissociate a molecule, and then a second femtosecond pulse is fired at an interval after the pulse. The frequency of the second pulse is set at an absorption of one of the free fragmentation products, so its absorption is a measure of the abundance of the dissociation product. For example, when ICN is dissociated by the first pulse, the emergence of CN can be monitored by watching the growth of the free CN absorption. In this way it has been found that the CN signal remains zero until the fragments have separated by about 600 pm, which takes about 205 fs.

Some sense of the progress that has been made in the study of the intimate mechanism of chemical reactions can be obtained by considering the decay of the ion pair Na^+I^-. Absorption of energy from the femtosecond laser by the ionic species leads to redistribution of electrons and forms a state that corresponds to a covalently bonded NaI molecule. The probe pulse examines the system at an absorption frequency either of the free Na atom or at a frequency at which the atom absorbs when it is a part of the complex. The latter frequency depends on the Na–I distance, so an absorption is obtained each time the vibration of the complex returns it to that separation.

A typical set of results is shown in the illustration. The bound Na absorption intensity shows up as a series of pulses that recur in about 1 ps, showing that the complex vibrates about that period. The decline in intensity shows the rate at which the complex can dissociate as the two atoms swing away from each other. The free Na absorption also grows in an oscillating manner, showing the periodicity of the vibration of the complex, each swing of which gives it a chance to dissociate. The precise period of the oscillation in NaI is 1.25 ps. The complex survives

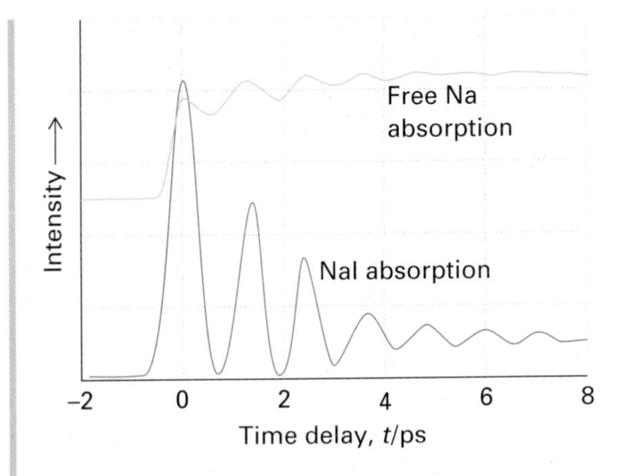

The absorption spectra of the species NaI and Na immediately after a femtosecond flash. The oscillations show how the species incipiently form then reform their precursors before finally forming products. (Adapted from A. H. Zewail, *Science* **242**, 1645 (1988).)

for about ten oscillations. By contrast, although the oscillation frequency of NaBr is similar, it barely survives one oscillation.

Femtochemistry techniques have also been used to examine analogues of the activated complex involved in bimolecular reactions. As an example, consider the weakly bound complex (also called a 'van der Waals molecule'), IH···OCO. The HI bond can be dissociated by a femtosecond pulse, and the H atom is ejected towards the O atom of the neighbouring CO_2 molecule to form HOCO. Hence, the complex is a source of a species that resembles the activated complex of the reaction

$$H + CO_2 \rightarrow [HOCO]^\ddagger \rightarrow HO + CO$$

The probe pulse is tuned to the OH radical, which enables the evolution of $[HOCO]^\ddagger$ to be studied in real time. Femtosecond techniques have also been used to study more complex reactions, such as the Diels–Alder reaction, nucleophilic substitution reactions, and pericyclic addition and cleavage reactions. Biological processes that are open to study by femtochemistry include the photo-stimulated processes of vision (Box 20.1) and the energy-converting processes of photosynthesis (Box 20.2). In other experiments, the photoejection of carbon monoxide from myoglobin and the attachment of O_2 to the exposed site have been studied to obtain rate constants for the two processes.

Exercise 1 Consult literature sources and list the observed time-scales during which the following processes occur: proton transfer reactions, the initial event of vision, energy transfer in photosynthesis, the initial electron transfer events of photosynthesis, the helix-to-coil transition in polypeptides, harpoon reactions, and collisions in liquids.

Exercise 2 Laser flash photolysis is often used to measure the binding rate of CO to haem proteins, such as myoglobin (Mb), because CO dissociates from the bound state relatively easily upon absorption of energy from an intense and narrow pulse of light. The reaction is usually run under pseudofirst-order conditions (see Section 10.6). For a reaction in which $[Mb]_0 = 10$ mmol dm^{-3}, [CO] = 400 mmol dm^{-3}, and the rate constant is 5.8×10^5 mol^{-1} s^{-1}, plot a curve of [Mb] against time. The observed reaction is Mb + CO → MbCO.

of the activated complex. The principal goal of transition state theory is to write an expression for the rate constant by tracking the history of the activated complex from its formation by encounters between the reactants to its decay into product. Here we outline the steps involved in the calculation, with an eye towards gaining insight into the molecular events that optimize the rate constant.

The activated complex $C^\ddagger$ is formed from the reactants A and B and it is supposed—without much justification—that there is an equilibrium between the concentrations of A, B, and $C^\ddagger$:

$$A + B \rightleftharpoons C^\ddagger \qquad K^\ddagger = \frac{[C^\ddagger]}{[A][B]}$$

At the transition state, motion along the reaction coordinate corresponds to some complicated collective vibration-like motion of all the atoms in the complex (and the motion of the solvent molecules if they are involved too). However, it is possible that not every motion along the reaction coordinate takes the complex through the transition state and to the product P. By taking into account the equilibrium between A, B, and $C^\ddagger$ and the rate of successful passage of $C^‡$ through the transition state, it is possible to derive the **Eyring equation** for the rate constant k_{TS}:[4]

$$k_{TS} = \kappa \times \frac{kT}{h} \times K^‡ \quad (10.23)$$

where $k = R/N_A = 1.381 \times 10^{-23}$ J K^{-1} is Boltzmann's constant and $h = 6.626 \times 10^{-34}$ J s is Planck's constant (which we meet in Chapter 12). The factor κ is the **transmission coefficient**, which takes into account the fact that the activated complex does not always pass through to the transition state. In the absence of information to the contrary, κ is assumed to be about 1.

The term kT/h in eqn 10.23 (which has the dimensions of a frequency, as kT is an energy, and division by Planck's constant turns an energy into a frequency; with kT in joules, kT/h has the units s^{-1}) arises from consideration of the motions of atoms that lead to the decay of $C^‡$ into products, as specific bonds are broken and formed. It follows that one way in which an increase in temperature enhances the rate is by causing more vigorous motion in the activated complex, facilitating the rearrangement of atoms and the formation of new bonds.

Calculation of the equilibrium constant $K^‡$ is very difficult, except in certain simple model cases. For example, if we suppose that the reactants are two structureless atoms and that the activated complex is a diatomic molecule of bond length R, then k_{ACT} turns out to be the same as for collision theory provided we interpret the collision cross-section in eqn 10.22 as πR^2.

It is more useful to express the Eyring equation in terms of thermodynamic parameters and to discuss reactions in terms of their empirical values. Thus, we saw in Section 7.3 that an equilibrium constant may be expressed in terms of the standard reaction Gibbs energy ($-RT \ln K = \Delta_r G^{\ominus}$). In this context, the Gibbs energy is called the **activation Gibbs energy**, and written $\Delta^‡ G$. It follows that

$$\Delta^‡ G = -RT \ln K^‡ \quad \text{and} \quad K^‡ = e^{-\Delta^‡ G/RT}$$

Therefore, by writing

$$\Delta^‡ G = \Delta^‡ H - T\Delta^‡ S \quad (10.24)$$

we conclude that (with $\kappa = 1$)

$$k_{TS} = \frac{kT}{h} e^{-(\Delta^‡ H - T\Delta^‡ S)/RT}$$

$$= \left(\frac{kT}{h} e^{\Delta^‡ S/R}\right) e^{-\Delta^‡ H/RT} \quad (10.25)$$

Useful relations involving exponentials include:

$e^{x+y} = e^x e^y \qquad e^{x-y} = e^x/e^y$

This expression has the form of the Arrhenius expression, eqn 10.19, if we identify the **enthalpy of activation**, $\Delta^‡ H$, with the activation energy and the term in parentheses, which depends on the **entropy of activation**, $\Delta^‡ S$, with the pre-exponential factor.

The advantage of transition state theory over collision theory is that it is applicable to reactions in solution as well as in the gas phase. It also gives some clue to the calculation of the steric factor P, as the orientation requirements are carried in the entropy of activation. Thus, if there are strict orientation requirements (for example, in the approach of a substrate molecule to an enzyme), then the entropy of activation will be strongly negative (representing a decrease in disorder when the activated complex forms), and the pre-exponential factor will be small. In practice, it is occasionally possible to estimate the sign and magnitude of the entropy of activation and hence to estimate the rate constant. The general importance of transition state theory is that it shows that even a complex series of events—not only a collisional encounter in the gas phase—displays Arrhenius-like behaviour, and that the concept of activation energy is applicable.

Self-test 10.10

In a particular reaction in water, it is proposed that two ions of opposite charge come together to form an electrically neutral activated complex. Is the contribution of the solvent to the entropy of activation likely to be positive or negative?

[*Answer:* positive, as H_2O is less organized around the neutral species]

[4] Be very careful to distinguish the Boltzmann constant k from the symbol for a rate constant. In transition state theory, we always denote the rate constant k_{TS}. In some expositions, you will see Boltzmann's constant denoted k_B to emphasize its significance.

CHECKLIST OF KEY IDEAS

You should now be familiar with the following concepts:

☐ 1 The rates of chemical reactions are measured by using techniques that monitor the concentrations of species present in the reaction mixture (Table 10.1).

☐ 2 Spectrophotometry is the measurement of the absorption of light by a material.

☐ 3 The Beer–Lambert law relates the absorbance of a sample to the concentration of an absorbing species, $A = \varepsilon[\mathrm{J}]l$ with $A = \log(I_0/I)$.

☐ 4 Techniques include real-time and quenching procedures, flow and stopped-flow techniques, and flash photolysis.

☐ 5 The instantaneous rate of a reaction is the slope of the tangent to the graph of concentration against time (expressed as a positive quantity).

☐ 6 A rate law is an expression for the reaction rate in terms of the concentrations of the species that occur in the overall chemical reaction.

☐ 7 For a rate law of the form rate $= k[\mathrm{A}]^a[\mathrm{B}]^b \ldots$, the order with respect to A is a and the overall order is $a + b + \cdots$.

☐ 8 An integrated rate law is an expression for the rate of a reaction as a function of time.

☐ 9 The half-life of a first-order reaction is the time it takes for the concentration of a species to fall to half its initial value; $t_{1/2} = (\ln 2)/k$.

☐ 10 The temperature dependence of the rate constant of a reaction typically follows the Arrhenius law, $\ln k = \ln A - E_a/RT$.

☐ 11 The larger the activation energy, the more sensitive the rate constant is to the temperature.

☐ 12 In collision theory, it is supposed that the rate is proportional to the collision frequency, a steric factor, and the fraction of collisions that occur with at least the kinetic energy E_a along their lines of centres.

☐ 13 In transition state theory, it is supposed that an activated complex is in equilibrium with the reactants, and that the rate at which that complex forms products depends on the rate at which it passes through a transition state. The result is the Eyring equation, $k_{TS} = \kappa(kT/h)K^{\ddagger}$.

☐ 14 The rate constant may be parameterized in terms of the Gibbs energy, entropy, and enthalpy of activation, $k_{TS} = (kT/h)\,e^{\Delta^{\ddagger}S/R}\,e^{-\Delta^{\ddagger}H/RT}$.

DISCUSSION QUESTIONS

10.1 Describe the main features, including advantages and disadvantages, of the following experimental methods for determining the rate law of a reaction: the isolation method, the method of initial rates, and fitting data to integrated rate law expressions.

10.2 Distinguish between zeroth-order, first-order, second-order, and pseudofirst-order reactions.

10.3 Define the terms in and limit the generality of the expression $\ln k = \ln A - E_a/RT$.

10.4 Describe the formulation of the Eyring equation.

EXERCISES

The symbol ‡ indicates that calculus is required.

10.5 The molar absorption coefficient of cytochrome P450, an enzyme involved in the breakdown of harmful substances in the liver and small intestine, at 522 nm is 291 $dm^3 mol^{-1} cm^{-1}$. When light of that wavelength passes through a cell of length 6.5 mm containing a solution of the solute, 39.8 per cent of the light is absorbed. What is the molar concentration of the solution?

10.6 Consider a solution of two unrelated substances A and B. Let their molar absorption coefficients be equal at a certain wavelength, and write their total absorbance *A*. Show that we can infer the concentrations of A and B from the total absorbance at some other wavelength provided we know the molar absorption coefficients at that different wavelength. (See eqn 10.4.)

10.7 The molar absorption coefficients of tryptophan and tyrosine at 240 nm are 2.00×10^3 $dm^3 mol^{-1} cm^{-1}$ and 1.12×10^4 $dm^3 mol^{-1} cm^{-1}$, respectively, and at 280 nm they are 5.40×10^3 $dm^3 mol^{-1} cm^{-1}$ and 1.50×10^3 $dm^3 mol^{-1} cm^{-1}$, respectively. The absorbance of a sample obtained by hydrolysis of a protein was measured in a cell of thickness 1.00 cm, and was found to be 0.660 at 240 nm and 0.221 at 280 nm. What are the concentrations of the two amino acids?

10.8 A solution was prepared by dissolving tryptophan and tyrosine in 0.15 M NaOH(aq) and a sample was transferred to a cell of length 1.00 cm. The two amino acids share the same molar absorption coefficient at 294 nm (2.38×10^3 $dm^3 mol^{-1} cm^{-1}$) and the absorbance of the solution at that wavelength is 0.468. At 280 nm the molar absorption coefficients are 5.23×10^3 $dm^3 mol^{-1} cm^{-1}$ and 1.58×10^3 $dm^3 mol^{-1} cm^{-1}$, respectively, and the total absorbance of the solution is 0.676. What are the concentrations of the two amino acids? *Hint.* It would be sensible to use the result derived in Exercise 10.6, but this specific example could be worked through without using that general case.

10.9 The rate of formation of C in the reaction 2 A + B $\rightarrow$ 3 C + 2 D is 2.2 mol $dm^{-3} s^{-1}$. State the rates of formation and consumption of A, B, and D.

10.10 The rate law for the reaction in Exercise 10.9 was reported as rate = *k*[A][B][C] with the molar concentrations in moles per cubic decimetre and the time in seconds. What are the units of *k*?

10.11 If the rate laws are expressed with (a) concentrations in numbers of molecules per cubic metre (molecules m^{-3}), (b) pressures in kilopascals, what are the units of the second-order and third-order rate constants?

10.12 The following initial-rate data were obtained on the rate of binding of glucose with the enzyme hexokinase (obtained from yeast) present at a concentration of 1.34 mmol dm^{-3}. What is (a) the order of reaction with respect to glucose, (b) the rate constant?

$[C_6H_{12}O_6]$/(mmol dm^{-3})	1.00	1.54	3.12	4.02
Initial rate/(mol $dm^{-3} s^{-1}$)	5.0	7.6	15.5	20.0

10.13 The following data were obtained on the initial rates of a reaction of a *d*-metal complex in aqueous solution. What is (a) the order of reaction with respect to the complex and the reactant Y, (b) the rate constant? For the experiments (a), [Y] = 2.7 mmol dm^{-3} and for experiments (b) [Y] = 6.1 mmol dm^{-3}.

[Complex]/(mmol dm^{-3})		8.01	9.22	12.11
Rate/(mol $dm^{-3} s^{-1}$)	(a)	125	144	190
	(b)	640	730	960

10.14 The rate constant for the first-order decomposition of N_2O_5 in the reaction 2 N_2O_5(g) $\rightarrow$ 4 NO_2(g) + O_2(g) is $k = 3.38 \times 10^{-5}$ s^{-1} at 25°C. What is the half-life of N_2O_5? What will be the total pressure, initially 88.3 kPa for the pure N_2O_5 vapour, (a) 10 s, (b) 10 min after initiation of the reaction?

10.15 In a study of the alcohol dehydrogenase catalysed oxidation of ethanol, the molar concentration of ethanol decreased in a first-order reaction from 220 mmol dm^{-3} to 56.0 mmol dm^{-3} in 1.22×10^4 s. What is the rate constant of the reaction?

10.16 The elimination of carbon dioxide from pyruvate ions by a decarboxylase enzyme was monitored by measuring the partial pressure of the gas as it was formed in a 250 cm^3 flask at 20°C. In one experiment, the partial pressure increased from zero to 100 Pa in 522 s in a first-order reaction when the initial concentration of pyruvate ions in 100 cm^3 of solution was 3.23 mol dm^{-3}. What is the rate constant of the reaction?

10.17 In the study of a second-order gas-phase reaction, it was found that the molar concentration of a reactant fell from 220 mmol mol^{-1} to 56.0 mmol mol^{-1} in 1.22×10^4 s. What is the rate constant of the reaction?

10.18 Carbonic anhydrase is a zinc-based enzyme that catalyses the conversion of carbon dioxide to carbonic acid. In an experiment to study its effect, it was found that the molar concentration of carbon dioxide in solution decreased from 220 mmol dm^{-3} to 56.0 mmol dm^{-3} in 1.22×10^4 s. What is the rate constant of the reaction?

10.19 The formation of NOCl from NO in the presence of a large excess of chlorine is pseudosecond-order in NO. In an experiment to study the reaction, the partial pressure of NOCl increased from zero to 100 Pa in 522 s. What is the rate constant of the reaction given that the initial partial pressure of NO is 300 kPa?

10.20 A number of reactions that take place on the surfaces of catalysts are zero-order in the reactant. One example is the decomposition of ammonia on hot tungsten. In one experiment, the partial pressure of ammonia decreased from 21 kPa to 10 kPa in 770 s. (a) What is the rate constant for the zero-order reaction? (b) How long will it take all the ammonia to disappear?

10.21 The following kinetic data were obtained for the reaction $2\,ICl(g) + H_2(g) \rightarrow I_2(g) + 2\,HCl(g)$:

Experiment	$[ICl]_0$/ (mmol dm^{-3})	$[H_2]_0$/ (mmol dm^{-3})	Initial rate/ (mol dm^{-3} s^{-1})
1	1.5	1.5	3.7×10^{-7}
2	3.0	1.5	7.4×10^{-7}
3	3.0	4.5	22×10^{-7}
4	4.7	2.7	?

(a) Write the rate law for the reaction. (b) From the data, determine the value of the rate constant. (c) Use the data to predict the reaction rate for Experiment 4.

10.22 The following data were collected for the reaction $2\,HI(g) \rightarrow H_2(g) + I_2(g)$ at 580 K:

t/s	0	1000	2000	3000	4000
[HI]/(mol dm^{-3})	1.00	0.112	0.061	0.041	0.031

(a) Plot the data in an appropriate fashion to determine the order of the reaction. (b) From the graph, determine the rate constant.

10.23 The following data were collected for the reaction $H_2(g) + I_2(g) \rightarrow 2\,HI(g)$ at 780 K:

t/s	0	1	2	3	4
[HI]/(mol dm^{-3})	1	0.43	0.27	0.2	0.16

(a) Plot the data in an appropriate fashion to determine the order of the reaction. (b) From the graph, determine the rate constant.

10.24 The composition of a liquid-phase reaction $2\,A \rightarrow B$ was followed spectrophotometrically with the following results:

t/min	0	10	20	30	40	∞
[B]/(mol dm^{-3})	0	0.089	0.153	0.200	0.230	0.312

Determine the order of the reaction and its rate constant.

10.25 ‡Establish the integrated form of a third-order rate law of the form rate = $k[A]^3$. What would it be appropriate to plot to confirm that a reaction is third-order?

10.26 ‡Establish the integrated form of a second-order rate law of the form rate = $k[A][B]$ for a reaction $A + B \rightarrow$ products (a) with different initial concentrations of A and B, (b) with the same concentrations of the two reactants. *Hints*. Note that when the concentration of A falls to $[A]_0 - x$, the concentration of B falls to $[B]_0 - x$. Use these relations to show that the rate law may be written as

$$\frac{dx}{dt} = k([A]_0 - x)([B]_0 - x)$$

To make progress with integration of the rate law, use the form:

$$\int \frac{dx}{(a-x)(b-x)} = \frac{1}{b-a}\left(\ln\frac{1}{a-x} - \ln\frac{1}{b-x}\right) + \text{constant}$$

10.27 The half-life of pyruvic acid in the presence of an aminotransferase enzyme (which converts it to alanine) was found to be 221 s. How long will it take for the concentration of pyruvic acid to fall to $\frac{1}{64}$ of its initial value in this first-order reaction?

10.28 The half-life for the (first-order) radioactive decay of ^{14}C is 5730 a (1 a is the SI unit annum, for 1 year; the nuclide emits β particles, high-energy electrons, with an energy of 0.16 MeV). An archaeological sample contained wood that had only 69 per cent of the ^{14}C found in living trees. What is its age?

10.29 One of the hazards of nuclear explosions is the generation of ^{90}Sr and its subsequent incorporation in place of calcium in bones. This nuclide emits β particles of energy 0.55 MeV, and has a half-life of 28.1 a (1 a is the SI unit annum, for 1 year). Suppose 1.00 μg was absorbed by a newly born child. How much will remain after (a) 19 a, (b) 75 a if none is lost metabolically?

10.30 The second-order rate constant for the reaction $CH_3COOC_2H_5(aq) + OH^-(aq) \rightarrow CH_3CO_2^-(aq) + CH_3CH_2OH(aq)$ is 0.11 dm^3 mol^{-1} s^{-1}. What is the concentration of ester after (a) 15 s, (b) 15 min when ethyl acetate is added to sodium hydroxide so that the initial concentrations are [NaOH] = 0.055 mol dm^{-3} and $[CH_3COOC_2H_5]$ = 0.150 mol dm^{-3}?

10.31 A reaction $2\,A \rightarrow P$ has a second-order rate law with k = 1.24 cm^3 mol^{-1} s^{-1}. Calculate the time required for the concentration of A to change from 0.260 mol dm^{-3} to 0.026 mol dm^{-3}.

10.32 A rate constant is 1.78×10^{-4} dm^3 mol^{-1} s^{-1} at 19°C and 1.38×10^{-3} dm^3 mol^{-1} s^{-1} at 37°C. Evaluate the Arrhenius parameters of the reaction.

10.33 The activation energy for the decomposition of benzene diazonium chloride is 99.1 kJ mol^{-1}. At what temperature will the rate be 10 per cent greater than its rate at 25°C?

10.34 Which reaction responds more strongly to changes of temperature, one with an activation energy of 52 kJ mol^{-1} or one with an activation energy of 25 kJ mol^{-1}?

10.35 The rate constant of a reaction increases by a factor of 1.23 when the temperature is increased from 20°C to 27°C. What is the activation energy of the reaction?

10.36 Make an appropriate Arrhenius plot of the following data for the conversion of cyclopropane to propene and calculate the activation energy for the reaction.

T/K	750	800	850	900
k/s^{-1}	1.8×10^{-4}	2.7×10^{-3}	3.0×10^{-2}	0.26

10.37 Food rots about 40 times more rapidly at 25°C than when it is stored at 4°C. Estimate the overall activation energy for the processes responsible for its decomposition.

10.38 Suppose that the rate constant of a reaction *decreases* by a factor of 1.23 when the temperature is increased from 20°C to 27°C. How should you report the activation energy of the reaction?

10.39 The enzyme urease catalyses the reaction in which urea is hydrolysed to ammonia and carbon dioxide. The half-life of urea in the pseudofirst-order reaction for a certain amount of urease doubles when the temperature is lowered from 20°C to 10°C and the Michaelis constant is largely unchanged. What is the activation energy of the reaction?

10.40 The activation energy of the first-order decomposition of dinitrogen oxide into N_2 and O is 251 kJ mol^{-1}. The half-life of the reactant is 6.5 Ms (1 Ms = 10^6 s) at 455°C. What will it be at 550°C?

10.41 Estimate the pre-exponential factor for the reaction between molecular hydrogen and ethene at 400°C.

10.42 Suppose an electronegative reactant needs to come to within 500 pm of a reactant with low ionization energy before an electron can flip across from one to the other (as in the harpoon mechanism). Estimate the reaction cross-section.

10.43 Estimate the activation Gibbs energy for the decomposition of urea in the reaction $CO(NH_2)_2(aq) + 2\ H_2O(l) \rightarrow 2\ NH_4^+(aq) + CO_3^{2-}(aq)$ for which the pseudofirst-order rate constant is $1.2 \times 10^{-7}\ s^{-1}$ at 60°C and $4.6 \times 10^{-7}\ s^{-1}$ at 70°C.

10.44 Calculate the entropy of activation of the reaction in Exercise 10.43 at the two temperatures.

Chapter 11

Accounting for the rate laws

Even quite simple rate laws can give rise to complicated behaviour. The sign that the heart maintains a steady pulse throughout a lifetime, but may break into fibrillation during a heart attack, is one sign of that complexity. On a less personal scale, reaction intermediates come and go, and all reactions approach equilibrium. However, the complexity of the behaviour of reaction rates means that the study of reaction rates can give deep insight into the way that reactions take place. As remarked in Chapter 10, rate laws are a window on to the mechanism, the sequence of elementary molecular events that lead from the reactants to the products, of the reactions they summarize.

Reaction schemes

So far, we have considered very simple rate laws, in which reactants are consumed or products formed. However, all reactions in fact proceed towards a state of equilibrium in which the reverse reaction becomes increasingly important. Moreover, many reactions proceed to products through a series of intermediates. In industry, one of the intermediates may be of crucial importance and the ultimate products may represent waste.

11.1 The approach to equilibrium

All forward reactions are accompanied by their reverse reactions. At the start of a reaction, when little or no product is present, the rate of the reverse reaction is negligible. However, as the concentration of products increases, the rate at which they decompose into reactants becomes greater. At equilibrium, the reverse rate matches the forward rate and the reactants and products are present in abundances given by the equilibrium constant for the reaction.

We can analyse this behaviour by thinking of a very simple reaction of the form

$$\text{Forward: A} \rightarrow \text{B} \quad \text{rate of formation of B} = k[\text{A}]$$

$$\text{Reverse: B} \rightarrow \text{A} \quad \text{rate of decomposition of B} = k'[\text{B}]$$

For instance, we could envisage this scheme as the interconversion of coiled (A) and uncoiled (B) DNA molecules. The *net* rate of formation of B, the difference of its rates of formation and decomposition, is

$$\text{Net rate of formation of B} = k[\text{A}] - k'[\text{B}]$$

When the reaction has reached equilibrium the concentrations of A and B are $[\text{A}]_{\text{eq}}$ and $[\text{B}]_{\text{eq}}$ and there is no net formation of either substance. It follows that

$$k[\text{A}]_{\text{eq}} = k'[\text{B}]_{\text{eq}}$$

and therefore that the equilibrium constant for the reaction is related to the rate constants by

$$K = \frac{[\text{B}]_{\text{eq}}}{[\text{A}]_{\text{eq}}} = \frac{k}{k'} \qquad (11.1)$$

If the forward rate constant is much larger than the reverse rate constant, then $K \gg 1$. If the opposite is true, then $K \ll 1$. This result is a crucial connection between the kinetics of a reaction and its equilibrium properties. It is also very useful in practice, as we may be able to measure the equilibrium constant and one of the rate constants, and can then calculate the missing rate constant from eqn 11.1. Alternatively, we can use the relation to calculate the equilibrium constant from kinetic measurements. This relation is valid even if the forward and reverse reactions have different orders.

Illustration 11.1

The relation between rate constants and equilibrium constants

The rates of the forward and reverse reactions for the dimerization of an antibacterial agent were found to be 8.1×10^8 dm^3 mol^{-1} s^{-1} (second-order) and 2.0×10^6 s^{-1} (first-order), respectively. The equilibrium constant for the dimerization is therefore

$$K = \frac{8.1 \times 10^8}{2.0 \times 10^6} = 4.0 \times 10^2$$

A note on good practice To ensure that the equilibrium constant is dimensionless and matches the conventions used in Chapters 7 and 8, we discard the units of the *k*s, provided the rate constants are expressed in moles per cubic decimetre and the same unit of time (typically seconds).

Equation 11.1 also gives us insight into the temperature dependence of equilibrium constants. First, we suppose that both the forward and reverse reactions show Arrhenius behaviour (Section 10.9). As we see from Fig. 11.1, for an exothermic reaction the activation energy of the forward reaction is smaller than that of the reverse reaction. Therefore, the forward rate constant increases less sharply with temperature than the reverse reaction does. Consequently, when we increase the temperature of a system at equilibrium, k' increases more steeply than k does, and the ratio k/k', and therefore K, decreases. This is exactly the conclusion we drew from the van 't Hoff equation (eqn 7.15), which was based on thermodynamic arguments.

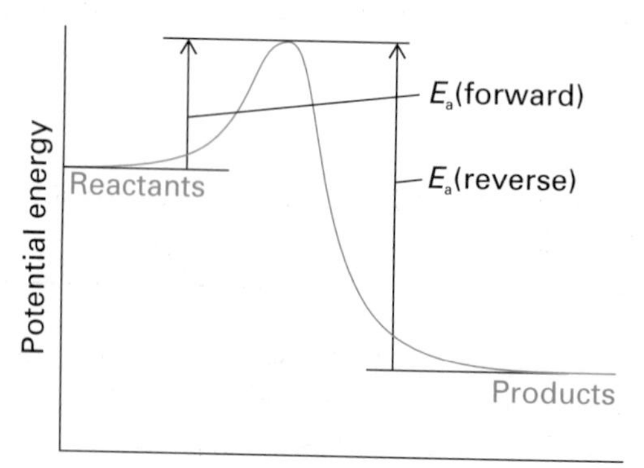

Fig. 11.1 The reaction profile for an exothermic reaction. The activation energy is greater for the reverse reaction than for the forward reaction, so the rate of the forward reaction increases less sharply with temperature. As a result, the equilibrium constant shifts in favour of the products as the temperature is raised.

Equation 11.1 tells us the ratio of concentrations after a long time has passed and the reaction has reached equilibrium. To find the concentrations at an intermediate stage, we need the integrated rate equation. If no B is present initially, we show in Derivation 11.1 that

$$[\mathrm{A}] = \frac{(k' + k\,\mathrm{e}^{-(k+k')t})[\mathrm{A}]_0}{k + k'} \qquad (11.2\mathrm{a})$$

$$[\mathrm{B}] = \frac{k(1 - \mathrm{e}^{-(k+k')t})[\mathrm{A}]_0}{k + k'} \qquad (11.2\mathrm{b})$$

where $[\mathrm{A}]_0$ is the initial concentration of A.

Derivation 11.1

The approach to equilibrium

The concentration of A is reduced by the forward reaction (at a rate $k[\mathrm{A}]$) but it is increased by the reverse reaction (at a rate $k'[\mathrm{B}]$). Therefore, the net rate of change is

$$\frac{\mathrm{d}[\mathrm{A}]}{\mathrm{d}t} = -k[\mathrm{A}] + k'[\mathrm{B}]$$

If the initial concentration of A is $[\mathrm{A}]_0$, and no B is present initially, then at all times $[\mathrm{A}] + [\mathrm{B}] = [\mathrm{A}]_0$. Therefore,

$$\frac{\mathrm{d}[\mathrm{A}]}{\mathrm{d}t} = -k[\mathrm{A}] + k'([\mathrm{A}]_0 - [\mathrm{A}])$$
$$= -(k + k')[\mathrm{A}] + k'[\mathrm{A}]_0$$

The solution of this differential equation is eqn 11.2a. To verify the result, differentiate eqn 11.2a by using the general relation

$$\frac{\mathrm{d}}{\mathrm{d}x}\mathrm{e}^{-ax} = -a\,\mathrm{e}^{-ax}$$

To obtain eqn 11.2b, we use eqn 11.2a and $[\mathrm{B}] = [\mathrm{A}]_0 - [\mathrm{A}]$.

As we see in Fig. 11.2, the concentrations start from their initial values and move gradually towards their final equilibrium values as t approaches infinity. We find the latter by setting t equal to infinity and using $\mathrm{e}^{-x} = 0$ at $x = \infty$:

$$[\mathrm{B}]_{\mathrm{eq}} = \frac{k[\mathrm{A}]_0}{k + k'} \qquad [\mathrm{A}]_{\mathrm{eq}} = \frac{k'[\mathrm{A}]_0}{k + k'} \qquad (11.3)$$

As may be verified, the ratio of these two expressions is the equilibrium constant in eqn 11.1.

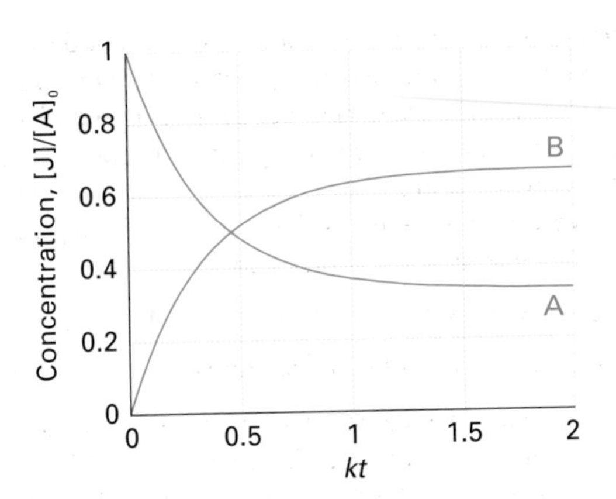

Fig. 11.2 The approach to equilibrium of a reaction that is first-order in both directions. Here we have taken $k = 2k'$. Note how, at equilibrium, the ratio of concentrations is 2:1, corresponding to $K = 2$.

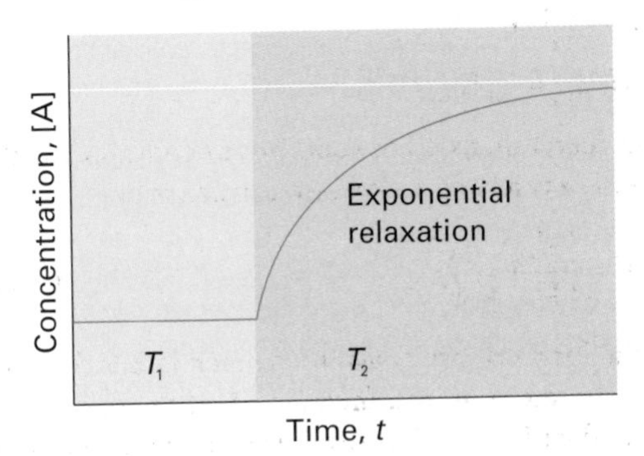

Fig. 11.3 The relaxation to the new equilibrium composition when a reaction initially at equilibrium at a temperature T_1 is subjected to a sudden change of temperature, which takes it to T_2.

11.2 Relaxation methods

The term **relaxation** denotes the return of a system to equilibrium. It is used in chemical kinetics to indicate that an externally applied influence has shifted the equilibrium position of a reaction, normally abruptly, and that the reaction is adjusting to the equilibrium composition characteristic of the new conditions (Fig. 11.3). We shall consider the response of reaction rates to a **temperature jump**, a sudden change in temperature. We know from Section 7.9 that the equilibrium composition of a reaction depends on the temperature (provided

$\Delta_r H^\ominus$ is non-zero), so a shift in temperature acts as a perturbation on the system. One way of achieving a temperature jump is to discharge a capacitor through a sample made conducting by the addition of ions, but laser or microwave discharges can also be used. Temperature jumps of between 5 and 10 K can be achieved in about 1 μs with electrical discharges. The high-energy output of pulsed lasers (Section 20.6) is sufficient to generate temperature jumps of between 10 and 30 K within nanoseconds in aqueous samples, making the technique suitable for the study of the events involved in protein folding (Box 11.1). Equilibria for which there is a change in volume between reactants and products are also sensitive to pressure, and **pressure-jump techniques** may then also be used.

Box 11.1 *Kinetics of protein unfolding*

Proteins are polymers that attain well-defined three-dimensional structures both in solution and in biological cells. They are *polypeptides* formed from different amino acids strung together by the *peptide link*, –CONH–. Hydrogen bonds between amino acids of a polypeptide give rise to stable helical or sheet structures, which may collapse into a random coil when certain conditions are changed. For example, the synthetic polypeptide poly-γ-benzyl-glutamate is helical in a non-hydrogen-bonding solvent, but in a hydrogen-bonding solvent it forms a random coil. The unwinding, or denaturation, of a helix into a random coil is a *cooperative transition*, in which the polymer becomes increasingly more susceptible to structural changes once the process has begun. Denaturation can be brought about by changes in either temperature or pH, and by reaction with certain compounds, such as urea or guanidinium hydrochloride, known as *denaturants*. Here we examine the kinetics of the helix–coil transition, focusing primarily on experimental strategies and some recent results.

Earlier work on folding and unfolding of small polypeptides and large proteins relied primarily on rapid mixing and stopped-flow techniques. In a typical stopped-flow experiment, a sample of the protein with a high concentration of a chemical denaturant is mixed with a solution containing a much lower concentration of the same denaturant. Upon entering the mixing chamber, the denaturant is diluted and the protein refolds. Unfolding is observed by mixing a sample of folded protein with a solution containing a high concentration of denaturant. These experiments are ideal for sorting out events in the millisecond time-scale, such as the formation of contacts between helical segments in a large protein. However, the available data also indicate that, in a number of proteins, a significant portion of the folding process occurs in less than 1 ms, a time-range not accessible by the stopped-flow technique. More recent temperature-jump and flash photolysis experiments have uncovered faster events. For example, at room temperature the formation of a loop between helical or sheet segments may be as fast as 1 μs and the formation of tightly packed cores with significant tertiary structure occurs in 10–100 μs. Among the fastest events are the formation of helices and sheets from fully unfolded peptide chains and we examine how the laser-induced temperature-jump technique has been used in the study of the helix–coil transition.

The laser-induced temperature-jump technique takes advantage of the fact that proteins unfold, or 'melt', at high temperatures and each protein has a characteristic melting temperature. Proteins also lose their native structures at very low temperatures, a process known as *cold denaturation*, and refold when the temperature in increased but kept significantly below the melting temperature. Hence, a temperature-jump experiment can be configured to monitor either folding or unfolding of a polypeptide, depending on the initial and final temperatures of the sample. The challenge of using melting or cold denaturation as the basis of kinetic measurements lies in increasing the temperature of the sample very quickly so that fast relaxation processes can be monitored. A number of clever strategies have been used. In one, a pulsed laser excites dissolved dye molecules that discard the extra energy largely by heat transfer to the solution. Another variation makes use of direct excitation of H_2O or D_2O with a pulsed infrared laser. The latter strategy leads to temperature jumps in a small irradiated volume of about 20 K in less than 100 ps. Relaxation of the sample can then be probed by a variety of spectroscopic techniques.

Much of the kinetic work on the helix–coil transition has been conducted in small synthetic polypeptides rich in alanine, an amino acid that is known to stabilize helical structures. Both experimental and theoretical results suggest that the mechanism of unfolding consists of at least two steps: a very fast step in which amino acids at either end of a helical segment undergo transitions to coil regions and a slower rate-determining step that corresponds to the cooperative melting of the rest of the chain and loss of helical content. Using h and c to denote an amino acid residue belonging to a helical and coil region, respectively, the mechanism may be summarized as follows:

$hhhh\ldots \rightarrow chhh\ldots$ very fast

$chhh\ldots \rightarrow cccc\ldots$ rate-determining step

The rate-determining step is thought to account for the relaxation time of 160 ns measured with a laser-induced temperature jump between 282.5 K and 300.6 K in an alanine-rich polypeptide containing 21 amino acids. It is thought that the limitation on the rate of the helix–coil transition in this peptide arises from an activation energy barrier of 1.7 kJ mol^{-1} associated with initial events of the form $\ldots hhhh\ldots \rightarrow \ldots hhch\ldots$ in the middle of the chain. Therefore, initiation is not only thermodynamically unfavourable but also kinetically slow. Theoretical models also suggest that a $hhhh\ldots \rightarrow chhh\ldots$ transition at either end of a helical segment has a significantly lower activation energy on account of the converting amino acid not being flanked by h regions.

The time constant for the helix–coil transition has also been measured in proteins. In apomyoglobin (myoglobin lacking the haem cofactor), the unfolding of the helices appears to have a relaxation time of about 50 ns, even shorter than in synthetic peptides. It is difficult to interpret these results because we do not yet know how the amino acid sequence or interactions between helices in a folded protein affect the helix–coil relaxation time.

Exercise 1 Consider a mechanism for the helix–coil transition in which initiation occurs in the middle of the chain:

$hhhh\ldots \rightleftarrows hchh\ldots$

$hchh\ldots \rightleftarrows cccc\ldots$

We saw above that this type of initiation is relatively slow, so neither step may be rate-determining. (a) Set up the rate equations for this alternative mechanism. (b) Apply the steady-state approximation and show that, under these circumstances, the mechanism is equivalent to $hhhh\ldots \rightleftarrows cccc\ldots$.

Exercise 2 Use your knowledge of experimental techniques and your results from the previous exercise to support or refute the following statement. It is very difficult to obtain experimental evidence for intermediates in protein folding by performing simple rate measurements and special time-resolved or trapping techniques must be used to detect intermediates directly.

When a sudden temperature increase is applied to a simple A $\rightleftharpoons$ B equilibrium that is first-order in each direction, the composition relaxes exponentially to the new equilibrium composition:

$$x = x_0\, e^{-t/\tau} \qquad \frac{1}{\tau} = k_a + k_b \tag{11.4}$$

where x is the departure from equilibrium at the new temperature, x_0 is the departure from equilibrium immediately after the temperature jump, and τ is the **relaxation time.**

Derivation 11.2

Relaxation to equilibrium

We need to keep track of the fact that rate constants depend on temperature. At the initial temperature, when the rate constants are k_a' and k_b', the net rate of change of [A] is

$$\frac{d[A]}{dt} = -k_a'[A] + k_b'[B]$$

At equilibrium under these conditions, we write the concentrations as $[A]'_{eq}$ and $[B]'_{eq}$ and

$$k_a'[A]'_{eq} = k_b'[B]'_{eq}$$

When the temperature is increased suddenly, the rate constants change to k_a and k_b, but the concentrations of A and B remain for an instant at their old equilibrium values. As the system is no longer at equilibrium, it readjusts to the new equilibrium concentrations, which are now given by

$$k_a[A]_{eq} = k_b[B]_{eq}$$

and it does so at a rate that depends on the new rate constants.

We write the deviation of [A] from its new equilibrium value as x, so $[A] = x + [A]_{eq}$ and $[B] = [B]_{eq} - x$. The concentration of A then changes as follows:

$$\frac{d[A]}{dt} = -k_a(x + [A]_{eq}) + k_b(-x + [B]_{eq})$$
$$= -(k_a + k_b)x$$

because the two terms involving the equilibrium concentrations cancel. From $[A] = x + [A]_{eq}$ it follows that $d[A]/dt = dx/dt$ and

$$\frac{dx}{dt} = -(k_a + k_b)x$$

To solve this equation we divide both sides by x and multiply by dt:

$$\frac{dx}{x} = -(k_a + k_b)\,dt$$

Now integrate both sides. When $t = 0$, $x = x_0$, its initial value, so the integrated equation has the form

$$\int_{x_0}^{x} \frac{dx}{x} = -(k_a + k_b)\int_0^t dt$$

The integral on the left is $\ln(x/x_0)$ (see Derivation 2.2), and that on the right is t. The integrated equation is therefore

$$\ln\frac{x}{x_0} = -(k_a + k_b)t$$

When antilogarithms are taken of both sides, the result is eqn 11.4.

Equation 11.4 shows that the concentrations of A and B relax into the new equilibrium at a rate determined by the *sum* of the two new rate constants. Because the equilibrium constant under the new conditions is $K = k_a/k_b$, its value may be combined with the relaxation time measurement to find the individual k_a and k_b.

11.3 Consecutive reactions

It is commonly the case that a reactant produces an intermediate, which subsequently decays into a product. Radioactive decay is often of this type, with one nuclide decaying into another, and then that nuclide decaying into a third:

$$^{239}\text{U} \xrightarrow{2.35\ \text{min}} {}^{239}\text{Np} \xrightarrow{2.35\ \text{days}} {}^{239}\text{Pu}$$

(The times are half-lives.) Biochemical processes are often elaborate versions of this simple model. For instance, the restriction enzyme EcoRI catalyses the cleavage of DNA and brings about the sequence of reactions

$$\text{Supercoiled DNA} \rightarrow \text{open-circle DNA} \rightarrow \text{linear DNA}$$

To illustrate the kinds of considerations involved, let's suppose that the reaction takes place in two steps, in one of which the intermediate I (the open-circle DNA, for instance) is formed from the reactant A (the supercoiled DNA) in a first-order reaction, and then I decays in a first-order reaction to form the product P (the linear DNA)

$$\text{A} \rightarrow \text{I} \qquad \text{rate of formation of I} = k_1[\text{A}]$$

$$\text{I} \rightarrow \text{P} \qquad \text{rate of formation of P} = k_2[\text{I}]$$

For simplicity, we are ignoring the reverse reactions, which is valid if they are slow. The first of these rate laws implies that the decay of A is first-order, and therefore that

$$[\text{A}] = [\text{A}]_0\, e^{-k_1 t} \qquad (11.5a)$$

The net rate of formation of I is the difference between its rate of formation and its rate of consumption, so we can write

$$\text{Net rate of formation of I} = k_1[\text{A}] - k_2[\text{I}]$$

with [A] given by eqn 11.5a. This equation is more difficult to solve, but it is a standard form with the following solution:

$$[\text{I}] = \frac{k_1}{k_2 - k_1}(e^{-k_1 t} - e^{-k_2 t})[\text{A}]_0 \qquad (11.5b)$$

Finally, because $[\text{A}] + [\text{I}] + [\text{P}] = [\text{A}]_0$ at all stages of the reaction, the concentration of P is

$$[\text{P}] = \left(1 + \frac{k_1 e^{-k_2 t} - k_2 e^{-k_1 t}}{k_2 - k_1}\right)[\text{A}]_0 \qquad (11.5c)$$

These solutions are illustrated in Fig. 11.4. We see that the intermediate grows in concentration initially, then decays as A is exhausted. Meanwhile, the concentration of P rises smoothly to its final value. As we see in Derivation 11.3, the intermediate reaches its maximum concentration at

$$t = \frac{1}{k_1 - k_2}\ln\frac{k_1}{k_2} \qquad (11.6)$$

This is the optimum time for a manufacturer trying to make the intermediate in a batch process to extract it. For instance, if $k_1 = 0.120\ \text{h}^{-1}$ and

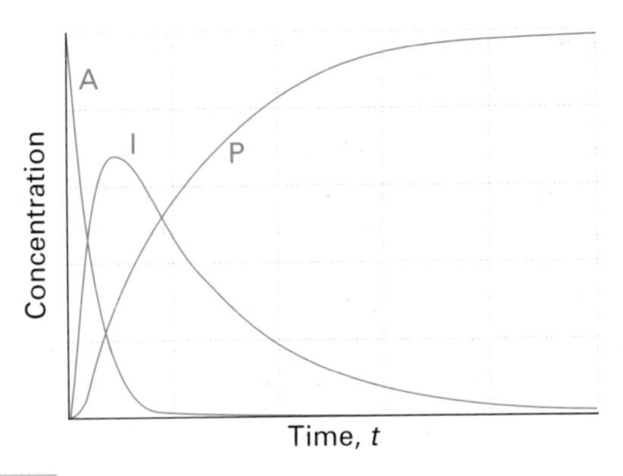

Fig. 11.4 The concentrations of the substances involved in a consecutive reaction of the form A → I → P, where I is an intermediate and P a product. We have used $k_1 = 5k_2$. Note how, at each time, the sum of the three concentrations is a constant.

$k_2 = 0.012\ \text{h}^{-1}$, then the intermediate is at a maximum at $t = 21$ h after the start of the process.

Derivation 11.3

The time of maximum concentration

To find the time corresponding to the maximum concentration of intermediate, we differentiate eqn 11.5b and look for the time at which $\text{d}[\text{I}]/\text{d}t = 0$. First, because $\text{d}e^{at}/\text{d}t = a\,e^{at}$, we obtain

$$\frac{\text{d}[\text{I}]}{\text{d}t} = \frac{k_1}{k_2 - k_1}(-k_1\,e^{-k_1 t} + k_2\,e^{-k_2 t})[\text{A}]_0 = 0$$

This equation is satisfied if

$$k_1\,e^{-k_1 t} = k_2\,e^{-k_2 t}$$

Because $e^{at}\,e^{bt} = e^{(a+b)t}$, this relation becomes

$$\frac{k_1}{k_2} = e^{(k_1 - k_2)t}$$

Taking logarithms of both sides leads to eqn 11.6.

Reaction mechanisms

We have seen how two simple types of reaction—approach to equilibrium and consecutive reactions—result in a characteristic dependence of the concentration on the time. We can suspect that other variations with time will act as the signatures of other reaction mechanisms.

11.4 Elementary reactions

Many reactions occur in a series of steps called **elementary reactions**, each of which involves only one or two molecules. We shall denote an elementary reaction by writing its chemical equation without displaying the physical state of the species, as in[1]

$$\text{H} + \text{Br}_2 \rightarrow \text{HBr} + \text{Br}$$

This equation signifies that a specific H atom attacks a specific Br_2 molecule to produce a molecule of HBr and a Br atom. Ordinary chemical equations summarize the overall stoichiometry of the reaction and do not imply any specific mechanism.

The **molecularity** of an elementary reaction is the number of molecules coming together to react. In a **unimolecular reaction** a single molecule shakes itself apart or its atoms into a new arrangement (Fig. 11.5). An example is the isomerization of cyclopropane into propene. The radioactive decay of nuclei (for example, the emission of a β particle from the nucleus of a tritium atom, which is used in mechanistic studies to follow the course of particular groups of atoms) is 'unimolecular' in the sense that a single nucleus shakes itself apart. In a **bimolecular reaction**, two molecules collide and exchange energy, atoms, or groups of atoms, or undergo some other kind of change, as in the reaction between H and F_2 or between H and Br_2 (Fig. 11.6).

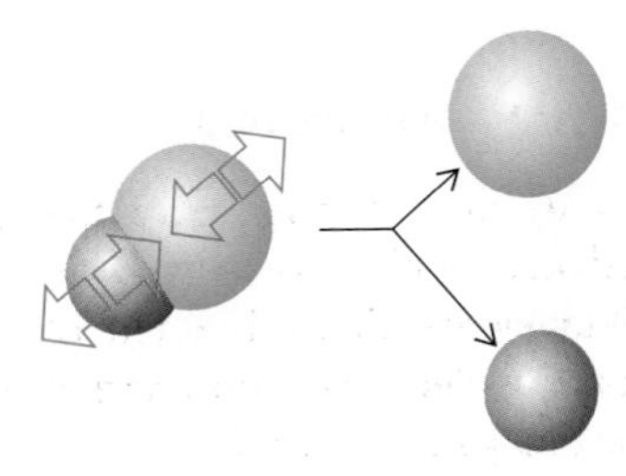

Fig. 11.5 In a unimolecular elementary reaction, an energetically excited species decomposes into products: it simply shakes itself apart.

[1] We have already used this convention without comment in some of the reactions discussed in Chapter 10.

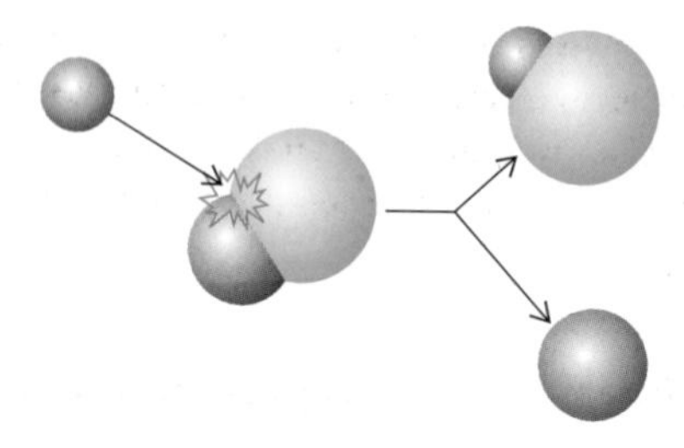

Fig. 11.6 In a bimolecular elementary reaction, two species are involved in the process.

It is important to distinguish molecularity from order: the *order* of a reaction is an empirical quantity, and is obtained by inspection of the experimentally determined rate law; the *molecularity* of a reaction refers to an individual elementary reaction that has been postulated as a step in a proposed mechanism. Many substitution reactions in organic chemistry (for instance, S_N2 nucleophilic substitutions) are bimolecular and involve an activated complex that is formed from two reactant species. Enzyme-catalysed reactions can be regarded, to a good approximation, as bimolecular in the sense that they depend on the encounter of a substrate molecule and an enzyme molecule.

We can write down the rate law of an elementary reaction from its chemical equation. First, consider a unimolecular reaction. In a given interval, 10 times as many A molecules decay when there are initially 1000 A molecules as when there are only 100 A molecules present. Therefore, the rate of decomposition of A is proportional to its concentration and we can conclude that *a unimolecular reaction is first-order*:

$$A \rightarrow \text{products} \qquad \text{rate} = k[A] \qquad (11.7)$$

The rate of a bimolecular reaction is proportional to the rate at which the reactants meet, which in turn is proportional to both their concentrations. Therefore, the rate of the reaction is proportional to the product of the two concentrations and *an elementary bimolecular reaction is second-order overall:*

$$A + B \rightarrow \text{products} \qquad \text{rate} = k[A][B] \qquad (11.8)$$

We must now explore how to string simple steps together into a mechanism and how to arrive at the corresponding overall rate law. For the present we emphasize that if the reaction is an elementary bimolecular process, then it has second-order kinetics; however, if the kinetics are second-order, then the reaction could be bimolecular but might be complex.

11.5 The formulation of rate laws

Suppose we propose that a particular reaction is the outcome of a sequence of elementary steps. How do we arrive at the rate law implied by the mechanism? We introduce the technique by considering the rate law for the gas-phase oxidation of nitric oxide (nitrogen monoxide, NO):

$$2\,NO(g) + O_2(g) \rightarrow 2\,NO_2(g)$$

Nitric oxide is a very important component of polluted atmospheres. It is formed in the hot exhausts of vehicles and the jet engines of aircraft and its oxidation is a step in the formation of acid rain. The compound is also a neurotransmitter involved in the physiological changes taking place during sexual arousal. Experimentally, the reaction is found to be third-order overall:

$$\text{Rate} = k[NO]^2[O_2]$$

One explanation of the observed reaction order might be that the reaction is a single termolecular (three-molecule) elementary step involving the simultaneous collision of two NO molecules and one O_2 molecule. However, such collisions occur very infrequently. Therefore, although termolecular collisions may contribute, the rate of reaction by this mechanism is so slow that another mechanism usually dominates.

The following mechanism has been proposed:

Step 1 Two NO molecules combine to form a dimer:

$$NO + NO \rightarrow N_2O_2$$

$$\text{rate of formation of } N_2O_2 = k_a[NO]^2$$

This step is plausible, because NO is an odd-electron species, a radical, and two radicals can form a covalent bond when they meet. That the N_2O_2 dimer is also known in the solid makes the suggestion plausible: it is often a good strategy to decide whether a proposed intermediate is the analogue of a known compound.

Step 2 The N_2O_2 dimer decomposes into NO molecules:

$$N_2O_2 \rightarrow NO + NO$$
$$\text{rate of decomposition of } N_2O_2 = k_a'[N_2O_2]$$

This step, the reverse of step 1, is a unimolecular decay: the dimer shakes itself apart. We adopt the convention in which the rate constant of a reverse reaction is marked with a prime (as in k_a for the forward reaction and k_a' for its reverse).

Step 3 Alternatively, an O_2 molecule collides with the dimer and results in the formation of NO_2:

$$N_2O_2 + O_2 \rightarrow NO_2 + NO_2$$
$$\text{rate of consumption of } N_2O_2 = k_b[N_2O_2][O_2]$$

Now we proceed to derive the rate law on the basis of this proposed mechanism. The rate of formation of product comes directly from step 3:

$$\text{rate of formation of } NO_2 = 2k_b[N_2O_2][O_2]$$

The 2 appears in the rate law because two NO_2 molecules are formed in each reaction event, so the concentration of NO_2 increases at twice the rate that the concentration of N_2O_2 decays. However, this expression is not an acceptable overall rate law because it is expressed in terms of the concentration of the intermediate N_2O_2: an acceptable rate law for an overall reaction is expressed solely in terms of the species that appear in the overall reaction. Therefore, we need to find an expression for the concentration of N_2O_2. To do so, we consider the net rate of formation of the intermediate, the difference between its rates of formation and decay. Because N_2O_2 is formed by step 1 but decays by steps 2 and 3, its net rate of formation is

$$\text{Net rate of formation of } N_2O_2$$
$$= k_a[NO]^2 - k_a'[N_2O_2] - k_b[N_2O_2][O_2]$$

Note that formation terms occur with a positive sign and decay terms occur with a negative sign because they reduce the net rate of formation.

If we could solve this equation for the concentration of N_2O_2 in terms of the concentrations of NO and O_2, we could substitute the result into the preceding expression and obtain the overall rate law. However, this involves solving a very difficult differential equation, and will give an enormously complex expression. In fact, even in this relatively simple case, we can obtain only a numerical solution using a computer. To make progress towards obtaining a simple formula, we must make an approximation.

11.6 The steady-state approximation

It is common at this stage of formulating a rate law to introduce the **steady-state approximation**, in which we suppose that *the concentrations of all intermediates remain constant and small throughout the reaction* (except right at the beginning and right at the end). An **intermediate** is any species that does not appear in the overall reaction but that has been invoked in the mechanism. For our mechanism the intermediate is N_2O_2, so we write

$$\text{Net rate of formation of } N_2O_2 = 0$$

which implies that

$$k_a[NO]^2 - k_a'[N_2O_2] - k_b[N_2O_2][O_2] = 0$$

We can rearrange this equation into an expression for the concentration of N_2O_2:

$$[N_2O_2] = \frac{k_a[NO]^2}{k_a' + k_b[O_2]}$$

It follows that the rate of formation of NO_2 is

$$\text{Rate of formation of } NO_2 = 2k_b[N_2O_2][O_2]$$
$$= \frac{2k_ak_b[NO]^2[O_2]}{k_a' + k_b[O_2]} \qquad (11.9)$$

At this stage, the rate law is more complex than the observed law, but the numerator resembles it. The two expressions become identical if we suppose that the rate of decomposition of the dimer is much greater than its rate of reaction with oxygen, as then $k_a'[N_2O_2] \gg k_b[N_2O_2][O_2]$, or, after cancelling the $[N_2O_2]$, $k_a' \gg k_b[O_2]$. When this condition is satisfied, we can approximate the denominator in the overall rate law by k_a' alone and conclude that

$$\text{Rate of formation of } NO_2$$
$$= \left(\frac{2k_ak_b}{k_a'}\right)[NO]^2[O_2] \qquad (11.10)$$

This expression has the observed overall third-order form. Moreover, we can identify the observed rate constant as the following combination of rate constants for the elementary reactions:

$$k = \frac{2k_a k_b}{k'_a} \quad (11.11)$$

Self-test 11.1

An alternative mechanism that may apply when the concentration of O_2 is high and that of NO is low is one in which the first step is $NO + O_2 \rightarrow NO\cdots O_2$ and its reverse, followed by $NO\cdots O_2 + NO \rightarrow NO_2 + NO_2$. Confirm that this mechanism also leads to the observed rate law when the concentration of NO is low.

[*Answer:* rate $= 2k_a k_b[NO]^2[O_2]/(k'_a + k_b[NO]) \approx (2k_a k_b/k'_a)[NO]^2[O_2]$]

One feature to note is that although each of the rate constants in eqn 11.11 increases with temperature, that might not be true of k itself. Thus, if the rate constant k'_a increases more rapidly than the product $k_a k_b$ increases, then k will decrease with increasing temperature and the reaction will go more slowly as the temperature is raised. The physical reason is that the dimer N_2O_2 shakes itself apart so quickly at the higher temperature that its reaction with O_2 is less able to take place, and products are formed more slowly. Mathematically, we would say that the composite reaction had a 'negative activation energy'. We have to be very cautious about making predictions about the effect of temperature on reactions that are the outcome of several steps.

Self-test 11.2

Suppose that each rate constant in eqn 11.11 exhibits an Arrhenius temperature dependence, and show that k is also Arrhenius-like with the possibility that the overall activation energy is negative.

[*Answer:* $A = 2A_a A_b/A'_a$, $E_a = E_{a,a} + E_{a,b} - E'_{a,a} < 0$ if $E'_{a,a} > E_{a,a} + E_{a,b}$]

11.7 The rate-determining step

The oxidation of nitrogen monoxide introduces another important concept. Let's suppose that step 3 is very fast, so k'_a may be neglected relative to $k_b[O_2]$ in eqn 11.9. One way to achieve this condition is to increase the concentration of O_2 in the reaction mixture. Then the rate law simplifies to

$$\text{Rate of formation of } NO_2 = \frac{2k_a k_b[NO]^2[O_2]}{k_b[O_2]} = 2k_a[NO]^2 \quad (11.12)$$

Now the reaction is second-order in NO and the concentration of O_2 does not appear in the rate law. The physical explanation is that the rate of reaction of N_2O_2 is so great, on account of the high concentration of O_2 in the system, that N_2O_2 reacts as soon as it is formed. Therefore, under these conditions, the rate of formation of NO_2 is determined by the rate at which N_2O_2 is formed. This step is an example of a **rate-determining step**, the slowest step in a reaction mechanism, which controls the rate of the overall reaction.

The rate-determining step is not just the slowest step: it must be slow *and* be a crucial gateway for the formation of products. If a faster reaction can also lead to products, then the slowest step is irrelevant because the slow reaction can then be side-stepped (Fig. 11.7). The rate-determining step is like a slow ferry crossing between two fast highways: the overall rate at which traffic can reach its destination is

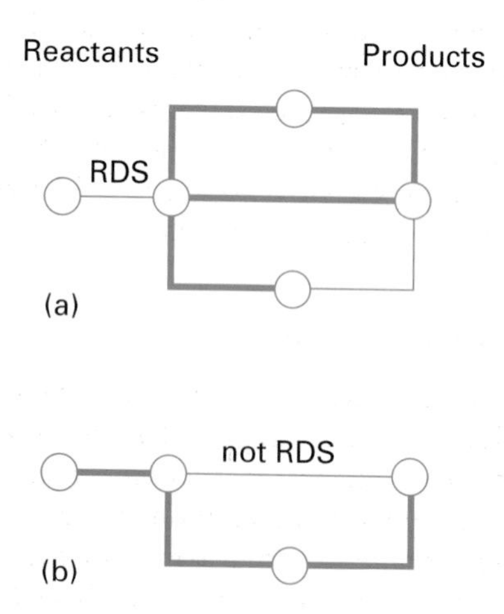

Fig. 11.7 The rate-determining step (RDS) is the slowest step of a reaction *and* acts as a bottleneck. In this schematic diagram, fast reactions are represented by heavy lines (freeways) and slow reactions by thin lines (country lanes). Circles represent substances. (a) The first step is rate-determining. (b) Although the second step is the slowest, it is not rate-determining because it does not act as a bottleneck (there is a faster route that circumvents it).

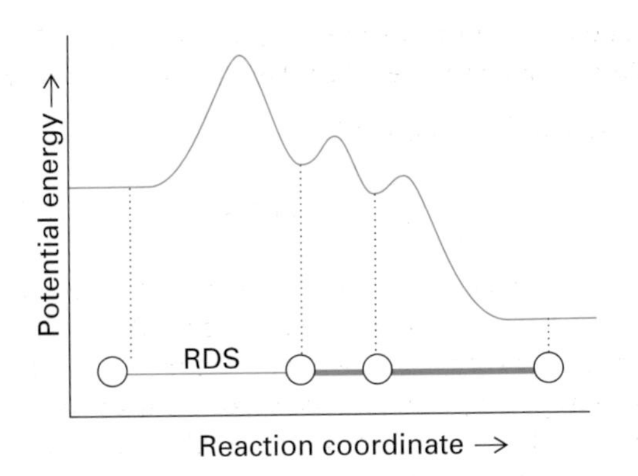

Fig. 11.8 The reaction profile for a mechanism in which the first step is the rate-determining step (RDS).

determined by the rate at which it can make the ferry crossing. If a bridge is built that circumvents the ferry, the ferry remains the slowest step but it is no longer rate-determining.

The rate law of a reaction that has a rate-determining step can often be written down almost by inspection. If the first step in a mechanism is rate-determining, then the rate of the overall reaction is equal to the rate of the first step because all subsequent steps are so fast that once the first intermediate is formed it results immediately in the formation of products. Figure 11.8 shows the reaction profile for a mechanism of this kind in which the slowest step is the one with the highest activation energy. Once over the initial barrier, the intermediates cascade into products.

11.8 Kinetic control

In some cases reactants can give rise to a variety of products, as in nitrations of mono-substituted benzene, when various proportions of the ortho-, meta-, and para-substituted products are obtained, depending on the directing power of the original substituent. Suppose two products, P_1 and P_2, are produced by the following competing reactions:

$A + B \rightarrow P_1$ rate of formation of $P_1 = k_1[A][B]$

$A + B \rightarrow P_2$ rate of formation of $P_2 = k_2[A][B]$

The relative proportion in which the two products have been produced at a given stage of the reaction (before it has reached equilibrium) is given by the ratio of the two rates, and therefore to the two rate constants:

$$\frac{[P_2]}{[P_1]} = \frac{k_2}{k_1} \tag{11.13}$$

This ratio represents the **kinetic control** over the proportions of products, and is a common feature of the reactions encountered in organic chemistry, where reactants are chosen that facilitate pathways favouring the formation of a desired product. If a reaction is allowed to reach equilibrium, then the proportion of products is determined by thermodynamic rather than kinetic considerations, and the ratio of concentrations is controlled by considerations of the standard Gibbs energies of all the reactants and products.

11.9 Unimolecular reactions

A number of gas-phase reactions follow first-order kinetics, as in the isomerization of cyclopropane mentioned earlier, in which the strained triangular molecule bursts open into an acyclic alkene:

$$cyclo\text{-}C_3H_6 \rightarrow CH_3CH{=}CH_2$$

$$\text{rate} = k[cyclo\text{-}C_3H_6]$$

The problem with reactions like this is that the reactant molecule presumably acquires the energy it needs to react by collisions with other molecules. Collisions, though, are simple *bimolecular* events, so how can they result in a first-order rate law? First-order gas-phase reactions are widely called 'unimolecular reactions' because (as we shall see) the rate-determining step is an elementary unimolecular reaction in which the reactant molecule changes into the product. This term must be used with caution, however, because the composite mechanism has bimolecular as well as unimolecular steps.

The first successful explanation of unimolecular reactions is ascribed to Frederick Lindemann in 1921. The **Lindemann mechanism** is as follows:

Step 1 A reactant molecule A becomes energetically excited (denoted A*) by collision with another A molecule:

$$A + A \rightarrow A^* + A$$

$$\text{rate of formation of } A^* = k_a[A]^2$$

Step 2 The energized molecule might lose its excess energy by collision with another molecule:

$A^* + A \rightarrow A + A$

rate of deactivation of $A^* = k_a'[A^*][A]$

Step 3 Alternatively, the excited molecule might shake itself apart and form products P. That is, it might undergo the unimolecular decay

$A^* \rightarrow P$

rate of formation of $P = k_b[A^*]$

rate of consumption of $A^* = k_b[A^*]$

If the unimolecular step, Step 3, is slow enough to be the rate-determining step, the overall reaction will have first-order kinetics, as observed. We can demonstrate this conclusion explicitly by applying the steady-state approximation to the net rate of formation of the intermediate A* and find that

Rate of formation of $P = k[A]$,

$$\text{with } k = \frac{k_a k_b}{k_a'} \qquad (11.14)$$

This rate law is first-order, as we set out to show.

Derivation 11.4

The Lindemann mechanism

First, we write down the expression for the net rate of formation of A*, and set this rate equal to zero:

Net rate of formation of A*

(Formation) (Deactivation) (Reaction)

$$= k_a[A]^2 - k_a'[A^*][A] - k_b[A^*] = 0$$

(Steady state)

The solution of this equation is

$$[A^*] = \frac{k_a[A]^2}{k_b + k_a'[A]}$$

It follows that the rate law for the formation of products is

$$\text{Rate of formation of P} = k_b[A^*] = \frac{k_a k_b[A]^2}{k_b + k_a'[A]}$$

At this stage the rate law is not first-order in A. However, we can suppose that the rate of deactivation of A* by (A*,A) collisions is much greater than the rate of unimolecular decay of A* to products. That is, we suppose that the unimolecular decay of A* is the rate-determining step. Then $k_a'[A^*][A] \gg k_b[A^*]$, which corresponds to $k_a'[A] \gg k_b$. If that is the case, we can neglect k_b in the denominator of the rate law and obtain eqn 11.14.

Self-test 11.3

Suppose that an inert gas M is present and dominates the excitation of A and de-excitation of A*. Derive the rate law for the formation of products.

[*Answer:* rate $= k_a k_b[A][M]/(k_b + k_a'[M])$]

Reactions in solution

We now turn specifically to reactions in solution, where the reactant molecules do not fly freely through a gaseous medium and collide with each other, but wriggle past their closely packed neighbours as gaps open up in the structure.

11.10 Activation control and diffusion control

The concept of the rate-determining step plays an important role in reactions in solution, where it leads to the distinction between 'diffusion control' and 'activation control'. To develop this point, let's suppose that a reaction between two solute molecules A and B occurs by the following mechanism. First, we assume that A and B drift into each other's vicinity by the process of diffusion, and form an **encounter pair**, AB, at a rate proportional to each of their concentrations:

$A + B \rightarrow AB$ rate of formation of $AB = k_d[A][B]$

The 'd' subscript reminds us that this process is diffusional. The encounter pair persists for some time as a result of the **cage effect**, the trapping of A and B near each other by their inability to escape rapidly through the surrounding solvent molecules. However, the encounter pair can break up when A and B have the opportunity to diffuse apart, so we must allow for the following process:

$AB \rightarrow A + B$ rate of loss of $AB = k_d'[AB]$

We suppose that this process is first-order in AB. Competing with this process is the reaction between A and B while they exist as an encounter pair. This process depends on their ability to acquire sufficient energy to react. That energy might come from the jostling of the thermal motion of the solvent molecules. We assume that this step is first-order in AB, but if the solvent molecules are involved it is more accurate to regard it as pseudofirst-order with the solvent molecules in great and constant excess. In any event, we can suppose that the reaction is

$$\text{AB} \rightarrow \text{products}$$

$$\text{rate of reactive loss of AB} = k_a[\text{AB}]$$

The 'a' subscript reminds us that this process is activated in the sense that it depends on the acquisition by AB of at least a minimum energy.

Now we use the steady-state approximation to set up the rate law for the formation of products and find

$$\text{Rate of formation of products} = k[\text{A}][\text{B}]$$

$$k = \frac{k_a k_d}{k_a + k_d'} \tag{11.15}$$

Derivation 11.5

Diffusion control

The net rate of formation of AB is

$$\text{Net rate of formation of AB} = k_d[\text{A}][\text{B}] - k_d'[\text{AB}] - k_a[\text{AB}]$$

In a steady state, this rate is zero, so we can write

$$k_d[\text{A}][\text{B}] - k_d'[\text{AB}] - k_a[\text{AB}] = 0$$

which we can rearrange to find [AB]:

$$[\text{AB}] = \frac{k_d[\text{A}][\text{B}]}{k_a + k_d'}$$

The rate of formation of products (which is the same as the rate of reactive loss of AB) is therefore

$$\text{Rate of formation of products} = k_a[\text{AB}] = \frac{k_a k_d[\text{A}][\text{B}]}{k_a + k_d'}$$

This expression is the same as eqn 11.15.

Now we distinguish two limits. Suppose the rate of reaction is much faster than the rate at which the encounter pair breaks up. In this case, $k_a \gg k_d'$ and we can neglect k_d' in the denominator of the expression for k in eqn 11.15. The k_a in the numerator and denominator then cancel and we are left with

$$\text{Rate of formation of products} = k_d[\text{A}][\text{B}]$$

In this **diffusion-controlled limit**, the rate of the reaction is controlled by the rate at which the reactants diffuse together (as expressed by k_d), as once they have encountered each other, the reaction is so fast that they will certainly go on to form products rather than diffuse apart before reacting. Alternatively, we may suppose that the rate at which the encounter pair accumulated enough energy to react is so low that it is highly likely that the pair will break up. In this case, we can set $k_a \ll k_d'$ in the expression for k, and obtain

$$\text{Rate of formation of products} = \frac{k_a k_d}{k_d'}[\text{A}][\text{B}] \tag{11.16}$$

In this **activation-controlled limit**, the reaction rate depends on the rate at which energy accumulates in the encounter pair (as expressed by k_a).

A lesson to learn from this analysis is that the concept of the rate-determining stage is rather subtle. Thus, in the diffusion-controlled limit, the condition for the encounter rate to be rate-determining is not that it is the slowest step, but that the reaction rate of the encounter pair is much greater than the rate at which the pair breaks up. In the activation-controlled limit, the condition for the rate of energy accumulation to be rate-determining is likewise a competition between the rate of reaction of the pair and the rate at which it breaks up, and all three rate constants control the overall rate. The best way to analyse competing rates is to do as we have done here: set up the overall rate law, and then analyse how it simplifies as we allow particular elementary processes to dominate others.

A detailed analysis of the rates of diffusion of molecules in liquids shows that the rate constant k_d is related to the **coefficient of viscosity**, η (eta), of the medium by

$$k_d = \frac{8RT}{3\eta} \tag{11.17}$$

We see that the higher the viscosity, then the smaller the diffusional rate constant, and therefore the slower the reaction of a diffusion-controlled reaction.

Illustration 11.2

The diffusion-controlled rate constant

For a diffusion-controlled reaction in water, for which $\eta = 8.9 \times 10^{-4}$ kg m^{-1} s^{-1} at 25°C, we find

$$k_d = \frac{8 \times (8.3145 \text{ J K}^{-1}\text{ mol}^{-1}) \times (298 \text{ K})}{3 \times (8.9 \times 10^{-4} \text{ kg m}^{-1}\text{ s}^{-1})}$$

(R, T and η are labelled in callouts.)

$$= \frac{8 \times 8.3145 \times 298}{3 \times 8.9 \times 10^{-4}} \frac{\text{J mol}^{-1}}{\text{kg m}^{-1}\text{ s}^{-1}}$$

(J is labelled in a callout.)

$$= 7.4 \times 10^{6} \frac{\text{kg m}^2\text{ s}^{-2}\text{ mol}^{-1}}{\text{kg m}^{-1}\text{ s}^{-1}}$$

$$= 7.4 \times 10^{6} \text{ m}^3\text{ s}^{-1}\text{ mol}^{-1}$$

Because 1 m^3 = 10^3 dm^3, this result can be written k_d = 7.4 × 10^9 dm^3 mol^{-1} s^{-1}, which is a useful approximate estimate to keep in mind for such reactions.

11.11 Diffusion

Diffusion plays such a central role in the processes involved in reactions in solution that we need to examine it more closely. The picture to hold in mind is that a molecule in a liquid is surrounded by other molecules and can move only a fraction of a diameter, perhaps because its neighbours move aside momentarily, before colliding. Molecular motion in liquids is a series of short steps, with incessantly changing directions, like people in an aimless, milling crowd.

The process of migration by means of a random jostling motion through a fluid (a gas as well as a liquid) is called **diffusion**. We can think of the motion of the molecule as a series of short jumps in random directions, a so-called **random walk**. If there is an initial concentration gradient in the liquid (for instance, a solution may have a high concentration of solute in one region), then the rate at which the molecules spread out is proportional to the concentration gradient, $\Delta c/\Delta x$, and we write

$$\text{Rate of diffusion} \propto \text{concentration gradient}$$

To express this relation mathematically, we introduce the **flux**, J, which is the number of particles passing through an imaginary window in a given time interval, divided by the area of the window and the duration of the interval:

$$J = \frac{\text{number of particles passing through window}}{\text{area of window} \times \text{time interval}} \qquad (11.18a)$$

Then,

$$J = -D \times \text{concentration gradient} \qquad (11.18b)$$

Equation 11.18b is a verbal interpretation of the equation

$$J = -D\frac{dc}{dx}$$

where dc/dx is the gradient of the number concentration c.

Equation 11.18b is called **Fick's first law** of diffusion (see *Further information* 11.1 for a derivation and the precise mathematical form). The coefficient D, which has the dimensions of area divided by time (with units m^2 s^{-1}), is called the **diffusion coefficient**: if D is large, molecules diffuse rapidly. Some values are given in Table 11.1. The negative sign in eqn 11.18b simply means that if the concentration gradient is negative (down from left to right, Fig. 11.9), then the flux is positive (flowing from left to right). To get the number of molecules passing through a given window in a given time interval, we multiply the flux by the area of the window and the time interval. If the concentration in eqn 11.18b is

Table 11.1

Diffusion coefficients at 25°C, $D/(10^{-9}$ m^2 s$^{-1})$

Ar in tetrachloromethane	3.63
$C_{12}H_{22}O_{11}$ (sucrose) in water	0.522
CH_3OH in water	1.58
H_2O in water	2.26
NH_2CH_2COOH in water	0.673
O_2 in tetrachloromethane	3.82

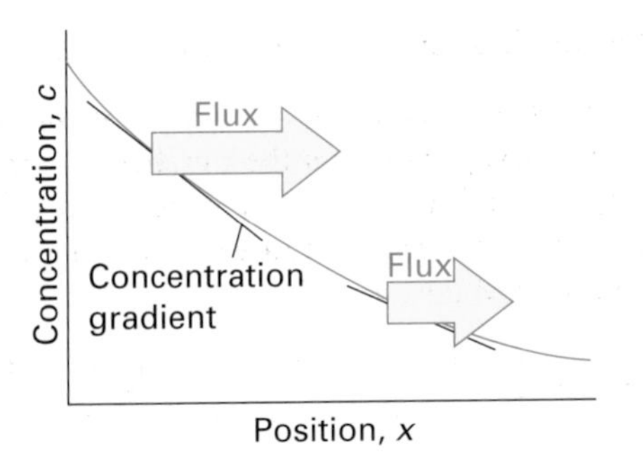

Fig. 11.9 The flux of solute particles is proportional to the concentration gradient. Here we see a solution in which the concentration falls from left to right. The gradient is negative (down from left to right) and the flux is positive (towards the right). The greatest flux is found where the gradient is steepest (towards the left).

a molar concentration, then the flux is expressed in moles rather than numbers of molecules.

Illustration 11.3

Estimating the flux of molecules

Suppose that in a region of an unstirred aqueous solution of sucrose the molar concentration gradient is -0.10 mol dm^{-3} cm^{-1}, then the flux arising from this gradient is

$$J = -(0.522 \times 10^{-9}\ \text{m}^2\ \text{s}^{-1}) \times (-0.10\ \text{mol dm}^{-3}\ \text{cm}^{-1})$$

$$= 5.22 \times 10^{-11}\ \frac{\text{m}^2\ \text{s}^{-1}\ \text{mol}}{\text{dm}^3\ \text{cm}}$$

$$= 5.22 \times 10^{-11}\ \frac{\text{m}^2\ \text{s}^{-1}\ \text{mol}}{(10^{-3}\ \text{m}^3) \times (10^{-2}\ \text{m})}$$

$$= 5.22 \times 10^{-11} \times 10^5\ \text{m}^{-2}\ \text{s}^{-1}\ \text{mol}$$

$$= 5.2 \times 10^{-6}\ \text{mol m}^{-2}\ \text{s}^{-1}$$

The amount of sucrose molecules passing through a 1.0-cm square window in 10 minutes is therefore

$$n = JA\Delta t$$

$$= (5.2 \times 10^{-6}\ \text{mol m}^{-2}\ \text{s}^{-1}) \times (1.0 \times 10^{-2}\ \text{m})^2 \times (10 \times 60\ \text{s})$$

$$= 3.1 \times 10^{-7}\ \text{mol}$$

The diffusion of molecules may be assisted—and normally greatly dominated—by bulk motion of the fluid as a whole (as when a wind blows in the atmosphere and currents flow in lakes). This motion is called **convection**. Because diffusion is so slow, we speed up the spread of solute molecules by inducing convection by stirring a fluid, turning on an extractor fan, or relying on natural phenomena such as winds and storms.

One of the most important equations in the physical chemistry of fluids is the **diffusion equation**, which enables us to predict the rate at which the concentration of a solute changes in a non-uniform solution. In essence, the diffusion equation expresses the fact that wrinkles in the concentration tend to disperse. The formal (but still verbal) statement of the diffusion equation, which is also known as **Fick's second law** of diffusion, is:

Rate of change of concentration in a region
$= D \times$ (curvature of the concentration in the region) (11.19)

The 'curvature' is a measure of the wrinkliness of the concentration (see below). The derivation of this expression is given in *Further information* 11.1, which shows how to derive this law from Fick's first law. The concentrations on the left and right of this equation may be either number concentration (molecules m^{-3}, for instance) or molar concentration.

The mathematical form of the diffusion equation is

$$\frac{dc}{dt} = D\frac{d^2c}{dx^2}$$

We are interpreting the second derivative d^2c/dx^2 as a measure of the curvature of the concentration c. Because the concentration is a function of both time and location, the derivatives are in fact *partial* derivatives; but we are not using that notation in this book.

The diffusion equation tells us that a uniform concentration and a concentration with unvarying slope through the region result in no net change in concentration because the rate of influx through one wall of the region is equal to the rate of efflux through the opposite wall. Only if the slope of the concentration varies through the region—only if the concentration is wrinkled—is there a change in concentration. Where the curvature is positive (a dip, Fig. 11.10) the change in concentration is positive: the dip tends to fill. Where the curvature is negative (a heap), the change in concentration is negative: the heap tends to spread.

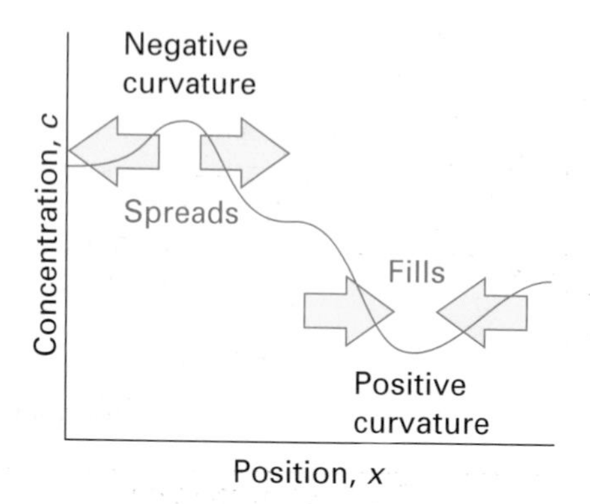

Fig. 11.10 Nature abhors a wrinkle. The diffusion equation tells us that peaks in a distribution (regions of negative curvature) spread and troughs (regions of positive curvature) fill in.

We can understand the nature of diffusion more deeply by considering it as the outcome of a random walk, a series of steps in random directions and (in general) through random distances. Although a molecule undergoing a random walk may take many steps in a given time, it has only a small probability of being found far from its starting point because some of the steps lead it away from the starting point but others lead it back. The net distance travelled in a time t from the starting point is measured by the **root mean square distance**, d,[2] with

$$d = (2Dt)^{1/2} \qquad (11.20)$$

Thus, the net distance increases only as the square root of the time, so for a particle to be found twice as far (on average) from its starting point, we must wait four times as long.

Self-test 11.4

The diffusion coefficient of H_2O in water is $2.26 \times 10^{-9}\ m^2\ s^{-1}$ at 25°C. How long does it take for an H_2O molecule to travel (a) 1.0 cm, (b) 2.0 cm from its starting point in a sample of unstirred water?

[*Answer:* (a) 6.1 h, (b) 25 h]

The relation between the diffusion coefficient and the rate at which the molecule takes its steps and the distance of each step is called the **Einstein–Smoluchowski equation**:

$$D = \frac{\lambda^2}{2\tau} \qquad (11.21)$$

where λ (lambda) is the length of each step (which in the model is assumed to be the same for each step) and τ (tau) is the time each step takes. This equation tells us that a molecule that takes rapid, long steps has a high diffusion coefficient. We can interpret τ as the average lifetime of a molecule near another molecule before it makes a sudden jump to its next position.

Self-test 11.5

Suppose an H_2O molecule moves through one molecular diameter (about 200 pm) each time it takes a step in a random walk. What is the time for each step at 25°C?

[*Answer:* 9 ps]

The diffusion coefficient increases with temperature because an increase in temperature enables a molecule to escape more easily from the attractive forces exerted by its neighbours. If we suppose that the rate ($1/\tau$) of the random walk follows an Arrhenius temperature dependence with an activation energy E_a, then the diffusion coefficient will follow the relation

$$D = D_0\, e^{-E_a/RT} \qquad (11.22)$$

The rate at which particles diffuse through a liquid is related to the viscosity, and we should expect a high diffusion coefficient to be found for fluids that have a low viscosity. That is, we can suspect that $\eta \propto 1/D$, where η is the coefficient of viscosity. In fact, the **Einstein relation** states that

$$D = \frac{kT}{6\pi\eta a} \qquad (11.23)$$

where a is the radius of the molecule. It follows that[3]

$$\eta = \eta_0\, e^{E_a/RT} \qquad (11.24)$$

[2] The formal definition of the root mean square distance is $\{\langle d^2\rangle - \langle d\rangle^2\}^{1/2}$, where $\langle\ldots\rangle$ denotes an average value.

[3] Note the change in sign of the exponent: viscosity decreases as the temperature is raised. We are supposing that the strong temperature dependence of the exponential term dominates the weak linear dependence on T in the numerator of eqn 11.23.

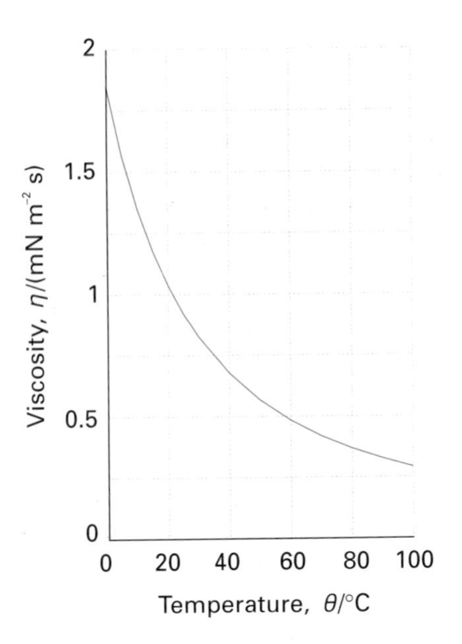

Fig. 11.11 The experimental temperature dependence of the viscosity of water. As the temperature is increased, more molecules are able to escape from the potential wells provided by their neighbours, so the liquid becomes more fluid.

This temperature dependence is observed, at least over reasonably small temperature ranges (Fig. 11.11). The intermolecular potentials govern the magnitude of E_a, but the problem of calculating it is immensely difficult and still largely unsolved.

Self-test 11.6

Estimate the activation energy for the viscosity of water from the graph in Fig. 11.11, by using the viscosities at 40°C and 80°C. *Hint.* Use an equation like eqn 11.24 to formulate an expression for the logarithm of the ratio of the two viscosities.

[*Answer:* 19 kJ mol^{-1}]

Catalysis

A **catalyst** is a substance that accelerates a reaction but undergoes no net chemical change. The catalyst lowers the activation energy of the reaction by providing an alternative path that avoids the slow, rate-determining step of the uncatalysed reaction (Fig. 11.12). Catalysts can be very effective; for

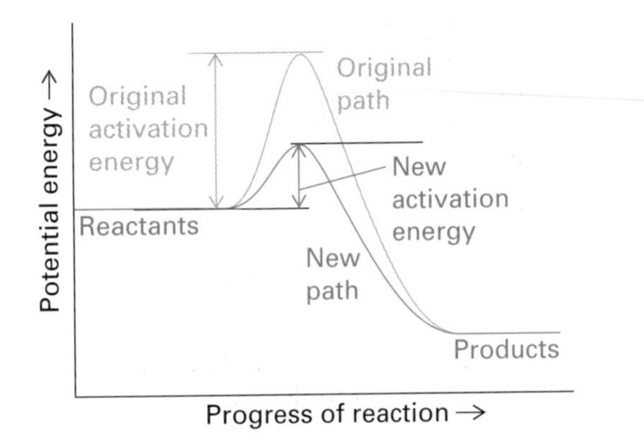

Fig. 11.12 A catalyst acts by providing a new reaction pathway between reactants and products, with a lower activation energy than the original pathway.

instance, the activation energy for the decomposition of hydrogen peroxide in solution is 76 kJ mol^{-1}, and the reaction is slow at room temperature. When a little iodide ion is added, the activation energy falls to 57 kJ mol^{-1} and the rate constant increases by a factor of 2000. **Enzymes**, which are biological catalysts, are very selective and can have a dramatic effect on the reactions they control. For example, the enzyme catalase reduces the activation energy for the decomposition of hydrogen peroxide to 8 kJ mol^{-1}, corresponding to an acceleration of the reaction by a factor of 10^{15} at 298 K.

11.12 Homogeneous catalysis

A **homogeneous catalyst** is a catalyst in the same phase as the reaction mixture. For example, the decomposition of hydrogen peroxide in aqueous solution is catalysed by bromide ion or catalase. A **heterogeneous catalyst** is a catalyst in a different phase from the reaction mixture. For example, the hydrogenation of ethene to ethane, a gas-phase reaction, is accelerated in the presence of a solid catalyst such as palladium, platinum, or nickel. The metal provides a surface upon which the reactants bind; this binding facilitates encounters between reactants and increases the rate of the reaction. We examine heterogeneous catalysis in Chapter 16 and consider only homogeneous catalysis here.

In **acid catalysis** the crucial step is the transfer of a proton to the substrate:

$$X + HA \rightarrow HX^+ + A^- \qquad HX^+ \rightarrow \text{products}$$

Acid catalysis is the primary process in keto–enol tautomerism:

$$CH_3COCH_2CH_3 \xrightleftharpoons{H^+} CH_3C(OH){=}CHCH_3$$

In **base catalysis**, a proton is transferred from the substrate to a base, as in the hydrolysis of esters:

$$CH_3COOCH_2CH_3 + H_2O \xrightarrow{OH^-} CH_3COOH \text{ (as } CH_3CO_2^-) + CH_3CH_2OH$$

11.13 Enzymes

One of the earliest descriptions of the action of enzymes is the **Michaelis–Menten mechanism.** The proposed mechanism, with all species in an aqueous environment, is as follows.[4]

Step 1 The bimolecular formation of a combination, ES, of the enzyme and the substrate:

$$E + S \rightarrow ES \qquad \text{rate of formation of ES} = k_a[E][S]$$

Step 2 The unimolecular decomposition of the complex:

$$ES \rightarrow E + S$$

$$\text{rate of decomposition of ES} = k_a'[ES]$$

Step 3 The unimolecular formation of products and the release of the enzyme from its combination with the substrate:

$$ES \rightarrow P + E \qquad \text{rate of formation of P} = k_b[ES]$$

$$\text{rate of consumption of ES} = k_b[ES]$$

The rate law for the rate of formation of product in terms of the concentrations of enzyme and substrate then turns out to be

$$\text{Rate of formation of P} = k[E]_0,$$

$$\text{with } k = \frac{k_b[E]_0[S]}{[S] + K_M} \qquad (11.25)$$

where the **Michaelis constant,** K_M (which has the dimensions of a concentration), is

$$K_M = \frac{k_a' + k_b}{k_a} \qquad (11.26)$$

and $[E]_0$ is the total concentration of enzyme (both bound and unbound).

Derivation 11.6

The Michaelis–Menten rate law

The product is formed (irreversibly) in step 3, so we begin by writing

$$\text{Rate of formation of P} = k_b[ES]$$

To calculate the concentration [ES] we set up an expression for the net rate of formation of ES allowing for its formation in step 1 and its removal in steps 2 and 3. Then we set that net rate equal to zero:

$$\text{Net rate of formation of ES} = k_a[E][S] - k_a'[ES] - k_b[ES] = 0$$

It follows that

$$[ES] = \frac{k_a[E][S]}{k_a' + k_b}$$

However, [E] and [S] are the molar concentrations of the *free* enzyme and *free* substrate. If $[E]_0$ is the total concentration of enzyme, then

$$[E] + [ES] = [E]_0$$

Because only a little enzyme is added, the free substrate concentration is almost the same as the total substrate concentration and we can ignore the fact that [S] differs slightly from [S] + [ES]. Therefore,

$$[ES] = \frac{k_a([E]_0 - [ES])[S]}{k_a' + k_b}$$

Multiplication by $k_a' + k_b$ gives first

$$k_a'[ES] + k_b[ES] = k_a[E]_0[S] - k_a[ES][S]$$

and then

$$(k_a' + k_b + k_a[S])[ES] = k_a[E]_0[S]$$

Division by k_a turns this expression into

$$\left(\frac{k_a' + k_b}{k_a} + [S]\right)[ES] = [E]_0[S]$$

We recognize the first term inside the parentheses as K_M, so this expression rearranges to

$$[ES] = \frac{[E]_0[S]}{[S] + K_M}$$

It follows from the first equation in this Derivation that the rate of formation of product is given by eqn 11.25.

[4] Michaelis and Menten derived their rate law in 1913 in a more restrictive way, by assuming a rapid equilibrium. The approach we take is a generalization using the steady-state approximation made by Briggs and Haldane in 1925.

According to eqn 11.25, the rate of enzymolysis is first-order in the enzyme concentration, but the effective rate constant k depends on the concentration of substrate. When $[S] \ll K_M$, the effective rate constant is equal to $k_b[S]/K_M$. Therefore, the rate increases linearly with [S] at low concentrations. When $[S] \gg K_M$, the effective rate constant is equal to k_b, and the rate law in eqn 11.25 reduces to

$$\text{Rate of formation of P} = k_b[E]_0 \qquad (11.27)$$

The rate is independent of the concentration of S because there is so much substrate present that it remains at effectively the same concentration even though products are being formed. Under these conditions, the rate of formation of product is a maximum, and $k_b[E]_0$ is called the **maximum velocity**, v_{max}, of the enzymolysis:

$$v_{max} = k_b[E]_0 \qquad (11.28)$$

The constant k_b is called the **maximum turnover number**. The rate-determining step is step 3, because there is ample ES present (because S is so abundant), and the rate is determined by the rate at which ES reacts to form the product.

It follows from eqns 11.25 and 11.28 that the reaction rate v at a general substrate composition is related to the maximum velocity by

$$v = \frac{[S]v_{max}}{[S] + K_M} \qquad (11.29)$$

This relation is illustrated in Fig. 11.13. Equation 11.29 is the basis of the analysis of enzyme kinetic data by using a **Lineweaver–Burk plot**, a graph of $1/v$ (the reciprocal of the reaction rate) against $1/[S]$ (the reciprocal of the substrate concentration). If we take the reciprocal of both sides of eqn 11.29 it becomes

$$\frac{1}{v} = \frac{[S] + K_M}{[S]v_{max}} = \frac{1}{v_{max}} + \left(\frac{K_M}{v_{max}}\right)\frac{1}{[S]} \qquad (11.30)$$

Because this expression has the form

$$y = \text{intercept} + \text{slope} \times x$$

with $y = 1/v$ and $x = 1/[S]$, we should obtain a straight line when we plot $1/v$ against $1/[S]$. The slope of the straight line is K_M/v_{max} and the extrapolated intercept at $1/[S] = 0$ is equal to $1/v_{max}$ (Fig. 11.14). Therefore, the intercept can be used to find v_{max}, and then that value combined with the slope to find the value of K_M. Alternatively, note that the extrapolated intercept with the horizontal axis (where $1/v = 0$) occurs at $1/[S] = -1/K_M$.

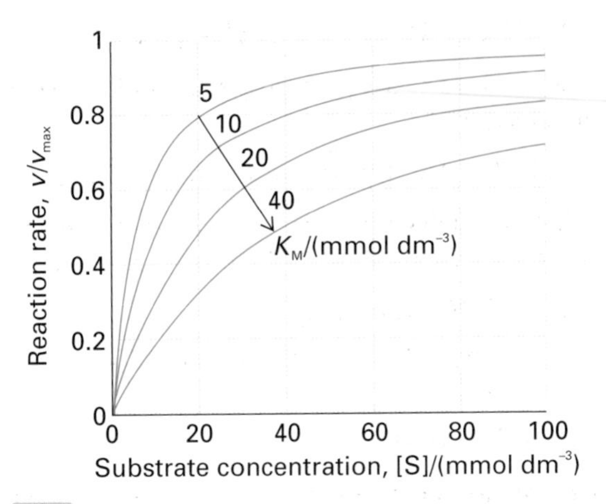

Fig. 11.13 The variation of the rate of an enzyme-catalysed reaction with concentration of the substrate according to the Michaelis–Menten model. When $[S] \ll K_M$, the rate is proportional to [S]; when $[S] \gg K_M$, the rate is independent of [S].

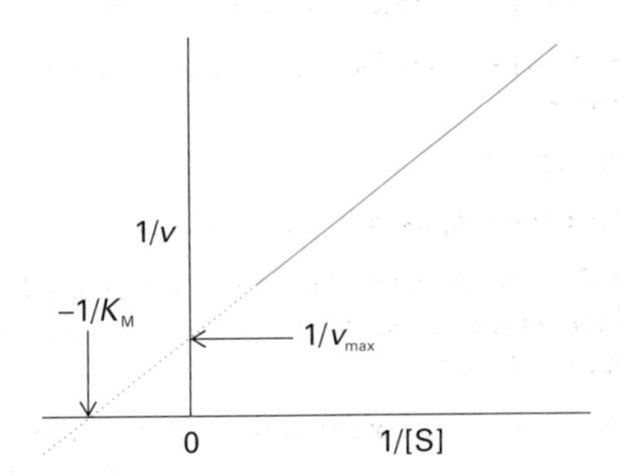

Fig. 11.14 A Lineweaver–Burk plot is used to analyse kinetic data on enzyme-catalysed reactions. The reciprocal of the rate of formation of products ($1/v$) is plotted against the reciprocal of the substrate concentration (1/[S]). All the data points (which typically lie in the full region of the line) correspond to the same overall enzyme concentration, $[E]_0$. The intercept of the extrapolated (dotted) straight line with the horizontal axis is used to obtain the Michaelis constant, K_M. The intercept with the vertical axis is used to determine $v_{max} = k_b[E]_0$, and hence k_b. The slope may also be used, as it is equal to K_M/v_{max}.

Example 11.1

Analysing a Lineweaver–Burk plot

The enzyme carbonic anhydrase catalyses the hydration of CO_2 in red blood cells to give hydrogencarbonate ion:

$$CO_2 + H_2O \rightarrow HCO_3^- + H^+$$

The following data were obtained for the reaction at pH = 7.1, 273.5 K, and an enzyme concentration of 2.3 nmol dm^{-3}:

$[CO_2]$/(mmol dm^{-3})	1.25	2.5
v/(mmol dm^{-3} s^{-1})	2.78×10^{-2}	5.00×10^{-2}
$[CO_2]$/(mmol dm^{-3})	5	20
v/(mmol dm^{-3} s^{-1})	8.33×10^{-2}	1.67×10^{-1}

Determine the maximum velocity and the Michaelis constant for the reaction.

Strategy We construct a Lineweaver–Burk plot by drawing up a table of 1/[S] and $1/v$. The intercept at 1/[S] = 0 is v_{max} and the slope of the line through the points is K_M/v_{max}, so K_M is found from the slope divided by the intercept.

Solution We draw up the following table:

$1/([CO_2]$/(mmol dm^{-3}))	0.8	0.4	0.2	0.05
$1/(v$/(mmol dm^{-3} s^{-1}))	36.0	20.0	12.0	5.99

The data are plotted in Fig. 11.15. A least squares analysis gives an intercept at 4.00 and a slope of 40.0. It follows that

$$v_{max}/(\text{mmol dm}^{-3}\ \text{s}^{-1}) = \frac{1}{\text{intercept}} = \frac{1}{4.00} = 0.250$$

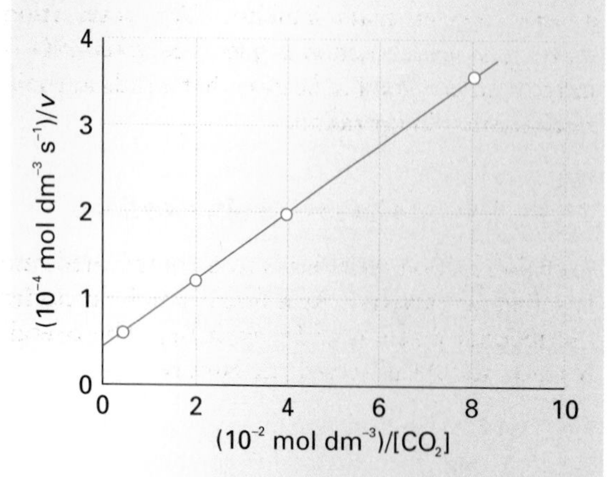

Fig. 11.15 The Lineweaver–Burke plot based on the data in Example 11.1.

and

$$K_M/(\text{mmol dm}^{-3}) = \frac{\text{slope}}{\text{intercept}} = \frac{40.0}{4.00} = 10.0$$

A note on good practice The slope and the intercept are unit-less: as we have remarked previously, all graphs should be plotted as pure numbers.

Self-test 11.7

The enzyme α-chymotrypsin is secreted in the pancreas of mammals and cleaves peptide bonds made between certain amino acids. Several solutions containing the small peptide *N*-glutaryl-L-phenylalanine-*p*-nitroanilide at different concentrations were prepared and the same small amount of α-chymotrypsin was added to each one. The following data were obtained on the initial rates of the formation of product:

[S]/(mmol dm^{-3})	0.334	0.450	0.667
v/(mmol dm^{-3} s^{-1})	0.152	0.201	0.269
[S]/(mmol dm^{-3})	1.00	1.33	1.67
v/(mmol dm^{-3} s^{-1})	0.417	0.505	0.667

Determine the maximum velocity and the Michaelis constant for the reaction.

[*Answer:* 2.80 mmol dm^{-3} s^{-1}, 5.89 mmol dm^{-3}]

The action of an enzyme may be partially suppressed by the presence of a foreign substance, which is called an **inhibitor.** An inhibitor may be a poison that has been administered to the organism, or it may be a substance that is naturally present in a cell and involved in its regulatory mechanism. In **competitive inhibition** the inhibitor competes for the active site and reduces the ability of the enzyme to bind the substrate (Fig. 11.16). In **non-competitive inhibition**

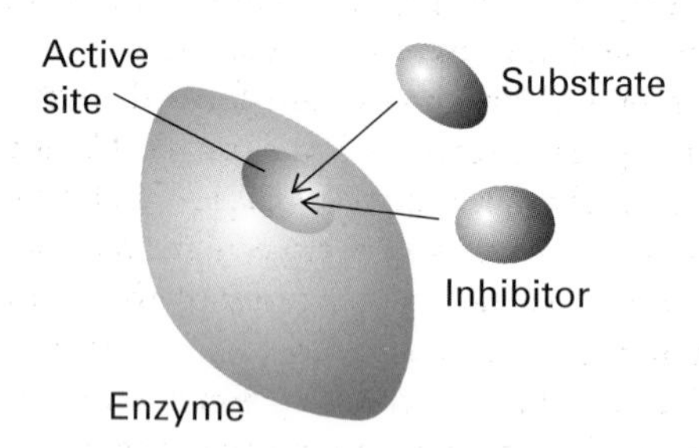

Fig. 11.16 In competitive inhibition, both the substrate (the egg shape) and the inhibitor compete for the active site, and reaction ensues only if the substrate is successful in attaching there.

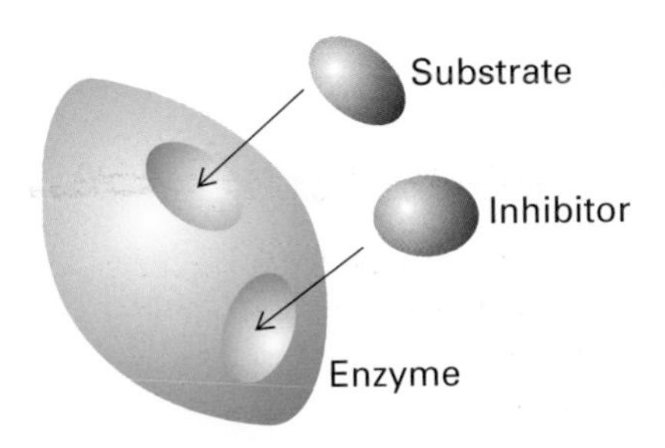

Fig. 11.17 In one version of non-competitive inhibition, the substrate and the inhibitor attach to distant sites of the enzyme molecule, and a complex in which they are both attached does not lead to the formation of product.

the inhibitor attaches to another part of the enzyme molecule, thereby distorting it and reducing its ability to bind the substrate (Fig. 11.17).

Chain reactions

Many gas-phase reactions and liquid-phase polymerization reactions are **chain reactions**, reactions in which an intermediate produced in one step generates a reactive intermediate in a subsequent step, then that intermediate generates another reactive intermediate, and so on.

11.14 The structure of chain reactions

The intermediates responsible for the propagation of a chain reaction are called **chain carriers**. In a **radical chain reaction** the chain carriers are radicals. Ions may also propagate chains, and in nuclear fission the chain carriers are neutrons.

The first chain carriers are formed in the **initiation step** of the reaction. For example, Cl atoms are formed by the dissociation of Cl_2 molecules either as a result of vigorous intermolecular collisions in a thermolysis reaction or as a result of absorption of a photon in a photolysis reaction. The chain carriers produced in the initiation step attack other reactant molecules in the propagation steps, and each attack gives rise to a new chain carrier. An example is the attack of a methyl radical on ethane:

$$\cdot CH_3 + CH_3CH_3 \rightarrow CH_4 + \cdot CH_2CH_3$$

The dot signifies the unpaired electron and marks the radical, which in this section we need to emphasize. In some cases the attack results in the production of more than one chain carrier. An example of such a **branching step** is

$$\cdot O \cdot + H_2O \rightarrow HO\cdot + HO\cdot$$

where the attack of one O atom on an H_2O molecule forms two $\cdot OH$ radicals (Box 11.2).[5]

The chain carrier might attack a product molecule formed earlier in the reaction. Because this attack decreases the net rate of formation of product, it is called a **retardation step**. For example, in a light-initiated reaction in which HBr is formed from H_2 and Br_2, an H atom might attack an HBr molecule, leading to H_2 and Br:

$$\cdot H + HBr \rightarrow H_2 + \cdot Br$$

Retardation does not end the chain, because one radical ($\cdot H$) gives rise to another ($\cdot Br$), but it does deplete the concentration of the product. Elementary reactions in which radicals combine and end the chain are called **termination steps**, as in

$$CH_3CH_2\cdot + \cdot CH_2CH_3 \rightarrow CH_3CH_2CH_2CH_3$$

In an **inhibition step**, radicals are removed other than by chain termination, such as by reaction with the walls of the vessel or with foreign radicals:

$$CH_3CH_2\cdot + \cdot R \rightarrow CH_3CH_2R$$

The NO molecule has an unpaired electron and is a very efficient chain inhibitor. The observation that a gas-phase reaction is quenched when NO is introduced is a good indication that a radical chain mechanism is in operation.

11.15 The rate laws of chain reactions

A chain reaction often leads to a complicated rate law (but not always). As a first example, consider the thermal reaction of H_2 with Br_2. The overall reaction and the observed rate law are

[5] In the notation to be introduced in Section 13.11, an O atom has the configuration $[He]2s^22p^4$, with two unpaired electrons.

Box 11.2 *Explosions*

A *thermal explosion* is due to the rapid increase of reaction rate with temperature. If the energy released in an exothermic reaction cannot escape, the temperature of the reaction system rises, and the reaction goes faster. The acceleration of the rate results in a faster rise of temperature, and so the reaction goes even faster—catastrophically fast. A *chain-branching explosion* may occur when there are chain-branching steps in a reaction, because then the number of chain carriers grows exponentially and the rate of reaction may cascade into an explosion.

An example of both types of explosion is provided by the reaction between hydrogen and oxygen:

$$2\,H_2(g) + O_2(g) \rightarrow 2\,H_2O(g)$$

Although the net reaction is very simple, the mechanism is very complex and has not yet been fully elucidated. It is known that a chain reaction is involved, and that the chain carriers include $\cdot H$, $\cdot O\cdot$, $\cdot OH$, and $\cdot O_2H$. Some steps are:

Initiation: $H_2 + \cdot(O_2)\cdot \rightarrow \cdot OH + \cdot OH$

Propagation: $H_2 + \cdot OH \rightarrow \cdot H + H_2O$

$\cdot(O_2)\cdot + \cdot H \rightarrow \cdot O\cdot + \cdot OH$ (branching)

$\cdot O\cdot + H_2 \rightarrow \cdot OH + \cdot H$ (branching)

$\cdot H + \cdot(O_2)\cdot + M \rightarrow \cdot HO_2 + M^*$

The two branching steps can lead to a chain-branching explosion.

The occurrence of an explosion depends on the temperature and pressure of the system, and the *explosion regions* for the reaction are shown in the illustration. At very low pressures, the system is outside the explosion region and the mixture reacts smoothly. At these pressures the chain carriers produced in the branching steps can reach the walls of the container where they combine (with an efficiency that depends on the composition of the walls). Increasing the pressure of the mixture along the vertical line in the illustration takes the system through the *lower explosion limit* (provided that the temperature is greater than about 730 K). The mixture then explodes because the chain carriers react before reaching the walls and the branching reactions are explosively efficient. The reaction is smooth when the pressure is above the *upper explosion limit*. The concentration of molecules in the gas is then so great that the radicals produced in the branching reaction combine in the body of the gas, and gas-phase reactions such as $\cdot(O_2)\cdot + \cdot H \rightarrow \cdot O_2H$ can occur. Recombination reactions like this are facilitated by three-body collisions, because the third body (M) can remove the excess energy and allow the formation of a bond:

$$\cdot(O_2)\cdot + \cdot H + M \rightarrow \cdot O_2H + M^*$$

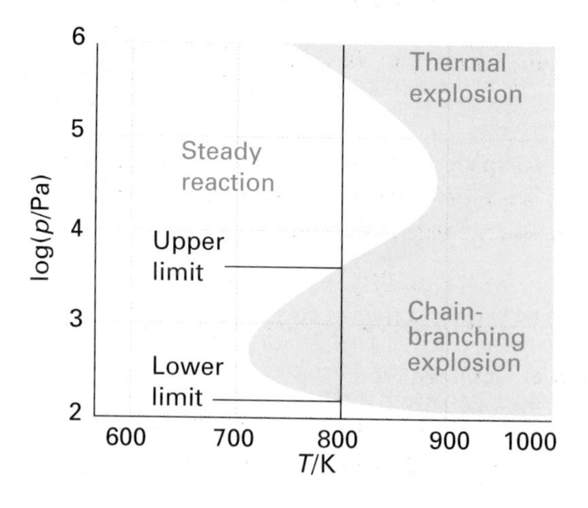

The explosion limits of the H_2/O_2 reaction. In the explosive regions the reaction proceeds explosively when heated homogeneously.

The radical $\cdot OH_2$ is relatively unreactive and can reach the walls, where it is removed. At low pressures three-particle collisions are unimportant and recombination is much slower. At higher pressures, when three-particle collisions are important, the explosive propagation of the chain by the radicals produced in the branching step is partially quenched because $\cdot O_2H$ is formed in place of $\cdot O\cdot$ and $\cdot OH$. If the pressure is increased to above the third explosion limit the reaction rate increases so much that a thermal explosion occurs.

Exercise 1 Refer to the illustration and determine the pressure range for a chain-branching explosion in the hydrogen–oxygen reaction at (a) 700 K, (b) 900 K.

Exercise 2 Suppose that a reaction mechanism (such as that for the reaction of hydrogen and oxygen) gives the following expressions for the time dependence of the concentration of H atoms:

Low O_2 concentration:

$$[H] = \frac{v_{\text{initiation}}}{k_{\text{termination}} - k_{\text{branching}}}\left\{1 - e^{-(k_{\text{termination}}-k_{\text{branching}})t}\right\}$$

High O_2 concentration:

$$[H] = \frac{v_{\text{initiation}}}{k_{\text{termination}} - k_{\text{branching}}}\left\{1 - e^{(k_{\text{termination}}-k_{\text{branching}})t}\right\}$$

where $v_{\text{initiation}}$ is the rate at which H atoms are formed in an initiation step. Plot graphs of these functions and identify the conditions for an explosion.

$$H_2(g) + Br_2(g) \rightarrow 2\,HBr(g)$$

$$\text{Rate of formation of HBr} = \frac{k[H_2][Br_2]^{3/2}}{[Br_2] + k'[HBr]} \qquad (11.31)$$

The complexity of the rate law suggests that a complicated mechanism is involved. The following radical chain mechanism has been proposed:

Step 1 Initiation: $Br_2 \rightarrow Br\cdot + Br\cdot$

rate of consumption of $Br_2 = k_a[Br_2]$

Step 2 Propagation:

$Br\cdot + H_2 \rightarrow HBr + H\cdot$ rate $= k_b[Br][H_2]$

$H\cdot + Br_2 \rightarrow HBr + Br\cdot$ rate $= k_b'[H][Br_2]$

In this and the following steps, 'rate' means either the rate of formation of one of the products or the rate of consumption of one of the reactants. We shall specify the species only if the rates differ.

Step 3 Retardation:

$H\cdot + HBr \rightarrow H_2 + Br\cdot$ rate $= k_c[H][HBr]$

Step 4 Termination:

$Br\cdot + \cdot Br + M \rightarrow Br_2 + M$

rate of formation of $Br_2 = k_d[Br]^2$

The 'third body', M, a molecule of an inert gas, removes the energy of recombination; the constant concentration of M has been absorbed into the rate constant k_d. Other possible termination steps include the recombination of H atoms to form H_2 and the combination of H and Br atoms; however, it turns out that only Br atom recombination is important.

Now we establish the rate law for the reaction. The experimental rate law is expressed in terms of the rate of formation of product, HBr, so we start by writing an expression for its net rate of formation. Because HBr is formed in step 2 (by both reactions) and consumed in step 3,

$$\text{Net rate of formation of HBr} = k_b[Br][H_2] + k_b'[H][Br_2] - k_c[H][HBr] \qquad (11.32)$$

To make progress, we need the concentrations of the intermediates Br and H. Therefore, we set up the expressions for their net rate of formation and apply the steady-state assumption to both:

$$\text{Net rate of formation of H} = k_b[Br][H_2] - k_b'[H][Br_2] - k_c[H][HBr] = 0$$

$$\text{Net rate of formation of Br} = 2k_a[Br_2] - k_b[Br][H_2] + k_b'[H][Br_2] + k_c[H][HBr] - 2k_d[Br]^2 = 0$$

The steady-state concentrations of the intermediates are found by solving these two equations and are

$$[Br] = \left(\frac{k_a[Br_2]}{k_d}\right)^{1/2}$$

$$[H] = \frac{k_b(k_a/k_d)^{1/2}[H_2][Br_2]^{1/2}}{k_b'[Br_2] + k_c[HBr]}$$

When we substitute these concentrations into eqn 11.32 we obtain

$$\text{Rate of formation of HBr} = \frac{2k_b(k_a/k_d)^{1/2}[H_2][Br_2]^{3/2}}{[Br_2] + (k_c/k_b')[HBr]} \qquad (11.33)$$

This equation has the same form as the empirical rate law, and we can identify the two empirical rate coefficients as

$$k = 2k_b\left(\frac{k_a}{k_d}\right)^{1/2} \qquad k' = \frac{k_c}{k_b'} \qquad (11.34)$$

We can conclude that the proposed mechanism is at least consistent with the observed rate law. Additional support for the mechanism would come from the detection of the proposed intermediates (by spectroscopy), and the measurement of individual rate constants for the elementary steps and confirming that they correctly reproduced the observed composite rate constants.

CHECKLIST OF KEY IDEAS

You should now be familiar with the following concepts:

☐ 1 The equilibrium constant for a reaction is equal to the ratio of the forward and reverse rate constants, $K = k/k'$.

☐ 2 In relaxation methods of kinetic analysis, the equilibrium position of a reaction is first shifted suddenly and then allowed to readjust the equilibrium composition characteristic of the new conditions.

☐ 3 The molecularity of an elementary reaction is the number of molecules coming together to react.

☐ 4 An elementary unimolecular reaction has first-order kinetics; and an elementary bimolecular reaction has second-order kinetics.

☐ 5 In the steady-state approximation, it is assumed that the concentrations of all reaction intermediates remain constant and small throughout the reaction.

☐ 6 The rate-determining step is the slowest step in a reaction mechanism that controls the rate of the overall reaction.

☐ 7 Provided a reaction has not reached equilibrium, the products of competing reactions are controlled by kinetics, with $[P_2]/[P_1] = k_2/k_1$.

☐ 8 A reaction in solution may be diffusion-controlled ($k = k_d$) or activation-controlled ($k = k_a k_d / k'_d$).

☐ 9 The Lindemann mechanism of 'unimolecular' reactions is a theory that accounts for the first-order kinetics of gas-phase reactions.

☐ 10 Fick's first law of diffusion states that the flux is proportional to the concentration gradient.

☐ 11 Fick's second law of diffusion, the diffusion equation, states that the rate of change of concentration in a region is proportional to the curvature of the concentration in the region.

☐ 12 Diffusion takes place in a random walk; the net distance travelled in a time t from the starting point is $d = (2Dt)^{1/2}$.

☐ 13 The Einstein–Smoluchowski equation, $D = \lambda^2/2\tau$, expresses the diffusion coefficient in terms of the rate at which the molecule takes its steps and the distance of each step.

☐ 14 Catalysts are substances that accelerate reactions but undergo no net chemical change.

☐ 15 A homogeneous catalyst is a catalyst in the same phase as the reaction mixture.

☐ 16 Enzymes are homogeneous, biological catalysts.

☐ 17 The Michaelis–Menten mechanism of enzyme kinetics accounts for the dependence of rate on the concentration of the substrate, $v = v_{max}[S]/([S] + K_M)$.

☐ 18 A Lineweaver–Burk plot, based on $1/v = 1/v_{max} + (K_M/v_{max})(1/[S])$, is used to determine the parameters that occur in the Michaelis–Menten mechanism.

☐ 19 In a chain reaction, an intermediate (the chain carrier) produced in one step generates a reactive intermediate in a subsequent step.

FURTHER INFORMATION 11.1

Fick's laws of diffusion

Fick's first law of diffusion. Consider the arrangement in Fig. 11.18. Let's suppose that in an interval Δt the number of molecules passing through the window of area A from the left is proportional to the number in the slab of thickness l and area A, and therefore volume lA, just to the left of the window where the average (number) concentration is $c(x - \frac{1}{2}l)$ and to the length of the interval Δt:

$$\text{Number coming from left} \propto c(x - \tfrac{1}{2}l)lA\,\Delta t$$

Likewise, the number coming from the right in the same interval is

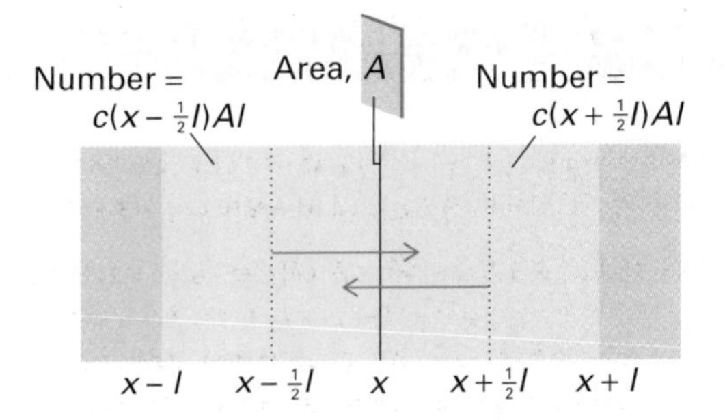

Fig. 11.18 The calculation of the rate of diffusion considers the net flux of molecules through a plane of area A as a result of arrivals from on average a distance $\frac{1}{2}l$ in each direction.

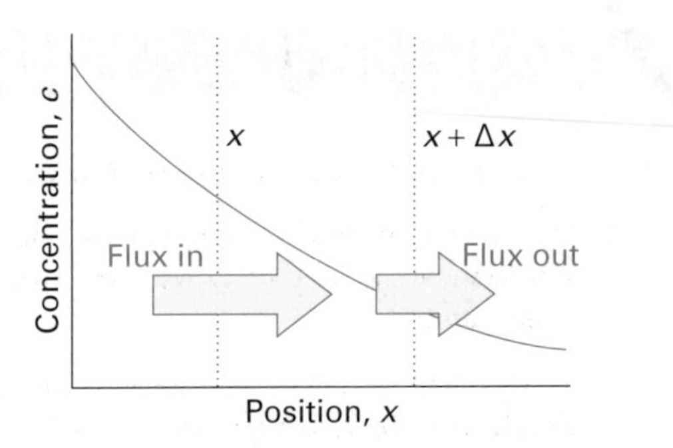

Fig. 11.19 To calculate the change in concentration in the region between the two walls, we need to consider the net effect of the influx of particles from the left and their efflux towards the right. Only if the slope of the concentrations is different at the two walls will there be a net change.

$$\text{Number coming from right} \propto c(x+\tfrac{1}{2}l)lA\Delta t$$

The net flux is therefore the difference in these numbers divided by the area and the time interval:

$$J \propto \frac{c(x-\frac{1}{2}l)lA\Delta t - c(x+\frac{1}{2}l)lA\Delta t}{A\Delta t}$$
$$= \{c(x-\tfrac{1}{2}l) - c(x+\tfrac{1}{2}l)\}l$$

We now express the two concentrations in terms of the concentration at the window itself, $c(x)$, and the concentration gradient, $\Delta c/\Delta x$, as follows:

$$c(x+\tfrac{1}{2}l) = c(x) + \tfrac{1}{2}l \times \frac{\Delta c}{\Delta x}$$

$$c(x-\tfrac{1}{2}l) = c(x) - \tfrac{1}{2}l \times \frac{\Delta c}{\Delta x}$$

From which it follows that

$$J \propto \left\{\left(c(x) - \tfrac{1}{2}l\frac{\Delta c}{\Delta x}\right) - \left(c(x) + \tfrac{1}{2}l\frac{\Delta c}{\Delta x}\right)\right\}l$$
$$\propto -l^2\frac{\Delta c}{\Delta x}$$

On writing the constant of proportionality as D (and absorbing l^2 into it), we obtain eqn 11.18b.

Fick's second law. Consider the arrangement in Fig. 11.19. The number of solute particles passing through the window of area A located at x in an interval Δt is $J(x)A\Delta t$, where $J(x)$ is the flux at the location x. The number of particles passing out of the region through a window of area A at a short distance away, at $x + \Delta x$, is $J(x + \Delta x)A\Delta t$, where $J(x + \Delta x)$ is the flux at the location of this window. The flux in and the flux out will be different if the concentration gradients are different at the two windows. The net change in the number of solute particles in the region between the two windows is

$$\text{Net change in number} = J(x)A\Delta t - J(x+\Delta x)A\Delta t$$
$$= \{J(x) - J(x+\Delta x)\}A\Delta t$$

Now we express the flux at $x + \Delta x$ in terms of the flux at x and the gradient of the flux, $\Delta J/\Delta x$:

$$J(x+\Delta x) = J(x) + \frac{\Delta J}{\Delta x} \times \Delta x$$

It follows that

$$\text{Net change in number} = -\frac{\Delta J}{\Delta x} \times \Delta x \times A\,\Delta t$$

The change in concentration inside the region between the two windows is the net change in number divided by the volume of the region (which is $A\Delta x$), and the net rate of change is obtained by dividing that change in concentration by the time interval Δt. Therefore, on dividing by both $A\,\Delta x$ and Δt, we obtain

$$\text{Rate of change of concentration} = -\frac{\Delta J}{\Delta x}$$

Finally, we express the flux by using Fick's first law:

$$\text{Rate of change of concentration}$$
$$= -\frac{\Delta(-D \times (\text{concentration gradient}))}{\Delta x}$$
$$= D\frac{\Delta(\text{concentration gradient})}{\Delta x}$$

The 'gradient of the gradient' of the concentration is what we have called the 'curvature' of the concentration, and thus we obtain eqn 11.19.

Slightly more formally, on writing the concentration as $\Delta c/\Delta x$ and the rate of change of concentration as $\Delta c/\Delta t$, the last expression becomes

$$\frac{\Delta c}{\Delta t} = D\frac{\Delta(\Delta c/\Delta x)}{\Delta x} = D\frac{\Delta^2 c}{(\Delta x)^2}$$

This expression becomes more exact as the intervals Δx and Δt become smaller, and in the limit of them becoming infinitesimal it becomes

$$\frac{dc}{dt} = D\frac{d^2 c}{dx^2}$$

which is the mathematical statement of eqn 11.19.

DISCUSSION QUESTIONS

11.1 Sketch, without carrying out the calculation, the variation of concentration with time for the approach to equilibrium when both forward and reverse reactions are second-order. How does your graph differ from that in Fig. 11.2?

11.2 Assess the validity of the following statement: the rate-determining step is the slowest step in a reaction mechanism.

11.3 Limit the generality of the expression $k = k_a k_b[A]/(k_b + k_a'[A])$ for the effective rate constant of a unimolecular reaction $A \rightarrow P$ with the mechanism shown below. Suggest an experimental procedure that may either support or refute the mechanism.

$A + A \rightarrow A^* + A$ rate of formation of $A^* = k_a[A]^2$

$A^* + A \rightarrow A + A$ rate of deactivation of $A^* = k_a'[A^*][A]$

$A^* \rightarrow P$ rate of formation of $P = k_b[A^*]$

rate of consumption of $A^* = k_b[A^*]$

11.4 Discuss the features, advantages, and limitations of the Michaelis–Menten mechanism of enzyme action.

EXERCISES

The symbol ‡ indicates that calculus is required.

11.5 The equilibrium constant for the attachment of a substrate to the active site of an enzyme was measured as 235. In a separate experiment, the rate constant for the second-order attachment was found to be 7.4×10^7 dm^3 mol^{-1} s^{-1}. What is the rate constant for the loss of the unreacted substrate from the active site?

11.6 ‡Confirm (by differentiation) that the expressions in eqn 11.2 are the correct solutions of the rate laws for approach to equilibrium.

11.7 ‡Find the solutions of the same rate laws that led to eqn 11.2, but for some B present initially. Go on to confirm that the solutions you find reduce to those in eqn 11.2 when $[B]_0 = 0$.

11.8 ‡Confirm (by differentiation) that the three expressions in eqn 11.5 are correct solutions of the rate laws for consecutive first-order reactions.

11.9 ‡Confirm that at the time given by eqn 11.6 the intermediate reaches its *maximum* concentration.

11.10 Two radioactive nuclides decay by successive first-order processes:

$$X \xrightarrow{22.5\ \text{days}} Y \xrightarrow{33.0\ \text{days}} Z$$

(The times are half-lives in days.) Suppose that Y is an isotope that is required for medical applications. At what stage after X is first formed will Y be most abundant?

11.11 Two products are formed in reactions in which there is kinetic control of the ratio of products. The activation energy for the reaction leading to Product 1 is greater than that leading to Product 2. Will the ratio of product concentrations $[P_1]/[P_2]$ increase or decrease if the temperature is raised?

11.12 Calculate the magnitude of the diffusion-controlled rate constant at 298 K for a species in (a) water, (b) pentane. The viscosities are 1.00×10^{-3} kg m^{-1} s^{-1} and 2.2×10^{-4} kg m^{-1} s^{-1}, respectively.

11.13 What is (a) the flux of nutrient molecules down a concentration gradient of 0.10 mol dm^{-3} m^{-1}, (b) the amount of molecules (in moles) passing through an area of 5.0 mm^2 in 1.0 min? Take for the diffusion coefficient the value for sucrose in water (5.22×10^{-10} m^2 s^{-1}).

11.14 How long does it take a sucrose molecule in water at 25°C to diffuse (a) 1 mm, (b) 1 cm, (c) 1 m from its starting point?

11.15 The mobility of species through fluids is of the greatest importance for nutritional processes. (a) Estimate the diffusion coefficient for a molecule that leaps 150 pm each 1.8 ps. (b) What would be the diffusion coefficient if the molecule travelled only half as far on each step?

11.16 How long will it take a small molecule to diffuse across a phospholipid bilayer of thickness 0.50 nm at 37°C if the viscosity within the bilayer is 0.010 kg m^{-1} s^{-1}?

11.17 Is diffusion important in lakes? How long would it take a small pollutant molecule about the size of H_2O to diffuse across a lake of width 100 m?

11.18 Pollutants spread through the environment by convection (winds and currents) and by diffusion. How many steps must a molecule take to be 1000 step-lengths away from its origin if it undergoes a one-dimensional random walk?

11.19 The viscosity of water at 20°C is 1.0019 mN s m^{-2} and at 30°C it is 0.7982 mN s m^{-2}. What is the activation energy for the motion of water molecules?

11.20 Calculate the ratio of rates of catalysed to non-catalysed reactions at 37°C given that the Gibbs energy of activation for a particular reaction is reduced from 100 kJ mol^{-1} to 10 kJ mol^{-1}.

11.21 The reaction $2\,H_2O_2(aq) \rightarrow 2\,H_2O(l) + O_2(g)$ is catalysed by Br^- ions. If the mechanism is:

$H_2O_2 + Br^- \rightarrow H_2O + BrO^-$ (slow)

$BrO^- + H_2O_2 \rightarrow H_2O + O_2 + Br^-$ (fast)

give the predicted order of the reaction with respect to the various participants.

11.22 The reaction mechanism

$A_2 \rightleftharpoons A + A$ (fast)

$A + B \rightarrow P$ (slow)

involves an intermediate A. Deduce the rate law for the formation of P.

11.23 Consider the following mechanism for formation of a double helix from its strands A and B:

$A + B \rightleftharpoons$ unstable helix (fast)

unstable helix $\rightarrow$ stable double helix (slow)

Derive the rate equation for the formation of the double helix and express the rate constant of the reaction in terms of the rate constants of the individual steps.

11.24 The following mechanism has been proposed for the decomposition of ozone in the atmosphere:

Step 1 $O_3 \rightarrow O_2 + O$ and its reverse (k_1, k_1')

Step 2 $O + O_3 \rightarrow O_2 + O_2$ (k_2; the reverse reaction is negligibly slow)

Use the steady-state approximation, with O treated as the intermediate, to find an expression for the rate of decomposition of O_3. Show that if step 2 is slow, then the rate is second-order in O_3 and –1 order in O_2.

11.25 The condensation reaction of acetone, $(CH_3)_2CO$ (propanone), in aqueous solution is catalysed by bases, B, that react reversibly with acetone to form the carbanion $C_3H_5O^-$. The carbanion then reacts with a molecule of acetone to give the product. A simplified version of the mechanism is

Step 1 $AH + B \rightarrow BH^+ + A^-$

Step 2 $A^- + BH^+ \rightarrow AH + B$

Step 3 $A^- + HA \rightarrow$ product

where AH stands for acetone and A^- its carbanion. Use the steady-state approximation to find the concentration of the carbanion and derive the rate equation for the formation of the product.

11.26 Consider the acid-catalysed reaction

$HA + H^+ \rightleftharpoons HAH^+$ (fast)

$HAH^+ + B \rightarrow BH^+ + AH$ (slow)

Deduce the rate law and show that it can be made independent of the specific term $[H^+]$.

11.27 As remarked in Footnote 4, Michaelis and Menten derived their rate law by assuming a rapid pre-equilibrium of E, S, and ES. Derive the rate law in this manner, and identify the conditions under which it becomes the same as that based on the steady-state approximation (eqn 11.25).

11.28 The enzyme-catalysed conversion of a substrate at 25°C has a Michaelis constant of 0.045 mol dm^{-3}. The rate of the reaction is 1.15 mmol dm^{-3} s^{-1} when the substrate concentration is 0.110 mol dm^{-3}. What is the maximum velocity of this enzymolysis?

11.29 Find the condition for which the reaction rate of an enzymolysis that follows Michaelis–Menten kinetics is half its maximum value.

11.30 Show that a plot of the rate of enzymolysis, v, plotted against $v/[S]$ is an alternative route to the determination of the value of K_M.

11.31 The rate, v, of an enzyme-catalysed reaction was measured when various amounts of substrate S were present and the concentration of enzyme was 12.5 μmol dm^{-3}. The following results were obtained:

[S]/(mmol dm^{-3})	1.0	2.0	3.0	4.0	5.0
v/(μmol dm^{-3} s^{-1})	1.1	1.8	2.3	2.6	2.9

Determine the Michaelis–Menten constant, the maximum velocity of the reaction, and the maximum turnover number of the enzyme.

11.32 The following results were obtained for the action of an ATPase on ATP at 20°C, when the concentration of the ATPase was 20 nmol dm^{-3}:

[ATP]/(μmol dm^{-3})	0.60	0.80	1.4	2.0	3.0
v/(μmol dm^{-3} s^{-1})	0.81	0.97	1.30	1.47	1.69

Determine the Michaelis–Menten constant, the maximum velocity of the reaction, and the maximum turnover number of the enzyme.

11.33 Consider the following chain mechanism:

(1) $AH \rightarrow A\cdot + H\cdot$

(2) $A\cdot \rightarrow B\cdot + C$

(3) $AH + B\cdot \rightarrow A\cdot + D$

(4) $A\cdot + B\cdot \rightarrow P$

Identify the initiation, propagation, and termination steps, and use the steady-state approximation to deduce that the decomposition of AH is first-order in AH.

11.34 Consider the following mechanism for the thermal decomposition of R_2:

(1) $R_2 \rightarrow R + R$

(2) $R + R_2 \rightarrow P_B + R'$

(3) $R' \rightarrow P_A + R$

(4) $R + R \rightarrow P_A + P_B$

where R_2, P_A, and P_B are stable hydrocarbons and R and R′ are radicals. Find the dependence of the rate of decomposition of R_2 on the concentration of R_2.

11.35 (a) Confirm eqn 11.31 for the rate of formation of HBr. (b) What are the orders of the reaction (with respect to each species) when the concentration of HBr is (i) very low, (ii) very high? Suggest an interpretation in each case.

Chapter 12

Quantum theory

The phenomena of chemistry cannot be understood thoroughly without a firm understanding of the principal concepts of quantum mechanics, the most fundamental description of matter that we currently possess. The same is true of nearly all the spectroscopic techniques that are now so central to investigations of composition and structure. Present-day techniques for studying chemical reactions have progressed to the point where the information is so detailed that quantum mechanics has to be used in its interpretation. And, of course, the very currency of chemistry—the electronic structures of atoms and molecules—cannot be discussed without making use of quantum mechanical concepts.

The role—indeed, the existence—of quantum mechanics was appreciated only during the twentieth century. Until then it was thought that the motion of atomic and subatomic particles could be expressed in terms of the laws of classical mechanics introduced in the seventeenth century by Isaac Newton (see Appendix 3), as these laws were very successful at explaining the motion of planets and everyday objects such as pendulums and projectiles. However, towards the end of the nineteenth century, experimental evidence accumulated showing that classical mechanics failed when it was applied to very small particles, such as individual atoms, nuclei, and electrons, and when the transfers of energy were very small. It took until 1926 to identify the appropriate concepts and equations for describing them.

The failures of classical physics

In this section, we see how it came to be realized that classical mechanics has severe shortcomings, particularly when applied to systems in which only small energies are transferred. To appreciate these shortcomings, we need to know that classical physics is based on three 'obvious' assumptions:

1 A particle travels in a **trajectory**, a path with a precise position and momentum at each instant.

> The linear momentum, p, is the product of mass, m, and velocity, v: $p = mv$.

2 Any type of motion can be excited to a state of arbitrary energy.

3 Waves and particles are distinct concepts.

These assumptions agree with everyday experience. For example, a pendulum swings with a precise oscillating motion and can be made to oscillate with any energy simply by pulling it back to an arbitrary angle and then letting it swing freely. Classical mechanics lets us predict the angle of the pendulum and the speed at which it is swinging at any instant. Everyday experience, however, does not extend to the behaviour of individual atoms and subatomic particles. Careful experiments of the type described below have shown that the laws of classical mechanics, and particularly the three basic assumptions, fail to account for the observed behaviour of very small particles. Classical mechanics is in fact only an *approximate* description of the motion of particles, and the approximation is invalid when it is applied to molecules, atoms, and electrons.

12.1 Black-body radiation

In classical physics, light is described as electromagnetic radiation, which is understood in terms of the **electromagnetic field**, an oscillating electric and magnetic disturbance that spreads as a harmonic wave through empty space, the vacuum. Such waves are generated by the acceleration of electric charge, as in the oscillating motion of electrons in the antenna of a radio transmitter. The wave travels at a constant speed called the *speed of light*, c, which is

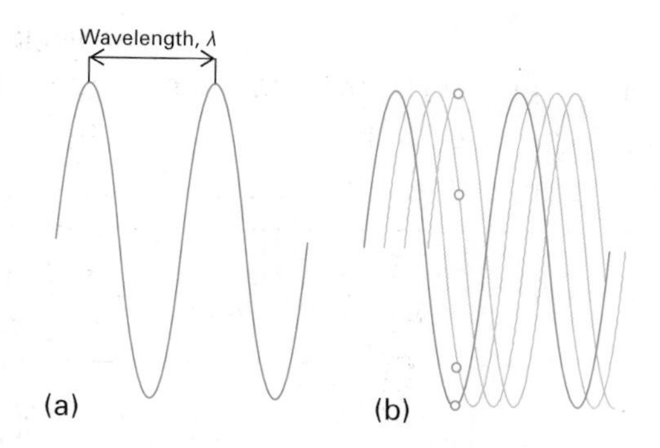

Fig. 12.1 (a) The wavelength, λ, of a wave is the peak-to-peak distance. (b) The wave is shown travelling to the right at a speed c. At a given location, the instantaneous amplitude of the wave changes through a complete cycle (the four dots show half a cycle). The frequency, ν, is the number of cycles per second that occur at a given point.

about 3×10^8 m s^{-1}. As its name suggests, an electromagnetic field has two components, an **electric field** that acts on charged particles (whether stationary or moving) and a **magnetic field** that acts only on moving charged particles. The electromagnetic field is characterized by a **wavelength**, λ (lambda), the distance between the neighbouring peaks of the wave, and its **frequency**, ν (nu), the number of times per second at which its displacement at a fixed point returns to its original value (Fig. 12.1). The frequency is measured in *hertz*, Hz, where 1 Hz = 1 s^{-1}. The wavelength and frequency of an electromagnetic wave are related by

$$\lambda\nu = c \quad (12.1)$$

Therefore, the shorter the wavelength, the higher the frequency.

> The physics of waves is reviewed in Appendix 3.

The **electromagnetic spectrum**, the description and classification of the electromagnetic field according to its frequency and wavelength, is summarized in Fig. 12.2. White light is a mixture of electromagnetic radiation with wavelengths ranging from about 380 nm to about 700 nm (1 nm = 10^{-9} m). Our eyes perceive different wavelengths of radiation in this range as different colours, so it can be said that white light is a mixture of light of all different colours.

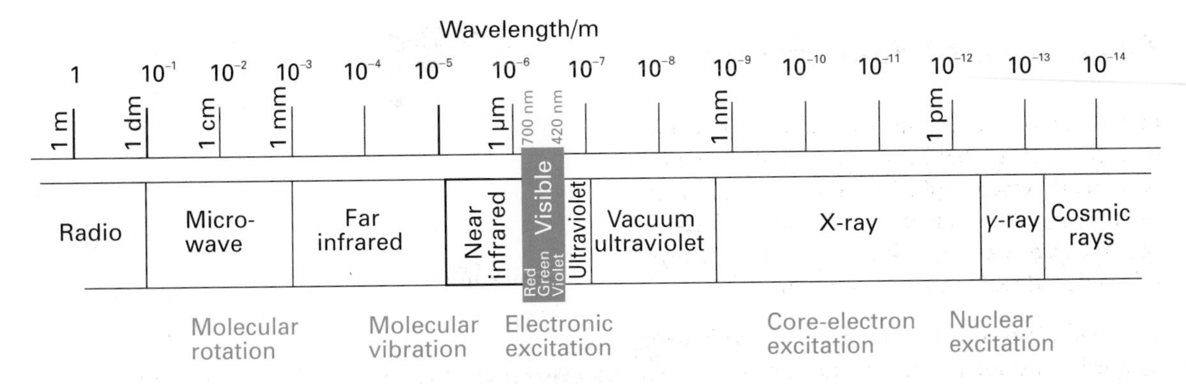

Fig. 12.2 The electromagnetic spectrum and the classification of the spectral regions.

A hot object emits electromagnetic radiation because its atoms and electrons are ceaselessly being accelerated: the atoms vibrate around their mean positions and their electrons are moved from location to location. At high temperatures, an appreciable proportion of the radiation is in the visible region of the spectrum. A higher proportion of short-wavelength blue light is generated as the temperature is raised. We observe this behaviour when an iron bar glowing red hot becomes white hot when heated further, because then more blue light mixes into the red light and changes the perceived colour towards white. The precise dependence is illustrated in Fig. 12.3, which shows how the energy output varies with wavelength at a series of temperatures. The curves are those of an ideal emitter called a **black body**, which is a body capable of emitting and absorbing all frequencies of radiation. A good approximation to a black body is a pinhole in a container, because the radiation leaking out of the hole has been absorbed and re-emitted inside the container so many times that it has come to thermal equilibrium with the walls.[1]

We shall consider the **energy density** of the radiation in a cavity, the total energy in the cavity divided by the volume of the cavity,[2] and in particular the contribution to the total energy density from radiation of different wavelengths. Figure 12.3 shows two main features. The first is that shorter wavelengths contribute more to the energy density as the temperature is raised. As a result, the perceived colour shifts towards the blue, as already mentioned. An analysis of the data led Wilhelm Wien (in

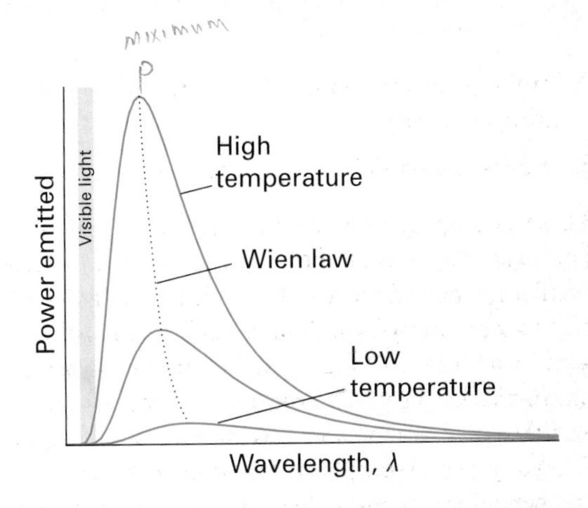

Fig. 12.3 The power emitted by a black body at three temperatures. Note how the power increases in the visible region (the tinted range of wavelengths) as the temperature is raised, and how the peak maximum moves to shorter wavelengths. The total power (the area under the curve) increases as the temperature is increased (as T^4).

1893) to summarize this shift by a statement now known as **Wien's displacement law:**

$$T\lambda_{max} = \text{constant} \qquad (12.2)$$

where the value of the constant is 2.9 mm K. In this expression, λ_{max} is the wavelength of the radiation that makes the greatest contribution to the energy

[1] Thermal equilibrium in the sense that the temperature of the radiation-filled space inside the container is the same as that of the walls.

[2] Just as we calculate the mass of an object by multiplying its volume by its mass density, so we calculate the total energy in a container by multiplying the energy density by the volume of the container.

density when the (absolute) temperature is T. Wien's law implies that as T increases, λ_{max} decreases enough to preserve the value of $T\lambda_{max}$.

Illustration 12.1

Using Wien's law

One application of Wien's law is to the estimation of the temperatures of stars, and other inaccessible hot objects. For example, the maximum emission of the Sun occurs at $\lambda_{max} \approx 490$ nm, so its surface temperature must be close to

$$T = \frac{\text{constant}}{\lambda_{max}} = \frac{2.9 \times 10^{-3}\ \text{m K}}{4.9 \times 10^{-7}\ \text{m}} = 5.9 \times 10^{3}\ \text{K}$$

or about 6000 K.

Self-test 12.1

Estimate the wavelength at the maximum energy output of an incandescent lamp if the filament is at 3000°C.

[*Answer:* 890 nm]

The second feature of black-body radiation had been noticed in 1879 by Josef Stefan, who considered the sharp rise in the **emittance**, M, the total power emitted by a black body divided by the surface area of the body, as the temperature is raised. He established what is now called the **Stefan–Boltzmann law:**

$$M = aT^4 \qquad (12.3)$$

The rate of change of energy is the power, expressed as joules per second, or *watts*, W, where 1 W = 1 J s^{-1}.

with $a = 56.7$ nW m^{-2} K^{-4} (where 1 nW = 10^{-9} W). This law implies that each square centimetre of the surface of a black body at 1000 K radiates about 5.7 W when all wavelengths are taken into account. It radiates $3^4 = 81$ times that power (460 W) when the temperature is increased by a factor of 3, to 3000 K. The law is the basis of seeking as high a temperature as possible for an incandescent lamp because then the emission is as strong as possible.

Self-test 12.2

Suppose technological advances made it possible to produce a ceramic material that could be used as a filament at 3800°C instead of 3000°C. By what factor would the power output of a lamp that used the new material increase?

[*Answer:* 2.4]

The physicist Lord Rayleigh studied black-body radiation from a classical viewpoint. In his day (at the end of the nineteenth century), electromagnetic radiation was regarded as waves in a ubiquitous 'ether'. The idea of the time was that, if the ether could oscillate at a certain frequency ν, then radiation of that frequency would be present. Rayleigh took the view that the ether could oscillate with any frequency, so waves could exist in it of any wavelength. With minor help from James Jeans, Rayleigh arrived at the **Rayleigh–Jeans law,** which predicted that the density of energy in a region of the electromagnetic field due to radiation of wavelength λ is proportional to $1/\lambda^4$.

You should immediately see a problem. Because the power emitted at a particular wavelength is proportional to the density of energy at that wavelength, then as λ decreases, the power increases without limit (Fig. 12.4). The law therefore predicts that oscillations of very short wavelength (high

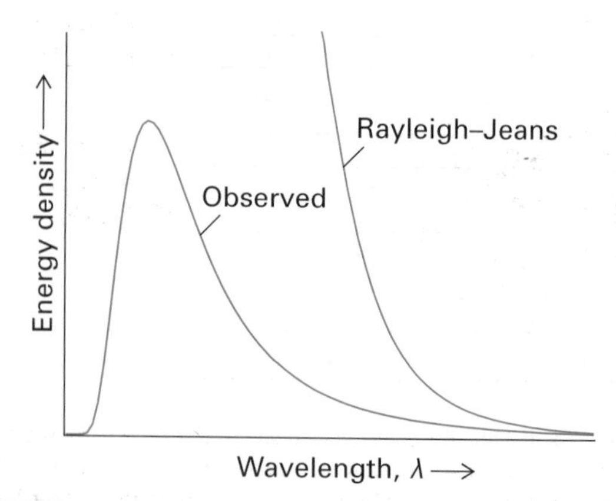

Fig. 12.4 The Rayleigh–Jeans law leads to an infinite energy density at short wavelengths and gives rise to the ultraviolet catastrophe.

frequency, corresponding to ultraviolet radiation, X-rays, and even γ-rays) are excited even at room temperature. So, according to classical physics, every time you strike a match, you blast the surroundings with γ-rays! This absurd result is called the **ultraviolet catastrophe.** It is a direct and unavoidable consequence of applying classical ideas to the electromagnetic field.

In 1900, the German physicist Max Planck found that he could account for the characteristics of black-body radiation by proposing that *the energy of each electromagnetic oscillator is limited to discrete values and cannot be varied arbitrarily*. Thus, the oscillation of the electromagnetic field that corresponds to yellow light, for instance, can be stimulated only if a certain energy is provided. This limitation of the energy to discrete values is called the **quantization of energy**. Specifically, Planck proposed that the energy of an oscillator of frequency ν is restricted to an integral multiple of the quantity $h\nu$, where h is a fundamental constant now known as **Planck's constant:**

$$E = nh\nu \qquad n = 0, 1, 2, \ldots \qquad (12.4)$$

with $h = 6.626 \times 10^{-34}$ J s (Fig. 12.5).

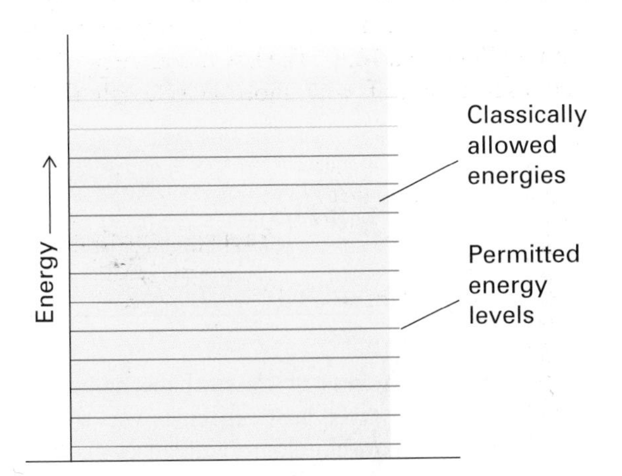

Fig. 12.5 According to classical physics, an oscillator (including the oscillators that correspond to vibrations of the electromagnetic field and correspond to radiation of a particular frequency) can have any energy (as depicted by the tinted range of energies). Planck's proposal implied that an oscillator could be excited only in discrete steps, as it can possess only certain energies (those depicted by the horizontal lines in the illustration).

Self-test 12.3

What is the minimum energy that can be used to excite an oscillator corresponding to yellow light of frequency 5.2×10^{14} Hz?

[*Answer:* 3.4×10^{-19} J]

When Planck calculated the energy density using his quantization postulate, he obtained an expression like Rayleigh's except for an additional factor that at short wavelengths is approximately $e^{-hc/\lambda kT}$. When λ is very short, this factor is very small, so it overcomes the rise predicted by Rayleigh's formula and the ultraviolet catastrophe is avoided. Figure 12.6 shows a plot of Planck's equation: it compares very favourably with the experimental curve shown in Fig. 12.4.

What is the physical reason for the success of Planck's quantization hypothesis? The atoms in the walls of the black body undergo thermal motion, and this motion excites the oscillators of the electromagnetic field. According to classical mechanics,

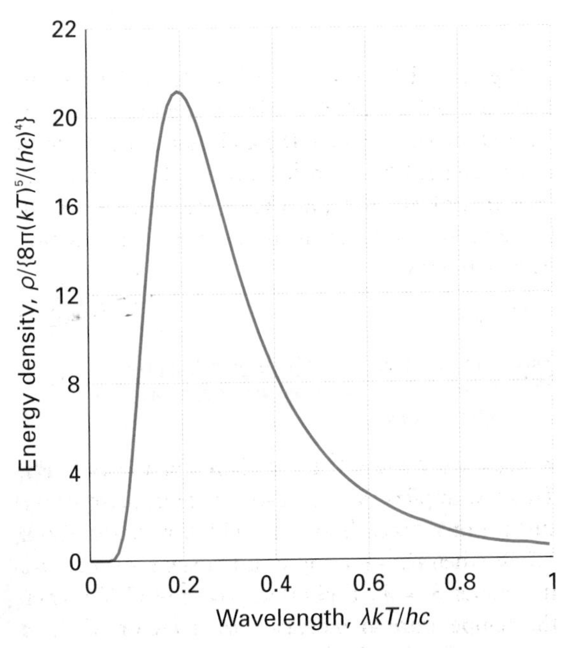

Fig. 12.6 The Planck distribution results in a very low energy density (ρ) for high-frequency, short-wavelength oscillators and is in excellent agreement with experiment.

all the electromagnetic oscillators are excited, even those of very high frequency, and the corresponding wavelengths of radiation are emitted, including radiation of very short wavelength. According to quantum mechanics, however, the oscillators are excited only if they can acquire an energy of at least $h\nu$. This minimum energy is too large for the walls to supply in the case of the high-frequency oscillators, so the latter remain unexcited. The effect of quantization is to quench the contribution from the high-frequency oscillators, as they cannot be excited with the energy available, and hence the very short wavelength radiation is not emitted.

Planck's result accounts quantitatively for the Stefan–Boltzmann and Wien laws. Thus, when the area under the graph in Fig. 12.6 is calculated (to obtain the total energy density over the entire wavelength range), the resulting expression is proportional to T^4, just as the Stefan–Boltzmann law asserts. Similarly, when we calculate the wavelength λ_{max} corresponding to the maximum point of the curve, we find that its value is inversely proportional to the temperature, which is in agreement with Wien's law.

12.2 Heat capacities

Even before Planck did his work, there was experimental information around that, had people been alert, would have led them to the quantum theory before him. In Section 2.4 we saw that heat capacity, C, is the constant of proportionality between the rise in temperature, ΔT, of a sample and the heat, q, supplied:

$$q = C\,\Delta T$$

On the basis of somewhat slender experimental evidence, the French scientists Pierre-Louis Dulong and Alexis-Thérèse Petit had proposed in 1819 that the molar heat capacity of all monatomic solids —such as metals—was equal (in modern units) to about 25 J K^{-1} mol^{-1}. Classical physics was able to account for this value quite readily, because if we assume that the atomic oscillators can be excited to any energy, then the predicted molar heat capacity is $3R$, where R is the gas constant, and $3R = 25$ J K^{-1} mol^{-1}.[3]

Derivation 12.1

The heat capacity of a monatomic solid

Each of the N atoms of a solid can oscillate in any of three perpendicular directions (Fig. 12.7). The solid is therefore equivalent to a collection of $3N$ oscillators. According to the *equipartition theorem* of classical physics, at a temperature T, the average energy of any oscillator is kT, where k is Boltzmann's constant. It follows that the total energy of the N vibrating atoms is $3N \times kT$. The energy per mole of atoms is therefore $3N_AkT$, or $3RT$, because the number of atoms per mole is N_A. Finally, we note that because the molar energy is $3RT$, then when the temperature of the sample increases by ΔT, the molar energy increases by $3R\,\Delta T$. This increase in energy must be supplied as heat from the surroundings, so the heat required to raise the temperature by ΔT is $3R\,\Delta T$. It follows by comparison with the definition of molar heat capacity ($q = C_m\,\Delta T$) that $C_m = 3R$.

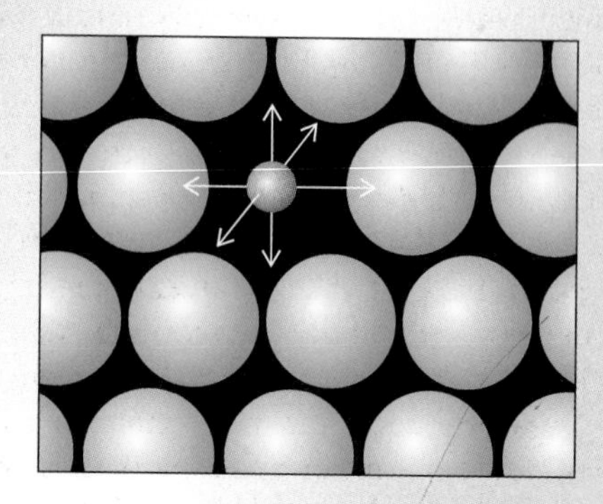

Fig. 12.7 An atom in a solid can oscillate about its position in three perpendicular directions, and when a solid is heated, the vigour of the motion increases. This illustration depicts a view of one layer of atoms in a solid and shows the oscillations of one of the atoms (which is drawn smaller for clarity).

The apparent success of classical mechanics in accounting for observed heat capacities was short-lived because, when technological advances made it possible to measure heat capacities at low temperatures, all substances were found to have values significantly lower than 25 J K^{-1} mol^{-1}. At very

[3] We have already remarked that the gas constant crops up in expressions for all manner of 'non-gas' properties. It is in fact a more fundamental constant (Boltzmann's constant, k) in disguise ($R = N_Ak$).

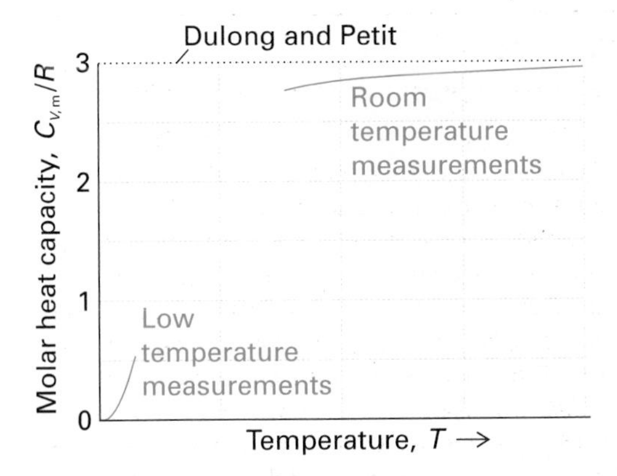

Fig. 12.8 The Dulong and Petit law implies that the heat capacity should be the same at all temperatures. However, all solids have a lower heat capacity as the temperature is lowered, and as T approaches zero, the heat capacity approaches zero too.

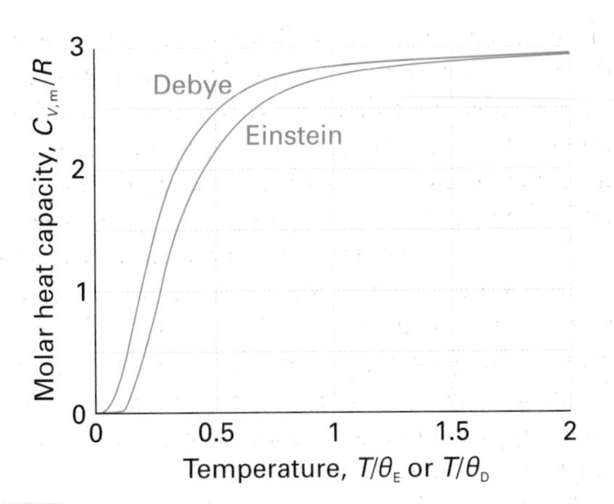

Fig. 12.9 The Einstein formula predicts the general temperature dependence quite well, but is everywhere too low. Debye's modification of Einstein's calculation gives very good agreement with experiment ($\theta_E = h\nu/k$; $\theta_D = h\nu_{max}/k$).

low temperatures, the heat capacity was found to approach zero (Fig. 12.8). Even some quite common substances at room temperature were found to have molar heat capacities well below the expected value: the value for diamond, for instance, is only 6.1 J K^{-1} mol^{-1} at 25°C. That value could have been determined at the start of the nineteenth century and quantum theory could have been invented then.

In 1905 Albert Einstein set out to explain these observations. He took the view that each atom oscillates about its mean position with a single frequency ν. He then borrowed Planck's hypothesis and asserted that the permitted energy of any oscillating atom is an integral multiple of $h\nu$ (exactly as for electromagnetic oscillators). On the basis of this model, Einstein deduced that instead of $C_m = 3R$, a better formula is

$$C_m = 3Rf(T) \qquad (12.5)$$

where $f(T) \rightarrow 0$ as $T \rightarrow 0$ and $f(T) \rightarrow 1$ as T becomes large (such as room temperature).[4] This expression is plotted in Fig. 12.9. We see that it does indeed predict a decrease in heat capacity as the temperature is lowered and, because of the behaviour of the factor $f(T)$, that C_m approaches zero as T approaches zero.

The physical reason for the success of Einstein's model is that an atom can start to oscillate only if it can acquire a certain minimum energy ($h\nu$). At low temperatures there is only enough energy available for a few atoms to be able to oscillate. Because so few atoms can be involved in taking up energy, the solid cannot absorb heat readily and consequently its heat capacity is low. At higher temperatures there is enough energy available for all the oscillators to become active: all $3N$ oscillators contribute, and the molar heat capacity approaches its classical value of $3R$. Tightly-bonded, light atoms oscillate relative to their neighbours at high frequencies, so we expect them to have widely spaced energy levels and to show the effects of quantization even at quite high temperatures. That is the case for diamond, which approaches its classical heat capacity only for temperatures above about 1800 K. Lead, on the contrary, has loosely bonded heavy atoms: their vibrational frequencies are low, the energy separation between neighbouring levels is small, and the heat capacity is close to its classical value down to temperatures as low as about 90 K.

The Dutch physicist Peter Debye carried out a more refined approach to the calculation. He allowed for the atoms to oscillate with a range of frequencies rather than the single frequency supposed by Einstein. The graph of his more complicated expression is similar to Einstein's, but the numerical agreement with the experimental data is better (see Fig. 12.9).

[4] For completeness, $f(T) = \dfrac{(h\nu/kT)^2 \, e^{h\nu/kT}}{(e^{h\nu/kT} - 1)^2}$.

An important practical conclusion from Debye's calculation is that at low temperatures, the heat capacity of a solid is expected to be proportional to T^3. This dependence, which is called the **Debye T^3 law**, is used to extrapolate measurements of heat capacities to $T = 0$ in the experimental determination of entropies (Section 4.5).

12.3 The photoelectric effect

So far, we have seen that two observations—on the electromagnetic field and the heat capacities of solids—have led to the overthrow of the classical view that oscillators can have any energy. We shall now see how three other experimental observations upset another central concept of classical physics, the distinction between waves and particles.

Planck's discovery that an electromagnetic oscillator of frequency ν can possess only the energies 0, $h\nu$, $2h\nu$, ... inspired a new view of the nature of electromagnetic radiation. Instead of thinking of radiation of a given frequency as the excitement of the electromagnetic field to one of its permitted states of oscillation at that frequency, we can think of it as a stream of 0, 1, 2, ... particles travelling at the speed c, each particle having an energy $h\nu$. When there is only one such particle present, the energy of the radiation is $h\nu$, when there are two particles of that frequency, their total energy is $2h\nu$, and so on. These particles of electromagnetic radiation are now called **photons**. According to the photon picture of radiation, a ray of light of frequency ν consists of a stream of photons, each one having an energy $h\nu$ and speed c. As the intensity of the ray is increased, the number of photons increases, but each one continues to have the energy $h\nu$. An intense beam of monochromatic (single-frequency) radiation consists of a dense stream of identical photons; a weak beam of radiation of the same frequency consists of a relatively small number of the same type of photons.

Example 12.1

Calculating the number of photons

Calculate the number of photons emitted by a 100 W yellow lamp in 10.0 s. Take the wavelength of yellow light as 560 nm and assume 100 per cent efficiency.

Strategy The total energy emitted by a lamp in a given interval is its power multiplied by the time interval of interest (1 J = 1 W s). The number of photons emitted in that time is therefore the total energy divided by the energy of one photon. We calculate the energy of a single photon from the formula $E = h\nu$ which, after using eqn 12.1, becomes $E = hc/\lambda$.

Solution The electromagnetic energy, $E_{emitted}$, emitted by the lamp of power P switched on for a time t (assuming all the energy it consumes is converted into radiation of a single frequency) is

$$E_{emitted} = Pt$$

(Later we substitute $P = 100$ W and $t = 10.0$ s.) Each photon has energy

$$E_{photon} = h\nu \overset{\nu = c/\lambda}{=} \frac{hc}{\lambda}$$

(Later we substitute $\lambda = 560$ nm, 5.60×10^{-7} m.) The number of photons required to carry away the total energy is therefore the total energy divided by the energy of one photon:

$$N_{photons} = \frac{E_{emitted}}{E_{photon}} = \frac{Pt}{(hc/\lambda)} = \frac{Pt\lambda}{hc}$$

At this point we substitute the data:

$$N_{photons} = \frac{(100\ \text{J s}^{-1}) \times (10.0\ \text{s}) \times (5.60 \times 10^{-7}\ \text{m})}{(6.626 \times 10^{-34}\ \text{J s}) \times (2.998 \times 10^{8}\ \text{m s}^{-1})}$$

$$= \frac{100 \times 10.0 \times 5.60 \times 10^{-7}}{6.626 \times 2.998 \times 10^{-26}} \frac{\text{J s m s}^{-1}}{\text{J s m s}^{-1}}$$

$$= 2.82 \times 10^{21}$$

A note on good practice. It is a good idea to carry out a calculation in terms of symbols as far as possible, and to put in the numerical data at the last stage. In that way, you can use the equation you derive for different data, and the opportunity for numerical error, including rounding errors, is reduced.

Self-test 12.4

How many 1000 nm photons does a 1 mW infrared rangefinder emit in 0.1 s?

[*Answer:* 5×10^{14}]

Evidence that confirmed the view that radiation can be interpreted as a stream of particles comes from the **photoelectric effect**, the ejection of electrons

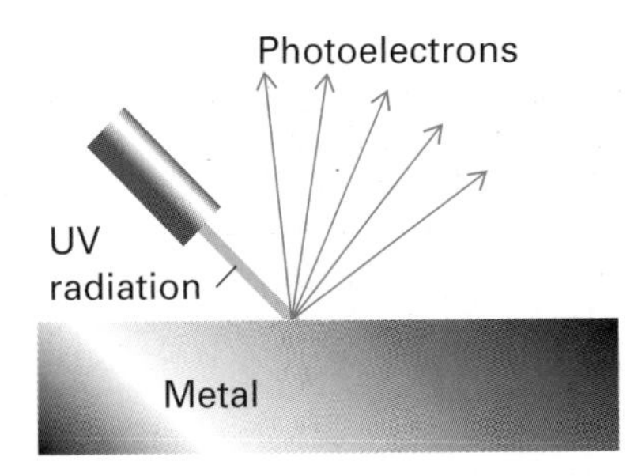

Fig. 12.10 The experimental arrangement to demonstrate the photoelectric effect. A beam of ultraviolet radiation is used to irradiate a patch of the surface of a metal, and electrons are ejected from the surface if the frequency of the radiation is above a threshold value that depends on the metal.

from metals when they are exposed to ultraviolet radiation (Fig. 12.10). The characteristics of the photoelectric effect are as follows:

1 No electrons are ejected, regardless of the intensity of the radiation, unless the frequency exceeds a threshold value characteristic of the metal.
2 The kinetic energy of the ejected electrons varies linearly with the frequency of the incident radiation but is independent of its intensity.

> We say that y *varies linearly* with x if the relation between them is $y = a + bx$; we say that y is *proportional* to x if the relation is $y = bx$.

3 Even at low light intensities, electrons are ejected immediately if the frequency is above the threshold value.

These observations strongly suggest an interpretation of the photoelectric effect in which an electron is ejected in a collision with a particle-like projectile, provided the projectile carries enough energy to expel the electron from the metal. If we suppose that the projectile is a photon of energy $h\nu$, where ν is the frequency of the radiation, then the conservation of energy requires that the kinetic energy of the electron (which is equal to $\frac{1}{2}m_e v^2$, when the speed of the electron is v) should be equal to the energy supplied by the photon less the energy Φ (uppercase phi) required to remove the electron from the metal (Fig. 12.11):

$$E_K = h\nu - \Phi \tag{12.6}$$

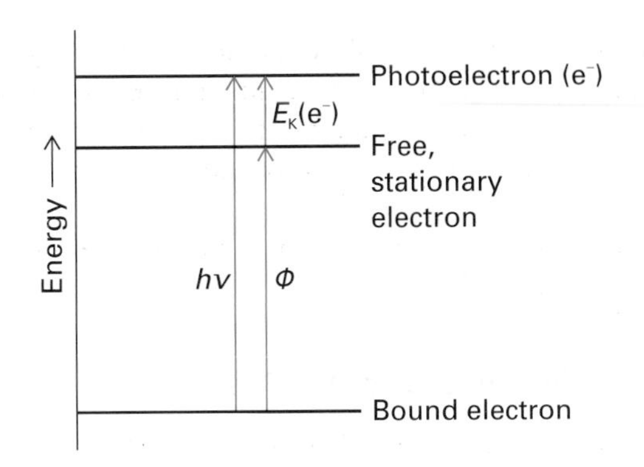

Fig. 12.11 In the photoelectric effect, an incoming photon brings a definite quantity of energy, $h\nu$. It collides with an electron close to the surface of the metal target, and transfers its energy to it. The difference between the work function, Φ, and the energy $h\nu$ appears as the kinetic energy of the ejected electron.

The quantity Φ is called the **work function** of the metal, the analogue of the ionization energy of an atom.

> **Self-test 12.5**
>
> The work function of rubidium is 2.09 eV (1 eV = 1.60×10^{-19} J). Can blue (470 nm) light eject electrons from the metal?
>
> [*Answer:* yes]

When $h\nu < \Phi$, photoejection (the ejection of electrons by light) cannot occur because the photon supplies insufficient energy to expel the electron: this conclusion is consistent with observation 1. Equation 12.6 predicts that the kinetic energy of an ejected electron should increase linearly with the frequency, in agreement with observation 2. When a photon collides with an electron, it gives up all its energy, so we should expect electrons to appear as soon as the collisions begin, provided the photons carry sufficient energy: this conclusion agrees with observation 3. Thus, the photoelectric effect is strong evidence for the existence of photons.

12.4 The diffraction of electrons

The photoelectric effect shows that light has certain properties of particles. Although contrary to the

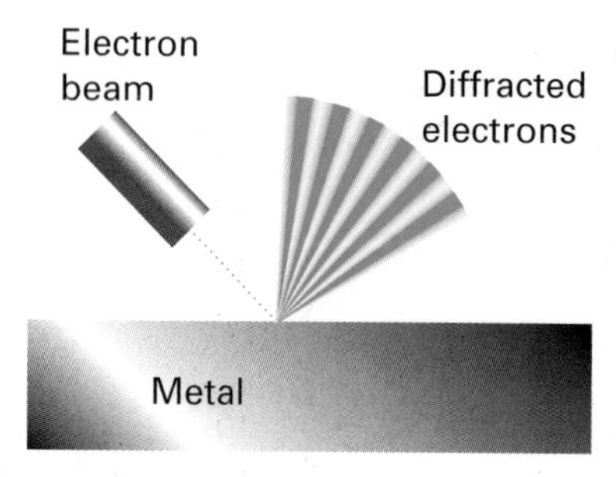

Fig. 12.12 In the Davisson–Germer experiment, a beam of electrons was directed on a single crystal of nickel, and the scattered electrons showed a variation in intensity with angle that corresponded to the pattern that would be expected if the electrons had a wave character and were diffracted by the layers of atoms in the solid.

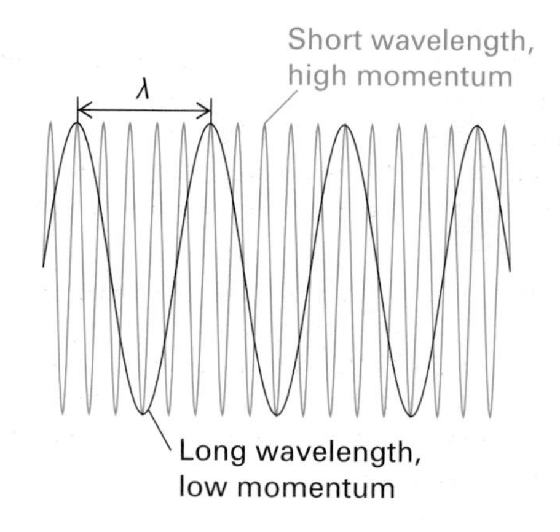

Fig. 12.13 According to the de Broglie relation, a particle with low momentum has a long wavelength whereas a particle with high momentum has a short wavelength. A high momentum can result either from a high mass or from a high velocity (because $p = mv$). Macroscopic objects have such large masses that, even if they are travelling very slowly, their wavelengths are undetectably short.

long-established wave theory of light, a similar view had been held before, but discarded. No significant scientist, however, had taken the view that matter is wave-like. Nevertheless, experiments carried out in 1925 forced people to doubt even that conclusion. The crucial experiment was performed by the American physicists Clinton Davisson and Lester Germer, who observed the diffraction of electrons by a crystal (Fig. 12.12). **Diffraction** is the interference between waves caused by an object in their path, and results in a series of bright and dark fringes where the waves are detected. It is a typical characteristic of waves (see Appendix 3).

The Davisson–Germer experiment, which has since been repeated with other particles (including molecular hydrogen), shows clearly that 'particles' have wave-like properties. We have also seen that 'waves' have particle-like properties. Thus we are brought to the heart of modern physics. When examined on an atomic scale, the concepts of particle and wave melt together, particles taking on the characteristics of waves, and waves the characteristics of particles. This joint wave–particle character of matter and radiation is called **wave–particle duality**.

As these concepts emerged there was an understandable confusion—which continues to this day—about how to combine both aspects of matter into a single description. Some progress was made by Louis de Broglie when, in 1924, he suggested that any particle travelling with a linear momentum, p, should have (in some sense) a wavelength λ given by the **de Broglie relation**:

$$\lambda = \frac{h}{p} \qquad (12.7)$$

The wave corresponding to this wavelength, what de Broglie called a 'matter wave', has the mathematical form $\sin(2\pi x/\lambda)$. The de Broglie relation implies that the wavelength of a 'matter wave' should decrease as the particle's speed increases (Fig. 12.13). The relation also implies that, for a given speed, heavy particles should be associated with waves of shorter wavelengths than those of lighter particles. Equation 12.7 was confirmed by the Davisson–Germer experiment, as the wavelength it predicts for the electrons they used in their experiment agrees with the details of the diffraction pattern they observed. We shall build on the relation, and understand it more, in the next section.

Example 12.2

Estimating the de Broglie wavelength

Estimate the wavelength of electrons that have been accelerated from rest through a potential difference of 1.00 kV.

Strategy To use the de Broglie relation, we need to know the linear momentum, because we can combine these two expressions and rearrange them into p =

$(2m_eE_K)^{1/2}$. Finally, we need to know that the kinetic energy acquired by an electron accelerated from rest by falling through a potential difference V is eV, where $e = 1.602 \times 10^{-19}$ C is the magnitude of its charge (see Appendix 3), so we can write $E_K = eV$ and obtain $p = (2m_eeV)^{1/2}$.

Solution From $E_K = \frac{1}{2}m_e\upsilon^2$ it follows that $\upsilon = (2E_K/m_e)^{1/2}$, and from $p = m_e\upsilon$, we get first $p = m_e(2E_K/m_e)^{1/2}$, and then $p = (2m_eE_K)^{1/2}$. Next, because the kinetic energy of the accelerated electron is eV, we obtain $p = (2m_eeV)^{1/2}$. This is the expression we can use in de Broglie's relation, which becomes

$$\lambda = \frac{h}{(2m_eeV)^{1/2}}$$

At this stage, all we need to do is to substitute the data and use the relations 1 C V = 1 J and 1 J = 1 kg m^2 s^{-2}:

$$\lambda = \frac{6.626 \times 10^{-34}\ \text{J s}}{\{2 \times (9.110 \times 10^{-31}\ \text{kg}) \times (1.602 \times 10^{-19}\ \text{C}) \times (1.00 \times 10^3\ \text{V})\}^{1/2}}$$

$$= 3.88 \times 10^{-11}\ \text{m}$$

The wavelength of 38.8 pm is comparable to typical bond lengths in molecules (about 100 pm). Electrons accelerated in this way are used in the technique of *electron diffraction*, in which the diffraction pattern generated by interference when a beam of electrons passes through a sample is interpreted in terms of the locations of the atoms.

Self-test 12.6

Calculate the wavelength of an electron in a 10 MeV particle accelerator (1 MeV = 10^6 eV).

[*Answer:* 0.39 pm]

12.5 Atomic and molecular spectra

The most directly compelling evidence for the quantization of energy comes from the frequencies of radiation absorbed or emitted by atoms and molecules. We shall only mention this point here, and leave it for a much more complete treatment later (Chapters 19 and 20). Figure 12.14 shows a typical atomic emission spectrum and Fig. 12.15 shows a typical molecular absorption spectrum. The obvious feature of both is that *radiation is emitted (or absorbed) at a series of discrete frequencies*. The emission of light at discrete frequencies can be understood if the energy of the atoms or molecules is also confined to discrete values, as then energy can be discarded only in packets (Fig. 12.16). For example, if the energy of an atom decreases by ΔE, then the energy is carried away as a photon of that energy, and therefore of frequency $\nu = \Delta E/h$. As a result, radiation of frequency ν, a so-called **spectroscopic line**, appears in the spectrum.

Classical mechanics failed completely in its attempts to account for the existence of discrete spectroscopic lines, just as it failed to account for

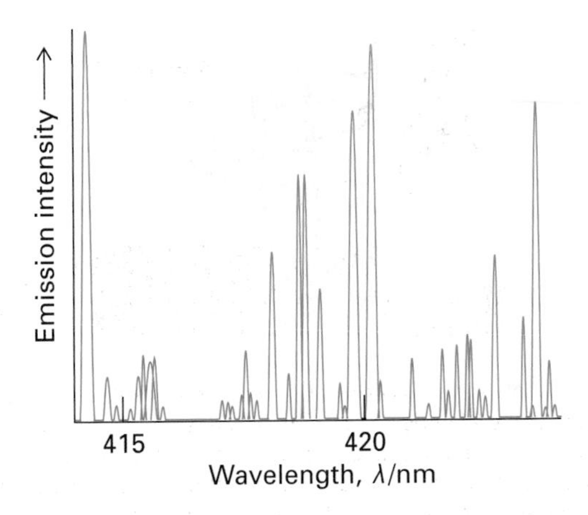

Fig. 12.14 A region of the spectrum of radiation emitted by excited iron atoms consists of radiation at a series of discrete wavelengths (or frequencies).

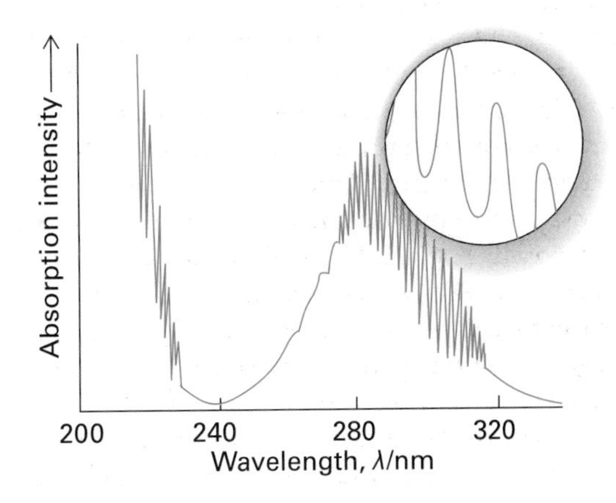

Fig. 12.15 When a molecule changes its state, it does so by absorbing radiation at definite frequencies. This spectrum is part of that due to sulfur dioxide (SO_2) molecules. This observation suggests that molecules can possess only discrete energies, not a continuously variable energy.

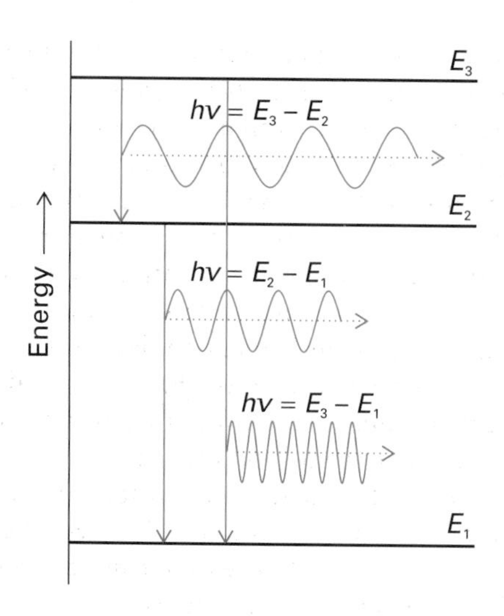

Fig. 12.16 Spectral lines can be accounted for if we assume that a molecule emits a photon as it changes between discrete energy levels. High-frequency radiation is emitted when the two states involved in the transition are widely separated in energy; low-frequency radiation is emitted when the two states are close in energy.

the other experiments described above. Such total failure showed that the basic concepts of classical mechanics were false. A new mechanics, which in due course came to be known as *quantum mechanics*, had to be devised to take its place.

The dynamics of microscopic systems

We shall take the de Broglie relation as our starting point, and abandon the classical concept of particles moving along trajectories. From now on, we adopt the quantum mechanical view that *a particle is spread through space like a wave*. As for a wave in water where the water accumulates in some places but is low in others, there are regions where the particle is more likely to be found than others. To describe this distribution, we introduce the concept of **wavefunction**, ψ (psi), in place of the trajectory, and then set up a scheme for calculating and interpreting ψ. A 'wavefunction' is the modern term for de Broglie's 'matter wave'. To a very crude first approximation, we can visualize a wavefunction as

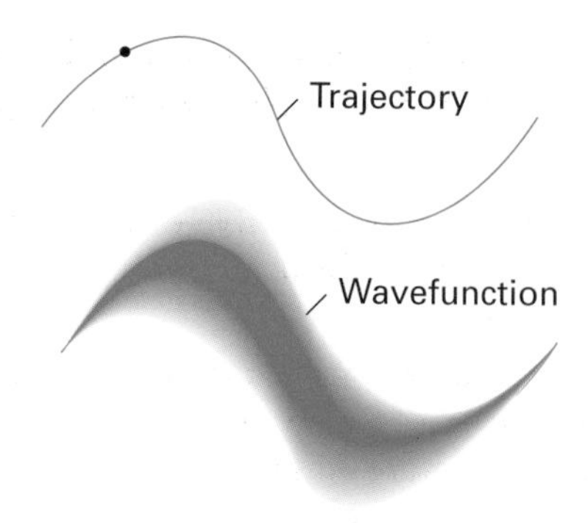

Fig. 12.17 According to classical mechanics, a particle may have a well-defined trajectory, with a precisely specified position and momentum at each instant (as represented by the precise path in the diagram). According to quantum mechanics, a particle cannot have a precise trajectory; instead, there is only a probability that it may be found at a specific location at any instant. The wavefunction that determines its probability distribution is a kind of blurred version of the trajectory. Here, the wavefunction is represented by areas of shading: the darker the area, the greater the probability of finding the particle there.

a blurred version of a trajectory (Fig. 12.17); however, we refine this picture in the following sections.

12.6 The Schrödinger equation

In 1926, the Austrian physicist Erwin Schrödinger proposed an equation for calculating wavefunctions. The **Schrödinger equation** for a single particle of mass m moving with energy E in one dimension is

$$-\frac{\hbar^2}{2m}\frac{d^2\psi}{dx^2} + V\psi = E\psi \qquad (12.8)$$

In this expression, V, which may depend on the position x of the particle, is the potential energy; $\hbar$ (which is read h-bar) is a convenient modification of Planck's constant:

$$\hbar = \frac{h}{2\pi} = 1.054\,59 \times 10^{-34}\ \mathrm{J\,s}$$

The fact that the Schrödinger equation is a 'differential equation', an equation in terms of the derivatives of a function, should not cause too much consternation. We provide a justification of the form of the equation in *Further information 12.1*. The rare cases where we need to see the explicit forms of its solution will involve very simple functions. For example (and to become familiar with the form of wavefunctions in three simple cases, but not putting in various constants):

1 The wavefunction for a freely moving particle is $\sin x$ (exactly as for de Broglie's matter wave, $\sin(2\pi x/\lambda)$).
2 The wavefunction for a particle free to oscillate to and fro near a point is e^{-x^2}, where x is the displacement from the point.
3 The wavefunction for an electron in a hydrogen atom is e^{-r}, where r is the distance from the nucleus.

As can be seen, none of these wavefunctions is particularly complicated mathematically.

One feature of the solution of any given Schrödinger equation, a feature common to all differential equations, is that an infinite number of possible solutions are allowed mathematically. For instance, if $\sin x$ is a solution of the equation, then so too is $a \sin bx$, where a and b are arbitrary constants, with each solution corresponding to a particular value of E. However, it turns out that only some of these solutions are acceptable physically. To be acceptable, a solution must satisfy certain constraints called **boundary conditions** that we describe shortly (Fig. 12.18). Suddenly, we are at the heart of quantum mechanics: *the fact that only some solutions are acceptable, together with the fact that each solution corresponds to a characteristic value of E, implies that only certain values of the energy are acceptable*. That is, *when the Schrödinger equation is solved subject to the boundary conditions that the solutions must satisfy, we find that the energy of the system is quantized*. Planck and his immediate successors had to postulate the quantization of energy for each system they considered: now we see that quantization is an automatic feature of a single equation, the Schrödinger equation, which is applicable to all systems. Later in this chapter and the next we shall see exactly which energies are allowed in a variety of systems, the most important of which (for chemistry) are atoms.

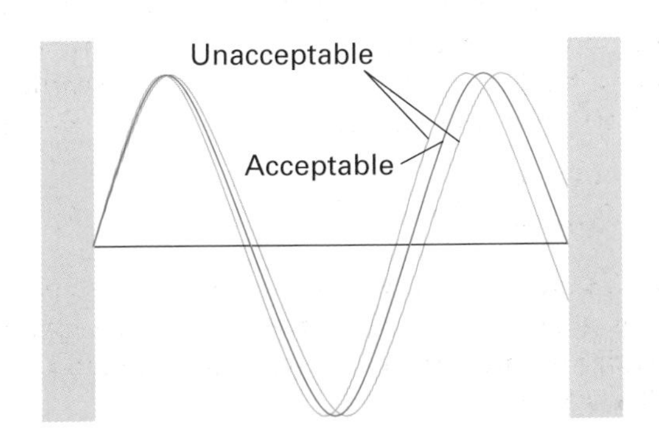

Fig. 12.18 Although an infinite number of solutions of the Schrödinger equation exist, not all of them are physically acceptable. Acceptable wavefunctions have to satisfy certain boundary conditions, which vary from system to system. In the example shown here, where the particle is confined between two impenetrable walls, the only acceptable wavefunctions are those that fit between the walls (like the vibrations of a stretched string). Because each wavefunction corresponds to a characteristic energy, and the boundary conditions rule out many solutions, only certain energies are permissible.

12.7 The Born interpretation

Before going any further, it will be helpful to understand the physical significance of a wavefunction. The interpretation of ψ that is widely used is based on a suggestion made by the German physicist Max Born. He made use of an analogy with the wave theory of light, in which the square of the amplitude of an electromagnetic wave is interpreted as its intensity and therefore (in quantum terms) as the number of photons present. The **Born interpretation** asserts that:

The probability of finding a particle in a small region of space of volume δV is proportional to $\psi^2 \delta V$, where ψ is the value of the wavefunction in the region.

In other words, ψ^2 is a **probability density**. As for other kinds of density, such as mass density (ordinary 'density'), we get the probability itself by multiplying the probability density by the volume of the region of interest.

The Born interpretation implies that wherever ψ^2 is large, there is a high probability of finding the particle. Wherever ψ^2 is small, there is only a small chance of finding the particle. The density of shading in Fig. 12.19 represents this **probabilistic interpretation**, an interpretation that accepts that we can make predictions only about the probability of finding a particle somewhere. This interpretation is in contrast to classical physics, which claims to be able to predict precisely that a particle will be at a given point on its path at a given instant.

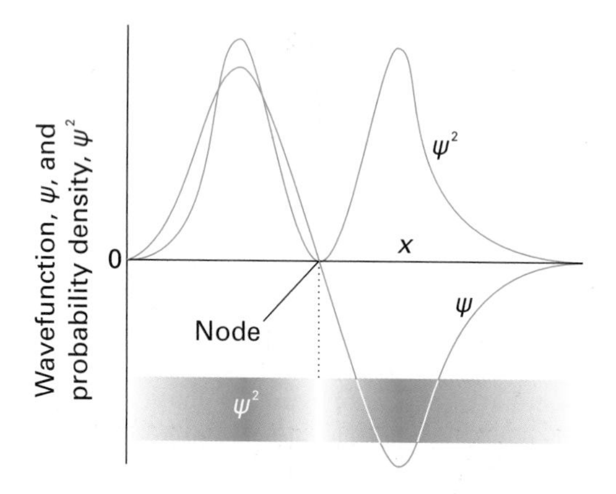

Fig. 12.19 A wavefunction does not have a direct physical interpretation. However, its square (its square modulus if it is complex) tells us the probability of finding a particle at each point. The probability density implied by the wavefunction shown here is depicted by the density of shading.

Example 12.3

Interpreting a wavefunction

The wavefunction of an electron in the lowest energy state of a hydrogen atom is proportional to e^{-r/a_0}, with a_0 = 52.9 pm and r the distance from the nucleus (Fig. 12.20). Calculate the relative probabilities of finding the electron inside a small volume located at (a) the nucleus, (b) a distance a_0 from the nucleus.

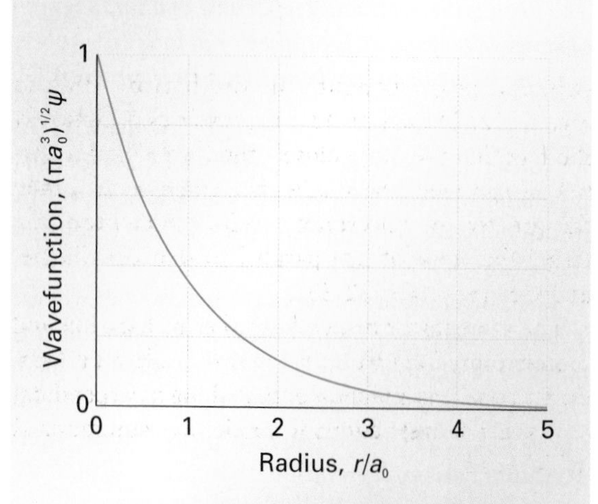

Fig. 12.20 The wavefunction for an electron in the ground state of a hydrogen atom is an exponentially decaying function of the form e^{-r/a_0}, where a_0 is the Bohr radius.

Strategy The probability is proportional to $\psi^2\delta V$ evaluated at the specified location. The volume of interest is so small (even on the scale of the atom) that we can ignore the variation of ψ within it and write

$$\text{Probability} \propto \psi^2\delta V$$

with ψ evaluated at the point in question.

Solution (a) At the nucleus, $r = 0$, so there $\psi^2 \propto 1.0$ (because $e^0 = 1$) and the probability is proportional to $1.0 \times \delta V$. (b) At a distance $r = a_0$ in an arbitrary direction, $\psi^2 \propto e^{-2} \times \delta V = 0.14 \times \delta V$. Therefore, the ratio of probabilities is $1.0/0.14 = 7.1$. It is more probable (by a factor of 7.1) that the electron will be found at the nucleus than in the same tiny volume located at a distance a_0 from the nucleus.

Self-test 12.7

The wavefunction for the lowest energy state in the ion He^+ is proportional to e^{-2r/a_0}. Repeat the calculation for this ion. Any comment?

[*Answer:* 55; a more compact wavefunction on account of the higher nuclear charge]

12.8 The uncertainty principle

We have seen that, according to the de Broglie relation, a wave of constant wavelength, the wavefunction $\sin(2\pi x/\lambda)$, corresponds to a particle with a definite linear momentum $p = h/\lambda$. However, a wave does not have a definite location at a single point in space, so we cannot speak of the precise position of the particle if it has a definite momentum. Indeed, because a sine wave spreads throughout the whole of space we cannot say anything about the location of the particle: because the wave spreads everywhere, the particle may be found anywhere in the whole of space. This statement is one half of the **uncertainty principle** proposed by Werner Heisenberg in 1927, in one of the most celebrated results of quantum mechanics:

It is impossible to specify simultaneously, with arbitrary precision, both the momentum and the position of a particle.

Before discussing the principle further, we must establish the other half: that if we know the position of a particle exactly, then we can say nothing about its momentum. If the particle is at a definite

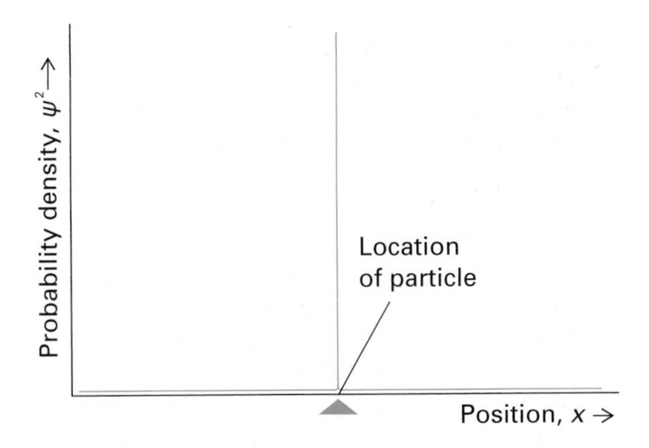

Fig. 12.21 The wavefunction for a particle with a well-defined position is a sharply spiked function that has zero amplitude everywhere except at the particle's position.

location, then its wavefunction must be non-zero there and zero everywhere else (Fig. 12.21). We can simulate such a wavefunction by forming a **superposition** of many wavefunctions; that is, by adding together the amplitudes of a large number of sine functions (Fig. 12.22). This procedure is successful because the amplitudes of the waves add together at one location to give a non-zero total amplitude, but cancel everywhere else. In other words, we can create a sharply localized wavefunction by adding together wavefunctions corresponding to many different wavelengths, and therefore, by the de Broglie relation, of many different linear momenta.

The superposition of a few sine functions gives a broad, ill-defined wavefunction. As the number of functions increases, the wavefunction becomes sharper because of the more complete interference between the positive and negative regions of the components. When an infinite number of components are used, the wavefunction is a sharp, infinitely narrow spike like that in Fig. 12.21, which corresponds to perfect localization of the particle. Now the particle is perfectly localized, but at the expense of discarding all information about its momentum.

The quantitative version of the position–momentum uncertainty relation is

$$\Delta p \, \Delta x \geq \tfrac{1}{2}\hbar \qquad (12.9)$$

The quantity Δp is the 'uncertainty' in the linear momentum and Δx is the uncertainty in position

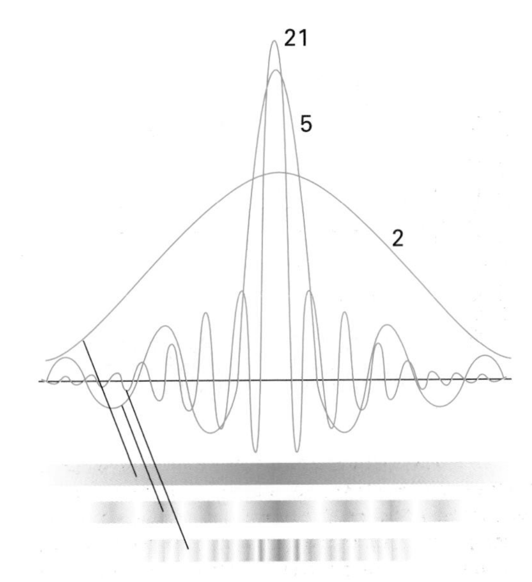

Fig. 12.22 The wavefunction for a particle with an ill-defined location can be regarded as the sum (superposition) of several wavefunctions of different wavelengths that interfere constructively in one place but destructively elsewhere. As more waves are used in the superposition, the location becomes more precise at the expense of uncertainty in the particle's momentum. An infinite number of waves are needed to construct the wavefunction of a perfectly localized particle. The numbers against each curve are the number of sine waves used in the superpositions.

(which is proportional to the width of the peak in Fig. 12.22).[5] Equation 12.9 expresses quantitatively the fact that the more closely the location of a particle is specified (the smaller the value of Δx), then the greater the uncertainty in its momentum (the larger the value of Δp) parallel to that coordinate, and vice versa (Fig. 12.23).

The uncertainty principle applies to location and momentum *along the same axis*. It is silent on location on one axis and momentum along a perpendicular axis. The restrictions it implies are summarized in Table 12.1.

[5] Strictly, the uncertainty in momentum is the root mean square (rms) deviation of the momentum from its mean value, $\Delta p = (\langle p^2\rangle - \langle p\rangle^2)^{1/2}$, where the angle brackets denote mean values. Likewise, the uncertainty in position is the rms deviation in the mean value of position, $\Delta x = (\langle x^2\rangle - \langle x\rangle^2)^{1/2}$.

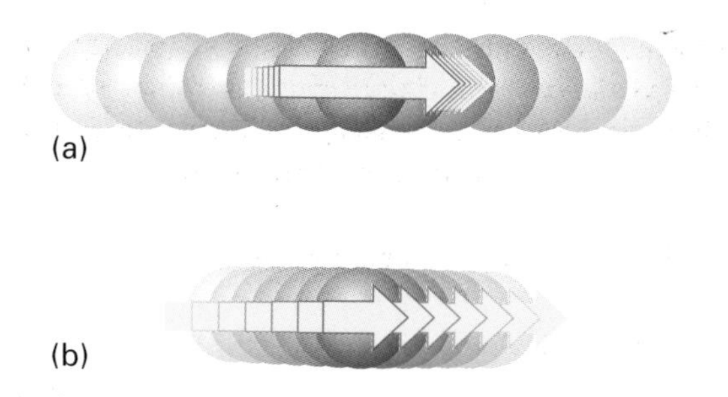

Fig. 12.23 A representation of the content of the uncertainty principle. The range of locations of a particle is shown by the circles, and the range of momenta by the arrows. In (a), the position is quite uncertain, and the range of momenta is small. In (b), the location is much better defined, and now the momentum of the particle is quite uncertain.

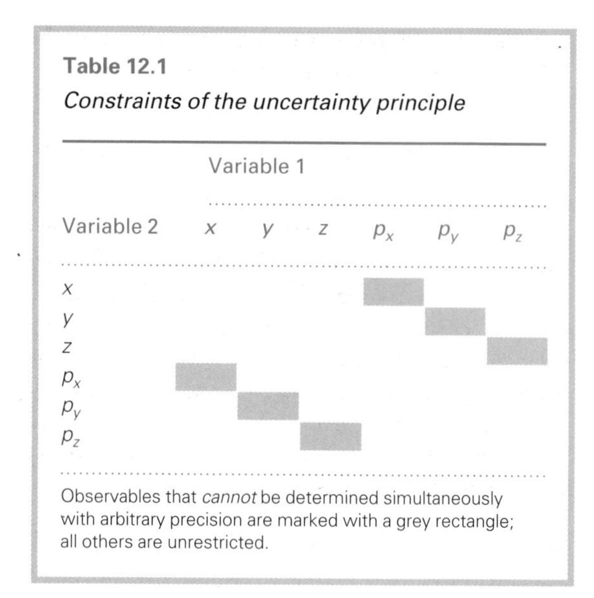

Table 12.1
Constraints of the uncertainty principle

Variable 2	Variable 1 x	y	z	p_x	p_y	p_z
x				■		
y					■	
z						■
p_x	■					
p_y		■				
p_z			■			

Observables that *cannot* be determined simultaneously with arbitrary precision are marked with a grey rectangle; all others are unrestricted.

Example 12.4
Using the uncertainty principle

The speed of a certain projectile of mass 1.0 g is known to within 1.0×10^{-6} m s^{-1}. What is the minimum uncertainty in its position along its line of flight?

Strategy We can estimate Δp from $m\,\Delta v$, where Δv is the uncertainty in the speed; then we use eqn 12.9 to estimate the minimum uncertainty in position, Δx, where x is the direction in which the projectile is travelling.

Solution From $\Delta p\,\Delta x \geq \frac{1}{2}\hbar$, the uncertainty in position is

$$\Delta x \geq \frac{\hbar}{2\,\Delta p} = \frac{1.054 \times 10^{-34}\ \mathrm{J\,s}}{2 \times (1.0 \times 10^{-3}\ \mathrm{kg}) \times (1.0 \times 10^{-6}\ \mathrm{m\,s^{-1}})}$$
$$= 5.3 \times 10^{-26}\ \mathrm{m}$$

This degree of uncertainty is completely negligible for all practical purposes. However, when the mass is that of an electron, the same uncertainty in speed implies an uncertainty in position far larger than the diameter of an atom, so the concept of a trajectory—the simultaneous possession of a precise position and momentum—is untenable.

Self-test 12.8

Estimate the minimum uncertainty in the speed of an electron in a hydrogen atom (taking its diameter as 100 pm).

[*Answer:* 580 km s^{-1}]

The uncertainty principle epitomizes the difference between classical and quantum mechanics. Classical mechanics supposed, falsely as we now know, that the position and momentum of a particle can be specified simultaneously with arbitrary precision. However, quantum mechanics shows that position and momentum are **complementary**; that is, not simultaneously specifiable. Quantum mechanics requires us to make a choice: we can specify position at the expense of momentum, or momentum at the expense of position.

Applications of quantum mechanics

We shall now illustrate some of the concepts that have been introduced and gain some familiarity with the implications and interpretation of quantum mechanics. We shall encounter many other illustrations in the following chapters, as quantum mechanics pervades the whole of chemistry. Just to set the scene, here we describe three basic types of motion: translation (motion in a straight line), rotation, and vibration. It turns out that the wavefunctions for free translational and rotational motion can be constructed directly from the de Broglie relation, without solving the Schrödinger equation itself, and we shall take that simple route. That is not possible for vibrational motion where the motion is more complicated, so there we shall have to use the Schrödinger equation to find the wavefunctions.

12.9 Translation: motion in one dimension

Here we consider translational motion of a particle in one dimension. We shall see that when the particle is confined to move within two infinitely high walls, only certain wavefunctions and their corresponding energies are acceptable. However, when the walls are of finite height, the solutions of the Schrödinger equation reveal surprising features of particles, especially their ability to tunnel into and through regions where classical physics would forbid them to be found.

(a) A particle in a box

First, we consider the translational motion of a 'particle in a box', a particle of mass m that can travel in a straight line in one dimension (along the x axis) but is confined between two walls separated by a distance L. The potential energy of the particle is zero inside the box but rises abruptly to infinity at the walls (Fig. 12.24). The particle might be a bead free to slide along a horizontal wire between two stops. Although this problem is very elementary, there has been a resurgence of research interest in it now that nanometre-scale structures are used to trap electrons in cavities resembling square wells.

The boundary conditions for this system are the requirement that each acceptable wavefunction of the particle must fit inside the box exactly, like the vibrations of a violin string (as in Fig. 12.18).[6] It follows that the wavelength, λ, of the permitted wavefunctions must be one of the values

$$\lambda = 2L, L, \tfrac{2}{3}L, \ldots \quad \text{or} \quad \lambda = \frac{2L}{n},$$

with $n = 1, 2, 3, \ldots$

Each wavefunction is a sine wave with one of these wavelengths; therefore, because a sine wave of wavelength λ has the form $\sin(2\pi x/\lambda)$, the permitted wavefunctions are

$$\psi_n = N \sin \frac{n\pi x}{L} \qquad n = 1, 2, \ldots \qquad (12.10)$$

The constant N is called the **normalization constant.** It is chosen so that the total probability of finding the particle inside the box is 1, and has the value $N = (2/L)^{1/2}$.

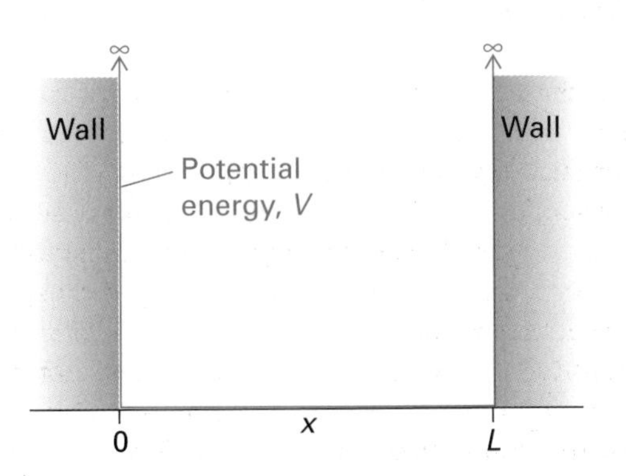

Fig. 12.24 A particle in a one-dimensional region with impenetrable walls at either end. Its potential energy is zero between $x = 0$ and $x = L$ and rises abruptly to infinity as soon as the particle touches either wall.

Derivation 12.2

The normalization constant

According to the Born interpretation, the probability of finding a particle in the infinitesimal region of length dx at the point x, given that its normalized wavefunction has the value ψ at that point, is equal to $\psi^2\,dx$. Therefore, the total probability of finding the particle between $x = 0$ and $x = L$ is the sum (integral) of all the probabilities of its being in each infinitesimal region. That total probability is 1 (the particle is certainly in the range somewhere), so we know that

$$\int_0^L \psi^2\,dx = 1$$

Substitution of the form of the wavefunction turns this expression into

$$N^2 \int_0^L \sin^2 \frac{n\pi x}{L}\,dx = 1$$

Our task is to solve this equation for N. Because

$$\int \sin^2 ax\,dx = \tfrac{1}{2}x - \frac{\sin 2ax}{4a} + \text{constant}$$

[6] More precisely, the boundary conditions stem from the requirement that the wavefunction is continuous everywhere: because the wavefunction is zero outside the box, it must therefore be zero at $x = 0$ and at $x = L$.

it follows that, because $\sin b\pi = 0$ ($b = 0, 1, 2, \ldots$), the sine term is zero at $x = 0$ and $x = L$,

$$\int_0^L \sin^2 \frac{n\pi x}{L}\, dx = \tfrac{1}{2}L$$

Therefore,

$$N^2 \times \tfrac{1}{2}L = 1$$

and hence $N = (2/L)^{1/2}$. Note that, in this case but not in general, the same normalization factor applies to all the wavefunctions regardless of the value of n.

It is a simple matter to find the permitted energy levels because the only contribution to the energy is the kinetic energy of the particle: the potential energy is zero everywhere inside the box, and the particle is never outside the box. First, we note that it follows from the de Broglie relation, eqn 12.7, that the only acceptable values of the linear momentum are

$$p = \frac{h}{\lambda} \overset{\lambda = 2L/n}{=} \frac{nh}{2L} \qquad n = 1, 2, \ldots$$

Then, because the kinetic energy of a particle of momentum p and mass m is $E = p^2/2m$, it follows that the permitted energies of the particle are

$$E_n = \frac{n^2h^2}{8mL^2} \qquad n = 1, 2, \ldots \qquad (12.11)$$

As we see in eqns 12.10 and 12.11, the energies and wavefunctions of a particle in a box are labelled with the number n. A **quantum number**, of which n is an example, is an integer (in certain cases, as we shall see in Chapter 13, a half-integer) that labels the state of the system. As well as acting as a label, a quantum number specifies certain physical properties of the system: in the present example, n specifies the energy of the particle through eqn 12.11.

The permitted energies of the particle are shown in Fig. 12.25 together with the shapes of the wavefunctions for $n = 1$ to 6. All the wavefunctions except the one of lowest energy ($n = 1$) possess points called **nodes** where the function passes through zero.[7] The number of nodes in the wavefunctions shown in the illustration increases from 0 (for $n = 1$) to 5 (for $n = 6$), and is $n - 1$ for a particle in a box in general. It is a general feature of quantum mechanics that the wavefunction corresponding to the state of lowest energy has no nodes, and as the number of nodes in the wavefunctions increases, the energy increases too.

The solutions of a particle in a box introduce another important general feature of quantum mechanics. Because the quantum number n cannot be zero (for this system), the lowest energy that the particle may possess is not zero, as would be allowed by classical mechanics, but $h^2/8mL^2$ (the energy when $n = 1$). This lowest, irremovable energy is called the **zero-point energy**. The existence of a zero-point energy is consistent with the uncertainty principle. If a particle is confined to a finite region, its location is not completely indefinite; consequently its momentum cannot be specified precisely as zero, and therefore its kinetic energy cannot be precisely zero either. The zero-point energy is not a special, mysterious kind of energy. It is simply the last remnant of energy that a particle cannot give up. For a particle in a box it can be interpreted as the energy arising from a ceaseless fluctuating motion of the particle between the two confining walls of the box.

The energy difference between adjacent levels is

$$\Delta E = E_{n+1} - E_n = (n+1)^2\frac{h^2}{8mL^2} - n^2\frac{h^2}{8mL^2}$$

$$= (2n+1)\frac{h^2}{8mL^2} \qquad (12.12)$$

This expression shows that the difference decreases as the length L of the box increases, and that it becomes zero when the walls are infinitely far apart (Fig. 12.26). Atoms and molecules free to move in laboratory-sized vessels may therefore be treated as though their translational energy is not quantized, because L is so large. The expression also shows that the separation decreases as the mass of the particle

[7] Passing *through* zero is an essential part of the definition; just becoming zero is not sufficient. The points at the edges of the box where $\psi = 0$ are not nodes, because the wavefunction does not pass through zero there.

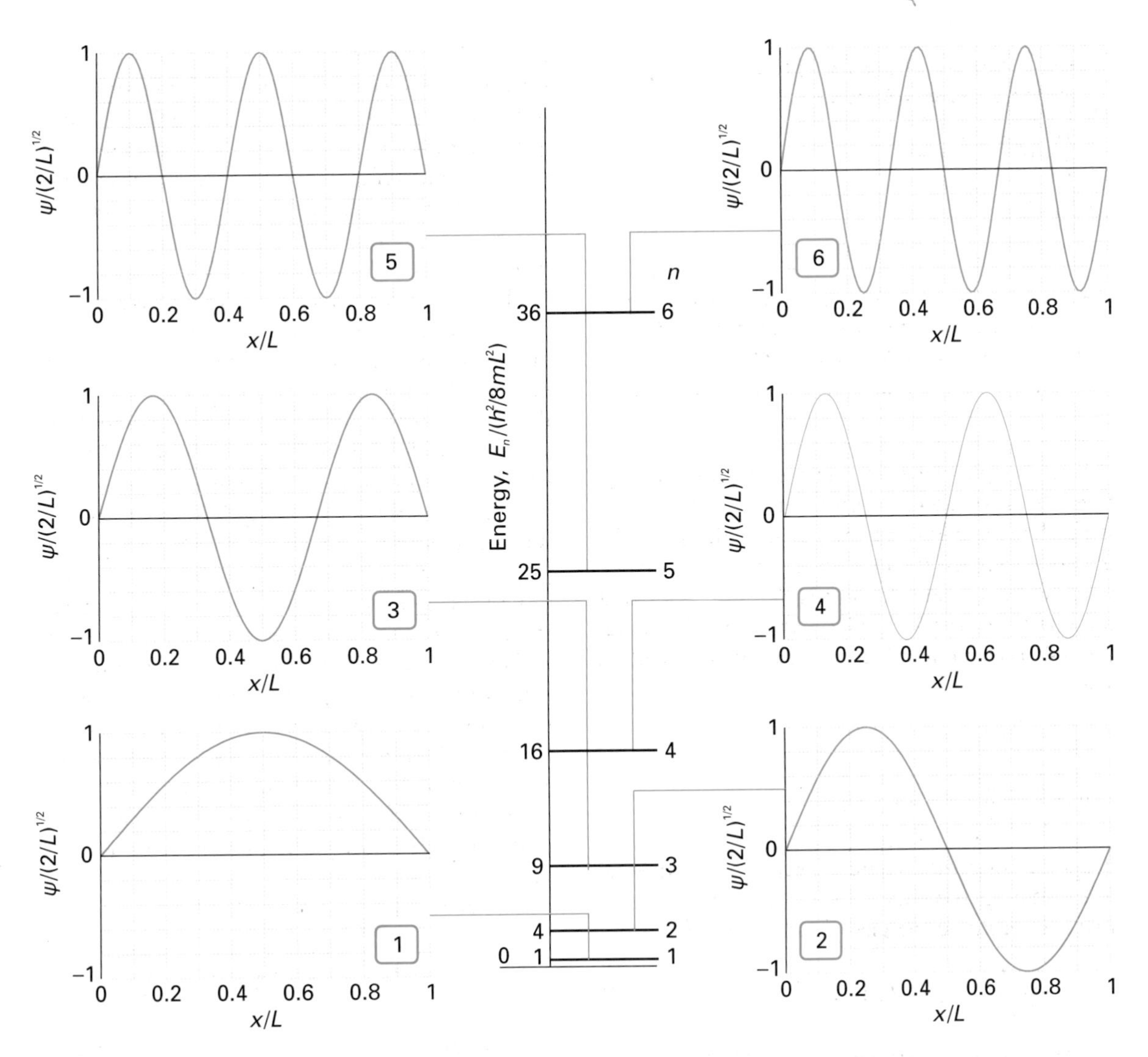

Fig. 12.25 The allowed energy levels and the corresponding (sine wave) wave functions for a particle in a box. Note that the energy levels increase as n^2, and so their spacing increases as n increases. Each wavefunction is a standing wave, and successive functions possess one more half wave and a correspondingly shorter wavelength.

increases. Particles of macroscopic mass (like balls and planets, and even minute specks of dust) behave as though their translational motion is unquantized. Both these conclusions are true in general:

1 The greater the size of the system, the less important are the effects of quantization.

2 The greater the mass of the particle, the less important are the effects of quantization.

Self-test 12.9

Consider an electron that is a part of a conjugated polyene (such as a carotene molecule) of length 2.0 nm. Treat the long molecule as a one-dimensional box and the electron as a particle confined to the box. What is the energy in electronvolts (1 eV = 1.602×10^{-19} J) to excite it from the level with $n = 5$ to the next higher level?

[*Answer:* 1.0 eV]

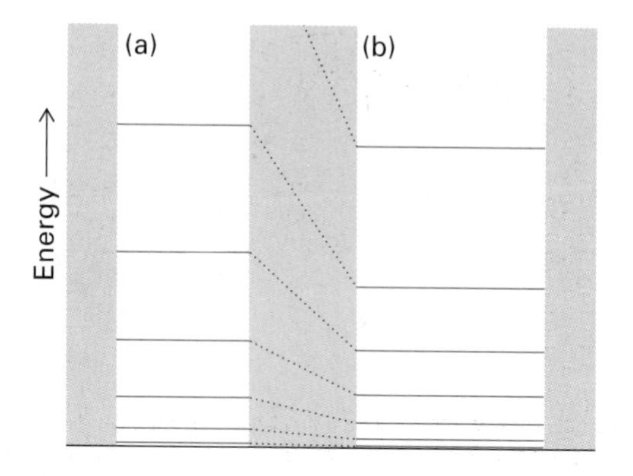

Fig. 12.26 (a) A narrow box has widely spaced energy levels; (b) a wide box has closely spaced energy levels. (In each case, the separations depend on the mass of the particle too.)

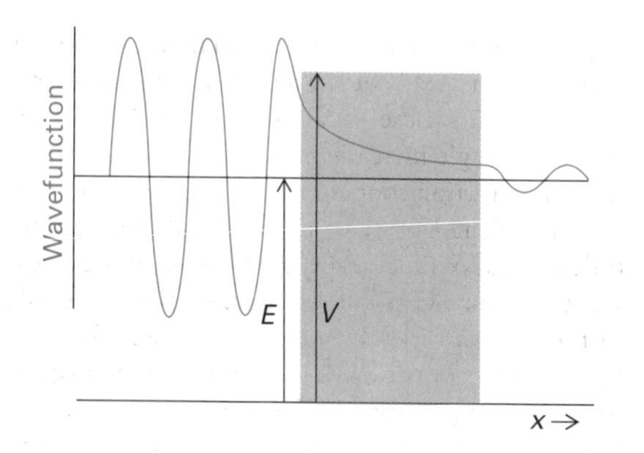

Fig. 12.27 A particle incident on a barrier from the left has an oscillating wavefunction, but inside the barrier there are no oscillations (for $E < V$). If the barrier is not too thick, the wavefunction is non-zero at its opposite face, and so oscillation begins again there.

(b) Tunnelling

If the potential energy of a particle does not rise to infinity when it is in the walls of the container, and $E < V$, the wavefunction does not decay abruptly to zero. If the walls are thin (so that the potential energy falls to zero again after a finite distance) and the particle is very light, the wavefunction oscillates inside the box (eqn 12.10), varies smoothly inside the region representing the wall, and oscillates again on the other side of the wall outside the box (Fig. 12.27). Hence the particle might be found on the outside of a container even though according to classical mechanics it has insufficient energy to escape. Such leakage by penetration through classically forbidden zones is called **tunnelling**. Tunnelling is a consequence of the wave character of matter. Just as radio waves pass through walls and X-rays penetrate soft tissue, so can 'matter waves' tunnel through walls.

The Schrödinger equation can be used to determine the probability of tunnelling of a particle incident on a finite barrier, but here we only summarize the result of the calculation.[8] It turns out that the tunnelling probability decreases sharply with the thickness of the wall and with the mass of the particle. Hence, tunnelling is very important for electrons, moderately important for protons, and less important for heavier particles. The very rapid equilibration of proton transfer reactions (Chapter 8) is also a manifestation of the ability of protons to tunnel through barriers and transfer quickly from an acid to a base. Tunnelling of protons between acidic and basic groups is also an important feature of the mechanism of some enzyme-catalysed reactions. Electron tunnelling is one of the factors that determine the rates of electron transfer reactions at electrodes and in biological systems. The important technique of 'scanning tunnelling microscopy' relies on the dependence of electron tunnelling on the thickness of the region between a point and a surface (Section 16.2).

12.10 Rotation: a particle on a ring

The discussion of translational motion focused on linear momentum, p. When we turn to rotational motion we have to focus instead on the analogous **angular momentum**, J. The magnitude of the angular momentum of a particle that is travelling on a circular path of radius r is defined as

$$J = pr \qquad (12.13)$$

where p is its linear momentum ($p = mv$) at any instant. A particle that is travelling at high speed in a circle has a higher angular momentum than a particle of the same mass travelling more slowly. An object with a high angular momentum (like a

[8] For details of the calculation, see P. Atkins and J. de Paula, Physical chemistry, 7th edn, Oxford University Press/W.H. Freeman (2002).

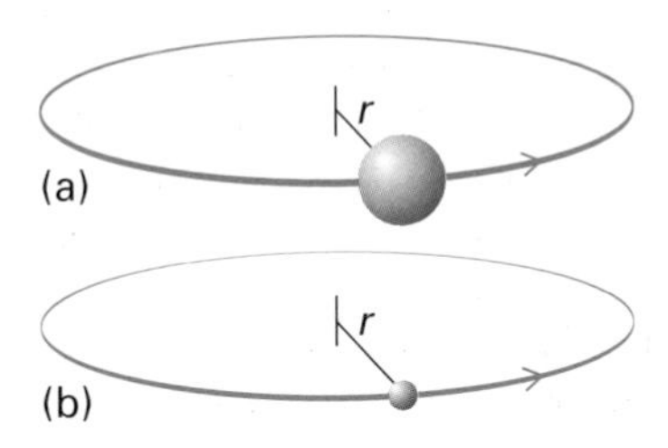

Fig. 12.28 A particle travelling on a circular path has a moment of inertia I that is given by mr^2. (a) This heavy particle has a large moment of inertia about the central point; (b) this light particle is travelling on a path of the same radius, but it has a smaller moment of inertia. The moment of inertia plays a role in circular motion that is the analogue of the mass for linear motion: a particle with a high moment of inertia is difficult to accelerate into a given state of rotation, and requires a strong braking force to stop its rotation.

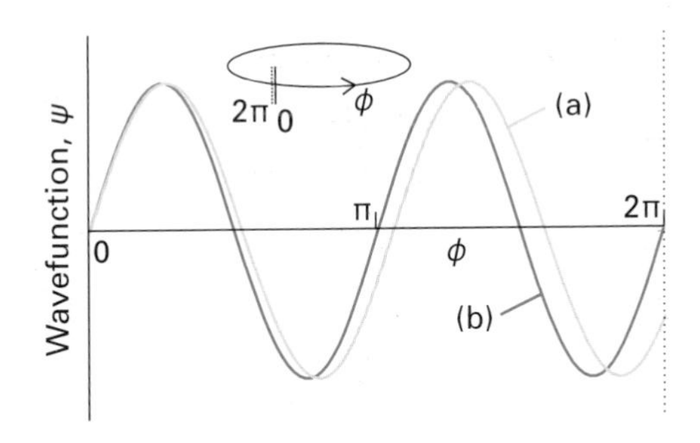

Fig. 12.29 Two solutions of the Schrödinger equation for a particle on a ring. The circumference has been opened out into a straight line; the points at $\phi = 0$ and 2π are identical. The solution in (a) is unacceptable because it has different values after each circuit, and so interferes destructively with itself. The solution in (b) is acceptable because it reproduces itself on successive circuits.

flywheel) requires a strong braking force (more precisely, a strong torque) to bring it to a standstill.

To see what quantum mechanics tells us about rotational motion, we consider a particle of mass m moving in a horizontal circular path of radius r. The energy of the particle is entirely kinetic because the potential energy is constant and can be set equal to zero everywhere. We can therefore write $E = p^2/2m$. By using eqn 12.13, we can express this energy in terms of the angular momentum as

$$E = \frac{J_z^2}{2mr^2}$$

where J_z is the angular momentum for rotation around the z-axis (the axis perpendicular to the plane). The quantity mr^2 is the **moment of inertia** of the particle about the z-axis, and denoted I: a heavy particle in a path of large radius has a large moment of inertia (Fig. 12.28). It follows that the energy of the particle is

$$E = \frac{J_z^2}{2I} \tag{12.14}$$

Now we use the de Broglie relation to see that the energy of rotation is quantized. To do so, we express the angular momentum in terms of the wavelength of the particle:

$$J_z = pr = \frac{hr}{\lambda}$$

Suppose for the moment that λ can take an arbitrary value. In that case, the amplitude of the wavefunction depends on the angle as shown in Fig. 12.29. When the angle increases beyond 2π (that is, 360°), the wavefunction continues to change. For an arbitrary wavelength it gives rise to a different amplitude at each point and the interference between the waves on successive circuits cancels the amplitude of the wave on its previous circuit. Thus, this particular arbitrary wave cannot survive in the system. An acceptable solution is obtained only if the wavefunction reproduces itself on successive circuits: we say that the wavefunction must satisfy **cyclic boundary conditions**. Specifically, acceptable wavefunctions match after each circuit, and therefore have wavelengths that are given by the expression

$$\lambda = \frac{2\pi r}{n} \qquad n = 0, 1, \ldots$$

where the value $n = 0$, which gives an infinite wavelength, corresponds to a uniform amplitude. It follows that the permitted energies are

$E = J_z^2/2I$, $J_z = hr/\lambda$; $\lambda = 2\pi r/n$; $h/2\pi = \hbar$

$$E_n = \frac{(hr/\lambda)^2}{2I} = \frac{(nh/2\pi)^2}{2I} = \frac{n^2\hbar^2}{2I}$$

with $n = 0, \pm1, \pm2, \ldots$.

We need to make two points about the expression for the energy before we use it. One is that a particle

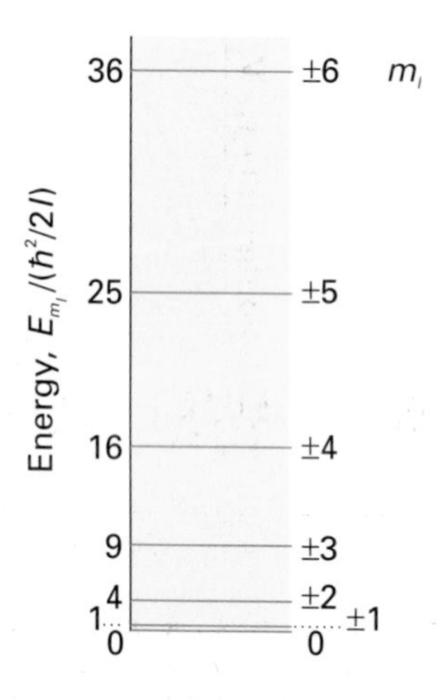

Fig. 12.30 The energy levels of a particle that can move on a circular path. Classical physics allowed the particle to travel with any energy (as represented by the continuous tinted band); quantum mechanics, however, allows only discrete energies. Each energy level, other than the one with $m_l = 0$, is doubly degenerate, because the particle may rotate either clockwise or counterclockwise with the same energy.

can travel either clockwise or counterclockwise around a ring. We represent these different directions by positive and negative values of n, with positive values representing clockwise rotation seen from below (like a right-handed screw), and negative values representing counterclockwise rotation. The energy depends on n^2, so the difference in sign—the direction of rotation—has no effect on the energy. Second, in the discussion of rotational motion it is conventional to denote the quantum number by m_l in place of n.[9] Therefore, the final expression for the energy levels is

$$E_{m_l} = \frac{m_l^2 \hbar^2}{2I} \qquad m_l = 0, \pm 1, \ldots \qquad (12.15)$$

These energy levels are drawn in Fig. 12.30.

As we have remarked, the occurrence of m_l^2 in the expression for the energy means that two states of motion, such as those with $m_l = +1$ and $m_l = -1$, both correspond to the same energy. Such a condition, in which more than one state has the same energy, is called **degeneracy**. All the states with $|m_l| > 0$ are doubly degenerate because two states correspond to the same energy for each value of $|m_l|$. The state with $m_l = 0$, the lowest energy state of the particle, is **non-degenerate**, meaning that only one state has a particular energy (in this case, zero).

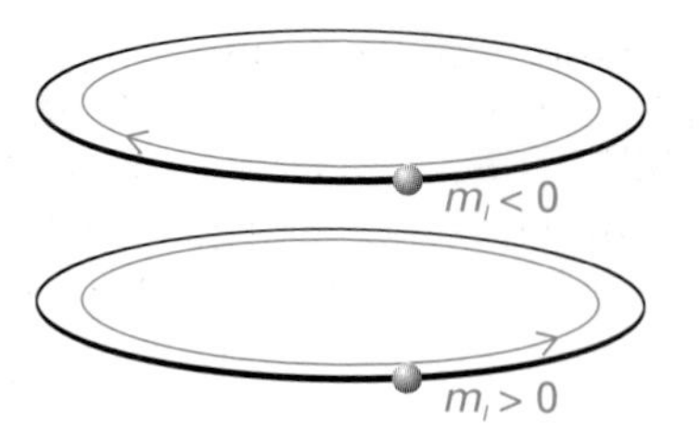

Fig. 12.31 The significance of the sign of m_l. When $m_l < 0$, the particle travels in a counterclockwise direction as viewed from below; then $m_l > 0$, the motion is clockwise.

An important additional conclusion is that *the angular momentum of the particle is quantized*. We can use the relation between angular momentum and linear momentum (angular momentum = pr), and between linear momentum and the allowed wavelengths of the particle ($\lambda = 2\pi r/m_l$), to conclude that the angular momentum of a particle around the z-axis is confined to the values

$$J_z = pr = \frac{hr}{\lambda} = \frac{hr}{2\pi r/m_l} = m_l \times \frac{h}{2\pi}$$

That is, the angular momentum of the particle around the axis is confined to the values

$$J_z = m_l \hbar \qquad (12.16)$$

with $m_l = 0, \pm 1, \pm 2, \ldots$. Positive values of m_l correspond to clockwise rotation (as seen from below) and negative values correspond to counterclockwise rotation (Fig. 12.31). The quantized motion can be thought of in terms of the rotation of a bicycle wheel that can rotate only with a discrete series of angular momenta, so that as the wheel is accelerated, the angular momentum jerks from the values 0 (when the wheel is stationary) to $\hbar$, $2\hbar$, ... but can have no intermediate value.

A final point concerning the rotational motion of a particle is that it does not have a zero-point energy: m_l may take the value 0, so E may be zero. This conclusion is also consistent with the uncertainty principle. Although the particle is certainly between the angles 0 and 360° on the ring, that

[9] This convention is elaborated in Chapter 13.

range is equivalent to not knowing anything about where it is on the ring. Consequently, the angular momentum may be specified exactly, and a value of zero is possible. When the angular momentum is zero precisely, the energy of the particle is also zero precisely.

Self-test 12.10

Consider an electron that is part of a cyclic, aromatic molecule (such as benzene). Treat the molecule as a ring of diameter 280 pm and the electron as a particle that moves only along the perimeter of the ring. What is the energy in electronvolts (1 eV = 1.602×10^{-19} J) required to excite the electron from the level with $m_l = \pm 1$ to the next higher level?

[*Answer:* 5.83 eV]

12.11 Vibration: the harmonic oscillator

In the type of vibrational motion known as **harmonic oscillation**, a particle vibrates backwards and forwards, restrained by a spring that obeys **Hooke's law** of force. Hooke's law states that the restoring force is proportional to the displacement, x:

$$\text{Restoring force} = -kx \qquad (12.17a)$$

The constant of proportionality k is called the **force constant**: a stiff spring has a high force constant and a weak spring has a low force constant. The potential energy of a particle subjected to this force increases as the square of the displacement, and specifically

$$V(x) = \tfrac{1}{2}kx^2 \qquad (12.17b)$$

The variation of V with x is shown in Fig. 12.32: it has the shape of a parabola (a curve of the form $y = ax^2$), and we say that a particle undergoing harmonic motion has a 'parabolic potential energy'.

Derivation 12.3

Potential energy and force

In classical mechanics (and in quantum mechanics) the force is the negative slope of the potential energy:

$$F = -\frac{dV}{dx}$$

Because the infinitesimal quantities may be treated as any other quantity in algebraic manipulations, we rearrange the expression into

$$dV = -F\,dx$$

and then integrate both sides from $x = 0$, where the potential energy is $V(0)$, to x, where the potential energy is $V(x)$:

$$V(x) - V(0) = -\int_0^x F\,dx$$

Now substitute $F = -kx$:

$$V(x) - V(0) = -\int_0^x (-kx)\,dx = k\int_0^x x\,dx = \tfrac{1}{2}kx^2$$

We are free to choose $V(0) = 0$, which then gives eqn 12.17b.

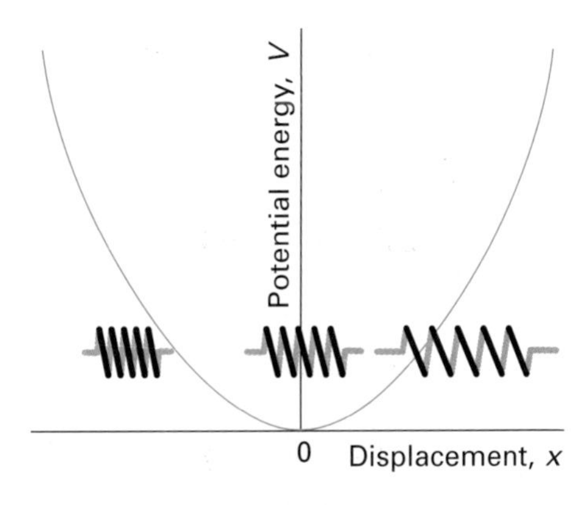

Fig. 12.32 The parabolic potential energy characteristic of an harmonic oscillator. Positive displacements correspond to extension of the spring; negative displacements correspond to compression of the spring.

Unlike the earlier cases we considered, the potential energy varies with position, so we have to use $V(x)$ in the Schrödinger equation. Then we have to select the solutions that satisfy the boundary equations, which in this case means that they must fit into the parabola representing the potential energy.[10] The solutions of the equation are quite hard to find, but once found they turn out to be very simple. For instance, the energies of the solutions that satisfy the boundary conditions are

[10] More precisely, the wavefunctions must all go to zero for large displacements from $x = 0$: they do not have to go abruptly to zero at the edges of the parabola.

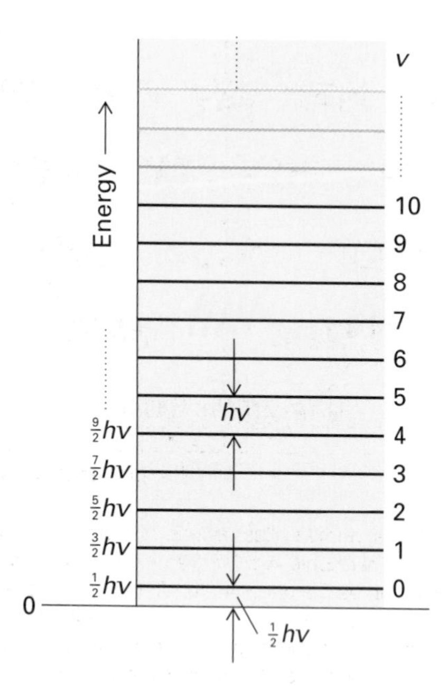

Fig. 12.33 The array of energy levels of a harmonic oscillator (the levels continue upwards to infinity). The separation depends on the mass and the force constant. Note the zero-point energy.

$$E_v = (v + \tfrac{1}{2})h\nu \qquad v = 0, 1, 2, \ldots$$

$$\nu = \frac{1}{2\pi}\left(\frac{k}{m}\right)^{1/2} \qquad (12.18)$$

where m is the mass of the particle and v is the **vibrational quantum number.**[11] These energies form a uniform ladder of values separated by $h\nu$ (Fig. 12.33). The quantity ν is a frequency (in cycles per second, or hertz, Hz), and is in fact the frequency that a classical oscillator of mass m and force constant k would be calculated to have. In quantum mechanics, though, ν tells us (through $h\nu$) the separation of any pair of adjacent energy levels. The separation is large for stiff springs and high masses.

Illustration 12.2

Molecular vibrations

The force constant for an H–Cl bond is 516 N m^{-1}, where the newton (N) is the SI unit of force (1 N = 1 kg m s^{-2}). If we suppose that, because the chlorine atom is relatively very heavy, only the hydrogen atom moves, we take m as the mass of the H atom (1.67 × 10^{-27} kg for ^{1}H). We find

$$\nu = \frac{1}{2\pi}\left(\frac{k}{m}\right)^{1/2} = \frac{1}{2\pi}\left(\frac{516\ \text{N m}^{-1}}{1.67\times10^{-27}\ \text{kg}}\right)^{1/2}$$
$$= 8.85\times10^{13}\ \text{Hz}$$

The separation between adjacent levels is h times this frequency, or 5.86 × 10^{-20} J.

Figure 12.34 shows the shapes of the first few wavefunctions of a harmonic oscillator. The ground-state wavefunction (corresponding to $v = 0$ and

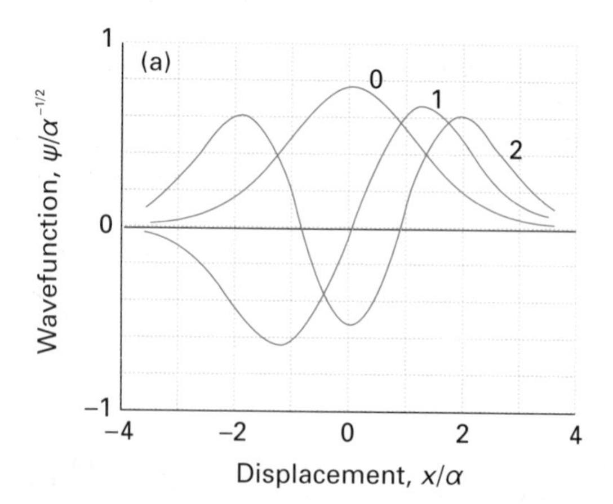

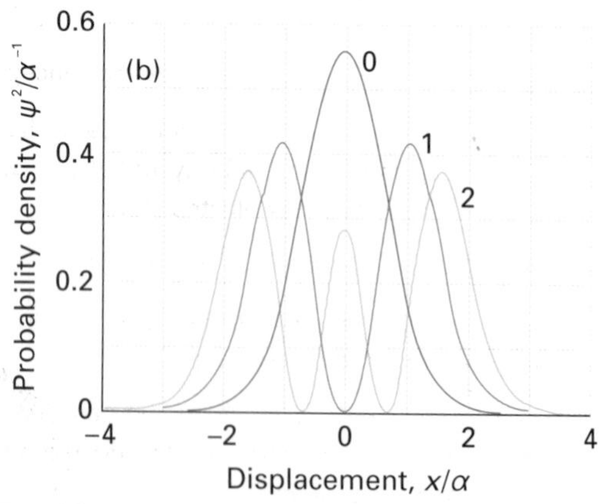

Fig. 12.34 (a) The wavefunctions and (b) the probability densities of the first three states of a harmonic oscillator. Note how the probability of finding the oscillator at large displacements increases as the state of excitation increases. The wavefunctions and displacements are expressed in terms of the parameter $\alpha = (\hbar^2/mk)^{1/4}$.

[11] Be very careful to distinguish the quantum number v (italic vee) from the frequency ν (Greek nu).

having the zero-point energy $\frac{1}{2}h\nu$) is a bell-shaped curve, a curve of the form e^{-x^2} (a Gaussian function; see Section 1.6), with no nodes. This shape shows that the particle is most likely to be found at $x = 0$ (zero displacement), but may be found at greater displacements with decreasing probability. The first excited wavefunction has a node at $x = 0$ and peaks on either side. Therefore, in this state, the particle will be found most probably with the 'spring' stretched or compressed to the same amount. However, the wavefunctions extend beyond the limits of motion of a classical oscillator (Fig. 12.35), another example of quantum mechanical tunnelling.

The relevance of the harmonic oscillator itself to chemistry is that atoms vibrate relative to one another in molecules, with the bond acting like a spring. Therefore, eqn 12.18 describes the allowed vibrational energy levels of molecules. The equation is enormously important for the interpretation of vibrational (infrared) spectroscopy, as we see in Chapter 17.

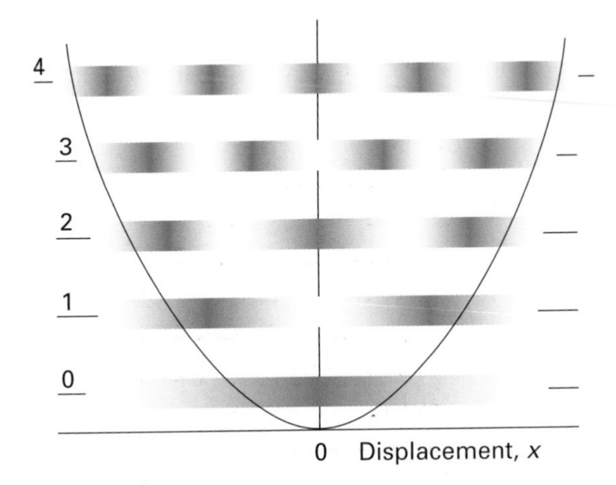

Fig. 12.35 A schematic illustration of the probability density for finding a harmonic oscillator at a given displacement. Classically, the oscillator cannot be found at displacements at which its total energy is less than its potential energy (because the kinetic energy cannot be negative). A quantum oscillator, however, may tunnel into regions that are classically forbidden.

CHECKLIST OF KEY IDEAS

You should now be familiar with the following concepts:

☐ 1 Early evidence for quantum theory came from the investigation of black-body radiation, heat capacities, and the photoelectric effect.

☐ 2 Wien's law states that $T\lambda_{max}$ = constant.

☐ 3 The Stefan–Boltzmann law states that the emissivity of a black body is proportional to T^4.

☐ 4 Planck proposed that electromagnetic oscillators of frequency ν could acquire or discard energy in quanta of magnitude $h\nu$.

☐ 5 Einstein proposed that atoms oscillating in a solid with frequency ν could acquire or discard energy in quanta of magnitude $h\nu$.

☐ 6 The photoelectric effect is the ejection of electrons when radiation of greater than a threshold frequency is incident on a metal; the kinetic energy of the ejected electrons and frequency of the incident radiation are related by $E_K = h\nu - \Phi$, where Φ is the work function of the metal.

☐ 7 The wave-like character of electrons was demonstrated by the Davisson–Germer diffraction experiment.

☐ 8 The joint wave–particle character of matter and radiation is called wave–particle duality.

☐ 9 The de Broglie relation for the wavelength, λ, of a particle of linear momentum p is $\lambda = h/p$.

☐ 10 A wavefunction, ψ, contains all the dynamical information about a system and is found by solving the appropriate Schrödinger equation, $-(\hbar^2/2m)d^2\psi/dx^2 + V\psi = E\psi$, subject to the constraints on the solutions known as boundary conditions.

☐ 11 According to the Born interpretation, the probability of finding a particle in a small region of space of volume δV is proportional to $\psi^2 \delta V$, where ψ is the value of the wavefunction in the region.

☐ 12 According to the Heisenberg uncertainty principle, it is impossible to specify simultaneously, with arbitrary precision, both the momentum and the position of a particle: $\Delta p\,\Delta x \geq \frac{1}{2}\hbar$.

- ☐ 13 The energy levels of a particle of mass m in a box of length L are $E_n = n^2h^2/8mL^2$, with $n = 1, 2, \ldots$, and the wavefunctions are $\psi_n(x) = (2/L)^{1/2}\sin(n\pi x/L)$.
- ☐ 14 The zero-point energy is the lowest permissible energy of a system; for a particle in a box, the zero-point energy is $E_1 = h^2/8mL^2$.
- ☐ 15 Because wavefunctions do not, in general, decay abruptly to zero, particles may tunnel into classically forbidden regions.
- ☐ 16 The energy levels of a particle of mass m on a circular ring of radius r are $E_{m_l} = m_l^2\hbar^2/2I$, where I is the moment of inertia, $I = mr^2$ and $m_l = 0, \pm1, \pm2, \ldots$.
- ☐ 17 The angular momentum of a particle on a ring is quantized and confined to the values $J_z = m_l\hbar$, $m_l = 0, \pm1, \pm2, \ldots$.
- ☐ 18 A particle undergoes harmonic motion if it is subjected to a Hooke's-law restoring force (a force proportional to the displacement) and has a parabolic potential energy, $V(x) = \frac{1}{2}kx^2$.
- ☐ 19 The energy levels of a harmonic oscillator are $E_\upsilon = (\upsilon + \frac{1}{2})h\nu$, where $\nu = (1/2\pi)(k/m)^{1/2}$ and $\upsilon = 0, 1, 2, \ldots$.

FURTHER INFORMATION 12.1

A justification of the Schrödinger equation

We can justify the form of the Schrödinger equation to a certain extent by showing that it implies the de Broglie relation for a freely moving particle. By free motion we mean motion in a region where the potential energy is zero ($V = 0$ everywhere). Then, eqn 12.8 simplifies to:

$$-\frac{\hbar^2}{2m}\frac{d^2\psi}{dx^2} = E\psi$$

and a solution is

$$\psi = \sin kx \qquad k = \frac{(2mE)^{1/2}}{\hbar}$$

as may be verified by substitution of the solution into both sides of the equation and using

$$\frac{d}{dx}\sin kx = k\cos kx \qquad \frac{d}{dx}\cos kx = -k\sin kx$$

The function $\sin kx$ is a wave of wavelength $\lambda = 2\pi/k$, as we can see by comparing $\sin kx$ with $\sin(2\pi x/\lambda)$, the standard form of a harmonic wave with wavelength λ (Fig. 12.36). Next, we note that the energy of the particle is entirely kinetic (because $V = 0$ everywhere), so the total energy of the particle is just its kinetic energy:

$$E = E_K = \frac{p^2}{2m}$$

Because E is related to k by

$$E = \frac{k^2\hbar^2}{2m}$$

it follows from a comparison of the two equations that $p = k\hbar$. Therefore, the linear momentum is related to the wavelength of the wavefunction by

$$p = \frac{2\pi}{\lambda} \times \frac{h}{2\pi} = \frac{h}{\lambda}$$

which is the de Broglie relation. We see, in the case of a freely moving particle, that the Schrödinger equation has led to an experimentally verified conclusion.

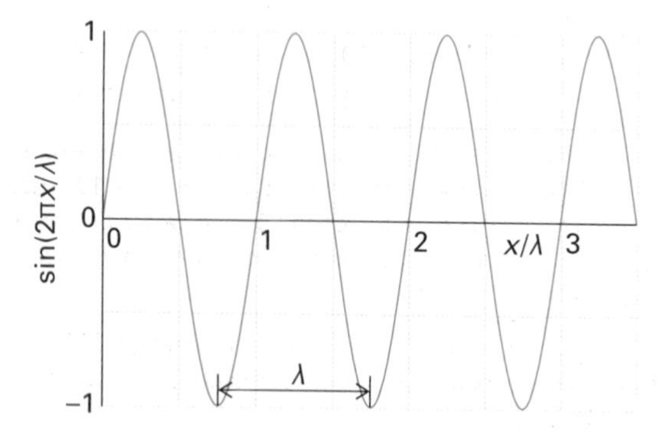

Fig. 12.36 The wavelength of a harmonic wave of the form $\sin(2\pi x/\lambda)$. The amplitude of the wave is the maximum height above the centre line.

DISCUSSION QUESTIONS

12.1 Summarize the evidence that led to the introduction of quantum theory.

12.2 Discuss the physical origin of quantization energy for a particle confined to moving inside a one-dimensional box or on a ring.

12.3 Define, justify, and provide examples of zero-point energy.

12.4 Discuss the physical origins of quantum mechanical tunnelling. Why is tunnelling more likely to contribute to the mechanisms of electron transfer and proton transfer processes than to mechanisms of group transfer reactions, such as A–B + C → A + B–C (where A, B, and C are large molecular groups)?

EXERCISES

The symbol ‡ indicates that calculus is required.

12.5 In early 1999 it was thought that the first planet outside the solar system had been photographed; by midsummer of that year, the 'planet' had been reclassified as a cool star with surface temperature 2500°C. What is the wavelength of its maximum emission?

12.6 A photodetector produces 0.68 μW when exposed to radiation of wavelength 245 nm. How many photons does it detect per second?

12.7 A glow-worm emits red light of wavelength 650 nm. If that were radiation from a hot source, what would be the temperature of the source? What is your conclusion?

12.8 Incandescent lamps are a common feature of everyday life. Calculate the total power radiated by a 5.0 cm × 2.0 cm section of the surface of a hot body at 3000 K.

12.9 The wavelength of the emission maximum from a small pinhole in an electrically heated container was determined at a series of temperatures, and the results are given below. Deduce a value for Planck's constant.

θ/°C	1000	1500	2000	2500	3000	3500
λ_{max}/nm	2181	1600	1240	1035	878	763

12.10 Calculate the size of the quantum involved in the excitation of (a) an electronic motion of frequency 1.0×10^{15} Hz, (b) a molecular vibration of period 20 fs, (c) a pendulum of period 0.50 s. Express the results in joules and in kilojoules per mole.

12.11 A certain lamp emits blue light of wavelength 350 nm. How many photons does it emit each second if its power is (a) 1.00 W, (b) 100 W?

12.12 An FM radio transmitter broadcasts at 98.4 MHz with a power of 45 kW. How many photons does it generate per second?

12.13 The workfunction for metallic caesium is 2.14 eV. Calculate the kinetic energy and the speed of the electrons ejected by light of wavelength (a) 750 nm, (b) 250 nm.

12.14 A diffraction experiment requires the use of electrons of wavelength 550 pm. Calculate the velocity of the electrons.

12.15 Calculate the de Broglie wavelength of (a) a mass of 1.0 g travelling at 1.0 m s^{-1}, (b) the same, travelling at 1.00×10^5 km s^{-1}, (c) a He atom travelling at 1000 m s^{-1} (a typical speed at room temperature).

12.16 Calculate the de Broglie wavelength of an electron accelerated from rest through a potential difference, V, of (a) 1.00 V, (b) 1.00 kV, (c) 100 kV. (*Hint.* The electron is accelerated to a kinetic energy equal to eV.)

12.17 Calculate the de Broglie wavelength of yourself travelling at 8 km h^{-1}. What does your wavelength become when you stop?

12.18 Calculate the linear momentum of photons of wavelength (a) 725 nm, (b) 75 pm, (c) 20 m.

12.19 Calculate the energy per photon and the energy per mole of photons for radiation of wavelength (a) 600 nm (red), (b) 550 nm (yellow), (c) 400 nm (violet), (d) 200 nm (ultraviolet), (e) 150 pm (X-ray), (f) 1.0 cm (microwave).

12.20 How fast would a particle of mass 1.0 g need to travel to have the same linear momentum as a photon of radiation of wavelength 300 nm?

12.21 Suppose that you designed a spacecraft to work by photon pressure. The sail was a completely absorbing fabric of area 1.0 km^2 and you directed a 1.0 kW red laser beam of wavelength 650 nm on to it from a base on the Moon. What is (a) the force, (b) the pressure exerted by the radiation on the sail? (c) Suppose the mass of the spacecraft was 1.0 kg. Given that, after a period of acceleration from standstill, speed = (force/mass) × time, how long would it take for the craft to accelerate to a speed of 1.0 m s^{-1}?

12.22 The energy required for the ionization of a certain atom is 3.44 aJ (1 aJ = 10^{-18} J; a denotes 'atto'). The absorption of a photon of unknown wavelength ionizes the atom and ejects an electron with velocity 1.03×10^6 m s^{-1}. Calculate the wavelength of the incident radiation.

12.23 In an X-ray photoelectron experiment, a photon of wavelength 150 pm ejects an electron from the inner shell of an atom and it emerges with a speed of 2.24×10^7 m s^{-1}. Calculate the binding energy of the electron.

12.24 Calculate the probability that an electron will be found (a) between $x = 0.1$ and 0.2 nm, (b) between 4.9 and 5.2 nm in a box of length $L = 10$ nm when its wavefunction is $\psi = (2/L)^{1/2}\sin(2\pi x/L)$. (*Hint*. Treat the wavefunction as a constant in the small region of interest and interpret δV as δx.)

12.25 ‡Repeat Exercise 12.24, but allow for the variation of the wavefunction in the region of interest. What are the percentage errors in the procedure used in Exercise 12.24? (*Hint*. You will need to integrate $\psi^2 dx$ between the limits of interest. The indefinite integral you require is given in Derivation 12.2.)

12.26 ‡What is the probability of finding a particle of mass m in (a) the left-hand one-third, (b) the central one-third, (c) the right-hand one-third of a box of length L when it is in the state with $n = 1$?

12.27 The speed of a certain proton is 350 km s^{-1}. If the uncertainty in its momentum is 0.0100 per cent, what uncertainty in its location must be tolerated?

12.28 Calculate the minimum uncertainty in the speed of a ball of mass 500 g that is known to be within 5.0 μm of a certain point on a bat.

12.29 What is the minimum uncertainty in the position of a bullet of mass 5.0 g that is known to have a speed somewhere between 350.000 001 m s^{-1} and 350.000 000 m s^{-1}?

12.30 An electron is confined to a linear region with a length of the same order as the diameter of an atom (ca. 100 pm). Calculate the minimum uncertainties in its position and speed.

12.31 A hydrogen atom, treated as a point mass, is confined to an infinite one-dimensional square well of width 1.0 nm. How much energy does it have to give up to fall from the level with $n = 2$ to the lowest energy level?

12.32 The pores in zeolite catalysts are so small that quantum mechanical effects on the distribution of atoms and molecules within them can be significant. Calculate the location in a box of length L at which the probability of a particle being found is 50 per cent of its maximum probability when $n = 1$.

12.33 The blue solution formed when an alkali metal dissolves in liquid ammonia consists of the metal cations and electrons trapped in a cavity formed by ammonia molecules. (a) Calculate the spacing between the levels with $n = 4$ and $n = 5$ of an electron in a one-dimensional box of length 5.0 nm. (b) What is the wavelength of the radiation emitted when the electron makes a transition between the two levels?

12.34 A certain wavefunction is zero everywhere except between $x = 0$ and $x = L$, where it has the constant value A. Normalize the wavefunction.

12.35 As indicated in Self-test 12.9, the particle in a box is a crude model of the distribution and energy of electrons in conjugated polyenes, such as carotene and related molecules. Carotene is a molecule in which 22 single and double bonds alternate (11 of each) along a chain of carbon atoms. Take each CC bond length to be about 140 pm and suppose that the first possible upward transition (for reasons related to the Pauli principle, Section 13.9) is from $n = 11$ to $n = 12$. Estimate the wavelength of this transition.

12.36 Treat a rotating HI molecule as a stationary I atom around which an H atom circulates in a plane at a distance of 161 pm. Calculate (a) the moment of inertia of the molecule, (b) the greatest wavelength of the radiation that can excite the molecule into rotation.

12.37 A bee of mass 1 g lands on the end of a horizontal twig, which starts to oscillate up and down with a period of 1 s. Treat the twig as a massless spring, and estimate its force constant.

12.38 Treat a vibrating HI molecule as a stationary I atom with the H atom oscillating towards and away from the I atom. Given the force constant of the HI bond is 314 N m^{-1}, calculate (a) the vibrational frequency of the molecule, (b) the wavelength required to excite the molecule into vibration.

12.39 By what factor will the vibrational frequency of HI change when H is replaced by deuterium?

12.40 ‡The ground state wavefunction of a harmonic oscillator is proportional to $e^{-ax^2/2}$, where a depends on the mass and force constant. (a) Normalize this wavefunction. (b) At what displacement is the oscillator most likely to be found in its ground state? (*Hint*. For part (a), you will need the integral $\int_{-\infty}^{\infty} e^{-ax^2} dx = (\pi/a)^{1/2}$. For part (b), recall that the maximum (or minimum) of a function $f(x)$ occurs at the value of x for which $df/dx = 0$.)

Chapter 13

Atomic structure

Chapter 12 provided enough background for us to be able to move on to the discussion of the atomic structure. Atomic structure—the description of the arrangement of electrons in atoms—is an essential part of chemistry because it is the basis for understanding molecular and solid structures and all the physical and chemical properties of elements and their compounds.

A **hydrogenic atom** is a one-electron atom or ion of general atomic number *Z*. Hydrogenic atoms include H, He^{+}, Li^{2+}, C^{5+}, and even U^{91+}. Such very highly ionized atoms may be found in the outer regions of stars. A **many-electron atom** is an atom or ion that has more than one electron. Many-electron atoms include all neutral atoms other than H. For instance, helium, with its two electrons, is a many-electron atom in this sense. Hydrogenic atoms, and H in particular, are important because the Schrödinger equation can be solved for them and their structures can be discussed exactly. They provide a set of concepts that are used to describe the structures of many-electron atoms and (as we shall see in the next chapter) the structures of molecules too.

Hydrogenic atoms

Energetically excited atoms are produced when an electric discharge is passed through a gas or vapour or when an element is exposed to a hot flame. These atoms emit electromagnetic radiation of discrete frequencies as they discard energy and return to the **ground state**, their state of lowest energy (Fig. 13.1).

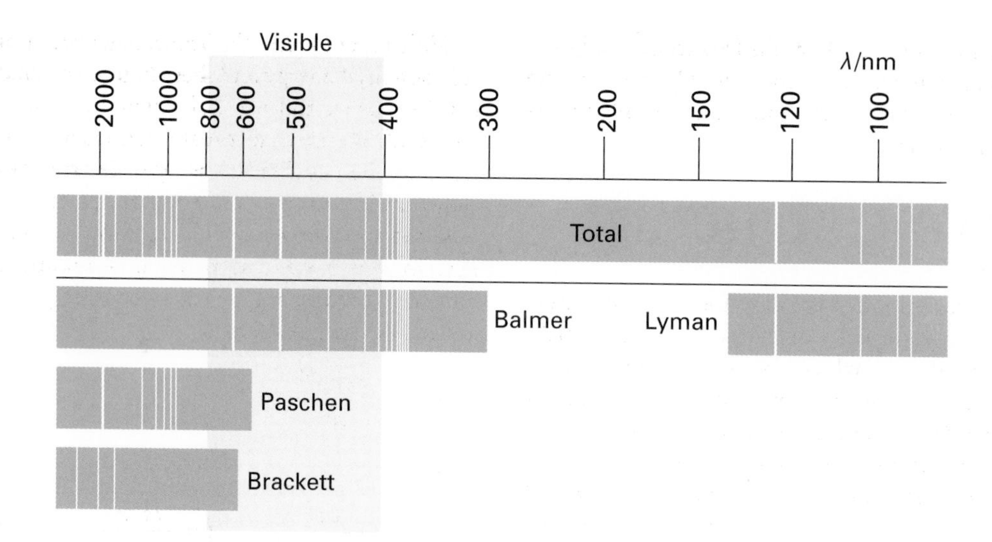

Fig. 13.1 The spectrum of atomic hydrogen. The spectrum is shown at the top, and is analysed into overlapping series below. The Balmer series lies largely in the visible region.

The record of frequencies, ν, wavenumbers ($\tilde{\nu} = \nu/c$), or wavelengths ($\lambda = c/\nu$), of the radiation emitted is called the **emission spectrum** of the atom. In its earliest form, the radiation was detected photographically as a series of lines (the focused image of the slit that the light was sampled through), and the components of radiation present in a spectrum are still widely referred to as spectroscopic 'lines'.

The essential properties of electromagnetic radiation are summarized in Section 12.1 and in Appendix 3.

13.1 The spectra of hydrogenic atoms

The first important contribution to understanding the spectrum of atomic hydrogen, which is observed when an electric discharge is passed through hydrogen gas, was made by the Swiss schoolteacher Johann Balmer. In 1885 he pointed out that (in modern terms) the wavenumbers of the light in the visible region of the electromagnetic spectrum fit the expression

$$\tilde{\nu} \propto \frac{1}{2^2} - \frac{1}{n^2}$$

with $n = 3, 4, \ldots$. The lines described by this expression are now called the **Balmer series** of the spectrum. Later, another set of lines was discovered in the ultraviolet region of the spectrum, and is called the **Lyman series**. Yet another set was discovered in the infrared region when detectors became available for that region, and is called the **Paschen series**. With this additional information available, the Swedish spectroscopist Johannes Rydberg noted (in 1890) that all the lines are described by the expression

$$\tilde{\nu} = R_H\left(\frac{1}{n_1^2} - \frac{1}{n_2^2}\right) \qquad (13.1)$$

with $n_1 = 1, 2, \ldots, n_2 = n_1 + 1, n_1 + 2, \ldots$, and $R_H =$ 109 677 cm^{-1}. The constant R_H is now called the **Rydberg constant** for hydrogen. The first five series of lines then correspond to n_1 taking the values 1 (Lyman), 2 (Balmer), 3 (Paschen), 4 (Brackett), and 5 (Pfund).

The existence of discrete spectroscopic lines strongly suggests that the energy of the electron in the hydrogen atom is quantized. The total energy is conserved when a **transition**, a change of state, occurs from one energy level to another. Therefore, when an atom changes its energy by ΔE, this difference must be carried away as a photon of frequency ν (as was illustrated in Fig. 12.16), where

$$\Delta E = h\nu \qquad (13.2)$$

This relation is called the **Bohr frequency condition.** It follows that we can expect to observe discrete lines if an electron in an atom can exist only in certain energy states.

13.2 The permitted energies of hydrogenic atoms

The quantum mechanical description of the structure of a hydrogenic atom is based on Rutherford's **nuclear model,** in which the atom is pictured as consisting of an electron outside a central nucleus of charge Ze. To derive the details of the structure of this type of atom, we have to set up and solve the Schrödinger equation in which the potential energy, V, is the Coulomb potential energy for the interaction between the nucleus of charge $+Ze$ and the electron of charge $-e$. In general, the **Coulombic potential energy** of a charge q_1 at a distance r from another charge q_2 is:

$$V = \frac{q_1 q_2}{4\pi\varepsilon_0 r} \tag{13.3a}$$

(V is used more commonly than E_p in this context.) The fundamental constant ε_0 is called the **vacuum permittivity.** It is a constant that ensures, in effect, that when the charges are expressed in coulombs (C) and their separation in metres (m), the energy is expressed in joules:

$$\varepsilon_0 = 8.854 \times 10^{-12}\ \mathrm{J^{-1}\ C^2\ m^{-1}}$$

Note that according to this expression, the potential energy of a charge is zero when it is at an infinite distance from the other charge. On setting $q_1 = +Ze$ and $q_2 = -e$

$$V = -\frac{Ze^2}{4\pi\varepsilon_0 r} \tag{13.3b}$$

The negative sign indicates that the potential energy falls (becomes more negative) as the distance between the nucleus and the electron decreases. We also need to identify the appropriate boundary conditions that the wavefunctions must satisfy in order to be acceptable. For the hydrogen atom, these conditions are that the wavefunction must not become infinite anywhere and that it must repeat itself (just like the particle on a ring) as we circle the nucleus either over the poles or round the equator.

With a lot of work, the Schrödinger equation with this potential energy and these boundary conditions can be solved, and we shall summarize the results. As usual, the need to satisfy boundary conditions leads to the conclusion that the electron can have only certain energies, which is qualitatively in accord with the spectroscopic evidence. Schrödinger found that, for a hydrogenic atom of atomic number Z with a nucleus of mass m_N, the allowed energy levels are given by the expression

$$E_n = -\frac{hcRZ^2}{n^2} \tag{13.4a}$$

where

$$hcR = \frac{\mu e^4}{32\pi^2\varepsilon_0^2\hbar^2} \qquad \mu = \frac{m_\mathrm{e} m_\mathrm{N}}{m_\mathrm{e} + m_\mathrm{N}} \tag{13.4b}$$

and $n = 1, 2, \ldots$. The quantity μ is the **reduced mass.** For all except the most precise considerations, the mass of the nucleus is so much bigger than the mass of the electron that the latter may be neglected in the denominator of μ, and then $\mu \approx m_\mathrm{e}$. The constant R (not the gas constant!) is numerically identical to the experimental Rydberg constant R_H when m_N is set equal to the mass of the proton. Schrödinger must have been thrilled to find that when he calculated R_H, the value he obtained was in almost exact agreement with the experimental value.[1]

Here we shall focus on eqn 13.4a, and unpack its significance. We shall examine (1) the role of n, (2) the significance of the negative sign, and (3) the appearance in the equation of Z^2.

The quantum number n is called the **principal quantum number.** We use it to calculate the energy of the electron in the atom by substituting its value into eqn 13.4a. The resulting energy levels are depicted in Fig. 13.2. Note how they are widely separated at low values of n, but then converge as n increases. At low values of n the electron is confined close to the nucleus by the pull between opposite charges and the energy levels are widely spaced like those of a particle in a narrow box. At high values of

[1] Niels Bohr had already derived the same expression for R_H, but his model of the atom—with an electron orbiting the nucleus—is now known to be erroneous. It had, however, an enormous impact on the development of quantum mechanics in the early twentieth century.

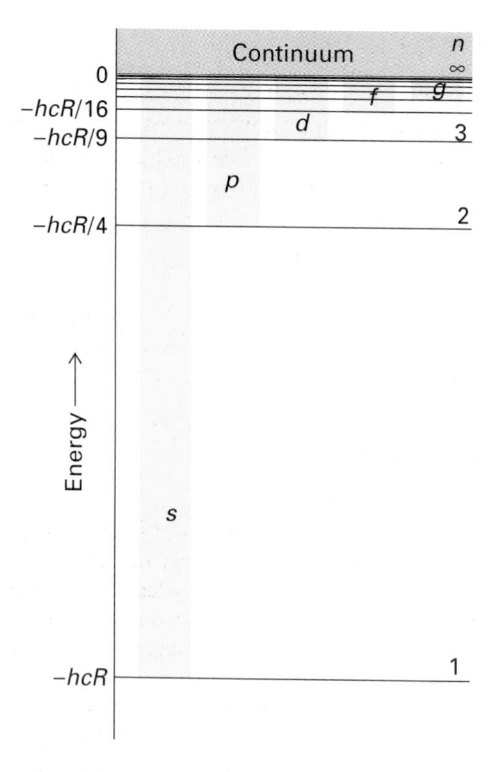

Fig. 13.2 The energy levels of the hydrogen atom. The energies are relative to a proton and an infinitely distant, stationary electron.

n, when the electron has such a high energy that it can travel out to large distances, the energy levels are close together, like those of a particle in a large box.

Now for the sign in eqn 13.4a. All the energies are negative, which signifies that an electron in an atom has a lower energy than when it is free. The zero of energy (which occurs at $n = \infty$) corresponds to the infinitely widely separated (so that the Coulomb potential energy is zero) and stationary (so that the kinetic energy is zero) electron and nucleus. The state of lowest, most negative, energy, the ground state of the atom, is the one with $n = 1$ (the lowest permitted value of n and hence the most negative value of the energy). The energy of this state is

$$E_1 = -hcRZ^2$$

The negative sign means that the ground state lies $hcRZ^2$ *below* the energy of the infinitely separated stationary electron and nucleus. The first excited state of the atom, the state with $n = 2$, lies at

$$E_2 = -\tfrac{1}{4}hcRZ^2$$

This energy level is $\tfrac{3}{4}hcRZ^2$ above the ground state.

These results allow us to explain the empirical expression for the spectroscopic lines observed in the spectrum of atomic hydrogen (for which $R = R_H$ and $Z = 1$). In a transition, an electron jumps from an energy level with one quantum number (n_2) to a level with a lower energy (with quantum number n_1). As a result, its energy changes by

$$\Delta E = \frac{hcR}{n_1^2} - \frac{hcR}{n_2^2}$$

This energy is carried away by a photon of energy $hc\tilde{\nu}$. By equating this energy to ΔE, we immediately obtain eqn 13.1.

Now consider the significance of Z^2 in eqn 13.4a. The fact that the energy levels are proportional to Z^2 stems from two effects. First, an electron at a given distance from a nucleus of charge Ze has a potential energy that is Z times more negative than an electron at the same distance from a proton (for which $Z = 1$). However, the electron is drawn in to the vicinity of the nucleus by the greater nuclear charge, so it is more likely to be found closer to the nucleus of charge Z than the proton. This effect is also proportional to Z, so overall the energy of an electron can be expected to be proportional to the square of Z, one factor representing the Z times greater strength of the nuclear field and the second factor representing the fact that the electron is Z times more likely to be found closer to the nucleus.

Self-test 13.1

The shortest wavelength transition in the Paschen series in hydrogen occurs at 821 nm; at what wavelength does it occur in Li^{2+}? (*Hint.* Think about the variation of energies with atomic number Z.)

[*Answer:* $\frac{1}{9} \times 821$ nm = 91.2 nm]

The minimum energy needed to remove an electron completely from an atom is called the **ionization energy**, I. For a hydrogen atom, the ionization energy is the energy required to raise the electron from the ground state (with $n = 1$ and energy $E_1 = -hcR_H$) to the state corresponding to complete removal of the electron (the state with $n = \infty$ and zero energy). Therefore, the energy that must be supplied is

$$I = hcR_H = 2.180 \times 10^{-18}\ \text{J}$$

which corresponds to 1312 kJ mol^{-1} or 13.59 eV.

Self-test 13.2

Predict the ionization energy of He^+ given that the ionization energy of H is 13.59 eV. (*Hint.* Decide how the energy of the ground state varies with *Z*.)

[*Answer:* $I_{He^+} = 4I_H = 54.36$ eV]

13.3 Quantum numbers

The wavefunction of the electron in a hydrogenic atom is called an **atomic orbital**. The name is intended to express something less definite than the 'orbit' of classical mechanics. An electron that is described by a particular wavefunction is said to 'occupy' that orbital. So, in the ground state of the atom, the electron occupies the orbital of lowest energy (that with $n = 1$).

We have remarked that there are three boundary conditions on the orbitals: that the wavefunctions must not become infinite, that they must match as we encircle the equator, and that they must match as we encircle the poles. Each boundary condition gives rise to a quantum number, so each orbital is specified by three quantum numbers that act as a kind of 'address' of the electron in the atom. We can suspect that the values allowed to the three quantum numbers are linked because, for instance, to get the right shape on a polar journey we also have to note how the wavefunction changes shape as we travel round the equator. It turns out that the relations between the allowed values are very simple.

One quantum number is the principal quantum number *n*, which we have already met. As we have seen, *n* determines the energy of the orbital through eqn 13.4 and is limited to the values

$$n = 1, 2, \ldots$$

without limit. Another quantum number is the **orbital angular momentum quantum number, *l*.**[2] This quantum number is restricted to the values

$$l = 0, 1, 2, \ldots, n-1$$

For a given value of *n*, there are *n* allowed values of *l*: all the values are positive (for example, if $n = 3$, then *l* may be 0, 1, or 2). The third quantum number is the **magnetic quantum number, m_l**. This quantum number is confined to the values

$$m_l = l, l-1, l-2, \ldots, -l$$

For a given value of *l*, there are $2l + 1$ values of m_l (for example, when $l = 3$, m_l may have any of the seven values +3, +2, +1, 0, −1, −2, −3).

Illustration 13.1

Counting orbitals

It follows from the restrictions on the values of the quantum numbers that there is only one orbital with $n = 1$, because when $n = 1$ the only value that *l* can have is 0, and that in turn implies that m_l can have only the value 0. Likewise, there are four orbitals with $n = 2$, because *l* can take the values 0 and 1, and in the latter case m_l can have the three values +1, 0, and −1. In general, there are n^2 orbitals with a given value of *n*.

A note on good practice Always give the sign of m_l, even when it is positive. So, write $m_l = +1$, not $m_l = 1$.

Although we need all three quantum numbers to specify a given orbital, eqn 13.4 reveals that for hydrogenic atoms—and, as we shall see, *only* for hydrogenic atoms—the energy depends only on the principal quantum number, *n*. Therefore, in hydrogenic atoms, and only in hydrogenic atoms, *all orbitals of the same value of n but different values of l and m_l have the same energy*. Recall from Section 12.10 that when we have more than one wavefunction corresponding to the same energy, we say that the wavefunctions are 'degenerate'; so, now we can say that in hydrogenic atoms all orbitals with the same value of *n* are degenerate. A second point is that the average distance of an electron from the nucleus of a hydrogenic atom of atomic number *Z* is

$$\langle r \rangle = n^2 \left\{ 1 + \tfrac{1}{2}\left(1 - \frac{l(l+1)}{n^2} \right) \right\} \frac{a_0}{Z} \qquad (13.5)$$

[2] This quantum number is also called by its older name, the *azimuthal quantum number*.

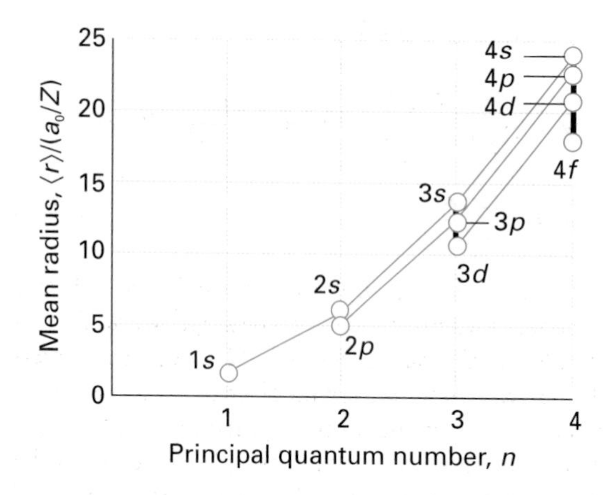

Fig. 13.3 The dependence of the mean radius of an atomic orbital on the values of the quantum numbers n and l for the first four shells of a hydrogenic atom.

As we see from Fig. 13.3, although there is some variation in the mean distance for orbitals with different values of l, the greatest differences arise from the value of n, and as n increases, so the average distance increases too. As Z increases, the mean radius is reduced because the increasing nuclear charge draws the electron closer in.

The degeneracy of all orbitals with the same value of n (remember from Illustration 13.1 that there are n^2 of them) and their similar mean radii is the basis of saying that they all belong to the same **shell** of the atom. It is common to refer to successive shells by letters:

n	1	2	3	4 ...
	K	L	M	N ...

Thus, all four orbitals of the shell with $n = 2$ form the L shell of the atom.

Orbitals with the same value of n but different values of l belong to different **subshells** of a given shell. These subshells are denoted by the letters s, p, ... using the following correspondence:

l	0	1	2	3 ...
	s	p	d	f ...

Only these four types of subshell are important in practice. For the shell with $n = 1$, there is only one subshell, the one with $l = 0$. For the shell with $n = 2$ (which allows $l = 0, 1$), there are two subshells,

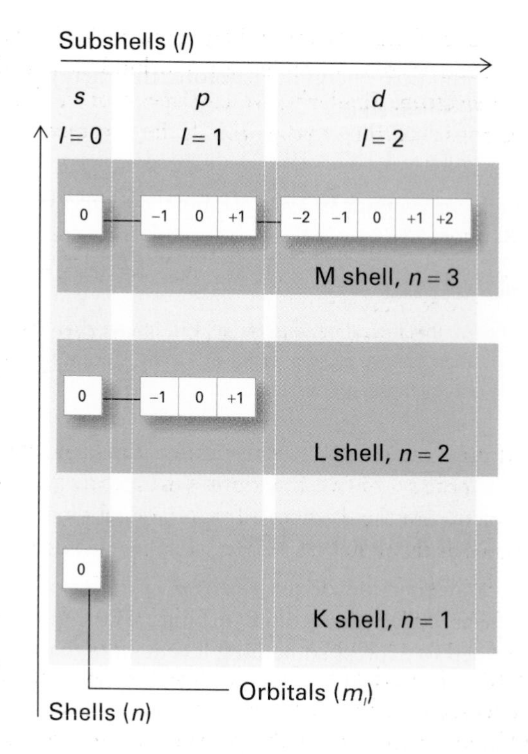

Fig. 13.4 The structures of atoms are described in terms of shells of electrons that are labelled by the principal quantum number n, and a series of n subshells of these shells, with each subshell of a shell being labelled by the quantum number l. Each subshell consists of $2l + 1$ orbitals.

namely the 2s subshell (with $l = 0$) and the 2p subshell (with $l = 1$). The general pattern of the first three shells and their subshells is shown in Fig. 13.4. In a hydrogenic atom, all the subshells of a given shell correspond to the same energy (because, as we have seen, the energy depends on n and not on l).

We have seen that if the orbital angular momentum quantum number is l, then m_l can take the $2l + 1$ values $m_l = 0, \pm1, \ldots, \pm l$. Therefore, each subshell contains $2l + 1$ individual orbitals (corresponding to the $2l + 1$ values of m_l for each value of l). It follows that in any given subshell, the number of orbitals is

s	p	d	f ...
1	3	5	7 ...

An orbital with $l = 0$ (and necessarily $m_l = 0$) is called an **s orbital**. A p subshell ($l = 1$) consists of three p **orbitals** (corresponding to $m_l = +1, 0, -1$). An electron that occupies an s orbital is called an s **electron**. Similarly, we can speak of p, d, … electrons according to the orbitals they occupy.

Self-test 13.3

How many orbitals are there in a shell with $n = 5$ and what is their designation?

[*Answer:* 25; one *s*, three *p*, five *d*, seven *f*, nine *g*]

It turns out that all atomic orbitals can be written as the product of two functions. One factor, $R(r)$, is a function of the distance r from the nucleus and is known as the **radial wavefunction.** Its form depends on the values of n and l but is independent of m_l: that is, all orbitals of the same subshell of a given shell have the same radial wavefunction. In other words, all p orbitals of a shell have the same radial wavefunction, all d orbitals of a shell likewise (but different from that of the p orbitals), and so on. The other factor, $Y(\theta,\phi)$, is called the **angular wavefunction**; it is independent of the distance from the nucleus but varies with the angles θ and ϕ. This factor, which we illustrate later, depends on the quantum numbers l and m_l. Therefore, regardless of the value of n, orbitals with the same value of l and m_l have the same angular wavefunction. In other words, for a given value of m_l, a d orbital has the same angular shape regardless of the shell to which it belongs. This 'separation' of the wavefunction means that any orbital with quantum numbers n, l, and m_l can be written

$$\psi_{n,l,m_l}(r,\theta,\phi) = Y_{l,m_l}(\theta,\phi)R_{n,l}(r) \qquad (13.6)$$

The advantage of this factorization is that we can discuss the radial and angular variation of wavefunctions separately and also expect to find, for a given l and m_l, the same angular variation (the same 'shape').

13.4 The wavefunctions: *s* orbitals

The mathematical form of a 1*s* orbital (the wavefunction with $n = 1$, $l = 0$, and $m_l = 0$) for a hydrogen atom is

$$\underbrace{\frac{1}{(4\pi)^{1/2}}}_{Y(\theta,\phi)}\;\underbrace{\left(\frac{4}{a_0^3}\right)^{1/2} e^{-r/a_0}}_{R(r)}$$

$$\psi = \frac{1}{(4\pi)^{1/2}}\left(\frac{4}{a_0^3}\right)^{1/2} e^{-r/a_0} = \frac{1}{(\pi a_0^3)^{1/2}}\, e^{-r/a_0}$$

$$a_0 = \frac{4\pi\varepsilon_0\hbar^2}{m_e e^2} \qquad (13.7)$$

In this case the angular wavefunction, $Y_{0,0} = 1/(4\pi)^{1/2}$, is a constant, independent of the angles θ and ϕ. You should recall that in Section 12.6 we anticipated that a wavefunction for an electron in a hydrogen atom has a wavefunction proportional to e^{-r}: this is its precise form. The constant a_0 is called the **Bohr radius** (because it occurred in Bohr's calculation of the properties of the hydrogen atom, footnote 1) and has the value 52.9177 pm. The wavefunction in eqn 13.7 is normalized to 1 (Section 12.9), so the probability of finding the electron in a small volume of magnitude δV at a given point is *equal* to $\psi^2\,\delta V$, with ψ evaluated at the point of interest.[3]

A 1*s* orbital depends only on the radius, r, of the point of interest and is independent of angle (the latitude and longitude of the point). Therefore, the orbital has the same amplitude at all points at the same distance from the nucleus regardless of direction. Because the probability of finding an electron is proportional to the square of the wavefunction, we now know that the electron will be found with the same probability in any direction (for a given distance from the nucleus). We summarize this angular independence by saying that a 1*s* orbital is **spherically symmetrical.** Because the same factor Y occurs in all orbitals with $l = 0$, all s orbitals have the same spherical symmetry.

The wavefunction in eqn 13.7 decays exponentially towards zero from a maximum value at the nucleus (Fig. 13.5). It follows that *the most probable point at which the electron will be found is at the nucleus itself*. A method of depicting the probability of finding the electron at each point in space is to represent ψ^2 by the density of shading in a diagram (Fig. 13.6). A simpler procedure is to show only the **boundary surface**, the shape that captures about 90 per cent of the electron probability. For the 1*s*

[3] We are supposing that the volume δV is so small that the wavefunction does not vary inside it.

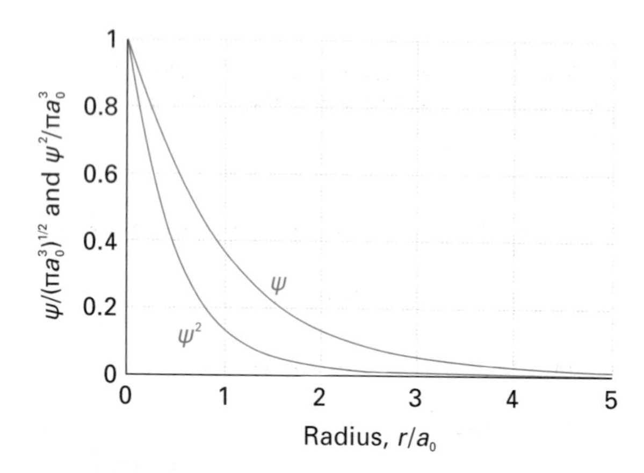

Fig. 13.5 The radial dependence of the wavefunction of a 1*s* orbital (n = 1, l = 0) and the corresponding probability density. The quantity a_0 is the Bohr radius (52.9 pm).

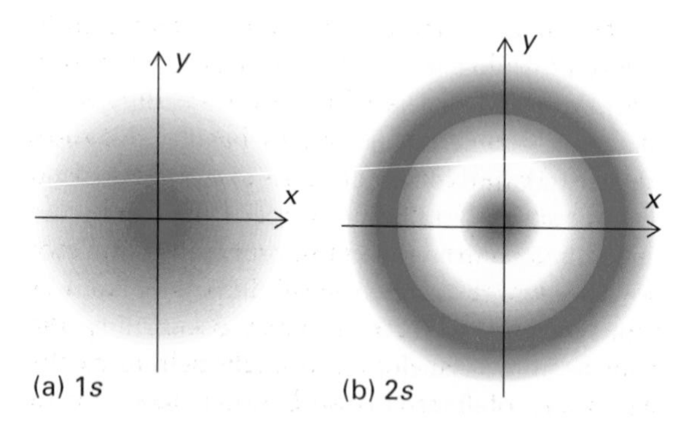

Fig. 13.6 Representations of the first two hydrogenic *s* orbitals, (a) 1*s*, (b) 2*s*, in terms of the electron densities (as represented by the density of shading).

orbital, the boundary surface is a sphere centred on the nucleus (Fig. 13.7).

Illustration 13.2
Electron probability

We can calculate the probability of finding the electron in a volume of 1.0 pm^3 centred on the nucleus in a hydrogen atom by setting $r = 0$ in the expression for ψ, using $e^0 = 1$, and taking $\delta V = 1.0$ pm^3. The value of ψ at the nucleus is $1/(\pi a_0^3)^{1/2}$. Therefore, $\psi^2 = 1/\pi a_0^3$ at the nucleus, and we can write

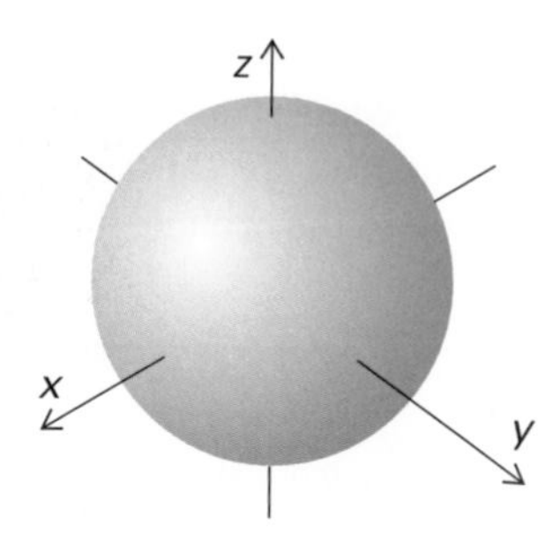

Fig. 13.7 The boundary surface of an *s* orbital within which there is a high probability of finding the electron.

$$\text{Probability} = \frac{1}{\pi a_0^3} \times \delta V = \frac{1}{\pi \times (52.9\ \text{pm})^3} \times (1.0\ \text{pm}^3)$$
$$= \frac{(1.0)^3}{\pi \times (52.9)^3} = 2.2 \times 10^{-6}$$

This result means that the electron will be found in the volume on one observation in 455 000.

Self-test 13.4

Repeat the calculation for finding the electron in the same volume located at the Bohr radius.

[*Answer:* 3.0×10^{-7}, 1 in 3 300 000 observations]

We often need to know the probability that an electron will be found at a given distance from a nucleus regardless of its angular position (Fig. 13.8). We can calculate this probability by combining the wavefunction in eqn 13.7 with the Born interpretation and find that, for an *s* orbital, the answer can be expressed as

$$\text{Probability} = P(r)\ \delta r$$
$$\text{with } P(r) = 4\pi r^2 \psi^2 \qquad (13.8a)$$

The function P is called the **radial distribution function**. The more general form, which also applies to orbitals that depend on angle, is

$$P(r) = r^2 R(r)^2 \qquad (13.8b)$$

where $R(r)$ is the radial wavefunction.

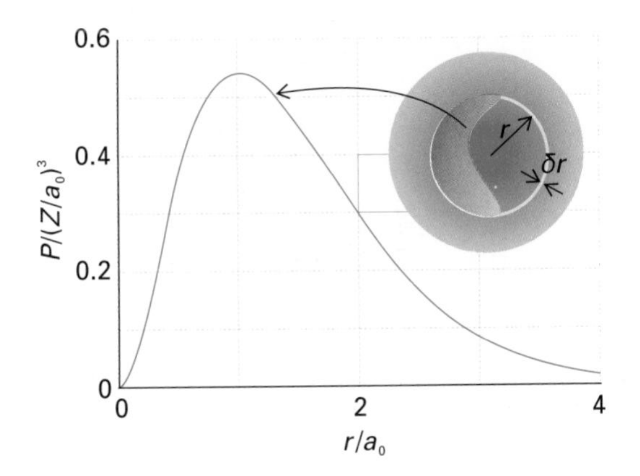

Fig. 13.8 The radial distribution function gives the probability that the electron will be found anywhere in a shell of radius r and thickness δr regardless of angle. The graph shows the output from an imaginary shell-like detector of variable radius and fixed thickness δr.

Derivation 13.1

The radial distribution function

Consider two spherical shells centred on the nucleus, one of radius r and the other of radius $r + \delta r$. The probability of finding the electron at a radius r regardless of its direction is equal to the probability of finding it between these two spherical surfaces. The volume of the region of space between the surfaces is equal to the surface area of the inner shell, $4\pi r^2$, multiplied by the thickness, δr, of the region, and is therefore $4\pi r^2\,\delta r$. According to the Born interpretation, the probability of finding an electron inside a small volume of magnitude δV is given, for a normalized wavefunction that is constant throughout the region, by the value of $\psi^2\,\delta V$. An s orbital has the same value at all angles at a given distance from the nucleus, so it is constant throughout the shell (provided δr is very small). Therefore, interpreting δV as the volume of the shell, we obtain

$$\text{Probability} = \psi^2 \times (4\pi r^2\,\delta r)$$

as in eqn 13.8a. The result we have derived is for any s orbital.

Illustration 13.3

The radial distribution function

To calculate the probability that the electron will be found between a shell of radius a_0 and a shell of radius 1.0 pm greater, we first substitute the wavefunction in eqn 13.7 into the expression for P in eqn 13.8a:

$$\text{Probability} = \underbrace{4\pi r^2\psi^2}_{P} \times \delta r = 4\pi r^2 \times \underbrace{\frac{1}{\pi a_0^3}\,e^{-2r/a_0}}_{\psi^2} \times \delta r$$

$$= \frac{4\,r^2}{a_0^3}\,e^{-2r/a_0} \times \delta r$$

Now we substitute $\delta r = 1.0$ pm and $r = a_0$:

$$\text{Probability} = \frac{4}{a_0}\,e^{-2} \times \delta r$$

$$= \frac{4}{52.9\ \text{pm}}\,e^{-2} \times (1.0\ \text{pm}) = 0.010$$

or about 1 inspection in 100.

The radial distribution function tells us the probability of finding an electron at a distance r from the nucleus regardless of its direction. Because r^2 increases from 0 as r increases but ψ^2 decreases towards 0 exponentially, P starts at 0, goes through a maximum, and declines to 0 again. The location of the maximum marks the most probable *radius* (not point) at which the electron will be found. For a 1s orbital of hydrogen, the maximum occurs at a_0, the Bohr radius. An analogy that might help to fix the significance of the radial distribution function for an electron is the corresponding distribution for the population of the Earth regarded as a perfect sphere. The radial distribution function is zero at the centre of the Earth and for the next 6400 km (to the surface of the planet), when it peaks sharply and then rapidly decays again to zero. It remains more or less zero for all radii more than about 10 km above the surface. Almost all the population will be found very close to $r = 6400$ km, and it is not relevant that people are dispersed non-uniformly over a very wide range of latitudes and longitudes. The small probability of finding people above and below 6400 km anywhere in the world corresponds to the population that happens to be down mines or living in places as high as Denver or Tibet at the time.

A 2s orbital (an orbital with $n = 2$, $l = 0$, and $m_l = 0$) is also spherical, so its boundary surface is a sphere. Because a 2s orbital spreads further out from the nucleus than a 1s orbital—because the

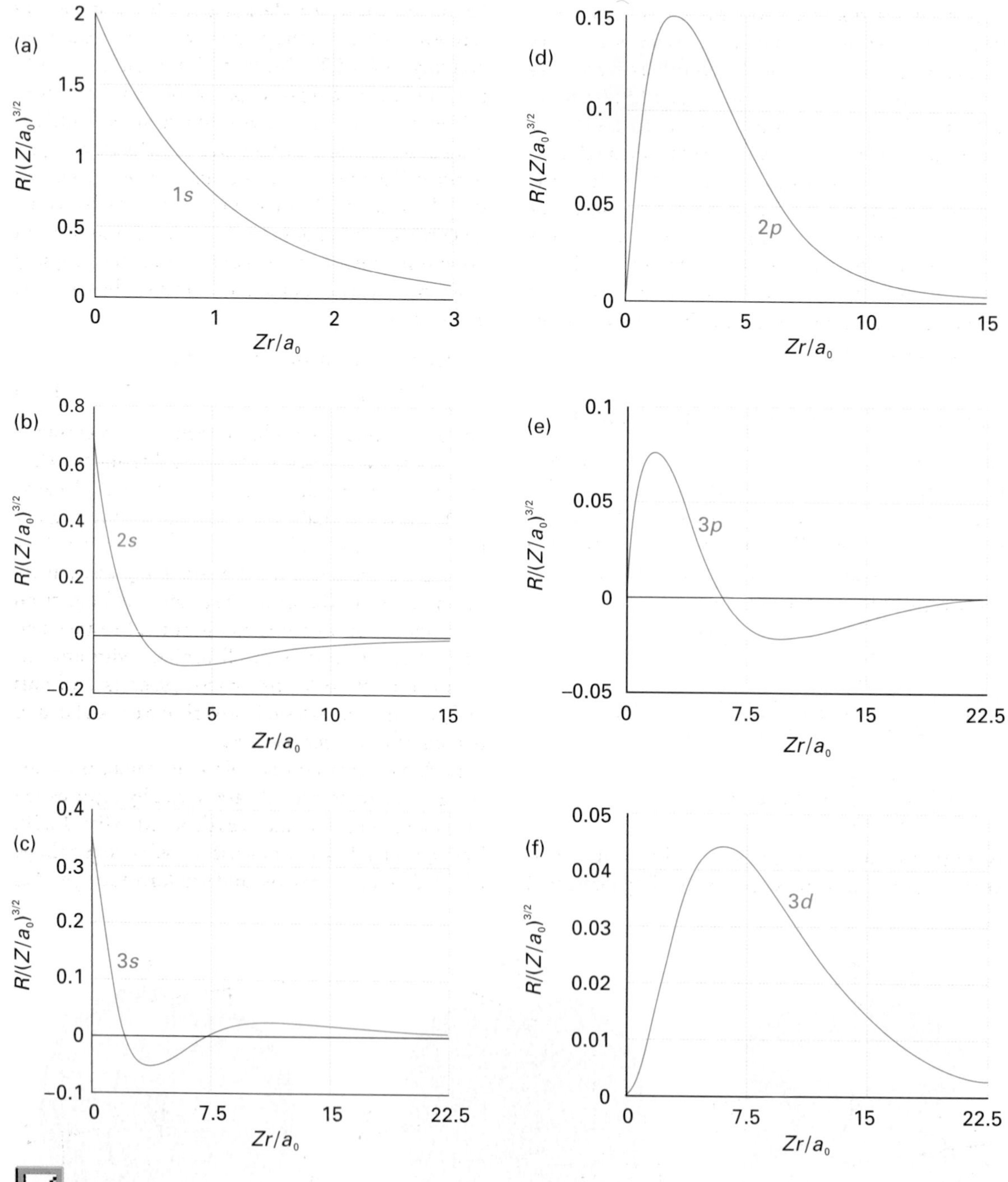

Fig. 13.9 The radial wavefunctions of the hydrogenic (a) 1*s*, (b) 2*s*, (c) 3*s*, (d) 2*p*, (e) 3*p*, and (f) 3*d* orbitals. Note that the *s* orbitals have a non-zero and finite value at the nucleus. The vertical scales are different in each case.

electron it describes has more energy to climb away from the nucleus—its boundary surface is a sphere of larger radius. The orbital also differs from a 1*s* orbital in its radial dependence (Fig. 13.9) because, although the wavefunction has a non-zero value at the nucleus (like all *s* orbitals), it passes through zero before commencing its exponential decay towards zero at large distances. We summarize the fact that the wavefunction passes through zero everywhere at a certain radius by saying that the orbital has a **radial node**. A 3*s* orbital has two radial nodes, a 4*s* orbital has three radial nodes. In general, an *ns* orbital has $n - 1$ radial nodes.

13.5 The wavefunctions: *p* and *d* orbitals

All *p* orbitals (orbitals with $l = 1$) have a double-lobed appearance like that shown in Fig. 13.10. The two lobes are separated by a **nodal plane** that cuts through the nucleus. There is zero probability density for an electron on this plane. Here, for instance, is the explicit form of the $2p_z$ orbital:

$$\psi = \underbrace{\left(\frac{3}{4\pi}\right)^{1/2} \cos\theta}_{Y(\theta,\phi)} \times \underbrace{\tfrac{1}{2}\left(\frac{1}{6a_0^3}\right)^{1/2} \frac{r}{a_0} e^{-r/2a_0}}_{R(r)}$$

$$= \left(\frac{1}{32\pi a_0^5}\right)^{1/2} r\cos\theta\, e^{-r/2a_0}$$

Note that because ψ is proportional to r, it is zero at the nucleus, so there is zero probability density of finding the electron at the nucleus. The orbital is also zero everywhere on the plane with $\cos\theta = 0$, corresponding to $\theta = 90°$. The p_x and p_y orbitals are similar, but have nodal planes perpendicular to this one.

The exclusion of the electron from the nucleus is a common feature of all atomic orbitals except *s* orbitals. To understand its origin, we need to know that the value of the quantum number *l* tells us the magnitude of the angular momentum of the electron around the nucleus (in classical terms, how rapidly it is circulating around the nucleus) through the expression

$$\text{Magnitude of angular momentum} = \{l(l+1)\}^{1/2}\hbar \tag{13.9}$$

For an *s* orbital, the orbital angular momentum is zero (because $l = 0$), and in classical terms the electron does not circulate around the nucleus. Because $l = 1$ for a *p* orbital, the magnitude of the angular momentum of a *p* electron is $2^{1/2}\hbar$. As a result, a *p* electron—in classical terms—is flung away from the nucleus by the centrifugal force arising from its motion, but an *s* electron is not. The same centrifugal effect appears in all orbitals with angular momentum (those for which $l > 0$), such as *d* orbitals and *f* orbitals, and all such orbitals have nodal planes that cut through the nucleus.

Each *p* subshell consists of three orbitals ($m_l = +1, 0, -1$). The three orbitals are normally represented by their boundary surfaces, as depicted in Fig. 13.10. The p_x orbital has a symmetrical double-lobed shape directed along the *x*-axis, and similarly the p_y and p_z

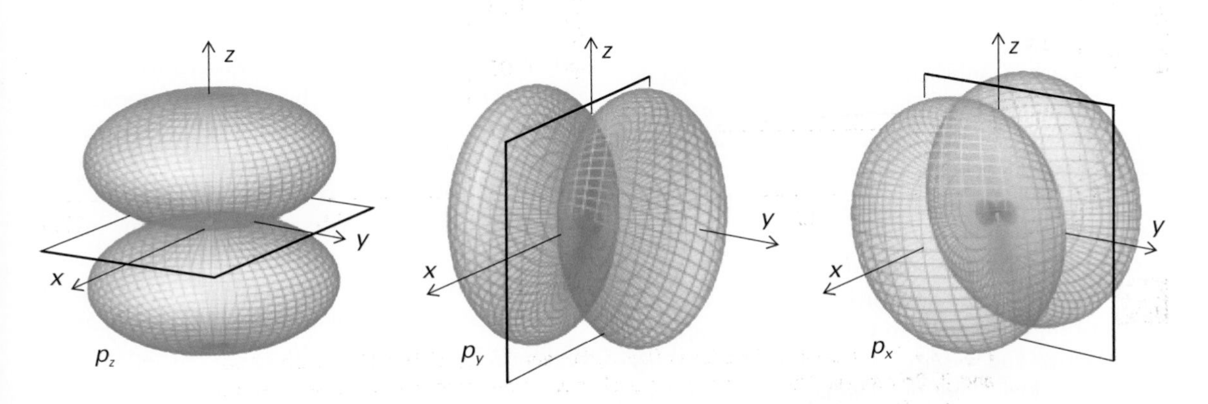

Fig. 13.10 The boundary surfaces of *p* orbitals. A nodal plane passes through the nucleus and separates the two lobes of each orbital.

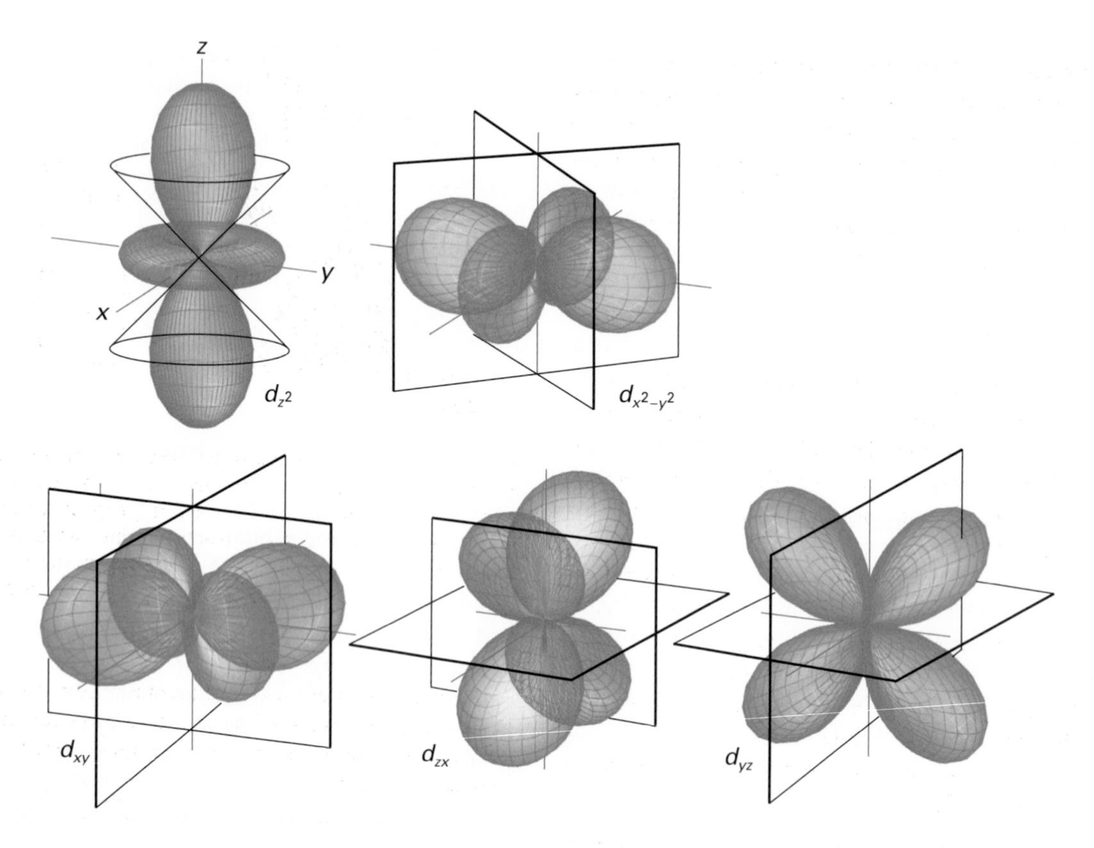

Fig. 13.11 The boundary surfaces of d orbitals. Two nodal planes in each orbital intersect at the nucleus and separate the four lobes of each orbital.

orbitals are directed along the y- and z-axes, respectively. As n increases, the p orbitals become bigger (for the same reason as s orbitals) and have $n - 2$ radial nodes.[4] However, their boundary surfaces retain the double-lobed shape shown in the illustration. Each d subshell consists of five orbitals ($m_l = +2, +1, 0, -1, -2$). These five orbitals are normally represented by the boundary surfaces shown in Fig. 13.11 and labelled as shown there.

We can now explain the physical significance of the quantum number m_l. It indicates the component of the electron's orbital angular momentum around an arbitrary axis passing through the nucleus. Positive values of m_l correspond to clockwise motion seen from below and negative values correspond to counter clockwise motion. The larger the value of $|m_l|$, the higher the orbital angular momentum around the arbitrary axis. Specifically:

$$\text{Component of orbital angular momentum} = m_l\hbar \qquad (13.10)$$

An s electron has $m_l = 0$, and has no orbital angular momentum about any axis. A p electron can circulate clockwise about an axis as seen from below ($m_l = +1$). Of its total orbital angular momentum of $2^{1/2}\hbar = 1.414\hbar$, an amount $\hbar$ is due to motion around the selected axis (the rest is due to motion around the other two axes). A p electron can also circulate counterclockwise as seen from below ($m_l = -1$), or not at all ($m_l = 0$) about that selected axis. An electron in the d subshell can circulate with five different amounts of orbital angular momentum about an arbitrary axis ($+2\hbar, +\hbar, 0, -\hbar, -2\hbar$).

[4] The radial wavefunction is zero at $r = 0$, but that is not a radial node because the wavefunction does not pass *through* zero there.

Except for orbitals with $m_l = 0$, there is not a one-to-one correspondence between the value of m_l and the orbitals shown in the illustrations: we cannot say, for instance, that a p_x orbital has $m_l = +1$. For technical reasons, the orbitals we draw are combinations of orbitals with opposite values of m_l (p_x, for instance, is the sum of the orbitals with $m_l = +1$ and -1).

13.6 Electron spin

To complete the description of the state of a hydrogenic atom, we need to introduce one more concept, that of electron spin. The **spin** of an electron is an *intrinsic* angular momentum that every electron possesses and that cannot be changed or eliminated (just like its mass or its charge). The name 'spin' is evocative of a ball spinning on its axis, and (so long as it is treated with caution) this classical interpretation can be used to help to visualize the motion. However, in fact, spin is a purely quantum mechanical phenomenon and has no classical counterpart, so the analogy must be used with care.

We shall make use of two properties of electron spin (Fig. 13.12):

1. Electron spin is described by a **spin quantum number,** s (the analogue of l for orbital angular momentum), with s fixed at the single (positive) value of $\frac{1}{2}$ for all electrons at all times.
2. The spin can be clockwise or counterclockwise; these two states are distinguished by the **spin magnetic quantum number,** m_s, which can take the values $+\frac{1}{2}$ or $-\frac{1}{2}$ but no other values.

An electron with $m_s = +\frac{1}{2}$ is called an **α electron** and commonly denoted α or ↑; an electron with $m_s = -\frac{1}{2}$ is called a **β electron** and denoted β or ↓.

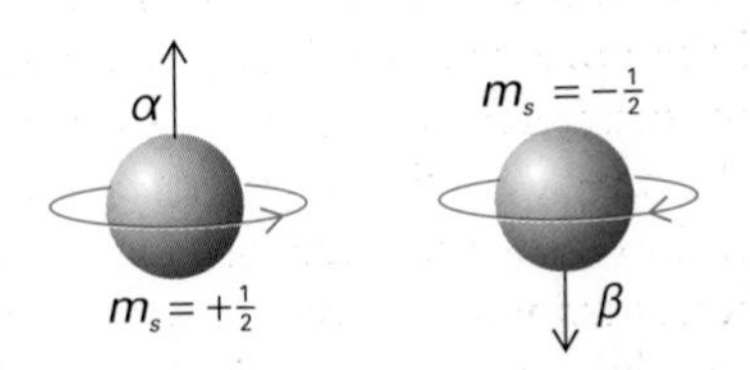

Fig. 13.12 A classical representation of the two allowed spin states of an electron. The magnitude of the spin angular momentum is $(3^{1/2}/2)\hbar$ in each case, but the directions of spin are opposite.

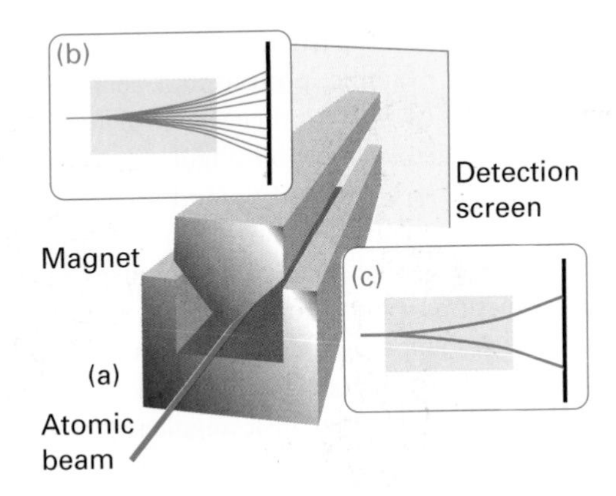

Fig. 13.13 (a) The experimental arrangement for the Stern–Gerlach experiment: the magnet is the source of an inhomogeneous field. (b) The classically expected result, when the orientations of the electron spins can take all angles. (c) The observed outcome using silver atoms, when the electron spins can adopt only two orientations (↑ and ↓).

> ***A note on good practice*** The quantum number s is equal to $\frac{1}{2}$ for electrons. You will occasionally see its value written incorrectly as $s = +\frac{1}{2}$ or $s = -\frac{1}{2}$. For the projection, use m_s.

The existence of electron spin was confirmed by an experiment performed by Otto Stern and Walther Gerlach in 1921, who shot a beam of silver atoms through a strong magnetic field (Fig. 13.13). A silver atom has 47 electrons, and (for reasons that will become clear later) 23 of the spins are ↑ and 23 spins are ↓; the one remaining spin may be either ↑ or ↓.[5] Because the spin angular momenta of the ↑ and ↓ electrons cancel each other, the atom behaves as if it had the spin of a single electron. The idea behind the Stern–Gerlach experiment was that a rotating, charged body—in this case an electron—behaves like a magnet and interacts with the applied field. Because the magnetic field pushes or pulls the electron according to the orientation of the electron's spin, the initial beam of atoms should split into two beams, one corresponding to atoms with ↑ spin and the other to atoms with ↓ spin. This result was observed.

[5] As will probably be familiar from introductory chemistry, 46 of the electrons are paired and occupy orbitals in accord with the building-up principle.

Other fundamental particles also have characteristic spins. For example, protons and neutrons are **spin-$\frac{1}{2}$ particles** (that is, for them $s = \frac{1}{2}$) so invariably spin with a single, irremovable angular momentum. Because the masses of a proton and a neutron are so much greater than the mass of an electron, yet they all have the same spin angular momentum, the classical picture of proton and neutron spin would be of particles spinning much more slowly than an electron. Some elementary particles have $s = 1$ and therefore have a higher intrinsic angular momentum than an electron. For our purposes the most important **spin-1 particle** is the photon. It is a very deep feature of nature, that the fundamental particles from which matter is built have half-integral spin (such as electrons and quarks, all of which have $s = \frac{1}{2}$). The particles that transmit forces between these particles, so binding them together into entities such as nuclei, atoms, and planets, all have integral spin (such as $s = 1$ for the photon, which transmits the electromagnetic interaction between charged particles). Fundamental particles with half-integral spin are called **fermions**; those with integral spin are called **bosons**. Matter therefore consists of fermions bound together by bosons.

13.7 Spectral transitions and selection rules

We have already seen that, when an electron makes a transition from an orbital in a shell with a principal quantum number n_2 into an orbital of a shell with principal quantum number n_1, the excess energy is emitted as a photon and contributes to one of the spectral lines given by the Rydberg formula, eqn 13.1. We can think of the sudden change in the distribution of the electron as it changes its spatial distribution from one orbital to another orbital as jolting the electromagnetic field into oscillation, and that oscillation corresponds to the generation of a photon of light.

It turns out, however, that not all transitions between all available orbitals are possible. For example, it is not possible for an electron in a 3*d* orbital to make a transition to a 1*s* orbital. Transitions are classified as either **allowed**, if they can contribute to the spectrum, or **forbidden**, if they cannot. The allowed or forbidden character of a transition can be traced to the role of the photon spin, which we mentioned above. When a photon, with its one unit of angular momentum, is generated in a transition, the angular momentum of the electron must change by one unit to compensate for the angular momentum carried away by the photon. That is, the angular momentum must be conserved—neither created nor destroyed—just as linear momentum is conserved in collisions. Thus, an electron in a *d* orbital (with $l = 2$) cannot make a transition into an *s* orbital (with $l = 0$) because the photon cannot carry away enough angular momentum. Similarly, an *s* electron cannot make a transition to another *s* orbital, because then there is no change in the electron's angular momentum to make up for the angular momentum carried away by the photon.

A **selection rule** is a statement about which spectroscopic transitions are allowed. They are derived (for atoms) by identifying the transitions that conserve angular momentum when a photon is emitted or absorbed. The selection rules for hydrogenic atoms are

$$\Delta l = \pm 1 \qquad \Delta m_l = 0, \pm 1$$

The principal quantum number n can change by any amount consistent with the Δl for the transition because it does not relate directly to the angular momentum.

Illustration 13.4

Using the selection rules

To identify the orbitals to which an electron in a 4*d* electron may make spectroscopic transitions we apply the selection rules, principally the rule concerning l. Because $l = 2$, the final orbital must have $l = 1$ or 3. Thus, an electron may make a transition from a 4*d* orbital to any *np* orbital (subject to $\Delta m_l = 0, \pm 1$) and to any *nf* orbital (subject to the same rule). However, it cannot undergo a transition to any other orbital, so a transition to any *ns* orbital or another *nd* orbital is forbidden.

Self-test 13.5

To what orbitals may a 4*s* electron make spectroscopic transitions?

[*Answer: np* orbitals only]

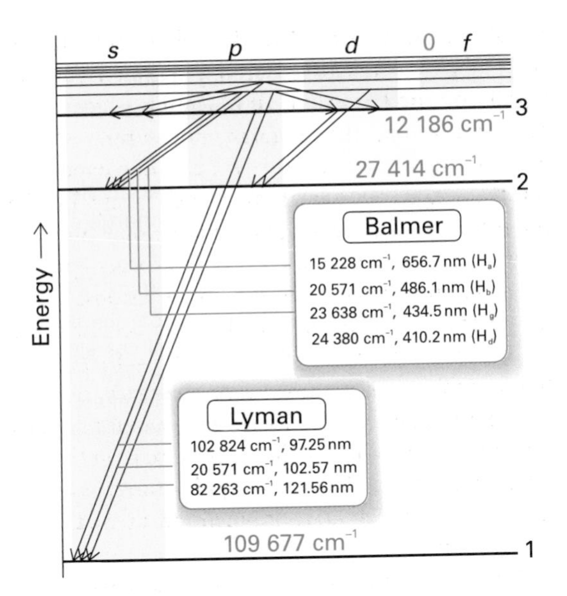

Fig. 13.14 A Grotrian diagram that summarizes the appearance and analysis of the spectrum of atomic hydrogen.

Selection rules enable us to construct a **Grotrian diagram** (Fig. 13.14), which is a diagram that summarizes the energies of the states and the allowed transitions between them. The thickness of a transition line in the diagram is sometimes used to indicate in a general way its relative intensity in the spectrum.

The structures of many-electron atoms

The Schrödinger equation for a many-electron atom is highly complicated because all the electrons interact with one another. Even for a He atom, with its two electrons, no mathematical expression for the orbitals and energies can be given and we are forced to make approximations. Modern computational techniques, however, are able to refine the approximations we are about to make, and permit highly accurate numerical calculations of energies and wavefunctions.

13.8 The orbital approximation

In the **orbital approximation** we suppose that a reasonable first approximation to the exact wavefunction is obtained by letting each electron occupy its 'own' orbital, and writing

$$\psi = \psi(1)\psi(2)\ldots \qquad (13.11)$$

where $\psi(1)$ is the wavefunction of electron 1, $\psi(2)$ that of electron 2, and so on. We can think of the individual orbitals as resembling the hydrogenic orbitals, but with nuclear charges that are modified by the presence of all the other electrons in the atom. This description is only approximate, but it is a useful model for discussing the properties of atoms, and is the starting point for more sophisticated descriptions of atomic structure.

Illustration 13.5

A many-electron wavefunction

If we consider only the interaction of each electron with the nucleus and disregard their mutual repulsion, and further assume that both electrons occupy the same 1*s* orbital, the wavefunction for each electron in helium is $\psi = (8/\pi a_0^3)^{1/2}\,e^{-2r/a_0}$. If electron 1 is at a radius r_1 and electron 2 is at a radius r_2 (and at any angle), then the overall wavefunction for the two-electron atom is

$$\psi = \psi(1)\psi(2) = \left(\frac{8}{\pi a_0^3}\right)^{1/2} e^{-2r_1/a_0} \times \left(\frac{8}{\pi a_0^3}\right)^{1/2} e^{-2r_2/a_0}$$

$$= \left(\frac{8}{\pi a_0^3}\right) e^{-2(r_1+r_2)/a_0}$$

The orbital approximation allows us to express the electronic structure of an atom by reporting its **configuration**, the list of occupied orbitals (usually, but not necessarily, in its ground state). For example, because the ground state of a hydrogen atom consists of a single electron in a 1*s* orbital, we report its configuration as $1s^1$ (read 'one s one'). A helium atom has two electrons. We can imagine forming the atom by adding the electrons in succession to the orbitals of the bare nucleus (of charge 2*e*). The first electron occupies a hydrogenic 1*s* orbital, but because $Z = 2$, the orbital is more compact than in H itself. The second electron joins the first in the same

1*s* orbital, and so the electron configuration of the ground state of He is $1s^2$ (read 'one s two').

13.9 The Pauli exclusion principle

Lithium, with $Z = 3$, has three electrons. Two of its electrons occupy a 1*s* orbital drawn even more closely than in He around the more highly charged nucleus. The third electron, however, does not join the first two in the 1*s* orbital because a $1s^3$ configuration is forbidden by a fundamental feature of nature summarized by the **Pauli exclusion principle:**

No more than two electrons may occupy any given orbital, and if two electrons do occupy one orbital, then their spins must be paired.

Electrons with **paired spins**, denoted ↑↓, have zero net spin angular momentum because the spin angular momentum of one electron is cancelled by the spin of the other. The exclusion principle is the key to understanding the structures of complex atoms, to chemical periodicity, and to molecular structure. It was proposed by the Austrian Wolfgang Pauli in 1924 when he was trying to account for the absence of some lines in the spectrum of helium. In *Further information* 13.1 we see that the exclusion principle is a consequence of an even deeper statement about wavefunctions.

Lithium's third electron cannot enter the 1*s* orbital because that orbital is already full: we say the K shell is **complete** and that the two electrons form a **closed shell.** Because a similar closed shell occurs in the He atom, we denote it [He]. The third electron is excluded from the K shell ($n = 1$) and must occupy the next available orbital, which is one with $n = 2$ and hence belonging to the L shell. However, we now have to decide whether the next available orbital is the 2*s* orbital or a 2*p* orbital, and therefore whether the lowest energy configuration of the atom is $[\mathrm{He}]2s^1$ or $[\mathrm{He}]2p^1$.

13.10 Penetration and shielding

Unlike in hydrogenic atoms, in many-electron atoms the 2*s* and 2*p* orbitals (and, in general, all the subshells of a given shell) are not degenerate. For reasons we shall now explain, *s* electrons generally lie lower in energy than *p* electrons of a given shell, and *p* electrons lie lower than *d* electrons.

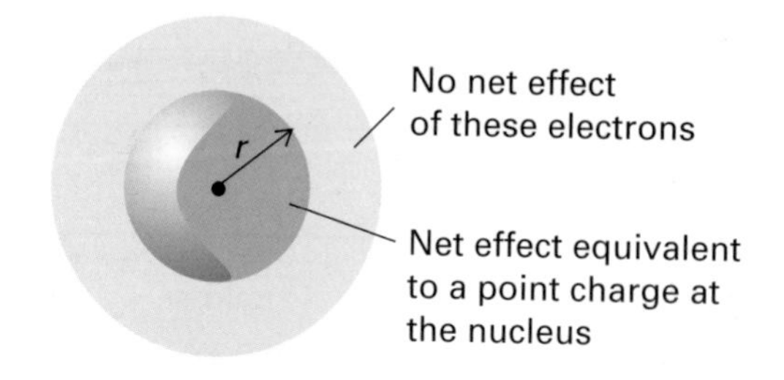

Fig. 13.15 An electron at a distance r from the nucleus experiences a Coulombic repulsion from all the electrons within a sphere of radius r and which is equivalent to a point negative charge located on the nucleus. The effect of the point charge is to reduce the apparent nuclear charge of the nucleus from Ze to $Z_{\mathrm{eff}}e$.

An electron in a many-electron atom experiences a Coulombic repulsion from all the other electrons present. When the electron is at a distance r from the nucleus, the repulsion it experiences from the other electrons can be modelled by a point negative charge located on the nucleus and having a magnitude equal to the charge of the electrons within a sphere of radius r (Fig. 13.15). The effect of the point negative charge is to lower the full charge of the nucleus from Ze to $Z_{\mathrm{eff}}e$, the **effective nuclear charge.**[6] To express the fact that an electron experiences a nuclear charge that has been modified by the other electrons present, we say that the electron experiences a **shielded nuclear charge.** The electrons do not in fact 'block' the full Coulombic attraction of the nucleus: the effective charge is simply a way of expressing the net outcome of the nuclear attraction and the electronic repulsions in terms of a single equivalent charge at the centre of the atom.

The effective nuclear charges experienced by *s* and *p* electrons are different because the electrons have different wavefunctions and therefore different distributions around the nucleus (Fig. 13.16). An *s* electron has a greater **penetration** through inner shells than a *p* electron of the same shell in the sense that an *s* electron is more likely to be found close to

[6] Commonly, Z_{eff} itself is referred to as the 'effective nuclear charge', although strictly that quantity is $Z_{\mathrm{eff}}e$.

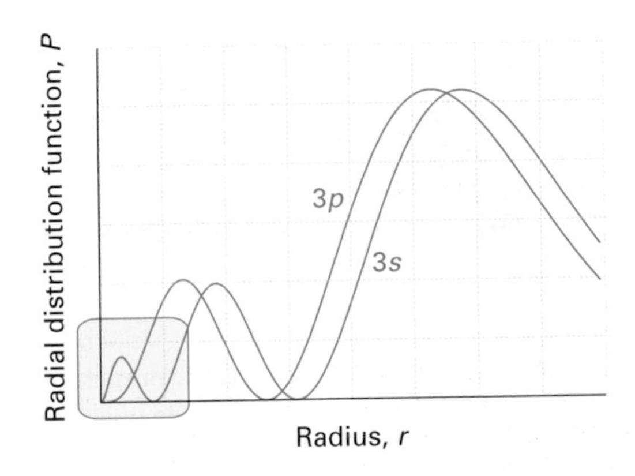

Fig. 13.16 An electron in an *s* orbital (here a 3*s* orbital) is more likely to be found close to the nucleus than an electron in a *p* orbital of the same shell. Hence it experiences less shielding and is more tightly bound.

the nucleus than a *p* electron of the same shell (the *p* orbital, remember, has an angular node passing through the nucleus). As a result of this greater penetration, an *s* electron experiences less shielding than a *p* electron of the same shell and therefore experiences a larger Z_{eff}. Consequently, by the combined effects of penetration and shielding, an *s* electron is more tightly bound than a *p* electron of the same shell. Similarly, a *d* electron penetrates less than a *p* electron of the same shell, and it therefore experiences more shielding and an even smaller Z_{eff}.

The consequence of penetration and shielding is that, in general, the energies of orbitals in the same shell of a many-electron atom lie in the order

$$s < p < d < f$$

The individual orbitals of a given subshell (such as the three *p* orbitals of the *p* subshell) remain degenerate because they all have the same radial characteristics and so experience the same effective nuclear charge.

We can now complete the Li story. Because the shell with $n = 2$ has two non-degenerate subshells, with the 2*s* orbital lower in energy than the three 2*p* orbitals, the third electron occupies the 2*s* orbital. This arrangement results in the ground state configuration $1s^2 2s^1$, or $[He]2s^1$. It follows that we can think of the structure of the atom as consisting of a central nucleus surrounded by a complete helium-like shell of two 1*s* electrons, and around that a more diffuse 2*s* electron. The electrons in the outermost shell of an atom in its ground state are called the **valence electrons** because they are largely responsible for the chemical bonds that the atom forms (and, as we shall see, the extent to which an atom can form bonds is called its 'valence'). Thus, the valence electron in Li is a 2*s* electron, and lithium's other two electrons belong to its core, where they take little part in bond formation.

13.11 The building-up principle

The extension of the procedure used for H, He, and Li to other atoms is called the **building-up principle.**[7] The building-up principle specifies an order of occupation of atomic orbitals that reproduces the experimentally determined ground-state configurations of neutral atoms.

We imagine the bare nucleus of atomic number *Z*, and then feed into the available orbitals *Z* electrons one after the other. The first two rules of the building-up principle are:

1 The order of occupation of orbitals is[8]

   1*s* 2*s* 2*p* 3*s* 3*p* 4*s* 3*d*
   4*p* 5*s* 4*d* 5*p* 6*s* 5*d* 4*f*
   6*p* ...

2 According to the Pauli exclusion principle, each orbital may accommodate up to two electrons.

The order of occupation is approximately the order of energies of the individual orbitals, because, in general, the lower the energy of the orbital, the lower the total energy of the atom as a whole when that orbital is occupied. An *s* subshell is complete as soon as two electrons are present in it. Each of the three *p* orbitals of a shell can accommodate two electrons, so a *p* subshell is complete as soon as six electrons are present in it. A *d* subshell, which consists of five orbitals, can accommodate up to 10 electrons.

[7] The building-up principle is still widely called the *Aufbau principle*, from the German word for building up.

[8] This order is best remembered by noting that it follows the layout of the periodic table.

As an example, consider a carbon atom. Because $Z = 6$ for carbon, there are six electrons to accommodate. Two enter and fill the 1*s* orbital, two enter and fill the 2*s* orbital, leaving two electrons to occupy the orbitals of the 2*p* subshell. Hence its ground configuration is $1s^2 2s^2 2p^2$, or more succinctly $[\mathrm{He}]2s^2 2p^2$, with [He] the helium-like $1s^2$ core. However, it is possible to be more specific. On electrostatic grounds, we can expect the last two electrons to occupy different 2*p* orbitals, as they will then be farther apart on average and repel each other less than if they were in the same orbital. Thus, one electron can be thought of as occupying the $2p_x$ orbital and the other the $2p_y$ orbital, and the lowest-energy configuration of the atom is $[\mathrm{He}]2s^2 2p_x^1 2p_y^1$. The same rule applies whenever degenerate orbitals of a subshell are available for occupation. Therefore, another rule of the building-up principle is:

3 Electrons occupy different orbitals of a given subshell before doubly occupying any one of them.

It follows that a nitrogen atom ($Z = 7$) has the configuration $[\mathrm{He}]2s^2 2p_x^1 2p_y^1 2p_z^1$. Only when we get to oxygen ($Z = 8$) is a 2*p* orbital doubly occupied, giving the configuration $[\mathrm{He}]2s^2 2p_x^2 2p_y^1 2p_z^1$.

An additional point arises when electrons occupy degenerate orbitals (such as the three 2*p* orbitals) singly, as they do in C, N, and O, as there is then no requirement that their spins should be paired. We need to know whether the lowest energy is achieved when the electron spins are the same (both ↑, for instance, denoted ↑↑, if there are two electrons in question, as in C) or when they are paired (↑↓). This question is resolved by **Hund's rule:**

4 In its ground state, an atom adopts a configuration with the greatest number of unpaired electrons.

The explanation of Hund's rule is complicated, but it reflects the quantum mechanical property of **spin correlation**, that electrons in different orbitals with parallel spins have a quantum-mechanical tendency to stay well apart (a tendency that has nothing to do with their charge: even two 'uncharged electrons' would behave in the same way). Their mutual avoidance allows the atom to shrink slightly, so the electron–nucleus interaction is improved when the spins are parallel. We can now conclude that in the ground state of a C atom, the two 2*p* electrons have the same spin, that all three 2*p* electrons in an N atom have the same spin, and that the two electrons that singly occupy different 2*p* orbitals in an O atom have the same spin (the two in the $2p_x$ orbital are necessarily paired).

Neon, with $Z = 10$, has the configuration $[\mathrm{He}]2s^2 2p^6$, which completes the L ($n = 2$) shell. This closed-shell configuration is denoted [Ne], and acts as a core for subsequent elements. The next electron must enter the 3*s* orbital and begin a new shell, and so a Na atom, with $Z = 11$, has the configuration $[\mathrm{Ne}]3s^1$. Like lithium with the configuration $[\mathrm{He}]2s^1$, sodium has a single *s* electron outside a complete core.

Self-test 13.6

Predict the ground-state electron configuration of sulfur.

[*Answer:* $[\mathrm{Ne}]3s^2 3p_x^2 3p_y^1 3p_z^1$]

This analysis has brought us to the origin of chemical periodicity. The L shell is completed by eight electrons, and so the element with $Z = 3$ (Li) should have similar properties to the element with $Z = 11$ (Na). Likewise, Be ($Z = 4$) should be similar to Mg ($Z = 12$), and so on up to the noble gases He ($Z = 2$), Ne ($Z = 10$), and Ar ($Z = 18$).

13.12 The occupation of *d* orbitals

Argon has complete 3*s* and 3*p* subshells, and as the 3*d* orbitals are high in energy, the atom effectively has a closed-shell configuration. Indeed, the 4*s* orbitals are so lowered in energy by their ability to penetrate close to the nucleus that the next electron (for potassium) occupies a 4*s* orbital rather than a 3*d* orbital and the K atom resembles a Na atom. The same is true of a Ca atom, which has the configuration $[\mathrm{Ar}]4s^2$, resembling that of its congener Mg, which is $[\mathrm{Ne}]3s^2$.

Ten electrons can be accommodated in the five 3*d* orbitals, which accounts for the electron configurations of scandium to zinc. The building-up principle has less clear-cut predictions about the ground-state configurations of these elements and a

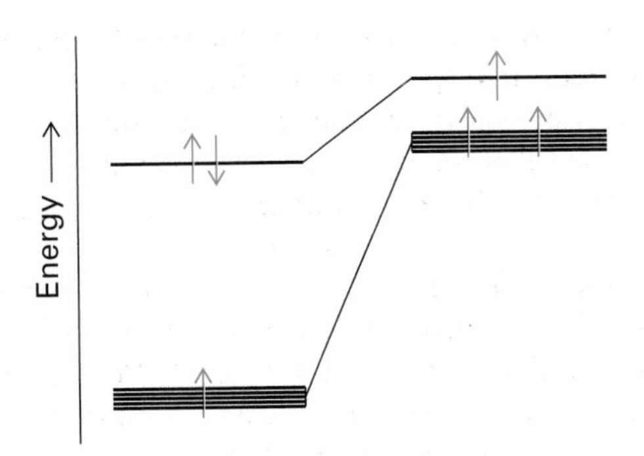

Fig. 13.17 Strong electron–electron repulsions in the 3*d* orbitals are minimized in the ground state of a scandium atom if the atom has the configuration $[Ar]3d^1 4s^2$ (shown on the left) instead of $[Ar]3d^2 4s^1$ (shown on the right). The total energy of the atom is lower when it has the configuration $[Ar]3d^1 s^2$ despite the cost of populating the high-energy 4*s* orbital.

simple analysis no longer works. Calculations show that for these atoms the energies of the 3*d* orbitals are always lower than the energy of the 4*s* orbital. However, spectroscopic results show that Sc has the configuration $[Ar]3d^1 4s^2$, instead of $[Ar]3d^3$ or $[Ar]3d^2 4s^1$. To understand this observation, we have to consider the nature of electron–electron repulsions in 3*d* and 4*s* orbitals. The most probable distance of a 3*d* electron from the nucleus is less than that for a 4*s* electron, so two 3*d* electrons repel each other more strongly than two 4*s* electrons. As a result, Sc has the configuration $[Ar]3d^1 4s^2$ rather than the two alternatives, because then the strong electron–electron repulsions in the 3*d* orbitals are minimized. The total energy of the atom is least despite the cost of allowing electrons to populate the high-energy 4*s* orbital (Fig. 13.17). The effect just described is generally true for scandium through zinc, so their electron configurations are of the form $[Ar]3d^n 4s^2$, where $n = 1$ for scandium and $n = 10$ for zinc.

At gallium, the energy of the 3*d* orbitals has fallen so far below those of the 4*s* and 4*p* orbitals that they (the full 3*d* orbitals) can be largely ignored, and the building-up principle can be used in the same way as in preceding periods. Now the 4*s* and 4*p* subshells constitute the valence shell, and the period terminates with krypton. Because 18 electrons have intervened since argon, this period is the first **long period** of the periodic table. The existence of the ***d* block** (the 'transition metals') reflects the stepwise occupation of the 3*d* orbitals, and the subtle shades of energy differences along this series gives rise to the rich complexity of inorganic (and bioinorganic) *d*-metal chemistry. A similar intrusion of the *f* orbitals in Periods 6 and 7 accounts for the existence of the ***f* block** of the periodic table (the lanthanoids and actinoids).

13.13 The configurations of cations and anions

The configurations of cations of elements in the *s*, *p*, and *d* blocks of the periodic table are derived by removing electrons from the ground-state configuration of the neutral atom in a specific order. First, we remove any valence *p* electrons, then the valence *s* electrons, and then as many *d* electrons as are necessary to achieve the stated charge. For instance, because the configuration of Fe is $[Ar]3d^6 4s^2$, an Fe^{3+} cation has the configuration $[Ar]3d^5$.

The configurations of anions are derived by continuing the building-up procedure and adding electrons to the neutral atom until the configuration of the next noble gas has been reached. Thus, the configuration of an O^{2-} ion is achieved by adding two electrons to $[He]2s^2 2p^4$, giving $[He]2s^2 2p^6$, the configuration of Ne.

Self-test 13.7

Predict the electron configurations of (a) a Cu^{2+} ion and (b) an S^{2-} ion.

[*Answer:* (a) $[Ar]3d^9$, (b) $[Ne]3s^2 3p^6$]

Periodic trends in atomic properties

The periodic recurrence of analogous ground-state electron configurations as the atomic number increases accounts for the periodic variation in the properties of atoms. Here we concentrate on two aspects of atomic periodicity: atomic radius and ionization energy. Both can be correlated with the

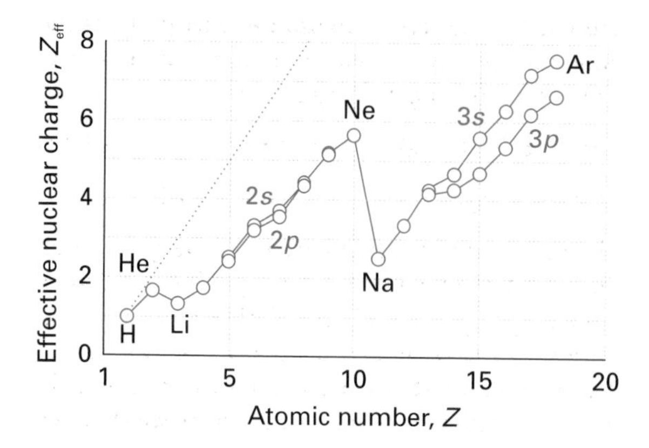

Fig. 13.18 The variation of the effective atomic number with actual atomic number for the elements of the first three periods. The value of Z_{eff} depends on the identity of the orbital occupied by the electron: we show the values only for the valence electrons.

Table 13.1
Atomic radii of main-group elements, r/pm

Li 157	**Be** 112	**B** 88	**C** 77	**N** 74	**O** 66	**F** 64
Na 191	**Mg** 160	**Al** 143	**Si** 118	**P** 110	**S** 104	**Cl** 99
K 235	**Ca** 197	**Ga** 153	**Ge** 122	**As** 121	**Se** 117	**Br** 114
Rb 250	**Sr** 215	**In** 167	**Sn** 158	**Sb** 141	**Te** 137	**I** 133
Cs 272	**Ba** 224	**Tl** 171	**Pb** 175	**Bi** 182	**Po** 167	

effective nuclear charge, and Fig. 13.18 shows how this quantity varies through the first three periods.

The textbook's web site contains links to databases of atomic properties.

13.14 Atomic radius

The **atomic radius** of an element is half the distance between the centres of neighbouring atoms in a solid (such as Cu) or, for non-metals, in a homonuclear molecule (such as H_2 or S_8). It is of great significance in chemistry, because the size of an atom is one of the most important controls on the number of chemical bonds the atom can form. Moreover, the size and shape of a molecule depend on the sizes of the atoms of which it is composed, and molecular shape and size are crucial aspects of a molecule's biological function. Atomic radius also has an important technological aspect, because the similarity of the atomic radii of the *d*-block elements is the main reason why they can be blended together to form so many different alloys, particularly varieties of steel. If there is one single attribute of an element that determines its chemical properties (either directly, or indirectly through the variation of other properties), then it is atomic radius.

In general, atomic radii decrease from left to right across a period and increase down each group

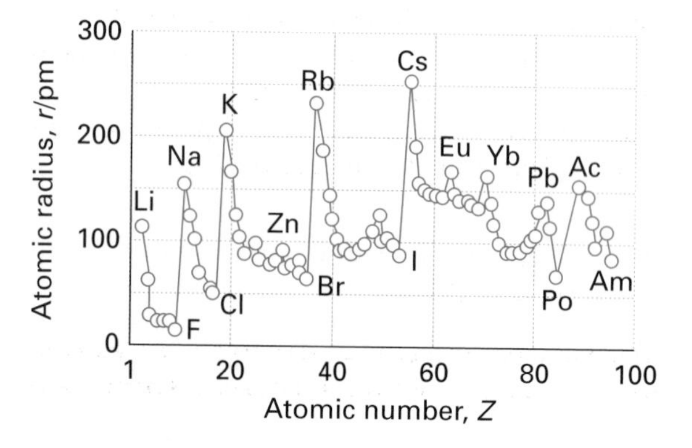

Fig. 13.19 The variation of atomic radius through the periodic table. Note the contraction of radius following the lanthanoids in Period 6 (following Yb, ytterbium).

(Table 13.1 and Fig. 13.19). The decrease across a period can be traced to the increase in nuclear charge, which draws the electrons in closer to the nucleus. The increase in nuclear charge is partly cancelled by the increase in the number of electrons, but because electrons are spread over a region of space, one electron does not fully shield one nuclear charge, so the increase in nuclear charge dominates. The increase in atomic radius down a group (despite the increase in nuclear charge) is explained by the fact that the valence shells of successive periods correspond to higher principal quantum numbers. That is, successive periods correspond to the start and then completion of successive (and more distant) shells of the atom that surround each other like the successive layers of an onion. The need to occupy a more distant shell leads to a larger atom despite the increased nuclear charge.

A modification of the increase down a group is encountered in Period 6, as the radii of the atoms late in the *d* block and in the following regions of the *p* block are not as large as would be expected by simple extrapolation down the group. The reason can be traced to the fact that in Period 6 the *f* orbitals are in the process of being occupied. An *f* electron is a very inefficient shielder of nuclear charge (for reasons connected with its radial extension) and, as the atomic number increases from La to Yb, there is a considerable contraction in radius. By the time the *d* block resumes (at lutetium, Lu), the poorly shielded but considerably increased nuclear charge has drawn in the surrounding electrons, and the atoms are compact. They are so compact, that the metals in this region of the periodic table (iridium to lead) are very dense. The reduction in radius below that expected by extrapolation from preceding periods is called the **lanthanide contraction.**

13.15 Ionization energy and electron affinity

The minimum energy necessary to remove an electron from a many-electron atom is its **first ionization energy**, I_1. The **second ionization energy**, I_2, is the minimum energy needed to remove a second electron (from the singly charged cation):

$$E(g) \rightarrow E^{+}(g) + e^{-}(g) \qquad I_1 = E(E^{+}) - E(E) \qquad (13.12)$$

$$E^{+}(g) \rightarrow E^{2+}(g) + e^{-}(g) \qquad I_2 = E(E^{2+}) - E(E^{+})$$

The variation of the first ionization energy through the periodic table is shown in Fig. 13.20 and some numerical values are given in Table 13.2. The ionization energy of an element plays a central role in determining the ability of its atoms to participate in bond formation (as bond formation, as we shall see

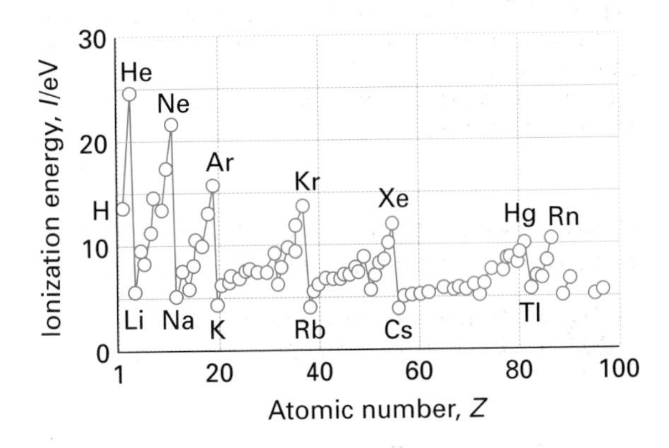

Fig. 13.20 The periodic variation of the first ionization energies of the elements.

Table 13.2 *First ionization energies of main-group elements, I/eV* *

H 13.60							**He** 24.59
Li 5.32	**Be** 9.32	**B** 8.30	**C** 11.26	**N** 14.53	**O** 13.62	**F** 17.42	**Ne** 21.56
Na 5.14	**Mg** 7.65	**Al** 5.98	**Si** 8.15	**P** 10.49	**S** 10.36	**Cl** 12.97	**Ar** 15.76
K 4.34	**Ca** 6.11	**Ga** 6.00	**Ge** 7.90	**As** 9.81	**Se** 9.75	**Br** 11.81	**Kr** 14.00
Rb 4.18	**Sr** 5.70	**In** 5.79	**Sn** 7.34	**Sb** 8.64	**Te** 9.01	**I** 10.45	**Xe** 12.13
Cs 3.89	**Ba** 5.21	**Tl** 6.11	**Pb** 7.42	**Bi** 7.29	**Po** 8.42	**At** 9.64	**Rn** 10.78

* 1 eV = 96.485 kJ mol^{-1}. See also Table 3.2.

in Chapter 14, is a consequence of the relocation of electrons from one atom to another). After atomic radius, ionization energy is the most important property for determining an element's chemical characteristics.

Lithium has a low first ionization energy: its outermost electron is well-shielded from the weakly charged nucleus by the core ($Z_{eff} = 1.3$ compared with $Z = 3$) and it is easily removed. Beryllium has a higher nuclear charge than lithium, and its outermost electron (one of the two 2*s* electrons) is more difficult to remove: its ionization energy is larger. The ionization energy decreases between beryllium and boron because in the latter the outermost electron occupies a 2*p* orbital and is less strongly bound than if it had been a 2*s* electron. The ionization energy increases between boron and carbon because the latter's outermost electron is also 2*p* and the nuclear charge has increased. Nitrogen has a still higher ionization energy because of the further increase in nuclear charge.

There is now a kink in the curve because the ionization energy of oxygen is lower than would be expected by simple extrapolation. At oxygen a 2*p* orbital must become doubly occupied, and the electron–electron repulsions are increased above what would be expected by simple extrapolation along the row. (The kink is less pronounced in the next row, between phosphorus and sulfur, because their orbitals are more diffuse.) The values for oxygen, fluorine, and neon fall roughly on the same line, the increase of their ionization energies reflecting the increasing attraction of the nucleus for the outermost electrons.

The outermost electron in sodium is 3*s*. It is far from the nucleus, and the latter's charge is shielded by the compact, complete neon-like core. As a result, the ionization energy of sodium is substantially lower than that of neon. The periodic cycle starts again along this row, and the variation of the ionization energy can be traced to similar reasons.

The **electron affinity**, E_{ea}, is the difference in energy between a neutral atom and its anion. It is the energy *released* in the process

$$E(g) + e^-(g) \rightarrow E^-(g)$$

$$E_{ea} = E(E) - E(E^-) \qquad (13.13a)$$

The electron affinity is positive if the anion has a lower energy than the neutral atom. Care should be taken to distinguish the electron affinity from the electron-gain enthalpy (Section 3.2): they have very similar numerical values but differ in sign:

Table 13.3 *Electron affinities of main-group elements, E_{ea}/eV* *

H +0.75							He <0†
Li +0.62	Be −0.19	B +0.28	C +1.26	N −0.07	O +1.46	F +3.40	Ne −0.30†
Na +0.55	Mg −0.22	Al +0.46	Si +1.38	P +0.46	S +2.08	Cl +3.62	Ar −0.36†
K +0.50	Ca −1.99	Ga +0.3	Ge +1.20	As +0.81	Se +2.02	Br +3.37	Kr −0.40†
Rb +0.49	Sr +1.51	In +0.3	Sn +1.20	Sb +1.05	Te +1.97	I +3.06	Xe −0.42†
Cs +0.47	Ba −0.48	Tl +0.2	Pb +0.36	Bi +0.95	Po +1.90	At +2.80	Rn −0.42†

* 1 eV = 96.485 kJ mol^{-1}. See also Table 3.3.
† Calculated.

$$E(g) + e^-(g) \rightarrow E^-(g)$$

$$\Delta_{eg}H^{\ominus} = H^{\ominus}_m(E^-) - H^{\ominus}_m(E) \quad (13.13b)$$

Electron affinities (Table 13.3) vary much less systematically through the periodic table than ionization energies. Broadly speaking, however, the highest electron affinities are found close to fluorine. In the halogens, the incoming electron enters the valence shell and experiences a strong attraction from the nucleus. The electron affinities of the noble gases are negative—which means that the anion has a higher energy than the neutral atom—because the incoming electron occupies an orbital outside the closed valence shell. It is then far from the nucleus and repelled by the electrons of the closed shells. The first electron affinity of oxygen is positive for the same reason as for the halogens. However, the second electron affinity (for the formation of O^{2-} from O^-) is strongly negative because, although the incoming electron enters the valence shell, it experiences a strong repulsion from the net negative charge of the O^- ion.

The spectra of complex atoms

The spectra of many-electron atoms can be very complicated, yet that complexity contains a great deal of detailed information about the interactions between electrons. Here we consider the notation used to specify the states of atoms. Chemists need to know how to designate the states of atoms when they are describing photochemical events in the atmosphere and the chemical composition of stars (Box 13.1). We also describe an interaction that has important consequences in molecular spectroscopy and magnetism.

The textbook's web site contains links to databases of atomic spectra.

13.16 Term symbols

For historical reasons, the energy level of an atom is called a **term** and the notation used to specify the term is called a **term symbol**. A term symbol looks like $^3D_2$, with each component (the 3, the D, and the 2) telling us something about the angular momentum of the electrons in the atom.

The letter (D, for instance) tells us the total orbital angular momentum of the electrons in the atom. To find it, we work out the **total orbital angular momentum quantum number**, L, in the manner described below, and then we use the following code:

L	0	1	2	3...
	S	P	D	F...

Note that the code is the same as for orbitals, but we use upper-case Roman letters. To find L we identify the orbital angular momentum quantum numbers (l_1 and l_2 for instance) of the electrons in the valence shell of the atom, and then form the following series:

$$L = l_1 + l_2, l_1 + l_2 - 1, \ldots, |l_1 - l_2|$$

This and the analogous series introduced later are called **Clebsch–Gordan series**. The modulus signs (|...|) simply mean that the series terminates at a positive value. The highest total orbital angular momentum occurs when the two electrons are orbiting in the same direction (in classical terms, like the planets round the Sun); the lowest occurs when they are orbiting in opposite directions.

Illustration 13.6

The terms of a configuration

Suppose we are considering the excited-state configuration of carbon [He]$2s^22p^13p^1$ in which a $2p$ electron has been promoted to a $3p$ orbital. We concentrate on the p electrons because the s electrons have no orbital angular momentum. For each electron $l = 1$ (that is, $l_1 = 1$ and $l_2 = 1$ for the two electrons we are considering). It follows that

$$L = 1 + 1, 1 + 1 - 1, \ldots, |1 - 1| = 2, 1, 0$$

It follows that the configuration gives rise to D, P, and S terms, corresponding to the three allowed values of the total orbital angular momentum.

Next, we consider the total **spin angular momentum quantum number**, S. This quantum number is obtained in the same way as L, by adding together the individual spin angular momentum quantum numbers:

Box 13.1 *Spectroscopy of stars*

The bulk of stellar material consists of neutral and ionized forms of hydrogen and helium atoms, with helium being the product of 'hydrogen burning' by nuclear fusion. However, nuclear fusion also makes heavier elements. It is generally accepted that the outer layers of stars are composed of lighter elements, such as H, He, C, N, O, and Ne in both neutral and ionized forms. Heavier elements, including neutral and ionized forms of Si, Mg, Ca, S, and Ar, are found closer to the stellar core. The core itself contains the heaviest elements and ^{56}Fe is particularly abundant because it is very stable. All of these elements are in the gas phase on account of the very high temperatures in stellar interiors. For example, the temperature is estimated to be 3.6 MK (1 MK = 10^6 K) halfway to the centre of the Sun.

Astronomers use spectroscopic techniques to determine the chemical composition of stars because each element, and indeed each isotope of an element, has a characteristic spectral signature that is transmitted through space by the star's light. To understand the spectra of stars, we must first know why they shine. Nuclear reactions in the dense stellar interior generate radiation that travels to less dense outer layers. Absorption and re-emission of photons by the atoms and ions in the interior give rise to a quasi-continuum of radiation energy that is emitted into space by a thin layer of gas called the *photosphere*. To a good approximation, the distribution of energy emitted from a star's photosphere resembles the Planck distribution for a very hot black body (Section 12.1). For example, the energy distribution of our Sun's photosphere may be modelled by a Planck distribution with an effective temperature of 5800 K. Superimposed on the black-body radiation continuum are sharp absorption and emission lines from neutral atoms and ions present in the photosphere. Analysis of stellar radiation with a spectrometer mounted onto a telescope, such as the Hubble Space Telescope, yields the chemical composition of the star's photosphere by comparison with known spectra of the elements. The data can also reveal the presence of small molecules, such as CN, C_2, TiO, and ZrO, in certain 'cold' stars, which are stars with relatively low effective temperatures.

The two outermost layers of a star are the *chromosphere*, a region just above the photosphere, and the *corona*, a region above the chromosphere that can be seen (with proper care) during eclipses. The photosphere, chromosphere, and corona comprise a star's 'atmosphere'. Our Sun's chromosphere is much less dense than its photosphere and its temperature is much higher, rising to about 10 kK (1 kK = 10^3 K). The reasons for this increase in temperature are not fully understood. The temperature of our Sun's corona is very high, rising up to 1.5 MK, so black-body emission is strong from the X-ray to the radiofrequency region of the spectrum. The spectrum of the Sun's corona is dominated by emission lines from electronically excited species, such as neutral atoms and a number of highly ionized species. The most intense emission lines in the visible range are from the Fe^{13+} ion at 530.3 nm, the Fe^{9+} ion at 637.4 nm, and the Ca^{4+} ion at 569.4 nm.

Because our telescopes detect only light from the outer layers of stars, their overall chemical composition must be inferred from theoretical work on their interiors and from spectral analysis of their atmospheres. Data on our Sun indicate that it is 92 per cent hydrogen and 7.8 per cent helium. The remaining 0.2 per cent is due to heavier elements, among which C, N, O, Ne, and Fe are the most abundant. More advanced analysis of spectra also permits the determination of other properties of stars, such as their relative speeds and their effective temperatures.

Exercise 1 Hydrogen is the most abundant element in all stars (and hence in the Universe). However, neither absorption nor emission lines due to neutral hydrogen are found in the spectra of stars with effective temperatures higher than 25 000 K. Account for this observation.

Exercise 2 The distribution of isotopes of an element may yield clues about the nuclear reactions that occur in the interior of a star. Show that it is possible to use spectroscopy to confirm the presence of both $^4He^+$ and $^3He^+$ in a star by calculating the wavenumbers of the $n = 3 \rightarrow n = 2$ and of the $n = 2 \rightarrow n = 1$ transitions for each isotope.

$$S = s_1 + s_2, s_1 + s_2 - 1, \ldots, |s_1 - s_2|$$

For electrons, $s = \frac{1}{2}$, so for two electrons

$$S = \tfrac{1}{2} + \tfrac{1}{2}, \tfrac{1}{2} + \tfrac{1}{2} - 1, \ldots, |\tfrac{1}{2} - \tfrac{1}{2}| = 1, 0$$

Then the value of S is represented in the term symbol by writing the **multiplicity** of the term, the value of $2S + 1$, as a left superscript. The higher the multiplicity of a term, the more electrons there are in the atom that are spinning in the same direction.

Illustration 13.7

Singlet and triplet terms

For the excited configuration of carbon, $[He]2s^22p^13p^1$, that we are considering, the two p electrons each have $s = \frac{1}{2}$, so $S = 1, 0$. The corresponding multiplicities are $2 \times 1 + 1 = 3$ (a 'triplet' term) and $2 \times 0 + 1 = 1$ (a 'singlet' term). The corresponding term symbols are

Triplet terms: $^3D, ^3P, ^3S$ Singlet terms: $^1D, ^1P, ^1S$

A note on good practice Except in casual conversation, the name 'state' should not be used in place of 'term'. As we shall see, in general a term consists of a number of different states.

Finally, we come to the right subscript. This label is the **total angular momentum quantum number,** J, the total angular momentum being the sum of the orbital angular momentum and the spin angular momentum. We find J (a positive number) by forming the series

$$J = L + S, L + S - 1, \ldots, |L - S|$$

If there are many electrons having spins in the same direction as their orbital motion, then J is large. If the spins are aligned against the orbital motion, then J is small. Each value of J corresponds to a particular **level** of a term.

Illustration 13.8

Identifying the levels

The levels that occur in the ^3D term are found by setting $L = 2$ and $S = 1$; then

$$J = 2 + 1, 2 + 1 - 1, \ldots, |2 - 1| = 3, 2, 1$$

That is, the levels of the ^3D term are $^3D_3$, $^3D_2$, and $^3D_1$ (note that there are three levels for this triplet term). In the $^3D_3$ level, not only are the two p electrons orbiting in the same sense, the two spins are spinning in the same direction as each other, and the total spin is in the same direction as the orbital angular momentum. In $^3D_1$ the total spin is aligned oppositely to the total orbital momentum and the overall total angular momentum is relatively low.

A note on good practice 'Levels' are still not 'states'. Each level with a quantum number J consists of $2J + 1$ individual states distinguished by the quantum number M_J.

Self-test 13.8

What terms and levels can arise from the configuration $\ldots 4p^13d^1$?

[*Answer:* $^1F_3$, $^1D_2$, $^1P_1$, $^3F_{4,3,2}$, $^3D_{3,2,1}$, $^3P_{2,1,0}$]

The terms of a configuration in general have different energies because they correspond to the occupation of different orbitals and to different numbers of electrons with parallel spins. Typically, Hund's rule enables us to identify the term of lowest energy as the one with the greatest number of parallel spins (Section 13.11), as parallel spins tend to stay apart and that allows the atom to shrink slightly. In other words,

The term with the greatest multiplicity lies lowest in energy.

In our example, the triplet terms lie lower than the singlet terms, so one of the terms ^3D, ^3P, ^3S lies lowest. It is also commonly found that, having sorted the terms by multiplicity,

The term with the greatest orbital angular momentum lies lowest in energy.

Classically, we can think of the term with the greatest orbital angular momentum as having electrons circulating in the same direction, like cars on a traffic circle, and therefore being able to stay far apart. We therefore predict that the ^3D term will lie lowest of all the terms arising from the

$[He]2s^22p^13p^1$ configuration. To find which of the three *levels* of this term lies lowest, we need another concept.

13.17 Spin–orbit coupling

An electron is a charged particle, so its orbital angular momentum gives rise to a magnetic field, just as an electric current in a loop gives rise to a magnetic field in an electromagnet. That is, an electron with orbital angular momentum acts like a tiny bar magnet. An electron also has a spin angular momentum, and this intrinsic 'spinning motion' means that it also acts as a tiny bar magnet. The magnet arising from the spin interacts with the magnet arising from the orbital motion and gives rise to the interaction called **spin–orbit coupling.**

The two magnets have a higher energy when they are parallel than when they are antiparallel (Fig. 13.21). However, because the relative orientation of the magnets reflects the relative orientation of the orbital and spin angular momenta, the energy of the atom depends on the total angular momentum quantum number J (because its value also reflects the relative orientation of the two kinds of momentum). A low energy is obtained when the angular momenta, and therefore the bar magnets, are antiparallel to each other. That arrangement of angular momenta corresponds to a low value of J. Therefore, we can predict that the level with the lowest value of J will lie lowest in energy. In our current example, we predict that the lowest level of the ^3D term is $^3D_1$. A more general statement, which applies to many-electron systems, is as follows:

For atoms with shells that are less than half full, the level with lowest J lies lowest in energy; for atoms with shells that are more than half full, the level with highest J lies lowest.

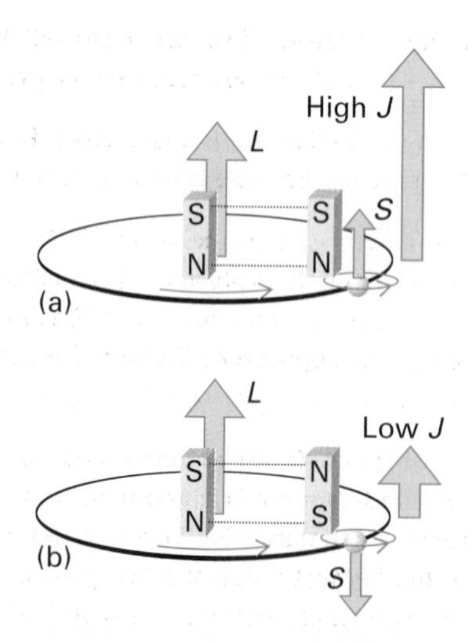

Fig. 13.21 The magnetic interaction responsible for spin–orbit coupling. (a) A high total angular momentum corresponds to a parallel arrangements of magnetic moments (represented by the bar magnets), and hence a high energy. (b) A low total angular momentum corresponds to an antiparallel arrangements of magnetic moments, and hence a low energy. Note that the difference in energy is not due *directly* to the differences in total angular momentum: the total simply tells us the relative orientations of the two magnetic moments.

The strength of the spin–orbit coupling increases sharply with atomic number. In Period 2 atoms it gives rise to splittings between levels of the order of 10^2 cm^{-1}, but in Period 3 the difference approaches 10^3 cm^{-1}. We can understand this increase by thinking about the source of the orbital magnetic field. To do so, imagine that we are riding on the electron as it orbits the nucleus. From our viewpoint, the nucleus appears to orbit around us (rather as the pre-Copernicans thought the Sun revolved around the Earth). If the nucleus has a high atomic number it will have a high charge, we shall be at the centre of a strong electric current, and we experience a strong magnetic field. If the nucleus has a low atomic number, we experience a feeble magnetic field arising from the low current that encircles us.

Spin–orbit coupling has important consequences in photochemistry and in particular for the existence of the property of 'phosphorescence', which we discuss in Chapter 18.

13.18 Selection rules

Now that we have described the energy levels of complex atoms, we can decide which spectroscopic transitions are allowed or forbidden. We have seen that spectroscopic selection rules arise from the conservation of angular momentum during a transition and from the fact that a photon has a spin of 1. They can therefore be expressed in terms of the term symbols, because the latter carry information about angular momentum. A detailed analysis leads to the following rules:[9]

$$\Delta S = 0 \qquad \Delta L = 0, \pm 1 \quad \Delta l = \pm 1$$

$$\Delta J = 0, \pm 1, \text{ but } J = 0 \leftrightarrow J = 0 \text{ is forbidden}$$

The rule about ΔS (no change of overall spin) stems from the fact that the light does not affect the spin directly. The rules about ΔL and Δl express the fact that the orbital angular momentum of an individual electron must change (so $\Delta l = \pm 1$), but whether or not this results in an overall change of orbital momentum depends on the coupling of angular momenta.

[9] These selection rules apply strictly for relatively light atoms, those near the top of the periodic table. As the atomic number increases, the rules progressively fail on account of significant spin–orbit coupling. So, for example, transitions between singlet and triplet states are allowed in heavy atoms.

CHECKLIST OF KEY IDEAS

You should now be familiar with the following concepts:

☐ 1 Hydrogenic atoms are atoms with a single electron; their energies are given by $E_n = -hcRZ^2/n^2$, with $n = 1, 2, \ldots$.

☐ 2 The wavefunctions of hydrogenic atoms are labelled with three quantum numbers, the principal quantum number $n = 1, 2, \ldots$, the orbital angular momentum quantum number $l = 0, 1, \ldots, n-1$, and the magnetic quantum number $m_l = l, l-1, \ldots, -l$.

☐ 3 s Orbitals are spherically symmetrical and have non-zero amplitude at the nucleus.

☐ 4 A radial distribution function, $P(r)$, is the probability density for finding an electron between r and $r + \delta r$, and for s orbitals $P(r) = 4\pi r^2\psi^2$.

☐ 5 The magnitude of the orbital angular momentum of an electron is $\{l(l+1)\}^{1/2}\hbar$ and the component of angular momentum about an axis is $m_l\hbar$.

☐ 6 An electron possesses an intrinsic angular momentum, its spin, which is described by the quantum numbers $s = \frac{1}{2}$ and $m_s = \pm\frac{1}{2}$.

☐ 7 A selection rule is a statement about which spectroscopic transitions are allowed; for hydrogenic atoms, $\Delta l = \pm 1$ and $\Delta m_l = 0, \pm 1$.

☐ 8 In the orbital approximation, each electron in a many-electron atom is supposed to occupy its own orbital.

☐ 9 The Pauli exclusion principle states that no more than two electrons may occupy any given orbital and if two electrons do occupy one orbital, then their spins must be paired.

☐ 10 In a many-electron atom, the orbitals of a given shell lie in the order $s < p < d < f$ as a result of the effects of penetration and shielding.

☐ 11 Atomic radii decrease from left to right across a period and increase down a group.

☐ 12 Ionization energies increase from left to right across a period and decrease down a group.

☐ 13 Electron affinities are highest towards the top right of the periodic table (near fluorine).

☐ 14 A term symbol has the form ${}^{2S+1}\{L\}_J$, where $2S + 1$ is the multiplicity and $\{L\}$ is a letter denoting the value of L; the values of S, L, and J are given by the appropriate Clebsch–Gordan series of the form $j = j_1 + j_2, j_1 + j_2 - 1, \ldots, |j_1 - j_2|$.

☐ 15 For a given configuration (and most reliably for the ground-state configuration) the term with the greatest multiplicity lies lowest in energy, that with the highest value of L lies lowest, and for atoms with shells that are less than half full, the level with the lowest J lies lowest.

☐ 16 Different levels of a term have different energies on account of spin–orbit coupling, and the strength of spin–orbit coupling increases sharply with increasing atomic number.

☐ 17 The selection rules for spectroscopic transitions in complex atoms are: $\Delta S = 0$, $\Delta L = 0, \pm 1$, $\Delta l = \pm 1$, $\Delta J = 0, \pm 1$, but $J = 0 \leftrightarrow J = 0$ is forbidden.

FURTHER INFORMATION 13.1

The Pauli principle

The Pauli exclusion principle is a special case of a general statement called the *Pauli principle*:

When the labels of any two identical fermions are exchanged, the total wavefunction changes sign. When the labels of any two identical bosons are exchanged, the total wavefunction retains the same sign.

A *fermion* is a particle with half-integral spin (such as electrons, protons, and neutrons); a *boson* is a particle with integral spin (such as photons, which have spin 1). The Pauli *exclusion* principle applies only to fermions. By 'total wavefunction' is meant the entire wavefunction, including the spin of the particles.

Consider the wavefunction for two electrons $\Psi(1,2)$. The Pauli principle implies that it is a fact of nature that the wavefunction must change sign if we interchange the labels 1 and 2 wherever they occur in the function: $\Psi(2,1) = -\Psi(1,2)$. Suppose the two electrons in an atom occupy an orbital ψ, then in the orbital approximation the overall wavefunction is $\psi(1)\psi(2)$. To apply the Pauli principle, we must deal with the total wavefunction, the wavefunction including spin. There are several possibilities for two spins: the state $\alpha(1)\alpha(2)$ corresponds to parallel spins whereas (for technical reasons related to the cancellation of each spin's angular momentum by the other) the combination $\alpha(1)\beta(2) - \beta(1)\alpha(2)$ corresponds to paired spins. The total wavefunction of the system is one of the following:

Parallel spins: $\psi(1)\psi(2)\alpha(1)\alpha(2)$

Paired spins: $\psi(1)\psi(2)\{\alpha(1)\beta(2) - \beta(1)\alpha(2)\}$

The Pauli principle, however, asserts that for a wavefunction to be acceptable (for electrons), it must change sign when the electrons are exchanged. In each case, exchanging the labels 1 and 2 converts the factor $\psi(1)\psi(2)$ into $\psi(2)\psi(1)$, which is the same, because the order of multiplying the functions does not change the value of the product. The same is true of $\alpha(1)\alpha(2)$. Therefore, the first combination is not allowed, because it does not change sign. The second combination, however, changes to

$$\psi(2)\psi(1)\{\alpha(1)\beta(2) - \beta(1)\alpha(2)\}$$
$$= -\psi(1)\psi(2)\{\alpha(1)\beta(2) - \beta(1)\alpha(2)\}$$

This combination does change sign (it is 'antisymmetric'), and is therefore acceptable.

Now we see that the only possible state of two electrons in the same orbital allowed by the Pauli principle is the one that has paired spins. This is the content of the Pauli exclusion principle. The exclusion principle is irrelevant when the orbitals occupied by the electrons are different, and both electrons may then have (but need not have) the same spin state. Nevertheless, even then the overall wavefunction must still be antisymmetric overall, and must still satisfy the Pauli principle itself.

DISCUSSION QUESTIONS

13.1 List and describe the significance of the quantum numbers needed to specify the internal state of a hydrogenic atom.

13.2 Explain the significance of (a) a boundary surface and (b) the radial distribution function for hydrogenic orbitals.

13.3 Describe the orbital approximation for the wavefunction of a many-electron atom. What are the limitations of the approximation?

13.4 Specify and account for the selections rules for transitions in (a) hydrogenic atoms and (b) many-electron atoms.

EXERCISES

The symbol ‡ indicates that calculus is required.

13.5 Calculate the wavelength of the line with $n = 5$ in the Balmer series of the spectrum of atomic hydrogen.

13.6 The frequency of one of the lines in the Paschen series of the spectrum of atomic hydrogen is 2.7415×10^{15} Hz. Identify the principal quantum number of the upper state in the transition.

13.7 One of the terms of the H atom is at 27 414 cm^{-1}. What is (a) the wavenumber, (b) the energy of the term with which it combines to produce light of wavelength 486.1 nm?

13.8 The Rydberg constant, eqn 13.4, depends on the mass of the nucleus. What is the difference in wavenumbers of the $2p \rightarrow 1s$ transition in hydrogen and deuterium?

13.9 What transition in He^+ has the same frequency (disregarding mass differences) as the $2p \rightarrow 1s$ transition in H?

13.10 Predict the ionization energy of Li^{2+} given that the ionization energy of He^+ is 54.36 eV.

13.11 How many orbitals are present in the N shell of an atom?

13.12 The 'Humphreys series' is another group of lines in the spectrum of atomic hydrogen. It begins at 12 368 nm and has been traced to 3281.4 nm. (a) What are the transitions involved? (b) What are the wavelengths of the intermediate transitions?

13.13 At what wavelength would you expect the longest wavelength transition of the Humphreys series to occur in He^+? (*Hint.* The energy levels of hydrogenic atoms and ions are proportional to Z^2.)

13.14 A series of lines in the spectrum of atomic hydrogen lies at 656.46, 486.27, 434.17, and 410.29 nm. (a) What is the wavelength of the next line in the series? (b) What is the ionization energy of the atom when it is in the lower state of the transitions?

13.15 The Li^{2+} ion is hydrogenic and has a Lyman series at 740 747, 877 924, 925 933 cm^{-1}, and beyond. (a) Show that the energy levels are of the form $-hcR_{Li}/n^2$ and find the value of R_{Li} for this ion. (b) Go on to predict the wavenumbers of the two longest wavelength transitions of the Balmer series of the ion and (c) find the ionization energy of the ion.

13.16 At what radius does the probability of finding an electron in a small volume located at a point in the ground state of an H atom fall to 25 per cent of its maximum value?

13.17 At what radius in the H atom does the radial distribution function of the ground state have (a) 25 per cent, (b) 10 per cent of its maximum value?

13.18 What is the probability of finding an electron anywhere in one lobe of a *p* orbital given that it occupies the orbital?

13.19 What is the probability of finding the electron in a volume of 5.0 pm^3 centred on the nucleus in (a) a hydrogen atom, (b) a He^+ ion?

13.20 ‡What is the most probable distance of an electron from the nucleus in a hydrogen atom? (*Hint.* Look for a maximum in the radial distribution function.)

13.21 The (normalized) wavefunction for a 2*s* orbital in hydrogen is

$$\psi = \left(\frac{1}{32\pi a_0^3}\right)^{1/2}\left(2 - \frac{r}{a_0}\right)e^{-r/2a_0}$$

Calculate the probability of finding an electron that is described by this wavefunction in a volume of 1.0 pm^3 (a) centred on the nucleus, (b) at the Bohr radius, (c) at twice the Bohr radius.

13.22 Construct an expression for the radial distribution function of a hydrogenic 2*s* electron (see Exercise 13.21 for the form of the orbital), and plot the function against *r*. What is the most probable radius at which the electron will be found?

13.23 ‡For a more accurate determination of the most probable radius at which an electron will be found in an H2*s* orbital (Exercise 13.21), differentiate the radial distribution function to find where it is a maximum.

13.24 Locate the radial nodes in (a) the 3*s* orbital, (b) the 4*s* orbital of an H atom which is proportional to $24 - 36\rho + 12\rho^2 - \rho^3$, with $\rho = r/2a_0$.

13.25 The wavefunction of one of the *d* orbitals is proportional to $\sin\theta\cos\theta\cos\phi$. At what angles does it have nodal planes?

13.26 What is the orbital angular momentum (as multiples of $\hbar$) of an electron in the orbitals (a) 1*s*, (b) 3*s*, (c) 3*d*, (d) 2*p*, (e) 3*p*? Give the numbers of angular and radial nodes in each case.

13.27 State the orbital degeneracy of the levels in the hydrogen atom that have energy (a) $-hcR_H$, (b) $-\frac{1}{9}hcR_H$, and (c) $-\frac{1}{49}hcR_H$.

13.28 How many electrons can occupy subshells with the following values of *l*: (a) 0, (b) 3, (c) 5?

13.29 How is the ionization energy of an anion related to the electron affinity of the parent atom?

13.30 When ultraviolet radiation of wavelength 58.4 nm from a helium lamp is directed on to a sample of krypton, electrons are ejected with a speed of 1.59×10^6 m s^{-1}. Calculate the ionization energy of krypton.

13.31 If we lived in a four-dimensional world, there would be one *s* orbital, four *p* orbitals, and nine *d* orbitals in their respective subshells. (a) Suggest what form the periodic table might take for the first 24 elements. (b) Which elements (using their current names) would be noble gases?

13.32 What terms (expressed as S, D, etc.) can arise from the $[He]2s^22p^13d^1$ excited configuration of carbon?

13.33 What are the total spin angular momenta (reported as the value of S) that can arise from four electrons? (*Hint.* Use the Clebsch–Gordan series successively.)

13.34 What levels can the following terms possess: (a) ^1S, (b) ^3F, (c) ^5S, (d) ^5P?

13.35 The ground-state configuration of a Ti^{2+} ion is [Ar]$3d^2$. (a) What is the term of lowest energy and which level of that term lies lowest? (b) How many states belong to that lowest level?

13.36 Which of the following transitions are allowed in the normal electronic emission spectrum of an atom: (a) $2s \rightarrow 1s$, (b) $2p \rightarrow 1s$, (c) $3d \rightarrow 2p$, (d) $5d \rightarrow 2s$, (e) $5p \rightarrow 3s$?

13.37 To what orbitals may a $5f$ electron make spectroscopic transitions?

Chapter 14

The chemical bond

The **chemical bond**, a link between atoms, is central to all aspects of chemistry. Reactions make them and break them, and the structures of solids and individual molecules depend on them. The physical properties of individual molecules and of bulk samples of matter also stem in large part from the shifts in electron density that take place when atoms form bonds. The theory of the origin of the numbers, strengths, and three-dimensional arrangements of chemical bonds between atoms is called **valence theory**.

Valence theory is an attempt to explain the properties of molecules ranging from the smallest to the largest. For instance, it explains why N_2 is so inert that it acts as a diluent for the aggressive oxidizing power of atmospheric oxygen. At the other end of the scale, valence theory deals with the structural origins of the function of protein molecules and the molecular biology of DNA. The description of chemical bonding has become highly developed through the use of computers, and it is now possible to compute details of the electron distribution in molecules of almost any complexity. However, much can also be achieved in terms of a simple qualitative understanding of bond formation, and that is the initial focus of this chapter.

There are two major approaches to the calculation of molecular structure, **valence bond** (VB) **theory** and **molecular orbital** (MO) **theory**. Almost all modern computational work makes use of MO theory, and we concentrate on it in this chapter. VB theory, however, has left its imprint on the language of chemistry, and it is important to know the significance of terms that chemists use every day. The structure of this chapter is therefore as follows. First, we set out a few concepts common to all levels of description. Then we present the concepts of VB theory that continue to be used in chemistry (such as hybridization and resonance). Next, we present the basic ideas of MO theory, and finally we see how computational techniques pervade all current discussions of molecular structure.

Introductory concepts

Certain ideas of valence theory will be well known from introductory chemistry. This section reviews this background.

14.1 The classification of bonds

We distinguish between two types of bond:

An ionic bond is formed by the transfer of electrons from one atom to another and the consequent attraction between the ions so formed.

A covalent bond is formed when two atoms share a pair of electrons.

The character of a covalent bond, which we concentrate on in this chapter, was identified by G. N. Lewis (in 1916, before quantum mechanics was fully developed). We shall assume that Lewis's ideas are familiar, but for convenience they are reviewed in Appendix 4.2. In this chapter we develop the modern theory of chemical bond formation in terms of the quantum mechanical properties of electrons and set Lewis's ideas in a modern context. We shall see that ionic and covalent bonds are two extremes of a single type of bond. However, because there are certain aspects of ionic solids that require special attention, we treat them separately in Chapter 15.

Lewis's original theory was unable to account for the shapes adopted by molecules. The most elementary (but qualitatively quite successful) explanation of the shapes adopted by molecules is the **valence-shell electron pair repulsion** (VSEPR) **model** in which we suppose that the shape of a molecule is determined by the repulsions between electron pairs in the valence shell. This model is fully discussed in introductory chemistry texts, but we give a brief review of it in Appendix 4.3. Once again, the purpose of this chapter is to extend these elementary arguments and to indicate some of the contributions that quantum theory has made to understanding why a molecule adopts its characteristic shape.

14.2 Potential energy curves

All theories of molecular structure adopt the **Born–Oppenheimer approximation.** In this approximation, it is supposed that the nuclei, being so much heavier than an electron, move relatively slowly and may be treated as stationary while the electrons move around them. We can therefore think of the nuclei as being fixed at arbitrary locations, and then solve the Schrödinger equation for the electrons alone. The approximation is quite good for molecules in their electronic ground states, as calculations suggest that (in classical terms) the nuclei in H_2 move through only about 1 pm while the electron speeds through 1000 pm.

By invoking the Born–Oppenheimer approximation, we can select an internuclear separation in a diatomic molecule and solve the Schrödinger equation for the electrons for that nuclear separation. Then we can choose a different separation and repeat the calculation, and so on. In this way we can explore how the energy of the molecule varies with bond length and obtain a **molecular potential energy curve**, a graph showing how the molecular energy depends on the internuclear separation (Fig. 14.1). The graph is called a *potential* energy curve because the nuclei are stationary and contribute no kinetic

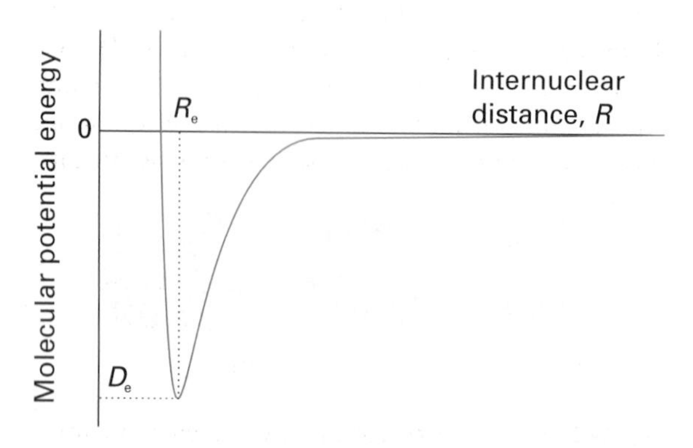

Fig. 14.1 A molecular potential energy curve. The equilibrium bond length R_e corresponds to the energy minimum D_e.

energy. Once the curve has been calculated, we can identify the **equilibrium bond length**, R_e, the internuclear separation at the minimum of the curve, and D_e, the depth of the minimum below the energy of the infinitely widely separated atoms. In Chapter 19 we shall also see that the narrowness of the potential well is an indication of the stiffness of the bond. Similar considerations apply to polyatomic molecules, where bond angles may be varied as well as bond lengths.

We shall now see how quantum mechanics can account for the features of the curve shown in Fig. 14.1. In particular, we shall justify the presence of a potential energy minimum, which is a manifestation of the energetic advantage of making a chemical bond.

Valence bond theory

In valence bond theory, a bond is regarded as forming when an electron in an atomic orbital on one atom pairs its spin with that of an electron in an atomic orbital on another atom (Fig. 14.2). To understand why this pairing leads to bonding, we have to examine the wavefunction for the two electrons that form the bond.

14.3 Diatomic molecules

We begin by considering the simplest possible chemical bond, the one in molecular hydrogen, H–H. When the two ground-state H atoms are far apart, we can be confident that electron 1 is in the 1*s* orbital of atom A, which we denote $\psi_A(1)$, and electron 2 is in the 1*s* orbital of atom B, which we denote $\psi_B(2)$. It is a general rule in quantum mechanics that the wavefunction for several non-interacting particles is the product of the wavefunctions for each particle, so we can write

$$\psi(1,2) = \psi_A(1)\psi_B(2)$$

When the two atoms are at their bonding distance, it may still be true that electron 1 is on A and electron 2 is on B. However, an equally likely arrangement is for electron 1 to escape from A and be found on B and for electron 2 to be on A. In this case the wavefunction is

$$\psi(1,2) = \psi_A(2)\psi_B(1)$$

Whenever two outcomes are equally likely, the rules of quantum mechanics tell us to add together the two corresponding wavefunctions. Therefore, the (unnormalized) wavefunction for the two electrons in a hydrogen molecule is

$$\psi_{H\text{–}H}(1,2) = \psi_A(1)\psi_B(2) + \psi_A(2)\psi_B(1) \qquad (14.1)$$

This expression is the VB wavefunction for the bond in molecular hydrogen. It expresses the idea that we cannot keep track of either electron, and that their distributions blend together. The wavefunction is only an approximation, because when the two atoms are close together, it is not true that the electrons do not interact. However, this approximate wavefunction is a reasonable starting point for all discussions of the VB theory of bonding.

For technical reasons related to the Pauli exclusion principle, we show in Derivation 14.1 that the wavefunction in eqn 14.1 can exist only if the two electrons it describes have opposite spins. It follows that the merging of orbitals that gives rise to a bond is accompanied by the pairing of the two electrons that contribute to it. Bonds do not form *because* electrons tend to pair: bonds are *allowed* to form by the electrons pairing their spins.

Because ψ is built from the merging of H1*s* orbitals, we can expect the overall distribution of the electrons in the molecule to be sausage-shaped (as in Fig. 14.2). A VB wavefunction with cylindrical symmetry around the internuclear axis is called a **σ bond.**[1] All VB wavefunctions are constructed in a similar way, by using the atomic orbitals available on the participating atoms. In general, therefore, the (unnormalized) VB wavefunction for an A–B bond is

$$\psi_{A\text{–}B}(1,2) = \psi_A(1)\psi_B(2) + \psi_A(2)\psi_B(1) \qquad (14.2)$$

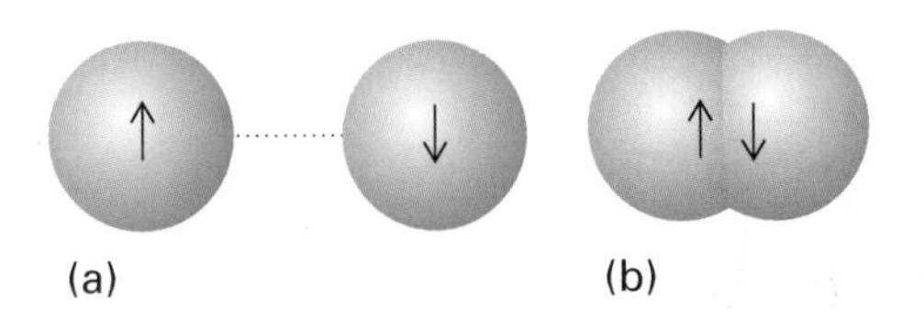

Fig. 14.2 In the valence bond theory, a σ bond is formed when two electrons in orbitals on neighbouring atoms pair (a) and the orbitals merge to form a cylindrical electron cloud (b).

Derivation 14.1

The Pauli principle and bond formation

The VB wavefunction for an A–B bond is given in eqn 14.2:

$$\psi_{A\text{-}B}(1,2) = \psi_A(1)\psi_B(2) + \psi_A(2)\psi_B(1)$$

This spatial component of the total wavefunction does not change sign when the labels 1 and 2 are interchanged. To formulate a wavefunction that obeys the Pauli principle (*Further information* 13.1) and changes sign when the labels 1 and 2 are interchanged, we must combine this symmetric spatial wavefunction with the antisymmetric spin function $\alpha(1)\beta(2) - \beta(1)\alpha(2)$ and write

$$\psi_{A\text{-}B}(2,1) = \{\psi_A(1)\psi_B(2) + \psi_A(2)\psi_B(1)\} \times \{\alpha(1)\beta(2) - \beta(1)\alpha(2)\}$$

This is the only permitted combination, and because $\alpha(1)\beta(2) - \beta(1)\alpha(2)$ represents a spin-paired state of the two electrons, we see that the Pauli principle requires the two electrons in the bond to be paired (↑↓).

To calculate the energy of a molecule for a series of internuclear separations R, we substitute the VB wavefunction into the Schrödinger equation for the molecule and carry out the necessary mathematical manipulations to calculate the corresponding values of the energy. When this energy is plotted against R, we get the curve shown in Fig. 14.1. As R decreases from infinity, the energy falls below that of two separated H atoms as each electron becomes free to migrate to the other atom. As can be seen from Fig. 14.3, as the two atoms approach each other, there is an accumulation of electron density between the two nuclei. The electrons attract the two nuclei, and the potential energy is lowered. However, this decrease in energy is counteracted by an increase in energy from the Coulombic repulsion between the two positively charged nuclei of charges Z_Ae and Z_Be, which has the form

$$V_{\text{nuc,nuc}} = \frac{Z_A Z_B e^2}{4\pi\varepsilon_0 R} \qquad (14.3)$$

(For H_2, $Z_A = Z_B = 1$.) This positive contribution to the energy becomes large as R becomes small. As a result, the total energy curve passes through a minimum and then climbs to a strongly positive value as the two nuclei are pressed together.

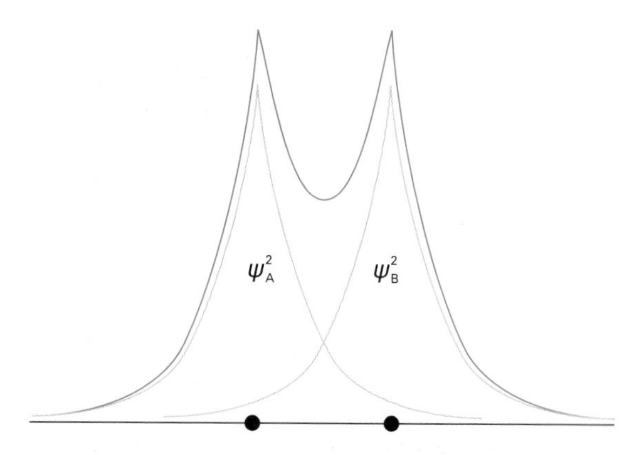

Fig. 14.3 The electron density in H_2 according to the valence bond model of the chemical bond and the electron densities corresponding to the contributing atomic orbitals. The nuclei are denoted by large dots on the horizontal line. Note the accumulation of electron density in the internuclear region.

The Coulomb interaction between two charges q_1 and q_2 separated by a distance r is described by the *Coulombic potential energy*: $E_P = q_1q_2/4\pi\varepsilon_0 r$, where $\varepsilon_0 = 8.854 \times 10^{-12}$ J^{-1} C^2 m^{-1} is the vacuum permittivity.

We can use a similar description for molecules built from atoms that contribute more than one electron to the bonding. For example, to construct the VB description of N_2, we consider the valence electron configuration of each atom, which is $2s^22p_x^12p_y^12p_z^1$. It is conventional to take the z-axis to be the internuclear axis, so we can imagine each atom as having a $2p_z$ orbital pointing towards a $2p_z$ orbital on the other atom, with the $2p_x$ and $2p_y$ orbitals perpendicular to the axis (Fig. 14.4). Each of these p orbitals is occupied by one electron, so we can think of bonds as being formed by the merging of matching orbitals on neighbouring atoms and the pairing of the electrons that occupy them. We get a cylindrically symmetric σ bond from the merging of the two $2p_z$ orbitals and the pairing of the electrons they contain. However, the remaining p orbitals cannot merge to give σ bonds because they do not have cylindrical symmetry around the internuclear axis. Instead, the $2p_x$ orbitals merge and the two

[1] The bond is so called because, when viewed along the internuclear axis it resembles a pair of electrons in an s orbital (and σ, sigma, is the Greek equivalent of s).

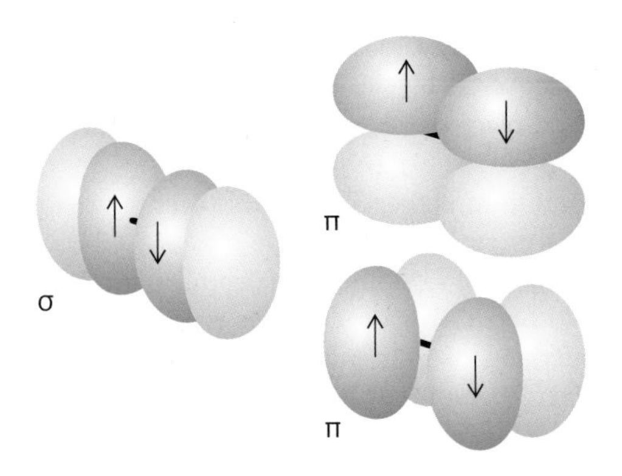

Fig. 14.4 The bonds in N_2 are built by allowing the electrons in the N2*p* orbitals to pair. However, only one orbital on each atom can form a σ bond: the orbitals perpendicular to the axis form π bonds.

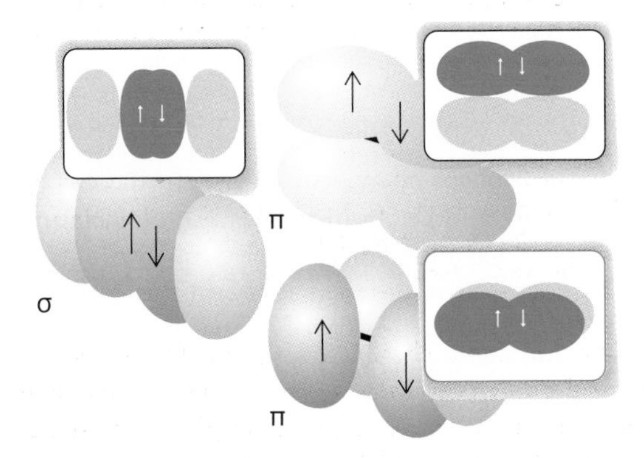

Fig. 14.5 The electrons in the 2*p* orbitals of two neighbouring N atoms merge to form σ and π bonds. The electrons in the N2p_z orbitals pair to form a bond of cylindrical symmetry. Electrons in the N2*p* orbitals that lie perpendicular to the axis also pair to form two π bonds.

electrons pair to form a **π bond**.[2] Similarly, the $2p_y$ orbitals merge and their electrons pair to form another π bond. In general, a π bond arises from the merging of two *p* orbitals that approach side-by-side and the pairing of the electrons that they contain. It follows that the overall bonding pattern in N_2 is a σ bond plus two π bonds (Fig. 14.5), which is consistent with the Lewis structure :N≡N: in which the atoms are linked by a triple bond.

Self-test 14.1

Describe the VB ground state of a Cl_2 molecule.

[*Answer:* one σ(Cl3p_z,Cl3p_z) bond]

14.4 Polyatomic molecules

We can extend these concepts to polyatomic species. Each σ bond in a polyatomic molecule is formed by the merging of orbitals with cylindrical symmetry about the internuclear axis and the pairing of the spins of the electrons they contain. Likewise, π bonds are formed by pairing electrons that occupy atomic orbitals of the appropriate symmetry. A simple description of the electronic structure of H_2O should make this clear.

Illustration 14.1

The VB description of H_2O

The valence electron configuration of an O atom is $2s^22p_x^22p_y^12p_z^1$. The two unpaired electrons in the O2*p* orbitals can each pair with an electron in an H1*s* orbital, and each combination results in the formation of a σ bond (each bond has cylindrical symmetry about the respective O–H internuclear distance). Because the $2p_y$ and $2p_z$ orbitals lie at 90° to each other, the two σ bonds they form also lie at 90° to each other (Fig. 14.6). We predict, therefore, that H_2O should be an angular molecule, which it is. However, the model predicts a bond angle of 90°, whereas the actual bond angle is 104°.

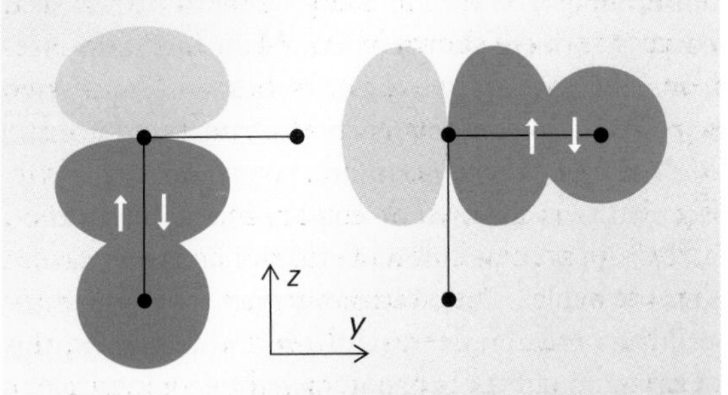

Fig. 14.6 The bonding in an H_2O molecule can be pictured in terms of the pairing of an electron belonging to one H atom with an electron in an O2*p* orbital; the other bond is formed likewise, but using a perpendicular O2*p* orbital. The predicted bond angle is 90°, which is in poor agreement with the experimental bond angle (104°).

[2] A π bond is so called because, viewed along the internuclear axis, it resembles a pair of electrons in a *p* orbital (and π is the Greek equivalent of p).

Self-test 14.2

Give a VB description of NH_3, and predict the bond angle of the molecule on the basis of this description. The experimental bond angle is 107°.

[*Answer:* three σ(N2*p*,H1*s*) bonds; 90°]

While broadly correct, VB theory seems to have two deficiencies. One is the poor estimate it provides for the bond angle in H_2O (and other molecules, such as NH_3). Indeed, the theory appears to make worse predictions than the qualitative VSEPR model, which predicts HOH and HNH bond angles of slightly less than 109° in H_2O and NH_3, respectively. The second major deficiency is the apparent inability of VB theory to account for the number of bonds that atoms can form, and in particular the tetravalence of carbon. To appreciate the latter problem, we note that the ground-state valence configuration of a carbon atom is $2s^22p_x^12p_y^1$, which suggests that it should be capable of forming only two bonds, not four.

14.5 Promotion and hybridization

Two modifications solve all these problems. First, we allow a valence electron to be **promoted** from a full atomic orbital to an empty atomic orbital as a bond is formed: that results in two unpaired electrons instead of two paired electrons, and each unpaired electron can participate in bond formation. In carbon, for example, the promotion of a 2*s* electron to a 2*p* orbital leads to the configuration $2s^12p_x^12p_y^12p_z^1$, with four unpaired electrons in separate orbitals. These electrons may pair with four electrons in orbitals provided by four other atoms (such as four H1*s* orbitals if the molecule is CH_4), and as a result the atom can form four σ bonds. Promotion is worthwhile if the energy it requires can be more than recovered in the greater strength or number of bonds that can be formed.

We can now see why tetravalent carbon is so common. The promotion energy of carbon is small because the promoted electron leaves a doubly occupied 2*s* orbital and enters a vacant 2*p* orbital, hence significantly relieving the electron–electron repulsion it experiences in the former. Furthermore, the energy required for promotion is more than recovered by the atom's ability to form four bonds in place of the two bonds of the unpromoted atom.

Promotion, however, appears to imply the presence of three σ bonds of one type (in CH_4, from the merging of H1*s* and C2*p* orbitals) and a fourth σ bond of a distinctly different type (formed from the merging of H1*s* and C2*s*). It is well known, however, that all four bonds in methane are exactly equivalent in terms of both their chemical properties and their physical properties (their lengths, strengths, and stiffnesses).

A characteristic property of waves is that they interfere with one another, resulting in a greater displacement where peaks or troughs coincide, giving rise to *constructive interference*, and a smaller displacement where peaks coincide with troughs, giving rise to *destructive interference*. The physics of waves is reviewed in Appendix 3.

This problem is overcome in VB theory by drawing on another technical feature of quantum mechanics that allows the same electron distribution to be described in different ways. In this case, we can describe the electron distribution in the promoted atom either as arising from four electrons in one *s* and three *p* orbitals, or as arising from four electrons in four different *mixtures* of these orbitals. Mixtures (more formally, linear combinations) of atomic orbitals on the same atom are called **hybrid orbitals**. We can picture them by thinking of the four original atomic orbitals, which are waves centred on a nucleus, as being like ripples spreading from a single point on the surface of a lake. These waves interfere destructively or constructively in different regions and give rise to four new shapes. The specific linear combinations that give rise to four equivalent hybrid orbitals are

$$h_1 = s + p_x + p_y + p_z$$
$$h_2 = s - p_x - p_y + p_z$$
$$h_3 = s - p_x + p_y - p_z$$
$$h_4 = s + p_x - p_y - p_z$$

In general, a linear combination of two functions *f* and *g* is $c_1f + c_2g$, where c_1 and c_2 are numerical coefficients, so a linear combination is a more general term than 'sum'. In a sum, $c_1 = c_2 = 1$.

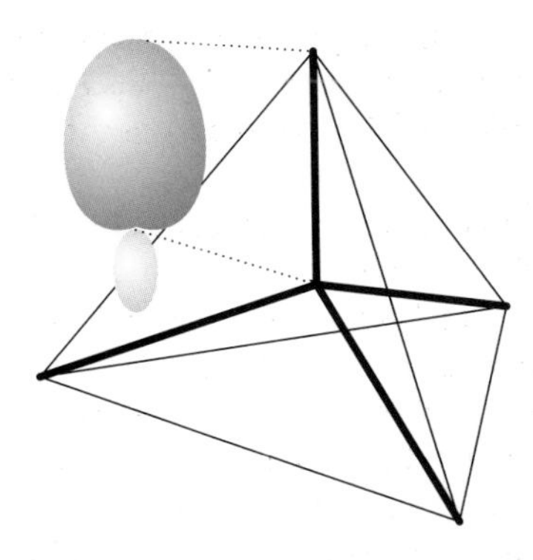

Fig. 14.7 The $2s$ and three $2p$ orbitals of a carbon atom hybridize, and the resulting hybrid orbitals point towards the corners of a regular tetrahedron.

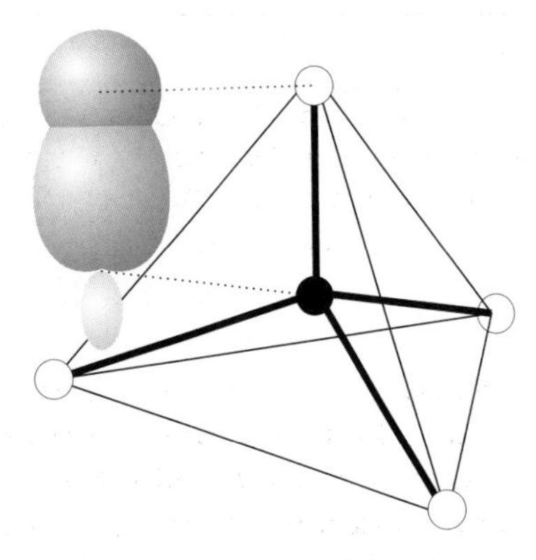

Fig. 14.8 The valence bond description of the structure of CH_4. Each σ bond is formed by the pairing of an electron in an H1s orbital with an electron in one of the hybrid orbitals shown in Fig. 14.7. The resulting molecule is regular tetrahedral.

As a result of the constructive and destructive interference between the positive and negative regions of the component orbitals, each hybrid orbital has a large lobe pointing towards one corner of a regular tetrahedron (Fig. 14.7). Because each hybrid is built from one s orbital and three p orbitals, it is called an **sp^3 hybrid orbital.**

It is now easy to see how the valence bond description of the methane molecule leads to a tetrahedral molecule containing four equivalent C–H bonds. It is energetically favourable (in the end, after bonding has been taken into account) for the carbon atom to undergo promotion. The promoted configuration has a distribution of electrons that is equivalent to one electron occupying each of four tetrahedral hybrid orbitals. Each hybrid orbital of the promoted atom contains a single unpaired electron; a hydrogen 1s electron can pair with each one, giving rise to a σ bond pointing in a tetrahedral direction. Because each sp^3 hybrid orbital has the same composition, all four σ bonds are identical apart from their orientation in space (Fig. 14.8).

Hybridization is also used in the VB description of alkenes. An ethene molecule is planar, with HCH and HCC bond angles close to 120°. To reproduce this σ-bonding structure, we think of each C atom as being promoted to a $2s^12p_x^12p_y^12p_z^1$ configuration. However, instead of using all four orbitals to form hybrids, we form **sp^2 hybrid orbitals** by allowing the s orbital and two of the p orbitals to interfere. As shown in Fig. 14.9, the three hybrid orbitals

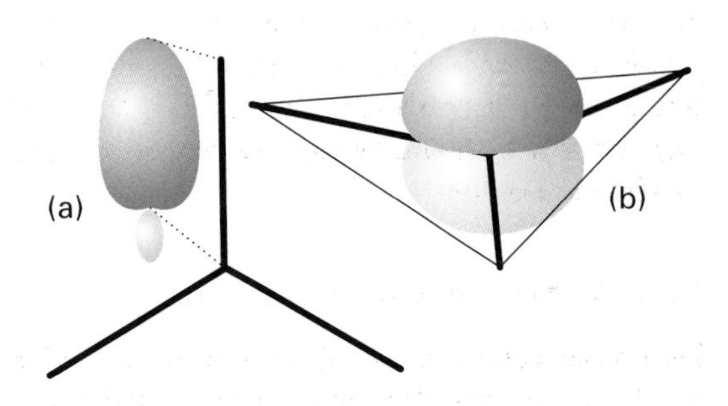

Fig. 14.9 (a) Trigonal planar hybridization is obtained when an s and two p orbitals are hybridized. The three lobes lie in a plane and make an angle of 120° to each other. (b) The remaining p orbital in the valence shell of an sp^2-hybridized atom lies perpendicular to the plane of the three hybrids.

$$h_1 = s + 2^{1/2}p_x$$
$$h_2 = s + (\tfrac{3}{2})^{1/2}p_x - (\tfrac{1}{2})^{1/2}p_y$$
$$h_3 = s - (\tfrac{3}{2})^{1/2}p_x - (\tfrac{1}{2})^{1/2}p_y$$

lie in a plane and point towards the corners of an equilateral triangle. The third $2p$ orbital ($2p_z$) is not included in the hybridization, and its axis is perpendicular to the plane in which the hybrids lie. The coefficients $2^{1/2}$, etc. in the hybrids have been chosen to give the correct directional properties of the hybrids. The *squares* of the coefficients give the proportion of each atomic orbital in the hybrid. All three hybrids have s and p orbitals in the ratio 1:2, as indicated by the label sp^2.

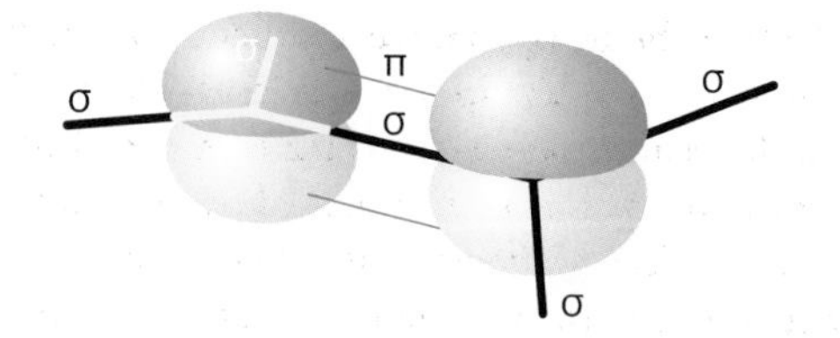

Fig. 14.10 The valence bond description of the structure of a carbon–carbon double bond, as in ethene. The electrons in the two sp^2 hybrids that point towards each other pair and form a σ bond. Electrons in the two *p* orbitals that are perpendicular to the plane of the hybrids pair, and form a π bond. The electrons in the remaining hybrid orbitals are used to form bonds to other atoms (in ethene itelf, to H atoms).

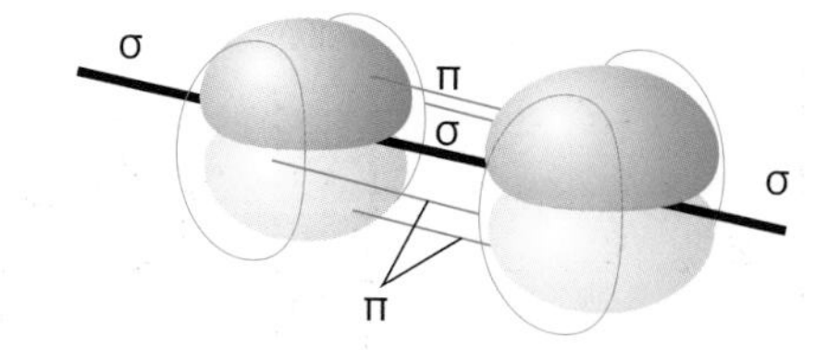

Fig. 14.11 The electronic structure of ethyne (acetylene). The electrons in the two *sp* hybrids on each atom pair to form σ bonds either with the other C atom or with an H atom. The remaining two unhybridized 2*p* orbitals on each atom are perpendicular to the axis: the electrons in corresponding orbitals on each atom pair to form two π bonds. The overall electron distribution is cylindrical.

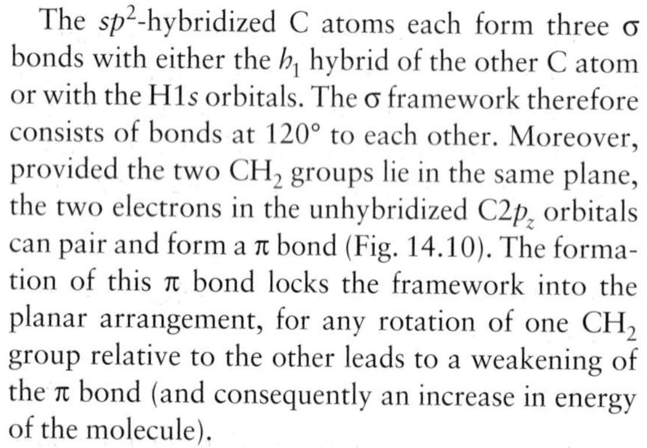

The sp^2-hybridized C atoms each form three σ bonds with either the h_1 hybrid of the other C atom or with the H1*s* orbitals. The σ framework therefore consists of bonds at 120° to each other. Moreover, provided the two CH_2 groups lie in the same plane, the two electrons in the unhybridized $C2p_z$ orbitals can pair and form a π bond (Fig. 14.10). The formation of this π bond locks the framework into the planar arrangement, for any rotation of one CH_2 group relative to the other leads to a weakening of the π bond (and consequently an increase in energy of the molecule).

A similar description applies to a linear ethyne (acetylene) molecule, H–C≡C–H. Now the carbon atoms are ***sp* hybridized**, and the σ bonds are built from hybrid atomic orbitals of the form

$$h_1 = s + p_z$$
$$h_2 = s - p_z$$

Note that the *s* and *p* orbitals contribute in equal proportions. The two hybrids lie along the *z*-axis. The electrons in them pair either with an electron in the corresponding hybrid orbital on the other C atom or with an electron in the H1*s* orbitals. Electrons in the two remaining *p* orbitals on each atom, which are perpendicular to the molecular axis, pair to form two perpendicular π bonds (as in Fig. 14.11).

Other hybridization schemes, particularly those involving *d* orbitals, are often invoked to account for (or at least be consistent with) other molecular geometries (Table 14.1). An important point to note is that *the hybridization of N atomic orbitals always results in the formation of N hybrid orbitals.* For example, sp^3d^2 hybridization results in six equivalent hybrid orbitals pointing towards the corners of a regular octahedron. This octahedral hybridization scheme is sometimes invoked to account for the structure of octahedral molecules, such as SF_6.

Self-test 14.3

Describe the bonding in a PCl_5 molecule in VB terms.

[*Answer:* five σ bonds formed from sp^3d hybrids on the central P atom]

The 'pure' schemes in Table 14.1 are not the only possibilities: it is possible to form hybrid orbitals with intermediate proportions of atomic orbitals. For example, as more *p*-orbital character is included in an *sp*-hybridization scheme, the hybridization changes towards sp^2 and the angle between the

Table 14.1
Hybrid orbitals

Number	Shape	Hybridization*
2	Linear	sp
3	Trigonal planar	sp^2
4	Tetrahedral	sp^3
5	Trigonal bipyramidal	sp^3d
6	Tetrahedral	sp^3d^2

* Other combinations are possible.

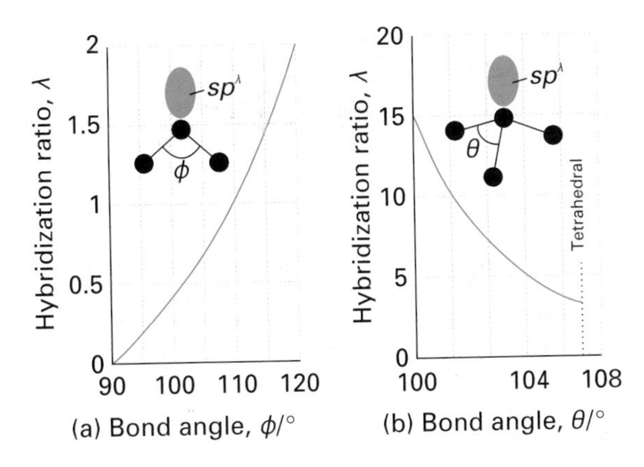

Fig. 14.12 The variation of hybridization with bond angle in (a) angular, (b) trigonal pyramidal molecules. The vertical axis gives the ratio of *p* to *s* character, so high values indicate mostly *p* character.

hybrids changes continuously from 180° for pure *sp* hybridization to 120° for pure sp^2 hybridization. If the proportion of *p* character continues to be increased (by reducing the proportion of *s* orbital), then the hybrids eventually become pure *p* orbitals at an angle of 90° to each other (Fig. 14.12). Now we can account for the structure of H_2O, with its bond angle of 104°. Each O–H σ bond is formed from an O atom hybrid orbital with a composition that lies between pure *p* (which would lead to a bond angle of 90°) and pure sp^2 (which would lead to a bond angle of 120°). The actual bond angle and hybridization adopted are found by calculating the energy of the molecule as the bond angle is varied, and looking for the angle at which the energy is a minimum.

14.6 Resonance

Another term introduced by VB theory into chemistry is **resonance**, the superposition of the wavefunctions representing different electron distributions in the same nuclear framework. To understand what this means, consider the VB description of a purely covalently bonded HCl molecule, which could be written

$$\psi_{H-Cl}(1,2) = \psi_H(1)\psi_{Cl}(2) + \psi_H(2)\psi_{Cl}(1)$$

We have supposed that the bond is formed by the spin pairing of electrons in the H1*s* orbital, ψ_H, and the Cl2p_z orbital, ψ_{Cl}. However, there is something wrong with this description: it allows electron 1 to be on the H atom when electron 2 is on the Cl atom, and vice versa, but it does not allow for unequal sharing of electron density between the atoms. On physical grounds, we should expect the purely covalent character of HCl to be an incomplete description of the molecule: because the Cl atom has higher ionization energy and electron affinity than the H atom, we can expect the ionic form H^+Cl^- to play a role. The wavefunction for this ionic structure, in which both electrons are in the Cl2p_z orbital, is

$$\psi_{H^+Cl^-}(1,2) = \psi_{Cl}(1)\psi_{Cl}(2)$$

However, this wavefunction alone is unrealistic, because HCl is not an ionic species. A better description of the wavefunction for the molecule is as a superposition of the covalent and ionic descriptions, and we write (with a slightly simplified notation)

$$\psi_{HCl} = \psi_{H-Cl} + \lambda\psi_{H^+Cl^-}$$

with λ (lambda) some numerical coefficient. In general, we write

$$\psi = \psi_{covalent} + \lambda\psi_{ionic} \quad (14.4)$$

where $\psi_{covalent}$ is the wavefunction for the purely covalent form of the bond and ψ_{ionic} is the wavefunction for the ionic form of the bond. According to the general rules of quantum mechanics, in which probabilities are related to squares of wavefunctions, we interpret the square of λ as the relative proportion of the ionic contribution. If λ^2 is very small, the covalent description is dominant. If λ^2 is very large, the ionic description is dominant.

We find the numerical value of λ by using the **variation theorem**. First, we write down a plausible wavefunction, a **trial wavefunction**, for the molecule, such as the wavefunction in eqn 14.4 where λ is variable parameter. The variation theorem then states that:

The energy of a trial wavefunction is never less than the true energy.

The theorem implies that if we vary λ until we achieve the lowest energy, then the wavefunction with that value of λ is the best available of that particular kind.

The approach summarized by eqn 14.4, in which we express a wavefunction as the sum of wavefunctions corresponding to a variety of structures *with the nuclei in the same locations*, is called **resonance.** In this case, where one structure is pure covalent and the other pure ionic, it is called **ionic–covalent resonance.** The interpretation of the wavefunction, which is called a **resonance hybrid,** is that if we were to inspect the molecule, then the proportion of the time that it would be found with an ionic structure is proportional to λ^2. Resonance is not a flickering between the contributing states: it is a blending of their characteristics, much as a mule is a blend of a horse and a donkey. For instance, we might find that the lowest energy is reached when $\lambda = 0.1$, so the best description of the bond in the molecule in terms of a wavefunction like that in eqn 14.4 is a resonance structure described by the wavefunction $\psi = \psi_{\text{covalent}} + 0.1\psi_{\text{ionic}}$. This wavefunction implies that the probabilities of finding the molecule in its covalent and ionic forms are in the ratio 100:1 (because $0.1^2 = 0.01$).

One of the most famous examples of resonance is in the VB description of benzene, where the wavefunction of the molecule is written as a superposition of the wavefunctions of the two covalent Kekulé structures (**1**) and (**2**):

1 **2**

$$\psi = \psi_{\text{Kek1}} + \psi_{\text{Kek2}} \tag{14.5}$$

The two contributing structures have identical energies, so they contribute equally to the superposition. The effect of resonance (which is represented by a double-headed arrow) in this case is to distribute double-bond character around the ring and to make the lengths and strengths of all the carbon–carbon bonds identical. Because the wavefunction is improved by allowing resonance, it follows from the variation theorem that the energy of the molecule is lowered relative to either Kekulé structure alone. This lowering is called the **resonance stabilization** of the molecule and, in the context of VB theory, is largely responsible for the unusual stability of aromatic rings. Resonance always lowers the energy (because it improves the wavefunction), and the lowering is greatest when the contributing structures have similar energies. The wavefunction of benzene is improved still further, in the sense that the calculated energy of the molecule is lowered further still, if we allow ionic–covalent resonance too, by allowing a small admixture of structures such as that shown in (**3**).

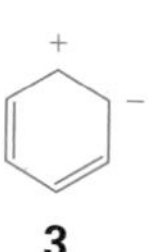

3

Resonance should not be regarded as a physical oscillation between the contributing structures. It is only a mathematical device for achieving a closer approximation to the true wavefunction of the molecule than that represented by any single contributing structure alone.

Molecular orbitals

In molecular orbital theory, electrons are treated as spreading throughout the entire molecule: every electron contributes to the strength of every bond. This theory has been more fully developed than valence bond theory and provides the language that is widely used in modern discussions of bonding in small inorganic molecules, *d*-metal complexes, and solids. To introduce it, we follow the same strategy as in Chapter 13, where the one-electron hydrogen atom was taken as the fundamental species for discussing atomic structure, and then developed into a description of many-electron atoms. In this section we use the simplest molecule of all, the one-electron hydrogen molecule–ion, H_2^+, to introduce the essential features of bonding, and then use it as a guide to the structures of more complex systems.

14.7 Linear combinations of atomic orbitals

A **molecular orbital** is a one-electron wavefunction for an electron that spreads throughout the molecule. The mathematical forms of such orbitals are highly complicated, even for such a simple species as H_2^+, and they are unknown in general. All modern work builds approximations to the true molecular orbital by formulating models based on linear combinations of the atomic orbitals on the atoms in the molecule.

First, we recall the general principle of quantum mechanics that, if there are several possible outcomes, then we add together the wavefunctions that represent those outcomes.[3] In H_2^+, there are two possible outcomes: an electron may be found either in an atomic orbital centred on A, ψ_A, or it may be found in an orbital centred on B, ψ_B. Therefore, we write

$$\psi = c_A\psi_A + c_B\psi_B \tag{14.6a}$$

where c_A and c_B are numerical coefficients. This wavefunction is called a **linear combination of atomic orbitals** (LCAO). The squares of the coefficients tell us the relative proportions of the atomic orbitals contributing to the molecular orbital. In a homonuclear diatomic molecule, an electron can be found with equal probability in orbital A or orbital B, so the *squares* of the coefficients must be equal, which implies that $c_B = \pm c_A$. The two possible wavefunctions are therefore[4]

$$\psi = \psi_A \pm \psi_B \tag{14.6b}$$

First, we consider the LCAO with the plus sign,

$$\psi = \psi_A + \psi_B \tag{14.7}$$

as this molecular orbital will turn out to have the lower energy of the two. The form of this orbital is shown in Fig. 14.13. It is called a **σ orbital** because it resembles an *s* orbital when viewed along the axis.[5] Because (as we shall see) it is the σ orbital of lowest energy, it is labelled 1σ. An electron that occupies a σ orbital is called a **σ electron**. In the ground state of the H_2^+ ion, there is a single 1σ electron, so we report the ground-state configuration of H_2^+ as $1\sigma^1$.

We can see the origin of the lowering of energy that is responsible for the formation of the bond by examining the LCAO-MO. The two atomic orbitals are like waves centred on adjacent nuclei. In the internuclear region, the amplitudes interfere constructively and the wavefunction has an enhanced amplitude there (Fig. 14.14). Because the amplitude is increased, there is an increased probability of finding the electron between the two nuclei, where it is in a good position to interact strongly with both of them. Hence the energy of the molecule is lower than that of the separate atoms, where each electron can interact strongly with only one nucleus. In elementary MO theory, the bonding effect of an electron that occupies a molecular orbital is ascribed to its accumulation in the internuclear region as a result of the constructive interference of the contributing atomic orbitals.

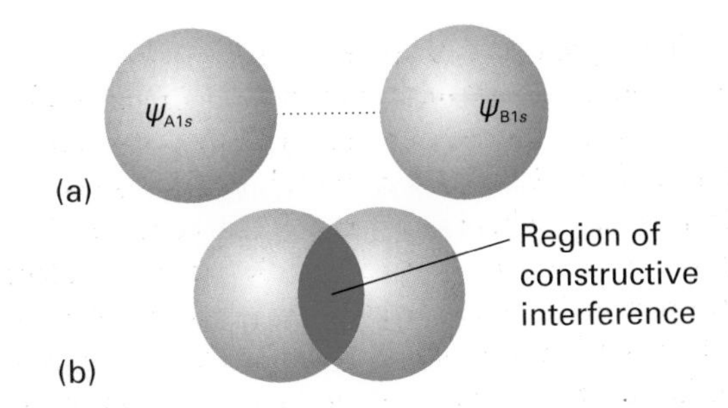

Fig. 14.13 The formation of a bonding molecular orbital (a σ orbital). (a) Two H1*s* orbitals come together. (b) The atomic orbitals overlap, interfere constructively, and give rise to an enhanced amplitude in the internuclear region. The resulting orbital has cylindrical symmetry about the internuclear axis. When it is occupied by two paired electrons, to give the configuration σ^2, we have a σ bond.

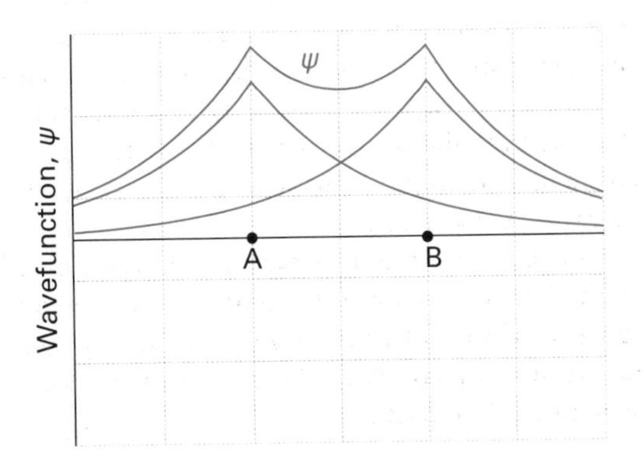

Fig. 14.14 The bonding molecular orbital wavefunction along the internuclear axis. Note that there is an enhancement of amplitude between the nuclei, so there is an increased probability of finding the bonding electrons in that region.

[3] We used this principle to construct valence bond wavefunctions.

[4] For simplicity, we are ignoring the overall normalization factor.

[5] More precisely, it is so called because an electron that occupies a σ orbital has zero orbital angular momentum around the internuclear axis, just as an *s* electron has zero orbital angular momentum around an axis passing through the nucleus.

14.8 Bonding and antibonding orbitals

A 1σ orbital is an example of a **bonding orbital**, a molecular orbital that, if occupied, contributes to the strength of a bond between two atoms. As in VB theory, we can substitute the wavefunction in eqn 14.7 into the Schrödinger equation for the molecule–ion with the nuclei at a fixed separation R and solve the equation for the energy. The molecular potential energy curve obtained by plotting the energy against R is very similar to the one drawn in Fig. 14.1. The energy of the molecule falls as R is decreased from large values because the electron is increasingly likely to be found in the internuclear region as the two atomic orbitals interfere more effectively. However, at small separations, there is too little space between the nuclei for significant accumulation of electron density there. In addition, the nucleus–nucleus repulsion $V_{\text{nuc,nuc}}$ (eqn 14.3) becomes large. As a result, after an initial decrease, at small internuclear separations the potential energy curve passes through a minimum and then rises sharply to high values. Calculations on H_2^+ give the equilibrium bond length as 130 pm and the bond dissociation energy as 171 kJ mol^{-1}; the experimental values are 106 pm and 250 kJ mol^{-1}, so this simple LCAO-MO description of the molecule, while inaccurate, is not absurdly wrong.

Now consider the alternative LCAO, the one with a minus sign:

$$\psi = \psi_A - \psi_B \tag{14.8}$$

Because this wavefunction is also cylindrically symmetrical around the internuclear axis it is also a σ orbital, which we denote as 1σ* (Fig. 14.15). When substituted into the Schrödinger equation, we find that it has a higher energy than the bonding 1σ orbital and, indeed, it has a higher energy than either of the two atomic orbitals.

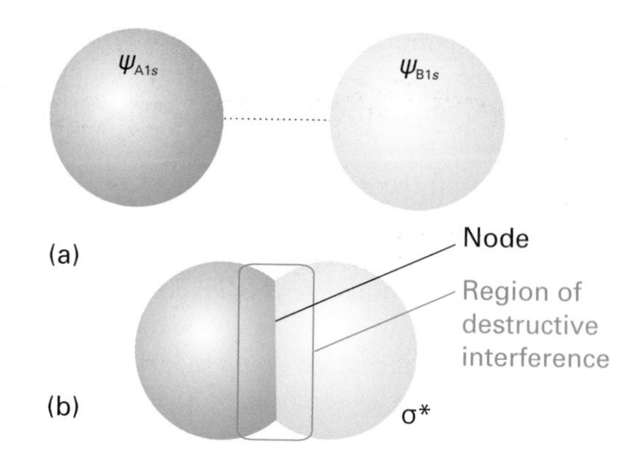

Fig. 14.15 The formation of an antibonding molecular orbital (a σ* orbital). (a) Two H1s orbitals come together. (b) The atomic orbitals overlap with opposite signs (as depicted by different shades of colour), interfere destructively, and give rise to a decreased amplitude in the internuclear region. There is a nodal plane exactly halfway between the nuclei, on which any electrons that occupy the orbital will not be found.

Self-test 14.4

Show that the molecular orbital written above is zero on a plane cutting through the internuclear axis at its midpoint. Take each atomic orbital to be of the form e^{-r/a_0}, with r_A measured from nucleus A and r_B measured from nucleus B.

[*Answer:* the atomic orbitals cancel for values equidistant from the two nuclei]

We can trace the origin of the high energy of the 1σ* orbital to the existence of a **nodal plane**, a plane on which the wavefunction passes through zero. This plane lies halfway between the nuclei and cuts through the internuclear axis. The two atomic orbitals cancel on this plane as a result of their destructive interference, because they have opposite signs. In drawings like those in Figs 14.13 and 14.15, we represent overlap of orbitals with the same sign (as in the formation of 1σ) by shading of the same tint; the overlap of orbitals of opposite sign (as in the formation of 1σ*) is represented by one orbital of a light tint (or white) and another orbital of a dark tint.

The 1σ* orbital is an example of an **antibonding orbital**, an orbital that, if occupied, decreases the strength of a bond between two atoms. The antibonding character of the 1σ* orbital is partly a result of the exclusion of the electron from the internuclear region and its relocation outside the bonding region where it helps to pull the nuclei apart rather than pulling them together (Fig. 14.16). An antibonding orbital is often slightly more strongly antibonding than the corresponding bonding orbital is bonding: although the 'gluing' effect of a bonding electron and the 'anti-gluing' effect of an antibonding electron are similar, the nuclei repel each other

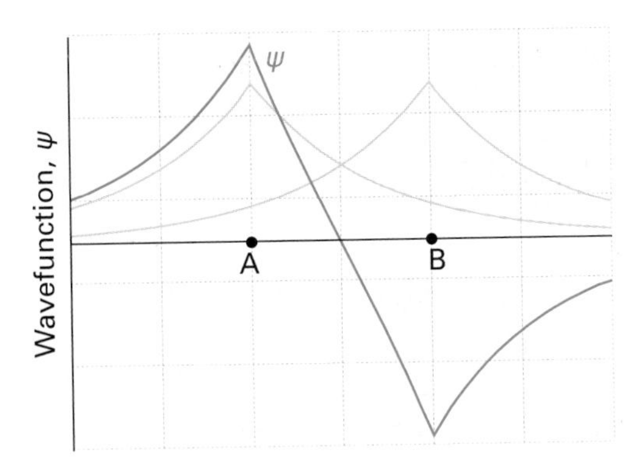

Fig. 14.16 The antibonding molecular orbital wavefunction along the internuclear axis. Note that there is a decrease in amplitude between the nuclei, so there is a decreased probability of finding the bonding electrons in that region.

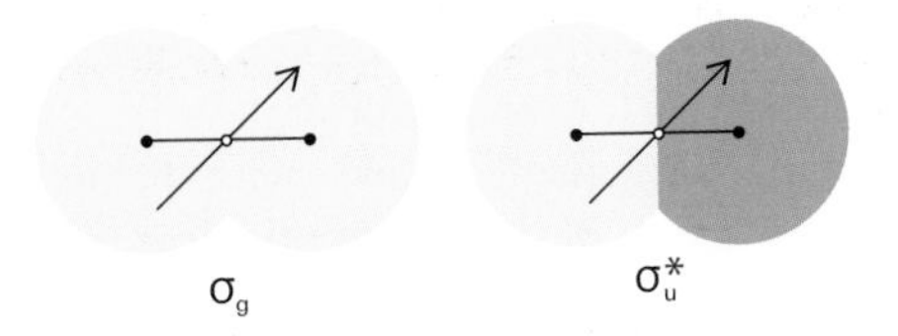

Fig. 14.17 The gerade/ungerade character of σ bonding and antibonding orbitals.

in both cases, and this repulsion pushes both levels up in energy.

We need to make a few points about notation. For homonuclear diatomic molecules, it is helpful to identify the inversion symmetry of a molecular orbital, especially when discussing electronic transitions (Chapter 18). By 'inversion symmetry' is meant the behaviour of a wavefunction when it is inverted through the centre (more formally, the centre of inversion) of the molecule. Thus, if we consider any point of the σ bonding orbital, and then project it through the centre of the molecule and out an equal distance on the other side, then we arrive at an identical value of the wavefunction (Fig. 14.17). This so-called ***gerade* symmetry** (from the German word for 'even') is denoted by a subscript g, as in σ_g. The same procedure applied to the antibonding σ^* orbital results in the same size but opposite sign of the wavefunction. This ***ungerade* symmetry** ('odd symmetry') is denoted by a subscript u, as in σ_u. This inversion symmetry classification (or 'parity') is not applicable to heteronuclear diatomic molecules (like CO) as they do not have a centre of inversion.

14.9 The structures of diatomic molecules

In Chapter 13 we used the hydrogenic atomic orbitals and the building-up principle to deduce the ground electronic configurations of many-electron atoms. Here we use the same procedure for many-electron diatomic molecules (such as H_2 with two electrons and even Br_2 with 70), but using the H_2^+ molecular orbitals as a basis. The general procedure is as follows:

1 Construct molecular orbitals by forming linear combinations of all suitable valence atomic orbitals supplied by the atoms (the meaning of 'suitable' will be explained shortly); N atomic orbitals result in N molecular orbitals.

2 Accommodate the valence electrons supplied by the atoms so as to achieve the lowest overall energy subject to the constraint of the Pauli exclusion principle, that no more than two electrons may occupy a single orbital (and then must be paired).

3 If more than one molecular orbital of the same energy is available, add the electrons to each individual orbital before doubly occupying any one orbital (because that minimizes electron–electron repulsions).

4 Take note of Hund's rule (Section 13.11), that if electrons occupy different degenerate orbitals, then they do so with parallel spins.

The following sections show how these rules are used in practice.

Self-test 14.5

How many molecular orbitals can be built from the valence shell orbitals in O_2?

[*Answer:* 8]

14.10 Hydrogen and helium molecules

The first step in the discussion of H_2, the simplest many-electron diatomic molecule, is to build the molecular orbitals. Because each H atom of H_2 contributes a 1*s* orbital (as in H_2^+), we can form the 1σ and $1\sigma^*$ bonding and antibonding orbitals from them, as we have seen already. At the equilibrium

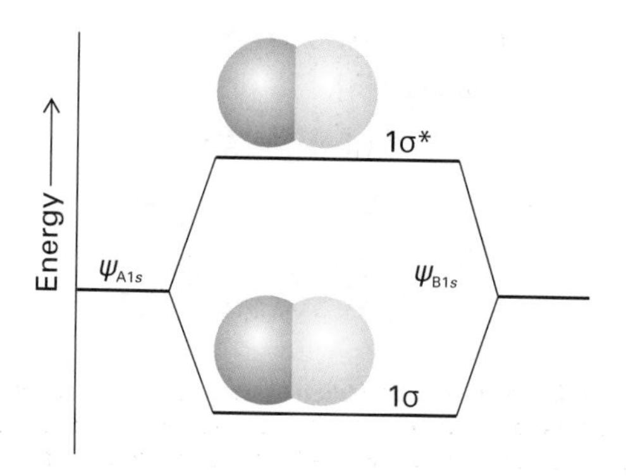

Fig. 14.18 A molecular orbital energy level diagram for orbitals constructed from (1*s*,1*s*)-overlap, the separation of the levels corresponding to the equilibrium bond length.

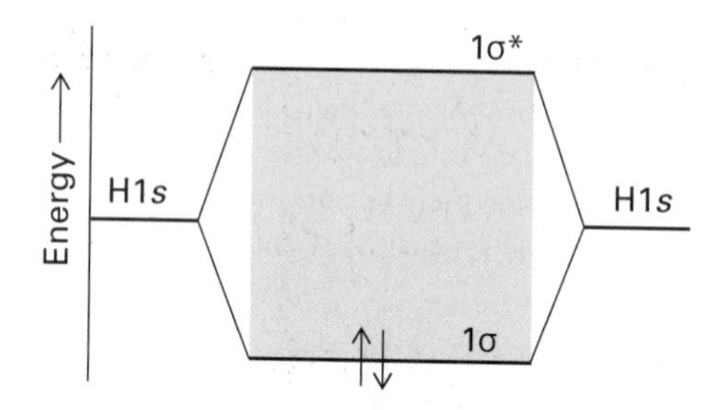

Fig. 14.19 The ground electronic configuration of H_2 is obtained by accommodating the two electrons in the lowest available orbital (the bonding orbital).

internuclear separation these orbitals will have the energies represented by the horizontal lines in Fig. 14.18.

There are two electrons to accommodate (one from each atom). Both can enter the 1σ orbital by pairing their spins (Fig. 14.19). The ground-state configuration is therefore $1\sigma^2$, and the atoms are joined by a bond consisting of an electron pair in a bonding σ orbital. These two electrons bind the two nuclei together more strongly and closely than the single electron in H_2^+, and the bond length is reduced from 106 pm to 74 pm. A pair of electrons in a σ orbital is called a **σ bond**, and is very similar to the σ bond of VB theory. The two differ in certain details of the electron distribution between the two atoms joined by the bond, but both have an accumulation of density between the nuclei.

We can conclude that *the importance of an electron pair in bonding stems from the fact that two is*

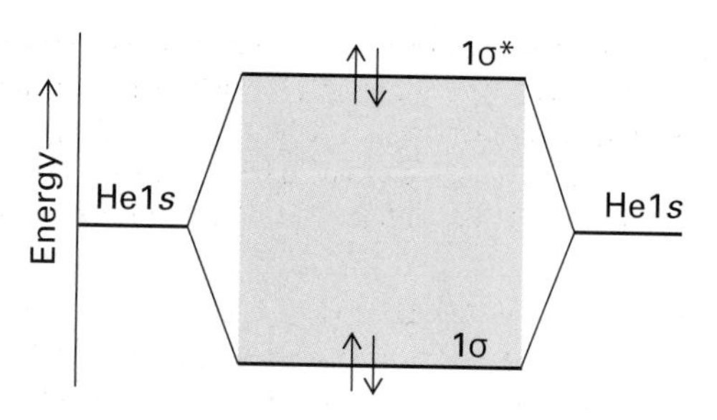

Fig. 14.20 The ground electronic configuration of the four-electron molecule He_2 has two bonding electrons and two antibonding electrons. It has a higher energy than the separated atoms, and so He_2 is unstable relative to two He atoms.

the maximum number of electrons that can enter each bonding molecular orbital. Electrons do not 'want' to pair: they pair because in that way they are able to occupy a low-energy orbital.

A similar argument shows why helium is a monatomic gas. Consider a hypothetical He_2 molecule. Each He atom contributes a 1*s* orbital to the linear combination used to form the molecular orbitals, and so we can construct 1σ and $1\sigma^*$ molecular orbitals. They differ in detail from those in H_2 because the He1*s* orbitals are more compact, but the general shape is the same, and for qualitative discussions we can use the same molecular orbital energy level diagram as for H_2. Because each atom provides two electrons, there are four electrons to accommodate. Two can enter the 1σ orbital, but then it is full (by the Pauli exclusion principle). The next two electrons must enter the antibonding $1\sigma^*$ orbital (Fig. 14.20). The ground electronic configuration of He_2 is therefore $1\sigma^2 1\sigma^{*2}$. Because an antibonding orbital is slightly more antibonding than a bonding orbital is bonding, the He_2 molecule has a higher energy than the separated atoms and is unstable. Hence, two ground-state He atoms do not form bonds to each other, and helium is a monatomic gas.

Example 14.1

Judging the stability of diatomic molecules

Decide whether Li_2 is likely to exist on the assumption that only the valence *s* orbitals contribute to its molecular orbitals.

Strategy Decide what molecular orbitals can be formed from the available valence orbitals, rank them in order of energy, then feed in the electrons supplied by the valence orbitals of the atoms. Judge whether there is a net bonding or net antibonding effect between the atoms.

Solution Each molecular orbital is built from 2*s* atomic orbitals, which give one bonding and one antibonding combination (1σ and 1σ*, respectively). Each Li atom supplies one valence electron; the two electrons fill the 1σ orbital, to give the configuration $1\sigma^2$, which is bonding.

Self-test 14.6

Is LiH likely to exist if the Li atom uses only its 2*s* orbital for bonding?

[*Answer:* yes, $\sigma(\text{Li}2s,\text{H}1s)^2$]

14.11 Period 2 diatomic molecules

We shall now see how the concepts we have introduced apply to other homonuclear diatomic molecules, such as N_2 and Cl_2, and diatomic ions such as O_2^{2-}. In line with the building-up procedure, we first consider the molecular orbitals that may be formed from the valence orbitals and do not (at this stage) trouble about how many electrons are available.

In Period 2, the valence orbitals are 2*s* and 2*p*. Suppose first that we consider these two types of orbital separately. Then the 2*s* orbitals on each atom overlap to form bonding and antibonding combinations that we denote 1σ and 1σ*, respectively. Likewise, the two $2p_z$ orbitals (by convention, the internuclear axis is the *z*-axis) have cylindrical symmetry around the internuclear axis. They may therefore participate in σ-orbital formation to give the bonding and antibonding combinations 2σ and 2σ*, respectively (Fig. 14.21). The resulting energy levels of the σ orbitals are shown in the MO energy level diagram in Fig. 14.22. Both bonding σ orbitals have g symmetry and both antibonding σ orbitals have u symmetry.

Strictly, we should not consider the *s* and p_z orbitals separately, because both of them can contribute to the formation of σ orbitals. Therefore, in a more advanced treatment, we should combine all four orbitals together to form four σ molecular orbitals, each one of the form

$$\psi = c_1\psi_{A2s} + c_2\psi_{B2s} + c_3\psi_{A2p_z} + c_4\psi_{B2p_z}$$

We find the four coefficients, which represent the different contributions that each atomic orbital makes to the overall molecular orbital, by using the variation theorem. However, in practice, the two lowest energy combinations of this kind are very

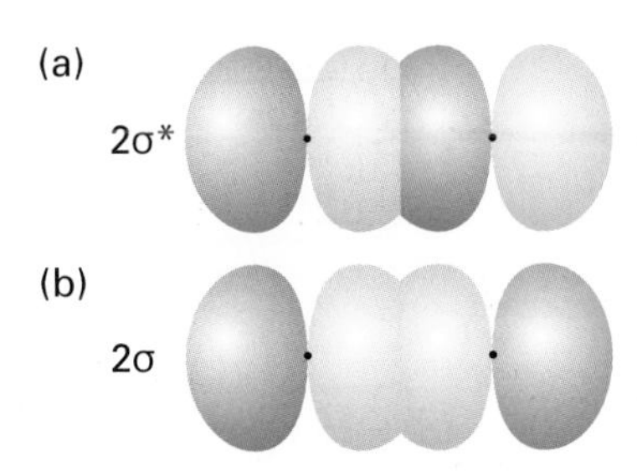

Fig. 14.21 (a) The interference leading to the formation of a σ bonding orbital and (b) the corresponding antibonding orbital when two *p* orbitals overlap along an internuclear axis.

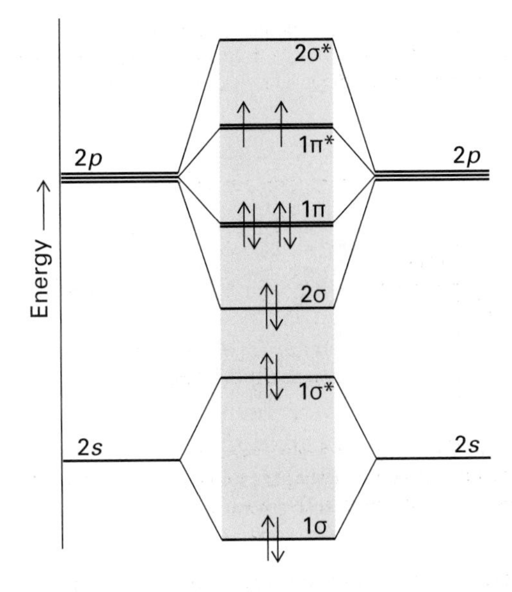

Fig. 14.22 A typical molecular orbital energy level diagram for Period 2 homonuclear diatomic molecules. the valence atomic orbitals are drawn in the columns on the left and the right; the molecular orbitals are shown in the middle. Note that the π orbitals form doubly degenerate pairs. The sloping lines joining the molecular orbitals to the atomic orbitals show the principal composition of the molecular orbitals. This diagram is suitable for O_2 and F_2; the configuration of O_2 is shown.

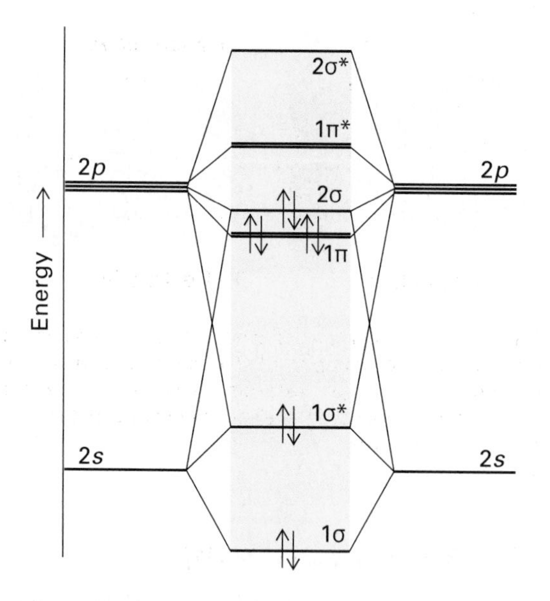

Fig. 14.23 A typical molecular orbital energy level diagram for Period 2 homonuclear diatomic molecules up to and including N_2.

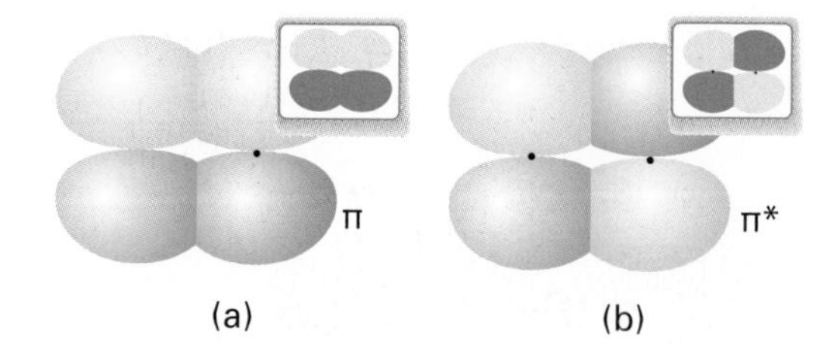

Fig. 14.24 (a) The interference leading to the formation of a π bonding orbital and (b) the corresponding antibonding orbital.

similar to the combination 1σ and 1σ* of 2*s* orbitals that we have described, and the two highest energy combinations are very similar to the 2σ and 2σ* combinations of $2p_z$ orbitals. In each case there will be small differences: the 1σ* orbital, for instance, will be contaminated by some $2p_z$ character and the 2σ orbital will be contaminated by some 2*s* character, and their energies will be slightly shifted from where they would be if we considered only the 'pure' combinations. Nevertheless, the changes are not great, and we can continue to think of 1σ and 1σ* as being one bonding and antibonding pair, and of 2σ and 2σ* as being another pair. The four orbitals are shown in the centre column of Fig. 14.23. There is no guarantee that 1σ* and 2σ will be in the exact location shown in the illustration and the locations shown in Fig. 14.22 are found in some molecules (see below).

There is one further point in this connection. As soon as we allow all four atomic orbitals to contribute to an LCAO it is no longer clear—except by appealing to the form of the simple pairwise LCAOs that each one resembles—whether a particular combination is bonding or antibonding: all we can say is that the four linear combinations have successively increasing energies. However, the parity classification is unaffected, and the orbitals can still be classified as g or u; in homonuclear diatomic molecules, inversion symmetry is a more fundamental classification scheme than bonding and antibonding.

Now consider the $2p_x$ and $2p_y$ orbitals of each atom, which are perpendicular to the internuclear axis and may overlap side-by-side. This overlap may be constructive or destructive and results in a bonding and an antibonding **π orbital**, which we label 1π and 1π*, respectively. The notation π is the analogue of *p* in atoms because, when viewed along the axis of the molecule, a π orbital looks like a *p* orbital (Fig. 14.24).[6] The two $2p_x$ orbitals overlap to give a bonding and an antibonding π orbital, as do the two $2p_y$ orbitals too. The two bonding combinations have the same energy; likewise, the two antibonding combinations have the same energy. Hence, each π energy level is doubly degenerate and consists of two distinct orbitals. Two electrons in a π orbital constitute a **π bond**: such a bond resembles a π bond of valence bond theory, but the details of the electron distribution are slightly different.

The inversion-symmetry classification also applies to π orbitals. As we see from Fig. 14.25, a bonding π orbital changes sign on inversion, and is therefore classified as u. The antibonding π* orbital does not change sign, and is therefore g. The bonding and antibonding combinations can therefore be denoted $1\pi_u$ and $1\pi_g$. The relative order of the σ and π orbitals in a molecule cannot be predicted without detailed calculation and varies with the energy separation between the 2*s* and 2*p* orbitals of the atoms; in some molecules the order shown in Fig. 14.22

[6] More precisely, an electron in a π orbital has one unit of orbital angular momentum about the internuclear axis.

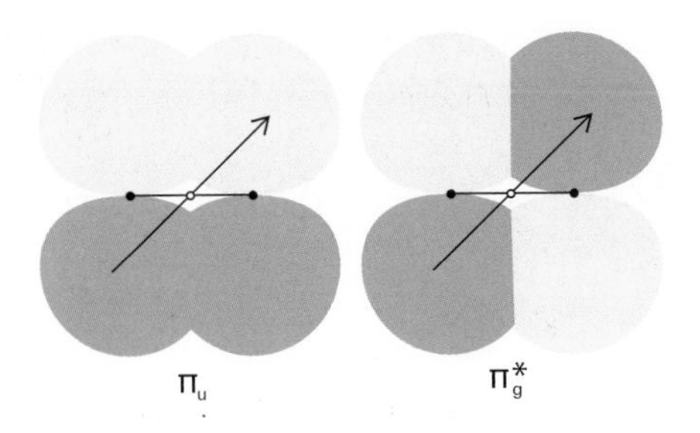

Fig. 14.25 The gerade/ungerade character of π bonding and antibonding orbitals.

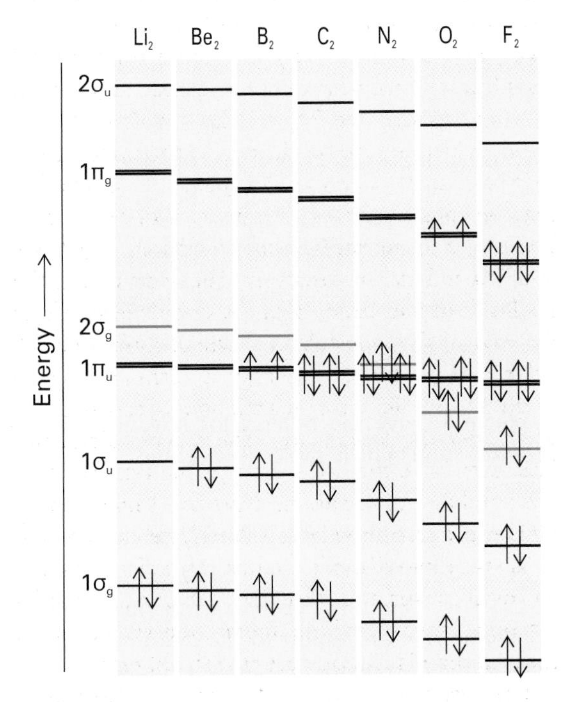

Fig. 14.26 The variation of the orbital energies of Period 2 homonuclear diatomic molecules. Only the valence-shell orbitals are shown.

applies, whereas others have the order shown in Fig. 14.23. The change in order can be seen in Fig. 14.26, which shows the calculated energy levels for the Period 2 homonuclear diatomic molecules. A useful rule is that, for neutral molecules, the order shown in Fig. 14.22 is valid for O_2 and F_2, whereas the order shown in Fig. 14.23 is valid for the preceding elements of the period.

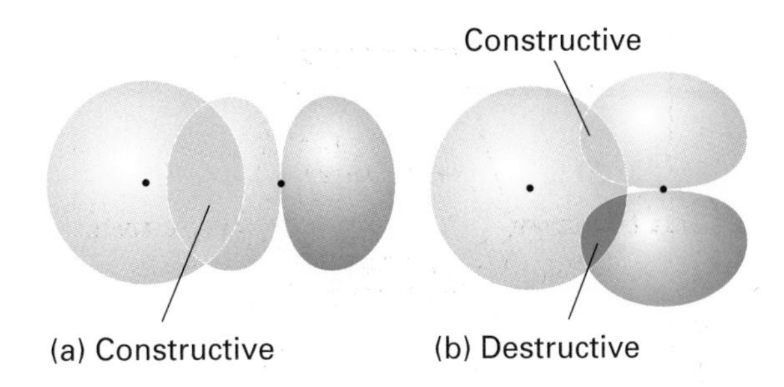

Fig. 14.27 Overlapping *s* and *p* orbitals. (a) End-on overlap leads to non-zero overlap and to the formation of an axially symmetric σ orbital. (b) Broadside overlap leads to no net accumulation or reduction of electron density and does not contribute to bonding.

14.12 Symmetry and overlap

One central feature of molecular orbital theory can now be addressed. We have seen that *s* and p_z orbitals may contribute to the formation of σ orbitals, and that p_x and p_y orbitals may contribute to π orbitals. However, we never have to consider orbitals formed by the overlap of *s* and p_x orbitals (or p_y orbitals). When building molecular orbitals, *we need consider linear combinations only of atomic orbitals of the same symmetry with respect to the internuclear axis*. Because an *s* orbital has cylindrical symmetry around the internuclear axis, but a p_x orbital does not, the two atomic orbitals cannot contribute to the same molecular orbital. The reason for this distinction based on symmetry can be understood by considering the interference between an *s* orbital and a p_x orbital (Fig. 14.27): although there is constructive interference between the two orbitals on one side of the axis, there is an exactly compensating amount of destructive interference on the other side of the axis, and the net bonding or antibonding effect is zero.

Derivation 14.2

Overlap integrals

The extent to which two orbitals overlap is measured by the **overlap integral**, *S*:

$$S = \int \psi_A \psi_B \, d\tau$$

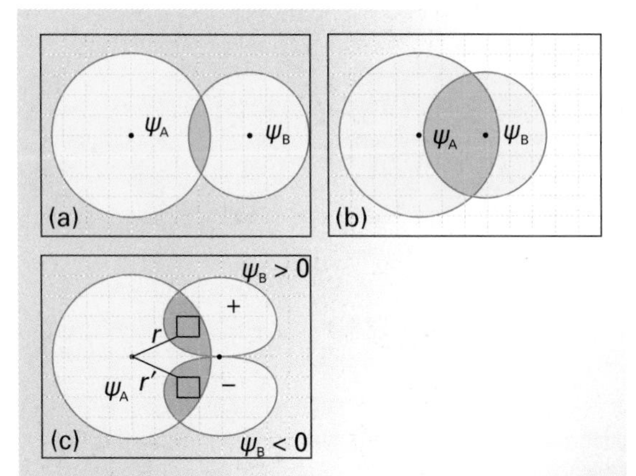

Fig. 14.28 A schematic representation of the contributions to the overlap integral. (a) $S \approx 0$ because the orbitals are far apart and their product is always small. (b) S is large (but less than 1) because the product $\psi_A\psi_B$ is large over a substantial region. (c) $S = 0$ because the positive region of overlap is exactly cancelled by the negative region.

In quantum mechanics, it is conventional to use $d\tau$ (where τ is tau) to represent an infinitesimal volume. In cartesian coordinates, $d\tau = dx\,dy\,dz$. In spherical coordinates, $d\tau = r^2\,dr \sin\theta\,d\theta\,d\phi$.

where the integration is over all space. If the atomic orbital ψ_A on A is small wherever the orbital ψ_B on B is large, or vice versa, then the product of their amplitudes is everywhere small and the integral—the sum of these products—is small (Fig. 14.28a). If ψ_A and ψ_B are simultaneously large in some region of space, then S may be large (Fig. 14.28b). If the two atomic orbitals are identical (for example, 1*s* orbitals on the same nucleus), $S = 1$. The overlap integral between two H1*s* orbitals separated by a distance R turns out to be

$$S = \left\{1 + \frac{R}{a_0} + \frac{1}{3}\left(\frac{R}{a_0}\right)^2\right\} e^{-R/a_0}$$

where a_0 is the Bohr radius. This function is plotted in Fig. 14.29: note how the exponential factor ensures that S approaches zero for large separations. Typical values for orbitals with $n = 2$ are in the range 0.2 to 0.3.

Now consider the arrangement in Fig. 14.28c in which an *s* orbital overlaps a p_x orbital of a different atom. At some point the product $\psi_A\psi_B$ may be large. However, there is a point where $\psi_A\psi_B$ has exactly the same magnitude but an opposite sign. When the integral is evaluated, these two contributions are added together and cancel. For every point in the upper half of the diagram, there is a point in the lower half that cancels it, so $S = 0$. Therefore, for symmetry reasons, there is no net overlap between the *s* and *p* orbitals in this arrangement.

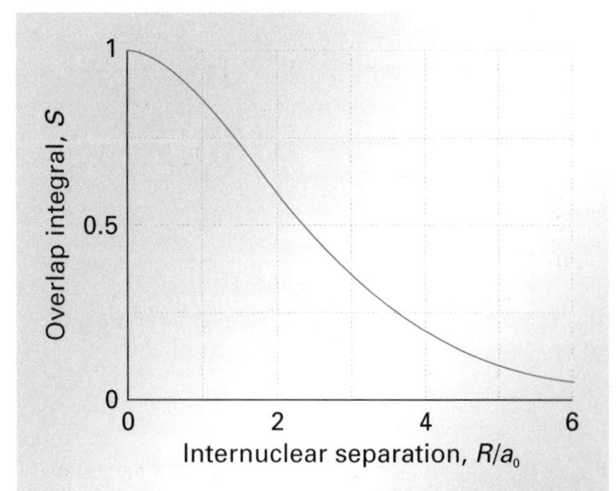

Fig. 14.29 The variation of the overlap integral with internuclear distance for two H1*s* orbitals.

We now have the criteria for selecting atomic orbitals from which molecular orbitals are to be built:

1. Use all available valence orbitals from both atoms (in polyatomic molecules, from all the atoms).
2. Classify the atomic orbitals as having σ and π symmetry with respect to the internuclear axis, and build σ and π orbitals from all atomic orbitals of a given symmetry.
3. From N_σ atomic orbitals of σ symmetry, N_σ σ orbitals can be built with progressively higher energy from strongly bonding to strongly antibonding.
4. From N_π atomic orbitals of π symmetry, N_π π orbitals can be built with progressively higher energy from strongly bonding to strongly antibonding. The π orbitals occur in doubly degenerate pairs.

As a general rule, the energy of each type of orbital (σ or π) increases with the number of internuclear nodes. The lowest energy orbital of a given species

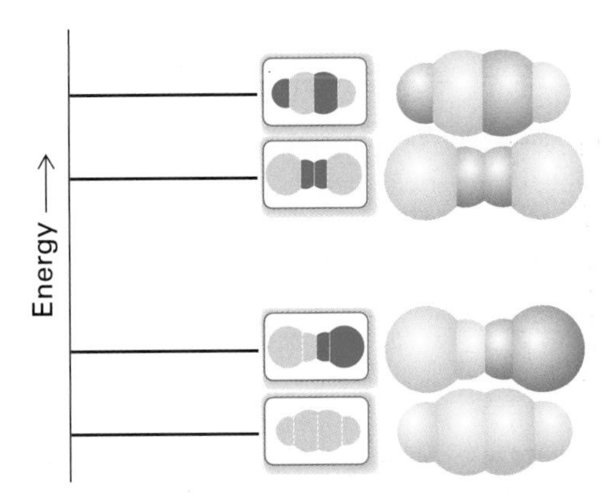

Fig. 14.30 A schematic representation of the four molecular orbitals that can be formed from four *s* orbitals in a chain of four atoms. The lowest energy combination (the bottom diagram) is formed from atomic orbitals with the same sign, and there are no internuclear nodes. The next higher orbital has one node (at the centre of the molecule). The next higher orbital has two internuclear nodes, and the uppermost, highest energy orbital, has three internuclear nodes, one between each neighbouring pair of atoms, and is fully antibonding. The sizes of the spheres reflect the contributions of each atom to the molecular orbital; the shading represents different signs.

has no internuclear nodes and the highest energy orbital has a nodal plane between each pair of adjacent atoms (Fig. 14.30).

Example 14.2

Assessing the contribution of d orbitals

Can *d* orbitals contribute to σ and π orbitals in diatomic molecules?

Strategy We need to assess the symmetry of *d* orbitals with respect to the internuclear *z*-axis: orbitals of the same symmetry can contribute to a given molecular orbital.

Solution A d_{z^2} orbital has cylindrical symmetry around *z* and so can contribute to σ orbitals. The d_{zx} and d_{yz} orbitals have π symmetry with respect to the axis (Fig. 14.31), so they can contribute to π orbitals.

Self-test 14.7

Sketch the 'δ orbitals' (orbitals that resemble four-lobed *d* orbitals when viewed along the internuclear axis) that may be formed by the remaining two *d* orbitals (and

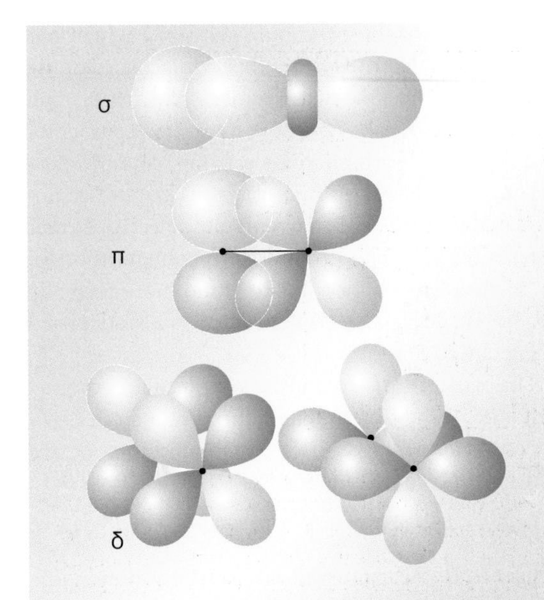

Fig. 14.31 The types of molecular orbital to which *d* orbitals can contribute. The σ and π combinations can be formed with *s*, *p*, and *d* orbitals of the appropriate symmetry, but the δ orbitals can be formed only by the *d* orbitals of the two atoms.

which contribute to bonding in some *d*-metal cluster compounds). Give their inversion-symmetry classification.

[*Answer:* see Fig. 14.31: bonding are g, antibonding are u]

14.13 The electronic structures of homonuclear diatomic molecules

Figures 14.22 and 14.23 show the general layout of the valence-shell atomic orbitals of Period 2 atoms on the left and right. The lines in the middle are an indication of the energies of the molecular orbitals that can be formed by overlap of atomic orbitals. From the eight valence shell orbitals (four from each atom), we can form eight molecular orbitals: four are σ orbitals and four, in two pairs, are doubly degenerate π orbitals. With the orbitals established, we derive the ground-state electron configurations of the molecules by adding the appropriate number of electrons to the orbitals and following the building-up rules. Charged species (such as the peroxide ion, O_2^{2-}, and C_2^+) need either more or fewer electrons (for anions and cations, respectively) than the neutral molecules.

We illustrate the procedure with N_2, which has 10 valence electrons; for this molecule we use Fig. 14.22. The first two electrons pair, enter, and fill the 1σ orbital. The next two electrons enter and fill the 1σ* orbital. Six electrons remain. There are two 1π orbitals, so four electrons can be accommodated in them. The two remaining electrons enter the 2σ orbital. The ground-state configuration of N_2 is therefore $1\sigma^2 1\sigma^{*2} 1\pi^4 2\sigma^2$ (and more formally $1\sigma_g^2 1\sigma_u^2 1\pi_u^4 2\sigma_g^2$). This configuration is also depicted in Fig. 14.23.

The strength of a bond in a molecule is the net outcome of the bonding and antibonding effects of the electrons in the orbitals. The **bond order**, *b*, in a diatomic molecule is defined as

$$b = \tfrac{1}{2}(n - n^*) \qquad (14.9)$$

where n is the number of electrons in bonding orbitals and n^* is the number of electrons in antibonding orbitals (as judged by their resemblance to the simple pairwise LCAOs). Each electron pair in a bonding orbital increases the bond order by 1 and each pair in an antibonding orbital decreases it by 1. For H_2, $b = 1$, corresponding to a single bond between the two atoms: this bond order is consistent with the Lewis structure H–H for the molecule. In He_2, which has equal numbers of bonding and antibonding electrons (with $n = 2$ and $n^* = 2$), the bond order is $b = 0$, and there is no bond. In N_2, 1σ, 3σ, and 1π are bonding orbitals, and $n = 2 + 2 + 4 = 8$; however, 2σ* (the antibonding partner of 1σ) is antibonding, so $n^* = 2$ and the bond order of N_2 is $b = \tfrac{1}{2}(8 - 2) = 3$. This value is consistent with the Lewis structure :N≡N:, in which there is a triple bond between the two atoms.

The bond order is a useful parameter for discussing the characteristics of bonds, because it correlates with bond length, and the greater the bond order between atoms of a given pair of atoms, the shorter the bond. The bond order also correlates with bond strength, and the greater the bond order, the greater the strength. The high bond order of N_2 is consistent with its high dissociation energy (942 kJ mol^{-1}).

Example 14.3

Writing the electron configuration of a diatomic molecule

Write the ground-state electron configuration of O_2 and calculate the bond order.

Strategy Decide which MO energy level diagram to use (Fig. 14.22 or Fig. 14.23). Count the valence electrons and accommodate them by using the building-up principle.

Solution Figure 14.22 is appropriate for oxygen. There are 12 valence electrons to accommodate. The first 10 electrons recreate the N_2 configuration (with a reversal of the order of the 3σ and 1π orbitals); the remaining two electrons must occupy the 2π* orbitals. The configuration and bond order are therefore $1\sigma^2 1\sigma^{*2} 2\sigma^2 1\pi^4 1\pi^{*2}$ and more formally $1\sigma_g^2 1\sigma_u^2 2\sigma_g^2 1\pi_u^4 1\pi_g^2$. This configuration is also depicted in Fig. 14.22. Because 1σ, 2σ, and 1π are regarded as bonding and 1σ* and 1π* as antibonding, the bond order is $b = \tfrac{1}{2}(8 - 4) = 2$. This bond order accords with the classical view that oxygen has a double bond.

Self-test 14.8

Write the electron configuration of F_2 and deduce its bond order.

[*Answer:* $1\sigma_g^2 1\sigma_u^2 2\sigma_g^2 1\pi_u^4 1\pi_g^4$, $b = 1$]

We see from Example 14.3 that the electron configuration of O_2 is $1\sigma^2 1\sigma^{*2} 2\sigma^2 1\pi^4 1\pi^{*2}$. According to the building-up principle, the two 1π* electrons in O_2 will occupy different orbitals. One enters the 1π* orbital formed by overlap of $2p_x$. The other enters its degenerate partner, the 1π* orbital formed from overlap of the $2p_y$ orbitals. Because the two electrons occupy different orbitals, by Hund's rule they will have parallel spins (↑↑). Consequently, an O_2 molecule is sometimes regarded as a biradical, a species with two unpaired electrons.[7] Molecular orbital theory therefore suggests—correctly—that O_2 is a reactive component of the Earth's atmosphere; its most important biological role is as an oxidizing agent. By contrast, N_2, the major component of the air we breathe, is so unreactive that nitrogen fixation, the reduction of

[7] A true biradical has two electron spins with random relative orientations; in O_2 the two spins are parallel.

atmospheric N_2 to NH_3 by certain microorganisms, is among the most thermodynamically demanding of biological processes in the sense that it requires a great deal of energy derived from metabolic processes.

A radical is a molecular species containing one or more unpaired electrons; most radicals are highly reactive and must be studied by special techniques, such as those discussed in Section 10.2.

The electronic configuration of O_2 also suggests that it will be magnetic because the magnetic fields generated by the two unpaired spins do not cancel. Specifically, O_2 is predicted to be a **paramagnetic** substance, a substance that is drawn into a magnetic field. Most substances (those with paired electron spins) are **diamagnetic**, and are pushed out of a magnetic field. That O_2 is in fact a paramagnetic gas is a striking confirmation of the superiority of the molecular orbital description of the molecule over the Lewis and VB descriptions (which require all the electrons to be paired). The property of paramagnetism is used to monitor the oxygen content of incubators by measuring the magnetism of the gases they contain.

An F_2 molecule has two more electrons than an O_2 molecule, so its configuration is $1\sigma^2 1\sigma^{*2} 2\sigma^2 1\pi^4 1\pi^{*4}$ and its bond order is 1. We conclude that F_2 is a singly bonded molecule, in agreement with its Lewis structure :F̤̈–F̤̈:. The low bond order is consistent with the low dissociation energy of F_2 (154 kJ mol^{-1}). A hypothetical Ne_2 molecule would have two further electrons: its configuration would be $1\sigma^2 1\sigma^{*2} 2\sigma^2 1\pi^4 1\pi^{*4} 2\sigma^{*2}$ and its bond order 0. The bond order of zero—which implies that two neon atoms do not bond together—is consistent with the monatomic character of neon.

Example 14.4

Judging the relative bond strengths of molecules and ions

The superoxide ion, O_2^-, plays an important rôle in the ageing processes that take place in organisms. Judge whether O_2^- is likely to have a larger or smaller dissociation energy than O_2.

Strategy Because a species with the larger bond order is likely to have the larger dissociation energy, we should compare their electronic configurations, and assess their bond orders.

Solution From Fig. 14.22,

O_2 $\quad 1\sigma^2 1\sigma^{*2} 1\pi^4 2\sigma^2 1\pi^2 \quad b = 2$

O_2^- $\quad 1\sigma^2 1\sigma^{*2} 1\pi^4 2\sigma^1 1\pi^3 \quad b = 1.5$

Because the anion has the smaller bond order, we expect it to have the smaller dissociation energy.

Self-test 14.9

Which can be expected to have the higher dissociation energy, F_2 or F_2^+?

[*Answer:* F_2^+]

14.14 Heteronuclear diatomic molecules

A **heteronuclear diatomic molecule** is a diatomic molecule formed from atoms of two different elements, such as CO and HCl. The electron distribution in the covalent bond between the atoms is not symmetrical between the atoms because it is energetically favourable for a bonding electron pair to be found closer to one atom rather than the other. This imbalance results in a **polar bond**, which is a covalent bond in which the electron pair is shared unequally by the two atoms. The **electronegativity**, χ (chi), of an element is the power of its atoms to draw electrons to itself when it is part of a compound, so we can expect the polarity of a bond to depend on the relative electronegativities of the elements.

Linus Pauling formulated a numerical scale of electronegativity based on considerations of bond dissociation energies, E(A–B):

$$|\chi_A - \chi_B| = 0.102 \times \{\Delta E/(\text{kJ mol}^{-1})\}^{1/2} \qquad (14.10a)$$

with

$$\Delta E = E(\text{A–B}) - \tfrac{1}{2}\{E(\text{A–A}) + E(\text{B–B})\} \qquad (14.10b)$$

Table 14.2 lists values for the main-group elements. Robert Mulliken proposed an alternative definition in terms of the ionization energy, I, and the electron affinity, E_{ea}, of the element expressed in electronvolts:

Table 14.2

Electronegativities of the main-group elements

H						
2.1						
Li	**Be**	**B**	**C**	**N**	**O**	**F**
1.01	1.5	2.0	2.5	3.0	3.5	4.0
Na	**Mg**	**Al**	**Si**	**P**	**S**	**Cl**
0.9	1.2	1.5	1.8	2.1	2.5	3.0
K	**Ca**	**Ga**	**Ge**	**As**	**Se**	**Br**
0.8	1.0	1.6	1.8	2.0	2.4	2.8
Rb	**Sr**	**In**	**Sn**	**Sb**	**Te**	**I**
0.8	1.0	1.7	1.8	1.9	2.1	2.5
Cs	**Ba**	**Tl**	**Pb**	**Bi**	**Po**	
0.7	0.9	1.8	1.8	1.9	2.0	

$$\chi = \tfrac{1}{2}(I + E_{ea}) \qquad (14.11)$$

This relation is plausible, because an atom that has a high electronegativity is likely to be one that has a high ionization energy (so that it is unlikely to lose electrons to another atom in the molecule) and a high electron affinity (so that it is energetically favourable for an electron to move towards it). The Mulliken electronegativities are broadly in line with the Pauling electronegativities. Electronegativities show a periodicity, and the elements with the highest electronegativities are those close to fluorine in the periodic table.

The location of the bonding electron pair close to one atom in a heteronuclear molecule results in that atom having a net negative charge, which is called a **partial negative charge** and denoted δ−. There is a compensating **partial positive charge**, δ+, on the other atom. In a typical heteronuclear diatomic molecule, the more electronegative element has the partial negative charge and the more electropositive element has the partial positive charge.

Self-test 14.10

Predict the (weak) polarity of a C–H bond.

[*Answer:* $^{\delta-}$C–H$^{\delta+}$]

Molecular orbital theory takes polar bonds into its stride. A polar bond consists of two electrons in an orbital of the form

$$\psi = c_A\psi_A + c_B\psi_B \qquad (14.12)$$

with c_B^2 no longer equal to c_A^2. If $c_B^2 > c_A^2$, the electrons spend more time on B than on A and the molecule is polar in the sense $^{\delta+}$A–B$^{\delta-}$. A non-polar bond, a covalent bond in which the electron pair is shared equally between the two atoms and there are zero partial charges on each atom, has $c_A^2 = c_B^2$. A pure ionic bond, in which one atom has obtained almost sole possession of the electron pair (as in Cs^+F^-, to a first approximation), has one coefficient zero (so that A^+B^- would have $c_A^2 = 0$ and $c_B^2 = 1$).

A general feature of molecular orbitals between dissimilar atoms is that the atomic orbital with the lower energy (that belonging to the more electronegative atom) makes the larger contribution to the lowest energy molecular orbital. The opposite is true of the highest (most antibonding) orbital, for which the principal contribution comes from the atomic orbital with higher energy (the less electronegative atom):

Bonding orbitals: for $\chi_A > \chi_B$, $c_A^2 > c_B^2$

Antibonding orbitals: for $\chi_A > \chi_B$, $c_A^2 < c_B^2$

Figure 14.32 shows a schematic representation of this point.

These features of polar bonds can be illustrated by considering HF. The general form of the molecular orbitals of HF is

$$\psi = c_H\psi_H + c_F\psi_F \qquad (14.13)$$

where ψ_H is an H1*s* orbital and ψ_F is an F2p_z orbital. Because the ionization energy of a hydrogen atom is 13.6 eV, we know that the energy of the H1*s* orbital is −13.6 eV. As usual, the zero of energy is the infinitely separated electron and proton (Fig. 14.33). Similarly, from the ionization energy of fluorine, which is 18.6 eV, we know that the energy of the F2p_z orbital is −18.6 eV, about 5 eV lower than the H1*s* orbital. It follows that the bonding σ orbital in HF is mainly F2p_z and the antibonding σ orbital is mainly H1*s* orbital in character. The two electrons in the bonding orbital are most likely to be found in the F2p_z orbital, so there is a partial negative charge

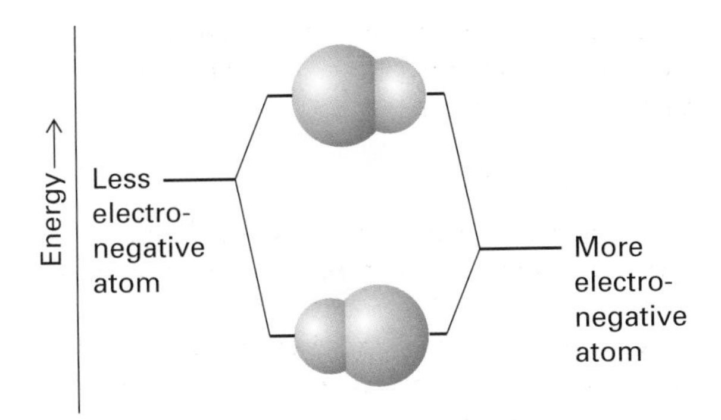

Fig. 14.32 A schematic representation of the relative contributions of atoms of different electronegativities to bonding and antibonding molecular orbitals. In the bonding orbital, the more electronegative atom makes the greater contribution (represented by the larger sphere), and the electrons of the bond are more likely to be found on that atom. The opposite is true of an antibonding orbital. An antibonding orbital is of high energy partly because the electrons that occupy it are likely to be found on the more electropositive atom.

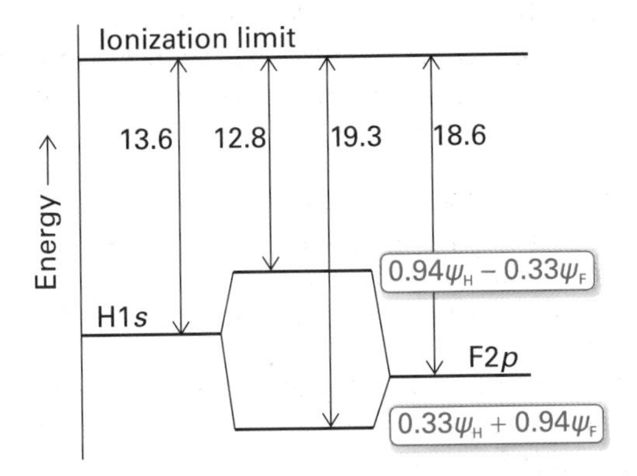

Fig. 14.33 The atomic orbital energy levels of H and F atoms and the molecular orbitals they form. The bonding orbital has predominantly F atom character and the antibonding orbital has predominantly H atom character. Energies are in electronvolts.

on the F atom and a partial positive charge on the H atom.

A systematic way of finding the coefficients in the linear combinations is to use the variation theorem and to look for the values of the coefficients that result in the lowest energy (Section 14.2). For example, when the variation principle is applied to an H_2 molecule, the calculated energy is lowest when the two H1*s* orbitals contribute equally to a bonding

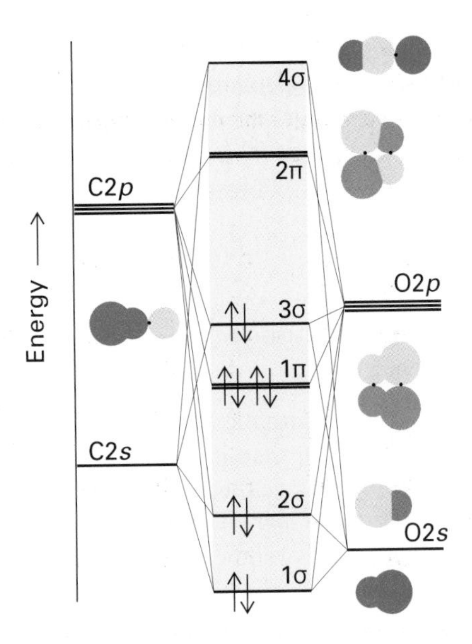

Fig. 14.34 The molecular orbital energy level diagram for CO.

orbital. However, when we apply the principle to HF, the lowest energy is obtained for the orbital

$$\psi = 0.33\psi_H + 0.94\psi_F$$

We see that indeed the F2p_z orbital does make the greater contribution to the bonding σ orbital.

Self-test 14.11

What percentage of its time does a σ electron in HF spend in an F2p_z orbital?

[*Answer:* 88 per cent (= $(0.94)^2 \times 100$ per cent)]

Figure 14.34 shows the bonding scheme in CO and illustrates a number of points we have made. The ground configuration is $1\sigma^2 2\sigma^2 1\pi^4 3\sigma^2$. (The g,u designation is inapplicable because the molecule is heteronuclear.) The lowest energy orbitals are predominantly of O character as that is the more electronegative element. The **highest occupied molecular orbital** (HOMO) is 3σ, which is a largely non-bonding orbital centred on C, so the two electrons that occupy it can be regarded as a lone pair on the C atom. The **lowest unoccupied molecular orbital** (LUMO) is 2π, which is largely a doubly degenerate orbital of 2*p* character on carbon. This combination of a lone pair orbital on C and a pair of empty π orbitals also largely on C is at the root of the importance of carbon monoxide in *d*-block chemistry, because it enables it to form an extensive series of carbonyl complexes by a combination of electron donation from the 3σ orbital and electron acceptance into the 2π orbitals.

14.15 The structures of polyatomic molecules

The bonds in polyatomic molecules are built in the same way as in diatomic molecules, the only difference being that we use more atomic orbitals to construct the molecular orbitals, and these molecular orbitals spread over the entire molecule, not just the adjacent atoms of the bond. In general, a molecular orbital is a linear combination of all the atomic orbitals of all the atoms in the molecule. In H_2O, for instance, the atomic orbitals are the two H1*s* orbitals, the O2*s* orbital, and the three O2*p* orbitals (if we consider only the valence shell). From these six atomic orbitals we can construct six molecular orbitals that spread over all three atoms. The molecular orbitals differ in energy. The lowest-energy, most strongly bonding orbital has the least number of nodes between adjacent atoms. The highest-energy, most strongly antibonding orbital has the greatest numbers of nodes between neighbouring atoms.

According to MO theory, the bonding influence of a single electron pair is distributed over all the atoms, and each electron pair (the maximum number of electrons that can occupy any single molecular orbital) helps to bind all the atoms together. In the LCAO approximation, each molecular orbital is modelled as a sum of atomic orbitals, with atomic orbitals contributed by all the atoms in the molecule. Thus, a typical molecular orbital in H_2O constructed from H1*s* orbitals (denoted ψ_A and ψ_B) and O2*s* and O2*p* orbitals (denoted ψ_{Os} and ψ_{Op}) will have the composition

$$\psi = c_1\psi_A + c_2\psi_{Os} + c_3\psi_{Op} + c_4\psi_B \qquad (14.14)$$

Because four atomic orbitals are being used to form the LCAO, there will be four possible molecular orbitals of this kind: the lowest-energy (most bonding) orbital will have no internuclear nodes and the

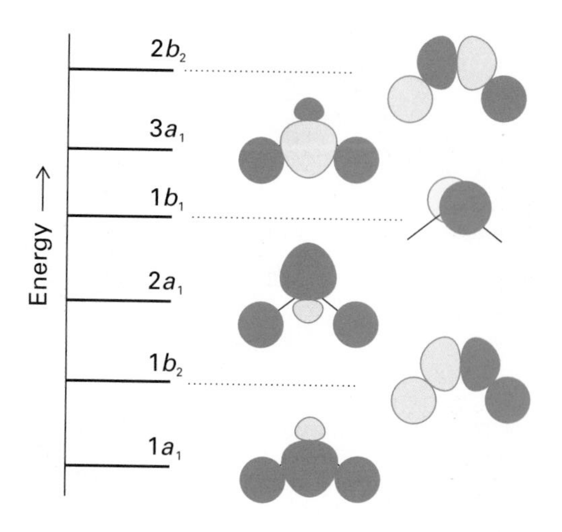

Fig. 14.35 Schematic form of the molecular orbitals of H_2O.

highest-energy (most antibonding) orbital will have a node between each pair of neighbouring nuclei (Fig. 14.35).

An important example of the application of MO theory is to the orbitals that may be formed from the *p* orbitals perpendicular to the molecular plane of benzene, C_6H_6. Because there are six such atomic orbitals, it is possible to form six molecular orbitals of the form

$$\psi = c_1\psi_1 + c_2\psi_2 + c_3\psi_3 + c_4\psi_4 + c_5\psi_5 + c_6\psi_6 \qquad (14.15)$$

The lowest-energy, most strongly bonding orbital has no internuclear nodes, and has the form[8]

$$\psi = \psi_1 + \psi_2 + \psi_3 + \psi_4 + \psi_5 + \psi_6$$

This orbital is illustrated at the bottom of Fig. 14.36. It is strongly bonding because the constructive interference between neighbouring *p* orbitals results in a good accumulation of electron density between the nuclei (but slightly off the internuclear axis, as in the π bonds of diatomic molecules). The most antibonding orbital has the form

$$\psi = \psi_1 - \psi_2 + \psi_3 - \psi_4 + \psi_5 - \psi_6$$

[8] We are ignoring normalization factors, for clarity. In this and the following case it would be $(\frac{1}{6})^{1/2}$ if we ignore overlap.

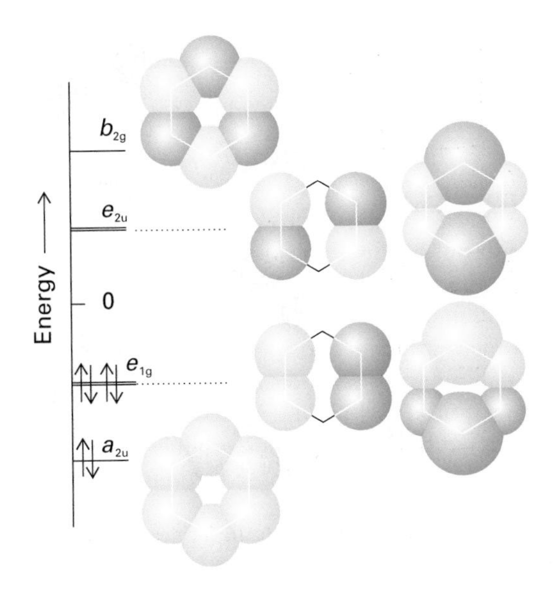

Fig. 14.36 The π orbitals of benzene. The lowest-energy orbital is fully bonding between neighbouring atoms but the uppermost orbital is fully antibonding. The two pairs of doubly degenerate molecular orbitals have an intermediate number of internuclear nodes. As usual, light and dark shading represents different signs of the wavefunction. The orbitals have opposite signs below the plane of the ring. The symmetry designations are those appropriate to a hexagonal molecule.

The alternation of signs in the linear combination results in destructive interference between neighbours, and the molecular orbital has a nodal plane between each pair of neighbours, as shown in the illustration. The remaining four molecular orbitals are more difficult to establish by qualitative arguments, but they have the form shown in Fig. 14.36, and lie in energy between the most bonding and most antibonding orbitals. Note that the four intermediate orbitals form two doubly degenerate pairs, one net bonding and the other net antibonding.

We find the energies of the six π molecular orbitals in benzene by solving the Schrödinger equation; they are also shown in the molecular orbital energy level diagram. There are six electrons to be accommodated (one is supplied by each C atom), and they occupy the lowest three orbitals (Fig. 14.37). The resulting electron distribution is like a double doughnut. It is an important feature of the configuration that the only molecular orbitals occupied have a net bonding character, as this is one con-

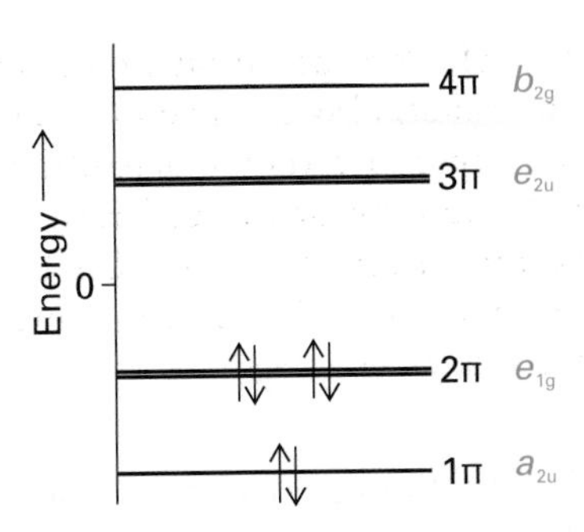

Fig. 14.37 The π molecular orbital energy level diagram for benzene, and the configuration in its ground state.

tribution to the stability (in the sense of low energy) of the benzene molecule. It may be helpful to note the similarity between the molecular orbital energy level diagram for benzene and that for N_2 (see Fig. 14.23): the strong bonding in benzene is echoed in the strong bonding in nitrogen.

A feature of the molecular orbital description of benzene is that each molecular orbital spreads either all round or partially round the C_6 ring. That is, π bonding is **delocalized**, and each electron pair helps to bind together several or all of the C atoms. The delocalization of bonding influence is a primary feature of molecular orbital theory and we shall encounter it in its extreme form when we come to consider the electronic structures of solids.

Computational chemistry

Computational chemistry is now a standard part of chemical research. One major application is in pharmaceutical chemistry, where the likely pharmacological activity of a molecule can be assessed computationally from its shape and electron density distribution before expensive *in vivo* trials are started. Commercial software is now widely available for calculating the electronic structures of molecules and displaying the results graphically. All such calculations work within the Born–Oppenheimer approximation and express the molecular orbitals as LCAOs.

There are two principal approaches to solving the Schrödinger equation for many-electron polyatomic molecules. In the **semi-empirical methods**, certain expressions that occur in the Schrödinger equation are set equal to parameters that have been chosen to lead to the best fit to experimental quantities, such as enthalpies of formation. Semi-empirical methods are applicable to a wide range of molecules with an almost limitless number of atoms, and are widely popular. In the more fundamental ***ab initio* methods**, an attempt is made to calculate structures from first principles, using only the atomic numbers of the atoms present. Such an approach is intrinsically more reliable than a semi-empirical procedure.

Both types of procedure typically adopt a **self-consistent field** (SCF) procedure, in which an initial guess about the composition of the LCAO is successively refined until the solution remains unchanged in a cycle of calculation. For example, the potential energy of an electron at a point in the molecule depends on the locations of the nuclei and all the other electrons. Initially, we do not know the locations of those electrons (more specifically, we do not know the detailed form of the wavefunctions that describe their locations, the molecular orbitals they occupy). First, then, we guess the form of those wavefunctions—we guess the values of the coefficients in the LCAO used to build the molecular orbitals—and solve the Schrödinger equation for the electron of interest on the basis of that guess. Now we have a first approximation to the molecular orbital of our electron (a reasonable estimate of the coefficients for its LCAO) and we repeat the procedure for all the other molecular orbitals in the molecule. At this stage, we have a new set of molecular orbitals that, in general, will have coefficients that differ from our first guess, and we also have an estimate of the energy of the molecule. We use that refined set of molecular orbitals to repeat the calculation and calculate a new energy. In general, the coefficients in the LCAOs and the energy will differ from the new starting point. However, there comes a stage when repetition of the calculation leaves the coefficients and energy unchanged. The orbitals are now said to be self-consistent, and we accept them as a description of the molecule.

14.16 Semi-empirical methods

Semi-empirical methods have grown in sophistication. All of them are based on a manipulation of the Schrödinger equation, which gives a series of simultaneous equations for the coefficients in the LCAO used to build the molecular orbitals:

$$(H_{AA} - ES_{AA})c_A + (H_{AB} - ES_{AB})c_B + \cdots = 0$$
$$(H_{BA} - ES_{BA})c_A + (H_{BB} - ES_{BB})c_B + \cdots = 0$$

and so on. In this expression, the H_{JK} are expressions that include various contributions to the energy, including the repulsion between electrons and their attractions to the nuclei; the S_{JK} are the overlap integrals introduced in Derivation 14.2 between orbitals J and K. The coefficients and the energies of the corresponding orbitals are found by solving these simultaneous equations by making various approximations.

The first and most primitive procedure was proposed in 1931 by Erich Hückel for the π orbitals of hydrocarbons. He took an extreme view: all the overlap integrals were ignored ($S_{JK} = 0$ if $J \neq K$) unless the two orbitals belonged to the same atom ($S_{JJ} = 1$); all the H_{JK} were set equal to zero unless J and K were the same ($H_{JJ} = \alpha$) or were on neighbouring atoms ($H_{JK} = \beta$). The parameters α and β are then chosen to give agreement with selected experimental quantities, such as bond strengths and spectroscopic excitation energies. For instance, α is commonly set equal to the ionization energy of carbon and β is commonly taken as about -0.8 eV (-75 kJ mol^{-1}).

Illustration 14.2

The Hückel approximation

Consider the ethene molecule, $CH_2{=}CH_2$. The π orbitals are built from a *p* orbital on each C atom, so the LCAOs have the form $\psi = c_A\psi_A + c_B\psi_B$ where ψ_A and ψ_B are the two *p* orbitals perpendicular to the molecular plane. The two simultaneous equations we have to solve are therefore

$$(H_{AA} - ES_{AA})c_A + (H_{AB} - ES_{AB})c_B = 0$$
$$(H_{BA} - ES_{BA})c_A + (H_{BB} - ES_{BB})c_B = 0$$

According to the Hückel approximation, we simplify these equations to

$$(\alpha - E)c_A + \beta c_B = 0$$
$$\beta c_A + (\alpha - E)c_B = 0$$

The solutions of these equations are $E = \alpha \pm \beta$ and $c_B = \pm c_A$. Therefore, the orbitals and their energies are

$$\psi = c_A(\psi_A + \psi_B) \qquad E = \alpha + \beta$$

$$\psi = c_A(\psi_A - \psi_B) \qquad E = \alpha - \beta$$

The first of this pair lies lower in energy because β is negative.

Self-test 14.12

Solve the simultaneous equations $(\alpha - E)c_A + \beta c_B = 0$ and $\beta c_A + (\alpha - E)c_B = 0$ and verify the results from Illustration 14.2. (*Hint.* If you are not familiar with the use of determinants to solve simultaneous equations, begin by dividing the first equation by $(\alpha - E)$ and the second by $-\beta$. Then add the two equations and proceed to the solution, remembering that neither c_A nor c_B can be zero.)

The removal of the restriction of the Hückel method to planar hydrocarbon systems was achieved with the introduction of the **extended Hückel theory** (EHT) in about 1963. In heteroatomic nonplanar systems (such as *d*-metal complexes) the separation of orbitals into π and σ is no longer appropriate and each type of atom has a different value of H_{JJ} (which in Hückel theory is set equal to α for all atoms). In this approximation, the overlap integrals are not set equal to zero but are calculated explicitly. Furthermore, the H_{JK}, which in Hückel theory are set equal to β, in EHT are made proportional to the overlap integral between the orbitals J and K.

The web site contains links to sites from which free software for Hückel and EHT calculations can be downloaded.

Further approximations of the Hückel method were removed with the introduction of the 'complete neglect of differential overlap' (CNDO) method which is a slightly more sophisticated method for dealing with the terms H_{JK} that appear in the simultaneous equations for the coefficients. The introduction of CNDO opened the door to an avalanche of similar but improved methods and their accompanying acronyms, such as 'intermediate neglect of differential overlap' (INDO), 'modified neglect of differential overlap' (MNDO), and the 'Austin Model 1' (AM1, version 2 of MINDO). Software for all these procedures is now readily available, and reasonably sophisticated calculations can be run even on hand-held computers.

14.17 *Ab initio* methods and density functional theory

The *ab initio* methods also simplify the calculations, but they do so by setting up the problem in a different manner, avoiding the need to estimate parameters by appeal to experimental data. In these methods, sophisticated techniques are used to solve the Schrödinger equation numerically. The difficulty with this procedure is the enormous time it takes to carry out the detailed calculation. That time can be reduced by replacing the hydrogenic atomic orbitals used to form the LCAO by a **gaussian-type orbital** (GTO) in which the exponential function e^{-r} characteristic of actual orbitals is replaced by a sum of gaussian functions of the form e^{-r^2} (recall the relative shapes of exponential and gaussian functions shown in Fig. 1.7).

A technique that has gained considerable ground in recent years to become one of the most widely used techniques for the calculation of molecular structure is **density functional theory** (DFT). Its advantages include less demanding computational effort, less computer time, and—in some cases, particularly *d*-metal complexes—better agreement with experimental values than is obtained from other procedures. The central focus of DFT is the electron density, ρ (rho), rather than the wavefunction ψ. When the Schrödinger equation is expressed in terms of ρ, it becomes a set of equations called the **Kohn–Sham equations**. Like the Schrödinger equation, the Kohn–Sham equations are solved iteratively and self-consistently. First, we guess the electron density. For this step it is common to use a superposition of atomic electron densities. Next, the Kohn–Sham equations are solved to obtain an initial set of orbitals. This set of orbitals is used to obtain a better approximation to the electron density and the process is repeated until the density and the energy are constant to within some tolerance.

The 'functional' part of the name DFT comes from the fact that the energy of the molecule is a function of the electron density, written $E[\rho]$, and the electron density is itself a function of position, $\rho(\boldsymbol{r})$, and in mathematics a function of a function is called a 'functional'.

The web site contains links to sites where you may perform semi-empirical and *ab initio* calculations on simple molecules directly from your web browser.

14.18 Graphical output

One of the most significant developments in computational chemistry has been the introduction of graphical representations of molecular orbitals and electron densities. The raw output of a molecular structure calculation is a list of the coefficients of the atomic orbitals in each molecular orbital and the energies of these orbitals. The graphical representation of a molecular orbital uses stylized shapes to represent the basis set, and then scales their size to indicate the value of the coefficient in the LCAO. Different signs of the wavefunctions are represented by different colours: in the illustrations shown here (Fig. 14.38), we use different shades of grey and colour.

Once the coefficients are known, we can build up a representation of the electron density in the molecule by noting which orbitals are occupied and then forming the squares of those orbitals. The total electron density at any point is then the sum of the squares of the wavefunctions evaluated at that point. The outcome is commonly represented by an **isodensity surface**, a surface of constant total electron density (Fig. 14.39). There are several styles of representing an isodensity surface, as a solid form, as a transparent form with a ball-and-stick representation of the molecule within, or as a mesh. A related representation is a **solvent-accessible surface** in which the shape represents the shape of the molecule by imagining a sphere representing a solvent molecule rolling across the surface and plotting the locations of the centre of that sphere.

One of the most important aspects of a molecule other than its geometrical shape is the distribution of charge over its surface. A common procedure begins with calculation of the net electric charge at each point on an isodensity surface by subtracting the charge due to the electron density at that point from the charge due to the nuclei. Then the potential energy of interaction between each charge on the surface and a 'probe' charge located away from the molecule is computed. The result is an **electrostatic potential surface** (an 'elpot surface') in which (in full colour renditions) net positive potential is shown in one colour and net negative potential is shown in another, with intermediate gradations of colour (Fig. 14.40).

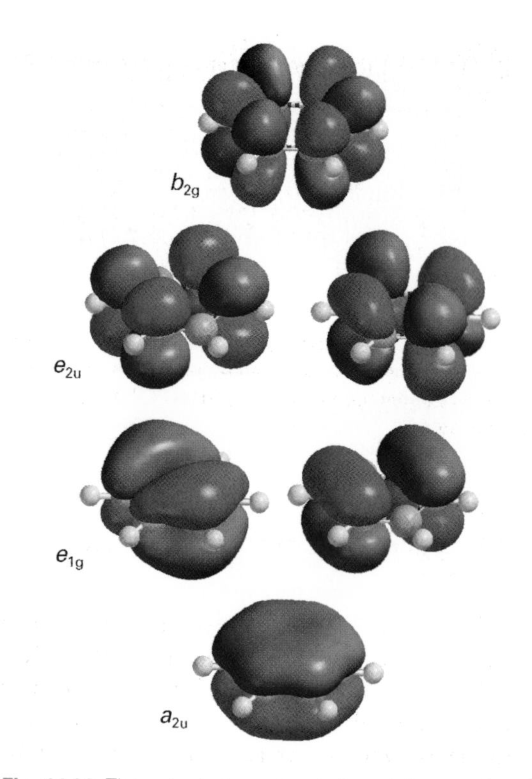

Fig. 14.38 The output of a computation of the π orbitals of benzene: opposite signs of the wavefunctions are represented by different colours. Compare these molecular orbitals with the more diagrammatic representation in Fig. 14.36.

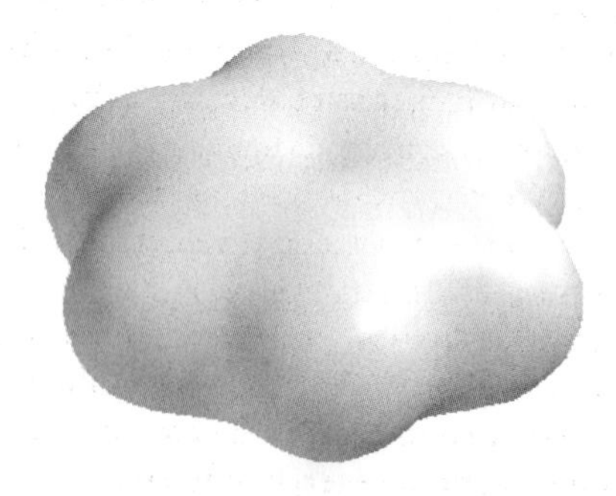

Fig. 14.39 The isodensity surface of benzene obtained by using the same software as in Fig. 14.38.

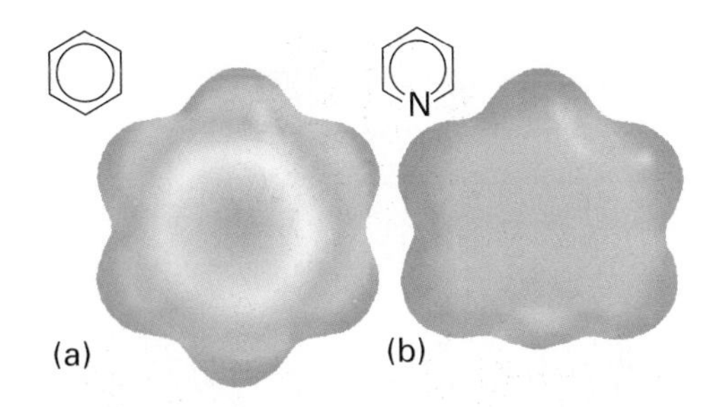

Fig. 14.40 The electrostatic potential surfaces of (a) benzene and (b) pyridine. There is an accumulation of electron density on the nitrogen atom of pyridine at the expense of the other atoms.

14.19 **Applications of computational chemistry**

Our description of quantum mechanical methods has been punctuated by remarks to the effect that the calculated energies and wavefunctions of molecules are only approximate. Deviations from experimental values increase with the number of electrons in the molecule, so one goal of computational chemistry—at least when applied to large molecules—is to gain insight into trends in molecular properties without necessarily striving for ultimate accuracy. We have already encountered one example of this approach in Section 3.6, where we saw that quantum mechanical methods may be used to estimate the standard enthalpies of formation of molecules. We noted that good agreement between calculated and experimental values is relatively rare and computational chemistry is more useful in the search for the most thermodynamically stable conformation of a flexible molecule, although it is often not possible to predict the correct magnitude of the conformational energy difference.

Molecular orbital calculations may also be used to predict trends in electrochemical properties, such as standard potentials (Chapter 9). Several experimental and computational studies of aromatic hydrocarbons indicate that decreasing the energy of the LUMO enhances the ability of a molecule to accept an electron into the LUMO, with an attendant increase in the value of the molecule's standard potential.

We remarked in Chapter 12 that a molecule can absorb or emit a photon of energy hc/λ, resulting in a transition between two quantized molecular energy levels. The transition of lowest energy (and longest wavelength) occurs between the HOMO and the LUMO. We can use calculations based on semi-empirical, *ab initio*, and DFT methods to correlate the HOMO–LUMO energy gap with the wavelength of absorption. For example, consider the linear polyenes shown in Table 14.3, all of which absorb in the ultraviolet region of the spectrum. The table shows that, as expected, the wavelength of the lowest-energy electronic transition decreases as the energy separation between the HOMO and LUMO increases. We also see that the smallest HOMO–LUMO gap and longest wavelength of absorption correspond to octatetraene, the longest polyene in the group. It follows that the wavelength of the transition increases with increasing number of conjugated double bonds in linear polyenes. Extrapolation of the trend suggests that a sufficiently long linear polyene should absorb light in the visible region of the electromagnetic spectrum. This is indeed the case for β-carotene (**4**), which absorbs light with $\lambda \approx 450$ nm. The ability of β-carotene to absorb visible light is part of the strategy used by plants to harvest solar energy for use in photosynthesis (Box 20.2).

4 β-Carotene

There are several ways in which molecular orbital calculations lend insight into reactivity. For example, electrostatic potential surfaces may be used to visualize an electron-poor region of a molecule that is susceptible to association with or chemical attack by an electron-rich region of another molecule. Such considerations are important for assessing the pharmacological activity of potential drugs.

An attractive feature of computational chemistry is its ability to model species that may be too unstable or short-lived to be studied experimentally. For this reason, quantum mechanical methods are often used to study the transition state, with an eye toward describing factors that stabilize it and increase the reaction rate. Systems as complex as enzymes are amenable to study by computational methods.

Table 14.3 *Summary of* ab initio *calculations and spectroscopic data for four linear polyenes*

	$\Delta E_{HOMO-LUMO}/eV$	$\lambda_{transition}/nm$
Ethene (C_2H_4)	18.1	163
Butadiene (C_4H_6)	14.5	217
Hexatriene (C_6H_8)	12.7	252
Octatetraene (C_8H_{10})	11.6	304

1 eV = 1.602 × 10^{-19} J.

CHECKLIST OF KEY IDEAS

You should now be familiar with the following concepts:

☐ **1** The classification of bonds as covalent and ionic.

☐ **2** The Born–Oppenheimer approximation and molecular potential energy curves.

☐ **3** Valence bond theory and the concepts of σ and π bonds, promotion, hybridization, and resonance.

☐ **4** Molecular orbital theory and the construction of molecular orbitals as linear combinations of atomic orbitals.

☐ **5** Bonding and antibonding atomic orbitals and inversion (g,u) symmetry.

☐ **6** The building-up principle for constructing the electron configuration of molecules on the basis of their molecular orbital energy level diagram.

☐ **7** The concepts of σ and π orbitals and the role of symmetry and the similarity of energy in the construction of molecular orbitals.

☐ **8** The bond order of a molecule, $b = \frac{1}{2}(n - n^*)$.

☐ **9** The concept of electronegativity and the Pauling and Mulliken definitions.

☐ **10** The MO description of polar bonds, $\psi = c_A\psi_A + c_B\psi_B$.

☐ **11** The concept of self-consistent field and the distinction between semi-empirical and *ab initio* methods of computation.

☐ **12** The Hückel method for the estimation of the energies of molecular orbitals.

☐ **13** Applications of molecular orbital calculations to the prediction of reactivity and thermochemical, electrochemical, and spectroscopic properties.

DISCUSSION QUESTIONS

14.1 Compare the approximations built into valence bond theory and molecular orbital theory.

14.2 Discuss the steps involved in the construction of sp^3, sp^2, and sp hybrid orbitals.

14.3 Distinguish between the Pauling and Mulliken electronegativity scales.

14.4 Distinguish between semi-empirical, *ab initio*, and density functional theory methods of electronic structure determination.

EXERCISES

The symbol ‡ indicates that calculus is required.

14.5 Give the valence bond description of a P_2 molecule. Why is P_4 a more stable form of molecular phosphorus?

14.6 Write down the valence bond wavefunction for a nitrogen molecule.

14.7 Calculate the molar energy of repulsion between two hydrogen nuclei at the separation in H_2 (74.1 pm). The result is the energy that must be overcome by the attraction from the electrons that form the bond.

14.8 Give the valence bond description of SO_2 and SO_3 molecules.

14.9 The structure of the visual pigment retinal is shown in (**5**). Label each atom with its state of hybridization and specify the composition of each of the different types of bond.

CHO

5 11-*cis*-Retinal

14.10 ‡Show that the orbitals $h_1 = s + p_x + p_y + p_z$ and $h_2 = s - p_x - p_y + p_z$ do not overlap ($S = 0$; see Derivation 14.2). (*Hint*. Each atomic orbital is individually normalized to 1. Also, note that (i) s and p orbitals do not overlap and (ii) p orbitals with perpendicular orientations do not overlap.)

14.11 ‡Show that the sp^2 hybrid orbital $(s + 2^{1/2}p)/3^{1/2}$ is normalized to 1 if the s and p orbitals are each normalized to 1.

14.12 ‡Find another sp^2 hybrid orbital that has zero overlap with the hybrid orbital in the preceding problem.

14.13 ‡Normalize the wavefunction $\psi = \psi_{\text{covalent}} + \lambda\psi_{\text{ionic}}$ in terms of the parameter λ and the overlap integral S between the covalent and ionic wavefunctions.

14.14 Before doing the following calculation, sketch how the overlap between an s orbital and a $2p$ orbital can be expected to depend on their separation. The overlap integral between an H1s orbital and an H2p orbital on nuclei separated by a distance R is $S = (R/a_0)\{1 + (R/a_0) + \frac{1}{3}(R/a_0)^2\}\, e^{-R/a_0}$. Plot this function, and find the separation for which the overlap is a maximum.

14.15 ‡Suppose that a molecular orbital has the form $N(0.145A + 0.844B)$. Find a linear combination of the orbitals A and B that is orthogonal to this combination.

14.16 A normalized valence bond wavefunction turned out to have the form $\psi = 0.989\,\psi_{\text{covalent}} + 0.150\,\psi_{\text{ionic}}$. What is the chance that, in 1000 inspections of the molecule, both electrons of the bond will be found on one atom?

14.17 Suppose that the function $\psi = A\,e^{-ar^2}$, with A being the normalization constant and a being an adjustable parameter, is used as a trial wavefunction for the 1s orbital of the hydrogen atom. The energy of this trial wavefunction is

$$E = \frac{3a\hbar^2}{2\mu} - 2e^2\left(\frac{2a}{\pi}\right)^{1/2}$$

where e is the electron charge, and μ is the effective mass of the H atom. Draw a graph of E as a function of a and identify the minimum energy associated with this trial wavefunction.

14.18 ‡A more accurate procedure than that in Exercise 14.17 is to find the minimum of E by differentiation. Do so.

14.19 Benzene is commonly regarded as a resonance hybrid of the two Kekulé structures, but other possible structures can also contribute. Draw three other structures in which there are only covalent π bonds (allowing for bonding between some non-adjacent C atoms) and two structures in which there is one ionic bond. Why may these structures be ignored in simple descriptions of the molecule?

14.20 ‡Show, if overlap is ignored, (a) that any molecular orbital expressed as a linear combination of two atomic orbitals may be written in the form $\psi = \psi_A \cos\theta + \psi_B \sin\theta$, where θ is a parameter that varies between 0 and $\frac{1}{2}\pi$, and (b) that if ψ_A and ψ_B are orthogonal and normalized to 1, then ψ is also normalized to 1. (c) To what values of θ do the bonding and antibonding orbitals in a homonuclear diatomic molecule correspond?

14.21 Draw diagrams to show the various orientations in which a *p* orbital and a *d* orbital on adjacent atoms may form bonding and antibonding molecular orbitals.

14.22 Give the ground-state electron configurations of (a) Li_2, (b) Be_2, and (c) C_2.

14.23 Give the ground-state electron configurations of (a) H_2^-, (b) N_2, and (c) O_2. For heteronuclear diatomic molecules, a good first approximation is that the energy level diagram is much the same as for homonuclear diatomic molecules.

14.24 Three diatomic species that are biologically important because they either promote or inhibit life are (a) CO, (b) NO, and (c) CN^-. The first binds to haemoglobin, the second is a neurotransmitter, and the third interrupts the respiratory electron-transfer chain. Their biochemical action is a reflection of their orbital structure. Deduce their ground-state electron configurations.

14.25 From the ground-state electron configurations of B_2 and C_2, predict which molecule should have the greater dissociation energy.

14.26 Some chemical reactions proceed by the initial loss or transfer of an electron to a diatomic species. Which of the molecules N_2, NO, O_2, C_2, F_2, and CN would you expect to be stabilized by (a) the addition of an electron to form AB^-, (b) the removal of an electron to form AB^+?

14.27 From the ground-state electron configurations of B_2 and C_2, predict which molecule should have the greater bond dissociation energy.

14.28 The existence of compounds of the noble gases was once a great surprise and stimulated a great deal of theoretical work. Sketch the molecular orbital energy level diagram for XeF and deduce its ground-state electron configurations. Is XeF likely to have a shorter bond length than XeF^+?

14.29 Where it is appropriate, give the parity of (a) $1\pi^*$ in F_2, (b) 2σ in NO, (c) 1δ in Tl_2, (d) $1\delta^*$ in Fe_2.

14.30 Give the (g,u) parities of the first four levels of a particle-in-a-box wavefunction.

14.31 (a) Give the parities of the wavefunctions for the first four levels of a harmonic oscillator. (b) How may the parity be expressed in terms of the quantum number v?

14.32 State the parities of the six π orbitals of benzene (see Fig. 14.36).

14.33 Two diatomic molecules that are important for the welfare of humanity are NO and N_2: the former is both a pollutant and a neurotransmitter, and the latter is the ultimate source of the nitrogen of proteins and other biomolecules. Use the electron configurations of NO and N_2 to predict which is likely to have the shorter bond length.

14.34 Put the following species in order of increasing bond length: F_2^-, F_2, F_2^+.

14.35 Arrange the species O_2^+, O_2, O_2^-, O_2^{2-} in order of increasing bond length.

14.36 Construct the molecular orbital energy level diagrams of (a) ethene (ethylene) and (b) ethyne (acetylene) on the basis that the molecules are formed from the appropriately hybridized CH_2 or CH fragments.

14.37 Predict the electronic configurations of (a) the benzene anion, (b) the benzene cation.

14.38 Many of the colours of vegetation are due to electronic transitions in conjugated π-electron systems. In the *free-electron molecular orbital* (FEMO) theory, the electrons in a conjugated molecule are treated as independent particles in a box of length *L*. Sketch the form of the two occupied orbitals in butadiene predicted by this model and predict the minimum excitation energy of the molecule. The tetraene $CH_2{=}CHCH{=}CHCH{=}CHCH{=}CH_2$ can be treated as a box of length $8R$, where $R = 140$ pm (as in this case, an extra half bond-length is often added at each end of the box). Calculate the minimum excitation energy of the molecule and sketch the HOMO and LUMO.

Chapter 15

Metallic, ionic, and covalent solids

Modern chemistry is closely concerned with the properties of solids. Apart from their intrinsic usefulness for construction, modern solids have made possible the semiconductor revolution and recent advances in ceramics have given rise to the hope that we may now be on the verge of a superconductor revolution. Advances in our understanding of electron mobility in solids are also useful in biology, where electron transport processes are responsible for many biochemical processes, particularly photosynthesis and respiration.

The principal technique for investigating the arrangements of atoms in condensed phases, primarily crystalline solids, is X-ray diffraction, but nuclear magnetic resonance (NMR, Chapter 21) is now also making significant contributions. Information from X-ray diffraction and NMR is the basis of much of molecular biology, so the material presented here is the foundation for our discussion of biomolecular structures in Chapter 18. In each case, the observed crystal structure is nature's solution to the problem of condensing objects of various shapes into an aggregate of minimum energy and, for temperatures above zero, of minimum Gibbs energy.

Bonding in solids

The bonding within a solid may be of various kinds. Simplest of all (in principle) is the bonding in a **metallic solid**, in which electrons are delocalized over arrays of identical cations and bind the whole together into a rigid but malleable structure. Because the delocalized electrons can accommodate bonding patterns with very little directional character, the crystal structures of metals are determined largely by the geometrical problem of packing spherical atoms into a dense, orderly array. In an **ionic solid**, the ions (in general, of different radii, and not always spherical) are held together by their Coulombic interaction, and pack together to give an electrically neutral structure. In a **covalent solid** (or *network solid*), covalent bonds in a definite spatial orientation link the atoms in a network extending through the crystal. The stereochemical demands of valence now override the geometrical problem of packing spheres together, and elaborate and extensive structures may be formed. Important examples of covalent solids are diamond and graphite. **Molecular solids**, which are the subject of the overwhelming majority of modern structural determinations, consist of discrete molecules attracted to one another by the interactions described in Chapter 16.

Some solids—notably the metals—conduct electricity because they have mobile electrons. These **electronic conductors** are classified on the basis of the variation of their electrical conductivity with temperature (Fig. 15.1). A **metallic conductor** is an electronic conductor with a conductivity that *decreases* as the temperature is raised. Metallic conductors include the metallic elements, their alloys, and graphite. Some organic solids are metallic conductors. A **semiconductor** is an electronic conductor with a conductivity that *increases* as the temperature is raised. Semiconductors include silicon, diamond, and gallium arsenide. A semiconductor generally has a lower conductivity than that typical of metals, but the magnitude of the conductivity is not relevant to the distinction. It is conventional to classify substances with very low electrical conductivities, such as most ionic solids, as **insulators**. We shall use this term, but it is one of convenience rather than one of fundamental significance. **Superconductors** are substances that conduct electricity with zero resistance. The mechanism of superconductivity in metals at very low (liquid helium) temperatures is well understood: that of the potentially more useful **high-temperature superconductors** (HTSCs), which are ceramic mixed oxides such as $YBa_2Cu_3O_7$, is still unresolved.

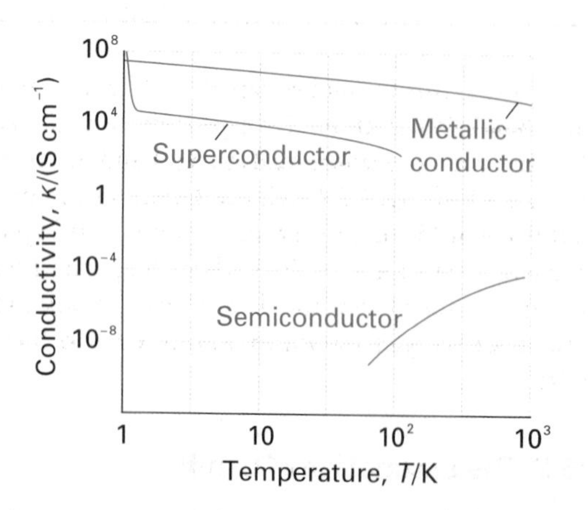

Fig. 15.1 The typical variation with temperature of the electrical conductivities of different classes of electronic conductor.

15.1 The band theory of solids

Metallic and ionic solids can both be treated by molecular orbital theory. The advantage of that approach is that we can then see both types of solid as two extremes of a single kind. In each case, the electrons responsible for the bonding are delocalized throughout the solid (as in a benzene molecule, but on a much bigger scale). In an elemental metal, the electrons can be found on all the atoms with equal probability, which matches the elementary picture of a metal as consisting of cations embedded in a nearly uniform electron 'sea'. In an ionic solid the wavefunctions occupied by the delocalized electrons are almost entirely concentrated on the anions.

We shall consider initially a single, infinitely long line of identical atoms, each one having one *s* orbital available for forming molecular orbitals (as in sodium). One atom of the solid contributes one *s* orbital with a certain energy (Fig. 15.2). When a second atom is brought up it forms a bonding and an antibonding orbital. The orbital of the third atom overlaps its nearest neighbour (and only slightly the next-nearest), and three molecular orbitals are formed from these three atomic orbitals. The fourth atom leads to the formation of a fourth molecular orbital. At this stage we can begin to see that the general effect of bringing up successive atoms is to spread the range of energies covered by the molecular orbitals, and also to fill in the range of energies with more and more orbitals (one more for each

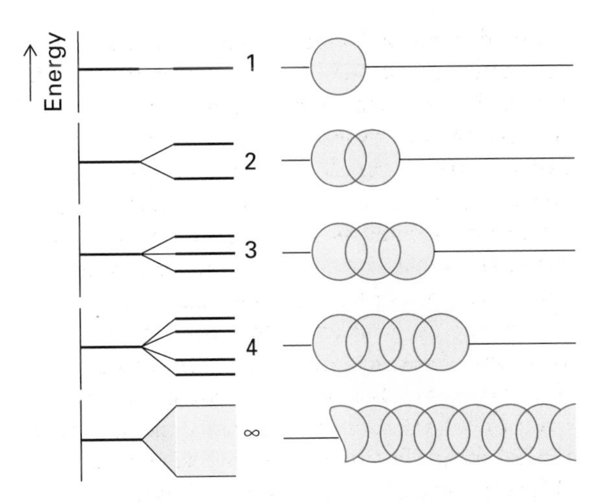

Fig. 15.2 The formation of a band of N molecular orbitals by successive addition of N atoms to a line. Note that the band remains of finite width, and although it looks continuous when N is large, it consists of N different orbitals.

additional atom). When N atoms have been added to the line, there are N molecular orbitals covering a band of finite width. When N is infinitely large, the difference between neighbouring energy levels in the band is infinitely small, but the band still has finite width. This band consists of N different molecular orbitals, the lowest-energy orbital being fully bonding, and the highest-energy orbital being fully antibonding between adjacent atoms (Fig. 15.3). In the

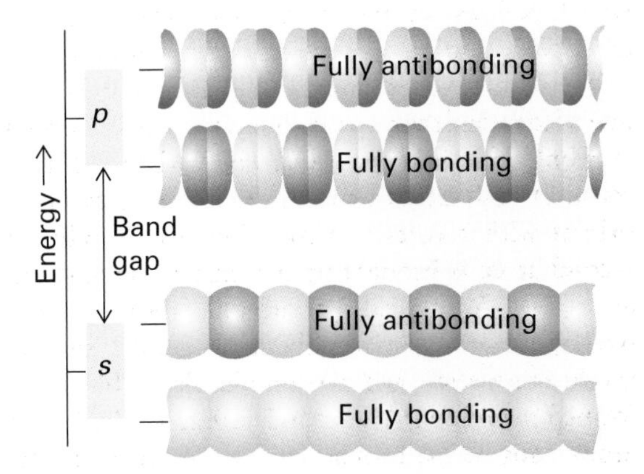

Fig. 15.3 The overlap of s orbitals gives rise to an s band, and the overlap of p orbitals gives rise to a p band. In this case the s and p orbitals of the atoms are so widely spaced that there is a band gap. In many cases the separation is less, and the bands overlap.

Hückel approximation (Section 14.16), their energies are given by

$$E_k = \alpha + 2\beta \cos \frac{k\pi}{N+1} \qquad k = 1, 2, \dots, N \qquad (15.1)$$

As N becomes infinite, the separation between neighbouring levels, $E_{k+1} - E_k$, goes to zero but, as shown in Derivation 15.1, the width of the band, $E_N - E_1$, becomes 4β, a finite quantity.

Derivation 15.1

The width of a band

The energy of the level with $k = 1$ is

$$E_1 = \alpha + 2\beta \cos \frac{\pi}{N+1}$$

As N becomes infinite, the cosine term becomes cos 0, which is equal to 1. Therefore, in this limit

$$E_1 = \alpha + 2\beta$$

When k has its maximum value of N,

$$E_N = \alpha + 2\beta \cos \frac{N\pi}{N+1}$$

As N approaches infinity, we can ignore the 1 in the denominator, and the cosine term becomes cos π, which is equal to −1. Therefore, in this limit

$$E_N = \alpha - 2\beta$$

The difference between the upper and lower energies of the band is therefore 4β.

A band formed from overlap of s orbitals is called an **s band**. If the atoms have p orbitals available, then the same procedure leads to a **p band** (as in the upper half of Fig. 15.3, with different values of α and β in eqn 15.1). If the atomic p orbitals lie higher in energy than the s orbitals, then the p band lies higher than the s band, and there may be a **band gap**, a range of energies for which no molecular orbitals exist.

15.2 The occupation of bands

Now consider the electronic structure of a solid formed from atoms each of which is able to contribute one electron (for example, the alkali metals).

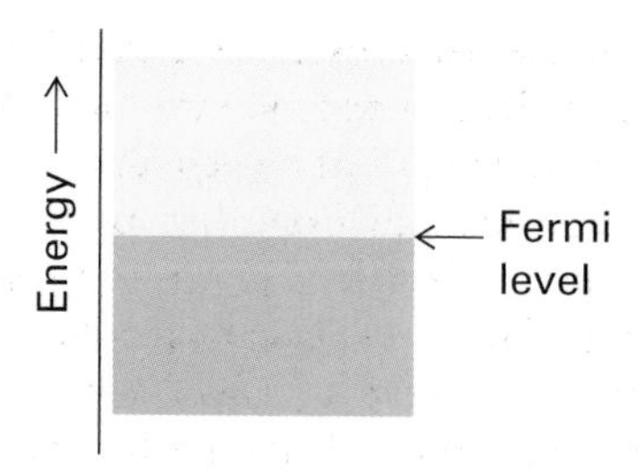

Fig. 15.4 When N electrons occupy a band of N orbitals, it is only half full and the electrons near the Fermi level (the top of the filled levels) are mobile.

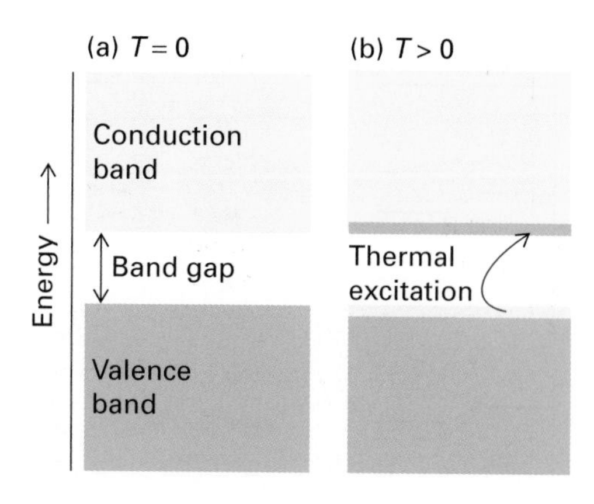

Fig. 15.5 (a) When $2N$ electrons are present, the band is full and the material is an insulator at $T = 0$. (b) At temperatures above $T = 0$, electrons populate the levels of the conduction band at the expense of the valence band, and the solid is a semiconductor.

There are N atomic orbitals and therefore N molecular orbitals squashed into a band of finite width. There are N electrons to accommodate, and they pair and enter the lowest $\frac{1}{2}N$ molecular orbitals (Fig. 15.4). The highest occupied molecular orbital is called the **Fermi level**. However, unlike in the discrete molecules we considered in Chapter 14, there are empty orbitals just above and very close in energy to the Fermi level, so it requires hardly any energy to excite the uppermost electrons. Some of the electrons are therefore very mobile and give rise to electrical conductivity.

As we have remarked, metallic conductivity is characterized by a decrease in electrical conductivity with increasing temperature. This behaviour is accommodated in the present model because an increase in temperature causes more vigorous thermal motion of the atoms, with the result that there are more collisions between the moving electrons and the atoms. That is, at high temperatures the electrons are scattered out of their paths through the solid and are less efficient at transporting charge.

When each atom provides two electrons, the $2N$ electrons fill the N orbitals of the s band. The Fermi level now lies at the top of the band and there is a gap before the next band begins (Fig. 15.5a). As the temperature is increased, electrons can populate the empty orbitals of the upper band (Fig. 15.5b). They are now mobile, and the solid has become an electronic conductor. In fact, it is a *semiconductor*, because the electrical conductivity depends on the number of electrons that are promoted across the gap and that number increases, and the electrical conductivity increases accordingly, as the temperature is raised.

If the gap is large, very few electrons will be excited across it at ordinary temperatures and the conductivity will remain close to zero, giving an insulator. Thus, the conventional distinction between an insulator and a semiconductor is related to the size of the band gap and is not absolute like the distinction between a metal (incomplete bands at $T = 0$) and a semiconductor (full bands at $T = 0$).

Another method of increasing the number of charge carriers and enhancing the semiconductivity of a solid is to implant foreign atoms into an otherwise pure material. If these **dopants** can trap electrons (as indium or gallium atoms can in silicon, because In and Ga atoms have one fewer valence electron than Si), then they withdraw electrons from the filled band, leaving holes that allow the remaining electrons to move (Fig. 15.6a). This doping procedure gives rise to **p-type semiconductivity**, the p indicating that the holes are positive relative to the electrons in the band. Alternatively, a dopant might carry excess electrons (for example, phosphorus atoms introduced into germanium), and these additional electrons occupy otherwise empty bands, giving **n-type semiconductivity** (Fig. 15.6b), where n denotes the negative charge of the carriers.[1]

[1] The preparation of doped but otherwise ultrapure materials is described in Box 6.2.

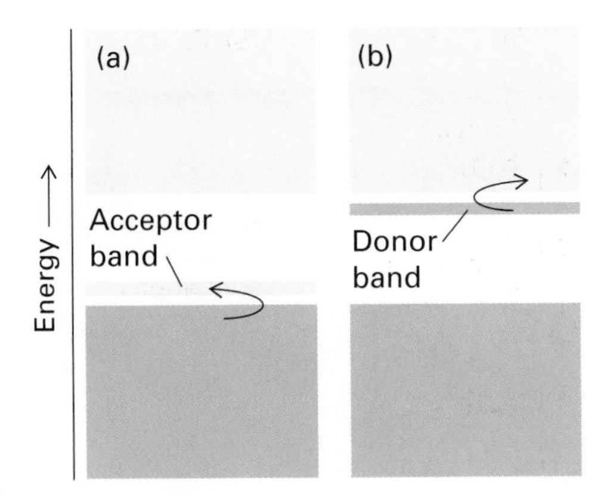

Fig. 15.6 (a) A dopant with fewer electrons than its host can form a narrow band that accepts electrons from the valence band. The holes in the valence band are mobile, and the substance is a *p-type semiconductor.* (b) A dopant with more electrons than its host forms a narrow band that can supply electrons to the conduction band. The electrons it supplies are mobile, and the substance is an *n-type semiconductor.*

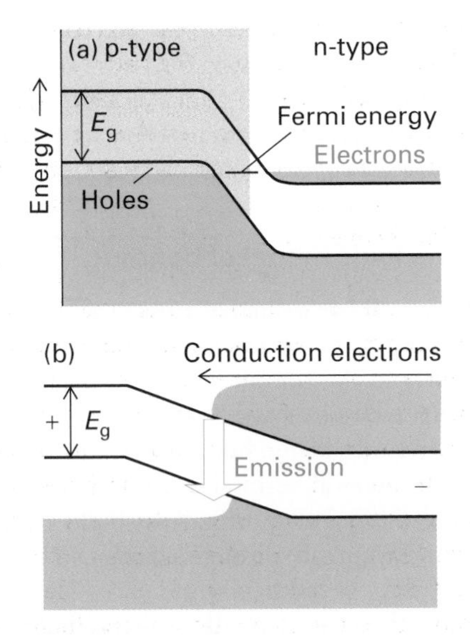

Fig. 15.7 The structure of a diode junction (a) without bias, (b) with bias.

15.3 The optical properties of junctions

In this section we need to consider the properties of a **p–n junction**, the interface of the two types of semiconductor. The band structure of such a junction is shown in Fig. 15.7. When electrons are supplied through an external circuit to the n side of the junction, the electrons in the conduction band of the n-type semiconductor fall into the holes in the valence band of the p-type semiconductor.

As the electrons fall from the upper band into the lower, they release energy. In some solids the wavelengths of the wavefunctions in the upper and lower states are different, which means that the linear momenta (through the de Broglie relation, $p = h/\lambda$) of the electron in the initial and final states are different. As a result, the transition can occur only if the electron transfers linear momentum to the lattice and the device becomes warm as the atoms are stimulated to vibrate. This is the case for silicon semiconductors, and is one reason why computers need efficient cooling systems.

In some materials, most notably gallium arsenide, GaAs, the wavefunctions of the initial and final states of the electron have the same wavelengths and correspond to the same linear momentum. As a result, transitions can occur without the lattice needing to participate by mopping up the difference in linear momenta. The energy difference is therefore emitted as light. Practical **light-emitting diodes** of this kind are widely used in electronic displays. Gallium arsenide itself emits infrared light, but the width of the band gap is increased by incorporating phosphorus, and a material of composition approximately $GaAs_{0.6}P_{0.4}$ emits light in the red region of the spectrum.

15.4 Superconductivity

Following the discovery by the Dutch physicist Heike Kamerlingh Onnes in 1911 that mercury is a superconductor below the **critical temperature**, T_c, of 4.2 K, the boiling point of liquid helium, physicists and chemists made slow but steady progress in the discovery of superconductors with higher critical temperatures. Metals, such as tungsten, mercury, and lead, tend to have critical temperatures below about 10 K. Intermetallic compounds, such as Nb_3X (X = Sn, Al, or Ge), and alloys, such as Nb/Ti and Nb/Zr, have critical temperatures between 10 K and 23 K. In 1986, however, an entirely new range of HTSCs was discovered with critical temperatures well above 77 K, the boiling point of the inexpensive refrigerant liquid nitrogen. For example, $HgBa_2Ca_2Cu_2O_8$ has $T_c = 153$ K.

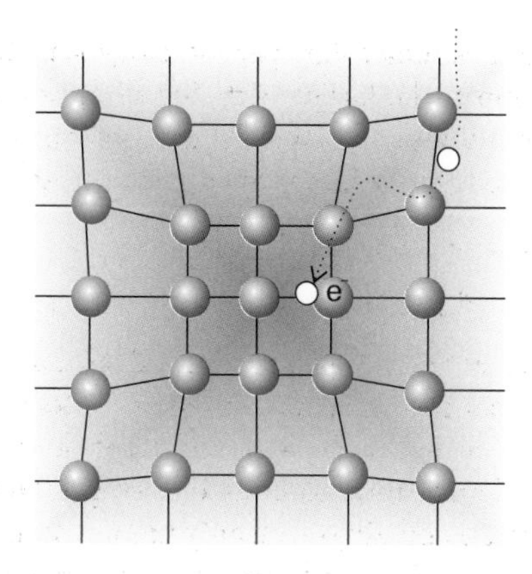

Fig. 15.8 The formation of a Cooper pair. One electron distorts the crystal lattice and the second electron has a lower energy if it goes to that region. These electron–lattice interactions effectively bind the two electrons into a pair.

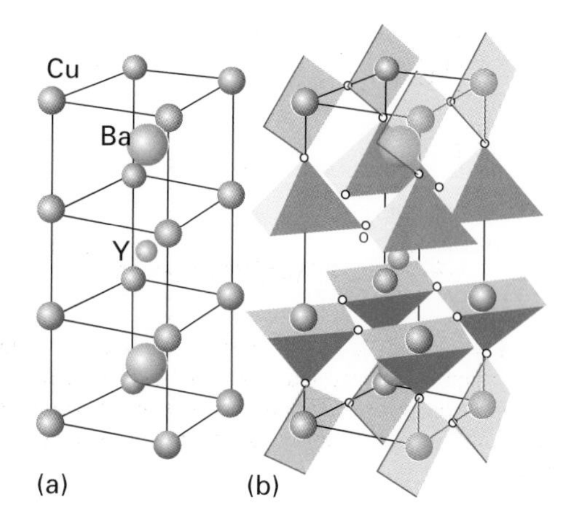

Fig. 15.9 The structure of the $YBa_2Cu_3O_7$ superconductor. (a) Metal atom positions. (b) The polyhedra show the position of oxygen atoms and indicate that the metal ions are in square-planar and square-pyramidal coordination environments.

The central concept of low-temperature superconductivity is the existence of a **Cooper pair**, a pair of electrons that exists on account of the indirect electron–electron interactions mediated by the nuclei of the atoms in the lattice. Thus, if one electron is in a particular region of a solid, the nuclei there move towards it and give rise to a distorted local structure (Fig. 15.8). Because that local distortion is rich in positive charge, it is favourable for a second electron to join the first. Hence, there is a virtual attraction between the two electrons, and they move together as a pair. A Cooper pair undergoes less scattering than an individual electron as it travels through the solid because the distortion caused by one electron can attract back the other electron should it be scattered out of its path in a collision. Because the Cooper pair is stable against scattering, it can carry charge freely through the solid, and hence give rise to superconductivity. The local distortion is disrupted by thermal motion of the ions in the solid, so the virtual attraction occurs only at very low temperatures.

The Cooper pairs responsible for low-temperature superconductivity are likely to be important in HTSCs, but the mechanism for pairing is hotly debated. Consider $YBa_2Cu_3O_7$, one of the most widely studied superconductors, which features layers of square-pyramidal CuO_5 units and almost flat sheets of square-planar CuO_4 units (Fig. 15.9). It is believed that movement of electrons along the linked CuO_4 units accounts for superconductivity, whereas the linked CuO_5 units act as 'charge reservoirs' that maintain an appropriate number of electrons in the superconducting layers.

15.5 The ionic model of bonding

Suppose we have a line of atoms with different electronegativities, such as a one-dimensional array of sodium and chlorine atoms rather than the identical atoms treated so far. Each sodium atom contributes an *s* orbital and one electron. Each chlorine atom contributes a *p* orbital and its one electron.

We use the *s* and *p* orbitals to build molecular orbitals that spread throughout the solid. Now, however, there is a crucial difference. The orbitals on the two types of atom have markedly different energies, so (just as in the construction of molecular orbitals for diatomic molecules, Section 14.12) we consider them separately. The Cl3*p* orbitals interact to form one band and the higher energy Na3*s* orbitals interact to form another band. However, because the sodium atoms have very little overlap with one another (they are separated by a chlorine atom), the Na3*s* band is very narrow; so is the Cl3*p* band, for a similar reason. As a result, there is a big gap between two narrow bands (Fig. 15.10).

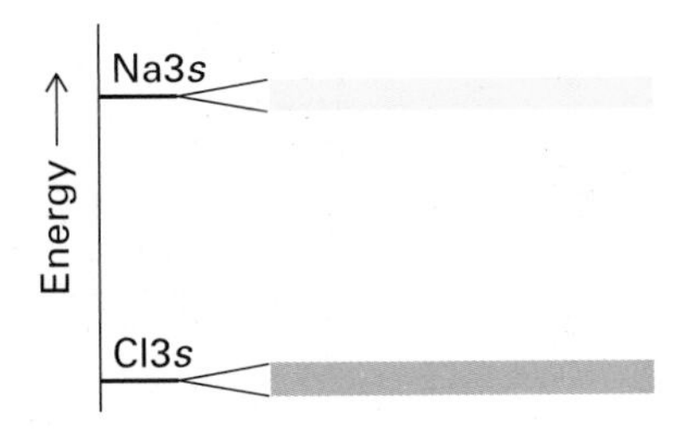

Fig. 15.10 The bands formed from two elements of widely different electronegativity (such as sodium and chlorine): they are widely separated and narrow. If each atom provides one electron, the lower band is full and the substance is an insulator.

Now consider the occupation of the bands. If there are N sodium atoms and N chlorine atoms, there will be $2N$ electrons to accommodate. These electrons occupy and fill the lower Cl3p band. As a result of the big band gap, the substance is an insulator before the Na3s band becomes available. Moreover, because only the Cl3p band is occupied, the electron density is almost entirely on the chlorine atoms. In other words, we can treat the solid as composed of Na^+ cations and Cl^- anions, just as in an elementary picture of ionic bonding.

Now that we know where the electron density is largely located, we can adopt a much simpler model of the solid. Instead of expressing the structure in terms of molecular orbitals, we treat it as a collection of cations and anions. This simplification is the basis of the **ionic model** of bonding.

15.6 Lattice enthalpy

The strength of a covalent bond is measured by its dissociation energy, the energy needed to separate the two atoms joined by the bond. For thermodynamic applications we express this energy in terms of the bond enthalpy (Section 3.2). The strength of an ionic bond is measured similarly, but now we have to take into account the energy required to separate *all* the ions of a solid sample from one another and, for thermodynamic applications, express this energy as a change in enthalpy. The **lattice enthalpy**, $\Delta H_L^\ominus$, is the standard enthalpy change accompanying the separation of the species that compose the solid (such as ions if the solid is ionic, and molecules if the solid is molecular) per mole of formula units. For example, the lattice enthalpy of an ionic solid such as sodium chloride is the standard molar enthalpy change accompanying the process[2,3]

$$NaCl(s) \rightarrow Na^+(g) + Cl^-(g)$$
$$\Delta H_L^\ominus = 786 \text{ kJ mol}^{-1}$$

Lattice enthalpies of solids are determined from other experimental data by using a **Born–Haber cycle**, which is a cycle (a closed path) of steps that includes lattice formation as one stage. The value of the lattice enthalpy—the only unknown in a well-chosen cycle—is found from the requirement that the sum of the enthalpy changes round a complete cycle is zero (because enthalpy is a state property).[4] A typical cycle for an ionic compound has the form shown in Fig. 15.11. Example 15.1 illustrates how the cycle is used and Table 15.1 gives characteristic values.

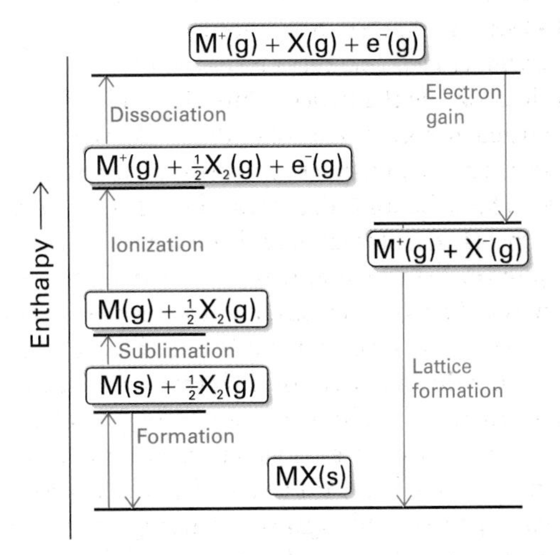

Fig. 15.11 The Born–Haber cycle for the determination of one of the unknown enthalpies, most commonly the lattice enthalpy. Upward-pointing arrows denote positive changes in enthalpy; downward-pointing arrows denote negative enthalpy changes. All the steps in the cycle correspond to the same temperature.

[2] Because the lattice enthalpy is invariably a positive quantity, it is normally reported without its + sign.

[3] The lattice enthalpy of a molecular solid, such as ice, is the standard molar enthalpy of sublimation; the lattice enthalpy of a metal is its enthalpy of atomization.

[4] All the data must be for a single temperature.

Table 15.1 *Lattice enthalpies, $\Delta H_L^{\ominus}/(kJ\ mol^{-1})$*

LiF	1037	LiCl	852	LiBr	815	LiI	761
NaF	926	NaCl	786	NaBr	752	NaI	705
KF	821	KCl	717	KBr	689	KI	649
MgO	3850	CaO	3461	SrO	3283	BaO	3114
MgS	3406	CaS	3119	SrS	2974	BaS	2832
Al_2O_3	15 900						

Example 15.1

Using a Born–Haber cycle to determine a lattice enthalpy

Calculate the lattice enthalpy of KCl(s) using a Born–Haber cycle and the following information, which is all for 25°C.

Process	$\Delta H^{\ominus}/(kJ\ mol^{-1})$
Sublimation of K(s)	+89
Ionization of K(g)	+418
Dissociation of Cl_2(g)	+244
Electron attachment to Cl(g)	−349
Formation of KCl(s)	−437

Strategy First, draw the cycle, showing the atomization of the elements, their ionization, and the formation of the solid lattice; then complete the cycle (for the step *solid compound → original elements*) by using the enthalpy of formation. The sum of enthalpy changes round the cycle is zero, so include the numerical data and set the sum of all the terms equal to zero; then solve the equation for the one unknown (the lattice enthalpy).

Solution Figure 15.12 shows the cycle required. The first step is the sublimation (atomization) of solid potassium:

	$\Delta H^{\ominus}/(kJ\ mol^{-1})$
K(s) → K(g)	+89 (the enthalpy of sublimation or atomization of potassium)

Chlorine atoms are formed by dissociation of Cl_2:

$\frac{1}{2}Cl_2(g) \rightarrow Cl(g)$	+122 (half the bond enthalpy of Cl–Cl)

Now, potassium ions are formed by ionization of the gas-phase atoms:

$K(g) \rightarrow K^+(g) + e^-(g)$	+418 (the ionization enthalpy of potassium)

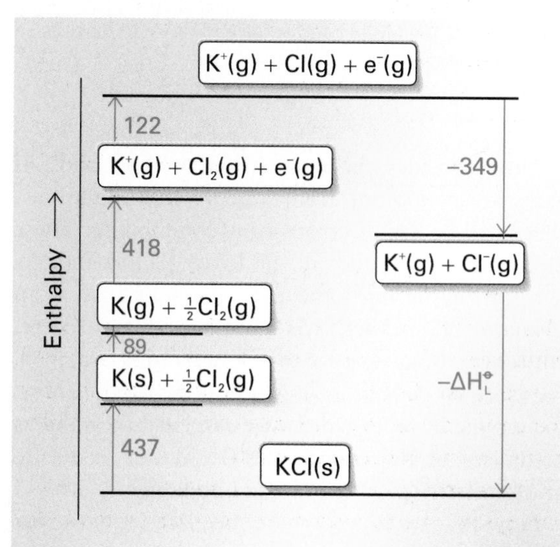

Fig. 15.12 The Born–Haber cycle for the calculation of the lattice enthalpy of potassium chloride. The sum of the enthalpy changes around the cycle is zero. The numerical values are in kilojoules per mole.

and chloride ions are formed from the chlorine atoms:

$Cl(g) + e^-(g) \rightarrow Cl^-(g)$	−349 (the electron-gain enthalpy of chlorine)

The solid is now formed:

$K^+(g) + Cl^-(g) \rightarrow KCl(s)$	$-\Delta H_L^{\ominus}$ (the enthalpy change when the lattice *forms* is the negative of the lattice enthalpy)

and the cycle is completed by decomposing KCl(s) into its elements:

$KCl(s) \rightarrow K(s) + \frac{1}{2}Cl_2(g)$	+437 (the negative of the enthalpy of formation of KCl)

The sum of the enthalpy changes is $-\Delta H_L^{\ominus} + 717$ kJ mol^{-1}; however, the sum must be equal to zero, so $\Delta H_L^{\ominus} = 717$ kJ mol^{-1}.

Self-test 15.1

Calculate the lattice enthalpy of magnesium bromide from the following data and the information in the *Data section*.

Process	$\Delta H^{\ominus}$/(kJ mol^{-1})
Sublimation of Mg(s)	+148
Ionization of Mg(g) to Mg^{2+}(g)	+2187
Dissociation of Br_2(g)	+193
Electron attachment to Br(g)	−325

[*Answer*: 2402 kJ mol^{-1}]

15.7 The origin of lattice enthalpy

Our next task is to account for the values of lattice enthalpies. The dominant interaction in an ionic lattice is the Coulombic interaction between ions, which is far stronger than any other attractive interaction, so we concentrate on that.

The starting point is the Coulombic potential energy for the interaction of two ions of charge numbers z_1 and z_2 (with cations having positive charge numbers and anions negative charge numbers) with centres separated by a distance r_{12}:

$$V_{12} = \frac{(z_1 e) \times (z_2 e)}{4\pi\varepsilon_0 r_{12}} \tag{15.2}$$

where ε_0 is the vacuum permittivity (see Appendix 3). To calculate the total potential energy of all the ions in a crystal, we have to sum this expression over all the ions present. Nearest neighbours (which have opposite signs) attract and contribute a large negative term, second-nearest neighbours (which have the same sign) repel and contribute a slightly weaker positive term, and so on (Fig. 15.13). The overall result, however, is that there is a net attraction between the cations and anions and a favourable (negative) contribution to the energy of the solid. For instance, for a uniformly spaced line of alternating cations and anions for which $z_1 = +z$ and $z_2 = -z$, with d the distance between the centres of adjacent ions, we find

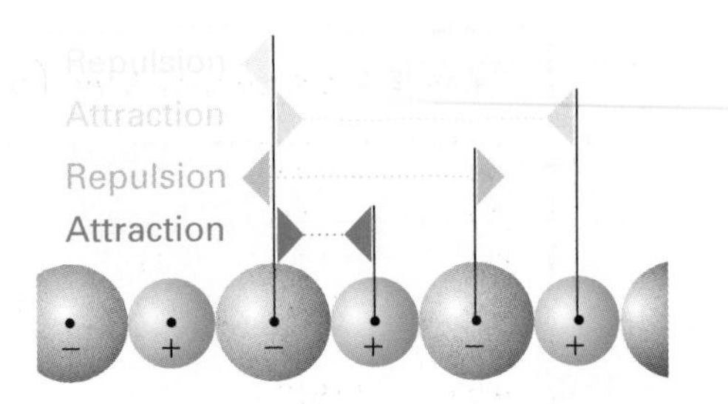

Fig. 15.13 There are alternating positive and negative contributions to the potential energy of a crystal lattice on account of the repulsions between ions of like charge and attractions of ions of opposite charge. The total potential energy is negative, but the sum might converge quite slowly.

$$V = -\frac{z^2 e^2}{4\pi\varepsilon_0 d} \times 2 \ln 2 \tag{15.3}$$

Derivation 15.2

The lattice energy of a one-dimensional crystal

Consider a line of alternating cations and anions extending in an infinite direction to the left and right of the ion of interest. The Coulombic potential energy of interaction with the ions on the right is the following sum of terms, where the negative terms represent attractions between ions of charge opposite to that of the ion of interest and the positive terms represent repulsions between ions of the same charge:

(Attraction, Repulsion, Attraction, Repulsion)

$$V = \frac{1}{4\pi\varepsilon_0} \times \left(-\frac{z^2e^2}{d} + \frac{z^2e^2}{2d} - \frac{z^2e^2}{3d} + \frac{z^2e^2}{4d} - \cdots \right)$$

$$= -\frac{z^2e^2}{4\pi\varepsilon_0 d} \times \left(1 - \tfrac{1}{2} + \tfrac{1}{3} - \tfrac{1}{4} + \cdots\right)$$

(ln 2)

$$= -\frac{z^2e^2}{4\pi\varepsilon_0 d} \times \ln 2$$

In the last step we have used

$$1 - \tfrac{1}{2} + \tfrac{1}{3} - \tfrac{1}{4} + \cdots = \ln 2$$

It is often useful to express a function as a sum of terms called a *Taylor expansion*. For example, the function ln x can be expanded as

$$\ln x = (x-1) - \tfrac{1}{2}(x-1)^2 + \tfrac{1}{3}(x-1)^3 - \tfrac{1}{4}(x-1)^4 + \cdots.$$

The interaction of the ion of interest with the ions to its left is the same, so the total potential energy of interaction is twice this expression for V, which is eqn 15.3.

Table 15.2
Madelung constants

Structural type	A
Caesium chloride	1.763
Fluorite	2.519
Rock salt	1.748
Rutile	2.408

When the calculation is repeated for more realistic, three-dimensional arrays of ions it is also found that the potential energy depends on the charge numbers of the ions and the value of a single parameter d, which may be taken as the distance between the centres of nearest neighbours:

$$V = \frac{e^2}{4\pi\varepsilon_0} \times \frac{z_1 z_2}{d} \times A \qquad (15.4)$$

where A is a number called the **Madelung constant.** The value of the Madelung constant for a single line of ions is $2 \ln 2 = 1.386\ldots$ as we have already seen; Table 15.2 gives the computed values of the constant for a variety of lattices with structures that we describe later in the chapter. Because the charge number of cations is positive and that of anions is negative, the product $z_1 z_2$ is negative. Therefore, V is also negative, which corresponds to a lowering in potential energy relative to the gas of widely separated ions.

So far, we have considered only the Coulombic interaction between ions. However, regardless of their signs, the ions repel each other when they are pressed together and their wavefunctions overlap. These additional repulsions work against the net Coulombic attraction between ions, so they raise the energy of the solid. When their effect is taken into account, it turns out that the lattice enthalpy is given by the **Born–Meyer equation:**

$$\Delta H_L^\ominus = |z_1 z_2| \times \frac{N_A e^2}{4\pi\varepsilon_0 d} \times \left(1 - \frac{d^*}{d}\right) \times A \qquad (15.5)$$

where d^* is an empirical parameter that is often taken as 34.5 pm (simply because that value is found to give reasonable agreement with experiment). The modulus signs ($|\ldots|$) mean that we should remove any minus sign from the product of z_1 and z_2, which results in a positive value for the lattice enthalpy. The important feature of this expression is that it shows that $\Delta H_L^\ominus \propto |z_1 z_2|/d$, which implies that *the lattice enthalpy increases with increasing charge number of the ions and with decreasing ionic radius.* The second conclusion follows from the fact that the smaller the ionic radii, the smaller the value of d. This feature is in accord with the variation in the experimental values in Table 15.1.

Self-test 15.2

Which can be expected to have the greater lattice enthalpy, magnesium oxide or strontium oxide?

[*Answer:* MgO]

15.8 Covalent networks

We have already noted that covalent bonds in a definite spatial orientation link the atoms in covalent network solids. Covalent solids are typically hard and often unreactive. Examples include silicon, red phosphorus, boron nitride, and—very importantly—diamond and graphite, which we discuss in detail.

Diamond and graphite are two allotropes of carbon. In diamond each sp^3-hybridized carbon is bonded tetrahedrally to its four neighbours (Fig. 15.14). The network of strong C–C bonds is repeated throughout the crystal and, as a result, diamond is the hardest known substance.

Allotropes are distinct forms of an element that differ in the way that the atoms are linked. For example, oxygen has two allotropes: O_2 and O_3 (ozone).

In graphite, σ bonds between sp^2-hybridized carbon atoms form hexagonal rings that, when repeated throughout a plane, give rise to sheets (Fig. 15.15). Because the sheets can slide against

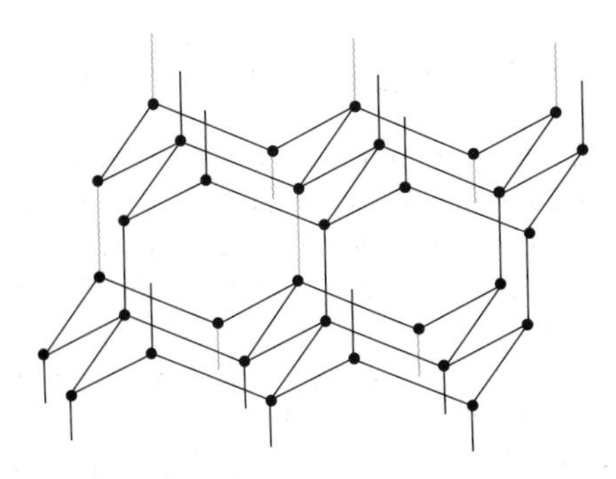

Fig. 15.14 A fragment of the structure of diamond. Each carbon atom is tetrahedrally bonded to four neighbours. This framework-like structure results in a rigid crystal with a high thermal conductivity.

each other (especially when impurities are present), graphite is used widely as a lubricant.

The electrical properties of diamond and graphite are determined by differences in the bonding patterns in these solids. Graphite is an electronic conductor because electrons are free to move from one carbon atom to another through bands formed by the overlap of partially filled, unhybridized p orbitals in a sheet. This band model explains the experimental observation that graphite conducts electricity well within the planar sheets, but less well between sheets. The electrical conductivity of graphite-like sheets of carbon atoms is now being considered in the design of nanometre-sized electronic devices (Box 15.1). We see from Fig. 15.14 that delocalized σ or π networks are not possible in diamond, which—in contrast to graphite—is an insulator (more precisely, a large band gap semiconductor).

15.9 Magnetic properties of solids

The magnetic properties of a solid are determined by interactions between the spins of its electrons. Some materials are magnetic and others may become magnetized when placed in an external magnetic field. A bulk sample exposed to a magnetic field of strength $\mathcal{H}$ acquires a **magnetization,** $\mathcal{M}$, which is proportional to $\mathcal{H}$:

$$\mathcal{M} = \chi \mathcal{H} \qquad (15.6)$$

An electric field acts on charged particles, whether stationary or moving, whereas a magnetic field acts only on moving charged particles. The strength of a magnetic field is denoted by $\mathcal{H}$ and has units of ampere per metre (A m^{-1}).

where χ is the dimensionless **volume magnetic susceptibility** (Table 15.3). A typical paramagnetic volume susceptibility is about 10^{-3}. We can think of the magnetization as contributing to the density of lines of force in the material (Fig. 15.16). Materials

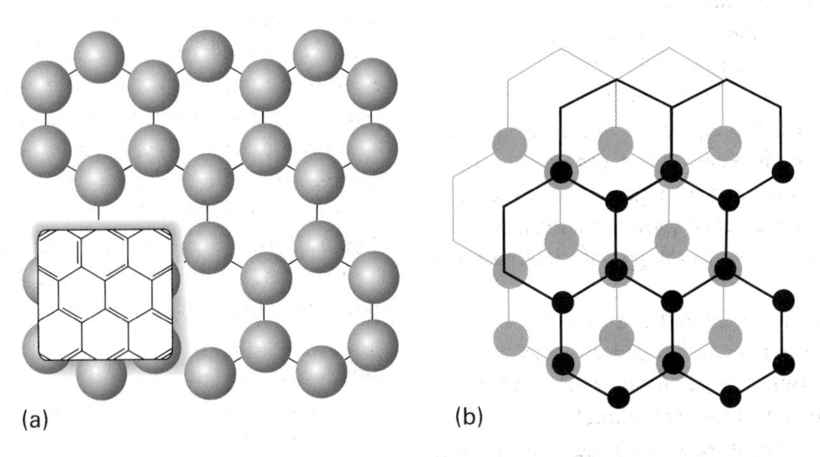

Fig. 15.15 Graphite consists of flat planes of hexagons of carbon atoms lying above one another. (a) The arrangement of carbon atoms in a sheet; (b) the relative arrangement of neighbouring sheets. When impurities are present, the planes can slide over one another easily. Graphite conducts well within the planes but less well perpendicular to the planes.

Box 15.1 *Nanowires*

A great deal of research effort is now being expended in the fabrication of nanometre-sized assemblies of atoms and molecules that can be used as tiny building blocks in a variety of technological applications. The future economic impact of nanotechnology, the aggregate of applications of devices built from nanometre-sized components, could be very significant. For example, increased demand for very small digital electronic devices has driven the design of ever smaller and more powerful microprocessors. However, there is an upper limit on the density of electronic circuits that can be incorporated into silicon-based chips with current fabrication technologies. As the ability to process data increases with the number of circuits in a chip, it follows that soon chips and the devices that use them will have to become bigger if processing power is to increase indefinitely. One way to circumvent this problem is to fabricate devices from nanometre-sized components. Another advantage of making nanometre-sized electronic devices, or *nanodevices*, is the possibility of using quantum mechanical effects. For example, electron tunnelling between two conducting regions separated by a thin insulating region can increase the speed of electron conduction and, consequently, the data processing speed in a digital nanoprocessor.

The study of nanodevices can also advance our basic understanding of chemical reactions. Nanometre-sized chemical reactors can serve as laboratories for the study of chemical reactions in constrained environments. Some of these reactions could comprise the foundation for the construction of nanometre-sized chemical sensors, with potential applications in medicine. For example, nanodevices with carefully designed biochemical properties could replace viruses and bacteria as the active species in vaccines.

A number of techniques have already been developed for the fabrication of nanometre-sized structures. The synthesis of *nanowires*, nanometre-sized atomic assemblies that conduct electricity, is a major step in the fabrication of nanodevices. An important type of nanowire is based on *carbon nanotubes*, thin cylinders of carbon atoms that are both mechanically strong and highly conducting. In recent years, methods for selective synthesis of nanotubes have been developed and they consist of different ways to condense a carbon plasma either in the presence or in the absence of a catalyst. The simplest structural motif is called a *single-walled nanotube* (SWNT) and in shown in the first illustration. In an SWNT, sp^2-hybridized carbon atoms form hexagonal rings reminiscent of the structure of the carbon sheets found in graphite (see Fig. 15.15). The tubes have diameters of between 1 and 2 nm and lengths of several micrometres. The features shown in the illustration have been confirmed by direct visualization with scanning tunnelling microscopy. A *multiwalled nanotube* (MWNT) consists of several concentric SWNTs and its diameter varies between 2 and 25 nm.

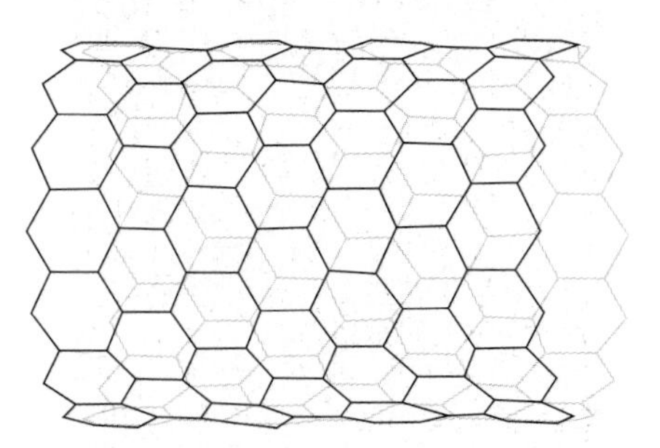

In a single-walled nanotube (SWNT), sp^2-hybridized carbon atoms form hexagonal rings that grow as tubes with diameters between 1 and 2 nm and lengths of several micrometres.

The origin of electrical conductivity in carbon nanotubes is the delocalization of π electrons that occupy unhydridized *p* orbitals, just as in graphite (Section 15.8). Recent studies have shown a correlation between structure and conductivity in SWNTs. The illustration above shows an SWNT that is a semiconductor. If the hexagons are rotated by 60°, the resulting SWNT is a metallic conductor.

Silicon nanowires can be made by focusing a pulsed laser beam on to a solid target composed of silicon and iron. The laser ejects Fe and Si atoms from the surface of the target, forming a vapour phase that can condense into liquid $FeSi_n$ nanoclusters at sufficiently low temperatures. The phase diagram for this complex mixture shows that solid silicon and liquid $FeSi_n$ coexist at temperatures higher than 1473 K. Hence, it is possible to precipitate solid silicon from the mixture if the experimental conditions are controlled to maintain the $FeSi_n$ nanoclusters in a liquid state that is saturated with silicon. It is observed that the silicon precipitate consists of nanowires with diameters of about 10 nm and lengths greater than 1 μm.

Nanowires are also fabricated by *molecular beam epitaxy* (MBE), in which gaseous atoms or molecules are sprayed onto a crystalline surface in an evacuated

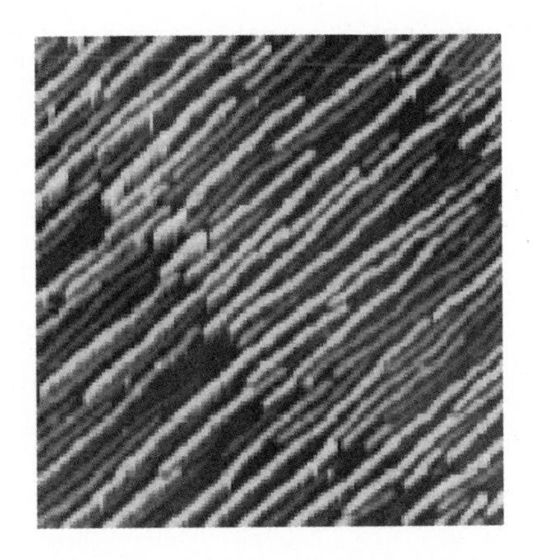

Germanium nanowires fabricated onto a silicon surface by molecular beam epitaxy and imaged by atomic force microscopy. Reproduced with permission from T. Ogino *et al.*, *Acc. Chem. Res.* **32**, 447 (1999).

chamber. Through careful control of the chamber temperature and of the spraying process, it is possible to create nanometre-sized assemblies with specific shapes. For example, the second illustration shows an image of germanium nanowires on a silicon surface. The wires are about 2 nm high, 10–32 nm wide, and 10–600 nm long. It is also possible to deposit *quantum dots*, nanometre-sized boxes or spheres of atoms, on a surface. Semiconducting quantum dots could be important building blocks of nanometre-sized lasers.

Direct manipulation of atoms on a surface also leads to the formation of nanowires. The Coulomb attraction between an atom and the tip of a scanning tunnelling microscope can be exploited to move atoms along a surface, arranging them into patterns, such as wires.

Exercise 1 Prepare a brief report on the design of a nanometre-sized transistor that uses a carbon nanotube as a component. A useful starting point is the work summarized by Tans *et al.*, *Nature* **393**, 49 (1998).

Exercise 2 The movement of atoms and ions on a surface depends on their ability to leave one position and stick to another, and therefore on the energy changes that occur. As an illustration, consider a two-dimensional square lattice of univalent positive and negative ions separated by 200 pm, and consider a cation on top of this array. Calculate, by direct summation, its Coulombic interaction when it is in an empty lattice point directly above an anion.

Table 15.3

Magnetic suceptibilities at 298 K

	$\chi/10^{-6}$	$\chi_m/(10^{-5}\ cm^3\ mol^{-1})$
Al(s)	+22	+2.2
Cu(s)	−9.6	−6.8
$CuSO_4\cdot 5H_2O$(s)	+176	+1930
H_2O(l)	−9.06	−160
$MnSO_4\cdot 4H_2O$(s)	+2640	+2790
NaCl(s)	−13.9	−38
S(s)	−12.9	−2.0

χ is the dimensionless magnetic susceptibility; χ_m is the molar magnetic susceptibility. The two are related by $\chi_m = \chi V_m$, where V_m is the molar volume of the sample.

for which χ is negative are called **diamagnetic** and tend to move out of a magnetic field; the density of lines of force is lower than in a vacuum. Materials for which χ is positive are called **paramagnetic;** they tend to move into a magnetic field and the density of lines of force in them is greater than in a vacuum.

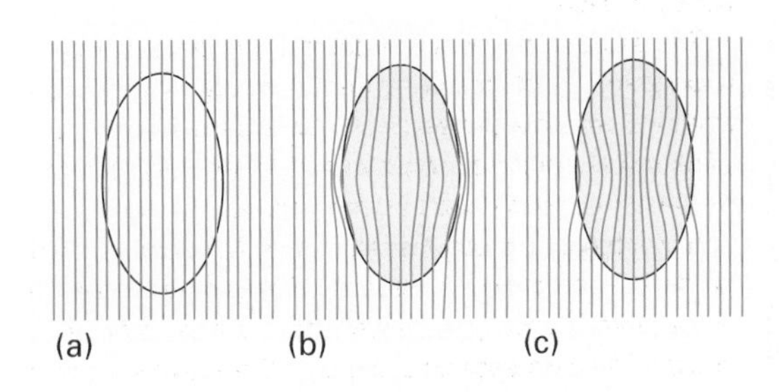

Fig. 15.16 (a) In a vacuum, the strength of a magnetic field can be represented by the density of lines of force. (b) In a diamagnetic material, the lines of force are reduced. (c) In a paramagnetic material, the lines of force are increased.

Diamagnetism arises from the effect of the magnetic field on the electrons of molecules. Specifically, an applied magnetic field induces the circulation of electronic currents, which give rise to a magnetic field that usually opposes the applied field and reduces the density of lines of force, and so the substance is diamagnetic. The great majority of molecules with no unpaired electron spins are diamagnetic. In these cases, the induced electron currents occur within the orbitals of the molecule that are occupied in its ground state. In a few cases the induced field augments the applied field and increases the density of lines of force within the material. The substance is then paramagnetic even though it has no unpaired electrons. In these cases, the induced electron currents arise from migration of electrons through unoccupied orbitals, so this kind of paramagnetism occurs only if the excited states are low in energy (as in some *d*- and *f*-block complexes). The much more common kind of paramagnetism arises from unpaired electron spins, which behave like tiny bar magnets that tend to line up with the applied field. The more that can line up in this way, the greater the lowering of the energy and the sample tends to move into the applied field. Many compounds of the *d*-block elements are paramagnetic because they have various numbers of unpaired *d*-electrons. Molecules, specifically radicals, with unpaired electrons are paramagnetic. Examples include the brown gas nitrogen dioxide (NO_2) and the peroxyl radical (HO_2), which plays a role in atmospheric chemistry.

Self-test 15.3

After reviewing concepts from Chapters 13 and 14, identify each of the following species as diamagnetic or paramagnetic: Mg, Fe, Zn, N_2, O_2, NO.

[*Answer:* Mg, Zn, and N_2 are diamagnetic; Fe, O_2, and NO are paramagnetic]

At low temperatures, some paramagnetic solids make a transition to a phase in which large domains of electron spins align with parallel orientations. This cooperative alignment gives rise to a very strong magnetization—in some cases millions of times greater—and is called **ferromagnetism** (Fig. 15.17). In other cases, the cooperative effect leads to alternating spin orientations: the spins are locked into a low-magnetization arrangement to give an **antiferromagnetic phase** that has a zero magnetization because the contributions from different spins cancel. The transition to the ferromagnetic phase occurs at the **Curie temperature**, and the transition to the antiferromagnetic occurs at the **Néel temperature**.

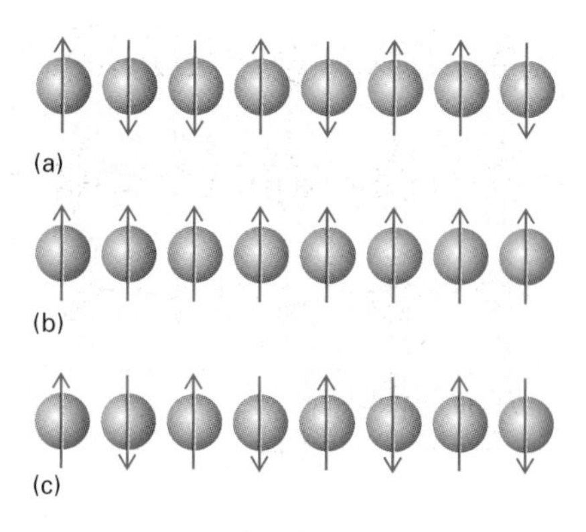

Fig. 15.17 (a) In a paramagnetic material, the electron spins are aligned at random in the absence of an applied magnetic field. (b) In a ferromagnetic material, the electron spins are locked into a parallel alignment over large domains. (c) In an antiferromagnetic material, the electron spins are locked into an antiparallel arrangement. The latter two arrangements survive even in the absence of an applied field.

Superconductors have unique magnetic properties. Some superconductors, classed as Type I, show abrupt loss of superconductivity when an applied magnetic field exceeds a critical value $\mathcal{H}_c$ characteristic of the material. Type I superconductors are also completely diamagnetic—the lines of force are completely excluded—below $\mathcal{H}_c$. This exclusion of a magnetic field in a material is known as the **Meissner effect**, which can be demonstrated by the levitation of a superconductor above a magnet. Type II superconductors, which include the HTSCs, show a gradual loss of superconductivity and diamagnetism with increasing magnetic field.

Crystal structure

Now we turn to the structures adopted by atoms and ions when they stack together to give a crystalline solid. The structures of crystals are of considerable practical importance, as they have implications for geology, materials, technologically advanced materials such as semiconductors and high-temperature superconductors, and in biology. The first, and often very demanding, step in an X-ray structural analysis of biological macromolecules is to form crystals in which the large molecules lie in orderly ranks. On the contrary, the crystallization of

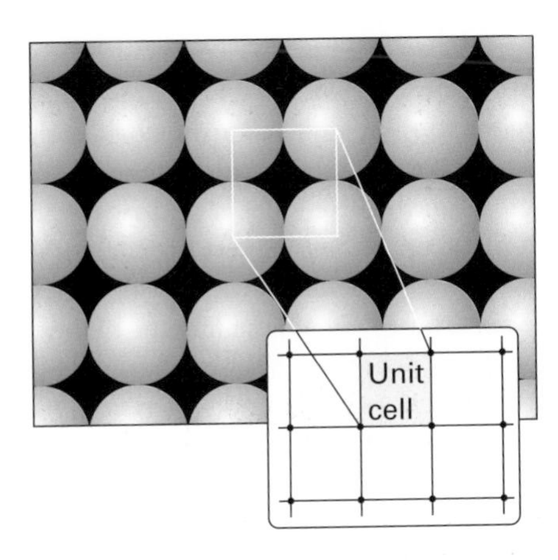

Fig. 15.18 A crystal consists of a uniform array of atoms, molecules, or ions, as represented by these spheres. In many cases, the components of the crystal are far from spherical, but this diagram illustrates the general idea. The location of each atom, molecule, or ion can be represented by a single point; here (for convenience only), the locations are denoted by a point at the centre of the sphere. The unit cell, which is shown shaded in the inset, is the smallest block from which the entire array of points can be constructed without rotating or otherwise modifying the block.

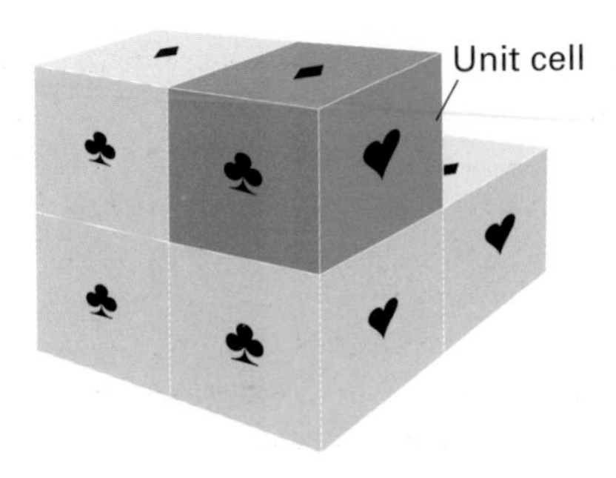

Fig. 15.19 A unit cell, here shown in three dimensions, is like a brick used to construct a wall. Once again, only pure translations are allowed in the construction of the crystal. (Some bonding patterns for actual walls use rotations of bricks, so for these patterns a single brick is not a unit cell.)

a virus particle would take it out of circulation, and one of the strategies adopted by viruses for avoiding this kind of entombment makes unconscious use of the geometry of crystal packing.

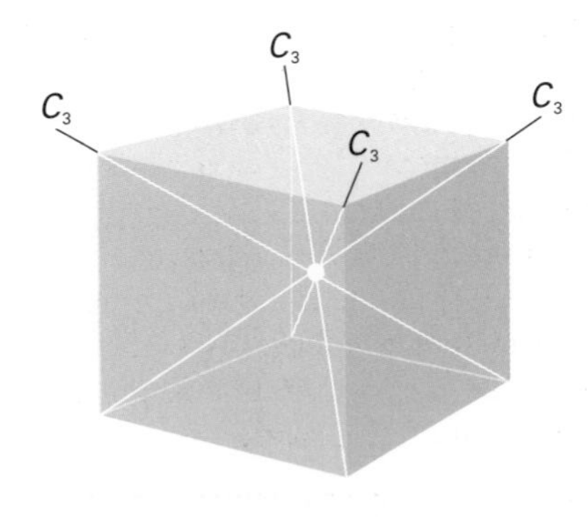

Fig. 15.20 A unit cell belonging to the cubic system has four threefold axes (denoted C_3) arranged tetrahedrally.

15.10 Unit cells

The pattern that atoms, ions, or molecules adopt in a crystal is expressed in terms of an array of points making up the **lattice** that identify the locations of the individual species (Fig. 15.18). A **unit cell** of a crystal is the small three-dimensional figure obtained by joining typically eight of these points, and which may be used to construct the entire crystal lattice by purely translational displacements, much as a wall may be constructed from bricks (Fig. 15.19). An infinite number of different unit cells can describe the same structure, but it is conventional to choose the cell with sides that have the shortest lengths and are most nearly perpendicular to one another.

Unit cells are classified into one of seven **crystal systems** according to the symmetry they possess under rotations about different axes. The *cubic system*, for example, has four threefold axes (Fig. 15.20). A threefold axis is an axis of a rotation that restores the unit cell to the same appearance three times during a complete revolution, after rotations through 120°, 240°, and 360°. The four axes of a cube make the tetrahedral angle to each other. The *monoclinic system* has one twofold axis (Fig. 15.21). A twofold axis is an axis of a rotation that leaves the cell apparently unchanged twice during a complete revolution, after rotations through 180° and 360°. The **essential symmetries**, the properties that must be present for the unit cell to belong to a particular system, are listed in Table 15.4.

A unit cell may have lattice points other than at its corners, so each crystal system can occur in a number of different varieties. For example, in some cases points may occur on the faces and in the body of the cell without destroying the cell's essential symmetry.

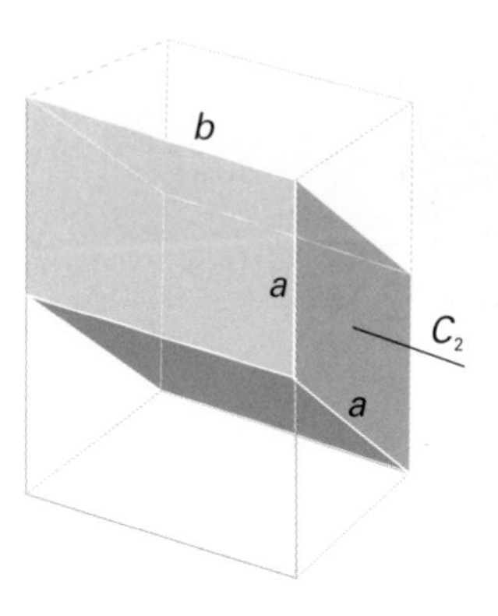

Fig. 15.21 A unit cell belonging to the monoclinic system has one twofold (denoted C_2) axis (along b).

Table 15.4

The essential symmetries of the seven crystal systems

The system	Essential symmetries
Triclinic	None
Monoclinic	One twofold axis
Orthorhombic	Three perpendicular twofold axes
Rhombohedral	One threefold axis
Tetragonal	One fourfold axis
Hexagonal	One sixfold axis
Cubic	Four threefold axes in a tetrahedral arrangement

These various possibilities give rise to 14 distinct types of unit cell, which define the **Bravais lattices** (Fig. 15.22).

15.11 The identification of crystal planes

The identification of the type of unit cell specifies the internal symmetry of the crystal. To specify a unit cell fully, we also need to know its size, such as the lengths of its sides. There is a useful relation between the spacing of the planes passing through the lattice points, which (as we shall see) we can measure, and the lengths we need to know.

Because two-dimensional arrays of points are easier to visualize than three-dimensional arrays, we shall introduce the concepts we need by referring to two dimensions initially, and then extend the conclusions to three dimensions. Consider the two-dimensional rectangular lattice formed from a rectangular unit cell of sides a and b (Fig. 15.23). We can distinguish the four sets of planes shown in the illustration by the distances at which they intersect the axes. One way of labelling the planes would therefore be to denote each set by the smallest intersection distances. For example, we could denote the four sets in the illustration as $(1a,1b)$, $(3a,2b)$, $(-1a,1b)$, and $(\infty a,1b)$. If, however, we agreed always to quote distances along the axes as multiples of the lengths of the unit cell, then we could omit the a and b and label the planes more simply as $(1,1)$, $(3,2)$, $(-1,1)$, and $(\infty,1)$.

Now let's suppose that the array in Fig. 15.23 is the top view of a three-dimensional rectangular lattice in which the unit cell has a length c in the z direction. All four sets of planes intersect the z-axis at infinity, so the full labels of the sets of planes of lattice points are $(1,1,\infty)$, $(3,2,\infty)$, $(-1,1,\infty)$, and $(\infty,1,\infty)$.

The presence of infinity in the labels is inconvenient. We can eliminate it by taking the reciprocals of the numbers in the labels; this step also turns out to have further advantages, as we shall see. The resulting **Miller indices**, (hkl), are the reciprocals of the numbers in the parentheses with fractions cleared. For example, the $(1,1,\infty)$ planes in Fig. 15.23 are the (110) planes in the Miller notation (because $\frac{1}{1} = 1$ and $\frac{1}{\infty} = 0$). Similarly, the $(3,2,\infty)$ planes become first $(\frac{1}{3}, \frac{1}{2},0)$ when reciprocals are formed, and then $(2,3,0)$ when fractions are cleared by multiplication through by 6, so they are referred to as the (230) planes. We write negative indices with a bar over the number: Fig. 15.23c shows the $(\bar{1}10)$ planes. Figure 15.24 shows some planes in three dimensions, including an example of a lattice with axes that are not mutually perpendicular.

Self-test 15.4

A representative member of a set of planes in a crystal intersects the axes at $3a$, $2b$, and $2c$; what are the Miller indices of the planes?

[*Answer:* (233)]

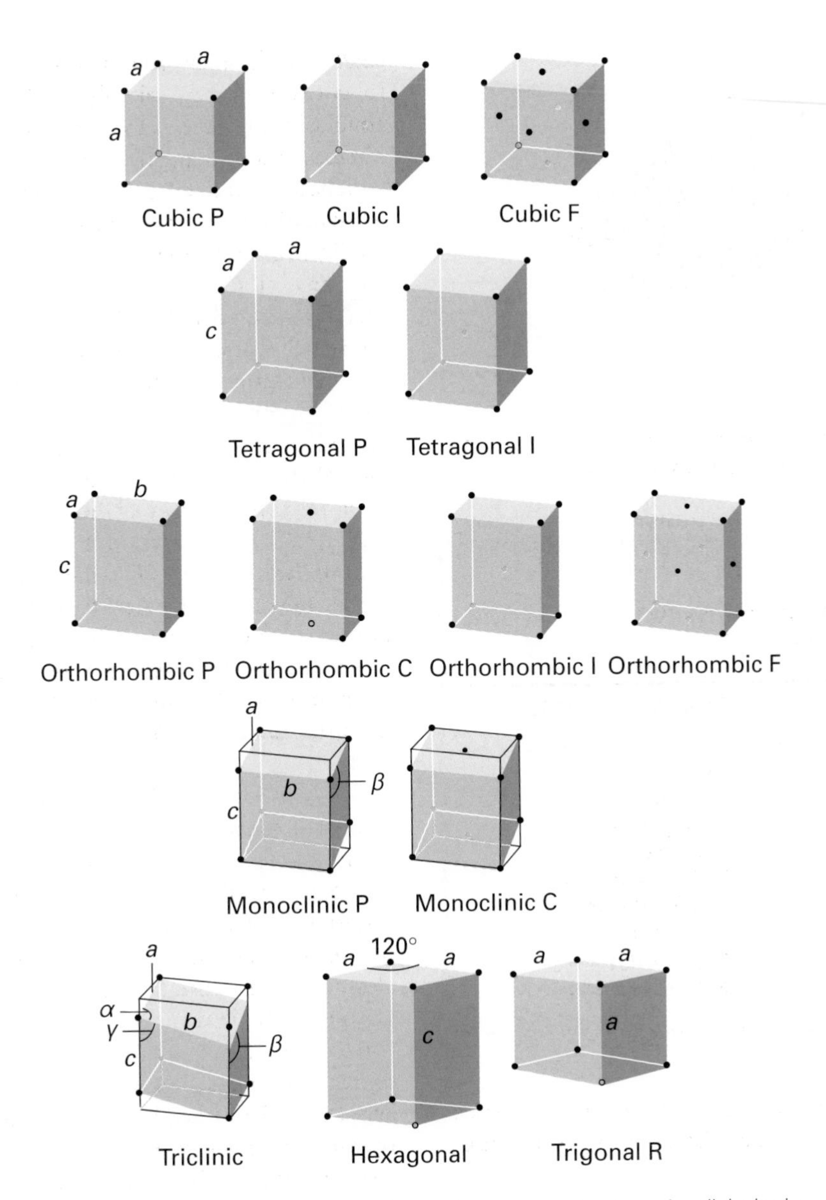

Fig. 15.22 The 14 Bravais lattices. The letter P denotes a primitive unit cell, I a body-centred unit cell, F a face-centred unit cell, and C (or A or B) a cell with lattice points on two opposite faces.

It is helpful to keep in mind the fact, as illustrated in Fig. 15.23, that the smaller the value of h in the Miller index (hkl), the more nearly parallel the plane is to the a axis. The same is true of k and the b axis and l and the c axis. When $h = 0$, the planes intersect the a axis at infinity, so the $(0kl)$ planes are parallel to the a axis. Similarly, the $(h0l)$ planes are parallel to b and the $(hk0)$ planes are parallel to c.

The Miller indices are very useful for calculating the separation of planes. For instance, we show in Derivation 15.3 that they can be used to derive the following very simple expression for the separation, d, of the (hkl) planes:

$$\frac{1}{d^2} = \frac{h^2}{a^2} + \frac{k^2}{b^2} + \frac{l^2}{c^2} \tag{15.7}$$

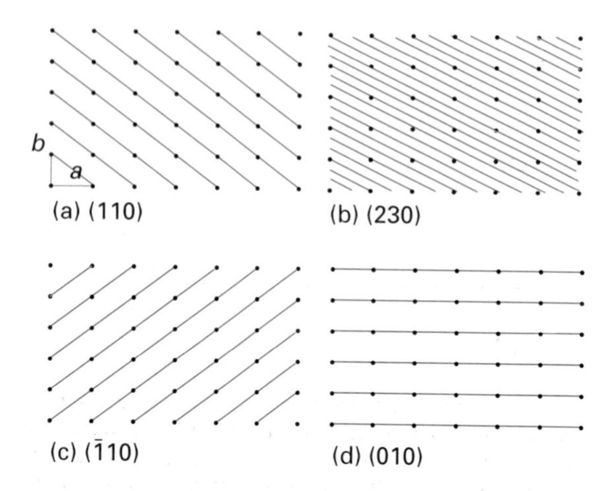

Fig. 15.23 Some of the planes that can be drawn through the points of the space lattice and their corresponding Miller indices (*hkl*).

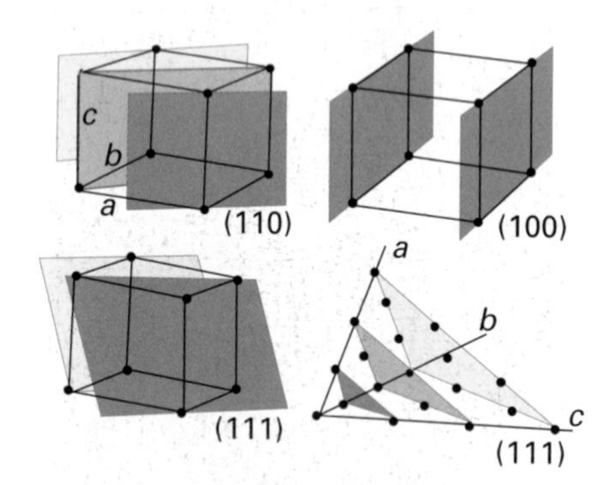

Fig. 15.24 Some representative planes in three dimensions and their Miller indices. Note that a 0 indicates that a plane is parallel to the corresponding axis, and that the indexing may also be used for unit cells with non-orthogonal axes.

Derivation 15.3
The separation of lattice planes

Consider the (*hk*0) planes of a rectangular lattice built from an orthorhombic unit cell of sides of lengths *a* and *b* (Fig. 15.25). We can write the following trigonometric expressions for the angle ϕ shown in the illustration:

$$\sin\phi = \frac{d}{(a/h)} = \frac{hd}{a} \qquad \cos\phi = \frac{d}{(b/k)} = \frac{kd}{b}$$

Then, because $\sin^2\phi + \cos^2\phi = 1$, we obtain

$$\frac{h^2d^2}{a^2} + \frac{k^2d^2}{b^2} = 1$$

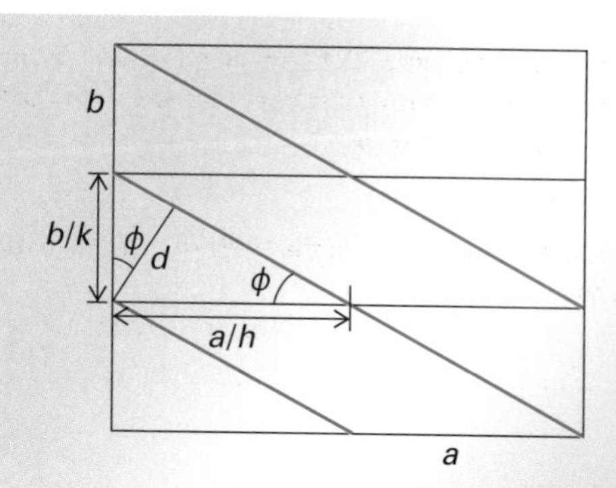

Fig. 15.25 The geometrical construction used to relate the separation of planes to the dimensions of the unit cell.

which we can rearrange into

$$\frac{1}{d^2} = \frac{h^2}{a^2} + \frac{k^2}{b^2}$$

In three dimensions, this expression generalizes to eqn 15.7.

Example 15.2
Using the Miller indices

Calculate the separation of (a) the (123) planes and (b) the (246) planes of an orthorhombic cell with $a = 0.82$ nm, $b = 0.94$ nm, and $c = 0.75$ nm.

Strategy For the first part, we simply substitute the information into eqn 15.7. For the second part, instead of repeating the calculation, we should examine how *d* in eqn 15.7 changes when all three Miller indices are multiplied by 2 (or by a more general factor, *n*).

Solution Substituting the data into eqn 15.7 gives

$$\frac{1}{d^2} = \frac{1^2}{(0.82\text{ nm})^2} + \frac{2^2}{(0.94\text{ nm})^2} + \frac{3^2}{(0.75\text{ nm})^2}$$
$$= \frac{22}{\text{nm}^2}$$

It follows that $d = 0.21$ nm. When the indices are all increased by a factor of 2, the separation becomes

$$\frac{1}{d^2} = \frac{(2\times 1)^2}{(0.82\text{ nm})^2} + \frac{(2\times 2)^2}{(0.94\text{ nm})^2} + \frac{(2\times 3)^2}{(0.75\text{ nm})^2}$$
$$= 4 \times \frac{22}{\text{nm}^2}$$

So, for these planes $d = 0.11$ nm. In general, increasing the indices uniformly by a factor n decreases the separation of the planes by n.

Self-test 15.5

Calculate the separation of the (133) and (399) planes in the same lattice.

[*Answer:* 0.19 nm, 0.063 nm]

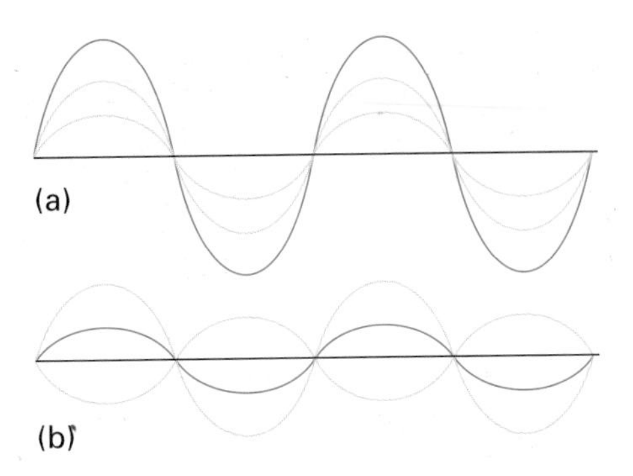

Fig. 15.26 When two waves (drawn as thin lines) are in the same region of space they interfere. Depending on their relative phase, they may interfere (a) constructively, to give an enhanced amplitude, or (b) destructively, to give a smaller amplitude.

15.12 The determination of structure

One of the most important techniques for the determination of the structures of crystals is **X-ray diffraction.** In its simplest form, the technique is used to identify the lattice type and the separation of the planes of lattice points (and hence the distance between the centres of atoms and ions). In its most sophisticated version, X-ray diffraction provides detailed information about the location of all the atoms in a molecule, even those as complicated as proteins. Special techniques are also available for the study of structural changes that accompany chemical reactions. The current considerable success of modern molecular biology has stemmed from X-ray diffraction techniques that have grown in sensitivity and scope as computing techniques have become more powerful. Here we concentrate on the principles of the technique and illustrate how it may be used to determine the spacing of atoms in a crystal.

The physics of waves is reviewed in Appendix 3.

A characteristic property of waves is that they **interfere** with one another, which means that they give a greater amplitude where their displacements add and a smaller amplitude where their displacements subtract (Fig. 15.26). Because the intensity of electromagnetic radiation is proportional to the square of the amplitude of the waves, the regions of constructive and destructive interference show up as regions of enhanced and diminished intensities. The phenomenon of **diffraction** is the interference caused by an object in the path of waves, and the pattern of varying intensity that results is called the **diffraction pattern** (Fig. 15.27).[5] Diffraction occurs when the dimensions of the diffracting object are comparable to the wavelength of the radiation. Sound waves, with wavelengths of the order of 1 m, are diffracted by macroscopic objects. Light waves, with wavelengths of the order of 500 nm, are diffracted by narrow slits.

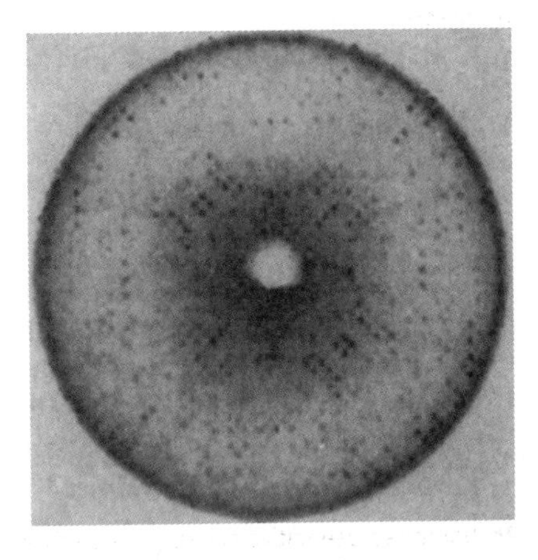

Fig. 15.27 A typical diffraction pattern obtained in a version of the X-ray diffraction technique. The black dots are the reflections, the points of maximum constructive interference, that are used to determine the structure of the crystal.

X-rays have wavelengths comparable to bond lengths in molecules and the spacing of atoms in crystals (about 100 pm), so they are diffracted by them. By analysing the diffraction pattern, it is possible to draw up a detailed picture of the location of

[5] We first encountered diffraction in Section 12.4 in connection with the wave properties of electrons.

atoms. Electrons moving at about 2×10^4 km s^{-1} (after acceleration through about 4 kV) have wavelengths of about 20 pm (recall Example 12.2), and may also be diffracted by molecules. Neutrons generated in a nuclear reactor, and then slowed to thermal velocities (that is, bouncing off the nuclei of atoms until their kinetic energy has become the same as that of the targets), have similar wavelengths and may also be used for diffraction studies.

The short-wavelength electromagnetic radiation we call X-rays is produced by bombarding a metal with high-energy electrons. The electrons decelerate as they plunge into the metal and generate radiation with a continuous range of wavelengths. This radiation is called **bremsstrahlung.**[6] Superimposed on the continuum are a few high-intensity, sharp peaks. These peaks arise from the interaction of the incoming electrons with the electrons in the inner shells of the atoms. A collision expels an electron (Fig. 15.28), and an electron of higher energy drops into the vacancy, emitting the excess energy as an X-ray photon. An example of the process is the expulsion of an electron from the K shell (the shell with $n = 1$) of a copper atom, followed by the transition of an outer electron into the vacancy. The energy so released gives rise to copper's K_α radiation of wavelength 154 pm. Currently, however, there is a major shift in emphasis to using **synchrotron radiation** as a source of high-intensity, monochromatic X-rays. Synchrotron radiation is produced when electrons move at high speed in a circle, as accelerated charges generate electromagnetic radiation, and the high speeds achieved in the particle accelerators known as *synchrotrons* result in the production of very high frequency radiation. The principal drawback is that synchrotron sources are costly and must be built as national facilities.

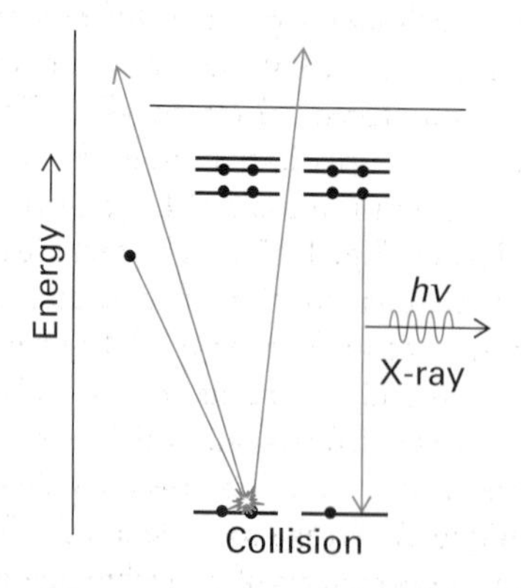

Fig. 15.28 The formation of X-rays. When a metal is subjected to a high-energy electron beam, an electron in an inner shell of an atom is ejected. When an electron falls into the vacated orbital from an orbital of much higher energy, the excess energy is released as an X-ray photon.

In 1923, the German physicist Max von Laue suggested that X-rays might be diffracted when passed through a crystal, as the wavelengths of X-rays are comparable to the separation of atoms, and diffraction occurs when the wavelength of radiation is comparable to the dimensions of a target. Laue's suggestion was confirmed almost immediately by Walter Friedrich and Paul Knipping, and then developed by William and Lawrence Bragg, who later jointly received the Nobel Prize. X-ray diffraction has grown since then into a technique of extraordinary power.

15.13 The Bragg law

The earliest approach to the analysis of X-ray diffraction patterns treated a plane of atoms as a semitransparent mirror and modelled the crystal as stacks of reflecting planes of separation d (Fig. 15.29). The model makes it easy to calculate the angle the crystal must make to the incoming beam of X-rays for constructive interference to occur. It has also given rise to the name **reflection** to denote an intense spot arising from constructive interference.

The path-length difference of the two rays shown in the illustration is

$$AB + BC = 2d \sin \theta$$

where θ is the **glancing angle.** When the path-length difference is equal to one wavelength ($AB + BC = \lambda$), the reflected waves interfere constructively. It follows that a reflection should be observed when the glancing angle satisfies the **Bragg law:**

$$\lambda = 2d \sin \theta \qquad (15.8)$$

The primary use of the Bragg law is to determine the spacing between the layers of atoms because, once the angle θ corresponding to a reflection has been determined, d may readily be calculated.

[6] *Bremse* is German for brake, *Strahlung* for ray.

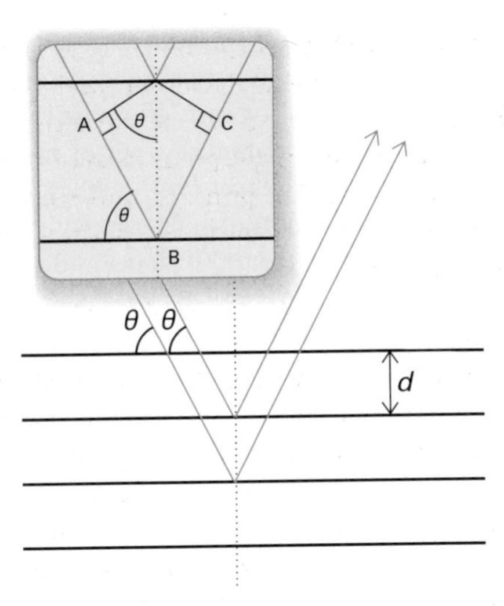

Fig. 15.29 The derivation of the Bragg law treats each lattice plane as reflecting the incident radiation. The path lengths differ by AB + BC, which depends on the glancing angle θ. Constructive interference (a 'reflection') occurs when AB + BC is equal to an integral number of wavelengths.

Example 15.3

Using the Bragg law

A reflection from the (111) planes of a cubic crystal was observed at a glancing angle of 11.2° when Cu K_α X-rays of wavelength 154 pm were used. What is the length of the side of the unit cell?

Strategy We can find the separation, d, of the lattice planes from eqn 15.8 and the data. Then we find the length of the side of the unit cell by using eqn 15.7. Because the unit cell is cubic, $a = b = c$, so eqn 15.7 simplifies to

$$\frac{1}{d^2} = \frac{h^2 + k^2 + l^2}{a^2}$$

which rearranges to

$$a = d \times (h^2 + k^2 + l^2)^{1/2}$$

Solution According to the Bragg law, the separation of the (111) planes responsible for the diffraction is

$$d = \frac{\lambda}{2\sin\theta} = \frac{154\text{ pm}}{2\sin 11.2°}$$

It then follows that with $h = k = l = 1$,

$$a = \frac{154\text{ pm}}{2\sin 11.2°} \times 3^{1/2} = 687\text{ pm}$$

Self-test 15.6

Calculate the angle at which the same lattice will give a reflection from the (123) planes.

[*Answer*: 24.8°]

15.14 Experimental techniques

Laue's original method consisted of passing a beam of X-rays of a wide range of wavelengths into a single crystal, and recording the diffraction pattern photographically. The idea behind the approach was that a crystal might not be suitably orientated to act as a diffraction grating for a single wavelength, but whatever its orientation the Bragg law would be satisfied for at least one of the wavelengths when a range of wavelengths is present in the beam.

An alternative technique was developed by Peter Debye and Paul Scherrer and independently by Albert Hull. They used monochromatic (single-frequency) X-rays and a powdered sample. When the sample is a powder, we can be sure that some of the randomly distributed crystallites will be orientated so as to satisfy the Bragg law. For example, some of them will be orientated so that their (111) planes, of spacing d, give rise to a reflection at a particular angle and others will be orientated so that their (230) planes give rise to a reflection at a different angle. Each set of (hkl) planes gives rise to reflections at a different angle. In the modern version of the technique, which uses a **powder diffractometer**, the sample is spread on a flat plate and the diffraction pattern is monitored electronically. The major application is for qualitative analysis because the diffraction pattern is a kind of fingerprint and may be recognizable (Fig. 15.30). The technique is also used for the characterization of substances that cannot be crystallized or for the initial determination of the dimensions and symmetries of unit cells.

Modern X-ray diffraction, which uses an **X-ray diffractometer** (Fig. 15.31), is now a highly sophisticated technique. By far the most detailed information comes from developments of the techniques pioneered by the Braggs, in which a single crystal is used as the diffracting object and a monochromatic beam of X-rays is used to generate the diffraction pattern. The single crystal (which may be only a fraction of a

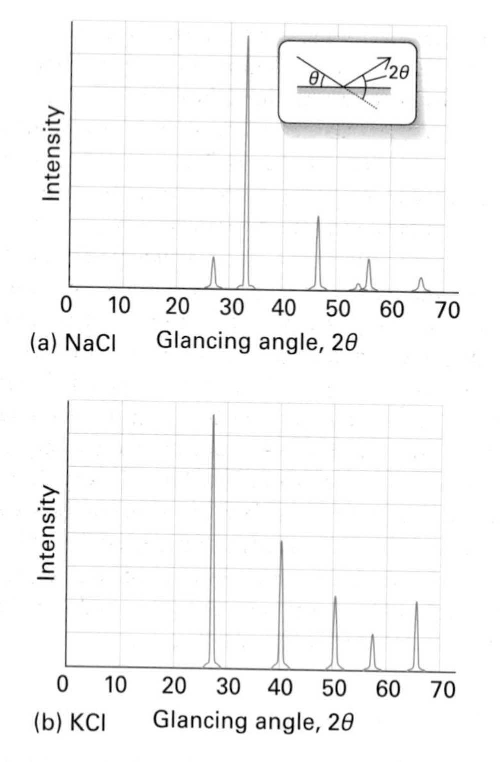

Fig. 15.30 Typical X-ray powder diffraction patterns that can be used to identify the material and determine the size of its unit cell. (a) Sodium chloride; (b) potassium chloride.

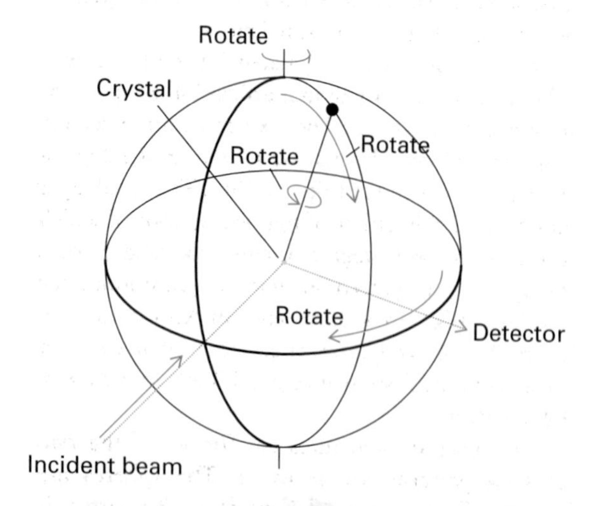

Fig. 15.31 A four-circle diffractometer. The settings of the orientations of the components is controlled by computer; each reflection is monitored in turn, and their intensities are recorded.

millimetre in length) is rotated relative to the beam, and the diffraction pattern is monitored and recorded electronically for each crystal orientation. The primary data are therefore a set of intensities arising from the Miller planes (hkl), with each set of planes giving a reflection of intensity I_{hkl}. For our purposes, we focus on the ($h00$) planes and write the intensities I_h.

To derive the structure of the crystal from the intensities we need to convert them to the *amplitude* of the wave responsible for the signal. Because the intensity of electromagnetic radiation is given by the square of the amplitude, we need to form the **structure factors** $F_h = (I_h)^{1/2}$. Here is the first difficulty: we do not know the sign to take. For instance, if $I_h = 4$, then F_h can be either +2 or −2. This ambiguity is the **phase problem** of X-ray diffraction. However, once we have the structure factors, we can calculate the electron density $\rho(x)$ by forming the following sum:

$$\rho(x) = \frac{1}{V}\left\{F_0 + 2\sum_{h=1}^{\infty} F_h \cos(2h\pi x)\right\} \qquad (15.9)$$

A *Fourier synthesis*, of which eqn 15.9 is an example, is a reconstruction of a repetitive function as a superposition of sine or cosine waves. Long-wavelength waves account for the general features of the structure, and the details are gradually filled in by incorporating shorter-wavelength waves.

where V is the volume of the unit cell. This expression is called a **Fourier synthesis** of the electron density: we show how it is used in Illustration 15.1. The point to note is that low values of the index h give the major features of the structure (they correspond to long-wavelength cosine terms) whereas the high values give the fine detail (short-wavelength cosine terms). Clearly, if we do not know the sign of F_h, we do not know whether the corresponding term in the sum is positive or negative and we get different electron densities, and hence crystal structures, for different choices of sign.

Illustration 15.1

The determination of crystal structure

The following intensities were obtained in an experiment on an organic solid:

h	0	1	2	3	4	5	6	7	8	9
I_h	256	100	5	1	50	100	8	10	5	10

h	10	11	12	13	14	15
I_h	40	25	9	4	4	9

To find the structure factors, we take square-roots of the intensities:

h	0	1	2	3	4	5	6	7
F_h	±16	±10	±2.2	±1	±7.1	±10	±2.8	±3.2

h	8	9	10	11	12	13	14	15
F_h	±2.2	±3.2	±6.3	±5	±3	±2	±2	±3

Suppose the signs alternate $+-+-\cdots$; then the electron density is

$$V\rho(x) = 16 - 20\cos(2\pi x) + 4.4\cos(4\pi x) - \cdots - 6\cos(30\pi x)$$

This function is shown in Fig. 15.32a, and the locations of several types of atom are easy to identify as peaks in the electron density. If we use + signs up to $h = 5$ and − signs thereafter; the electron density is

$$V\rho(x) = 16 + 20\cos(2\pi x) + 4.4\cos(4\pi x) + \cdots - 6\cos(30\pi x)$$

This density is shown in Fig. 15.32b. This structure has more regions of illegal negative electron density, so is less plausible than the structure obtained from the first choice of phases.

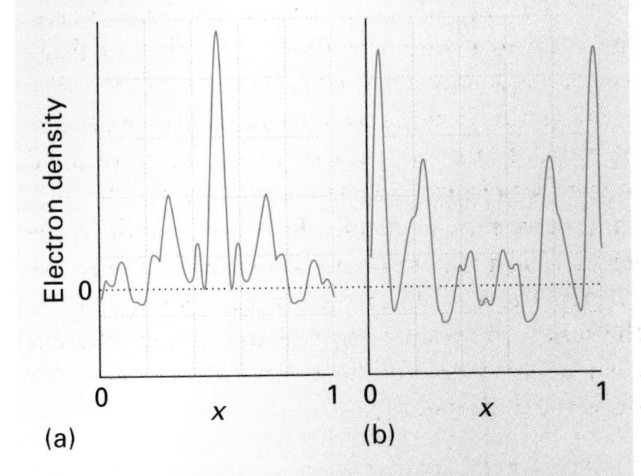

Fig. 15.32 The Fourier synthesis of the electron density of a one-dimensional crystal using the data in Illustration 15.1. (a) Using alternating signs for the structure factors; (b) using positive signs for h up to 5, then negative signs.

The phase problem can be overcome to some extent by the method of **isomorphous replacement**, in which heavy atoms are introduced into the crystal. The technique relies on the fact that the scattering of X-rays is caused by the oscillations an incoming electromagnetic wave generates in the electrons of atoms, and heavy atoms give rise to stronger scattering than light atoms. So heavy atoms dominate the diffraction pattern and greatly simplify its interpretation. The phase problem can also be resolved by judging whether the calculated structure is chemically plausible, whether the electron density is positive throughout, and by using more refined mathematical techniques. Huge numbers of crystal structures have been determined in this way. In the following sections we review how some of them can be rationalized. For metals and monatomic ions we can model the atoms and ions as hard spheres, and consider how such spheres can be stacked together in a regular, electrically neutral array.

15.15 Metal crystals

Most metallic elements crystallize in one of three simple forms, two of which can be explained in terms of stacking spheres to give the closest possible packing. In such **close-packed structures** the spheres representing the atoms are packed together with least waste of space and each sphere has the greatest possible number of nearest neighbours.

We can form a close-packed layer of identical spheres, one with maximum utilization of space, as shown in Fig. 15.33a. Then we can form a second close-packed layer by placing spheres in the depressions of the first layer (Fig. 15.33b). The third layer may be added in either of two ways, both of which result in the same degree of close packing. In one, the spheres are placed so that they reproduce the first layer (Fig. 15.33c), to give an ABA pattern of layers. Alternatively, the spheres may be placed over the gaps in the first layer (Fig. 15.33d), so giving an ABC pattern.

Two types of structures are formed if the two stacking patterns are repeated. The spheres are **hexagonally close-packed** (hcp) if the ABA pattern is repeated to give the sequence of layers ABABAB.... The name reflects the symmetry of the unit cell (Fig. 15.34). Metals with hcp structures include

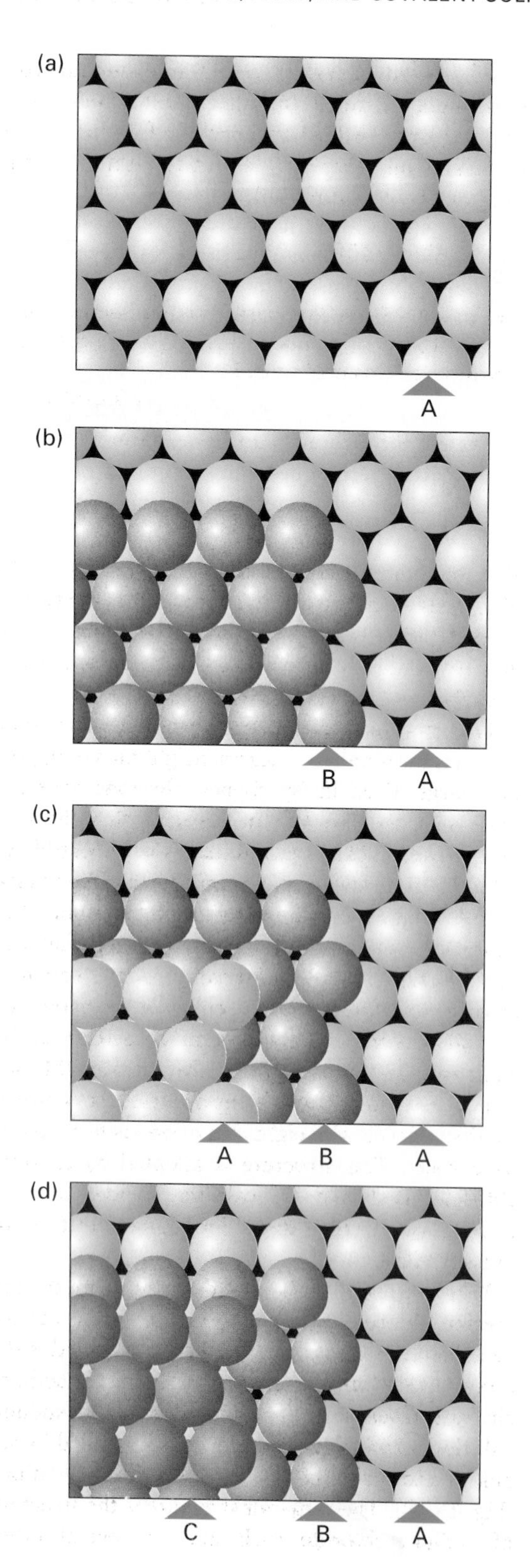

Fig. 15.33 The close-packing of identical spheres. (a) The first layer of close-packed spheres. (b) The second layer of close-packed spheres occupies the dips of the first layer. The two layers are the AB component of the structure. (c) The third layer of close-packed spheres might occupy the dips lying directly above the spheres in the first layer, resulting in an ABA structure. (d) Alternatively, the third layer might lie in the dips that are not above the spheres in the first layer, resulting in an ABC structure.

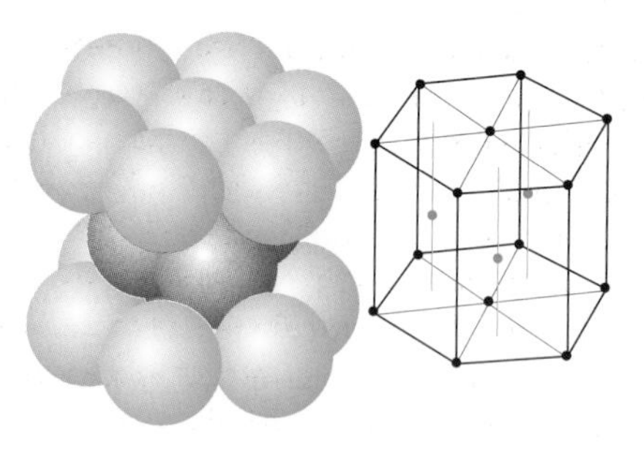

Fig. 15.34 A hexagonal close-packed structure. The tinting of the spheres (denoting the three layers of atoms) is the same as in Fig. 15.33.

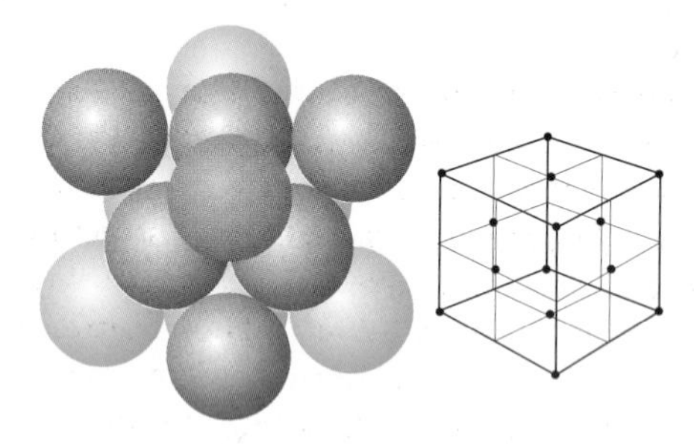

Fig. 15.35 A cubic close-packed structure. The tinting of the spheres is the same as in Fig. 15.33.

beryllium, cadmium, cobalt, manganese, titanium, and zinc. Solid helium (which forms only under pressure) also adopts this arrangement of atoms. Alternatively, the spheres are **cubic close-packed** (ccp) if the ABC pattern is repeated to give the sequence of layers ABCABC.... Here too, the name reflects the symmetry of the unit cell (Fig. 15.35). Metals with this structure include silver, aluminium, gold, calcium, copper, nickel, lead, and platinum. The noble gases other than helium also adopt a ccp structure.

The compactness of the ccp and hcp structures is indicated by their **coordination number**, the number of atoms immediately surrounding any selected atom, which is 12 in both cases. Another measure of their compactness is the **packing fraction**, the fraction of space occupied by the spheres, which is 0.740. That is, in a close-packed solid of identical hard spheres, 74.0 per cent of the available space is occupied and only 26.0 per cent of the total volume is empty space.

The fact that many metals are close-packed accounts for one of their common characteristics, their high density. However, there is a difference between ccp and hcp metals. In cubic close packing, the faces of the cubes extend throughout the solid, and give rise to a **slip plane**. Careful analysis of the ccp structure shows that there are eight slip planes in various orientations whereas an hcp structure has only one set of slip planes. When the metal is under stress, the layers of atoms may slip past one another along a slip plane. Because a ccp metal has more slip planes than an hcp metal, a ccp metal is more malleable than an hcp metal. Thus, copper, which is highly malleable, is ccp, but zinc, which is hcp, is more brittle.

A number of common metals adopt structures that are not close-packed, which suggests that directional covalent bonding between neighbouring atoms is beginning to influence the structure and impose a specific geometrical arrangement. One such arrangement results in a **body-centred cubic** (bcc) lattice, with one sphere at the centre of a cube formed by eight others (Fig. 15.36). The bcc structure is adopted by a number of common metals, including barium, caesium, chromium, iron, potassium, and tungsten. The coordination number of a bcc lattice is 8 and its packing fraction is only 0.68, showing that only about two-thirds of the available space is occupied.

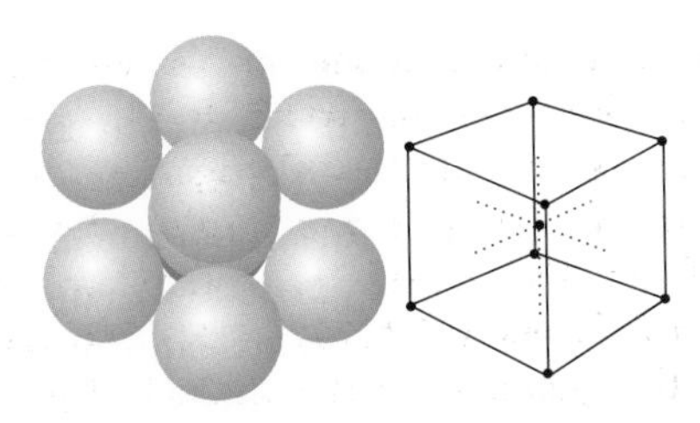

Fig. 15.36 A body-centred cubic unit cell. The spheres on the corners touch the central sphere but the packing pattern leaves more empty space than in the two close-packed structures.

Self-test 15.7

What is the coordination number and the packing fraction of a primitive cubic lattice in which there is a lattice point at each corner of a cube?

[*Answer*: 6, 0.52]

15.16 Ionic crystals

To model the structures of ionic crystals by stacks of spheres we must allow for the fact that the two or more types of ion present in the compound have different radii (generally with the cations smaller than the anions) and different charges.

The **coordination number** of an ion in an ionic crystal is the number of nearest neighbours of opposite charge. Even if, by chance, the ions have the same size, the problem of ensuring that the unit cells are electrically neutral makes it impossible to achieve 12-coordinate close-packed structures (which is one reason why ionic solids are generally less dense than metals). The closest packing that can be achieved is the 8-coordination of the **caesium-chloride structure** in which each cation is surrounded by eight anions and each anion is surrounded by eight cations (Fig. 15.37). In the caesium-chloride structure, an ion of one charge occupies the centre of a cubic unit cell with eight ions of opposite charge at its corners. This structure is adopted by caesium chloride itself and by calcium sulfide, caesium cyanide (with some distortion), and one type of brass (CuZn).

When the radii of the ions differ by more than in caesium chloride, even 8-coordinate packing cannot be achieved. One common structure adopted is the 6-coordinated **rock-salt structure** typified by sodium chloride (rock salt is a mineral form of sodium chloride) in which each cation is surrounded by six anions and each anion is surrounded by six cations (Fig. 15.38). The rock-salt structure is the structure of sodium chloride itself and of several other

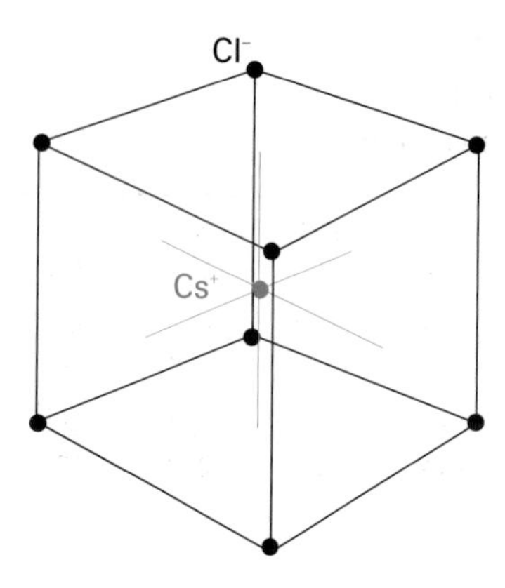

Fig. 15.37 The caesium-chloride structure consists of two interpenetrating simple cubic lattices, one of cations and the other of anions, so that each cube of ions of one kind has a counterion at its centre. This illustration shows a single unit cell with a Cs^+ ion at the centre. By imagining eight of these unit cells stacked together to form a bigger cube, it should be possible to imagine an alternative form of the unit cell with Cs^+ at the corners and a Cl^- ion at the centre.

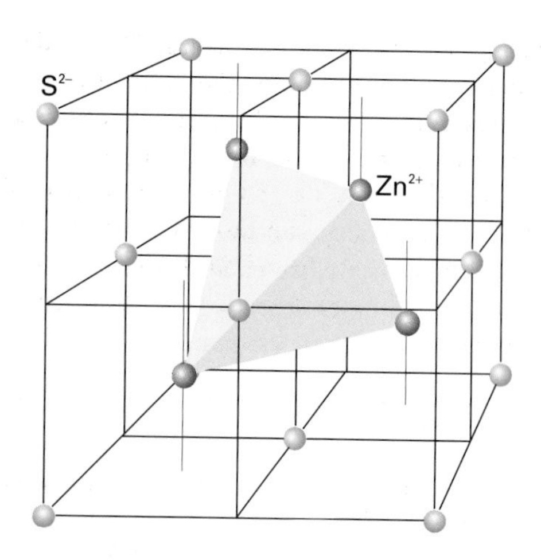

Fig. 15.39 The sphalerite (zinc-blende, ZnS) structure. This structure is typical of ions that have markedly different radii and equal but opposite charges.

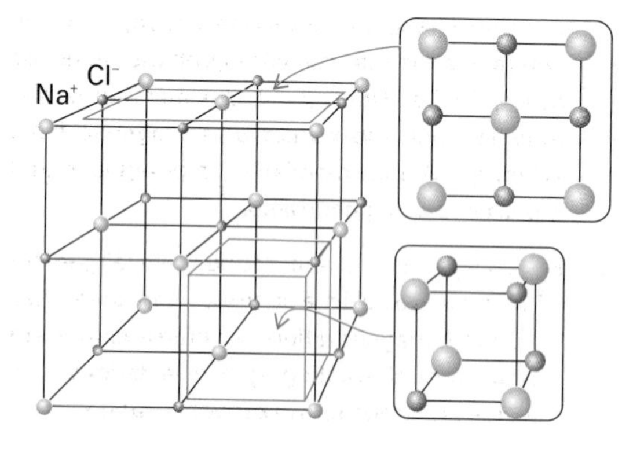

Fig. 15.38 The rock-salt (NaCl) structure consists of two mutually interpenetrating slightly expanded face-centred cubic lattices. The additional diagrams in this illustration show various details of the structure.

compounds of formula MX, including potassium bromide, silver chloride, and magnesium oxide.

The switch from the caesium-chloride structure to the rock-salt structure (in a number of examples) can be correlated with the **radius ratio**

$$\gamma = \frac{r_{\text{smaller}}}{r_{\text{larger}}} \qquad (15.10)$$

The two radii are those of the smaller and larger ions in the crystal. The **radius-ratio rule**, which is derived by analysing the geometrical problem of stacking together spheres of different radii, states that the caesium-chloride structure should be expected when

$$\gamma > 3^{1/2} - 1 = 0.732$$

and that the rock-salt structure should be expected when

$$2^{1/2} - 1 = 0.414 < \gamma < 0.732$$

For $\gamma < 0.414$, when the two types of ions have markedly different radii (like oranges and grapefruit), the most efficient packing leads to four-coordination of the type exhibited by the sphalerite (zinc blende) form of zinc sulfide, ZnS (Fig. 15.39). The radius-ratio rule is moderately well supported by observation. The deviation of a structure from the prediction is often taken to be an indication of a shift from ionic towards covalent bonding.

The **ionic radii** used to calculate γ, and wherever else it is important to know the sizes of ions, are derived from the distance between the centres of adjacent ions in a crystal. However, in a diffraction experiment we measure the distance between the centres of ions. It is necessary to apportion that total distance by defining the radius of one ion and reporting all others on that basis. One scale that is widely used is based on the value 140 pm for the radius of the O^{2-} ion (Table 15.5). Other scales are also available (such as one based on F^- for discussing halides), and it is essential not to mix values from different scales. Because ionic radii are so arbitrary, predictions based on them (such as those made by using the radius-ratio rule) must be viewed cautiously.

Self-test 15.8

Is sodium iodide likely to have a rock-salt or caesium-chloride structure?

[*Answer:* rock salt]

Table 15.5

Ionic radii, r/pm

Li^+	Be^{2+}	B^{3+}	N^{3-}	O^{2-}	F^-
159	27	12	171	140	133
Na^+	Mg^{2+}	Al^{3+}	P^{3-}	S^{2-}	Cl^-
102	72	53	212	184	181
K^+	Ca^{2+}	Ga^{3+}	As^{3-}	Se^{2-}	Br^-
138	100	62	222	198	196
Rb^+	Sr^{2+}				
149	116				
Cs^+	Ba^{2+}				
170	136				

CHECKLIST OF KEY IDEAS

You should now be familiar with the following concepts:

☐ 1 Solids are classified as metallic, ionic, covalent, and molecular.

☐ 2 Electronic conductors are classified as metallic conductors or semiconductors according to the temperature dependence of their conductivities; a superconductor is an electronic conductor with zero resistance.

☐ 3 According to the band theory, electrons occupy molecular orbitals formed from the overlap of atomic orbitals: full bands are called valence bands and empty bands are called conduction bands.

☐ 4 Semiconductors are classified as p-type or n-type according to whether conduction is due to holes in the valence band or electrons in the conduction band.

☐ 5 The lattice enthalpy is the change in enthalpy (per mole of formula units) accompanying the complete separation of the components of the solid.

☐ 6 The electrostatic contribution to the lattice enthalpy is expressed by the Born–Meyer equation, $\Delta H_L^\ominus = |z_1z_2|(N_Ae^2/4\pi\varepsilon_0 d)(1 - d^*/d)A$, where A is the Madelung constant and d is the separation between the centres of neighbouring ions.

☐ 7 A bulk sample exposed to a magnetic field of strength $\mathcal{H}$ acquires a magnetization, $\mathcal{M} = \chi\mathcal{H}$, where χ is the dimensionless volume magnetic susceptibility. When $\chi < 0$, the material is diamagnetic and moves out of a magnetic field. When $\chi > 0$, the material is paramagnetic and moves into a magnetic field.

☐ 8 Ferromagnetism is the cooperative alignment of electron spins in a material and gives rise to strong magnetization. Antiferromagnetism results from alternating spin orientations in a material and leads to weak magnetization.

☐ 9 Type I superconductors show abrupt loss of superconductivity when an applied magnetic field exceeds a critical value $\mathcal{H}_c$ characteristic of the material. They are also completely diamagnetic below $\mathcal{H}_c$. Type II superconductors show a gradual loss of superconductivity and diamagnetism with increasing magnetic field.

☐ 10 Unit cells are classified into seven crystal systems according to their rotational symmetries.

☐ 11 Crystal planes are specified by a set of Miller indices (hkl) and the separation of neighbouring planes in a rectangular lattice is given by $1/d^2 = h^2/a^2 + k^2/b^2 + l^2/c^2$.

☐ 12 The Bragg law relating the glancing angle θ to the separation of lattice planes is $\lambda = 2d \sin \theta$, where λ is the wavelength of the radiation.

☐ 13 Many elemental metals have close-packed structures with coordination number 12; close-packed structures may be either cubic (ccp) or hexagonal (hcp).

☐ 14 Representative ionic structures include the caesium-chloride, rock-salt, and zinc-blende structures.

☐ 15 The radius-ratio rule may be used cautiously to predict which of these three structures is likely.

DISCUSSION QUESTIONS

15.1 Explain how metallic conductors, semiconductors, and insulators are identified and explain their properties in terms of band theory.

15.2 Describe the phase problem in X-ray diffraction and explain how it may be overcome.

15.3 Describe the structures of elemental metallic solids in terms of the packing of hard spheres.

15.4 Describe the caesium-chloride and rock-salt structures in terms of the occupation of holes in expanded close-packed lattices.

EXERCISES

The symbol ‡ indicates that calculus is required.

15.5 Classify as n-type or p-type a semiconductor formed by doping (a) germanium with phosphorus, (b) germanium with indium.

15.6 The electrical resistance of a sample increased from 100 Ω to 120 Ω when the temperature was changed from 0°C to 100°C. Is the substance a metallic conductor or a semiconductor?

15.7 Describe the bonding in magnesium oxide, MgO, in terms of bands composed of Mg and O atomic orbitals. How does this model justify the ionic model of this compound?

15.8 Use eqn 15.1 to find an expression for the separation between neighbouring levels in a band of N atoms and show that the separation goes to zero as N increases to infinity.

15.9 ‡Calculate the density of states for a long line of atoms, where the density of state is the quantity $\rho(k)$ in the expression $dE = \rho(k)dk$ and draw a graph of $\rho(k)$. Where is the density of states greatest? (*Hint*. Use eqn 15.1 and form dE/dk.)

15.10 Estimate the lattice enthalpy of magnesium oxide from the data in the *Data section* and the ionization and electron gain enthalpies in Chapter 3.

15.11 Estimate the lattice enthalpy of calcium chloride, $CaCl_2$, from thermodynamic data.

15.12 Calculate the potential energy of an ion at the centre of a diffuse 'spherical crystal' in which concentric spheres of ions of opposite charge surround the ion and the numbers of ions on the spherical surfaces fall away rapidly with distance. Let successive spheres lie at radii d, $2d$, ... and the number of ions (all of the same charge) on each successive sphere is inversely proportional to the radius of the sphere. You will need the following sum:

$$1 - \frac{1}{2^2} + \frac{1}{3^2} - \frac{1}{4^2} + \cdots = \frac{\pi^2}{12}$$

15.13 Estimate the ratio of the lattice enthalpies of SrO and CaO from the Born–Meyer equation by using the ionic radii in Table 15.5.

15.14 Type I superconductors show abrupt loss of superconductivity when an applied magnetic field exceeds a critical value $\mathcal{H}_c$ that depends on temperature and T_c as

$$\mathcal{H}_c(T) = \mathcal{H}_c(0)\left(1 - \frac{T^2}{T_c^2}\right)$$

where $\mathcal{H}_c(0)$ is the value of $\mathcal{H}_c$ as $T \rightarrow 0$. Lead has $T_c = 7.19$ K and $\mathcal{H}_c = 63\,901$ A m^{-1}. At what temperature does lead become superconducting in a magnetic field of 20 000 A m^{-1}?

15.15 Draw a set of points as a rectangular array based on unit cells of side a and b, and mark the planes with Miller indices (10), (01), (11), (12), (23), (41), $(4\bar{1})$.

15.16 Repeat Exercise 15.15 for an array of points in which the *a* and *b* axes make 60° to each other.

15.17 In a certain unit cell, planes cut through the crystal axes at (2*a*, 3*b*, *c*), (*a*, *b*, *c*), (6*a*, 3*b*, 3*c*), (2*a*, −3*b*, −3*c*). Identify the Miller indices of the planes.

15.18 Draw an orthorhombic unit cell and mark on it the (100), (010), (001), (011), (101), and $(10\bar{1})$ planes.

15.19 Draw a triclinic unit cell and mark on it the (100), (010), (001), (011), (101), and $(10\bar{1})$ planes.

15.20 Calculate the separations of the planes (111), (211), and (100) in a crystal in which the cubic unit cell has sides of length 532 pm.

15.21 Calculate the separations of the planes (123) and (236) in an orthorhombic crystal in which the unit cell has sides of lengths 0.754, 0.623, and 0.433 nm.

15.22 The glancing angle of a Bragg reflection from a set of crystal planes separated by 97.3 pm is 19.85°. Calculate the wavelength of the X-rays.

15.23 The separation of (100) planes of lithium metal is 350 pm and its density is 0.53 g cm^{-3}. Is the structure of lithium fcc or bcc?

15.24 Copper crystallizes in an fcc structure with unit cells of side 361 pm. (a) Predict the appearance of the powder diffraction pattern using 154 pm radiation. (b) Calculate the density of copper on the basis of this information.

15.25 Construct the electron density along the *x*-axis of a crystal given the following structure factors:

h	0	1	2	3	4	5	6	7
F_h	+30.0	+8.2	+6.5	+4.1	+5.5	−2.4	+5.4	+3.2

h	8	9	10	11	12	13	14	15
F_h	−1.0	+1.1	+6.5	+5.2	−4.3	−1.2	+0.1	+2.1

15.26 Calculate the packing fraction of a stack of cylinders.

15.27 Calculate the packing fraction of a cubic close-packed structure.

15.28 Suppose a virus can be regarded as a sphere and that it stacks together in a hexagonal close-packed arrangement. If the density of the virus is the same as that of water (1.00 g cm^{-3}), what is the density of the solid?

15.29 How many (a) nearest neighbours, (b) next-nearest neighbours are there in a body-centred cubic structure? What are their distances if the side of the cube is 500 nm?

15.30 How many (a) nearest neighbours, (b) next-nearest neighbours are there in a cubic close-packed structure? What are their distances if the side of the cube is 500 nm?

15.31 The thermal and mechanical processing of materials is an important step in ensuring that they have the appropriate physical properties for their intended application. Suppose a metallic element underwent a phase transition in which its crystal structure changed from cubic close-packed to body-centred cubic. (a) Would it become more or less dense? (b) By what factor would its density change?

15.32 The compound Rb_3TlF_6 has a tetragonal unit cell with dimensions *a* = 651 pm and *c* = 934 pm. Calculate the volume of the unit cell and the density of the solid.

15.33 The orthorhombic unit cell of $NiSO_4$ has the dimensions *a* = 634 pm, *b* = 784 pm, and *c* = 516 pm, and the density of the solid is estimated as 3.9 g cm^{-3}. Determine the number of formula units per unit cell and calculate a more precise value of the density.

15.34 The unit cells of $SbCl_3$ are orthorhombic with dimensions *a* = 812 pm, *b* = 947 pm, and *c* = 637 pm. Calculate the spacing of (a) the (321) planes, (b) the (642) planes.

15.35 Use the radius-ratio rule to predict the kind of crystal structure expected for magnesium oxide.

Chapter 16

Solid surfaces

Processes at solid surfaces govern the viability of industry both constructively, as in catalysis, and destructively, as in corrosion. Chemical reactions at solid surfaces may differ sharply from reactions in the bulk, as reaction pathways of much lower activation energy may be provided, and hence result in catalysis. The concept of a solid surface has been extended in recent years with the availability of microporous materials as catalysts.

Although we start the chapter with a discussion of clean surfaces, you should not lose sight of the fact that for chemists, the important aspects of a surface are the attachment of substances to it and the reactions that take place there. Also of interest are surfaces immersed in solvents and in gases at high pressure. Moreover, the structure and even the elemental composition at the surface may be entirely different from that of the bulk, as in the presence of an oxide layer on aluminium. As the reactions that take place at a surface typically involve only a few surface layers, the reactivity of a surface may be determined solely by this peculiar composition.

Reactions at surfaces include the processes that lie at the heart of electrochemistry. Therefore, in the final part of the chapter we revisit the topics treated in Chapter 9, but focus on the dynamics of electrode processes rather than the equilibrium properties treated there.

The growth and structure of surfaces

The attachment of molecules to a surface is called **adsorption**. The substance that adsorbs is the **adsorbate** and the underlying material that we are concerned with in this section is the **adsorbent** or **substrate**. The reverse of adsorption is **desorption**.

16.1 Surface growth

A simple picture of a perfect crystal surface is as a tray of oranges in a grocery store (Fig. 16.1). A gas molecule that collides with the surface can be imagined as a ping-pong ball bouncing erratically over the oranges. The molecule loses energy as it bounces under the influence of intermolecular forces, but it is likely to escape from the surface before it has lost enough kinetic energy to be trapped. The same is true, to some extent, of an ionic crystal in contact with a solution. There is little energy advantage for an ion in solution to discard some of its solvating molecules and stick at an exposed position on a flat surface.

The picture changes when the surface has defects, because then there are ridges of incomplete layers of atoms or ions. A typical type of surface defect is a **step** between two otherwise flat layers of atoms called **terraces** (Fig. 16.2). A step defect might itself have defects, including kinks. When an atom settles on a terrace it bounces across it under the influence of the intermolecular potential, and might come to a step or a corner formed by a kink. Instead of interacting with a single terrace atom, the molecule now interacts with several, and the interaction may be strong enough to trap it. Likewise, when ions deposit from solution, the loss of the solvation interaction is offset by a strong Coulombic interaction between the arriving ions and several ions at the surface defect.

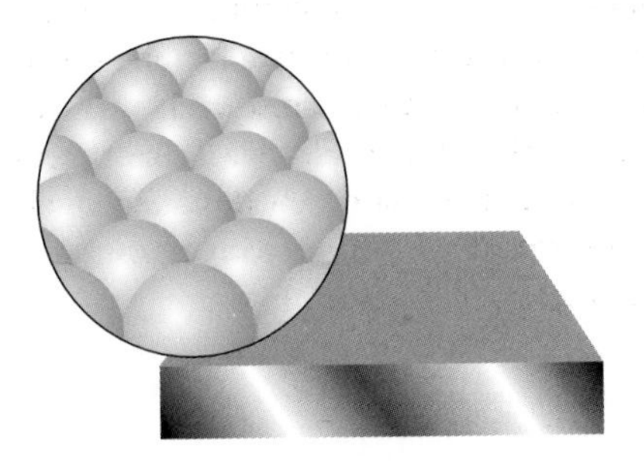

Fig. 16.1 A schematic diagram of the flat surface of a solid. This primitive model is largely supported by scanning tunnelling microscope images.

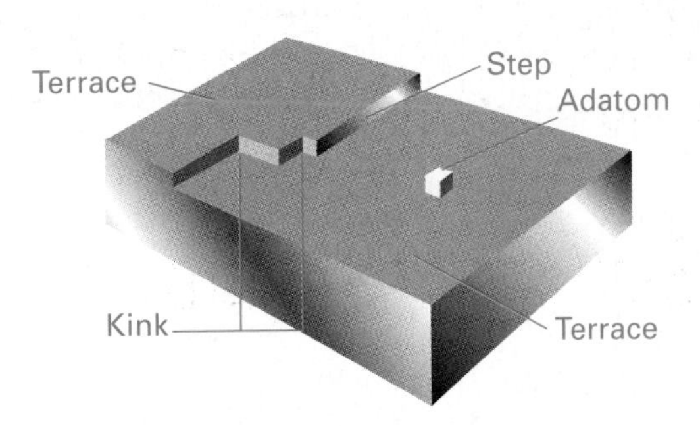

Fig. 16.2 Some of the kinds of defects that may occur on otherwise perfect terraces. Defects play an important role in surface growth and catalysis.

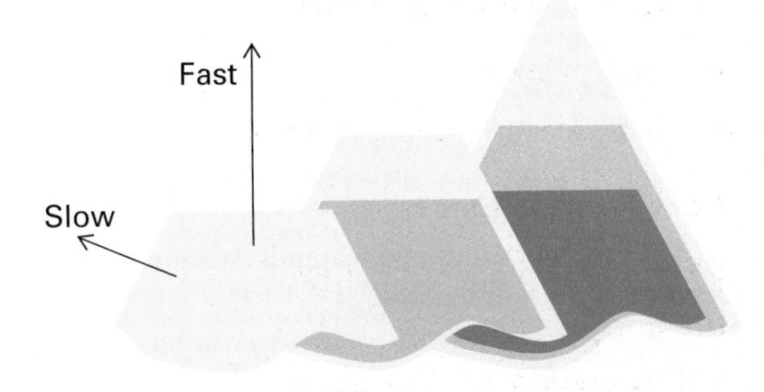

Fig. 16.3 The slower-growing faces of a crystal dominate its final external appearance. Three successive stages of the growth are shown.

The rapidity of growth depends on the crystal plane concerned, and the slowest growing faces dominate the appearance of the crystal. This feature is explained in Fig. 16.3, where we see that although the horizontal face grows forward most rapidly, it grows itself out of existence, and the more slowly growing faces survive.

16.2 Surface composition and structure

Under normal conditions, a surface exposed to a gas is constantly bombarded with molecules and a freshly prepared surface is covered very quickly. Just how quickly can be estimated by using the kinetic theory of gases and the following expression for the **collision flux**, Z_W, the number of hits on a region of a surface during an interval divided by the area of the region and the duration of the interval:

$$Z_W = \frac{p}{(2\pi mkT)^{1/2}} \tag{16.1}$$

where m is the mass of the molecules. For air at 1 atm and 25°C the collision flux is $3 \times 10^{27}\ m^{-2}\ s^{-1}$. Because 1 m^2 of metal surface consists of about 10^{19} atoms, each atom is struck about 10^8 times each second. Even if only a few collisions leave a molecule adsorbed to the surface, the time for which a freshly prepared surface remains clean is very short.

The obvious way to retain cleanliness is to reduce the pressure. When it is reduced to 0.1 mPa (as in a simple vacuum system) the collision flux falls to about $10^{18}\ m^{-2}\ s^{-1}$, corresponding to one hit per surface atom in each 0.1 s. Even that is too brief in most experiments, and in **ultra-high vacuum** (UHV) techniques pressures as low as 0.1 μPa (when $Z_W = 10^{15}\ m^{-2}\ s^{-1}$) are reached on a routine basis, and 1 nPa (when $Z_W = 10^{13}\ m^{-2}\ s^{-1}$) with special care. These collision fluxes correspond to each surface atom being hit once every 10^5 to 10^6 s, or about once a day.

The chemical composition of a surface can be determined by a variety of ionization techniques. The same techniques can be used to detect any remaining contamination after cleaning and to detect layers of material adsorbed later in the experiment. One technique that may be used is **photoemission spectroscopy**, a derivative of the photoelectric effect, which uses X-rays (for XPS) or hard (short-wavelength) ultraviolet (for UPS) ionizing radiation to eject electrons from adsorbed species. The kinetic energies of the electrons ejected from their orbitals are measured and the pattern of energies is a fingerprint of the material present (Fig. 16.4). UPS, which examines electrons ejected from valence shells, is also used to establish the bonding characteristics and the details of valence shell electronic structures of substances on the surface. Its usefulness is its ability to reveal which orbitals of the adsorbate are involved in the bond to the substrate. For instance, the principal difference between the photoemission results on free benzene and benzene adsorbed on

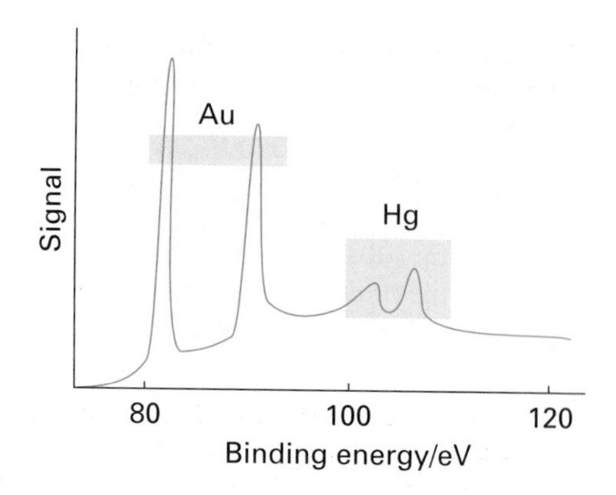

Fig. 16.4 The X-ray photoelectron emission spectrum of a sample of gold contaminated with a surface layer of mercury. (M. W. Roberts and C. S. McKee, *Chemistry of the metal–gas interface*, Oxford, 1978.)

palladium is in the energies of the π electrons. This difference is interpreted as meaning that the C_6H_6 molecules lie parallel to the surface and are attached to it by their π orbitals. By contrast, pyridine (C_6H_5N) stands almost perpendicular to the surface, and is attached by a σ bond formed by the nitrogen lone pair.

Auger electron spectroscopy (AES) is an important technique that is widely used in the microelectronics industry. The **Auger** (pronounced oh-zhey) **effect** is the emission of a second electron after high-energy radiation has expelled another electron. The first electron to depart leaves a hole in a low-lying orbital, and an upper electron falls into it. The energy released in this transition may result either in the generation of radiation, which is called **X-ray fluorescence** (Fig. 16.5a), or in the ejection of another electron (Fig. 16.5b). The latter is the secondary electron of the Auger effect. The energies of the secondary electrons are characteristic of the material present, so the Auger effect effectively takes a fingerprint of the sample (Fig. 16.6). In practice, the Auger spectrum is normally obtained by irradiating the sample with an electron beam rather than electromagnetic radiation. In **scanning Auger electron microscopy** (SAM), the finely focused electron beam is scanned over the surface and a map of composition is compiled; the resolution can reach to below about 50 nm.

One of the most informative techniques for determining the arrangement of the atoms close to and

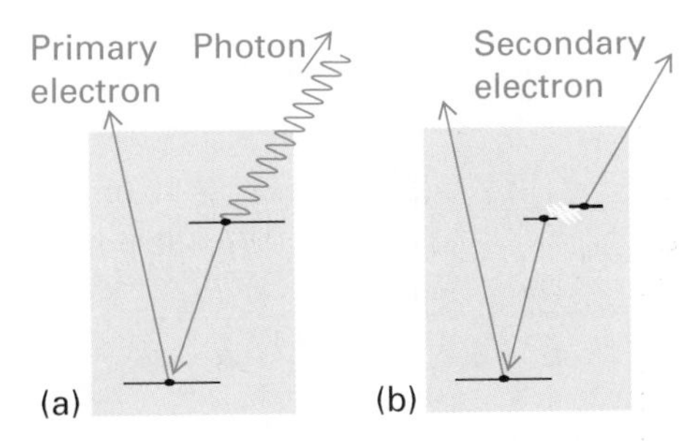

Fig. 16.5 When an electron is expelled from a solid (a) an electron of higher energy may fall into the vacated orbital and emit an X-ray photon to produce X-ray fluorescence. Alternatively, (b) the electron falling into the orbital may give up its energy to another electron, which is ejected in the Auger effect.

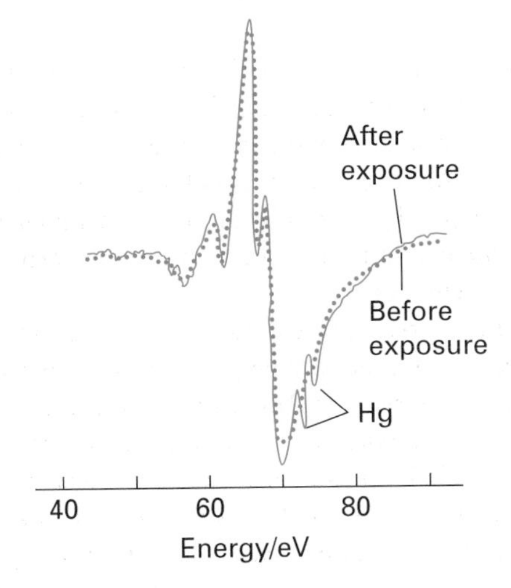

Fig. 16.6 An Auger spectrum of the same sample used for Fig. 16.4 taken before and after deposition of mercury. (M. W. Roberts and C. S. McKee, *Chemistry of the metal–gas interface*, Oxford, 1978.)

adsorbed on the surface is **low-energy electron diffraction** (LEED). This technique is like X-ray diffraction but uses the wave character of electrons, and the sample is now the surface of a solid. The use of low-energy electrons (with energies in the range 10–200 eV, corresponding to wavelengths in the range 100–400 pm) ensures that the diffraction is caused only by atoms on and close to the surface. The experimental arrangement is shown in Fig. 16.7, and typical LEED patterns, obtained by photographing the fluorescent screen through the viewing port, are shown in Fig. 16.8.

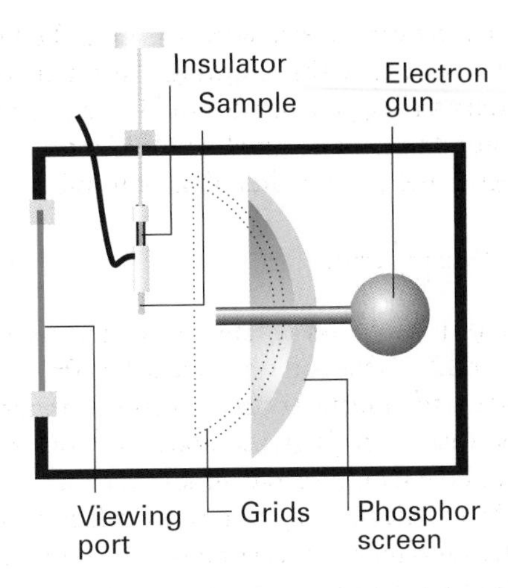

Fig. 16.7 A schematic diagram of the apparatus used for a LEED experiment. The electrons diffracted by the surface layers are detected by the fluorescence they cause on the phosphor screen.

(a)

(b)

Fig. 16.8 LEED photographs of (a) a clean platinum surface and (b) after its exposure to propyne, $CH_3C{\equiv}CH$. (Photographs provided by Professor G. A. Somorjai.)

Example 16.1
Interpreting a LEED pattern

The LEED pattern from a clean unreconstructed (110) face of palladium is shown in (a) below. The reconstructed surface gives the LEED pattern shown as (b). What can be inferred about the structure of the reconstructed surface?

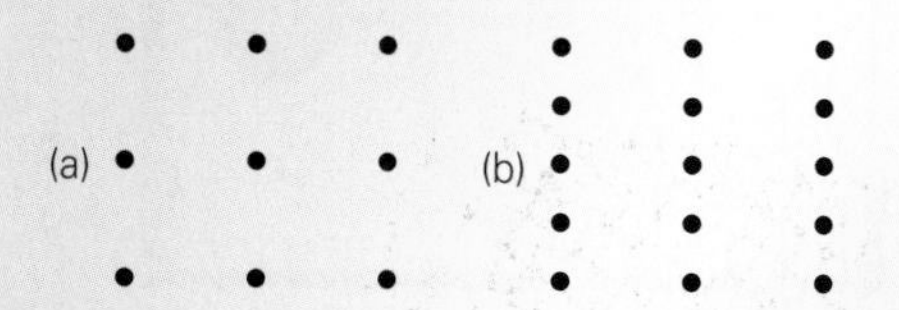

Strategy Recall from the Bragg law (Section 15.13), $\lambda = 2d \sin \theta$, that for a given wavelength, the smaller the separation d of the layers, the greater the scattering angle (so that $2d \sin \theta$ remains constant). In terms of the LEED pattern, the farther apart the atoms responsible for the pattern, the closer the spots appear in the pattern. Twice the separation between the atoms corresponds to half the separation between the spots, and vice versa. Therefore, inspect the two patterns and identify how the new pattern relates to the old.

Solution The horizontal separation between spots is unchanged, which indicates that the atoms remain in the same position in that dimension when reconstruction occurs. However, the vertical spacing is halved, which suggests that the atoms are twice as far apart in that direction as they are in the unreconstructed surface.

Self-test 16.1

Sketch the LEED pattern for a surface that was reconstructed from that shown in (a) above by tripling the vertical separation between atoms.

[*Answer:* ● ● ● ● ● ● ● / ● ● ● ● ● ● ● / ● ● ● ● ● ● ●]

LEED experiments show that the surface of a crystal rarely has exactly the same form as a slice through the bulk. As a general rule, it is found that metal surfaces are often simply truncations of the bulk lattice, but the distance between the top layer of atoms and the one below is contracted by around 5 per cent. Semiconductors generally have surfaces reconstructed to a depth of several layers. Reconstruction occurs in ionic solids. For example, in lithium fluoride the Li^+ and F^- ions close to the surface apparently lie on slightly different planes. An example of the detail that can now be obtained from refined LEED techniques is shown in Fig. 16.9 for CH_3C– adsorbed on a (111) plane of rhodium.

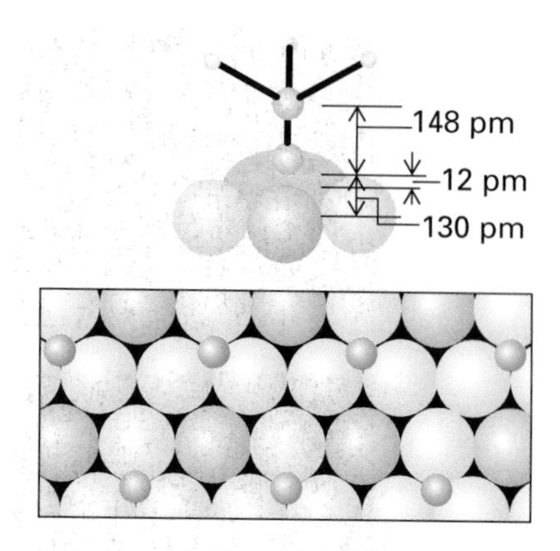

Fig. 16.9 The structure of a surface close to the point of attachment of CH_3C– to the (110) surface of rhodium at 300 K and the changes in positions of the metal atoms that accompany chemisorption.

The presence of terraces, steps, and kinks in a surface shows up in LEED patterns, and their surface density (the number of defects in a region divided by the area of the region) can be estimated. Three examples of how steps and kinks affect the pattern are shown in Fig. 16.10. The samples used were obtained by cleaving a crystal at different angles to a plane of atoms. Only terraces are produced when the cut is parallel to the plane, and the density of steps increases as the angle of the cut increases. The observation of additional structure in the LEED patterns, rather than blurring, shows that the steps are arrayed regularly.

Terraces, steps, kinks, and dislocations on a surface may be observed by **scanning tunnelling microscopy** (STM) and **atomic force microscopy** (AFM), two techniques that have revolutionized the study of surfaces. In STM a platinum–rhodium or tungsten needle is scanned across the surface of a conducting solid. When the tip of the needle is brought very close to the surface, electrons tunnel across the intervening space (Fig. 16.11). In the *constant-current mode* of operation, the stylus moves up and down corresponding to the form of the

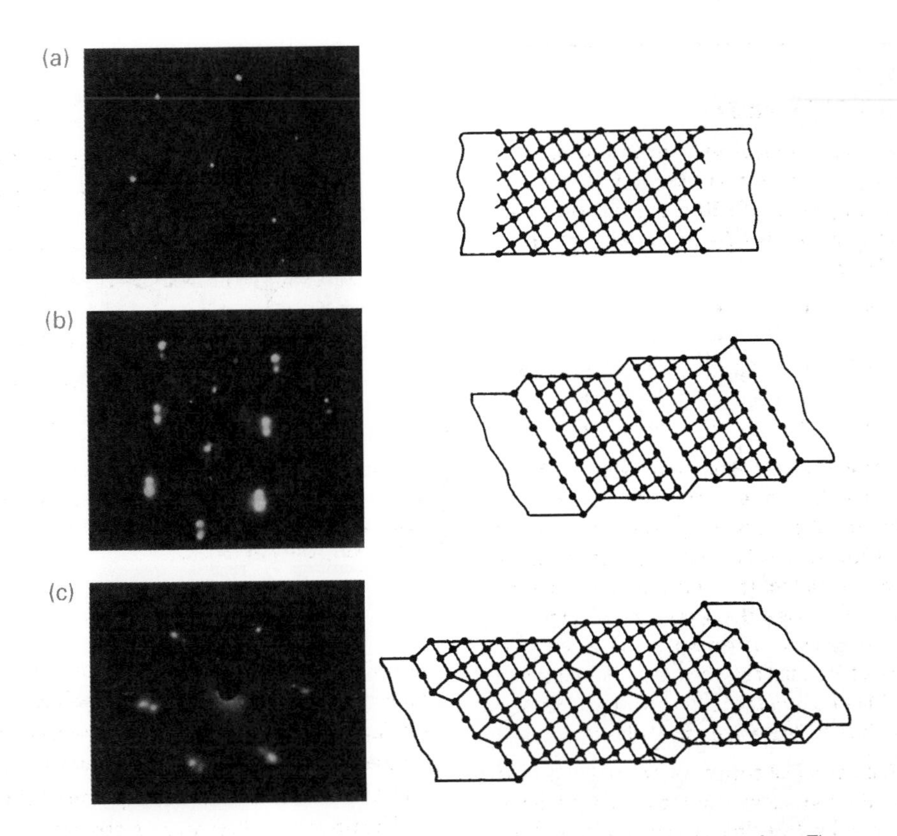

Fig. 16.10 LEED patterns may be used to assess the defect density of a surface. The photographs correspond to a platinum surface with (a) low defect density, (b) regular steps separated by about six atoms, and (c) regular steps with kinks. (Photographs provided by Professor G. A. Samorjai.)

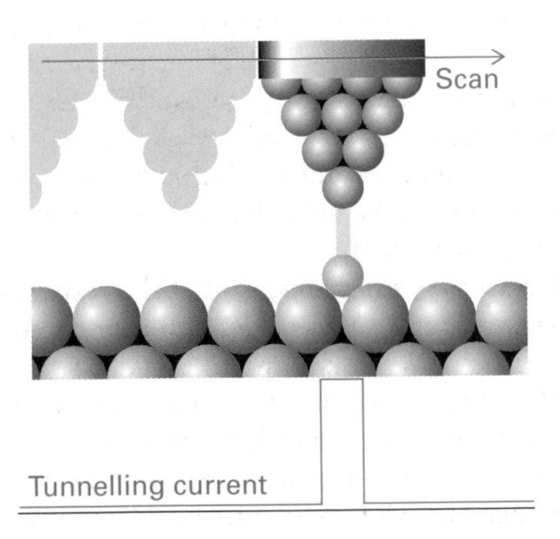

Fig. 16.11 A scanning tunnelling microscope makes use of the current of electrons that tunnel between the surface and the tip. That current is very sensitive to the distance of the tip above the surface.

surface, and the topography of the surface, including any adsorbates, can be mapped on an atomic scale. The vertical motion of the stylus is achieved by fixing it to a piezoelectric cylinder that contracts or expands according to the potential difference it experiences. In the *constant-z mode*, the vertical position of the stylus is held constant and the current is monitored. Because the tunnelling probability is very sensitive to the size of the gap, the microscope can detect tiny, atom-scale variations in the height of the surface. An example of the kind of image obtained with a clean surface is shown in Fig. 16.12, where the cliff is only one atom high. Figure 16.13 shows the dissociation of SiH_3 adsorbed onto a Si(001) surface into adsorbed SiH_2 units and H atoms. The tip of the scanning tunnelling microscope can also be used to manipulate adsorbed

Fig. 16.12 An STM image of caesium atoms on a gallium arsenide surface.

atoms on a surface, making possible the fabrication of complex and yet very tiny structures, such as nanometre-sized electronic devices (Box 15.1).

In AFM a sharpened stylus attached to a beam is scanned across the surface. The force exerted by the surface and any adsorbate pushes or pulls on the stylus and deflects the beam (Fig. 16.14). The deflection is monitored by using a laser beam. Because no current is needed between the sample and the probe, the technique can be applied to non-conducting surfaces too. A spectacular demonstration of the power of AFM is given in Fig. 16.15, which shows individual DNA molecules on a solid surface.

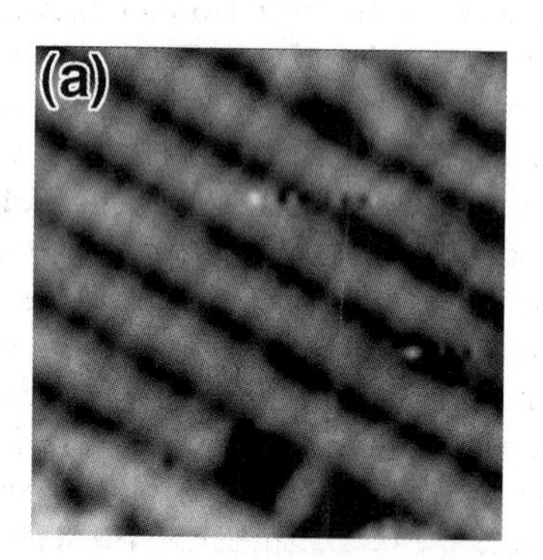

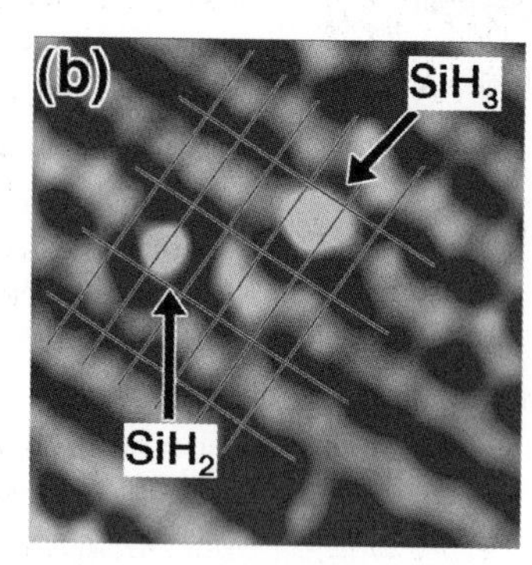

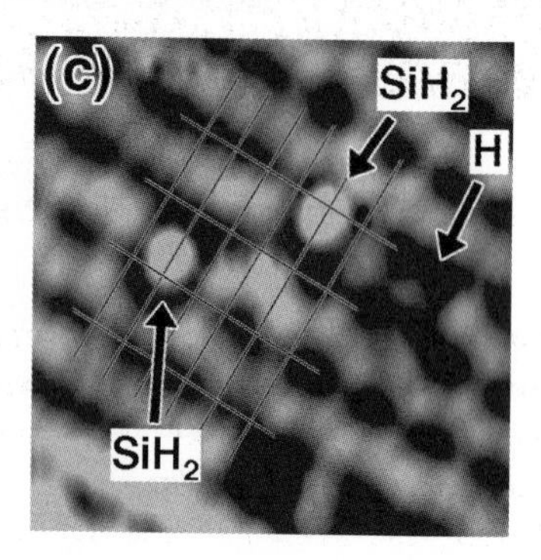

Fig. 16.13 Visualization by STM of the reaction $SiH_3 \rightarrow SiH_2 + H$ on a 4.7 nm × 4.7 nm area of a Si(001) surface. (a) The Si(001) surface before exposure to $Si_2H_6(g)$. (b) Adsorbed Si_2H_6 dissociates into SiH_2(surface) and SiH_3(surface). (c) After 8 min, SiH_3(surface) dissociates into SiH_2(surface) and H(surface). (Reproduced with permission from Y. Wang, M. J. Bronikowski, and R. J. Hamers, *Surface Science* **64**, 311 (1994).)

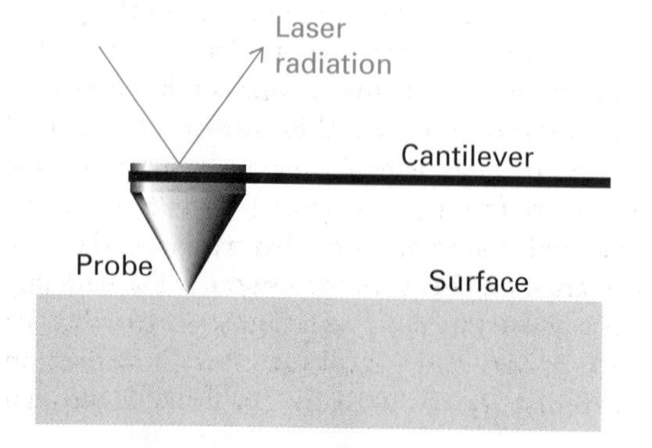

Fig. 16.14 In atomic force microscopy, a laser beam is used to monitor the tiny changes in the position of a probe as it is attracted to or repelled from atoms on a surface.

The extent of adsorption

The extent of surface coverage is normally expressed as the **fractional coverage, θ** (theta):

$$\theta = \frac{\text{number of adsorption sites occupied}}{\text{number of adsorption sites available}} \qquad (16.2)$$

The fractional coverage is often expressed in terms of the volume of adsorbate adsorbed by $\theta = V/V_\infty$, where V_∞ is the volume of adsorbate corresponding to complete monolayer coverage. In each case, the volume in the definition of θ is that of the free gas measured under standard conditions of temperature and pressure, not the volume the adsorbed gas

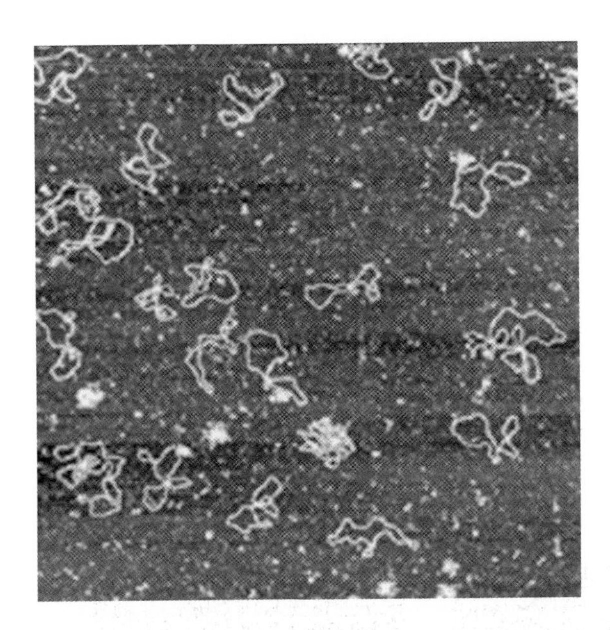

Fig. 16.15 An AFM image of bacterial DNA plasmids on a mica surface. (Courtesy of Veeco Instruments.)

occupies when attached to the surface. The **rate of adsorption** is the rate of change of surface coverage, and can be determined by observing the change in fractional coverage with time.

Among the principal techniques for measuring the rate of desorption are flow methods, in which the sample itself acts as a pump because adsorption removes molecules from the gas. One commonly used technique is therefore to monitor the rates of flow of gas into and out of the system: the difference is the rate of gas uptake by the sample. In **flash desorption** the sample is suddenly heated (electrically) and the resulting rise in pressure is interpreted in terms of the amount of adsorbate originally on the sample. The interpretation may be confused by the desorption of a compound (for example, WO_3 from oxygen on tungsten). **Surface plasmon resonance** (SPR) is a technique in which the kinetics and thermodynamics of surface processes, particularly of biological systems, are monitored by detecting the effect of adsorption and desorption on the refractive index of a gold substrate. **Gravimetry**, in which the sample is weighed on a microbalance during the experiment, can also be used. A common instrument for gravimetric measurements is the **quartz crystal microbalance** (QCM), in which the mass of a sample laid on the surface of a quartz crystal is related to changes in the crystal's mechanical properties. The key principle behind the operation of a QCM is the ability of a quartz crystal to vibrate at a characteristic frequency when an oscillating electric field is applied. The vibrational frequency decreases when material is spread over the surface of the crystal and the change in frequency is proportional to the mass of material. Masses as small as a few nanograms (1 ng = 10^{-9} g) can be measured reliably in this way.

16.3 Physisorption and chemisorption

Molecules and atoms can attach to surfaces in two ways, although there is no clear frontier between the two types of adsorption. In **physisorption** (an abbreviation of 'physical adsorption'), there is a van der Waals interaction between the adsorbate and the substrate (for example, a dispersion or a dipolar interaction, Section 17.5, of the kind responsible for the condensation of vapours to liquids). The energy released when a molecule is physisorbed is of the same order of magnitude as the enthalpy of condensation. Such small energies can be absorbed as vibrations of the lattice and dissipated as thermal motion, and a molecule bouncing across the surface will gradually lose its energy and finally adsorb to it in the process called **accommodation**. The enthalpy of physisorption can be measured by monitoring the rise in temperature of a sample of known heat capacity,[1] and typical values are in the region of 20 kJ mol^{-1} (Table 16.1). This small enthalpy change is insufficient to lead to bond breaking, so a physisorbed molecule retains its identity, although it might be distorted by the presence of the surface.

In **chemisorption** (an abbreviation of 'chemical adsorption'), the molecules (or atoms) adsorb to the surface by forming a chemical (usually covalent) bond, and tend to find sites that maximize their coordination number with the substrate. The enthalpy of chemisorption is very much greater than that for physisorption, and typical values are in the region of 200 kJ mol^{-1} (Table 16.2). The distance between

[1] They may also be measured by observing the temperature dependence of the parameters that occur in the adsorption isotherm (see Section 16.4).

Table 16.1
Maximum observed enthalpies of physisorption, $\Delta_{ads}H^{\ominus}/(kJ\ mol^{-1})$

CH_4	−21
CO	−25
H_2	−84
H_2O	−59
N_2	−21
NH_3	−38
O_2	−21

Table 16.2
Enthalpies of chemisorption, $\Delta_{ads}H^{\ominus}/(kJ\ mol^{-1})$

Adsorbate	Adsorbent (substrate)			
	Cr	Fe	Ni	Pt
C_2H_4	−427	−285	−243	
CO		−192		
H_2	−188	−134		
NH_3		−188	−155	
O_2				−293

the surface and the closest adsorbate atom is also typically shorter for chemisorption than for physisorption. A chemisorbed molecule may be torn apart at the demand of the unsatisfied valencies of the surface atoms, and the existence of molecular fragments on the surface as a result of chemisorption is one reason why solid surfaces catalyse reactions.

An example of chemisorption that has received much attention recently is the formation of **self-assembled monolayers** (SAMs), which are ordered molecular aggregates that form a single layer of organic material on a surface. To understand the formation of SAMs, consider the result of exposing molecules such as alkyl thiols, RSH, where R represents an alkyl chain, to a gold surface. The thiols chemisorb onto the surface, forming RS–Au(I) adducts. If we represent the atoms close to the adsorption site as Au_n, then we can write the attachment as

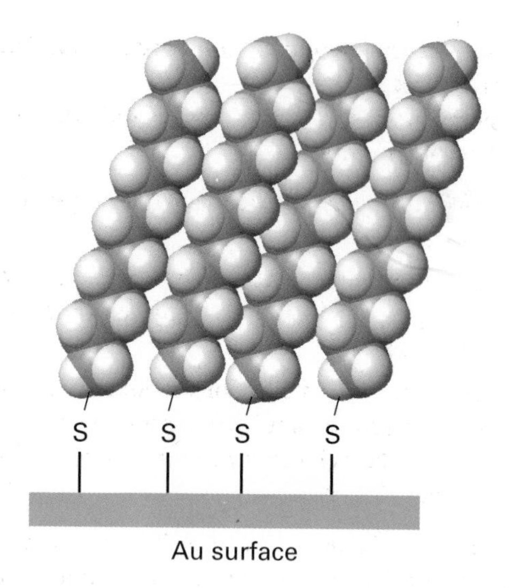

Fig. 16.16 Self-assembled monolayers of alkylthiols formed onto a gold surface by chemisorption of the thiol groups and aggregation of the alkyl chains.

$$RSH + Au_n \rightarrow RS\text{–}Au(I)\cdot Au_{n-1} + \tfrac{1}{2}H_2(g)$$

If R has a sufficiently long chain, van der Waals interactions between the adsorbed RS– units lead to the formation of a highly ordered monolayer on the surface (Fig. 16.16).

The principal test for distinguishing chemisorption from physisorption used to be the enthalpy of adsorption. Values less negative than -25 kJ mol^{-1} were taken to signify physisorption, and values more negative than about -40 kJ mol^{-1} were taken to signify chemisorption. However, this criterion is by no means foolproof or any longer of particular interest, and spectroscopic techniques that identify the state of the adsorbed species are now available and more fundamental.

16.4 Adsorption isotherms

The free gas A and the adsorbed gas are in a dynamic equilibrium of the form

$$A(g) + M(surface) \rightleftharpoons AM(surface)$$

and the fractional coverage, θ, of the surface depends on the pressure of the overlying gas. The variation of

θ with pressure at a chosen temperature is called the **adsorption isotherm**.

The simplest physically plausible isotherm is based on three assumptions:

1 Adsorption cannot proceed beyond monolayer coverage.

2 All sites are equivalent and the surface is uniform (that is, the surface is perfectly flat on a microscopic scale).

3 There are no interactions between adsorbed molecules, so the ability of a molecule to adsorb at a given site is independent of the occupation of neighbouring sites.

We show in Derivation 16.1 that the relation between the fractional coverage θ and the partial pressure of A, p, that results from application of these three assumptions is the **Langmuir isotherm**:

$$\theta = \frac{Kp}{1+Kp} \qquad K = \frac{k_a}{k_d} \tag{16.3}$$

where k_a and k_b are, respectively, the rate constants for adsorption and desorption. This expression is plotted for various values of K (which has the dimensions of 1/pressure) in Fig. 16.17. We see that as the partial pressure of A increases, the fractional coverage increases towards 1. Half the surface is covered when $p = 1/K$.

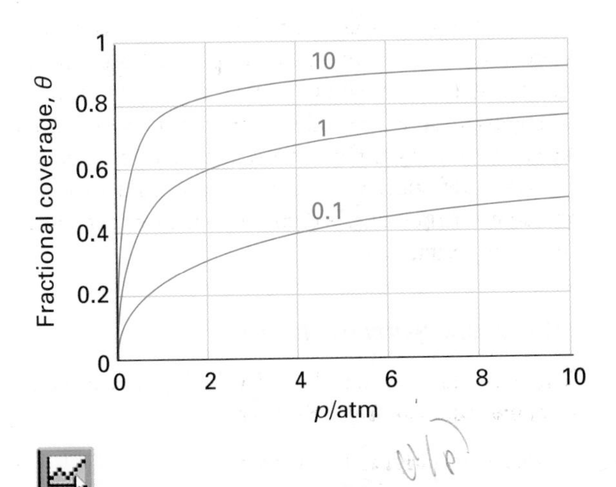

Fig. 16.17 The Langmuir isotherm for non-dissociative adsorption for different values of K.

Derivation 16.1

The Langmuir isotherm

To obtain the Langmuir isotherm, we suppose that the rate at which A adsorbs to the surface is proportional to the partial pressure (because the rate at which molecules strike the surface is proportional to the pressure), and to the number of sites that are not occupied at the time, which is $(1-\theta)N$:

$$\text{Rate of adsorption} = k_a N(1-\theta)p$$

where k_a is the adsorption rate constant. The rate at which the adsorbed molecules leave the surface is proportional to the number currently on the surface ($N\theta$):

$$\text{Rate of desorption} = k_d N\theta$$

where k_d is the desorption rate constant. At equilibrium, the two rates are equal, so we can write

$$k_a N(1-\theta)p = k_d N\theta$$

The Ns cancel and, using $K = k_a/k_d$, we obtain

$$Kp(1-\theta) = \theta$$

which rearranges into eqn 16.3.

Example 16.2

Using the Langmuir isotherm

The data given below are for the adsorption of CO on charcoal at 273 K. Confirm that they fit the Langmuir isotherm, and find the constant K and the volume corresponding to complete coverage. In each case V has been corrected to 1.00 atm (more precisely, to 101.325 kPa).

p/kPa	13.3	26.7	40.0	53.3	66.7	80.0	93.3
V/cm^3	10.2	18.6	25.5	31.5	36.9	41.6	46.1

Strategy From eqn 16.3,

$$\frac{1}{\theta} = \frac{1+Kp}{Kp} = \frac{1}{Kp} + 1$$

Then, by substituting $\theta = V/V_\infty$, where V_∞ is the volume corresponding to complete coverage (as measured at 273 K and 1.00 atm)

$$\frac{V_\infty}{V} = \frac{1}{Kp} + 1$$

Division of both sides by V_∞ and multiplication by p then gives

$$\frac{p}{V} = \frac{1}{KV_\infty} + \frac{p}{V_\infty}$$

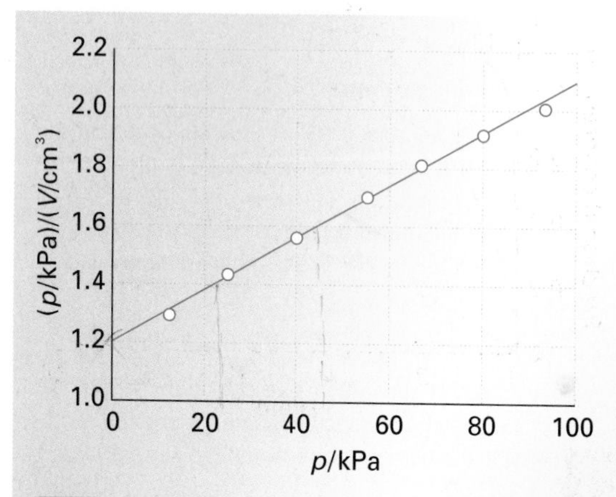

Fig. 16.18 The plot of the data in Example 16.2. As illustrated here, the Langmuir isotherm predicts that a straight line should be obtained when p/V is plotted against p.

Hence, a plot of p/V against p should give a straight line of slope $1/V_\infty$ and intercept $1/KV_\infty$.

Solution The data for the plot are as follows:

p/kPa	13.3	26.7	40.0	53.3	66.7
$(p$/kPa$)/(V$/cm$^3)$	1.30	1.44	1.57	1.69	1.81

p/kPa	80.0	93.3
$(p$/kPa$)/(V$/cm$^3)$	1.92	2.02

The points are plotted in Fig. 16.18. The (least-squares) slope is 0.00900, so V_∞ = 111 cm^3. The intercept at $p = 0$ is 1.20, so

$$K = \frac{1}{(111\text{ cm}^3)\times(1.20\text{ kPa cm}^{-3})} = 7.51\times10^{-3}\text{ kPa}^{-1}$$

A note on good practice. To analyse data graphically, it is usually sensible to look for combinations of the data that give a straight line. The resulting graph allows you to detect any rogue points, but use a linear regression (least-squares) analysis to obtain the intercept and slope.

Self-test 16.2

Repeat the calculation for the following data:

p/kPa	13.3	26.7	40.0	53.3	66.7	80.0	93.3
V/cm^3	10.3	19.3	27.3	34.1	40.0	45.5	48.0

[*Answer:* 128 cm^3, 6.70 × 10^{-3} kPa^{-1}]

A further point is that because K is essentially an equilibrium constant, then its temperature dependence is given by the van 't Hoff equation (Section 7.9):

$$\ln K = \ln K' - \frac{\Delta H^\ominus}{R}\left(\frac{1}{T} - \frac{1}{T'}\right) \qquad (16.4)$$

It follows that if we plot $\ln K$ against $1/T$, then the slope of the graph is equal to $-\Delta_{ads}H^\ominus/R$, where $\Delta_{ads}H^\ominus$ is the standard enthalpy of adsorption. However, because this quantity might vary with the extent of surface coverage either because the adsorbate molecules interact with each other or because adsorption occurs at a sequence of different sites, care must be taken to measure K at the same value of the fractional coverage. The resulting value of $\Delta_{ads}H^\ominus$ is called the **isosteric enthalpy of adsorption.** The variation of $\Delta_{ads}H^\ominus$ with θ allows us to explore the validity of the Langmuir assumptions.

Example 16.3

The isosteric enthalpy of adsorption

The pressure of nitrogen gas in equilibrium with a layer of nitrogen adsorbed on rutile (TiO_2) with a fractional coverage of $\theta = 0.10$ varied with temperature as follows:

T/K	220	240	260	280	300
p/kPa	2.8	7.7	17.0	38.0	68.0

Determine the isosteric enthalpy of adsorption at $\theta = 0.10$.

Strategy First, find the relation between K in the Langmuir isotherm and p for a given fractional coverage. Then use the van 't Hoff equation, which predicts that a plot of $\ln K$ against $1/T$ should be a straight line of slope $-\Delta_{ads}H^\ominus/R$.

Solution We rearrange eqn 16.3 into

$$K = \frac{\theta}{1-\theta}\times\frac{1}{p}$$

and then, on taking logarithms,

$$\ln K = \ln\left(\frac{\theta}{1-\theta}\right) + \ln\frac{1}{p} = \text{constant} - \ln p$$

The constant term will not affect the slope of the plot, so we can plot $-\ln p$ against $1/T$. To do so, we draw up the following table:

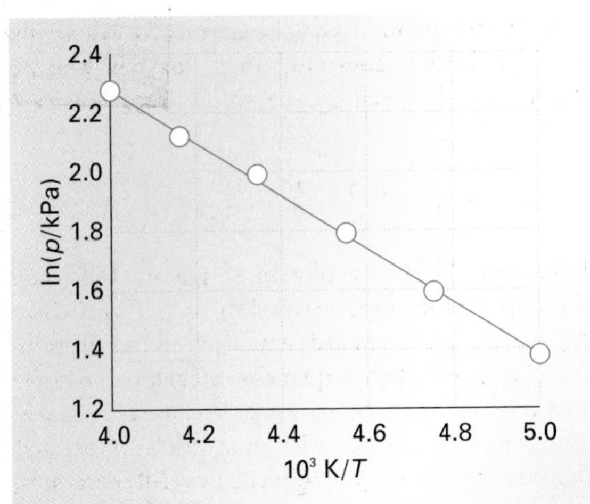

Fig. 16.19 The isosteric enthalpy of adsorption can be obtained from the slope of the plot of ln p against $1/T$, where p is the pressure needed to achieve the specified surface coverage. The data used are from Example 16.3.

$(10^3\ \mathrm{K})/T$	4.55	4.17	3.85	3.57	3.33
$-\ln(p/\mathrm{kPa})$	−1.03	−2.04	−2.83	−3.64	−4.22

The points are plotted in Fig. 16.19. The (least-squares) slope of the straight line is −0.381, so

$$\frac{\Delta_{\mathrm{ads}}H^{\ominus}}{R} = -0.381 \times 10^3\ \mathrm{K}$$

Therefore,

$$\Delta_{\mathrm{ads}}H^{\ominus} = (-0.381 \times 10^3\ \mathrm{K}) \times (8.3147\ \mathrm{J\ K^{-1}\ mol^{-1}})$$
$$= -3.17 \times 10^3\ \mathrm{J\ mol^{-1}}$$

or $-3.17\ \mathrm{kJ\ mol^{-1}}$.

A note on good practice The graph, like all graphs, is plotted using dimensionless variables, so the slope is a pure number. Although a graph is a good way of identifying rogue points, use a least-squares linear regression procedure to calculate the slope. Take care in interpreting the slope, because at that stage the units (and the appropriate power of 10) must be reinstated.

Self-test 16.3

The data below show the pressures of CO needed for the volume of adsorption (corrected to 1.00 atm and 273 K) to be 10.0 cm³. Calculate the adsorption enthalpy at this surface coverage.

T/K	200	210	220	230	240	250
p/kPa	4.00	4.95	6.03	7.20	8.47	9.85

[*Answer:* $-7.52\ \mathrm{kJ\ mol^{-1}}$]

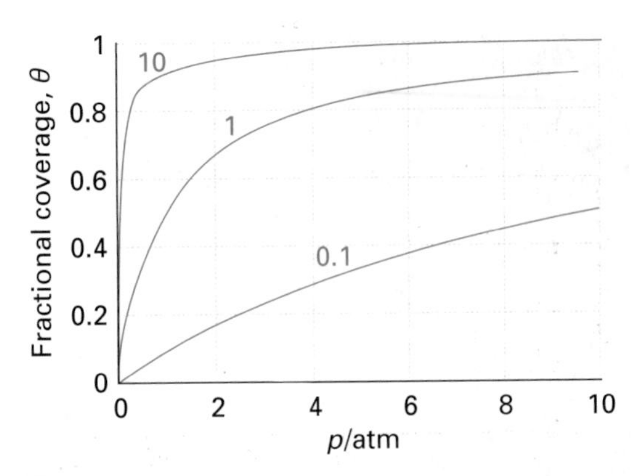

Fig. 16.20 The Langmuir isotherm for dissociative adsorption, $X_2(g) \rightarrow 2\,X(\text{surface})$, for different values of K.

There are two modifications of the Langmuir isotherm that should be noted. Suppose the substrate dissociates on adsorption, as in

$$A_2(g) + M(\text{surface}) \rightleftharpoons A\text{–}M(\text{surface}) + A\text{–}M(\text{surface})$$

We show in Derivation 16.2 that the resulting isotherm is

$$\theta = \frac{(Kp)^{1/2}}{1 + (Kp)^{1/2}} \qquad (16.5)$$

The surface coverage now depends on the square root of the pressure in place of the pressure itself (Fig. 16.20).

Derivation 16.2

The effect of substrate dissociation on the Langmuir isotherm

When the substrate dissociates on adsorption, the rate of adsorption is proportional to the pressure and to the probability that *both* atoms will find sites, which is proportional to the square of the number of vacant sites:

$$\text{Rate of adsorption} = k_a p\{N(1-\theta)\}^2$$

The rate of desorption is proportional to the frequency of encounters of atoms on the surface, and is therefore second-order in the number of atoms present:

$$\text{Rate of desorption} = k_a(N\theta)^2$$

The condition for no net change is

$$k_a p\{N(1-\theta)\}^2 = k_d(N\theta)^2$$

After using $K = k_a/k_d$, cancelling the Ns, and taking the square root of both sides of the expression, we obtain

$$(Kp)^{1/2}(1-\theta) = \theta$$

which rearranges into eqn 16.5.

The second modification we need to consider deals with a mixture of two gases A and B that compete for the same sites on the surface. It is left as an exercise (Exercise 16.18) for you to show that if A and B both follow Langmuir isotherms, and adsorb without dissociation, then

$$\theta_A = \frac{K_A p_A}{1 + K_A p_A + K_B p_B}$$

$$\theta_B = \frac{K_B p_B}{1 + K_A p_A + K_B p_B} \quad (16.6)$$

where K_J is the ratio of adsorption and desorption rate constants for species J, p_J is its partial pressure in the gas phase, and θ_J is the fraction of total sites occupied by J. Coadsorption of this kind is important in catalysis and we use these isotherms later.

If the initial adsorbed layer can act as a substrate for further (for example, physical) adsorption, then instead of the isotherm levelling off to some saturated value at high pressures, it can be expected to rise indefinitely as more and more molecules condense on to the surface, just like water vapour can condense indefinitely onto the surface of liquid water. The most widely used isotherm dealing with multilayer adsorption was derived by Stephen Brunauer, Paul Emmett, and Edward Teller, and is called the **BET isotherm**:

$$\frac{V}{V_{mon}} = \frac{cz}{(1-z)\{1-(1-c)z\}}$$

$$\text{with } z = \frac{p}{p^*} \quad (16.7a)$$

In this expression, p^* is the vapour pressure above a layer of adsorbate that is more than one molecule thick and can therefore be taken to be the vapour pressure of the bulk liquid, V_{mon} is the volume corresponding to monolayer coverage, and c is a constant that is large when the enthalpy of desorption from a monolayer is large compared with the enthalpy of vaporization of the liquid adsorbate.

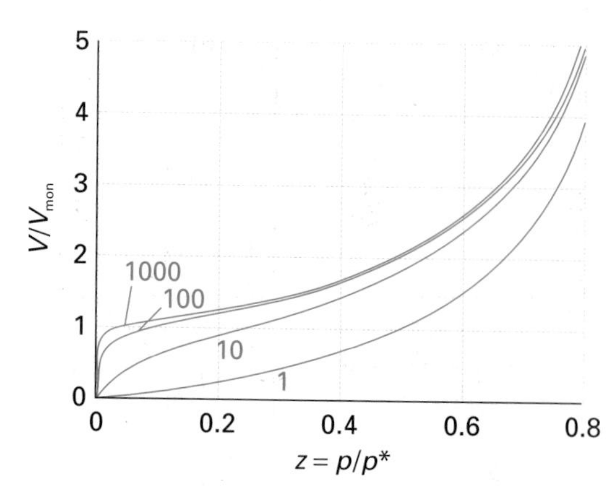

Fig. 16.21 Plots of the BET isotherm for different values of c. The value of V/V_{mon} rises indefinitely because the adsorbate may condense on the covered substrate surface.

Figure 16.21 illustrates the shapes of BET isotherms. They rise indefinitely as the pressure is increased because there is no limit to the amount of material that may condense when multilayer coverage may occur. A BET isotherm is not accurate at all pressures, but it is widely used in industry to determine the surface areas of solids. When $c \gg 1$, the BET isotherm takes the simpler form

$$\frac{V}{V_{mon}} = \frac{1}{1-z} \quad (16.7b)$$

This expression is applicable to unreactive gases on polar surfaces, for which $c \approx 10^2$.

16.5 The rates of surface processes

Figure 16.22 shows how the potential energy of a molecule varies with its distance above the adsorption site. As the molecule approaches the surface its potential energy decreases as it becomes physisorbed into the **precursor state** for chemisorption. Dissociation into fragments often takes place as a molecule moves into its chemisorbed state and, after an initial increase in energy as the bonds stretch, there is a sharp decrease as the adsorbate–substrate bonds

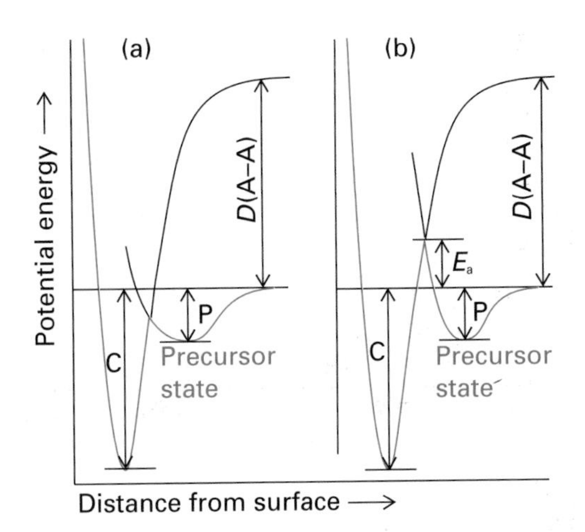

Fig. 16.22 The potential energy profiles for the dissociative chemisorption of an A_2 molecule. In each case, P is the enthalpy of (non-dissociative) physisorption and C that for chemisorption (at $T = 0$). The relative locations of the curves determine whether the chemisorption is (a) not activated or (b) activated.

reach their full strength. Even if the molecule does not fragment, there is likely to be an initial increase in potential energy as the bonds adjust when the molecule approaches the surface.

In most cases, therefore, we can expect there to be a potential energy barrier separating the precursor and chemisorbed states. This barrier, however, might be low and might not rise above the energy of a distant, stationary molecule (as in Fig. 16.22a). In this case, chemisorption is not an activated process and can be expected to be rapid. Many gas adsorptions on clean metals appear to be non-activated. In some cases the barrier rises above the zero axis (as in Fig. 16.22b); such chemisorptions are activated and slower than the non-activated kind. An example is the adsorption of H_2 on copper, which has an activation energy in the region of 20–40 kJ mol^{-1}.

One point that emerges from this discussion is that rates are not good criteria for distinguishing between physisorption and chemisorption. Chemisorption can be fast if the activation energy is small or zero, but it may be slow if the activation energy is large. Physisorption is usually fast, but it can appear to be slow if adsorption is taking place on a porous medium.

The rate at which a surface is covered by adsorbate depends on the ability of the substrate to dissipate the energy of the incoming molecule as thermal motion as it crashes onto the surface. If the energy is not dissipated quickly, the molecule migrates over the surface until a vibration expels it into the overlying gas or it reaches an edge. The proportion of collisions with the surface that successfully lead to adsorption is called the **sticking probability**, s:

$$s = \frac{\text{rate of adsorption of particles by the surface}}{\text{rate of collision of particles with the surface}} \qquad (16.8)$$

The denominator can be calculated from kinetic theory (by using eqn 16.1), and the numerator can be measured by observing the rate of change of pressure. Values of s vary widely. For example, at room temperature CO has s in the range 0.1–1.0 for several d-metal surfaces, suggesting that almost every collision sticks, but for N_2 on rhenium $s < 10^{-2}$, indicating that more than a hundred collisions are needed before one molecule sticks successfully.

Desorption is always an activated process because the molecules have to be lifted from the foot of a potential well. A physisorbed molecule vibrates in its shallow potential well, and might shake itself off the surface after a short time. The temperature dependence of the first-order rate of departure can be expected to be Arrhenius-like,

$$k_d = A\,e^{-E_d/RT} \qquad (16.9)$$

where A is a pre-exponential factor (obtained from the intercept of an Arrhenius plot, Section 10.9, at $1/T = 0$) and the activation energy for desorption, E_d, is likely to be comparable to the enthalpy of physisorption. In the discussion of half-lives of first-order reactions (Section 10.8) we saw that $t_{1/2} = (\ln 2)/k$; so for desorption, the half-life for remaining on the surface has a temperature dependence given by

$$t_{1/2} = \frac{\ln 2}{k_d} = \tau_0\,e^{E_d/RT} \qquad \tau_0 = \frac{\ln 2}{A} \qquad (16.10)$$

(Note the positive sign in the exponent.) If we suppose that $1/\tau_0$ is approximately the same as the vibrational frequency of the weak molecule–surface bond (about 10^{12} Hz) and $E_d \approx 25$ kJ mol^{-1}, then residence half-lives of around 10 ns are predicted at room temperature. Lifetimes close to 1 s are obtained only by lowering the temperature to about 100 K. For chemisorption, with $E_d = 100$ kJ mol^{-1} and guessing that $\tau_0 = 10^{-14}$ s (because the adsorbate–substrate bond is quite stiff), we expect a residence half-life of about 3×10^3 s (about an hour) at room temperature, decreasing to 1 s at about 350 K.

One way to measure the desorption activation energy is to monitor the rate of increase in pressure when the sample is maintained at a series of temperatures, and to attempt to make an Arrhenius plot. A more sophisticated technique is **temperature programmed desorption** (TPD) or **thermal desorption spectroscopy** (TDS). The basic observation is a surge in desorption rate (as monitored by a mass spectrometer) when the temperature is raised linearly to the temperature at which desorption occurs rapidly; but once the desorption has occurred there is no more adsorbate to escape from the surface, so the desorption flux falls again as the temperature continues to rise. The TPD spectrum, the plot of desorption flux against temperature, therefore shows a peak, the location of which depends on the desorption activation energy. There are three maxima in the example shown in Fig. 16.23, indicating the presence of three adsorption sites with different activation energies.

In many cases only a single desorption activation energy (and a single peak in the TPD spectrum) is observed. When several peaks are observed they might correspond to adsorption on different crystal planes or to multilayer adsorption. For instance, Cd atoms on tungsten show two desorption activation energies, one of 18 kJ mol^{-1} and the other of 90 kJ mol^{-1}. The explanation is that the more tightly bound Cd atoms are attached directly to the substrate, and the less strongly bound are in a layer (or layers) above the primary overlayer. Another example of a system showing two desorption activation energies is CO on tungsten, the values being 120 kJ mol^{-1} and 300 kJ mol^{-1}. The explanation is believed to be the existence of two types of metal–adsorbate binding site, one involving a simple M–CO bond, the other adsorption with dissociation into individually adsorbed C and O atoms.

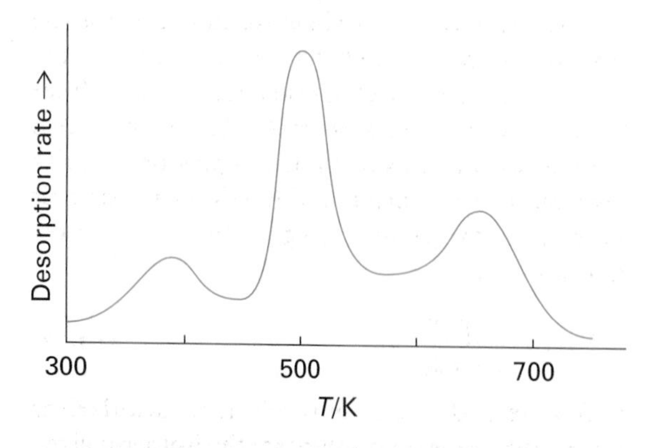

Fig. 16.23 The flash desorption spectrum of H_2 on the (100) face of tungsten. The three peaks indicate the presence of three sites with different adsorption enthalpies and therefore different desorption activation energies. (P. W. Tamm and L. D. Schmidt, *J. Chem. Phys.* **51**, 5352 (1969).)

Catalytic activity at surfaces

We saw in Chapter 11 that a catalyst acts by providing an alternative reaction path with a lower activation energy. A catalyst does not disturb the final equilibrium composition of the system, only the rate at which that equilibrium is approached. In this section we shall consider **heterogeneous catalysis**, in which the catalyst and the reagents are in different phases. A common example is a solid introduced as a heterogeneous catalyst into a gas-phase reaction. Many industrial processes make use of heterogeneous catalysts, which include platinum, rhodium, zeolites (Section 16.7), and various metal oxides, but attention is turning increasingly to homogeneous catalysts, partly because they are easier to cool. However, their use typically requires additional separation steps, and such catalysts are generally immobilized on a support, in which case they become heterogeneous.

A metal acts as a heterogeneous catalyst for certain gas-phase reactions by providing a surface to which a reactant can attach by chemisorption. For example, hydrogen molecules may attach as atoms to a nickel surface, and these atoms react much more readily with another species (such as an alkene) than the original molecules. The chemisorption step therefore results in a reaction pathway with a lower activation energy than in the absence of the catalyst.

16.6 Mechanisms of heterogeneous catalysis

Heterogeneous catalysis normally depends on at least one reactant being adsorbed (usually chemisorbed) and modified to a form in which it readily undergoes reaction. Often this modification takes the form of a fragmentation of the reactant molecules.

The decomposition of phosphine (PH_3) on tungsten is first-order at low pressures and zeroth-order at high pressures. To account for these observations, we write down a plausible rate law in terms of an adsorption isotherm and explore its form in the limits of high and low pressure. If the rate is supposed to be proportional to the surface coverage and we suppose that θ is given by the Langmuir isotherm, we would write

$$\text{Rate} = k\theta = \frac{kKp}{1+Kp} \qquad (16.11)$$

where p is the pressure of phosphine. When the pressure is so low that $Kp \ll 1$, we can neglect Kp in the denominator and obtain

$$\text{Rate} = kKp \qquad (16.12a)$$

and the decomposition is first-order. When $Kp \gg 1$, we can neglect the 1 in the denominator, whereupon the Kp terms cancel and we are left with

$$\text{Rate} = k \qquad (16.12b)$$

and the decomposition is zeroth-order. Many heterogeneous reactions are first-order, which indicates that the rate-determining stage is the adsorption process.

Self-test 16.4

Suggest the form of the rate law for the deuteration of NH_3 in which D_2 adsorbs dissociatively but not extensively (that is, $Kp \ll 1$, with p the partial pressure of D_2), and NH_3 (with partial pressure p') adsorbs at different sites.

[*Answer:* rate = $k(Kp)^{1/2}K'p'/(1 + K'p')$]

In the **Langmuir–Hinshelwood mechanism** (LH mechanism) of surface-catalysed reactions, the reaction takes place by encounters between molecular fragments and atoms adsorbed on the surface. We therefore expect the rate law to be overall second-order in the extent of surface coverage:

$$A + B \rightarrow P \qquad \text{rate} = k\theta_A\theta_B$$

Insertion of the appropriate isotherms for A and B then gives the reaction rate in terms of the partial pressures of the reactants. For example, if A and B follow the adsorption isotherms given in eqn 16.5, then the rate law can be expected to be

$$\text{Rate} = \frac{kK_AK_Bp_Ap_B}{(1 + K_Ap_A + K_Bp_B)^2} \qquad (16.13)$$

The parameters K in the isotherms and the rate constant k are all temperature dependent, so the overall temperature dependence of the rate may be strongly non-Arrhenius, in the sense that the reaction rate is unlikely to be proportional to $e^{-E_a/RT}$. The LH mechanism is dominant for the catalytic oxidation of CO to CO_2 on the (111) surface of platinum.

In the **Eley–Rideal mechanism** (ER mechanism) of a surface-catalysed reaction, a gas-phase molecule collides with another molecule already adsorbed on the surface. We can therefore expect the rate of formation of product to be proportional to the partial pressure, p_B, of the non-adsorbed gas B and the extent of surface coverage, θ_A, of the adsorbed gas A. It follows that the rate law should be

$$A + B \rightarrow P \qquad \text{rate} = kp_B\theta_A$$

The rate constant, k, might be much larger than for the uncatalysed gas-phase reaction because the reaction on the surface has a low activation energy and the adsorption itself is often not activated. If we know the adsorption isotherm for A, we can express the rate law in terms of its partial pressure, p_A. For example, if the adsorption of A follows a Langmuir isotherm in the pressure range of interest, then the rate law would be

$$\text{Rate} = \frac{kKp_Ap_B}{1 + Kp_A} \qquad (16.14)$$

If A were a diatomic molecule that adsorbed as atoms, then we would substitute the isotherm given in eqn 16.4 instead.

According to eqn 16.14, when the partial pressure of A is high (in the sense $Kp_A \gg 1$) there is almost complete surface coverage, and the rate law is

$$\text{Rate} \approx \frac{kKp_A p_B}{Kp_A} = kp_B$$

Now the rate-determining step is the collision of B with the adsorbed fragments. When the pressure of A is low ($Kp_A \ll 1$), perhaps because of its reaction, the rate law becomes

$$\text{Rate} \approx \frac{kKp_A p_B}{1} = kKp_A p_B$$

Now the extent of surface coverage is rate-determining.

Almost all thermal surface-catalysed reactions are thought to take place by the LH mechanism, but a number of reactions with an ER mechanism have also been identified from molecular beam investigations. For example, the reaction between H(g) and D(ad) to form HD(g) is thought to be by an ER mechanism involving the direct collision and pick-up of the adsorbed D atom by the incident H atom. However, the two mechanisms should really be thought of as ideal limits, and all reactions lie somewhere between the two and show features of each one.

16.7 Examples of catalysis

Almost the whole of modern chemical industry depends on the development, selection, and application of catalysts (Table 16.3). All we can hope to do in this section is to give a brief indication of some of the problems involved. Other than the ones we consider, these problems include the danger of the catalyst being poisoned by by-products or impurities, and economic considerations relating to cost and lifetime.

The activity of a catalyst depends on the strength of chemisorption as indicated by the 'volcano' curve in Fig. 16.24 (which is so called on account of its general shape). To be active, the catalyst should be extensively covered by adsorbate, which is the case if chemisorption is strong. However, if the strength of the substrate–adsorbate bond becomes too great, then the activity declines either because the other reactant molecules cannot react with the adsorbate

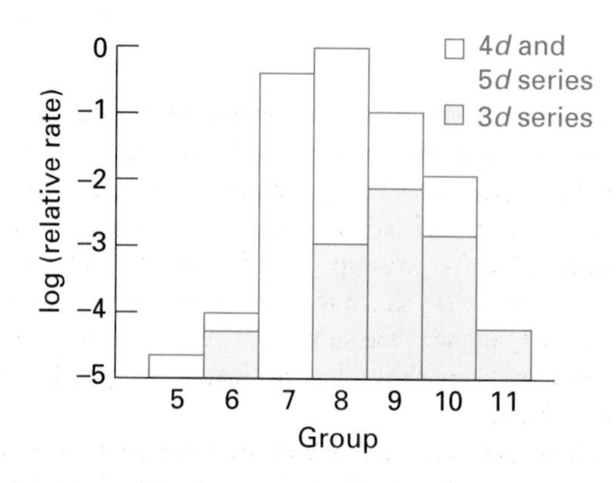

Fig. 16.24 A volcano curve of catalytic activity arises because although the reactants must adsorb reasonably strongly, they must not adsorb so strongly that they are immobilized. The tinted and white rectangles correspond to the 3*d* and (4*d*, 5*d*) series of metals, respectively. The group numbers relate to the periodic table (see inside back cover).

Table 16.3 *Properties of catalysts*

Catalyst	Function	Examples
Metals	Hydrogenation Dehydrogenation	Fe, Ni, Pt, Ag
Semiconducting oxides and sulfides	Oxidation Desulfurization	NiO, ZnO, MgO Bi_2O_3/MoO_3, MoS_2
Insulating oxides	Dehydration	Al_2O_3, SiO_2, MgO
Acids	Polymerization Isomerization Cracking Alkylation	H_3PO_4, H_2SO_4 SiO_2/Al_2O_3, zeolites

Table 16.4 *Chemisorption abilities*

	O_2	C_2H_2	C_2H_4	CO	H_2	CO_2	N_2
Ti, Cr, Mo, Fe	+	+	+	+	+	+	+
Ni, Co	+	+	+	+	+	+	–
Pd, Pt	+	+	+	+	+	–	–
Mn, Cu	+	+	+	+	±	–	–
Al, Au	+	+	+	+	–	–	–
Li, Na, K	+	+	–	–	–	–	–
Mg, Ag, Zn, Pb	+	–	–	–	–	–	–

+, Strong chemisorption; ± chemisorption; – no chemisorption.

or because the adsorbate molecules are immobilized on the surface. This pattern of behaviour suggests that the activity of a catalyst should initially increase with strength of adsorption (as measured, for instance, by the enthalpy of adsorption) and then decline, and that the most active catalysts should be those lying near the summit of the volcano. Most active metals are those that lie close to the middle of the *d* block.

Many metals are suitable for adsorbing gases, and the general order of adsorption strengths decreases along the series O_2, C_2H_2, C_2H_4, CO, H_2, CO_2, N_2. Some of these molecules adsorb dissociatively (for example, H_2). Elements from the *d* block, such as iron, vanadium, and chromium, show a strong activity towards all these gases, but manganese and copper are unable to adsorb N_2 and CO_2. Metals towards the left of the periodic table (for example, magnesium and lithium) can adsorb (and, in fact, react with) only the most active gas (O_2). These trends are summarized in Table 16.4.

As an example of catalytic action, consider the hydrogenation of alkenes. The alkene (**1**) adsorbs by forming two bonds with the surface (**2**), and on the same surface there may be adsorbed H atoms. When an encounter occurs, one of the alkene–surface bonds is broken (forming **3** or **4**) and later an encounter with a second H atom releases the fully hydrogenated hydrocarbon, which is the thermodynamically more stable species. The evidence for a two-stage reaction is the appearance of different isomeric alkenes in the mixture. The formation of isomers comes about because, while the hydrocarbon chain is waving about over the surface of the metal, an atom in the chain might chemisorb again to form (**5**) and then desorb to (**6**), an isomer of the original molecule. The new alkene would not be formed if the two hydrogen atoms attached simultaneously.

1

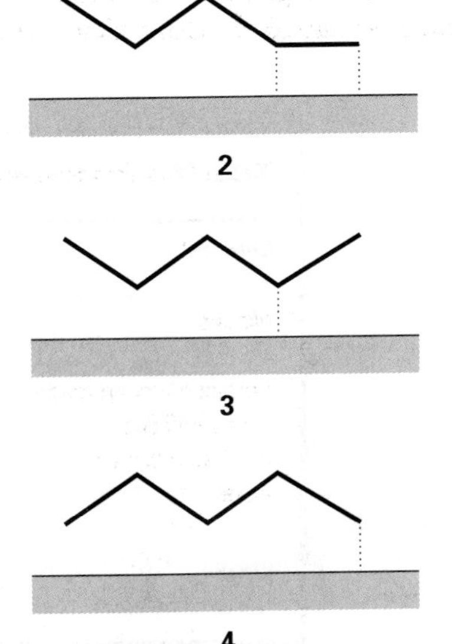

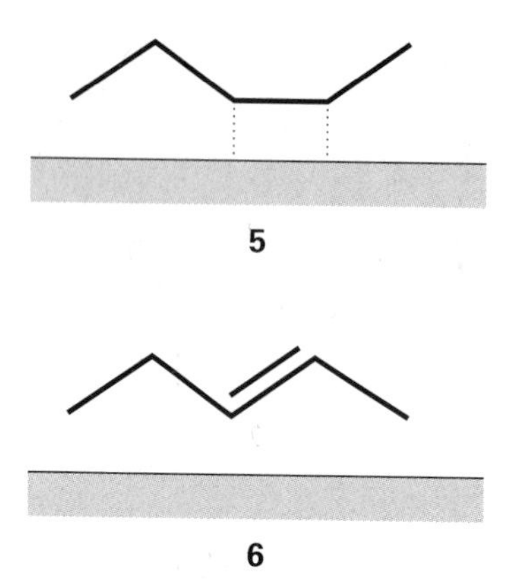

Catalytic oxidation is widely used in industry and in pollution control. Although in some cases it is desirable to achieve complete oxidation (as in the production of nitric acid from ammonia), in others partial oxidation is the aim. For example, the complete oxidation of propene to carbon dioxide and water is wasteful, but its partial oxidation to propenal (acrolein, CH_2=CHCHO) is the start of important industrial processes. Likewise, the controlled oxidations of ethene to ethanol, ethanal (acetaldehyde), and (in the presence of chlorine) to chloroethene (vinyl chloride, for the manufacture of PVC), are the initial stages of very important chemical industries.

Some of these reactions are catalysed by *d*-metal oxides of various kinds. The physical chemistry of oxide surfaces is very complex, as can be appreciated by considering what happens during the oxidation of propene to propenal on bismuth molybdate. The first stage is the adsorption of the propene molecule with loss of a hydrogen to form the propenyl (allyl) radical, CH_2=$CHCH_2$·. An O atom in the surface can now transfer to this radical, leading to the formation of propenal and its desorption from the surface. The H atom also escapes with a surface O atom, and goes on to form H_2O, which leaves the surface. The surface is left with vacancies and metal ions in lower oxidation states. These vacancies are attacked by O_2 molecules in the overlying gas, which then chemisorb as O_2^- ions, so reforming the catalyst. This sequence of events, which is called the **Mars van Krevelen mechanism**, involves great upheavals of the surface, and some materials break up under the stress.

Many of the small organic molecules used in the preparation of all kinds of chemical products come from petroleum. These small building blocks of polymers, perfumes, and petrochemicals in general are usually cut from the long-chain hydrocarbons drawn from the Earth as petroleum. The catalytically induced fragmentation of the long-chain hydrocarbons is called **cracking**, and is often brought about on silica–alumina catalysts. These catalysts act by forming unstable carbocations that dissociate and rearrange to more highly branched isomers. These branched isomers burn more smoothly and efficiently in internal combustion engines, and are used to produce higher octane fuels.

Catalytic **reforming** uses a dual-function catalyst, such as a dispersion of platinum and acidic alumina. The platinum provides the metal function, and brings about dehydrogenation and hydrogenation. The alumina provides the acidic function, being able to form carbocations from alkenes. The sequence of events in catalytic reforming shows up very clearly the complications that must be unravelled if a reaction as important as this is to be understood and improved. The first step is the attachment of the long-chain hydrocarbon by chemisorption to the platinum. In this process first one and then a second H atom is lost, and an alkene is formed. The alkene migrates to a Brønsted acid site, where it accepts a proton and attaches to the surface as a carbocation. This carbocation can undergo several different reactions. It can break into two, isomerize into a more highly branched form, or undergo varieties of ring closure. Then the adsorbed molecule loses a proton, escapes from the surface, and migrates (possibly through the gas) as an alkene to a metal part of the catalyst where it is hydrogenated. We end up with a rich selection of smaller molecules that can be withdrawn, fractionated, and then used as raw materials for other products.

The concept of a solid surface has been extended in recent years with the availability of **microporous materials**, in which the surface effectively extends deep inside the solid. Zeolites are microporous aluminosilicates with the general formula $\{[M^{n+}]_{x/n}\cdot[H_2O]_m\}\{[AlO_2]_x[SiO_2]_y\}^{x-}$, where M^{n+} cations and H_2O molecules bind inside the cavities, or pores, of the Al–O–Si framework (Fig. 16.25). Small neutral molecules, such as CO_2, NH_3, and hydrocarbons

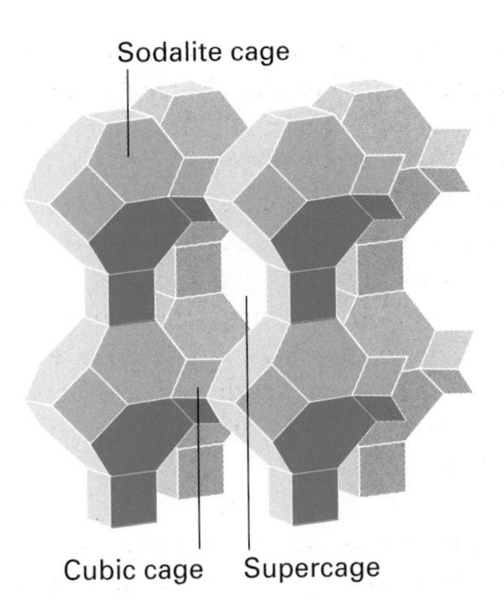

Fig. 16.25 A framework representation of the general layout of the Si, Al, and O atoms in a zeolite material. Each vertex corresponds to a Si or Al atom and each edge corresponds to the approximate location of an O atom. Note the large central pore, which can hold cations, water molecules, or other small molecules.

7

$-H_2O$

8

(including aromatic compounds), can also adsorb to the internal surfaces and we shall see that this partially accounts for the utility of zeolites as catalysts.

Some zeolites for which $M = H^+$ are very strong acids and catalyse a variety of reactions that are of particular importance to the petrochemical industry. Examples include the dehydration of methanol to form hydrocarbons such as gasoline and other fuels:

$$x\,CH_3OH \xrightarrow{\text{zeolite}} (CH_2)_x + x\,H_2O$$

and the isomerization of 1,3-dimethylbenzene (*m*-xylene) to 1,4-dimethylbenzene (*p*-xylene). The catalytically important form of these acidic zeolites may be either a Brønsted acid (**7**) or a Lewis acid (**8**). Like enzymes, a zeolite catalyst with a specific composition and structure is very selective towards certain reactants and products because only molecules of certain sizes can enter and exit the pores in which catalysis occurs. It is also possible that zeolites derive their selectivity from the ability to bind and to stabilize only transition states that fit properly in the pores. The analysis of the mechanism of zeolite catalysis is greatly facilitated by computer simulation of microporous systems, which shows how molecules fit in the pores, migrate through the connecting tunnels, and react at the appropriate active sites.

Processes at electrodes

A very special kind of surface is that of an electrode in contact with an electrolyte. Studies of processes on electrode surfaces are of enormous importance in electrochemistry, where they give information about the rate of electron transfer between the electrode and electroactive species in solution, and are essential to the improvement of the performance of batteries and fuel cells (Box 9.2). Detailed knowledge of the factors that determine the rate of electron transfer leads to a better understanding of power production in batteries and of electron conduction in metals, semiconductors, and nanometre-sized electronic devices. Indeed, the economic consequences of electrode processes are almost incalculable. Most of the modern methods of generating electricity are inefficient, and the development of fuel cells could enhance our production and deployment of energy, not least by the reduction of the generation of polluting nitrogen oxides. Today we produce energy inefficiently to produce goods that then decay by corrosion. Each step of this wasteful sequence could be improved by discovering more about the kinetics of electrochemical processes. Similarly, the techniques of organic and inorganic electrosynthesis, where an electrode is an active component of an industrial process, depend on intimate understanding of the kinetics of the processes taking place at electrodes.

16.8 The electrode–solution interface

Whereas most of the preceding discussion focused on the gas–solid interface, we now have to turn our attention to a metal immersed in an aqueous solution of ions. The most primitive model of the boundary between the solid and liquid phases is an **electrical double layer**, which consists of a sheet of positive charge at the surface of the electrode and a sheet of negative charge next to it in the solution (or vice versa). This arrangement creates an electrical potential difference, called the **Galvani potential difference**, between the bulk of the metal electrode and the bulk of the solution. For simplicity in the following, we shall identify the Galvani potential difference with what in Chapter 9 we called the electrode potential.[2]

We can construct a more detailed picture of the interface by speculating about the arrangement of ions and electric dipoles in the solution. In the **Helmholtz layer model** of the interface the solvated ions arrange themselves along the surface of the electrode but are held away from it by their hydration spheres (Fig. 16.26). The location of the sheet of ionic charge, which is called the **outer Helmholtz plane** (OHP), is identified as the plane running through the solvated ions. In this simple model, the electrical potential changes linearly within the layer bounded by the electrode surface on one side and the OHP on the other. In a refinement of this model, ions that have discarded their solvating molecules and have become attached to the electrode surface by chemical bonds are regarded as forming the **inner Helmholtz plane** (IHP). The Helmholtz layer model ignores the disrupting effect of thermal motion, which tends to break up and disperse the rigid outer plane of charge. In the **Gouy–Chapman model** of the **diffuse double layer**, the disordering effect of thermal motion is taken into account in much the same way as the Debye–Hückel model describes the ionic atmosphere of an ion (Section 9.1) with the latter's single central ion replaced by an infinite, plane electrode (Fig. 16.27).

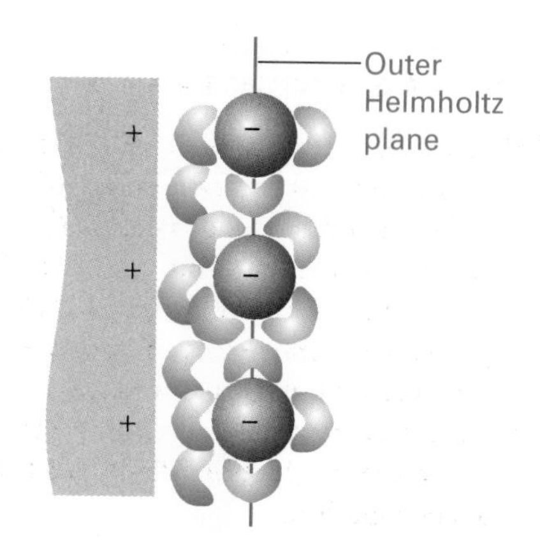

Fig. 16.26 A simple model of the electrode–solution interface treats it as two rigid planes of charge. One plane, the outer Helmholtz plane (OHP), is due to the ions with their solvating molecules and the other plane is that of the electrode itself.

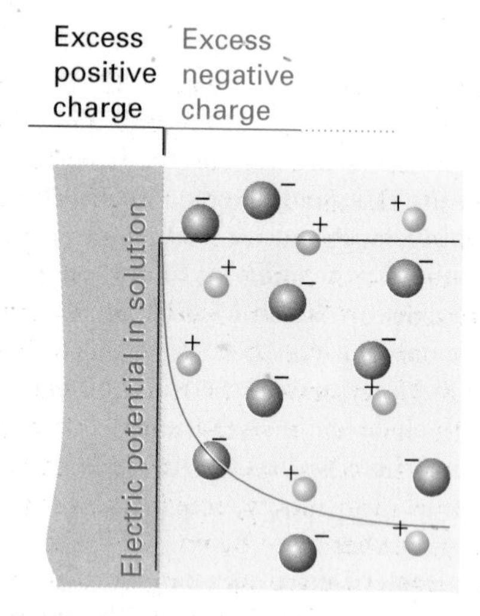

Fig. 16.27 The Gouy–Chapman model of the electrical double layer treats the outer region as an atmosphere of counter-charge, similar to the Debye–Hückel theory of ion atmospheres. The plot of electrical potential against distance from the electrode surface shows the meaning of the diffuse double layer (see text for details).

[2] In a more detailed treatment we would have to allow for them to differ by a constant.

16.9 The rate of electron transfer

We shall consider a reaction at the electrode in which an ion is reduced by the transfer of a single electron in the rate-determining step.[3] The quantity we focus on is the **current density**, j, the electric current flowing through a region of an electrode divided by the area of the region. An analysis of the effect of the Galvani potential difference at the electrode on the current density using a version of transition-state theory (Section 10.11) leads to the **Butler–Volmer equation:**[4]

$$j = j_0\{e^{(1-\alpha)f\eta} - e^{-\alpha f\eta}\} \quad (16.15)$$

We have written $f = F/RT$, where F is Faraday's constant (Section 9.7; at 298 K, $f = 38.9\ V^{-1}$). The quantity η (eta) is the **overpotential:**

$$\eta = E' - E$$

where E is the electrode potential at equilibrium, when there is no net flow of current, and E' is the electrode potential when a current is being drawn from the cell. The quantity α is the **transfer coefficient**, and is an indication of where the transition state between the reduced and oxidized forms of the electroactive species in solution is reactant-like ($\alpha = 0$) or product-like ($\alpha = 1$): typical values are close to 0.5. The quantity j_0 is the **exchange-current density**, the magnitude of the equal but opposite current densities when the electrode is at equilibrium. As usual in chemistry, equilibrium is dynamic, so even though there may be no net flow of current at an electrode, there are matching inward and outward flows of electrons. Figure 16.28 shows how eqn 16.15 predicts the current density to depend on the overpotential for different values of the transfer coefficient.

When the overpotential is so small that $f\eta \ll 1$ (in practice, η less than about 0.01 V) the exponentials in eqn 16.15 can be expanded by using $e^x = 1 + x + \cdots$ to give

$$j = j_0\{1 + (1-\alpha)f\eta + \cdots - (1 - \alpha f\eta + \cdots)\} \approx j_0 f\eta \quad (16.16)$$

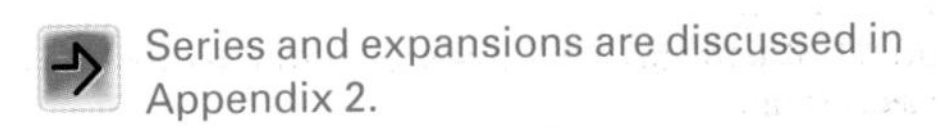

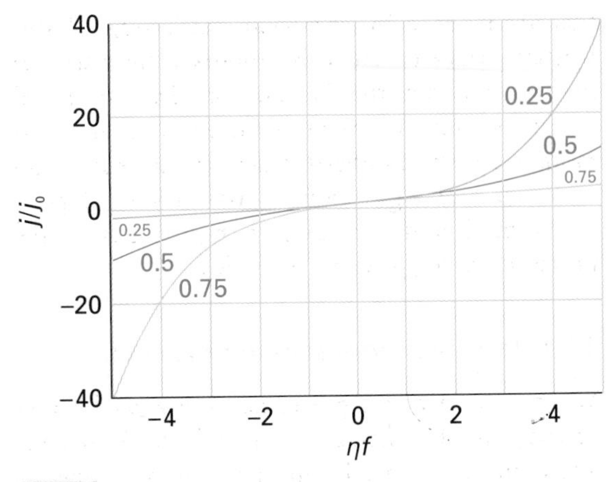

Fig. 16.28 The dependence of the current density on the overpotential for different values of the transfer coefficient.

This equation shows that the current density is proportional to the overpotential, so at low overpotentials the interface behaves like a conductor that obeys Ohm's law.

Ohm's law states that $V = IR$, where V is the potential difference, I is the current, and R is the resistance. Additional concepts of electrostatics are discussed in Appendix 3.

Self-test 16.5

The exchange current density of a Pt(s)|H_2(g)|H^+(aq) electrode at 298 K is 0.79 mA cm^{-2}. What is the current through an electrode of total area 5.0 cm^2 when the overpotential is +5.0 mV?

[*Answer:* 0.77 mA]

When the overpotential is large and positive (in practice, $\eta \geq 0.12$ V), the second exponential in eqn 16.15 is much smaller than the first, and may be neglected. For instance, if $\eta = 0.2$ V and $\alpha = 0.5$,

[3] The last phrase is important: in the deposition of cadmium, for instance, only one electron is transferred in the rate-determining step even though overall the deposition involves the transfer of two electrons.

[4] For a derivation of this equation, see P. Atkins and J. de Paula, *Physical Chemistry*, 7th edn, Oxford University Press/W.H. Freeman (2002).

$e^{-\alpha f\eta} = 0.02$ whereas $e^{(1-\alpha)f\eta} = 49$. Then (ignoring signs, which indicate the direction of the current)

$$j = j_0 \, e^{(1-\alpha)f\eta}$$

By taking logarithms of both sides we obtain

$$\ln j = \ln j_0 + (1-\alpha)f\eta \qquad (16.17a)$$

If, instead, the overpotential is large but negative (in practice, $\eta \le -0.12$ V), the first exponential in eqn 16.15 may be neglected. Then

$$j = j_0 \, e^{-\alpha f\eta}$$

so

$$\ln j = \ln j_0 - \alpha f\eta \qquad (16.17b)$$

The plot of the logarithm of the current density against the overpotential is called a **Tafel plot.** The slope gives the value of α and the intercept at $\eta = 0$ gives the exchange-current density.

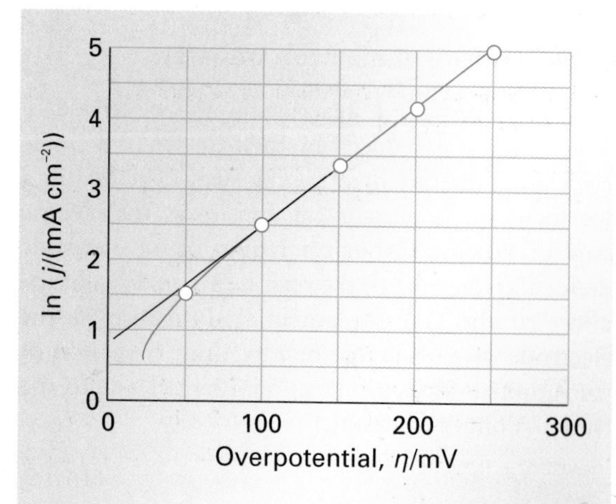

Fig. 16.29 A Tafel plot is used to measure the exchange-current density (given by the extrapolated intercept at $\eta = 0$) and the transfer coefficient (from the slope). The data are from Example 16.4.

Example 16.4

Interpreting a Tafel plot

The data below refer to the anodic current through a platinum electrode of area 2.0 cm^2 in contact with an Fe^{3+},Fe^{2+} aqueous solution at 298 K. Calculate the exchange-current density and the transfer coefficient for the electrode process.

η/mV	50	100	150	200	250
I/mA	8.8	25.0	58.0	131	298

Strategy The anodic process is the oxidation Fe^{2+}(aq) → Fe^{3+}(aq) + e^-. To analyse the data, we make a Tafel plot (of ln j against η) using the anodic form (eqn 16.17a). The intercept at $\eta = 0$ is ln j_0 and the slope is $(1-\alpha)f$.

Solution Draw up the following table:

η/mV	50	100	150	200	250
j/(mA cm^{-2})	4.4	12.5	29.0	65.5	149
ln(j/(mA cm^{-2}))	1.48	2.53	3.37	4.18	5.00

The points are plotted in Fig. 16.29. The high overpotential region gives a straight line of intercept 0.88 and slope 0.0165. From the former it follows that ln(j_0/(mA cm^{-2})) = 0.88, so j_0 = 2.4 mA cm^{-2}. From the latter,

$$(1-\alpha)\frac{F}{RT} = 0.0165 \text{ mV}^{-1}$$

so $\alpha = 0.58$. Note that the Tafel plot is non-linear for $\eta < 100$ mV; in this region $\alpha f\eta = 2.3$ and the approximation that $\alpha f\eta \gg 1$ fails.

Self-test 16.6

Repeat the analysis using the following cathodic current data:

η/mV	−50	−100	−150	−200	−250	−300
I/mA	0.3	1.5	6.4	27.6	118.6	510

[*Answer:* $\alpha = 0.75$, $j_0 = 0.041$ mA cm^{-2}]

Some experimental values for the Butler–Volmer parameters are given in Table 16.5. From them we can see that exchange-current densities vary over a very wide range. For example, the N_2,N_3^- couple on platinum has $j_0 = 10^{-76}$ A cm^{-2}, whereas the H^+,H_2 couple on platinum has $j_0 = 8 \times 10^{-4}$ A cm^{-2}, a difference of 73 orders of magnitude. Exchange currents are generally large when the redox process involves no bond breaking (as in the $[Fe(CN)_6]^{3-}$, $[Fe(CN)_6]^{4-}$ couple) or if only weak bonds are broken (as in Cl_2,Cl^-). They are generally small when more than one electron needs to be transferred, or when multiple or strong bonds are broken, as in the N_2,N_3^- couple and in redox reactions of organic compounds.

Electrodes with potentials that change only slightly when a current passes through them are classified

Table 16.5

Exchange current densities and transfer coefficients at 298 K

Reaction	Electrode	$j/(\mathrm{A\ cm^{-2}})$	α
$2\,H^+ + 2\,e^- \rightarrow H_2$	Pt	7.9×10^{-4}	
	Ni	6.3×10^{-6}	0.58
	Pb	5.0×10^{-12}	
	Hg	7.9×10^{-13}	0.50
$Fe^{3+} + e^- \rightarrow Fe^{2+}$	Pt	2.5×10^{-3}	0.58
$Ce^{4+} + e^- \rightarrow Ce^{3+}$	Pt	4.0×10^{-5}	0.75

as **non-polarizable.** Those with strongly current-dependent potentials are classified as **polarizable.** From the linearized equation (eqn 16.16) it is clear that the criterion for low polarizability is high exchange-current density (so η may be small even though j is large). The calomel and H_2/Pt electrodes are both highly non-polarizable, which is one reason why they are so extensively used as reference electrodes in electrochemistry.

16.10 Voltammetry

One of the assumptions in the derivation of the Butler–Volmer equation is the negligible conversion of the electroactive species at low current densities, resulting in uniformity of concentration near the electrode. This assumption fails at high current densities because the consumption of electroactive species close to the electrode results in a concentration gradient. The diffusion of the species towards the electrode from the bulk is slow and may become rate-determining; a larger overpotential is then needed to produce a given current. This effect is called **concentration polarization.** Concentration polarization is important in the interpretation of **voltammetry,** the study of the current through an electrode as a function of the applied potential difference.

The kind of output from **linear-sweep voltammetry** is illustrated in Fig. 16.30. Initially, the absolute value of the potential is low, and the current is due to the migration of ions in the solution. However, as the potential approaches the reduction potential

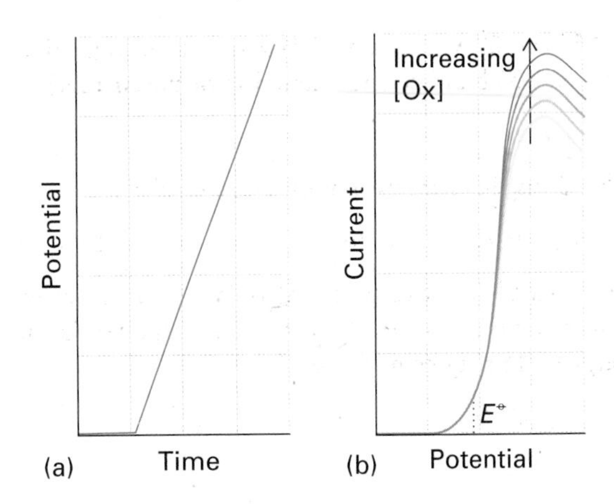

Fig. 16.30 (a) The change of potential with time and (b) the resulting current/potential curve in a voltammetry experiment. The peak value of the current density is proportional to the concentration of electroactive species (for instance, [Ox]) in solution.

of the reducible solute, the current grows. Soon after the potential exceeds the reduction potential the current rises and reaches a maximum value. This maximum current is proportional to the molar concentration of the species, so that concentration can be determined from the peak height after subtraction of an extrapolated baseline.

In **cyclic voltammetry** the potential is applied in a sawtooth manner and the current is monitored. A typical cyclic voltammogram is shown in Fig. 16.31.

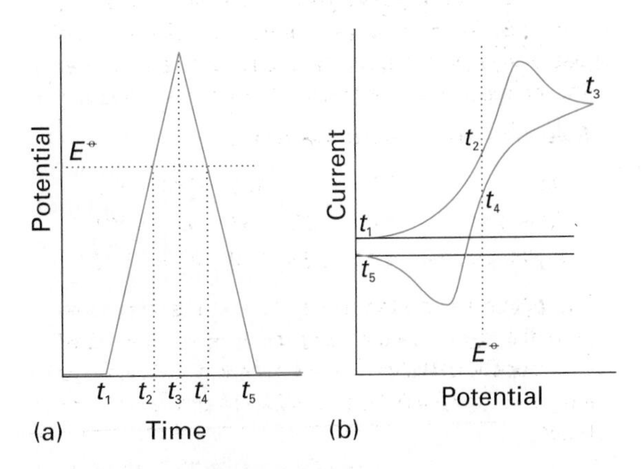

Fig. 16.31 (a) The change of potential with time and (b) the resulting current/potential curve in a cyclic voltammetry experiment.

The shape of the curve is initially like that of a linear sweep experiment, but after reversal of the sweep there is a rapid change in current on account of the high concentration of oxidizable species close to the electrode that was generated on the reductive sweep. When the potential is close to the value required to oxidize the reduced species, there is a substantial current until all the oxidation is complete, and the current returns to zero. Cyclic voltammetry data are obtained at scan rates of about 50 mV s^{-1}, so a scan over a range of 2 V takes about 80 s.

When the reduction reaction at the electrode can be reversed, as in the case of the $[Fe(CN)_6]^{3-}$/$[Fe(CN)_6]^{4-}$ couple, the cyclic voltammogram is broadly symmetric about the standard potential of the couple (as in Fig. 16.31). The scan is initiated with $[Fe(CN)_6]^{3-}$ present in solution, and as the potential approaches $E^{\ominus}$ for the couple, the $[Fe(CN)_6]^{3-}$ near the electrode is reduced and current begins to flow. As the potential continues to change, the current begins to decline again because all the $[Fe(CN)_6]^{3-}$ near the electrode has been reduced and the current reaches its limiting value. The potential is now returned linearly to its initial value, and the reverse series of events occurs with the $[Fe(CN)_6]^{4-}$ produced during the forward scan now undergoing oxidation. The peak of current lies on the other side of $E^{\ominus}$, so the species present and its standard potential can be identified, as indicated in the illustration, by noting the locations of the two peaks.

The overall shape of the curve gives details of the kinetics of the electrode process and the change in shape as the rate of change of potential is altered gives information on the rates of the processes involved. For example, the matching peak on the return phase of the sawtooth change of potential may be missing, which indicates that the oxidation (or reduction) is irreversible. The appearance of the curve may also depend on the time-scale of the sweep, because if the sweep is too fast some processes might not have time to occur. This style of analysis is illustrated in the following example.

Example 16.5

Analysing a cyclic voltammetry experiment

The electroreduction of *p*-bromonitrobenzene in liquid ammonia is believed to occur by the following mechanism:

$$BrC_6H_4NO_2 + e^- \rightarrow BrC_6H_4NO_2^-$$
$$BrC_6H_4NO_2^- \rightarrow \cdot C_6H_4NO_2 + Br^-$$
$$\cdot C_6H_4NO_2 + e^- \rightarrow C_6H_4NO_2^-$$
$$C_6H_4NO_2^- + H^+ \rightarrow C_6H_5NO_2$$

Suggest the likely form of the cyclic voltammogram expected on the basis of this mechanism.

Strategy Decide which steps are likely to be reversible on the time-scale of the potential sweep: such processes will give symmetrical voltammograms. Irreversible processes will give unsymmetrical shapes as reduction (or oxidation) might not occur. However, at fast sweep rates, an intermediate might not have time to react, and a reversible shape will be observed.

Solution At slow sweep rates, the second reaction has time to occur, and a curve typical of a two-electron reduction will be observed, but there will be no oxidation peak on the second half of the cycle because the product, $C_6H_5NO_2$, cannot be oxidized (Fig. 16.32a). At fast sweep rates, the second reaction does not have time to take place before oxidation of the $BrC_6H_4NO_2^-$ intermediate starts to occur during the reverse scan, so the voltammogram will be typical of a reversible one-electron reduction (Fig. 16.32b).

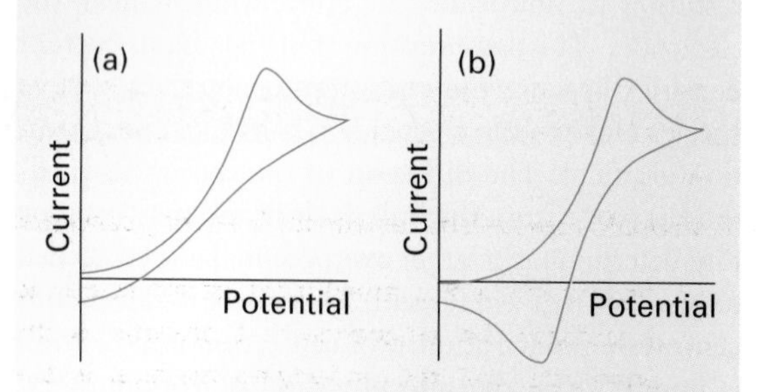

Fig. 16.32 (a) When a non-reversible step in a reaction mechanism has time to occur, the cyclic voltammogram may not show the reverse oxidation or reduction peak. (b) However, if the rate of sweep is increased, the return step may be caused to occur before the irreversible step has had time to intervene, and a typical 'reversible' voltammogram is obtained.

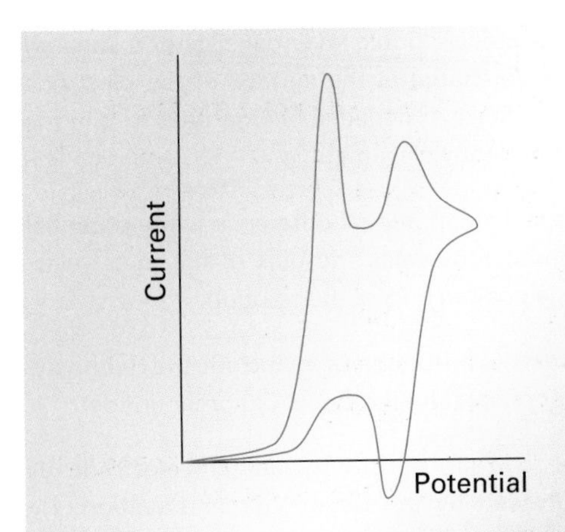

Fig. 16.33 The cyclic voltammogram referred to in Self-test 16.7.

Self-test 16.7

Suggest an interpretation of the cyclic voltammogram shown in Fig. 16.33. The electroactive material is ClC_6H_4CN in acid solution; after reduction to $ClC_6H_4CN^-$, the radical anion may form C_6H_5CN irreversibly.

[*Answer:* $ClC_6H_4CN + e^- \rightleftharpoons ClC_6H_4CN^-$, $ClC_6H_4CN^- + H^+ + e^- \rightarrow C_6H_5CN + Cl^-$, $C_6H_5CN + e^- \rightleftharpoons C_6H_5CN^-$]

16.11 Electrolysis

To induce current to flow through an electrolytic cell and bring about a non-spontaneous cell reaction, the applied potential difference must exceed the cell emf by at least the **cell overpotential**. The cell overpotential is the sum of the overpotentials at the two electrodes and the ohmic drop (IR_s, where R_s is the internal resistance of the cell) due to the current through the electrolyte. The additional potential needed to achieve a detectable rate of reaction may need to be large when the exchange-current density at the electrodes is small.

The rate of gas evolution or metal deposition during electrolysis can be estimated from the Butler–Volmer equation and tables of exchange-current densities. The exchange-current density depends strongly on the nature of the electrode surface, and changes in the course of the electrodeposition of one metal on another. A very crude criterion is that significant evolution or deposition occurs only if the overpotential exceeds about 0.6 V.

A glance at Table 16.5 shows the wide range of exchange-current densities for a metal/hydrogen electrode. The most sluggish exchange currents occur for lead and mercury, and the value of 1 pA cm^{-2} corresponds to a monolayer of atoms being replaced in about 5 a (a is the SI symbol for annum, year). For such systems, a high overpotential is needed to induce significant hydrogen evolution. By contrast, the value for platinum (1 mA cm^{-2}) corresponds to a monolayer being replaced in 0.1 s, so gas evolution occurs for a much lower overpotential.

CHECKLIST OF KEY IDEAS

You should now be familiar with the following concepts:

☐ 1 Adsorption is the attachment of molecules to a surface; the substance that adsorbs is the adsorbate and the underlying material is the adsorbent or substrate. The reverse of adsorption is desorption.

☐ 2 The collision flux, Z_W, is related to the pressure by $Z_W = p/(2\pi mkT)^{1/2}$.

☐ 3 Techniques for studying surface composition and structure include scanning tunnelling microscopy (STM), atomic force microscopy (AFM), photoemission spectroscopy, Auger electron spectroscopy (AES), and low-energy electron diffraction (LEED).

☐ 4 The fractional coverage, θ, is the ratio of the number of occupied sites to the number of available sites.

☐ 5 Techniques for studying the rates of surface processes include flash desorption, surface plasmon resonance (SPR), and gravimetry by using a quartz crystal microbalance (QCM).

☐ 6 Physisorption is adsorption by a van der Waals interaction; chemisorption is adsorption by formation of a chemical (usually covalent) bond.

☐ 7 The Langmuir isotherm is a relation between the fractional coverage and the partial pressure of the adsorbate: $\theta = Kp/(1 + Kp)$.

☐ 8 The isosteric enthalpy of adsorption is determined from a plot of ln K against $1/T$.

☐ 9 The BET isotherm is an isotherm applicable when multilayer adsorption is possible:

$$V/V_{mon} = cz/(1-z)\{1-(1-c)z\}, \text{ with } z = p/p^*.$$

☐ 10 The sticking probability, s, is the proportion of collisions with the surface that successfully lead to adsorption.

☐ 11 Desorption is an activated process with half-life $t_{1/2} = \tau_0 e^{E_d/RT}$; the desorption activation energy is measured by temperature programmed desorption (TPD) or thermal desorption spectroscopy (TDS).

☐ 12 In the Langmuir–Hinshelwood (LH) mechanism of surface-catalysed reactions, the reaction takes place by encounters between molecular fragments and atoms adsorbed on the surface.

☐ 13 In the Eley–Rideal (ER) mechanism of a surface-catalysed reaction, a gas-phase molecule collides with another molecule already adsorbed on the surface.

☐ 14 An electrical double layer consists of a sheet of positive charge at the surface of the electrode and a sheet of negative charge next to it in the solution (or vice versa).

☐ 15 The Galvani potential difference is the potential difference between the bulk of the metal electrode and the bulk of the solution.

☐ 16 Models of the double layer include the Helmholtz layer model and the Gouy–Chapman model.

☐ 17 The current density, j, at an electrode is expressed by the Butler–Volmer equation, $j = j_0\{e^{(1-\alpha)f\eta} - e^{-\alpha f\eta}\}$, where η is the overpotential, $\eta = E' - E$, α is the transfer coefficient, and j_0 is the exchange-current density.

☐ 18 A Tafel plot is a plot of the logarithm of the current density against the overpotential: the slope gives the value of α and the intercept at $\eta = 0$ gives the exchange-current density.

☐ 19 Voltammetry is the study of the current through an electrode as a function of the applied potential difference.

☐ 20 To induce current to flow through an electrolytic cell and bring about a non-spontaneous cell reaction, the applied potential difference must exceed the cell emf by at least the cell overpotential.

DISCUSSION QUESTIONS

16.1 Distinguish between the Langmuir and BET isotherms.

16.2 Describe the essential features of the Langmuir–Hinshelwood, Eley–Rideal, and Mars van Krevelen mechanisms for surface-catalysed reactions.

16.3 Define the terms in and limit the generality of the following expressions: (a) $j = j_0 f\eta$, (b) $j = j_0 e^{(1-\alpha)f\eta}$, and (c) $j = j_0 e^{-\alpha f\eta}$.

16.4 Discuss the technique of cyclic voltammetry and account for the characteristic shape of a cyclic voltammogram, such as those shown in Figs 16.31 and 16.32.

EXERCISES

The symbol ‡ indicates that calculus is necessary.

16.5 Calculate the frequency of molecular collisions per square centimetre of surface in a vessel containing (a) hydrogen, (b) propane at 25°C when the pressure is (i) 100 Pa, (ii) 0.10 μTorr.

16.6 What pressure of argon gas is required to produce a collision rate of 4.5×10^{20} s^{-1} at 425 K on a circular surface of diameter 1.5 mm?

16.7 Calculate the average rate at which He atoms strike a Cu atom in a surface formed by exposing a (100) plane in metallic copper to helium gas at 80 K and a pressure of 35 Pa. Crystals of copper are face-centred cubic with a cell edge of 361 pm.

16.8 The rate, v, at which electrons tunnel through a potential barrier of height 2 eV, like that in a scanning tunnelling microscope, and thickness d can be expressed as $v = A\,e^{-d/l}$, with $A = 5 \times 10^{14}$ s^{-1} and $l = 70$ pm. (a) Calculate the rate at which electrons tunnel across a barrier of width 750 pm. (b) By what factor is the current reduced when the probe is moved away by a further 100 pm?

16.9 ‡We saw in Chapter 9 that the potential energy of interaction between two charges q_1 and q_2 separated by a distance r is $V = q_1q_2/4\pi\varepsilon_0 r$. To get an idea of the magnitudes of forces measured by AFM, calculate the force acting between two electrons separated by 0.50 nm. By what factor does the force drop if the distance between the electrons increases to 0.60 nm? (*Hint.* The relation between force and potential energy is $F = -dV/dr$.)

16.10 A monolayer of CO molecules is adsorbed on the surface of 1.00 g of an Fe/Al_2O_3 catalyst at 77 K, the boiling point of liquid nitrogen. Upon warming, the carbon monoxide occupies 4.25 cm^3 at 0°C and 1.00 bar. What is the surface area of the catalyst?

16.11 The adsorption of a gas is described by the Langmuir isotherm with $K = 0.85$ kPa^{-1} at 25°C. Calculate the pressure at which the fractional surface coverage is (a) 0.15, (b) 0.95.

16.12 Show that the Langmuir isotherm (eqn 16.3) implies that the constant K can be determined experimentally by plotting $1/\theta$ against $1/p$.

16.13 The following data are for the chemisorption of hydrogen on copper powder at 25°C. Confirm that they fit the Langmuir isotherm at low coverages. Then find the value of K for the adsorption equilibrium and the adsorption volume corresponding to complete coverage.

p/Pa	25	129	253	540	1000	1593
V/cm^3	0.042	0.163	0.221	0.321	0.411	0.471

16.14 The values of K for the adsorption of CO on charcoal are 1.0×10^{-3} Torr^{-1} at 273 K and 2.7×10^{-3} Torr^{-1} at 250 K. Estimate the enthalpy of adsorption. (*Hint.* Recall the van 't Hoff equation, eqn 7.14.)

16.15 The following data show the pressures of CO needed for the volume of adsorption (corrected to 1.00 atm and 273 K) to be 10.0 cm^3 using the same sample as in Example 16.2. Calculate the adsorption enthalpy at this surface

T/K	200	210	220	230	240	250
p/kPa	4.32	5.59	7.07	8.80	10.67	12.80

16.16 ‡The differential form of the van 't Hoff equation for the temperature dependence of equilibrium constants is $d(\ln K)/dT = \Delta_r H^{\ominus}/RT^2$. Find the corresponding expression for the temperature dependence of the pressure corresponding to a given fractional coverage on the basis of the Langmuir isotherm.

16.17 How does the pressure depend on the fractional coverage for an adsorbate that dissociates? (*Hint.* Rearrange eqn 16.5 into an expression for p as a function of θ.)

16.18 Confirm that the adsorption isotherms for two reactants A and B that compete for the same sites on a surface is given by eqn 16.6.

16.19 The data for the adsorption of ammonia on barium fluoride at 0°C, when $p^* = 429.6$ kPa, are reported below. Confirm that they fit a BET isotherm and find values of c and V_{mon}.

p/kPa	14.0	37.6	65.6	79.2	82.7	100.7	106.4
V/cm^3	11.1	13.5	14.9	16.0	15.5	17.3	16.5

16.20 The enthalpy of adsorption of ammonia on a nickel surface is found to be −155 kJ mol^{-1}. Estimate the mean lifetime of an NH_3 molecule on the surface at 500 K.

16.21 The average time for which an oxygen atom remains adsorbed on to a tungsten surface is 0.36 s at 2548 K and 3.49 s at 2362 K. (a) Find the activation energy for desorption. (b) What is the pre-exponential factor for these tightly chemisorbed atoms?

16.22 In an experiment on the adsorption of oxygen on tungsten it was found that the same volume of oxygen was desorbed in 27 min at 1856 K and 2.0 min at 1978 K. What is the activation energy of desorption? How long would it take for the same amount to desorb at (a) 298 K, (b) 3000 K?

16.23 Hydrogen iodide is very strongly adsorbed on gold but only slightly adsorbed on platinum. Assume the adsorption follows the Langmuir isotherm and predict the order of the HI decomposition reaction on each of the two metal surfaces.

16.24 According to the Langmuir–Hinshelwood mechanism of surface-catalysed reactions, the rate of reaction between A and B depends on the rate at which the adsorbed species meet. (a) Write the rate law for the reaction according to this mechanism. (b) Find the limiting form of the rate law when the partial pressures of the reactants are low. (c) Could this mechanism ever account for zero-order kinetics?

16.25 The transfer coefficient of a certain electrode in contact with M^{2+} and M^{3+} in aqueous solution at 25°C is 0.42. The current density is found to be 17.0 mA cm^{-2} when the overpotential is 105 mV. What is the overpotential required for a current density of 7255 mA cm^{-2}?

16.26 Determine the exchange-current density from the information given in Exercise 16.25.

16.27 A typical exchange-current density, that for H^+ discharge at platinum, is 0.79 mA cm^{-2} at 25°C. What is the current density at an electrode when its overpotential is (a) 10 mV, (b) 100 mV, (c) −5.0 V? Take $\alpha = 0.5$.

16.28 How many electrons or protons are transported through the double layer in each second when the Pt,H_2|H^+, Pt|Fe^{3+},Fe^{2+}, and Pb,H_2|H^+ electrodes are at equilibrium at 25°C? Take the area as 1.0 cm^2 in each case. Estimate the number of times each second a single atom on the surface takes part in a electron transfer event, assuming an electrode atom occupies about (280 pm)^2 of the surface.

16.29 In an experiment on the Pt|H_2|H^+ electrode in dilute H_2SO_4 the following current densities were observed at 25°C. Evaluate α and j_0 for the electrode.

η/mV	50	100	150	200	250
j/(mA cm^{-2})	2.66	8.91	29.9	100	335

How would the current density at this electrode depend on the overpotential of the same set of magnitudes but of opposite sign?

16.30 The following current–voltage data are for an indium anode relative to a standard hydrogen electrode at 293 K:

$-E$/V	0.388	0.365	0.350	0.335
j/(A m^{-2})	0	0.590	1.438	3.507

Use the data to calculate the transfer coefficient and the exchange-current density. What is the cathodic current density when the potential is 0.365 V?

16.31 The following data are for the overpotential for H_2 evolution with a mercury electrode in dilute aqueous solutions of H_2SO_4 at 25°C. Determine the exchange-current density and transfer coefficient, α.

η/V	0.60	0.65	0.73	0.79	0.84	0.89
j/(mA m^{-2})	2.9	6.3	28	100	250	630

η/V	0.93	0.96
j/(mA m^{-2})	1650	3300

Explain any deviations from the result expected from the Tafel equation.

16.32 The following illustrations are four different examples of voltammograms. Identify the processes occurring in each system. In each case the vertical axis is the current and the horizontal axis is the (negative) electrode potential.

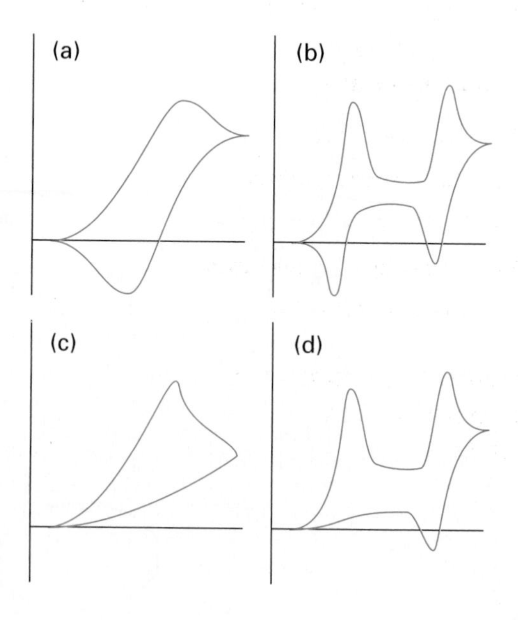

Chapter 17

Molecular interactions

Atoms and molecules with complete valence shells are still able to interact with one another even though all their valences are satisfied. They attract one another over the range of several atomic diameters and they repel one another when pressed together. These residual interactions are highly important. They account, for instance, for the condensation of gases to liquids and the structures of molecular solids. All organic liquids and solids, ranging from small molecules like benzene to virtually infinite cellulose and the polymers from which fabrics are made, are bound together by the cohesive interactions we explore in this chapter. These interactions are also responsible for the structural organization of biological macromolecules as they pin molecular building blocks—such as polypeptides, polynucleotides, and lipids—together in the arrangement essential to their proper physiological function.

In this chapter we present the basic theory of molecular interactions and then explore how they play a role in the properties of liquids. In the following chapter, we explore how the same interactions contribute to the properties of macromolecules and molecular aggregates.

van der Waals interactions

The interactions between molecules include the attractive and repulsive interactions between the partial electric charges of polar molecules and of polar functional groups in macromolecules and the repulsive interactions that prevent the complete collapse of matter to densities as high as those characteristic of atomic nuclei. The repulsive interactions arise from the exclusion of electrons from regions of space where the orbitals of closed-shell species overlap. One class of interactions, those proportional to the inverse sixth power of the separation, are called **van der Waals interactions**. A general point is that most of the following discussion is in terms of the *potential energy* arising from the interaction: the intermolecular *force* typically depends inversely on one higher power of the separation, so a van der Waals force is proportional to the inverse seventh power of the separation.

If the potential energy is denoted V, then the force is $-\mathrm{d}V/\mathrm{d}r$ (see Appendix 3). So, if $V = -C/r^6$, the magnitude of the force is

$$\frac{\mathrm{d}}{\mathrm{d}r}\left(-\frac{C}{r^6}\right) = \frac{6C}{r^7}$$

where we have used

$$\frac{\mathrm{d}}{\mathrm{d}x}\left(\frac{1}{x^n}\right) = -\frac{n}{x^{n+1}}$$

It follows that for a Coulomb interaction between two charges, which is proportional to $1/r$, the force is proportional to $1/r^2$.

17.1 Interactions between partial charges

Atoms in molecules in general have partial charges. Table 17.1 gives the partial charges typically found on the atoms in peptides. If these charges were separated by a vacuum, they would attract or repel each other in accord with Coulomb's law (see Chapter 9) and we would write

Table 17.1
Partial charges in polypeptides

Atom	Partial charge/e
C(=O)	+0.45
C(–CO)	+0.06
H(–C)	+0.02
H(–N)	+0.18
H(–O)	+0.42
N	−0.36
O	−0.38

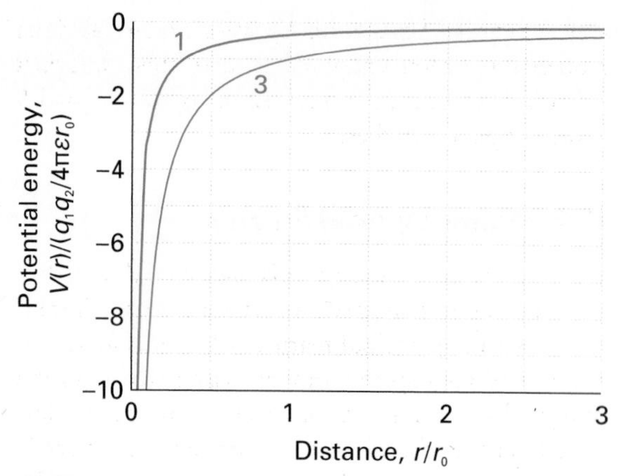

Fig. 17.1 The Coulomb potential for two charges and its dependence on their separation. The two curves correspond to different relative permittivities (1 for a vacuum, 3 for a fluid). The r_0 is an arbitrary length common to both axes.

$$V = \frac{q_1 q_2}{4\pi\varepsilon_0 r} \qquad (17.1a)$$

where q_1 and q_2 are the partial charges and r is their separation. However, we should take into account the possibility that other parts of the molecule, or other molecules, lie between the charges, and decrease the strength of the interaction. The simplest procedure for taking into account these very complicated effects is to treat the medium as a uniform continuum and to write

$$V = \frac{q_1 q_2}{4\pi\varepsilon r} \qquad (17.1b)$$

where ε is the **permittivity** of the medium lying between the charges. The permittivity is usually expressed as a multiple of the vacuum permittivity by writing $\varepsilon = \varepsilon_r\varepsilon_0$, where ε_r is the **relative permittivity**.[1] The effect of the medium can be very large: for water at 25°C, $\varepsilon_r = 78$, so the potential energy of two charges separated by bulk water is reduced by nearly two orders of magnitude compared to the value it would have if the charges were separated by a vacuum (Fig. 17.1). The problem is made worse in calculations on polypeptides and nucleic acids by the fact that two partial charges may have water and

[1] The relative permittivity is still widely called the *dielectric constant*.

a biopolymer chain lying between them. Various models have been proposed to take this awkward effect into account, the simplest being to set $\varepsilon_r = 3.5$ and to hope for the best.

17.2 Electric dipole moments

When the molecules or groups that we are considering are widely separated, it turns out to be simpler to express the principal features of their interaction in terms of the dipole moments associated with the charge distributions rather than with each individual partial charge. At its simplest, an **electric dipole** consists of two charges q and $-q$ separated by a distance l. The product ql is called the **electric dipole moment**, μ. We represent dipole moments by an arrow with a length proportional to μ and pointing from the negative charge to the positive charge (**1**).[2] Because a dipole moment is the product of a charge (in coulombs, C) and a length (in metres, m), the SI unit of dipole moment is the coulomb-metre (C m). However, it is often much more convenient to report a dipole moment in **debye**, D, where

$$1\ \text{D} = 3.335\ 64 \times 10^{-30}\ \text{C m}$$

because then experimental values for molecules are close to 1 D (Table 17.2).[3] The dipole moment of charges e and $-e$ separated by 100 pm is 1.6×10^{-29} C m, corresponding to 4.8 D. Dipole moments of small molecules are typically smaller than that, at about 1 D, confirming that the charge separation in simple molecules is only partial.

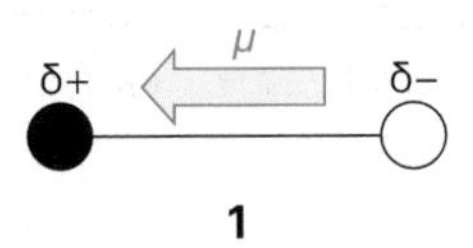

1

A **polar molecule** has a permanent electric dipole moment arising from the partial charges on its atoms (Section 14.14). A **non-polar molecule** has no permanent electric dipole moment. All heteronuclear diatomic molecules are polar because the difference in electronegativities of their two atoms results in non-zero partial charges. Typical dipole moments are 1.08 D for HCl and 0.42 D for HI (Table 17.2). A very approximate relation between the dipole moment and the difference in Pauling electronegativities (Table 14.2) of the two atoms, $\Delta\chi$, is

$$\mu/\text{D} \approx \Delta\chi \qquad (17.2)$$

Table 17.2

Dipole moments (μ) and mean polarizability volumes (α′)

	μ/D	$\alpha'/(10^{-30}\ \text{m}^3)$
Ar	0	1.66
CCl_4	0	10.5
C_6H_6	0	10.4
H_2	0	0.819
H_2O	1.85	1.48
NH_3	1.47	2.22
HCl	1.08	2.63
HBr	0.80	3.61
HI	0.42	5.45

Illustration 17.1

Estimating dipole moments

The electronegativities of hydrogen and bromine are 2.1 and 2.8, respectively. The difference is 0.7, so we predict an electric dipole moment of about 0.7 D for HBr. The experimental value is 0.80 D.

Because it attracts the electrons more strongly, the more electronegative atom is usually the negative end of the dipole. However, there are exceptions, particularly when antibonding orbitals are occupied. Thus, the dipole moment of CO is very small (0.12 D) but the negative end of the dipole is on the C atom even though the O atom is more electronegative. This apparent paradox is resolved as soon as we realize that antibonding orbitals are occupied in CO (see Fig. 14.34), and because electrons in antibonding orbitals tend to be found closer to the less electronegative atom, they contribute a negative partial charge to that atom. If this contribution is larger than the opposite contribution from the electrons in bonding orbitals, then the net effect will

[2] Be careful with this convention: for historical reasons the opposite convention is still widely adopted.

[3] The unit is named after Peter Debye, the Dutch pioneer of the study of dipole moments of molecules.

μ δ+ δ+ μ
δ− δ−

2 Ozone, O_3

be a small negative partial charge on the *less* electronegative atom.

Molecular symmetry is of the greatest importance in deciding whether a polyatomic molecule is polar or not. Indeed, molecular symmetry is more important than the question of whether or not the atoms in the molecule belong to the same element. Homonuclear polyatomic molecules may be polar if they have low symmetry and the atoms are in inequivalent positions. For instance, the angular molecule ozone, O_3 (**2**), is homonuclear; however, it is polar because the central O atom is different from the outer two (it is bonded to two atoms, they are bonded only to one); moreover, the dipole moments associated with each bond make an angle to each other and do not cancel. Heteronuclear polyatomic molecules may be non-polar if they have high symmetry, because individual bond dipoles may then cancel. The heteronuclear linear triatomic molecule CO_2, for example, is non-polar because, although there are partial charges on all three atoms, the dipole moment associated with the OC bond points in the opposite direction to the dipole moment associated with the CO bond, and the two cancel (**3**).

δ− μ δ+ δ+ μ δ−

3 Carbon dioxide, CO_2

Self-test 17.1

Use the VSEPR model, which is reviewed in Appendix 4, to judge whether ClF_3 is polar or non-polar. (*Hint.* Predict the structure first.)

[*Answer:* polar]

To a first approximation, it is possible to resolve the dipole moment of a polyatomic molecule into contributions from various groups of atoms in the molecule and the directions in which these individual contributions lie (Fig. 17.2). Thus,

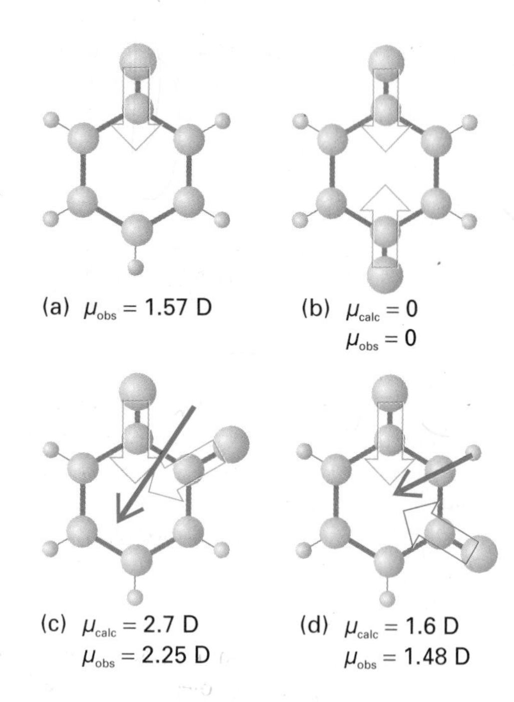

Fig. 17.2 The dipole moments of the dichlorobenzene isomers can be obtained approximately by vectorial addition of two chlorobenzene dipole moments (1.57 D).

1,4-dichlorobenzene is non-polar by symmetry on account of the cancellation of two equal but opposing C–Cl moments (exactly as in carbon dioxide). 1,2-Dichlorobenzene, however, has a dipole moment that is approximately the resultant of two chlorobenzene dipole moments arranged at 60° to each other. This technique of 'vector addition' can be applied with fair success to other series of related molecules, and the resultant μ_{res} of two dipole moments μ_1 and μ_2 that make an angle θ to each other (**4**) is approximately

$$\mu_{res} \approx (\mu_1^2 + \mu_2^2 + 2\mu_1\mu_2 \cos \theta)^{1/2} \qquad (17.3)$$

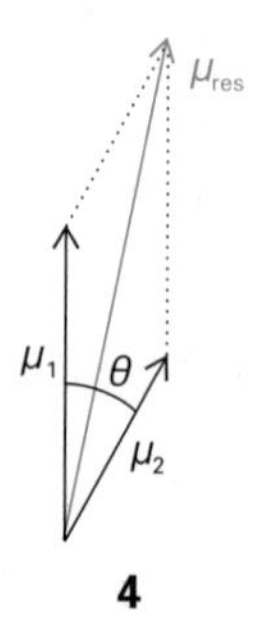

4

A vector is a quantity with both magnitude and direction. It is possible to add, subtract, and obtain products of vectors, as described in Appendix 2, where eqn 17.3 is derived.

Self-test 17.2

Estimate the ratio of the electric dipole moments of *ortho* (1,2-) and *meta* (1,3-) disubstituted benzenes.

[*Answer*: $\mu(ortho)/\mu(meta) = 1.7$]

A better approach to the calculation of dipole moments is to take into account the locations and magnitudes of the partial charges on all the atoms. These partial charges are included in the output of many molecular structure software packages. The programs calculate the dipole moments of the molecules by noting that an electric dipole moment is actually a vector, $\boldsymbol{\mu}$, with three components, μ_x, μ_y, and μ_z (5). The direction of $\boldsymbol{\mu}$ shows the orientation of the dipole in the molecule and the length of the vector is the magnitude, μ, of the dipole moment. In common with all vectors, the magnitude is related to the three components by

$$\mu = (\mu_x^2 + \mu_y^2 + \mu_z^2)^{1/2} \qquad (17.4a)$$

In three dimensions, a vector μ has components μ_x, μ_y, and μ_z along the x-, y-, and z-axes, respectively. The direction of each of the components is denoted with a plus sign or minus sign. For example, if $\mu_x = -1.0$ D, the x-component of the vector μ has a magnitude of 1.0 D and points in the $-x$ direction.

To calculate μ we need to calculate the three components and then substitute them into this expression. To calculate the x-component, for instance, we need to know the partial charge on each atom and the atom's x-coordinate relative to a point in the molecule and form the sum

$$\mu_x = \sum_J q_J x_J \qquad (17.4b)$$

where q_J is the partial charge of atom J, x_J is the x-coordinate of atom J, and the sum is over all the atoms in the molecule. Analogous expressions are used for the y- and z-components. For an electrically neutral molecule, the origin of the coordinates is arbitrary, so it is best chosen to simplify the measurements.

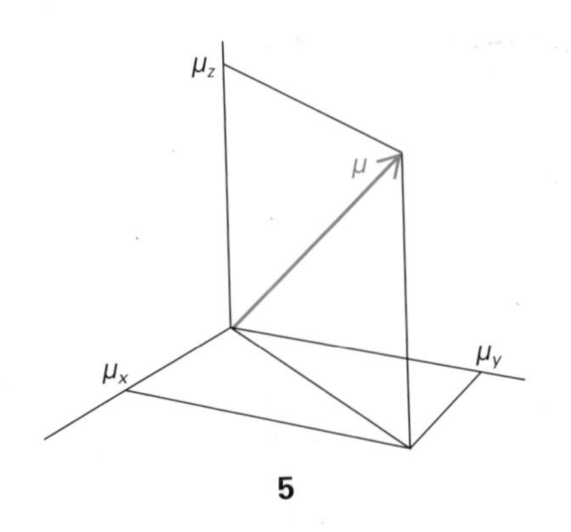

5

Example 17.1

Calculating a molecular dipole moment

Estimate the electric dipole moment of the peptide group using the partial charges (as multiples of e) in Table 17.1 and the locations of the atoms shown in (**6**).

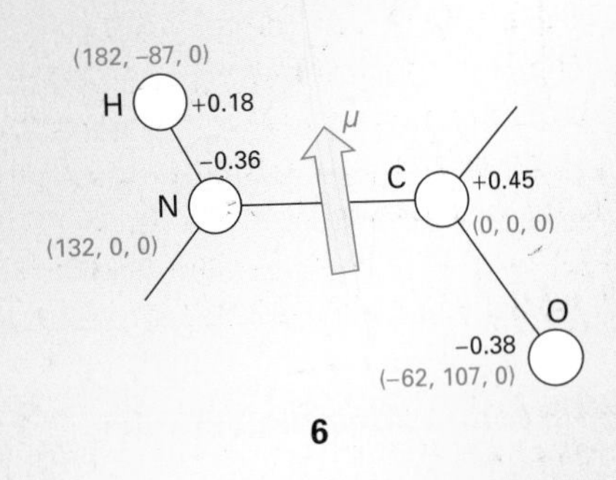

6

Strategy We use eqn 17.4b to calculate each of the components of the dipole moment and then eqn 17.4a to assemble the three components into the magnitude of the dipole moment. Note that the partial charges are multiples of the fundamental charge, $e = 1.609 \times 10^{-19}$ C (see inside front cover).

Solution The expression for μ_x is

$$\begin{aligned}\mu_x &= (-0.36e) \times (132\text{ pm}) + (0.45e) \times (0\text{ pm}) \\ &\quad + (0.18e) \times (182\text{ pm}) + (-0.38e) \times (-62.0\text{ pm}) \\ &= 8.8e\text{ pm} \\ &= 8.8 \times (1.609 \times 10^{-19}\text{ C}) \times (10^{-12}\text{ m}) \\ &= 1.4 \times 10^{-30}\text{ C m}\end{aligned}$$

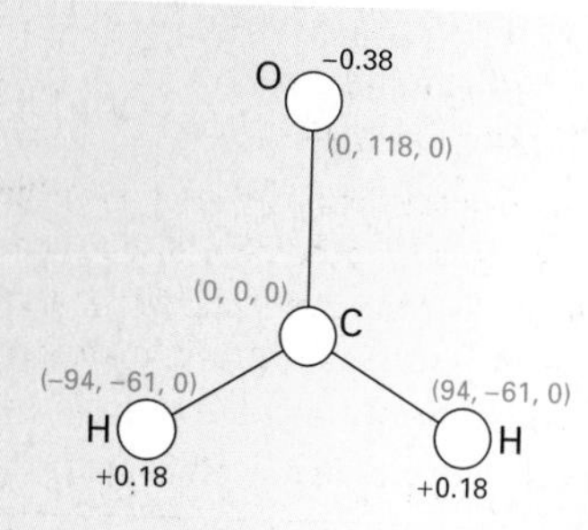

7 Methanal, formaldehyde, HCHO

corresponding to $\mu_x = 0.42$ D. The expression for μ_y is:

$$\mu_y = (-0.36e) \times (0 \text{ pm}) + (0.45e) \times (0 \text{ pm}) + (0.18e) \times (-86.6 \text{ pm}) + (-0.38e) \times (107 \text{ pm}) = -56e \text{ pm} = -9.1 \times 10^{-30} \text{ C m}$$

It follows that $\mu_y = -2.7$ D. Therefore, because $\mu_z = 0$,

$$\mu = \{(0.42 \text{ D})^2 + (-2.7 \text{ D})^2\}^{1/2} = 2.7 \text{ D}$$

We can find the orientation of the dipole moment by arranging an arrow of length 2.7 units of length to have x-, y-, and z-components of 0.42, −2.7, and 0 units; the orientation is superimposed on (**6**).

Self-test 17.3

Calculate the electric dipole moment of formaldehyde, using the information in (**7**).

[*Answer:* −3.2 D]

17.3 Interactions between dipoles

The potential energy of a dipole μ_1 in the presence of a charge q_2 is calculated by taking into account the interaction of the charge with the two partial charges of the dipole, one resulting in a repulsion and the other an attraction. The result for the arrangement shown in (**8**) is:

$$V = -\frac{q_2\mu_1}{4\pi\varepsilon_0 r^2} \qquad (17.5a)$$

Derivation 17.1

The interaction of a charge with a dipole

When the charge and dipole are collinear, as in (**8**), the potential energy is

(Repulsion between $+q_1$ and q_2) (Attraction between $-q_1$ and q_2)

$$V = \frac{q_1q_2}{4\pi\varepsilon_0(r+\frac{1}{2}l)} - \frac{q_1q_2}{4\pi\varepsilon_0(r-\frac{1}{2}l)} = \frac{q_1q_2}{4\pi\varepsilon_0 r\left(1+\frac{l}{2r}\right)} - \frac{q_1q_2}{4\pi\varepsilon_0 r\left(1-\frac{l}{2r}\right)}$$

Next, we suppose that the separation of charges in the dipole is much smaller than the distance of the charge q_2 in the sense that $l/2r \ll 1$. Then we can use

$$\frac{1}{1+x} \approx 1-x \qquad \frac{1}{1-x} \approx 1+x$$

The expansions used in this chapter are:

$$\frac{1}{1+x} = 1-x+x^2-\cdots \qquad \frac{1}{1-x} = 1+x+x^2+\cdots$$

If $x \ll 1$, then $(1+x)^{-1} \approx 1-x$, and $(1-x)^{-1} \approx 1+x$. See Appendix 2 for more information about expansions.

to write

$$V = \frac{q_1q_2}{4\pi\varepsilon_0 r}\left\{\left(1-\frac{l}{2r}\right)-\left(1+\frac{l}{2r}\right)\right\} = -\frac{q_1q_2 l}{4\pi\varepsilon_0 r^2}$$

Now we recognize that $q_2 l = \mu_2$, the dipole moment of molecule 2, and obtain eqn 17.5a.

A similar calculation for the more general orientation shown in (**9**) gives

$$V = -\frac{\mu_1 q_2 \cos\theta}{4\pi\varepsilon_0 r^2} \qquad (17.5b)$$

If q_2 is positive, the energy is lowest when $\theta = 0$ (and $\cos\theta = 1$), because then the partial negative charge of the dipole lies closer than the partial positive

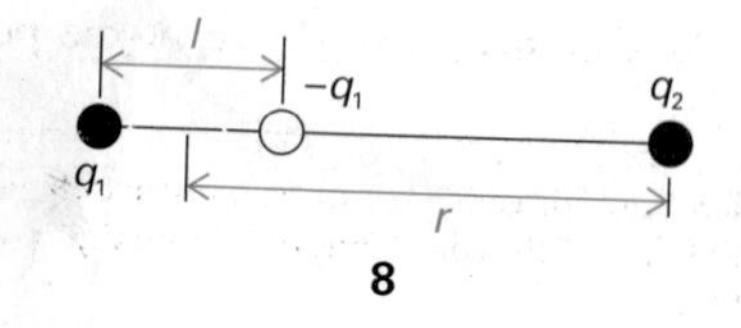

8

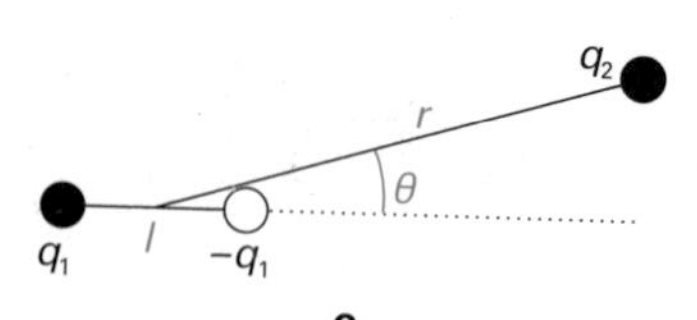

9

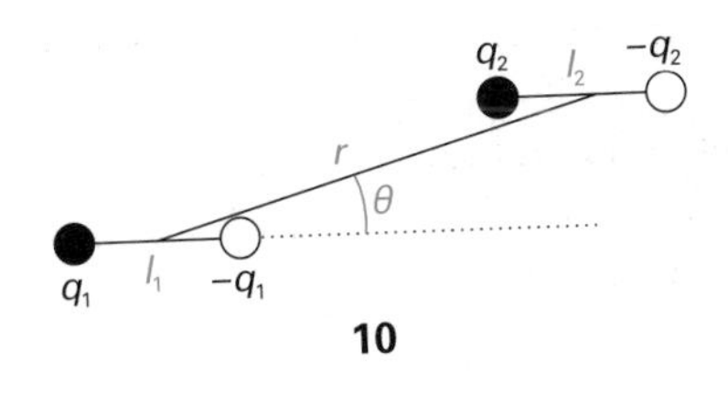

10

charge to the point charge and the attraction outweighs the repulsion. This interaction energy decreases more rapidly with distance than that between two point charges (as $1/r^2$ rather than $1/r$) because, from the viewpoint of the single charge, the partial charges of the point dipole seem to merge and cancel as the distance r increases.

We can calculate the interaction energy between two dipoles μ_1 and μ_2 in the orientation shown in (**10**) in a similar way, by taking into account all four charges of the two dipoles. The outcome is[4]

$$V = \frac{\mu_1\mu_2(1 - 3\cos^2\theta)}{4\pi\varepsilon_0 r^3} \qquad (17.6)$$

This potential energy decreases even more rapidly than in eqn 17.5 (as $1/r^3$ instead of $1/r^2$) because the charges of *both* dipoles seem to merge as the separation of the dipoles increases. The angular factor takes into account how the like or opposite charges come closer to one another as the relative orientation of the dipoles is changed. The energy is lowest when $\theta = 0$ or 180° (when $1 - 3\cos^2\theta = -2$), because opposite partial charges then lie closer together than like partial charges. The potential energy is negative (attractive) in some orientations when $\theta < 54.7°$ (the angle at which $1 - 3\cos^2\theta = 0$, corresponding to $\cos\theta = (\frac{1}{3})^{1/2}$) because opposite charges are closer than like charges. It is positive (repulsive) when $\theta > 54.7°$ because then like charges are closer than unlike charges. The potential energy is zero on the lines at 54.7° and 180 − 54.7 = 123.3° because at those angles the two attractions and the two repulsions cancel (**11**).

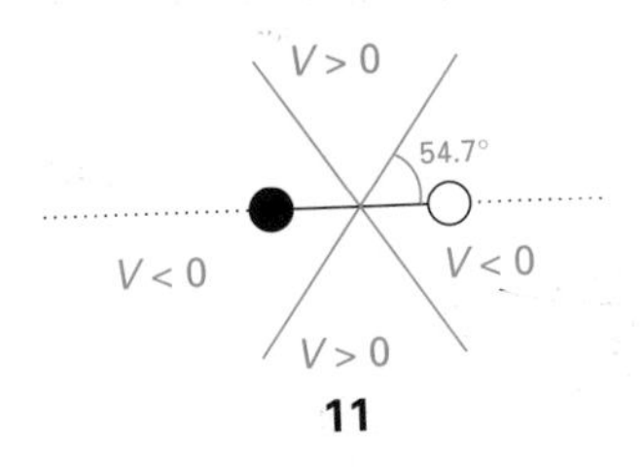

11

Illustration 17.2

Calculating a dipole–dipole interaction energy

To calculate the molar potential energy of the dipolar interaction between two peptide links separated by 3.0 nm in different regions of a polypeptide chain with $\theta = 180°$, we take $\mu_1 = \mu_2 = 2.7$ D, corresponding to 9.1×10^{-30} C m, and find

$$V = \frac{(9.1\times10^{-30}\ \text{C m})^2 \times (-2)}{4\pi \times (8.854\times10^{-12}\ \text{J}^{-1}\ \text{C}^2\ \text{m}^{-1}) \times (3.0\times10^{-9}\ \text{m})^3}$$

$$= \frac{(9.1\times10^{-30})^2 \times (-2)}{4\pi \times (8.854\times10^{-12}) \times (3.0\times10^{-9})^3}\ \frac{\text{C}^2\ \text{m}^2}{\text{J}^{-1}\ \text{C}^2\ \text{m}^{-1}\ \text{m}^3}$$

$$= -5.6\times10^{-23}\ \text{J}$$

This value corresponds (after multiplication by Avogadro's constant) to −34 J mol^{-1}.

A note on good practice We reiterate the importance of including the units at every stage of the calculation, in part because the correct cancellation helps to monitor whether the calculation has been set up and carried out correctly.

The average potential energy of interaction between polar molecules that are freely rotating in a fluid (a gas or liquid) is zero because the attractions and repulsions cancel. However, because the potential energy of a dipole near another dipole depends on their relative orientations, the molecules exert forces on each other and therefore do not in fact rotate completely freely, even in a gas. As a result, the lower energy orientations are marginally favoured, so there is a non-zero interaction between rotating polar molecules (Fig. 17.3). The detailed calculation of the average interaction energy is quite complicated, but the final answer is very simple:

$$V = -\frac{2\mu_1^2\mu_2^2}{3(4\pi\varepsilon_0)^2 kTr^6} \qquad (17.7)$$

The important features of this expression are the dependence of the average interaction energy on the inverse sixth power of the separation and its inverse dependence on the temperature. The inverse sixth power of the distance dependence of the potential

[4] For a derivation of eqn 17.6, see P. Atkins and J. de Paula, *Physical chemistry*, 7th edn, Oxford University Press/W.H. Freeman (2002).

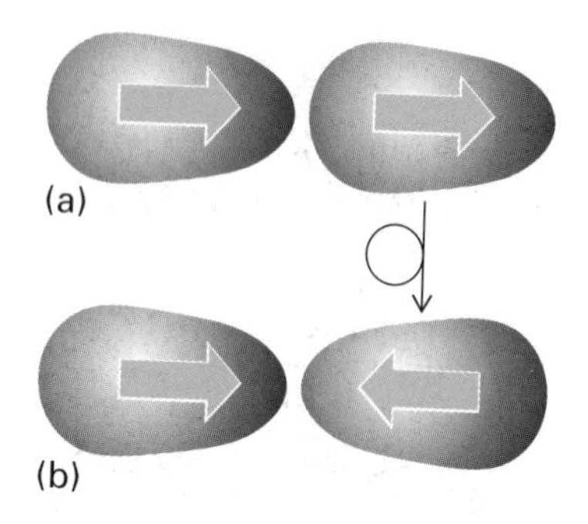

Fig. 17.3 A dipole–dipole interaction. When a pair of molecules can adopt all relative orientations with equal probability, the favourable orientations (a) and the unfavourable ones (b) cancel, and the average interaction is zero. In an actual fluid, the interactions in (a) predominate slightly.

energy identifies it as a van der Waals interaction. The temperature dependence reflects the way that the greater thermal motion overcomes the mutual orientating effects of the dipoles at higher temperatures. At 25°C the average interaction energy for pairs of molecules with $\mu = 1$ D is about -1.4 kJ mol^{-1} when the separation is 0.3 nm. This energy should be compared with the average molar kinetic energy of $\frac{3}{2}RT = 3.7$ kJ mol^{-1} at the same temperature: the two are not very dissimilar, but they are both much less than the energies involved in the making and breaking of chemical bonds.

17.4 Induced dipole moments

A non-polar molecule may acquire a temporary **induced dipole moment,** μ^*, as a result of the influence of an electric field generated by a nearby ion or polar molecule. The field distorts the electron distribution of the molecule, and gives rise to an electric dipole. The molecule is said to be *polarizable*. The magnitude of the induced dipole moment is proportional to the strength of the electric field, $\mathcal{E}$, and we write

$$\mu^* = \alpha\mathcal{E} \tag{17.8}$$

The proportionality constant α is the **polarizability** of the molecule. The larger the polarizability of the molecule, the greater is the distortion caused by a given strength of electric field. If the molecule has few electrons (such as N_2), they are tightly controlled by the nuclear charges and the polarizability of the molecule is low. If the molecule contains large atoms with electrons some distance from the nucleus (such as I_2), the nuclear control is less and the polarizability of the molecule is greater. The polarizability also depends on the orientation of the molecule with respect to the field unless the molecule is tetrahedral (such as CCl_4), octahedral (such as SF_6), or icosahedral (such as C_{60}). Atoms, tetrahedral, octahedral, and icosahedral molecules have isotropic (orientation-independent) polarizabilities; all other molecules have anisotropic (orientation-dependent) polarizabilities.

The polarizabilities reported in Table 17.2 are given as **polarizability volumes,** α':

$$\alpha' = \frac{\alpha}{4\pi\varepsilon_0} \tag{17.9}$$

The polarizability volume has the dimensions of volume (hence its name) and is comparable in magnitude to the volume of the molecule.

Self-test 17.4

What strength of electric field is required to induce an electric dipole moment of 1.0 μD in a molecule of polarizability volume 1.1×10^{-31} m^3 (like CCl_4)?

[*Answer:* 2.7 kV cm^{-1}]

A polar molecule with dipole moment μ_1 can induce a dipole moment in a polarizable molecule (which may itself be either polar or non-polar) because the partial charges of the polar molecule give rise to an electric field that distorts the second molecule. That induced dipole interacts with the permanent dipole of the first molecule, and the two are attracted together (Fig. 17.4). The formula for the **dipole–induced-dipole interaction energy** is

$$V = -\frac{\mu_1^2\alpha_2}{\pi\varepsilon_0 r^6} \tag{17.10}$$

where α_2 is the polarizability of molecule 2. The negative sign shows that the interaction is attractive. For a molecule with $\mu = 1$ D (such as HCl) near a molecule of polarizability volume $\alpha' = 1.0 \times 10^{-31}$ m^3 (such as benzene, Table 17.2) the average interaction energy is about -0.8 kJ mol^{-1} when the separation is 0.3 nm. The inverse sixth-power dependence of the potential energy identifies it

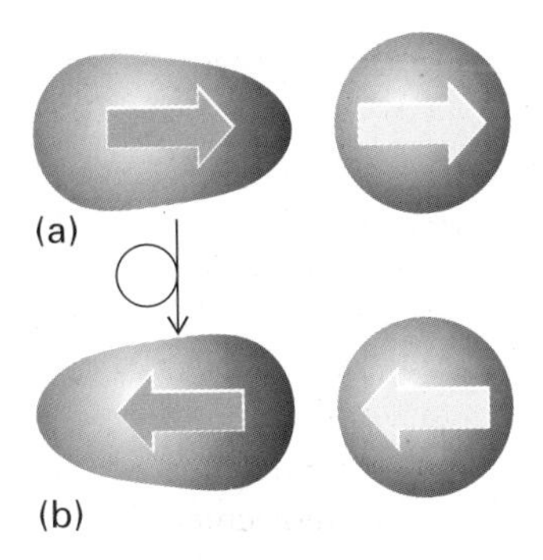

Fig. 17.4 A dipole–induced-dipole interaction. The induced dipole (light arrows) follows the changing orientation of the permanent dipole (dark arrows).

as another contribution to the van der Waals interaction.

17.5 Dispersion interactions

Finally, we consider the interactions between species that have neither a net charge nor a permanent electric dipole moment (such as two Xe atoms in a gas or two non-polar groups on the peptide residues of a protein). Despite their absence of partial charges, we know that uncharged, non-polar species can interact because they form condensed phases, such as benzene, liquid hydrogen, and liquid xenon.

The **dispersion interaction**, or **London force**, between non-polar species arises from the transient dipoles that they possess as a result of fluctuations in the instantaneous positions of their electrons (Fig. 17.5). Suppose, for instance, that the electrons in one molecule flicker into an arrangement that results in partial positive and negative charges and thus gives it an instantaneous dipole moment μ_1. While it exists, this dipole can polarize the other molecule and induce in it an instantaneous dipole moment μ_2. The two dipoles attract each other and the potential energy of the pair is lowered. Although the first molecule will go on to change the size and direction of its dipole (perhaps within 10^{-16} s), the second will follow it; that is, the two dipoles are *correlated* in direction like two meshing gears, with a positive partial charge on one molecule appearing close to a negative partial charge on the other molecule and vice versa. Because of this correlation of the relative positions of the partial charges, and their resulting attractive interaction, the attraction between the two instantaneous dipoles does not average to zero. Instead, it gives rise to a net attractive interaction. Polar molecules interact by a dispersion interaction as well as by dipole–dipole interactions, with the dispersion interaction often dominant.

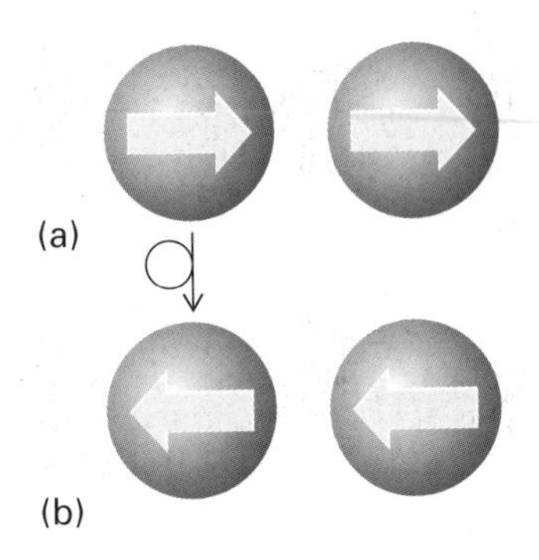

Fig. 17.5 In the dispersion interaction, an instantaneous dipole on one molecule induces a dipole on another molecule, and the two dipoles then interact to lower the energy. The directions of the two instantaneous dipoles are correlated and, although they occur in different orientations at different instants, the interaction does not average to zero.

The strength of the dispersion interaction depends on the polarizability of the first molecule because the magnitude of the instantaneous dipole moment μ_1 depends on the looseness of the control that the nuclear charge has over the outer electrons. If that control is loose, the electron distribution can undergo relatively large fluctuations. Moreover, if the control is loose, then the electron distribution can also respond strongly to applied electric fields and hence have a high polarizability. It follows that a high polarizability is a sign of large fluctuations in local charge density. The strength also depends on the polarizability of the second molecule, as that polarizability determines how readily a dipole can be induced in molecule 2 by molecule 1. We therefore expect $V \propto \alpha_1\alpha_2$. The actual calculation of the dispersion interaction is quite involved, but a reasonable approximation to the interaction energy is the **London formula:**

$$V = -\frac{2}{3} \times \frac{\alpha_1'\alpha_2'}{r^6} \times \frac{I_1 I_2}{I_1 + I_2} \tag{17.11}$$

where I_1 and I_2 are the ionization energies of the two molecules. Once again, the potential energy of interaction turns out to be proportional to the inverse sixth power of the separation, so it is a third contribution to the van der Waals interaction. For two CH_4 molecules, $V \approx -5$ kJ mol^{-1} when $r = 0.3$ nm.

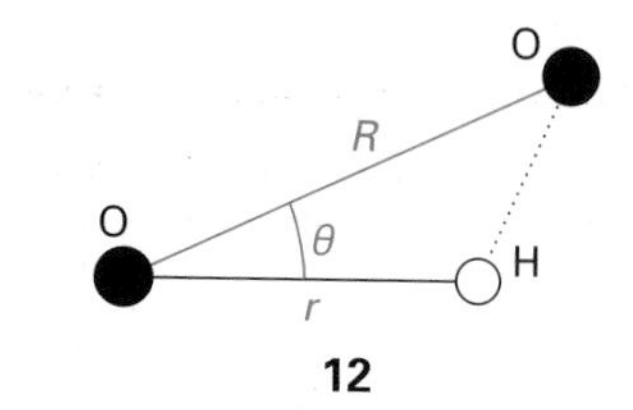

The total interaction

The van der Waals interactions are attractive interactions that vary as the inverse sixth power of the separation. However, there are several other types of interaction, both attractive and repulsive, some of which dominate the van der Waals interactions when they are present.

17.6 Hydrogen bonding

The strongest intermolecular interaction arises from the formation of a **hydrogen bond**, in which a hydrogen atom lies between two strongly electronegative atoms and binds them together. The bond is normally denoted X–H···Y, with X and Y being nitrogen, oxygen, or fluorine. Unlike the other interactions we have considered, hydrogen bonding is not universal, but is restricted to molecules that contain these atoms. A common hydrogen bond is formed between O–H groups and O atoms, as in liquid water and ice. The distance dependence of the hydrogen bond is quite different from the other interactions we have considered, and is best regarded as a 'contact' interaction, which turns on when the X–H group is in direct contact with the Y atom.

The most elementary description of the formation of a hydrogen bond is that it is the result of a Coulombic interaction between the partly exposed positive charge of a proton bound to an electron-withdrawing X atom (in the fragment X–H) and the negative charge of a lone pair on the second atom Y, as in $^{\delta-}$X–H$^{\delta+}$···:Y$^{\delta-}$. In Exercise 17.28, you are invited to use the electrostatic model to calculate the dependence of the molar potential energy of interaction on the OOH angle, denoted θ in (**12**), and the results are plotted in Fig. 17.6. We see that at $\theta = 0$, when the OHO atoms lie in a straight line, the potential energy is -19 kJ mol^{-1}. Note how sharply the energy depends on angle: it is negative only with $\pm 12°$ of linearity.

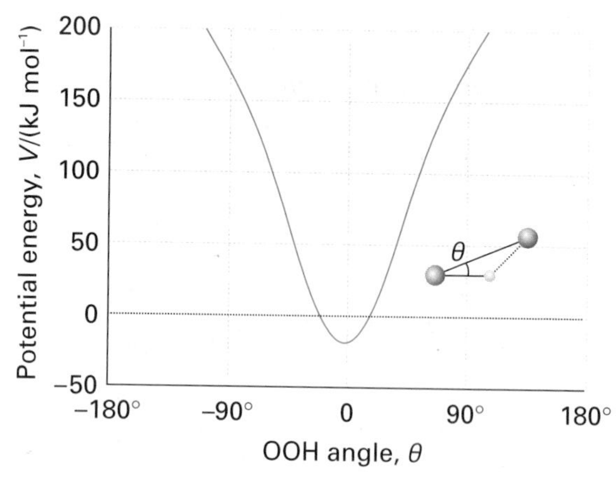

Fig. 17.6 The variation of the energy of interaction (on the electrostatic model) of a hydrogen bond as the angle between the O–H and :O groups is changed.

Molecular orbital theory provides an alternative description that is more in line with the concept of delocalized bonding and the ability of an electron pair to bind more than one pair of atoms (Section 14.15). Thus, if the X–H bond is regarded as formed from the overlap of an orbital on X, ψ_X, and a hydrogen 1*s* orbital, ψ_H, and the lone pair on Y occupies an orbital on Y, ψ_Y, then when the two molecules are close together, we can build three molecular orbitals from the three basis orbitals:

$$\psi = c_1\psi_X + c_2\psi_H + c_3\psi_Y$$

One of the molecular orbitals is bonding, one almost non-bonding, and the third antibonding (Fig. 17.7). These three orbitals need to accommodate four electrons (two from the original X–H bond and two from the lone pair of Y), so two enter the bonding orbital and two enter the non-bonding orbital. Because the antibonding orbital remains empty, the net effect—depending on the precise location of the almost non-bonding orbital—may be a lowering

Table 17.3 *Interaction potential energies*

Interaction type	Distance dependence of potential energy	Typical energy (kJ mol^{-1})	Comment
Ion–ion	$1/r$	250	Only between ions
Ion–dipole	$1/r^2$	15	
Dipole–dipole	$1/r^3$	2	Between stationary polar molecules
	$1/r^6$	0.3	Between rotating polar molecules
London (dispersion)	$1/r^6$	2	Between all types of molecules and ions

The energy of a hydrogen bond X–H···Y is typically 20 kJ mol^{-1} and occurs on contact for X, Y = N, O, or F.

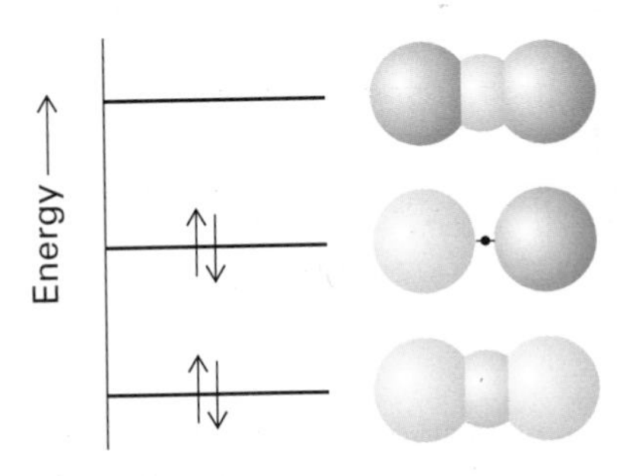

Fig. 17.7 A schematic portrayal of the molecular orbitals that can be formed from an X, H, and Y orbital and which gives rise to an X–H···Y hydrogen bond. The lowest-energy combination is fully bonding, the next non-bonding, and the uppermost is antibonding. The antibonding orbital is not occupied by the electrons provided by the X–H bond and the :Y lone pair, so the configuration shown may result in a net lowering of energy in certain cases (namely when the X and Y atoms are N, O, or F).

of energy. Recent experiments suggest that the hydrogen bonds in ice have significant covalent character and are best described by a molecular orbital treatment.

Hydrogen bond formation, which has a typical strength of the order of 20 kJ mol^{-1},[5] dominates the van der Waals interactions when it can occur. It accounts for the rigidity of molecular solids such as sucrose and ice, the low vapour pressure, high viscosity, and surface tension of liquids such as water, the secondary structure of proteins (the formation of helices and sheets of polypeptide chains), the structure of DNA and hence the transmission of genetic information, and the attachment of drugs to receptors sites in proteins (Box 17.1). Hydrogen bonding also contributes to the solubility in water of species such as ammonia and compounds containing hydroxyl groups and to the hydration of anions. In this last case, even ions such as Cl^- and HS^- can participate in hydrogen bond formation with water, as their charge enables them to interact with the hydroxylic protons of H_2O.

Table 17.3 summarizes the strengths and distance dependence of the attractive interactions that we have considered so far.

17.7 The hydrophobic effect

There is one further type of interaction that we need to consider: it is an *apparent* force that influences the shape of a macromolecule mediated by the properties of the solvent, water. First, we need to understand why hydrocarbon molecules do not dissolve appreciably in water. Experiments indicate that the transfer of a hydrocarbon molecule from a non-polar solvent into water is often exothermic ($\Delta H < 0$). Therefore, the fact that dissolving is not spontaneous must mean that entropy change is negative ($\Delta S < 0$). For example, the process

$$CH_4(\text{in } CCl_4) \rightarrow CH_4(aq)$$

has $\Delta G = +12$ kJ mol^{-1}, $\Delta H = -10$ kJ mol^{-1}, and $\Delta S = -75$ J K^{-1} mol^{-1} at 298 K. Substances characterized

[5] This figure is approximately half the enthalpy of vaporization of water: in water, there is an average of two hydrogen bonds per H_2O molecule.

Box 17.1 *Molecular recognition*

Molecular interactions are responsible for the assembly of many biological structures. Hydrogen bonding and hydrophobic interactions are primarily responsible for the three-dimensional structures of biopolymers, such as proteins, nucleic acids, and cell membranes. The binding of a ligand, or *guest*, to a biopolymer, or *host*, is also governed by molecular interactions. Examples of biological *host–guest complexes* include enzyme–substrate complexes, antigen–antibody complexes, and drug–receptor complexes. In all these cases, a site on the guest contains functional groups that can interact with complementary functional groups of the host. For example, a hydrogen bond donor group of the guest must be positioned near a hydrogen bond acceptor group of the host for tight binding to occur. It is generally true that many specific intermolecular contacts must be made in a biological host–guest complex and, as a result, a guest binds only chemically similar hosts. The strict rules governing molecular recognition of a guest by a host control every biological process, from metabolism to immunological response, and provide important clues for the design of effective drugs for the treatment of disease.

Interactions between non-polar groups can be important in the binding of a guest to a host. For example, many active sites of enzymes have hydrophobic pockets that bind non-polar groups of a substrate. In addition to dispersion, repulsive, and hydrophobic interactions, so-called *π-stacking interactions* are also possible, in which the planar π systems of aromatic macrocycles lie one on top of the other, in a nearly parallel orientation. Such interactions are responsible for the stacking of hydrogen-bonded base pairs in DNA, as shown in the illustration. Some drugs with planar π systems, shown as a rectangle in the illustration, are effective because they intercalate between base pairs through π-stacking interactions, causing the helix to unwind slightly and altering the function of DNA.

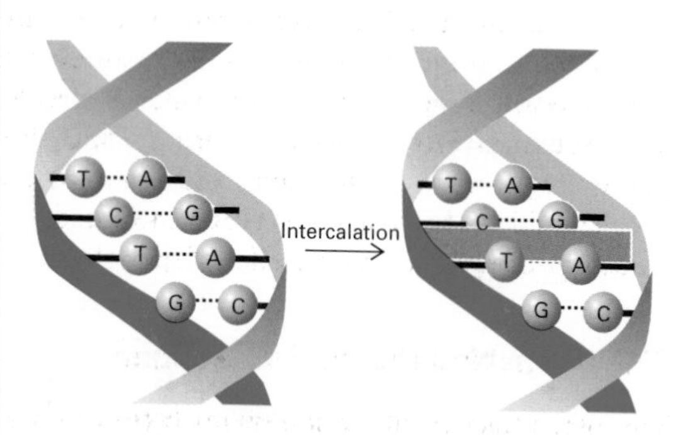

Some drugs with planar π systems, shown by a coloured rectangle, intercalate between the base pairs of DNA.

Coulombic interactions can be important in the interior of a biopolymer host, where the relative permittivity can be much lower than that of the aqueous exterior. For example, at physiological pH, amino acid side chains containing carboxylic acid or amine groups are negatively and positively charged, respectively, and can attract each other. Dipole–dipole interactions are also possible because many of the building blocks of biopolymers are polar, including the peptide link, –CONH– (see Exercise 2). However, hydrogen bonding interactions are by far the most prevalent in a biological host–guest complexes. Many effective drugs on the market bind tightly and inhibit the action of enzymes that are associated with the progress of a disease. In many cases, a successful inhibitor will be able to form the same hydrogen bonds with the binding site that the normal substrate of the enzyme can form, except that the drug is chemically inert towards the enzyme. This strategy has been used in the design of drugs for the treatment of acquired immunodeficiency syndrome (AIDS), caused by the human immunodeficiency virus (HIV) (see Exercise 2).

Exercise 1 Molecular orbital calculations may be used to predict structures of intermolecular complexes. Hydrogen bonds between purine and pyrimidine bases are responsible for the double-helix structure of DNA. Consider methyladenine (**B1**, with R = CH_3) and methylthymine (**B2**, with R = CH_3) as models of two bases that can form hydrogen bonds in DNA. (a) Using molecular modelling software, calculate the atomic charges of all atoms in methyladenine and methylthymine. (b) Based on your tabulation of atomic charges, identify the atoms in methyladenine and methylthymine that are likely to participate in hydrogen bonds. (c) Draw all possible adenine–thymine

R
N N
H_2N N
HN

B1

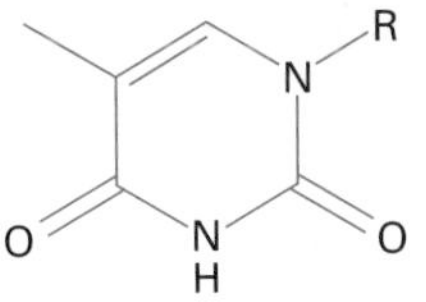

B2

pairs that can be linked by hydrogen bonds, keeping in mind that linear arrangements of the A–H···B fragments are preferred in DNA. For this step, you may want to use your molecular modelling software to align the molecules properly. (d) Consult a biochemistry textbook and determine which of the pairs that you drew in part (c) occur naturally in DNA molecules.

Exercise 2 For mature HIV particles to form in cells of the host organism, several large proteins coded for by the viral genetic material must be cleaved by a protease enzyme. The drug Crixivan (**B3**) is a competitive inhibitor

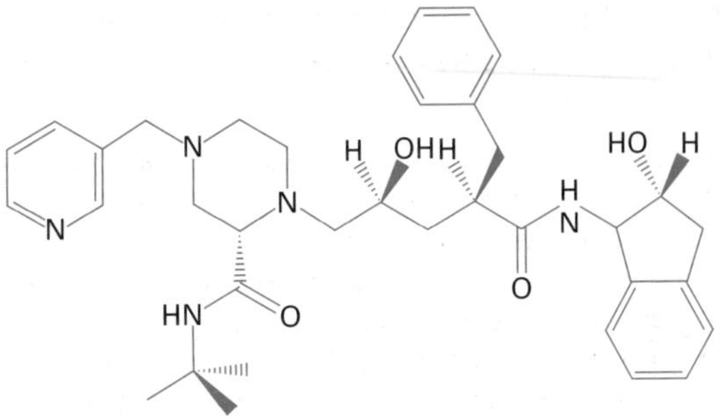

B3 Crixivan

of HIV protease and has several molecular features that optimize binding to the active site of the enzyme. Consult the current literature and prepare a brief report summarizing molecular interactions between Crixivan and HIV protease that are thought to be responsible for the drug's efficacy. (*Hint*. A good starting point is R. E. Babine and S. L. Bender, *Chem. Rev.* **97**, 1359–1472 (1997).)

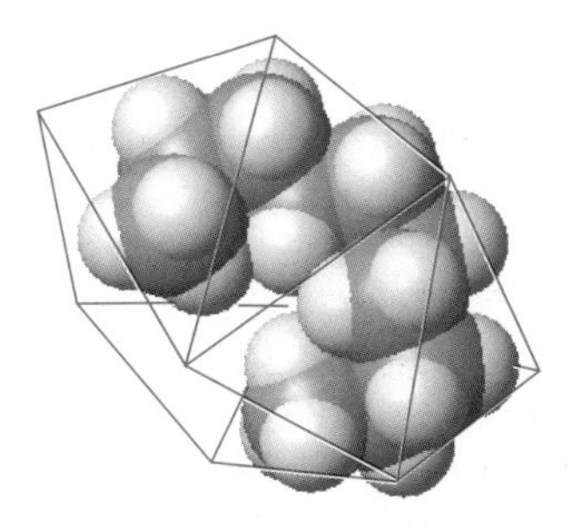

Fig. 17.8 When a hydrocarbon molecule is surrounded by water, the water molecules form a clathrate cage. As a result of this acquisition of structure, the entropy of the water decreases, so the dispersal of the hydrocarbon into water is entropy-opposed; the coalescence of the hydrocarbon into a single large blob is entropy-favoured.

by a positive Gibbs energy of transfer from a non-polar to a polar solvent are classified as **hydrophobic**.

The origin of the decrease in entropy that prevents hydrocarbons from dissolving in water is the formation of a solvent cage around the hydrophobic molecule (Fig. 17.8). The formation of this cage decreases the entropy of the system because the water molecules must adopt a less disordered arrangement than in the bulk liquid. However, when many solute molecules cluster together, fewer (albeit larger) cages are required and more solvent molecules are free to move. The net effect of formation of large clusters of hydrophobic molecules is then a decrease in the organization of the solvent and therefore a net *increase* in entropy of the system. This increase in entropy of the solvent is large enough to render spontaneous the association of hydrophobic molecules in a polar solvent.

The increase in entropy that results from the decrease in structural demands on the solvent is the origin of the **hydrophobic effect**, which tends to encourage the clustering of hydrophobic groups in micelles and biopolymers. Thus, the presence of hydrophobic groups in polypeptides results in an increase in structure of the surrounding water and a decrease in entropy. The entropy can increase if the hydrophobic groups are twisted into the interior of the molecule, which liberates the water molecules and results in an increase in their disorder. The hydrophobic interaction is an example of an ordering process, a kind of virtual force, that is mediated by a tendency towards greater disorder of the solvent.

17.8 Modelling the total interaction

The total attractive interaction energy between rotating molecules that cannot participate in hydrogen bonding is the sum of the contributions from the

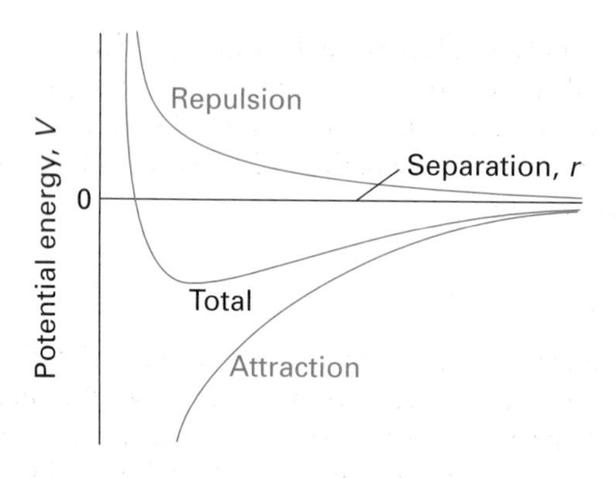

Fig. 17.9 The general form of an intermolecular potential energy curve (the graph of the potential energy of two closed-shell species as the distance between them is changed). The attractive (negative) contribution has a long range, but the repulsive (positive) interaction increases more sharply once the molecules come into contact. The overall potential energy is shown by the line labelled Total.

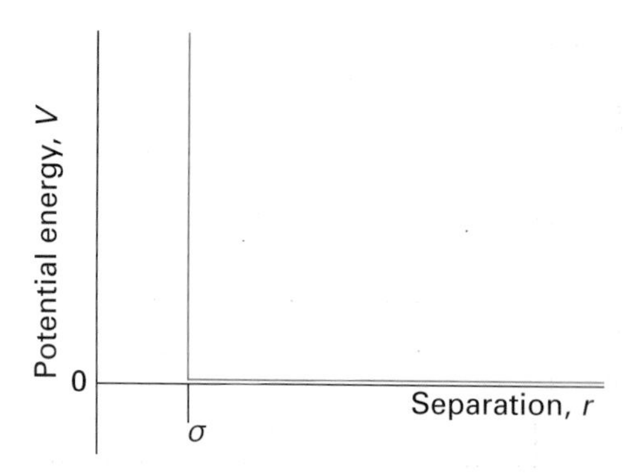

Fig. 17.10 The true intermolecular potential can be modelled in a variety of ways. One of the simplest is this *hard-sphere potential*, in which there is no potential energy of interaction until the two molecules are separated by a distance σ when the potential energy rises abruptly to infinity as the impenetrable hard spheres repel each other.

dipole–dipole, dipole–induced-dipole, and dispersion interactions. Only the dispersion interaction contributes if both molecules are non-polar. All three interactions vary as the inverse sixth power of the separation, so we may write the total van der Waals interaction energy as

$$V = -\frac{C}{r^6} \qquad (17.12)$$

where C is a coefficient that depends on the identity of the molecules and the type of interaction between them.

Repulsive terms become important and begin to dominate the attractive forces when molecules are squeezed together (Fig. 17.9), for instance, during the impact of a collision, under the force exerted by a weight pressing on a substance, or simply as a result of the attractive forces drawing the molecules together. These repulsive interactions arise in large measure from the Pauli exclusion principle, which forbids pairs of electrons being in the same region of space. The repulsions increase steeply with decreasing separation in a way that can be deduced only by very extensive, complicated molecular structure calculations. In many cases, however, progress can be made by using a greatly simplified representation of the potential energy, where the details are ignored and the general features expressed by a few adjustable parameters.

One such approximation is the **hard-sphere potential**, in which it is assumed that the potential energy rises abruptly to infinity as soon as the particles come within some separation σ (Fig. 17.10):

$$V = \begin{cases} \infty & \text{for } r \le \sigma \\ 0 & \text{for } r > \sigma \end{cases} \qquad (17.13)$$

This very simple potential is surprisingly useful for assessing a number of properties.

Another widely used approximation is to express the short-range repulsive potential energy as inversely proportional to a high power of r:

$$V = +\frac{C^*}{r^n} \qquad (17.14)$$

where C^* is another constant (the star signifies repulsion). Typically, n is set equal to 12, in which case the repulsion dominates the $1/r^6$ attractions strongly at short separations because then $C^*/r^{12} \gg C/r^6$. The sum of the repulsive interaction with $n = 12$ and the attractive interaction given by eqn 17.12 is called the **Lennard-Jones (12,6)-potential.** It is normally written in the form

$$V = 4\varepsilon\left\{\left(\frac{\sigma}{r}\right)^{12} - \left(\frac{\sigma}{r}\right)^{6}\right\} \qquad (17.15)$$

and is drawn in Fig. 17.11. The two parameters are now ε (epsilon), the depth of the well, and σ, the separation at which $V = 0$. Some typical values are

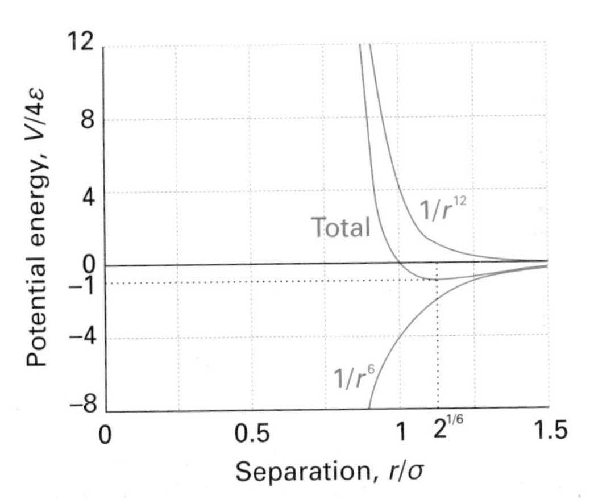

Fig. 17.11 The Lennard-Jones potential is another approximation to the true intermolecular potential energy curves. It models the attractive component by a contribution that is proportional to $1/r^6$, and the repulsive component by a contribution that is proportional to $1/r^{12}$. Specifically, these choices result in the Lennard-Jones (12,6)-potential. Although there are good theoretical reasons for the former, there is plenty of evidence to show that $1/r^{12}$ is only a very poor approximation to the repulsive part of the curve.

Table 17.4

Lennard-Jones parameters for the (12,6)-potential

	$\varepsilon/(\text{kJ mol}^{-1})$	σ/pm
Ar	128	342
Br_2	536	427
C_6H_6	454	527
Cl_2	368	412
H_2	34	297
He	11	258
Xe	236	406

listed in Table 17.4. The well minimum occurs at $r = 2^{1/6}\sigma$. Although the (12,6)-potential has been used in many calculations, there is plenty of evidence to show that $1/r^{12}$ is a very poor representation of the repulsive potential, and that the exponential form $e^{-r/\sigma}$ is superior. An exponential function is more faithful to the exponential decay of atomic wavefunctions at large distances, and hence to the distance dependence of the overlap that is responsible for repulsion. However, a disadvantage of the exponential form is that it is slower to compute, which is important when considering the interactions between the large numbers of atoms in liquids and macromolecules.[6]

17.9 Molecules in motion

The intermolecular interactions we have described govern the shapes that complicated molecules adopt and the motion of molecules in liquids. We deal with the structural aspects of these interaction in the next chapter. In this section, we consider how to take the interactions into account to describe molecular motion.

In a **molecular dynamics** simulation, the molecule is set in motion by heating it to a specified temperature and the possible trajectories of all atoms under the influence of the intermolecular forces are calculated from Newton's laws of motion. For instance, if the interaction is described by a Lennard-Jones potential, eqn 17.15, the force along the line of centres of two neighbouring molecules is

$$F = -24\varepsilon\left\{\frac{2\sigma^{12}}{r^{13}} - \frac{\sigma^6}{r^7}\right\} \tag{17.16}$$

The equations of motion are solved numerically, allowing the molecules to adjust their locations and velocities in femtosecond steps (1 fs = 10^{-15} s). The calculation is repeated for tens of thousands of such steps.

The same technique can be used to examine the internal motion of macromolecules, such as the proteins we consider in Chapter 18, and software packages are available that calculate the trajectories of a large number of atoms in three dimensions. The trajectories correspond to the conformations that the molecule can sample at the temperature of the simulation. At very low temperatures, the neighbouring components of the molecule are trapped in wells like that in Fig. 17.9, the atomic motion is restricted, and only a few conformations are possible. At high temperatures, more potential energy barriers can be overcome and more conformations are possible.

[6] A further computational advantage of the (12,6)-potential is that once r^6 has been calculated, r^{12} is obtained by taking the square.

In the **Monte Carlo method**, the atoms of a macromolecule or the molecules of a liquid are moved through small but otherwise random distances, and the change in potential energy is calculated. If the potential energy is not greater than before the change, then the new arrangement is accepted. However, if the potential energy is greater than before the change, it is necessary to use a criterion for rejecting or accepting it. To establish this criterion, we use the Boltzmann distribution (Section 22.1), which states that at equilibrium at a temperature T the ratio of populations of two states that differ in energy by ΔE is $e^{-\Delta E/kT}$, where k is Boltzmann's constant. In the Monte Carlo method, the exponential factor is calculated for the new atomic arrangement and compared with a random number between 0 and 1; if the factor is larger than the random number, the new arrangement is accepted; if the factor is not larger, then the new arrangement is rejected and another one is generated instead.

CHECKLIST OF KEY IDEAS

You should now be familiar with the following concepts:

☐ 1 A van der Waals force is an attractive interaction between closed-shell molecules with a potential energy that is inversely proportional to the sixth power of the separation.

☐ 2 A polar molecule is a molecule with a permanent electric dipole moment; the magnitude of a dipole moment is the product of the partial charge and the separation.

☐ 3 Dipole moments are approximately additive (as vectors, eqn 17.3).

☐ 4 The potential energy of the dipole–dipole interaction between two fixed (non-rotating) molecules is proportional to $\mu_1\mu_2/r^3$ and between molecules that are free to rotate is proportional to $\mu_1^2\mu_2^2/kTr^6$.

☐ 5 The dipole–induced-dipole interaction between two molecules is proportional to $\mu_1^2\alpha_2/r^6$, where α is the polarizability.

☐ 6 The polarizability is a measure of the ability of an electric field to induce a dipole moment in a molecule ($\mu = \alpha\mathcal{E}$).

☐ 7 The potential energy of the dispersion (or London) interaction is proportional to $\alpha_1\alpha_2/r^6$.

☐ 8 A hydrogen bond is an interaction of the form X–H···Y, where X and Y are N, O, or F.

☐ 9 The hydrophobic interaction is an ordering process mediated by a tendency towards greater disorder of the solvent: it causes hydrophobic groups to cluster together.

☐ 10 The Lennard-Jones (6,12)-potential, $V = 4\varepsilon\{(\sigma/r)^{12} - (\sigma/r)^6\}$, is a model of the total intermolecular potential energy.

☐ 11 A molecular dynamics calculation uses Newton's laws of motion to calculate the motion of molecules in a fluid (and the motion of atoms in macromolecules).

☐ 12 A Monte Carlo simulation uses a selection criterion for accepting or rejecting a new arrangement of atoms or molecules.

DISCUSSION QUESTIONS

17.1 Explain how the permanent dipole moment and the polarizability of a molecule arise.

17.2 Describe the formation of a hydrogen bond in terms of (a) an electrostatic interaction and (b) molecular orbital theory.

17.3 Account for the hydrophobic effect and discuss its manifestations.

17.4 Outline the procedures used to calculate the motion of molecules in fluids and atoms in molecules.

EXERCISES

The symbol ‡ indicates that calculus is required.

17.5 Estimate the dipole moment of an HCl molecule from the electronegativities of the elements and express the answer in debye and coulomb-metres.

17.6 Use the VSEPR model to judge whether SF_4 is polar.

17.7 The electric dipole moment of toluene (methylbenzene) is 0.40 D. Estimate the dipole moments of the three xylenes (dimethylbenzenes). Which value can you be sure about?

17.8 From the information in the preceding problem, estimate the dipole moments of (a) 1,2,3-trimethylbenzene, (b) 1,2,4-trimethylbenzene, and (c) 1,3,5-trimethylbenzene. Which value can you be sure about?

17.9 Calculate the resultant of two dipoles of magnitude 1.50 D and 0.80 D that make an angle 109.5° to each other.

17.10 At low temperatures a substituted 1,2-dichloroethane molecule can adopt the three conformations (**13**), (**14**), and (**15**) with different probabilities. Suppose that the dipole moment of each bond is 1.50 D. Calculate the mean dipole moment of the molecule when (a) all three conformations are equally likely, (b) only conformation (**14**) occurs, (c) the three conformations occur with probabilities in the ratio 2:1:1 and (d) 1:2:2.

Cl
Cl
13

Cl
Cl
14

Cl
Cl
15

17.11 Calculate the electric dipole moment of a glycine molecule using the partial charges in Table 17.1 and the locations of the atoms shown in (**16**).

(−86, 118, 37) H
(34, 146, −98) H
C (−195, 70, −38)
C (199, 16, −38)
O
N
H (−199, −1, −100)
H (−80, −110, −111)
O (49, −107, 88)
O (82, −15, 34)
H (129, −146, 126)

16 Glycine

17.12 (a) Plot the magnitude of the electric dipole moment of hydrogen peroxide as the H–OO–H (azimuthal) angle ϕ changes. Use the dimensions shown in (**17**). (b) Devise a way for depicting how the angle as well as the magnitude changes.

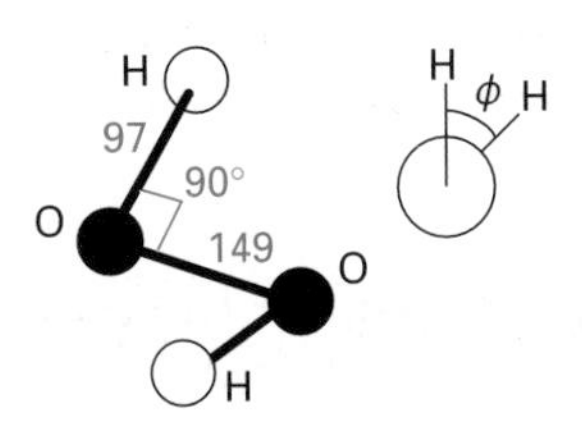

17 Hydrogen peroxide

17.13 Calculate the molar energy required to reverse the direction of a water molecule located (a) 100 pm, (b) 300 pm from a Li^+ ion. Take the dipole moment of water as 1.85 D.

17.14 Show, by following the procedure in Derivation 17.1, that eqn 17.6 describes the potential energy of two electric dipole moments in the orientation shown in (**10**) in the text.

17.15 What is the contribution to the total molar energy of (a) the kinetic energy, (b) the potential energy of interaction between hydrogen chloride molecules in a gas at 298 K when 1.00 mol of molecules is confined to 10 dm^3? Is the kinetic theory of gases justifiable in this case?

17.16 (a) What are the units of the polarizability α? (b) Show that the units of polarizability volume are cubic metres (m^3).

17.17 The electric field at a distance r from a point charge q is equal to $q/4\pi\varepsilon_0 r^2$. How close to a water molecule (of polarizability volume 1.48×10^{-30} m^3) must a proton approach before the dipole moment it induces is equal to the permanent dipole moment of the molecule (1.85 D)?

17.18 Phenylanine (Phe, **18**) is a naturally occurring amino acid with a benzene ring. What is the energy of interaction between its benzene ring and the electric dipole moment of a neighbouring peptide group? Take the distance between the groups as 4.0 nm and treat the benzene ring as benzene itself. Take the dipole moment of the peptide group as 2.7 D.

O
H_2N
OH

18 Phenylalanine

17.19 Now consider the London interaction between the benzene rings of two Phe residues (see Exercise 17.18). Estimate the potential energy of attraction between two such rings (treated as benzene molecules) separated by 4.0 nm. For the ionization energy, use $I = 5.0$ eV.

17.20 In a region of the oxygen-storage protein myoglobin, the OH group of a tyrosine residue is hydrogen bonded to the N atom of a histidine residue in the geometry shown in (**19**). Use the partial charges in Table 17.1 to estimate the potential energy of this interaction.

19

17.21 Given that force is the negative slope of the potential, calculate the distance dependence of the force acting between two non-bonded groups of atoms in a polypeptide chain that have a London dispersion interaction with each other. What is the separation at which the force is zero? (*Hint.* Calculate the slope by considering the potential energy at R and $R + \delta R$, with $\delta R \ll R$, and evaluating $\{V(R+\delta R) - V(R)\}/\delta R$. You should use the expansion in Derivation 17.1 together with

$$(1 \pm x + \cdots)^6 = 1 \pm 6x + \cdots \qquad (1 \pm x + \cdots)^{12} = 1 \pm 12x + \cdots$$

At the end of the calculation, let δR become vanishingly small.)

17.22 ‡Repeat Exercise 17.21 by noting that $F = -\mathrm{d}V/\mathrm{d}r$ and differentiating the expression for V.

17.23 Acetic acid vapour contains a proportion of planar, hydrogen-bonded dimers (**20**). The apparent dipole moment of molecules in pure gaseous acetic acid increases with increasing temperature. Suggest an interpretation of this observation.

20 $(CH_3COOH)_2$

17.24 The coordinates of the atoms of an acetic acid dimer are set out in more detail in (**21**). Consider only the Coulombic interactions between the partial charges indicated by the dotted lines and their symmetry-related equivalents. At what distance R does the attraction become attractive?

21 $(CH_3COOH)_2$

17.25 The potential energy of a CH_3 group in ethane as it is rotated around the C–C bond can be written $V = \frac{1}{2}V_0(1 + \cos 3\phi)$, where ϕ is the azimuthal angle (**22**) and $V_0 = 11.6$ kJ mol^{-1}. (a) What is the change in potential energy between the trans and fully eclipsed conformations? (b) Show that for small variations in angle, the torsional (twisting) motion around the C–C bond can be expected to be that of a harmonic oscillator. (c) Estimate the vibrational frequency of this torsional oscillation.

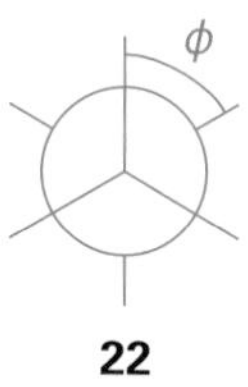

22

17.26 Suppose you distrusted the Lennard-Jones (12,6)-potential for assessing a particular polypeptide conformation, and replaced the repulsive term by an exponential function of the form $e^{-r/\sigma}$. Sketch the form of the potential energy and locate the distance at which it is a minimum.

17.27 ‡Use calculus to identify the distance at which the exponential-6 potential described in Exercise 7.26 is a minimum.

17.28 Consider the arrangement shown in (**12**) for a system consisting of an O–H group and an O atom, and then use the electrostatic model of the hydrogen bond to calculate the dependence of the molar potential energy of interaction on the angle θ. Set the partial charges on H and O to $0.45e$ and $-0.83e$, respectively, and take $R = 200$ pm and $r = 95.7$ pm.

Chapter 18

Macromolecules and aggregates

Naturally occurring macromolecules include polysaccharides such as cellulose, polypeptides such as protein enzymes, and polynucleotides such as deoxyribonucleic acid (DNA). Synthetic macromolecules include **polymers** such as nylon and polystyrene that are manufactured by stringing together and (in some cases) cross-linking smaller units known as **monomers**.

Macromolecules give rise to special problems that include the shapes and the lengths of polymer chains, the determination of their sizes, and the large deviations from ideality of their solutions. Natural macromolecules differ in certain respects from synthetic macromolecules, particularly in their composition and the resulting structure, but the two share a number of common properties. We concentrate on these common properties here. Another level of complexity arises when small molecules aggregate into large particles in a process called 'self-assembly' and give rise to aggregates. One example is the assembly of haemoglobin from four myoglobin-like polypeptides. A similar type of aggregation gives rise to a variety of **disperse phases**, which include colloids. The properties of these disperse phases resemble to a certain extent the properties of solutions of macromolecules, and we describe their common attributes in the second part of this chapter.

Synthetic and biological macromolecules

Macromolecules provide an interesting and important illustration of how the interactions described in Chapter 17 jointly determine the shape of a molecule and its properties. The overall shape of a polypeptide, for instance, is sustained by a variety of molecular interactions, including van der Waals interactions, hydrogen bonding, and the hydrophobic effect.

18.1 Determination of size and shape

X-ray diffraction (Section 15.12) can reveal the position of almost every heavy atom (that is, every atom other than hydrogen) even in very large molecules. However, there are several reasons why other techniques must also be used. In the first place, the sample might be a mixture of molecules with different chain lengths and extent of cross-linking, in which case sharp X-ray images are not obtained. Even if all the molecules in the sample are identical, it might prove impossible to obtain a single crystal. Furthermore, although work on proteins and DNA has shown how immensely interesting and motivating the data can be, the information is incomplete. For instance, what can be said about the shape of the molecule in its natural environment, a biological cell? What can be said about the response of its shape to changes in its environment?

Many proteins (and specifically protein enzymes) are **monodisperse**, meaning that they have a single, definite molar mass.[1] A synthetic polymer, however, is **polydisperse**, in the sense that a sample is a mixture of molecules with various chain lengths and molar masses. The various techniques that are used to measure molar masses result in different types of mean values of polydisperse systems. The **number-average molar mass**, $\bar{M}_n$, is the value obtained by weighting each molar mass by the number of molecules of that mass present in the sample:

$$\bar{M}_n = \frac{1}{N}\sum_i N_i M_i \qquad (18.1)$$

where N_i is the number of molecules with molar mass M_i and there are N molecules in all. The **weight-average molar mass**, $\bar{M}_w$, is the average calculated by weighting the molar masses of the molecules by the mass of each one present in the sample:

$$\bar{M}_w = \frac{1}{m}\sum_i m_i M_i \qquad (18.2)$$

In this expression, m_i is the total mass of molecules of molar mass M_i and m is the total mass of the sample. In general, these two averages are different and the ratio $\bar{M}_w/\bar{M}_n$ is called the **heterogeneity index** (or 'polydispersity index'). In the determination of protein molar masses we expect the various averages to be the same because the sample is monodisperse (unless there has been degradation). A synthetic polymer normally spans a range of molar masses and the different averages yield different values. Typical synthetic materials have $\bar{M}_w/\bar{M}_n \approx 4$. The term 'monodisperse' is conventionally applied to synthetic polymers in which this index is less than 1.1; commercial polyethylene samples might be much more heterogeneous, with a ratio close to 30. One consequence of a narrow molar mass distribution for synthetic polymers is often a higher degree of three-dimensional long-range order in the solid and therefore higher density and melting point. The spread of values is controlled by the choice of catalyst and reaction conditions.

Example 18.1

Determining the heterogeneity index of a polymer sample

Determine the heterogeneity index of a sample of poly(vinyl chloride) from the following data:

Molar mass interval/ (kg mol^{-1})	Average molar mass within interval/ (kg mol^{-1})	Mass of sample within interval/g
5–10	7.5	9.6
10–15	12.5	8.7
15–20	17.5	8.9
20–25	22.5	5.6
25–30	27.5	3.1
30–35	32.5	1.7

[1] There may be small variations, such as one amino acid replacing another, depending on the source of the sample.

Strategy We begin by calculating the number-average and weight-average molar masses from eqns 18.1 and 18.2, respectively. To do so, we weight the molar mass within each interval by the number and mass, respectively, of the molecule in each interval. We obtain the amount in each interval by dividing the mass of the sample in each interval by the average molar mass for that interval. Because number of molecules is proportional to amount of substance (the number of moles), the number-weighted average can be obtained directly from the amounts in each interval. Finally, we use the average molar masses to calculate the heterogeneity index of the sample as the ratio $\bar{M}_w/\bar{M}_n$.

Solution The amounts in each interval are as follows:

Interval	5–10	10–15	15–20
Molar mass/(kg mol^{-1})	7.5	12.5	17.5
Amount/mmol	1.30	0.70	0.51

Interval	20–25	25–30	30–35
Molar mass/(kg mol^{-1})	22.5	27.5	32.5
Amount/mmol	0.25	0.11	0.052

Total amount/mmol: 2.92

The number-average molar mass is therefore

$$\bar{M}_n/(\text{kg mol}^{-1}) = \frac{1}{2.92}(1.3\times 7.5 + 0.70\times 12.5 + 0.51$$
$$\times 17.5 + 0.25\times 22.5 + 0.11\times 27.5 + 0.052\times 32.5) = 13$$

The weight-average molar mass is calculated directly from the data by first noting that adding the masses in each interval gives the total mass of the sample, 37.6 g. It follows that:

$$\bar{M}_w/(\text{kg mol}^{-1}) = \frac{1}{37.6}(9.6\times 7.5 + 8.7\times 12.5 + 8.9$$
$$\times 17.5 + 5.6\times 22.5 + 3.1\times 27.5 + 1.7\times 32.5) = 16$$

The heterogeneity index is $\bar{M}_w/\bar{M}_n = 1.2$.

Self-test 18.1

The *Z-average molar mass* is defined as

$$\bar{M}_Z = \frac{\sum_i N_i M_i^3}{\sum_i N_i M_i^2}$$

and can be interpreted in terms of the mean cubic molar mass. Evaluate the *Z*-average molar mass of the sample described in Example 18.1.

[*Answer:* 19 kg mol^{-1}]

Number-average molar masses may be determined by measuring the osmotic pressure of polymer solutions (Section 6.8). The upper limit for the reliability of membrane osmometry is about 1000 kDa (1 kDa = 1 kg mol^{-1}). A major problem for macromolecules of relatively low molar mass (less than about 10 kDa), however, is their ability to percolate through the membrane. One consequence of this partial permeability is that membrane osmometry tends to overestimate the average molar mass of a polydisperse mixture. Techniques for the determination of molar mass and polydispersity that are not limited in this way include mass spectrometry, laser light scattering, ultracentrifugation, electrophoresis, and chromatography.

Mass spectrometry is among the most accurate techniques for the determination of molar masses. The procedure consists of ionizing the sample in the gas phase and then measuring the mass-to-charge number ratio (m/z) of all ions. Macromolecules present a challenge because it is difficult to produce gaseous ions of large species without fragmentation. However, **matrix-assisted laser desorption/ionization** (MALDI) has overcome this problem. In this technique, the macromolecule is embedded in a solid matrix composed of an organic material and inorganic salts, such as sodium chloride or silver trifluoroacetate. This sample is then irradiated with a pulsed laser. The laser energy ejects electronically excited matrix ions, cations, and neutral macromolecules, thus creating a dense gas plume above the sample surface. The macromolecule is ionized by collisions and complexation with small cations, such as H^+, Na^+, and Ag^+, and the masses of the resulting ions are determined in a mass spectrometer.

Figure 18.1 shows the MALDI mass spectrum of a polydisperse sample of poly(butylene adipate) (PBA, **1**). The MALDI technique produces mostly singly charged molecular ions that are not fragmented. Therefore, the multiple peaks in the spectrum arise from polymers of different lengths (different 'n-mers'), with the intensity of each peak being proportional to the abundance of each n-mer in the sample. Values of $\bar{M}_n$, $\bar{M}_w$, and the heterogeneity index can be calculated from the data. It is also possible to use the mass spectrum to verify the structure of a polymer, as shown in the following example.

Example 18.2

Interpreting the mass spectrum of a polymer

The mass spectrum in Fig. 18.1 consists of peaks spaced by 200 g mol^{-1}. The peak at 4113 g mol^{-1} corresponds to the polymer for which $n = 20$. From these data, verify that the sample consists of polymers with the general structure given by (**1**).

1 Poly(butylene adipate)

Strategy Because each peak corresponds to a different value of n, the molar mass difference, ΔM, between peaks corresponds to the molar mass, M, of the repeating unit (the group inside the brackets in **1**). Furthermore, the molar mass of the terminal groups (the groups outside the brackets in **1**) may be obtained from the molar mass of any peak, by using

$$M(\text{terminal groups}) = M(n\text{-mer}) - n\,\Delta M - M(\text{cation})$$

where the last term corresponds to the molar mass of the cation that attaches to the macromolecule during ionization.

Solution The value of ΔM is consistent with the molar mass of the repeating unit shown in (**1**), which is 200 g mol^{-1}. The molar mass of the terminal group is calculated by recalling that Na^+ is the cation in the matrix:

$$\begin{aligned} &M(\text{terminal group}) \\ &= 4113\text{ g mol}^{-1} - 20(200\text{ g mol}^{-1}) - 23\text{ g mol}^{-1} \\ &= 90\text{ g mol}^{-1} \end{aligned}$$

The result is consistent with the molar mass of the $-O(CH_2)_4OH$ terminal group (89 g mol^{-1}) plus the molar mass of the $-H$ terminal group (1 g mol^{-1}).

Self-test 18.2

What would be the molar mass of the $n = 20$ polymer if silver trifluoroacetate were used instead of NaCl in the preparation of the matrix?

[*Answer:* 4.2 kg mol^{-1}]

In a gravitational field, heavy particles settle towards the foot of a column of solution by the process called **sedimentation.** The rate of sedimentation depends on the strength of the field and on the masses and shapes of the particles. Spherical molecules (and compact molecules in general) sediment faster than rod-like or extended molecules. For example, DNA helices sediment much faster when they are collapsed into a random coil, so sedimentation rates can be used to study denaturation (the loss of structure). Sedimentation is normally very slow, but it can be accelerated by **ultracentrifugation,** a technique that replaces the gravitational field with a centrifugal field. The effect is achieved in an ultracentrifuge, which is essentially a cylinder that can be rotated at high speed about its axis with a sample in a cell near its periphery (Fig. 18.2). Modern ultracentrifuges can produce accelerations equivalent to about 10^5 that of gravity ('10^5 g'). Initially the sample is uniform, but the 'top' (innermost) boundary of the solute moves outwards as sedimentation proceeds and the rate at which it recedes can be interpreted in terms of the number-average molar mass. In an alternative 'equilibrium' version of the technique, the weight-average molar mass can be obtained from the ratio of concentrations c of the macromolecules at two different radii in a centrifuge operating at angular frequency ω:

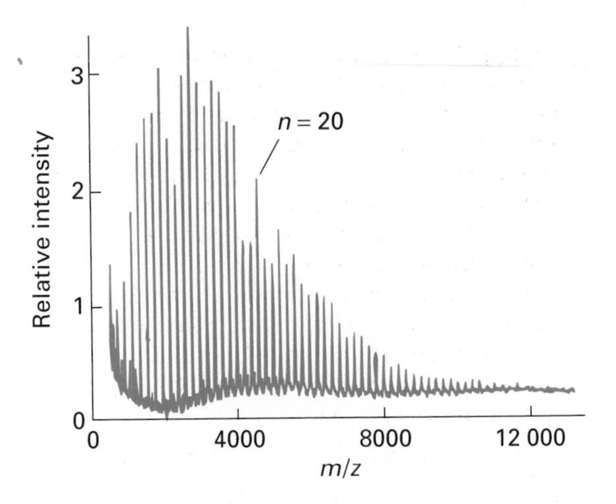

Fig. 18.1 MALDI-TOF spectrum of a sample of poly(butylene adipate) with $\bar{M}_n$ = 4525 g mol^{-1}. (Adapted from D. C. Muddiman *et al., J. Chem. Educ.* **74**, 1288 (1997).)

$$\bar{M}_w = \frac{2RT}{(r_2^2 - r_1^2)b\omega^2} \ln \frac{c_2}{c_1} \qquad (18.3)$$

where b is a correction factor that takes into account the buoyancy of the medium. The centrifuge is run

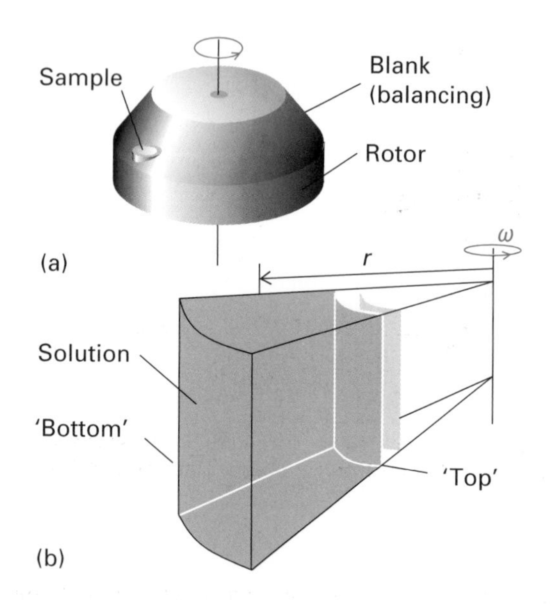

Fig. 18.2 (a) An ultracentrifuge head. The sample on one side is balanced by a blank diametrically opposite. (b) Detail of the sample cavity: the 'top' surface is the inner surface, and the centrifugal force causes sedimentation towards the outer surface; a particle at a radius r experiences a force of magnitude $mr\omega^2$.

more slowly in this technique than in the sedimentation rate method to avoid having all the solute pressed in a thin film against the bottom of the cell. At these slower speeds, several days may be needed for equilibrium to be reached.

Many macromolecules, such as DNA, are charged and move in response to an electric field. This motion is called **electrophoresis**. Electrophoretic mobility is a result of a constant drift speed reached by an ion when the electrical driving force is matched by the frictional drag force. Electrophoresis is a very valuable tool in the separation of biopolymers from complex mixtures, such as those resulting from fractionation of biological cells. In **gel electrophoresis**, migration takes place through a gel slab. In **capillary electrophoresis**, the sample is dispersed in a medium (such as methylcellulose) and held in a thin glass or plastic tube with diameters ranging from 20 to 100 μm. The small size of the apparatus makes it easy to dissipate heat when large electric fields are applied. Excellent separations may be effected in minutes rather than hours. Each polymer fraction emerging from the capillary can be characterized further by other techniques, such as MALDI.

Light scattering measurements of polymer size are based on the observation that large particles scatter light very efficiently. A familiar example is the light scattered by specks of dust in a sunbeam. Analysis of the intensity of light scattered by a sample at different angles relative to the incident radiation (typically from a laser beam at a single wavelength) yields the size and molar mass of a polymer, large aggregate (such as a colloid; see Section 18.6), or biological system ranging in size from a protein to a virus. A special laser scattering technique, **dynamic light scattering**, can be used to investigate the diffusion of polymers in solution. Consider two polymer molecules being irradiated by a laser beam. Suppose that at a time t the scattered waves from these particles interfere constructively at the detector, leading to a large signal. However, as the molecules move through the solution, the scattered waves may interfere destructively at another time t' and result in no signal. When this behaviour is extended to a very large number of molecules in solution, it results in fluctuations in light intensity that can be analysed to reveal the molar mass and diffusion coefficient of the polymer. Unlike mass spectrometry, laser light scattering measurements may be performed in nearly intact samples; often the only preparation required is filtration.

18.2 Models of structure: random coils

The most likely conformation of a chain of identical units not capable of forming hydrogen bonds or any other type of specific bond is a **random coil**. Polyethylene is a simple example. The random coil model is a helpful starting point for estimating the orders of magnitude of the properties of polymers and denatured proteins in solution.

The simplest model of a random coil is a **freely jointed chain**,[2] in which any bond is free to make any angle with respect to the preceding one (Fig. 18.3). We assume that the residues occupy zero volume, so different parts of the chain can occupy

[2] Be alert in this section to the similarities between the discussion of a random coil and the random walk used as a discussion of diffusion in Section 11.11: the two are mathematically equivalent.

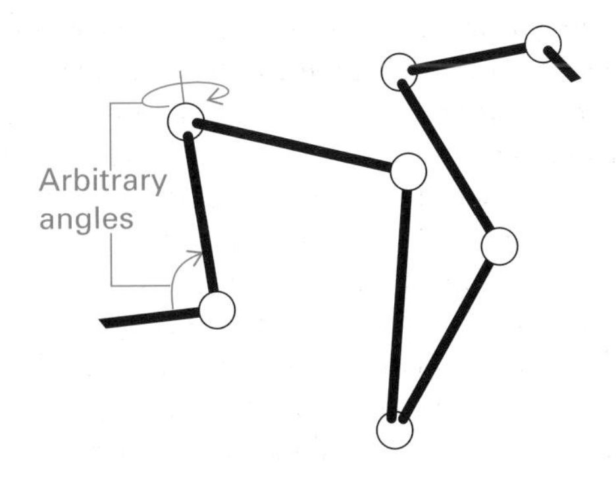

Fig. 18.3 A freely-jointed chain is like a three-dimensional random walk, each step being in an arbitrary direction but of the same length.

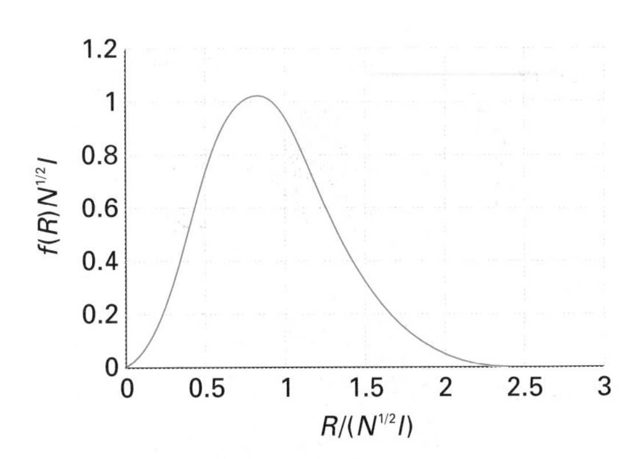

Fig. 18.4 The probability distribution for the separation of the ends of a three-dimensional random coil of N links of length l.

the same region of space. The model is obviously an oversimplification because a bond is in fact constrained to a cone of angles around a direction defined by its neighbour. In a hypothetical one-dimensional freely jointed chain all the residues lie in a straight line, and the angle between neighbours is either 0° or 180°. The residues in a three-dimensional freely jointed chain are not restricted to lie in a line or a plane.

The probability that the ends of a three-dimensional freely jointed chain of N monomer units each of length l lie in the range R to $R + \delta R$ is written $f(R)\delta R$, with

$$f(R) = 4\pi\left(\frac{a}{\pi^{1/2}}\right)^3 R^2\, e^{-a^2R^2} \qquad a = \left(\frac{3}{2Nl^2}\right)^{1/2} \tag{18.4}$$

This function is plotted in Fig. 18.4. Note that it is very unlikely that the two ends will be found either very close together ($R = 0$), because the factor R^2 vanishes, or stretched out in an almost straight line because the exponential factor then vanishes. The function $f(R)$ describes the average separation of the ends: in some coils, the ends may be far apart whereas in others their separation is small. An alternative interpretation of eqn 18.4 is to regard each coil in a sample as ceaselessly writhing from one conformation to another; then $f(R)\delta R$ is the probability that at any instant the chain will be found with the separation of its ends between R and $R + \delta R$.

There are several measures of the geometrical size of a random coil. The **root mean square separation,** R_{rms}, is a measure of the average separation of the ends of a random coil (see Derivation 18.1):

$$R_{rms} = N^{1/2}l \tag{18.5a}$$

We see that as the number of monomer units increases, the root mean square separation of its end increases as $N^{1/2}$, and consequently the volume of the coil increases as $N^{3/2}$. The **contour length,** R_c, is the length of the macromolecule measured along its backbone from atom to atom:

$$R_c = Nl \tag{18.5b}$$

The **radius of gyration,** R_G, of a macromolecule is the radius of a thin shell (think of a table-tennis ball) that has the same mass as the molecule and the same moment of inertia. The radius of gyration of a table-tennis ball is the same as its actual radius; that of a solid sphere of radius r is $R_G = (\frac{3}{5})^{1/2}r$. The radius of gyration of a random coil is

$$R_G = \left(\frac{N}{6}\right)^{1/2} l \tag{18.5c}$$

Derivation 18.1

The root mean square separation of the ends of a freely jointed chain

The root mean square separation, R_{rms}, is the square root of the mean value of R^2, $\langle R^2\rangle$, calculated by weighting each possible value of R^2 with the probability that R

occurs. The general expression for the mean nth power of the end-to-end separation is

$$\langle R^n \rangle = \int_0^\infty R^n f(R)\,\mathrm{d}R$$

To calculate R_{rms}, we first determine $\langle R^2 \rangle$ by using $n = 2$ and $f(R)$ from eqn 18.4:

$$\langle R^2 \rangle = 4\pi\left(\frac{a}{\pi^{1/2}}\right)^3 \int_0^\infty R^4\,\mathrm{e}^{-a^2R^2}\,\mathrm{d}R$$

$$= 4\pi\left(\frac{a}{\pi^{1/2}}\right)^3 \times \frac{3\pi^{1/2}}{8a^5} = \frac{3}{2a^2}$$

We have used the standard integral

$$\int_0^\infty x^4\,\mathrm{e}^{-a^2x^2}\,\mathrm{d}x = \frac{3\pi^{1/2}}{8a^5}$$

Equation 18.5a then follows once we introduce the expression for a in eqn 18.4 and take the square root of the resulting equation.

Illustration 18.1

Calculating the dimensions of a polymer coil

Consider a polyethylene chain with $M = 56$ kDa, corresponding to $N = 4000$. Because $l = 154$ pm for a C–C bond, we find (by using 10^3 pm = 1 nm)

From eqn 18.5a: $R_{\mathrm{rms}} = (4000)^{1/2} \times 154\ \mathrm{pm} = 9.74\ \mathrm{nm}$

From eqn 18.5b: $R_{\mathrm{c}} = 4000 \times 154\ \mathrm{pm} = 616\ \mathrm{nm}$

From eqn 18.5c: $R_{\mathrm{G}} = \left(\frac{4000}{6}\right)^{1/2} \times 154\ \mathrm{pm} = 3.98\ \mathrm{nm}$

The random coil model ignores the role of the solvent: a poor solvent will tend to cause the coil to tighten so that solute–solvent contacts are minimized; a good solvent does the opposite. Therefore, calculations based on this model are better regarded as lower bounds to the dimensions for a polymer in a good solvent and as upper bounds for a polymer in a poor solvent. The model is most reliable for a polymer in a bulk solid sample, where the coil is likely to have its natural dimensions.

A random coil is the least structured conformation of a polymer chain in the sense that it can be achieved in the greatest possible number of ways (in

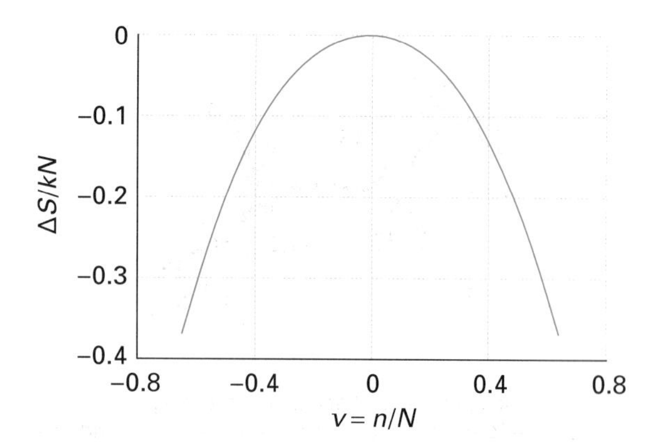

Fig. 18.5 The change in molar entropy of a perfect elastomer as its extension changes; $\nu = 1$ corresponds to complete extension; $\nu = 0$, the conformation of highest entropy, corresponds to the random coil.

contrast, for instance, to the straight-chain conformation, which can be achieved in only one way) and corresponds to the state of greatest entropy. Any stretching of the coil introduces order and reduces the entropy. Conversely, the formation of a random coil from a more extended form is a spontaneous process (provided enthalpy contributions do not interfere). The change in **conformational entropy**, the entropy arising from the arrangement of bonds, when a coil containing N bonds of length l is stretched or compressed by nl is

$$\Delta S = -\tfrac{1}{2}kN\ln\{(1+\nu)^{1+\nu}(1-\nu)^{1-\nu}\} \qquad \nu = n/N \qquad (18.6)$$

where k is Boltzmann's constant. This function is plotted in Fig. 18.5, and we see that minimum extension—fully coiled—corresponds to maximum entropy. This spontaneous tendency to form a coil is responsible for the tendency of rubber (or at least, an ideal rubber with no intermolecular interactions) to spring back into shape after being stretched.

18.3 Models of structure: polypeptides and polynucleotides

Polypeptides are almost at the opposite end of the scale of structure from random coils, as they can become highly ordered: they need to be, because structure in biology is almost synonymous with function. We need to distinguish four levels of structure. The **primary structure** of a biopolymer is the

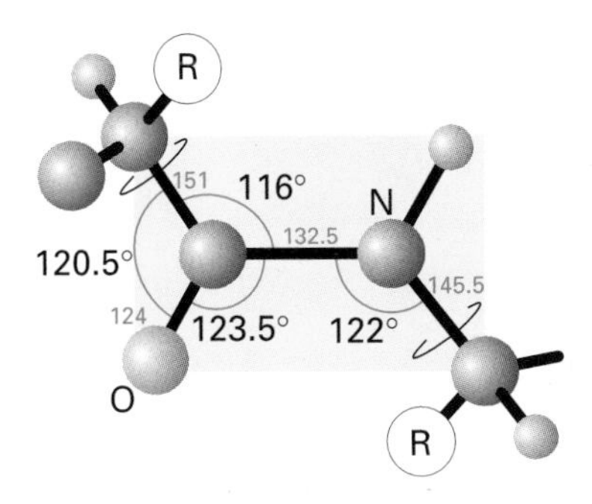

Fig. 18.6 The dimensions that characterize the peptide link. The C–NH–CO–C atoms define a plane (the C–N bond has partial double-bond character), but there is rotational freedom around the C–CO and N–C bonds.

sequence of its monomer units: this sequence is determined by valence forces in the sense that the monomers are linked by covalent bonds. For polypeptides, which we consider here, the primary structure is an ordered list of the amino acid residues. The **secondary structure** of a polypeptide is the spatial arrangement of the polypeptide chain—its twisting into a specific shape—under the influence of interactions between the various peptide residues (the amino acid groups).

We can rationalize the secondary structures of proteins in large part in terms of the hydrogen bonds between the –NH– and –CO– groups of the peptide links (Fig. 18.6). These bonds lead to two principal structures. One, which is stabilized by hydrogen bonding between peptide links of the same chain, is the **α helix**. The other, which is stabilized by hydrogen bonding links to different chains or more distant parts of the same chain, is the **β sheet.**[3]

The α helix is illustrated in Fig. 18.7. Each turn of the helix contains 3.6 amino acid residues, so there are 18 residues in five turns of the helix. The pitch of a single turn (the lateral movement corresponding to one complete rotation) is 544 pm. The N–H···O bonds lie parallel to the axis and link every fifth group (so residue i is linked to residues $i-4$ and $i+4$). There is freedom for the helix to be arranged as either a right- or a left-handed screw, but the overwhelming majority of natural polypeptides are right-handed on account of the preponderance of the L-configuration of the naturally occurring amino acids. It turns out, in agreement with experience,

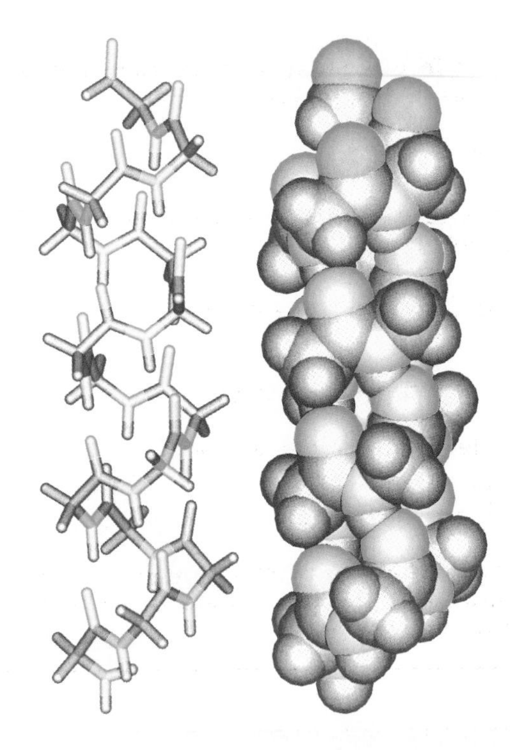

Fig. 18.7 The polypeptide α helix, with poly-L-glycine as an example. Carbon atoms are shown in grey, with nitrogen and oxygen atoms both in colour, and hydrogen atoms in white. See the web site for a full-colour version. There are 3.6 residues per turn, and a translation along the helix of 150 pm per residue, giving a pitch of 540 pm. The diameter (ignoring side chains) is about 600 pm.

that a right-handed α helix of L-amino acids has a marginally lower energy than a left-handed helix of the same acids.

A β sheet is formed by hydrogen bonding between two extended polypeptide chains. Some of the side chains lie above the sheet and some lie below it. Two types of structures can be distinguished from the pattern of hydrogen bonding between the constituent chains. In an **antiparallel β sheet** (Fig. 18.8), the N–H···O atoms of the hydrogen bonds form a straight line. This arrangement is a consequence of the antiparallel arrangement of the chains: each N–H bond on one chain is aligned with a C–O bond from another chain. Antiparallel β sheets are very common in proteins. In a **parallel**

[3] The β sheet is still widely known by its former name, the *β-pleated sheet.*

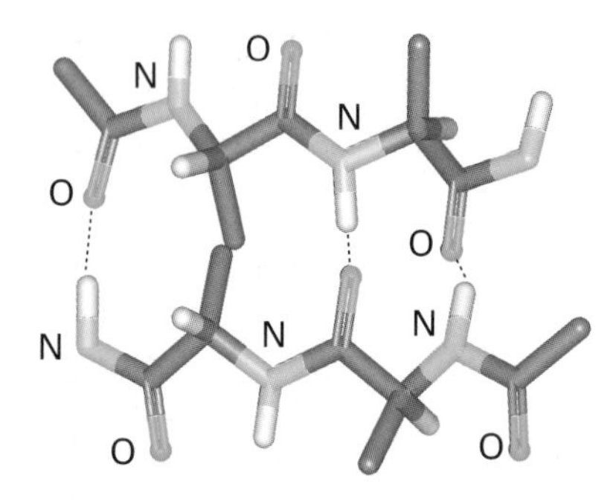

Fig. 18.8 An antiparallel β sheet ($\phi = -139°$, $\psi = 113°$) in which the N–H–O atoms of the hydrogen bonds form a straight line.

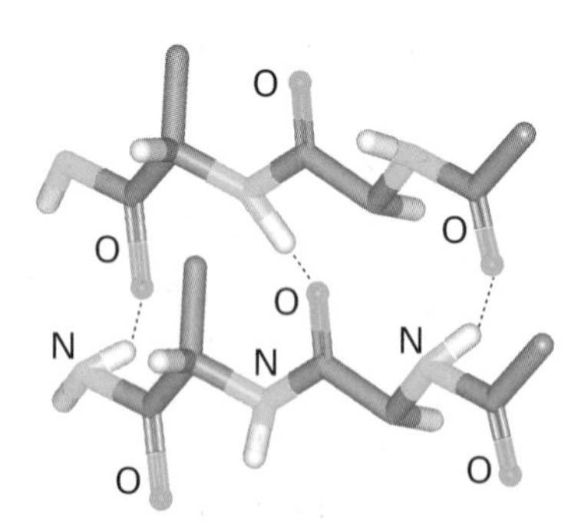

Fig. 18.9 A parallel β sheet ($\phi = -119°$, $\psi = 113°$) in which the N–H–O atoms of the hydrogen bonds are not perfectly aligned.

β sheet (Fig. 18.9), the N–H···O atoms of the hydrogen bonds are not perfectly aligned. This arrangement is a result of the parallel arrangement of the chains: each N–H bond on one chain is aligned with an N–H bond of another chain and, as a result, each C–O bond of one chain is aligned with a C–O bond of another chain. These structures are not common in proteins.

Helical and sheet-like polypeptide chains are folded into a **tertiary structure** if there are other bonding influences between the residues of the chain that are strong enough to overcome the interactions responsible for the secondary structure. The folding influences include –S–S– **disulfide links**, van der Waals interactions, hydrophobic interactions, ionic interactions (which depend on the pH), and strong hydrogen bonds (such as O–H···O).

Proteins with $M > 50$ kDa are often found to be aggregates of two or more polypeptide chains.

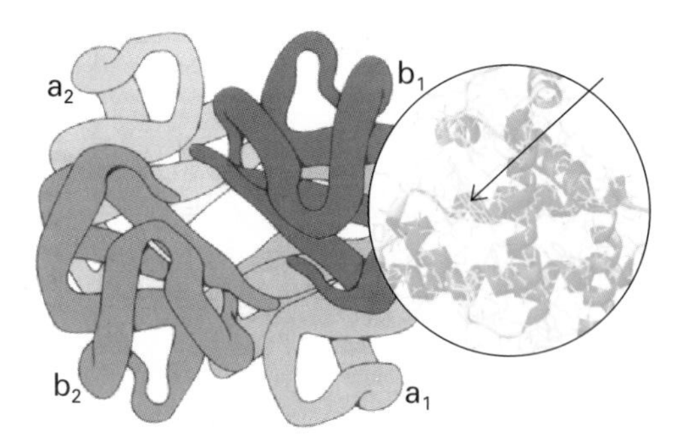

Fig. 18.10 A haemoglobin molecule consists of four myoglobin-like units. An O_2 molecule attaches to the iron atom in the haem group indicated by the arrow.

The possibility of such **quaternary structure** often confuses the determination of their molar masses because different techniques might give values differing by factors of 2 or more. Haemoglobin, which consists of four myoglobin-like chains (Fig. 18.10), is an example of a quaternary structure. Myoglobin is an oxygen-storage protein. The subtle differences that arise when four such molecules coalesce to form haemoglobin result in the latter being an oxygen transport protein, able to load O_2 cooperatively and to unload it cooperatively too (see Box 7.1).

Both deoxyribonucleic acid (DNA) and ribonucleic acid (RNA), which are key components of the mechanism of storage and transfer of genetic information in biological cells, are *polynucleotides* (**2**), in which base–sugar–phosphate units are linked by phosphodiester bonds. In RNA the sugar is β-D-ribose and in DNA it is β-D-2-deoxyribose (as shown in **2**). The most common bases are adenine (A, **3**), cytosine (C, **4**), guanine (G, **5**), thymine (T, found in DNA only, **6**), and uracil (U, found in RNA only, **7**). Under physiological conditions, each phosphate group of the chain carries a negative charge and the bases are deprotonated and neutral. This charge distribution leads to two important properties. One is that the polynucleotide chain is a **polyelectrolyte**, a macromolecule with many charged sites, with a large and negative overall charge. The second is that the bases can interact by hydrogen bonding, as shown for A–T (**8**) and C–G base pairs (**9**).

The secondary and tertiary structures of DNA and RNA arise primarily from the pattern of interactions between bases of one or more chains. In

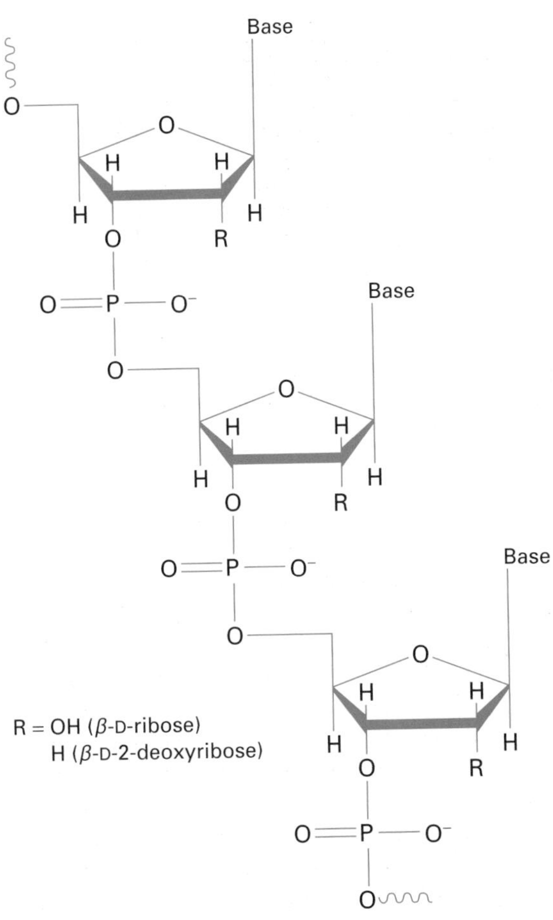

R = OH (β-D-ribose)
H (β-D-2-deoxyribose)

2 The general form of a polynucleotide

3 Adenine

4 Cytosine

5 Guanine

6 Thymine

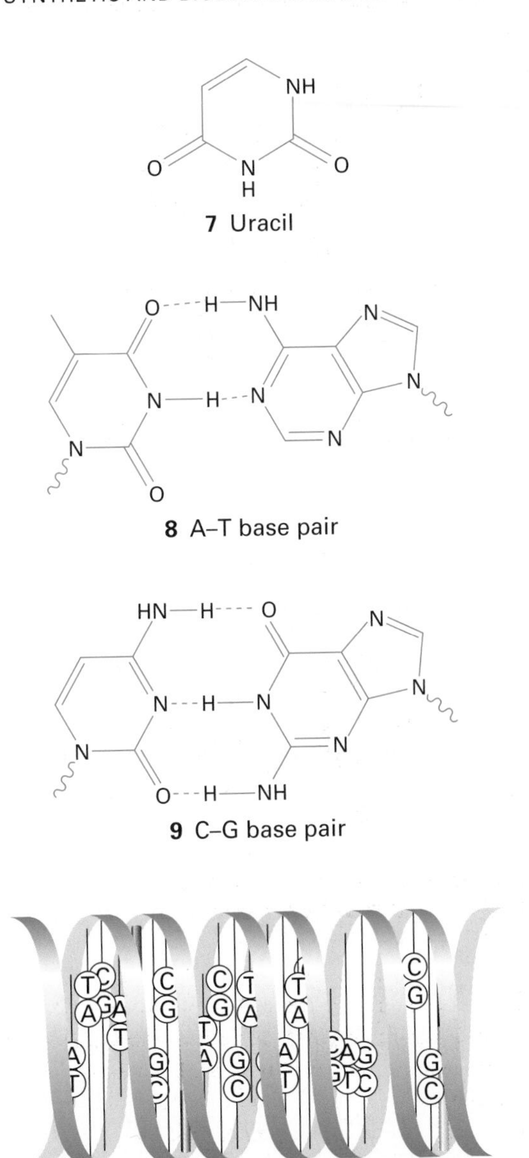

7 Uracil

8 A–T base pair

9 C–G base pair

Fig. 18.11 DNA double helix, in which two polynucleotide chains are linked together by hydrogen bonds between adenine (A) and thymine (T) and between cytosine (C) and guanine (G).

DNA, two polynucleotide chains wind around each other to form a double helix (Fig. 18.11). The chains are held together by links involving A–T and C–G base pairs that lie parallel to each other and perpendicular to the major axis of the helix. The structure is stabilized further by the π stacking interactions mentioned in Box 17.1. In B-DNA, the most

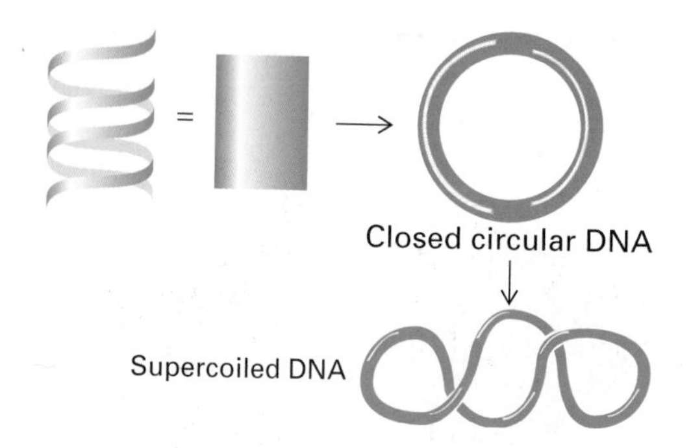

Fig. 18.12 A long section of DNA may form closed circular DNA (ccDNA) by covalent linkage of the two ends of the chain. Twisting of ccDNA leads to the formation of supercoiled DNA.

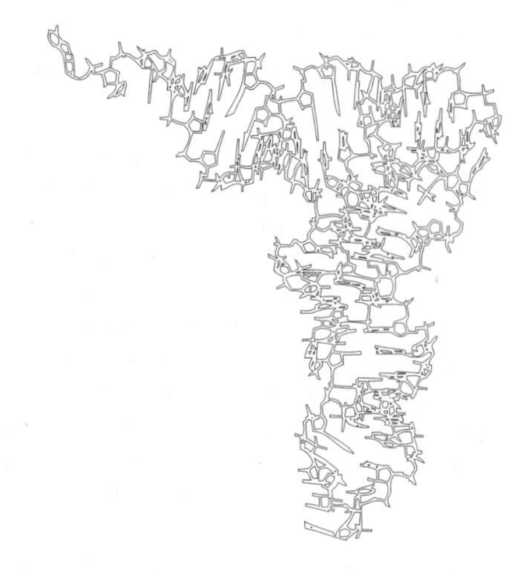

Fig. 18.13 The structure of a transfer RNA (tRNA).

common form of DNA found in biological cells, the helix is right-handed with a diameter (the distance between the centres of the atoms directly across the helix) of 2.0 nm and a pitch (the distance between the centres of atoms related by one turn of the helix) of 3.4 nm. Long stretches of DNA can fold further into a variety of tertiary structures. Two examples are shown in Fig. 18.12. Supercoiled DNA is found in the chromosome and can be visualized as the twisting of closed circular DNA (ccDNA), much like the twisting of a rubber band.

The extra –OH group in β-D-ribose imparts enough steric strain to a polynucleotide chain to prevent the formation of a stable RNA double helix. Therefore, RNA exists primarily as single chains that can fold into complex structures by formation of A–U and G–C base pairs. One example of this structural influence is the structure of transfer RNA (tRNA), shown schematically in Fig. 18.13, in which base-paired regions are connected by loops and coils. Transfer RNAs help to assemble polypeptide chains during protein synthesis in the cell.

Biopolymer **denaturation**, or loss of structure, can be caused by several means, and different aspects of structure may be affected. Denaturation at the secondary level is brought about by agents that destroy hydrogen bonds. Thermal motion may be sufficient, in which case denaturation is a kind of intramolecular melting. When eggs are cooked the albumin is denatured irreversibly, and the protein collapses into a structure resembling a random coil. The **helix–coil transition** of polypeptides is sharp, like ordinary melting, because it is a cooperative process in the sense that when one hydrogen bond has been broken it is easier to break its neighbours, and then even easier to break theirs, and so on. The disruption cascades down the helix, and the transition occurs sharply. Denaturation may also be brought about chemically. For instance, a solvent that forms stronger hydrogen bonds than those within the helix will compete successfully for the NH and CO groups. Acids and bases can cause denaturation by protonation or deprotonation of various groups.

In contemporary physical chemistry and molecular biophysics, a great deal of work is being done on the rationalization and prediction of the structures of biomolecules such as the polypeptides and nucleic acids described here, using the interactions described in Chapter 17 (Box 18.1).

18.4 Mechanical properties of polymers

Synthetic polymers are classified broadly as *elastomers*, *fibres*, and *plastics*, depending on their **crystallinity**, the degree of three-dimensional long-range order attained in the solid state.

An **elastomer** is a flexible polymer that can expand or contract easily upon application of an external force. Elastomers are polymers with numerous cross-links that pull them back into their original shape when a stress is removed. The weak directional constraints on silicon–oxygen bonds is

Box 18.1 *The prediction of protein structure*

A polypeptide chain adopts a conformation corresponding to a minimum Gibbs energy, which depends on the *conformational energy*, the energy of interaction between different parts of the chain, and the energy of interaction between the chain and surrounding solvent molecules. In the aqueous environment of biological cells, the outer surface of a protein molecule is covered by a mobile sheath of water molecules, and its interior contains pockets of water molecules. These water molecules play an important role in determining the conformation that the chain adopts through hydrophobic interactions and hydrogen bonding to amino acids in the chain.

The simplest calculations of the conformational energy of a polypeptide chain ignore entropy and solvent effects and concentrate on the total potential energy of all the interactions between non-bonded atoms. For example, as remarked in the text, these calculations predict that a right-handed α helix of L-amino acids is marginally more stable than a left-handed helix of the same amino acids.

To calculate the energy of a conformation, we need to make use of many of the molecular interactions described in Chapter 17, and also of some additional interactions:

1 *Bond stretching.* Bonds are not rigid, and it may be advantageous for some bonds to stretch and others to be compressed slightly as parts of the chain press against one another. If we liken the bond to a spring, then the potential energy takes the form (see Section 12.11)

$$V_{\text{stretch}} = \tfrac{1}{2}k_{\text{stretch}}(R - R_{\text{e}})^2$$

where R_{e} is the equilibrium bond length and k_{stretch} is the force constant, a measure of the stiffness of the bond in question.

2 *Bond bending.* An O–C–H bond angle (or some other angle) may open out or close in slightly to enable the molecule as a whole to fit together better. If the equilibrium bond angle is θ_{e}, we write

$$V_{\text{bend}} = \tfrac{1}{2}k_{\text{bend}}(\theta - \theta_{\text{e}})^2$$

where k_{bend} is the force constant, a measure of how difficult it is to change the bond angle.

3 *Bond torsion.* There is a barrier to internal rotation of one bond relative to another (just like the barrier to internal rotation in ethane). Because the planar peptide link is relatively rigid, the geometry of a polypeptide chain can be specified by the two angles that two neighbouring planar peptide links make to each other. The first illustration shows the two angles ϕ and ψ commonly used to specify this relative orientation. The sign convention is that a

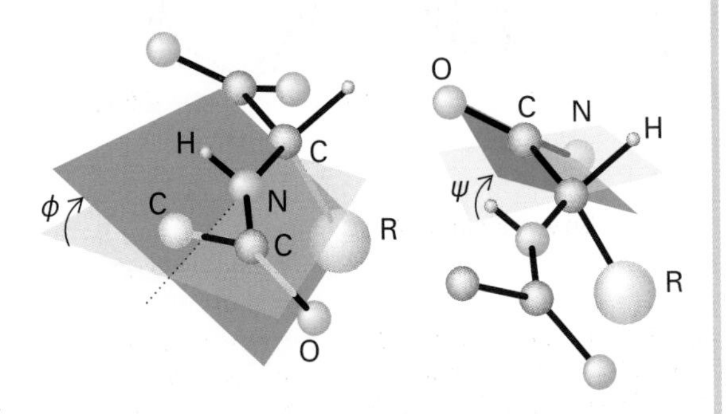

The definition of the torsional angles ψ and ϕ between two peptide units.

positive angle means that the front atom must be rotated clockwise to bring it into an eclipsed position relative to the rear atom. For an all-*trans* form of the chain, all ϕ and ψ are 180°. A helix is obtained when all the ϕ are equal and when all the ψ are equal. For a right-handed α helix, all $\phi = -57°$ and all $\psi = -47°$. For a left-handed α helix, both angles are positive. For an antiparallel β sheet, $\phi = -139°$, $\psi = 113°$. The torsional contribution to the total potential energy is

$$V_{\text{torsion}} = A(1 + \cos 3\phi) + B(1 + \cos 3\psi)$$

in which A and B are constants of the order of 1 kJ mol^{-1}. Because only two angles are needed to specify the conformation of a helix, and they range from −180° to +180°, the torsional potential energy of the entire molecule can be represented on a *Ramachandran plot*, a contour diagram in which one axis represents ϕ and the other represents ψ.

4 *Interaction between partial charges.* If the partial charges q_i and q_j on the atoms i and j are known, a Coulombic contribution of the form $1/r$ can be included:

$$V_{\text{Coulomb}} = \frac{q_i q_j}{4\pi\varepsilon r}$$

where ε is the permittivity of the medium in which the charges are embedded. Charges of $-0.28e$ and $+0.28e$ are assigned to N and H, respectively, and $-0.39e$ and $+0.39e$ to O and C, respectively. The interaction between partial charges does away with the need to take dipole–dipole interactions into account, as they are taken care of by dealing with each partial charge explicitly.

5 *Dispersive and repulsive interactions.* The interaction energy of two atoms separated by a distance r (which we

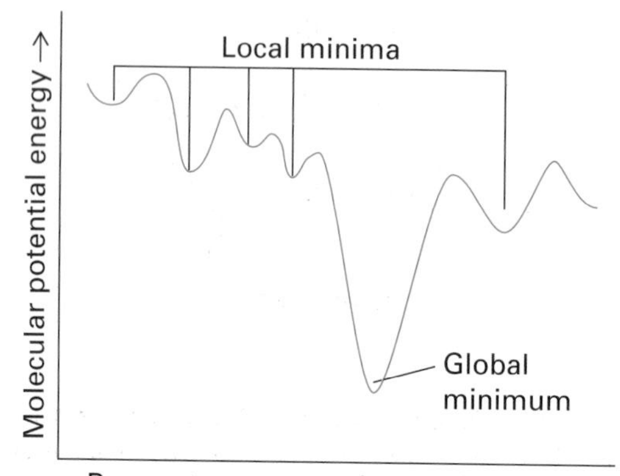

For large molecules, a plot of potential energy against the molecular geometry often shows several local minima and a global minimum.

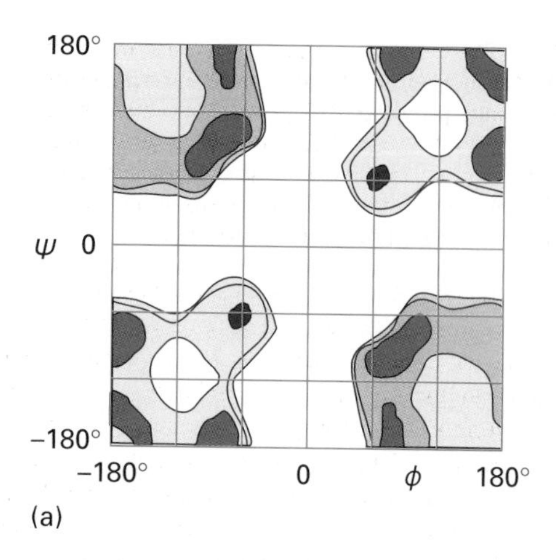

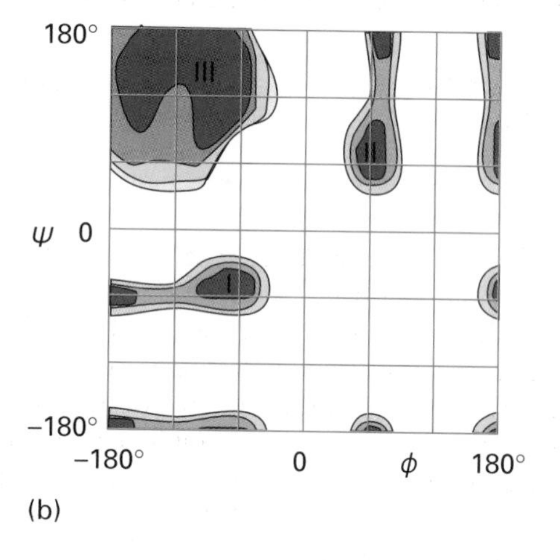

Contour plots of potential energy against the torsional angles ψ and ϕ, also known as Ramachandran diagrams, for (a) a glycyl residue of a polypeptide chain and (b) an alanyl residue. The darker the shading is, the lower the potential energy. The glycyl diagram is symmetrical, but regions I and II in the alanine diagram, which correspond to right- and left-handed helices, are unsymmetrical, and the minimum in region I lies lower than that in region II. (After D. A. Brant and P. J. Flory, *J. Mol. Biol.* 23, 47 (1967).)

know once ϕ and ψ are specified) can be given by the Lennard-Jones (12,6) form (Section 17.8):

$$V_{\mathrm{LJ}} = \frac{C}{r^{12}} - \frac{D}{r^{6}}$$

6 *Hydrogen bonding.* In some models of structure, the interaction between partial charges is judged to take into account the effect of hydrogen bonding. In other models, hydrogen bonding is added as another interaction of the form

$$V_{\mathrm{H\ bonding}} = \frac{E}{r^{12}} - \frac{F}{r^{10}}$$

The total potential energy of a given conformation (ϕ,ψ) can be calculated by summing the contributions given by the preceding equations for all bond angles (including torsional angles) and pairs of atoms in the molecule. The procedure is known as a *molecular mechanics* simulation and is automated in commercially available molecular modelling software. For large molecules, plots of potential energy versus bond distance or bond angle often show several local minima and a global minimum (see the second illustration). The software packages include schemes for modifying the locations of the atoms and searching for these minima systematically.

The third illustration shows the potential energy contours for the helical form of polypeptide chains formed from the non-chiral amino acid glycine (R = H) and the chiral amino acid L-alanine (R = CH_3). The contours were computed by summing all the contributions described above for each choice of angles, and then plotting contours of equal potential energy. The glycine map is symmetrical, with minima of equal depth at $\phi = -80°$, $\psi = +90°$ and at $\phi = +80°$, $\psi = -90°$. By contrast, the map for L-alanine is unsymmetrical, and there are three distinct low-energy conformations (marked I, II, III). The minima of regions I and II lie close to the angles typical of right- and left-handed α helices, but the former has a lower minimum, which is consistent with the formation of right-handed helices from the naturally occurring L-amino acids.

The web site contains links to sites where you may predict the secondary structure of a polypeptide by molecular mechanics simulations. There are also links to sites where you may visualize the structures of proteins and nucleic acids that have been obtained by experimental and theoretical methods.

The structure corresponding to the global minimum of a molecular mechanics simulation is a snapshot of the molecule at $T = 0$ because only the potential energy is included in the calculation; contributions to the total energy from kinetic energy are excluded. In a *molecular dynamics* simulation, the molecule is set in motion by heating it to a specified temperature as described in Section 17.9. Therefore, molecular dynamics calculations are useful tools for the visualization of the flexibility of polymers.

Lumiflavin

Exercise 1 Theoretical studies have estimated that the lumiflavin isoalloazine ring system has an energy minimum at the bending angle of 15°, but that it requires only 8.5 kJ mol^{-1} to increase the angle to 30°. If there are no other compensating interactions, what is the force constant for lumiflavin bending?

Exercise 2 The equilibrium bond length of a carbon–carbon single bond is 152 pm. Given a C–C force constant of 400 N m^{-1}, how much energy, in kilojoules per mole, would it take to stretch the bond to 165 pm?

responsible for the high elasticity of silicones. A **perfect elastomer**, a polymer in which the internal energy is independent of the extension of the random coil, can be modelled as a freely jointed chain.

We saw in Section 18.2 that the contraction of an extended chain to a random coil is spontaneous in the sense that it corresponds to an increase in entropy; the entropy change of the surroundings is zero because no energy is released when the coil forms. In Derivation 18.2 we see how to use the conformational entropy to deduce that the restoring force, F, of a one-dimensional perfect elastomer at a temperature T is

$$F = \frac{kT}{2l}\ln\left(\frac{1+\nu}{1-\nu}\right) \qquad \nu = n/N \tag{18.7}$$

where N is the total number of bonds of length l and the polymer is stretched or compressed by nl (k is Boltzmann's constant). This function is plotted in Fig. 18.14. At low extensions, when $\nu \ll 1$, we show in Derivation 18.2 that

$$F \approx \frac{\nu kT}{l} = \frac{nkT}{Nl} \tag{18.8}$$

and the sample obeys Hooke's law: the restoring force is proportional to the displacement (which is proportional to n). For small displacements, therefore, the whole coil shakes with simple harmonic motion.

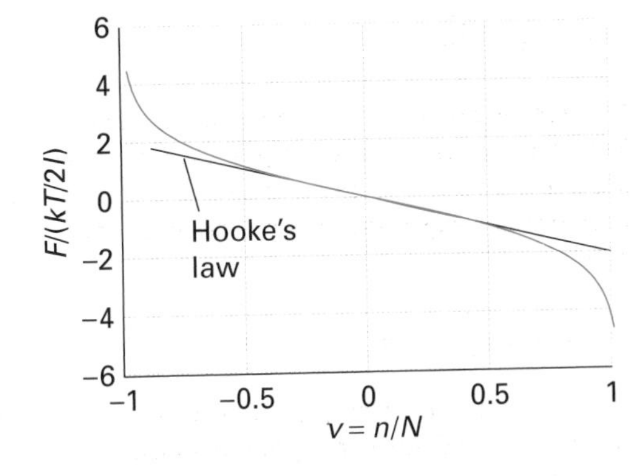

Fig. 18.14 The restoring force, F, of a one-dimensional perfect elastomer. For small strains, F is linearly proportional to the extension, corresponding to Hooke's law.

Derivation 18.2

The force required to stretch a polymer

The work done on an elastomer when it is extended through an infinitesimal distance dx is $F dx$, where F is the restoring force. From the infinitesimal form of eqn 2.8 ($dU = dq + dw$, with $dq = T dS$ and $dw = -p dV + F dx$) it follows that the change in internal energy is

$$dU = T\,dS - p\,dV + F\,dx$$

Provided the temperature and volume are constant (for instance, the sample is supposed to contract laterally as it is stretched), we can set $dV = 0$, treat T as a constant, and divide through by dx to obtain

$$\frac{dU}{dx} = T\frac{dS}{dx} + F$$

In a perfect elastomer, as in a perfect gas, the internal energy is independent of the dimensions (at constant temperature), so the term on the left is zero. The restoring force is therefore related to the change of entropy with extension as follows:

$$F = -T\frac{dS}{dx}$$

If we now substitute eqn 18.6 into this expression, we obtain

$$F \overset{dx = l\,dn}{=} -\frac{T}{l}\frac{dS}{dn} \overset{n = N\nu}{=} -\frac{T}{Nl}\frac{dS}{d\nu} \overset{\text{eqn 18.6}}{=} \frac{kT}{2l}\ln\left(\frac{1+\nu}{1-\nu}\right)$$

as in eqn 18.7. When ν is small we can use the expansions

$$\ln(1+\nu) = \nu - \tfrac{1}{2}\nu^2 + \cdots$$
$$\ln(1-\nu) = -\nu - \tfrac{1}{2}\nu^2 - \cdots$$

to write

$$\ln\left(\frac{1+\nu}{1-\nu}\right) = \ln(1+\nu) - \ln(1-\nu)$$
$$= (\nu - \tfrac{1}{2}\nu^2 + \cdots) - (-\nu - \tfrac{1}{2}\nu^2 - \cdots)$$
$$= 2\nu + \cdots$$

with the unwritten terms of order ν^3 being negligible for small extensions. Substitution of this result into eqn 18.7 gives eqn 18.8.

A **fibre** is a polymeric material with such a low degree of branching that the molecules can be made to lie parallel to one another and acquire strength from the interactions between them. One example is nylon-66 (Fig. 18.15). In contrast to elastomers, fibres need to have a resistance to stretching, which requires the chains to be nearly fully extended and for there to be strong interactions between them. Hydrogen bonding between chains, as in nylon, is one way to achieve this resistance, and side chains are undesirable as they hinder the formation of ordered microcrystalline regions. Under certain conditions, nylon-66 can be prepared in a state of high crystallinity, in which hydrogen bonding between the peptide links of neighbouring chains results in an ordered array.

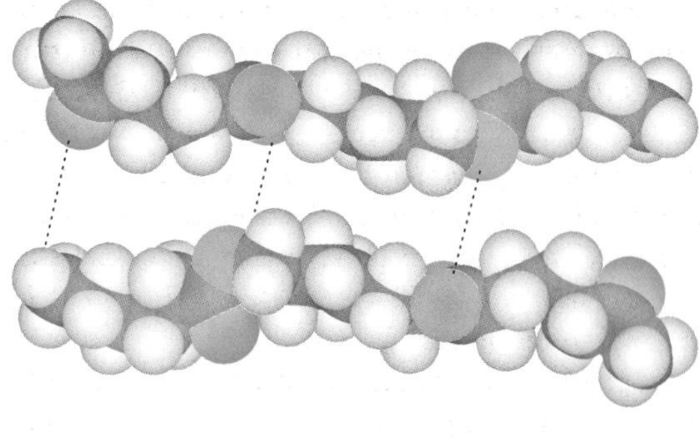

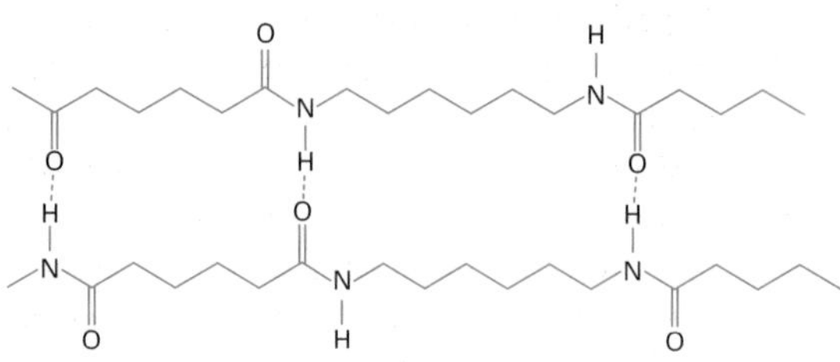

Fig. 18.15 A fragment of two nylon-66 polymer chains showing the pattern of hydrogen bonds that are responsible for the cohesion between the chains.

A **plastic** is a polymer that can attain only a limited degree of crystallinity and, as a result, is neither as strong as a fibre nor as resilient as an elastomer. Certain materials, such as nylon-66, can be prepared either as a fibre or as a plastic. A sample of plastic nylon-66 may be visualized as consisting of crystalline hydrogen-bonded regions of varying size interspersed among amorphous, random coil regions. A single type of polymer may exhibit more than one characteristic because, to display fibrous character, the polymers need to be aligned; if the chains are not aligned, then the substance may be plastic. That is the case with nylon, poly(vinyl chloride), and the siloxanes.

The crystallinity of synthetic polymers can be destroyed by thermal motion at sufficiently high temperatures. This loss of crystallinity may be thought of as a kind of intramolecular melting from a crystalline solid to a more fluid-like random coil. Polymer melting also occurs at a specific **melting temperature,** T_m, which increases with the strength and number of intermolecular interactions in the material. Thus, polyethylene, which has chains that interact only weakly in the solid, has $T_m = 414$ K, and nylon-66 fibres, in which there are strong hydrogen bonds between chains, has $T_m = 530$ K. High melting temperatures are desirable in most practical applications involving fibres and plastics.

All synthetic polymers undergo a transition from a state of high to low chain mobility at the **glass transition temperature,** T_g. To visualize the glass transition, we consider what happens to an elastomer as we lower its temperature. There is sufficient energy available at normal temperatures for limited bond rotation to occur and the flexible chains writhe about. At lower temperatures, the amplitudes of the writhing motion decrease until a specific temperature, T_g, is reached at which motion is frozen completely and the sample forms a glass. Glass transition temperatures well below 300 K are desirable in elastomers that are to be used at normal temperatures.

These concepts are mirrored by natural polymers. For instance, the 'melting' of biopolymers from an ordered structure, such as a helix or sheet, to a flexible random coil, also occurs at a specific temperature, T_m, which increases with the strength and number of intermolecular interactions in the material. The melting temperature, and therefore the thermal stability, of DNA increases with the number of G–C base pairs in the sequence because each G–C base pair has three hydrogen bonds whereas each A–T base pair has only two. More energy is required to unravel a double helix that, on average, has more hydrogen bonding interactions per base pair.

Mesophases and disperse systems

A **mesophase** is a bulk phase that is intermediate in character between a solid and a liquid. The most important type of mesophase is a **liquid crystal,** which is a substance having liquid-like imperfect long-range order in some directions but some aspects of crystal-like short-range order in other directions. Liquid crystals can be used as models of biological membranes and studied to gain insight into the process of transport of molecules into and out of cells. They are also of considerable technological importance for their use in displays on electronic equipment. A **disperse system** is a dispersion of small particles of one material in another. The small particles are commonly called **colloids.** In this context, 'small' means something less than about 500 nm in diameter (about the wavelength of light). In general, they are aggregates of numerous atoms or molecules, but are too small to be seen with an ordinary optical microscope. They pass through most filter papers, but can be detected by light-scattering, sedimentation, and osmosis.

18.5 Liquid crystals

There are three important types of liquid crystal; they differ in the type of long-range order that they retain. One type of retained long-range order gives rise to a **smectic phase** (from the Greek word for soapy), in which the molecules align themselves in layers (Fig. 18.16). Other materials, and some smectic liquid crystals at higher temperatures, lack the layered structure but retain a parallel alignment (Fig. 18.17): this mesophase is the **nematic phase** (from the Greek for thread). The strongly anisotropic optical properties of nematic liquid crystals, and their response to electric fields, is the

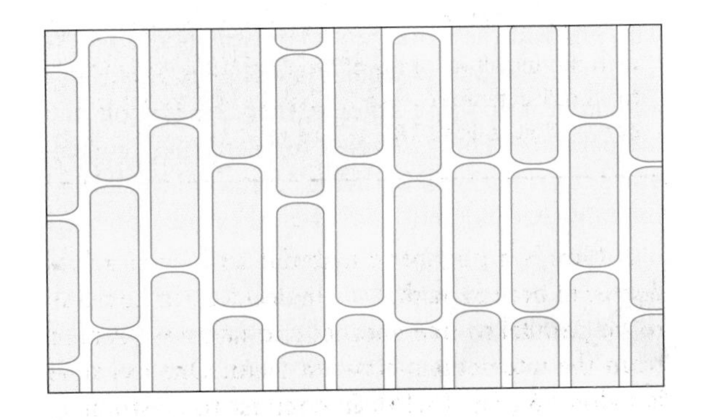

Fig. 18.16 The arrangement of molecules in the smectic phase of a liquid crystal.

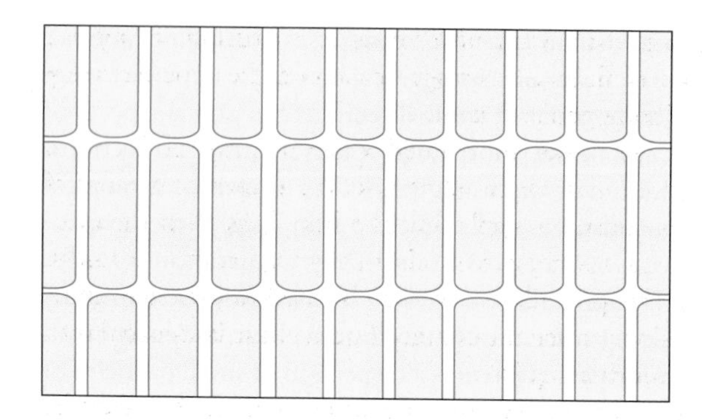

Fig. 18.17 The arrangement of molecules in the nematic phase of a liquid crystal.

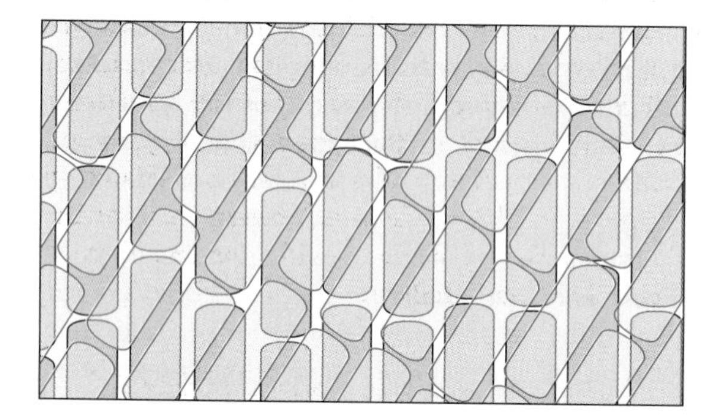

Fig. 18.18 The arrangement of molecules in the cholesteric phase of a liquid crystal. Two layers are shown: the relative orientation of these layers is repeated in successive layers to give a helical structure.

basis of their use as data displays. In the **cholesteric phase**, which is so-called because some derivatives of cholesterol form them, the molecules lie in sheets at angles that change slightly between neighbouring sheets (Fig. 18.18), so forming helical structures. The pitch of the helix varies with temperature. As a result, cholesteric liquid crystals diffract light and appear to have colours that depend on the temperature. They are used for detecting temperature distributions in living material, including human patients, and have even been incorporated into fabrics.

In a 'twisted nematic' liquid crystal display (LCD), the liquid crystal is held between two flat plates about 10 μm apart. The inner surface of each plate is coated with a transparent conducting material, such as indium/tin oxide. The plates also have a surface that causes the liquid crystal to adopt a

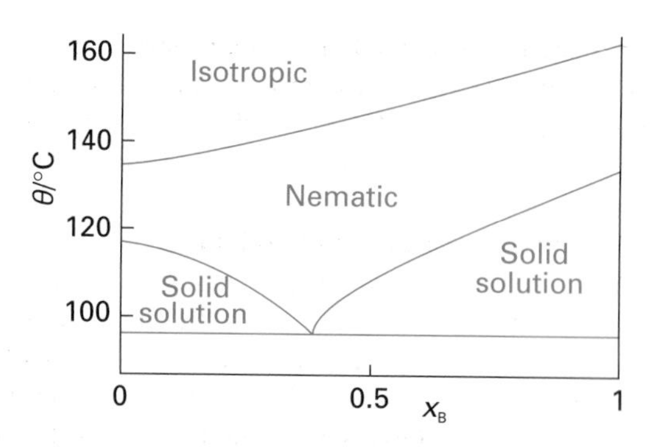

Fig. 18.19 The phase diagram at 1 atm of a binary system of two liquid crystalline materials, 4,4-dimethoxyazoxybenzene (A) and 4,4-diethoxyazoxybenzene (B).

particular orientation at its interface and are typically set at 90° to each other but 270° in a 'supertwist' arrangement. The entire assembly lies between polarizing filters. The incident light passes through the outer polarizer, then its plane of polarization is rotated as it passes through the twisted nematic and, depending on the setting of the second polarizer, will pass through (if that is how the second polarizer is arranged). When a potential difference is applied across the cell, the helical arrangement is lost and the plane of the light is no longer rotated and will be blocked by the second polarizer.

The polarization of light is discussed in Appendix 3.

Although there are many liquid crystalline materials, some difficulty is often experienced in achieving a technologically useful temperature range for the existence of the mesophase. To overcome this difficulty, mixtures can be used. An example of the type of phase diagram that is then obtained is shown in Fig. 18.19. As can be seen, the mesophase exists over a wider range of temperatures than either liquid crystalline material alone.

18.6 Classification of disperse systems

The name given to a disperse system depends on the nature of the substances involved. A **sol** is a dispersion of a solid in a liquid (such as clusters of gold atoms in water) or of a solid in a solid (such as ruby glass, which is a gold-in-glass sol, and achieves its colour by scattering). An **aerosol** is a dispersion of a liquid in a gas (like fog and many sprays) and of a solid in a gas (such as smoke): the particles are often large enough to be seen with a microscope. An **emulsion** is a dispersion of a liquid in a liquid (such as milk and some paints).

A further classification of colloids is as **lyophilic** (solvent attracting) and **lyophobic** (solvent repelling); in the case of water as solvent, the terms **hydrophilic** and **hydrophobic** are used instead. Lyophobic colloids include the metal sols. Lyophilic colloids generally have some chemical similarity to the solvent, such as OH groups able to form hydrogen bonds. A **gel** is a system in which at least one component has a low rigidity (such as a cross-linked polymer or a lipid bilayer) and at least one component has a high mobility (for example, the solvent).

The preparation of aerosols can be as simple as sneezing (which produces an aerosol). Laboratory and commercial methods make use of several techniques. Material (for example, quartz) may be ground in the presence of the dispersion medium. Passing a heavy electric current through a cell may lead to the crumbling of an electrode into colloidal particles; arcing between electrodes immersed in the support medium also produces a colloid. Chemical precipitation sometimes results in a colloid. A precipitate (for example, silver iodide) already formed may be converted to a colloid by the addition of a **peptizing agent**, a substance that disperses a colloid. An example of a peptizing agent is potassium iodide, which provides ions that adhere to the colloidal particles and cause them to repel one another. Clays may be peptized by alkalis, the OH^- ion being the active agent.

Emulsions are normally prepared by shaking the two components together, although some kind of **emulsifying agent** has to be used to stabilize the product. This emulsifier may be a soap (a long-chain fatty acid), a surfactant, or a lyophilic sol that forms a protective film around the dispersed phase. In milk, which is an emulsion of fats in water, the emulsifying agent is casein, a protein containing phosphate groups. That casein is not completely successful in stabilizing milk is apparent from the formation of cream: the dispersed fats coalesce into oily droplets that float to the surface. This separation may be prevented by ensuring that the emulsion is dispersed very finely initially: violent agitation with ultrasonics or extrusion through a very fine mesh brings this about, the product being 'homogenized' milk.

Aerosols are formed when a spray of liquid is torn apart by a jet of gas. The dispersal is aided if a charge is applied to the liquid, as then the electrostatic repulsions blast the jet apart into droplets. This procedure may also be used to produce emulsions, when the charged liquid phase is squirted into another liquid.

Disperse systems are often purified by **dialysis**, which uses osmosis to remove small impurities from solutions of macromolecules. The aim is to remove much (but not all, for reasons explained later) of the ionic material that may have accompanied their formation. A membrane (for instance, cellulose) is selected that is permeable to solvent and ions but not to the bigger colloid particles. Dialysis is very slow, and is normally accelerated by applying an electric field and making use of the charge carried by many colloids; the technique is then called **electrodialysis**.

18.7 Surface, structure, and stability

The principal feature of colloids is the very great surface area of the dispersed phase in comparison with the same amount of ordinary material. For example, a cube of side 1 cm has a surface area of 6 cm^2. When it is dispersed as 10^{18} little 10 nm cubes the total surface area is 6×10^6 cm^2 (about the size of a tennis court). This dramatic increase in area means that surface effects are of dominating importance in the chemistry of disperse systems.

As a result of their great surface area, many colloids are thermodynamically unstable with respect to the bulk: that is, many colloids have a thermodynamic tendency to reduce their surface area (like a liquid). Their apparent stability must therefore be a consequence of the kinetics of collapse: such disperse systems are kinetically non-labile, not thermodynamically stable. At first sight, however, even the kinetic argument seems to fail: colloidal particles attract one another over large distances by the dispersion interaction, so there is a long-range force tending to collapse them down into a single blob.

Several factors oppose the long-range dispersion attraction. There may be a protective film at the surface of the colloid particles that stabilizes the interface and cannot be penetrated when two particles touch. For example, the surface atoms of a platinum sol in water react chemically and are turned into $-Pt(OH)_3H_3$, and this layer encases the particle like a shell. A fat can be emulsified by a soap because the long hydrocarbon tails penetrate the oil droplet but the $-CO_2^-$ head groups (or other hydrophilic groups in detergents) surround the surface, form hydrogen bonds with water, and give rise to a shell of negative charge that repels a possible approach from another similarly charged particle.

By a **surfactant** we mean a species that accumulates at the interface of two phases or substances (one of which may be air) and modifies the properties of the surface. An effective surfactant accumulates at the interface between the phases and does not dissolve well in either of the bulk phases. A typical surfactant consists of a long hydrocarbon tail that dissolves in hydrocarbon and other non-polar materials, and a hydrophilic **head group**, such as a carboxylate group, $-CO_2^-$, that dissolves in a polar solvent (typically water). In other words, a surfactant is an **amphipathic** substance,[4] meaning that it has both hydrophobic and hydrophilic regions. Soaps, for example, consist of the alkali metal salts of long-chain carboxylic acids, and the surfactant in detergents is typically a long-chain benzenesulfonic acid ($R-C_6H_4SO_3H$). The mode of action of a surfactant in a detergent, and of soap, is to dissolve in both the aqueous phase and the hydrocarbon phase where their surfaces are in contact, and hence to solubilize the hydrocarbon phase so that it can be washed away (Fig. 18.20).

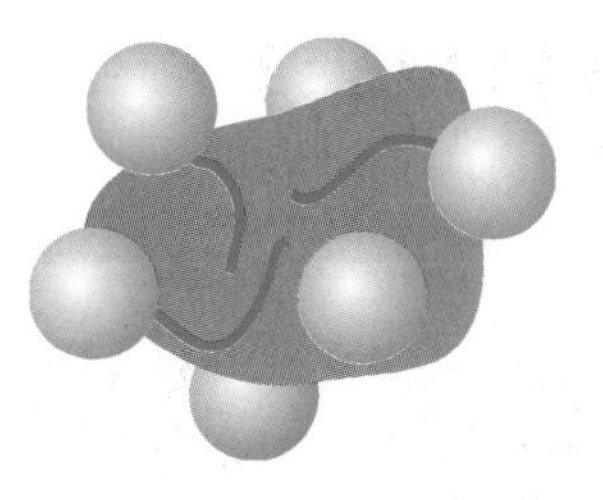

Fig. 18.20 A surfactant molecule in a detergent or soap acts by sinking its hydrophobic hydrocarbon tail into the grease, so leaving its hydrophilic head groups on the surface of the grease where they can interact attractively with the surrounding water.

Surfactant molecules can group together as **micelles**, colloid-sized clusters of molecules, even in the absence of grease droplets, as their hydrophobic tails tend to congregate, and their hydrophilic heads provide protection (Fig. 18.21). Micelles form only above the **critical micelle concentration** (CMC) and above the **Krafft temperature**. Non-ionic surfactant molecules may cluster together in swarms of 1000 or more, but ionic species tend to be disrupted by the Coulomb repulsions between head groups and are normally limited to groups of between 10 and 100 molecules. The shapes of the individual micelles vary with concentration. Although spherical micelles do occur, they are more commonly flattened spheres close to the CMC, and rod-like at higher concentrations. The interior of a micelle is like a droplet of oil, and magnetic resonance shows that the hydrocarbon tails are mobile, but slightly more restricted than in the bulk.

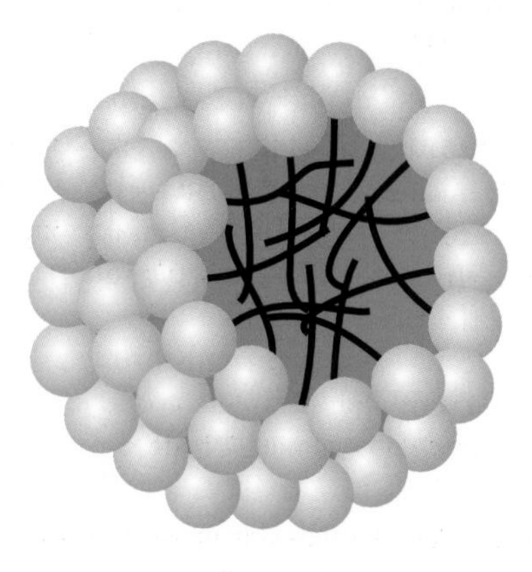

Fig. 18.21 A representation of a spherical micelle. The hydrophilic groups are represented by spheres, and the hydrophobic hydrocarbon chains are represented by the stalks; the latter are mobile.

Micelles are important in industry and biology on account of their solubilizing function: matter can be transported by water after it has been dissolved in their hydrocarbon interiors. For this reason, micellar systems are used as detergents and drug carriers, and for organic synthesis, froth flotation, and petroleum recovery. They can be perceived as a part of a family of similar structures formed

[4] The *amphi-* part of the name is from the Greek word for both, and the *-pathic* part is from the same root as sympathetic (meaning 'feeling').

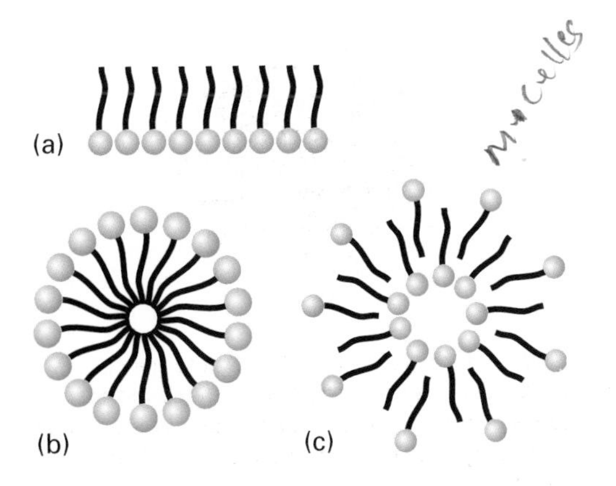

Fig. 18.22 Amphipathic molecules form a variety of related structures in water: (a) a monolayer; (b) a spherical micelle; (c) a bilayer vesicle.

when amphipathic substances are present in water (Fig. 18.22). A **monolayer** forms at the air–water interface, with the hydrophilic head groups facing the water. Micelles are like monolayers that enclose a region. A **bilayer vesicle** is like a double-micelle, with an inward pointing inner surface of molecules surrounded by an outward pointing outer layer. The 'flat' version of a bilayer vesicle is the analogue of a cell membrane (Box 18.2).

The thermodynamics of micelle formation shows that the enthalpy of formation in aqueous systems is probably positive (that is, that they are endothermic) with $\Delta H \approx$ 1–2 kJ per mole of surfactant molecules. That they do form above the CMC indicates that the entropy change accompanying their formation must then be positive (in order for the Gibbs energy accompanying the formation process to be negative), and measurements suggest a value of about +140 J K^{-1} mol^{-1} at room temperature. That the entropy change is positive even though the molecules are clustering together shows that there must be a contribution to the entropy from the solvent and this is ascribed to the hydrophobic effect (Section 17.7).

Box 18.2 *Biological membranes*

Some micelles at concentrations well above the CMC form extended parallel sheets, called *lamellar micelles*, two molecules thick. The individual molecules lie perpendicular to the sheets, with hydrophilic groups on the outside in aqueous solution and on the inside in non-polar media. Such lamellar micelles show a close resemblance to biological membranes, and are often a useful model on which to base investigations of biological structures.

Although lamellar micelles are convenient models of cell membranes, actual membranes are highly sophisticated structures. The basic structural element of a membrane is a phospholipid, such as phosphatidyl choline, which contains long hydrocarbon chains (typically in the range C_{14}–C_{24}) and a variety of polar groups, such as $-CH_2CH_2N(CH_3)_3^+$. The hydrophobic chains stack together to form an extensive bilayer about 5 nm across. The lipid molecules form layers instead of spherical micelles because the hydrocarbon chains are too bulky to allow packing into nearly spherical clusters.

The bilayer is a highly mobile structure. Not only are the hydrocarbon chains ceaselessly twisting and turning in the region between the polar groups, but the phospholipid and other molecules inserted into the bilayer migrate over the surface. It is better to think of the membrane as a viscous fluid rather than a permanent structure, with a viscosity about 100 times that of water. In common with diffusional behaviour in general (Section 11.11), the average distance a phospholipid molecule diffuses is proportional to the square root of the time.[5] Typically, a phospholipid molecule migrates through about 1 μm (the diameter of a cell) in about 1 min.

Phosphatidyl choline

Peripheral proteins are proteins attached to the bilayer. *Integral proteins* are proteins immersed in the mobile but viscous bilayer. These proteins may span the depth of the bilayer and consist of tightly packed α helices or, in some

[5] For a molecule confined to a two-dimensional plane, the average distance travelled in a time t is equal to $(4Dt)^{1/2}$.

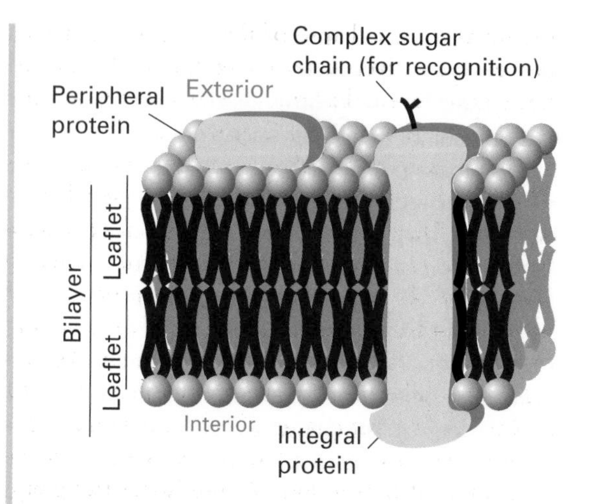

In the fluid mosaic model of a biological cell membrane, integral proteins diffuse through the lipid bilayer. In the alternative lipid raft model, a number of lipid and cholesterol molecules envelope and transport the protein around the membrane.

cases, β sheets containing hydrophobic residues that sit comfortably within the hydrocarbon region of the bilayer. There are two views of the motion of integral proteins in the bilayer. In the *fluid mosaic model* shown in the illustration the proteins are mobile, but their diffusion coefficients are much smaller than those of the lipids. In the *lipid raft model*, a number of lipid and cholesterol molecules form ordered structures, or 'rafts', that envelope proteins and help to carry them to specific parts of the cell.

The mobility of the bilayer enables it to flow round a molecule close to the outer surface, to engulf it, and incorporate it into the cell by the process of *endocytosis*. Alternatively, material from the cell interior wrapped in cell membrane may coalesce with the cell membrane itself, which then withdraws and ejects the material in the process of *exocytosis*. The function of the proteins embedded in the bilayer, however, is to act as devices for transporting matter into and out of the cell in a more subtle manner. By providing hydrophilic channels through an otherwise alien hydrophobic environment, some proteins act as *ion channels* and *ion pumps* (Box 9.1).

All lipid bilayers undergo a transition from a state of high to low chain mobility at a temperature that depends on the structure of the lipid. To visualize the transition, we consider what happens to a membrane as we lower its temperature. There is sufficient energy available at normal temperatures for limited bond rotation to occur and the flexible chains writhe. However, the membrane still has a great deal of order in the sense that the bilayer structure does not come apart and the system is best described as a liquid crystal. At lower temperatures, the amplitudes of the writhing motion decrease until a specific temperature is reached at which motion is largely frozen. The membrane is said to exist as a gel. Biological membranes exist as liquid crystals at physiological temperatures.

The web site contains links to databases of thermodynamic properties of lipids.

Interspersed among the phospholipids of biological membranes are sterols, such as cholesterol, which is largely hydrophobic but does contain a hydrophilic –OH group. Sterols, which are present in different proportions in different types of cells, prevent the hydrophobic chains of lipids from 'freezing' into a gel and, by disrupting the packing of the chains, spread the melting point of the membrane over a range of temperatures.

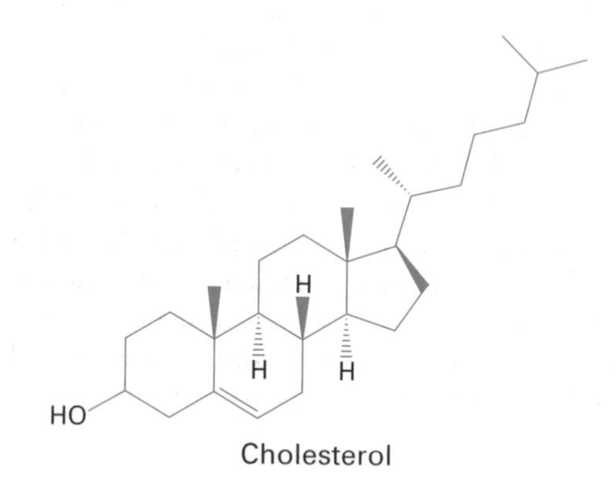

Cholesterol

Exercise 1 Lipid diffusion in a cell plasma membrane occurs with a diffusion constant of 1.0×10^{-8} cm^2 s^{-1} and the same lipid in a lipid bilayer has a diffusion constant of 1.0×10^{-7} cm^2 s^{-1}. How long will it take the lipid to diffuse 10 nm in a plasma membrane and a lipid bilayer?

Exercise 2 Organisms are capable of biosynthesizing lipids of different composition so that cell membranes have melting temperatures close to the ambient temperature. Keeping in mind that structural elements that prevent alignment of the hydrophobic chains in the gel phase lead to low melting temperatures, explain why bacterial and plant cells grown at low temperatures synthesize more phospholipids with unsaturated chains (chains containing C=C bonds) than do cells grown at higher temperatures.

18.8 The electric double layer

Apart from the physical stabilization of disperse systems, a major source of kinetic non-lability is the existence of an electric charge on the surfaces of the colloidal particles. Because of this charge, ions of opposite charge tend to cluster nearby.

Two regions of charge must be distinguished. First, there is a fairly immobile layer of ions that stick tightly to the surface of the colloidal particle, and which may include water molecules (if that is the support medium). The radius of the sphere that captures this rigid layer is called the **radius of shear**, and is the major factor determining the mobility of the particles (Fig. 18.23). The electric potential at the radius of shear relative to its value in the distant, bulk medium is called the **zeta potential**, ζ (zeta), or the **electrokinetic potential**. The charged unit attracts an oppositely charged ionic atmosphere. The inner shell of charge and the outer atmosphere jointly constitute the **electric double layer**.

At high concentrations of ions of high charge number, the atmosphere is dense and the potential falls to its bulk value within a short distance. In this case there is little electrostatic repulsion to hinder the close approach of two colloid particles. As a result, **flocculation**, the aggregation of the colloidal particles, occurs as a consequence of the van der Waals forces. Flocculation is often reversible, and should be distinguished from **coagulation**, which is the irreversible collapse of the colloid into a bulk phase. When river water containing colloidal clay flows into the sea, the brine induces coagulation and is a major cause of silting in estuaries.

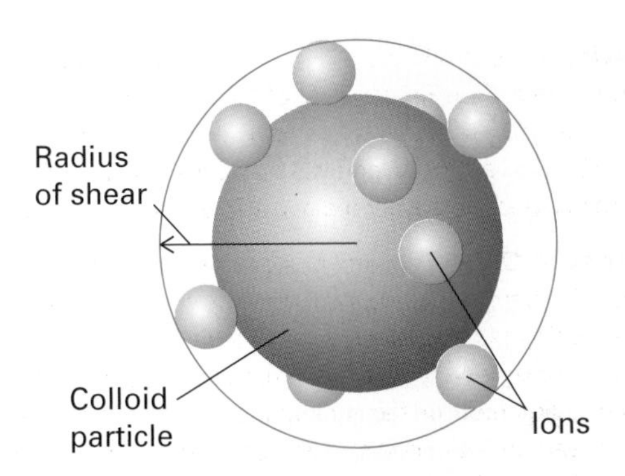

Fig. 18.23 The definition of the radius of shear for a colloidal particle. The spheres are ions attached to the surface of the particle.

Metal oxide and sulfide sols have charges that depend on the pH; sulfur and the noble metals tend to be negatively charged. Naturally occurring macromolecules also acquire a charge when dispersed in water, and an important feature of proteins and other natural macromolecules is that their overall charge depends on the pH of the medium. For instance, in acid environments protons attach to basic groups and the net charge of the macromolecule is positive; in basic media the net charge is negative as a result of proton loss. At the **isoelectric point**, the pH is such that there is no net charge on the macromolecule.

The primary role of the electric double layer is to render the colloid kinetically non-labile. Colliding colloidal particles break through the double layer and coalesce only if the collision is sufficiently energetic to disrupt the layers of ions and solvating molecules, or if thermal motion has stirred away the surface accumulation of charge. This kind of disruption of the double layer may occur at high temperatures, which is one reason why sols precipitate when they are heated. The protective role of the double layer is the reason why it is important not to remove all the ions (other than those needed to ensure overall electrical neutrality) when a colloid is being purified by dialysis, and why proteins coagulate most readily at their isoelectric point.

The presence of charge on colloidal particles and natural macromolecules also permits us to control their motion, as in dialysis and electrophoresis. Apart from its application to the determination of molar mass, electrophoresis has several analytical and technological applications. One analytical application is to the separation of different macromolecules, as discussed in Section 18.1. Technical applications include silent ink-jet printers, the painting of objects by airborne charged paint droplets, and electrophoretic rubber forming by deposition of charged rubber molecules on anodes formed into the shape of the desired product (for example, surgical gloves).

CHECKLIST OF KEY IDEAS

You should now be familiar with the following topics:

- ☐ 1 Many proteins (specifically protein enzymes) are monodisperse, a synthetic polymer is polydisperse.
- ☐ 2 The number-average molar mass, $\bar{M}_n$, is the value obtained by weighting each molar mass by the number of molecules of that mass present in the sample: $\bar{M}_n = (1/N)\sum_i N_i M_i$.
- ☐ 3 The weight-average molar mass, $\bar{M}_w$, is the average calculated by weighting the molar masses of the molecules by the mass of each one present in the sample: $\bar{M}_w = (1/m)\sum_i m_i M_i$.
- ☐ 4 Techniques for the determination of the mean molar masses of macromolecules include osmometry, mass spectrometry (as MALDI), sedimentation rates and equilibria, gel and capillary electrophoresis, and laser light scattering.
- ☐ 5 The least structured model of a macromolecule is as a random coil; for a freely jointed random coil of contour length Nl, the root mean square separation is $N^{1/2}l$ and the radius of gyration is $R_G = (N/6)^{1/2}l$.
- ☐ 6 The primary primary structure of a biopolymer is the sequence of its monomer units.
- ☐ 7 The secondary structure of a protein is the spatial arrangement of the polypeptide chain and includes the α helix and β sheet.
- ☐ 8 Helical and sheet-like polypeptide chains are folded into a tertiary structure by bonding influences between the residues of the chain.
- ☐ 9 Some macromolecules have a quaternary structure as aggregates of two or more polypeptide chains.
- ☐ 10 Protein denaturation is loss of structure; a helix–coil transition is a cooperative process.
- ☐ 11 Synthetic polymers are classified as elastomers, fibres, and plastics.
- ☐ 12 A perfect elastomer is a polymer in which the internal energy is independent of the extension of the random coil; for small extensions a random coil model obeys a Hooke's law restoring force, $F = nkT/Nl$.
- ☐ 13 Synthetic polymers undergo a transition from a state of high to low chain mobility at the glass transition temperature, T_g.
- ☐ 14 A mesophase is a bulk phase that is intermediate in character between a solid and a liquid.
- ☐ 15 A disperse system is a dispersion of small particles of one material in another.
- ☐ 16 Liquid crystals are classified as smectic, nematic, or cholesteric.
- ☐ 17 Colloids are classified as lyophilic (solvent attracting, specifically hydrophilic for water) and lyophobic (solvent repelling, specifically hydrophobic for water).
- ☐ 18 A surfactant is a species that accumulates at the interface of two phases or substances and modifies the properties of the surface.
- ☐ 19 The radius of shear is the radius of the sphere that captures the rigid layer of charge attached to a colloid particle.
- ☐ 20 The zeta potential is the electric potential at the radius of shear relative to its value in the distant, bulk medium.
- ☐ 21 The inner shell of charge and the outer atmosphere jointly constitute the electric double layer.
- ☐ 22 Many colloid particles are thermodynamically unstable but kinetically non-labile.

DISCUSSION QUESTIONS

18.1 Distinguish between number-average and weight-average molar masses.

18.2 Distinguish between contour length, root mean square separation, and radius of gyration of a random coil.

18.3 Identify the terms in and limit the generality of the following expressions: (a) $\Delta S = -\frac{1}{2}kN \ln\{(1+\nu)^{1+\nu}(1-\nu)^{1-\nu}\}$, (b) $F = (kT/2l)\ln\{(1+\nu)/(1-\nu)\}$, (c) $R_{rms} = N^{1/2}l$, and (d) $R_g = (N/6)^{1/2}l$.

18.4 Cotton consists of the polymer cellulose, which is a linear chain of glucose molecules. The chains are held together by hydrogen bonding. When a cotton shirt is ironed, it is first moistened, then heated under pressure. Explain this process.

18.5 Some polymers can form liquid crystal mesophases with unusual physical properties. For example, liquid crystalline Kevlar (**10**) is strong enough to be the material of choice for bulletproof vests and is stable at temperatures up to 600 K. What molecular interactions contribute to the formation, thermal stability, and mechanical strength of liquid crystal mesophases in Kevlar?

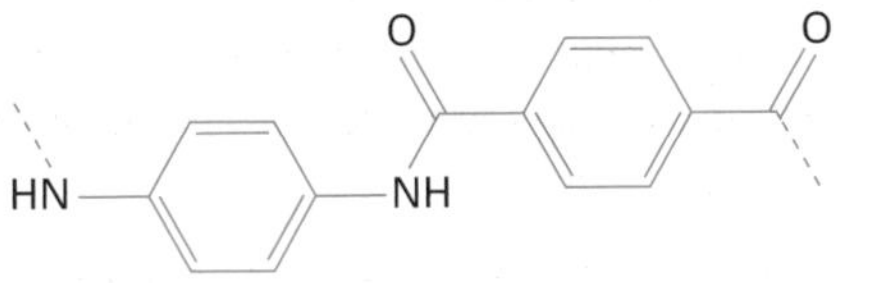

HN NH O O

10

18.6 Disc-like molecules, such as (**11**), can form *discotic* liquid crystal mesophases that resemble a column, with the aromatic rings stacked one on top of the other and separated by very small distances (less than 0.5 nm). It has been proposed that such liquid crystals can act as 'molecular wires' for the conduction of electrons along the column. Explain the rationale for this proposal.

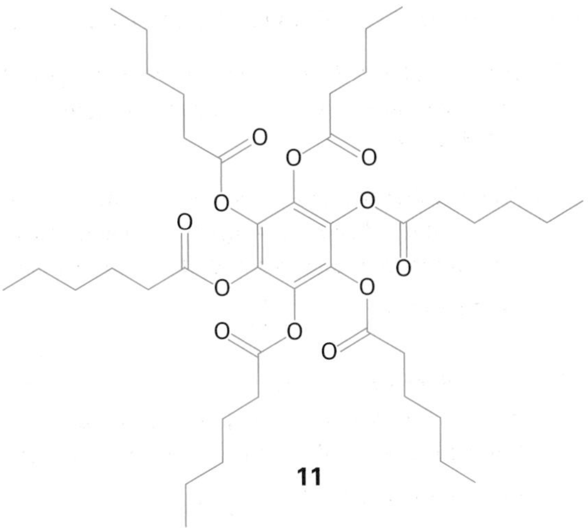

11

18.7 Explain the physical origins of surface activity by surfactant molecules.

18.8 It is observed that the critical micelle concentration of sodium dodecyl sulfate in aqueous solution decreases as the concentration of added sodium chloride increases. Explain this effect.

18.9 The fluidity of a lipid bilayer dispersed in aqueous solution depends on temperature and there are two important melting transitions. One transition is from a 'solid crystalline' state, in which the hydrophobic chains are packed together tightly (hence move very little), to a 'liquid crystalline state', in which there is increased but still limited movement of the of the chains. The second transition, which occurs at a higher temperature than the first, is from the liquid crystalline state to a liquid state, in which the hydrophobic interactions holding the aggregate together are largely disrupted. It is observed that the transition temperatures increase with the hydrophobic chain length and decrease with the number of C=C bonds in the chain. Explain these observations.

EXERCISES

The symbol ‡ indicates that calculus is required.

18.10 Calculate the number-average molar mass and the mass-average molar mass of a mixture of equal amounts of two polymers, one having $M = 62\ \text{kg mol}^{-1}$ and the other $M = 78\ \text{kg mol}^{-1}$.

18.11 A solution consists of solvent, 30 per cent by mass of a dimer with $M = 30\ \text{kg mol}^{-1}$ and its monomer. What average molar mass would be obtained from measurement of (a) osmotic pressure, (b) light scattering?

18.12 Determine the heterogeneity index of a sample of polystyrene from the following data:

Molar mass interval/ (kg mol^{-1})	Average molar mass within interval/ (kg mol^{-1})	Mass of sample within interval/g
5–10	7.5	18
10–15	12.5	22
15–20	17.5	17.5
20–25	22.5	14.2
25–30	27.5	9.7
30–35	32.5	4.5

18.13 Polystyrene is a synthetic polymer with the structure $-(CH_2CH(C_6H_5))_n-$. A batch of polydisperse polystyrene was prepared by initiating the polymerization with the *t*-butyl free radical. As a result, the *t*-butyl group is expected to be covalently attached to the end of the final products. A sample from this batch was embedded in an organic matrix containing silver trifluoroacetate and the resulting MALDI-TOF spectrum consisted of a large number of peaks separated by $104\ \text{g mol}^{-1}$, with the most intense peak at $25\,578\ \text{g mol}^{-1}$. Comment on the purity of this sample and determine the number of $-CH_2CH(C_6H_5)-$ units in the species that gives rise to the most intense peak in the spectrum.

18.14 The data from a sedimentation equilibrium experiment performed at 300 K on a macromolecular solute in aqueous solution show that a graph of $\ln c$ against r^2 is a straight line with a slope of $729\ \text{cm}^{-2}$. The rotational rate of the centrifuge was 50 000 rpm (revolutions per minute). The specific volume of the solute is $v_s = 0.61\ \text{cm}^3\ \text{g}^{-1}$. Calculate the molar mass of the solute. (*Hint.* Use eqn 18.3; you need to know that the buoyancy correction is $b = 1 - \rho v_s$; take $\rho = 1.00\ \text{g cm}^{-3}$.)

18.15 Calculate the speed of operation (in rpm) of an ultracentrifuge needed to obtain a readily measurable concentration gradient in a sedimentation equilibrium experiment. Take that gradient to be a concentration at the bottom of the cell about five times greater than that at the top. Use $r_{top} = 5.0$ cm, $r_{bottom} = 7.0$ cm, $M \approx 10^5\ \text{g mol}^{-1}$, $\rho v_s \approx 0.75$, $T = 298$ K.

18.16 To determine the weight-average molar mass of a polymer by laser light scattering, we measure the intensity I_θ of scattered radiation as a function of the angle θ between the scattered and incident beams. It is customary to form the *Rayleigh ratio* $R_\theta = (I_\theta/I_0) \times r^2$, where I_0 is the intensity of incident light and r is the distance between the sample and the detector. For an ideal solution of a polymer, the dependence of R_θ on θ is given by:

$$\frac{1}{R_\theta} = \frac{1}{Kc_P\bar{M}_w} + \left(\frac{16\pi^2R_g^2}{3\lambda^2}\right)\left(\frac{1}{R_\theta}\sin^2\tfrac{1}{2}\theta\right)$$

where c_P is the mass concentration of the polymer, λ is wavelength of the incident laser radiation, $\bar{M}_w$ is the weight-average molar mass of the polymer, K is an instrumental parameter held constant during the experiment, and R_g is the radius of gyration of the macromolecule. The following data for an aqueous solution of a polymer with $c_P = 2.0\ \text{kg m}^{-3}$ were obtained at 20°C with laser light at $\lambda = 532$ nm:

$\theta/°$	15.0	45.0	70.0	85.0	90.0
R_θ	23.8	22.9	21.6	20.7	20.4

In a separate experiment, it was determined that $K = 2.40 \times 10^{-2}\ \text{mol m}^3\ \text{kg}^{-2}$. From this information, calculate R_g and M for the protein.

18.17 A polymer chain consists of 700 segments, each 0.90 nm long. If the chain were ideally flexible, what would be the root mean square separation of the ends of the chain?

18.18 Calculate the contour length (the length of the extended chain) and the root mean square separation (the end-to-end distance) for polyethylene with a molar mass of $280\ \text{kg mol}^{-1}$.

18.19 The radius of gyration of a long-chain molecule is found to be 7.3 nm. The chain consists of C–C links. Assume the chain is randomly coiled and estimate the number of links in the chain.

18.20 ‡Use eqn 18.4 to deduce expressions for (a) the root mean square separation of the ends of the chain, (b) the mean separation of the ends, and (c) their most probable separation. Evaluate these three quantities for a fully flexible chain with $N = 4000$ and $l = 154$ pm.

18.21 Construct a two-dimensional random walk by using a random number generating routine with mathematical software or electronic spreadsheet. Construct a walk of 50 and 100 steps. If there are many people working on the problem, investigate the mean and most probable separations in the plots by direct measurement. Do they vary as $N^{1/2}$?

18.22 Use the following information and the expression for the radius of gyration of a solid sphere to classify the species listed as globular or rod-like. The specific volume, v_s, is the reciprocal of the density.

	$M/(\text{g mol}^{-1})$	$v_s/(\text{cm}^3\ \text{g}^{-1})$	R_g/nm
Serum albumin	66×10^3	0.752	2.98
Bushy stunt virus	10.6×10^6	0.741	12.0
DNA	4×10^6	0.556	117.0

18.23 Estimate the force required to expand a random coil (a perfect elastomer) consisting of 1000 links by 10 per cent of its fully coiled state at 300 K.

18.24 The melting temperature of a DNA molecule can be determined by differential scanning calorimetry (Box 2.1). The following data were obtained in aqueous solutions containing 1.0×10^{-2} mol dm^{-3} Na_3PO_4(s) for a series of DNA molecules with varying base pair composition, with f the fraction of G–C base pairs:

f	0.375	0.509	0.589	0.688	0.750
T_m/K	339	344	348	351	354

(a) Estimate the melting temperature of a DNA molecule containing 40.0 per cent G–C base pairs. (b) Provide a molecular interpretation for the observation that the melting temperature increases with the fraction of G–C base pairs.

18.25 The following table lists the glass transition temperatures, T_g, of several polymers. Discuss the reasons why the structure of the monomer unit has an effect on the value of T_g.

Polymer	Poly(oxymethylene)	Polyethylene
Structure	$-(OCH_2)_n-$	$-(CH_2CH_2)_n-$
T_g/K	198	253
Polymer	Poly(vinyl chloride)	Polystyrene
Structure	$-(CH_2CHCl)_n-$	$-(CH_2CH(C_6H_5))_n-$
T_g/K	354	381

Chapter 19

Molecular rotations and vibrations

Spectroscopy is the analysis of the electromagnetic radiation emitted, absorbed, or scattered by atoms and molecules. We saw in Chapter 13 that photons act as messengers from inside atoms and that we can use atomic spectra to obtain detailed information about electronic structure. Photons of radiation ranging from radio waves to the ultraviolet also bring information to us about molecules. The difference between molecular and atomic spectroscopy, however, is that the energy of a molecule can change not only as a result of electronic transitions but also because it can make transitions between its rotational and vibrational states. Molecular spectra are more complicated but they contain more information, including electronic energy levels, bond lengths, bond angles, and bond strength. Molecular spectroscopy is used to analyse materials and to monitor changing concentrations in kinetic studies (Section 10.1).

This and the next two chapters survey several principal types of spectroscopy, using radiation that ranges over eight orders of magnitude, from radiofrequencies (10^8 Hz) up to the ultraviolet (10^{16} Hz).

General features of spectroscopy

In **emission spectroscopy**, a molecule undergoes a transition from a state of higher energy, E_2, to a state of lower energy, E_1, and emits the excess energy as a photon (Fig. 19.1). In **absorption spectroscopy**, the absorption of radiation is monitored as the frequency of the radiation is swept over a range. In **Raman spectroscopy**, an intense, monochromatic

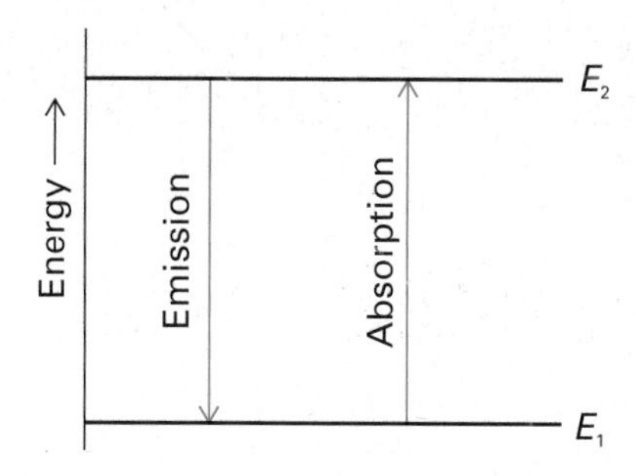

Fig. 19.1 In emission spectroscopy, a molecule returns to a lower state (typically the ground state) from an excited state, and emits the excess energy as a photon. The same transition may be observed in absorption, when the incident radiation supplies a photon that can excite the molecule from its ground state to an excited state.

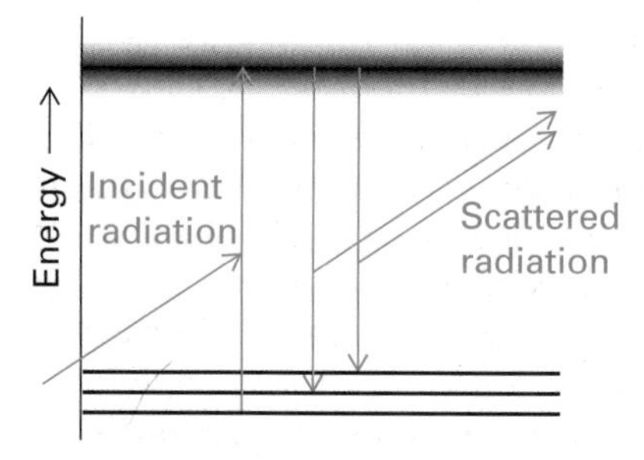

Fig. 19.2 In Raman spectroscopy, an incident photon is scattered from a molecule with either an increase in frequency (if the radiation collects energy from the molecule) or—as shown here—with a lower frequency if it loses energy to the molecule. The process can be regarded as taking place by an excitation of the molecule to a wide range of states (represented by the shaded band), and the subsequent return of the molecule to a lower state; the net energy change is then carried away by the photon.

(single-frequency) incident beam is passed through the sample and we record the frequencies present in the radiation scattered by the sample (Fig. 19.2).

The energy of a photon emitted or absorbed, and therefore the frequency, ν (nu), of the radiation emitted or absorbed, is given by the Bohr frequency condition (Section 13.1):

$$h\nu = |E_1 - E_2| \qquad (19.1)$$

Here E_1 and E_2 are the energies of the two states between which the transition occurs and h is Planck's constant.[1] This relation is often expressed in terms of the wavelength, λ (lambda), of the radiation by using the relation

$$\lambda = \frac{c}{\nu} \qquad (19.2a)$$

where c is the speed of light, or in terms of the wavenumber, $\tilde{\nu}$ (nu tilde):

$$\tilde{\nu} = \frac{1}{\lambda} = \frac{\nu}{c} \qquad (19.2b)$$

The units of wavenumber are almost always chosen as reciprocal centimetres (cm^{-1}), so we can picture the wavenumber of radiation as the number of complete wavelengths per centimetre. The chart in Fig. 12.2 summarized the frequencies, wavelengths, and wavenumbers of the various regions of the electromagnetic spectrum.

A note on good practice You will often hear people speak of a frequency as 'so many wavenumbers'. This usage is doubly wrong. First, *frequency* and *wavenumber* are two distinct physical observables with different units, and should be distinguished. Second, 'wavenumber' is not a unit, it is an observable with the dimensions of 1/length and commonly reported in reciprocal centimetres (cm^{-1}).

19.1 Experimental techniques

Emission, absorption, and Raman spectroscopy give the same information about energy level separations, but practical considerations generally determine which technique is used. In this chapter we concentrate on absorption and Raman spectroscopy. Emission spectroscopy is discussed in Chapter 20.

(a) Absorption spectroscopy

A **spectrometer** is an instrument that detects the characteristics of light scattered, emitted, or absorbed by atoms and molecules. Figure 19.3 shows the general layout of an absorption spectrometer. Radiation from an appropriate source is directed towards a sample. In most spectrometers, light

[1] Raman scattering is a special case, and we deal with it later.

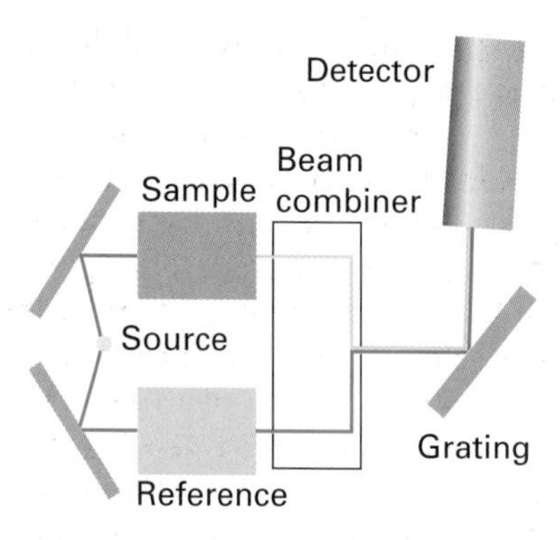

Fig. 19.3 The layout of a typical absorption spectrometer. The beams pass alternately through the sample and reference cells, and the detector is synchronized with them so that the relative absorption can be determined.

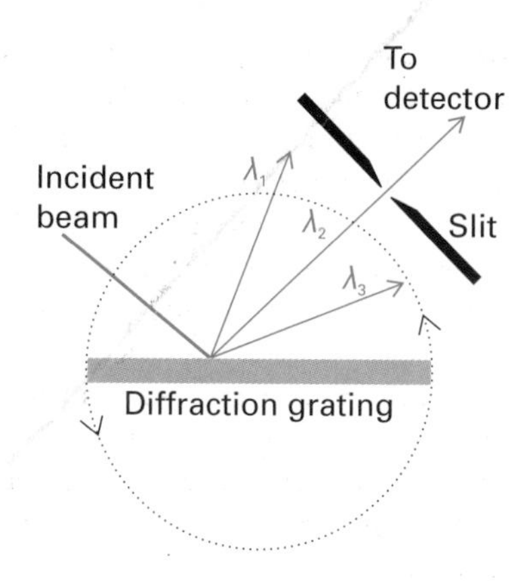

Fig. 19.4 A beam of light is dispersed by a diffraction grating into three component wavelengths λ_1, λ_2, and λ_3. In the configuration shown, only radiation with λ_2 passes through a narrow slit and reaches the detector. Rotating the diffraction grating in the direction shown by the arrows allows λ_3 to reach the detector.

transmitted, emitted, or scattered by the sample is collected by mirrors or lenses and strikes a dispersing element that separates radiation into different frequencies. The intensity of light at each frequency is then analysed by a suitable detector.

The source in a spectrometer typically produces radiation spanning a range of frequencies, but in a few cases (including lasers) it generates nearly monochromatic radiation. For the far-infrared ($35\ \text{cm}^{-1} < \tilde{\nu} < 200\ \text{cm}^{-1}$), the source is commonly a mercury arc inside a quartz envelope, most of the radiation being generated by the hot quartz. A *Nernst filament* or *globar* is used to generate radiation in the mid-infrared ($200\ \text{cm}^{-1} < \tilde{\nu} < 4000\ \text{cm}^{-1}$): it consists of a heated ceramic filament containing rare-earth (lanthanoid) oxides, and emits radiation closely resembling that of a hot black body (Section 12.1). For the visible region of the spectrum, a *tungsten–iodine lamp* is used, which gives out intense white light. The halogen combines with any vaporized tungsten atoms, and the resulting halide decomposes on the hot filament, so restoring the tungsten and lengthening the life of the filament. A discharge through deuterium gas or xenon in quartz is still widely used for the near-ultraviolet. A *klystron* (which is also used in radar installations and microwave ovens) or, more commonly now, a semiconductor device known as a *Gunn diode*, is used to generate microwaves. Radiofrequency radiation is generated by causing an electric current to oscillate in a coil of wire.

The simplest dispersing element is a glass or quartz prism, but modern instruments use a *diffraction grating*, a glass or ceramic plate into which fine grooves have been cut about 1000 nm apart (a spacing comparable to the wavelength of visible light) and covered with a reflective aluminium coating. The grating causes interference between waves reflected from its surface, and constructive interference occurs at specific angles that depend on the frequency of the radiation being used. Thus, each wavelength of light is directed into a specific direction (Fig. 19.4). In a *monochromator*, a narrow exit slit allows only a narrow range of wavelengths to reach the detector. Turning the grating around an axis perpendicular to the incident and diffracted beams allows different wavelengths to be analysed; in this way, the absorption spectrum is built up one narrow wavelength range at a time. In a *polychromator*, there is no slit and a broad range of wavelengths can be analysed simultaneously by *array detectors*, such as those discussed below.

Modern spectrometers, particularly those operating in the infrared and near-infrared, now almost always use Fourier-transform techniques of spectral detection and analysis. The heart of a Fourier-transform spectrometer is a *Michelson interferometer*, a device for analysing the frequencies present in a composite signal. The total signal from a sample is like a chord played on a piano, and the Fourier transform of the signal is equivalent to the separation of the chord into its individual notes, its spectrum. A major advantage of the Fourier-transform procedure is that all the radiation emitted by the source is monitored continuously. This is in contrast to a spectrometer in which a monochromator discards most of the generated radiation. As a result, Fourier-transform spectrometers have a higher sensitivity than conventional spectrometers.

The detector is a device that converts radiation into an electric current or voltage for appropriate signal processing and display. Detectors may consist of a single radiation-sensing element or of several small elements arranged in one- or two-dimensional arrays. A common detector is a *photodiode*, a solid-state device that conducts electricity when struck by photons because light-induced electron transfer reactions in the detector material create mobile charge carriers (negatively charged electrons and positively charged 'holes'). With appropriate choice of material, photodiodes can be used to detect radiation spanning a wide range of wavelengths. For example, silicon is sensitive in the visible region and germanium is used in most spectrometers operating in the near-infrared region of the spectrum, including Fourier-transform Raman spectrometers.

A *charge-coupled device* (CCD) is a two-dimensional array of several million photodiode detectors. With a CCD, a wide range of wavelengths that emerge from a polychromator are detected simultaneously, thus eliminating the need to measure light intensity one narrow wavelength range at a time. CCD detectors are used widely to monitor absorption, emission, and Raman scattering.

The most common detectors found in commercial infrared spectrometers are sensitive in the mid-infrared region. An example is the mercury–cadmium–telluride (MCT) detector, a *photovoltaic device* for which the potential difference changes upon exposure to infrared radiation.

A microwave detector is typically a *crystal diode* consisting of a tungsten tip in contact with a semiconductor, such as germanium, silicon, or gallium arsenide. In microwave spectroscopy, as in other applications where the optical signal is very weak, the intensity of the radiation arriving at the detector is usually modulated, because alternating signals are easier to amplify than a steady signal. In most cases the beam is chopped by a rotating shutter.

A spectrometer's resolution is the smallest observable separation between two closely spaced spectral bands. The highest resolution is obtained when the sample is gaseous and of such low pressure that collisions between the molecules are infrequent. Gaseous samples are essential for rotational (microwave) spectroscopy, because only in that phase can molecules rotate freely. For infrared spectroscopy, the sample is typically a liquid held between windows of sodium chloride (which is transparent down to 700 cm^{-1}) or potassium bromide (down to 400 cm^{-1}). Other ways of preparing the sample include grinding it into a paste with 'Nujol', a hydrocarbon oil, or pressing it into a solid disc, perhaps with powdered potassium bromide.

(b) Raman spectroscopy

In **Raman spectroscopy**, molecular energy levels are explored by examining the frequencies present in the radiation scattered by molecules. In a typical experiment, a monochromatic incident laser beam is passed through the sample and the radiation scattered from the front face of the sample is monitored (Fig. 19.5). This detection geometry allows for the study of gases, pure liquids, solutions, suspensions, and solids. About 1 in 10^7 of the incident photons collide with the molecules, give up some of their energy, and emerge with a lower energy. These scattered photons constitute the lower-frequency

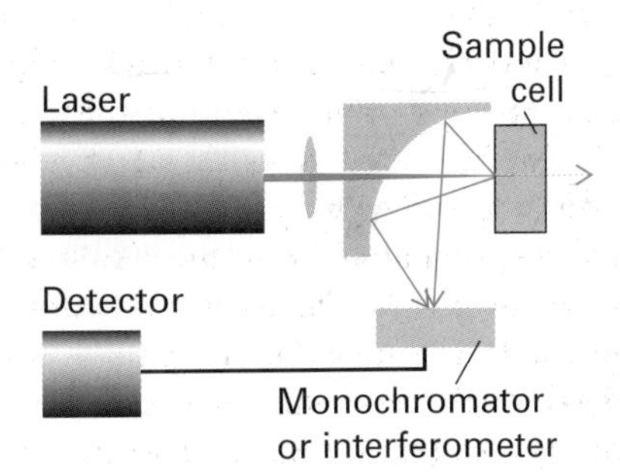

Fig. 19.5 A common arrangement adopted in Raman spectroscopy. A laser beam first passes through a lens and then through a small hole in a mirror with a curved reflecting surface. The focused beam strikes the sample and scattered light is both deflected and focused by the mirror. The spectrum is analysed by a monochromator or an interferometer.

Stokes radiation from the sample. Other incident photons may collect energy from the molecules (if they are already excited), and emerge as higher-frequency **anti-Stokes radiation.** The component of radiation scattered into the forward direction without change of frequency is called **Rayleigh radiation.**

Lasers are used as the radiation sources in Raman spectrometers for two reasons. First, the shifts in frequency of the scattered radiation from the incident radiation are quite small, so highly monochromatic radiation from a laser is required if the shifts are to be observed. Second, the intensity of scattered radiation is low, so intense incident beams, such as those from a laser, are needed. Raman spectra may be examined by using visible and ultraviolet lasers, in which case a diffraction grating is used to distinguish between Rayleigh, Stokes, and anti-Stokes radiation. In Fourier-transform Raman spectrometers, radiation scattered by the sample passes through a Michelson interferometer.

19.2 Measures of intensity

We now return to absorption spectroscopy. In Section 10.1, we introduced the **Beer–Lambert law,** which relates the intensity of absorption of radiation at a particular wavelength to the concentration [J] of the absorbing species:

$$A = \log \frac{I_0}{I} = \varepsilon[\mathrm{J}]l \qquad (19.3)$$

In this originally empirical expression, but which is justified theoretically in *Further information* 19.1, A is the **absorbance** of the sample, I_0 and I are the incident and transmitted intensities, respectively, l is the length of the sample, and ε (epsilon) is the **molar absorption coefficient,** with dimensions of 1/(concentration × length); the logarithm is to base 10. It is common to report the absorption of radiation in terms of the **transmittance,** T, of a sample at a given frequency, where

$$T = \frac{I}{I_0} \qquad (19.4)$$

The molar absorption coefficient depends on the frequency of the incident radiation and is greatest where the absorption is most intense. Typical values of ε for strong transitions are of the order of

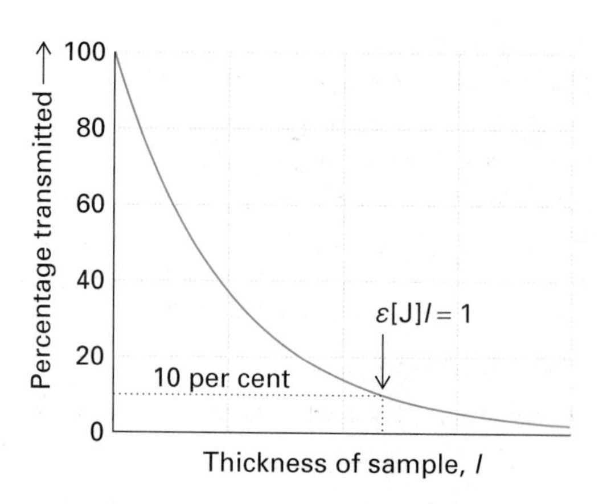

Fig. 19.6 The intensity of light transmitted by an absorbing sample decreases exponentially with the path length through the sample.

10^4–10^5 dm^3 mol^{-1} cm^{-1}, indicating that in a solution of molar concentration 0.01 mol dm^{-3} the intensity of light (of frequency corresponding to the maximum absorption) falls to 10 per cent of its initial value after passing through about 0.1 mm of solution (Fig. 19.6).

Example 19.1

The molar absorption coefficient

Radiation of wavelength 256 nm passed through 1.0 mm of a solution that contained benzene in a transparent solvent at a concentration of 0.050 mol dm^{-3}. The light intensity is reduced to 16 per cent of its initial value (so $T = 0.16$). Calculate the absorbance and the molar absorption coefficient of the benzene. What would be the transmittance through a cell of thickness 2.0 mm?

Strategy For the calculation of ε we use the relation $\log x^{-1} = -\log x$ to rearrange eqn 19.4:

$$A = -\log \frac{I}{I_0} = -\log T$$

It follows from this expression and eqn 19.3 that

$$\varepsilon = -\frac{\log T}{[\mathrm{J}]l}$$

For the transmittance through the thicker cell, we use the value of ε calculated here and $T = 10^{-A}$.

Solution The molar absorption coefficient is

$$\varepsilon = -\frac{\log 0.16}{(0.050\ \text{mol dm}^{-3}) \times (1.0\ \text{mm})}$$
$$= 16\ \text{dm}^3\ \text{mol}^{-1}\ \text{mm}^{-1}$$

These units are convenient for the rest of the calculation (but the outcome could be reported as $1.6 \times 10^2\ \text{dm}^3\ \text{mol}^{-1}\ \text{cm}^{-1}$ if desired). The absorbance is

$$A = -\log 0.16 = 0.80$$

The absorbance of a sample of length 2.0 mm is

$$A = \varepsilon[\text{J}]l$$
$$= (16\ \text{dm}^3\ \text{mol}^{-1}\ \text{mm}^{-1}) \times (0.050\ \text{mol dm}^{-3}) \times (2.0\ \text{mm})$$
$$= 1.6$$

It follows that the transmittance is then

$$T = 10^{-A} = 10^{-1.6} = 0.025$$

That is, the emergent light is reduced to 2.5 per cent of its incident intensity.

Self-test 19.1

The transmittance of an aqueous solution that contained Cu^{2+} ions at a molar concentration of 0.10 mol dm^{-3} was measured as 0.30 at 600 nm in a cell of length 5.0 mm. Calculate the molar absorption coefficient of Cu^{2+}(aq) at that wavelength, and the absorbance of the solution. What would be the transmittance through a cell of length 1.0 mm?

[*Answer:* $10\ \text{dm}^3\ \text{mol}^{-1}\ \text{cm}^{-1}$, $A = 0.52$, $T = 0.79$]

The maximum value of the molar absorption coefficient, ε_{max}, is an indication of the intensity of a transition. However, because absorption bands generally spread over a range of wavenumbers, the absorption at a single wavenumber might not give a true indication of the intensity. The latter is best reported as the **integrated absorption coefficient**, $\mathcal{A}$, the area under the plot of the molar absorption coefficient against wavenumber (Fig. 19.7).

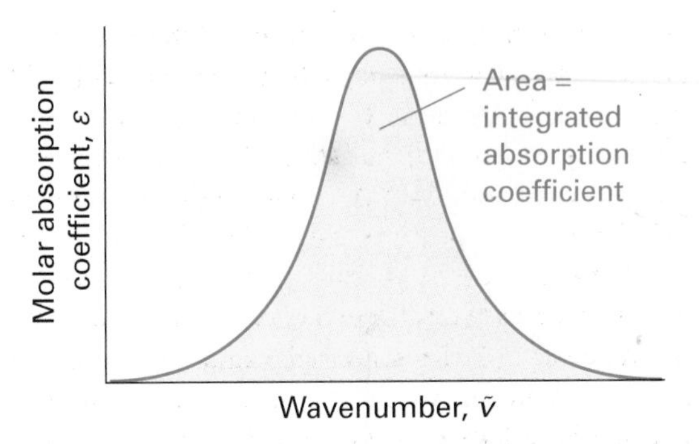

Fig. 19.7 The integrated absorption coefficient of a transition is the area under a plot of the molar absorption coefficient against the wavenumber of the incident radiation.

As we discuss in *Further information* 19.1, the intensity of a spectral line also depends on the number of molecules that are in the initial state and the strength with which individual molecules are able to interact with the electromagnetic field and generate or absorb photons. If we confine our attention to vibrational and electronic spectroscopy, then the situation is very simple: *almost all vibrational absorptions and all electronic absorptions occur from the ground state of a molecule*, because that is the only state populated at room temperature. However, molecules can be prepared in short-lived excited states as a result of chemical reaction, electric discharge, or photolysis. In these cases the populations may be quite different from those at thermal equilibrium, and absorption and emission spectra—if they can be recorded quickly enough—then arise from transitions from all the populated levels.

19.3 Selection rules

Whether or not a transition can be driven by or can drive the oscillations of the surrounding electromagnetic field depends on a quantity called the **transition dipole moment**. This quantity is a measure of the dipole moment associated with the shift of electric charge that accompanies a transition (Fig. 19.8). The intensity of the transition is proportional to the square of the associated transition dipole moment. A large transition dipole moment indicates that the transition gives a strong 'thump' to the electromagnetic field, and conversely that the electromagnetic field interacts strongly with the molecule.

A **selection rule** is a statement about when a transition dipole is non-zero. There are two parts to a selection rule. A **gross selection rule** specifies the general features that a molecule must have if it is to have a spectrum of a given kind. For instance, we shall see that a molecule gives a rotational spectrum

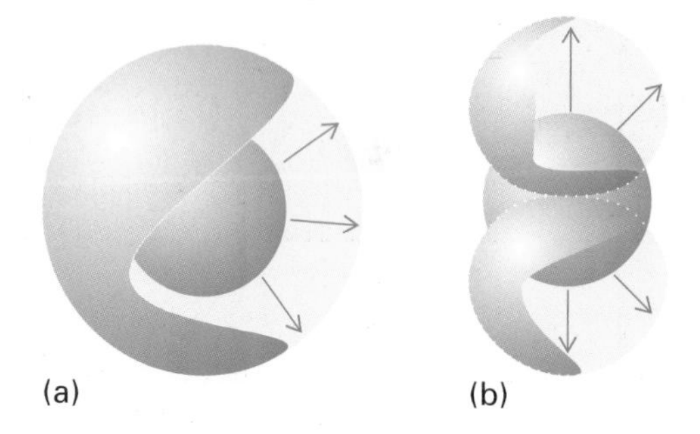

Fig. 19.8 The transition moment is a measure of the magnitude of the shift in charge during a transition. (a) A spherical redistribution of charge as in this transition has no associated dipole moment, and does not give rise to electromagnetic radiation. (b) This redistribution of charge has an associated dipole moment.

only if it has a permanent electric dipole moment. Once the gross selection rule has been recognized, we consider the **specific selection rule**, a statement about which changes in quantum number may occur in a transition. We have already encountered examples of specific selection rules when discussing atomic spectra, such as the rule $\Delta l = \pm 1$ for the angular momentum quantum number.

A transition that is permitted by a specific selection rule is classified as **allowed.** Transitions that are disallowed by a specific selection rule are called **forbidden.** Forbidden transitions sometimes occur weakly because the selection rule is based on an approximation that turns out to be slightly invalid.

19.4 Linewidths

In condensed media, an electronic transition may spread over several thousand reciprocal centimetres: its width stems from the simultaneous excitation of molecular vibrations, with the individual spectral lines blending together to give a broad band. An important broadening process in gaseous samples is the **Doppler effect,** in which radiation is shifted in frequency when the source is moving towards or away from the observer. When a source emitting radiation of frequency ν recedes with a speed s, the observer detects radiation of frequency

$$\nu' = \left(\frac{1 - s/c}{1 + s/c}\right)^{1/2} \nu \qquad (19.5a)$$

where c is the speed of the radiation (the speed of light for electromagnetic radiation, the speed of sound for sound waves). A source approaching the observer appears to be emitting radiation of frequency

$$\nu' = \left(\frac{1 + s/c}{1 - s/c}\right)^{1/2} \nu \qquad (19.5b)$$

Similar expressions apply to the wavenumber of the radiation.

Self-test 19.2

A laser line occurs at 628.443 cm^{-1}. What wavenumber will an observer detect when approaching the laser at (a) 1 m s^{-1}, (b) 1000 m s^{-1}?

[*Answer:* (a) 628.443 cm^{-1}, (b) 628.445 cm^{-1}]

Molecules reach high speeds in all directions in a gas, and a stationary observer detects the corresponding Doppler-shifted range of frequencies. Some molecules approach the observer, some move away; some move quickly, others slowly. The detected spectroscopic 'line' is the absorption or emission profile arising from all the resulting Doppler shifts. The profile reflects the Maxwell distribution of molecular speeds (Section 1.6) towards or away from the observer, and the outcome is that we observe a bell-shaped Gaussian curve (a curve of the form e^{-x^2}, Fig. 19.9). When the temperature is

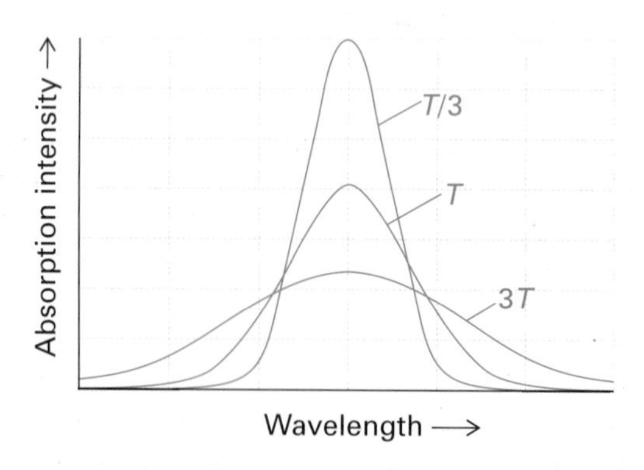

Fig. 19.9 The shape of a Doppler-broadened spectral line reflects the Maxwell distribution of speeds in the sample at the temperature of the experiment. Note that the line broadens as the temperature is increased. The width at half-height is given by eqn 19.6.

T and the molar mass of the molecule is M, the width of the line at half its maximum height (the 'width at half-height') is

$$\delta\lambda = \frac{2\lambda}{c}\left(\frac{2RT \ln 2}{M}\right)^{1/2} \tag{19.6}$$

The Doppler width increases with temperature because the molecules acquire a wider range of speeds. Therefore, to obtain spectra of maximum sharpness, it is best to work with cold gaseous samples.

Self-test 19.3

The Sun emits radiation at 677.4 nm that has been identified as arising from a transition in highly ionized ^{57}Fe. Its width at half-height is 5.3 pm. What is the temperature of the Sun's surface?

[*Answer:* 6.8×10^3 K]

Another source of line broadening is the finite lifetime of the states involved in the transition. When the Schrödinger equation is solved for a system that is changing with time, it is found that the states of the system do not have precisely defined energies. If the time-constant for the decay of a state is τ (tau), which is called the **lifetime** of the state,[2] then its energy levels are blurred by δE, where

$$\delta E \approx \frac{\hbar}{\tau} \tag{19.7a}$$

We see that the shorter the lifetime of a state, the less well defined is its energy. The energy spread inherent to the states of systems that have finite lifetimes is called **lifetime broadening.**[3] When we express the energy spread as a wavenumber by writing $\delta E = hc\delta\tilde{\nu}$ and use the values of the fundamental constants, the practical form of this relation becomes

$$\delta\tilde{\nu} \approx \frac{5.3\ \text{cm}^{-1}}{\tau/\text{ps}} \tag{19.7b}$$

Only if τ is infinite can the energy of a state be specified exactly (with $\delta E = 0$). However, no excited state has an infinite lifetime; therefore, all states are subject to some lifetime broadening, and the shorter the lifetimes of the states involved in a transition, the broader the spectral lines.

Self-test 19.4

What is the width (expressed as a wavenumber) of a transition from a state with a lifetime of 5.0 ps?

[*Answer:* 1.1 cm^{-1}]

Two processes are principally responsible for the finite lifetimes of excited states, and hence for the widths of transitions to or from them. The dominant one is **collisional deactivation**, which arises from collisions between molecules or with the walls of the container. If the collisional lifetime is τ_{col}, then the resulting collisional linewidth is $\delta E_{col} \approx \hbar/\tau_{col}$. In gases, the collisional lifetime can be lengthened, and the broadening minimized, by working at low pressures. The second contribution is **spontaneous emission**, the emission of radiation when an excited state collapses into a lower state. The rate of spontaneous emission depends on details of the wavefunctions of the excited and lower states. Because the rate of spontaneous emission cannot be changed (without changing the molecule), it is a natural limit to the lifetime of an excited state. The resulting lifetime broadening is the **natural linewidth** of the transition.

The natural linewidth of a transition cannot be changed by modifying the temperature or pressure. Natural linewidths depend strongly on the transition frequency ν (they increase as ν^3), so low-frequency transitions (such as the microwave transitions of rotational spectroscopy) have very small natural linewidths; for such transitions, collisional and Doppler line-broadening processes are dominant. The natural lifetimes of electronic transitions are very much shorter than for vibrational transitions, so the natural linewidths of electronic transitions are much greater than those of vibrational and rotational transitions. For example, a typical electronic excited state natural lifetime is about 10^{-8} s (10^4 ps), corresponding to a natural width of about 5×10^{-4} cm^{-1} (equivalent to 15 MHz).

[2] The decay of the state is assumed to be exponential and proportional to $e^{-t/\tau}$.

[3] Lifetime broadening is also called *uncertainty broadening*.

Rotational spectroscopy

The energy levels of molecules free to rotate are quantized, and transitions between these levels give rise to the **rotational spectrum** of a molecule. Very little energy is needed to change the state of rotation of a molecule, and the electromagnetic radiation emitted or absorbed lies in the microwave region, with wavelengths of the order of 0.1–1 cm and frequencies close to 10 GHz. The rotational spectroscopy of gas-phase samples is therefore also known as **microwave spectroscopy**. To achieve sufficient absorption, the path lengths of gaseous samples must be very long, of the order of metres. Long path lengths are achieved by multiple passage of the beam between two parallel mirrors at each end of the sample cavity.

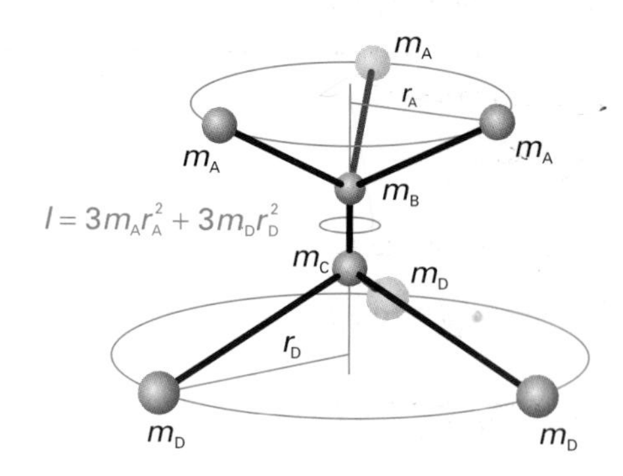

Fig. 19.10 The definition of moment of inertia. In this molecule there are three identical atoms attached to the B atom and three different but mutually identical atoms attached to the C atom. In this example, the centre of mass lies on an axis passing through the B and C atoms, and the perpendicular distances are measured from this axis.

19.5 The rotational energy levels of molecules

To a first approximation, the rotational states of molecules are based on a model system called a **rigid rotor**, a body that is not distorted by the stress of rotation. The simplest type of rigid rotor is called a **linear rotor**, and corresponds to a linear molecule, such as HCl, CO_2, or HC≡CH, that is supposed not to be able to bend or stretch under the stress of rotation. When the Schrödinger equation is solved for a linear rotor (see *Further information* 19.2), the energies are found to be

$$E_J = hBJ(J+1) \qquad J = 0, 1, 2, \ldots \tag{19.8}$$

where J is the **rotational quantum number**. The constant B (a frequency, with the units hertz, Hz) is called the **rotational constant** of the molecule, and is defined as

$$B = \frac{\hbar}{4\pi I} \tag{19.9}$$

where I is the **moment of inertia** of the molecule. The moment of inertia of a molecule is the mass of each atom multiplied by the square of its distance from the axis of rotation (Fig. 19.10):

$$I = \sum_i m_i r_i^2 \tag{19.10}$$

The moment of inertia plays a role in rotation analogous to the role played by mass in translation. A body with a high moment of inertia (like that of a flywheel or a heavy molecule) undergoes only a small rotational acceleration when a twisting force (a torque) is applied, but a body with a small moment of inertia undergoes a large acceleration when subjected to the same torque. Table 19.1 gives the expressions for the moments of inertia of various types of molecules in terms of the masses of their atoms and their bond lengths and bond angles.

Illustration 19.1

Calculating the moment of inertia of a molecule

To calculate the moment of inertia of a $^{12}C^{16}O_2$ molecule, we take the axis of rotation through the C atom (the centre of mass of the molecule). It follows that

$$I = m_O R^2 + 0 + m_O R^2 = 2m_O R^2$$

where R is the CO bond length. We now use $m_O = 16.00$ u (where the atomic mass unit is 1 u = $1.660\,54 \times 10^{-27}$ kg) and $R = 116$ pm, and find

$$\begin{aligned} I &= 2 \times (16.00\ \text{u}) \times (1.16 \times 10^{-10}\ \text{m})^2 \\ &= 2 \times (16.00 \times 1.660\,54 \times 10^{-27}\ \text{kg}) \times (1.16 \times 10^{-10}\ \text{m})^2 \\ &= 7.15 \times 10^{-46}\ \text{kg m}^2 \end{aligned}$$

A note on good practice To calculate the moment of inertia precisely, we need to specify the nuclide. Also, the mass to use is the actual atomic mass, not the element's molar mass; don't forget to convert from atomic mass units (u, formerly amu) to kilograms.

Table 19.1 *Moments of inertia*

1 *Diatomic molecules*

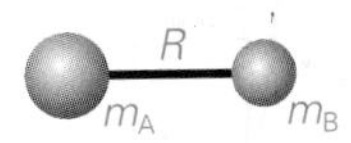

$$I = \mu R^2 \qquad \mu = \frac{m_A m_B}{m}$$

2 *Triatomic linear rotors*

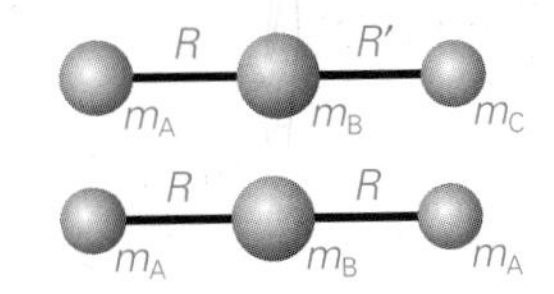

$$I = m_A R^2 + m_C R'^2 - \frac{(m_A R - m_C R')^2}{m}$$

$$I = 2m_A R^2$$

3 *Symmetric rotors*

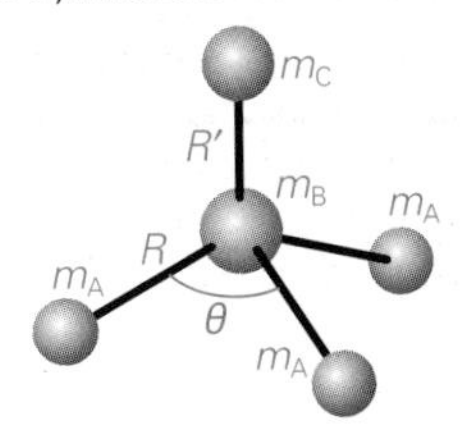

$$I_{\parallel} = 2m_A(1 - \cos\theta)R^2$$

$$I_{\perp} = m_A(1 - \cos\theta)R^2 + \frac{m_A}{m}(m_B + m_C)(1 + 2\cos\theta)R^2 + \frac{m_C}{m}\{(3m_A + m_B)R' + 6m_A R[\tfrac{1}{3}(1 + 2\cos\theta)]^{1/2}\}R'$$

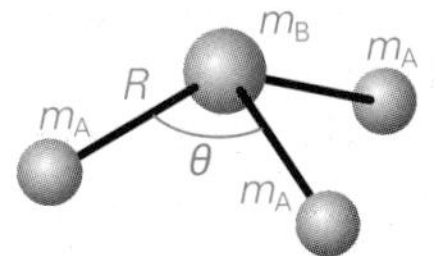

$$I_{\parallel} = 2m_A(1 - \cos\theta)R^2$$

$$I_{\perp} = m_A(1 - \cos\theta)R^2 + \frac{m_A m_B}{m}(1 + 2\cos\theta)R^2$$

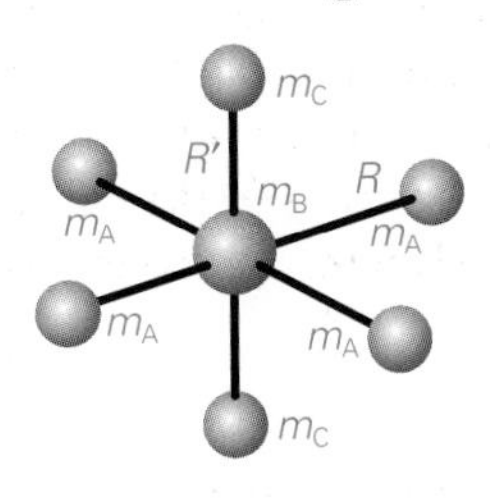

$$I_{\parallel} = 4m_A R^2$$

$$I_{\perp} = 2m_A R^2 + 2m_C R'^2$$

4 *Spherical rotors*

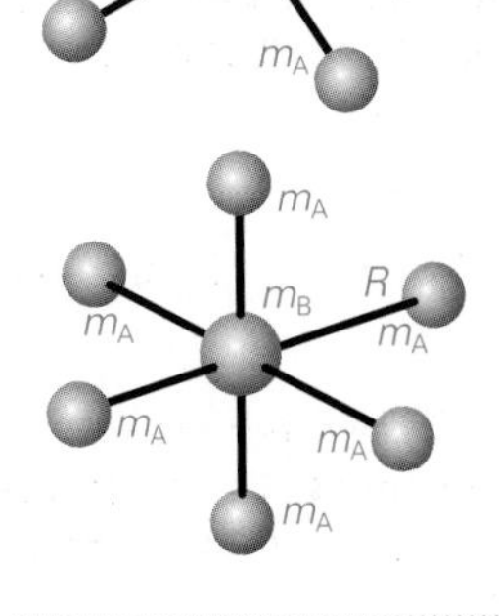

$$I = \tfrac{8}{3}m_A R^2$$

$$I = 4m_A R^2$$

In each case, m is the total mass of the molecule.

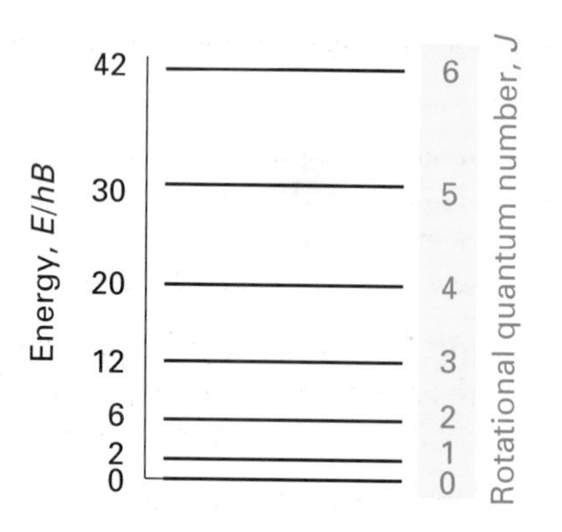

Fig. 19.11 The energy levels of a linear rigid rotor as multiples of hB.

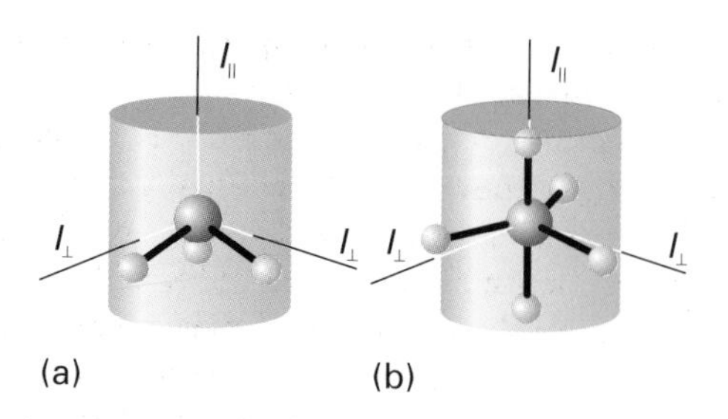

Fig. 19.12 The two different moments of inertia of (a) a trigonal pyramidal molecule and (b) a trigonal bipyramidal molecule.

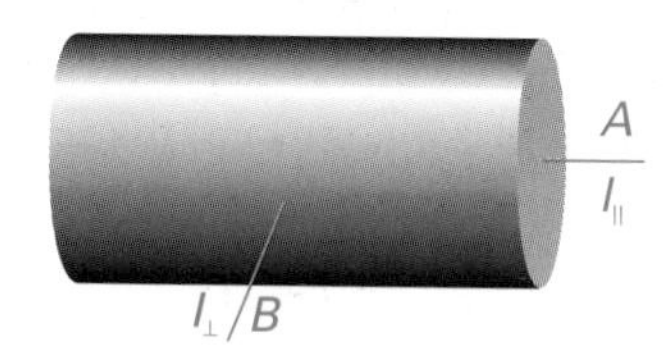

Fig. 19.13 The two rotational constants of a symmetric rotor, which are inversely proportional to the moments of inertia parallel and perpendicular to the axis of the molecule.

Figure 19.11 shows the energy levels predicted by eqn 19.8: note that the separation of neighbouring levels increases with J. Note also that, because J may be 0, the lowest possible energy is 0: there is no zero-point rotational energy for molecules. The rotational quantum number also specifies the angular momentum of the molecule (classically, a measure of its rate of rotation): a molecule with $J = 0$ has zero angular momentum, and as J increases, so does the molecule's angular momentum. In general, the rotational angular momentum is $\{J(J+1)\}^{1/2}\hbar$, the same relation as that between the orbital angular momentum of an electron and the quantum number l.

A number of non-linear molecules can be modelled as a **symmetric rotor**, a rigid rotor in which the moments of inertia about two axes are the same, but different from a third (and all three are non-zero).[4] An example is ammonia, NH_3, and another is phosphorus pentachloride, PCl_5 (Fig. 19.12). As shown in *Further information* 19.2, the energy levels of a symmetric rotor are determined by two quantum numbers, J and K, and are

$$E_{J,K} = hBJ(J+1) + h(A-B)K^2$$
$$J = 0, 1, 2, \ldots \qquad K = J, J-1, \ldots, -J \qquad (19.11)$$

The rotational constants A and B are inversely proportional to the moments of inertia parallel and perpendicular to the axis of the molecule (Fig. 19.13):

$$A = \frac{\hbar}{4\pi I_{\parallel}} \qquad B = \frac{\hbar}{4\pi I_{\perp}} \qquad (19.12)$$

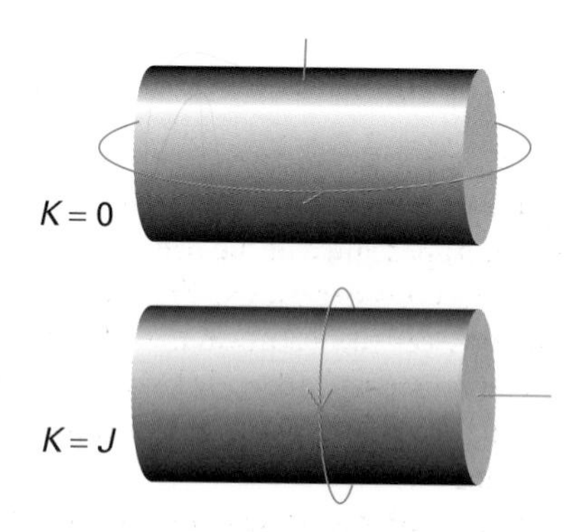

Fig. 19.14 When $K = 0$ for a symmetric rotor, the entire motion of the molecule is around an axis perpendicular to the symmetry axis of the rotor. When the value of $|K|$ is close to J, almost all the motion is around the symmetry axis.

The quantum number K tells us, through $K\hbar$, the component of angular momentum around the molecular axis (Fig. 19.14). When $K = 0$, the molecule is rotating end-over-end and not at all around its own axis. When $K = \pm J$ (the greatest values in its range), the molecule is rotating mainly about its axis.

[4] The formal criterion of a molecule being a symmetric rotor is that it has an axis of threefold or higher symmetry.

Intermediate values of K correspond to a combination of the two modes of rotation.

A special case of a symmetric rotor is a **spherical rotor**, a rigid body with three equal moments of inertia (like a sphere). Tetrahedral, octahedral, and icosahedral molecules (CH_4, SF_6, and C_{60}, for instance) are spherical rotors. Their energy levels are very simple: when $I_{\parallel} = I_{\perp}$, the rotational constants A and B are equal and eqn 19.11 simplifies to eqn 19.8.

There is one final remark. Molecules are not really *rigid* rotors: they distort under the stress of rotation. As their bond lengths increase, their energy levels become slightly closer together. This effect is taken into account by supposing that eqn 19.8 can be modified to

$$E_J = hBJ(J+1) - hDJ^2(J+1)^2 \qquad (19.13)$$

The parameter D is the **centrifugal distortion constant.** It is large when the bond is easily stretched, and so its magnitude is related to the force constants of bonds.

19.6 The populations of rotational states

The question we now address is the relative numbers of molecules in each rotational state, as that will affect the appearance of the rotational spectrum. There are two considerations: first, whether there are restrictions on the rotational state in which a molecule can exist; and second, how the molecules are distributed over the permitted rotational states at a given temperature.

Not all the rotational states of symmetrical molecules, like H_2 and CO_2, are permitted. The elimination of certain states is a consequence of the Pauli exclusion principle that, as we saw in Chapter 13, also forbids the occurrence of certain atomic states (such as those with three electrons in one orbital, or two electrons with the same spin in the same orbital). The restriction on the permitted rotational states due to the Pauli principle can be traced to the effect of nuclear spin and is called **nuclear statistics.**

To understand how the Pauli exclusion principle excludes certain rotational states, we need to express the principle in a more general way than in *Further information* 13.1, which referred only to electrons. The most general form of the Pauli principle states

When any two indistinguishable fermions are interchanged, the wavefunction must change sign; when any two indistinguishable bosons are interchanged, the wavefunction must remain the same.

(Bosons are particles with integral spin; fermions are particles with half-integral spin; see Section 13.6.) In short, if A and B are indistinguishable particles, then

$$\text{For fermions:} \quad \psi(B,A) = -\psi(A,B)$$

$$\text{For bosons:} \quad \psi(B,A) = \psi(A,B)$$

The 'fermion' part of this principle implies the Pauli *exclusion* principle, as we saw in Chapter 13. However, in this form it is more general and has wider implications.

Consider a CO_2 molecule, which we denote O_ACO_B. When the molecule rotates through 180°, it becomes O_BCO_A, with the two O atoms interchanged. The nuclear spin of oxygen-16 is zero, so it is a boson, and therefore the wavefunction must remain unchanged by this interchange. However, when *any* molecule is rotated through 180°, its wavefunction changes by a factor of $(-1)^J$. To see why that is so, we have drawn the first few wavefunctions for a particle travelling on a ring in Fig. 19.15, and we see that a rotation of 180° leaves wavefunctions with $J = 0, 2, \ldots$ unchanged but changes the sign of those with $J = 1, 3, \ldots$. The only way for the two requirements (that the wavefunction does not change sign and the fact that it changes by a factor of $(-1)^J$) to be consistent is for J to be restricted to even values. That is, a CO_2 molecule can exist only in the rotational states with $J = 0, 2, 4, \ldots$.

The analysis of the implications is more complex for molecules in which the nuclei have non-zero spin

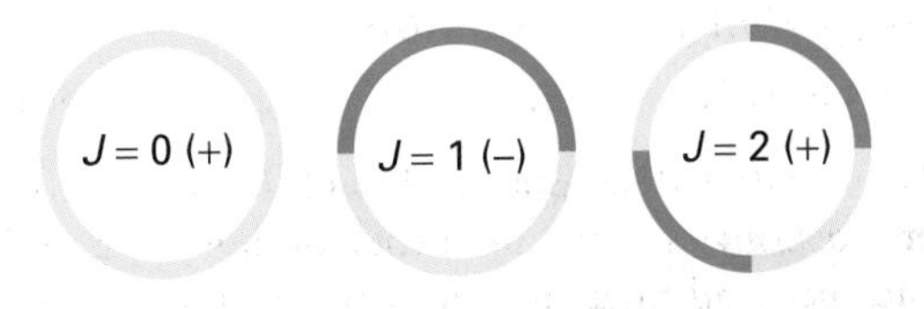

Fig. 19.15 The phases of the wavefunctions of a particle on a ring for the first few states: note that the parity of the wavefunction (its behaviour under inversion through the centre of the ring) is even, odd, even, ...

(which includes H_2, with its spin-$\frac{1}{2}$ nuclei) because the permitted rotational states depend on the relative orientation of the nuclear spins. However, the results can be expressed quite simply:

$$\frac{\text{Number of ways of achieving odd } J}{\text{Number of ways of achieving even } J} = \begin{cases} (I+1)/I & \text{for half-integral spin nuclei} \\ I/(I+1) & \text{for integral spin nuclei} \end{cases}$$

where I is the nuclear spin quantum number. For H_2, with its spin-$\frac{1}{2}$ nuclei ($I = \frac{1}{2}$), the ratio is 3:1. For D_2 and N_2, with their spin-1 nuclei ($I = 1$, where D is deuterium, ^{2}H), the ratio is 1:2.

The even-J rotational states of H_2 are allowed when the two nuclear spins are antiparallel (↑↓) and the odd-J states are allowed when the nuclear spins are parallel (↑↑). Different relative nuclear spin orientations change into one another only very slowly, so an H_2 molecule with parallel nuclear spins remains distinct from one with paired nuclear spins for long periods. The two forms of hydrogen can be separated by physical techniques, and stored. The form with parallel nuclear spins is called *ortho-hydrogen* and the form with paired nuclear spins is called *para-hydrogen* (remember: *para* for *paired*). Because *ortho*-hydrogen cannot exist in a state with $J = 0$, it continues to rotate at very low temperatures and has an effective rotational zero-point energy (Fig. 19.16). This energy is of some concern to manufacturers of liquid hydrogen, as the slow conversion of *ortho*-hydrogen into *para*-hydrogen (which can exist with $J = 0$) as nuclear spins slowly realign releases rotational energy, which vaporizes the liquid. Techniques are used to accelerate the conversion of *ortho*-hydrogen to *para*-hydrogen to avoid this problem. One such technique is to pass hydrogen over a metal surface: the molecules adsorb on the surface as atoms, which then recombine in the lower energy *para*-hydrogen form.

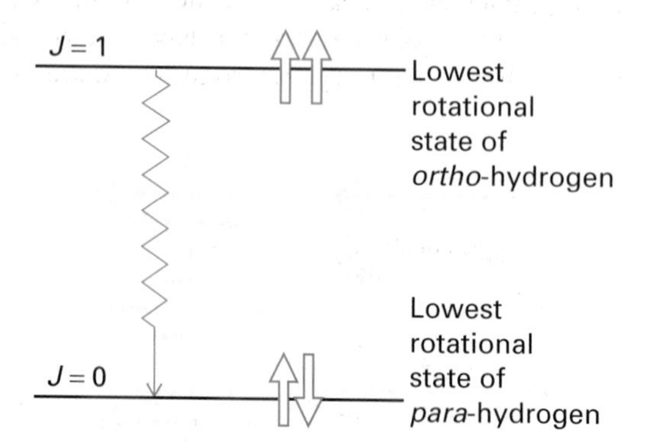

Fig. 19.16 When hydrogen is cooled, the molecules with parallel nuclear spins accumulate in their lowest available rotational state, the one with $J = 1$. They can enter the lowest rotational state ($J = 0$) only if the spins change their relative orientation and become antiparallel. This is a slow process under normal circumstances, so energy is released slowly.

Next, we need to consider how the permitted rotational states are populated. Because the rotational states of molecules are close together in energy, we can expect many states to be occupied at ordinary temperatures. However, we have to take into account the degeneracy of the rotational levels because, although a given *state* may have a low population, there may be many states of the same energy, and the total population of an *energy level* may be quite large.

For a linear molecule, which is all we consider (but see Exercise 19.25), the angular momentum of the molecule may have $2J + 1$ different orientations with respect to an external axis, each designated by the value of the quantum number $M_J = J, J - 1, \ldots, -J$ (Fig. 19.17, just as in atoms, there are $2l + 1$ orientations of the orbital angular momentum, one corresponding to each permitted value of m_l). The energy of the molecule is independent of its plane of rotation, so all $2J + 1$ states have the same energy, and therefore a level with a given value of J is $(2J + 1)$-fold degenerate. We shall see in Section 22.1 that

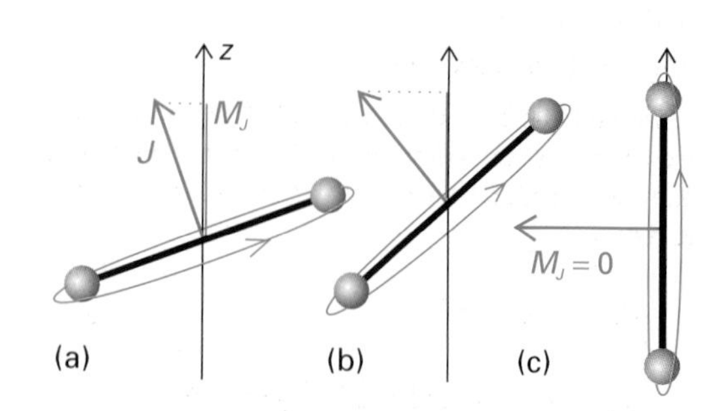

Fig. 19.17 The significance of the quantum number M_J: it indicates the orientation of the molecular rotational angular momentum with respect to an external axis. (a) $M_J \approx J$, (b) $M_J \approx J - 1$, (c) $M_J = 0$.

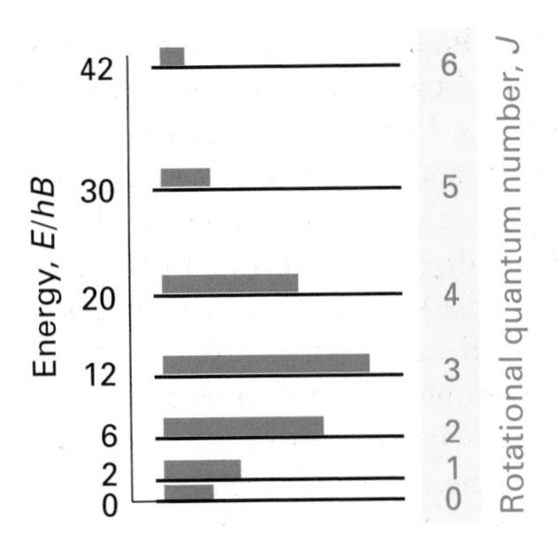

Fig. 19.18 The thermal equilibrium relative populations of the rotational energy levels of a linear rotor.

each of these individual states has a population that is proportional to $e^{-E_J/kT}$, with $E_J = hBJ(J+1)$, so the total population of a given *level* is

$$P_J \propto (2J+1)\,e^{-hBJ(J+1)/kT} \qquad (19.14)$$

Figure 19.18 shows how this population varies with J. As shown in Derivation 19.1, it passes through a maximum at

$$J_{max} = \left(\frac{kT}{2hB}\right)^{1/2} - \frac{1}{2} \qquad (19.15)$$

For a typical linear molecule (for example, OCS, with $B = 6$ GHz) at room temperature, $J_{max} = 22$. Broadly speaking, then, the absorption spectrum of the molecule should show a similar distribution of intensities.

Derivation 19.1

The most populated level

Here we need to find the value of J for which P_J is a maximum, so we differentiate the right-hand side of eqn 19.14 with respect to J and set the result equal to zero:

$$\frac{d}{dJ}(2J+1)\,e^{-hBJ(J+1)/kT}$$

$$= 2\,e^{-hBJ(J+1)/kT} - \frac{hB(2J+1)^2}{kT}\,e^{-hBJ(J+1)/kT}$$

$$= \left\{2 - \frac{hB(2J+1)^2}{kT}\right\} e^{-hBJ(J+1)/kT} = 0$$

To evaluate the derivative, we have used the following two results:

$$\frac{d}{dx}uv = \frac{du}{dx}v + u\frac{dv}{dx}$$

$$\frac{d}{dx}e^{ax} = a\,e^{ax}$$

To find the value of x corresponding to the extremum (maximum or minimum) of any function $f(x)$, we differentiate the function, set the result equal to zero, and solve the equation for x.

Therefore, we need to solve

$$2 - \frac{hB(2J+1)^2}{kT} = 0$$

which gives eqn 19.15.

19.7 Rotational transitions: microwave spectroscopy

The gross selection rule for rotational transitions is that *the molecule must be polar*. The classical basis of this rule is that a stationary observer watching a rotating polar molecule sees its partial charges moving backwards and forwards and their motion shakes the electromagnetic field into oscillation (Fig. 19.19). Because the molecule must be polar, it follows that tetrahedral (CH_4, for instance), octahedral (SF_6), symmetric linear (CO_2), and homonuclear diatomic (H_2) molecules do not have rotational spectra. On the contrary, heteronuclear diatomic

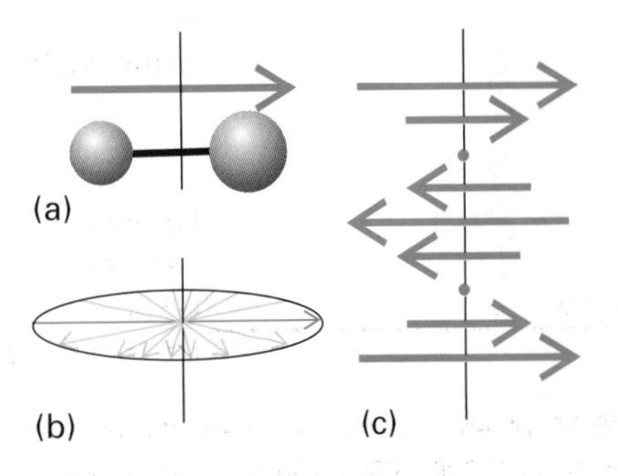

Fig. 19.19 To an external observer, (a) a rotating polar molecule has (b) an electric dipole (the arrow) that (c) appears to oscillate. This oscillating dipole can interact with the electromagnetic field.

(HCl) and less symmetrical polar polyatomic molecules (NH_3) are polar and do have rotational spectra. We say that polar molecules are **rotationally active** whereas non-polar molecules are **rotationally inactive**.

The specific selection rules for rotational transitions are

$$\Delta J = \pm 1 \qquad \Delta K = 0$$

The first of these selection rules can be traced, like the rule $\Delta l = \pm 1$ for atoms (Section 13.7), to the conservation of angular momentum when a photon is absorbed or created. A photon is a spin-1 particle, and when one is absorbed or created the angular momentum of the molecule must change by a compensating amount. Because J is a measure of the angular momentum of the molecule, J can change only by ± 1 (for pure rotational transitions, $\Delta J = +1$ corresponds to absorption, $\Delta J = -1$ to emission). The second selection rule ($\Delta K = 0$; that is, the quantum number K may not change) can be traced to the fact that the dipole moment of a polar molecule does not move when a molecule rotates around its symmetry axis (think of NH_3 rotating around its threefold axis). As a result, there can be no acceleration or deceleration of the rotation of the molecule about that axis by the absorption or emission of electromagnetic radiation.

When a rigid molecule changes its rotational quantum number from J to $J + 1$ in an absorption, the change in rotational energy of the molecule is

$$\Delta E = E_{J+1} - E_J = hB(J + 1)(J + 2) - hBJ(J + 1) = 2hB(J + 1)$$

The energies of these transitions are $2hB$, $4hB$, $6hB$, ... The frequency of the radiation absorbed in a transition starting from the level J is therefore

$$\nu_J = 2B(J + 1) \qquad (19.16a)$$

and the lines occur at $2B$, $4B$, $6B$, ... The intensity distribution will be like that in Fig. 19.20 with a maximum intensity at $\nu_{J_{max}}$, with J_{max} given by eqn 19.15. A rotational spectrum of a polar linear molecule (HCl) and of a polar symmetric rotor (NH_3) therefore consists of a series of lines at frequencies separated by $2B$. If centrifugal distortion is significant, then we use eqn 19.13 in the same way, and find

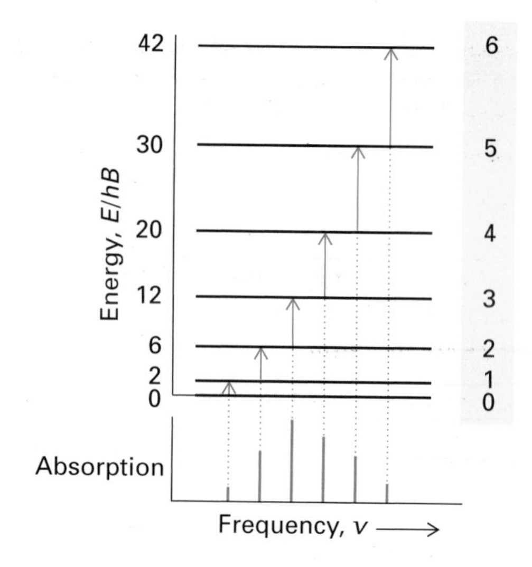

Fig. 19.20 The allowed rotational transitions (shown as absorptions) for a linear molecule.

$$\nu_J = 2B(J + 1) - 4D(J + 1)^3 \qquad (19.16b)$$

Now the lines converge as J increases. To determine B and D, we divide both sides by $J + 1$, to obtain

$$\frac{\nu_J}{J + 1} = 2B - 4D(J + 1)^2 \qquad (19.17)$$

Therefore, by plotting the $\nu_J/(J + 1)$ against $(J + 1)^2$, we should get a straight line with intercept $2B$ and slope $-4D$ (see Exercise 19.33).

A note on good practice It is often sensible to formulate an expression that, when plotted, results in a straight line. Then deviations—and deficiencies in the model—are easiest to identify. If the straight line looks plausible, the data should be analysed statistically, by doing a linear regression (least-squares) analysis of the data.

Example 19.2

Estimating the frequency of a rotational transition

Estimate the frequency of the $J = 0 \rightarrow 1$ transition of the $^1H^{35}Cl$ molecule. The masses of the two atoms are 1.673×10^{-27} kg and 5.807×10^{-26} kg, respectively, and the equilibrium bond length is 127.4 pm.

Strategy The calculation depends on the value of B, which we obtain by substituting the data into eqn 19.9. The frequency of the transition is $2B$.

Solution The moment of inertia of the molecule is

$$I = \mu R^2$$
$$= \frac{(1.673 \times 10^{-27}\,\text{kg}) \times (5.807 \times 10^{-26}\,\text{kg})}{(1.673 \times 10^{-27}\,\text{kg}) + (5.807 \times 10^{-26}\,\text{kg})} \times (1.274 \times 10^{-10}\,\text{m})^2$$
$$= 2.639 \times 10^{-47}\,\text{kg m}^2$$

Therefore, the rotational constant is

$$B = \frac{\hbar}{4\pi I}$$
$$= \frac{1.054\,57 \times 10^{-34}\,\text{J s}}{4\pi \times (2.639 \times 10^{-47}\,\text{kg m}^2)} = 3.180 \times 10^{11}\,\text{s}^{-1}$$

or 318.0 GHz (1 GHz = 10^9 Hz). It follows that the frequency of the transition is

$$\nu = 2B = 636.0\,\text{GHz}$$

This frequency corresponds to the wavelength 0.4712 mm.

Self-test 19.5

What is the frequency and wavelength of the same transition in the $^2H^{35}Cl$ molecule? The mass of ^2H is 3.344×10^{-27} kg. Before commencing the calculation, decide whether the frequency should be higher or lower than for $^1H^{35}Cl$.

[*Answer:* 327.0 GHz, 0.9167 mm]

Once we have measured the separation between adjacent lines in a rotational spectrum of a molecule and converted it to B, we can use the value of B to obtain a value for the moment of inertia $I_\perp$. For a diatomic molecule, we can convert that value to a value of the bond length, R, by using eqn 19.10. Highly accurate bond lengths can be obtained in this way. In some cases, isotopic substitution can help. A classic case is the determination of the two bond lengths in the molecule OCS. Analysis of the microwave spectrum of this linear molecule gives a single quantity, the rotational constant, and from this single quantity we cannot deduce the two different bond lengths. However, by recording the absorption of the two isotopomers $^{16}O^{12}C^{33}S$ and $^{16}O^{12}C^{34}S$ and assuming that isotopic substitution leaves the bond lengths unchanged, we get two pieces of information, the moment of inertia of each isotopomer, and it is now possible to determine the two bond lengths (see Exercise 19.34).

19.8 Rotational Raman spectra

The gross selection rule for rotational Raman spectra is that *the polarizability of the molecule must be anisotropic*. We saw in Section 17.4 that the polarizability of a molecule is a measure of the extent to which an applied electric field can induce an electric dipole moment ($\mu = \alpha\mathcal{E}$). The *anisotropy* of this polarizability is its variation with the orientation of the molecule. Tetrahedral (CH_4), octahedral (SF_6), and icosahedral (C_{60}) molecules, like all spherical rotors, have the same polarizability regardless of their orientations, so these molecules are **rotationally Raman inactive**: they do not have rotational Raman spectra. All other molecules, including homonuclear diatomic molecules such as H_2, are **rotationally Raman active.**

The specific selection rules for the rotational Raman transitions of linear molecules (the only ones we consider) are

$\Delta J = +2$ (Stokes lines)

$\Delta J = -2$ (anti-Stokes lines)

It follows that the change in energy when a rigid rotor makes the transition $J \to J + 2$ is

$$\Delta E = hB(J+2)(J+3) - hBJ(J+1) = 2hB(2J+3) \qquad (19.18)$$

Therefore, when a photon scatters from molecules in the rotational states $J = 0, 1, 2, \ldots$, and transfers some of its energy to the molecule, the energy of the photon is decreased by $6hB$, $10hB$, $14hB$, ... and its frequency is reduced by $6B$, $10B$, $14B$, ... from the frequency of the incident radiation. If the photon acquires energy during the collision, then a similar argument shows that the anti-Stokes lines occur with frequencies $6B$, $10B$, $14B$, ... higher than the incident radiation (Fig. 19.21). It follows that from a measurement of the separation of the Raman lines, we can determine the value of B and hence calculate the bond length. Because homonuclear diatomic species are rotationally Raman active, this technique

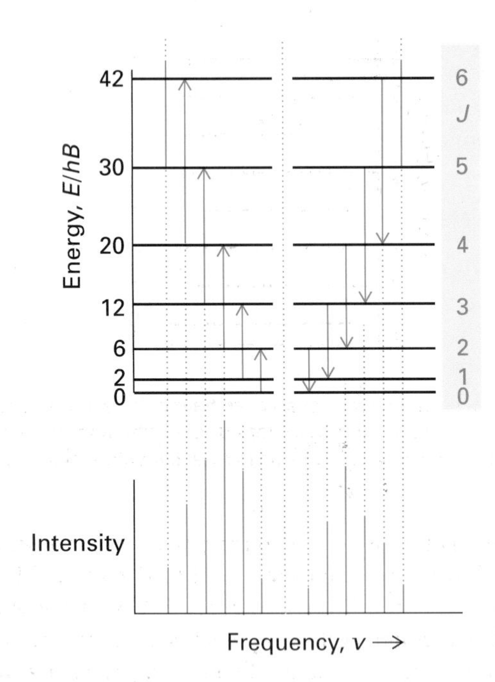

Fig. 19.21 The transitions responsible for the Stokes and anti-Stokes lines of a rotational Raman spectrum of a linear molecule.

can be applied to them as well as to heteronuclear species.

There is an important qualification of these remarks for symmetrical molecules, such as H_2 and CO_2. We saw in Section 19.6 that nuclear statistics either rules out certain states or leads to an alternation of populations. We saw, for instance, that CO_2 can exist only in states with even values of J. As a result, its rotational Raman spectrum consists of lines at $6B$, $14B$, $22B$, ... and separated by $8B$ because the lines starting from odd values of J are missing. For molecules with non-zero nuclear spin, all the Raman lines are present but they show an alternation of intensities: for H_2, the odd-J lines are three times more intense than the even-J lines, whereas for D_2 and N_2, even-J lines are twice as intense as the odd-J lines.

Vibrational spectra

All molecules are capable of vibrating, and complicated molecules may do so in a large number of different modes. Even a benzene molecule, with 12 atoms, can vibrate in 30 different modes, some of which involve the periodic swelling and shrinking of the ring and others its buckling into various distorted shapes. A molecule as big as a protein can vibrate in tens of thousands of different ways, twisting, stretching, and buckling in different regions and in different manners. Vibrations can be excited by the absorption of electromagnetic radiation. Observing the frequencies at which this absorption occurs gives very valuable information about the identity of the molecule and provides quantitative information about the flexibility of its bonds.

19.9 The vibrations of molecules

We base our discussion on Fig. 19.22, which shows a typical potential energy curve (it is a reproduction of Fig. 14.1) of a diatomic molecule as its bond is lengthened by pulling one atom away from the other or pressing it into the other. In regions close to the equilibrium bond length R_e (at the minimum of the curve) we can approximate the potential energy by a parabola (a curve of the form $y = x^2$), and write

$$V = \tfrac{1}{2}k(R - R_e)^2 \qquad (19.19)$$

where k is the force constant of the bond (units: newton per metre, N m^{-1}), as in the discussion of vibrations in Section 12.11. The steeper the walls of the potential (the stiffer the bond), the greater the force constant (Fig. 19.23).

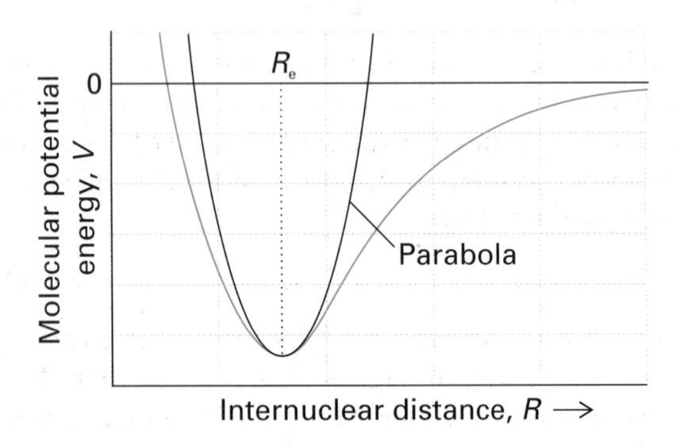

Fig. 19.22 A molecular potential energy curve can be approximated by a parabola near the bottom of the well. A parabolic potential results in harmonic oscillation. At high vibrational excitation energies the parabolic approximation is poor.

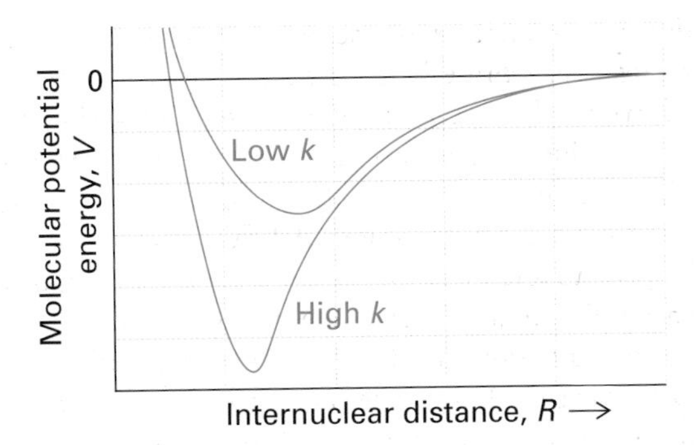

Fig. 19.23 A low value of k indicates a loose bond; a high value indicates a stiff bond. Although the value of k is not directly related to the strength of the bond, this illustration indicates that it is likely that a strong bond (one with a deep minimum) has a large force constant.

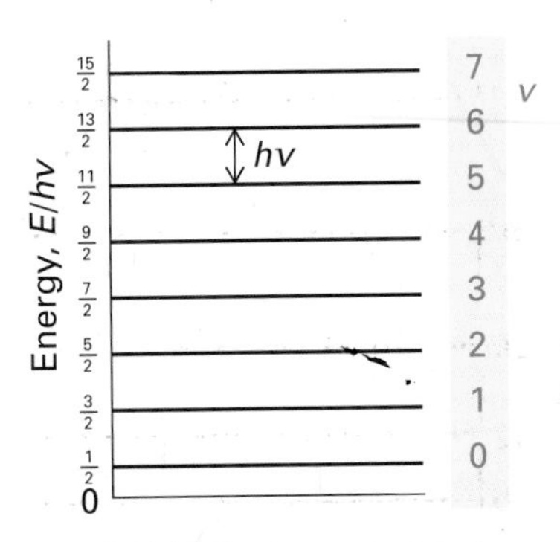

Fig. 19.24 The energy levels of an harmonic oscillator. The quantum number v ranges from 0 to infinity, and the permitted energy levels form a uniform ladder with spacing $h\nu$.

The potential energy in eqn 19.19 has the same form as that for the harmonic oscillator (Section 12.11), so we can use the solutions of the Schrödinger equation given there. The only complication is that both atoms joined by the bond move, so the 'mass' of the oscillator has to be interpreted carefully. Detailed calculation shows that for two atoms of masses m_A and m_B joined by a bond of force constant k, the energy levels are[5]

$$E_v = (v + \tfrac{1}{2})h\nu \qquad v = 0, 1, 2, \ldots \qquad (19.20a)$$

where

$$\nu = \frac{1}{2\pi}\left(\frac{k}{\mu}\right)^{1/2} \qquad \mu = \frac{m_A m_B}{m_A + m_B} \qquad (19.20b)$$

and μ is called the **effective mass** of the molecule (some call it the *reduced mass*). Vibrational transitions are commonly expressed as a wavenumber (in reciprocal centimetres), so it is often convenient to write eqn 19.20a as

$$E_v = (v + \tfrac{1}{2})hc\tilde{\nu} \qquad v = 0, 1, 2, \ldots \qquad (19.20c)$$

with $\tilde{\nu} = \nu/c$. Figure 19.24 illustrates these energy levels (a repeat of Fig. 12.33): we see that they form a uniform ladder of separation $hc\tilde{\nu}$ between neighbours.

At first sight it might be puzzling that the effective mass appears rather than the total mass of the two atoms. However, the presence of μ is physically plausible. If atom A were as heavy as a brick wall, it would not move at all during the vibration and the vibrational frequency would be determined by the lighter, mobile atom. Indeed, if A were a brick wall, we could neglect m_B compared with m_A in the denominator of μ and find $\mu \approx m_B$, the mass of the lighter atom. This is approximately the case in HI, for example, where the I atom barely moves and $\mu \approx m_H$. In the case of a homonuclear diatomic molecule, for which $m_A = m_B = m$, the effective mass is half the mass of one atom: $\mu = \tfrac{1}{2}m$.

Self-test 19.6

An $^{1}H^{35}Cl$ molecule has a force constant of 516 N m^{-1}, a reasonably typical value. Calculate (a) the vibrational frequency, ν, and (b) the wavenumber, $\tilde{\nu}$, of the molecule and (c) the energy separation between any two neighbouring vibrational energy levels.

[*Answer*: (a) 89.7 THz; (b) 2992 cm^{-1}, (c) 59.4 zJ]

19.10 Vibrational transitions

Because a typical vibrational excitation energy is of the order of 10^{-20}–10^{-19} J, the frequency of the radiation should be of the order of 10^{13}–10^{14} Hz (from $\Delta E = h\nu$). This frequency corresponds to infrared radiation, so vibrational transitions are observed by **infrared spectroscopy**. As we have remarked,

[5] We have previously warned about the importance of distinguishing between the quantum number v (vee) and the frequency ν (nu).

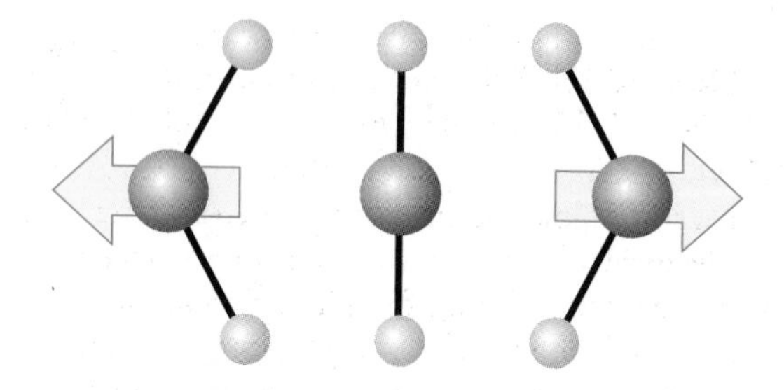

Fig. 19.25 The oscillation of a molecule, even if it is non-polar, may result in an oscillating dipole that can interact with the electromagnetic field. Here we see a representation of a bending mode of CO_2. The arrow represents the molecular dipole moment.

in infrared spectroscopy, transitions are normally expressed in terms of their wavenumbers and lie typically in the range 300–3000 cm^{-1}.

The gross selection rule for vibrational spectra is that *the electric dipole moment of the molecule must change during the vibration*. The basis of this rule is that the molecule can shake the electromagnetic field into oscillation only if it has an electric dipole moment that oscillates as the molecule vibrates (Fig. 19.25). The molecule need not have a permanent dipole: the rule requires only a *change* in dipole moment, possibly from zero. The stretching motion of a homonuclear diatomic molecule does not change its electric dipole moment from zero, so the vibrations of such molecules neither absorb nor generate radiation. We say that homonuclear diatomic molecules are **infrared inactive**, because their dipole moments remain zero however long the bond. Heteronuclear diatomic molecules, which have a dipole moment that changes as the bond lengthens and contracts, are **infrared active**.

Example 19.3

Using the gross selection rule

State which of the following molecules are infrared active: N_2, CO_2, OCS, H_2O, $CH_2{=}CH_2$, C_6H_6.

Strategy Molecules that are infrared active (that is, have vibrational spectra) have dipole moments that change during the course of a vibration. Therefore, judge whether a distortion of the molecule can change its dipole moment (including changing it from zero).

Solution All the molecules except N_2 possess at least one vibrational mode that results in a change of dipole moment, so all except N_2 are infrared active. It should be noted that not all the modes of complicated molecules are infrared active. For example, a vibration of CO_2 in which the O–C–O bonds stretch and contract symmetrically is inactive because it leaves the dipole moment unchanged (at zero). A bending motion of the molecule, however, is active and can absorb radiation.

Self-test 19.7

Repeat the question for H_2, NO, N_2O.

[*Answer:* NO, N_2O.]

The specific selection rule for vibrational transitions is

$$\Delta v = \pm 1$$

The change in energy for the transition from a state with quantum number v to one with quantum number $v+1$ is

$$\Delta E = (v + \tfrac{3}{2})hc\tilde{\nu} - (v + \tfrac{1}{2})hc\tilde{\nu} = hc\tilde{\nu} \qquad (19.21)$$

It follows that absorption occurs when the incident radiation provides photons with this energy, and therefore when the incident radiation has a wavenumber given by eqn 19.20c. Molecules with stiff bonds (large k) joining atoms with low masses (small μ) have high vibrational wavenumbers. Bending modes are usually less stiff than stretching modes, so bends tend to occur at lower wavenumbers than stretches in the spectrum.

At room temperature, almost all the molecules are in their vibrational ground states initially (the state with $v = 0$). Therefore, the most important spectral transition is from $v = 0$ to $v = 1$.

Illustration 19.2

Vibrational transition wavenumbers

It follows from the calculation of $\tilde{\nu}$ for HCl (in Self-test 19.6), that $\tilde{\nu} = 2992$ cm^{-1}, so the infrared spectrum of the molecule will be an absorption at that frequency. The corresponding frequency and wavelength are 89.7 THz (1 THz = 10^{12} Hz) and 3.34 μm, respectively.

Self-test 19.8

The force constant of the bond in the CO group of a peptide link is approximately 1.2 kN m^{-1}. At what wavenumber would you expect it to absorb? (*Hint.* For the effective mass, treat the group as a $^{12}C^{16}O$ molecule.)

[*Answer:* at approximately 1720 cm^{-1}]

19.11 Anharmonicity

The vibrational terms in eqn 19.21 are only approximate because they are based on a parabolic approximation to the actual potential energy curve. A parabola cannot be correct at all extensions because it does not allow a molecule to dissociate. At high vibrational excitations the swing of the atoms (more precisely, the spread of vibrational wavefunction) allows the molecule to explore regions of the potential energy curve where the parabolic approximation is poor. The motion then becomes **anharmonic**, in the sense that the restoring force is no longer proportional to the displacement. Because the actual curve is less confining than a parabola, we can anticipate that the energy levels become less widely spaced at high excitation.

The convergence of levels at high vibrational quantum numbers is expressed by replacing eqn 19.21 by

$$E_v = (v + \tfrac{1}{2})hc\tilde{\nu} - (v + \tfrac{1}{2})^2 hc\tilde{\nu}x_e + \cdots \qquad (19.22)$$

where x_e is the **anharmonicity constant**. Anharmonicity also accounts for the appearance of additional weak absorption lines called **overtones** corresponding to the transitions with $\Delta v = +2, +3, \ldots$. These overtones appear because the usual selection rule is derived from the properties of harmonic oscillator wavefunctions, which are only approximately valid when anharmonicity is present.

19.12 Vibrational Raman spectra of diatomic molecules

In **vibrational Raman spectroscopy** the incident photon leaves some of its energy in the vibrational modes of the molecule it strikes, or collects additional energy from a vibration that has already been excited.

The gross selection rule for vibrational Raman transitions is that *the molecular polarizability must change as the molecule vibrates.* The polarizability plays a role in vibrational Raman spectroscopy because the molecule must be squeezed and stretched by the incident radiation so that a vibrational excitation may occur during the photon–molecule collision. Both homonuclear and heteronuclear diatomic molecules swell and contract during a vibration, and the control of the nuclei over the electrons, and hence the molecular polarizability, changes too. Both types of diatomic molecule are therefore vibrationally Raman active.

The specific selection rule for vibrational Raman transitions is the same as for infrared transitions ($\Delta v = \pm 1$). The photons that are scattered with a lower wavenumber than that of the incident light, the Stokes lines, are those for which $\Delta v = +1$. The Stokes lines are more intense than the anti-Stokes lines (for which $\Delta v = -1$), because very few molecules are in an excited vibrational state initially.

The information available from vibrational Raman spectra adds to that from infrared spectroscopy because homonuclear diatomic molecules can also be studied. The spectra can be interpreted in terms of the force constants, dissociation energies, and bond lengths, and some of the information obtained is included in Table 19.2.

Table 19.2

Properties of diatomic molecules

	$\tilde{\nu}/cm^{-1}$	R_e/pm	$k/(N\ m^{-1})$	$D/(kJ\ mol^{-1})$
$^{1}H_2^+$	2333	106	160	256
$^{1}H_2$	4401	74	575	432
$^{2}H_2$	3118	74	577	440
$^{1}H^{19}F$	4138	92	955	564
$^{1}H^{35}Cl$	2991	127	516	428
$^{1}H^{81}Br$	264	141	412	363
$^{1}H^{127}I$	2308	161	314	295
$^{14}N_2$	235S	110	2294	942
$^{16}O_2$	158	121	1177	494
$^{19}F_2$	892	142	445	154
$^{35}Cl_2$	560	199	323	239

19.13 The vibrations of polyatomic molecules

How many modes of vibration are there in a polyatomic molecule? We can answer this question by thinking about how each atom may change its location, and we show in Derivation 19.2 that

Non-linear molecules:

number of vibrational modes = $3N - 6$

Linear molecules:

number of vibrational modes = $3N - 5$

Derivation 19.2

The number of vibrational modes

Each atom may move along any of three perpendicular axes. Therefore, the total number of such displacements in a molecule consisting of N atoms is $3N$. Three of these displacements correspond to movement of the centre of mass of the molecule, so these three displacements correspond to the translational motion of the molecule as a whole. The remaining $3N - 3$ displacements are 'internal' modes of the molecule that leave its centre of mass unchanged. Three angles are needed to specify the orientation of a non-linear molecule in space (Fig. 19.26). Therefore, three of the $3N - 3$ internal displacements leave all bond angles and bond lengths unchanged but change the orientation of the molecule as a whole. These three displacements are therefore rotations. That leaves $3N - 6$ displacements that change neither the centre of mass of the molecule nor the orientation of the molecule in space. These $3N - 6$ displacements are the vibrational modes. A similar calculation for a linear molecule, which requires only two angles to specify its orientation in space, gives $3N - 5$ as the number of vibrational modes.

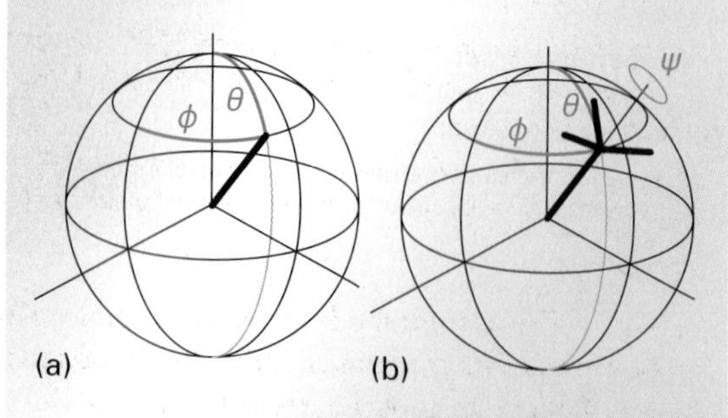

Fig. 19.26 (a) The orientation of a linear molecule requires the specification of two angles (the latitude and longitude of its axis). (b) The orientation of a non-linear molecule requires the specification of three angles (the latitude and longitude of its axis and the angle of twist—the torsional angle—around that axis).

Illustration 19.3

The number of vibrational modes

A water molecule, H_2O, is triatomic and non-linear, and has three modes of vibration. Naphthalene, $C_{10}H_8$, has 48 distinct modes of vibration. Any diatomic molecule ($N = 2$) has one vibrational mode; carbon dioxide ($N = 3$) has four vibrational modes.

The description of the vibrational motion of a polyatomic molecule is much simpler if we consider combinations of the stretching and bending motions of individual bonds. For example, although we could describe two of the four vibrations of a CO_2 molecule as individual carbon–oxygen bond stretches, ν_L and ν_R in Fig. 19.27, the description of the motion is much simpler if we use two combinations of these vibrations. One combination is ν_1 in Fig. 19.28: this combination is the **symmetric stretch**. The other combination is ν_3, the **antisymmetric stretch**, in

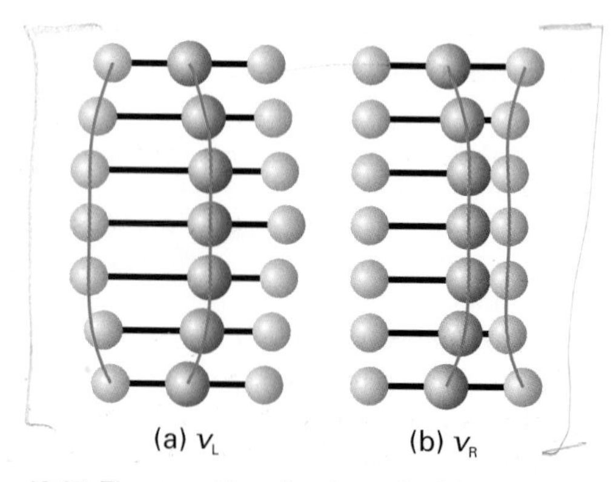

Fig. 19.27 The stretching vibrations of a CO_2 molecule can be represented in a number of ways. In this representation, (a) one O=C bond vibrates and the remaining O atom is stationary, and (b) the C=O bond vibrates while the other O atom is stationary. Because the stationary atom is linked to the C atom, it does not remain stationary for long. That is, if one vibration begins, it rapidly stimulates the other to occur.

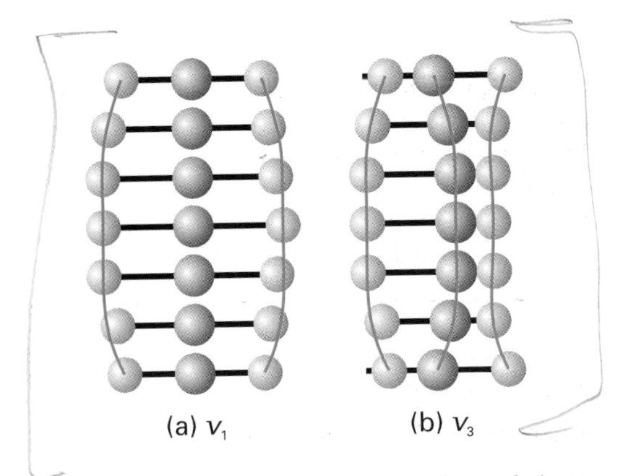

Fig. 19.28 Alternatively, linear combinations of the two modes can be taken to give these two normal modes of the molecule. The mode in (a) is the symmetric stretch and that in (b) is the antisymmetric stretch. The two modes are independent, and if either of them is stimulated, the other remains unexcited. Normal modes greatly simplify the description of the vibrations of the molecule.

which the two O atoms always move in the same directions and opposite to the C atom. The two modes are independent in the sense that if one is excited, then its motion does not excite the other. They are two of the four 'normal modes' of the molecule, its independent, collective vibrational displacements. The two other normal modes are the **bending modes**, ν_2. In general, a **normal mode** is an independent, synchronous motion of atoms or groups of atoms that may be excited without leading to the excitation of any other normal mode.

Self-test 19.9

How many normal modes of vibration are there in (a) ethyne (HC≡CH) and (b) a protein molecule of 4000 atoms?

[*Answer:* (a) 7, (b) 11 994]

The four normal modes of CO_2, and the $3N - 6$ (or $3N - 5$) normal modes of polyatomic molecules in general, are the key to the description of molecular vibrations. Each normal mode behaves like an independent harmonic oscillator and the energies of the vibrational levels are given by the same expression as in eqn 19.20, but with an effective mass that depends on the extent to which each of the atoms contributes to the vibration. Atoms that do not move, such as the C atom in the symmetric stretch of CO_2, do not contribute to the effective mass. The force constant also depends in a complicated way on the extent to which bonds bend and stretch during a vibration. Typically, a normal mode that is largely a bending motion has a lower force constant (and hence a lower frequency) than a normal mode that is largely a stretching motion.

The gross selection rule for the infrared activity of a normal mode is that *the motion corresponding to a normal mode must give rise to a changing dipole moment*. Deciding whether this is so can sometimes be done by inspection. For example, the symmetric stretch of CO_2 leaves the dipole moment unchanged (at zero), so this mode is infrared inactive and makes no contribution to the molecule's infrared spectrum. The antisymmetric stretch, however, changes the dipole moment because the molecule becomes unsymmetrical as it vibrates, so this mode is infrared active. The fact that the mode does absorb infrared radiation enables carbon dioxide to act as a 'greenhouse gas' by absorbing infrared radiation emitted from the surface of the Earth (Box 19.1). Because the dipole moment change is parallel to the molecular axis in the antisymmetric stretching mode, the transitions arising from this mode are classified as **parallel bands** in the spectrum. Both bending modes are also infrared active: they are accompanied by a changing dipole perpendicular to the molecular axis (as in Fig. 19.25), so transitions involving them lead to a **perpendicular band** in the spectrum.

Self-test 19.10

State the ways in which the infrared spectrum of dinitrogen oxide (nitrous oxide, N_2O) will differ from that of carbon dioxide.

[*Answer:* different frequencies on account of different atomic masses and force constants; all four modes infrared active]

Some of the normal modes of organic molecules can be regarded as motions of individual functional groups. Others cannot be regarded as localized in this way and are better regarded as collective motions of the molecule as a whole. The latter are generally of relatively low frequency, and occur at wavenumbers below about 1500 cm^{-1} in the spectrum. The resulting whole-molecule region of the absorption spectrum is called the **fingerprint**

Box 19.1 *Global warming**

Solar energy strikes the top of the Earth's atmosphere at a rate of 343 W m^{-2}. About 30 per cent of this energy is reflected back into space by the Earth or the atmosphere. The Earth–atmosphere system absorbs the remaining energy and re-emits it into space as black-body radiation, with most of the intensity being carried by infrared radiation in the range 200–2500 cm^{-1} (4–50 μm). The Earth's average temperature is maintained by an energy balance between solar radiation absorbed by the Earth and black-body radiation emitted by the Earth.

The trapping of infrared radiation by certain gases in the atmosphere is known as the *greenhouse effect*, so-called because it warms the Earth as if the planet were enclosed in a huge greenhouse. The result is that the natural greenhouse effect raises the average surface temperature well above the freezing point of water and creates an environment in which life is possible. The major constituents of the Earth's atmosphere, O_2 and N_2, do not contribute to the greenhouse effect because homonuclear diatomic molecules cannot absorb infrared radiation. However, the minor atmospheric gases water vapour and CO_2 do absorb infrared radiation and hence are responsible for the greenhouse effect (see the first illustration). Water vapour absorbs strongly in the ranges 1300–1900 cm^{-1} (5.3–7.7 μm) and 3550–3900 cm^{-1} (2.6–2.8 μm), whereas CO_2 shows strong absorption in the ranges 500–725 cm^{-1} (14–20 μm) and 2250–2400 cm^{-1} (4.2–4.4 μm).

Increases in the levels of greenhouse gases, which also include methane, dinitrogen oxide, ozone, and certain chlorofluorocarbons, as a result of human activity have the potential to enhance the natural greenhouse effect, leading to significant warming of the planet. This problem is referred to as *global warming*, which we now explore in some detail.

The concentration of water vapour in the atmosphere has remained steady over time, but concentrations of some other greenhouse gases are rising. From about the year 1000 until about 1750, the CO_2 concentration remained fairly stable, but, since then, it has increased by 28 per cent. The concentration of methane, CH_4, has more than doubled during this time and is now at its highest level for 160 000 years (160 ka; a is the SI unit denoting 1 year). Studies of air pockets in ice cores taken from Antarctica show that increases in the concentration of both atmospheric CO_2 and CH_4 over the past 160 ka correlate well with increases in the global surface temperature.

Human activities are primarily responsible for the rising concentrations of atmospheric CO_2 and CH_4. Most of the atmospheric CO_2 comes from the burning of hydrocarbon fuels, which began on a large scale with the Industrial Revolution in the middle of the nineteenth century. The additional methane comes mainly from the petroleum industry and from agriculture.

The temperature of the surface of the Earth has increased by about 0.5 K since the late-nineteenth century (see the second illustration). If we continue to rely on hydrocarbon fuels and current trends in population growth and energy are not reversed, then by the middle of the twenty-first century, the concentration of CO_2 in the atmosphere will be about twice its value prior to the Industrial Revolution. The Intergovernmental Panel on Climate Change (IPCC) estimated in 1995 that, by the year 2100, the Earth will undergo an increase in temperature of 3 K. Furthermore, the rate of temperature change is likely to be greater than at any time in the past 10 ka. To place a temperature rise of 3 K in perspective, it is useful to consider that the average temperature of the Earth during the last ice age was only 6 K colder than at present. Just as cooling the planet (for example, during an ice age)

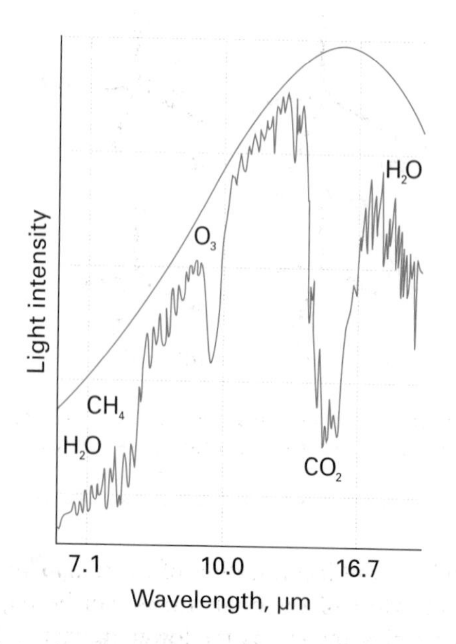

The intensity of infrared radiation that would be lost from the Earth in the absence of greenhouse gases is shown by the smooth line. The jagged line is the intensity of the radiation actually emitted. The maximum wavelength of radiation absorbed by each greenhouse gas is indicated.

* This box is based on a similar contribution initially prepared by Loretta Jones and appearing in P. Atkins and L. Jones, *Chemical principles*, W.H. Freeman and Co., New York (2005).

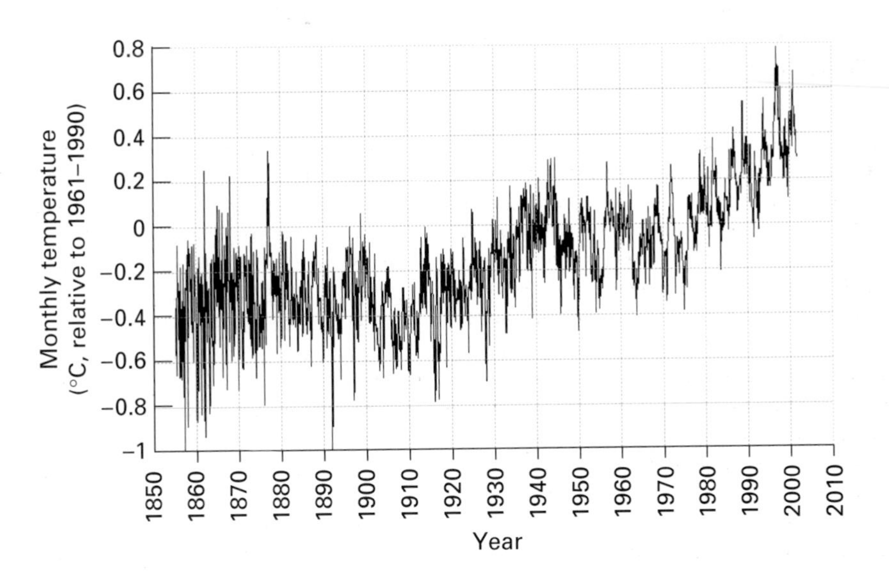

The average change in surface temperature of the Earth from 1855 to 2002.

can lead to detrimental effects on ecosystems, so too can a dramatic warming of the globe. One example of a significant change in the environment caused by a temperature increase of 3 K is a rise in sea level by about 0.5 m, which is sufficient to alter weather patterns and submerge current coastal ecosystems.

Computer projections for the next 200 years predict further increases in atmospheric CO_2 levels and suggest that, to maintain CO_2 at its current concentration, we would have to reduce hydrocarbon fuel consumption immediately by about 50 per cent. Clearly, to reverse global warming trends, we need to develop alternatives to fossil fuels, such as hydrogen (which can be used in fuel cells, Box 9.2) and solar energy technologies.

Exercise 1 Use the data given in the first paragraph of this box and the Stefan–Boltzmann law (eqn 12.3) to calculate the average black-body temperature of the Earth. This temperature would be the surface temperature of the planet in the absence of a greenhouse effect. What is the wavelength of the most plentiful of the Earth's black-body radiation?

Exercise 2 The following illustration shows the vibrational normal modes of CH_4. Which of these modes are infrared active and which are infrared inactive?

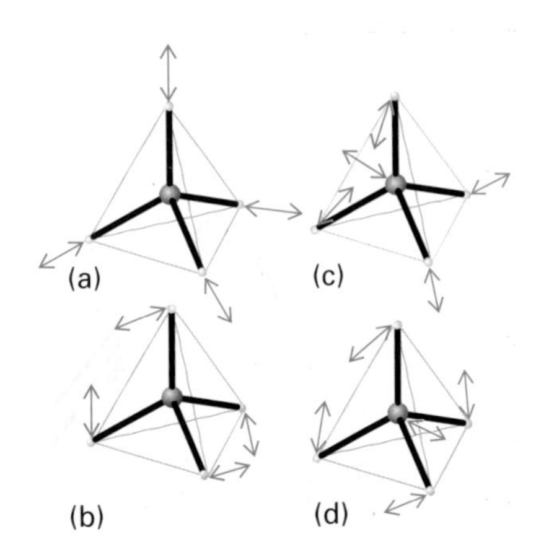

Normal modes of vibration of CH_4. An arrow indicates the direction of motion of an atom during the vibration.

region of the spectrum, as it is characteristic of the molecule. The matching of the fingerprint region with a spectrum of a known compound in a library of infrared spectra is a very powerful way of confirming the presence of a particular substance.

The characteristic vibrations of functional groups that occur outside the fingerprint region are very useful for the identification of an unknown compound. Most of these vibrations can be regarded as stretching modes, as the lower frequency bending modes usually occur in the fingerprint region and so are less readily identified. The characteristic wavenumbers of some functional groups are listed in Table 19.3.

Table 19.3
Typical vibrational wavenumbers

Vibration type	$\tilde{\nu}$/cm^{-1}
C–H	2850–2960
C–H	1340–1465
C–C stretch, bend	700–1250
C=C stretch	1620–1680
C≡C stretch	2100–2260
O–H stretch	3590–3650
C=O stretch	1640–1780
C≡N stretch	2215–2275
N–H stretch	3200–3500
Hydrogen bonds	3200–3570

Example 19.4

Interpreting an infrared spectrum

The infrared spectrum of an organic compound is shown in Fig. 19.29. Suggest an identification.

Strategy Some of the features at wavenumbers above 1500 cm^{-1} can be identified by comparison with the data in Table 19.3.

Solution (a) C–H stretch of a benzene ring, indicating a substituted benzene; (b) carboxylic acid O–H stretch, indicating a carboxylic acid; (c) the strong absorption of a conjugated C≡C group, indicating a substituted alkyne; (d) this strong absorption is also characteristic of a carboxylic acid that is conjugated to a carbon–carbon multiple bond; (e) a characteristic vibration of a benzene ring, confirming the deduction drawn from (a); (f) a characteristic absorption of a nitro group (–NO_2) connected to a multiply bonded carbon–carbon system, suggesting a nitro-substituted benzene. The molecule contains as components a benzene ring, an aromatic carbon–carbon bond, a –COOH group, and a –NO_2 group. The molecule is in fact $O_2N–C_6H_4–C≡C–COOH$. A more detailed analysis and comparison of the fingerprint region shows it to be the 1,4-isomer.

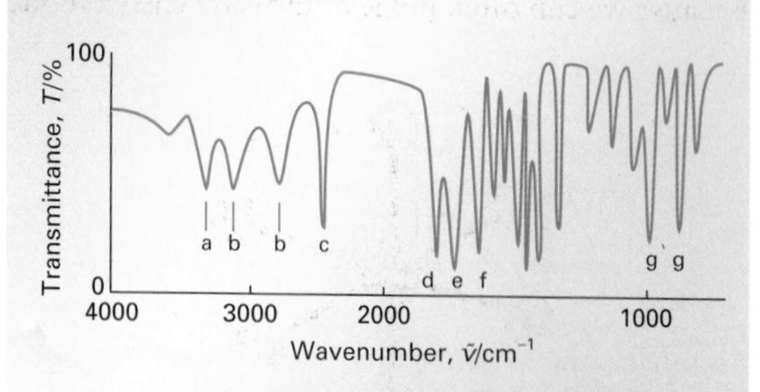

Fig. 19.29 A typical infrared absorption spectrum taken by forming a sample into a disc with potassium bromide. As explained in the example, the substance can be identified as $O_2N–C_6H_4–C≡C–COOH$.

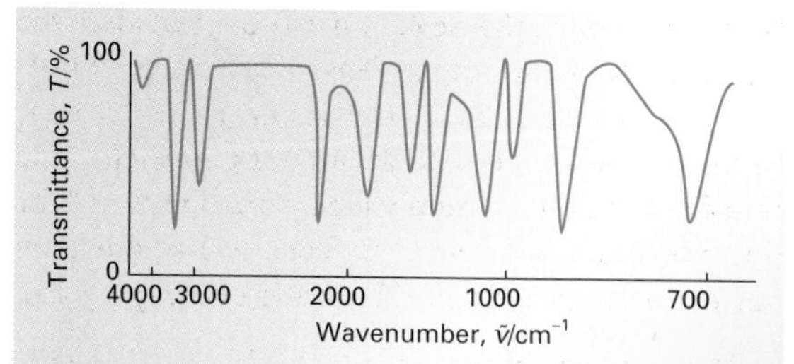

Fig. 19.30 The spectrum considered in Self-test 19.11.

Self-test 19.11

Suggest an identification of the organic compound responsible for the spectrum shown in Fig. 19.30. (*Hint.* The molecular formula of the compound is C_3H_5ClO.)

[*Answer:* CH_2=CClCH$_2$OH]

19.14 Vibration–rotation spectra

The vibrational spectra of gas-phase molecules are more complicated than this discussion implies, because the excitation of a vibration also results in the excitation of rotation. The effect is rather like what happens when ice-skaters throw out or draw in their arms: they rotate more slowly or more rapidly. The effect on the spectrum is to break the single line resulting from a vibrational transition into a multitude of lines with separations between neighbours that depend on the rotational constant of the molecule.

To establish the so-called 'band structure' of a vibrational transition, we begin by writing the expressions for the vibrational and rotational levels. For a linear molecule (the only type we consider), we combine eqns 19.8 and 19.20 and write[6]

$$E_{v,J} = (v + \tfrac{1}{2})h\nu + hBJ(J+1) \qquad (19.23)$$

[6] For this part of the discussion it is simpler to express vibrational transitions as frequencies rather than wavenumbers, but the conversion between them is straightforward.

Next, we apply the selection rules. Provided the molecule is polar, or at least acquires a dipole moment in a vibrational transition (as when CO_2 bends or undergoes an asymmetric stretch), the rotational quantum number may change by ±1 or (in some cases, see below) 0. The absorptions then fall into three groups called **branches** of the spectrum.

P branch, transitions with $\Delta J = -1$: $\nu_J = \nu - 2BJ$

Q branch, transitions with $\Delta J = 0$: $\nu_J = \nu$

R branch, transitions with $\Delta J = +1$:

$$\nu_J = \nu + 2B(J+1)$$

Figure 19.31 shows the resulting appearance of the branches of a typical spectrum. In this case (for HCl), there is no Q branch, because a *Q branch is allowed only when there is angular momentum around the axis of a linear molecule*. For instance, the vibrational spectrum of NO has a Q branch because its single π electron is a source of electronic orbital angular momentum. The asymmetric stretch of CO_2 does not have a Q branch, but the bending vibration does, because the bent molecule can rotate around what used to be its linear axis.

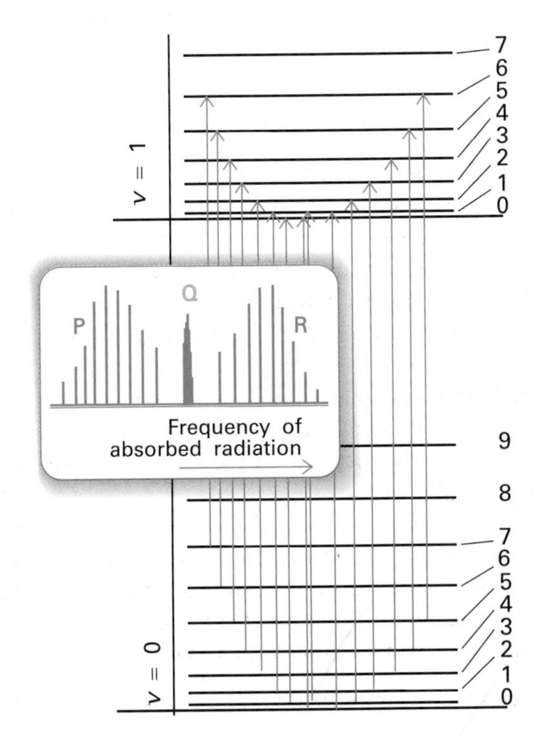

Fig. 19.31 The formation of P, Q, and R branches in a vibration–rotation spectrum. The intensities reflect the populations of the initial rotational levels.

The separation between the lines in the P and R branches of a vibrational transition is $2B$. Therefore, the bond length can be deduced without needing to take a pure rotational microwave spectrum. However, the latter is more precise.

19.15 Vibrational Raman spectra of polyatomic molecules

The gross selection rule for the vibrational Raman spectrum of a polyatomic molecule is that *the normal mode of vibration is accompanied by a changing polarizability*. However, it is often quite difficult to judge by inspection when this is so. The symmetric stretch of CO_2, for example, alternately swells and contracts the molecule: this motion changes its polarizability, so the mode is Raman active. The other modes of CO_2 leave the polarizability unchanged (although that is hard to justify pictorially), so they are Raman inactive.

In some cases it is possible to make use of a very general rule about the infrared and Raman activity of vibrational modes. The **exclusion rule** states:

If the molecule has a centre of inversion, then no modes can be both infrared and Raman active.

(A mode may be inactive in both.) A molecule has a centre of inversion if it looks unchanged when each atom is projected through a single point and out an equal distance on the other side (Fig. 19.32). Because we can often judge intuitively when a mode

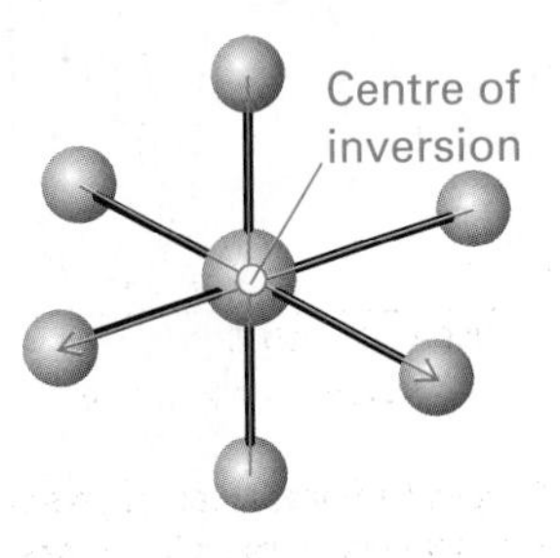

Fig. 19.32 In an inversion operation, we consider every point in a molecule, and project them all through the centre of the molecule out to an equal distance on the other side.

changes the molecular dipole moment, we can use this rule to identify modes that are not Raman active. The rule applies to CO_2 but to neither H_2O nor CH_4 because they have no centre of symmetry.

Self-test 19.12

One vibrational mode of benzene is a 'breathing mode' in which the ring alternately expands and contracts. Can it be vibrationally Raman active?

[Answer: yes]

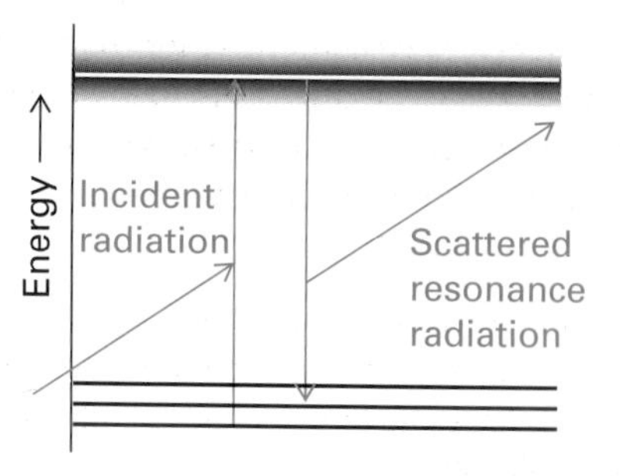

Fig. 19.33 In the *resonance Raman effect*, the incident radiation has a frequency corresponding to an actual electronic excitation of the molecule. A photon is emitted when the excited state returns to a state close to the ground state.

A modification of the basic Raman effect involves using incident radiation that nearly coincides with the frequency of an electronic transition of the sample (Fig. 19.33; compare with Fig. 19.2, where the incident radiation does not coincide with an electronic transition). The technique is then called **resonance Raman spectroscopy**. It is characterized by a much greater intensity in the scattered radiation. Furthermore, because it is often the case that only a few vibrational modes contribute to the more intense scattering, the spectrum is greatly simplified. Resonance Raman spectroscopy is used to study biological molecules that absorb strongly in the ultraviolet and visible regions of the spectrum. Examples include the haem co-factors in haemoglobin and the cytochromes and the pigments β-carotene and chlorophyll, which capture solar energy during plant photosynthesis.

CHECKLIST OF KEY IDEAS

You should now be familiar with the following concepts:

☐ 1 A spectrometer consists of a source of radiation, a dispersing element, and a detector.

☐ 2 One contribution to the linewidth is the Doppler effect, which can be minimized by working at low temperatures.

☐ 3 Another contribution is lifetime broadening: $\delta E \approx \hbar/\tau$, where τ is the lifetime of the state.

☐ 4 The intensity of a transition is proportional to the square of the transition dipole moment.

☐ 5 A selection rule is a statement about when the transition dipole is non-zero.

☐ 6 A gross selection rule specifies the general features that a molecule must have if it is to have a spectrum of a given kind.

☐ 7 A specific selection rule is a statement about which changes in quantum number may occur in a transition.

☐ 8 The rotational energy levels of a linear rotor and a spherical rotor are given by $E_J = hBJ(J+1)$ with $J = 0, 1, 2, \ldots$, where $B = \hbar/4\pi I$ is the rotational constant of a molecule with moment of inertia I.

☐ 9 The Pauli principle states for fermions $\psi(\mathrm{B,A}) = -\psi(\mathrm{A,B})$ and for bosons $\psi(\mathrm{B,A}) = \psi(\mathrm{A,B})$. The consequences of the Pauli principle for rotational states are called nuclear statistics.

☐ 10 The populations of rotational energy levels are given by the Boltzmann distribution in connection with noting the degeneracy of each level.

☐ 11 The gross selection rule for rotational transitions is that the molecule must be polar.

☐ 12 The specific selection rules for rotational transitions are $\Delta J = \pm 1$, $\Delta K = 0$; a rotational spectrum of a polar linear molecule and of a polar symmetric rotor consists of a series of lines at frequencies separated by $2B$.

☐ 13 In a Raman spectrum lines shifted to lower frequency than the incident radiation are called Stokes lines and lines shifted to higher frequency are called anti-Stokes lines.

☐ 14 The gross selection rule for rotational Raman spectra is that the polarizability of the molecule must be anisotropic.

☐ 15 The specific selection rules for the rotational Raman transitions of linear molecules are $\Delta J = +2$ (Stokes lines), $\Delta J = -2$ (anti-Stokes lines).

☐ 16 The vibrational energy levels of a molecule are $E_v = (v + \frac{1}{2})hc\tilde{\nu}$ with $v = 0, 1, 2, \ldots$, where $\tilde{\nu} = (1/2\pi c)(k/\mu)^{1/2}$ and $\mu = m_A m_B/(m_A + m_B)$.

☐ 17 The gross selection rule for vibrational spectra is that the electric dipole moment of the molecule must change during the vibration.

☐ 18 The specific selection rule for vibrational transitions is $\Delta v = \pm 1$.

☐ 19 The number of vibrational modes of non-linear molecules is $3N - 6$; for linear molecules the number is $3N - 5$.

☐ 20 Rotational transitions accompany vibrational transitions and split the spectrum into a P branch ($\Delta J = -1$), a Q branch ($\Delta J = 0$), and an R branch ($\Delta J = +1$). A Q branch is observed only when the molecule possesses angular momentum around its axis.

☐ 21 The gross selection rule for the vibrational Raman spectrum of a polyatomic molecule is that the normal mode of vibration is accompanied by a changing polarizability.

☐ 22 The exclusion rule states that if the molecule has a centre of inversion, then no modes can be both infrared and Raman active.

☐ 23 In resonance Raman spectroscopy, radiation that nearly coincides with the frequency of an electronic transition is used to excite the sample and the result is a much greater intensity in the scattered radiation.

FURTHER INFORMATION 19.1

Intensities in absorption spectroscopy

Derivation of the Beer–Lambert law

The Beer–Lambert law is an empirical result. However, it is simple to account for its form. We think of the sample as consisting of a stack of infinitesimal slices, like sliced bread (Fig. 19.34). The thickness of each layer is dx. The change in intensity, dI, that occurs when electromagnetic radiation passes through one particular slice is proportional to the thickness of the slice, the concentration of the absorber J, and the intensity of the incident radiation at that slice of the sample, so $dI \propto [J]I\,dx$. Because dI is negative (the intensity is reduced by absorption), we can write

$$dI = -\kappa[J]I\,dx$$

where κ (kappa) is the proportionality coefficient. Division by I gives

$$\frac{dI}{I} = -\kappa[J]\,dx$$

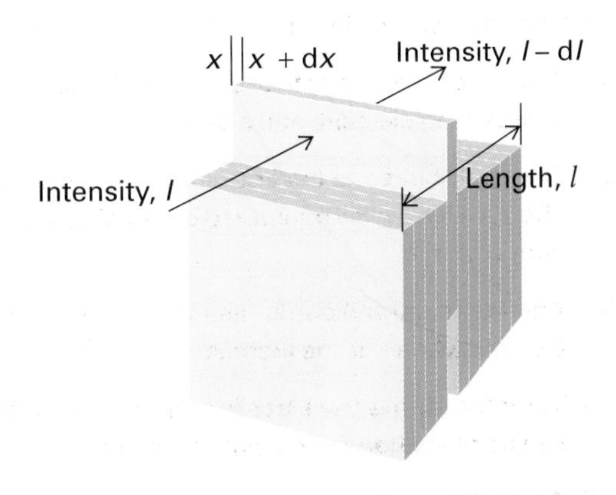

Fig. 19.34 To establish the Beer–Lambert law, the sample is supposed to be sliced into a large number of planes. The reduction in intensity caused by one plane is proportional to the intensity incident on it (after passing through the preceding planes), the thickness of the plane, and the concentration of absorbing species.

This expression applies to each successive slice. To obtain the intensity that emerges from a sample of thickness l when the intensity incident on one face of the sample is I_0, we sum all the successive changes. Because a sum over infinitesimally small increments is an integral, we write:

$$\int_{I_0}^{I} \frac{\mathrm{d}I}{I} = -\kappa \int_0^l [\mathrm{J}]\,\mathrm{d}x$$

If the concentration is uniform, [J] is independent of location and may be taken outside the integral on the right; the expression then integrates to

$$\ln \frac{I}{I_0} = -\kappa[\mathrm{J}]l$$

Because the relation between natural and common logarithms is $\ln x = (\ln 10) \log x$, we can write $\varepsilon = \kappa/\ln 10$ and obtain

$$\log \frac{I}{I_0} = -\varepsilon[\mathrm{J}]l$$

which, on substituting $A = \log(I_0/I) = -\log(I/I_0)$, is the Beer–Lambert law (eqn 19.3).

Absorption intensities

The intensity of an absorption line is related to the rate at which energy from electromagnetic radiation at a specified frequency is absorbed by a molecule. Einstein identified three contributions to the rates of transitions between states. *Stimulated absorption* is the transition from a low-energy state to one of higher energy that is driven by the electromagnetic field oscillating at the transition frequency. He reasoned that the more intense the electromagnetic field (the more intense the incident radiation), the greater the rate at which transitions are induced and hence the stronger the absorption by the sample, so he wrote the rate of stimulated absorption as

$$\text{Rate of stimulated absorption} = NB\rho$$

where N is the number of molecules in the lower state, the constant B is the *Einstein coefficient of stimulated absorption*, and $\rho\delta\nu$ is the energy density of radiation in the frequency range ν to $\nu + \delta\nu$, with ν as the frequency of the transition. For the time being, we can treat B as an empirical parameter that characterizes the transition: if B is large, then a given intensity of incident radiation will induce transitions strongly and the sample will be strongly absorbing.

Einstein considered that the radiation was also able to induce the molecule in the upper state to undergo a transition to the lower state, and hence to generate a photon of frequency ν. Thus, he wrote the rate of this stimulated emission as

$$\text{Rate of stimulated emission} = N'B'\rho$$

where N' is the number of molecules in the excited state and B' is the *Einstein coefficient of stimulated emission.* Note that only radiation of the same frequency as the transition can stimulate an excited state to fall to a lower state. However, he realized that stimulated emission was not the only means by which the excited state could generate radiation and return to the lower state, and suggested that an excited state could undergo *spontaneous emission* at a rate that is independent of the intensity of the radiation (of any frequency) that is already present. Einstein therefore wrote the total rate of transition from the upper to the lower state as

$$\text{Overall rate of emission} = N'(A + B'\rho)$$

The constant A is the *Einstein coefficient of spontaneous emission.* It can be shown that the coefficients of stimulated absorption and emission are equal, and that the coefficient of spontaneous emission is related to them by

$$A = \left(\frac{8\pi h\nu^3}{c^3}\right)B$$

The equality of the coefficients of stimulated emission and absorption implies that if two states happen to have equal populations, then the rate of stimulated emission is equal to the rate of stimulated absorption, and there is then no net absorption. The drop in the value of A with decreasing frequency implies that spontaneous emission can be largely ignored at the relatively low frequencies of rotational and vibrational transitions, and the intensities of these transitions can be discussed in terms of stimulated emission and absorption. Then the net rate of absorption is given by

$$\begin{aligned}\text{Net rate of absorption} &= NB\rho - N'B'\rho\\ &= (N - N')B\rho\end{aligned}$$

and is proportional to the population difference of the two states involved in the transition. In Chapter 22, we shall see that the ratio of populations of states of energies E and E' is given by:

$$\frac{N'}{N} = \mathrm{e}^{-\Delta E/kT} \qquad \Delta E = E' - E$$

It follows that for a constant energy difference ΔE, the population difference $(N - N')$ and the intensity of absorption increase with decreasing temperature. Also, for a specified temperature, the population difference and the intensity of absorption increase with increasing energy separation between the states.

FURTHER INFORMATION 19.2

The rotational energy levels of molecules

The starting point for this derivation is the classical expression for the kinetic energy, E_K, of rotation of a body of moment of inertia I and angular velocity ω (in radians per second):

$$E_K = \tfrac{1}{2}I\omega^2$$

When the body is able to rotate round all three perpendicular axes, its total kinetic energy is the sum of three contributions:

$$E_K = \tfrac{1}{2}I_{xx}\omega_x^2 + \tfrac{1}{2}I_{yy}\omega_y^2 + \tfrac{1}{2}I_{zz}\omega_z^2$$

(For technical reasons, moments of inertia are given two subscripts to denote direction.) We can rewrite this expression in terms of the angular momentum $J_q = I_{qq}\omega_q$ around each axis:

$$E_K = \frac{J_x^2}{2I_{xx}} + \frac{J_y^2}{2I_{yy}} + \frac{J_z^2}{2I_{zz}}$$

If the molecule is a symmetric rotor, we can write $I_{xx} = I_{yy} = I_\perp$ and $I_{zz} = I_\parallel$, and obtain

$$E_K = \frac{J_x^2}{2I_\perp} + \frac{J_y^2}{2I_\perp} + \frac{J_z^2}{2I_\parallel} = \frac{J_x^2 + J_y^2}{2I_\perp} + \frac{J_z^2}{2I_\parallel}$$

It is convenient to write this expression in terms of the magnitude of the angular momentum $J^2 = J_x^2 + J_y^2 + J_z^2$:

$$E_K = \frac{J^2}{2I_\perp} + \left(\frac{1}{2I_\parallel} - \frac{1}{2I_\perp}\right)J_z^2$$

At this point, we make the transition from classical to quantum mechanics. According to quantum mechanics, the square of the magnitude of angular momentum is $J(J+1)\hbar^2$, with $J = 0, 1, 2, \ldots$ and any component (such as J_z) is limited to the values $K\hbar$ with $K = J, J-1, \ldots, -J$. (The quantum number K is used in place of M_J for the component on an internally defined axis.) It follows that the quantum mechanical expression for the energy of a symmetric rotor is

$$E_K = \frac{J(J+1)\hbar^2}{2I_\perp} + \left(\frac{1}{2I_\parallel} - \frac{1}{2I_\perp}\right)K^2\hbar^2$$

For a linear rotor, only the value $K = 0$ is allowed because the molecule cannot rotate around its axis, and we obtain eqn 19.8. For a spherical rotor, the two moments of inertia are the same, and the second term disappears to give eqn 19.18 again. For a symmetric rotor, with A and B defined as in eqn 19.12, we obtain eqn 19.11.

DISCUSSION QUESTIONS

19.1 Describe the physical origins of linewidths in the absorption and emission spectra of gases, liquids, and solids.

19.2 Discuss the physical origins of the gross selection rules for: (a) microwave spectroscopy, (b) rotational Raman spectroscopy, (c) infrared spectroscopy, and (d) vibrational Raman spectroscopy.

19.3 Consider a diatomic molecule that is highly susceptible to centrifugal distortion in its ground vibrational state. Do you expect excitation to high rotational energy levels to change the equilibrium bond length of this molecule? Justify your answer.

19.4 Suppose that you wish to characterize the normal modes of benzene in the gas phase. Why is it important to obtain both infrared absorption and Raman spectra of your sample?

EXERCISES

For these exercises, use $m(^1H) = 1.0078$ u, $m(^2H) = 2.0140$ u, $m(^{12}C) = 12.0000$ u, $m(^{13}C) = 13.0034$ u, $m(^{16}O) = 15.9949$ u, $m(^{19}F) = 18.9984$ u, $m(^{32}S) = 31.9721$ u, $m(^{34}S) = 33.9679$ u, $m(^{127}I) = 126.9045$ u.

The symbol ‡ indicates that calculus is required.

19.5 Express a wavelength of 670 nm as (a) a frequency, (b) a wavenumber.

19.6 What is (a) the wavenumber, (b) the wavelength of the radiation used by an FM radio transmitter broadcasting at 92.0 MHz?

19.7 The molar absorption coefficient of a substance dissolved in hexane is known to be 743 $dm^3\ mol^{-1}\ cm^{-1}$ at 285 nm. Calculate the percentage reduction in intensity when light of that wavelength passes through 2.5 mm of a solution of concentration 3.25 mmol dm^{-3}.

19.8 When light of wavelength 410 nm passes through 2.5 mm of a solution of the dye responsible for the yellow of daffodils at a concentration 0.433 mmol dm^{-3}, the transmission is 71.5 per cent. Calculate the molar absorption coefficient of the colouring matter at this wavelength and express the answer in centimetre-squared per mole ($cm^2\ mol^{-1}$).

19.9 ‡The Beer–Lambert law is derived on the basis that the concentration of absorbing species is uniform (see Further information 19.1). Suppose, instead, that the concentration falls exponentially as $[J] = [J]_0\, e^{-x/\lambda}$. Derive an expression for the variation of I with sample length: suppose that $l \gg \lambda$. (*Hint*. Work through Derivation 19.1, but use this expression for the concentration.)

19.10 The following data were obtained for the absorption by Br_2 in carbon tetrachloride using a cell of length 2.0 mm. Calculate the molar absorption coefficient (ε) of bromine at the wavelength used:

$[Br_2]/(mol\ dm^{-3})$	0.0010	0.0050	0.0100	0.0500
T/(per cent)	81.4	35.6	12.7	3.0×10^{-3}

19.11 A cell of length 2.0 mm was filled with a solution of benzene in a non-absorbing solvent. The concentration of the benzene was 0.010 mol dm^{-3} and the wavelength of the radiation was 256 nm (where there is a maximum in the absorption). Calculate the molar absorption coefficient of benzene at this wavelength given that the transmission was 48 per cent. What will the transmittance be in a cell of length 4.0 mm at the same wavelength?

19.12 A swimmer enters a gloomier world (in one sense) on diving to greater depths. Given that the mean molar absorption coefficient of sea water in the visible region is $6.2 \times 10^{-5}\ dm^3\ mol^{-1}\ cm^{-1}$, calculate the depth at which a diver will experience (a) half the surface intensity of light, (b) one-tenth that intensity.

19.13 What is the Doppler-shifted wavelength of a red (660 nm) traffic light approached at 55 m.p.h.? At what speed would it appear green (520 nm)?

19.14 A spectral line of $^{48}Ti^{8+}$ in a distant star was found to be shifted from 654.2 nm to 706.5 nm and to be broadened to 61.8 pm. What is the speed of recession and the surface temperature of the star?

19.15 Estimate the lifetime of a state that gives rise to a line of width (a) 0.1 cm^{-1}, (b) 1 cm^{-1}, (c) 1.0 GHz.

19.16 A molecule in a liquid undergoes about 1×10^{13} collisions in each second. Suppose that (a) every collision is effective in deactivating the molecule vibrationally and (b) that one collision in 200 is effective. Calculate the width (in cm^{-1}) of vibrational transitions in the molecule.

19.17 The kinetic energy of a bicycle wheel rotating once per second is about 0.2 J. To what rotational quantum number does that correspond? For the moment of inertia, let the mass of the wheel (which is concentrated in its rim) be 0.75 kg and its radius be 70 cm.

19.18 Calculate the moment of inertia of (a) $^1H_2$, (b) $^2H_2$, (c) $^{12}C^{16}O_2$, (d) $^{13}CO_2$. Use $R_e(CO) = 112$ pm.

19.19 Calculate the rotational constants of the molecules in Exercise 19.18; express your answer in hertz (Hz).

19.20 (a) Express the moment of inertia of an octahedral AB_6 molecule in terms of its bond lengths and the masses of the B atoms. (b) Calculate the rotational constant of $^{32}S^{19}F_6$, for which the S–F bond length is 158 pm.

19.21 (a) Derive expressions for the two moments of inertia of a square-planar AB_4 molecule in terms of its bond lengths and the masses of the B atoms.

19.22 Suppose you were seeking the presence of (planar) SO_3 molecules in the microwave spectra of interstellar gas clouds. (a) You would need to know the rotational constants A and B. Calculate these parameters for $^{32}S^{16}O_3$, for which the S–O bond length is 143 pm. (b) Could you use microwave spectroscopy to distinguish the relative abundances of $^{32}S^{16}O_3$ and $^{33}S^{16}O_3$?

19.23 Which of the following molecules can have a pure rotational spectrum? (a) HCl, (b) N_2O, (c) O_3, (d) SF_4, (e) XeF_4.

19.24 Which of the molecules in Exercise 19.23 can have a rotational Raman spectrum?

19.25 A rotating methane molecule is described by the quantum numbers J, M_J, and K. How many rotational states have an energy equal to $hBJ(J+1)$ with $J=10$?

19.26 Suppose the methane molecule in Exercise 19.25 is replaced by chloromethane. How many rotational states now have an energy equal to $hBJ(J+1)$ with $J=10$?

19.27 ‡The most populated rotational energy level of a linear rotor is given in eqn 19.15. What is the most populated rotational level of a spherical rotor, given that its degeneracy is $(2J+1)^2$?

19.28 The rotational constant of $^1H^{35}Cl$ is 318.0 GHz. What is the separation of the lines in its pure rotational spectrum (a) in gigahertz, (b) in reciprocal centimetres?

19.29 The rotational constant of $^1H^{35}Cl$ is 318.0 GHz. What is the separation of the lines in its rotational Raman spectrum (a) in gigahertz, (b) in reciprocal centimetres?

19.30 Suppose that hydrogen is replaced by deuterium in $^1H^{35}Cl$. Would you expect the $J=1 \rightarrow 0$ transition to move to higher or lower wavenumber?

19.31 The rotational constant of $^{12}C^{16}O_2$ (from Raman spectroscopy) is 11.70 GHz. What is the CO bond length in the molecule?

19.32 The microwave spectrum of $^1H^{127}I$ consists of a series of lines separated by 384 GHz. Compute its bond length. What would be the separation of the lines in $^2H^{127}I$?

19.33 The following wavenumbers are observed in the rotational spectrum of OCS: 1.217 105 4 cm^{-1}, 1.1.622 800 5 cm^{-1}, 2.028 488 3 cm^{-1}, and 2.434 170 8 cm^{-1}. Use the graphical procedure implied by eqn 19.17 to infer the values of B and D for this molecule.

19.34 The microwave spectrum of $^{16}O^{12}CS$ gave absorption lines (in GHz) as follows:

J	1	2	3	4
^{32}S	24.325 92	36.488 82	48.651 64	60.814 08
^{34}S	23.732 33		47.462 40	

Assume that the bond lengths are unchanged by substitution and calculate the CO and CS bond lengths in OCS. (*Hint*. The moment of inertia of a linear molecule of the form ABC is

$$I = m_A R_{AB}^2 + m_C R_{BC}^2 - \frac{(m_A R_{AB} - m_C R_{BC})^2}{m_A + m_B + m_C}$$

where r_{AB} and r_{BC} are the A–B and B–C bond lengths, respectively.)

19.35 Suppose the C=O group in a peptide bond can be regarded as isolated from the rest of the molecule. Given the force constant of the bond in a carbonyl group is 908 N m^{-1}, calculate the vibrational frequency of (a) $^{12}C{=}^{16}O$, (b) $^{13}C{=}^{16}O$.

19.36 The wavenumber of the fundamental vibrational transition of Cl_2 is 565 cm^{-1}. Calculate the force constant of the bond.

19.37 The hydrogen halides have the following fundamental vibrational wavenumbers:

	HF	HCl	HBr	HI
$\tilde{\nu}/cm^{-1}$	4141.3	2988.9	2649.7	2309.5

Calculate the force constants of the hydrogen–halogen bonds.

19.38 From the data in Exercise 19.37, predict the fundamental vibrational wavenumbers of the deuterium halides.

19.39 Infrared absorption by $^1H^{81}Br$ gives rise to an R branch from $v=0$. What is the wavenumber of the line originating from the rotational state with $J=2$?

19.40 Which of the following molecules may show infrared absorption spectra: (a) H_2, (b) HCl, (c) CO_2, (d) H_2O, (e) CH_3CH_3, (f) CH_4, (g) CH_3Cl, (h) N_2?

19.41 How many normal modes of vibration are there for (a) NO_2, (b) N_2O, (c) cyclohexane, (d) hexane?

19.42 Consider the vibrational mode that corresponds to the uniform expansion of the benzene ring. Is it (a) Raman, (b) infrared active?

Chapter 20

Electronic transitions and photochemistry

The energy needed to change the distribution of an electron in a molecule is of the order of several electronvolts. Consequently, the photons emitted or absorbed when such changes occur lie in the visible and ultraviolet regions of the spectrum, which spread from about 14 000 cm^{-1} for red light to 21 000 cm^{-1} for blue, and on to 50 000 cm^{-1} for ultraviolet radiation (Table 20.1). Indeed, many of the colours of the objects in the world around us, including the green of vegetation, the colours of flowers and of synthetic dyes, and the colours of pigments and minerals, stem from transitions in which an electron migrates from one orbital of a molecule or ion into another. The change in location of an electron that takes place when chlorophyll absorbs red and blue light (leaving green to be reflected) is the primary energy-harvesting step by which our planet captures energy from the Sun and uses it to drive the non-spontaneous reactions of photosynthesis. In some cases the relocation of an electron may be so extensive that it results in the breaking of a bond and the dissociation of the molecule: such processes give rise to the numerous reactions of photochemistry, including the reactions that sustain or damage the atmosphere.

An electronvolt is the energy acquired by an electron when it falls through a potential difference of 1 V; 1 eV corresponds to 8065.5 cm^{-1} and 96.485 kJ mol^{-1}.

Table 20.1 *Colour, frequency, and energy of light*

Colour	λ/nm	$\nu/(10^{14}\ \text{Hz})$	$\tilde{\nu}/(10^4\ \text{cm}^{-1})$	E/eV	$E/(\text{kJ mol}^{-1})$
Infrared	1000	3.00	1.00	1.24	120
Red	700	4.28	1.43	1.77	171
Orange	620	4.84	1.61	2.00	193
Yellow	580	5.17	1.72	2.14	206
Green	530	5.66	1.89	2.34	226
Blue	470	6.38	2.13	2.64	254
Violet	420	7.14	2.38	2.95	285
Near-ultraviolet	300	10.0	3.33	4.15	400
Far-ultraviolet	200	15.0	5.00	6.20	598

Ultraviolet and visible spectra

White light is a mixture of light of all different colours. The removal, by absorption, of any one of these colours from white light results in the complementary colour being observed. For instance, the absorption of red light from white light by an object results in that object appearing green, the complementary colour of red. Conversely, the absorption of green light results in the object appearing red. The pairs of complementary colours are neatly summarized by the artist's colour wheel shown in Fig. 20.1, where complementary colours lie opposite one another along a diameter.

It should be stressed, however, that the perception of colour is a very subtle phenomenon. Although an object may appear green because it absorbs red light, it may also appear green because it absorbs all colours from the incident light *except* green. This is the origin of the colour of vegetation, because chlorophyll absorbs in two regions of the spectrum, leaving green to be reflected (Fig. 20.2). Moreover, an absorption band may be very broad, and although it may be a maximum at one particular wavelength, it may have a long tail that spreads into other regions (Fig. 20.3). In such cases, it is very difficult to predict the perceived colour from the location of the absorption maximum.

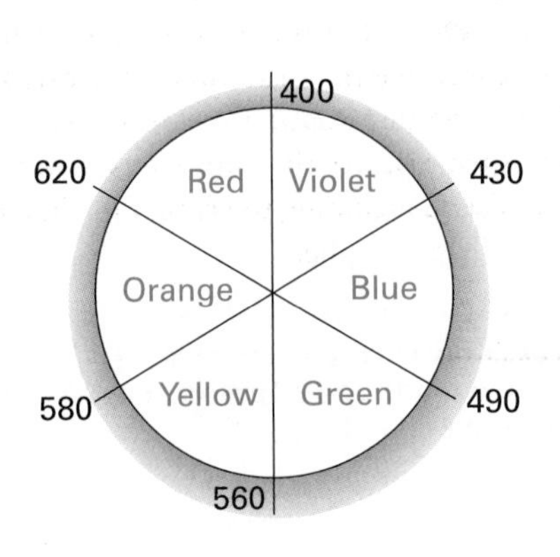

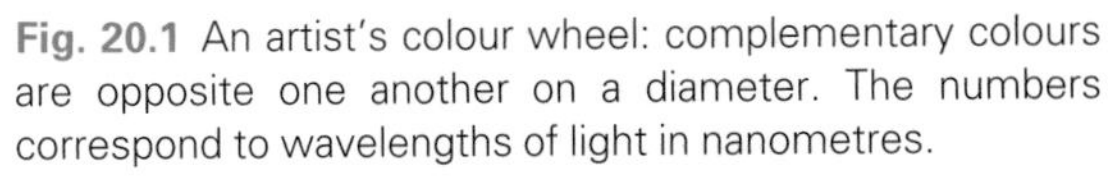
Fig. 20.1 An artist's colour wheel: complementary colours are opposite one another on a diameter. The numbers correspond to wavelengths of light in nanometres.

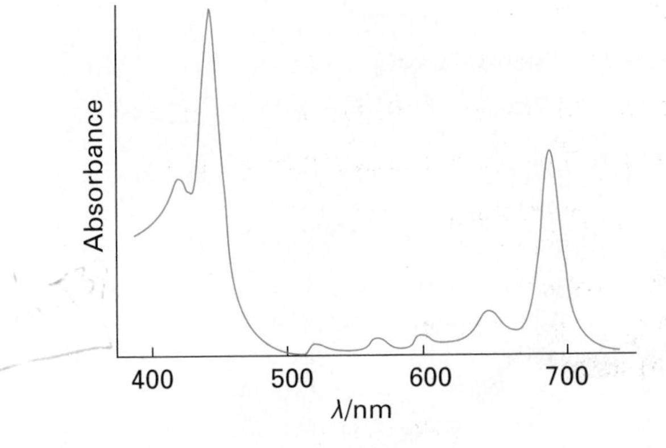

Fig. 20.2 The absorption spectrum of chlorophyll in the visible region. Note that it absorbs in the red and blue regions, and that green light is not absorbed.

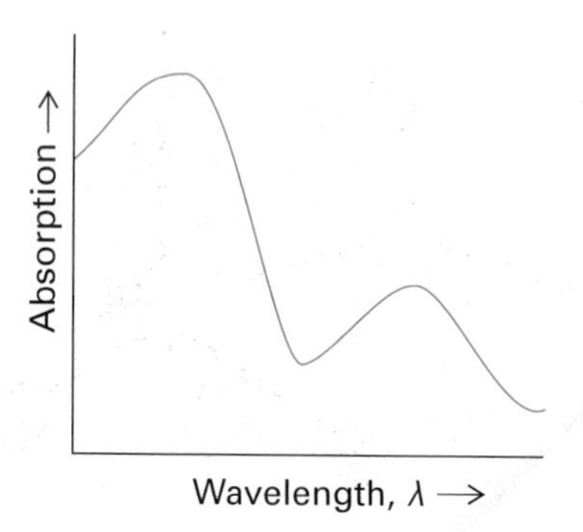

Fig. 20.3 An electronic absorption of a species in solution is typically very broad and consists of several broad bands.

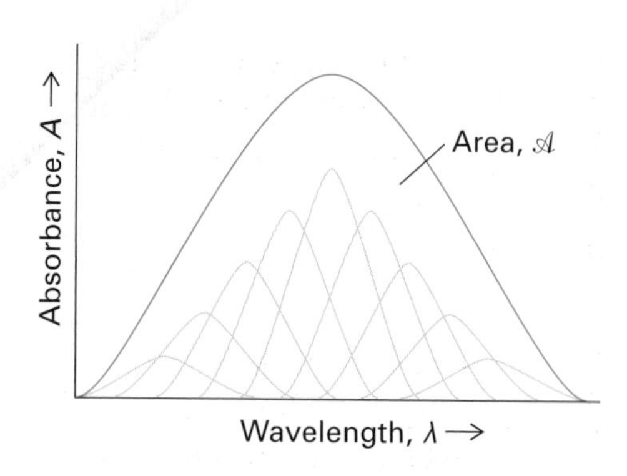

Fig. 20.4 An electronic absorption band consists of many superimposed bands that merge together to give a single broad band with unresolved vibrational structure.

In Chapter 19 we discussed the general principles that determine the extent of absorption of electromagnetic radiation by a sample and contribute to the linewidths of absorption spectra. Here we apply those principles to electronic transitions in the ultraviolet and visible regions of the electromagnetic spectrum.

20.1 The Franck–Condon principle

We now consider the intensity of an electronic transition and the shape of the absorption band. The central point is that whenever an electronic transition takes place, it is accompanied by the excitation of vibrations of the molecule. In the electronic ground state of a molecule, the nuclei take up locations in response to the Coulombic forces acting on them. These forces arise from the electrons and the other nuclei. After an electronic transition, when an electron has migrated to a different part of the molecule, the nuclei are subjected to different Coulombic forces from the surrounding electrons. The molecule may respond to the change in forces by bursting into vibration. As a result, some of the energy used to redistribute an electron is in fact used to stimulate the vibrations of the absorbing molecules. Therefore, instead of a single, sharp, and purely electronic absorption line being observed, the absorption spectrum consists of many lines. This **vibrational structure** of an electronic transition can be resolved if the sample is gaseous, but in a liquid or solid the lines usually merge together and result in a broad, almost featureless band (Fig. 20.4).

The vibrational structure of a band is explained by the **Franck–Condon principle:**

Because nuclei are so much more massive than electrons, an electronic transition takes place faster than the nuclei can respond.

In an electronic transition, electron density is lost rapidly from some regions of the molecule and is built up rapidly in others. As a result, the initially stationary nuclei suddenly experience a new force field. They respond by beginning to vibrate, and (in classical terms) swing backwards and forwards from their original separation, which they maintained during the rapid electronic excitation. The equilibrium separation of the nuclei in the initial electronic state therefore becomes a **turning point**, one of the end points of a nuclear swing, in the final electronic state (Fig. 20.5). To predict the most likely final vibrational state we draw a vertical line from the minimum of the lower curve (the starting point for the transition) up to the point at which the line intersects the curve representing the upper electronic state (the turning point of the newly stimulated vibration). This procedure gives rise to the term **vertical transition** for a transition in accord with the Franck–Condon principle. In practice, the electronically excited molecule may be formed in one of several excited vibrational states, so the absorption occurs at several different frequencies. As remarked above, in a condensed medium, the individual transitions merge together to give a broad, largely featureless band of absorption.

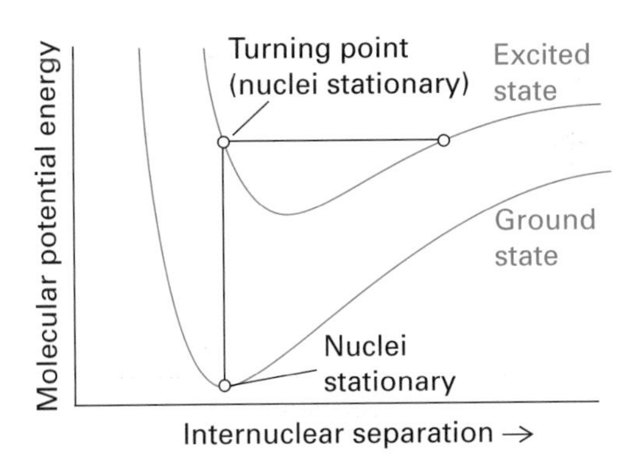

Fig. 20.5 According to the Franck–Condon principle, the most intense electronic transition is from the ground vibrational state to the vibrational state that lies vertically above it in the upper electronic state. Transitions to other vibrational levels also occur, but with lower intensity.

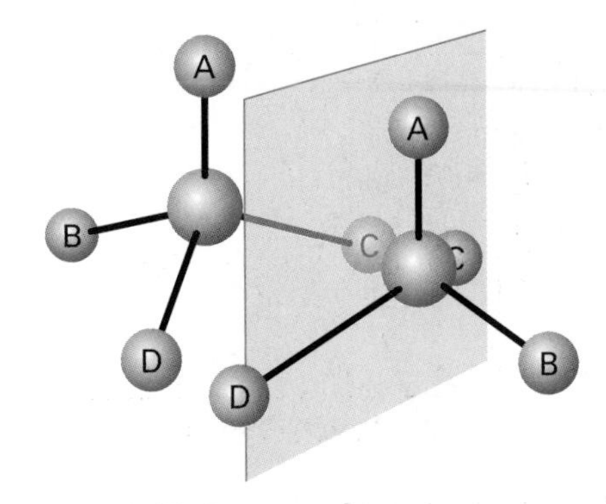

Fig. 20.7 A chiral molecule is one that is not superimposable to its mirror image. A carbon atom attached to four different groups is an example of a chiral centre in a molecule. Such molecules are optically active.

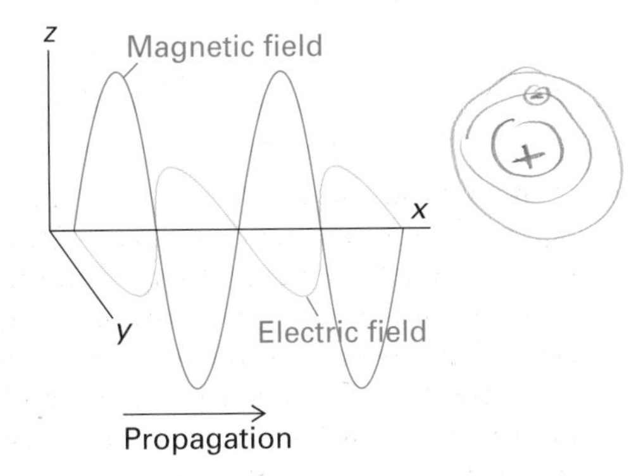

Fig. 20.6 Electromagnetic radiation consists of a wave of electric and magnetic fields perpendicular to the direction of propagation (in this case the *x*-direction), and mutually perpendicular to each other. This illustration shows a plane-polarized wave, with the electric and magnetic fields oscillating in the *xy* and *xz* planes, respectively.

20.2 Circular dichroism

Electromagnetic radiation is **plane polarized** when the electric and magnetic fields each oscillate in a single plane (Fig. 20.6). The plane of polarization may be oriented in any direction around the direction of propagation (the *x*-direction in Fig. 20.6), with the electric and magnetic fields perpendicular to that direction and perpendicular to each other. An alternative mode of polarization is **circular polarization**, in which the electric and magnetic fields rotate around the direction of propagation in either a clockwise or a counterclockwise sense but remain perpendicular to it and each other.

When plane-polarized radiation passes through samples of certain kinds of matter, the plane of polarization is rotated. This rotation is the phenomenon of **optical activity**. Optical activity is observed when the molecules in the sample are **chiral**, which means distinguishable from their mirror image (Fig. 20.7). In many cases, organic chiral compounds are easy to identify, because they contain a carbon atom to which are bonded four different groups. The amino acid alanine, $NH_2CH(CH_3)COOH$, is an example. Mirror image pairs of chiral molecules, which are called **enantiomers**, rotate light of a given frequency through exactly the same angle but in opposite directions.

Chiral molecules have a second characteristic: they absorb left and right circularly polarized light to different extents. In a circularly polarized ray of light, the electric field describes a helical path as the wave travels through space (Fig. 20.8), and the rotation may be either clockwise or counterclockwise. The differential absorption of left- and right-circularly polarized light is called **circular dichroism** (CD). In terms of the absorbances for the two components, A_L and A_R, the circular dichroism of a sample of molar concentration [J] is reported as

$$\Delta\varepsilon = \varepsilon_L - \varepsilon_R = \frac{A_L - A_R}{[J]l} \qquad (20.1)$$

where l is the path length of the sample.

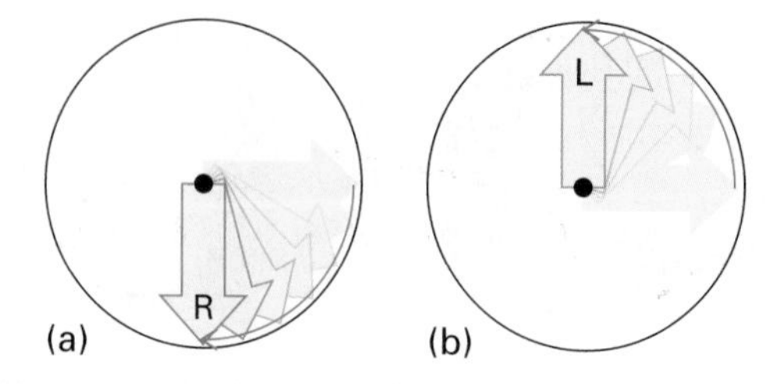

Fig. 20.8 In circularly polarized light, the electric field at different points along the direction of propagation rotates. The arrays of arrows in these illustrations show the view of the electric field when looking towards the oncoming ray: (a) right-circularly polarized, (b) left-circularly polarized light.

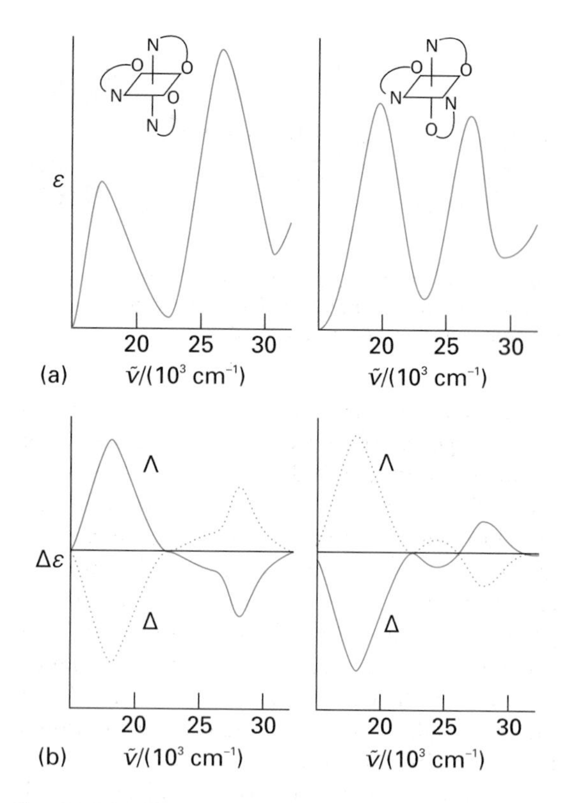

Fig. 20.9 (a) The absorption spectra of two isomers of $[Co(ala)_3]$, where ala is the conjugate base of alanine, and (b) the corresponding CD spectra. The left- and right-handed forms of these isomers, labelled Λ and Δ, give identical absorption spectra. However, the CD spectra are distinctly different, and the absolute configurations have been assigned by comparison with the CD spectra of a complex of known absolute configuration.

Circular dichroism is a useful adjunct to visible and UV spectroscopy. For example, the CD spectra of the enantiomeric pairs of chiral *d*-metal complexes are distinctly different, whereas there is little difference between their absorption spectra (Fig. 20.9). Moreover, CD spectra can be used to assign the absolute configuration of complexes by comparing the observed spectrum with the CD spectrum of a similar complex of known handedness. The CD spectra of polypeptides and nucleic acids give similar structural information. In these cases the spectrum of the polymer chain arises from the chirality of individual monomer units and, in addition, a contribution from the helical structure of the polymer itself. By subtracting the CD spectra of a mixture of monomers, the remaining structure is due largely to the secondary structure of the polymer, and in this can its conformation can be investigated. Circular dichroism can also be used to identify and follow changes in the conformation of biological macromolecules (Fig. 20.10).

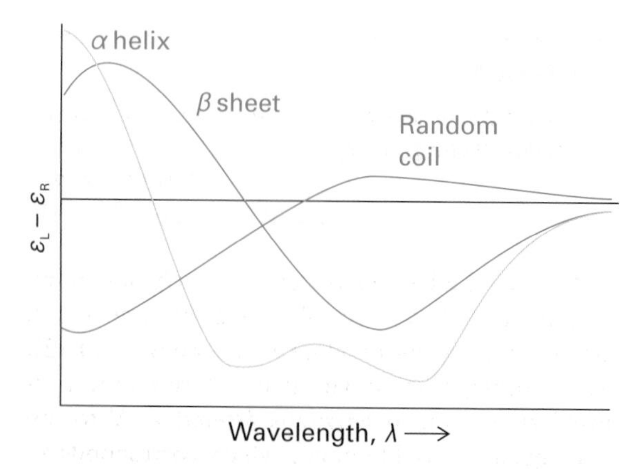

Fig. 20.10 CD spectra typical of a polypeptide in three different conformations.

20.3 Specific types of transitions

The absorption of a photon can often be traced to the excitation of an electron that is localized on a small group of atoms. For example, an absorption at about 290 nm is normally observed when a carbonyl group is present. Groups with characteristic optical absorptions are called **chromophores** (from the Greek for 'colour bringer'), and their presence often accounts for the colours of many substances.

A *d*-metal complex may absorb light as a result of the transfer of an electron from the ligands into

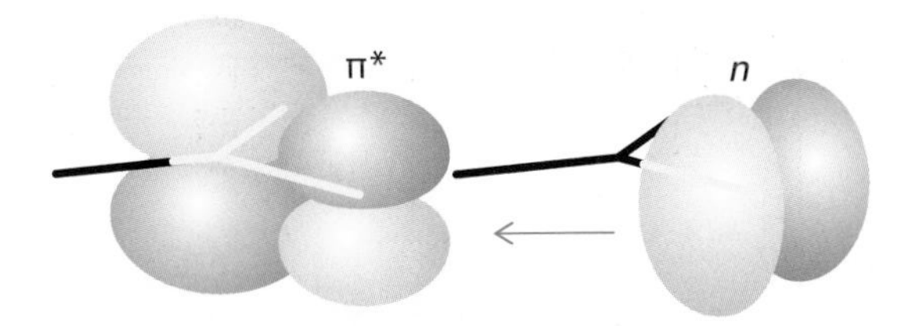

Fig. 20.11 A carbonyl group acts as a chromophore primarily because of the excitation of a non-bonding O lone-pair electron to an antibonding CO π* orbital.

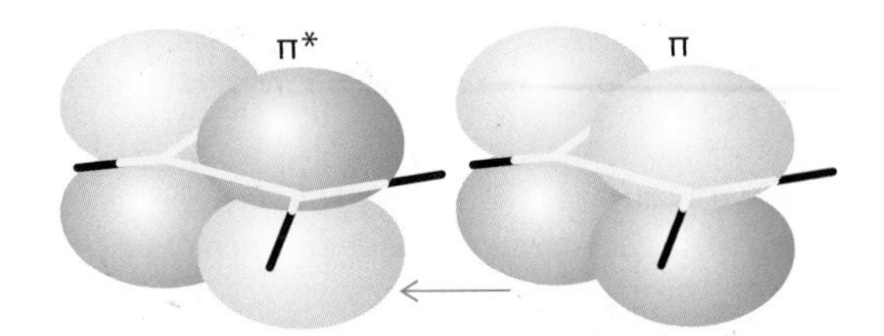

Fig. 20.12 A carbon–carbon double bond acts as a chromophore. One of its important transitions is the π-to-π* transition illustrated here, in which an electron is promoted from a π orbital to the corresponding antibonding orbital.

the *d* orbitals of the central atom, or vice versa. In such **charge-transfer transitions** the electron moves through a considerable distance, which means that the redistribution of charge as measured by the transition dipole moment may be large and the absorption correspondingly intense. This mode of chromophore activity is shown by the permanganate ion, MnO_4^-: the charge redistribution that accompanies the migration of an electron from the O atoms to the central Mn atom accounts for its intense purple colour (resulting from absorption in the range 420–700 nm).

The transition responsible for absorption in carbonyl compounds can be traced to the lone pairs of electrons on the O atom. One of these electrons may be excited into an empty π* orbital of the carbonyl group (Fig. 20.11), which gives rise to an ***n*-to-π* transition**, where *n* denotes a non-bonding orbital (an orbital that is neither bonding nor antibonding, such as that occupied by a lone pair). Typical absorption energies are about 4 eV.

Self-test 20.1

Estimate the wavelength of maximum absorption for a transition of energy 4.3 eV.

[*Answer:* 288 nm]

A C=C double bond acts as a chromophore because the absorption of a photon excites a π electron into an antibonding π* orbital (Fig. 20.12). The chromophore activity is therefore due to a **π-to-π* transition.** Its energy is around 7 eV for an unconjugated double bond, which corresponds to an absorption at 180 nm (in the ultraviolet). When the double bond is part of a conjugated chain, the energies of the molecular orbitals lie closer together and the transition shifts into the visible region of the spectrum. Many of the reds and yellows of vegetation are due to transitions of this kind. For example, the carotenes that are present in green leaves (but are concealed by the intense absorption of the chlorophyll until the latter decays in the autumn) collect some of the solar radiation incident on the leaf by a π-to-π* transition in their long conjugated hydrocarbon chains. A similar type of absorption is responsible for the primary process of vision (Box 20.1).

Radiative and non-radiative decay

In most cases, the excitation energy of a molecule that has absorbed a photon is degraded into the disordered thermal motion of its surroundings in a process known as **internal conversion.** However, one process by which an electronically excited molecule can discard its excess energy is by **radiative decay,** in which an electron relaxes back into a lower energy orbital and in the process generates a photon. As a result, an observer sees the sample glowing (if the emitted radiation is in the visible region of the spectrum).

There are two principal modes of radiative decay, fluorescence and phosphorescence (Fig. 20.13). In **fluorescence,** the spontaneously emitted radiation ceases very soon after the exciting radiation is extinguished. In **phosphorescence,** the spontaneous emission may persist for long periods (even hours, but characteristically seconds or fractions of a

Box 20.1 *Vision*

The eye is an exquisite photochemical organ that acts as a transducer, converting radiant energy into electrical signals that travel along neurons. Here we concentrate on the events taking place in the human eye, but similar processes occur in all animals. Indeed, a single type of protein, rhodopsin, is the primary receptor for light throughout the animal kingdom, which indicates that vision emerged very early in evolutionary history, no doubt because of its enormous value for survival.

Photons enter the eye through the cornea, pass through the ocular fluid that fills the eye, and fall on the retina. The ocular fluid is principally water, and passage of light through this medium is largely responsible for the *chromatic aberration* of the eye, the blurring of the image as a result of different frequencies being brought to slightly different focuses. The chromatic aberration is reduced to some extent by the tinted region called the *macular pigment* that covers part of the retina. The pigments in this region are the carotene-like xanthophylls (**1**), which remove some of the blue light and hence help to sharpen the image. They also protect the photoreceptor molecules from too great a flux of potentially dangerous high-energy photons. The xanthophylls have delocalized electrons that spread along the chain of conjugated double bonds, and the π-to-π* transition lies in the visible.

1 A xanthophyll

About 57 per cent of the photons that enter the eye reach the retina; the rest are scattered or absorbed by the occular fluid. Here the primary act of vision takes place, in which the chromophore of a rhodopsin molecule absorbs a photon in another π-to-π* transition. A rhodopsin molecule consists of an opsin protein molecule to which is attached an 11-*cis*-retinal molecule (**2**). The latter resembles half a carotene molecule, showing Nature's economy in its use of available materials. The attachment

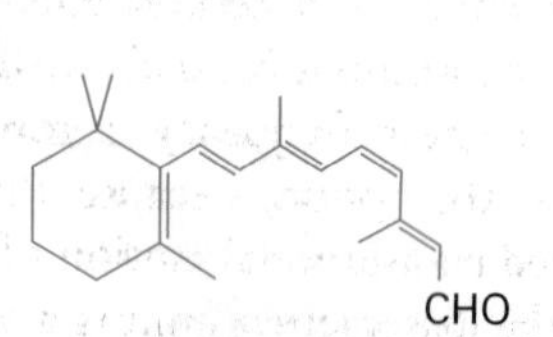

2 11-*cis*-Retinal

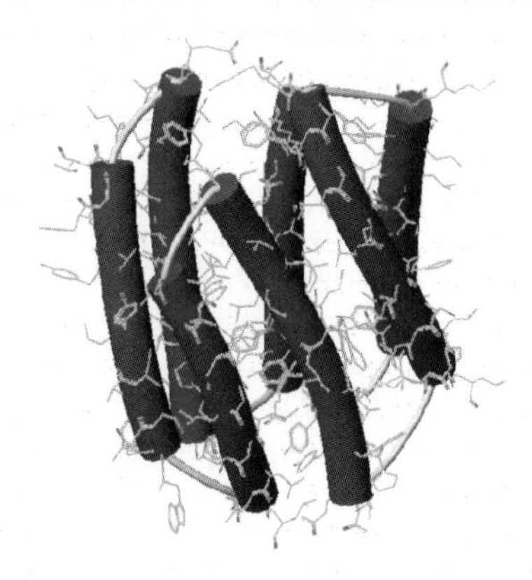

The structure of the rhodopsin molecule, consisting of an opsin protein to which is attached an 11-*cis*-retinal molecule embedded in the space surrounded by the helical regions (depicted as cylinders).

is by the formation of a Schiff's base, using the –CHO group of the chromophore. The free 11-*cis*-retinal molecule absorbs in the ultraviolet, but attachment to the opsin protein molecule shifts the absorption into the visible region. The rhodopsin molecules are situated in the membranes of special cells (the 'rods' and the 'cones') that cover the retina. The opsin molecule is anchored into the cell membrane by two hydrophobic groups and largely surrounds the chromophore (see illustration).

Immediately after the absorption of a photon, the 11-*cis*-retinal molecule undergoes photoisomerization into all-*trans*-retinal (**3**). Photoisomerization takes about 200 fs and about 67 pigment molecules isomerize for every 100 photons that are absorbed. The process is able to occur because the π-to-π* excitation of an electron loosens one of the π bonds (the one indicated by the arrow in the diagram), its torsional rigidity is lost, and one part of the molecule swings round into its new position. At that point, the molecule returns to its ground state, but is now trapped in its new conformation. The straightened tail of all-*trans*-retinal results in the molecule taking up more space than 11-*cis*-retinal did, so the molecule

3 All-*cis*-retinal

presses against the coils of the opsin molecule that surrounds it. Thus, in about 0.25–0.50 ms from the initial absorption event, the rhodopsin molecule is activated.

Now a sequence of biochemical events—the *biochemical cascade*—converts the altered configuration of the rhodopsin molecule into a pulse of electric potential that travels through the optical nerve into the optical cortex, where it is interpreted as a signal and incorporated into the web of events we call 'vision'. At the same time, the resting state of the rhodopsin molecule is restored by a series of non-radiative chemical events powered by ATP. The process involves the escape of all-*trans*-retinal as all-*trans*-retinol (in which $-CHO$ has been reduced to $-CH_2OH$) from the opsin molecule by a process catalysed by the enzyme rhodopsin kinase and the attachment of another protein molecule, arrestin. The free all-*trans*-retinol molecule now undergoes enzyme-catalysed isomerization into 11-*cis*-retinol followed by dehydrogenation to form 11-*cis*-retinal, which is then delivered back into an opsin molecule. At this point, the cycle of excitation, photoisomerization, and regeneration is ready to begin again.

Exercise 1 The flux of visible photons reaching Earth from the North Star is about $4 \times 10^3\ mm^{-2}\ s^{-1}$. Of these photons, 30 per cent are absorbed or scattered by the atmosphere and 25 per cent of the surviving photons are scattered by the surface of the cornea of the eye. A further 9 per cent are absorbed inside the cornea. The area of the pupil at night is about 40 mm^2 and the response time of the eye is about 0.1 s. Of the photons passing through the pupil, about 43 per cent are absorbed in the ocular medium. How many photons from the North Star are focused on to the retina in 0.1 s? For a continuation of this story, see R. W. Rodieck, *The first steps in seeing*, Sinauer (1998).

Exercise 2 In the free-electron molecular orbital theory of electronic structure, the π electrons in a conjugated molecule are treated as non-interacting particles in a box of length equal to the length of the conjugated system. On the basis of this model, at what wavelength would you expect all-*trans*-retinal to absorb? Take the mean carbon–carbon bond length to be 140 pm.

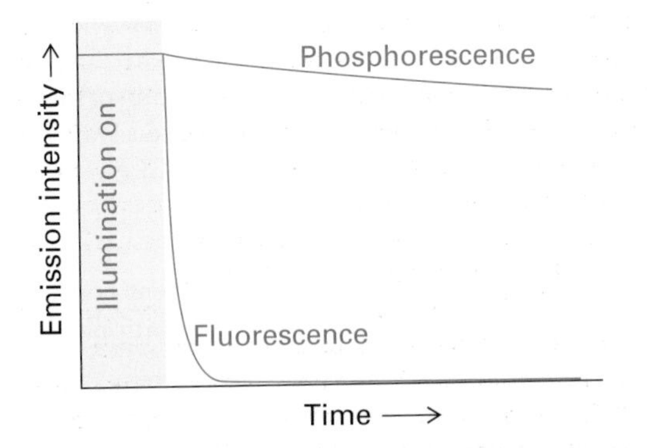

Fig. 20.13 The empirical (observation-based) distinction between fluorescence and phosphorescence is that the former is extinguished very quickly after the exciting source is removed, whereas the latter continues with relatively slowly diminishing intensity.

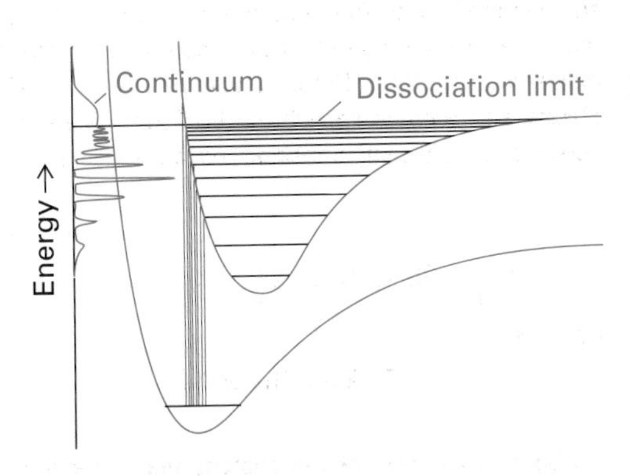

Fig. 20.14 When absorption occurs to unbound states of the upper electronic state, the molecule dissociates and the absorption is a continuum. Below the dissociation limit the electronic spectrum has a normal vibrational structure.

second). The difference suggests that fluorescence is an immediate conversion of absorbed light into re-emitted radiant energy and that phosphorescence involves the storage of energy in a reservoir from which it slowly leaks.

Other than thermal degradation, a non-radiative fate for an electronically excited molecule is **dissociation**, or fragmentation (Fig. 20.14). The onset of dissociation can be detected in an absorption spectrum by seeing that the vibrational structure of a band terminates at a certain energy. Absorption occurs in a continuous band above this **dissociation limit**, the highest frequency before the onset of continuous absorption, because the final state is unquantized translational motion of the fragments. Locating the dissociation limit is a valuable way of determining the bond dissociation energy.

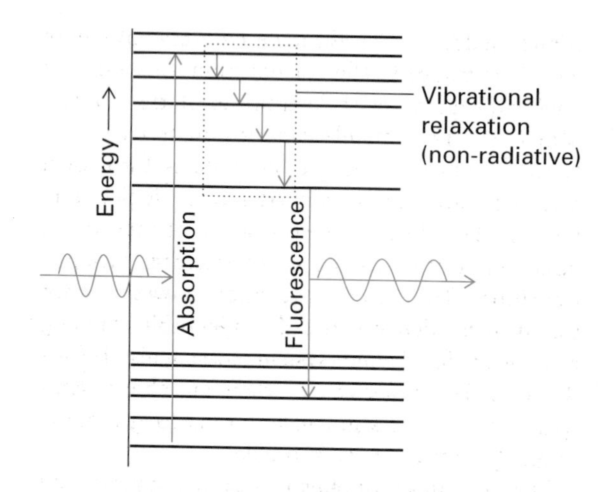

Fig. 20.15 A Jablonski diagram showing the sequence of steps leading to fluorescence. After the initial absorption the upper vibrational states undergo radiationless decay—the process of vibrational relaxation—by giving up energy to the surroundings. A radiative transition then occurs from the ground state of the upper electronic state. In practice, the separation of the ground states of the electronic states is 10 to 100 times greater than the separation of the vibrational levels.

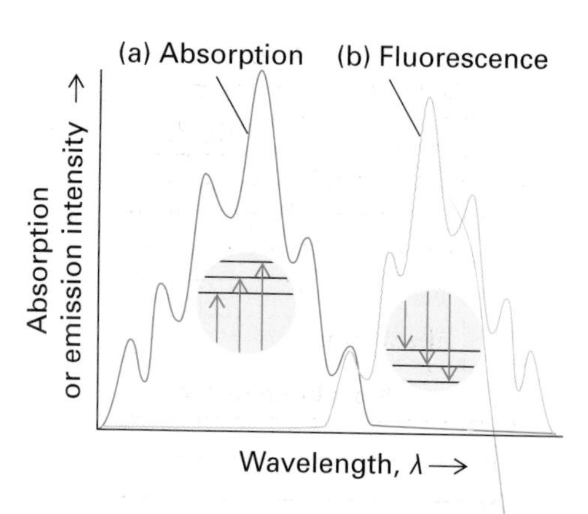

Fig. 20.16 The absorption spectrum (a) shows a vibrational structure characteristic of the upper state. The fluorescence spectrum (b) shows a structure characteristic of the lower state; it is also displaced to lower frequencies and resembles a mirror image of the absorption.

20.4 Fluorescence

Figure 20.15 is a simple example of a **Jablonski diagram**, a schematic portrayal of molecular electronic and vibrational energy levels, which shows the sequence of steps involved in fluorescence. The initial absorption takes the molecule to an excited electronic state, and if the absorption spectrum were monitored it would look like the one shown in Fig. 20.16a. The excited molecule is subjected to collisions with the surrounding molecules, and as it gives up energy it steps down the ladder of vibrational levels. The surrounding molecules, however, might be unable to accept the larger energy needed to lower the molecule to the ground electronic state. The excited state might therefore survive long enough to generate a photon and emit the remaining excess energy as radiation. The downward electronic transition is **vertical**, which means in accord with the Franck–Condon principle, and the fluorescence spectrum has a vibrational structure characteristic of the lower electronic state (Fig. 20.16b).

Fluorescence occurs at a lower frequency than that of the incident radiation because the fluorescence radiation is emitted after some vibrational energy has been discarded into the surroundings. The vivid oranges and greens of fluorescent dyes are an everyday manifestation of this effect: they absorb in the ultraviolet and fluoresce in the visible. The mechanism also suggests that the intensity of the fluorescence ought to depend on the ability of the solvent molecules to accept the electronic and vibrational quanta. It is indeed found that a solvent composed of molecules with widely spaced vibrational levels (such as water) may be able to accept the large quantum of electronic energy and so decrease the intensity of the solute's fluorescence.

20.5 Phosphorescence

Figure 20.17 is a Jablonski diagram showing the events leading to phosphorescence. The first steps are the same as in fluorescence, but the presence of a triplet state plays a decisive role. A **triplet state** is a state in which two electrons in different orbitals have parallel spins: the ground state of O_2, which was discussed in Section 14.13, is an example. The name 'triplet' reflects the (quantum mechanical) fact that the total spin of two parallel electron spins (↑↑) can adopt only three orientations with respect to an axis. An ordinary spin-paired state (↑↓) is called a

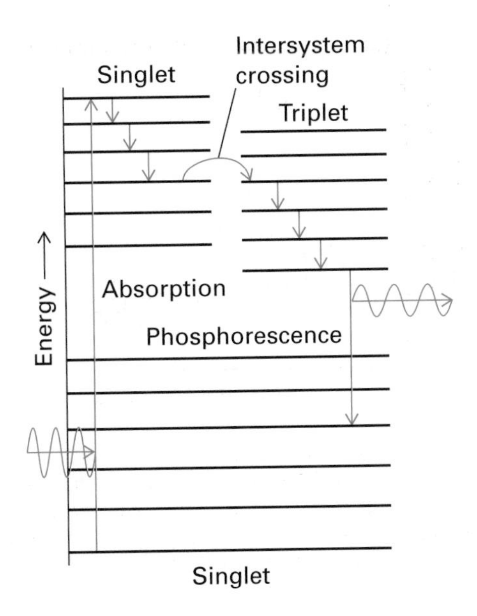

Fig. 20.17 The sequence of steps leading to phosphorescence. The important step is the intersystem crossing from an excited singlet to an excited triplet state. The triplet state acts as a slowly radiating reservoir because the return to the ground state is very slow.

singlet state because there is only one orientation in space for such a pair of spins.[1]

The ground state of a typical phosphorescent molecule is a singlet because its electrons are all paired; the excited state to which the absorption excites the molecule is also a singlet. The peculiar feature of a phosphorescent molecule, however, is that it possesses an excited triplet state of an energy similar to that of the excited singlet state and into which the excited singlet state may convert. Hence, if there is a mechanism for unpairing two electron spins (and so converting ↑↓ into ↑↑), then the molecule may undergo **intersystem crossing** and become a triplet state. The unpairing of electron spins is possible if the molecule contains a heavy atom, such as an atom of sulfur, with strong spin–orbit coupling (Section 13.17). Then the angular momentum needed to convert a singlet state into a triplet state may be acquired from the orbital motion of the electrons.

After an excited singlet molecule crosses into a triplet state, it continues to discard energy into the surroundings and to step down the ladder of vibrational states. However, it is now stepping down the triplet's ladder, and at the lowest vibrational energy level it is trapped. The solvent cannot extract the final, large quantum of electronic excitation energy. Moreover, the molecule cannot radiate its energy because return to the ground state is forbidden: a triplet state cannot convert into a singlet state because the spin of one electron cannot reverse in direction relative to the other electron during a transition.[2] The radiative transition, however, is not totally forbidden because the spin–orbit coupling responsible for the intersystem crossing also breaks this rule. The molecules are therefore able to emit weakly and the emission may continue long after the original excited state was formed.

The mechanism of phosphorescence summarized in Fig. 20.17 accounts for the observation that the excitation energy seems to become trapped in a slowly leaking reservoir. It also suggests (as is confirmed experimentally) that phosphorescence should be most intense from solid samples: energy transfer is then less efficient and the intersystem crossing has time to occur as the singlet excited state loses vibrational energy. The mechanism also suggests that the phosphorescence efficiency should depend on the presence of a moderately heavy atom (with its ability to flip electron spins), which is in fact the case.

20.6 Lasers

The word *laser* is an acronym formed from *l*ight *a*mplification by *s*timulated *e*mission of *r*adiation. As this name suggests, it is a process that depends on *stimulated* emission as distinct from the spontaneous emission processes characteristic of fluorescence and phosphorescence. In **stimulated emission**, an excited state is stimulated to emit a photon by the presence of radiation of the same frequency, and the more photons there are present, the greater the probability of the emission. To picture the process, we can think of the oscillations of the electromagnetic field as periodically distorting the excited molecule at the frequency of the transition and hence encouraging the molecule to generate a

[1] In the language introduced in Section 13.16, a triplet state has $S = 1$ and the corresponding magnetic quantum number M_S has one of the three values +1, 0, and −1; a singlet state has $S = 0$ and M_S has the single value 0.

[2] A selection rule valid for light atoms is $\Delta S = 0$.

photon of the same frequency. The essential feature of laser action is the strong **gain**, or growth of intensity, that results: the more photons present of the appropriate frequency, the more photons of that frequency the excited molecules will be stimulated to form, and so the laser medium fills with photons and can escape either continuously or in pulses.

Example 20.1

Relating the power and energy of a laser

A laser rated at 0.10 J can generate radiation in 3.0 ns pulses at a pulse repetition rate of 10 Hz. Assuming that the pulses are rectangular, calculate the peak power output and the average power output of this laser.

Strategy The power output is the energy released in an interval divided by the duration of the interval, and is expressed in watts ($1\ W = 1\ J\ s^{-1}$). To calculate the peak power output, P_{peak}, we divide the energy released during the pulse by the duration of the pulse. The average power output, $P_{average}$, is the total energy released by a large number of pulses divided by the duration of the time interval over which the total energy was measured. So, the average power is simply the energy released by one pulse multiplied by the pulse repetition rate.

Solution From the data,

$$P_{peak} = \frac{\overbrace{0.10\ J}^{\text{Energy of pulse}}}{\underbrace{3.0 \times 10^{-9}\ s}_{\text{Duration of pulse}}} = 3.3 \times 10^{7}\ J\ s^{-1}$$

That is, the peak power output is 33 MW. The pulse repetition rate is 10 Hz, so that ten pulses are emitted by the laser for every second of operation. It follows that the average power output is

$$P_{average} = 0.10\ J \times 10\ s^{-1} = 1.0\ J\ s^{-1} = 1.0\ W$$

The peak power is much higher than the average power because this laser emits light for only 3.0×10^{-8} s during each second of operation.

Self-test 20.2

Calculate the peak power and average power output of a laser with a pulse energy of 2.0 mJ, a pulse duration of 30 ps ($1\ ps = 1 \times 10^{-12}\ s$), and a pulse repetition rate of 38 MHz.

[*Answer:* $P_{peak} = 67\ MW$, $P_{average} = 76\ kW$]

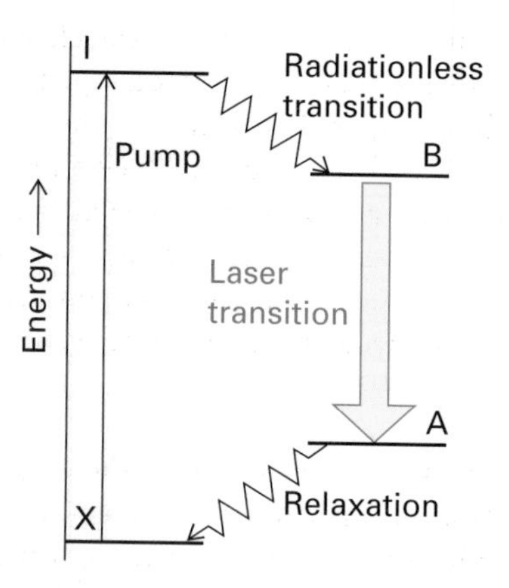

Fig. 20.18 The transitions involved in a four-level laser. Because the laser transition terminates in an excited state (A), the population inversion between A and B is much easier to achieve than when the lower state of the laser transition is the ground state.

One requirement for laser action is the existence of an excited state that has a long enough lifetime for it to participate in stimulated emission. Another requirement is the existence of a greater population in the upper state than in the lower state where the transition terminates. Because at thermal equilibrium the population is greater in the lower energy state, it is necessary to achieve a **population inversion** in which there are more molecules in the upper state than in the lower.

Figure 20.18 illustrates one way to achieve population inversion indirectly through an intermediate state I. Thus, the molecule is excited to I, which then gives up some of its energy non-radiatively (by passing energy on to vibrations of the surroundings) and changes into a lower state B; the laser transition is the return of B to a lower state A. Because four levels are involved overall, this arrangement leads to a **four-level laser**. The transition from X to I is caused by an intense flash of light in the process called **pumping**. In some cases the pumping flash is achieved with an electric discharge through xenon or with the radiation from another laser.

The web site for this text contains links to databases on the optical properties of laser materials.

In practice, the laser medium is confined to a cavity that ensures that only certain photons of a particular frequency, direction of travel, and state of polarization are generated abundantly. The cavity is essentially a region between two mirrors, which reflect the light back and forth. This arrangement can be regarded as a version of the particle in a box, with the particle now being a photon. As in the treatment of a particle in a box (Section 12.9(a)), the only wavelengths that can be sustained satisfy

$$n \times \tfrac{1}{2}\lambda = L \qquad (20.2)$$

where n is an integer and L is the length of the cavity. That is, only an integral number of half-wavelengths fit into the cavity; all other waves undergo destructive interference with themselves. In addition, not all wavelengths that can be sustained by the cavity are amplified by the laser medium (many fall outside the range of frequencies of the laser transitions), so only a few contribute to the laser radiation. These wavelengths are the **resonant modes** of the laser.

Photons with the correct wavelength for the resonant modes of the cavity and the correct frequency to stimulate the laser transition are highly amplified. One photon might be generated spontaneously, and travel through the medium. It stimulates the emission of another photon, which in turn stimulates more (Fig. 20.19). The cascade of energy builds up rapidly, and soon the cavity is an intense reservoir of radiation at all the resonant modes it can sustain. Some of this radiation can be withdrawn if one of the mirrors is partially transmitting.

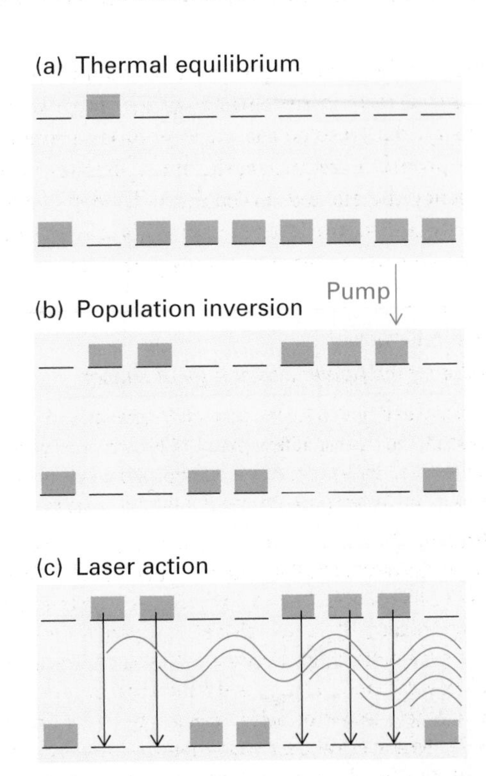

Fig. 20.19 A schematic illustration of the steps leading to laser action. (a) At thermal equilibrium, more atoms are in the ground state. (b) When the initial state absorbs, the populations are inverted (the atoms are pumped to the excited state). (c) A cascade of radiation then occurs, as one emitted photon stimulates another atom to emit, and so on. The radiation is coherent (phases in step).

The resonant modes of the cavity have various natural characteristics, and to some extent may be selected. Only photons that are travelling strictly parallel to the axis of the cavity undergo more than a couple of reflections, so only they are amplified, all others simply vanishing into the surroundings. Hence, laser light generally forms a beam with very low divergence. It may also be polarized, with its electric vector in a particular plane (or in some other state of polarization), by including a polarizing filter into the cavity or by making use of polarized transitions in a solid medium.

The requirements for laser action can be satisfied by using a variety of different systems. A *solid-state laser* is one in which the active medium is in the form of a single crystal or a glass. The first successful laser, the *ruby laser* built by Theodore Maiman in 1960, is an example (Fig. 20.20). Ruby is Al_2O_3 containing a small proportion of Cr^{3+} ions[3]. The population inversion results from pumping a majority of the Cr^{3+} ions into an excited state by using an intense flash from another source, followed by a radiationless transition to another, lower excited state. The transition from the lower of the two excited states to the ground state is the laser transition, and gives rise to red 694 nm radiation.

A *neodymium laser* is an example of a four-level laser (Fig. 20.21). In one form it consists of Nd^{3+} ions at low concentration in yttrium aluminium garnet (YAG, specifically $Y_3Al_5O_{12}$), and is then known as

[3] The normal green of Cr^{3+} is modified to red by the distortion of the local crystal field stemming from the replacement of an Al^{3+} ion by a slightly larger Cr^{3+} ion.

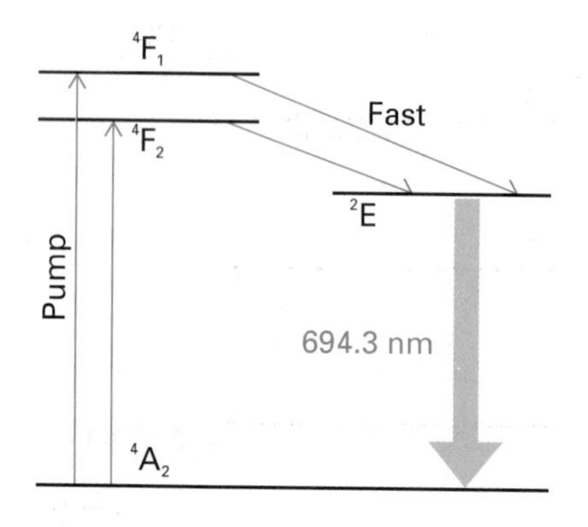

Fig. 20.20 The transitions involved in a ruby laser. The laser medium, ruby, consists of Al_2O_3 doped with Cr^{3+} ions.

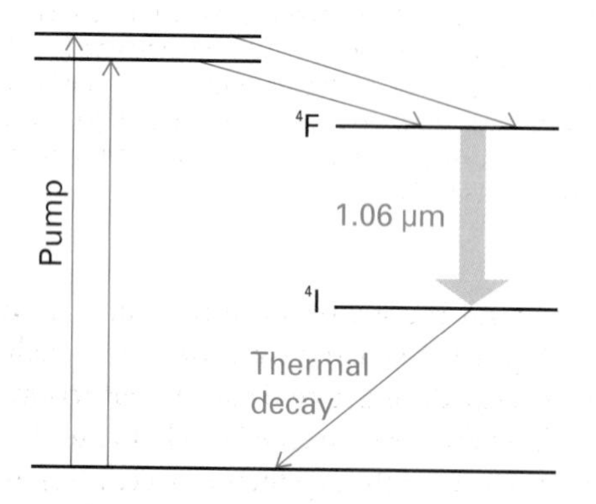

Fig. 20.21 The transitions involved in a neodymium laser. The laser action takes place between two excited states, and the population inversion is easier to achieve than in the ruby laser.

a Nd-YAG laser. A neodymium laser operates at a number of wavelengths in the infrared, the band at 1064 nm being most common. The transition at 1064 nm is very efficient and the laser is capable of substantial power output. The power is great enough that focusing the beam on to a material may lead to the observation of **non-linear optical phenomena,** which arise from changes in the optical properties of the substance in the presence of an intense electric field from electromagnetic radiation. A useful non-linear optical phenomenon is **frequency doubling,** or *second harmonic generation,* in which an intense laser beam is converted to radiation with twice (and in general a multiple) of its initial frequency as it passes though a suitable material. Frequency doubling and tripling of a Nd-YAG laser produce green light at 532 nm and ultraviolet light at 355 nm, respectively.

A *titanium sapphire laser* consists of Ti^{3+} ions at low concentration in a crystal of sapphire (Al_2O_3). The emission spectrum of Ti^{3+} in sapphire is very broad and laser action occurs over a wide range of wavelengths (700–1000 nm). The titanium sapphire laser is usually pumped by another laser, such as a neodymium laser, and can be operated in both continuous or pulsed modes, in which case very intense and short (20–100 fs, 1 fs = 10^{-15} s) flashes of light can be produced. When considered together with broad wavelength tunability, these features of the titanium sapphire laser justify its wide use in modern spectroscopy and photochemistry.

In *diode lasers,* of the type used in CD players and bar-code readers, the light emission at a p–n junction (Section 15.3) is sustained by sweeping away the electrons that fall into the holes of the p-type semiconductor. This process is arranged to occur in a cavity formed by making use of the abrupt difference in refractive index between the different components of the junction, and the radiation trapped in the cavity enhances the production of more radiation. One widely used material is GaAs doped with aluminium, which produces infrared laser radiation and is widely used in CD players.

Because *gas lasers* can be cooled by a rapid flow of the gas through the cavity, they can be used to generate high powers. The pumping is normally achieved using a gas that is different from the gas responsible for the laser emission itself. In the helium–neon laser the active medium is a mixture of helium and neon in a mole ratio of about 5:1 (Fig. 20.22). The initial step is the excitation of an He atom to the long-lived $1s^12s^1$ configuration by using an electric discharge (the collisions of electrons and ions cause transitions that are not restricted by electric-dipole selection rules). The excitation energy of this transition happens to match an excitation energy of neon, and during an He–Ne collision efficient transfer of energy may occur, leading to the production of highly excited, long-lived Ne atoms with unpopulated intermediate states. Laser action generating 633 nm radiation (among about 100 other lines) then occurs.

The *argon-ion laser* (Fig. 20.23), one of a number of 'ion lasers', consists of argon at about 1 Torr,

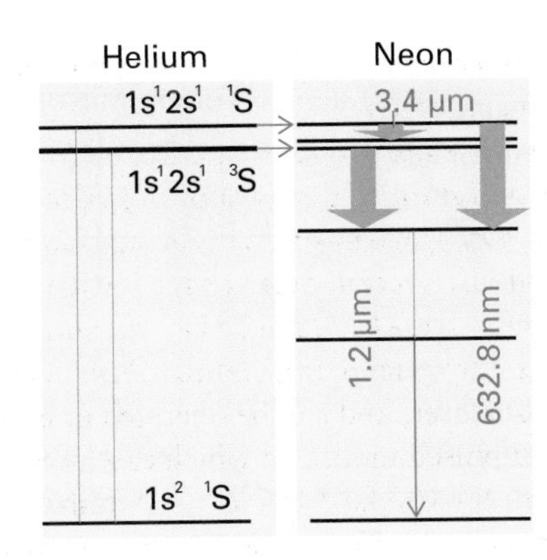

Fig. 20.22 The transitions involved in a helium–neon laser. The pumping (of the neon) depends on a coincidental matching of the helium and neon energy separations, so excited He atoms can transfer their excess energy to Ne atoms during a collision.

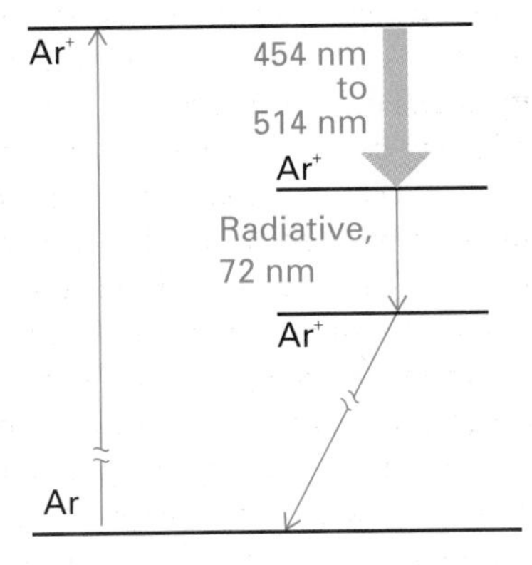

Fig. 20.23 The transitions involved in an argon-ion laser.

through which an electric discharge is passed. The discharge results in the formation of Ar^+ and Ar^{2+} ions in excited states, which undergo a laser transition to a lower state. These ions then revert to their ground states by emitting hard ultraviolet radiation (at 72 nm), and are then neutralized by a series of electrodes in the laser cavity. The *carbon dioxide laser* works on a slightly different principle (Fig. 20.24), as its radiation (between 9.2 μm and 10.8 μm, with the strongest emission at 10.6 μm, in the infrared) arises from vibrational transitions. Most of the working gas is nitrogen, which becomes vibrationally excited by electronic and ionic collisions in an electric discharge. The vibrational levels happen to

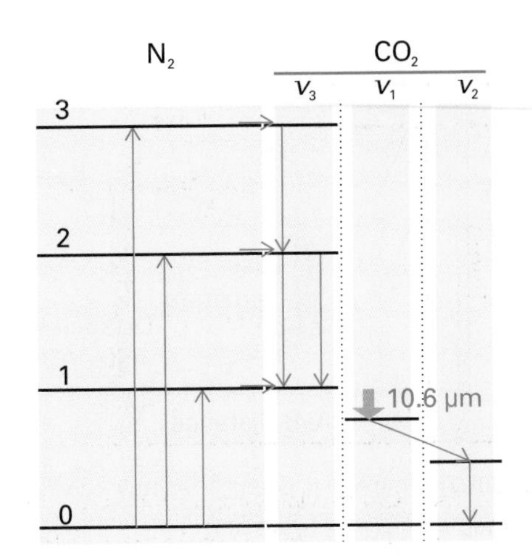

Fig. 20.24 The transitions involved in a carbon dioxide laser. The pumping also depends on the coincidental matching of energy separations; in this case the vibrationally excited N_2 molecules have excess energies that correspond to a vibrational excitation of the antisymmetric stretch of CO_2. The laser transition is from $v_3 = 1$ to $v_1 = 1$.

coincide with the ladder of antisymmetric stretch (ν_3, see Fig. 19.28) energy levels of CO_2, which pick up the energy during a collision. Laser action then occurs from the lowest excited level of ν_3 to the lowest excited level of the symmetric stretch (ν_1), which has remained unpopulated during the collisions.

Chemical reactions may also be used to generate molecules with non-equilibrium, inverted populations. For example, the photolysis of Cl_2 leads to the formation of Cl atoms that attack H_2 molecules in the mixture and produce HCl and H. The latter then attacks Cl_2 to produce vibrationally excited ('hot') HCl molecules. Because the newly formed HCl molecules have non-equilibrium vibrational populations, laser action can result as they return to lower states. Such processes are remarkable examples of the direct conversion of chemical energy into coherent electromagnetic radiation.

The population inversion needed for laser action is achieved in a more underhand way in *exciplex lasers*,[4] because in these (as we shall see) the lower state does not effectively exist. This odd situation is

[4] The term 'excimer laser' is also widely encountered and used loosely when 'exciplex laser' is more appropriate. An exciplex has the form AB* whereas an excimer, an excited dimer, is AA*.

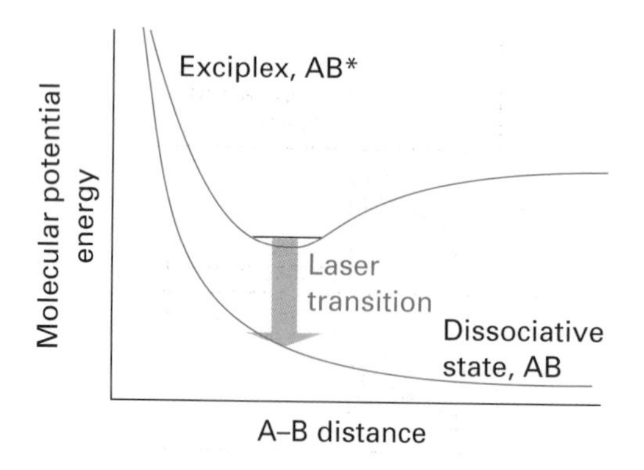

Fig. 20.25 The molecular potential energy curves for an exciplex. The species can survive only as an excited state, because on discarding its energy it enters the lower, dissociative state. Because only the upper state can exist, there is never any population in the lower state.

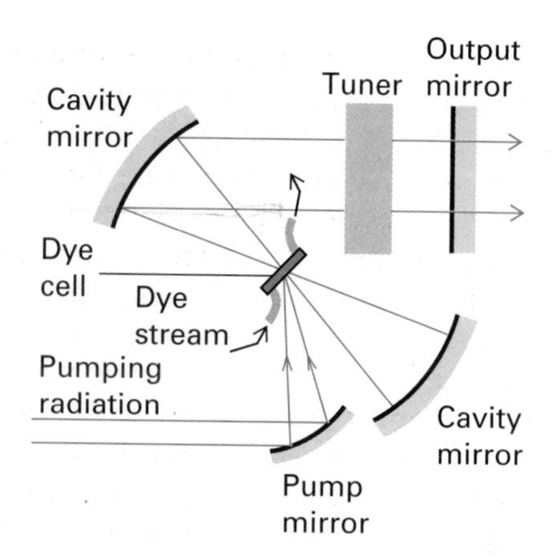

Fig. 20.26 The configuration used for a dye laser. The dye is flowed through the cell inside the laser cavity. The flow helps to keep it cool and prevents degradation.

achieved by forming an **exciplex**, a combination of two atoms (or molecules) that survives only in an excited state and dissociates as soon as the excitation energy has been discarded. An example is a mixture of xenon, chlorine, and neon. An electric discharge through the mixture produces excited Cl atoms that attach to the Xe atoms to give the exciplex XeCl*. The exciplex survives for about 10 ns, which is time for it to participate in laser action at 308 nm (in the ultraviolet). As soon as XeCl* has discarded a photon, the atoms separate because the molecular potential energy curve of the ground state is dissociative, and the ground state of the exciplex cannot become populated (Fig. 20.25).

Gas lasers and most solid-state lasers operate at discrete frequencies, and although the frequency required may be selected by suitable optics, the laser cannot be tuned continuously. The tuning problem can be overcome by using a *dye laser*, which has broad spectral characteristics because the solvent broadens the vibrational structure of the transitions into bands. Hence, it is possible to scan the wavelength continuously (by rotating the diffraction grating in the cavity) and achieve laser action at any chosen wavelength. As the gain is very high, only a short length of the optical path need be through the dye. The excited states of the active medium, the dye, are sustained by another laser or a flash lamp, and the dye solution is flowed through the laser cavity to avoid thermal degradation (Fig. 20.26).

20.7 Applications of lasers in chemistry

Laser radiation has a number of advantages for applications in chemistry. One advantage is its highly monochromatic character, which enables very precise spectroscopic observations to be made. Another advantage is the ability of laser radiation to be produced in very short pulses (currently, as brief as about 1 fs): as a result, very fast chemical events, such as the individual transfers of atoms during a chemical reaction, can be followed (see Box 10.1). Laser radiation is also very intense, which reduces the time needed for spectroscopic observations. Raman spectroscopy (Chapter 19) was revitalized by the introduction of lasers because the intense beam increases the intensity of scattered radiation, so the use of laser sources increases the sensitivity of Raman spectroscopy. A well-defined beam also implies that the detector can be designed to collect only the radiation that has passed through a sample, and can be screened much more effectively against the stray scattered light that can obscure the Raman signal. The monochromaticity of laser radiation is also a great advantage, as it makes possible the observation of scattered light that differs by only fractions of reciprocal centimetres from the incident radiation. Such high resolution is particularly useful for observing the rotational structure of Raman lines because rotational transitions are of the order of a few reciprocal centimetres.

The large number of photons in an incident beam generated by a laser gives rise to a qualitatively different branch of spectroscopy, as the photon density is so high that more than one photon may be absorbed by a single molecule and give rise to **multiphoton processes.** Because the selection rules for multiphoton processes are different, states inaccessible by conventional one-photon spectroscopy become observable.

The monochromatic character of laser radiation is a very powerful characteristic because it allows us to excite specific states with very high precision. One consequence of state-specificity is that the illumination of a sample may be efficient in stimulating a photochemical reaction, because its frequency can be tuned exactly to an absorption. The specific excitation of a particular excited state of a molecule may greatly enhance the rate of a reaction even at low temperatures. As we saw in Chapter 10, the rate of a reaction is increased by raising the temperature because the energies of the various modes of motion of the molecule are enhanced. However, this enhancement increases the energy of all the modes, even those that do not contribute appreciably to the reaction rate. With a laser we can excite the kinetically significant mode, so rate enhancement is achieved most efficiently. An example is the reaction

$$BCl_3 + C_6H_6 \rightarrow C_6H_5\text{–}BCl_2 + HCl$$

which normally proceeds only above 600°C in the presence of a catalyst; exposure to 10.6 μm CO_2 laser radiation results in the formation of products at room temperature without a catalyst. The commercial potential of this procedure is considerable (provided laser photons can be produced sufficiently cheaply) because heat-sensitive compounds, such as pharmaceuticals, may perhaps be made at lower temperatures than in conventional reactions.

The state-selectivity of lasers is also of considerable potential for laser isotope separation. Isotope separation is possible because two isotopomers (species that differ only in their isotopic composition) have slightly different energy levels and hence slightly different absorption frequencies. At least two absorption processes are required. In the first step, a photon excites an atom to a higher state; in the second step, a photon achieves photoionization from that state (Fig. 20.27). The energy separation between the two states involved in the first step depends on the nuclear mass. Therefore, if the laser radiation is tuned to the appropriate frequency, only one of the isotopomers will undergo excitation and hence be available for photoionization in the second step. An example of this procedure is the photoionization of uranium vapour, in which the incident laser is tuned to excite ^{235}U but not ^{238}U. The ^{235}U atoms in the atomic beam are ionized in the two-step process; they are then attracted to a negatively charged electrode, and may be collected (Fig. 20.28). This procedure is being used in the latest generation of uranium separation plants.

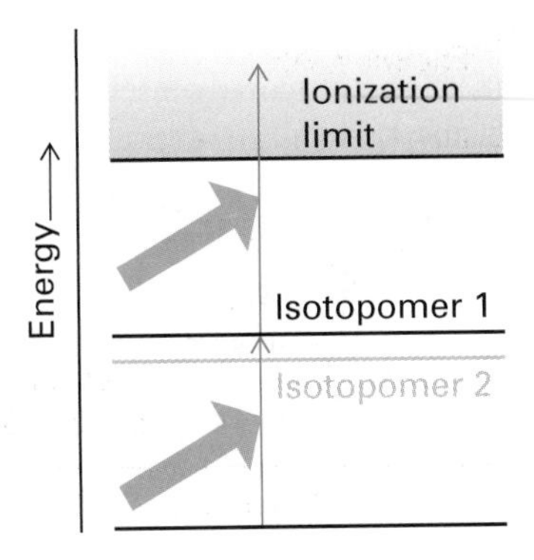

Fig. 20.27 In one method of isotope separation, one photon excites an isotopomer to an excited state, and then a second photon achieves photoionization. The success of the first step depends on the nuclear mass.

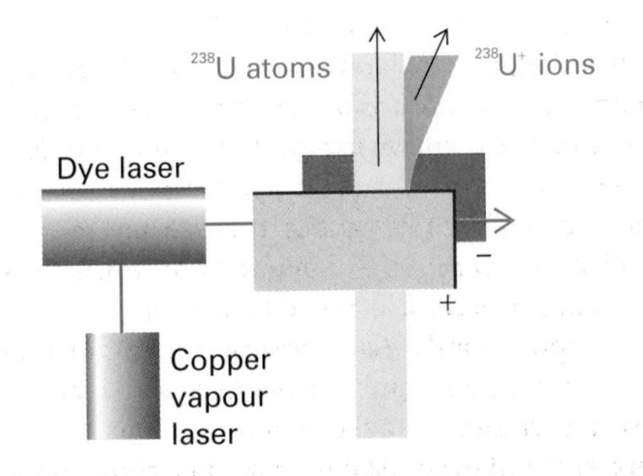

Fig. 20.28 An experimental arrangement for isotope separation. The dye laser, which is pumped by a copper-vapour laser, photoionizes the U atoms selectively according to their mass, and the ions are deflected by the electric field applied between the plates.

The ability of lasers to produce pulses of very short duration is particularly useful in chemistry when we want to monitor processes in time. In **time-resolved spectroscopy**, laser pulses are used to obtain the absorption, emission, or Raman spectrum of reactants, intermediates, products, and even transition states of reactions. Lasers that produce nanosecond pulses are generally suitable for the observation of reactions with rates controlled by the speed with which reactants can move through a fluid medium. However, femtosecond to picosecond laser pulses are needed to study energy transfer, molecular rotations, vibrations, and conversion from one mode of motion to another. The arrangement shown in Fig. 20.29 is often used to study ultrafast chemical reactions that can be initiated by light. An intense but brief laser pulse, the *pump*, promotes a molecule A to an excited electronic state A* that can either emit a photon (as fluorescence or phosphorescence) or react with another species B to yield a product C:

$$A + h\nu \rightarrow A^* \qquad \text{(absorption)}$$

$$A^* \rightarrow A \qquad \text{(emission)}$$

$$A^* + B \rightarrow [AB] \rightarrow C \qquad \text{(reaction)}$$

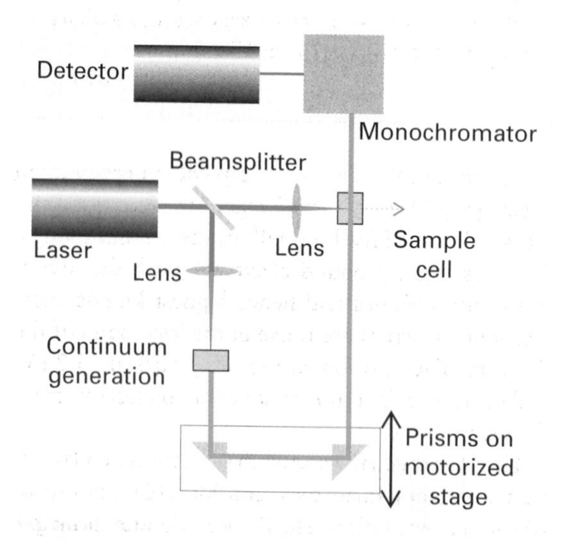

Fig. 20.29 A configuration used for time-resolved absorption spectroscopy, in which the same pulsed laser is used to generate a monochromatic pump pulse and, after continuum generation in a suitable liquid, a 'white' light probe pulse. The time delay between the pump and probe pulses may be varied.

Here [AB] denotes either an intermediate or an activated complex. The rates of appearance and disappearance of the various species are determined by observing time-dependent changes in the absorption spectrum of the sample during the course of the reaction. This observation is made by passing a weak pulse of white light, the *probe*, through the sample at different times after the laser pulse. Pulsed 'white' light can be generated directly from the laser pulse by the non-linear optical phenomenon of *continuum generation*, in which focusing an ultrashort laser pulse on a vessel containing a liquid such as water or carbon tetrachloride results in an outgoing beam with a wide distribution of frequencies. A time delay between the strong laser pulse and the 'white' light pulse can be introduced by allowing one of the beams to travel a longer distance before reaching the sample. For example, a difference in travel distance of $\Delta d = 3$ mm corresponds to a time delay $\Delta t = \Delta d/c \approx 10$ ps between two beams, where c is the speed of light. The relative distances travelled by the two beams in Fig. 20.29 are controlled by directing the 'white' light beam to a motorized stage carrying a pair of mirrors.

Variations of the arrangement in Fig. 20.29 allow for the observation of fluorescence decay kinetics of A* and time-resolved Raman spectra during the course of the reaction. The fluorescence lifetime of A* can be determined by exciting A as before and measuring the decay of the fluorescence intensity after the pulse with a fast photodetector system. In this case, continuum generation is not necessary. Time-resolved resonance Raman spectra of A, A*, B, [AB], or C can be obtained by initiating the reaction with a strong laser pulse of a certain wavelength and then, some time later, irradiating the sample with another laser pulse that can excite the resonance Raman spectrum of the desired species. Also in this case continuum generation is not necessary. Instead, the Raman excitation beam may be generated in a dye laser.

Photoelectron spectroscopy

The exposure of a molecule to high-frequency radiation can result in the ejection of an electron. This **photoejection** is the basis of another type of

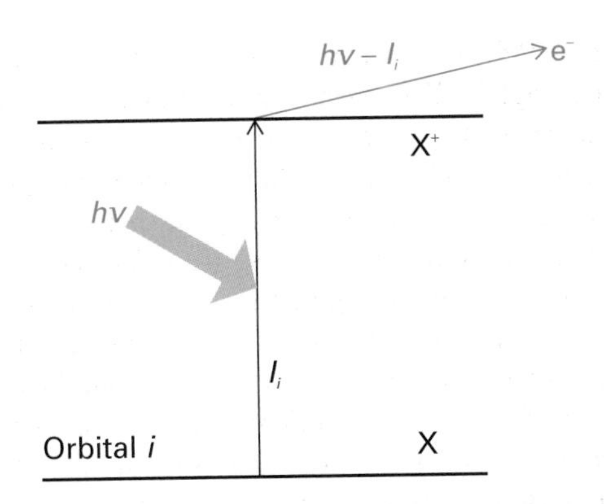

Fig. 20.30 The basic principle of photoelectron spectroscopy. An incoming photon of known energy collides with an electron in one of the orbitals and expels it with a kinetic energy that is equal to the difference between the energy supplied by the photon and the ionization energy from the occupied orbital. An electron from an orbital with a low ionization energy will emerge with a high kinetic energy (and high speed) whereas an electron from an orbital with a high ionization energy will be ejected with a low kinetic energy (and low speed).

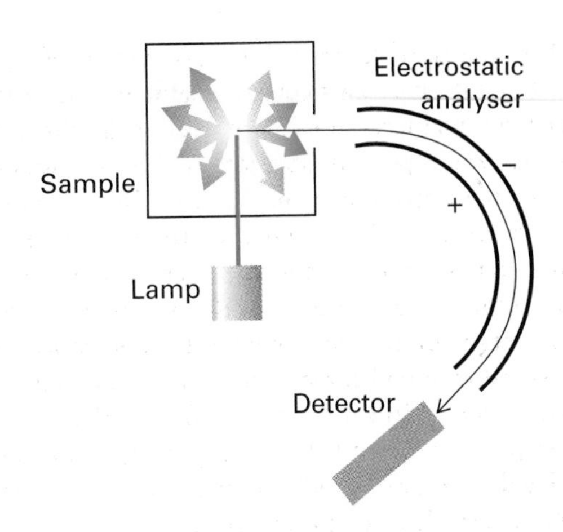

Fig. 20.31 A photoelectron spectrometer consists of a source of ionizing radiation, such as a helium discharge lamp for ultraviolet photoelectron spectroscopy (UPS) and an X-ray source for X-ray photoelectron spectroscopy (XPS), an electrostatic analyser, and an electron detector. The deflection of the path of the electron caused by the analyser depends on their speed.

spectroscopy in which we monitor the energies of the ejected photoelectrons. If the incident radiation has frequency ν, the photon that causes photoejection has energy $h\nu$. If the ionization energy of the molecule is I, the difference in energy, $h\nu - I$, is carried away as kinetic energy. Because the kinetic energy of an electron of speed v is $\frac{1}{2}m_e v^2$, we can write

$$h\nu = I + \tfrac{1}{2}m_e v^2 \qquad (20.3)$$

Therefore, by monitoring the velocity of the photoelectron, and knowing the frequency of the incident radiation, we can determine the ionization energy of the molecule and hence the strength with which the electron was bound (Fig. 20.30). In this context the 'ionization energy' of the molecule has different values depending on the orbital that the photoelectron occupied, and the slower the ejected electron, the lower in energy the orbital from which it was ejected. The apparatus is a modification of a mass spectrometer (Fig. 20.31), in which the velocity of the photoelectrons is measured by determining the strength of the electric field required to bend their paths on to the detector.

Self-test 20.3

What is the velocity of photoelectrons that are ejected from a molecule with radiation of energy 21 eV (from a helium discharge lamp) and are known to come from an orbital of ionization energy 12 eV?

[*Answer:* 1.8×10^3 km s^{-1}]

Figure 20.32 shows a typical photoelectron spectrum (of HBr). If we disregard the fine structure, we see that the HBr lines fall into two main groups. The least tightly bound electrons (with the lowest ionization energies and hence highest kinetic energies when ejected) are those in the lone pairs of the Br atom. The next ionization energy lies at 15.2 eV, and corresponds to the removal of an electron from the HBr σ bond.

The HBr spectrum shows that ejection of a σ electron is accompanied by a considerable amount of vibrational excitation. The Franck–Condon principle would account for this observation if ejection were accompanied by an appreciable change in equilibrium bond length between HBr and HBr^+. When that is so, the ion is formed in a bond-compressed state, which is consistent with the important bonding

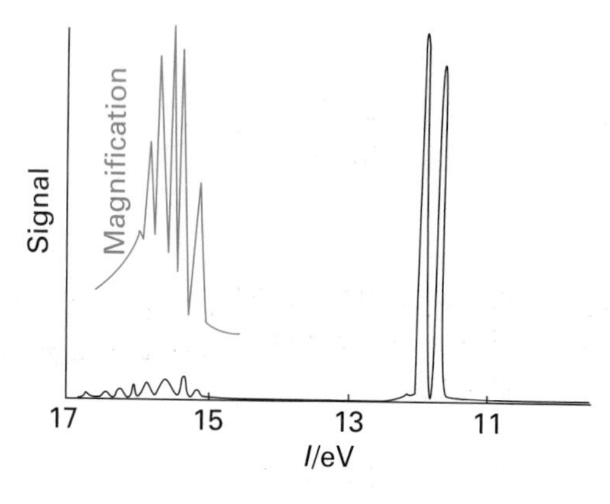

Fig. 20.32 The photoelectron spectrum of HBr. The lowest ionization energy band corresponds to the ionization of a Br lone-pair electron. The higher ionization energy band corresponds to the ionization of a bonding electron. The structure on the latter is due to the vibrational excitation of HBr^+ that results from the ionization.

effect of the σ electrons. The lack of much vibrational structure in the other band is consistent with the non-bonding role of the Br4p_x and Br4p_y lone-pair electrons, because the equilibrium bond length is little changed when one is removed.

Example 20.2

Interpreting a UV photoelectron spectrum

The highest kinetic energy electrons in the spectrum of H_2O using 21.22 eV He radiation are at about 9 eV and show a large vibrational spacing of 0.41 eV. The symmetric stretching mode of the neutral H_2O molecule lies at 3652 cm^{-1}. What conclusions can be drawn from the nature of the orbital from which the electron is ejected?

Strategy To convert from electronvolts to reciprocal centimetres, use 1 eV = 8065.5 cm^{-1}. If the vibrational separation in the ion is similar to that in the molecule, then the ejected electron had little influence on bonding in the molecule. A lot of vibrational structure would suggest that the electron had been heavily involved in bonding.

Solution Because 0.41 eV corresponds to 3.3×10^3 cm^{-1}, which is similar to the 3652 cm^{-1} of the non-ionized molecule, we can suspect that the electron is ejected from an orbital that has little influence on the bonding in the molecule. That is, photoejection is from a largely non-bonding orbital.

Self-test 20.4

In the same spectrum of H_2O, the band near 7.0 eV shows a long vibrational series with spacing 0.125 eV. The bending mode of H_2O lies at 1596 cm^{-1}. What conclusions can you draw about the characteristics of the orbital occupied by the photoelectron?

[*Answer:* The electron contributes to long-distance HH bonding across the molecule]

Photochemistry

Photochemical reactions are initiated by the absorption of light. The most important of all are the photochemical processes that capture the Sun's radiant energy. Some of these reactions lead to the heating of the atmosphere during the daytime by absorption in the ultraviolet region as a result of reactions like those depicted in Fig. 20.33. Others include the absorption of red and blue light by chlorophyll and the subsequent use of the energy to bring about the synthesis of carbohydrates from carbon dioxide and water (Box 20.2). Indeed, without photochemical processes the world would be simply a warm, sterile, rock.

20.8 Quantum yield

A molecule acquires enough energy to react by absorbing a photon. However, not every excited molecule may form a specific primary product (atoms, radicals, or ions, for instance) because there are many ways in which the excitation may be lost other than by dissociation or ionization. We therefore speak of the **primary quantum yield, ϕ** (phi), which is the number of events (physical changes or chemical reactions) that lead to primary products (photons, atoms, or ions, for instance) divided by the number of photons absorbed by the molecule in the same time interval:

$$\phi = \frac{\text{number of events}}{\text{number of photons absorbed}} \qquad (20.4)$$

If each molecule that absorbs a photon undergoes dissociation (for instance), then $\phi = 1$. If none does, because the excitation energy is lost before the molecule has time to dissociate, then $\phi = 0$.

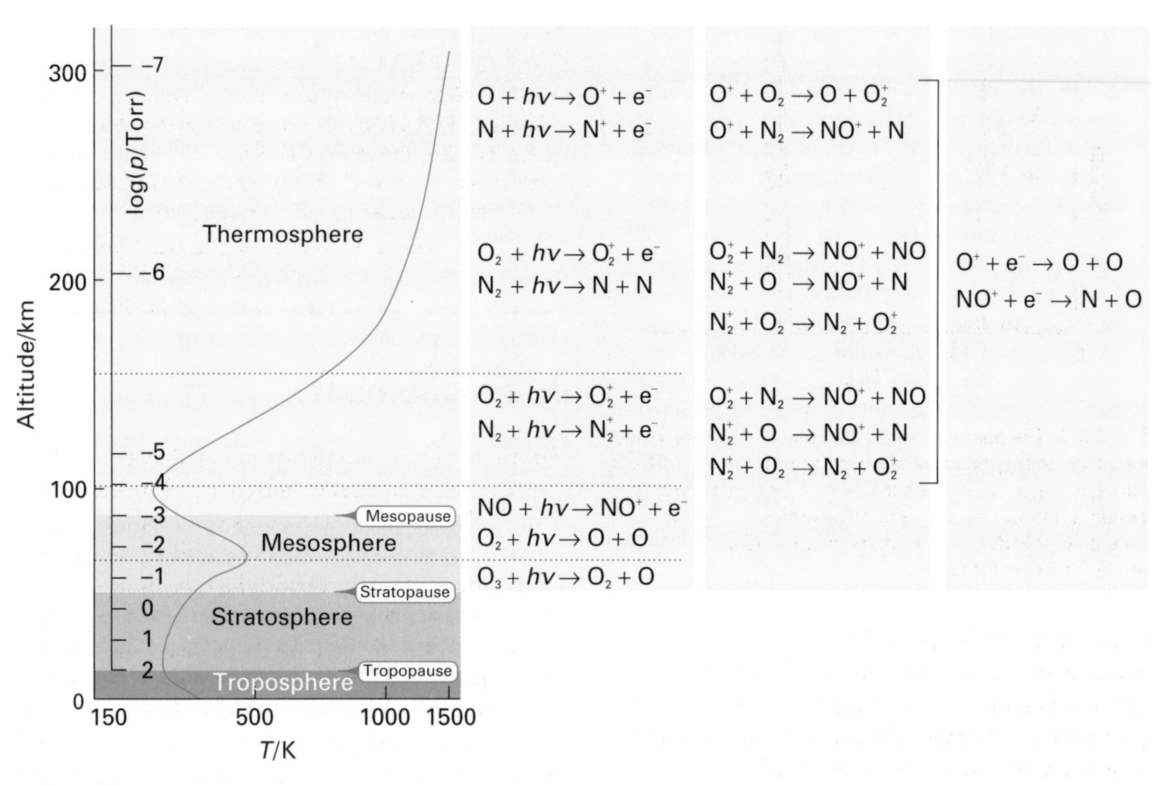

Fig. 20.33 The temperature profile through the atmosphere and some of the reactions that take place in each region.

Box 20.2 *Photosynthesis*

Up to 1 kW m^{-2} of radiation from the Sun reaches the Earth's surface, with the exact intensity depending on latitude, time of day, and weather. A large proportion of solar radiation with wavelengths below 400 nm and above 1000 nm is absorbed by atmospheric gases such as ozone and O_2, which absorb ultraviolet radiation, and CO_2 and H_2O, which absorb infrared radiation. As a result, plants, algae, and some species of bacteria evolved photosynthetic apparatus that captures visible and near-infrared radiation. Plants use radiation in the wavelength range 400–700 nm to drive the endergonic reduction of CO_2 to glucose, with concomitant oxidation of water to O_2 ($\Delta_r G^{\ominus} = +2880$ kJ mol^{-1}).

Plant photosynthesis takes place in the *chloroplast*, a special organelle of the plant cell. Electrons flow from reductant to oxidant via a series of electrochemical reactions that are coupled to the synthesis of ATP. In the chloroplast, chlorophylls *a* and *b* and carotenoids (of which *β*-carotene is an example) bind to proteins called *light-harvesting complexes*, which absorb solar energy and transfer it to protein complexes known as *reaction centres*, where light-induced electron-transfer reactions occur. The combination of a light-harvesting complex and a reaction centre complex is called a *photosystem*, and plants have two: photosystem I and photosystem II.

In photosystems I and II, absorption of a photon raises a chlorophyll or carotenoid molecule to an excited singlet state. The initial energy- and electron-transfer events of photosynthesis are under tight kinetic control and the efficient capture of solar energy stems from rapid quenching of the excited singlet state of chlorophyll by processes that occur with relaxation times that are much shorter than the fluorescence lifetime, which is about 5 ns in diethyl ether at room temperature. Time-resolved spectroscopic data show that within 0.1–5 ps of absorption of light by a chlorophyll molecule in a light-harvesting complex, the energy hops to a nearby pigment via the Förster mechanism. About 100–200 ps later, which corresponds to thousands of hops within the complex, more than 90 per cent of the absorbed energy reaches the reaction centre. The absorption of energy from light decreases the reduction potential of special dimers of chlorophyll *a* molecules known as P700 (in photosystem I) and P680 (in photosystem II). In their excited states, P680 and P700 initiate electron-transfer reactions that culminate in the oxidation of water to O_2 and the reduction of $NADP^+$ to NADPH. The initial electron-transfer steps are fast and compete effectively with chlorophyll fluorescence. For example, the transfer of an electron from the excited singlet state of P680 to its immediate electron acceptor occurs within 3 ps. Once the excited state of P680 has been quenched efficiently by this first reaction, subsequent steps that lead to the oxidation of water occur more slowly, with reaction times varying from 200 ps to 1 ms. Experiments show that for each molecule of NADPH formed in the chloroplast of green plants, one molecule of ATP is synthesized. Finally, the ATP and NADPH molecules participate in the *Calvin–Benson cycle*, a sequence of enzyme-controlled reactions that leads to the reduction of CO_2 to glucose in the chloroplast.

In summary, plant photosynthesis uses solar energy to transfer electrons from a poor reductant (water) to carbon dioxide. In the process, high-energy molecules (carbohydrates, such as glucose) are synthesized in the cell. Animals feed on the carbohydrates derived from photosynthesis. The O_2 released by photosynthesis as a waste product is used to oxidize carbohydrates to CO_2. This drives biological processes, such as biosynthesis, muscle contraction, cell division, and nerve conduction. Hence, the sustenance of life on Earth depends on a tightly regulated carbon–oxygen cycle that is driven by solar energy.

Exercise 1 The light-induced electron-transfer reactions in photosynthesis occur because chlorophyll molecules (whether in monomeric or dimeric forms) are better reducing agents in their electronic excited states. Justify this observation with the help of molecular orbital theory.

Exercise 2 The photosynthetic oxidation of water to O_2 occurs in an enzyme that contains four manganese ions, each of which can exist in oxidation states ranging from +2 to +4. The electrochemical production of one molecule of O_2 requires the oxidation of two molecules of water by a total of four electrons. However, the excited state of P680 can donate only one electron at a time to plastoquinone. Explain how electron transfer mediated by P680 can lead to the formation of a molecule of O_2 in photosystem II. (*Hint.* See V. A. Szalai and G. W. Brudvig, How plants produce dioxygen. *American Scientist* **86**, 542 (1998).)

If we divide the numerator and denominator of eqn 20.4 by the time interval during which the photochemical event occurs, we see that the primary quantum yield is also the rate of radiation-induced primary events divided by the rate of photon absorption. Furthermore, if we equate the rate of photon absorption with the intensity, I_{abs}, of light absorbed by the molecule, we may write

$$\phi = \frac{\text{Rate}}{I_{abs}} \tag{20.5}$$

A molecule in an excited state must either decay to the ground state or form a photochemical product. Therefore, the total number of molecules deactivated by radiative processes, non-radiative processes, and photochemical reactions must be equal to the number of excited species produced by absorption of light. We conclude that the sum of primary quantum yields ϕ_i for *all* physical changes and photochemical reactions i must be equal to 1, regardless of the number of reactions involving the excited state. It follows that

$$\sum_i \phi_i = \sum_i \frac{\text{Rate}_i}{I_{abs}} = 1 \tag{20.6}$$

One successfully excited molecule might initiate the consumption of more than one reactant molecule. We therefore need to introduce the **overall quantum yield**, Φ (uppercase phi), which is the number of reactant molecules that react for each photon absorbed. In the photolysis of HI, for example, the processes are

$$HI + h\nu \rightarrow H + I$$

$$H + HI \rightarrow H_2 + I$$

$$I + I + M \rightarrow I_2$$

The overall quantum yield is 2 because the absorption of one photon leads to the destruction of two HI molecules. In a photochemically initiated chain reaction, Φ may be very large, and values of about 10^4 are common. In such cases the chain reaction acts as a chemical amplifier of the initial absorption step.

Example 20.3

Using the quantum yield

The overall quantum yield for the formation of ethene from 4-heptanone with 313 nm light is 0.21. How many molecules of 4-heptanone per second, and what chemical amount per second, are destroyed when the sample is irradiated with a 50 W, 313 nm source under conditions of total absorption?

Strategy We need to determine the rate of emission of photons of the lamp as the number of photons emitted by the lamp per second. Because all photons are absorbed (by assertion), this quantity is also I_{abs}, which we calculate by dividing the power (joules per second) by the energy of a single photon ($E = h\nu$, with $\nu = c/\lambda$). From eqn 20.5, the rate of the photochemical reaction (the number of molecules destroyed per second) is I_{abs} multiplied by the overall quantum yield, Φ.

Solution A source of power P (the rate at which energy is supplied) generates photons at a rate given by P divided by the energy of each photon, E. The energy of a photon of wavelength λ is $E = hc/\lambda$. Therefore,

$$\text{Rate of photon production} = I_{abs} = \overbrace{\frac{P}{\underbrace{(hc/\lambda)}_{\text{Energy of photon}}}}^{\text{Rate of energy production}} = \frac{P\lambda}{hc}$$

$$= \frac{(50\ \text{J s}^{-1}) \times (313 \times 10^{-9}\ \text{m})}{(6.626\ 08 \times 10^{-34}\ \text{J s}) \times (2.997\ 92 \times 10^{8}\ \text{m s}^{-1})}$$

$$= 7.9 \times 10^{19}\ \text{s}^{-1}$$

The number of 4-heptanone molecules destroyed per second is therefore 0.21 times this quantity, or $1.7 \times 10^{19}\ \text{s}^{-1}$, corresponding (after division by N_A) to $2.8 \times 10^{-5}\ \text{mol s}^{-1}$.

Self-test 20.5

The overall quantum yield for another reaction at 290 nm is 0.30. For what length of time must irradiation with a 100 W source continue in order to destroy 1.0 mol of molecules?

[*Answer:* 3.8 h]

20.9 Mechanisms of photochemical reactions

As an example of how to incorporate the photochemical activation step into a mechanism, consider the photochemical activation of the reaction

$$H_2(g) + Br_2(g) \rightarrow 2\ HBr(g)$$

which we described in Section 11.13. In place of the first step in the thermal reaction we have

$$Br_2 + h\nu \rightarrow Br + Br$$

$$\text{Rate of consumption of } Br_2 = \text{rate of photon absorption} = I_{abs}$$

Because the thermal reaction mechanism had $k_a[Br_2]$ in place of I_{abs} for the equivalent of this step, it follows that I_{abs} should take the place of $k_a[Br_2]$ in the rate law we derived for the thermal reaction scheme. Therefore, from eqn 11.24 we can write

$$\text{Rate of formation of HBr} = \frac{2k_b(1/k_d)^{1/2}[H_2][Br_2]I_{abs}^{1/2}}{[Br_2] + (k_c/k_b')[HBr]} \qquad (20.7)$$

Although the details of this expression are complicated, the essential prediction is clear: the reaction rate should depend on the square root of the absorbed light intensity. This prediction is confirmed experimentally.

20.10 The kinetics of decay of excited states

In many cases, proper description of the rates and mechanisms of photochemical reactions also requires knowledge of such processes as fluorescence and phosphorescence that can deactivate an excited state before the reaction has a chance to occur. Let us consider the time-scales of light absorption and emission. Electronic transitions caused by absorption of ultraviolet and visible radiation occur within 10^{-16}–10^{-15} s. We expect, then, that the upper limit for the rate constant of a first-order photochemical reaction is about $10^{16}\ \text{s}^{-1}$. Fluorescence is slower than absorption, with typical time constants of 10^{-12}–10^{-6} s. Therefore, the excited singlet state can initiate very fast photochemical reactions in the femtosecond (10^{-15} s) to picosecond (10^{-12} s) time-scale. Examples of such ultrafast reactions are the initial events of vision (Box 20.1) and photosynthesis (Box 20.2). Typical intersystem crossing (ISC) and phosphorescence time constants for large organic molecules are 10^{-12}–10^{-4} s and 10^{-6}–10^{-1} s, respectively. As a consequence, excited triplet states are photochemically important. Indeed, because phosphorescence decay is several orders of magnitude slower than most typical reactions, species in excited triplet states can undergo a very large number of collisions with other reactants before deactivation.

We begin our exploration of the interplay between reaction rates and excited state decay rates by considering the mechanism of deactivation of an excited singlet state in the absence of a chemical reaction. The following steps are involved:

Absorption: $S + h\nu_i \rightarrow S^*$

Rate of photon absorption $= I_{abs}$

Fluorescence: $S^* \rightarrow S + h\nu_f$

Rate of fluorescence $= k_f[S^*]$

Intersystem crossing: $S^* \rightarrow T^*$

Rate of intersystem crossing $= k_{ISC}[S^*]$

Internal conversion: $S^* \rightarrow S$

Rate of internal conversion $= k_{IC}[S^*]$

in which S is an absorbing species, S* an excited singlet state, T* an excited triplet state, and $h\nu_i$ and $h\nu_f$ are the energies of the incident and fluorescent photons, respectively. From the methods developed in Chapter 11 and the rates of the steps that form and destroy the excited singlet state S*, we write the rates of formation and decay of S* as:

Rate of formation of $S^* = I_{abs}$

$$\text{Rate of decay of } S^* = -k_f[S^*] - k_{ISC}[S^*] - k_{IC}[S^*]$$
$$= -(k_f + k_{ISC} + k_{IC})[S^*]$$

It follows that the excited state decays by a first-order process, so when the light is turned off, [S*] varies with time t as:

$$[S^*]_t = [S^*]_0 \, e^{-t/\tau_0} \quad (20.8)$$

where the **observed fluorescence lifetime**, τ_0, is defined as:

$$\tau_0 = \frac{1}{k_f + k_{ISC} + k_{IC}} \quad (20.9)$$

We show in Derivation 20.1 that the quantum yield of fluorescence is

$$\phi_f = \frac{k_f}{k_f + k_{ISC} + k_{IC}} \quad (20.10)$$

Derivation 20.1

The quantum yield of fluorescence

Most fluorescence measurements are conducted by illuminating a relatively dilute sample with a continuous and intense beam of light. It follows that [S*] is small and constant, so we may invoke the steady-state approximation (Section 11.6) and write:

$$\text{Rate of change of } [S^*] = I_{abs} - k_f[S^*] - k_{ISC}[S^*] - k_{IC}[S^*]$$
$$= I_{abs} - (k_f + k_{ISC} + k_{IC})[S^*] = 0$$

Consequently,

$$I_{abs} = (k_f + k_{ISC} + k_{IC})[S^*]$$

By using this expression and eqn 20.5, the quantum yield of fluorescence is written as:

$$\phi_f = \frac{\text{Rate of fluorescence}}{I_{abs}} = \frac{k_f[S^*]}{(k_f + k_{ISC} + k_{IC})[S^*]}$$

which simplifies to eqn 20.10.

We can visualize the process of fluorescence as follows. Under continuous illumination, an absorbing sample emits fluorescence photons with a constant intensity, I, which is proportional to $k_f[S^*]$ and hence also proportional to ϕ_f. There are many commercial instruments designed to make such steady-state fluorescence measurements of I and ϕ_f.

The observed fluorescence lifetime can be measured with a pulsed laser technique (Section 20.7). First, the sample is excited with a short light pulse from a laser at a wavelength where S absorbs strongly. Then, the exponential decay of the fluorescence intensity after the pulse is monitored with a fast detector system. From eqns 20.9 and 20.10, it follows that

$$\tau_0 = \frac{1}{k_f + k_{ISC} + k_{IC}}$$
$$= \left(\frac{k_f}{k_f + k_{ISC} + k_{IC}}\right) \times \frac{1}{k_f} = \frac{\phi_f}{k_f} \quad (20.11)$$

We see that the rate constant k_f can be determined through $k_f = \phi_f/\tau_0$, with ϕ_f measured with steady-state techniques and τ_0 measured with pulsed techniques.

20.11 Fluorescence quenching

Now we consider the kinetic information about photochemical processes that can be obtained by studying the effect of a molecule that can remove the excitation energy from the fluorescent molecule and therefore acts to **quench** the fluorescence.

Quenching may be either a desired process, such as in energy or electron transfer, or an undesired side reaction that can decrease the quantum yield of a desired photochemical process. Quenching effects may be studied by monitoring the fluorescence of a species involved in the photochemical reaction. The **Stern–Volmer equation** relates the fluorescence quantum yields ϕ_f and ϕ measured in the absence and presence, respectively, of a quencher Q at a molar concentration [Q]:

$$\frac{\phi_f}{\phi} = 1 + \tau_0 k_Q[Q] \qquad (20.12)$$

This equation tells us that a plot of ϕ_f/ϕ against [Q] is a straight line with slope $\tau_0 k_Q$. Such a plot is called a **Stern–Volmer plot** (Fig. 20.34). The method is quite general and may also be applied to the quenching of phosphorescence emission.

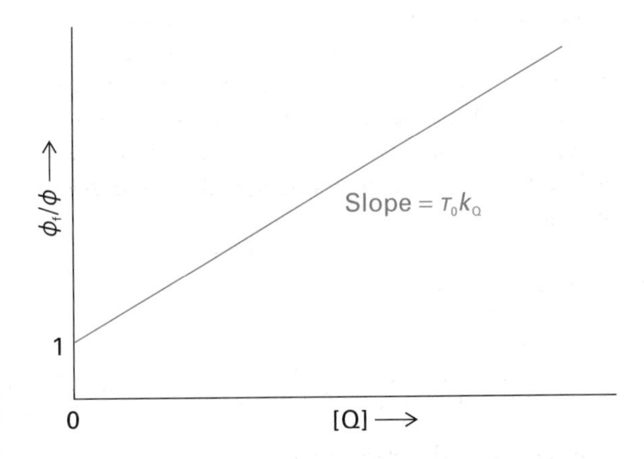

Fig. 20.34 The format of a Stern–Volmer plot and the interpretation of the slope in terms of the rate constant for quenching and the observed fluorescence lifetime in the absence of quenching.

Derivation 20.2

The Stern–Volmer equation

The addition of a quencher, Q, opens an additional channel for deactivation of S*:

Quenching: $S^* + Q \rightarrow S + Q$

Rate of quenching $= k_Q[Q][S^*]$

The steady-state approximation for [S*] now gives:

Rate of change of [S*]

$= I_{abs} - (k_f + k_{IC} + k_{ISC} + k_{IC} + k_Q[Q])[S^*] = 0$

and the fluorescence quantum yield in the presence of the quencher is:

$$\phi = \frac{k_f}{k_f + k_{ISC} + k_{IC} + k_Q[Q]}$$

It follows from this expression and eqn 20.10 that the ratio ϕ_f/ϕ is

$$\frac{\phi_f}{\phi} = \left(\frac{k_f}{k_f + k_{ISC} + k_{IC}}\right) \times \left(\frac{k_f + k_{ISC} + k_{IC} + k_Q[Q]}{k_f}\right)$$

$$= \frac{k_f + k_{ISC} + k_{IC} + k_Q[Q]}{k_f + k_{ISC} + k_{IC}}$$

$$= 1 + \frac{k_Q}{k_f + k_{ISC} + k_{IC}}[Q]$$

After using eqn 20.9, this expression simplifies to eqn 20.12.

Because the fluorescence intensity and lifetime are both proportional to the fluorescence quantum yield, plots of I_0/I and τ_0/τ (where the subscript 0 indicates a measurement in the absence of quencher) against [Q] should also be linear with the same slope and intercept as those shown for eqn 20.12.

Example 20.4

Determining the quenching rate constant

The molecule 2,2′-bipyridine (**4**) forms a complex with the Ru^{2+} ion. Ruthenium(II) tris-(2,2′-bipyridyl), $Ru(bpy)_3^{2+}$

N N

N N

4 2,2′-Bipyridine

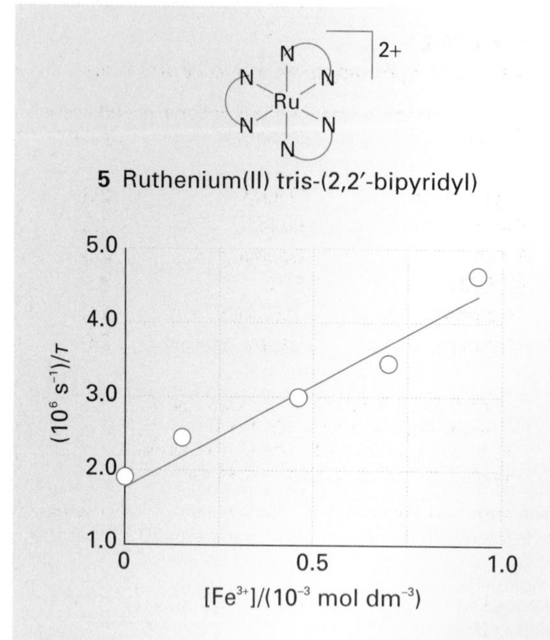

Fig. 20.35 The Stern–Volmer plot of the data for Example 20.4.

(5), has a strong charge-transfer transition at 450 nm. The quenching of the $Ru(bpy)_3^{2+}$ excited state by $Fe(H_2O)_6^{3+}$ in acidic solution was monitored by measuring emission lifetimes at 600 nm. Determine the quenching rate constant for this reaction from the following data:

$[Fe(H_2O)_6^{3+}]/(10^{-4}\ mol\ dm^{-3})$	0	1.6	4.7	7	9.4
$\tau/(10^{-7}\ s)$	6	4.05	3.37	2.96	2.17

Strategy We rewrite the Stern–Volmer equation (eqn 20.12) for use with lifetime data and then fit the data to a straight line.

Solution Upon substitution of τ_0/τ for ϕ_f/ϕ in eqn 20.12 and after rearrangement, we obtain:

$$\frac{1}{\tau} = \frac{1}{\tau_0} + k_Q[Q] \qquad (20.13)$$

Figure 20.35 shows a plot of $1/\tau$ against $[Fe^{3+}]$ and the results of a fit to eqn 20.13. The slope of the line is $k_Q = 2.8 \times 10^9\ dm^3\ mol^{-1}\ s^{-1}$.

Self-test 20.6

From the data above, predict the value of $[Fe^{3+}]$ required to decrease the intensity of $Ru(bpy)_3^{2+}$ emission to 50 per cent of the unquenched value.

[*Answer:* $6.0 \times 10^{-4}\ mol\ dm^{-3}$]

Three common mechanisms for quenching of an excited singlet (or triplet) state are:

Collisional deactivation: $S^* + Q \rightarrow S + Q$

Electron transfer: $S^* + Q \rightarrow S^+ + Q^-$ or $S^- + Q^+$

Resonance energy transfer: $S^* + Q \rightarrow S + Q^*$

Collisional quenching is particularly efficient when Q is a heavy species, such as the iodide ion, which receives energy from S* and then decays nonradiatively to the ground state. This fact may be used to determine the accessibility of amino acid residues of a folded protein to solvent. For example, fluorescence from a tryptophan residue ($\lambda_{abs} \approx 290$ nm, $\lambda_{fluor} \approx 350$ nm) is quenched by the iodide ion when the residue is on the surface of the protein and hence accessible to the solvent. Conversely, residues in the hydrophobic interior of the protein are not quenched effectively by I^-.

The quenching rate constant itself does not give much insight into the mechanism of quenching. For the system of Example 20.4, it is known that the quenching of the excited state of $Ru(bpy)_3^{2+}$ is a result of light-induced electron transfer to Fe^{3+}, but the quenching data do not allow us to prove the mechanism. However, there are some criteria that govern the relative efficiencies of energy and electron transfer.

According to the **Marcus theory** of electron transfer, which was proposed by R. A. Marcus in 1965, the rates of electron transfer (from ground or excited states) depend on:

1 The distance between the donor and acceptor, with electron transfer becoming more efficient as the distance between donor and acceptor decreases.

2 The reaction Gibbs energy, $\Delta_r G$, with electron transfer becoming more efficient as the reaction becomes more exergonic. For example, efficient photooxidation of S requires that the reduction potential of S* be lower than the reduction potential of Q.

3 The reorganization energy, the energy cost incurred by molecular rearrangements of donor, acceptor, and medium during electron transfer. The electron transfer rate is predicted to increase as this reorganization energy is matched closely by the reaction Gibbs energy.

Electron transfer can be studied by time-resolved spectroscopy (Section 20.7). The oxidized and reduced products often have electronic absorption spectra distinct from those of their neutral parent compounds. Therefore, the rapid appearance of such known features in the absorption spectrum after excitation by a laser pulse may be taken as indication of quenching by electron transfer.

Now we turn to resonance energy transfer. We visualize the process $S^* + Q \rightarrow S + Q^*$ as follows. The oscillating electric field of electromagnetic radiation induces an oscillating electric dipole moment in S. Energy will be absorbed by S if the frequency of the incident radiation, ν, is such that $\Delta E_S = h\nu$, where ΔE_S is the energy separation between the ground and excited electronic states of S and h is Planck's constant. This is the 'resonance condition' for absorption of radiation. The oscillating dipole on S now can affect electrons bound to a nearby Q molecule by inducing an oscillating dipole moment. If the frequency oscillation is such that $\Delta E_Q = h\nu$, then Q will absorb energy from S. The efficiency, E_T, of resonance energy transfer is defined as:

$$E_T = 1 - \frac{\phi}{\phi_f} \qquad (20.14)$$

According to the **Förster theory** of resonance energy transfer, which was proposed by T. Förster in 1959, energy transfer is efficient when:

1 The energy donor and acceptor are separated by a short distance, in the nanometre scale.

2 Photons emitted by the excited state of the donor can be absorbed directly by the acceptor.

For donor–acceptor systems that are held rigidly either by covalent bonds or by a protein 'scaffold', E_T increases with decreasing distance, R, according to

$$E_T = \frac{R_0^6}{R_0^6 + R^6} \qquad (20.15)$$

where R_0 is a parameter (with units of distance) that is characteristic of each donor–acceptor pair. Equation 20.15 has been verified experimentally and values of R_0 are available for a number of donor–acceptor pairs (Table 20.2).

The emission and absorption spectra of molecules span a range of wavelengths, so the second requirement of the Förster theory is met when the emission spectrum of the donor molecule overlaps significantly with the absorption spectrum of the acceptor. In the overlap region, photons emitted by the donor have the proper energy to be absorbed by the acceptor (Fig. 20.36).

In many cases, it is possible to prove that energy transfer is the predominant mechanism of quenching if the excited state of the acceptor fluoresces or phosphoresces at a characteristic wavelength. In a pulsed laser experiment, the rise in fluorescence intensity from Q^* with a time constant that is the

Table 20.2
Values of R_0 for some donor–acceptor pairs

Donor	Acceptor	R_0/nm
Naphthalene	Dansyl	2.2
Dansyl	ODR	4.3
Pyrene	Coumarin	3.9
IAEDANS	FITC	4.9
Tryptophan	IAEDANS	2.2
Tryptophan	Haem	2.9

Dansyl, 5-dimethylamino-l-naphthalenesulfonic; FITC, fluorescein-5-isothiocyanate; IEADANS, 5-((((2-iodoacetyl)amino)ethyl)amino)naphthalene-1-sulfonic acid; ODR, octadecyl-rhodamine.

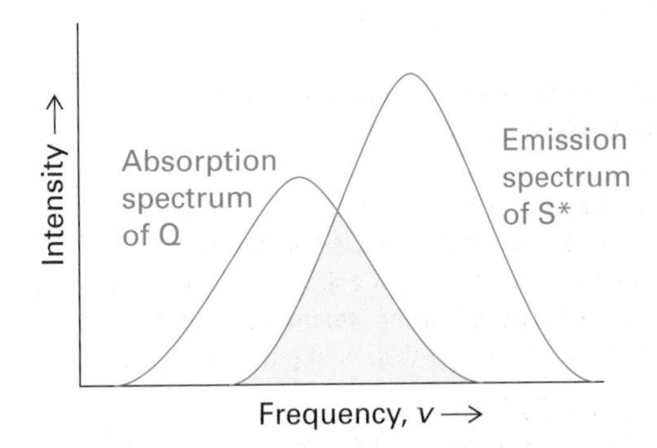

Fig. 20.36 According to the Förster theory, the rate of energy transfer from a molecule S* in an excited state to a quencher molecule Q is optimized at radiation frequencies in which the emission spectrum of S* overlaps with the absorption spectrum of Q, as shown in the shaded region.

same as that for the decay of the fluorescence of S* is often taken as indication of energy transfer from S to Q.

The dependence of E_T on R forms the basis of **fluorescence resonance energy transfer** (FRET), a technique that can be used to measure distances in biological systems. In a typical FRET experiment, a site on a biopolymer or membrane is labelled covalently with an energy donor and another site is labelled covalently with an energy acceptor. In certain cases, the donor or acceptor may be natural constituents of the system, such as amino acid groups, co-factors, or enzyme substrates. The distance between the labels is then calculated from the known value of R_0 and eqn 20.15. Several tests have shown that the FRET technique is useful for measuring distances ranging from 1 to 9 nm.

If donor and acceptor diffuse in solution or in the gas phase, Förster theory predicts that the efficiency of quenching by energy transfer increases as the average distance travelled between collisions of donor and acceptor decreases. That is, the quenching efficiency increases with concentration of quencher, as predicted by the Stern–Volmer equation.

Illustration 20.1

The energy donor 1.5-I AEDANS (**6**) has a fluorescence quantum yield of 0.75 in aqueous solution. The visual pigment 11-*cis*-retinal (Box 20.1) is a quencher of fluorescence and R_0 = 5.4 nm for the 1.5-I AEDANS/11-*cis*-retinal pair. When an amino acid on the surface of the protein rhodopsin, which binds 11-*cis*-retinal in its interior, was labelled covalently with 1.5-I AEDANS, the fluorescence quantum yield of the label decreased to 0.68. From eqn 20.14, we calculate $E_T = 1 - (0.68/0.75) = 0.093$ and from eqn 20.15 we calculate R = 7.9 nm, which is taken as the distance between the surface of the protein and 11-*cis*-retinal.

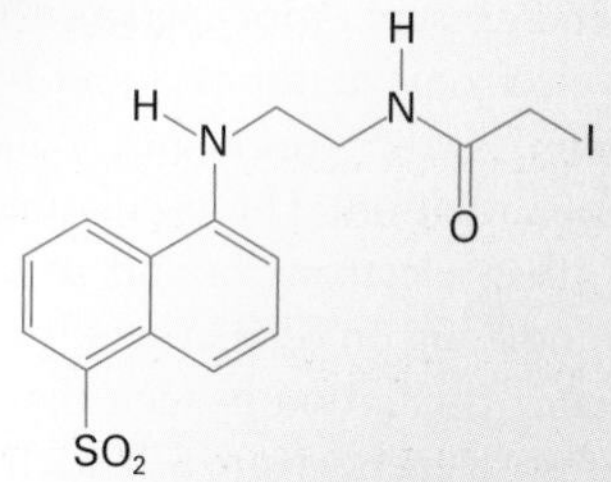

6 1,5-I AEDANS

CHECKLIST OF KEY IDEAS

You should now be familiar with the following concepts:

☐ 1 The Franck–Condon principle states that because nuclei are so much more massive than electrons, an electronic transition takes place faster than the nuclei can respond.

☐ 2 Chiral molecules may show optical activity and circular dichroism, the differential absorption of left- and right-circularly polarized light.

☐ 3 A chromophore is a group with characteristic optical absorption: examples are *d*-metal complexes, the carbonyl group, and the carbon–carbon double bond.

☐ 4 In fluorescence, the spontaneously emitted radiation ceases immediately after the exciting radiation is extinguished.

☐ 5 In phosphorescence, the spontaneous emission may persist for long periods; the process involves intersystem crossing into a triplet state.

☐ 6 Laser action depends on the achievement of population inversion and the stimulated emission of radiation.

☐ 7 Applications of lasers in chemistry include Raman spectroscopy, time-resolved spectroscopy, and the study of multiphoton and state-specific processes.

☐ 8 Photoelectron spectroscopy is based on the photoejection of an electron by ultraviolet radiation or X-rays; the kinetic energy of the photoelectron is related to the ionization energy and incident frequency by $h\nu = I + \frac{1}{2}m_e v^2$.

☐ 9 The primary quantum yield of a photochemical reaction is the number of reactant molecules producing specified primary products for each photon absorbed; the overall quantum yield is the number of reactant molecules that react for each photon absorbed.

☐ 10 The observed fluorescence lifetime is related to the quantum yield, ϕ_f, and rate constant, k_f, of fluorescence by $\tau_0 = \phi_f/k_f$.

☐ 11 A Stern–Volmer plot is used to analyse the kinetics of fluorescence quenching in solution. It is based on the Stern–Volmer equation, $\phi_f/\phi = 1 + \tau_0 k_Q[Q]$.

☐ 12 Collisional deactivation, electron transfer, and resonance energy transfer are common fluorescence quenching processes. The rate constants of electron and resonance energy transfer decrease with increasing separation between donor and acceptor molecules.

DISCUSSION QUESTIONS

20.1 Explain the origin of the Franck–Condon principle and how it leads to the appearance of vibrational structure in an electronic transition.

20.2 Explain how colour can arise from molecules.

20.3 Suppose that you are a colour chemist and had been asked to intensify the colour of a dye without changing the type of compound, and that the dye in question was a polyene. Would you choose to lengthen or to shorten the chain? Would the modification to the length shift the apparent colour of the dye towards the red or the blue?

20.4 The compound $CH_3CH{=}CHCHO$ has a strong absorption in the ultraviolet at 46 950 cm^{-1} and a weak absorption at 30 000 cm^{-1}. Justify these features in terms of the structure of the compound.

20.5 Figure 20.37 shows the UV–visible absorption spectra of a selection of amino acids. Suggest reasons for their different appearances in terms of the structures of the molecules.

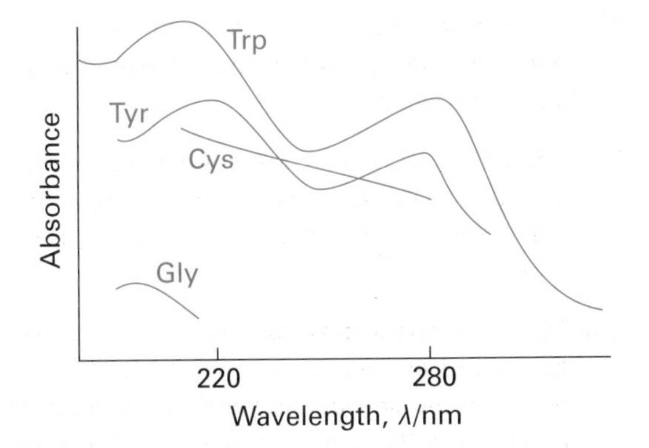

Fig. 20.37

20.6 Figure 20.38 shows the UV–visible absorption spectrum of a derivative of haemerythrin (Her) in the presence of different concentrations of CNS^- ions. What may be inferred from the spectrum?

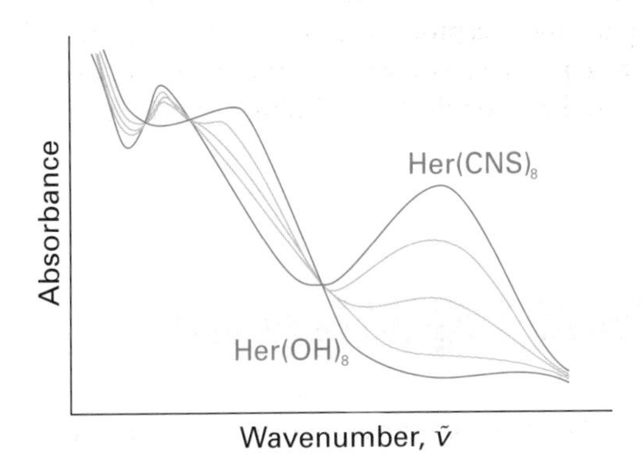

Fig. 20.38

20.7 The fluorescence spectrum of anthracene vapour shows a series of peaks of increasing intensity with individual maxima at 440 nm, 410 nm, 390 nm, and 370 nm followed by a sharp cut-off at shorter wavelengths. The absorption spectrum rises sharply form zero to a maximum at 360 nm with a trail of peaks of lessening intensity at 345 nm, 330 nm, and 305 nm. Account for these observations.

20.8 Describe the principle of laser action and the features of laser radiation that are applied to chemistry. Then, discuss two applications of lasers in chemistry.

20.9 Describe the mechanisms of photon emission by fluorescence and phosphorescence.

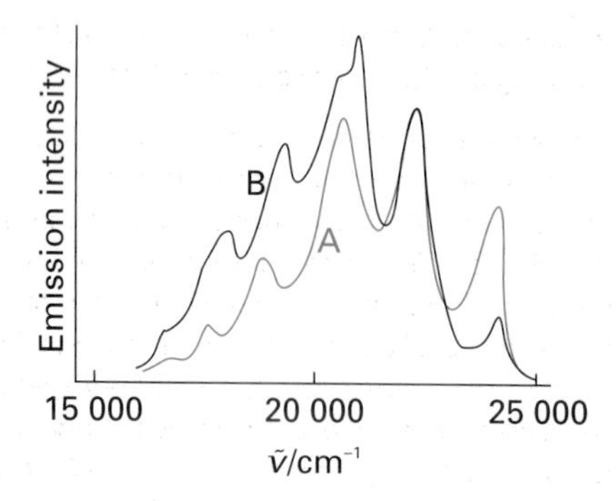

Fig. 20.39

20.10 The line marked A in Fig. 20.39 is the fluorescence spectrum of benzophenone in solid solution in ethanol at low temperatures observed when the sample is illuminated with 360 nm light. When naphthalene is illuminated with 360 nm light it does not absorb, but the line marked B in the illustration is the phosphorescence spectrum of a solid solution of a mixture of naphthalene and benzophenone in ethanol. Now a component of fluorescence from naphthalene can be detected. Account for this observation.

EXERCISES

20.11 An aqueous solution of a triphosphate derivative of molar mass 602 g mol^{-1} was prepared by dissolving 30.2 mg in 500 cm^3 of water and a sample was transferred to a cell of length 1.00 cm. The absorbance (optical density) was measured as 1.011. (a) Calculate the molar absorption coefficient. (b) Calculate the transmittance, expressed as a percentage, for a solution of twice the concentration.

20.12 A *Dubosq colorimeter* consists of a cell of fixed path length and a cell of variable path length. By adjusting the length of the latter until the transmission through the two cells is the same, the concentration of the second solution can be inferred from that of the former. Suppose that a plant dye of concentration 25 μg dm^{-3} is added to the fixed cell, the length of which is 1.55 cm. Then a solution of the same dye, but of unknown concentration, is added to the second cell. It is found that the same transmittance is obtained when the length of the second cell is adjusted to 1.18 cm. What is the concentration of the second solution?

20.13 What is the kinetic energy of an electron that has been accelerated through a potential difference of 5.0 eV?

20.14 What is the energy of an electron that has been ejected from an orbital of ionization energy of 11.0 eV by a photon of radiation of wavelength 100 nm?

20.15 In a particular photoelectron spectrum using 21.21 eV photons, electrons were ejected with kinetic energies of 11.01 eV, 8.23 eV, and 5.22 eV. Sketch the molecular orbital energy level diagram for the species, showing the ionization energies of the three identifiable orbitals.

20.16 Consider a unimolecular photochemical reaction with rate constant $k = 1.7 \times 10^4$ s^{-1} that involves a reactant with an observed fluorescence lifetime of 1.0 ns and an observed phosphorescence lifetime of 1.0 ms. Is the excited singlet state or the excited triplet state the most likely precursor of the photochemical reaction?

20.17 Derive an expression for the rate of disappearance of a species A in a photochemical reaction for which the mechanism is:

(1) initiation with light of intensity I, $A \rightarrow R\cdot + R\cdot$

(2) propagation, $A + R\cdot \rightarrow R\cdot + B$

(3) termination, $R\cdot + R\cdot \rightarrow R_2$

Hence, show that rate measurements will give only a combination of k_2 and k_3 if a steady state is reached, but that both may be obtained if a steady state is not reached.

20.18 In a photochemical reaction $A \rightarrow 2\,B + C$, the quantum efficiency with 500 nm light is 2.1×10^2 mol einstein^{-1} (1 einstein = 1 mol photons). After exposure of 300 mmol of A to the light, 2.28 mmol of B is formed. How many photons were absorbed by A?

20.19 In an experiment to measure the quantum efficiency of a photochemical reaction, the absorbing substance was exposed to 490 nm light from a 100 W source for 45 min. The intensity of the transmitted light was 40 per cent of the intensity of the incident light. As a result of irradiation, 0.344 mol of the absorbing substance decomposed. Determine the quantum efficiency.

20.20 When benzophenone is illuminated with ultraviolet light it is excited into a singlet state. This singlet changes rapidly into a triplet, which phosphoresces. Triethylamine acts as a quencher for the triplet. In an experiment in methanol as solvent, the phosphorescence intensity varied with amine concentration as shown below. A time-resolved laser spectroscopy experiment had also shown that the half-life of the fluorescence in the absence of quencher is 29 μs. What is the value of k_Q?

$[Q]/(\text{mol dm}^{-3})$	0.0010	0.0050	0.0100
I_f/(arbitrary units)	0.41	0.25	0.16

20.21 The quenching of tryptophan fluorescence by dissolved O_2 gas was monitored by measuring emission lifetimes at 348 nm in aqueous solutions. Determine the quenching rate constant for this process from the following data:

$[O_2]/(10^{-2}\text{ mol dm}^{-3})$	0	2.3	5.5	8	10.8
$\tau/(10^{-9}\text{ s})$	2.6	1.5	0.92	0.71	0.57

20.22 The fluorescence of a solution of a plant pigment illuminated by 330 nm radiation was studied in the presence of a quenching agent, with the following results:

$[Q]/(\text{mmol dm}^{-3})$	1.0	2.0	3.0	4.0	5.0
I_f/I_{abs}	0.31	0.18	0.13	0.10	0.081

In a second series of experiments, the incident radiation was extinguished and the lifetime of the decay of the fluorescence was observed:

$[Q]/(\text{mmol dm}^{-3})$	1.0	2.0	3.0	4.0	5.0
τ/ns	76	45	32	25	20

Determine the quenching rate constant and the half-life of the fluorescence.

20.23 The following data refer to a family of compounds with the general composition A–B_n–C in which the distance R between A and C was varied by increasing the number of B units in the linker:

R/nm	1.2	1.5	1.8	2.8	3.1	3.4	3.7
E_T	0.99	0.94	0.97	0.82	0.74	0.65	0.40

R/nm	4.0	4.3	4.6
E_T	0.28	0.24	0.16

Are the data described adequately by the Förster theory (eqn 20.15)? If so, what is the value of R_0 for the A–C pair?

20.24 The Beer–Lambert law states that the absorbance of a sample at a wavenumber $\tilde{\nu}$ is proportional to the molar concentration [J] of the absorbing species J and to the length l of the sample (eqn 19.3). In this problem you will show that the intensity of fluorescence emission from a sample of J is also proportional to [J] and l. Consider a sample of J that is illuminated with a beam of intensity $I_0(\tilde{\nu})$ at the wavenumber $\tilde{\nu}$. Before fluorescence can occur, a fraction of $I_0(\tilde{\nu})$ must be absorbed and an intensity $I(\tilde{\nu})$ will be transmitted. However, not all of the absorbed intensity is emitted and the intensity of fluorescence depends on the fluorescence quantum yield, ϕ_f, the efficiency of photon emission. The fluorescence quantum yield ranges from 0 to 1 and is proportional to the ratio of the integral of the fluorescence spectrum over the integrated absorption coefficient. Because of a Stokes shift of magnitude $\Delta\tilde{\nu}_{\text{Stokes}}$, fluorescence occurs at a wavenumber $\tilde{\nu}_f$, with $\tilde{\nu}_f + \Delta\tilde{\nu}_{\text{Stokes}} = \tilde{\nu}$. It follows that the fluorescence intensity at $\tilde{\nu}_f$, $I_f(\tilde{\nu}_f)$, is proportional to ϕ_f and to the intensity of exciting radiation that is absorbed by J, $I_{abs}(\tilde{\nu}) = I_0(\tilde{\nu}) - I(\tilde{\nu})$. (a) Use the Beer–Lambert law to express $I_{abs}(\tilde{\nu})$ in terms of $I_0(\tilde{\nu})$, [J], l, and $\varepsilon(\tilde{\nu})$, the molar absorption coefficient of J at $\tilde{\nu}$. (b) Use your result from part (a) to show that $I_f(\tilde{\nu}_f) \propto I_0(\tilde{\nu})\varepsilon(\tilde{\nu})\phi_f[\text{J}]l$.

20.25 Light-induced degradation of molecules, also called *photobleaching*, is a serious problem in *fluorescence microscopy*, in which a specimen (such as a biological cell) labelled with a fluorescent dye is observed under an optical microscope. A molecule of a dye commonly used to label biopolymers can withstand about 10^6 excitations by photons before light-induced reactions destroy its π system and the molecule no longer fluoresces. For how long will a single dye molecule fluoresce while being excited by 1.0 mW of 488 nm radiation from an argon-ion laser? You may assume that the dye has an absorption spectrum that peaks at 488 nm and that every photon delivered by the laser is absorbed by the molecule.

Chapter 21

Magnetic resonance

One of the most widely used and helpful forms of spectroscopy, and a technique that has transformed the practice of chemistry and its dependent disciplines, makes use of an effect that is familiar from classical physics. When two pendulums are joined by the same slightly flexible support and one is set in motion, the other is forced into oscillation by the motion of the common axle, and energy flows between the two. The energy transfer occurs most efficiently when the frequencies of the two oscillators are identical. The condition of strong effective coupling when the frequencies are identical is called **resonance**, and the excitation energy is said to 'resonate' between the coupled oscillators.

Resonance is the basis of a number of everyday phenomena, including the response of radios to the weak oscillations of the electromagnetic field generated by a distant transmitter. In this chapter we explore a spectroscopic application that when originally developed depended (and in some cases still does depend) on matching a set of energy levels to a source of monochromatic radiation in the radiofrequency and microwave ranges and observing the strong absorption by nuclei and electrons, respectively, that occurs at resonance.

Principles of magnetic resonance

The application of resonance that we describe here depends on the fact that electrons and many nuclei possess spin angular momentum (Table 21.1). An

Table 21.1

Nuclear constitution and the nuclear spin quantum number

Number of protons	Number of neutrons	I
Even	Even	0
Odd	Odd	Integer (1, 2, 3, ...)
Even	Odd	Half-integer ($\frac{1}{2}, \frac{3}{2}, \frac{5}{2}, \ldots$)
Odd	Even	Half-integer ($\frac{1}{2}, \frac{3}{2}, \frac{5}{2}, \ldots$)

electron (with spin quantum number $s = \frac{1}{2}$) in a magnetic field can take two orientations, corresponding to $m_s = +\frac{1}{2}$ (denoted α or ↑) and $m_s = -\frac{1}{2}$ (denoted β or ↓). A nucleus with **nuclear spin quantum number** I (the analogue of s for electrons, and which may be an integer or a half-integer) may take $2I + 1$ different orientations relative to an arbitrary axis. These orientations are distinguished by the quantum number m_I, which may take the values $m_I = I, I - 1, \ldots, -I$. A proton has $I = \frac{1}{2}$ (the same spin as an electron) and may adopt either of two orientations ($m_I = +\frac{1}{2}$ and $-\frac{1}{2}$). A ^{14}N nucleus has $I = 1$ and may adopt any of three orientations ($m_I = +1, 0, -1$). Spin-$\frac{1}{2}$ nuclei include protons (^{1}H), ^{13}C, ^{19}F, and ^{31}P nuclei. As for electrons, the state with $m_I = +\frac{1}{2}$ (↑) is denoted α, and that with $m_I = -\frac{1}{2}$ (↓) is denoted β.

21.1 Electrons and nuclei in magnetic fields

An electron possesses a magnetic moment due to its spin and this moment interacts with an external magnetic field. That is, an electron behaves like a tiny magnet. The orientation of this magnet is determined by the value of m_s and in a magnetic field $\mathcal{B}$ the two orientations have different energies. These energies are given by

$$E_{m_s} = -g_e \gamma \hbar \mathcal{B} m_s \tag{21.1}$$

where γ is the **magnetogyric ratio** of the electron

$$\gamma = -\frac{e}{2m_e} \tag{21.2}$$

and g_e is a factor, the **g-value of the electron**, which is close to 2.0023 for a free electron.[1] The energies are sometimes expressed in terms of the **Bohr magneton**

$$\mu_B = \frac{e\hbar}{2m_e} \qquad \mu_B = 9.274 \times 10^{-24}\ \mathrm{J\,T^{-1}} \tag{21.3}$$

a fundamental unit of magnetism,[2] in which case we write

$$E_{m_s} = g_e \mu_B \mathcal{B} m_s \tag{21.4}$$

For an electron, the β state lies below the α state.

Classically, the energy of a magnetic moment $\boldsymbol{m}$ in a magnetic field $\mathcal{B}$ is $E = -\boldsymbol{m}\cdot\mathcal{B}$. Equation 21.1 is the quantum mechanical version of the classical expression, with the field along the z-direction and the magnetic moment equal to $g_e \gamma s_z$ and $s_z = m_s \hbar$.

A nucleus with non-zero spin also has a magnetic moment and behaves like a tiny magnet. The orientation of this magnet is determined by the value of m_I, and in a magnetic field $\mathcal{B}$ the $2I + 1$ orientations of the nucleus have different energies. These energies are given by

$$E_{m_I} = -\gamma_N \hbar \mathcal{B} m_I \tag{21.5}$$

where γ_N is the **nuclear magnetogyric ratio.** For spin-$\frac{1}{2}$ nuclei with positive magnetogyric ratios (such as ^{1}H), the α state lies below the β state. The energy is sometimes written in terms of the **nuclear magneton,** μ_N, and an empirical constant called the **nuclear g-factor,** g_I:

$$\mu_N = \frac{e\hbar}{2m_p} \qquad \mu_N = 5.051 \times 10^{-27}\ \mathrm{J\,T^{-1}} \tag{21.6}$$

when it becomes

$$E_{m_I} = -g_N \mu_N \mathcal{B} m_I \tag{21.7}$$

Nuclear g-factors are experimentally determined dimensionless quantities with values typically between −6 and +6 (see Table 21.2). Positive values of γ_N (and g_I) indicate that the nuclear magnet lies in the same direction as the nuclear spin (this is the case for protons). Negative values indicate that the magnet points in the opposite direction. A nuclear

1 The 2 comes from Dirac's relativistic theory of the electron; the 0.0023 comes from additional correction terms.

2 The symbol T denotes the unit tesla, which is used to measure the intensity of a magnetic field (1 T = 1 kg s^{-2} A^{-1}).

Table 21.2 *Nuclear spin properties*

Nucleus	Natural abundance/per cent	Spin, I	$\gamma_N/(10^7\ T^{-1}\ s^{-1})$
^{1}H	99.98	$\frac{1}{2}$	26.752
^{2}H (D)	0.0156	1	4.1067
^{12}C	98.99	0	–
^{13}C	1.11	$\frac{1}{2}$	6.7272
^{14}N	99.64	1	1.9328
^{16}O	99.96	0	–
^{17}O	0.037	$\frac{5}{2}$	–3.627
^{19}F	100	$\frac{1}{2}$	25.177
^{31}P	100	$\frac{1}{2}$	10.840
^{35}Cl	75.4	$\frac{3}{2}$	2.624
^{37}Cl	24.6	$\frac{3}{2}$	2.184

magnet is about 2000 times weaker than the magnet associated with electron spin. Two very common nuclei, ^{12}C and ^{16}O, have zero spin and hence are not affected by external magnetic fields.

The energy separation of the two spin states of an electron (Fig. 21.1) is

$$\Delta E = E_\alpha - E_\beta = (\tfrac{1}{2})g_e\mu_B\mathcal{B} - (-\tfrac{1}{2}g_e\mu_B\mathcal{B}) = g_e\mu_B\mathcal{B} \qquad (21.8)$$

We shall see in Section 22.1 in the discussion of the Boltzmann distribution that the populations of the α and β states, N_α and N_β, are proportional to $e^{-E_\alpha/kT}$ and $e^{-E_\beta/kT}$, respectively, so the ratio of populations at equilibrium is

$$\frac{N_\alpha}{N_\beta} = e^{-(E_\alpha - E_\beta)/kT} \qquad (21.9a)$$

Because $E_\alpha - E_\beta > 0$ (for an electron the β state lies below the α state), $N_\alpha/N_\beta < 1$ and there are slightly more β spins than α spins. We show in Derivation 21.1 that

$$N_\beta - N_\alpha \approx \frac{Ng_e\mu_B\mathcal{B}}{2kT} \qquad (21.9b)$$

In a field of 1.0 T at 300 K, $(N_\beta - N_\alpha)N \approx 0.0022$, so there is an imbalance of populations of only about 2 electrons in a thousand (Exercise 21.11).

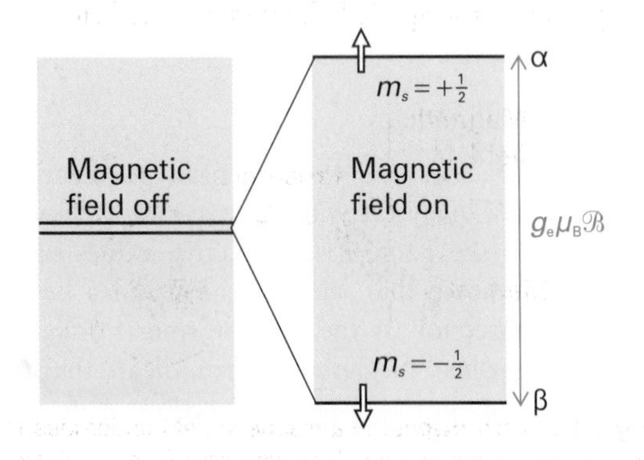

Fig. 21.1 The energy levels of an electron in a magnetic field. Resonance occurs when the energy separation of the levels matches the energy of the photons in the electromagnetic field.

Derivation 21.1

The population difference

To write an expression for the population difference, we begin with eqn 21.9a, written as

$$\frac{N_\alpha}{N_\beta} = e^{-(E_\alpha - E_\beta)/kT} \approx 1 - \frac{E_\alpha - E_\beta}{kT} = 1 - \frac{g_e\mu_B\mathcal{B}}{kT}$$

The expansion of an exponential function used here is $e^{-x} = 1 - x + \frac{1}{2}x^2 - \cdots$. If $x \ll 1$, then $e^{-x} \approx 1 - x$.

The expansion of the exponential term is appropriate for $\Delta E \ll kT$, a condition usually met for electron and nuclear spins. It follows that

$$\frac{N_\beta - N_\alpha}{N_\beta + N_\alpha} = \frac{N_\beta(1 - N_\alpha/N_\beta)}{N_\beta(1 + N_\alpha/N_\beta)} = \frac{1 - N_\alpha/N_\beta}{1 + N_\alpha/N_\beta}$$

$$\approx \frac{1 - (1 - g_e\mu_B\mathcal{B}/kT)}{1 + (1 - g_e\mu_B\mathcal{B}/kT)} \approx \frac{g_e\mu_B\mathcal{B}/kT}{2}$$

Then, with $N_\alpha + N_\beta = N$, the total number of spins, we have eqn 21.9b.

If the sample is exposed to radiation of frequency ν, the energy separations come into resonance with the radiation when the frequency satisfies the **resonance condition:**

$$h\nu = g_e\mu_B\mathcal{B} \qquad \text{or} \qquad \nu = \frac{g_e\mu_B\mathcal{B}}{h} \tag{21.10}$$

At resonance there is strong coupling between the electron spin and the radiation, and strong absorption occurs as the spins flip from β (low energy) to α (high energy).

The behaviour of nuclei is very similar. The energy separation of the two states of a spin-$\frac{1}{2}$ nucleus (Fig. 21.2) is

$$\Delta E = E_\beta - E_\alpha = \tfrac{1}{2}\gamma_N\hbar\mathcal{B} - (-\tfrac{1}{2}\gamma_N\hbar\mathcal{B})$$
$$= \gamma_N\hbar\mathcal{B} \tag{21.11}$$

Because for nuclei with positive γ_N the α state lies below the β state, $E_\beta - E_\alpha > 0$ and it follows from eqn 21.9 that $N_\beta/N_\alpha < 1$: there are slightly more α spins than β spins (the opposite of an electron) and in the same way as in Derivation 21.1 we can write

$$N_\alpha - N_\beta \approx \frac{N\gamma_N\hbar\mathcal{B}}{2kT} \tag{21.12}$$

For protons in a field of 10 T at 300 K, $(N_\alpha - N_\beta)/N \approx 3 \times 10^{-5}$, so even in such a strong field there is only a tiny imbalance of population of about 30 in a million.

As for electrons, if the sample is exposed to radiation of frequency ν, the energy separations come into resonance with the radiation when the frequency satisfies the resonance condition:

$$h\nu = \gamma_N\hbar\mathcal{B} \qquad \text{or} \qquad \nu = \frac{\gamma_N\mathcal{B}}{2\pi} \tag{21.13}$$

At resonance there is strong coupling between the nuclear spins and the radiation, and strong absorption occurs as the spins flip from α (low energy) to β (high energy).

It is sometimes useful to compare the quantum mechanical and classical pictures of magnetic nuclei pictured as tiny bar magnets. A bar magnet in an externally applied magnetic field undergoes the motion called **precession** as it twists round the direction of the field (Fig. 21.3). The rate of precession is proportional to the strength of the applied field, and is in fact equal to $(\gamma_N/2\pi)\mathcal{B}$, which in this context is called the **Larmor precession frequency**. That is, resonance absorption occurs when the Larmor precession frequency is the same as the frequency of the applied electromagnetic field.

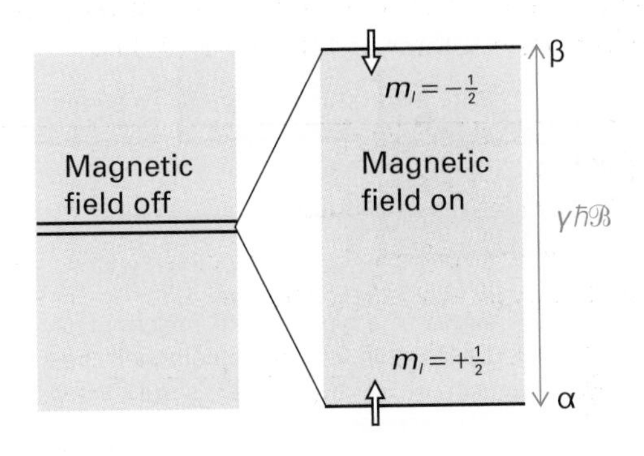

Fig. 21.2 The energy levels of a spin-$\frac{1}{2}$ nucleus (e.g. ^1H or ^{13}C) in a magnetic field. Resonance occurs when the energy separation of the levels matches the energy of the photons in the electromagnetic field.

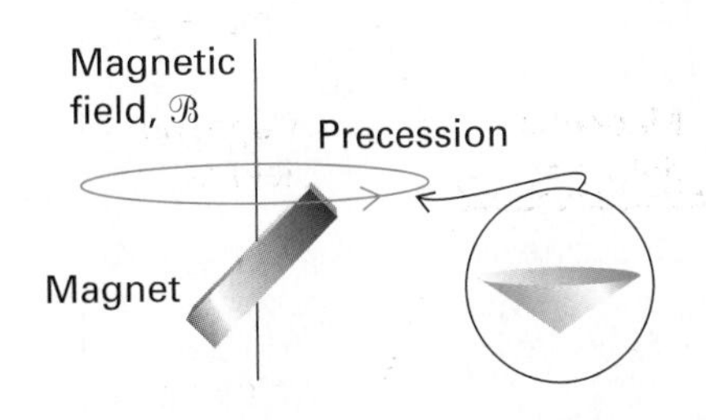

Fig. 21.3 A bar magnet in a magnetic field undergoes the motion called *precession*. A nuclear spin (and an electron spin) has an associated magnetic moment, and behaves in the same way. The frequency of precession is called the Larmor precession frequency, and is proportional to the applied field and the magnitude of the magnetic moment.

Self-test 21.1

Calculate the frequency at which radiation comes into resonance with proton spins in a 12 T magnetic field.

[*Answer:* 510 MHz]

The intensity of a nuclear magnetic resonance transition depends on a number of factors. We show in Derivation 21.2 that

$$\text{Intensity} \propto (N_\alpha - N_\beta)\mathcal{B} \propto \mathcal{B}^2 \qquad (21.14)$$

It follows that decreasing the temperature increases the intensity by increasing the population difference. The intensity can also be enhanced significantly by increasing the strength of the applied magnetic field. Similar arguments apply to electron spin resonance transitions.

Derivation 21.2

Intensities in NMR spectra

From the general considerations of transition intensities in *Further information* 19.1, we know that the rate of absorption of electromagnetic radiation is proportional to the population of the lower energy state (N_α in the case of a proton NMR transition) and the rate of stimulated emission is proportional to the population of the upper state (N_β). At the low frequencies typical of magnetic resonance, we can neglect spontaneous emission as it is very slow. Therefore, the net rate of absorption is proportional to the difference in populations, and we can write

$$\text{Rate of transition} \propto N_\alpha - N_\beta$$

The intensity of absorption, the rate at which energy is absorbed, is proportional to the product of the rate of transition (the rate at which photons are absorbed) and the energy of each photon, and the latter is proportional to the frequency v of the incident radiation. At resonance, this frequency is proportional to the applied magnetic field, so we can write

$$\text{Intensity of absorption} \propto (N_\alpha - N_\beta)\mathcal{B}$$

with the population difference proportional to the field (eqn 21.12).

21.2 The technique

In its simplest form, **nuclear magnetic resonance** (NMR) is the observation of the frequency at which magnetic nuclei in molecules come into resonance with an electromagnetic field when the molecule is exposed to a strong magnetic field. When applied to proton spins, the technique is occasionally called **proton magnetic resonance** (^{1}H NMR). In the early days of the technique the only nuclei that could be studied were protons (which behave like relatively strong magnets because γ_N is large), but now a wide variety of nuclei (especially ^{13}C and ^{31}P) are investigated routinely.

An NMR spectrometer consists of a magnet that can produce a uniform, intense field and the appropriate sources of radiofrequency radiation (Fig. 21.4). In simple instruments the magnetic field is provided by an electromagnet; for serious work, a superconducting magnet capable of producing fields of the order of 10 T and more is used.[3] The use of high magnetic fields has two advantages. One is that, as we have seen, the field increases the intensities of transitions. Second, a high field simplifies the appearance of certain spectra. Proton resonance occurs at about 400 MHz in fields of 9.4 T, so NMR is a radiofrequency technique (400 MHz corresponds to a wavelength of 75 cm).

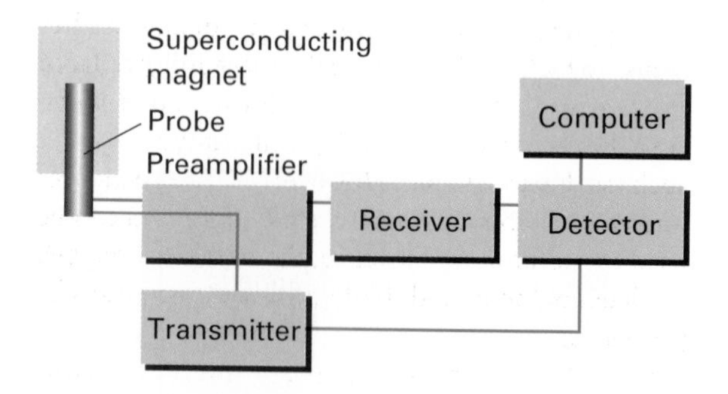

Fig. 21.4 The layout of a typical NMR spectrometer. The link from the transmitter to the detector indicates that the high frequency of the transmitter is subtracted from the high-frequency received signal to give a low-frequency signal for processing.

3 A magnetic field of 10 T is very strong: a small magnet, for example, gives a magnetic field of only a few millitesla.

Fourier transform NMR (FT-NMR) is the most common technique used in modern magnetic resonance. The sample is held in a strong magnetic field generated by a superconducting magnet and exposed to one or more carefully controlled brief bursts of radiofrequency radiation. This radiation changes the orientations of the nuclear spins in a controlled way, and the radiofrequency radiation they emit as they return to equilibrium is monitored and analysed mathematically (the latter is the 'Fourier transform' part of the technique). The detected radiation contains all the information in the spectrum obtained by the earlier technique, but it is a much more efficient way of obtaining the spectrum and hence is much more sensitive. Moreover, by choosing different sequences of exciting pulses, the data can be analysed much more closely.

The resonance technique for electrons in a magnetic field is called **electron paramagnetic resonance** (EPR) or **electron spin resonance** (ESR). Because electron magnetic moments are much bigger than nuclear magnetic moments, even quite modest fields can require high frequencies to achieve resonance. Much work is done using fields of about 0.3 T, when resonance occurs at about 9 GHz, corresponding to 3 cm ('X-band') microwave radiation, or at about 1 T, when resonance occurs at about 35 GHz, corresponding to about 9 mm ('Q-band') microwave radiation. Electron paramagnetic resonance is much more limited than NMR because it is applicable only to species with unpaired electrons, which include radicals (perhaps prepared by radiation damage or photolysis) and *d*-metal complexes, and also biologically active species such as haemoglobin. However, it gives valuable information about electron distributions and can be used to monitor, for instance, the uptake of oxygen by haemoglobin and biological electron transfer processes.

Both Fourier-transform (FT) and continuous wave (CW) EPR spectrometers are available. The FT-EPR instrument is like an FT-NMR spectrometer except that pulses of microwaves are used to excite electron spins in the sample. The layout of the more common CW-EPR spectrometer is shown in Fig. 21.5. It consists of a microwave source (a klystron or a Gunn oscillator), a cavity in which the sample is inserted in a glass or quartz container, a microwave detector, and an electromagnet with a field that can be varied in the region of 0.3 T (X-band) or 1 T (Q-band).

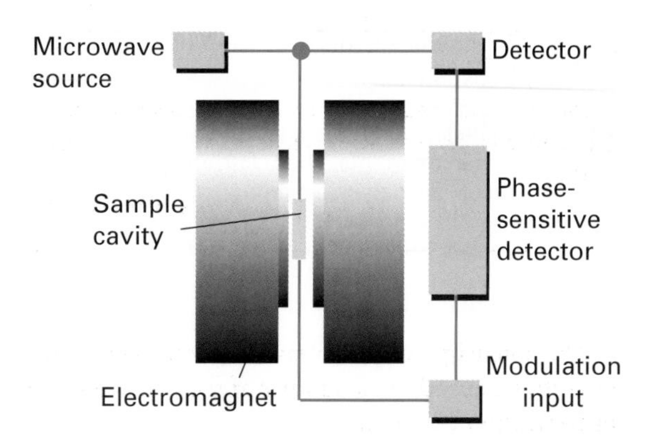

Fig. 21.5 The layout of a continuous-wave EPR spectrometer. A typical magnetic field is 0.3 T, which requires microwaves of frequency 9 GHz (wavelength 3 cm) for resonance.

The information in NMR spectra

Nuclear spins interact with the *local* magnetic field, the field in their immediate vicinity. The local field may differ from the applied field either because of the local electronic structure of the molecule or because there is another magnetic nucleus nearby.

21.3 The chemical shift

The applied magnetic field can induce a circulating motion of the electrons in the molecule, and that motion gives rise to a small additional magnetic field, $\mathcal{B}_{add}$. This additional field is proportional to the applied field, and it is conventional to express it as

$$\mathcal{B}_{add} = -\sigma\mathcal{B} \tag{21.15}$$

where the dimensionless quantity σ is the **shielding constant**. The shielding constant may be positive or negative according to whether the induced field adds to or subtracts from the applied field. The ability of the applied field to induce the circulation of electrons through the nuclear framework of the molecule depends on the details of the electronic structure near the magnetic nucleus of interest, so nuclei in different chemical groups have different shielding constants.

An applied magnetic field induces the circulation of electronic currents. These currents give rise to a magnetic field that, in diamagnetic substances, opposes the applied field and, in paramagnetic substances, augments the applied field.

Because the total local field is

$$\mathcal{B}_{\text{loc}} = \mathcal{B} + \mathcal{B}_{\text{add}} = (1 - \sigma)\mathcal{B}$$

the resonance condition is

$$\nu = \frac{\gamma_N \mathcal{B}_{\text{loc}}}{2\pi} = \frac{\gamma_N}{2\pi}(1 - \sigma)\mathcal{B} \qquad (21.16)$$

Because σ varies with the environment, different nuclei (even of the same element in different parts of a molecule) come into resonance at different frequencies.

The **chemical shift** of a nucleus is the difference between its resonance frequency and that of a reference standard. The standard for protons is the proton resonance in tetramethylsilane, $Si(CH_3)_4$, commonly referred to as TMS, which bristles with protons and dissolves without reaction in many solutions. Other references are used for other nuclei. For ^{13}C, the reference frequency is the ^{13}C resonance in TMS, and for ^{31}P it is the ^{31}P resonance in 85 per cent $H_3PO_4(aq)$. The separation of the resonance of a particular group of nuclei from the standard increases with the strength of the applied magnetic field because the induced field is proportional to the applied field, and the stronger the latter, the greater the shift.

Chemical shifts are reported on the **δ scale**, which is defined as

$$\delta = \frac{\nu - \nu^\circ}{\nu^\circ} \times 10^6 \qquad (21.17)$$

where ν° is the resonance frequency of the standard. The advantage of the δ scale is that shifts reported on it are independent of the applied field (because both numerator and denominator are proportional to the applied field). The resonance frequencies themselves, however, do depend on the applied field through

$$\nu = \nu^\circ + (\nu^\circ/10^6)\delta \qquad (21.18)$$

A note on good practice. In much of the literature, chemical shifts are reported in parts per million, ppm, in recognition of the factor of 10^6 in the definition; this is unnecessary. If you see 'δ = 10 ppm', interpret it, and use it in eqn 21.18, as $\delta = 10$.

Illustration 21.1

Using the chemical shift

A nucleus with $\delta = 1.00$ in a spectrometer operating at 500 MHz will have a shift relative to the reference equal to

$$\nu - \nu^\circ = (500\ \text{MHz}/10^6) \times 1.00$$
$$= (500\ \text{Hz}) \times 1.00 = 500\ \text{Hz}$$

because 1 MHz = 10^6 Hz. In a spectrometer operating at 100 MHz, the shift relative to the reference would be only 100 Hz.

Self-test 21.2

What is the shift of the resonance from TMS of a group of nuclei with $\delta = 3.50$ and an operating frequency of 350 MHz?

[*Answer:* 1.23 kHz]

If $\delta > 0$, we say that the nucleus is **deshielded**; if $\delta < 0$, then it is **shielded**. A positive δ indicates that the resonance frequency of the group of nuclei in question is higher than that of the standard. Hence $\delta > 0$ indicates that the local magnetic field is stronger than that experienced by the nuclei in the standard under the same conditions. Figure 21.6 shows some typical chemical shifts.

Illustration 21.2

The general appearance of a spectrum

The existence of a chemical shift explains the general features of the spectrum of ethanol shown in Fig. 21.7. The CH_3 protons form one group of nuclei with $\delta = 1$. The two CH_2 protons are in a different part of the molecule, experience a different local magnetic field, and hence resonate at $\delta = 3$. Finally, the OH proton is in another environment, and has a chemical shift of $\delta = 4$.

A note on good practice Traditionally, NMR spectra are plotted with δ increasing from right to left. Consequently, in a given applied magnetic field the resonance frequency also increases from right to left.

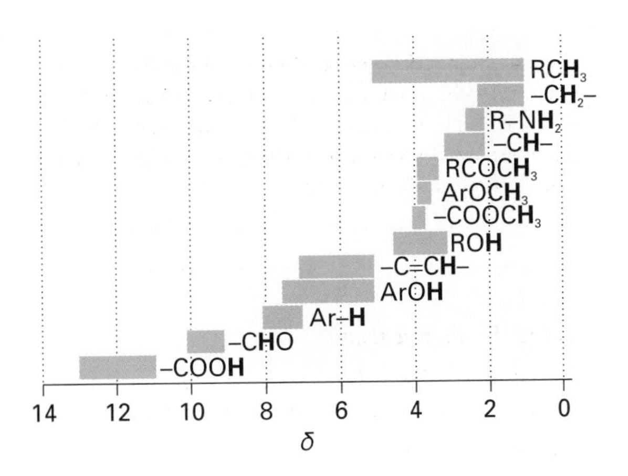

Fig. 21.6 The range of typical chemical shifts for ^{1}H resonances.

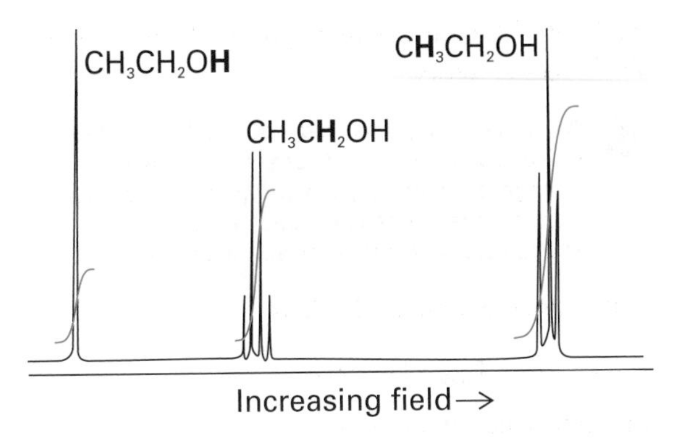

Fig. 21.7 The NMR spectrum of ethanol. The bold letters denote the protons giving rise to the resonance peak, and the step-like curves are the integrated signals for each group of lines.

We can use the relative intensities of the signal (the areas under the absorption lines) to help to distinguish which group of lines corresponds to which chemical group, and spectrometers can **integrate** the absorption—that is, determine the areas under the absorption signal—automatically (as is shown in Fig. 21.7). In ethanol the group intensities are in the ratio 3:2:1 because there are three CH_3 protons, two CH_2 protons, and one OH proton in each molecule. Counting the number of magnetic nuclei as well as noting their chemical shifts is valuable analytically because it helps us to identify the compound present in a sample and to identify substances in different environments (Box 21.1).

The observed shielding constant is the sum of three contributions:

$$\sigma = \sigma(\text{local}) + \sigma(\text{neighbour}) + \sigma(\text{solvent}) \quad (21.19)$$

The **local contribution**, σ(local), is essentially the contribution of the electrons of the atom that

Box 21.1 *Magnetic resonance imaging*

One of the most striking applications of nuclear magnetic resonance is in medicine. *Magnetic resonance imaging* (MRI) is a portrayal of the concentrations of protons in a solid object. The technique relies on the application of specific pulse sequences to an object in an inhomogeneous magnetic field (a field with values that vary inside the sample).

If an object containing hydrogen nuclei (a tube of water or a human body) is placed in an NMR spectrometer and exposed to a *homogeneous* magnetic field (a field that has the same value throughout the sample), then a single resonance signal will be detected. Now consider a flask of water in a magnetic field that varies linearly in the z-direction according to $\mathcal{B}_0 + G_z z$, where G_z if the field gradient along the z-direction (see the first illustration). Then the water protons will be resonant at the frequencies

$$\nu(z) = \frac{\gamma_N}{2\pi}(\mathcal{B}_0 + G_z z)$$

(similar equations may be written for gradients along the x and y directions). Exposing the sample to radiation with frequency $\nu(z)$ will result in a signal with an intensity that is proportional to the numbers of protons at the position z. This is an example of *slice selection*, the use of radiofrequency radiation that excites nuclei in a specific region, or slice, of the sample. It follows that the intensity of the NMR signal will be a projection of the numbers of protons on a line parallel to the field gradient. The image of a three-dimensional object such as a flask of water can be obtained if the slice selection technique is applied at different orientations (see the first illustration). In *projection reconstruction*, the projections can be analysed on a computer

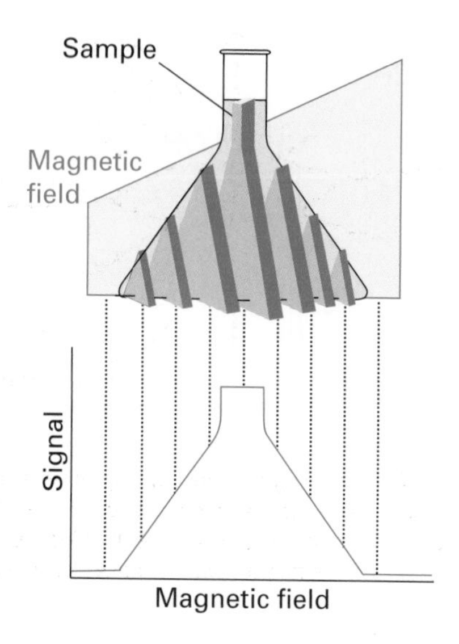

In a magnetic field that varies linearly over a sample, all the protons within a given slice (that is, at a given field value) come into resonance and give a signal of the corresponding intensity. The resulting intensity pattern is a map of the numbers in all the slices, and portrays the shape of the sample. Changing the orientation of the field shows the shape along the corresponding direction, and computer manipulation can be used to build up the three-dimensional shape of the sample.

to reconstruct the three-dimensional distribution of protons in the object.

A common problem with the techniques described above is image contrast, which must be optimized to show spatial variations in water content in the sample. One strategy for solving this problem takes advantage of the fact that the relaxation times of water protons are shorter for water in biological tissues than for the pure liquid. Furthermore, relaxation times from water protons are also different in healthy and diseased tissues. A *T_1-weighted image* is obtained by collecting data before spin–lattice relaxation can return the spins in the sample to equilibrium. Under these conditions, differences in signal intensities are directly related to differences in T_1. A *T_2-weighted image* is obtained by collecting data after the system has relaxed extensively, though not completely. In this way, signal intensities are strongly dependent on variations in T_2. However, allowing so much of the decay to occur leads to weak signals even for those protons with long spin–spin relaxation times. Another strategy involves the use of *contrast agents*, paramagnetic compounds that shorten the relaxation times of nearby protons. The

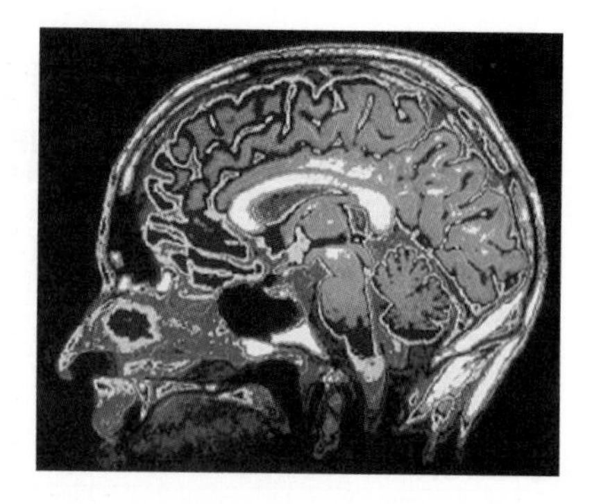

The great advantage of MRI is that it can display soft tissue, such as in this cross-section through a patient's head. (Courtesy of the University of Manitoba.)

technique is particularly useful in enhancing image contrast and in diagnosing disease if the contrast agent is distributed differently in healthy and diseased tissues.

The MRI technique is used widely to detect physiological abnormalities and to observe metabolic processes. With *functional MRI*, blood flow in different regions of the brain can be studied and related to the mental activities of the subject. The special advantage of MRI is that it can image *soft* tissues (see the second illustration), whereas X-rays are largely used for imaging hard, bony structures and abnormally dense regions, such as tumours. In fact, the invisibility of hard structures in MRI is an advantage, as it allows the imaging of structures encased by bone, such as the brain and the spinal cord. X-rays are known to be dangerous on account of the ionization they cause; the high magnetic fields used in MRI may also be dangerous, but apart from anecdotes about the extraction of loose fillings from teeth, there is no convincing evidence of their harmfulness, and the technique is considered safe.

Exercise 1 You are designing an MRI spectrometer. What field gradient (in microtesla per metre, $\mu T\ m^{-1}$) is required to produce a separation of 100 Hz between two protons separated by the long diameter of a human kidney (taken as 8 cm) given that they are in environments with $\delta = 3.4$? The radiofrequency field of the spectrometer is at 400 MHz and the applied field is 9.4 T.

Exercise 2 Suppose a uniform disc-shaped organ is in a linear field gradient, and that the MRI signal is proportional to the number of protons in a slice of width δx at each horizontal distance x from the centre of the disc. Sketch the shape of the absorption intensity for the MRI image of the disc before any computer manipulation has been carried out.

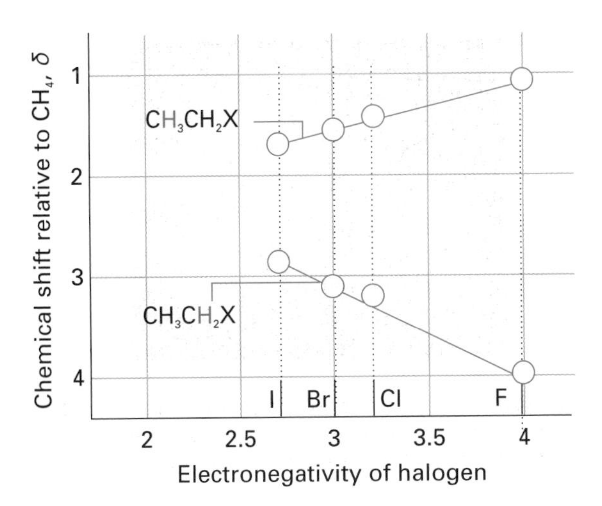

Fig. 21.8 The variation of chemical shift with the electronegativity of the halogen in the haloalkanes. Note that although the chemical shift of the immediately adjacent protons becomes more positive (the protons are deshielded) as the electronegativity increases, that of the next nearest protons decreases.

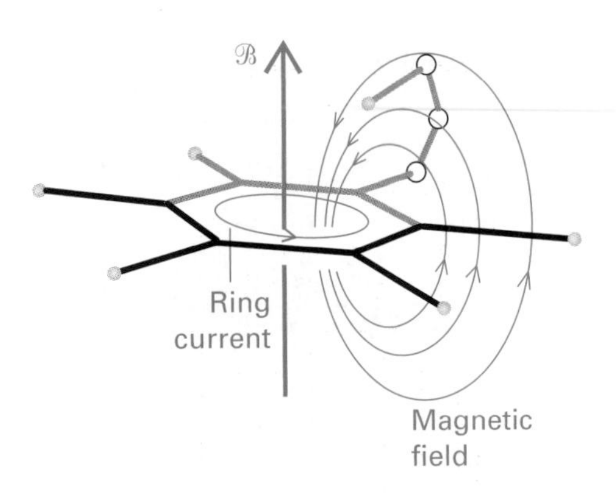

Fig. 21.9 The shielding and deshielding effects of the ring current induced in the benzene ring by the applied field. Protons attached to the ring are deshielded but a proton attached to a substituent that projects above the ring is shielded.

contains the nucleus in question. The **neighbouring group contribution,** σ(neighbour), is the contribution from the groups of atoms that form the rest of the molecule. The **solvent contribution,** σ(solvent), is the contribution from the solvent molecules.

The local contribution is broadly proportional to the electron density of the atom containing the nucleus of interest. It follows that the shielding is decreased if the electron density on the atom is reduced by the influence of an electronegative atom nearby. That reduction in shielding translates into an increase in deshielding, and hence to an increase in the chemical shift δ as the electronegativity of a neighbouring atom increases (Fig. 21.8). That is, as the electronegativity increases, δ decreases. Another contribution to σ(local) arises from the ability of the applied field to force the electrons to circulate through the molecule by making use of orbitals that are unoccupied in the ground state. This contribution is large in molecules with low-lying excited states and is dominant for atoms other than hydrogen. It is zero in free atoms and around the axes of linear molecules (such as ethyne, HC≡CH), where the electrons can circulate freely because a field applied along the internuclear axis is unable to force them into other orbitals.

The neighbouring group contribution arises from the currents induced in nearby groups of atoms. The strength of the additional magnetic field the proton experiences is inversely proportional to the cube of the distance r between H and X. A special case of a neighbouring group effect is found in aromatic compounds. The strong anisotropy of the magnetic susceptibility of the benzene ring is ascribed to the ability of the field to induce a **ring current,** a circulation of electrons around the ring, when it is applied perpendicular to the molecular plane. Protons in the plane are deshielded (Fig. 21.9), but any that happen to lie above or below the plane (as members of substituents of the ring) are shielded.

A solvent can influence the local magnetic field experienced by a nucleus in a variety of ways. Some of these effects arise from specific interactions between the solute and the solvent (such as hydrogen-bond formation and other forms of Lewis acid–base complex formation). The magnetic susceptibility of the solvent molecules, especially if they are aromatic, can also be the source of a local magnetic field. Moreover, if there are steric interactions that result in a loose but specific interaction between a solute molecule and a solvent molecule, then protons in the solute molecule may experience shielding or deshielding effects according to their location relative to the solvent molecule (Fig. 21.10). We shall see that the NMR spectra of species that contain

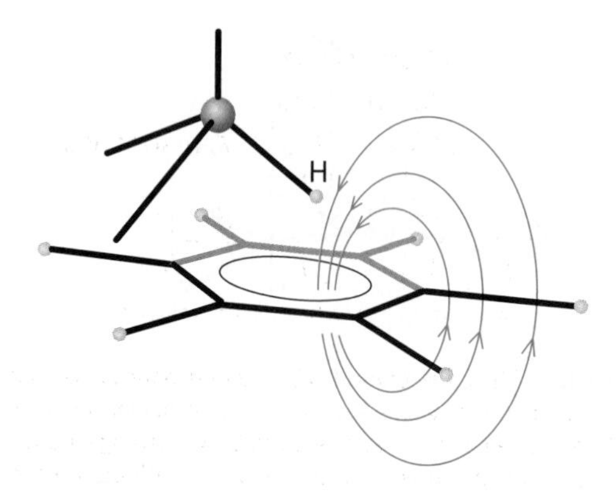

Fig. 21.10 An aromatic solvent (benzene here) can give rise to local currents that shield or deshield a proton in a solvent molecule. In this relative orientation of the solvent and solute, the proton on the solute molecule is shielded.

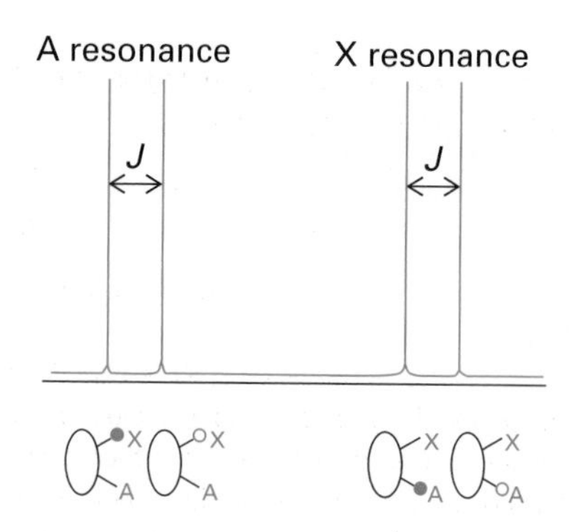

Fig. 21.11 The effect of spin–spin coupling on a NMR spectrum of two spin-$\frac{1}{2}$ nuclei with widely different chemical shifts. Each resonance is split into two lines separated by J. Full circles indicate α spins, open circles indicate β spins.

protons with widely different chemical shifts are easier to interpret than those in which the shifts are similar, so the appropriate choice of solvent may help to simplify the appearance and interpretation of a spectrum.

21.4 The fine structure

The splitting of the groups of resonances into individual lines in Fig. 21.7 is called the **fine structure** of the spectrum. It arises because each magnetic nucleus contributes to the local field experienced by the other nuclei and modifies their resonance frequencies. The strength of the interaction is expressed in terms of the **spin–spin coupling constant**, J, and reported in hertz (Hz). Spin coupling constants are an intrinsic property of the molecule and independent of the strength of the applied field.

Consider first a molecule that contains two spin-$\frac{1}{2}$ nuclei A and X. Suppose the spin of X is α; then A will resonate at a certain frequency as a result of the combined effect of the external field, the shielding constant, and the spin–spin interaction of nucleus A with nucleus X. As we show in Derivation 21.3, instead of a single line from A, we get a doublet of lines separated by a frequency J (Fig. 21.11). The same splitting occurs in the X resonance: instead of a single line it is a doublet with splitting J (the same value as for the splitting of A).

Derivation 21.3

The structure of an AX spectrum

First, neglect spin–spin coupling. The total energy of two protons in a magnetic field $\mathcal{B}$ is the sum of two terms like eqn 21.11 but with $\mathcal{B}$ modified to $(1-\sigma)\mathcal{B}$:

$$E = -\gamma_N \hbar(1-\sigma_A)\mathcal{B}m_A - \gamma_N \hbar(1-\sigma_X)\mathcal{B}m_X$$

Here σ_A and σ_X are the shielding constants of A and X. The four energy levels predicted by this formula are shown on the left of Fig. 21.12. The spin–spin coupling energy is normally written

$$E_{\text{spin-spin}} = hJm_Am_X$$

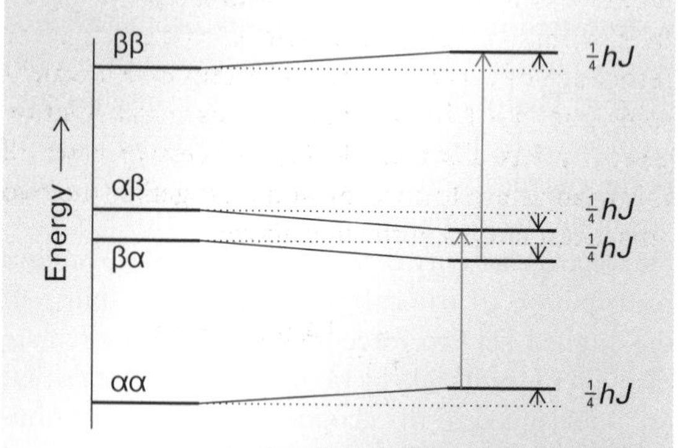

Fig. 21.12 The energy levels of a two-proton system in the presence of a magnetic field. The levels on the left apply in the absence of spin–spin coupling. Those on the right are the result of allowing for spin–spin coupling. The only allowed transitions differ in frequency by J.

There are four possibilities, depending on the values of the quantum numbers m_A and m_X:

	$\alpha_A\alpha_X$	$\alpha_A\beta_X$	$\beta_A\alpha_X$	$\beta_A\beta_X$
$E_{\text{spin-spin}}$	$+\frac{1}{4}hJ$	$-\frac{1}{4}hJ$	$-\frac{1}{4}hJ$	$+\frac{1}{4}hJ$

The resulting energy levels are shown on the right in Fig. 21.12.

Now consider the transitions. When an A nucleus changes its spin from α to β, the X nucleus remains in its same spin state, which may be either α or β. The two transitions are shown in the illustration and we see that they differ in frequency by J. Alternatively, the X nucleus can undergo a transition from α to β; now the A nucleus remains in its same spin state, which may be either α or β, and again there are two transitions differing in frequency by J.

If there is another X nucleus in the molecule with the same chemical shift as the first X (giving an AX_2 species), the resonance of A is split into a doublet by one X, and each line of the doublet is split again by the same amount by the second X (Fig. 21.13). This splitting results in three lines in the intensity ratio 1:2:1 (because the central frequency can be obtained in two ways). As in the AX case discussed above, the X resonance of the AX_2 species is split into a doublet by A.

Three equivalent X nuclei (an AX_3 species) split the resonance of A into four lines of intensity ratio 1:3:3:1 (Fig. 21.14). The X resonance remains a doublet as a result of the splitting caused by A. In general, N equivalent spin-$\frac{1}{2}$ nuclei split the resonance of a nearby spin or group of equivalent spins into $N+1$ lines with an intensity distribution given by Pascal's triangle (**1**). Successive rows of this triangle are formed by adding together the two adjacent numbers in the line above.

Fig. 21.13 The origin of the 1:2:1 triplet in the A resonance of an AX_2 species. The two X nuclei may have the $2^2 = 4$ spin arrangements (↑↑);(↑↓);(↓↑);(↓↓). The middle two arrangements are responsible for the coincident resonances of A.

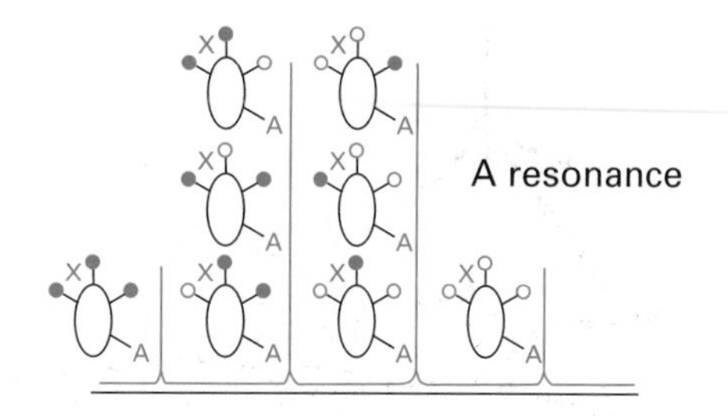

Fig. 21.14 The origin of the 1:3:3:1 quartet in the A resonance of an AX_3 species where A and X are spin-$\frac{1}{2}$ nuclei with widely different chemical shifts. There are $2^3 = 8$ arrangements of the spins of the three X nuclei, and their effects on the A nucleus give rise to four groups of resonances.

1

1 1

1 2 1

1 3 3 1

1 4 6 4 1

1 Pascal's triangle

Self-test 21.3

Complete the next line of Pascal's triangle, the pattern arising from five equivalent protons.

[*Answer:* 1:5:10:10:5:1]

Example 21.1

Accounting for the fine structure in a spectrum

Account for the fine structure in the ^1H NMR spectrum of the C–H protons of ethanol.

Strategy Refer to Pascal's triangle to determine the effect of a group of N equivalent protons on a proton, or (equivalently) a group of protons, of interest.

Solution The three protons of the CH_3 group split the single resonance of the CH_2 protons into a 1:3:3:1 quartet with a splitting J. Likewise, the two protons of the CH_2 group split the single resonance of the CH_3 protons into a 1:2:1 triplet. Each of these lines is split into a doublet to a small extent by the OH proton.

Self-test 21.4

What fine structure can be expected for the protons in $^{14}NH_4^+$? The nuclear spin quantum number of ^{14}N is 1.

[*Answer:* a 1:1:1 triplet from ^{14}N]

The spin–spin coupling constant of two nuclei joined by N bonds is normally denoted ^{N}J, with subscripts for the types of nuclei involved. Thus, $^{1}J_{CH}$ is the coupling constant for a proton joined directly to a ^{13}C atom, and $^{2}J_{CH}$ is the coupling constant when the two nuclei are separated by two bonds (as in ^{13}C–C–H). A typical value of $^{1}J_{CH}$ is between 10^2 and 10^3 Hz; the value of $^{2}J_{CH}$ is about 10 times less, between about 10 and 10^2 Hz. Both ^{3}J and ^{4}J give detectable effects in a spectrum, but couplings over larger numbers of bonds can generally be ignored.

Illustration 21.3

Interpreting the value of the spin–spin coupling constant

Figure 21.15 shows the ^{1}H NMR spectrum of diethyl ether, $(CH_3CH_2)_2O$. The resonance at $\delta = 3.4$ corresponds to CH_2 in an ether; that at $\delta = 1.2$ corresponds to CH_3 in CH_3CH_2. As we saw in Example 21.1, the fine structure of the CH_2 group (a 1:3:3:1 quartet) is characteristic of splitting caused by CH_3; the fine structure of the CH_3 resonance is characteristic of splitting caused by CH_2. The spin–spin coupling constant is $J = -60$ Hz (the same for each group). If the spectrum had been recorded with a spectrometer operating at five times the magnetic field strength, the groups of lines would have been observed to be five times further apart in frequency (but the same δ values). No change in spin–spin splitting would be observed.

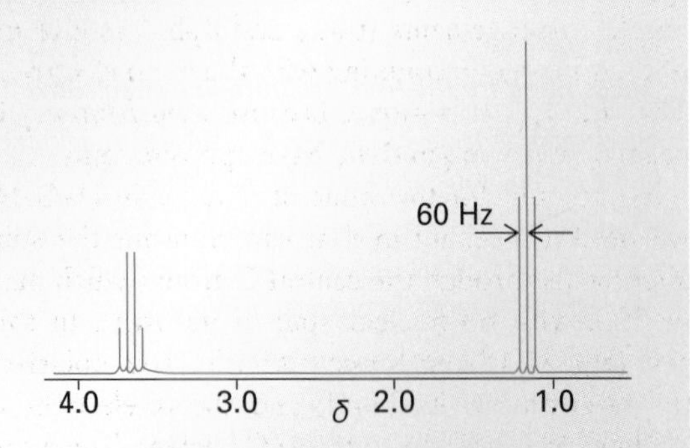

Fig. 21.15 The NMR spectrum considered in Illustration 21.3.

The magnitude of $^{3}J_{HH}$ depends on the dihedral angle, ϕ, between the two C–H bonds (**2**). The variation is expressed quite well by the **Karplus equation**:

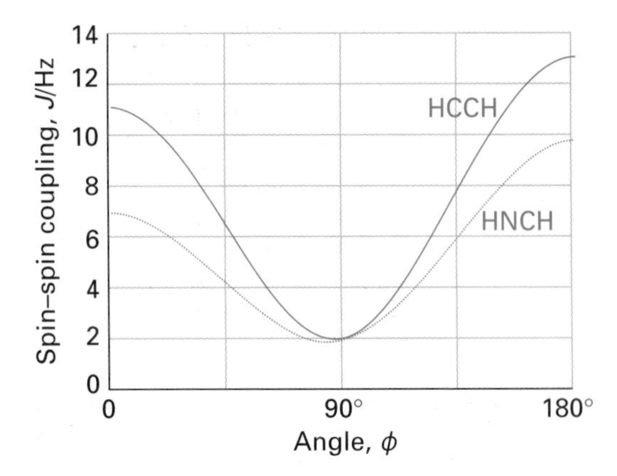

Fig. 21.16 The variation of $^{3}J_{HH}$ with angle, according to the Karplus equation for H–C–C–H and H–N–C–H.

2

$$^{3}J_{HH} = A + B\cos\phi + C\cos 2\phi \qquad (21.20)$$

Typical values of A, B, and C are +7 Hz, −1 Hz, and +5 Hz, respectively. Figure 21.16 shows the angular variation predicted by the equation. It follows that the measurement of $^{3}J_{HH}$ in a series of related compounds can be used to determine their conformations. The coupling constant $^{1}J_{CH}$ also depends on the hybridization of the C atom:

	sp	sp^2	sp^3
$^{1}J_{CH}$/Hz	250	160	125

Illustration 21.4

Determination of conformation

The investigation of H–N–C–H couplings in polypeptides can help to reveal their conformation. For $^{3}J_{HH}$ coupling in such a group, $A = +5.1$ Hz, $B = -1.4$ Hz, and $C = +3.2$ Hz. For an α helix, ϕ is close to 120°, which would give $^{3}J_{HH} \approx 4$ Hz. For a β sheet, ϕ is close to 180°, which would give $^{3}J_{HH} \approx 10$ Hz. Consequently, small coupling constants indicate an α helix whereas large couplings indicate a β sheet.

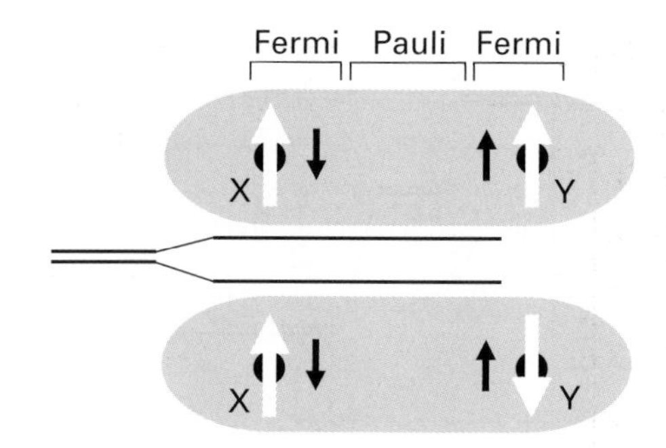

Fig. 21.17 The polarization mechanism for spin–spin coupling ($^1J_{HH}$). The two arrangements have slightly different energies. In this case, J is positive, corresponding to a lower energy when the nuclear spins are antiparallel.

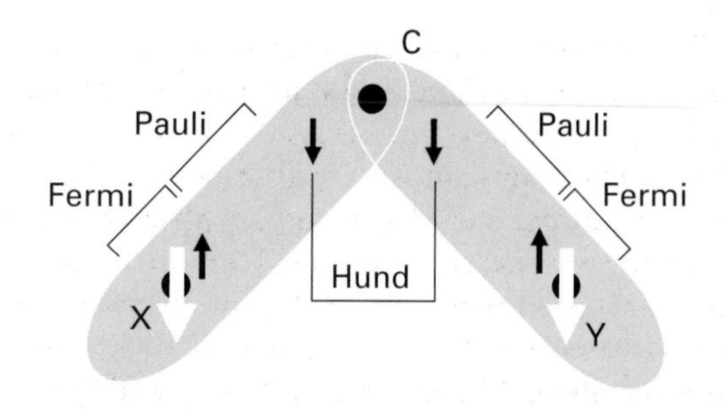

Fig. 21.18 The polarization mechanism for $^2J_{HH}$ spin–spin coupling. The spin information is transmitted from one bond to the next by a version of the mechanism that accounts for the lower energy of electrons with parallel spins in different atomic orbitals (Hund's rule of maximum multiplicity). In this case, $J < 0$, corresponding to a lower energy when the nuclear spins are parallel.

Spin–spin coupling in molecules in solution can be explained in terms of the **polarization mechanism**, in which the interaction is transmitted through the bonds. The simplest case to consider is that of $^1J_{XY}$ where X and Y are spin-$\frac{1}{2}$ nuclei joined by an electron-pair bond (Fig. 21.17). The coupling mechanism depends on the fact that in some atoms it is favourable for the nucleus and a nearby electron spin to be parallel (both α or both β), but in others it is favourable for them to be antiparallel (one α and the other β). The electron–nucleus coupling is magnetic in origin, and may be either a dipolar interaction between the magnetic moments of the electron and nuclear spins or a **Fermi contact interaction**, an interaction that depends on the very close approach of an electron to the nucleus and hence can occur only if the electron occupies an *s* orbital. We shall suppose that it is energetically favourable for an electron spin and a nuclear spin to be antiparallel (as is the case for a proton and an electron in a hydrogen atom), either $\alpha_e\beta_N$ or $\beta_e\alpha_N$, where we are using the labels e and N to distinguish the electron and nucleus spins.

If the X nucleus is α_X, a β electron of the bonding pair will tend to be found nearby (because that is energetically favourable for it). The second electron in the bond, which must have α spin if the other is β, will be found mainly at the far end of the bond (because electrons tend to stay apart to reduce their mutual repulsion). Because it is energetically favourable for the spin of Y to be antiparallel to an electron spin, a Y nucleus with β spin has a lower energy than a Y nucleus with α spin:

Low energy: $\alpha_X\beta_e \ldots \alpha_e\beta_Y$
High energy: $\alpha_X\beta_e \ldots \alpha_e\alpha_Y$

The opposite is true when X is β, because now the α spin of Y has the lower energy:

Low energy: $\beta_X\alpha_e \ldots \beta_e\alpha_Y$
High energy: $\beta_X\alpha_e \ldots \beta_e\beta_Y$

In other words, antiparallel arrangements of nuclear spins ($\alpha_X\beta_Y$ and $\beta_X\alpha_Y$) lie lower in energy than parallel arrangements ($\alpha_X\alpha_Y$ and $\beta_X\beta_Y$) as a result of their magnetic coupling with the bond electrons. That is, $^1J_{HH}$ is positive, because then hJm_Xm_Y is negative when m_X and m_Y have opposite signs.

To account for the value of $^2J_{XY}$, as in H–C–H, we need a mechanism that can transmit the spin alignments through the central C atom (which may be ^{12}C, with no nuclear spin of its own). In this case (Fig. 21.18), an X nucleus with α spin polarizes the electrons in its bond, and the α electron is likely to be found closer to the C nucleus. The more favourable arrangement of two electrons in different orbitals on the same atom is with their spins parallel (Hund's rule, Section 13.11), so the more favourable arrangement is for the α electron of the neighbouring bond to be close to the C nucleus. Consequently, the β electron of that bond is more likely to be found close to the Y nucleus, and therefore that nucleus will have a lower energy if it is α:

Low energy: $\alpha_X\beta_e \ldots \alpha_e[C]\alpha_e \ldots \beta_e\alpha_Y$
High energy: $\alpha_X\beta_e \ldots \alpha_e[C]\alpha_e \ldots \beta_e\beta_Y$

Low energy: $\beta_X\alpha_e \ldots \beta_e[C]\beta_e \ldots \alpha_e\beta_Y$
High energy: $\beta_X\alpha_e \ldots \beta_e[C]\beta_e \ldots \alpha_e\alpha_Y$

Hence, according to this mechanism, the energy of Y will be obtained if its spin is parallel ($\alpha_X\alpha_Y$ and $\beta_X\beta_Y$) to that of X. That is, ${}^2J_{HH}$ is negative, because then hJm_Xm_Y is negative when m_X and m_Y have the same sign.

The coupling of nuclear spin to electron spin by the Fermi contact interaction is most important for proton spins, but it is not necessarily the most important mechanism for other nuclei. These nuclei may also interact by a dipolar mechanism with the electron magnetic moments and with their orbital motion, and there is no simple way of specifying whether J will be positive or negative.

21.5 Spin relaxation

As resonant absorption continues, the population of the upper state rises to match that of the lower state. From eqn 21.13, we can expect the intensity of the absorption signal to decrease with time as the populations of the spin states equalize. This decrease due to the progressive equalization of populations is called **saturation**.

The fact that saturation is often not observed must mean that there are non-radiative processes by which β nuclear spins can become α spins again, and hence help to maintain the population difference between the two sites. The non-radiative return to an equilibrium distribution of populations in a system (eqn 21.9a) is an aspect of the process called **relaxation**. If we were to imagine forming a system of spins in which all the nuclei were in their β state, then the system returns exponentially to the equilibrium distribution (a small excess of α spins over β spins) with a time constant called the **spin–lattice relaxation time**, T_1 (Fig. 21.19).

However, there is another, more subtle aspect of relaxation. Let us imagine that somehow we have arranged all the spins in a sample to have exactly the same angle around the field direction at an instant. If each spin has a slightly different Larmor frequency (because they experience slightly different local magnetic fields), they will gradually fan out. At thermal equilibrium, all the bar magnets lie at *random* angles round the direction of the applied field, and the time constant for the exponential return of the system into this random arrangement is called the **spin–spin relaxation time**, T_2 (Fig. 21.20). For spins to be truly at thermal equilibrium, not only is the ratio of populations of the spin states given by eqn 21.9a but also the spin orientations must be random around the field direction.

What causes each type of relaxation? In each case the spins are responding to local magnetic fields that act to twist them into different orientations.

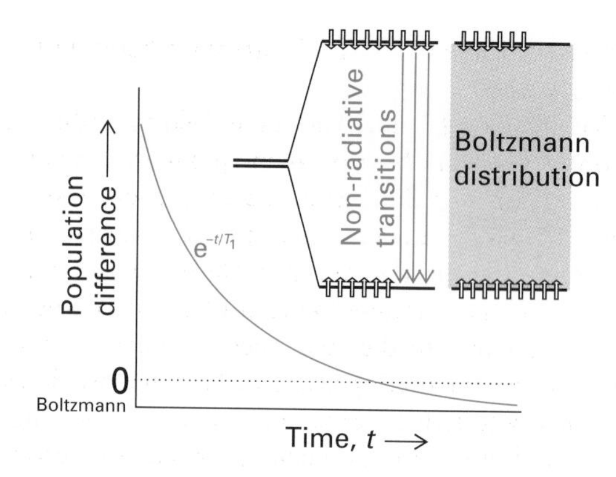

Fig. 21.19 The spin–lattice relaxation time is the time constant for the exponential return of the population of the spin states to their equilibrium (Boltzmann) distribution.

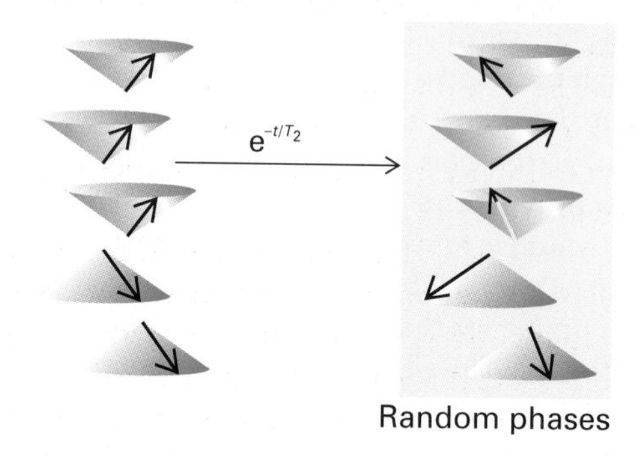

Fig. 21.20 The spin–spin relaxation time is the time constant for the exponential return of the spins to a random distribution around the direction of the magnetic field. No change in populations of the two spin states is involved in this type of relaxation, so no energy is transferred from the spins to the surroundings.

However, there is a crucial difference between the two processes.

The best kind of local magnetic field for inducing a transition from β to α (as in spin–lattice relaxation) is one that fluctuates at a frequency close to the resonance frequency. Such a field can arise from the tumbling motion of the molecule in the fluid sample. If the tumbling motion of the molecule is slow compared to the resonance frequency, it will give rise to a fluctuating magnetic field that oscillates too slowly to induce transitions, so T_1 will be long. If the molecule tumbles much faster than the resonance frequency, then it will give rise to a fluctuating magnetic field that oscillates too rapidly to induce transitions, so T_1 will again be long. Only if the molecule tumbles at about the resonance frequency will the fluctuating magnetic field be able to induce transitions effectively, and only then will T_1 be short. The rate of molecular tumbling increases with temperature and with reducing viscosity of the solvent, so we can expect a dependence like that shown in Fig. 21.21.

The best kind of local magnetic field for causing spin–spin relaxation is one that does not change very rapidly. Then each molecule in the sample lingers in its particular local magnetic environment for a long time, and the orientations of the spins have time to become randomized around the applied field direction. If the molecules move rapidly from one magnetic environment to another, the effects of different magnetic fields average out, and the

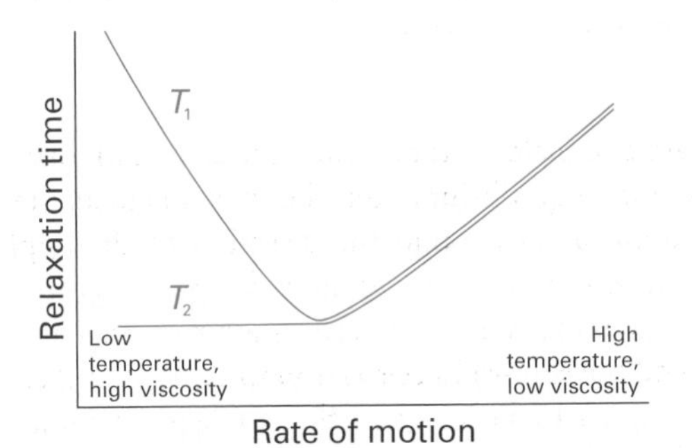

Fig. 21.21 The variation of the two relaxation times with the rate at which the molecules move (either by tumbling or migrating through the solution). The horizontal axis can be interpreted as representing temperature or viscosity. Note that at rapid rates of motion, the two relaxation times coincide.

randomization does not take place as quickly. In other words, slow molecular motion corresponds to short T_2 and fast motion corresponds to long T_2 (as shown in Fig. 21.21). Detailed calculation shows that when the motion is fast, the two relaxation times are equal, as has been drawn in the illustration.

Spin relaxation studies—using advanced techniques that make use of complicated sequences of pulses of radiofrequency energy to stimulate the spins into special orientations, and then monitoring their return to equilibrium—have two main applications. First, they reveal information about the mobility of molecules or parts of molecules. For example, by studying spin relaxation times of protons in the hydrocarbon chains of micelles and bilayers we can build up a detailed picture of the motion of these chains, and hence come to an understanding of the dynamics of cell membranes. Second, relaxation times depend on the separation of the nucleus from the source of the magnetic field that is causing its relaxation: that source may be another magnetic nucleus in the same molecule. By studying the relaxation times, we can determine the internuclear distances within the molecule and use them to build up a model of its shape.

21.6 Proton decoupling

Nuclear magnetic resonance spectroscopy is used widely to characterize newly synthesized organic compounds. Consequently, in addition to proton NMR spectra, carbon-13 NMR spectra are obtained routinely. Carbon-13 is a *dilute spin species* in the sense that it is unlikely that more than one ^{13}C nucleus will be found in any given small molecule (provided the sample has not been enriched with that isotope; the natural abundance of ^{13}C is only 1.1 per cent). Even in large molecules, although more than one ^{13}C nucleus may be present, it is unlikely that they will be close enough to give an observable splitting. Hence, it is not normally necessary to take into account ^{13}C–^{13}C spin–spin coupling within a molecule.

Protons are *abundant-spin species* in the sense that a molecule is likely to contain many of them. If we were observing a ^{13}C NMR spectrum, we would obtain a very complex spectrum on account of the coupling of the one ^{13}C nucleus with many of the protons that are present. To avoid this difficulty, ^{13}C NMR spectra are normally observed using the technique of **proton decoupling**. Thus, if the CH_3 protons of ethanol are irradiated with a second, strong, resonant radiofrequency pulse, they undergo rapid spin reorientations and the ^{13}C nucleus senses an average orientation. As a result, its resonance is a single line and not a 1:3:3:1 quartet. Proton decoupling has the additional advantage of enhancing sensitivity, because the intensity is concentrated into a single transition frequency instead of being spread over several transition frequencies. If care is taken to ensure that the other parameters on which the strength of the signal depends are kept constant, the intensities of proton-decoupled spectra are proportional to the number of ^{13}C nuclei present.

21.7 Conformational conversion and chemical exchange

The appearance of an NMR spectrum is changed if magnetic nuclei can jump rapidly between different environments. Consider a molecule, such as *N,N*-dimethylformamide, that can jump between conformations; in its case, the methyl shifts depend on whether they are *cis* or *trans* to the carbonyl group (Fig. 21.22). When the jumping rate is low, the spectrum shows two sets of lines, one each from molecules in each conformation. When the interconversion is fast, the spectrum shows a single line at the mean of the two chemical shifts. At intermediate inversion rates, the line is very broad. This maximum broadening occurs when the lifetime, τ (tau), of a conformation gives rise to a linewidth that is comparable to the difference of resonance frequencies, $\Delta\nu$, and both broadened lines blend

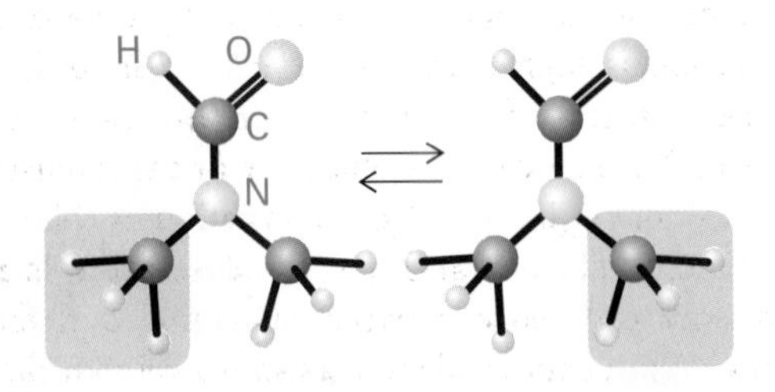

Fig. 21.22 When a molecule changes from one conformation to another, the positions of its protons are interchanged and jump between magnetically distinct environments.

together into a very broad line. Coalescence of the two lines occurs when

$$\tau = \frac{2^{1/2}}{\pi\Delta\nu} \qquad (21.21)$$

Example 21.2

Interpreting line broadening

The NO group in *N,N*-dimethylnitrosamine, $(CH_3)_2N\text{–}NO$, rotates about the N–N bond and, as a result, the magnetic environments of the two CH_3 groups are interchanged. In a 600 MHz spectrometer the two CH_3 resonances are separated by 390 Hz. At what rate of interconversion will the resonance collapse to a single line?

Strategy Use eqn 21.21 for the average lifetimes of the conformations. The rate of interconversion is the inverse of their lifetime.

Solution With $\Delta\nu = 390$ Hz,

$$\tau = \frac{2^{1/2}}{\pi \times (390\ \mathrm{s}^{-1})} = 1.2\ \mathrm{ms}$$

It follows that the signal will collapse to a single line when the interconversion rate exceeds about 830 s^{-1}.

Self-test 21.5

What would you deduce from the observation of a single line from the same molecule in a 300 MHz spectrometer?

[*Answer:* conformation lifetime less than 2.3 ms]

A similar explanation accounts for the loss of fine structure in solvents able to exchange protons with the sample. For example, hydroxyl protons are able to exchange with water protons. When this **chemical exchange** occurs, a molecule ROH with an α-spin proton (we write this ROH_α) rapidly converts to ROH_β and then perhaps to ROH_α again because the protons provided by the solvent molecules in successive exchanges have random spin orientations. Therefore, instead of seeing a spectrum composed of contributions from both ROH_α and ROH_β molecules (that is, a spectrum showing a doublet structure due to the OH proton) we see a spectrum that shows no splitting caused by coupling of the OH proton (as in Fig. 21.7). The effect is observed when the lifetime of a molecule due to this chemical exchange is so short that the lifetime broadening is greater than the doublet splitting. Because this splitting is often very small (a few hertz), a proton must remain attached to the same molecule for longer than about 0.1 s for the splitting to be observable. In water, the exchange rate is much faster than that, so alcohols show no splitting from the OH protons. In dry dimethylsulfoxide (DMSO), the exchange rate may be slow enough for the splitting to be detected.

21.8 The nuclear Overhauser effect

An effect that makes use of spin relaxation is of considerable usefulness for the determination of the conformations of proteins and other biological macromolecules in their natural aqueous environment. To introduce the effect, we consider a very simple AX system in which the two spins interact by a magnetic dipole–dipole interaction. We expect two lines in the spectrum, one from A and the other from X. However, when we irradiate the system with radiofrequency radiation at the resonance frequency of X using such a high intensity that we saturate the transition, we find that the A resonance is modified. It may be enhanced, diminished, or even converted into an emission rather than an absorption. That modification of one resonance by saturation of another is called the **nuclear Overhauser effect** (NOE).

To understand the effect, we need to think about the populations of the four levels of an AX system (Fig. 21.23). At thermal equilibrium, the population of the $\alpha_A\alpha_X$ level is the greatest, and that of the $\beta_A\beta_X$ level is the least; the other two levels have the same energy and an intermediate population. The thermal equilibrium absorption intensities reflect these populations, as the illustration shows. Now consider the combined effect of saturating the X transition and spin relaxation. When we saturate the X transition, the populations of the X levels are equalized, but at this stage there is no change in the populations of the A levels. If that were all there were to happen, all we would see would be the loss of the X resonance and no effect on the A resonance.

Now consider the effect of spin relaxation. Relaxation can occur in a variety of ways if there is a dipolar interaction between the A and X spins.

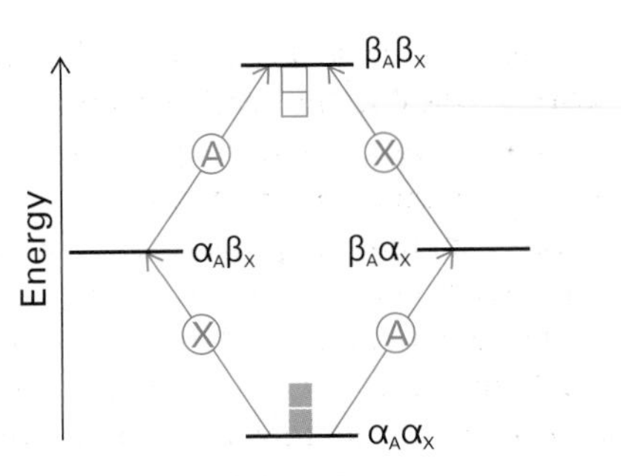

Fig. 21.23 The energy levels of an AX system and an indication of their relative populations. Each coloured square above the line represents an excess population and each white square below the line represents a population deficit. The transitions of A and X are marked.

One possibility is for the magnetic field acting between the two spins to cause them both to flop from β to α, so the $\alpha_A\alpha_X$ and $\beta_A\beta_X$ states regain their thermal equilibrium populations. However, the populations of the $\alpha_A\beta_X$ and $\beta_A\alpha_X$ levels remain unchanged at the values characteristic of saturation. As we see from Fig. 21.24, the population difference between the states joined by transitions of A is now greater than at equilibrium, so the resonance absorption is enhanced. Another possibility is for the dipolar interaction between the two spins to cause α to flip to β and β to flop to α. This transition equilibrates the populations of $\alpha_A\beta_X$ and $\beta_A\alpha_X$ but leaves the $\alpha_A\alpha_X$ and $\beta_A\beta_X$ populations unchanged (Fig. 21.25). Now we see from the illustration that the population differences in the states involved in the A transitions are decreased, so the resonance absorption is diminished.

Which effect wins? Does the NOE enhance the A absorption or does it diminish it? As in the discussion of relaxation times in Section 21.5, the efficiency of the intensity-enhancing $\beta_A\beta_X \leftrightarrow \alpha_A\alpha_X$ relaxation is high if the dipole field is modulated at the transition frequency, which in this case is close to 2ω; likewise, the efficiency of the intensity-diminishing $\alpha_A\beta_X \leftrightarrow \beta_A\alpha_X$ relaxation is high if the dipole field is stationary (because there is no frequency difference between the initial and final states). A large molecule rotates so slowly that there is very little motion at 2ω, so we expect intensity decrease (Fig. 21.26). A small molecule rotating rapidly can be expected to have substantial motion

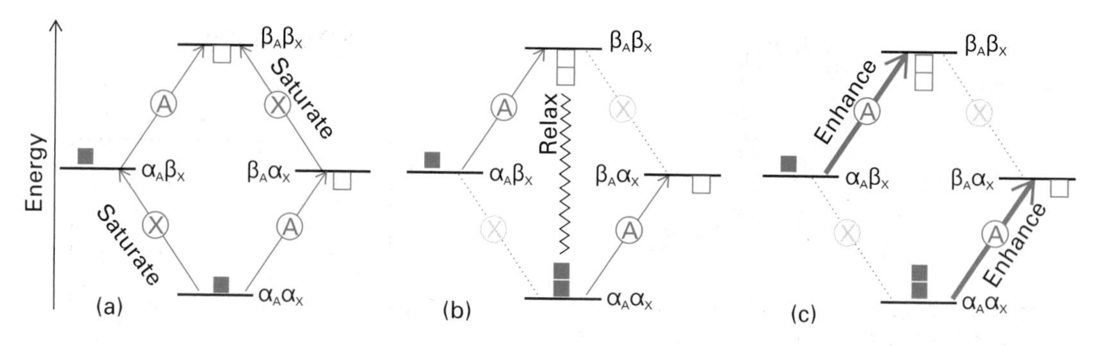

Fig. 21.24 (a) When the X transition is saturated, the populations of its two states are equalized and the population excess and deficit become as shown (using the same symbols as in Fig. 21.23). (b) Dipole–dipole relaxation relaxes the populations of the highest and lowest states, and they regain their original populations. (c) The A transitions reflect the difference in populations resulting from the preceding changes, and are enhanced compared with those shown in Fig. 21.23.

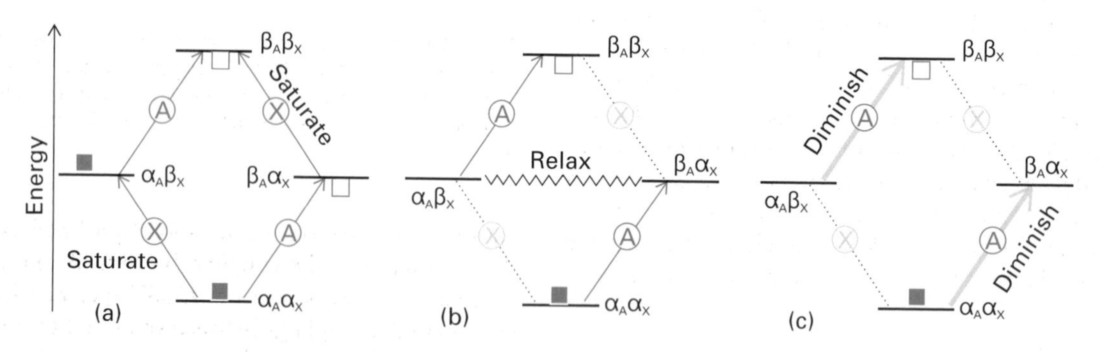

Fig. 21.25 (a) When the X transition is saturated, just as in Fig. 21.24 the populations of its two states are equalized and the population excess and deficit become as shown. (b) Dipole–dipole relaxation relaxes the populations of the two intermediate states, and they regain their original populations. (c) The A transitions reflect the difference in populations resulting from the preceding changes, and are diminished compared with those shown in Fig. 21.23.

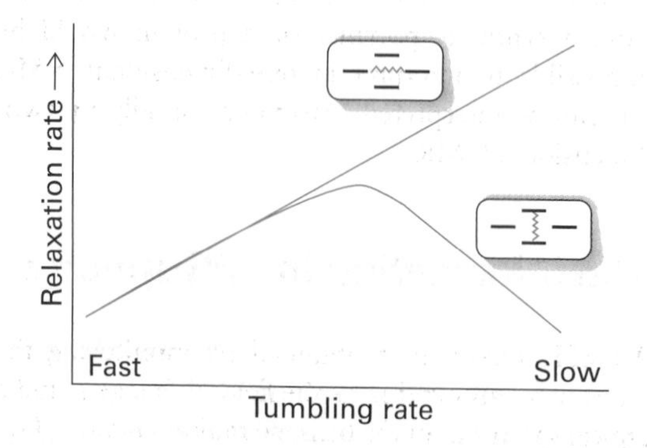

Fig. 21.26 The relaxation rates of the two types of relaxation (as indicated by the small diagrams) as a function of the tumbling rate of the molecule.

at 2ω, and a consequent enhancement of the signal. In practice, the enhancement lies somewhere between the two extremes and is reported in terms of the parameter η (eta), where

$$\eta = \frac{I - I_0}{I_0} \tag{21.22}$$

Here I_0 is the normal intensity and I is the NOE intensity of a particular transition; theoretically, η lies between -1 (diminution) and $+\frac{1}{2}$ (enhancement).

The value of η depends strongly on the separation of the two spins involved in the NOE, as the strength of the dipolar interaction between two spins separated by a distance r is proportional to

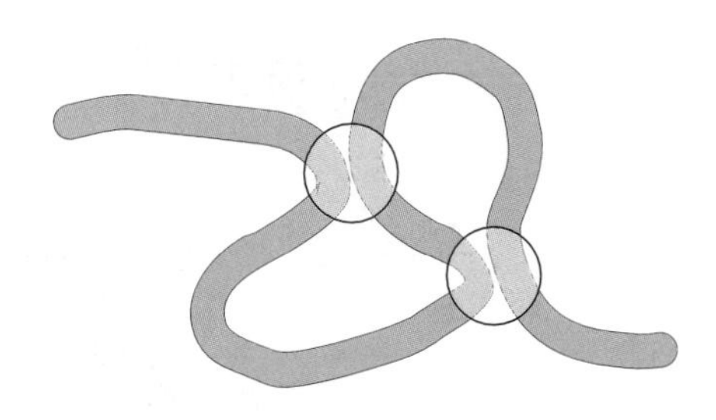

Fig. 21.27 If a NOE experiment shows that the protons within each of the two circles are coupled by a dipolar interaction, we can be confident that those protons are close together, and therefore infer the conformation of the polypeptide chain.

$1/r^3$ and its effect depends on the square of that strength, and therefore on $1/r^6$. This sharp dependence on separation is used to build up a picture of the conformation of a protein by using NOE to identify which nuclei can be regarded as neighbours (Fig. 21.27). The enormous importance of this procedure is that we can determine the conformation of polypeptides in an aqueous environment and do not need to try to make the single crystals that are essential for an X-ray diffraction investigation.

21.9 Two-dimensional NMR

An NMR spectrum contains a great deal of information and, if many spins are present, is very complex, as the fine structure of different groups of lines can overlap. The complexity would be reduced if we could use two axes to display the data, with resonances belonging to different groups lying at different locations on the second axis. This separation is essentially what is achieved in **two-dimensional NMR.**

Much modern NMR work makes use of techniques such as **correlation spectroscopy** (COSY) in which a clever choice of pulses and Fourier-transformation techniques makes it possible to determine all spin–spin couplings in a molecule. The COSY spectrum of an AX system contains four groups of signals centred on the two chemical shifts. Each group shows fine structure, consisting of a block of four signals separated by J_{AX}. The *diagonal peaks* are signals centred on (δ_A,δ_A) and (δ_X,δ_X) and lie along the diagonal. The *cross peaks* (or *off-diagonal peaks*)

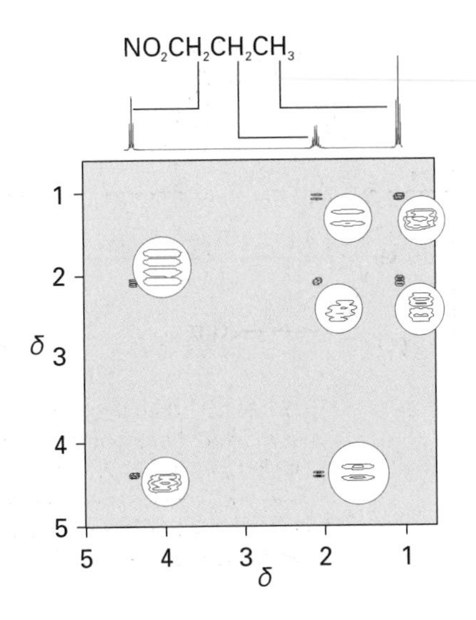

Fig. 21.28 Proton COSY spectrum of 1-nitropropane. The off-diagonal peaks show that the CH_3 protons are coupled to the central CH_2 protons, which in turn are coupled to the terminal CH_2NO_2 protons. (Spectrum provided by Professor G. Morris.)

are signals centred on (δ_A,δ_X) and (δ_X,δ_A) and owe their existence to the coupling between A and X. Consequently, cross peaks in COSY spectra allow us to map the couplings between spins and to trace out the bonding network in complex molecules. Figure 21.28 shows a simple example of a proton COSY spectrum of 1-nitropropane.

Although information from two-dimensional NMR spectroscopy is trivial in an AX system, it can be of enormous help in the interpretation of more complex spectra. For example, a complex spectrum from a synthetic polymer or a protein would be impossible to interpret in one-dimensional NMR but can be interpreted reasonably rapidly by two-dimensional NMR.

The information in EPR spectra

An EPR spectrum is obtained by monitoring the microwave absorption as the field is changed, and a typical spectrum (of the benzene radical anion, $C_6H_6^-$) is shown in Fig. 21.29. The peculiar appearance of the spectrum, which is in fact the first-derivative of the absorption, arises from the detection technique,

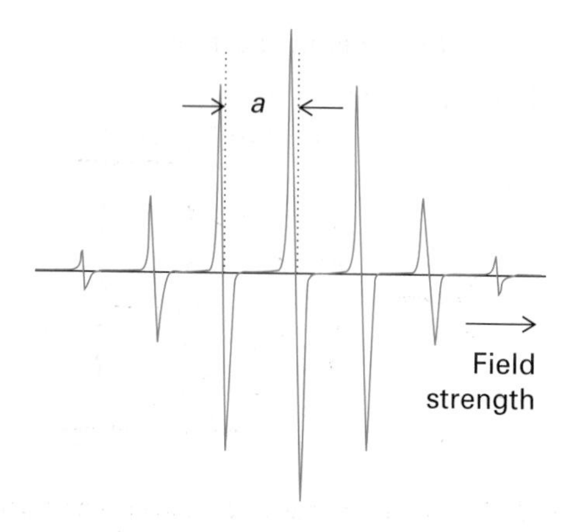

Fig. 21.29 The EPR spectrum of the benzene radical anion, $C_6H_6^-$, in fluid solution. *a* is the hyperfine splitting of the spectrum; the centre of the spectrum is determined by the *g*-value of the radical.

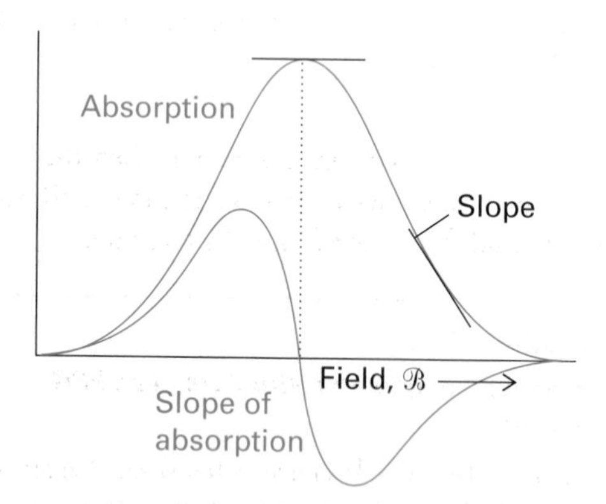

Fig. 21.30 When phase-sensitive detection is used, the signal is the first derivative of the absorption intensity. Note that the peak of the absorption corresponds to the point where the derivative passes through zero.

which is sensitive to the slope of the absorption curve (Fig. 21.30).

21.10 The *g*-value

Equation 21.10 gives the resonance frequency for a transition between the $m_s = -\frac{1}{2}$ and the $m_s = +\frac{1}{2}$ levels of a 'free' electron in terms of the *g*-value $g_e \approx 2.0023$. The magnetic moment of an unpaired electron in a radical also interacts with an external field, but the *g*-value is different from that of a free electron on account of local magnetic fields induced in the molecular framework of the radical. Consequently, the resonance condition is normally written as

$$h\nu = g\mu_B\mathcal{B} \tag{21.23}$$

where *g* is the **g-value** of the radical. Many organic radicals have *g*-values close to 2.0027; inorganic radicals have *g*-values typically in the range 1.9–2.1; paramagnetic *d*-metal complexes have *g*-values in a wider range (for example, 0 to 6).

The deviation of *g* from $g_e = 2.0023$ depends on the ability of the applied field to induce local electron currents in the radical, and therefore its value gives some information about electronic structure. In that sense, the *g*-value plays a role in EPR similar to the shielding constants in NMR. However, because that of *g*-values differ very little from g_e in many radicals (for instance, 2.003 for H, 1.999 for NO_2, and 2.01 for ClO_2), its main use in chemical applications is to aid the identification of the species present in a sample.

Illustration 21.5

Determining a g-value

The centre of the EPR spectrum of the methyl radical occurred at 329.40 mT in an X-band spectrometer operating at 9.2330 GHz. Its *g*-value is therefore

$$g = \frac{h\nu}{\mu_B\mathcal{B}} = \frac{(6.626\,08 \times 10^{-34}\ \text{J s}) \times \overbrace{(9.2330 \times 10^{9}\ \text{s}^{-1})}^{9.2330\ \text{GHz}}}{(9.2740 \times 10^{-24}\ \text{J T}^{-1}) \times (0.329\,40\ \text{T})}$$
$$= 2.0027$$

Self-test 21.6

At what magnetic field would the methyl radical come into resonance in a Q-band spectrometer operating at 34.000 GHz?

[*Answer:* 1.213 T]

21.11 Hyperfine structure

The most important features of EPR spectra are their **hyperfine structure**, the splitting of individual resonance lines into components. In general in spectroscopy, the term 'hyperfine structure' means the structure of a spectrum that can be traced to interactions of the electrons with nuclei other than as a result of the latter's point electric charge. The source of the hyperfine structure in EPR is the magnetic interaction between the electron spin and the magnetic dipole moments of the nuclei present in the radical.

Consider the effect on the EPR spectrum of a single H nucleus located somewhere in a radical. The proton spin is a source of magnetic field, and depending on the orientation of the nuclear spin, the field it generates adds to or subtracts from the applied field. The total local field is therefore

$$\mathcal{B}_{\text{loc}} = \mathcal{B} + am_I \qquad m_I = \pm\tfrac{1}{2} \tag{21.24}$$

where a is the **hyperfine coupling constant.** Half the radicals in a sample have $m_I = +\frac{1}{2}$, so half resonate when the applied field satisfies the condition

$$h\nu = g\mu_B(\mathcal{B} + \tfrac{1}{2}a), \quad \text{or } \mathcal{B} = \frac{h\nu}{g\mu_B} - \tfrac{1}{2}a \tag{21.25a}$$

The other half (which have $m_I = -\frac{1}{2}$) resonate when

$$h\nu = g\mu_B(\mathcal{B} - \tfrac{1}{2}a), \quad \text{or } \mathcal{B} = \frac{h\nu}{g\mu_B} + \tfrac{1}{2}a \tag{21.25b}$$

Therefore, instead of a single line, the spectrum shows two lines of half the original intensity separated by a and centred on the field determined by g (Fig. 21.31).

If the radical contains an ^{14}N atom ($I = 1$), its EPR spectrum consists of three lines of equal intensity, because the ^{14}N nucleus has three possible spin orientations, and each spin orientation is possessed by one-third of all the radicals in the sample. In general, a spin-I nucleus splits the spectrum into $2I + 1$ hyperfine lines of equal intensity.

When there are several magnetic nuclei present in the radical, each one contributes to the hyperfine structure. In the case of equivalent protons (for example, the two CH_2 protons in the radical CH_3CH_2) some of the hyperfine lines are coincident. It is not hard to show that if the radical contains N equivalent protons, then there are $N + 1$ hyperfine lines with an intensity distribution given by Pascal's triangle (Section 21.4). The spectrum of the benzene radical anion in Fig. 21.29, which has seven lines with intensity ratio 1:6:15:20:15:6:1, is consistent with a radical containing six equivalent protons. More generally, if the radical contains N equivalent nuclei with spin quantum number I, then there are $2NI + 1$ hyperfine lines with an intensity distribution given by modifications of Pascal's triangle.

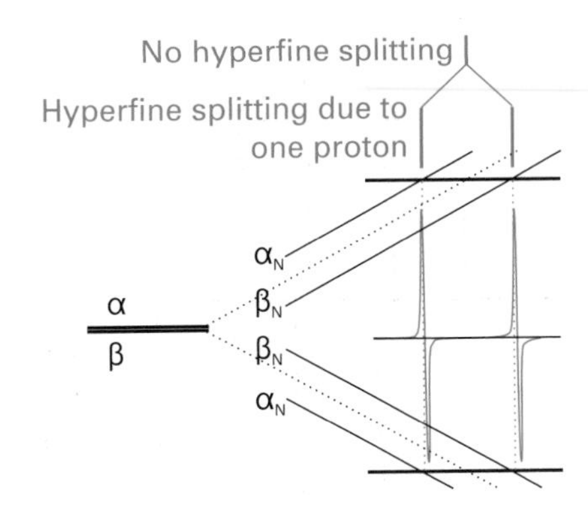

Fig. 21.31 The hyperfine interaction between an electron and a spin-$\frac{1}{2}$ nucleus results in four energy levels in place of the original two. As a result, the spectrum consists of two lines (of equal intensity) instead of one. The intensity distribution can be summarized by a simple stick diagram. The diagonal lines show the energies of the states as the applied field is increased, and resonance occurs when the separation of states matches the fixed energy of the microwave photon.

Example 21.3

Predicting the hyperfine structure of an EPR spectrum

A radical contains one ^{14}N nucleus ($I = 1$) with hyperfine constant 1.61 mT and two equivalent protons ($I = \frac{1}{2}$) with hyperfine constant 0.35 mT. Predict the form of the EPR spectrum.

Strategy We should consider the hyperfine structure that arises from each type of nucleus or group of equivalent nuclei in succession. So, split a line with one nucleus, then each of those lines is split by a second nucleus (or group of nuclei), and so on. It is best to start with the nucleus with the largest hyperfine splitting; however, any choice could be made, and the order in which nuclei are considered does not affect the conclusion.

Solution The ^{14}N nucleus gives three hyperfine lines of equal intensity separated by 1.61 mT. Each line is split into doublets of spacing 0.35 mT by the first proton, and each line of these doublets is split into doublets with the same 0.35 mT splitting (Fig. 21.32). The central lines of each split doublet coincide, so the proton

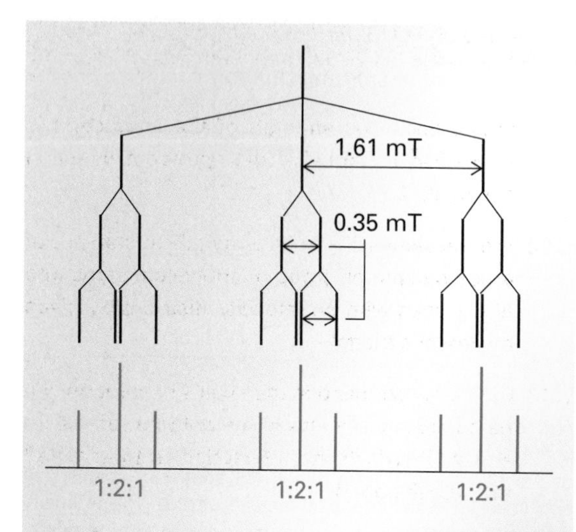

Fig. 21.32 The analysis of the hyperfine structure of radicals containing one ^{14}N nucleus ($I = 1$) and two equivalent protons.

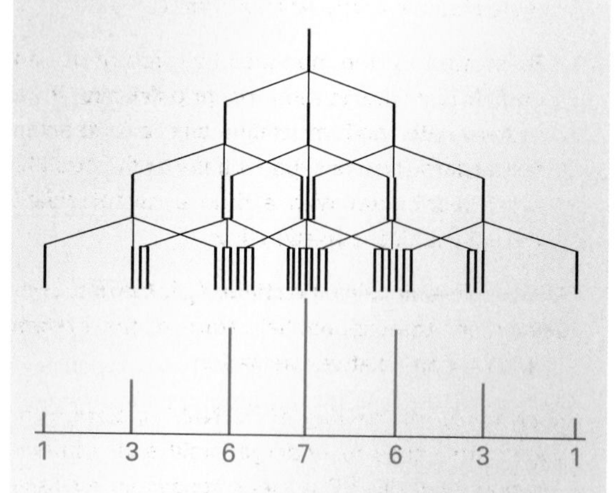

Fig. 21.33 The analysis of the hyperfine structure of radicals containing three equivalent ^{14}N nuclei.

splitting gives 1:2:1 triplets of internal splitting 0.35 mT. Therefore, the spectrum consists of three equivalent 1:2:1 triplets.

Self-test 21.7

Predict the form of the EPR spectrum of a radical containing three equivalent ^{14}N nuclei.

[*Answer:* Fig. 21.33]

The hyperfine structure of an EPR spectrum is a kind of fingerprint that helps to identify the radicals present in a sample. The interaction between the unpaired electron and the hydrogen nucleus responsible for hyperfine structure is either a dipolar interaction or the Fermi contact interaction described in Section 21.4. In the case of the contact interaction, the magnitude of the splitting depends on the distribution of the unpaired electron near the magnetic nuclei present, so the spectrum can be used to map the molecular orbital occupied by the unpaired electron. For example, because the hyperfine splitting in $C_6H_6^-$ is 0.375 mT, and one proton is close to a C atom with one-sixth the unpaired electron density (because the electron is spread uniformly around the ring), the hyperfine splitting caused by a proton in the electron spin entirely confined to a single adjacent C atom should be $6 \times 0.375\ \text{mT} = 2.25\ \text{mT}$. If in another aromatic radical we find a hyperfine splitting constant a, then the **spin density**, ρ, the probability that an unpaired electron is on the atom, can be calculated from the **McConnell equation:**

$$a = Q\rho \qquad (21.26)$$

with $Q = 2.25$ mT. In this equation, ρ is the spin density on a C atom and a is the hyperfine splitting observed for the H atom to which it is attached.

CHECKLIST OF KEY IDEAS

You should now be familiar with the following concepts

☐ 1 Resonance is the condition of strong effective coupling when the frequencies of two oscillators are identical.

☐ 2 The energy of an electron in a magnetic field $\mathcal{B}$ is $E_{m_s} = -g_e\gamma\hbar\mathcal{B}m_s$, where γ is the magnetogyric ratio of the electron.

☐ 3 The energy of a nucleus in a magnetic field $\mathcal{B}$ is $E_{m_I} = -\gamma_N\hbar\mathcal{B}m_I$, where γ_N is the nuclear magnetogyric ratio.

☐ 4 The resonance condition for an electron in a magnetic field is $h\nu = g_e\mu_B\mathcal{B}$.

☐ 5 The resonance condition for a nucleus in a magnetic field is $h\nu = \gamma_N\hbar\mathcal{B}$.

☐ 6 Nuclear magnetic resonance (NMR) is the observation of the frequency at which magnetic nuclei in molecules come into resonance with an electromagnetic field when the molecule is exposed to a strong magnetic field; NMR is a radiofrequency technique.

☐ 7 Electron paramagnetic resonance (EPR) or electron spin resonance (ESR) is the observation of the frequency at which an electron spin comes into resonance with an electromagnetic field when the molecule is exposed to a strong magnetic field; EPR is a microwave technique.

☐ 8 The intensity of an NMR or EPR transition increases with the difference in population of α and β states and the strength of the applied magnetic field (as $\mathcal{B}^2$).

☐ 9 The chemical shift of a nucleus is the difference between its resonance frequency and that of a reference standard; chemical shifts are reported on the δ scale, in which $\delta = (\nu - \nu^\circ) \times 10^6/\nu^\circ$.

☐ 10 The observed shielding constant is the sum of a local contribution, a neighbouring group contribution, and a solvent contribution.

☐ 11 The fine structure of an NMR spectrum is the splitting of the groups of resonances into individual lines; the strength of the interaction is expressed in terms of the spin–spin coupling constant, J.

☐ 12 N equivalent spin-$\frac{1}{2}$ nuclei split the resonance of a nearby spin or group of equivalent spins into $N + 1$ lines with an intensity distribution given by Pascal's triangle.

☐ 13 Spin–spin coupling in molecules in solution can be explained in terms of the polarization mechanism, in which the interaction is transmitted through the bonds.

☐ 14 The Fermi contact interaction is a magnetic interaction that depends on the very close approach of an electron to the nucleus and can occur only if the electron occupies an *s* orbital.

☐ 15 Relaxation is the non-radiative return to an equilibrium distribution of populations in a system with random relative spin orientations; the system returns exponentially to the equilibrium distribution with a time constant called the spin–lattice relaxation time, T_1.

☐ 16 The spin–spin relaxation time, T_2, is the time constant for the exponential return of the system into random relative orientations.

☐ 17 In proton decoupling of ^{13}C NMR spectra, protons are made to undergo rapid spin reorientations and the ^{13}C nucleus senses an average orientation. As a result, its resonance is a single line and not a group of lines.

☐ 18 Coalescence of the two lines occurs in conformational interchange or chemical exchange when the lifetime, τ, of the states is related to their resonance frequency difference, $\Delta\nu$, by $\tau = 2^{1/2}/\pi\Delta\nu$.

☐ 19 The nuclear Overhauser effect (NOE) is the modification of one resonance by the saturation of another.

☐ 20 In two-dimensional NMR, spectra are displayed in two axes, with resonances belonging to different groups lying at different locations on the second axis. An example of a two-dimensional NMR technique is correlation spectroscopy (COSY), in which all spin–spin couplings in a molecule are determined.

☐ 21 The EPR resonance condition is written $h\nu = g\mu_B\mathcal{B}$, where g is the g-value of the radical; the deviation of g from $g_e = 2.0023$ depends on the ability of the applied field to induce local electron currents in the radical.

☐ 22 The hyperfine structure of an EPR spectrum is its splitting of individual resonance lines into components by the magnetic interaction of the electron and nuclei with spin.

☐ 23 If a radical contains N equivalent nuclei with spin quantum number I, then there are $2NI + 1$ hyperfine lines with an intensity distribution given by a modification of Pascal's triangle.

☐ 24 The hyperfine structure due to a hydrogen attached to an aromatic ring is converted to spin density, ρ, on the neighbouring carbon atom by using the McConnell equation: $a = Q\rho$ with $Q = 2.25$ mT.

DISCUSSION QUESTIONS

21.1 Discuss the origins of the local, neighbouring group, and solvent contributions to the shielding constant.

21.2 Suggest a reason why the relaxation times of ^{13}C nuclei are typically much longer than those of ^{1}H nuclei.

21.3 Why does the removal of dissolved oxygen from a solution commonly increase the spin relaxation time of the solute?

21.4 Suggest a reason why the spin–lattice relaxation time of benzene (a small molecule) in a mobile, deuterated hydrocarbon solvent increases whereas that of a oligopeptide (a large molecule) decreases.

21.5 Discuss how the Fermi contact interaction and the polarization mechanism contribute to spin–spin couplings in NMR.

21.6 Explain how the EPR spectrum of an organic radical can be used to pinpoint the molecular orbital occupied by the unpaired electron.

EXERCISES

The symbol ‡ indicates that calculus is required.

21.7 Calculate the energy separation between the spin states of an electron in a magnetic field of 0.300 T.

21.8 The nucleus ^{32}S has a spin of $\frac{3}{2}$ and a nuclear g factor of 0.4289. Calculate the energies of the nuclear spin states in a magnetic field of 7.500 T.

21.9 Equations 21.5 and 21.7 define the g-value and the magnetogyric ratio of a nucleus. Given that g is a dimensionless number, what are the units of γ_N expressed in (a) tesla and hertz, (b) SI base units?

21.10 The magnetogyric ratio of ^{31}P is 1.0840×10^8 T^{-1} s^{-1}. What is the g-value of the nucleus?

21.11 Calculate the value of $(N_\beta - N_\alpha)/N$ for electrons in a field of (a) 0.30 T, (b) 1.1 T.

21.12 Calculate the resonance frequency and the corresponding wavelength for an electron in a magnetic field of 0.330 T, the magnetic field commonly used in EPR.

21.13 Calculate the value of $(N_\alpha - N_\beta)/N$ for (a) protons, (b) carbon-13 nuclei in a field of 10 T.

21.14 The magnetogyric ratio of ^{19}F is 2.5177×10^8 T^{-1} s^{-1}. Calculate the frequency of the nuclear transition in a field of 8.200 T.

21.15 Calculate the resonance frequency of a ^{14}N nucleus ($I = 1$, $g = 0.4036$) in a 15.00 T magnetic field.

21.16 Calculate the magnetic field needed to satisfy the resonance condition for unshielded protons in a 550.0 MHz radiofrequency field.

21.17 What is the shift of the resonance from TMS of a group of protons with $\delta = 6.33$ in a polypeptide in a spectrometer operating at 420 MHz?

21.18 The chemical shift of the CH_3 protons in acetaldehyde (ethanal) is $\delta = 2.20$ and that of the CHO proton is 9.80. What is the difference in local magnetic field between the two regions of the molecule when the applied field is (a) 1.5 T, (b) 6.0 T?

21.19 Using the information in Fig. 21.6, state the splitting (in hertz, Hz) between the methyl and aldehydic proton resonances in a spectrometer operating at (a) 300 MHz, (b) 550 MHz.

21.20 What would be the nuclear magnetic resonance spectrum for a proton resonance line that was split by interaction with seven identical protons?

21.21 What would be the nuclear magnetic resonance spectrum for a proton resonance line that was split by interaction with (a) two, (b) three equivalent nitrogen nuclei (the spin of a nitrogen nucleus is 1)?

21.22 Repeat Derivation 21.3 for an AX_2 spin-$\frac{1}{2}$ system and deduce the pattern of lines expected in the spectrum.

21.23 Sketch the appearance of the ^{1}H NMR spectrum of acetaldehyde (ethanal) using J = 2.90 Hz and the data in Fig. 21.6 in a spectrometer operating at (a) 300 MHz, (b) 550 MHz.

21.24 Sketch the form of the ^{19}F NMR spectra of a natural sample of $^{10}BF_4^-$ and $^{11}BF_4^-$.

21.25 Sketch the form of an $A_3M_2X_4$ spectrum, where A, M, and X are protons with distinctly different chemical shifts and $J_{AM} > J_{AX} > J_{MX}$.

21.26 ‡ Show that the coupling constant as expressed by the Karplus equation passes through a minimum when $\cos\phi = B/4C$. (*Hint*. Use calculus: evaluate the first derivative with respect to ϕ and set the result equal to 0. To confirm that the extremum is a minimum, go on to evaluate the second derivative and show that it is positive.)

21.27 A proton jumps between two sites with δ = 2.7 and δ = 4.8. At what rate of interconversion will the two signals collapse to a single line in a spectrometer operating at 550 MHz?

21.28 The centre of the EPR spectrum of atomic hydrogen lies at 329.12 mT in a spectrometer operating at 9.2231 GHz. What is the *g*-value of the atom?

21.29 A radical containing two equivalent protons shows a three-line spectrum with an intensity distribution 1:2:1. The lines occur at 330.2 mT, 332.5 mT, and 334.8 mT. What is the hyperfine coupling constant for each proton? What is the *g*-value of the radical given that the spectrometer is operating at 9.319 GHz?

21.30 Predict the intensity distribution in the hyperfine lines of the EPR spectra of (a) $\cdot CH_3$, (b) $\cdot CD_3$.

21.31 The benzene radical anion has g = 2.0025. At what field should you search for resonance in a spectrometer operating at (a) 9.302 GHz, (b) 33.67 GHz?

21.32 The EPR spectrum of a radical with two equivalent nuclei of a particular kind is split into five lines of intensity ratio 1:2:3:2:1. What is the spin of the nuclei?

21.33 The hyperfine coupling constants observed in the radical anions (**3**), (**4**), and (**5**) are shown (in millitesla, mT). Use the McConnell equation to map the probability of finding the unpaired electron in the π orbital on each C atom.

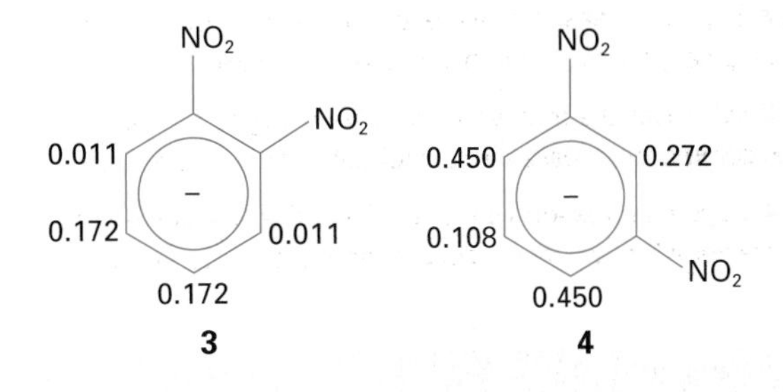

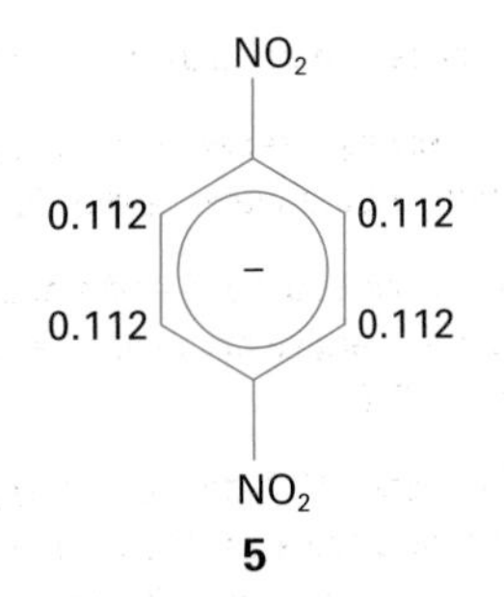

Chapter 22

Statistical thermodynamics

There are two great rivers in physical chemistry. One is the river of thermodynamics, which deals with the relations between bulk properties of matter, particularly properties related to the transfer of energy. The other is the river of molecular structure, including spectroscopy, which deals with the structures and properties of individual atoms and molecules. These two great rivers flow together in the part of physical chemistry called **statistical thermodynamics**, which shows how thermodynamic properties emerge from the properties of atoms and molecules. The first half of this book dealt with thermodynamic properties; the second half has dealt with atomic and molecular structure and its investigation. This is the chapter where the two great rivers merge.

A great problem with statistical thermodynamics is that it is highly mathematical.[1] Many of the derivations—even the most fundamental—are beyond the scope of this text.[2] All we can hope to see is some of the key concepts and the key results. Where possible the treatment will be qualitative.

The partition function

The key concept of quantum mechanics is the existence of a wavefunction that contains in principle all the dynamical information about a system,

[1] In this chapter, some *Examples*, *Self-tests*, and *Illustrations* require calculus: they are marked with the symbol ‡.

[2] See P. Atkins and J. de Paula, *Physical chemistry*, 7th edn, Oxford University Press/W.H. Freeman (2002), for details.

such as its energy, the electron density, the dipole moment, and so on. Once we know the wavefunction of an atom or molecule, we can extract from it all the dynamical information possible about the system—provided we know how to manipulate it. There is a similar concept in statistical thermodynamics. The **partition function**, q, contains all the *thermo*dynamic information about the system, such as its internal energy, entropy, heat capacity, and so on. Our task here is to see how to calculate the partition function and how to extract the information it contains.

22.1 The Boltzmann distribution

The single most important result in the whole of statistical thermodynamics is the **Boltzmann distribution**, the formula that tells us how to calculate the numbers of molecules in each state of a system at any temperature:[3]

$$N_i = \frac{N\,e^{-E_i/kT}}{q} \qquad (22.1)$$

Here N_i is the number of molecules in a state with energy E_i, N is the total number of molecules, k is Boltzmann's constant, a fundamental constant with the value 1.381×10^{-23} J K^{-1}, and T is the absolute temperature.[4] The term in the denominator, q, is the **partition function:**

$$q = \sum_i e^{-E_i/kT} = e^{-E_0/kT} + e^{-E_1/kT} + \ldots \qquad (22.2)$$

where the sum is over all the states of the system. We shall have much more to say about q later, and see how it can be calculated and given physical meaning.

The conceptual basis of the derivation of eqn 22.1 is very simple. We imagine a stack of energy levels arranged like bookshelves, one above the other. Then we imagine being blindfolded and throwing balls (the molecules) at the shelves (the energy levels) and letting them land on the available shelves entirely at random, apart from one condition. That condition is that the total energy, E, of the final arrangement must have the actual energy of the sample of matter we are seeking to describe. So, provided the temperature is above absolute zero, not all the balls are allowed to land on the bottom shelf, as that would give a total energy of zero. Some of the balls may land on the bottom shelf, but there

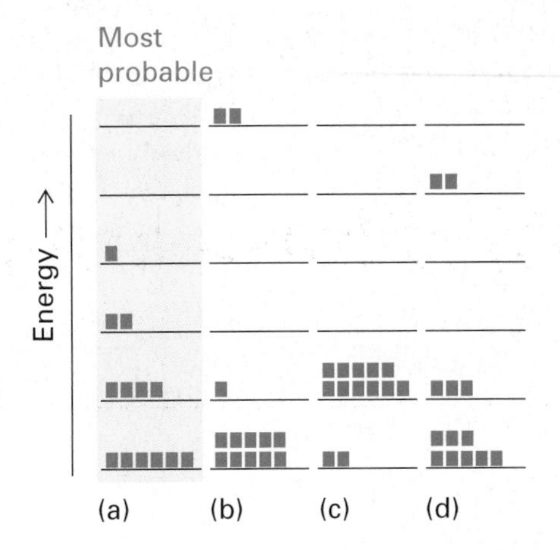

Fig. 22.1 The derivation of the Boltzmann distribution involves imagining that the molecules of a system (the squares) are distributed at random over the available energy levels subject to the requirements that the number of molecules and the total energy is constant, and then looking for the most probable arrangement. Of the four shown here, the numbers of ways of achieving each arrangement are (a) 181 180, (b) 858, (c) 78, (d) 12 870.[5] The number of ways of achieving (a) is by far the greatest, so this distribution is the most probable; it corresponds to the Boltzmann distribution.

must be others ending up on higher shelves to ensure that the total energy is E. If we imagine throwing 100 balls at a set of shelves, then we will end up with one particular valid distribution. If we repeated the experiment with the same number of balls, we would end up with a different but still valid distribution. If we went on repeating the experiment, we would get many different distributions, but some of them would occur more often than others (Fig. 22.1).

When this game is analysed mathematically, it turns out that the *most probable* distribution—the arrangement that turns up most often—is that given by eqn 22.1. In other words, *the Boltzmann distribution is the outcome of blind chance occupation of energy levels, subject to the requirement that the total energy has a particular value.* When we deal with about 10^{23} molecules and repeat the experiment

[3] Throughout this chapter 'molecules' will include single atoms or any other entities.

[4] The Boltzmann constant k and the gas constant R are related by $R = N_A k$, but k is arguably the more fundamental of the two constants. The gas constant is a 'molar Boltzmann constant'.

[5] To calculate the number of ways, W, of arranging N molecules with N_1 in state 1, N_2 in state 2, etc., use $W = N!/N_1!N_2!\ldots$, with $n! = n(n-1)(n-2)\ldots 1$, and $0! = 1$.

millions of times, the Boltzmann distribution turns out to be very accurate, and we can use it with confidence for all typical samples of matter.

The simplest application of the Boltzmann distribution is to calculate the relative numbers of molecules in two states separated in energy by ΔE. Suppose the energies of the two states are E_1 and E_2, then from eqn 22.1 we can write

$$\frac{N_2}{N_1} = \underbrace{\frac{N\,e^{-E_2/kT}/q}{N\,e^{-E_1/kT}/q}}_{\text{Boltzmann distribution}} = \frac{e^{-E_2/kT}}{e^{-E_1/kT}} = e^{-(E_2-E_1)/kT} = e^{-\Delta E/kT} \qquad (22.3)$$

where $\Delta E = E_2 - E_1$. This important result tells us that *the relative population of the upper state decreases exponentially with its energy above the lower state*. In this expression, the energy difference is in joules. If the energy difference is given in joules (or kilojoules) per mole, we simply use the gas constant in eqn 22.3 in place of Boltzmann's constant (because $R = kN_A$).

Illustration 22.1

Using the Boltzmann distribution

The boat conformation of cyclohexane (**1**) lies 22 kJ mol^{-1} higher in energy than the chair conformation (**2**). To find the relative populations of the two conformations in a sample of cyclohexane at 20°C, we set ΔE = 22 kJ mol^{-1} (that is, 22×10^3 J mol^{-1}) and T = 293 K and use eqn 22.3 with R in the exponent. We obtain:

$$\frac{N_{boat}}{N_{chair}} = e^{-\frac{22\times10^3\ \mathrm{J\,mol^{-1}}\ (\Delta E)}{(8.314\,47\ \mathrm{J\,K^{-1}\,mol^{-1}})\ (R) \times (293\ \mathrm{K})\ (T)}} = e^{-\frac{22\times10^3}{8.314\,47\times293}}$$

$$= 1.2 \times 10^{-4}$$

A note on good practice Note how the units cancel in the exponent: as always, you will avoid serious error by writing the units and ensuring that they cancel. Because exponentials are very sensitive to the numerical value of the exponent, do not round the intermediate steps but store them in your calculator until the last step of the calculation. Finally, note how the number of significant figures in the answer (two) does not exceed the number in the data.

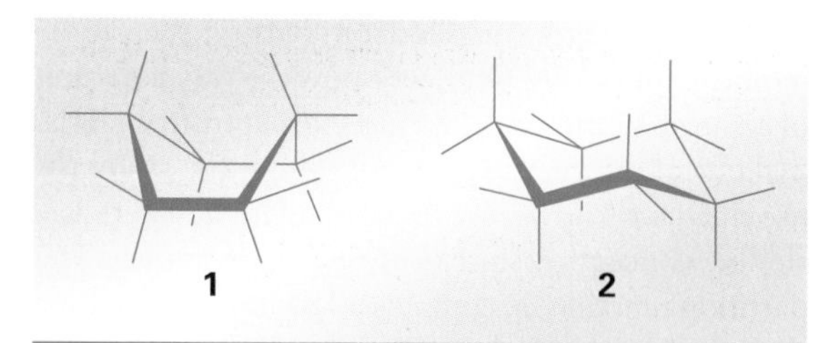

One very important feature of the Boltzmann distribution is that it applies to the populations of *states*. We have seen that in some cases (the hydrogen atom and rotating molecules are examples) several different states have the same energy. That is, some energy levels are *degenerate* (Section 12.10). The Boltzmann distribution can be used to calculate, for instance, the number of hydrogen atoms at a temperature T that have their electron in a $2p_x$ orbital. Because a $2p_y$ orbital has exactly the same energy, the number of atoms with an electron in a $2p_y$ orbital is the same as the number with an electron in a $2p_x$ orbital. The same is true of atoms with an electron in a $2p_z$ orbital. Therefore, if we want the *total* number of atoms with electrons in $2p$ orbitals, we have to multiply the number in *one* of them by a factor of 3. In general, if the degeneracy of an energy level (that is, the number of states of that energy) is g, we use a factor of g to get the population of the *level* (as distinct from an individual *state*). It is obviously very important to decide whether we wish to express the population of an individual state or the population of an entire degenerate energy level.

Illustration 22.2

Taking degeneracy into account

We saw in Section 19.5 that the rotational energy of a linear rotor is $hBJ(J+1)$ and that the degeneracy of each level is $2J+1$. Given that the degeneracy of the level with $J = 2$ (and energy $6hB$) is 5 and that of the level with $J = 1$ (and energy $2hB$) is 3, the relative number of molecules with $J = 2$ and 1 is

$$\frac{N_2}{N_1} = \underbrace{\frac{g_2 N\,e^{-E_2/kT}/q}{g_1 N\,e^{-E_1/kT}/q}}_{\text{Boltzmann distribution; Degeneracy, }2J+1} = \frac{g_2}{g_1}\,e^{-(E_2-E_1)/kT} = \tfrac{5}{3}\,e^{-4hB/kT}$$

(Energy, $hBJ(J+1)$)

For HCl, $B = 318.0$ GHz (corresponding to 318.0×10^{9} Hz $= 3.180 \times 10^{11}$ Hz), so at 25°C (corresponding to 298 K),

h B

$$\frac{N_2}{N_1} = \frac{5}{3} \times e^{-\frac{4 \times (6.626\,08 \times 10^{-34}\ \mathrm{J\,s}) \times (3.180 \times 10^{11}\ \mathrm{Hz})}{(1.380\,66 \times 10^{-23}\ \mathrm{J\,K^{-1}}) \times (298\ \mathrm{K})}}$$

k T

$$= \frac{5}{3} \times e^{-\frac{4 \times 6.626\,08 \times 10^{-34} \times 3.180 \times 10^{11}}{1.380\,66 \times 10^{-23} \times 298}} = 1.36$$

We see that there are *more* molecules in the level with $J = 2$ than in the level with $J = 1$, even though $J = 2$ corresponds to a higher energy. Each individual *state* with $J = 2$ has a lower population than each state with $J = 1$, but there are more states in the level with $J = 2$.

A note on good practice The energy of a state of a single molecule is in joules, so use Boltzmann's constant in the exponent of the Boltzmann distribution; if you are given energies in joules (or kilojoules) per mole, use the gas constant (and 1 kJ = 10^3 J).

One important convention that we adopt (largely for convenience) is that *all energies are measured relative to the ground state*. That is, we set the ground-state energy equal to zero, even if there is a zero-point energy. For instance, the energies of the states of a harmonic oscillator are measured from zero for the ground state:

Actual energies: $E = \frac{1}{2}h\nu, \frac{3}{2}h\nu, \ldots$

Our convention: $E = 0, h\nu, \ldots$

Likewise, the energies of the hydrogen atom are measured from zero for the 1*s* orbital:

Actual energies: $E = -hcR_{\mathrm{H}}, -\frac{1}{4}hcR_{\mathrm{H}}, \ldots$

Our convention: $E = 0, \frac{3}{4}hcR_{\mathrm{H}}, \ldots$

This convention greatly simplifies our interpretation of the significance of q.

22.2 The interpretation of the partition function

When we are interested only in the relative populations of levels and states, we do not need to know the partition function because it cancels in eqn 22.3. However, if we want to know the actual population of a state, then we use eqn 22.1, which requires us to know q. We also need to know q when we derive thermodynamic functions, as we shall see.

The definition of q is the sum over states (not levels), as given in eqn 22.2. We can write out the first few terms as follows:

$$q = 1 + e^{-E_1/kT} + e^{-E_2/kT} + e^{-E_3/kT} + \cdots$$

The first term is 1 because the energy of the ground state (E_0) is 0, according to our convention, and $e^0 = 1$. In principle, we just substitute the values of the energies, evaluate each term for the temperature of interest, and add them together to get q. However, that procedure does not give much insight.

To see the physical significance of q, let's suppose first that $T = 0$. Then, because $e^{-\infty} = 0$, all terms other than the first are equal to 0, and

$$q = 1$$

At $T = 0$ only the ground state is occupied and (provided that state is non-degenerate) $q = 1$. Now consider the other extreme: a temperature so high that all the $E_i/kT = 0$. Then, because $e^0 = 1$, the partition function is

$$q \approx 1 + 1 + 1 + 1 + \cdots = N$$

where N is the number of states of the molecule. That is, at very high temperatures, all the states of the system are thermally accessible. It follows that if the molecule has an infinite number of states, then q rises to infinity as T approaches infinity. We should begin to suspect that the partition function is telling us the number of states that are occupied at a given temperature.

Now consider an intermediate temperature, at which only some of the states are occupied significantly. Let's suppose that the temperature is such that kT is large compared to E_1 and E_2 but small compared to E_3 and all subsequent terms (Fig. 22.2). Because E_1/kT and E_2/kT are both small compared to 1, and $e^{-x} \approx 1$ when x is very small, the first three terms are all close to 1. However, because E_3/kT is large compared to 1, and $e^{-x} \approx 0$ when x is large, all the remaining terms are close to 0. Therefore,

$$q \approx 1 + 1 + 1 + 0 + \cdots = 3$$

Once again, we see that the partition function is telling us the number of significantly occupied states

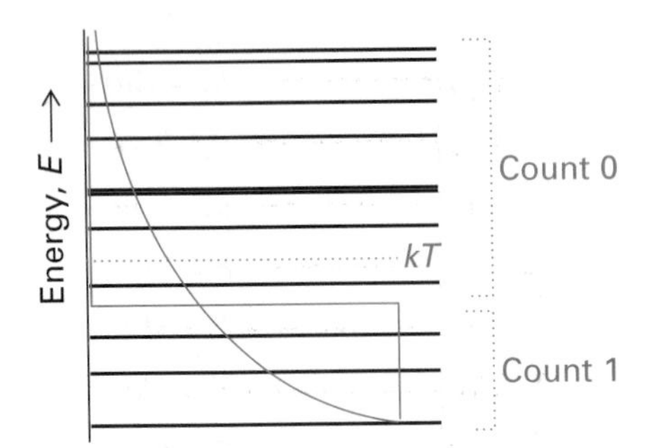

Fig. 22.2 The partition function is a measure of the number of thermally accessible states. Thus, for all states with $E < kT$ the exponential term is reasonably close to 1, whereas for all states with $E > kT$ the exponential term is close to 0. The states with $E < kT$ are significantly thermally accessible.

at the temperature of interest. That is the principal meaning of the partition function: *q tells us the number of thermally accessible states at the temperature of interest.*

Once we grasp the significance of q, statistical thermodynamics becomes much easier to understand. We can anticipate, even before we do any calculations, that q increases with temperature, because more states become accessible as the temperature is raised. At low temperatures q is small, and falls to 1 as the temperature approaches absolute zero (when only one state, the ground state, is accessible and we are supposing that that state is non-degenerate). Molecules with numerous, closely spaced energy levels (like the rotational states of bulky molecules) can be expected to have very large partition functions. Molecules with widely spaced energy levels can be expected to have small partition functions, because only the few lowest states will be occupied at low temperatures.

Example 22.1

Calculating a partition function

Calculate the partition function for the cyclohexane molecule, confining attention to the chair and boat conformations mentioned in Illustration 22.1. Show how the partition function varies with temperature.

Strategy Whenever calculating a partition function, start at the definition in eqn 22.2 and write out the individual terms. Remember to set the ground-state energy equal to 0. When the energies of states are given in joules (or kilojoules) per mole, replace the k in the definition of q by R.

Solution There are only two states, so the partition function has only two terms. The energy of the chair form is set at 0 and that of the boat form is $E = 22$ kJ mol^{-1}. Therefore:

$E_0 = 0$ $\quad E_1 = E$

$$q = 1 + e^{-E/RT}$$

E

$$= 1 + e^{-\frac{22\times10^{3}\ \mathrm{J\ mol^{-1}}}{(8.314\,47\ \mathrm{J\ K^{-1}\ mol^{-1}})\times T}} = 1 + e^{-\frac{2646\ \mathrm{K}}{T}}$$

R

A more general form of this function (for any value of E) is plotted in Fig. 22.3. We see that it rises from $q = 1$ (only the chair form is accessible at $T = 0$, when $(2646\ \mathrm{K})/T = \infty$ and $e^{-\infty} = 0$) to $q = 2$ at $T = \infty$ (when $(2646\ \mathrm{K})/T = 0$ and $e^{0} = 1$; both states are thermally accessible at high temperatures). At 20°C, $q = 1.0001$. As we saw in Illustration 22.1, the boat form is only slightly populated and so q differs very little from 1.

A note on good practice Note how the units are treated in the exponent: the units of E and R cancel apart from K^{-1} in the denominator, which becomes K in the numerator (in the form 2646 K), which will cancel

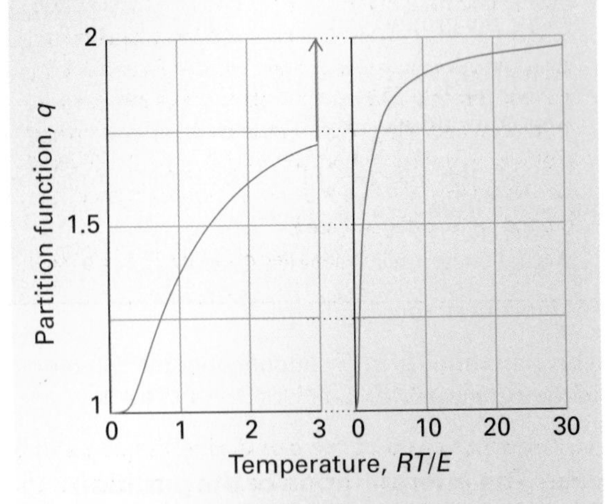

Fig. 22.3 The partition function for a two-level system with states at the energies 0 and E. At 20°C (293 K) and for $E = 22$ kJ mol^{-1}, $RT/E = 0.11$, where $q = 1.0001$. Note how the partition function rises from 1 and approaches 2 at high temperatures.

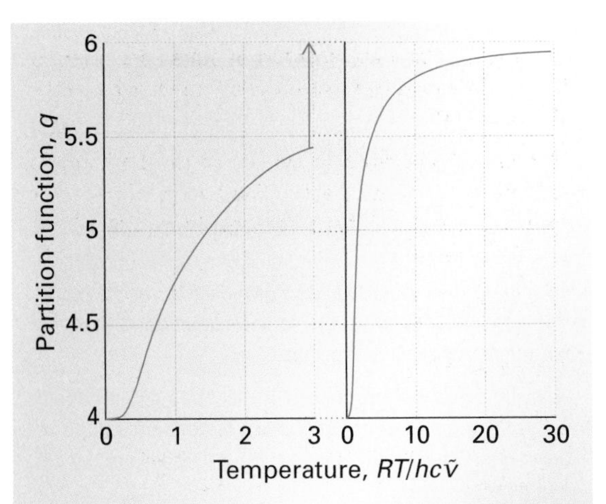

Fig. 22.4 The partition function for the six-level system treated in Self-test 22.1. Note how q rises from 4 (when only the four states of the $^3P_{3/2}$ level are occupied) and approaches 6 (when the two states of the $^3P_{1/2}$ level are also accessible). At 20°C, $kT/hc\tilde{\nu} = 0.504$, corresponding to $q = 5.21$.

the units K of T when values of the latter are introduced. You will sometimes see an expression like '$q = 1 + e^{-2646/T}$, with T in kelvins' (or, worse, 'with T the absolute temperature'); retention of the units, as we show, is completely unambiguous and therefore better practice.

Self-test 22.1

The ground configuration of a fluorine atom gives rise to a ^2P term with two levels,[6] the $J = \frac{3}{2}$ level (of degeneracy 4) and the $J = \frac{1}{2}$ level (of degeneracy 2) at an energy corresponding to 404.0 cm^{-1} above the ground state. Write down an expression for the partition function and plot it as a function of temperature. (*Hint.* Take $E = hc\tilde{\nu}$ for the energy of the upper level. In this instance, the ground state is degenerate.)

[*Answer:* $q = 4 + 2e^{-hc\tilde{\nu}/kT}$; Fig. 22.4]

22.3 Examples of partition functions

In a number of cases we can derive simple expressions for partition functions. For example, the energy levels of a harmonic oscillator form a simple ladder-like array (Fig. 22.5). If we set the energy of the lowest state equal to zero, the energies of the states are

$$E_0 = 0,\ E_1 = h\nu,\ E_2 = 2h\nu,\ E_3 = 3h\nu, \text{ etc.}$$

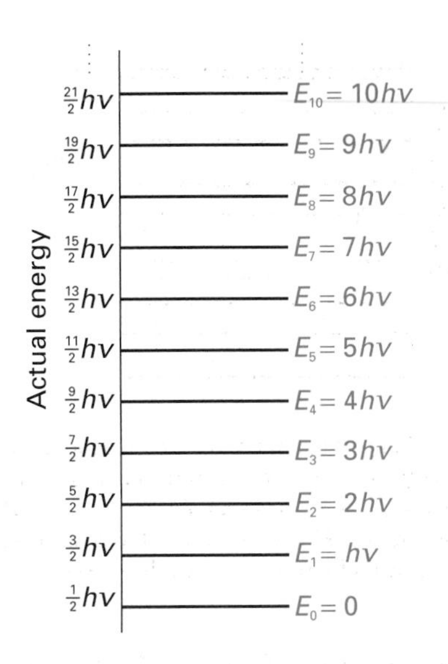

Fig. 22.5 The energy levels of a harmonic oscillator. When calculating a partition function, set the zero of energy at the lowest level, as shown on the right.

Therefore, the **vibrational partition function** is

$$q = 1 + e^{-h\nu/kT} + e^{-2h\nu/kT} + e^{-3h\nu/kT} + \cdots$$

The sum of this infinite series is

$$q = \frac{1}{1 - e^{-h\nu/kT}} \qquad (22.4)$$

If we set $x = e^{-h\nu/kT}$, the series is $1 + x + x^2 + x^3 + \cdots$, which sums to $1/(1 - x)$. In statistical thermodynamics there are three useful expansions to remember:

$$\frac{1}{1-x} = 1 + x + x^2 + \cdots$$

$$\frac{1}{1+x} = 1 - x + x^2 - \cdots$$

$$e^{-x} = 1 - x + \frac{x^2}{2!} - \cdots$$

where 'factorial n' is $n! = n(n-1)(n-2)\ldots 1$ (and $0! = 1$).

Equation 22.4 is the partition function for a harmonic oscillator, or any vibrating diatomic molecule. Figure 22.6 shows how q varies with temperature. Note that $q = 1$ at $T = 0$, when only the lowest state is occupied, and that as T becomes

[6] The notation used here was introduced in Section 13.16.

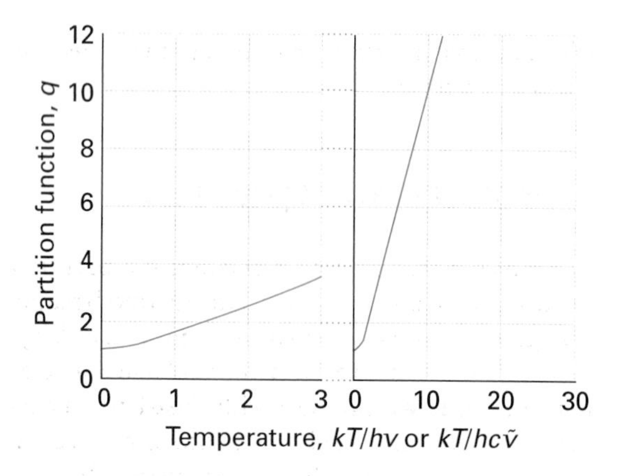

Fig. 22.6 The partition function for a harmonic oscillator. For an oscillator with $\tilde{\nu} = 1000\ \text{cm}^{-1}$, at 20°C, $kT/hc\tilde{\nu} = 0.204$, corresponding to $q = 1.01$.

high, so q becomes infinite because all the states of the infinite ladder are thermally accessible. At room temperature, and for typical molecular vibrational frequencies, q is very close to 1 because only the vibrational ground state is occupied (see Exercise 22.15).

We can carry out similar calculations for certain other types of motion. For example, suppose a molecule of mass m is confined in a flask of volume V at a temperature T, then (as shown in *Further information* 22.1) to a good approximation,[7] the **translational partition function** is

$$q = \frac{(2\pi mkT)^{3/2}V}{h^3} \tag{22.5}$$

We see that the partition function increases with temperature, as we have come to expect. However, note that q also increases with the volume of the flask. That we should expect too: the energy levels of a particle in a box become closer together as the size of the box increases (Section 12.9), so at a given temperature, more states are thermally accessible.

Illustration 22.3

Evaluating a translational partition function

Suppose we have an O_2 molecule (of mass 32 u) in a flask of volume 100 cm^3 at 20°C. Its translational partition function is

m   kT   V

$$q = \frac{(2\pi \times 32 \times (1.660\,54 \times 10^{-27}\ \text{kg}) \times (1.380\,66 \times 10^{-23}\ \text{J K}^{-1}) \times (298\ \text{K}))^{3/2} \times (1.00 \times 10^{-4}\ \text{m}^3)}{(6.626\,08 \times 10^{-34}\ \text{J s})^3}$$

$$= 9.67 \times 10^{25}$$

Note that a huge number of translational states are accessible at room temperature. This result is consistent with the derivation of eqn 22.5, which assumed that the translational energy levels form a near continuum in containers of macroscopic size.

A note on good practice All the units must cancel because all partition functions are dimensionless numbers. Here, because 1 J = 1 kg m^2 s^{-2}, the units cancel as follows:

$$\frac{(\text{kg J K}^{-1}\ \text{K})^{3/2}\ \text{m}^3}{(\text{J s})^3} = \frac{(\text{kg kg m}^2\ \text{s}^{-2})^{3/2}\ \text{m}^3}{(\text{kg m}^2\ \text{s}^{-2}\ \text{s})^3}$$

$$= \frac{(\text{kg m s}^{-1})^3\ \text{m}^3}{(\text{kg m}^2\ \text{s}^{-1})^3} = \frac{\text{kg}^3\ \text{m}^6\ \text{s}^{-3}}{\text{kg}^3\ \text{m}^6\ \text{s}^{-3}}$$

$$= 1$$

The **rotational partition function** can also be approximated when the temperature is high enough for many rotational states to be occupied. For a linear rotor it turns out (see *Further information* 22.1) that[8]

$$q = \frac{kT}{\sigma hB} \tag{22.6}$$

In this expression, B is the rotational constant (Section 17.3) and σ is the **symmetry number:** $\sigma = 1$ for an unsymmetrical linear rotor (such as HCl or HCN) and $\sigma = 2$ for a symmetrical linear rotor (such as H_2 or CO_2).[9] The rotational partition of HCl at 25°C works out to 19.6 (see Exercise 22.17), so about 20 rotational states[10] are significantly occupied at that temperature.

No closed form can be given for the **electronic partition function**, the partition function for the

[7] The approximation is valid for large containers and $T > 0$.

[8] This is an approximation valid for heavy molecules and $T > 0$.

[9] The symmetry number reflects the fact that an unsymmetrical molecule is distinguishable after rotation by 180° but a symmetrical molecule is not. When evaluating q we have to count only distinguishable states.

[10] *Not* levels: remember the $(2J + 1)$-fold degeneracy of each rotational level.

distribution of electrons over their available states. However, for closed-shell molecules the excited states are so high in energy that only the ground state is occupied, and for them $q = 1$. Special care has to be taken for atoms and molecules that do not have closed shells (as we saw in Self-test 22.1 for the fluorine atom).

22.4 The molecular partition function

The energy of a molecule can be approximated as the sum of contributions from its different modes of motion (translation, rotation, and vibration), the distribution of electrons, and the electronic and nuclear spin:

$$E_i = E_i^{T} + E_i^{R} + E_i^{V} + E_i^{E} + E_i^{S} \qquad (22.7)$$

where T denotes translation, R rotation, V vibration, E the electronic contribution, and S the spin contribution. The separation of the electronic and vibrational motions, for example, is justified by the Born–Oppenheimer approximation (Chapter 14), and the separation of the vibrational and rotational modes is valid to the extent that a molecule can be treated as a rigid rotor.

Given that the energy is a sum of independent contributions, the partition function is a product of contributions:

$$q = \sum_i e^{-E_i/kT} = \sum_i e^{-E_i^{T}/kT - E_i^{R}/kT - E_i^{V}/kT - E_i^{E}/kT - E_i^{S}/kT}$$

$$= \left(\sum_i e^{-E_i^{T}/kT}\right)\left(\sum_i e^{-E_i^{R}/kT}\right)\left(\sum_i e^{-E_i^{V}/kT}\right)\left(\sum_i e^{-E_i^{E}/kT}\right)\left(\sum_i e^{-E_i^{S}/kT}\right)$$

$$= q^{T}q^{R}q^{V}q^{E}q^{S} \qquad (22.8)$$

This result makes use of the fact that taking the exponential of a sum is the same as forming a product of each individual exponential: $e^{x+y+\cdots} = e^{x}e^{y}\ldots$. The inverse of this relation may be more familiar: the logarithm of a product is the sum of the logarithms of each factor: $\log xy\ldots = \log x + \log y + \cdots$.

The contribution from electronic spin is important in atoms or molecules containing unpaired electrons. For example, consider the Cs atom, which has one unpaired electron. We saw in Chapters 13 and 20 that the two spin states of this unpaired electron are equally occupied in the absence of any magnetic field, so it contributes a factor of 2 to the molecular partition function.

Thermodynamic properties

The principal reason for calculating the partition function is to use it to calculate thermodynamic properties of systems as small as atoms and as large as biopolymers. There are two fundamental relations we need. We can deal with First-Law quantities (such as heat capacity and enthalpy) once we know how to calculate the internal energy. We can deal with Second-Law quantities (such as the Gibbs energy and equilibrium constants) once we know how to calculate the entropy.

22.5 The internal energy and the heat capacity

To calculate the total energy, E, of the system, we note the energy of each state (E_i), multiply that energy by the number of molecules in the state (N_i), and then add together all these products:

$$E = N_0E_0 + N_1E_1 + N_2E_2 + \cdots = \sum_i N_iE_i$$

However, the Boltzmann distribution tells us the number of molecules in each state of a system, so we can replace the N_i in this expression by the expression in eqn 22.1:

Population of state i | Energy of state i | Sum over all states i

$$E = \sum_i \frac{N\,e^{-E_i/kT}}{q} \times E_i = \frac{N}{q}\sum_i E_i\,e^{-E_i/kT} \qquad (22.9)$$

If we know the individual energies of the states (from spectroscopy, for instance), then we just substitute their values into this expression. However, there is a much simpler method available when we have an expression for the partition function, such as those given in Section 22.3. In Derivation 22.1 we show that the energy is related to the slope of q plotted against T:

$$E = \frac{NkT^2}{q} \times \text{slope of } q \text{ plotted against } T \qquad (22.10)$$

Derivation 22.1

The internal energy from the partition function

The expression on the right of eqn 22.9 resembles the definition of the partition function, but differs from it by having the E_i factor multiplying each term. However, we can recognize that:

$$\frac{d}{dT}e^{-E_i/kT} = e^{-E_i/kT} \times \frac{d}{dT}\left(-\frac{E_i}{kT}\right) = \frac{E_i}{kT^2}e^{-E_i/kT}$$

 The *chain rule* states that for a function *f* of another function *g*, where *g* is itself a function of another variable *t*,

$$\frac{df}{dt} = \frac{df}{dg}\frac{dg}{dt}$$

In the present case the variable *t* is *T*, the function *f* is e^g, with $g = -E_i/kT$, so $df/dg = e^g$, and $g = -E_i/kT$, so $dg/dT = E_i/kT^2$.

In other words,

$$E_i e^{-E_i/kT} = kT^2\frac{d}{dT}e^{-E_i/kT}$$

With this substitution, the expression for the total energy becomes

$$E = \frac{N}{q}\sum_i kT^2\frac{d}{dT}e^{-E_i/kT} = \frac{NkT^2}{q}\frac{d}{dT}\sum_i e^{-E_i/kT}$$

because the sum of derivatives is the derivative of the sum. Magically (or more precisely, mathematically), the expression for the partition function has appeared, so we can write

$$E = \frac{NkT^2}{q}\frac{dq}{dT}$$

which is eqn 22.10.

The remarkable feature of eqn 22.10 is that it is an expression for the total energy in terms of the partition function alone. The partition function is starting to fulfil its promise to deliver all thermodynamic information about the system.

There is one more detail to take into account before we use eqn 22.10. Recall that we have set the zero of energy at the energy of the lowest state of the molecule. However, the internal energy of the system might be non-zero on account of zero-point energy, and the E in eqn 22.10 is the energy *above* the zero-point energy. That is, the internal energy at a temperature T is

$$U = U(0) + E \qquad (22.11)$$

with E given by eqn 22.10. For example, for a harmonic oscillator where we took the ground state energy as 0 rather than $\frac{1}{2}h\nu$, $U(0) = \frac{1}{2}Nh\nu$.

‡Example 22.2

Calculating the internal energy

Calculate the molar internal energy of a monatomic gas.

Strategy The only mode of motion of a monatomic gas is translation (we ignore electronic excitation). Therefore, substitute the translational partition function in eqn 22.5 into eqn 22.10 (using the precise mathematical form given in Derivation 22.1, and then insert the result into eqn 22.11. The partition function has the form $q = aT^{3/2}$, where a is a collection of constants.

Solution First, we need the slope (formally: the first derivative) of q with respect to T:

$$\overbrace{\frac{dq}{dT} = \frac{d}{dT}(aT^{3/2})}^{q=aT^{3/2}} = \tfrac{3}{2}aT^{1/2}$$

When we substitute this result into eqn 22.10 we get

$$E = \frac{NkT^2}{q}\overbrace{\frac{dq}{dT}}^{\frac{3}{2}aT^{1/2}} = \frac{NkT^2}{aT^{3/2}} \times \tfrac{3}{2}aT^{1/2} = \tfrac{3}{2}NkT \quad (q = aT^{3/2})$$

The molar internal energy is obtained by replacing N by Avogadro's constant and using eqn 22.11:

$$U_m = U_m(0) + \tfrac{3}{2}N_AkT = U_m(0) + \tfrac{3}{2}RT$$

The term $U_m(0)$ contains all the contributions from the binding energy of the electrons and of the nucleons in the nucleus. The term $\frac{3}{2}RT$ is the contribution to the internal energy from the translational motion of the atoms in their container.

Self-test 22.2

Calculate the molar internal energy of a gas of diatomic molecules. (*Hint.* Neglect the effect of vibrational motion and apply the rotational and translational contributions calculated in the example to eqn 22.8.)

[*Answer:* $U_m = U_m(0) + \frac{5}{2}RT$]

Once we have calculated the internal energy of a sample of molecules, it is a simple matter to calculate the heat capacity. It should be recalled that the heat capacity at constant volume, C_V, is defined as the slope of the plot of internal energy against temperature:

$$C_V = \frac{\Delta U}{\Delta T} \quad \text{at constant volume}$$

Therefore, all we need do is to evaluate the slope of the expression for U obtained from the partition function.

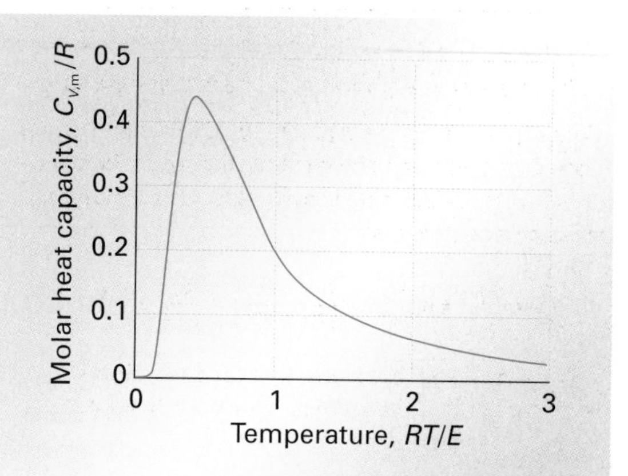

Fig. 22.7 The variation of the heat capacity of a two-level system with states at energies 0 and E. Note how the heat capacity is zero at $T = 0$, passes through a maximum at $T = 0.417E/R$, and approaches 0 at high temperatures.

‡Illustration 22.4

Calculating a heat capacity

The slope of U with respect to T is the first derivative:

$$C_V = \frac{dU}{dT} \quad \text{at constant volume}$$

The constant-volume molar heat capacity of a monatomic gas is therefore obtained by substituting the molar internal energy, $U_m = U_m(0) + \frac{3}{2}RT$, into this expression:

$$C_{V,m} = \frac{d}{dT}(U_m(0) + \tfrac{3}{2}RT) = \tfrac{3}{2}R$$

To calculate $C_{p,m}$, we use eqn 2.17 ($C_{p,m} - C_{V,m} = R$) and obtain $\frac{5}{2}R$.

‡Self-test 22.3

Calculate the contribution to the molar constant-volume heat capacity of a two-state system, like the chair–boat interconversion of cyclohexane (Illustration 22.1) and show how the heat capacity varies with temperature. (*Hint.* Distinguish between the internal energy (E in eqn 22.10) and the energy separation between the two conformations (E in Illustration 22.1). Also, note that for two functions f and g, $d(f/g)/dx = (1/g)df/dx - (f/g^2)dg/dx$.)

[*Answer:* $C_{V,m} = \dfrac{R(E/RT)^2 e^{E/RT}}{(1 + e^{E/RT})^2}$, Fig. 22.7]

22.6 The entropy and the Gibbs energy

The entry point into the calculation of properties arising from the Second Law of thermodynamics is the proposal made by Boltzmann that the entropy of a system can be calculated from the expression

$$S = k \ln W \tag{22.12}$$

Here W is the number of different ways in which the molecules of a system can be arranged yet result in the same total energy. This expression is the **Boltzmann formula** for the entropy. The entropy is zero if there is only one way of achieving a given total energy (because $\ln 1 = 0$). The entropy is high if there are many ways of achieving the same energy.

In most cases, $W = 1$ at $T = 0$ because there is only one way of achieving zero energy: put all the molecules into the same, lowest state. Therefore, $S = 0$ at $T = 0$, in accord with the Third Law of thermodynamics (Section 4.7). In certain cases, however, W may differ from 1 at $T = 0$. This is the case if disorder survives down to absolute zero because there is no energy advantage in adopting a particular orientation. For instance, there may be no energy difference between the arrangements ...AB AB AB... and ...BA AB BA..., so $W > 1$ even at $T = 0$. If $S > 0$ at $T = 0$ we say that the substance has a **residual entropy**. Ice has a residual entropy of 3.4 J K^{-1} mol^{-1}. It stems from the disorder in the hydrogen bonds between neighbouring water molecules: a given O atom has two short O–H bonds and two long O···H bonds to its neighbours, but there is a degree of randomness in which two bonds are short and which two are long.

Illustration 22.5

Calculating a residual entropy

Consider a sample of solid carbon monoxide containing N CO molecules. We saw in Section 17.2 that CO has a very small dipole moment. In fact, the dipolar interactions between CO molecules are so weak in a solid that even at $T = 0$ they lie either head-to-tail or head-to-head with approximately equal energies to give randomly orientated arrangements such as ...CO CO OC CO OC OC... with the same energy. Because each CO molecule can lie in either of two orientations (CO or OC) with equal energy, there are $2 \times 2 \times 2 \times \cdots = 2^N$ ways of achieving the same energy. The residual entropy of the sample, its entropy at $T = 0$, where there is this orientation disorder but no motional disorder, is therefore

$$S = k \ln 2^N = Nk \ln 2$$

(We have used $\ln x^a = a \ln x$.) The molar entropy is therefore

$$S_m = N_A k \ln 2 = R \ln 2$$

or 5.8 J K^{-1} mol^{-1}, which is close to the experimental value of 5 J K^{-1} mol^{-1}.

Boltzmann went on to show that there is a close relation between the entropy and the partition function: both are measures of the number of arrangements available to the molecules. The precise connection for *distinguishable* molecules (those locked in place in a solid) is

$$S = \frac{U - U(0)}{T} + Nk \ln q \qquad (22.13a)$$

The analogous term for *indistinguishable* molecules (identical molecules free to move, as in a gas) is

$$S = \frac{U - U(0)}{T} + Nk \ln q - Nk(\ln N - 1) \qquad (22.13b)$$

Because we can calculate the first term on the right from q, we now have a method for calculating the entropy of any system of non-interacting molecules once we know its partition function.

Example 22.3

Calculating the entropy

Calculate the contribution that rotational motion makes to the molar entropy of a gas of HCl molecules at 25°C.

Strategy We have already calculated the contribution to the internal energy (Self-test 22.2), and we have the rotational partition function in eqn 22.6 (with $\sigma = 1$). We need to combine the two parts. We use eqn 22.13a because we are concentrating on the internal motion (the rotation) of the molecules, not their translational motion.

Solution We substitute $U - U(0) = RT$ and $q = kT/hB$ into eqn 22.13a, and obtain[11]

$$S_m = \frac{RT}{T} + R \ln \frac{kT}{hB} = R\left(1 + \ln \frac{kT}{hB}\right)$$

Note that the entropy increases with temperature (Fig. 22.8). At a given temperature, the entropy is larger the smaller the value of B. That is, bulky molecules (which have large moments of inertia and therefore small rotational constants) have a higher rotational entropy than small molecules. Substitution of the numerical values gives $S_m = 3.98R$, or 33.1 J K^{-1} mol^{-1}.

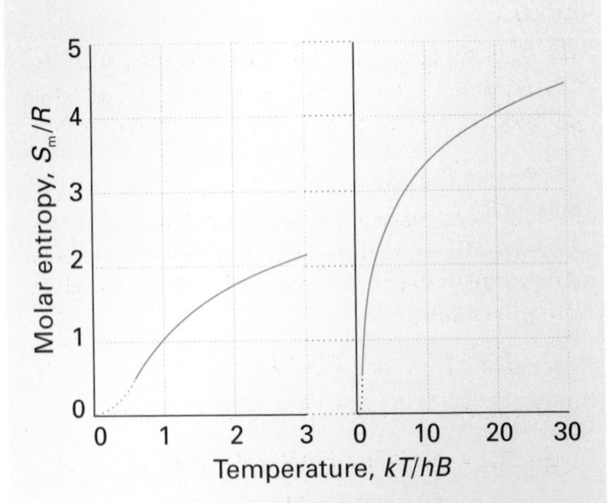

Fig. 22.8 The variation of the rotational contribution to the molar entropy with temperature. Note that eqn 22.6 is valid only for high temperatures, so the formula derived in Example 22.3 cannot be used at low temperatures (so we have terminated the curves before they become invalid). The dotted lines show the correct behaviour.

[11] This result is valid only for $T > 0$.

Self-test 22.4

The rotational partition function of an ethene molecule is 661 at 25°C. What is the contribution to its rotational entropy?

[*Answer:* 7.49*R*]

The Gibbs energy, G, was central to most of the thermodynamic discussions in the early chapters of this book, so to show that statistical thermodynamics is really useful we have to see how to calculate G from the partition function, q. We shall confine our attention to a perfect gas, because it is difficult to take molecular interactions into account, and in Derivation 22.2 we show that for a gas of N molecules

$$G - G(0) = -NkT \ln \frac{q}{N} \qquad (22.14)$$

Derivation 22.2

Calculating the Gibbs energy from the partition function

To set up the calculation, we go back to first principles. The Gibbs energy is defined as $G = H - TS$, and the enthalpy, H, is defined as $H = U + pV$. Therefore

$$G = U - TS + pV$$

For a perfect gas we can replace pV by $nRT = NkT$ (because $N = nN_A$ and $R = N_A k$), and note that at $T = 0$, $G(0) = U(0)$ (because the terms TS and NkT vanish at $T = 0$). Therefore,

$$G - G(0) = U - U(0) - TS + NkT$$

Now we substitute eqn 22.13b for S, and obtain

$$G - G(0) = -NkT \ln q + kT(N \ln N - N) + NkT$$
$$= -NkT(\ln q - \ln N)$$

Then, because $\ln q - \ln N = \ln(q/N)$, we obtain eqn 22.14.

We can convert eqn 22.14 into an expression for the molar Gibbs energy. First, we write $N = nN_A$, and eqn 22.14 becomes

$$G - G(0) = -nN_A kT \ln \frac{q}{nN_A}$$

Then we introduce the **molar partition function,** $q_m = q/n$, with units 1/mole (mol^{-1}). On dividing both sides of the preceding equation by n, we get

$$G_m - G_m(0) = -RT \ln \frac{q_m}{N_A} \qquad (22.15)$$

Example 22.4

Calculating the Gibbs energy

Calculate the molar Gibbs energy of a monatomic perfect gas and express it in terms of the pressure of the gas.

Strategy The calculation is based on eqn 22.15 with $q_m = q/n$. All we need to know is the translational partition function, which is given in eqn 22.5. Convert from V to p by using the perfect gas law.

Solution When we substitute $q = (2\pi mkT)^{3/2}V/h^3$ into eqn 22.15 we get

$$G_m - G_m(0) = -RT \ln \frac{\overbrace{(2\pi mkT)^{3/2}V/nh^3}^{q_m}}{N_A}$$

Next, we replace V by nRT/p (note that the ns cancel), and obtain (after a little tidying up, including writing $R = kN_A$)

$$G_m - G_m(0) = -RT \ln \frac{(2\pi m)^{3/2}(kT)^{3/2}}{nh^3 N_A} \frac{nN_A kT}{p}$$
$$= -RT \ln \frac{(2\pi m)^{3/2}(kT)^{5/2}}{ph^3} \qquad (22.16)$$
$$= RT \ln ap \qquad a = \frac{h^3}{(2\pi m)^{3/2}(kT)^{5/2}}$$

The Gibbs energy increases logarithmically (as $\ln p$) as p increases, just as we saw in Section 5.2 (eqn 5.2b).

Self-test 22.5

Ignore vibration and write the molar partition function of a diatomic molecule as $q_m^T q^R$ (see eqn 22.8). What is the molar Gibbs energy of such a gas?

[*Answer:* as in eqn 22.16, but with a replaced by $a\sigma hB/kT$]

The only further piece of information we require is the expression for the *standard* molar Gibbs energy, as that played such an important role in the discussion of equilibrium properties. All we need to do is to use the partition function calculated at $p^\ominus$. For instance, for a monatomic gas, we use $p = 1$ bar in eqn 22.16 and obtain the standard value of the molar Gibbs energy. In general, we write

$$G_m^{\ominus} - G_m^{\ominus}(0) = -RT \ln \frac{q_m^{\ominus}}{N_A} \qquad (22.17)$$

where the standard state sign on q simply reminds us to calculate its value at $p^{\ominus}$; to do so, we use $V_m^{\ominus} = RT/p^{\ominus}$ wherever it appears in $q_m^{\ominus}$.

22.7 The statistical basis of chemical equilibrium

We can obtain a deeper insight into the origin and significance of that most chemical of quantities, the equilibrium constant K, by considering the Boltzmann distribution of molecules over the available states of a system composed of reactants and products. When atoms can exchange partners, as in a reaction, the available states of the system include arrangements in which the atoms are present in the form of reactants and in the form of products: these arrangements have their characteristic sets of energy levels, but the Boltzmann distribution does not distinguish between their identities, only their energies. The atoms distribute themselves over both sets of energy levels in accord with the Boltzmann distribution (Fig. 22.9). At a given temperature, there will be a specific distribution of populations, and hence a specific composition of the reaction mixture.

It can be appreciated from Fig. 22.9 that if the reactants and products have similar arrays of molecular energy levels, then the dominant species in a reaction mixture at equilibrium will be the species with the lower set of energy levels. However, the fact that the equilibrium constant is related to the Gibbs energy ($\ln K = -\Delta_r G^{\ominus}/RT$) is a signal that entropy plays a role as well as energy. Its role can be appreciated by referring to Fig. 22.10. We see that although the B energy levels lie higher than the A energy levels, in this instance they are much more closely spaced. As a result, their total population may be considerable and B could even dominate in the reaction mixture at equilibrium. Closely spaced energy levels correlate with a high entropy (see eqn 22.13), so in this case we see that entropy effects dominate adverse energy effects. That is, a positive reaction enthalpy results in a lowering of the equilibrium constant (that is, an endothermic reaction

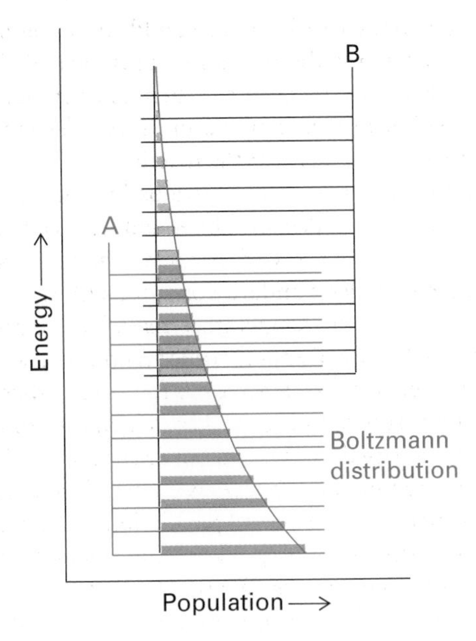

Fig. 22.9 The Boltzmann distribution of populations over the energy levels of two species A and B with similar densities of energy levels; the reaction A → B is endothermic in this example. The bulk of the population is associated with the species A, so that species is dominant at equilibrium.

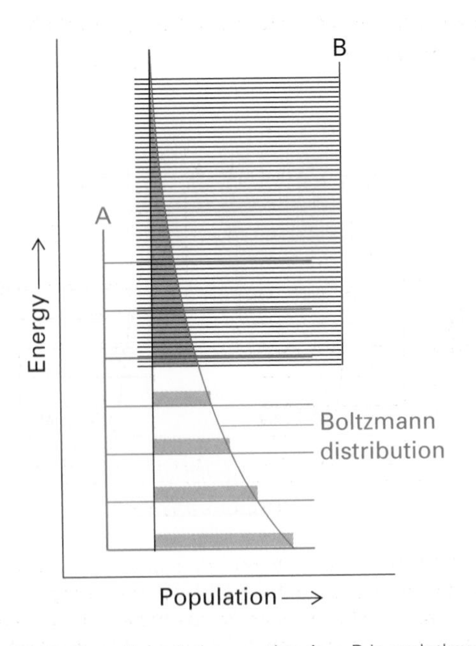

Fig. 22.10 Even though the reaction A → B is endothermic, the density of energy levels in B is so much greater than that in A, that the population associated with B is greater than that associated with A, so B is dominant at equilibrium.

can be expected to have an equilibrium composition that favours the reactants). However, if there is positive reaction entropy, then the equilibrium composition may favour the products, despite the endothermic character of the reaction.

Statistical principles also give us insight into the temperature dependence of the equilibrium constant. In Section 7.9, we saw that for a reaction that is exothermic under standard conditions ($\Delta_r H^{\ominus} < 0$), K decreases as the temperature rises. The opposite occurs in the case of endothermic reactions. The typical arrangement of energy levels for an endothermic reaction is shown in Fig. 22.11a. When the temperature is increased, the Boltzmann distribution adjusts and the populations change as shown. The change corresponds to an increased population of the higher energy states at the expense of the population of the lower energy states. We see that the states that arise from the B molecules become more populated at the expense of the A molecules. Therefore, the total population of B states increases, and B becomes more abundant in the equilibrium mixture. Conversely, if the reaction is exothermic (Fig. 22.11b), then an increase in temperature increases the population of the A states (which start at higher energy) at the expense of the B states, so the reactants become more abundant.

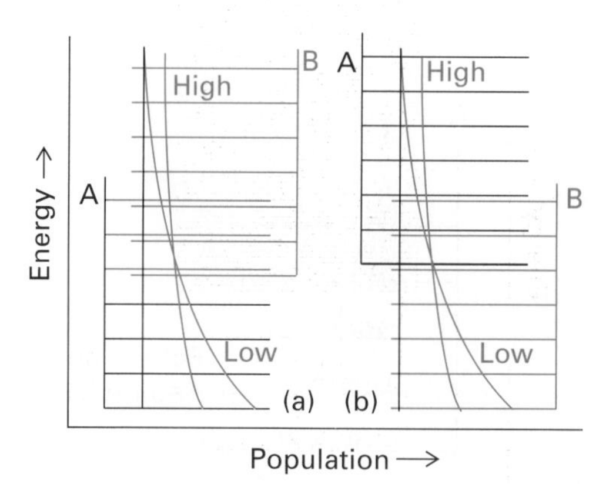

Fig. 22.11 The effect of temperature on a chemical equilibrium can be interpreted in terms of the change in the Boltzmann distribution with temperature and the effect of that change in the population of the species. (a) In an endothermic reaction, the population of B increases at the expense of A as the temperature is raised. (b) In an exothermic reaction, the opposite happens.

22.8 The calculation of the equilibrium constant

We can go beyond the qualitative picture developed above by writing a statistical thermodynamic expression for the equilibrium constant. We show in *Further information* 22.2 that, for the equilibrium $A(g) + B(g) \rightleftharpoons C(g)$,

$$K = \frac{q_m^{\ominus}(C)N_A}{q_m^{\ominus}(A)q_m^{\ominus}(B)} e^{-\Delta E/RT} \tag{22.18}$$

where ΔE is the difference in energy between the ground state of the product and that of the reactants. This expression is easy to remember: it has the same form as the equilibrium constant written in terms of the activities (Section 7.6), but with $q_m^{\ominus}/N_A$ replacing each activity (and an additional exponential factor).

Equation 22.18 is quite extraordinary as it provides a key link between partition functions, which can be derived from spectroscopy, and the equilibrium constant, which is central to the analysis of chemical reactions at equilibrium. It represents the merging of the two rivers that have flowed through this text.

Example 22.5

Calculating an equilibrium constant

Calculate the equilibrium constant for the gas-phase ionization $Cs(g) \rightleftharpoons Cs^+(g) + e^-(g)$ at 500 K.

Strategy This is a reaction of the form $A(g) \rightleftharpoons B(g) + C(g)$ rather than $A(g) + B(g) \rightleftharpoons C(g)$, so we need to modify eqn 22.18 slightly, but the form to use should be clear. Analyse each species individually, and write its partition function as the product of partition functions for each mode of motion. Evaluate these partition functions at the standard pressure (1 bar), and combine them as specified in eqn 22.18. For the difference in energy ΔE, use the ionization energy of Cs(g).

Solution The equilibrium constant is

$$K = \frac{q_m^{\ominus}(Cs^+,g)q_m^{\ominus}(e^-,g)}{q_m^{\ominus}(Cs,g)N_A} e^{-\Delta E/RT}$$

(Note how Avogadro's constant appears in the denominator: its units, mol^{-1}, ensure that K is dimensionless.) The electron has translational motion, so we need its translational partition function. We saw in Section 22.4 that the spin states contribute a factor of 2 to the molecular partition function. Therefore

$$q_m^{\ominus}(e^-,g) = 2 \times \frac{(2\pi m_e kT)^{3/2} V^{\ominus}}{nh^3} = \frac{2(2\pi m_e kT)^{3/2} RT}{p^{\ominus} h^3}$$

The Cs^+ ion, a closed-shell species, has only translational freedom:

$$q_m^{\ominus}(Cs^+,g) = \frac{(2\pi m_{Cs} kT)^{3/2} RT}{p^{\ominus} h^3}$$

The partition function of the Cs atom has a translational and a spin contribution:

$$q_m^{\ominus}(Cs,g) = 2 \times \frac{(2\pi m_{Cs} kT)^{3/2} RT}{p^{\ominus} h^3}$$

(We are not distinguishing the masses of the atoms Cs atom and the Cs^+ ion.) Then, with $\Delta E = I$, the ionization energy of the atom, we find

$$K = \frac{(2\pi m_{Cs} kT)^{3/2} RT / p^{\ominus} h^3 \times 2(2\pi m_e kT)^{3/2} RT / p^{\ominus} h^3}{2(2\pi m_{Cs} kT)^{3/2} RT / p^{\ominus} h^3 \times N_A} \times e^{-I/RT}$$

$$= \frac{(2\pi m_e kT)^{3/2} kT}{p^{\ominus} h^3} e^{-I/RT} = \frac{(2\pi m_e)^{3/2} (kT)^{5/2}}{p^{\ominus} h^3} e^{-I/RT}$$

When we substitute the data (only the ionization energy is specific to the element), we find:

$$K = \frac{(2\pi \times (9.10939 \times 10^{-31}\ \text{kg}))^{3/2} \times ((1.38066 \times 10^{-23}\ \text{J K}^{-1}) \times (1000\ \text{K}))^{5/2}}{(10^5\ \text{Pa}) \times (6.62608 \times 10^{-34}\ \text{J s})^3}$$

$$\times\, e^{-\frac{376 \times 10^3\ \text{J mol}^{-1}}{(8.31447\ \text{J K}^{-1}\ \text{mol}^{-1}) \times (1000\ \text{K})}}$$

$$= 2.42 \times 10^{-19}$$

A note on good practice Verify that the units do in fact all cancel (use 1 J = 1 kg m^2 s^{-2} and 1 Pa = 1 kg m^{-1} s^{-2}). The K calculated by the procedure described here is the thermodynamic equilibrium constant, which for gases is expressed in terms of the partial pressures of the reactants and products (relative to the standard pressure).

Self-test 22.6

Calculate the equilibrium constant for the dissociation $Na_2(g) \rightleftharpoons 2\,Na(g)$ at 1000 K. You will need the following information about $Na_2(g)$: $B = 46.38$ MHz, $\tilde{\nu} = 159.2$ cm^{-1}, and the dissociation energy is 70.4 kJ mol^{-1}. The ground state of a sodium atom is ^{2}S.

[*Answer:* 2.42]

CHECKLIST OF KEY IDEAS

You should now be familiar with the following concepts:

☐ 1 The Boltzmann distribution gives the numbers of molecules in each state of a system at any temperature: $N_i = N e^{-E_i/kT}/q$.

☐ 2 The partition function is defined as $q = \sum_i e^{-E_i/kT}$ and is an indication of the number of thermally accessible states at the temperature of interest.

☐ 3 The molecular partition function is the product of contributions from translation, rotation, vibration, electronic, and spin distributions: $q = q^T q^R q^V q^E q^S$.

☐ 4 The vibrational partition function is $q^V = 1/(1 - e^{-h\nu/kT})$.

☐ 5 The translational partition function is $q^T = (2\pi mkT)^{3/2} V/h^3$.

☐ 6 The rotational partition function is $q^R = kT/\sigma hB$, where $\sigma = 1$ for an unsymmetrical linear rotor and $\sigma = 2$ for a symmetrical linear rotor.

☐ 7 The electronic partition function is $q^E = 1$ for closed-shell molecules with high-energy excited states.

☐ 8 The internal energy is $U = U(0) + E$, with $E = (NkT^2/q) \times$ slope of q plotted against T.

☐ 9 The Boltzmann formula for the entropy is $S = k \ln W$, where W is the number of different ways in which the molecules of a system can be arranged while keeping the same total energy.

☐ 10 The entropy in terms of the partition function is $S = \{U - U(0)\}/T + Nk \ln q$ (distinguishable molecules) or $S = \{U - U(0)\}/T + Nk \ln q - Nk(\ln N - 1)$ (indistinguishable molecules).

☐ 11 The standard molar Gibbs energy is $G_m^\ominus - G_m^\ominus(0) = -RT \ln(q_m^\ominus/N_A)$.

☐ 12 The equilibrium constant for a chemical reaction

$A(g) + B(g) \rightleftharpoons C(g)$ is $K = \dfrac{q_m^\ominus(C)N_A}{q_m^\ominus(A)q_m^\ominus(B)} e^{-\Delta E/RT}$.

FURTHER INFORMATION 22.1

The calculation of partition functions

The translational partition function

We consider a particle of mass m in a rectangular box of sides X, Y, Z. Each direction can be treated independently and then the total partition function obtained by multiplying together the partition functions for each direction. The same strategy was used to write an expression for the molecular partition function by multiplying the contributions from (independent) modes of molecular motion.

The energy levels of a molecule of mass m in a container of length X are given by eqn 12.11 with $L = X$:

$$E_n = \frac{n^2h^2}{8mX^2} \qquad n = 1, 2, \ldots$$

The lowest level ($n = 1$) has energy $h^2/8mX^2$, so the energies relative to that level are

$$\varepsilon_n = (n^2 - 1)\varepsilon \qquad \varepsilon = h^2/8mX^2$$

The sum to evaluate is therefore

$$q_X = \sum_{n=1}^{\infty} e^{-(n^2-1)\varepsilon/kT}$$

The translational energy levels are very close together in a container the size of a typical laboratory vessel; therefore, the sum can be approximated by an integral:

$$q_X = \int_1^{\infty} e^{-(n^2-1)\varepsilon/kT}\, dn$$

The extension of the lower limit to $n = 0$ and the replacement of $n^2 - 1$ by n^2 introduces negligible error but turns the integral into standard form. We make the substitution $x^2 = n^2\varepsilon/kT$, implying $dn = dx/(\varepsilon/kT)^{1/2}$, and therefore that

$$q_X = \left(\frac{kT}{\varepsilon}\right)^{1/2} \int_0^{\infty} e^{-x^2}\, dx$$

$$= \left(\frac{kT}{\varepsilon}\right)^{1/2} \left(\frac{\pi^{1/2}}{2}\right) = \left(\frac{2\pi mkT}{h^2}\right)^{1/2} X$$

The same expression applies to the other dimensions of a rectangular box of sides Y and Z, so

$$q^T = q_X q_Y q_Z = \left(\frac{2\pi mkT}{h^2}\right)^{3/2} XYZ = \left(\frac{2\pi mkT}{h^2}\right)^{3/2} V$$

where $V = XYZ$ is the volume of the box.

The rotational partition function

The rotational partition function of a non-symmetrical (AB) linear rigid rotor is

$$q^R = \sum_J (2J + 1)\, e^{-hBJ(J+1)/kT}$$

where the sum is over the rotational energy levels and the factor $2J + 1$ takes into account the degeneracy of the levels. When many rotational states are occupied and kT is much larger than the separation between neighbouring states, we can approximate the sum by an integral:

$$q^R = \int_0^{\infty} (2J + 1)\, e^{-hBJ(J+1)/kT}\, dJ$$

Although this integral looks complicated, it can be evaluated without much effort by noting that it can also be written as

$$q^{rot} = -\frac{kT}{hB} \int_0^{\infty} \left(\frac{d}{dJ} e^{-hBJ(J+1)/kT}\right) dJ$$

Then, because the integral of a derivative of a function is the function itself,

$$q^R = -\frac{kT}{hB} e^{-hBJ(J+1)/kT}\Big|_0^{\infty} = \frac{kT}{hB}$$

For a homonuclear diatomic molecule, which looks the same after rotation by 180°, we have to divide this result by 2 to avoid double-counting of states, so in general

$$q^R = \frac{kT}{\sigma hB}$$

where $\sigma = 1$ for heteronuclear diatomic molecules and 2 for homonuclear diatomic molecules.

FURTHER INFORMATION 22.2

The equilibrium constant from the partition function

We know from thermodynamics (Section 7.6) that the equilibrium constant for a reaction is related to the standard reaction Gibbs energy by

$$\Delta_r G^{\ominus} = -RT \ln K$$

For the reaction A(g) + B(g) ⇌ C(g) we can use eqn 22.17 to write

$$\begin{aligned}\Delta_r G^{\ominus} &= G_m^{\ominus}(C) - \{G_m^{\ominus}(A) + G_m^{\ominus}(B)\}\\ &= \left\{G_m^{\ominus}(C,0) - RT\ln\frac{q_m^{\ominus}(C)}{N_A}\right\}\\ &\quad - \left[\left\{G_m^{\ominus}(A,0) - RT\ln\frac{q_m^{\ominus}(A)}{N_A}\right\}\right.\\ &\quad \left. + \left\{G_m^{\ominus}(B,0) - RT\ln\frac{q_m^{\ominus}(B)}{N_A}\right\}\right]\\ &= \{G_m^{\ominus}(C,0) - (G_m^{\ominus}(A,0) + G_m^{\ominus}(B,0))\}\\ &\quad - RT\left[\ln\frac{q_m^{\ominus}(C)}{N_A} - \left\{\ln\frac{q_m^{\ominus}(A)}{N_A} + \ln\frac{q_m^{\ominus}(B)}{N_A}\right\}\right]\end{aligned}$$

We can simplify this somewhat alarming expression. First, note that

$$\begin{aligned}&G_m^{\ominus}(C,0) - \{G_m^{\ominus}(A,0) + G_m^{\ominus}(B,0)\}\\ &\quad = U_m^{\ominus}(C,0) - \{U_m^{\ominus}(A,0) + U_m^{\ominus}(B,0)\} = \Delta E\end{aligned}$$

Next, we combine the logarithms using $\ln x - \ln y - \ln z = \ln(x/yz)$:

$$\ln\frac{q_m^{\ominus}(C)}{N_A} - \left\{\ln\frac{q_m^{\ominus}(A)}{N_A} + \ln\frac{q_m^{\ominus}(B)}{N_A}\right\} = \ln\frac{q_m^{\ominus}(C)N_A}{q_m^{\ominus}(A)q_m^{\ominus}(B)}$$

At this stage we have reached

$$\Delta_r G^{\ominus} = \Delta E - RT\ln\frac{q_m^{\ominus}(C)N_A}{q_m^{\ominus}(A)q_m^{\ominus}(B)}$$

When we use $\ln a + x = \ln a + \ln(e^x) = \ln(a\,e^x)$, this expression becomes

$$\Delta_r G^{\ominus} = -RT\ln\left\{\frac{q_m^{\ominus}(C)N_A}{q_m^{\ominus}(A)q_m^{\ominus}(B)}\,e^{-\Delta E/RT}\right\}$$

All we have to do now is to compare this expression with the thermodynamic expression, $\Delta_r G^{\ominus} = -RT \ln K$, and see that the term in parentheses is the expression for K (eqn 22.18).

DISCUSSION QUESTIONS

22.1 Describe the physical significance of the molecular partition function.

22.2 Identify the limits of the generality of the expressions $q^R = kT/hcB$, $q^V = kT/hc\tilde{\nu}$, and $q^E = g^E$, where g^E is the degeneracy of the ground electronic state of an atom or molecule.

22.3 Explain how the internal energy and entropy of a system composed of two levels vary with temperature.

22.4 Explain the reasoning behind the derivation of the entropy in terms of the partition function.

22.5 Explain the origin of the residual entropy.

22.6 Use concepts of statistical thermodynamics to describe the molecular features that determine the magnitudes of equilibrium constants and their variation with temperature.

EXERCISES

The symbol ‡ indicates that calculus is required.

22.7 Suppose polyethylene molecules in solution can exist either as a random coil or fully stretched out, with the latter conformation 2.4 kJ mol^{-1} higher in energy. What is the ratio of the two conformations at 20°C?

22.8 What is the ratio of populations of proton spin orientations in a magnetic field of (a) 1.5 T, (b) 15 T in a sample at 20°C? (*Hint.* For the energy difference, refer to Chapter 21.)

22.9 What is the ratio of populations of electron spin orientations in a magnetic field of 0.33 T in a sample at 20°C? (*Hint.* For the energy difference, refer to Chapter 21.)

22.10 Calculate the ratio of populations of CO_2 molecules with $J = 5$ and $J = 1$ at 20°C. The rotational constant of CO_2 is 11.70 GHz. (*Hint.* Molecular rotations are discussed in Section 19.5.)

22.11 Calculate the ratio of populations of CH_4 molecules with $J = 5$ and $J = 1$ at 20°C. The rotational constant of CH_4 is 157 GHz. (*Hint.* The degeneracy of a spherical rotor in a state with quantum number J is $(2J + 1)^2$.)

22.12 (a) Write down the expression for the partition function of a molecule that has three energy levels at 0, ε, and 3ε with degeneracies 1, 5, and 3, respectively. What are the values of q at (b) $T = 0$, (c) $T = \infty$?

22.13 The ground configuration of carbon gives rise to a triplet with the three levels $^3P_0$, $^3P_1$, and $^3P_2$ at wavenumbers 0, 16.4, and 43.5 cm^{-1}, respectively. Evaluate the partition function of carbon at (a) 10 K, (b) 298 K. (*Hint.* Remember that a level with quantum number J has $2J + 1$ states.)

22.14 The ground configuration of oxygen gives rise to the three levels $^3P_2$, $^3P_1$, and $^3P_0$ at wavenumbers 0, 158.5, and 226.5 cm^{-1}, respectively. (a) Before doing any calculation, state the value of the partition function at $T = 0$. (b) Evaluate the partition function at 298 K and confirm that its value at $T = 0$ is what you anticipated in (a).

22.15 Evaluate the vibrational partition function for $^{35}Cl_2$ at 298 K. For data, see Table 19.1.

22.16 Evaluate the translational partition function at 298 K of (a) a methane molecule trapped in the pore of a zeolite catalyst: take the pore to be spherical with a radius that allows the molecule to move through 1 nm in any direction (that is, the *effective* diameter is 1 nm), (b) a methane molecule in a flask of volume 100 cm^3.

22.17 Evaluate the rotational partition function at 298 K of (a) $^1H^{35}Cl$, for which the rotational constant is 318 GHz, (b) $^{12}C^{16}O_2$, for which the rotational constant is 11.70 GHz.

22.18 N_2O and CO_2 have similar rotational constants (12.6 and 11.7 GHz, respectively) but strikingly different rotational partition functions. Why?

22.19 Derive an expression for the internal energy of a collection of harmonic oscillators. (*Hint.* Substitute eqn 22.4 for the partition function into eqn 22.9 for the energy.)

22.20 Derive an expression for the energy of a molecule that has three energy levels at 0, ε, and 3ε with degeneracies 1, 5, and 3, respectively.

22.21 The states arising from the ground configuration of a carbon atom are described in Exercise 22.13. (a) Derive an expression for the electronic contribution to the molar internal energy and plot it as a function of temperature. (b) Evaluate the expression at 25°C?

22.22 (a) Derive an expression for the electronic contribution to the molar heat capacity of an oxygen atom and plot it as a function of temperature. (b) Evaluate the expression at 25°C. The structure of the atom is described in Exercise 22.14.

22.23 ‡(a) Deduce and then plot an expression for the mean energy of a harmonic oscillator from the partition function in eqn 22.4. (b) Determine the form that your result will have at high temperatures.

22.24 ‡Use the partition function in eqn 22.4 to derive an expression for the heat capacity of a harmonic oscillator, plot your result, and find the limiting value at high temperatures. What, precisely, is meant by 'high' in this case?

22.25 Suppose that the $FClO_3$ molecule can take up any of four orientations in the solid at $T = 0$. What is its residual molar entropy?

22.26 An average human DNA molecule has 5×10^8 base pairs (rungs on the DNA ladder) of four different kinds. If each rung were a random choice of one of these four possibilities, what would be the residual entropy associated with this typical DNA molecule?

22.27 Calculate the molar entropy of nitrogen (N_2) at 298 K. (*Hint.* Ignore the vibration of the molecule. Write the overall partition function as the product of the translational and rotational partition functions.) For data, see Table 19.1.

22.28 Estimate the change in molar entropy when a micelle consisting of 100 molecules disperses. (*Hint.* Treat the transition as the expansion of a gas-like substance that initially occupies a volume $V_{micelle}$ and spreads into a volume $V_{solution}$.)

22.29 The average end-to-end distance of a flexible polymer (such as a fully denatured polypeptide or a strand of DNA) is $N^{1/2}l$, where N is the number of groups (residues or bases) and l is the length of each group. Initially, therefore, one end of the polymer can be found anywhere within a sphere of radius $N^{1/2}l$ centred on the other end. When the ends join to form a circle, they are confined to a volume or radius l. What is the change in molar entropy? Plot the function you derive as a function of N.

22.30 Calculate the standard molar Gibbs energy of nitrogen (N_2) at 298 K relative to its value at $T = 0$.

22.31 Calculate the equilibrium constant for the ionization equilibrium of sodium atoms at 1000 K.

22.32 Calculate the equilibrium constant for the dissociation of I_2(g) at 500 K.

Appendix 1 Quantities and units

The result of a measurement is a **physical quantity** (such as mass or density) that is reported as a numerical multiple of an agreed **unit**:

Physical quantity = numerical value × unit

For example, the mass of an object may be reported as $m = 2.5$ kg and its density as $d = 1.010$ kg dm^{-3} where the units are, respectively, 1 kilogram (1 kg) and 1 kilogram per decimetre cubed (1 kg dm^{-3}). Units are treated like algebraic quantities, and may be multiplied, divided, and cancelled. Thus, the expression (physical quantity)/unit is simply the numerical value of the measurement in the specified units, and hence is a dimensionless quantity. For instance, the mass reported above could be denoted m/kg = 2.5 and the density as d/(kg dm^{-3}) = 1.01.

Physical quantities are denoted by italic or (sloping) Greek letters (as in m for mass and Π for osmotic pressure). Units are denoted by Roman letters (as in m for metre). In the **International System** of units (SI, from the French *Système International d'Unités*), the units are formed from seven **base units** listed in Table A1.1. All other physical quantities can be expressed as combinations of these physical quantities and reported in terms of **derived units**. Thus, volume is (length)^3 and may be reported as a multiple of 1 metre cubed (1 m^3), and density, which is mass/volume, may be reported as a multiple of 1 kilogram per metre cubed (1 kg m^{-3}).

A number of derived units have special names and symbols. The names of units derived from names of people are lower case (as in torr, joule, pascal, and kelvin), but their symbols are upper case (as in Torr, J, Pa, and K). The most important for our purposes are listed in Table A1.2. In all cases (both for base and derived quantities), the units may be modified by a prefix that denotes a factor of a power of 10. In a perfect world, Greek prefixes of units are upright (as in μm) and Greek symbols for physical properties are sloping (as in μ for chemical potential), but available typefaces are not always so obliging. Among the most common prefixes are those listed in Table A1.3. Examples of the use of these prefixes are

$$1\ \mathrm{nm} = 10^{-9}\ \mathrm{m} \quad 1\ \mathrm{ps} = 10^{-12}\ \mathrm{s} \quad 1\ \mu\mathrm{mol} = 10^{-6}\ \mathrm{mol}$$

The kilogram (kg) is anomalous: although it is a base unit, it is interpreted as 10^3 g, and prefixes are attached to the gram (as in 1 mg = 10^{-3} g). Powers of units apply to the prefix as well as the unit they modify:

$$1\ \mathrm{cm}^3 = 1\ (\mathrm{cm})^3 = 1\ (10^{-2}\ \mathrm{m})^3 = 10^{-6}\ \mathrm{m}^3$$

Note that 1 cm^3 does not mean 1 c(m^3). When carrying out numerical calculations, it is usually safest to write out the numerical value of an observable as powers of 10.

There are a number of units that are in wide use but are not a part of the International System. Some are exactly equal to multiples of SI units. These include the *litre* (L), which is exactly 10^3 cm^3 (or 1 dm^3) and the *atmosphere* (atm), which is exactly 101.325 kPa. Others rely on the values of fundamental constants, and hence are liable to change when the values of the fundamental constants are

Table A1.1
The SI base units

Physical quantity	Symbol for quantity	Base unit
Length	l	metre, m
Mass	m	kilogram, kg
Time	t	second, s
Electric current	I	ampere, A
Thermodynamic temperature	T	kelvin, K
Amount of substance	n	mole, mol
Luminous intensity	I	candela, cd

Table A1.2
A selection of derived units

Physical quantity	Derived unit*	Name of derived unit
Force	1 kg m s^{-2}	newton, N
Pressure	1 kg m^{-1} s^{-2}	pascal, Pa
	1 N m^{-2}	
Energy	1 kg m^2 s^{-2}	joule, J
	1 N m	
	1 Pa m^3	
Power	kg m^2 s^{-3}	watt, W
	1 J s^{-1}	

* Equivalent definitions in terms of derived units are given following the definition in terms of base units.

Table A1.3 *Common SI prefixes*

Prefix	z	a	f	p	n	μ	m
Name	zepto	atto	femto	pico	nano	micro	milli
Factor	10^{-21}	10^{-18}	10^{-15}	10^{-12}	10^{-9}	10^{-6}	10^{-3}
Prefix	c	d	k	M	G	T	
Name	centi	deci	kilo	mega	giga	tera	
Factor	10^{-2}	10^{-1}	10^{3}	10^{6}	10^{9}	10^{12}	

Table A1.4 *Some common units*

Physical quantity	Name of unit	Symbol for unit	Value
Time	minute	min	60 s
	hour	h	3600 s
	day	d	86 400 s
Length	ångström	Å	10^{-10} m
Volume	litre	L, l	1 dm^3
Mass	tonne	t	10^3 kg
Pressure	bar	bar	10^5 Pa
	atmosphere	atm	101.325 kPa
Energy	electronvolt	eV	$1.602\ 177\ 33 \times 10^{-19}$ J
			96.485 31 kJ mol^{-1}

All values in the final column are exact, except for the definition of 1 eV.

modified by more accurate or more precise measurements. Thus, the size of the energy unit *electronvolt* (eV), the energy acquired by an electron that is accelerated through a potential difference of exactly 1 V, depends on the value of the charge of the electron, and the present (2004) conversion factor is 1 eV = $1.602\ 177\ 33 \times 10^{-19}$ J. Table A1.4 gives the conversion factors for a number of these convenient units.

Appendix 2 Mathematical techniques

The art of doing mathematics correctly is to do nothing at each step of a calculation. That is, it is permissible to develop an equation by ensuring that the left-hand side of an expression remains equal to the right-hand side. There are several ways of modifying the *appearance* of an expression without upsetting its balance.

Basic procedures

We set the stage for the mathematical arguments in the text by reviewing a few basic procedures, such as manipulation of equations, graphs, logarithms, exponentials, and vectors.

A2.1 Algebraic equations and graphs

The simplest types of equation we have to deal with have the form

$$y = ax + b$$

This expression may be modified by subtracting b from both sides, to give

$$y - b = ax$$

It may be modified further by dividing both sides by a, to give

$$\frac{y-b}{a} = x$$

This series of manipulations is called **rearranging** the expression for y in terms of x to give an expression for x in terms of y. A short cut, as can be seen by inspecting these two steps, is that an added term can be moved through the equals sign provided that as it passes = it changes sign (that happened to b in the example). Similarly, a multiplying factor becomes a divisor (and vice versa) when it passes through the = sign (as happened to a).

There are several more complicated manipulations that are required in certain cases. For example, we can find the values of x that satisfy an equation of the form

$$ax^2 + bx + c = 0$$

or any equation that can be rearranged into this form by the steps we have already illustrated. An equation in which x occurs as its square is called a **quadratic equation.** Its solutions are found by inserting the values of the constants a, b, and c into the expression

$$x = \frac{-b \pm (b^2 - 4ac)^{1/2}}{2a} \qquad \text{(A2.1)}$$

where the two values of x given by this expression (one by using the + sign and the other by using the – sign) are called the two **roots** of the original quadratic equation.

A **function**, f, tells us how something changes as a variable is changed. For example, we might write

$$f(x) = ax + b$$

to show how a property f changes as x is changed. The variation of f with x is best shown by drawing a graph in which f is plotted on the vertical axis and x is plotted horizontally. The graph of the function we have just written is shown in Fig. A2.1. The important point about this graph is that it is **linear** (that is, it is a straight line); its **intercept** with the vertical axis (the value of f when $x = 0$) is b, and its **slope** is a. That is, a straight line has the form

$$f = \text{slope} \times x + \text{intercept}$$

A positive value of a indicates an upward slope from left to right (increasing x); a change of sign of a results in a negative slope, down from left to right. Strictly, we say that y *varies linearly* with x if the relation between them is $y = ax + b$; we say that y is *proportional* to x if the relation is $y = ax$.

The solutions of the equation $f(x) = 0$ can be visualized graphically: they are the values of x for which f cuts through the horizontal axis (the axis corresponding to $f = 0$). For example, the solution of the quadratic equation given earlier is depicted in Fig. A2.2. In general, a

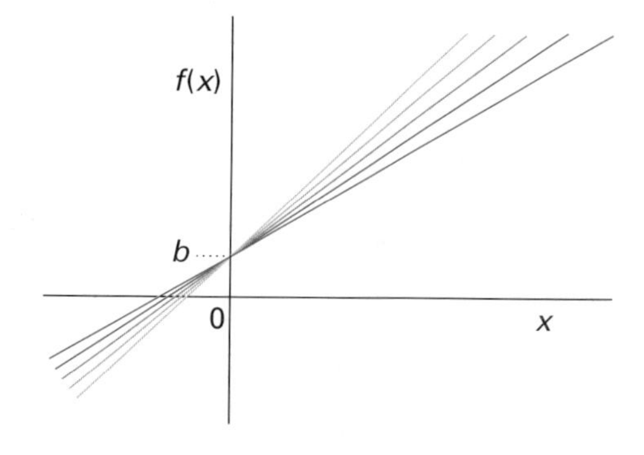

Fig. A2.1 A straight line is described by the equation $f(x) = ax + b$, where a is the slope and b is the intercept.

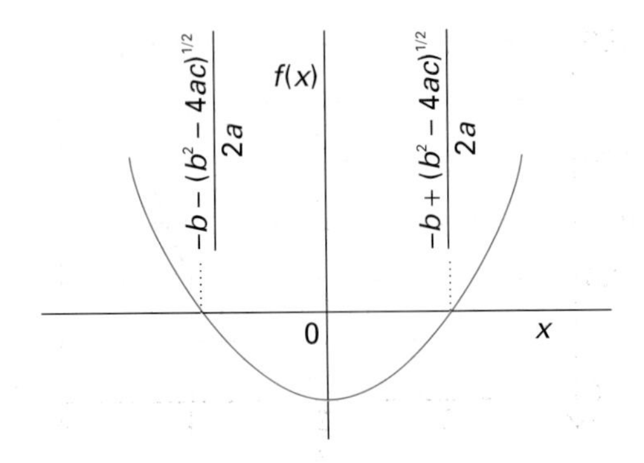

Fig. A2.2 The roots of a quadratic equation are given by the values of x where the parabola intersects the x-axis.

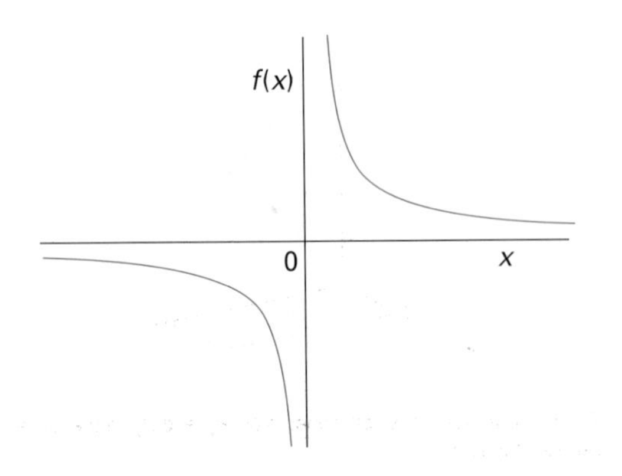

Fig. A2.3 The graph of the equation $f(x) = a/x$, where a is a constant, is a hyperbola. Shown in this figure is the case for $a > 0$.

quadratic equation has a graph that cuts through the horizontal axis at two points (the equation has two roots), a cubic equation (an equation in which x^3 is the highest power of x) cuts through it three times (the equation has three roots), and so on.

Another function that appears often in physical chemistry has the form

$$f(x) = \frac{a}{x}$$

(where a is a positive or negative constant) and its graph is a **hyperbola** (Fig. A2.3).We note that this equation does not have roots: $f(x)$ only approaches zero as x becomes very large and positive or very large and negative. Also, the absolute value of $f(x)$, its value after discarding its sign, approaches infinity as x approaches zero.

A2.2 Logarithms, exponentials, and powers

Some equations are most readily solved by using logarithms and related functions. The **natural logarithm** of a number x is denoted $\ln x$, and is defined as the power to which a certain number designated e must be raised for the result to be equal to x. The number e, which is equal to 2.718... may seem to be decidedly unnatural; however, it falls out naturally from various manipulations in mathematics and its use greatly simplifies calculations. On a calculator, $\ln x$ is obtained simply by entering the number x and pressing the 'ln' key or its equivalent. It follows from the definition of logarithms that

$$\ln x + \ln y = \ln xy \qquad \text{(A2.2a)}$$

$$\ln x - \ln y = \ln \frac{x}{y} \qquad \text{(A2.2b)}$$

$$a \ln x = \ln x^a \qquad \text{(A2.2c)}$$

Thus, $\ln 5 + \ln 3$ is the same as $\ln 15$ and $\ln 6 - \ln 2$ is the same as $\ln 3$, as may readily be checked with a calculator. The last of these three relations is very useful for finding an awkward root of a number. For example, suppose we wanted the fifth root of 28. We write the required root as x, with $x^5 = 28$. We take logarithms of both sides, which gives $\ln x^5 = \ln 28$, and then rewrite the left-hand side of this equation as $5 \ln x$. At this stage we see that we have to solve

$$5 \ln x = \ln 28$$

To do so, we divide both sides by 5, which gives

$$\ln x = \frac{\ln 28}{5} = 0.6664\ldots$$

All we need do at this stage is find the **antilogarithm** of the number on the right, the value of x for which the natural logarithm is the number quoted. The natural antilogarithm of a number is obtained by pressing the 'exp' key on a calculator (where 'exp' is an abbreviation for exponential), and in this case the answer is 1.947... .

There are a number of useful points to remember about logarithms, and they are summarized in Fig. A2.4. We see how logarithms increase only very slowly as x increases. For instance, when x increases from 1 to 1000, $\ln x$ increases from 0 to only 6.9. Another point is that the logarithm of 1 is 0: $\ln 1 = 0$. The logarithms of numbers less than 1 are negative, and in elementary mathematics the logarithms of negative numbers are not defined.[1]

[1] The logarithm of a negative number is complex (that is, involves i, the square root of −1): $\ln(-x) = i\pi + \ln x$.

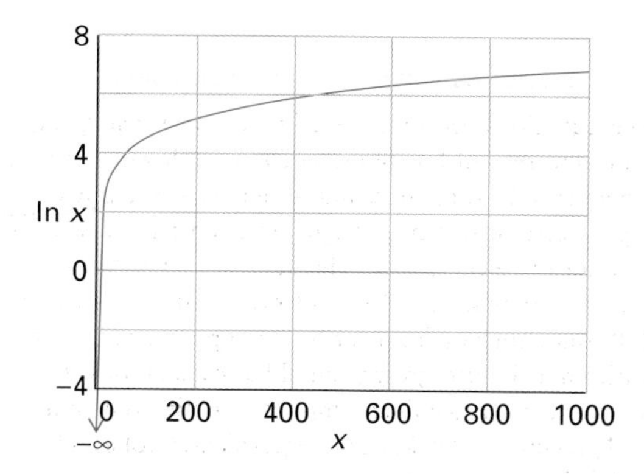

Fig. A2.4 The graph of ln x. Note that ln x approaches $-\infty$ as x approaches 0.

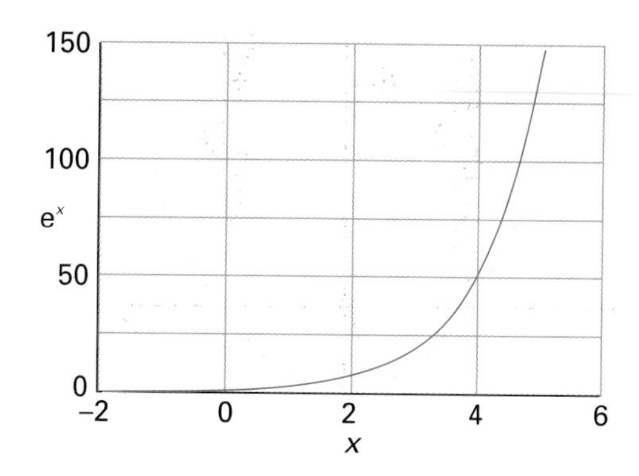

Fig. A2.5 The graph of e^x. Note that e^x approaches 0 as x approaches $-\infty$.

We also encounter the **common logarithm** of a number, the logarithm compiled with 10 in place of e; denoted log x. For example, log 5 is the power to which 10 must be raised to obtain 5, and is 0.698 97.... Common logarithms follow the same rules of addition and subtraction as natural logarithms. They are largely of historical interest now that calculators are so readily available, but they survive in the context of acid–base chemistry and pH. Common and natural logarithms (log and ln, respectively) are related by

$$\ln x = \ln 10 \times \log x = (2.303\ldots) \times \log x \quad \text{(A2.3)}$$

The **exponential function**, e^x, plays a very special role in the mathematics of chemistry. It is evaluated by entering x and pressing the 'exp' key on a calculator. The following properties are important:

$$e^x \times e^y = e^{x+y} \quad \text{(A2.4a)}$$

$$\frac{e^x}{e^y} = e^{x-y} \quad \text{(A2.4b)}$$

$$(e^x)^a = e^{ax} \quad \text{(A2.4c)}$$

(These relations are the analogues of the relations for logarithms.) A graph of e^x is shown in Fig. A2.5. As we see, it is positive for all values of x. It is less than 1 for all negative values of x, is equal to 1 when $x = 0$, and rises ever more rapidly towards infinity as x increases. This sharply rising character of e^x is the origin of the colloquial expression 'exponentially increasing' widely but loosely used in the media. (Strictly, a function increases exponentially if its rate of change is proportional to its current value.)

A2.3 Vectors

A vector quantity has both magnitude and direction. The vector $\boldsymbol{v}$ shown in Fig. A2.6 has components on the x, y, and z axes with magnitudes v_x, v_y, and v_z, respectively. The direction of each of the components is denoted with a plus sign or minus sign. For example, if $v_x = -1.0$, the x-component of the vector $\boldsymbol{v}$ has a magnitude of 1.0 and points in the $-x$ direction. The magnitude of the vector is denoted v or $|\boldsymbol{v}|$ and is given by

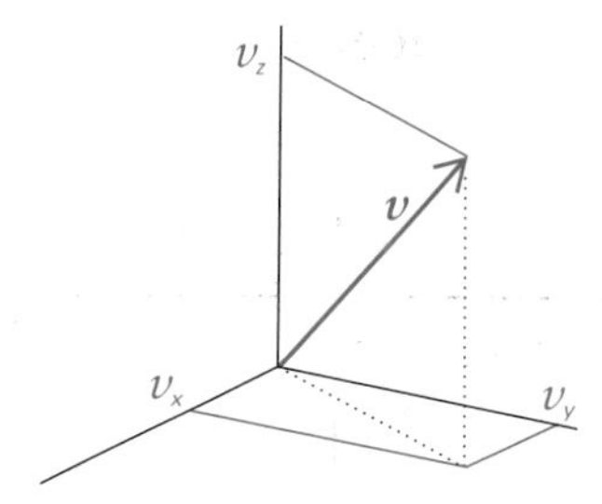

Fig. A2.6 The vector $\boldsymbol{v}$ has components $\boldsymbol{v}_x$, $\boldsymbol{v}_y$, and $\boldsymbol{v}_z$ on the x-, y-, and z-axes, respectively.

$$v = (v_x^2 + v_y^2 + v_z^2)^{1/2} \quad \text{(A2.5)}$$

Operations involving vectors are not as straightforward as those involving numbers. Here we describe a procedure for adding and subtracting two vectors because such vector operations are important for the discussion of atomic structure and molecular dipole moments.

Consider two vectors $\boldsymbol{v}_1$ and $\boldsymbol{v}_2$ making an angle θ (Fig. A2.7a). The first step in the addition of $\boldsymbol{v}_2$ to $\boldsymbol{v}_1$ consists of joining the tail of $\boldsymbol{v}_2$ to the head of $\boldsymbol{v}_1$, as shown in Fig. A2.7b. In the second step, we draw a vector $\boldsymbol{v}_{res}$, the **resultant vector**, originating from the tail of $\boldsymbol{v}_1$ to the head of $\boldsymbol{v}_2$, as shown in Fig. A2.7c.

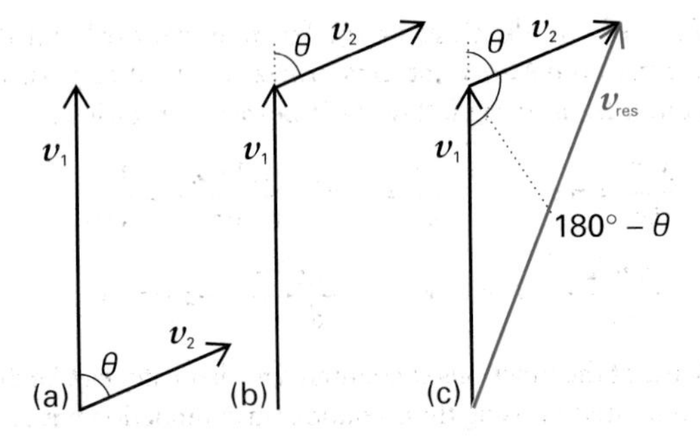

Fig. A2.7 (a) The vectors $\boldsymbol{v}_1$ and $\boldsymbol{v}_2$ make an angle θ. (b) To add $\boldsymbol{v}_2$ to $\boldsymbol{v}_1$, we first join the tail of $\boldsymbol{v}_2$ to the head of $\boldsymbol{v}_1$, making sure that the angle θ between the vectors remains unchanged. (c) To finish the process, we draw the resultant vector $\boldsymbol{v}_{res}$ by joining the tail of $\boldsymbol{v}_1$ to the head of $\boldsymbol{v}_2$.

Self-test A2.1

Using the same vectors shown in Fig. A2.7a, show that reversing the order of addition leads to the same result. That is, we obtain the same $\boldsymbol{v}_{res}$ whether we add $\boldsymbol{v}_2$ to $\boldsymbol{v}_1$ or $\boldsymbol{v}_1$ to $\boldsymbol{v}_2$.

[*Answer:* see Fig. A2.7c for the result of adding $\boldsymbol{v}_2$ to $\boldsymbol{v}_1$ and Fig. A2.8 for the result of adding $\boldsymbol{v}_1$ to $\boldsymbol{v}_2$]

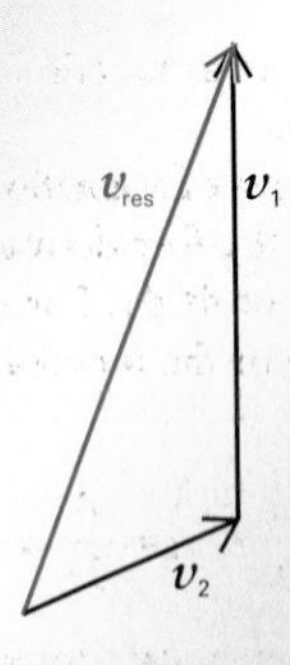

Fig. A2.8 The result of adding the vector $\boldsymbol{v}_1$ to the vector $\boldsymbol{v}_2$, with both vectors defined in Fig. A2.7a. Comparison with the result shown in Fig. A2.7c for the addition of $\boldsymbol{v}_2$ to $\boldsymbol{v}_1$ shows that reversing the order of vector addition does not affect the result.

To calculate the magnitude of $\boldsymbol{v}_{res}$, we note that $\boldsymbol{v}_1$, $\boldsymbol{v}_2$, and $\boldsymbol{v}_{res}$ form a triangle and that we know the magnitudes of two of its sides (v_1 and v_2) and of the angle between them ($180° - \theta$; see Fig. A2.7c). To calculate the magnitude of the third side, v_{res}, we make use of the *law of cosines*, which states that:

For a triangle with sides a, b, and c, and angle C facing side c:

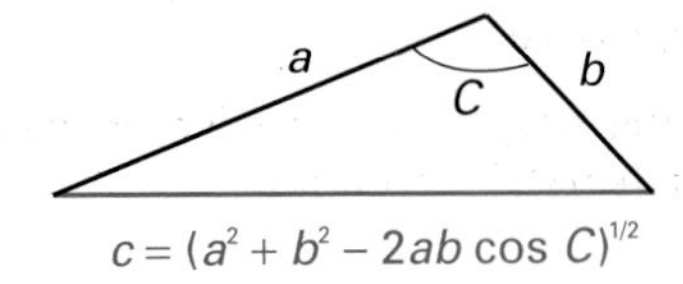

Fig. A2.9 The graphical representation of the law of cosines.

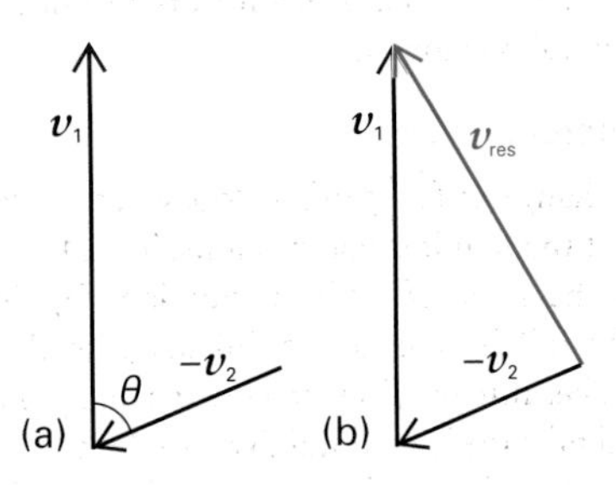

Fig. A2.10 The graphical method for subtraction of the vector $\boldsymbol{v}_2$ from the vector $\boldsymbol{v}_1$ (as shown in Fig. A2.7a) consists of two steps: (a) reversing the direction of $\boldsymbol{v}_2$ to form $-\boldsymbol{v}_2$, and (b) adding $-\boldsymbol{v}_2$ to $\boldsymbol{v}_1$.

$$c^2 = a^2 + b^2 - 2ab\cos C$$

This law is summarized graphically in Fig. A2.9 and its application to the case shown in Fig. A2.7c leads to the expression

$$v_{res}^2 = v_1^2 + v_2^2 - 2v_1v_2\cos(180° - \theta)$$

Because $\cos(180° - \theta) = -\cos\theta$, it follows after taking the square root of both sides of the preceding expression that

$$v_{res} = (v_1^2 + v_2^2 + 2v_1v_2\cos\theta)^{1/2} \qquad \text{(A2.6)}$$

which is the result used in Section 17.2 for the addition of two dipole moment vectors.

The subtraction of vectors follows the same principles outlined above for addition. Consider again the vectors shown in Fig. A2.7a. We note that subtraction of $\boldsymbol{v}_2$ from $\boldsymbol{v}_1$ amounts to addition of $-\boldsymbol{v}_2$ to $\boldsymbol{v}_1$. It follows that in the first step of subtraction we draw $-\boldsymbol{v}_2$ by reversing the direction of $\boldsymbol{v}_2$ (Fig. A2.10a). Then, the second step consists of adding the $-\boldsymbol{v}_2$ to $\boldsymbol{v}_1$ by using the strategy shown in Fig. A2.7c: we draw a resultant vector $\boldsymbol{v}_{res}$ by joining the tail of $-\boldsymbol{v}_2$ to the head of $\boldsymbol{v}_1$.

One procedure for multiplying vectors—and the only one we shall discuss here—consists of calculating the **scalar product** (or **dot product**) of two vectors $\boldsymbol{v}_1$ and $\boldsymbol{v}_2$ making an angle θ:[2]

[2] Another procedure involves calculation of the cross-product of two vectors. Vector division is not defined.

$$v_1 \cdot v_2 = v_1 v_2 \cos\theta \qquad (A2.7)$$

As its name suggests, the scalar product of two vectors is a scalar (a number) and not a vector.

Calculus

Now we turn to techniques of calculus, a branch of mathematics that is used to model a host of physical, chemical, and biological phenomena.

A2.4 Differentiation

Rates of change of functions—slopes—are best discussed in terms of the infinitesimal calculus. The slope of a function, like the slope of a hill, is obtained by dividing the rise of the hill by the horizontal distance (Fig. A2.11). However, because the slope may vary from point to point, we should take the horizontal distance between the points as small as possible. In fact, we let it become infinitesimally small—hence the name ***infinitesimal* calculus**. The values of a function f at two locations x and $x + \delta x$ are $f(x)$ and $f(x + \delta x)$, respectively. Therefore, the slope of the function f at x is the vertical distance, which we write δf, divided by the horizontal distance, which we write δx:

$$\text{Slope} = \frac{\text{rise in value}}{\text{horizontal distance}} = \frac{\delta f}{\delta x} = \frac{f(x+\delta x) - f(x)}{\delta x}$$

The slope exactly at x itself is obtained by letting the horizontal distance become zero, which we write $\lim \delta x \to 0$. In this limit, the δ is replaced by a d, and we write

$$\text{Slope at } x = \frac{\mathrm{d}f}{\mathrm{d}x} = \lim_{\delta x \to 0} \frac{f(x+\delta x) - f(x)}{\delta x}$$

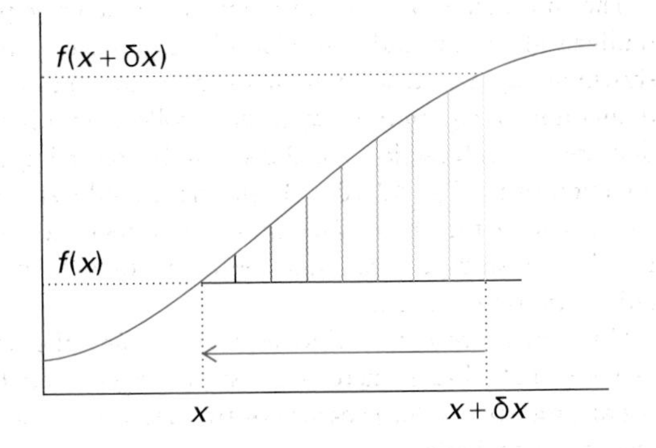

Fig. A2.11 The slope of $f(x)$ at x, $\mathrm{d}f/\mathrm{d}x$, is obtained by making a series of approximations to the value of $f(x+\delta x) - f(x)$ divided by change in x, denoted δx, and allowing δx to approach 0 (as denoted by the vertical lines getting closer to x).

To work out the slope of any function, we work out the expression on the right: this process is called **differentiation**. It leads to the following important expressions:

$$\frac{\mathrm{d}x^n}{\mathrm{d}x} = nx^{n-1} \qquad \frac{\mathrm{d}\,\mathrm{e}^{ax}}{\mathrm{d}x} = a\,\mathrm{e}^{ax} \qquad \frac{\mathrm{d}\ln ax}{\mathrm{d}x} = \frac{1}{x}$$

$$\frac{\mathrm{d}\sin ax}{\mathrm{d}x} = a\cos ax \qquad \frac{\mathrm{d}\cos ax}{\mathrm{d}x} = -a\sin ax$$

Most of the functions encountered in chemistry can be differentiated by using these relations in conjunction with the following rules:

Rule 1 For two functions f and g:

$$\mathrm{d}(f+g) = \mathrm{d}f + \mathrm{d}g \qquad (A2.8)$$

Rule 2 (the product rule). For two functions f and g:

$$\mathrm{d}(fg) = f\,\mathrm{d}g + g\,\mathrm{d}f \qquad (A2.9)$$

Rule 3 (the quotient rule). For two functions f and g:

$$\mathrm{d}\frac{f}{g} = \frac{1}{g}\mathrm{d}f - \frac{f}{g^2}\mathrm{d}g \qquad (A2.10)$$

Rule 4 (the chain rule). For a function $f = f(g)$, where $g = g(t)$,

$$\frac{\mathrm{d}f}{\mathrm{d}t} = \frac{\mathrm{d}f}{\mathrm{d}g}\frac{\mathrm{d}g}{\mathrm{d}t} \qquad (A2.11)$$

In the last rule, $f(g)$ is a 'function of a function', as in $\ln(1 + x^2)$ or $\ln(\sin x)$.

The second derivative of a function, denoted $\mathrm{d}^2f/\mathrm{d}x^2$, is calculated by taking the first derivative, $\mathrm{d}f/\mathrm{d}x$, and then taking the derivative of $\mathrm{d}f/\mathrm{d}x$. For example, to calculate the second derivative of the function $\sin ax$ (where a is a constant), we write

$$\frac{\mathrm{d}^2 \sin ax}{\mathrm{d}x^2} = \frac{\mathrm{d}}{\mathrm{d}x}\left(\frac{\mathrm{d}\sin ax}{\mathrm{d}x}\right) = \frac{\mathrm{d}}{\mathrm{d}x}(a\cos ax) = -a^2\sin ax$$

A very useful mathematical procedure involving differentiation consists of finding the value of x corresponding to the extremum (maximum or minimum) of any function $f(x)$. At an extremum the slope of the graph of the function is exactly zero (Fig. A2.12), so to find the value of x at which a maximum or minimum occurs we differentiate the function, set the result equal to zero, and solve the equation for x. For example, consider the function $4x^2 + 3x - 6$. The first derivative is zero when

$$\frac{\mathrm{d}}{\mathrm{d}x}(4x^2 + 3x - 6) = 8x + 3 = 0 \quad \text{or} \quad x = -\frac{3}{8}$$

To decide whether the function has a maximum or a minimum at this point, we note that the second derivative is an indication of the curvature of a function. Where $\mathrm{d}^2f/\mathrm{d}x^2$ is positive, the graph of the function has a $\cup$ shape;

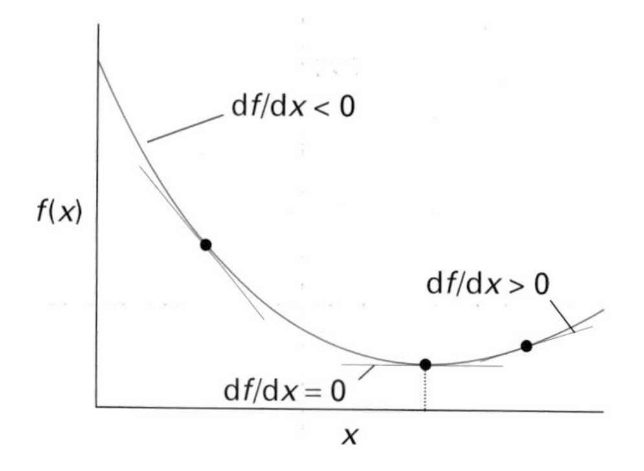

Fig. A2.12 At an extremum, the first derivative of a function is zero. The figure shows the case of a minimum.

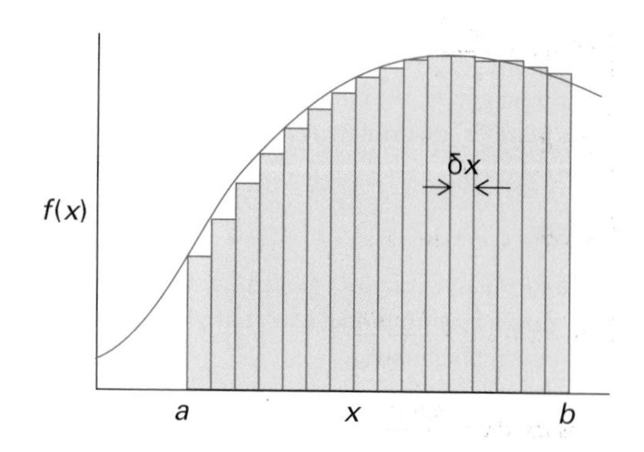

Fig. A2.13 The shaded area is equal to the definite integral of $f(x)$ between the limits a and b.

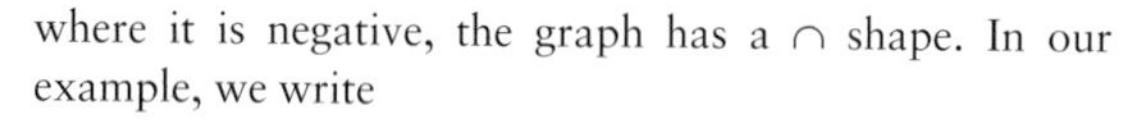

where it is negative, the graph has a ∩ shape. In our example, we write

$$\frac{d^2}{dx^2}(4x^2 + 3x - 6) = \frac{d}{dx}(8x + 3) = 8 > 0$$

It follows that the function $f(x) = 4x^2 + 3x - 6$ has a minimum at $x = -\frac{3}{8}$.

A2.5 Power series and Taylor expansions

A **power series** has the form

$$c_0 + c_1(x - a) + c_2(x - a)^2 + \cdots + c_n(x - a)^n + \cdots$$
$$= \sum_{n=0}^{\infty} c_n(x - a)^n \qquad \text{(A2.12)}$$

where c_n and a are constants. It is often useful to express a function $f(x)$ in the vicinity of $x = a$ as a special power series called the **Taylor series**, or **Taylor expansion**, which has the form:

$$f(x) = f(a) + \left(\frac{df}{dx}\right)_a (x - a) + \frac{1}{2!}\left(\frac{d^2f}{dx^2}\right)_a (x - a)^2$$
$$+ \cdots + \frac{1}{n!}\left(\frac{d^nf}{dx^n}\right)_a (x - a)^n$$
$$= \sum_{n=0}^{\infty} \frac{1}{n!}\left(\frac{d^nf}{dx^n}\right)_a (x - a)^n \qquad \text{(A2.13)}$$

where $n!$ denotes a **factorial** given by[3]

$$n! = n(n-1)(n-2) \cdots 1$$

The following Taylor expansions are often useful:

$$\frac{1}{1 + x} = 1 - x + x^2 \cdots$$

$$e^x = 1 + x + \tfrac{1}{2}x^2 + \cdots$$

$$\ln x = (x - 1) - \tfrac{1}{2}(x - 1)^2 + \tfrac{1}{3}(x - 1)^3 - \tfrac{1}{4}(x - 1)^4 + \cdots$$

$$\ln(1 + x) = x - \tfrac{1}{2}x^2 + \tfrac{1}{3}x^3 \cdots$$

If $x \ll 1$, then $(1 + x)^{-1} \approx 1 - x$, $e^x \approx 1 + x$, and $\ln(1 + x) \approx x$.

A2.6 Integration

The area under a graph of any function f is found by the techniques of **integration**. For instance, the area under the graph of the function f drawn in Fig. A2.13 can be written as the value of f evaluated at a point multiplied by the width of the region, δx, and then all those products $f(x)\,\delta x$ summed over all the regions:

$$\text{Area between } a \text{ and } b = \sum f(x)\,\delta x$$

When we allow δx to become infinitesimally small, written dx, and sum an infinite number of strips, we write

$$\text{Area between } a \text{ and } b = \int_a^b f(x)\,dx$$

The elongated S symbol on the right is called the **integral** of the function f. When written as $\int$ alone, it is the **indefinite integral** of the function. When written with limits (as in the expression above), it is the **definite integral** of the function. The definite integral is the indefinite integral evaluated at the upper limit (b) minus the indefinite integral evaluated at the lower limit (a).

Some important integrals are[4]

[3] By definition, $0! = 1$.

[4] Strictly, an indefinite integral should be written with an arbitrary constant on the right, so $\int x\,dx = \frac{1}{2}x^2 + \text{constant}$. However, tables of integrals commonly omit the constant. It cancels when the definite integral is evaluated.

$$\int x^n \, dx = \frac{x^{n+1}}{n+1}$$

$$\int e^{ax} \, dx = \frac{e^{ax}}{a}$$

$$\int \ln ax \, dx = x \ln ax - x$$

$$\int \sin ax \, dx = -\frac{\cos ax}{a}$$

$$\int \cos ax \, dx = \frac{\sin ax}{a}$$

It can be verified from these examples—and this is a very deep result of infinitesimal calculus—that *integration is the inverse of differentiation*. That is, if we integrate a function and then differentiate the result, we get back the original function.

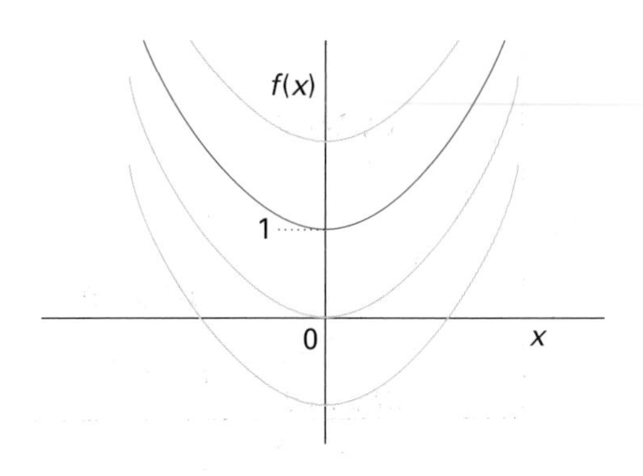

Fig. A2.14 The *general* solution of the differential equation $df/dx = ax$ is any one of the parabolas shown here (and others like them); the *particular* solution, which is identified by the boundary condition that f must satisfy, is shown by the dark line.

A2.7 Differential equations

An **ordinary differential equation** is a relation between derivatives of a function of one variable and the function itself. For example, if the slope of a function increases in proportion to x, we write

$$\frac{df}{dx} = ax$$

where a is a constant. To solve a differential equation, we have to look for the function f that satisfies it: the process is called **integrating** the equation. In this case we would multiply each side by dx, to obtain

$$df = ax \, dx$$

and then integrate both sides:

$$\int df = \int ax \, dx$$

The integral on the left is f (because integration is the inverse of differentiation) and that on the right is $\frac{1}{2}ax^2$ (plus a constant in each case). Therefore:

$$f(x) = \tfrac{1}{2}ax^2 + \text{constant}$$

This is the **general solution** of the equation (Fig. A2.14). To fix the value of the constant and to find the **particular solution,** we take note of the **boundary conditions** that the function must satisfy, the value that we know the function has at a particular point. Thus, if we know that $f(0) = 1$, then we can write

$$1 = \tfrac{1}{2}a + \text{constant}, \quad \text{so constant} = 1 - \tfrac{1}{2}a$$

The particular solution that satisfies the boundary condition is therefore

$$f(x) = \tfrac{1}{2}ax^2 + 1 - \tfrac{1}{2}a$$

In chemical kinetics, for instance, we may know that the reaction rate is proportional to the concentration of a reactant, and look for a general solution of the rate equation (a differential equation) that tells us how the concentration varies with time as the reaction proceeds. The particular solution is then obtained by making sure that the concentration has the correct value initially. A boundary condition is called an *initial condition* if the variable is time, as in a rate law.

A differential equation that is expressed in terms of first derivatives is a **first-order differential equation.** Rate laws are first-order differential equations.[5] A differential equation that is expressed in terms of second derivatives is a **second-order differential equation.** The Schrödinger equation is a second-order differential equation. The solution of differential equations is a very powerful technique in the physical sciences, but is often very difficult. All the second-order differential equations that occur in this text can be found tabulated in compilations of solutions or can be solved with mathematical software, and the specialized techniques that are needed to establish the form of the solutions may be found in mathematical texts.

[5] Do not confuse this use of the term 'order' with the order of the rate law: even a second-order rate law is a first-order differential equation!

Appendix 3 Concepts of physics

Throughout the text we use ideas of classical physics as the basis for discussion of energy exchanges during chemical reactions, atomic and molecular structure, molecular interactions, and spectroscopic techniques. Here we review the concepts the classical mechanics, electromagnetism, and electrostatics.

Classical mechanics

Classical mechanics describes the behaviour of particles in terms of two equations. One expresses the fact that the total energy is constant in the absence of external forces and the other expresses the response of particles to the forces acting on them.

A3.1 Energy

Kinetic energy, E_K, is the energy that a body (a block of matter, an atom, or an electron) possesses by virtue of its motion. The formula for calculating the kinetic energy of a body of mass m that is travelling at a speed v is

$$E_K = \tfrac{1}{2}mv^2 \qquad \text{(A3.1)}$$

This expression shows that a body may have a high kinetic energy if it is heavy (m large) and is travelling rapidly (v large). A stationary body ($v = 0$) has zero kinetic energy, whatever its mass. The energy of a sample of perfect gas is entirely due to the kinetic energy of its molecules: they travel more rapidly (on average) at high temperatures than at low, so raising the temperature of a gas increases the kinetic energy of its molecules.

Potential energy, E_P or V, is the energy that a body has by virtue of its position. A body on the surface of the Earth has a potential energy on account of the gravitational force it experiences: if the body is raised, then its potential energy is increased. There is no general formula for calculating the potential energy of a body because there are several kinds of force. For a body of mass m at a height h above (but close to) the surface of the Earth, the gravitational potential energy is

$$E_P = mgh$$

where g is the acceleration of free fall (g = 9.81 m s^{-2}). A heavy object at a certain height has a greater potential energy than a light object at the same height. One very important contribution to the potential energy is encountered when a charged particle is brought up to another charge. In this case the potential energy is inversely proportional to the distance between the charges (see Section A3.3):

$$E_P \propto \frac{1}{r} \quad \text{specifically, } E_P = \frac{q_1 q_2}{4\pi\varepsilon_0 r}$$

This **Coulomb potential energy** decreases with distance, and two infinitely widely separated charged particles have zero potential energy of interaction. The Coulomb potential energy plays a central role in the structures of atoms, molecules, and solids.

The **total energy**, E, of a body is the sum of its kinetic and potential energies. It is a central feature of physics that *the total energy of a body that is free from external influences is constant*. Thus, a stationary ball at a height h above the surface of the Earth has a potential energy of magnitude mgh; if it is released and begins to fall to the ground, it loses potential energy (as it loses height), but gains the same amount of kinetic energy (and therefore accelerates). Just before it hits the surface, it has lost all its potential energy, and all its energy is kinetic.

The SI unit of energy is the *joule* (J), which is defined as

$$1\ \text{J} = 1\ \text{kg m}^2\ \text{s}^{-2} \qquad \text{(A3.2)}$$

Calories (cal) and kilocalories (kcal) are still encountered in the chemical literature: by definition, 1 cal = 4.184 J. An energy of 1 cal is enough to raise the temperature of 1 g of water by 1°C.

The rate of change of energy is called the **power**, P, expressed as joules per second, or *watt*, W:

$$1\ \text{W} = 1\ \text{J s}^{-1} \qquad \text{(A3.3)}$$

A3.2 Force

Classical mechanics described the motion of a particle in terms of its **velocity**, $\boldsymbol{v}$, the rate of change of its position:

$$\boldsymbol{v} = \frac{d\boldsymbol{r}}{dt} \qquad \text{(A3.4)}$$

The velocity is a vector, with both direction and magnitude (see Appendix 2). The magnitude of the velocity is the **speed**, v. The **linear momentum**, $\boldsymbol{p}$, of a particle of mass m is related to its velocity, $\boldsymbol{v}$, by

$$\boldsymbol{p} = m\boldsymbol{v} \qquad \text{(A3.5)}$$

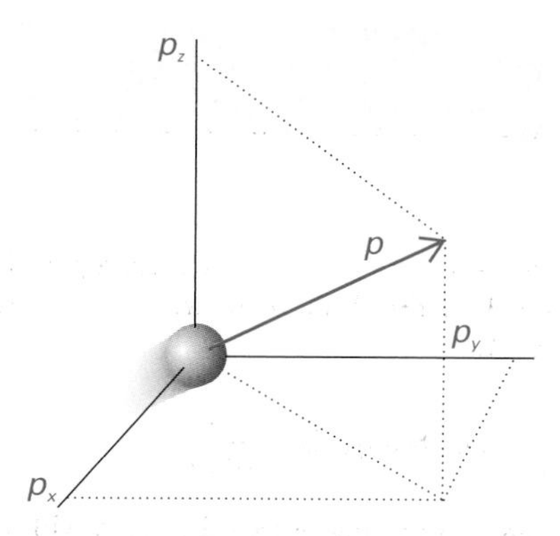

Fig. A3.1 The linear momentum of a particle is a vector property and points in the direction of motion.

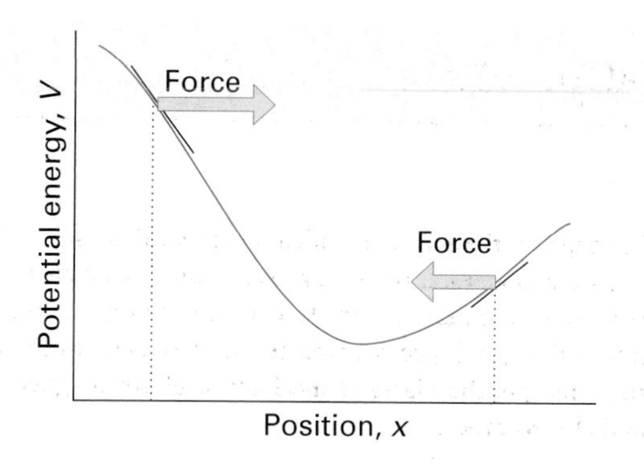

Fig. A3.2 The force acting on a particle is determined by the slope of the potential energy at each point. The force points in the direction of lower potential energy.

Like the velocity vector, the linear momentum vector points in the direction of travel of the particle (Fig. A3.2). In terms of the linear momentum, the kinetic energy of a particle is

$$E_K = \frac{p^2}{2m} \qquad \text{(A3.6)}$$

The state of motion of a particle is changed by a **force, *F***. According to Newton's second law of motion, a force changes the momentum of a particle such that the acceleration, a, of the particle (its rate of change of velocity, or dv/dt) is proportional to the strength of the force:

$$\text{Force} = \text{mass} \times \text{acceleration, or } F = ma = m\frac{dv}{dt} \qquad \text{(A3.7)}$$

We note that the force and acceleration, like the velocity and momentum, are vectors. The SI unit for expressing the magnitude of a force is the *newton* (N), which is defined as

$$1\ \text{N} = 1\ \text{kg m s}^{-2} \qquad \text{(A3.8)}$$

Equation A3.7 shows that a stronger force is required to accelerate a heavy particle by a given amount than to accelerate a light particle by the same amount. A force can be used to change the kinetic energy of a body, by accelerating the body to a higher speed. It may also be used to change the potential energy of a body by moving it to another position (for example, by raising it near the surface of the Earth). The force experienced by a particle free to move in one dimension is related to its potential energy, V, by

$$F = -\frac{dV}{dx} \qquad \text{(A3.9)}$$

This relation implies that the direction of the force is towards decreasing potential energy (Fig. A3.2).

The **work**, w, done on an object is the product of the distance, s, moved and the force opposing the motion:

$$w = -Fs \qquad \text{(A3.10a)}$$

It requires a lot of work to move a long distance against a strong opposing force (think of cycling into a strong wind). If the opposing force changes at different points on the path, then we consider the force as a function of position, $F(s)$, and write

$$w = -\int F(s)\, ds \qquad \text{(A3.10b)}$$

The integral is evaluated along the path traversed by the particle.

Electrostatics

Electrostatics is the study of the interactions of stationary electric charges. The elementary charge, the magnitude of charge carried by a single electron or proton, is $e \approx 1.60 \times 10^{-19}$ C. The magnitude of the charge per mole is Faraday's constant: $F = N_A e = 9.65 \times 10^4\ \text{C mol}^{-1}$.

A3.3 The Coulomb interaction

The fundamental expression in electrostatics is the Coulomb potential energy of one charge of magnitude q at a distance r from another charge q':

$$V = \frac{qq'}{4\pi\varepsilon_0 r} \qquad \text{(A3.11)}$$

That is, the potential energy is inversely proportional to the separation of the charges. The fundamental constant ε_0 is the **vacuum permittivity**; its value is

$$\varepsilon_0 = 8.854\ 187\ 816 \times 10^{-12}\ \text{J}^{-1}\ \text{C}^2\ \text{m}^{-1}$$

With r in metres and the charges in coulombs, the potential energy is in joules. The potential energy is equal to the work that must be done to bring up a charge q from infinity to a distance r from a charge q'. The implication is then that the *force* exerted by a charge q on a charge q' is inversely proportional to the *square* of their separation:

$$F = \frac{qq'}{4\pi\varepsilon_0 r^2} \quad \text{(A3.12)}$$

This expression is **Coulomb's inverse-square law of force.**

A3.4 The Coulomb potential

We can express the potential energy of a charge q in the presence of another charge q' in terms of the **Coulomb potential,**[1] ϕ, due to q':

$$V = q\phi, \qquad \phi = \frac{q'}{4\pi\varepsilon_0 r} \quad \text{(A3.13)}$$

The units of potential are joules per coulomb (J C^{-1}), so when ϕ is multiplied by a charge in coulombs, the result is in joules. The combination joules per coulomb occurs widely in electrostatics, and is called a *volt*, V:

$$1\ \text{V} = 1\ \text{J C}^{-1}$$

(which implies that 1 V C = 1 J). If there are several charges $q_1, q_2, \ldots$ present in the system, then the total potential experienced by the charge q is the sum of the potential generated by each charge:

$$\phi = \phi_1 + \phi_2 + \cdots$$

For example, the potential generated by a dipole is the sum of the potentials of the two equal and opposite charges: these potentials do not in general cancel because the point of interest is at different distances from the two charges (Fig. A3.3).

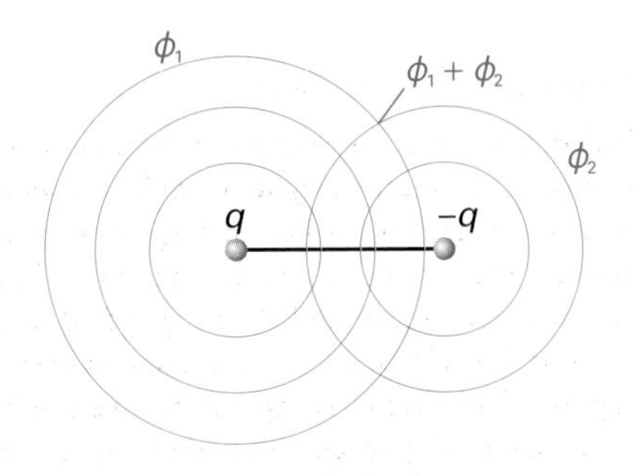

Fig. A3.3 The electric potential at a point is equal to the sum of the potentials due to each charge.

A3.5 Current, resistance, and Ohm's law

The motion of charge gives rise to an **electric current,** I. Electric current is measured in amperes, A, where

$$1\ \text{A} = 1\ \text{C s}^{-1}$$

If the electric charge is that of electrons (as it is through metals and semiconductors), then a current of 1 A represents the flow of 6×10^{18} electrons per second. If the current flows from a region of potential ϕ_i to ϕ_f, through a potential difference $\Delta\phi = \phi_f - \phi_i$, then the rate of doing work is the current (the rate of transfer of charge) multiplied by the potential difference, $I \times \Delta\phi$. The rate of doing work is called **power,** P, so

$$P = I\,\Delta\phi \quad \text{(A3.14)}$$

With current in amperes and the potential difference in volts, the power works out in joules per second, or watts, W (Section A3.1).

The total energy supplied in a time t is the power (the energy per second) multiplied by the time:

$$E = Pt = It\,\Delta\phi$$

The energy is obtained in joules with the current in amperes, the potential difference in volts, and the time in seconds.

The current flowing through a conductor is proportional to the potential difference between the ends of the conductor and inversely proportional to the **resistance,** R, of the conductor:

$$I = \frac{\Delta\phi}{R} \quad \text{(A3.15)}$$

This empirical relation is called **Ohm's law.** With the current in amperes and the potential difference in volts, the resistance is measured in *ohms*, Ω, with 1 Ω = 1 V A^{-1}.

Electromagnetic radiation

Waves are disturbances that travel through space with a finite velocity. Examples of disturbances include the collective motion of water molecules in ocean waves and of gas particles in sound waves. Waves can be characterized by a **wave equation,** a differential equation that describes the motion of the wave in space and time. **Harmonic waves** are waves with displacements that can be expressed as sine or cosine functions. These concepts are used in classical physics to describe the wave character of electromagnetic radiation, which is the focus of the following discussion.

[1] Distinguish potential from potential energy.

A3.6 The electromagnetic field

In classical physics, electromagnetic radiation is understood in terms of the **electromagnetic field,** an oscillating electric and magnetic disturbance that spreads as a harmonic wave through empty space, the vacuum. The wave travels at a constant speed called the *speed of light*, c, which is about 3×10^8 m s^{-1}. As its name suggests, an electromagnetic field has two components, an **electric field** that acts on charged particles (whether stationary or moving) and a **magnetic field** that acts only on moving charged particles. The electromagnetic field is characterized by a **wavelength,** λ (lambda), the distance between the neighbouring peaks of the wave, and its **frequency,** ν (nu), the number of times per second at which its displacement at a fixed point returns to its original value (Fig. A3.4). The frequency is measured in *hertz*, where 1 Hz = 1 s^{-1}. The wavelength and frequency of an electromagnetic wave are related by

$$\lambda\nu = c \tag{A3.16}$$

Therefore, the shorter the wavelength, the higher the frequency. The characteristics of a wave are also reported by giving the **wavenumber,** $\tilde{\nu}$ (nu tilde), of the radiation, where

$$\tilde{\nu} = \frac{\nu}{c} = \frac{1}{\lambda} \tag{A3.17}$$

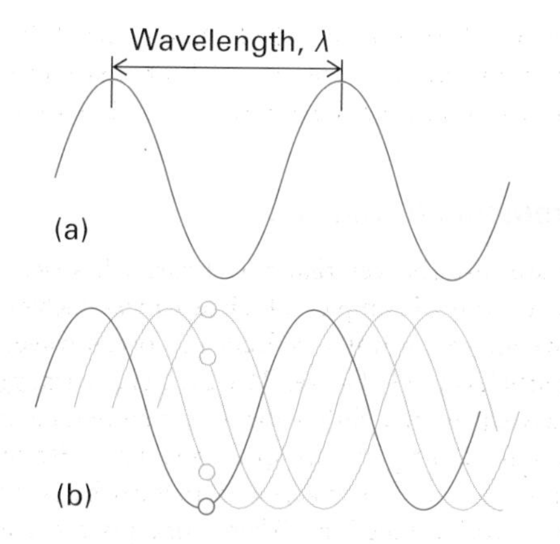

Fig. A3.4 (a) The wavelength, λ (lambda), of a wave is the peak-to-peak distance. (b) The wave is shown travelling to the right at a speed c. At a given location, the instantaneous amplitude of the wave changes through a complete cycle (the four dots show half a cycle) as it passes a given point. The frequency, ν (nu) is the number of cycles per second that occur at a given point. Wavelength and frequency are related by $\lambda\nu = c$.

Table A3.1
*The regions of the electromagnetic spectrum**

Region	Wavelength	Frequency/Hz
Radiofrequency	> 30 cm	$< 10^9$
Microwave	3 mm to 30 cm	10^9 to 10^{11}
Infrared	1000 nm to 3 mm	10^{11} to 3×10^{14}
Visible	400 nm to 800 nm	4×10^{14} to 8×10^{14}
Ultraviolet	3 nm to 300 nm	10^{15} to 10^{17}
X-rays, γ-rays	< 3 nm	$> 10^{17}$

* The boundaries of the regions are only approximate.

A wavenumber can be interpreted as the number of complete wavelengths in a given length. Wavenumbers are normally reported in reciprocal centimetres (cm^{-1}), so a wavenumber of 5 cm^{-1} indicates that there are five complete wavelengths in 1 cm. The classification of the electromagnetic field according to its frequency and wavelength is summarized in Table A3.1.

A3.7 Features of electromagnetic radiation

Consider an electromagnetic disturbance travelling along the x direction with wavelength λ and frequency ν. The functions that describe the oscillating electric field, $\mathcal{E}(x,t)$, and magnetic field, $\mathcal{B}(x,t)$, may be written as

$$\mathcal{E}(x,t) = \mathcal{E}_0 \cos\{2\pi\nu t - (2\pi/\lambda)x + \phi\} \tag{A3.18a}$$

$$\mathcal{B}(x,t) = \mathcal{B}_0 \cos\{2\pi\nu t - (2\pi/\lambda)x + \phi\} \tag{A3.18b}$$

where $\mathcal{E}_0$ and $\mathcal{B}_0$ are the amplitudes of the electric and magnetic fields, respectively, and the parameter ϕ is the **phase** of the wave, which varies from $-\pi$ to π and gives the relative location of the peaks of two waves. If two waves, in the same region of space, with the same wavelength are shifted by $\phi = \pi$ or $-\pi$ (so the peaks of one wave coincide with the troughs of the other), then the resultant wave will have diminished amplitudes. The waves are said to interfere destructively. A value of $\phi = 0$ (coincident peaks) corresponds to constructive interference, or the enhancement of the amplitudes. According to classical electromagnetic theory, the intensity of electromagnetic radiation is proportional to the square of the amplitude of the wave. For example, the light detectors discussed in Section 19.1 are based on the interaction between the electric field of the incident radiation and the detecting element, so light intensities are proportional to $\mathcal{E}_0^2$.

Equations A3.18a and A3.18b represent electromagnetic radiation that is **plane polarized;** it is so-called because the electric and magnetic fields each oscillate in a single plane (in this case the xy plane, Fig. A3.5). The

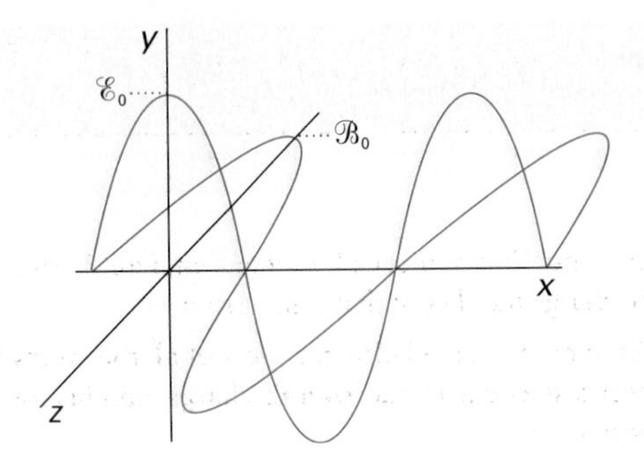

Fig. A3.5 Electromagnetic radiation consists of a wave of electric and magnetic fields perpendicular to the direction of propagation (in this case the x-direction), and mutually perpendicular to each other. This illustration shows a plane-polarized wave, with the electric and magnetic fields oscillating in the xy- and xz-planes, respectively.

plane of polarization may be orientated in any direction around the direction of propagation (the x-direction in Fig. A3.5), with the electric and magnetic fields perpendicular to that direction (and perpendicular to each other). An alternative mode of polarization is **circular polarization,** in which the electric and magnetic fields rotate around the direction of propagation in either a clockwise or a counterclockwise sense but remain perpendicular to it and each other.

According to quantum theory, a ray of frequency ν consists of a stream of **photons**, each one of which has energy

$$E = h\nu \qquad \text{(A3.19)}$$

where h is Planck's constant (Section 12.1). Thus, a photon of high-frequency radiation has more energy than a photon of low-frequency radiation. The greater the intensity of the ray, the greater the number of photons in it. In a vacuum, each photon travels with the speed of light. The frequency of the radiation determines the colour of visible light because different visual receptors in the eye respond to photons of different energy. The relation between colour and frequency is shown in Table A3.2, which also gives the energy carried by each type of photon.

Photons may also be polarized. A plane-polarized ray of light consists of plane-polarized photons and a circularly polarized ray consists of circularly polarized photons. The latter can be regarded as spinning either clockwise (for left-circularly polarized radiation) or counterclockwise (for right-circularly polarized radiation) about their direction of propagation.

Table A3.2 *Colour, frequency, and wavelength of light**

	Frequency/(10^{14} Hz)	Wavelength/nm	Energy of photon/(10^{-19} J)
X-rays and γ-rays	10^3 and above	3 and below	660 and above
Ultraviolet	10	300	6.6
Visible light			
Violet	7.1	420	4.7
Blue	6.4	470	4.2
Green	5.7	530	3.7
Yellow	5.2	580	3.4
Orange	4.8	620	3.2
Red	4.3	700	2.8
Infrared	3.0	1000	1.9
Microwaves and radiowaves	3×10^{-3} Hz and below	3×10^6 and above	2.0×10^{-22} J and below

* The values given are approximate but typical.

Appendix 4 Review of chemical principles

The concepts reviewed below are used throughout the text. They are usually covered in introductory chemistry texts, which should be consulted for further information.

A4.1 Oxidation numbers

A simple way of judging whether a monatomic species has undergone oxidation or reduction is to note if the charge number of the species has changed. For example, an increase in the charge number of a monatomic ion (which corresponds to electron loss), as in the conversion of Fe^{2+} to Fe^{3+}, is an oxidation. A decrease in charge number (to a less positive or more negative value, as a result of electron gain), as in the conversion of Br to Br^-, is a reduction.

It is possible to assign to an atom in a polyatomic species an effective charge number, called the **oxidation number**, ω. (There is no standard symbol for this quantity.) The oxidation number is defined so that an increase in its value ($\Delta\omega > 0$) corresponds to oxidation, and a decrease ($\Delta\omega < 0$) corresponds to reduction.

An oxidation number is assigned to an element in a compound by supposing that it is present as an ion with a characteristic charge; for instance, oxygen is present as O^{2-} in most of its compounds, and fluorine is present as F^- (Fig. A4.1). The more electronegative element is supposed to be present as the anion. This procedure implies that:

1 The oxidation number of an elemental substance is zero: $\omega(\text{element}) = 0$.

2 The oxidation number of a monatomic ion is equal to the charge number of that ion: $\omega(E^{z\pm}) = \pm z$.

3 The sum of the oxidation numbers of all the atoms in a species is equal to the overall charge number of the species.

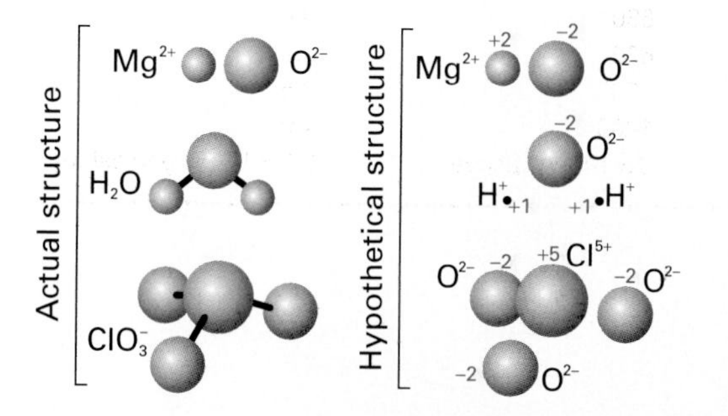

Fig. A4.1 To calculate the oxidation number of an element in an oxide or oxoacid, we suppose that each O atom is present as an O^{2-} ion, and then identify the charge of the element required to give the actual overall charge of the species. The more electronegative element plays a similar role in other compounds.

Thus, hydrogen, oxygen, iron, and all the elements have $\omega = 0$ in their elemental forms; $\omega(Fe^{3+}) = +3$ and $\omega(Br^-) = -1$. It follows that the conversion of Fe to Fe^{3+} is an oxidation (because $\Delta\omega > 0$) and the conversion of Br to Br^- is a reduction (because $\Delta\omega < 0$). The definition of oxidation number and its relation to oxidation and reduction are consistent with the definitions in terms of electron loss and gain.

As an illustration, consider the oxidation numbers of the elements in SO_2 and SO_4^{2-}. The sum of oxidation numbers of the atoms in SO_2 must be 0, so we can write

$$\omega(S) + 2\omega(O) = 0$$

Each O atom has $\omega = -2$. Hence,

$$\omega(S) + 2 \times (-2) = 0$$

which solves to $\omega(S) = +4$. Now consider SO_4^{2-}. The sum of oxidation numbers of the atoms in the ion is −2, so we can write

$$\omega(S) + 4\omega(O) = -2$$

Because $\omega(O) = -2$,

$$\omega(S) + 4 \times (-2) = -2$$

which solves to $\omega(S) = +6$. The sulfur is more highly oxidized in the sulfate ion than in sulfur dioxide.

Self-test A4.1

Calculate the oxidation numbers of the elements in (a) H_2S, (b) PO_4^{3-}, (c) NO_3^-.

[*Answer:* (a) $\omega(H) = +1$, $\omega(S) = -2$; (b) $\omega(P) = +5$, $\omega(O) = -2$; (c) $\omega(N) = +5$, $\omega(O) = -2$]

A4.2 The Lewis theory of covalent bonding

In his original formulation of a theory of the covalent bond, G. N. Lewis proposed that each bond consisted of one electron pair. Each atom in a molecule shared electrons until it had acquired an octet characteristic of a noble gas atom near it in the periodic table. (Hydrogen is an exception: it acquires a duplet of electrons.) Thus, to write down a Lewis structure:

1 Arrange the atoms as they are found in the molecule.
2 Add one electron pair (represented by dots, :) between each bonded atom.
3 Use the remaining electron pairs to complete the octets of all the atoms present either by forming lone pairs or by forming multiple bonds.
4 Replace bonding electron pairs by bond lines (—) but leave lone pairs as dots (:).

A Lewis structure does not (except in very simple cases) portray the actual geometrical structure of the molecule; it is a topological map of the arrangement of bonds.

As an example, consider the Lewis structure of methanol, CH_3OH, in which there are $4 \times 1 + 4 + 6 = 14$ valence electrons (and hence seven electron pairs) to accommodate. The first step is to write the atoms in the arrangement (1); the rectangles have been included to indicate which atoms are linked. The next step is to add electron pairs to denote bonds (2). The C atom now has a complete octet and all four H atoms have complete duplets. There are two unused electron pairs, which are used as lone pairs to complete the octet of the O atom (3). Finally, replace the bonding pairs by lines to indicate bonds (4). An example of a species with a multiple bond is acetic acid (5).

In some cases, more than one structure can be written in which the only difference is the location of multiple bonds or lone pairs. In such cases, the molecule's structure is interpreted as a **resonance hybrid**, a quantum mechanical blend, of the individual structures. Resonance is depicted by a double-headed arrow. For example, the ozone molecule, O_3, is a resonance hybrid of two structures (6). Resonance distributes multiple-bond character over the participating atoms.

1 **2** **3**

4 **5**

6

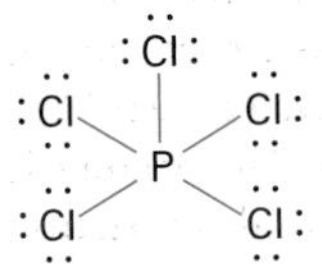

7 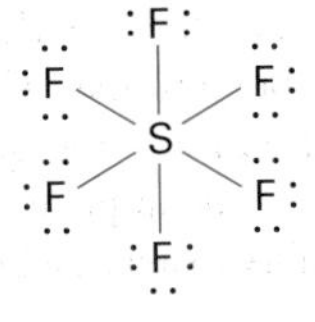 **8** 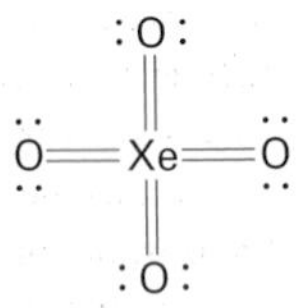 **9**

Many molecules cannot be written in a way that conforms to the octet rule. Those classified as **hypervalent molecules** require an expansion of the octet. Although it is often stated that octet expansion requires the involvement of *d* orbitals, and is therefore confined to Period 3 and subsequent elements, there is good evidence to suggest that octet expansion is a consequence of an atom's size, not its intrinsic orbital structure. Whatever the reason, octet expansion is needed to account for the structures of PCl_5 with expansion to 10 electrons (7), SF_6, expansion to 12 electrons (8), and XeO_4, expansion to 16 electrons (9). Octet expansion is also encountered in species that do not necessarily require it, but which, if it is permitted, may acquire a lower energy. Thus, of the structures (**10a**) and (**10b**) of the SO_4^{2-} ion, the second has a lower energy than the first. The actual structure of the ion is a resonance hybrid of both structures (together with analogous structures with double bonds in different locations), but the latter structure makes the dominant contribution.

Octet completion is not always energetically appropriate. Such is the case with boron trifluoride, BF_3. Two of the possible Lewis structures for this molecule are (**11a**) and (**11b**). In the former, the B atom has an **incomplete octet.**

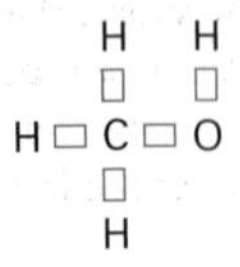

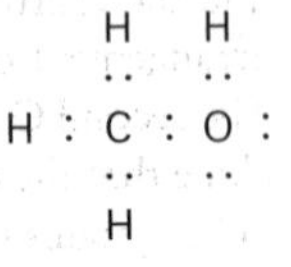

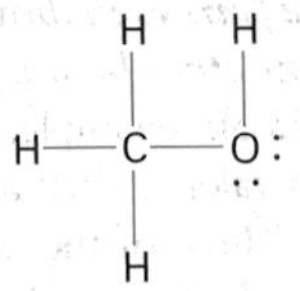

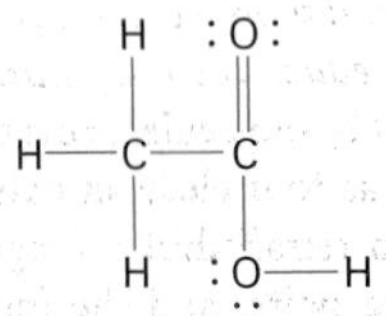

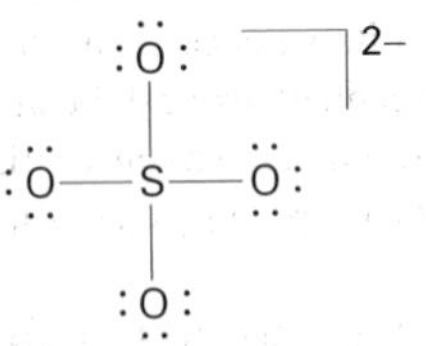

10a 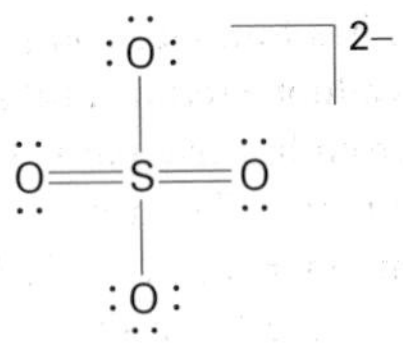 **10b**

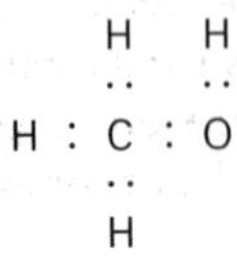

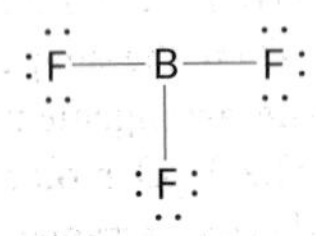

11a 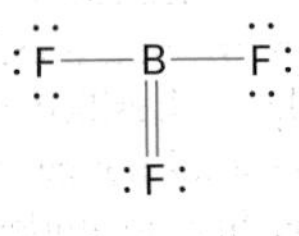 **11b**

Nevertheless, it has a lower energy than the other structure, because to form the latter structure one F atom has had to partially relinquish an electron pair, which is energetically demanding for such an electronegative element. The actual molecule is a resonance hybrid of the two structures (and of others with the double bond in different locations), but the overwhelming contribution is from the former structure. Consequently, we regard BF_3 as a molecule with an incomplete octet. This feature is responsible for its ability to act as a Lewis acid (an electron pair acceptor).

The Lewis approach fails for a class of **electron-deficient compounds**, which are molecules that have too few electrons for a Lewis structure to be written. The most famous example is diborane, B_2H_6, which requires at least seven pairs of electrons to bind the eight atoms together, but it has only 12 valence electrons in all. The structures of such molecules can be explained in terms of molecular orbital theory and the concept of delocalized electron pairs, in which the influence of an electron pair is distributed over several atoms.

A4.3 The VSEPR model

In the **valence-shell electron pair repulsion model** (VSEPR model) we focus on a single, central atom and consider the local arrangement of atoms that are linked to it. For example, in considering the H_2O molecule, we concentrate on the electron pairs in the valence shell of the central O atom. This procedure can be extended to molecules in which there is no obvious central atom, such as in benzene, C_6H_6, or hydrogen peroxide, H_2O_2, by focusing attention on a group of atoms, such as a C–CH–C fragment of benzene or an H–O–O fragment of hydrogen peroxide, and considering the arrangement of electron pairs around the central atom of the fragment.

The basic assumption of the VSEPR model is that *the valence-shell electron pairs of the central atom adopt positions that maximize their separations*. Thus, if the atom has four electron pairs in its valence shell, then the pairs adopt a tetrahedral arrangement around the atom; if the atom has five pairs, then the arrangement is trigonal bipyramidal. The arrangements adopted by electron pairs are summarized in Table A4.1.

Once the basic shape of the arrangement of electron pairs has been identified, the pairs are identified as bonding or non-bonding. For instance, in the H_2O molecule, two of the tetrahedrally arranged pairs are bonding pairs and two are non-bonding pairs. Then the shape of the molecule is classified by noting the arrangement of the atoms around the central atom. The H_2O molecule, for instance, has an underlying tetrahedral arrangement of lone pairs, but as only two of the pairs are bonding pairs, the molecule is classified as angular (Fig. A4.2) It is important to keep in mind the distinction between the arrangement of electron pairs and the shape of the resulting molecule: the latter is identified by noting the relative locations of the atoms, not the lone pairs (Fig. A4.3).

Table A4.1
Electron pair arrangements

Number of electron pairs	Arrangement
2	Linear
3	Trigonal planar
4	Tetrahedral
5	Trigonal bipyramidal
6	Octahedral
7	Pentagonal bipyramidal

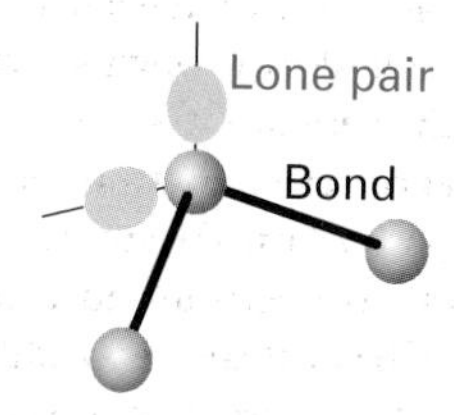

Fig. A4.2 The shape of a molecule is identified by noting the arrangement of its atoms, not its lone pairs. This molecule is angular even though the electron-pair distribution is tetrahedral.

For example, to predict the shape of an ethane molecule we concentrate on one of the C atoms initially. That atom has four electron pairs in its valence shell (in the molecule), and they adopt a tetrahedral arrangement. All four electron pairs are bonding: three bond H atoms and the fourth bonds the second C atom. Therefore, the arrangement of atoms is tetrahedral around the C atom. The second C atom has the same environment, so we conclude that the ethane molecule consists of two tetrahedral $-CH_3$ groups (**12**).

The next stage in the application of the VSEPR model is to accommodate the greater repelling effect of lone pairs compared with that of bonding pairs. That is, *bonding pairs tend to move away from lone pairs even though that might reduce their separation from other bonding pairs.* The NH_3 molecule provides a simple example. The N atom has four electron pairs in its valence shell and they adopt a tetrahedral arrangement. Three of the pairs are bonding pairs, and the fourth is a lone pair. The basic shape of the molecule is therefore trigonal pyramidal.

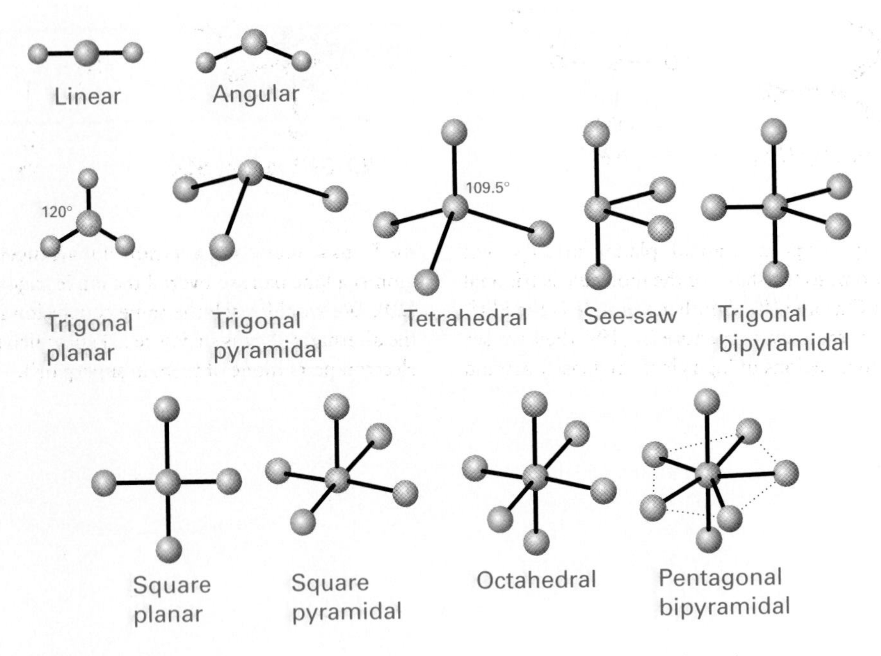

Fig. A4.3 The classification of molecular shapes according to the relative locations of atoms.

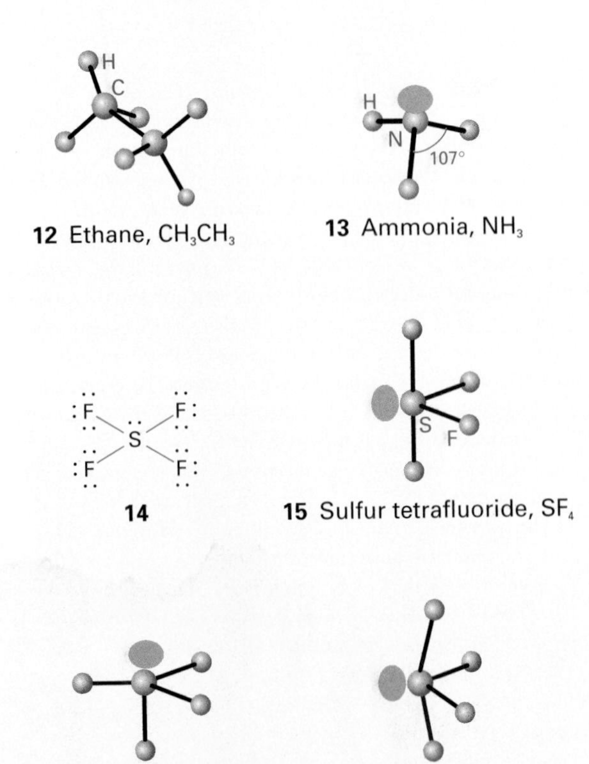

12 Ethane, CH_3CH_3

13 Ammonia, NH_3

14

15 Sulfur tetrafluoride, SF_4

16

17

However, a lower energy is achieved if the three bonding pairs move away from the lone pair, even though they are brought slightly closer together (**13**). We therefore predict an HNH bond angle of slightly less than the tetrahedral angle of 109.5°, which is consistent with the observed angle of 107°.

As an example, consider the shape of an SF_4 molecule. The first step is to write a Lewis (electron dot) structure for the molecule to identify the number of lone pairs in the valence shell of the S atom (**14**). This structure shows that there are five electron pairs on the S atom. Reference to Table A4.1 shows that the five pairs are arranged as a trigonal bipyramid. Four of the pairs are bonding pairs and one is a lone pair. The repulsions stemming from the lone pair are minimized if the lone pair is placed in an equatorial position: then it is close to the axial pairs (**15**), whereas if it had adopted an axial position it would have been close to three equatorial pairs (**16**). Finally, the four bonding pairs are allowed to relax away from the single lone pair, to give a distorted see-saw arrangement (**17**).

To take into account multiple bonds, each set of two or three electron pairs is treated as a single region of high electron density, a kind of 'superpair'. For example, each C atom in an ethene molecule, $CH_2{=}CH_2$, is regarded as having three pairs (one of them the superpair of two electrons pairs of the double bond); these regions of high

18 Ethene, $CH_2{=}CH_2$

19

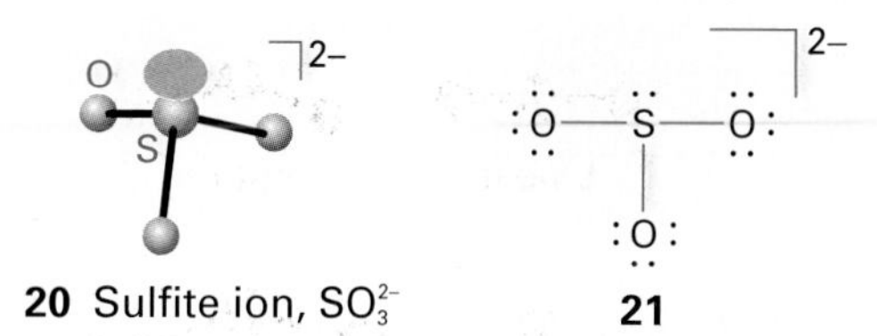

20 Sulfite ion, SO_3^{2-}

21

electron density adopt a trigonal planar arrangement around each atom, so the shape of the molecule is trigonal planar at each C atom (**18**). Another example is the SO_3^{2-} ion: if we adopt the Lewis structure in (**19**), then we see that there are four regions of high electron density around the S atom, indicating a tetrahedral arrangement. One region is a lone pair, so overall the ion is trigonal pyramidal (**20**). We would reach the same conclusion if we adopted the alternative Lewis structure (**21**) in which there are four electron pairs (none of them a 'superpair').

Data section

1 Thermodynamic data

Table D1.1 *Thermodynamic data for organic compounds (all values relate to 298.15 K)*

	M/ (g mol^{-1})	$\Delta_f H^\ominus$/ (kJ mol^{-1})	$\Delta_f G^\ominus$/ (kJ mol^{-1})	$S_m^\ominus$/ (J K^{-1} mol^{-1})	$C_{p,m}$/ (J K^{-1} mol^{-1})	$\Delta_c H^\ominus$/ (kJ mol^{-1})
C(s) (graphite)	12.011	0	0	5.740	8.527	−393.51
C(s) (diamond)	12.011	+1.895	+2.900	2.377	6.113	−395.40
CO_2(g)	44.010	−393.51	−394.36	213.74	37.11	
Hydrocarbons						
CH_4(g), methane	16.04	−74.81	−50.72	186.26	35.31	−890
CH_3(g), methyl	15.04	+145.69	+147.92	194.2	38.70	
C_2H_2(g), ethyne	26.04	+226.73	+209.20	200.94	43.93	−1300
C_2H_4(g), ethene	28.05	+52.26	+68.15	219.56	43.56	−1411
C_2H_6(g), ethane	30.07	−84.68	−32.82	229.60	52.63	−1560
C_3H_6(g), propene	42.08	+20.42	+62.78	267.05	63.89	−2058
C_3H_6(g), cyclopropane	42.08	+53.30	+104.45	237.55	55.94	−2091
C_3H_8(g), propane	42.10	−103.85	−23.49	269.91	73.5	−2220
C_4H_8(g), 1-butene	56.11	−0.13	+71.39	305.71	85.65	−2717
C_4H_8(g), *cis*-2-butene	56.11	−6.99	+65.95	300.94	78.91	−2710
C_4H_8(g), *trans*-2-butene	56.11	−11.17	+63.06	296.59	87.82	−2707
C_4H_{10}(g), butane	58.13	−126.15	−17.03	310.23	97.45	−2878
C_5H_{12}(g), pentane	72.15	−146.44	−8.20	348.40	120.2	−3537
C_5H_{12}(l)	72.15	−173.1				
C_6H_6(l), benzene	78.12	+49.0	+124.3	173.3	136.1	−3268
C_6H_6(g)	78.12	+82.93	+129.72	269.31	81.67	−3320
C_6H_{12}(l), cyclohexane	84.16	−156	+26.8		156.5	−3902
C_6H_{14}(l), hexane	86.18	−198.7		204.3		−4163
$C_6H_5CH_3$(g), methylbenzene (toluene)	92.14	+50.0	+122.0	320.7	103.6	−3953
C_7H_{16}(l), heptane	100.21	−224.4	+1.0	328.6	224.3	
C_8H_{18}(l), octane	114.23	−249.9	+6.4	361.1		−5471
C_8H_{18}(l), iso-octane	114.23	−255.1				−5461
$C_{10}H_8$(s), naphthalene	128.18	+78.53				−5157
Alcohols and phenols						
CH_3OH(l), methanol	32.04	−238.66	−166.27	126.8	81.6	−726
CH_3OH(g)	32.04	−200.66	−161.96	239.81	43.89	−764
C_2H_5OH(l), ethanol	46.07	−277.69	−174.78	160.7	111.46	−1368
C_2H_5OH(g)	46.07	−235.10	−168.49	282.70	65.44	−1409
C_6H_5OH(s), phenol	94.12	−165.0	−50.9	146.0		−3054
Carboxylic acids, hydroxy acids, and esters						
HCOOH(l), formic	46.03	−424.72	−361.35	128.95	99.04	−255
CH_3COOH(l), acetic	60.05	−484.5	−389.9	159.8	124.3	−875
CH_3COOH(aq)	60.05	−485.76	−396.46	178.7		

Table D1.1 *(continued)*

	M/(g mol^{-1})	$\Delta_f H^\ominus$/(kJ mol^{-1})	$\Delta_f G^\ominus$/(kJ mol^{-1})	$S_m^\ominus$/(J K^{-1} mol^{-1})	$C_{p,m}$/(J K^{-1} mol^{-1})	$\Delta_c H^\ominus$/(kJ mol^{-1})
$CH_3CO_2^-$(aq)	59.05	−486.01	−369.31	86.6	−6.3	
$(COOH)_2$(s), oxalic	90.04	−827.2			117	−254
C_6H_5COOH(s), benzoic	122.13	−385.1	−245.3	167.6	146.8	−3227
$CH_3CH(OH)COOH$(s), lactic	90.08	−694.0				−1344
$CH_3COOC_2H_5$(l), ethyl acetate	88.11	−479.0	−332.7	259.4	170.1	−2231
Alkanals and alkanones						
HCHO(g), methanal	30.03	−108.57	−102.53	218.77	35.40	−571
CH_3CHO(l), ethanal	44.05	−192.30	−128.12	160.2		−1166
CH_3CHO(g)	44.05	−166.19	−128.86	250.3	57.3	−1192
CH_3COCH_3(l), propanone	58.08	−248.1	−155.4	200.4	124.7	−1790
Sugars						
$C_6H_{12}O_6$(s), α-D-glucose	180.16	−1274				−2808
$C_6H_{12}O_6$(s), β-D-glucose	180.16	−1268	−910	212		
$C_6H_{12}O_6$(s), β-D-fructose	180.16	−1266				−2810
$C_{12}H_{22}O_{11}$(s), sucrose	342.30	−2222	−1543	360.2		−5645
Nitrogen compounds						
$CO(NH_2)_2$(s), urea	60.06	−333.51	−197.33	104.60	93.14	−632
CH_3NH_2(g), methylamine	31.06	−22.97	+32.16	243.41	53.1	−1085
$C_6H_5NH_2$(l), aniline	93.13	+31.1				−3393
$CH_2(NH_2)COOH$(s), glycine	75.07	−532.9	−373.4	103.5	99.2	−969

Table D1.2 *Thermodynamic data (all values relate to 298.15 K)**

	M/(g mol^{-1})	$\Delta_f H^\ominus$/(kJ mol^{-1})	$\Delta_f G^\ominus$/(kJ mol^{-1})	$S_m^\ominus$/(J K^{-1} mol^{-1})	$C_{p,m}$/(J K^{-1} mol^{-1})
Aluminium (aluminum)					
Al(s)	26.98	0	0	28.33	24.35
Al(l)	26.98	+10.56	+7.20	39.55	24.21
Al(g)	26.98	+326.4	+285.7	164.54	21.38
Al^{3+}(g)	26.98	+5483.17			
Al^{3+}(aq)	26.98	−531	−485	−321.7	
Al_2O_3(s, α)	101.96	−1675.7	−1582.3	50.92	79.04
$AlCl_3$(s)	133.24	−704.2	−628.8	110.67	91.84
Argon					
Ar(g)	39.95	0	0	154.84	20.786
Antimony					
Sb(s)	121.75	0	0	45.69	25.23
SbH_3(g)	153.24	+145.11	+147.75	232.78	41.05

Table D1.2 *(continued)*

	M/(g mol^{-1})	$\Delta_f H^\ominus$/(kJ mol^{-1})	$\Delta_f G^\ominus$/(kJ mol^{-1})	$S_m^\ominus$/(J K^{-1} mol^{-1})	$C_{p,m}$/(J K^{-1} mol^{-1})
Arsenic					
As(s, α)	74.92	0	0	35.1	24.64
As(g)	74.92	+302.5	+261.0	174.21	20.79
As_4(g)	299.69	+143.9	+92.4	314	
AsH_3(g)	77.95	+66.44	+68.93	222.78	38.07
Barium					
Ba(s)	137.34	0	0	62.8	28.07
Ba(g)	137.34	+180	+146	170.24	20.79
Ba^{2+}(aq)	137.34	−537.64	−560.77	+9.6	
BaO(s)	153.34	−553.5	−525.1	70.43	47.78
$BaCl_2$(s)	208.25	−858.6	−810.4	123.68	75.14
Beryllium					
Be(s)	9.01	0	0	9.50	16.44
Be(g)	9.01	+324.3	+286.6	136.27	20.79
Bismuth					
Bi(s)	208.98	0	0	56.74	25.52
Bi(g)	208.98	+207.1	+168.2	187.00	20.79
Bromine					
Br_2(l)	159.82	0	0	152.23	75.689
Br_2(g)	159.82	+30.907	+3.110	245.46	36.02
Br(g)	79.91	+111.88	+82.396	175.02	20.786
Br^-(g)	79.91	−219.07			
Br^-(aq)	79.91	−121.55	−103.96	+82.4	−141.8
HBr(g)	90.92	−36.40	−53.45	198.70	29.142
Cadium					
Cd(s, γ)	112.40	0	0	51.76	25.98
Cd(g)	112.40	+112.01	+77.41	167.75	20.79
Cd^{2+}(aq)	112.40	−75.90	−77.612	−73.2	
CdO(s)	128.40	−258.2	−228.4	54.8	43.43
$CdCO_3$(s)	172.41	−750.6	−669.4	92.5	
Caesium (cesium)					
Cs(s)	132.91	0	0	85.23	32.17
Cs(g)	132.91	+76.06	+49.12	175.60	20.79
Cs^+(aq)	132.91	−258.28	−292.02	+133.05	−10.5
Calcium					
Ca(s)	40.08	0	0	41.42	25.31
Ca(g)	40.08	+178.2	+144.3	154.88	20.786
Ca^{2+}(aq)	40.08	−542.83	−553.58	−53.1	
CaO(s)	56.08	−635.09	−604.03	39.75	42.80
$CaCO_3$(s) (calcite)	100.09	−1206.9	−1128.8	92.9	81.88
$CaCO_3$(s) (aragonite)	100.09	−1207.1	−1127.8	88.7	81.25
CaF_2(s)	78.08	1219.6	−1167.3	68.87	67.03
$CaCl_2$(s)	110.99	−795.8	−748.1	104.6	72.59
$CaBr_2$(s)	199.90	−682.8	−663.6	130	

Table D1.2 *(continued)*

	M/(g mol^{-1})	$\Delta_f H^\ominus$/(kJ mol^{-1})	$\Delta_f G^\ominus$/(kJ mol^{-1})	$S_m^\ominus$/(J K^{-1} mol^{-1})	$C_{p,m}$/(J K^{-1} mol^{-1})
Carbon (for 'organic' compounds of carbon, see Table D1.1)					
C(s) (graphite)	12.011	0	0	5.740	8.527
C(s) (diamond)	12.011	+1.895	+2.900	2.377	6.133
C(g)	12.011	+716.68	+671.26	158.10	20.838
C_2(g)	24.022	+831.90	+775.89	199.42	43.21
CO(g)	28.011	−110.53	−137.17	197.67	29.14
CO_2(g)	44.010	−393.51	−394.36	213.74	37.11
CO_2(aq)	44.010	−413.80	−385.98	117.6	
H_2CO_3(aq)	62.03	−699.65	−623.08	187.4	
HCO_3^-(aq)	61.02	−691.99	−586.77	+91.2	
CO_3^{2-}(aq)	60.01	−677.14	−527.81	−56.9	
CCl_4(l)	153.82	−135.44	−65.21	216.40	131.75
CS_2(l)	76.14	+89.70	+65.27	151.34	75.7
HCN(g)	27.03	+135.1	+124.7	201.78	35.86
HCN(l)	27.03	+108.87	+124.97	112.84	70.63
CN^-(aq)	26.02	+150.6	+172.4	+94.1	
Chlorine					
Cl_2(g)	70.91	0	0	223.07	33.91
Cl(g)	35.45	+121.68	+105.68	165.20	21.840
Cl^-(g)	35.45	−233.13			
Cl^-(aq)	35.45	−167.16	−131.23	+56.5	−136.4
HCl(g)	36.46	−92.31	−95.30	186.91	29.12
HCl(aq)	36.46	−167.16	−131.23	56.5	−136.4
Chromium					
Cr(s)	52.00	0	0	23.77	23.35
Cr(g)	52.00	+396.6	+351.8	174.50	20.79
CrO_4^{2-}(aq)	115.99	−881.15	−727.75	+50.21	
$Cr_2O_7^{2-}$(aq)	215.99	−1490.3	−1301.1	+261.9	
Copper					
Cu(s)	63.54	0	0	33.150	24.44
Cu(g)	63.54	+338.32	+298.58	166.38	20.79
Cu^+(aq)	63.54	+71.67	+49.98	+40.6	
Cu^{2+}(aq)	63.54	+64.77	+65.49	−99.6	
Cu_2O(s)	143.08	−168.6	−146.0	93.14	63.64
CuO(s)	79.54	−157.3	−129.7	42.63	42.30
$CuSO_4$(s)	159.60	−771.36	−661.8	109	100.0
$CuSO_4 \cdot H_2O$(s)	177.62	−1085.8	−918.11	146.0	134
$CuSO_4 \cdot 5H_2O$(s)	249.68	−2279.7	−1879.7	300.4	280
Deuterium					
D_2(g)	4.028	0	0	144.96	29.20
HD(g)	3.022	+0.318	−1.464	143.80	29.196
D_2O(g)	20.028	−249.20	−234.54	198.34	34.27
D_2O(l)	20.028	−294.60	−243.44	75.94	84.35
HDO(g)	19.022	−245.30	−233.11	199.51	33.81
HDO(l)	19.022	−289.89	−241.86	79.29	

Table D1.2 *(continued)*

	M/(g mol^{-1})	$\Delta_f H^{\ominus}$/(kJ mol^{-1})	$\Delta_f G^{\ominus}$/(kJ mol^{-1})	$S_m^{\ominus}$/(J K^{-1} mol^{-1})	$C_{p,m}$/(J K^{-1} mol^{-1})
Fluorine					
F_2(g)	38.00	0	0	202.78	31.30
F(g)	19.00	+78.99	+61.91	158.75	22.74
F^-(aq)	19.00	−332.63	−278.79	−13.8	−106.7
HF(g)	20.01	−271.1	−273.2	173.78	29.13
Gold					
Au(s)	196.97	0	0	47.40	25.42
Au(g)	196.97	+366.1	+326.3	180.50	20.79
Helium					
He(g)	4.003	0	0	126.15	20.786
Hydrogen (see also deuterium)					
H_2(g)	2.016	0	0	130.684	28.824
H(g)	1.008	+217.97	+203.25	114.71	20.784
H^+(aq)	1.008	0	0	0	0
H_2O(l)	18.015	−285.83	−237.13	69.91	75.291
H_2O(g)	18.015	−241.82	−228.57	188.83	33.58
H_2O_2(l)	34.015	−187.78	−120.35	109.6	89.1
Iodine					
I_2(s)	253.81	0	0	116.135	54.44
I_2(g)	253.81	+62.44	+19.33	260.69	36.90
I(g)	126.90	+106.84	+70.25	180.79	20.786
I^-(aq)	126.90	−55.19	−51.57	+111.3	−142.3
HI(g)	127.91	+26.48	+1.70	206.59	29.158
Iron					
Fe(s)	55.85	0	0	27.28	25.10
Fe(g)	55.85	+416.3	+370.7	180.49	25.68
Fe^{2+}(aq)	55.85	−89.1	−78.90	−137.7	
Fe^{3+}(aq)	55.85	−48.5	−4.7	−315.9	
Fe_3O_4(s) (magnetite)	231.54	−1184.4	−1015.4	146.4	143.43
Fe_2O_3(s) (haematite)	159.69	−824.2	−742.2	87.40	103.85
FeS(s, α)	87.91	−100.0	−100.4	60.29	50.54
FeS_2(s)	119.98	−178.2	−166.9	52.93	62.17
Krypton					
Kr(g)	83.80	0	0	164.08	20.786
Lead					
Pb(s)	207.19	0	0	64.81	26.44
Pb(g)	207.19	+195.0	+161.9	175.37	20.79
Pb^{2+}(aq)	207.19	−1.7	−24.43	+10.5	
PbO(s, yellow)	223.19	−217.32	−187.89	68.70	45.77
PbO(s, red)	223.19	−218.99	−188.93	66.5	45.81
PbO_2(s)	239.19	−277.4	−217.33	68.6	64.64

Table D1.2 *(continued)*

	M/(g mol^{-1})	$\Delta_f H^{\ominus}$/(kJ mol^{-1})	$\Delta_f G^{\ominus}$/(kJ mol^{-1})	$S_m^{\ominus}$/(J K^{-1} mol^{-1})	$C_{p,m}$/(J K^{-1} mol^{-1})
Lithium					
Li(s)	6.94	0	0	29.12	24.77
Li(g)	6.94	+159.37	+126.66	138.77	20.79
Li^+(aq)	6.94	−278.49	−293.31	+13.4	+68.6
Magnesium					
Mg(s)	24.31	0	0	32.68	24.89
Mg(g)	24.31	+147.70	+113.10	148.65	20.786
Mg^{2+}(aq)	24.31	−466.85	−454.8	−138.1	
MgO(s)	40.31	−601.70	−569.43	26.94	37.15
$MgCO_3$(s)	84.32	−1095.8	−1012.1	65.7	75.52
$MgCl_2$(s)	95.22	−641.32	−591.79	89.62	71.38
$MgBr_2$(s)	184.13	−524.3	−503.8	117.2	
Mercury					
Hg(l)	200.59	0	0	76.02	27.983
Hg(g)	200.59	+61.32	+31.82	174.96	20.786
Hg^{2+}(aq)	200.59	+171.1	+164.40	−32.2	
Hg_2^{2+}(aq)	401.18	+172.4	+153.52	+84.5	
HgO(s)	216.59	−90.83	−58.54	70.29	44.06
Hg_2Cl_2(s)	472.09	−265.22	−210.75	192.5	102
$HgCl_2$(s)	271.50	−224.3	−178.6	146.0	
HgS(s, black)	232.65	−53.6	−47.7	88.3	
Neon					
Ne(g)	20.18	0	0	146.33	20.786
Nitrogen					
N_2(g)	28.013	0	0	191.61	29.125
N(g)	14.007	+472.70	+455.56	153.30	20.786
NO(g)	30.01	+90.25	+86.55	210.76	29.844
N_2O(g)	44.01	+82.05	+104.20	219.85	38.45
NO_2(g)	46.01	+33.18	+51.31	240.06	37.20
N_2O_4(g)	92.01	+9.16	+97.89	304.29	77.28
N_2O_5(s)	108.01	−43.1	+113.9	178.2	143.1
N_2O_5(g)	108.01	+11.3	+115.1	355.7	84.5
HNO_3(l)	63.01	−174.10	−80.71	155.60	109.87
HNO_3(aq)	63.01	−207.36	−111.25	146.4	−86.6
NO_3^- (aq)	62.01	−205.0	−108.74	+146.4	−86.6
NH_3(g)	17.03	−46.11	−16.45	192.45	35.06
NH_3(aq)	17.03	−80.29	−26.50	113.3	
NH_4^+ (aq)	18.04	−132.51	−79.31	+113.4	+79.9
NH_2OH(s)	33.03	−114.2			
HN_3(l)	43.03	+264.0	+327.3	140.6	43.68
HN_3(g)	43.03	+294.1	+328.1	238.97	98.87
N_2H_4(l)	32.05	+50.63	+149.43	121.21	139.3
NH_4NO_3(s)	80.04	−365.56	−183.87	151.08	84.1
NH_4Cl(s)	53.49	−314.43	−202.87	94.6	

Table D1.2 *(continued)*

	M/(g mol^{-1})	$\Delta_f H^\ominus$/(kJ mol^{-1})	$\Delta_f G^\ominus$/(kJ mol^{-1})	$S_m^\ominus$/(J K^{-1} mol^{-1})	$C_{p,m}$/(J K^{-1} mol^{-1})
Oxygen					
O_2(g)	31.999	0	0	205.138	29.355
O(g)	15.999	+249.17	+231.73	161.06	21.912
O_3(g)	47.998	+142.7	+163.2	238.93	39.20
OH^-(aq)	17.007	−229.99	−157.24	−10.75	−148.5
Phosphorus					
P(s, wh)	30.97	0	0	41.09	23.840
P(g)	30.97	+314.64	+278.25	163.19	20.786
P_2(g)	61.95	+144.3	+103.7	218.13	32.05
P_4(g)	123.90	+58.91	+24.44	279.98	67.15
PH_3(g)	34.00	+5.4	+13.4	210.23	37.11
PCl_3(g)	137.33	−287.0	−267.8	311.78	71.84
PCl_3(l)	137.33	−319.7	−272.3	217.1	
PCl_5(g)	208.24	−374.9	−305.0	364.6	112.8
PCl_5(s)	208.24	−443.5			
H_3PO_3(s)	82.00	−964.4			
H_3PO_3(aq)	82.00	−964.8			
H_3PO_4(s)	94.97	−1279.0	−1119.1	110.50	106.06
H_3PO_4(l)	94.97	−1266.9			
H_3PO_4(aq)	94.97	−1277.4	−1018.7	−222	
PO_4^{3-}(aq)	94.97	−1277.4	−1018.7	−222	
P_4O_{10}(s)	283.89	−2984.0	−2697.0	228.86	211.71
P_4O_6(s)	219.89	−1640.1			
Potassium					
K(s)	39.10	0	0	64.18	29.58
K(g)	39.10	+89.24	+60.59	160.336	20.786
K^+(g)	39.10	+514.26			
K^+(aq)	39.10	−252.38	−283.27	+102.5	+21.8
KOH(s)	56.11	−424.76	−379.08	78.9	64.9
KF(s)	58.10	−576.27	−537.75	66.57	49.04
KCl(s)	74.56	−436.75	−409.14	82.59	51.30
KBr(s)	119.01	−393.80	−380.66	95.90	52.30
KI(s)	166.01	−327.90	−324.89	106.32	52.93
Silicon					
Si(s)	28.09	0	0	18.83	20.00
Si(g)	28.09	+455.6	+411.3	167.97	22.25
SiO_2(s,α)	60.09	−910.93	−856.64	41.84	44.43
Silver					
Ag(s)	107.87	0	0	42.55	25.351
Ag(g)	107.87	+284.55	+245.65	173.00	20.79
Ag^+(aq)	107.87	+105.58	+77.11	+72.68	+21.8
AgBr(s)	187.78	−100.37	−96.90	107.1	52.38
AgCl(s)	143.32	−127.07	−109.79	96.2	50.79
Ag_2O(s)	231.74	−31.05	−11.20	121.3	65.86
$AgNO_3$(s)	169.88	−124.39	−33.41	140.92	93.05

Table D1.2 *(continued)*

	$M/(g\ mol^{-1})$	$\Delta_f H^{\ominus}/(kJ\ mol^{-1})$	$\Delta_f G^{\ominus}/(kJ\ mol^{-1})$	$S_m^{\ominus}/(J\ K^{-1}\ mol^{-1})$	$C_{p,m}/(J\ K^{-1}\ mol^{-1})$
Sodium					
Na(s)	22.99	0	0	51.21	28.24
Na(g)	22.99	+107.32	+76.76	153.71	20.79
Na^{+}(aq)	22.99	−240.12	−261.91	+59.0	+46.4
NaOH(s)	40.00	−425.61	−379.49	64.46	59.54
NaCl(s)	58.44	−411.15	−384.14	72.13	50.50
NaBr(s)	102.90	−361.06	−348.98	86.82	51.38
NaI(s)	149.89	−287.78	−286.06	98.53	52.09
Sulfur					
S(s, α) (rhombic)	32.06	0	0	31.80	22.64
S(s, β) (monoclinic)	32.06	+0.33	+0.1	32.6	23.6
S(g)	32.06	+278.81	+238.25	167.82	23.673
S_2(g)	64.13	+128.37	+79.30	228.18	32.47
S^{2-}(aq)	32.06	+33.1	+85.8	−14.6	
SO_2(g)	64.06	−296.83	−300.19	248.22	39.87
SO_3(g)	80.06	−395.72	−371.06	256.76	50.67
H_2SO_4(l)	98.08	−813.99	−690.00	156.90	138.9
H_2SO_4(aq)	98.08	−909.27	−744.53	20.1	−293
SO_4^{2-}(aq)	96.06	−909.27	−744.53	+20.1	−293
HSO_4^{-}(aq)	97.07	−887.34	−755.91	+131.8	−84
H_2S(g)	34.08	−20.63	−33.56	205.79	34.23
H_2S(aq)	34.08	−39.7	−27.83	121	
HS^{-}(aq)	33.072	−17.6	+12.08	+62.08	
SF_6(g)	146.05	−1209	−1105.3	291.82	97.28
Tin					
Sn(s,β)	118.69	0	0	51.55	26.99
Sn(g)	118.69	+302.1	+267.3	168.49	20.26
Sn^{2+}(aq)	118.69	−8.8	−27.2	−17	
SnO(s)	134.69	−285.8	−256.8	56.5	44.31
SnO_2(s)	150.69	−580.7	+519.6	52.3	52.59
Xenon					
Xe(g)	131.30	0	0	169.68	20.786
Zinc					
Zn(s)	65.37	0	0	41.63	25.40
Zn(g)	65.37	+130.73	+95.14	160.98	20.79
Zn^{2+}(aq)	65.37	−153.89	−147.06	−112.1	+46
ZnO(s)	81.37	−348.28	−318.30	43.64	40.25

* Entropies and heat capacities of ions are relative to H^{+}(aq) and are given with a sign.

2 Standard potentials

Table D2.1a *Standard potentials at 298.15 K in electrochemical order*

Reduction half-reaction	*E*$^{\ominus}$/V	*Reduction half-reaction*	*E*$^{\ominus}$/V
Strongly oxidizing			
$H_4XeO_6 + 2H^+ + 2e^- \rightarrow XeO_3 + 3H_2O$	+3.0	$BrO^- + H_2O + 2e^- \rightarrow Br^- + 2OH^-$	+0.76
$F_2 + 2e^- \rightarrow 2F^-$	+2.87	$Hg_2SO_4 + 2e^- \rightarrow 2Hg + SO_4^{2-}$	+0.62
$O_3 + 2H^+ + 2e^- \rightarrow O_2 + H_2O$	+2.07	$MnO_4^{2-} + 2H_2O + 2e^- \rightarrow MnO_2 + 4OH^-$	+0.60
$S_2O_8^{2-} + 2e^- \rightarrow 2SO_4^{2-}$	+2.05	$MnO_4^- + e^- \rightarrow MnO_4^{2-}$	+0.56
$Ag^{2+} + e^- \rightarrow Ag^+$	+1.98	$I_2 + 2e^- \rightarrow 2I^-$	+0.54
$Co^{3+} + e^- \rightarrow Co^{2+}$	+1.81	$Cu^+ + e^- \rightarrow Cu$	+0.52
$HO_2 + 2H^+ + 2e^- \rightarrow 2H_2O$	+1.78	$I_3^- + 2e^- \rightarrow 3I^-$	+0.53
$Au^+ + e^- \rightarrow Au$	+1.69	$NiOOH + H_2O + e^- \rightarrow Ni(OH)_2 + OH^-$	+0.49
$Pb^{4+} + 2e^- \rightarrow Pb^{2+}$	+1.67	$Ag_2CrO_4 + 2e^- \rightarrow 2Ag + CrO_4^{2-}$	+0.45
$2HClO + 2H^+ + 2e^- \rightarrow Cl_2 + 2H_2O$	+1.63	$O_2 + 2H_2O + 4e^- \rightarrow 4OH^-$	+0.40
$Ce^{4+} + e^- \rightarrow Ce^{3+}$	+1.61	$ClO_4^- + H_2O + 2e^- \rightarrow ClO_3^- + 2OH^-$	+0.36
$2HBrO + 2H^+ + 2e^- \rightarrow Br_2 + 2H$	+1.60	$[Fe(CN)_6]^{3-} + e^- \rightarrow [Fe(CN)_6]^{4-}$	+0.36
$MnO_4^- + 8H^+ + 5e^- \rightarrow Mn^{2+} + 4H_2O$	+1.51	$Cu^{2+} + 2e^- \rightarrow Cu$	+0.34
$Mn^{3+} + e^- \rightarrow Mn^{2+}$	+1.51	$Hg_2Cl_2 + 2e^- \rightarrow 2Hg + 2Cl^-$	+0.27
$Au^{3+} + 3e^- \rightarrow Au$	+1.40	$AgCl + e^- \rightarrow Ag + Cl^-$	+0.22
$Cl_2 + 2e^- \rightarrow 2Cl^-$	+1.36	$Bi^{3+} + 3e^- \rightarrow Bi$	+0.20
$Cr_2O_7^{2-} + 14H^+ + 6e^- \rightarrow 2Cr^{3+} + 7H_2O$	+1.33	$Cu^{2+} + e^- \rightarrow Cu^+$	+0.16
$O_3 + H_2O + 2e^- \rightarrow O_2 + 2OH^-$	+1.24	$Sn^{4+} + 2e^- \rightarrow Sn^{2+}$	+0.15
$O_2 + 4H^+ + 4e^- \rightarrow 2H_2O$	+1.23	$AgBr + e^- \rightarrow Ag + Br^-$	+0.07
$ClO_4^- + 2H^+ + 2e^- \rightarrow ClO_3^- + H_2O$	+1.23	$Ti^{4+} + e^- \rightarrow Ti^{3+}$	0.00
$MnO_2 + 4H^+ + 2e^- \rightarrow Mn^{2+} + 2H_2O$	+1.23	$2H^+ + 2e^- \rightarrow H$	0, by definition
$Br_2 + 2e^- \rightarrow 2Br^-$	+1.09	$Fe^{3+} + 3e^- \rightarrow Fe$	−0.04
$Pu^{4+} + e^- \rightarrow Pu^{3+}$	+0.97	$O_2 + H_2O + 2e^- \rightarrow HO_2^- + OH^-$	−0.08
$NO_3^- + 4H^+ + 3e^- \rightarrow NO + 2H_2O$	+0.96	$Pb^{2+} + 2e^- \rightarrow Pb$	−0.13
$2Hg^{2+} + 2e^- \rightarrow Hg_2^{2+}$	+0.92	$In^+ + e^- \rightarrow In$	−0.14
$ClO^- + H_2O + 2e^- \rightarrow Cl^- + 2OH^-$	+0.89	$Sn^{2+} + 2e^- \rightarrow Sn$	−0.14
$Hg^{2+} + 2e^- \rightarrow Hg$	+0.86	$AgI + e^- \rightarrow Ag + I^-$	−0.15
$NO_3^- + 2H^+ + e^- \rightarrow NO_2 + H_2O$	+0.80	$Ni^{2+} + 2e^- \rightarrow Ni$	−0.23
$Ag^+ + e^- \rightarrow Ag$	+0.80	$Co^{2+} + 2e^- \rightarrow Co$	−0.28
$Hg_2^{2+} + 2e^- \rightarrow 2Hg$	+0.79	$In^{3+} + 3e^- \rightarrow In$	−0.34
$Fe^{3+} + e^- \rightarrow Fe^{2+}$	+0.77	$Tl^+ + e^- \rightarrow Tl$	−0.34
$Ti^{3+} + e^- \rightarrow Ti^{2+}$	−0.37	$PbSO_4 + 2e^- \rightarrow Pb + SO_4^{2-}$	−0.36
$Cd^{2+} + 2e^- \rightarrow Cd$	−0.40	$Ti^{2+} + 2e^- \rightarrow Ti$	−1.63
$In^{2+} + e^- \rightarrow In^+$	−0.40	$Al^{3+} + 3e^- \rightarrow Al$	−1.66
$Cr^{3+} + e^- \rightarrow Cr^{2+}$	−0.41	$U^{3+} + 3e^- \rightarrow U$	−1.79
$Fe^{2+} + 2e^- \rightarrow Fe$	−0.44	$Mg^{2+} + 2e^- \rightarrow Mg$	−2.36
$In^{3+} + 2e^- \rightarrow In^+$	−0.44	$Ce^{3+} + 3e^- \rightarrow Ce$	−2.48
$S + 2e^- \rightarrow S^{2-}$	−0.48	$La^{3+} + 3e^- \rightarrow La$	−2.52
$In^{3+} + e^- \rightarrow In^{2+}$	−0.49	$Na^+ + e^- \rightarrow Na$	−2.71
$U^{4+} + e^- \rightarrow U^{3+}$	−0.61	$Ca^{2+} + 2e^- \rightarrow Ca$	−2.87
$Cr^{3+} + 3e^- \rightarrow Cr$	−0.74	$Sr^{2+} + 2e^- \rightarrow Sr$	−2.89
$Zn^{2+} + 2e^- \rightarrow Zn$	−0.76	$Ba^{2+} + 2e^- \rightarrow Ba$	−2.91
$Cd(OH)_2 + 2e^- \rightarrow Cd + 2OH^-$	−0.81	$Ra^{2+} + 2e^- \rightarrow Ra$	−2.92
$2H_2O + 2e^- \rightarrow H_2 + 2OH^-$	−0.83	$Cs^+ + e^- \rightarrow Cs$	−2.92
$Cr^{2+} + 2e^- \rightarrow Cr$	−0.91	$Rb^+ + e^- \rightarrow Rb$	−2.93
$Mn^{2+} + 2e^- \rightarrow Mn$	−1.18	$K^+ + e^- \rightarrow K$	−2.93
$V^{2+} + 2e^- \rightarrow V$	−1.19	$Li^+ + e^- \rightarrow Li$	−3.05

Table D2.1b *Standard potentials at 298.15 K in alphabetical order*

Reduction half-reaction	$E^{\ominus}/V$	*Reduction half-reaction*	$E^{\ominus}/V$
Strongly reducing			
$Ag^+ + e^- \rightarrow Ag$	+0.80	$Co^{2+} + 2e^- \rightarrow Co$	−0.28
$Ag^{2+} + e^- \rightarrow Ag^+$	+1.98	$Co^{3+} + e^- \rightarrow Co^{2+}$	+1.81
$AgBr + e^- \rightarrow Ag + Br^-$	+0.0713	$Cr^{2+} + 2e^- \rightarrow Cr$	−0.91
$AgCl + e^- \rightarrow Ag + Cl^-$	+0.22	$Cr_2O_7^{2-} + 14H^+ + 6e^- \rightarrow 2Cr^{3+} + 7H_2O$	+1.33
$Ag_2CrO_4 + 2e^- \rightarrow 2Ag + CrO_4^{2-}$	+0.45	$Cr^{3+} + 3e^- \rightarrow Cr$	−0.74
$AgF + e^- \rightarrow Ag + F^-$	+0.78	$Cr^{3+} + e^- \rightarrow Cr^{2+}$	−0.41
$AgI + e^- \rightarrow Ag + I^-$	−0.15	$Cs^+ + e^- \rightarrow Cs$	−2.92
$Al^{3+} + 3e^- \rightarrow Al$	−1.66	$Cu^+ + e^- \rightarrow Cu$	+0.52
$Au^+ + e^- \rightarrow Au$	+1.69	$Cu^{2+} + 2e^- \rightarrow Cu$	+0.34
$Au^{3+} + 3e^- \rightarrow Au$	+1.40	$Cu^{2+} + e^- \rightarrow Cu^+$	+0.16
$Ba^{2+} + 2e^- \rightarrow Ba$	−2.91	$F_2 + 2e^- \rightarrow 2F^-$	+2.87
$Be^{2+} + 2e^- \rightarrow Be$	−1.85	$Fe^{2+} + 2e^- \rightarrow Fe$	−0.44
$Bi^{3+} + 3e^- \rightarrow Bi$	+0.20	$Fe^{3+} + 3e^- \rightarrow Fe$	−0.04
$Br_2 + 2e^- \rightarrow 2Br^-$	+1.09	$Fe^{3+} + e^- \rightarrow Fe^{2+}$	+0.77
$BrO^- + H_2O + 2e^- \rightarrow Br^- + 2OH^-$	+0.76	$[Fe(CN)_6]^{3-} + e^- \rightarrow [Fe(CN)_6]^{4-}$	+0.36
$Ca^{2+} + 2e^- \rightarrow Ca$	−2.87	$2H^+ + 2e^- \rightarrow H_2$	0, by definition
$Cd(OH)_2 + 2e^- \rightarrow Cd + 2OH^-$	−0.81	$2H_2O + 2e^- \rightarrow H_2 + 2OH^-$	−0.83
$Cd^{2+} + 2e^- \rightarrow Cd$	−0.40	$2HBrO + 2H^+ + 2e^- \rightarrow Br_2 + 2H_2O$	+1.60
$Ce^{3+} + 3e^- \rightarrow Ce$	−2.48	$2HClO + 2H^+ + 2e^- \rightarrow Cl_2 + 2H_2O$	+1.63
$Ce^{4+} + e^- \rightarrow Ce^{3+}$	+1.61	$H_2O_2 + 2H^+ + 2e^- \rightarrow 2H_2O$	+1.78
$Cl_2 + 2e^- \rightarrow 2Cl^-$	+1.36	$H_4XeO_6 + 2H^+ + 2e^- \rightarrow XeO_3 + 3H_2O$	+3.0
$ClO^- + H_2O + 2e^- \rightarrow Cl^- + 2OH^-$	+0.89	$Hg_2^{2+} + 2e^- \rightarrow 2Hg$	+0.79
$ClO_4^- + 2H^+ + 2e^- \rightarrow ClO_3^- + H_2O$	+1.23	$Hg_2Cl_2 + 2e^- \rightarrow 2Hg + 2Cl^-$	+0.27
$ClO_4^- + H_2O + 2e^- \rightarrow ClO_3^- + 2OH^-$	+0.36	$Hg^{2+} + 2e^- \rightarrow Hg$	+0.86
$2Hg^{2+} + 2e^- \rightarrow Hg_2^{2+}$	+0.92	$O_2 + 4H^+ + 4e^- \rightarrow 2H_2O$	+1.23
$Hg_2SO_4 + 2e^- \rightarrow 2Hg + SO_4^{2-}$	+0.62	$O_2 + e^- \rightarrow O_2^-$	−0.56
$I_2 + 2e^- \rightarrow 2I^-$	+0.54	$O_2 + H_2O + 2e^- \rightarrow HO_2^- + OH^-$	−0.08
$I_3^- + 2e^- \rightarrow 3I^-$	+0.53	$O_3 + 2H^+ + 2e^- \rightarrow O_2 + H_2O$	+2.07
$In^+ + e^- \rightarrow In$	−0.14	$O_3 + H_2O + 2e^- \rightarrow O_2 + 2OH^-$	+1.24
$In^{2+} + e^- \rightarrow In^+$	−0.40	$Pb^{2+} + 2e^- \rightarrow Pb$	−0.13
$In^{3+} + 2e^- \rightarrow In^+$	−0.44	$Pb^{4+} + 2e^- \rightarrow Pb^{2+}$	+1.67
$In^{3+} + 3e^- \rightarrow In$	−0.34	$PbSO_4 + 2e^- \rightarrow Pb + SO_4^{2-}$	−0.36
$In^{3+} + e^- \rightarrow In^{2+}$	−0.49	$Pt^{2+} + 2e^- \rightarrow Pt$	+1.20
$K^+ + e^- \rightarrow K$	−2.93	$Pu^{4+} + e^- \rightarrow Pu^{3+}$	+0.97
$La^{3+} + 3e^- \rightarrow La$	−2.52	$Ra^{2+} + 2e^- \rightarrow Ra$	−2.92
$Li^+ + e^- \rightarrow Li$	−3.05	$Rb^+ + e^- \rightarrow Rb$	−2.93
$Mg^{2+} + 2e^- \rightarrow Mg$	−2.36	$S + 2e^- \rightarrow S^{2-}$	−0.48
$Mn^{2+} + 2e^- \rightarrow Mn$	−1.18	$S_2O_8^{2-} + 2e^- \rightarrow 2SO_4^{2-}$	+2.05
$Mn^{3+} + e^- \rightarrow Mn^{2+}$	+1.51	$Sn^{2+} + 2e^- \rightarrow Sn$	−0.14
$MnO_2 + 4H^+ + 2e^- \rightarrow Mn^{2+} + 2H_2O$	+1.23	$Sn^{4+} + 2e^- \rightarrow Sn^{2+}$	+0.15
$MnO_4^- + 8H^+ + 5e^- \rightarrow Mn^{2+} + 4H_2O$	+1.51	$Sr^{2+} + 2e^- \rightarrow Sr$	−2.89
$MnO_4^- + e^- \rightarrow MnO_4^{2-}$	+0.56	$Ti^{2+} + 2e^- \rightarrow Ti$	−1.63
$MnO_4^{2-} + 2H_2O + 2e^- \rightarrow MnO_2 + 4OH^-$	+0.60	$Ti^{3+} + e^- \rightarrow Ti^{2+}$	−0.37
$Na^+ + e^- \rightarrow Na$	−2.71	$Ti^{4+} + e^- \rightarrow Ti^{3+}$	0.00
$Ni^{2+} + 2e^- \rightarrow Ni$	−0.23	$Tl^+ + e^- \rightarrow Tl$	−0.34
$NiOOH + H_2O + e^- \rightarrow Ni(OH)_2 + OH^-$	+0.49	$U^{3+} + 3e^- \rightarrow U$	−1.79
$NO_3^- + 2H^+ + e^- \rightarrow NO_2 + H_2O$	+0.80	$U^{4+} + e^- \rightarrow U^{3+}$	−0.61
$NO_3^- + 3H^+ + 3e^- \rightarrow NO + 2H_2O$	+0.96	$V^{2+} + 2e^- \rightarrow V$	−1.19
$NO_3^- + H_2O + 2e^- \rightarrow NO_2^- + 2OH^-$	+0.10	$V^{3+} + e^- \rightarrow V^{2+}$	−0.26
$O_2 + 2H_2O + 4e^- \rightarrow 4OH^-$	+0.40	$Zn^{2+} + 2e^- \rightarrow Zn$	−0.76

Answers to exercises

Answers to exercises can be found on the companion web site at:

www.oup.com/uk/booksites/chemistry

and

whfreeman.com/elements4e

Index